three californias

kim stanley robinson

TOR ◤ ESSENTIALS

A TOM DOHERTY ASSOCIATES BOOK

▪▪▪ *New York* ▪▪▪

THREE CALIFORNIAS

The Wild Shore © 1984 by Kim Stanley Robinson
The Gold Coast © 1988 by Kim Stanley Robinson
Pacific Edge © 1990 by Kim Stanley Robinson

"Triptych, with Softball" © 2020 by Francis Spufford

The Wild Shore maps by Mark Stein

All rights reserved.

A Tor Essentials Book
Published by Tom Doherty Associates
120 Broadway
New York, NY 10271

www.tor-forge.com

Tor® is a registered trademark of Macmillan Publishing Group, LLC.

Library of Congress Cataloging-in-Publication Data

Names: Robinson, Kim Stanley, author. | Robinson, Kim Stanley. The wild shore. |
    Robinson, Kim Stanley. The gold coast. | Robinson, Kim Stanley. Pacific edge.
Title: Three Californias / Kim Stanley Robinson.
Description: New York : Tor Essentials, 2020.
Identifiers: LCCN 2019042804 (print) | LCCN 2019042805 (ebook) |
    ISBN 9781250307569 (trade paperback) | ISBN 9781250758958 (ebook)
Classification: LCC PS3568.O2893 A6 2020 (print) | LCC PS3568.O2893 (ebook) |
    DDC 813/.54—dc23
LC record available at https://lccn.loc.gov/2019042804
LC ebook record available at https://lccn.loc.gov/2019042805

Our books may be purchased in bulk for promotional, educational, or business use. Please contact your local bookseller or the Macmillan Corporate and Premium Sales Department at 1-800-221-7945, extension 5442, or by email at MacmillanSpecialMarkets@macmillan.com.

First Edition: February 2020

Printed in the United States of America

0 9 8 7 6 5 4 3 2 1

contents

Triptych, With Softball

Francis Spufford

Triptych: a medieval painting made of three separate panels hinged together, so that as well as sharing a subject or a theme, the pictures can be turned to face each other, to start a silent conversation with each other. And that's what this is. It's a Californian triptych, with softball and surfing and hot-tubs, in which three very different futures for Orange County, just south of LA, are angled to face each other and to talk together.

Each of the three novels is complete in itself. Each of them, in fact, represents a separate triumph, and a separate *kind* of triumph.

The Wild Shore was Kim Stanley Robinson's very first novel, back in 1984, written during the anxious last years of the Cold War, when the nuclear-apocalypse story was making a comeback. In it, one of the great modern careers in SF was inaugurated with a portrait of a re-greened post-apocalypse America that might have come from the pen of Mark Twain. The world of *The Wild Shore* is a hard one, for sure. The valley at the edge of OC where it's set has a climate more like Alaska than the California we know, and there are only a handful of survivors eking out a livelihood from fishing and farming: but it's also a place of regained innocence, a place with the dew back on it, at least for seventeen-year-old Henry, the narrator. He tells us his story as if it were a boy's adventure, because for him, that's what it is: the adventure of his life, in which he gets to travel to the great city of San Diego (pop. 2000) along the old railroad track, and to swim for his life in the icy sea, and to wrestle with the claims of friendship, and to encounter love and death for the first time. For him, the tall tales he hears might be true, just as it might be true that Shakespeare was one of the greatest Americans. We know better; we notice, reading, that the women of Henry's village are quietly suffocating mutated babies, and that the secure little community he takes for granted is a very recent and fragile victory over chaos. But Henry's voice still fixes the mood for us, kind and decent and wide-eyed, giving us a ruined, primitive future that's close kin to a raft on the Mississippi.

Then in its successor *The Gold Coast,* we switch to excellence of another

sort altogether. This Orange County is an extrapolation of the present, with all
the existing trendlines of Southern Californian life soaring toward the vertical
and making a kind of asymptotic approach to dystopia. (An extrapolation of
the present it was written in thirty years ago, of course, rather than the present
in which you read it. This is a future with video tape but no CCTV, drugs delivered by eye-dropper but no hand-held devices. The military-industrial complex has a surviving USSR as its opponent, not China or Islamic State. In fact
the Soviet Union is still around well into the 21st century in all three novels;
for all three, inescapably, offer yesterday's tomorrows. But *prediction* is not the
business they were in anyway.) Now concrete condos, multilevel freeways, daz-
zle from mercury-vapor and xenon lighting, monster malls and five repeating
street-types have eaten the whole shore from LA to San Diego. The wild place of
The Wild Shore, the place that will be lovingly rewilded in the third novel, has
been subdued here by a narrow set of human desires, repeating and metastasiz-
ing until the precious land is gone—almost. And through this frantic tumor of a
town we travel along multiple tracks of experience, in multiple lives: four guys
in their twenties, partying on the last fumes of a high-school friendship and
diverging into different destinies as paramedic, drug dealer, Zen surfer, and lit-
erary slacker. But then beyond them, strands of viewpoint extend into defense
engineering, church work, Wang Wei–style poetic gestalts, and a through-
running history of OC. There's a central figure of young manhood, of course,
to stand as counterpart to Henry (and Kevin in the book yet to come) but the
hapless Jim holds the stage far less exclusively than the other two, for *The Gold
Coast* lacks the innocence of the first book and the single-minded calm the
last will possess. Its business is collage, is buzz, is the quick collection of glittering noisy impressions, from video sex to the blood on the metal of crashed
cars, with the novel's generous sympathy for all of the human stuff it contains
running under its surfaces like a piped and branching river. The result is one
of the great science-fictional pictures of city life, of a close-packed human hive.
Just as you could shelve *The Wild Shore* honorably next to *Huckleberry Finn*,
you could plant *The Gold Coast* to its credit beside the city-SF of William Gib-
son or Ian McDonald.

Pacific Edge on the other hand, third and last, would sit with honor in between *The Dispossessed* and *Woman on the Edge of Time*. For this one was, all
by itself, one of the deepest and subtlest utopias ever written from the political
left. Now Orange County is a warm, tended plain of fruit trees and eucalypts,
dotted with settlements as elegant as Italian hill towns. Transport is by bicycle or human-powered flying machine, with electric cars for hire on the few
remaining freeways. The laws and systems supporting this vision of the eco-
socialist good life are there in the novel for you, if you want to dig them out,
and there's a piece of politicking going on throughout, involving the intricacies

of the Californian water supply. But none of these dominate the foreground of the book. Where most utopias are thinly veiled guided tours, with a convenient outsider being marched in didactic fashion round the main features of the model society, usually receiving lectures as they go, this one is told from within, from perspectives that pretty much take utopia as read, and are busily engaged in an extroverted in-the-body Californian way with that year's softball season; with the soap opera of all small-town lives whether utopian or not; with a positively Shakespearean set of midsummer-night confusions. Above all, it turns out, with the heartbreak that no society, however good, can remove from human life. The nearest thing to the traditional outsider is the town's new lawyer, but he's not there to be educated, he's there to be a wise clown, and to offer wry, affectionate commentary on the population of bronzed gym-bunnies, and to cut the prevailing mellowness with a necessary dose of lemon juice. Instead as protagonist we get Kevin, builder of eco-houses, hammerer of nails, admirer of muscular knees on women, batter of a perfect thousand. Not stupid, exactly, but daringly close to it; insensible, maybe, to begin with, and waking from it as the book goes on, into astonished joy and then into deeper and deeper unhappiness. Until at the last sentence of the novel (a perfect last sentence, a sentence to crown most writers' entire output) we suddenly see Kevin's woe brought into proportion, tipped abruptly through one hundred and eighty degrees to become an exquisitely economical reflection on the space that different worlds allow to sorrow. Sorrow is personal, always; sorrow can be structural too, built into architectures of injustice, systems of woe. Utopia can do something about the second kind, but not about the first. Unhappiness (the mere personal kind) might be the exact thing that human history should be striving for. If we're lucky.

So: an apocalypse, an extrapolation, a utopia. Three different achievements, three different classic pleasures in store between these covers. But they also belong together. Separately great though they are, they become something greater still when joined, and allowed to converse.

Not of course that the triptych was (quite) designed as such, from beginning to end. It was clearly after the first book existed that Robinson saw the three-fold possibility. *The Wild Shore* reads unmistakably like the work of a new novelist holding nothing back, throwing in absolutely everything he cared about and wanted to say, with none of the strategic rationing writers go in for later. Alone among the three, it's not an active reflector of the other two, it doesn't know what it's in conversation with. But the other two books reach guilefully out to hook it into the pattern.

For a start, and most obviously, the triptych is unified by the character of Tom Barnard, grandfather-figure to all three of the protagonists, though he is only literally the biological grandfather of Kevin. Always aged eighty-one, though at three different 21st-century dates, always the voice for law and hope and the lessons of the past, he has been buffeted by three histories of the world into leading three disjoined lives. Sometimes he is even able to glimpse this. The version of him in *Pacific Edge,* the world-changing and successful lawyer now bereaved and hiding away as a hilltop hermit, thinks about how arbitrary it is "that the world had spun along to this sage sunlight," when he could "just as likely . . . have been raising bees in some bombed-out forest, or lying flat on his back in an old folks' home, choking for breath." Those are precisely the other two Toms of the other two books. Just as the world is most mangled in *The Wild Shore,* the counsel that the Tom there can offer Henry is the maddest and most unreliable (including his offer of a Green Card to Shakespeare). Just as Jim in *The Gold Coast* is the most lost of the three boys, so his Tom's advice is the most helpless and ineffectual. Tom is always a teacher, but who he teaches and what he can teach are harmonized differently in three different worlds, three different Californias.

Beyond that, there are common elements both large and small, in plain sight and hidden away. Look out for the common opening of the books with an excavation of some kind, the difference in what gets dug up signaling each world's particular relationship to its past. Look out for the common scene of communal bathing, the common timing of each story across a summer, the common insertion into each story of a contrasting other narrative, the common visit at a moment of romance to Swing Canyon, the common references to Shakespeare, the common attention to rock and salt water. The common attention, for that matter, to the getting of wisdom by young men, not because Kim Stanley Robinson takes the centering of male protagonists for granted or mistakes men for the default form of the human race but because, in the second half of the 1980s, he was specifically interested in how masculinity works. Masculinities in the plural, I suppose I should say, in line with the plurality of worlds that Henry, Kevin, and Jim are being men in, but they share a common situation on the uncertain boundary between boyhood and adulthood, not sure which childish things they should be putting away, or how.

After a while the search gets addictive. An easter-egg hunt, even. You can award yourself bonus points if you spot the appearance of the El Modena town hall in *Pacific Edge* as an El Torito restaurant in *The Gold Coast.* Can Ramona the horrible Stewart Lemon's secretary in *The Gold Coast* possibly be the same person as the Ramona who Kevin falls in love with? Can Hank the Zen carpenter in *Pacific Edge* conceivably be a middle-aged, chilled-out version of Henry from *The Wild Shore*, transplanted into utopia? If you want to get really, really meta about it, there is an anticipation of *Red Mars* buried somewhere in the trilogy, too.

But at the deepest level, what joins the triptych together is Orange County itself. "My God," realizes Jim in *The Gold Coast,* seeing by moonlight the last undeveloped parcel of his OC. "The land." The land, the geographical frame for all three of the human dramas. Here it is three times over, different but still recognizable every time: a dry yet fertile coastal plain with the salt water in front and the mountains and the desert behind. An edge-zone of North America. A habitat. The human existence that plays out in it can be a meager struggle for survival, as in *The Wild Shore*. It can be Robinson's best guess at a harmonious co-operation between place and human needs, as in *Pacific Edge*. Or it can be an orgy of appetite destroying its own substrate, as in *The Gold Coast*. But every time it is something molded by its presence on a specific patch of ground. Robinson is one of the great contemporary writers of place, in SF or in any other branch of literature. The traditions of nature-writing flow into his work—the commitment, starting all the way back with the Romantic poets and then traveling on down through Thoreau and John Muir, to paying such close sensory attention to rock and pebble and living things that they can be made present for the reader on the page, detail by detail, our senses waking up to act in partnership with the writing. These three books will all make you see, hear, touch, taste, smell more acutely. They will fill your nostrils with sagebrush and eucalyptus and pine needles, your ears with the exact sound-pattern of dripping water, your eyes with salt spray from the night-time sea glowing around the moon and making the black sky fuzzy. They will dip you in the Pacific breakers in three different moods of the ocean. (No, far more than three.) They will make you exclaim, along with Kevin, "What a glossy grainy surface to the massive rocky substance of the world!"

SF generally doesn't do this, despite being famously the kind of writing that treats the world as a character, that cares at least as much about setting as it does about character. On the whole, SF isn't a friend to the local, the immediate, the grounded. It prefers the widescreen, the new, the alien. But Kim Stanley Robinson *is* an SF writer: emphatically so. His imagination too responds fiercely to what is new and speculative, to what's invented rather than discovered, technological as well as biological, scientific as well as poetic, far off as well as close at hand. It's just that when he sends his imagination far away, the way it seems to take hold of what it finds there is by *making* it local; by understanding it, and rendering it every single time, whatever it is, as a dome of sense data oriented around particular human bodies, particular human feet on particular ground. He writes the dunes of the Martian north pole—black sand under a violet sky—in just the same way he writes sand at the mouth of San Onofre creek in *The Wild Shore,* criss-cross-cut by water flow. As if they were being *seen*. As if they were being registered, that very minute, there and then, by human eyes. As a result, he can make his invented worlds more solid than virtually any other SF writer. With Kim Stanley Robinson, there is *always* a "there" there.

But then comes the irony. As you read these books, you'll believe in the snowy pines of San Onofre, the spectrum-bend multi-level concrete of South Coast Plaza, the cloud-gel eco-houses of El Modena. But look up the satellite maps of the real OC, today, and you won't find any of them. With a curious pang of loss (and some relief, because uncomfortably close to our world though *The Gold Coast* is, we aren't quite there yet) you'll watch them all dissolve. What you took to be "the massive rocky substance of the world" was only the substance of three possibilities. And here we still are, all of us, on our one and only planet, made of atoms not words, with all our collective choices before us about our real future. So: what's it going to be then? Disaster? More of the same till we can hardly stand it? Or utopia? It's up to us.

the wild shore

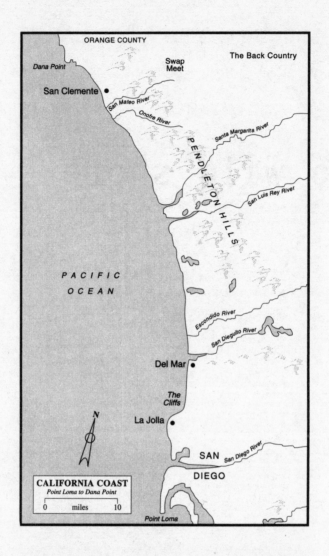

ORANGE COUNTY

The Back Country

Dana Point

Swap
Meet

San Clemente

San Mateo River

Onofre River

Santa Margarita River

P E N D L E T O N   H I L L S

San Luis Rey River

P A C I F I C
O C E A N

Escondido River

San Dieguito River

Del Mar

The
Cliffs

La Jolla

N

SAN   San Diego River

DIEGO

CALIFORNIA COAST
Point Loma to Dana Point
0   miles   10

Point Loma

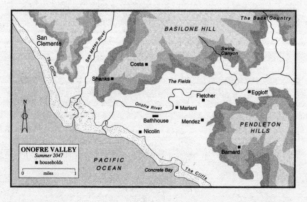

San
Clemente

San Mateo River

BASILONE HILL

The Back Country

Swing
Canyon

The Cliffs

Costa ■

Shanks ■

The Fields

Fletcher ■

Eggloff ■

Onofre River

Mariani ■

Bathhouse ■

Mendez ■

PENDLETON
HILLS

■ Nicolin

N

Barnard ■

ONOFRE VALLEY
Summer 2047
■ households
0   miles   1

PACIFIC
OCEAN

Concrete Bay

The Cliffs

part one

...SAN ONOFRE

... 1

"It wouldn't really be grave-robbing," Nicolin was explaining. "Just dig up a coffin and take the silver off the outside of it. Never open it up at all. Bury it again nice and proper—what could be wrong with that? Those silver coffin handles are going to waste in the ground."

The five of us considered it. Near sunset the cliffs at the mouth of our valley glow amber, and on the wide beach below, tangles of driftwood cast shadows all the way to the sandstone boulders at the foot of the cliff. Each clump of wood could have been a gravemarker, and I imagined digging under one to find what lay beneath it.

Gabby Mendez tossed a pebble at a gliding seagull. "Just exactly how is that not grave-robbing?" he demanded of Nicolin.

"It takes desecration of the body to make it grave-robbing." Nicolin winked at me; I was his partner in these sorts of things. "We aren't going to do any such thing. No searching for cuff links or belt buckles, no pulling off rings or dental work, nothing of the sort!"

"Ick," said Kristen Mariani.

We were on the point of the cliff above the rivermouth—Steve Nicolin and Gabby, Kristen and Mando Costa, Del Simpson and me—all old friends, grown up together, out on our point as we so often were at the end of a day, arguing and talking and making wild plans . . . that last being the specialty of Nicolin and me. Below us in the first bend of the river were the fishing boats, pulled up onto the tidal flats. It felt good to sit on the warm sand in the cool wind with my friends, watching the sun leak into the whitecaps, knowing my work for the day was done.

"Why, with that much silver we would be kings of the swap meet," Nicolin went on. "And queens," he said to Kristen. "We'd be able to buy anything there twice. Or travel up the coast if we wanted. Or across the country. Just generally do what we pleased."

And not what your father tells you to, I thought to myself. But I felt the pull of what he said, I admit it.

"How are you going to make sure that the coffin you take the trouble to dig up has got silver on it?" Gab asked, looking doubtful.

"You've heard the old man talk about funerals in the old time," Nicolin scolded. "Henry, you tell him."

"They were scared of death in an unnatural way," I said, like I was an authority. "So they made these huge funeral displays to distract themselves. Tom said a funeral might cost upward of five thousand dollars."

Steve nodded. "He says every coffin put down was crusted with silver."

"He says men walked on the moon, too," Gabby replied. "That don't mean I'm going to go there looking for footprints." But I had almost convinced him; he knew that Tom Barnard, who had taught us to read and write (taught Steve and Mando and me, anyway), would describe the wealth of the old time as quick as you might say, "Tell us—"

"So we just go up the freeway into the ruins," Nicolin went on, "and find a rich-looking tombstone in a cemetery, and there we have it."

"Tom says we shouldn't go up there," Kristen reminded us.

Nicolin laughed. "That's because he's scared of it." He looked more serious. "Of course that's understandable, given what he's been through. But there's no one up there but the wreckrats, and they won't be out at night."

He had no way to be sure of that, as we had never been up there day or night; but before Gabby could call him on it, Mando squeaked, "At *night?*"

"Sure!" Nicolin cried.

"I hear the scavengers will eat you if they can," Kristen said.

"Is your pa going to let you leave doctoring and farming during the day?" Nicolin asked Mando. "Well, it's the same with all of us, only more so. This gang has got to do its business at night." He lowered his voice: "That's the only time to be grave-robbing in a cemetery, anyway," laughing at the look on Mando's face.

"Grave-robbing at the beach you can do any time of day," I said, half to myself.

"I could get the shovels," Del said.

"And I could bring a lantern," Mando said quickly, to show he wasn't scared. And suddenly we were talking a plan. I perked up and paid more attention. Nicolin and I had outlined a number of schemes before: trapping a tiger in the back country, diving for sunken treasure on the concrete reef, extracting the silver contained in old railroad tracks by melting them. But most of these proposals had certain practical difficulties to them, and we let them slide. They were just talk. With this plan, however, all we had to do was sneak up into the ruins—something we always swore we really wanted to do—and dig. So we talked about which night the scavengers were least likely to be out and about (full moon, Nicolin assured Mando, when the ghosts were visible), who we might ask to come along, how we could chop the silver handles into tradeable discs, and so forth.

Then the ocean was lapping at the red rim of the sun, and it got a good deal colder. Gabby stood up and kneaded his butt.

"We're really going to do this one," Nicolin said intently. "And by God, I'm ready for it."

As we walked up from the point I took myself off from the rest and followed the cliff's edge. Down on the beach the tidal puddles streaking the sand were silver banded with red, little versions of the vast ocean surging beyond them. Behind me was our valley, winding up into the hills that crowded the sea. The trees of the forest blanketing the hills all waved their branches in the onshore wind, and their late spring greens were tinted pollen color by the drowning sun. For miles up and down the coast the forest tossed, fir and spruce and pine like the hair of a living creature, and as I walked I felt the wind toss my hair too. On the hillsides not one sign of man could be seen (though they were there), it was nothing but trees, tall and short, redwood and torrey pine and eucalyptus, dark green hills cascading into the sea, and as I walked the cliff's edge I was happy. I didn't have the slightest notion that my friends and I were starting a summer that would change us. As I write this account of those months, deep in the harshest winter I have ever known, I have the advantage of time passed, and I can see that this excursion in search of silver was the start of it—not so much because of what happened as what didn't happen, because of the ways in which we were deceived. Because of what it gave us a taste for. I was hungry; not just for food (that was a constant), but for a life that was more than fishing and hoeing weeds and checking snares. And Nicolin was hungrier than I.

But I'm getting ahead of my story. As I strolled the steep sandstone border between forest and sea, I was excited by the thought of an adventure. As I turned up the south path toward the little cabin that my pa and I shared, the smells of pine and sea salt raked the insides of my nose and made me drunk with hunger, and happily I imagined chips of silver the size of a dozen dimes. It occurred to me that my friends and I were for the very first time in our lives actually going to do what we had so often boastfully planned to do—and at the thought I felt a shiver of anticipation, I leaped from root to root in the trail: we were invading the territory of the scavengers, venturing north into the ruins of Orange County.

The night we picked to do it, fog was smoking off the ocean and gusting onshore, under a quarter moon that gave the white mist a faint glow. I waited inside the door of our cabin, ignoring Pa's snores. I had read him to sleep an hour before, and now he lay on his side, calloused fingers resting on the crease in the side of his head. Pa is lame, and simple, from tangling with a horse when I was young. My ma always used to read him to sleep, and when she died Pa sent me up to Tom's to carry on with my learning, saying in his slow way that it would be good for both of us.

I warmed my hands now and then over the coals of the stove fire, as I had the cabin door partway open, and it was cold. Outside, the eucalyptus down the path blew in and out of visibility. A clammy puff of fog drifted onto the house, smelling like the rivermouth flats.

W-whooo, w-whooo. Nicolin's call startled me from a doze. It was a pretty good imitation of the big canyon owls. I slipped out the door and hurried down the path to the eucalyptus. Nicolin had Del's two shovels over his shoulders; Del and Gabby stood behind him.

"We've got to get Mando," I said.

Del and Gabby looked at each other. "Costa?" Nicolin said.

I stared at him. "He'll be waiting for us." Mando and I were younger than the other three—me by one year, Mando by three—and I felt obliged to stick up for him.

"His house is on the way anyway," Nicolin told the others. We took the river path to the bridge, crossed and hiked up the hill path leading to the Costas'.

Doc Costa's weird oildrum house looked like a little black castle out of one of Tom's books—squat as a toad, and darker than anything natural in the fog. Nicolin made his call, and pretty soon Mando came out and hustled down to us.

"You still going to do it tonight?" he asked, peering around at the mist.

"Sure," I said quickly. "You got the lantern?"

"I forgot." He went back inside and got it. When he returned we walked back down to the old freeway and headed north.

We walked fast to warm up. The freeway was two pale ribbons in the mist, heavily cracked underfoot, black weeds in every crack. Quickly we crossed the ridge at the north end of our valley, then narrow San Mateo Valley immediately to the north. After that we were walking up and down the steep hills of San Clemente. We held close together and didn't say much. On each side of us ruins sat in the forest: walls of cement blocks, roofs held up by skeletal framing, tangles of wire looping from tree to tree. We knew the scavengers lived up here somewhere, and we hurried along silently. Fog licked over us as the freeway dropped into a broad canyon, and we couldn't see a thing but the broken surface of the road. Creaks emerged from the dark around us, as well as an occasional flurry of dripping, as if something had brushed against leaves.

Nicolin stopped to examine an offramp curving down to the right. "This is it," he hissed. "Cemetery's at the top of this valley."

"How do you know?" Gab said in his ordinary voice, which sounded awfully loud.

"I came up here and found it," Nicolin said. "How do you think I knew?"

We followed him off the highway. Down in the forest there were more buildings than trees, almost, and they were big buildings. They were falling down every way possible; windows and doors knocked out like teeth, with shrubs and ferns growing in every hole; walls slumped; roofs piled on the ground like barrows. The fog followed us up this street, rustling things so they sounded like scurrying feet. Wires looped over poles that sometimes tilted right down to the road; we had to step over them, and none of us touched the wires.

A coyote's bark chopped the silence and we froze. Coyote or scavenger? But nothing followed it, and we took off again. The street made some switchbacks at the head of the valley, and once we got up those we were on the canyon-cut plateau that once made up the top of San Clemente. Up here were houses, big ones, all set in rows like fish out to dry, as if there had been so many people that there wasn't room to give each family a decent garden. A lot of the houses were busted and overgrown, and some were gone entirely—just floors, with pipes sticking out of them like arms sticking up out of a grave.

Nicolin stopped at a street crossing filled with a bonfire pit. "Up here."

We followed him north, along a street on the plateau's edge. Below us the fog was like another ocean, putting us on the beach again so to speak, with occasional white waves running up over us. The houses lining the street stopped, and a fence began, metal rails connecting stone piles. Beyond the fence the rippling plateau was studded with squared stones sticking out of tall grass: the cemetery. We all stopped and looked. In the mist it was impossible to see where it ended. Finally we stepped over a break in the fence and walked in.

They had lined up the graves as straight as their houses. Suddenly Nicolin faced the sky and yowled his coyote yowl, *yip yip yoo-ee-oo-ee-oo-eeee.*

"Stop that," Gabby said, disgusted. "That's all we need is dogs howling at us."

"Or scavengers," Mando added fearfully.

Nicolin laughed. "Boys, we're standing in a silver mine, that's all." He crouched down to read a gravestone; too dark; he hopped over to another. "Look how big this one is." He put his face next to it and with the help of his fingers read it. "Here we got a Mister John Appleby. 1904–1984. *Nice* big stone, died the right time—living in one of the houses back there—rich for sure, right?"

"There should be a lot written on the stone," I said. "That's proof he was rich."

"There is a lot," Nicolin said. "Beloved father, I think . . . some other stuff. Want to give him a try?"

For a while no one answered. Then Gab said, "Good as any other."

"Better," Nicolin replied. He put down one shovel and hefted the other. "Let's get this grass out of the way." He started stabbing the shovel into the ground, making a line cut. Gabby and Del and Mando and I just stood and stared at him. He looked up. "Well?" he demanded quickly. "You want some of this silver?"

So I walked over and started cutting; I had wanted to before, but it made me nervous. When we had the grass pulled away so the dirt was exposed, we started digging in earnest. When we were in up to our knees we gave the shovels to Gabby and Del, panting some. I was sweating easily in the fog, and I cooled off fast. Clods of the wet clay squashed under my feet. Pretty soon Gabby said, "It's getting dark down here; better light the lantern." Mando got out his spark rasp and set to lighting the wick.

The lantern put out a ghastly yellow glare, dazzling me and making more shadows than anything else. I walked away from it to keep my night sight. My arms were spotted with dirt, and I felt more nervous than ever. From a distance the lantern's flame was larger and fainter, and my companions were black silhouettes, the ones with the shovels waist-deep in the earth. I came across a grave that had been dug up and left open, and I jumped and hustled back to the glow of the lantern.

Gabby looked up at me, his head just over the level of the dirt pile we were making. "They buried them deep," he said in an odd voice. He tossed up more dirt.

"Maybe this one's already dug up," Del suggested, looking into the hole at Mando, who was getting up a handful of dirt with every shovel toss.

"Sure," Nicolin scoffed. "Or maybe they buried him alive and he crawled out by himself."

"My hand hurts," Mando said. His shovel stock was a branch. Steve hopped into the hole to replace him, attacking the floor of the hole until the dirt flew into the mist.

It felt late. I was cold, and ravenous. The fog was thickening; the area wrapped around us looked clear, but quickly the mist became more visible, until several yards away it was all we could see—blank white. We were in a bubble of white, and at the edges of the bubble were shapes.

Thunk. One of Nicolin's stabs had hit something. He jabbed tentatively, *tunk tunk tunk*. "Got it," he said, and began to scrape dirt up again. After a bit he said, "Move the lantern down to this end." Mando picked it up and held it over the grave. By its light I saw the faces of my companions, sweaty and streaked with dirt, the whites of their eyes large.

Nicolin started to curse. Our hole, a good five feet long by three feet wide, had just nicked the end of the coffin. "The damn thing's buried *under* the head-stone!" It was still solidly stuck in the clay.

We argued a while about what to do, and the final plan—Nicolin's—was to scrape dirt away from the top and sides of the coffin, and haul it out into the hole we had made. After we had scraped away to the full reach of our arms, Nicolin said, "Henry, you've done the least digging so far, and you're long and skinny, so crawl down there and start pushing the dirt back to us."

I protested, but the others agreed I was the man for the job, so pretty soon I found myself lying on top of the coffin, with dripping clay an inch over my back and butt, tearing at the dirt with my fingers and slinging it out behind me. Only continuous cursing kept my mind off what was lying underneath the wood I was on, exactly parallel to my own body. The others yelled in encour-agements, like "Well, we're going home now," or "Oh, who's that coming?" or "Did you feel the coffin shake just then?" Finally I got my fingers over the far edge of the box, and I shimmied back out the hole, brushing the mud off me and muttering with disgust and fear. "Henry, I can always count on you," Steve said as he leaped into the grave. Then it was his and Del's turn to crawl around down there, tugging and grunting; and with a final jerk the coffin burst back into our hole, while Steve and Del fell down beside it.

It was made of black wood, with a greenish film on it that gleamed like pea-cock feathers in the lantern light. Gabby knocked the dirt off the handles, and then cleaned the gunk off the stripping around the coffin's lid: silver, all of it.

"Look at those handles," Del said reverently. There were six of them, three to a side, as bright and shiny as if they'd been buried the day before, instead of sixty years. I thought of us at the next swap meet, decked out like scavengers in fur coats and boots and feather hats, walking around with our pants al-most falling off from the weight of all those big chips of silver. We shouted and yowled and pounded each other on the back. Gabby rubbed a handle with his thumb; his nose wrinkled.

"Hey," he said. "Uh . . ." He grabbed the shovel leaning against the side of the hole, and poked the handle. *Thud,* it went. Not like metal on metal. And the blow left a gash in the handle. Gabby looked at Del and Steve, and crouched down to look close. He hit the handle again. Thud thud thud. He ran his hand over it.

"This ain't silver," he said. "It's cut. It's some kind of . . . some kind of plastic, I guess."

"God damn," said Nicolin. He jumped in the hole and grabbed the shovel, jabbed the stripping on the coffin lid, and cut it right in half.

We stared at the box. Nobody did any shouting.

"God damn that old liar," Nicolin said. He threw the shovel down. "He told us that every single one of those funerals cost a fortune. He said—" He paused; we all knew what the old man had said. "He told us there'd be silver."

He and Gabby and Del stood in the grave. Mando took the lantern to the headstone and put it down. "Should call this headstone a kneestone," he said, trying to lighten the mood a bit.

Nicolin heard him and scowled. "Should we go for his ring?"

"No!" Mando cried, and we all laughed at him.

"Go for his ring and belt buckle and dental work?" Nicolin said harshly, slipping a glance at Gabby. Mando shook his head furiously, looking like he was about to cry. Del and I laughed; Gabby climbed out of the hole, looking disgusted. Nicolin tilted his head back and laughed, short and sharp. "Let's bury this guy and then go bury the old man."

We shoveled dirt back in. The first clods hit the coffin with an awful hollow sound, *bonk bonk bonk*. It didn't take long to fill the hole. Mando and I put the grass back in place as best we could. When we were done it looked terrible. "Appears he's been bucking around down there," Gabby said.

We killed the lantern flame and took off. Fog flowed through the empty streets like water up a streambed, with us under the surface, down among drowned ruins and black seaweed. Back on the freeway it felt less submerged, but the fog swept hard across the road, and it was colder. We hiked south as fast as we could walk, none of us saying a word. When we warmed up we slowed down a little, and Nicolin began to talk. "You know, since they had those plastic handles colored silver, it must mean that some time before that people were buried with real silver handles—richer people, or people buried before 1984, or whatever." We all understood this as a roundabout way of proposing another dig, so no one agreed, although it appeared to make sense. Steve took offense at our silence and gained ground on us till he was just a mark in the mist. We were almost out of San Clemente.

"Some sort of plastic," Gabby was saying to Del. He started to laugh, harder and harder, until he was leaning an elbow on Del's shoulder. "Whoo, hoo hoo hoo . . . we just spent all night digging up five pounds of plastic."

All of a sudden a noise pierced the air—a howl, a singing screech that started low and got ever higher and louder. No living creature was behind that sound. It reached a peak of height and loudness, and wavered there between two tones, rising and falling, *oooooo-eeeeee-oooooo-eeeeee,* on and on and on, like the scream of the ghosts of every dead person ever buried in Orange County, or the final shrieks of all those killed by the bombs.

We all unstuck ourselves from our tracks and took off running. The noise continued, and appeared to follow us.

"What is it?" Mando cried.

"Scavengers!" Nicolin hissed. And the sound cranked up and down, closer to us than before. "Run faster!" Nicolin called over it. The breaks in the road surface gave us no trouble at all. Rocks began clattering off the concrete behind us. "Keep the shovels," I heard Del exclaim. I picked up a good-sized rock by the road, relieved in a way that it was only scavengers after us. Nothing but fog behind me, fog and the howl, but rocks came out of the whiteness at a good rate. I threw my rock at a dark shape and ran after the others, chased by some howls that were at least animal, and could have been human. But over them was the blast, rising and falling and rising. "Henry!" Steve shouted. The others were down the embankment with him. I jumped down and traversed through weeds, behind the rest. "Get rocks," Nicolin ordered. We picked up rocks, then turned and threw them onto the freeway behind us all at once. We got screams for a reply. "We got one!" Nicolin said. But there was no way of knowing. We rolled onto the freeway and ran again. The screech lost ground on us, and eventually we were into San Mateo Valley, on the way to Basilone Ridge and our own valley. Behind us the noise continued, fainter with distance and the muffling fog.

"That must be a siren," Nicolin said. "What they call a siren. Noise machine. We'll have to ask Rafael." We threw the rocks we had left in the general direction of the sound, and jogged over the ridge into Onofre.

"Those dirty scavengers," Nicolin said, when we were onto the river path, and had caught our breath. "I wonder how they found us."

"Maybe they were out wandering, and stumbled across us," I suggested.

"Doesn't seem likely."

"No." But I couldn't think of a likelier explanation, and I didn't hear Steve offering one.

"I'm going home," Mando said, a touch of relief in his voice. He sounded odd somehow, and I felt a chill run down me.

"Okay, you do that. We'll get those wreckrats another time."

Five minutes later we were at the bridge. Gabby and Del went upriver. Steve and I stood in the fork of the path. He started to discuss the night, cursing the scavengers, the old man, and John Appleby alike, and it was clear his blood was high. He was ready to talk till dawn, but I was tired. I didn't have his stamina, and I was still shaken by that noise. Siren or no, it had sounded deadly inhuman. So I said good night to Steve and slipped in the door of my cabin. Pa's snoring broke rhythm, resumed. I tore a piece of bread from the next day's loaf and stuffed it down, tasting dirt. I dipped my hands in the wash bucket and wiped them off, but they still felt grimy, and they stank of the grave. I gave up and lay on my bed, feeling gritty, and was asleep before I even warmed up.

... 2

I was dreaming of the moment when we had started to fill in the open grave. Dirt clods were hitting the coffin with that terrible sound, *bonk bonk bonk;* but in the dream the sound was a knocking from inside the coffin, getting louder and more desperate the faster we filled in the hole.

Pa woke me in the middle of this nightmare: "They found a dead man washed up on the beach this morning."

"What?" I cried, and jumped out of bed. Pa backed off. I leaned over the wash bucket and splashed my face. "What's this you say?"

"I say, they found one of those Chinamen. You're all covered with dirt. What's with you? You out again last night?"

I nodded. "We're building a hideout."

Pa shook his head, baffled and disapproving.

"I'm hungry," I added, going for the loaf of bread. I took a cup from the shelf and dipped it in the water bucket.

"We don't have anything but bread left."

"I know." I pulled some chunks from the loaf. Kathryn's bread was good even when a bit stale. I went to the door and opened it, and the gloom of our windowless cabin was split by a wedge of sunlight. I stuck my head out into the air: dull sun, trees along the river sopping wet. Inside the light fell on Pa's sewing table, the old machine burnished by years of handling. Beside it was the stove, and over that, next to the stovepipe that punctured the roof, the utensil shelf. That, along with table, chairs, wardrobe, and beds, made up the whole of our belongings.

"You better get down to the boats," Pa said sternly. "It's late, they'll be putting out."

"Umph." Still swallowing bread, I put on shirt and shoes. "Good luck!" Pa called as I ran out the door.

Crossing the freeway I was stopped by Mando, coming the other way. "Did you hear about the Chinaman washed up?" he called.

"Yeah! Did you see him?"

"Yes. Pa went down to look at him, and I tagged along."

"Was he shot?"

"Oh yeah. Four bullet holes, right in the chest."

"Man." A lot of them washed up like that. "I wonder what they're fighting about so hard out there."

Mando shrugged. "Pa says there's a coast guard offshore, keeping people out."

"I know," I said. "I just wonder if that's it." Big ships ghosted up and down the long coast, usually out near the horizon, sometimes nearer; and bodies washed ashore from time to time, riddled with bullets. But that was the extent of what we could say for sure about the world offshore. When I thought about it my curiosity became so intense it shaded into something like fury. Mando, on the other hand, was confident that his father (who was only echoing the old man) had the explanation. He accompanied me out to the cliff. Out to sea a bar of white cloud lay on the horizon: the fog bank, which would roll in later when the onshore wind got going. Down on the river flat they were loading nets onto the boats. "I've got to get on board," I said to Mando.

By the time I had descended the cliff they were launching the boats. I joined Steve by the smallest of them, which was still on the sand. John Nicolin, Steve's father, walked by and glared at me. "You two take the rods today. You won't be good for anything else." I kept my face wooden. He walked on to growl a command at the boat shoving off.

"He knows we were out?"

"Yeah." Steve's lip curled. "I fell over a drying rack when I snuck in."

"Did you get in trouble?"

He turned his head to show me a bruise in front of his ear. "What do you think?" He was in no mood to talk, and I went to help the men hauling the next boat over the flat. The cold water sluicing my feet woke me up for the first time that day. The little boat's turn came and Steve and I hopped in as it was shoved into the channel. We rowed lazily, relying on the current, and got over the breakers at the rivermouth without any trouble.

Once all the boats were out around the buoy marking the main reef, it was business as usual. The three big boats started their circling, spreading the purse net; Steve and I rowed south, the other rod boats rowed north. At the south end of the valley there is a small inlet, nearly filled by a reef made of concrete. Between the concrete reef and the larger reef offshore is a channel, one used by faster fish when the nets are dropped; rod fishing usually gets results when the nets are being worked. Steve and I dropped our anchor onto the main reef, and let the swell carry us in over the channel, almost to the curved white segments of the concrete reef. Then it was out with the rods. I knotted the shiny metal bar that was my lure onto the line. "Casket handle," I said to Steve, holding it up before I threw it over. He didn't laugh. I let it sink to the bottom, then started the slow reel up.

We fished. Lure to the bottom, reel it back up; throw it in again. Occasionally the rods would arc down, and a few minutes of struggling ended with the gaff work. Then it was back to it. To the north the netters were pulling up nets silver with flopping fish; the boats tilted in under the weight until sometimes it seemed their keels would show. Inland the hills seemed to rise and fall, rise and fall. Under the cloud-filmed sun the forest was a rich green, the cliff and the bare hilltops dull and gray.

Five years before, when I was twelve and Pa had first hired me out to John Nicolin, fishing had been a big deal. I had been excited by everything about it—the fishing itself, the moods of the ocean, the teamwork of the men, the entrancing view of the land from the sea. But a lot of days on the water had passed since then, a lot of fish hauled over the gunwale: big fish and small, no fish or so many fish that we exhausted our arms and wore our hands ragged; over slow swells, or wind-blown chop, or on water flat as a plate; and under skies hot and clear, or in rain that made the hills a gray mirage, or when it was stormy, with clouds scudding overhead like horses . . . mostly days like this day, however, moderate swell, sun fighting high clouds, medium number of fish. There had been a thousand days like this one, it seemed, and the thrill was long gone. It was just work to me now.

In between catches I dozed, lulled by the swell, waking up when my rod jerked into my stomach. Then I reeled the fish in, gaffed it, pulled it over the side, smacked its head, got the lure out and tossed it over again, and went back to sleep.

"Henry!"

"Yeah!" I said, sitting up and checking my rod automatically.

"We got quite a few fish here."

I glanced at the bonita and rock bass in the boat. "About a dozen."

"Good fishing. Maybe I'll be able to get away this afternoon," Steve said wistfully.

I doubted it, but I didn't say anything. The sun was obscured, and the water was gray. The fog bank had started its roll in. "Looks like we'll spend it on shore," I said.

"Yeah. We've got to go up and see Barnard; I want to beat the shit out of that old liar."

"Sure."

Then we both hooked big ones, and we had a time of it keeping our lines clear. We were still working them when the blare of Rafael's bugle floated over the water from the netters. We whooped and got our fish aboard without delay, slapped our oars into the oarlocks and beat it back to Rafael's boat. They parceled some fish out to us and we rowed into the rivermouth.

We pulled the boat up onto the sand and took our fish over to the cleaning tables. Gulls soused us repeatedly, screeching and flapping. When the boat was empty and pulled up to the cliff, Steve approached his father.

"Can I go now, Pa?" Steve asked. "Hanker and I need to do our lessons with Tom." Which was true.

"Nope," old Nicolin said, bent over and still inspecting the net. "You're going to help us fix this net. And then you're going to help your ma and sisters clean fish."

At first John had made Steve go to learn to read from the old man, because he figured it was a sign of family prosperity and distinction. Then when Steve got to liking it (which took a long time), his father started keeping him from it. John straightened, looked at Steve; a bit shorter than his son, but a lot thicker; both of them with the same squarish jaw, brown shock of hair, light blue eyes, straight strong nose. . . . They glared at each other, John daring Steve to talk back to him with all the men wandering around. For a second I thought it was going to happen, that Steve was going to defy him and begin who knows what kind of bloody dispute. But Steve turned away and stalked over to the cleaning tables. After a short wait to allow his anger to lose its first bloom, I followed him.

"I'll go on up and tell the old man you're coming later."

"All right," Steve said, not looking at me. "I'll be there when I can."

Old Nicolin gave me three rock bass and I hauled them up the cliff in a net bag. A gang of kids splashed clothes in the water, and farther upstream several women stood around the ovens at the Marianis'. I took the fish to Pa, who jumped up from his sewing machine hungrily. "Oh good. I'll get to work on these, one for tonight, dry the others." I told him I was going to the old man's and he nodded. "Eat this right after dark, okay?"

"Okay," I said, and was off.

The old man's home is on the steep ridge marking the southern end of our valley, on a flat spot just bigger than his house, about halfway to the peak of the tallest hill around. There isn't a better view from any home in Onofre. When I got up there the house, a four-roomed wooden box with a fine front window, was empty. I made my way carefully through the junk surrounding the house. Among the honey flats, the telephone wire cutters, the sundials, the rubber tires, the rain barrels with their canvas collecting funnels, the generator parts, the broken engines, the grandfather clocks and gas stoves and crates full of who knows what, there were big pieces of broken glass, and several varmint traps that he was constantly moving about, so that it was smart to watch out. Over at Rafael's house, machines like those scattered across Tom's little yard would be fixed and in working order, or stripped for their parts, but here they were just conversation pieces. Why have an automobile engine propped on sawhorses, and how had he gotten it up the ridge, anyway? That was just what Tom wanted you to wonder.

I kept going up the eroded path that ran the edge of the ridge. Near the peak of the spine the path turned and dropped into the crease south of it, a narrow canyon too small to hold a permanent stream, but there was a spring. The eucalyptus trees kept the ground clear of underbrush, and on a gentle slope of the crease the old man kept his beehives, a score of small white wooden domes. I spotted him standing among them, draped in his beekeeping clothes and hat. He moved pretty spryly, for a man over a hundred years old. He was ambling from dome to dome, pulling out trays and fingering them with a gloved hand, talking all the while. Tom talked to everything: people, himself, dogs, trees, the sky, fish on his plate, rocks he stubbed a toe on; naturally he talked to his bees. He shoved a flat back into a hive and looked around, suddenly wary; then he caught sight of me and waved.

"Get away from the hives, boy, you'll get stung."

"They aren't stinging you."

He took off his hat and waved a bee back toward its hive. "They won't sting me, they know who's taking care of them." The long white hair over his ears streamed back in the wind, mixing in my sight with the clouds. The fog was rising, forming quick cloud streams. Tom rubbed his freckled pate. "Let's get out of the wind, Henry my boy. It's so cold the bees are acting like idiots. Perhaps you'd have some tea with me."

"Sure." Tom's tea was so strong it was almost like having a meal.

"Have you got your lesson ready?"

"You bet. Say, did you hear about the dead man washed up?"

"I went down to look at him. Washed up just north of the rivermouth. A Japanese, I'd venture. We buried him at the back of the graveyard with the rest of them."

"What do you think happened to him?"

"Someone shot him!" He cackled at my expression. "I guess he was trying to visit the United States of America. But the United States of America is *out of bounds*." He navigated his yard and I followed him closely. We went into the house. "Obviously someone has declared us out of bounds, we are *beyond the pale,* boy, only in this case the pale is rather dark, those ships steaming back and forth out there are so black you can see them even on a moonless night, rather stupid of them if they wanted them truly invisible. I haven't seen a foreigner—a live foreigner, that is—since the day. That's too long for coincidence. So where are they?—since they *are* out there." He filled the teapot. "It's my hypothesis that declaring us off limits was the only way to avoid fighting over us. But I've outlined this particular guess to you before, eh?"

I nodded.

"And yet I don't even know who we're talking about, when you get right down to it."

"The Chinese, right?"

"Or the Japanese."

"So you think they really are out there on Catalina just to keep folks away?"

"Well I know *someone's* on Catalina, someone not like us. That's one thing I *know*. I've seen the lights from up here at night, blinking all over the island. You've seen them."

"I sure have," I said. "It's beautiful."

"Yeah, that Avalon must be a bustling little port these days. No doubt something bigger on the backside. It's a blessing to know something for sure, Henry. Surprisingly few things you can say that about. Knowledge is like quicksilver." He walked over to the fireplace. "But someone is on Catalina."

"We should go over and see who."

He shook his head, looking out his big window at the fast onshore streamers. "We wouldn't come back."

Subdued, he threw some twigs on the coals of the banked fire, and we sat before the window in two of his armchairs, waiting for the water to heat. The sea was a patchcloth, dark grays and light grays, with silver buttons scattered in a crooked line between us and the sun. It looked like it was going to rain rather than fog up; old Nicolin would be mighty annoyed, because you can fish in the rain. Tom pulled at his face, making a new pattern in the ten thousand wrinkles lining it. "Whatever happened to summertime," he sang, "yes when the living was eee-sy." I threw some more twigs on the fire, humming the little tune I had heard so often. Tom had told a lot of stories about the old time, and he was insistent that in those days our coastline had been a treeless, waterless desert. But looking out the window at the forest and the billowing clouds, feeling the fire warm the chill air of the room, remembering our adventure of the night before, I wondered if I could believe him. Half of his stories I could not confirm in his books.

He threw one of his packets of tea into the pot. I remembered once at a swap meet, when he came running up to Steve and Kathryn and me, drunk and excited, blabbing, "Look what I bought, look what I got!"—pulling us under a torch to show us a tatty old half an encyclopedia, opened to a picture of a black sky over white ground, on which stood two completely white figures and an American flag. "That's the *moon*, see? I *told* you we went there, and you wouldn't believe me." "I still don't believe you," Steve said, and nearly busted laughing at the fit the old man threw. "I bought this picture for four jars of honey to *prove* it to you skeptics, and you still won't believe me?" "No!" Kathryn and I laughed at the two of them—we were pretty drunk too. But he kept the picture (though he threw away the encyclopedia), and later I saw the blue ball of the Earth in the black sky, as small as the moon is in our sky. I must have stared at that picture for an hour. So one of the least likely of his claims was apparently true; and I was inclined to believe the rest of them, usually.

"All right," Tom said, handing me my cup full of the pungent tea. "Let's hear it."

I cleared my mind to imagine the page of the book Tom had assigned me to learn. The regular lines of the poetry made them easy to memorize, and I spoke them out as my mind's eye read them:

> "'Is this the region, this the soil, the clime,'
>   Said then the lost Archangel, 'this the seat
> That we must change for Heaven?
>   —this mournful gloom
> For that celestial light?'"

I went on easily, having a good time playing the part of defiant Satan. Some of the lines were especially good for thundering out:

> "'Farewell, happy fields,
> Where joy forever dwells! Hail, horrors! Hail,
> Infernal world! and thou, profoundest Hell,
> Receive thy new possessor—one who brings
> A mind not to be changed by place or time.
> The mind is its own place, and in itself
> Can make a Heaven of Hell, a Hell of Heaven.
> What matter where, if I be still the same,
> And what I should be, all but less than he
> Whom thunder hath made greater? Here at least
> We shall be free—'"

"All right, that's enough of that one," Tom said, looking satisfied as he stared out to sea. "Best lines he ever wrote, and half of them stolen from Virgil. What about the other piece?"

I started again:

"This royal throne of kings, this sceptered isle,
This earth of majesty, this seat of Mars,
This other Eden, demi-paradise,
This fortress built by Nature for herself
Against infection and the hand of war,
This happy breed of men, this little world,
This precious stone set in a silver sea
Which serves it in the office of a wall,
Or as a moat defensive to a house,
Against the envy of less happier lands,
This blessed plot, this earth, this realm, this England—"

"Enough!" Tom cried, chuckling and shaking his head. "Or too much. I don't know what I think. But I sure give you good stuff to memorize."

"Yeah," I said. "You can see why Shakespeare thought England was the best state."

"Yes, he was a great American. Maybe the greatest."

"But what does moat mean?"

"Moat? Why, it means a channel of water surrounding a place to make it hard to get to. Couldn't you figure it out by context?"

"If I could've, would I have asked you?"

He cackled. "Why, I heard that one out at one of the little back country swap meets, just last year. Some farmer. 'We're going to put a moat around the granary,' he said. Made me a bit surprised. But you hear odd words like that all the time. I heard someone at the swap meet say they were going to cozen up to someone, and someone else told me my sales pitch was a filibuster. It's amazing, how words stay in the spoken language. Bad news for the stomach is good news for the tongue, know what I mean?"

"No."

"Well, I'm surprised at you." He stood up, stiff and slow, and refilled the teapot. After he got it set on the rack over the fire he went to one of his bookshelves. The inside of his house was a bit like the yard: more clocks, cracked china plates, a collection of lanterns and lamps; but most of two walls were taken up by bookshelves, overflowing with stacks of mangy books. Now he brought one over and tossed it in my lap. "Time for some sight reading. Start where I have the marker, there."

I opened the slim mildewed book and began to read, an act that still gave me great trouble, great pleasure. "'Justice is in itself powerless: what rules by nature is *force*. To draw this over to the side of justice, so that by means of force justice rules—that is the problem of statecraft, and it is certainly a hard one; how hard you will realize if you consider what boundless egoism reposes in almost every human breast; and that it is many millions of individuals so constituted who have to be kept within the bounds of peace, order and legality. This being so, it is a wonder the world is on the whole as peaceful and law-abiding as we see it to be'"—this caused the old man to laugh—"'which situation, however, is brought about only by the machinery of the state. For the only thing that can produce an immediate effect is physical force, since this is the only thing which men as they generally are understand and respect—'"

"*Hey!*"

It was Nicolin, busting into the house like Satan into God's bedroom. "I'm going to kill you right here and now!" he cried, advancing on the old man.

Tom jumped up with a whoop: "Let's see you try!" he shouted. "You don't stand a chance!"—and the two of them grappled a bit in the middle of the room, Steve holding the old man by the shoulders at just enough distance so that Tom's fierce blows missed him.

"Just what do you mean filling our heads with lies, you old son of a bitch?" Nicolin demanded, shaking Tom back and forth with genuine anger.

"And what do you mean busting into my house like that. Besides"—losing his pleasure in their usual sport—"when did I ever lie to you?"

Steve snorted. "When didn't you? Telling us they used to bury their dead in silver-lined caskets. Well now we know that one's a lie, because we went up to San Clemente last night and dug one up, and the only thing it had on it was plastic."

"What's this?" Tom looked at me. "You did what?"

So I told him about the gang's expedition into San Clemente. When I got to the part about the coffin handles he began to laugh; he sat down in his chair and laughed, heee, heeee, hee hee, all through the rest of it, including the part about the scavengers' siren attack.

Nicolin stood over him, glowering. "So now we know you're lying, see?"

"Heeeeeee, hee hee hee." A cough or two. "No lies at all, boys. Only the truth from Tom Barnard. Listen here—why do you think that plastic on that coffin was silver-colored?" Steve gave me a significant look. "Because it usually *was* silver, of course. You just dug up some poor guy who died broke. Now, what were you doing digging up graves for, anyway?"

"We wanted the silver," Steve said.

"Bad luck." He got up to get another cup, poured it full. "I tell you, most of them were buried wrapped in the stuff. Sit down here, Stephen, and have some tea." Steve pulled up a little wooden chair, sat down. Tom curled in his chair and wrapped his knobby hands around his cup. "The really rich ones were buried in gold," he said slowly, looking down at the steam rising from his cup. "One of them had a gold mask, carved to look just like him, put over his dead face. In his burial chamber were gold statues of his wife, and dogs, and kids—he had on gold shoes, too, and little mosaic pictures of the important events of his life, made of precious stones, surrounding him on each wall of the chamber. . . ."

"Ah, come on," Nicolin protested.

"I'm serious! That's what it was like. You've been up there, now, and seen the ruins—are you going to tell me they didn't throw silver in the ground with their dead?"

"But why?" I asked. "Why that gold mask and all?"

"Because they were Americans." He sipped his tea. "That was the least of it, let me tell you." He stared out the window for a while. "Rain coming." After another minute's silent sipping: "What do you want silver so bad for, anyway?"

I let Nicolin answer that one, because it was his idea.

"To trade for things," Steve said. "To get what we want at the swap meets. To be able to go somewhere, down the coast maybe, and have something to trade for food." He glanced at the old man, who was watching him closely. "To be able to travel like you used to."

Tom ignored that. "You can get everything you want by trading what you make. Fish, in your case."

"But you can't go anywhere! You can't travel with fish on your back."

"You can't travel anyway. They blasted every important bridge in the country, from the looks of it. And if you did manage to get somewhere, the locals would take your silver and kill you, like as not. Or if they were just, you'd still run out of silver eventually, and you'd have to go to work where you were. Digging shit ditches or something."

The fire crackled as we sat there and watched it. Nicolin let out a long sigh, looking stubborn. The old man sipped his tea and went on. "We travel to the swap meet in three days, if the weather allows. That's farther than we used to travel, let me tell you. And we're meeting more new people than ever."

"Including scavengers," I said.

"You don't want to get in a feud with those young scavengers," Tom said.

"We already are," Steve replied.

Now it was Tom's turn to let out a sigh. "There's been too much of that already. So few people alive these days, there's no reason for it."

"They started it."

Big drops of rain hit the window. I watched them run down the glass, and wished my home had a window. Even with the door closed and dark clouds filling the sky, all the books and crockery and lanterns and even the walls gleamed silvery gray, as if they all contained a light of their own.

"I don't want you fighting at the swap meet," Tom said.

Steve shook his head. "We won't if we don't have to."

Tom frowned and changed the subject. "You got your lesson memorized?"

Steve shook his head. "I've had to work too much. I'm sorry."

After a bit I said, "You know what it looks like to me?"

"What what looks like," Tom asked.

"The coastline here. It looks like one time there was nothing but hills and valleys, all the way out to the horizon. Then one day some giant drew a straight line down it all, and everything west of the line fell down and the ocean came rushing in. Where the line crossed a hill there's a cliff, and where it crossed a valley there's a marsh and a beach. But always a straight line, see? The hills don't stick out into the ocean, and water doesn't come and fill in the valleys."

"That's a faultline," Tom said dreamily, eyes closed as if he were consulting books in his head. "The earth's surface is made up of big plates that are slowly sliding around. Truth! *Very* slowly—in your lifetime it might move an inch—in mine two, hee hee—and we're next to a fault where the plates meet. The Pacific plate is sliding north, and the land here south. That's why you get the straight line there. And earthquakes—you've felt them—those are the two plates slipping, grinding against each other. One time in the old time, there was an earthquake that shattered every city on this coast. Buildings fell like they did on the day. Fires burned and there was no water to put them out. Freeways like that one down there pointed at the sky, and no one could get in to help, at first. For a lot of people it was the end. But when the fires were burned out . . . they came from everywhere. They brought in giant machines and material, and they used the rubble that was all that was left of the cities. A month later every one of those cities was built back up again, just as they had been before, so exactly that you couldn't even tell there had been an earthquake."

"Ah come on," said Steve.

The old man shrugged. "That's what it was like."

We sat and looked through the slant-lines of water at the valley below. Black brooms of rain swept the whitecapped sea. Despite the years of work done in the valley, despite the square fields by the river, and the little bridge over it, despite the rooftops here and there, wood or tile or telephone wire—despite all of that, it was the freeway that was the main sign that humans lived in the valley . . . the freeway, cracked and dead and half silted over and worthless. The huge strips of concrete changed from whitish to wet gray as we watched. Many was the time when we had sat in Tom's house drinking tea and looking at it, Steve and me and Mando and Kathryn and Kristen, during our lessons or sitting out one shower or another, and many was the time that the old man had told us tales of America, pointing down at the freeway and describing the cars, until I could almost see them flashing back and forth, big metal machines of every color and shape flying along, weaving in and out amongst each other and missing dreadful crashes by an inch as they hurried to do business in San Diego or Los Angeles, red and white headlights glaring off the wet concrete and winking out over the hill, plumes of spray spiraling back and enveloping the cars following so that no one could see properly, and Death sat in every passenger seat, waiting for mistakes—so Tom would tell it, until it would actually seem strange to me to look down and see the road so empty.

But today Tom just sat there, letting out long breaths, looking over at Steve now and then and shaking his head. Sipping his tea in silence. It made me feel low; I wished he would tell another story. I would have to walk home in the rain, and Pa would have made the fire too small and our cabin would be chill, and long after our meal of bread and fish was done, I'd have to hunch over the coals to get warm, in the drafty dark. . . . Below us the freeway lay like a road of giants, gray in the wet green of the forest, and I wondered if cars would drive over it ever again.

...3

Swap meets brought out most of the people in Onofre, to get the caravan ready to go. A score of us stood on the freeway at the takeoff point on Basilone Ridge, some piling fish onto boat trailers, some still running down to the valley and back again with forgotten stuff, others yelling at the dogs, who were for once useful, as they pulled the trailers. Mostly we took fish to the swap meet—nine or ten trailers of them, fresh and dried—and my task was to help Rafael and Steve and Doc and Gabby to load the racks. Fish were slapping and dogs were yapping, and Steve was giving orders right and left to everyone but Kathryn, who would have kicked him, and overhead a flock of gulls screeched at us as they realized they weren't going to get a meal. It drove the dogs wild. It all reached a final pitch of yelling and we were off.

On the coast the sky was the color of sour milk, but as we turned off the freeway and moved inland up San Mateo Valley, the one just north of ours, the sun began to break through here and there, and splashes of sunlight made the hills blaze green. Our caravan stretched out as the road got thinner—it was an ancient asphalt thing, starred by potholes that we had filled with stones to make our travel easier.

Steve and Kathryn walked at the end of the line of trailers, arms around each other. Sitting on a trailer end, I watched them. I had known Kathryn Mariani for most of my life, and for most of my life I had been scared of her. The Marianis lived next to Pa and me, so I saw her all the time. She was the oldest of five girls, and when I was younger it seemed like she was always bossing us around, or giving someone a quick slap for trying to snatch bread. And she was big, too—after felling me with a kick of her heavy boot, as she had done more than once, her freckled ugly glare had inspected me from what seemed a tremendous height. I thought then that she was the meanest girl alive. It was only in the previous couple of years, when I grew as tall as her, that I got to the vantage point where I could see she was pretty. A snub nose doesn't look so good from below, nor a big wide mouth—but from level on she looked good. And the year before she and Steve had become lovers, so that the other girls snickered and wondered how long it would be before they had to get married. Steve was a lot happier on these trips, with his family left behind. When the dogs yelped he jogged up and tussled with them till they were grinning and simpering and slobbering over him again, ready to haul all day for the fun of it, because of the way Steve was laughing.

We made the swap meet about midday. The site was a grassy-floored meadow, filled with well-spaced eucalyptus and ironwood trees. When we got there the sun was out, more than half the attending villages were already there, and in the dappled light under the trees were colored canopies and flags, trailers and car bodies and long tables, scores of people in their finest clothes, and plumes of woodsmoke, breaking through the trees from a number of camp-fires. The dogs went wild.

We wound our way through the crowd to our campsite. After we said hello to the cowmen from Talega Canyon who camped next to us, I helped Rafael put up awnings over the fish trailers. The old man, staring raptly at the white canopy over the cowmen, pointed to it and said to Steve and me, "You know in the old time people used to string those things from their backs, and jump out of airplanes thousands of feet up. They floated all the way to the ground under them."

"Celebrating the meet a bit early, eh Tom?"

The dogs were a nuisance and we took them to the back of our site and tied them to trees. By the time we got back to the front of our camp the trading had already begun. We were the only seaside town at this meet, so we were popular. "Onofre's here," I heard someone calling. "Look at this abalone," someone else said, "I'm going to eat mine right now!" Rafael sang out his call: "Pescados. Pescados." Even the scavengers from Laguna came over to trade with us; they couldn't do their own fishing even with the ocean slapping them in the face. "I don't want your dimes, lady," Doc insisted. "I want boots, boots, and I know you've got them." "Take my dimes and buy the boots from someone else; I'm out today. Blue Book says one dime, one fish." Doc grumbled and made the sale. After moving the campfire wood off a trailer, I was done with my work for the day. Sometimes I had clothes to trade: I got them all tattered and torn from the scavengers, and then sold them whole again after Pa had sewn them up. But this time he hadn't patched a thing, because we hadn't had anything to trade for old clothes last month. So the day was mine, though I would keep an eye out for wrecked coats—and see them, too, but on people's backs. I walked to the front of our camp and sat down in the sun, on the edge of the main promenade. One woman in a long purple dress balanced a crate of chickens on her head as she walked by; she was trailed by two men in matching yellow and red striped pants, and blue long-sleeved shirts. Another woman wore a rainbow-stained pair of pants so stiff they had a crease fore and aft.

It wasn't just the clothes that distinguished the scavengers. They all talked loudly, all the time. Perhaps they did it to overcome the silence of the ruins. Tom often said that living in the ruins made the scavengers mad, and quite a few of them passing me had a look in their eye that made me think he was right—a wild look, as if they were searching for something to do that they couldn't quite find. I watched the younger ones closely, wondering if they were the ones who had run us out of San Clemente. We had had small fights with a group of them before, at the swap meets and in San Mateo Valley, where rocks had flown like bombs—but I didn't see any of the members of that crowd. A pair of them walked by dressed in pure white suits, with white hats to match. I had to grin. My blue jeans had had their knees patched countless times. All the folks from new towns and villages wore the same sort of thing, back country clothes kept together by needle and prayer, sometimes new things made up of scraps of cloth, or hides; wearing them was like having a badge saying you were healthy and normal. I suppose the scavengers' clothes were another sort of badge, saying that they were rich, and dangerous.

Then I saw Melissa Shanks walking out of our camp, carrying a basket of crabs. I hopped up without a thought and approached her. "Melissa!" I said, and gave her a fool's grin. "Want some help bringing back what you get for those pinchers?"

She raised her eyebrows. "What if I was out to get a pack of needles?"

"Well, um, I guess you wouldn't need much help."

"True. But lucky for you I'm out in search of a barrel half, so I'd be happy to have you along."

"Oh good." Melissa spent some time working at the ovens; she was a friend of Kathryn's younger sister Kristen. Other than the times I'd seen her at the ovens, I didn't know her. Her father, Addison Shanks, lived on Basilone Hill, and they didn't have much to do with the rest of the valley. "You'll be lucky to get a half cask for that many crabs," I went on, looking in her basket.

"I know. The Blue Book says it's possible, but I'll have to do some fast talking." She tossed back her long black hair confidently, and it gleamed in the sun, so glossy it seemed she wore jewelry. She was pretty: small teeth, a narrow nose, fine white skin. She had a whole series of careful, serious, haughty expressions, and that made her rare smiles all the sweeter. I stared at her too long, and bumped into an old woman going the other way.

"Carajo!"

"Sorry, mam, but I was made distract by this young maiden—"

"Well get a grip!"

"Indeed I'll try mam, goodbye," and took Melissa's arm in hand and we talked cheerily as we toured the meet on the main promenade, looking for a cooper. We eventually made for the Trabuco Canyon camp, agreeing that the farmers there were good woodworkers. A plume of smoke rose from their camp, floating through wedged sunbeams that turned the smoke seashell pink.

We smelled meat; they were roasting a steer half. A good crowd had gathered in their camp to join the feast. Melissa and I traded one of the crabs for a pair of ribs, and ate them standing, observing the antics of a slick trio of scavengers, who wanted six ribs for a box of safety pins. I was about to make a joke about them when I remembered Melissa's father. Addison did a lot of trading by night, to the north, and no one was sure how much he traded with scavengers, how much he stole from them, how much he worked for them. He was sort of a scavenger himself. I chewed the beef in silence, aware all of a sudden that I didn't know the girl at my side very well. She gnawed her rib clean as a dog's bone, looking at the sizzling meat over the fire. She sighed. "That was good, but I don't see any barrels. I guess we should look in the scavenger camps."

I agreed, although that would mean a tougher trade. We walked over to the north half of the park, where the scavengers stayed—keeping a clear route back home, perhaps. The camps and goods for trade were much different here: no food, except for several women guarding trays of spices and canned delicacies. We passed a man dressed in a shiny blue suit, trading tools that were spread out over a blanket on the grass. Some of the tools were rusty, others brighter than silver, each a different shape and size. We tried to guess what this or that tool had been for. One that gave us the giggles was two pairs of greenish metal clamps at each end of a wire in a tube of orange plastic. "That was to hold together husbands and wives who didn't get along," Melissa said.

"Nah, they'd need something stronger than those. They're probably a doorstop."

She crowed. "A *what?*" But she wouldn't let me explain. We walked on, past large displays of bright clothing and shiny shoes, and big rusty machines that were no use without electricity, and gun men with their crowd of spectators, on hand to watch the occasional big trade or demonstration shot. The seed exchange, on the border between the scavengers' camps and ours, was hopping as usual. Suddenly Melissa tugged on my arm. "There!" she said. Beyond the seed exchange was a woman in a scarlet dress, selling chairs, tables, and barrels.

"There you are," I said. I caught sight of Tom Barnard across the promenade. "I'm going to see what Tom's up to while you start your dealing."

"Good. I'll try the poor and innocent routine until you get there."

"Good luck." She didn't look all that innocent. I walked over to Tom, who was deep in discussion with another tool trader. When I stopped at his side he clapped a hand on my shoulder and went on talking.

"—industrial wastes, rotting wood, animal bodies, sometimes—"

"Bullshit," said the tool trader. ("That too," the old man got in.) "They made it from sugar cane and sugar beets; it says so right on the boxes. And sugar stays good forever, and it tastes just as good as your honey."

"There are no such things as sugar cane and sugar beets," Tom said scornfully. "You ever seen one of either? There are no such plants. Sugar companies made them up. Meanwhile they made their sugar out of sludge, and you'll pay for it with no end of dreadful diseases and deformities. But honey! Honey'll keep away colds and all ailments of the lungs, it'll get rid of gout and bad breath, it tastes ten times better than sugar, it'll help you live as long as me, and it's new and natural, not some sixty-year-old synthetic junk. Here, taste some of this, take a fingerful, I've been turning the whole meet on to it, no obligation in a fingerful."

The tool man dipped two fingers in the jar the old man held before him, and licked the honey off them.

"Yeah, it tastes good—"

"You bet it does! Now one God damned little lighter, of which you've got thousands up in O.C., is surely not much for two, twooooo jars of this delicious honey. Especially . . ." Tom cracked his palm against the side of his head to loosen the hinges of his memory. "Especially when you get the jars, too."

"The jars too, you say."

"Yes, I know it's generous of me, but you know how we Onofreans are, we'd give our pants away if people didn't mind our bare asses hanging out, besides I'm senile almost—"

"Okay, okay! You can shut up now, it's a deal. Give them over."

"All *right*, here they are young man," handing the jars to him. "You'll live to be as old as me eating this magic elixir, I swear."

"I'll pass on that if you don't mind," the scavenger said with a laugh. "But it'll taste good." He took the lighter, clear plastic with a metal cap, and gave it to the old man.

"See you again, now," Tom said, pocketing the lighter eagerly and pulling me away with him. Under the next tree he stopped. "See that, Henry? See that? A lighter for two little jars of honey? Was that a trade? Here, watch this. Could you believe my dealing? Watch this." He pulled out the lighter and held it before my face, pulled his thumb down the side. He let the flame stand for a second, then shut it off.

"That's nice," I said. "But you've already got a lighter."

He put his wrinkled face close to mine. "*Always* get these things when you see them, Henry. Always. They're about the most valuable thing the scavengers have to trade. They are the greatest invention of American technology." He rooted in his pack. "Here, have a drink." He offered me a small bottle of amber liquid.

"You've been to the liquor traders already?"

He grinned his gap-toothed grin. "First place I went to, of course. Have a drink of that. Hundred-year-old Scotch. Really fine."

I took a swallow, gasped.

"Take another, now, that first one just opens the gates. Feel that warmth down there?"

I traded swallows with him and pointed out Melissa, who looked like she wasn't making much headway with the barrel woman. "Ahh," said Tom, leering significantly. "Too bad she ain't dealing with a man."

I agreed. "Say, can I borrow a jar of honey from you? I'll work it off in the hives."

"Well, I don't know . . ."

"Ah come on, what else are you going to trade for today?"

"Lots of stuff," he protested.

"You already have the most important thing the scavengers own, right?"

"Oh, all right. I'll give you the little one. Have another drink before you go."

I got back to Melissa with my stomach burning and my head spinning. Melissa was saying slowly, like for the fourth time, "We just pulled them out of the live pen this morning. That's the way we always do it, everyone knows that. They all eat our crab and no one's got sick yet. The meat's good for a week if you keep it cool. It's the tastiest meat there is, as you know if you've ever eaten any."

"I've eaten it," the woman snapped. "But I'm sorry. Crab is good all right, but there's never enough of it to make a difference. These barrel halves are hard to find. You'd have it forever, and I'd get a few tastes of crab for a week."

"But if you don't sell them you're going to have to cart them back north," I interrupted in a friendly way. "Pushing them up all those hills and then making sure they don't roll down the other side . . . why we'd be doing you a favor to take one of them off your hands for free!—not that we want to do that, of course. Here—we'll throw in a jar of Barnard honey with these delicious pinchers, and really make it a steal for you." Melissa had been glaring at me for butting in on her deal, but now she smiled hopefully at the woman. The woman stared at the honey jar, but looked unconvinced.

"Blue Book says a barrel half is worth ten dollars," I said. "And these sidewalks are worth two dollars apiece. We've got seven of them, so you're already out-trading us four dollars' worth, not counting the honey."

"Everyone knows the Blue Book is full of shit," the woman said.

"Since when? It was scavengers made it up."

"Was not—it was you grubs did."

"Well, whoever made it up, everyone uses it, and they only call it shit when they're trying to deal someone dirty."

The woman hesitated. "Blue Book really says crabs are two dollars each?"

"You bet," I said, hoping there wasn't a copy nearby.

"Well," said the woman, "I do like the way that meat tastes."

Rolling the barrel half back to our camp, Melissa forgot about my rudeness. "Oh Henry," she sang, "how can I thank you?"

"Ah," I said, "no need." I stopped the barrel to let pass a quartet of shepherds with a giant table upside-down on their heads. Melissa wrapped her arms around me and gave me a good kiss. We stood there looking at each other before starting up again; her cheeks were flushed, her body warm against mine. As we started walking again she smacked her lips. "You been drinking, Henry?"

"Ah—old Barnard gave me a few sips back there."

"Oh yeah?" She looked over her shoulder. "Wouldn't mind some of that myself."

Back at camp Melissa went off to meet Kristen and I helped the end of the fish trading. Nicolin came by with a cigarette and we smoked it. Soon after that a fight started between a Pendleton cowboy and a scavenger, broken up by a crowd of big angry men whose job was keeping things peaceful. These meet sheriffs didn't like their authority ignored, and people fighting were always going to lose, slapped around hard by this gang. After that I nodded off for an hour or two, back with the sleeping dogs.

Rafael woke me when he came back to feed scraps to the perros. Only the western sky was still blue. I walked over to our fire, where a few people were still eating. I crouched beside Kathryn and ate some of the stew she offered me. "Where's Steve?"

"He's already in the scavenger camps. He said he'd be in the Mission Viejo one for the next hour or two."

"Ah," I said, wolfing down stew. "How come you aren't with him?"

"Well, Hanker, you know how it is. First of all, I had to stay here and help cook. But even if I could've gone, I can't keep up with Steve for an entire night. You know what that's like. I mean I could do it, but I wouldn't have any fun. Besides I think he likes being away from me at these things."

"Nah."

She shrugged. "I'm going to go hunt him down in a bit."

"How'd it go at the seed exchange?"

"Pretty good. Not like in the spring, but I did get a good packet of barley seed. That was a coup—everyone's interested in this barley 'cause it's doing so well in Talega, so the trading was hot, but our good elote did the trick. I'm going to plant that whole upper field with this stuff next week, and see how it does. I hope it's not too late."

"Your crew'll be busy."

"They're always busy."

"True." I finished the stew. "I guess I'll go look for Steve."

"Just go for the biggest noise. I'll see you over there."

Among the new town camps on the south side of the park it was dark and quiet, except for the eerie, piercing cries of the Trabuco peacocks, protesting their cages. Small fires here and there made the trees above them flicker and dance.

In the northern half of the park it was different. Bonfires roared in three clearings, making the colored awnings flap in the branches. Lanterns cast a mean white glare. I walked over to the Mission Viejo camp. A jar flew past me, spilling liquid and smashing against a tree. The bright colors of scavenged clothing wavered in the firelight, and every scavenger, man, woman and child, had gotten out their full collection of jewelry; they wore gold and silver necklaces, earrings, and wrist bracelets, all studded with gems. They were beautiful.

The Viejo camp had tables set end to end in long rows. The benches lining them were jammed with people drinking and talking and listening to the band at one end of the camp. I stood and looked, not seeing anyone I knew. Then Nicolin struck me in the arm, said, "Let's go hassle the old man, see he's over with Doc and the rest of the antiques."

Tom was set up at the end table with a few other survivors from the old time: Doc Costa, Leonard Sarowitz from Hemet, and George something from Cristianitos. The four of them were a familiar sight at swap meets, and were often joined by Odd Roger and other survivors old enough to remember what the old time was like. Tom was the senior member of this group by a long shot. He saw us and made a spot on the bench beside him. We had a drink from Leonard's jar; I gagged and sent half my swallow down my shirt. This put the four ancients in hysterics. Old Leonard's gums were as clear of teeth as a babe's.

"Is Fergie here?" Doc asked George, getting back to their conversation.

George shook his head. "He went west."

"Ah. Too bad."

"You know how fast this boy is?" Tom said, slapping me on the shoulder. Leonard shook his head, frowning. "Once I threw him a pitch and he hit a line drive past my ear—I turned around and saw the ball hit him in the ass as he slid into second."

The others laughed, but Leonard shook his head again. "Don't you distract me! You're trying to distract me!"

"What do you mean?"

"The point is—I was just telling him this, boys, and you should hear it too—the point is, if Eliot had fought back like an *American,* we wouldn't be in this fix right now."

"What fix is that?" Tom asked. "I'm doing okay as far as I can tell."

"Don't be facetious," Doc put in.

"Back at it again, I see," Steve observed, rolling his eyes and going for the jar.

"Why, I don't doubt we would be the strongest nation on Earth again, by God," Leonard went on.

"Now wait a second," Tom said. "There aren't enough Americans left alive to add up to a nation at all, much less the strongest on Earth. And what good would it do if we had blown the rest of the world into the same fix?"

Doc was so outraged he cut Leonard off and answered for him: "What good would it do?" he said. "It would mean there wouldn't be any God damned Chinese boating off the coast, watching us all the time and *bombing* every attempt we make to rebuild! That's what good it would do. That coward Eliot put America in a hole for good. We're the bottom of the world now, Tom Barnard, we're bears in the pit."

"Raarrrr," Steve growled, and took another drink. I took the next one.

"We were goners as soon as the bombs went off," Tom said. "Makes no difference what happened to the rest of the world. If Eliot had decided to push the button, that just would've killed more people and wrecked more countries. It wouldn't have done a thing for us. Besides, it wasn't the Russians or the Chinese that planted the bombs—"

"You don't think," Doc said.

"You know it wasn't! It was the God damned South Africans."

"The French!" George cried. "It was the French!"

"It was the Vietnamese," Leonard said.

"No it wasn't," Tom replied. "That poor country didn't even own a firecracker when we were done with it. And Eliot probably wasn't the man who decided not to retaliate, either. He probably died in the first moments of the day, like everyone else. It was some general in a plane who made the decision, you can bet your wooden teeth. And quite a surprise it must have been, too, even to him. Especially to him. Makes me wonder who he was."

Doc said, "Whoever it was, he was a coward and a traitor."

"He was a decent human being," said Tom. "If we had struck back at Russia and China, we'd be criminals and murderers. Anyway if we had done that the Russians would've sent their whole stockpile over here to answer ours, and then there wouldn't be a single *ant* left alive on North America today."

"Ants would still be alive," George said. Steve and I bent our heads to the table, giggling and pushing our fingers in each others' sides—"pushing the button," as the old men said. Tom was giving us a mean look, so we straightened up and drank some more to calm ourselves.

"—over five thousand nuclear blasts and survived," Doc was saying. Every meet the number went up. "We could have taken a few more. Our enemies deserved a few of them too, that's all I'm saying." Even though they had this argument every time they joined the other antiques, almost, Doc was still getting angry at Tom. Bitterly he cried, "If Eliot had pushed the button we'd all be in the same boat, and then we'd have a chance to rebuild. They won't let us rebuild, God damn it!"

"We are rebuilding, Ernest," Tom said jovially, trying to put the fun back in their argument. He waved at the surrounding scene.

"Get serious," Doc said. "I mean back to the way we were."

"I wouldn't want that," said Tom. "They'd likely blow us up again."

Leonard, however, was only listening to Doc: "We'd be in a race with the Communists to rebuild, and you know who would win that one. We would!"

"Yeah!" said George. "Or maybe the French. . . ."

Barnard just shook his head and grabbed the jar from Steve, who gave him a struggle for it. "As a doctor you should never wish such destruction on others, Ernest."

"As a doctor I know best what they did to us, and where they're keeping us," Doc replied fiercely. "We're bears in the pit."

"Let's get out of here," Steve said to me. "They're going to start deciding whether we belong to the Russians or the Chinese."

"Or the French," I said, and we slithered off the bench. I took a last gulp of the old man's liquor and he whacked me. "Out of here, you ungrateful wretches," he cried. "Not willing to listen to history without poking fun."

"We'll read the books," Steve said. "They don't get drunk."

"Listen to him," said Tom, as his cronies laughed. "I taught him to read, and he calls me a drunk."

"No wonder they're so mixed up, with you teaching them to read," Leonard said. "You sure you got the books turned right way up?"

We wandered off and made our way with some stumbling to the orange tree. This was a giant old oak, one of a half dozen or so in the park, that held in its branches gas lanterns wrapped in transparent orange plastic. It was the mark of the scavengers from central Orange County, and our gang used it as the meeting place later at night. We didn't see anyone from Onofre, so we sat on the grass and made ribald comments on the passing crowd. Steve waved down a man selling jars of liquor and gave him two dimes for a jar of tequila. "Jars back without a crack, else we put the crack in your back," the man intoned as he moved on. On the other side of the orange tree a small bike-powered generator was humming and crackling; a group of scavengers was using it to operate a small instant oven, cooking slabs of meat or whole potatoes in seconds. "Heat it and eat it," they cried. "See the miracle microwave! Heat it and eat it!" I took a sip of the tequila; it was strong stuff, but I was drunk enough to want to get drunker. "I am *drunk*," I told Steve. "I am *borracho*. I am *aplastaaaa-do*."

"Yes you are," Steve said. "Look at that silver." He pointed at one of the scavenger women's heavy necklaces. "Look at it!" He took a long swallow. "Hanker, these people are rich. Don't you think they could do just about anything they pleased? Go anywhere they pleased? Be anything they pleased? We've got to get some of that silver. Somehow we've got to. Life isn't just grunging for food in the same spot day after day, Henry. That's how animals live. But we're human beings, Hanker, that's what we are and don't you forget it, and Onofre ain't big enough for us, we can't live our whole lives in that valley like cows chewing cud. Give me another swallow of that, Hanker."

"The mind is its own place," I said as I gave him the jar. Neither of us needed any more, but when Gabby and Rebel and Kathryn and Kristen showed up, we were quick to help drink another jar. Steve forgot about silver for a while in favor of a kiss; Kathryn's red hair covered the sight. The band started again, a trumpet, a clarinet, two saxes, a drum and a bass fiddle, and we sang along with the tunes: "Waltzing Matilda," or "Oh Susannah," or "I've Just Seen a Face." Melissa showed up and sat down beside me. She'd been drinking and smoking. I put an arm around her, and over her shoulder Kathryn winked at me. More and more people crowded around the orange tree as the band heated up, and soon we couldn't see anything but legs. We played a game of guessing what town people were from by their legs alone, and then we danced around the tree with the rest of the crowd.

Much later we started our return to camp. I felt great. We staggered on the promenade, holding each other up and singing "High Hopes" all out of tune with the fading sound of the band. Halfway home we collided with a group coming out of the trees, and I was roughly shoved to the ground. "Chinga," I said, and scrambled up. There were shouts and scufflings, a few others hit the ground and rolled back up swinging and shouting angrily. "What the—" The two groups separated and stood facing each other belligerently; by the light of a distant lantern we saw that it was the gang from San Clemente, decked out in identical red and white striped shirts.

"Oh," said Nicolin, voice dripping with disgust, "it's them."

One of the leaders of their gang stepped into a shaft of light and grinned unpleasantly. His earlobes were all torn up from having on earrings in fights, but that hadn't stopped him; he still had two gold earrings in his left ear, and two silver ones in his right. "Little people shouldn't come into Clemente at night," he said.

"What's Clemente?" Nicolin asked casually. "Nothing north of us but ruins."

"Little people might get scared. They might hear a sound," and the guys behind him began to hum a rising tone, "uhnnnnnn-eeeeeehhhhhhh," the sound of the siren we had heard that night. When they stopped their leader said, "We don't like people like you in our town. Next time you won't get away so easy."

Nicolin cracked his crazy smile. "Found any good dead bodies to eat lately?"

he asked. With a rush they were on him, and Gabby and I had to come up on each side of him swinging hard to keep him from being surrounded, although with his heavy boots he was doing quite well on their kneecaps. As the fight broke out in earnest he started shouting happily "Vultures! Buzzards! Zopilotes!" and I had to look sharp because there were more of them than there were of us, and they seemed to have rings on every finger—

The sheriffs barged into us bellowing "What's this? Stop this—HEY!" I found myself on the dirt again, as did most of us. I started the laborious process of standing. "You kids get the fuck out of here," one of the sheriffs said. He was shaped like a barrel and was a foot taller than Steve, whom he held by the shirt. "We'll ban you from swap meets forever if we have to break up these fights again. Get out of here before we cave your faces in to make you think about it."

We rejoined the girls—Kristen and Rebel had been in the midst of the tussle, but the rest had stayed back—and trooped down the promenade. Behind us the Clemente gang started up the siren sound, "uhnnnnnnnnnnnneeeeeeee . . ."

"Damn!" Nicolin said, wrapping an arm around Kathryn. "We were going to pound those guys, too."

"They had you two to one," Kathryn pointed out.

"Oh Katie, don't you know that's just the way we wanted it?" We all agreed we had had them in a tight spot, and walked back to camp in a fine humor. Melissa found me and slipped under my arm. As we approached the camp she slowed down and we fell behind the others. Sensing something to this, I steered us off the promenade into the grove. I stopped and leaned back against a laurel.

"You looked good fighting," she said, and then we were kissing. After some long kisses she sort of let her weight go on me, and I slid down the tree with her, scraping my back on the bark. Once on the leaves I laid half on top, half beside her, a leg between hers, an awkward position, but it was making my blood pound. We were kissing without pause and I could feel her breathing fast. I tried to get my hand down her pants but couldn't get it far enough, so I pushed it up under her shirt and held her breast. She bit my neck and a jolt ran down that whole side of my body.

She pulled back. "Ohh," she sighed, "Henry. I told my dad I'd be right back. He'll start looking for me if I don't get back there pretty soon." She made a pout that I could just see in the dark, and I laughed and kissed it.

"That's okay. Some other time." I was too drunk to feel balked; five minutes before I hadn't been expecting anything like this, and it was easy to slip back to that. Anything was easy. I helped her to her feet and took a piece of bark out of my back. And laughed.

I walked Melissa into camp and with a final quick kiss left her near her father's set-up. I went back out in the grove to take a leak. Off through the treetrunks I could still see the scavengers' camps, bouncing in the firelight, and faintly I could hear a group of them singing "America the Beautiful." I sang along under my breath, a perfect harmony part that only I could hear, and the old tune filled my heart.

Back on the promenade I saw the old man, talking with two strangers dressed in dark coats. Tom was asking them questions. Wondering who they were I stumbled back to my sleeping spot. I laid down, head spinning, and looked up at black branches against the sky, every pine needle clear as an ink stroke. I figured I'd be out in a second. But when I settled down there was a noise; someone was crushing leaves over and over again, *crick, crick, crick, crick* . . . from where Steve slept. I started listening and before long I heard breathing. Kathryn's hums. My hard-on was back; I wasn't going to be able to fall asleep. After a minute's listening I felt strange, and got up and went out to the front of the camp, where the fire was a warm mass of coals. I sat watching them shift from gray to orange with every breath of wind, feeling horny and envious and drunk and happy.

All of a sudden the old man crashed into camp, looking drunker than I by a good deal. His scruff of hair flew around his head like smoke. He saw me and squatted by the fire. "Hank," he said, his voice uncommonly excited. "I've been talking with two men who were looking for me."

"I saw you out there with them. Who were they?"

He looked at me, his bloodshot eyes gleaming with reflected firelight. "They were from San Diego. And they came here—they talked to Recovery Simpson and followed us to the meet, to talk with me, ain't that nice—word gets around, you know, who a village elder is. Anyway . . ."

"The men."

"Yes! These men say they got from San Diego to Onofre *by train*."

We sat there staring at each other over the fire, and some little flames popped up. Light danced on his wild eyes. "They came by train."

... 4

A few days after the meet, Pa and I woke to the sound of a hard rain drumming on the roof. We ate a loaf of bread and made a big fire, and sat down to needle clothes, but the rain fisted the roof harder and harder, and when we looked out the door we could scarcely see the big eucalyptus. It looked like the ocean had decided to jump up and wash us down to it, and the young crops would be the first to go. Plants, stakes, the soil itself; they'd all be ripped away.

"Looks like we'll be putting the tarps down," Pa said.

"No doubt." We got out our rain gear and paced around the dark room. In a sheeting downpour we heard Rafael's bugle over the roar of the rain. We put on our gear and rushed out, and were drenched in seconds. "Whoo!" Pa cried, and ran for the bridge, splashing through puddles. At the bridge a few people were huddled under ponchos, waiting for the tarps to arrive. We went to the bathhouse beside the river path, now a little creek bordering the foaming brown river, dodging groups trundling along with one of the long tarps. At the bathhouse shed the Mendezes, Mando, Doc, and Steve and Kathryn were hauling out tarps and lifting them onto the shoulders of whoever was there. I jumped under the end of a roll and followed it off, spurred by Kathryn's sharp voice. It rained on us like the world was under a waterfall.

We helped run three tarps over the bridge and out to the fields, and then it was time to get them down. Mando and I got on one end of a roll—loosely rolled plastic it was, once clear, now opaque with mud. Gabby and Kristen were on the other end, and the four of us maneuvered it into position at the downhill end of some rows of cabbage. We unrolled it one lift at a time, grunting and shouting directions at each other, walking up the furrows ankle deep in water. The field sloped ahead of us black and lumpy. Gray pools of water bounced under the rain's onslaught where the grading was wrong. When we got to the end of the roll the ground between the cabbages was covered. Below us people were unfurling other tarps: the Hamishes, the Eggloffs, Manuel Reyes and the rest of Kathryn's farm crew, plus Rafael and Steve. Beyond them the river churned, a brown flood studded with an occasional tree stump. Thinner clouds rushed over and for a moment the light changed, so that everything glowed through the streaky veils of rain. Then just as suddenly it was twilight again.

The old man was at the bottom of the field helping to position the rest of the tarps, striding about under his shoulder umbrella, a plastic thing held over his head by two poles strapped to his back. I laughed and felt the rain in my mouth: "Now why can't he just wear a hat like everyone else?"

"That's just it," Mando said, hands clamped in his armpits for warmth. "He doesn't want to be like everyone else."

"He's already managed that."

Gabby and Kristen joined us at the bottom. Gabby had fallen and was completely covered with mud. We got another roll and began pulling it uphill. Wind hit the trees on the hill above and their branches bobbed as if the hillside were a big animal struggling under the storm, going *whoooo, whoooo,* and making the valley seem vast. Water poured down the tarps that were already laid. The drainage ditch at the bottom of the fields was overflowing, but it all spilled into the river anyway.

Tom came over to greet us. His sheltered face was as wet as anyone's. "Hello Gabriel, Henry. And Armando, Kristen. Kathryn says she needs help with the corn." The four of us hurried up the riverbank to the cornfields. Kathryn was at their foot, running around getting groups together, booting reluctant rolls uphill, pointing out slack in the tarps already tied down. She was as black with mud as Gabby. She shouted instructions at us, and hearing that shrill tone in her voice we ran.

The shoots of corn were about two hands high, and we couldn't just lay the tarps right on them without breaking them. There were cement blocks every few yards, therefore, and the tarps had to be tied down to these through grommet holes. So the blocks had to be perfectly placed to match the holes. I saw that Steve and John Nicolin were working together, heaving blocks and tying knots. Everyone out there was dripping black. Kathryn had sent us to the upper end of the field, and when we got there we found her two youngest sisters and Doc and Carmen Eggloff, struggling with one of the narrowest tarps. "Hey Dad, let's get this thing rolling," Mando said as we approached them.

"Go to it," Doc replied wearily. We got them to continue unrolling, while we tied the sides of the tarp down to the blocks. It took a lot of slipping around in the mud to get them right. Finally we got that tarp down, and hurried to start on another one.

Gusts of wind grabbed at the plastic and tore it away from my cold fingers. It hurt to hold on as hard as I had to. Tying the knots got almost impossible. Thicker clouds flowed over, and it got darker. The spread tarps shone. Kneeling in the muck, I looked up for a moment to see a field dotted with black figures, crouched or crawling or miserably bowed over, backs to the wind.

By the time we got our third tarp down, most of the cornfields were covered. We sloshed around our last tarp and down to the riverbank and Kathryn. The river took a torrey pine past us, tumbling in the flood with its needles still green, its roots white and naked.

Almost the whole crew had gathered by the drowned drainage channel: twenty of us or more, watching the Mendezes and Nicolins run around the tarps and crawl under them, tightening and letting slack. A few people made for the bathhouse; the rest of us stood around describing the unrolling to each other. The fields were now glistening, ridged plastic surfaces, and the rain hitting the tarps leaped back into the air, a score of droplets jumping up from each raindrop that fell. Sheets of water poured off the lower ends of the tarps into the drainage ditch, free of mud and our summer crops.

We trooped over the bridge to the bathhouse. Inside the big main room Rafael had been hard at work; it was already hot, and the baths were steaming. He was congratulated on his fire, "a nice controlled indoor bonfire," as Steve said. As I stripped my wet clothes off I admired for the hundredth time the complicated system of pipes and holding tanks and pumps that Rafael had constructed to heat the bath water. By the time I got in the dirt bath it was crowded. The dirt bath was the hotter of the two, and the air filled with the delighted moans and groans of scalded bathers. I couldn't feel my feet, but the rest of me burned. Then the heat penetrated the skin of my feet and they felt like one of Pa's pin cushions. I hooted loudly. The sheet metal of the bath bottom was hot to the touch, and most of us floated, bumping and splashing and discussing the storm.

The clean bath had wooden seats anchored in it, and soon folks hopped over and gathered around those. The boom of the rain on the corrugated metal roof washed over the chatter now and then. Some of the group had gone out to help spread the tarps before their own gardens were covered, and they had to put their clammy clothes back on (unless they kept spares at the bathhouse) and leave, promising that they would hurry back. We believed them.

The firelight cast dancing shadows of the pipe system across the roof, and the plank walls glowed the color of the fire. Everyone's skin was ruddy. The women were beautiful: Carmen Eggloff putting branches on the fire, the ribs of her back sticking out; the girls diving like seals around one of the seats; Kathryn standing before me to talk, thick and rounded, beads of water gleaming on her freckled skin; Mrs. Nicolin squealing as John splashed her in a rare display of playfulness. I sat in my usual corner listening to Kathryn and looking around contentedly: we were a room of fire-skinned animals, wet and steaming, crazy-maned, beautiful as horses.

Most of us were getting out, and Carmen was handing around her collection of towels, when a voice called from outside.

"*Hello there!* Hello in there!"

Talk stopped. In the silence (roof drumming) we heard it clearer: "Hello in there, I say! Greetings to you! We're travelers from the south! Americans!"

Automatically the women, and most of the men, went for their towels or clothes. I yanked on my cold muddy pants, and followed Steve to the door. Tom and Nat Eggloff were already there; Rafael joined us still naked, holding a pistol in his hand. John Nicolin bulled his way through us, still pulling up his shorts, and pushed out the door.

"What brings you here?" we heard him ask. The answer was inaudible. A second passed, and Rafael opened the door again. Two men wearing ponchos entered before John; they looked surprised to see Rafael. They were drenched, weary and bedraggled. One was a skinny man with a long nose and a black beard that was no more than a thin strip around his jaw. The other was short and stocky, wearing a soaked floppy hat. They took their ponchos off, revealing dark coats and wet pants. The shorter man saw Tom and said "Hello there. We met at the swap meet, remember?"

Tom said "Yes." The two visitors shook hands with all the men there. Without showing it much they looked around the room. All the women were dressed, or wrapped in towels, leaving a room filled with a fire, and steaming baths, and several naked men gleaming like fish among those of us with some cloth on. The shorter man did a sort of bow. "Thanks for taking us in. We're from San Diego, as Mr. Barnard here will tell you."

We stared at them.

"Did you get here by train?" Tom asked.

Both men nodded. "We brought the cars within five miles of here," he said. "We left our crew there and walked the rest of the way. We didn't want to work on the tracks closer to you until we talked with you about it."

"We thought we'd get here sooner," the shorter one said, "but the storm slowed us."

"Why'd you hike in a storm in the first place?" John Nicolin asked.

After some hesitation the short one said, "We prefer to hike under cloud cover. Can't be seen from above, then."

John tilted his head and squinted, not getting it.

"If you want to jump in that hot water," Tom said, "go right ahead."

Shaking his head the taller one said, "Thank you, but . . ." They looked at each other.

"Looks warm," the short one observed.

"True," the other said, nodding a few times. He was still shivering. He looked around at us shyly, then said to Tom, "Perhaps we'll just warm up by your fire, if that's all right. It's been a wet walk, and I'd like to get dry."

"Sure, sure. Do what you like."

John led the two men over to the fire, and Carmen threw on more wood. Steve nudged me. "Did you hear that? A train to San Diego? We can get a ride down there!"

"I guess we might," I replied. The men were introducing themselves: the taller one was Lee, the short one Jennings. Jennings took off his cap, revealing straggly blond hair, then removed his poncho, coat, shirt, boots, and socks. He laid his clothes over the drying racks and stood with his hands stretched out to the fire.

"We've been working on the rails north of Oceanside for a few weeks now," he told us. "The Mayor of San Diego has organized a bunch of work forces of various sorts, and our job is to establish better travel routes to the surrounding towns."

"Is it true that San Diego has a population of two thousand?" Tom asked. "I heard that at a swap meet."

"About that." Jennings nodded. "And since the Mayor began organizing things, we've accomplished a good deal. The settlements are scattered, but we have a train system between them now. All handcars, you understand, although we do have generators at home. There's a weekly swap meet, and a fishing fleet, and a militia. Naturally Lee and I are proudest of the exploration team. Why, we cleared highway eight all the way across the mountains to the Salton Sea, and shifted the train tracks onto it."

"The Salton Sea must be huge now," Tom said.

Lee nodded. "It's fresh water now, and filled with fish. People out there are doing pretty good."

"What brings you up here?" John Nicolin asked bluntly.

While Lee stared at John, Jennings looked around at his audience. Every face in the room was watching him closely. He appeared to like that. "Well, we had the rails going up to Oceanside," he explained, "and the ruined tracks extended north of that, so we decided to repair them."

"Why?" John persisted.

Jennings cocked his head to match the angle of John's. "Why? I guess you'd have to ask the Mayor that one. It was his idea. You see"—he glanced at Lee, as if getting permission to speak further—"you're all aware that the Japanese are guarding us on the west coast here?"

"Of course," John said.

"You could hardly miss that," Rafael added. He had put his pistol away, and was sitting on the edge of the bath.

"But I don't mean from just the ships offshore," Jennings said. "I mean from the sky. From satellites."

"You mean cameras?" Tom said.

"Sure. You've all seen the satellites?"

We had. Tom had pointed them out, swiftly moving points of light that were like stars cut loose. And he had told us that there were cameras in them, too. But—

"Those satellites carry cameras that can see things no bigger than a rat," said Jennings. "They really got the eye on us."

"You could look up and say 'go to hell!' and they'd read your lips," Lee added with a humorless laugh.

"That's right," Jennings said. "And at night they have heat sensitive cameras that could pick up something as small as this roof, if you had the fire in here lit on a rainless night."

People were shaking their heads in disbelief, but Tom and Rafael looked as if they believed it, and as people noticed this there were some angry comments made. "I *told* you," Doc said to Tom. Nat and Gabby and a couple others stared at the roof in dismay. To think we were being watched that closely . . . it was terrible, somehow.

Strangers are good for news, they say, but these two were really something. I wondered if Tom had known about this all along, and had never bothered to tell us, or if he had been ignorant of it too. From his look I guessed he might have known. I wasn't sure that such surveillance made any difference, but it felt awful, like a permanent trespass. At the same time it was fascinating. John looked to Tom for confirmation, and after a slight nod from him John said, "How do you know that? And what does that have to do with your coming this way, again?"

"We've learned some things from Catalina," Jennings said. "But that's not the end of it. Apparently the Japs' policy includes keeping our communities isolated. They don't want reunification on any scale whatsoever. When we put the tracks on highway eight we built some big bridges. One night around sunset, wham. They blew them up."

"What?" Tom cried.

"They don't do it in any big way," Jennings said. Lee snorted to hear this. "It's true. Always at dusk—a red streak out of the sky, and *thunk*, it's gone. No explosions."

"Burnt up?" Tom asked.

Lee nodded. "Tremendous heat. The tracks melt, the wood incinerates. Sometimes things around will catch fire, but usually not."

"We don't camp near our bridges much." Jennings cackled, but no one laughed with him. "Anyway, when the Mayor found out about this, he got mad.

He wanted to complete the tracks, no matter the bombings. Communications with other Americans is a God-given right! he said. Since they got the upper hand for the time being, and will bomb us when they see us, we'll just have to see to it that they don't see us."

"We work light," Lee said with sudden enthusiasm. "Most of the old pilings are still there for river bridges, and we just put beams across those and lay the rails across the beams. The handcars are light and don't need much support. After we've crossed we take the rails and beams across with us and hide them under trees, and there's no sign we've crossed. A few times for practice and we get so we can cross the easier rivers in a couple of hours."

The fact that these two men were struggling with the Japanese, even indirectly, silenced everyone in the room. John pursued his question: "And now that you've managed to get up here, what might your mayor want with us?"

Lee was eyeing John sharper and sharper, but Jennings replied in a perfectly friendly way: "Why, to say hello, I reckon. To show that we can get to each other quick if we need to. And he was hoping we could convince you to send one of your valley's officials to come down and talk about trade agreements and such. And then there's the matter of extending the tracks farther north—we'd need your permission and cooperation to do that, of course. The Mayor is mighty anxious to establish tracks up to the Los Angeles basin."

"The scavengers in Orange County would be a problem there," Rafael said.

"Our valley doesn't have *officials*," John said belligerently.

"Someone to speak for the rest of you, then," Jennings said mildly.

"The Mayor wants to talk about these scavengers, too," said Lee. "I take it you folks don't have much use for them?" No one answered. "We don't fancy them either. Appears they are helping the Japs."

Steve had been nudging me so often that my ribs were sore; now he almost busted them. "Did you hear that?" he said in a fierce whisper. "So that's where they get their silver!" Kathryn and I shushed him so we could hear the rest of the discussion.

Then the roof went silent. Those who wanted to go home found that Lee and Jennings planned to stay for a day or two, so several people gathered their ponchos and boots and left. Tom invited the San Diegans to stay up at his place, and they accepted. Pa came over to me.

"Is it okay with you if we go home and eat now?"

It looked like the talking was over, so I said, "Let's do it."

There was a sense of confusion to our departure. The strangers had told us so much we had never learned even at the swap meets that it filled us, and even finding dry clothes became difficult. After all the projects Lee and Jennings had listed the bathhouse didn't seem like much anymore. Pa and I got back into our wet clothes, as we had none to spare for the bathhouse, and we hurried home.

By the time we got there it was drizzling again. We got the fire going good and sat in our beds as we ate our dried fish and tortillas, gabbing about the San Diegans and their train. I fell asleep thinking of bridges made of nothing but train tracks.

The next morning I was fishing drowned greens out of our garden when I caught sight of Kathryn walking down the path, holding a bunch of scraggly young corn stalks in her hand. She'd been rolling up the tarps, and had a look at the damages. I could tell she was mad by the way she walked. The Mendezes' dog ran out barking playfully at her and she swung a foot at it with a curse. The dog yelped and ran back to its garden. Kathryn stood in the path cursing, and then kicked the base of the big eucalyptus with her heavy boot, *thump*.

Tom appeared from the other direction. "Henry!" he called. I waved to him as he approached.

He stood looking down at me with a twinkle in his eye. "Henry, what would you say to a trip to San Diego?"

"What?" I cried. "Sure, you bet! What?"

He laughed and sat down on the barrel half in our yard. "I was talking with John and Rafe and Carmen and the San Diegans last night, and we decided I'd go down there and talk with this Mayor of theirs. I want to take someone along, and the older men will all be working. So I thought you might not mind."

"Wouldn't mind!" I stalked around him. "Wouldn't mind!"

"I figured not. And we can make some sort of deal with your pa."

"Oh yeah?" Pa said as he came around the corner carrying two buckets of water. "What's this all about?"

"Well, Sky," Tom said, "I want to hire out your boy for a trip."

Pa put down the buckets and pulled his moustache while Tom told him about it. They wrangled over the value of a week of my work, both agreeing it wasn't much, until they'd worked out an agreement whereby Tom rented my services for whatever it took him to get a sewing machine that Pa had seen at the swap meet. "Even if the machine doesn't work, right?"

"Right," Pa said. "I want Rafe to strip it for parts, mostly."

And Tom was to deal with John Nicolin concerning my absence from the fishing.

"Hey!" I said. "You got to ask Steve to come too."

Tom looked at me. Fingering his beard, he said, "Yes. I suppose I do."

"Ha," said Pa.

"Aye. I don't know what John will say, but you're right, if I ask you I have to ask Steve. We'll see what happens."

I ran to the cliffs, singing San Diego, Sandy Dandy-ay-go. On the beach I shut up, and spent the afternoon fishing as usual. When we were back ashore I said to John, "Tom would like to talk with you about the train men, sir."

"Tell him to come by tonight," John said. "Come eat a meal with us. You come too."

"Thank you," I said. With a mysterious wink at Steve I was off up the cliff. I ran the river path home, splashing every puddle. To San Diego! To San Diego by train!

... 5

Late that afternoon the old man and I walked down the river path to the Nicolins'. The valley cupped us like a green bowl, tilted to spill us into the sea. The air smelled of wet earth and wet trees. Overhead crows cawed and dipped and lazily flapped their ways home. Above them there wasn't a cloud in the sky, just that pure dome of early evening blue. Naturally we were in high spirits. We skipped over puddles, cracked jokes. "I'm starved," the old man declared. "I haven't eaten a thing since you told me we were invited."

"But that was only a couple hours ago!"

"Sure, but I passed on tea."

We turned off the river path and climbed the trail leading to the Nicolins' house. Once over the freeway we could see it through the trees.

It was the biggest house in the valley, set on a fine patch of cleared land just behind the highest part of the beach cliff. The yard around the house had been planted with canyon grass, and the two-story, tile-roofed building stood on its green lawn like something from the old time. There were shutters bracketing glass windows, big eaves over the doors, and a brick chimney. Smoke lofted from this chimney, and lamps glowed in the windows. Tom and I gave each other a look and went to the door.

Before we got there Mrs. Nicolin threw it open, crying, "It's a mess in here but you'll just have to ignore it, come in."

"Thanks, Christy," Tom said. "The house may be a mess, but you're looking fine as always."

"Oh you liar," Mrs. Nicolin said, pulling back a loose strand of her thick black hair. But Tom was telling the truth; Christy Nicolin had a beautiful face, strong and kind, and she was tall and rangy, even after bearing seven kids. Steve took a lot of his features from her rather than from John: his height, his sharp-edged nose and jaw, his mouth. Now she waved us in the door past her, shaking her head at the ceiling to show us, as she always did, that her day had been too harried to be described or imagined. "They're cleaning up, they say. They've been building a butterchurn all afternoon, and right in my dining room."

Their house had a dozen or more rooms, but only the dining room had a giant set of windows facing west, so despite Mrs. Nicolin's protests it got used for everything that needed good light. All of the rooms we passed had fine furniture in them, beds and tables and chairs that John and Teddy, Steve's twelve-year-old brother, had built in imitation of old time stuff. To me the whole house looked like something out of books, and when I said that to Tom he agreed, saying it was more like houses used to be than any he'd ever seen: "Except they didn't have fireplaces in the kitchen, nor wooden walls and floors and ceilings in every single room."

When we got to the dining room the kids ran out of it yelling. Mrs. Nicolin sighed and led us in. John and Teddy were sweeping up splinters and chunks of wood. Tom and John shook hands, something they wouldn't do unless one was visiting the other at home. Through the big west windows we had a good view out to sea. Sunlight slanted in and lit the bottom of the east wall. I went to the kitchen and found Steve just outside it. He was out back, cleaning the inside of the new churn.

"What's up?" he asked.

I told him, as I couldn't think of any way to avoid it. "Jennings and Lee asked Tom if he would go back with them to talk to that mayor. Tom's going, and he wants to take us along!"

Steve let the churn fall to the grass. "Take us along? You and me?" He leaped over the churn, wiggled his arms in his victory shimmy dance. Suddenly he stopped and examined me. "How long will we be gone?"

"About a week, Tom says."

His eyes narrowed, and his wide mobile mouth became straight and tight. "What's the matter?"

"I just hope he'll let me go, that's all. Damn it! I'll just go anyway, no matter what he says." He picked up the churn again, and thumped the last chips out of it.

Soon Mrs. Nicolin called us all into the dining room, and got us seated around the big oak table: John and her at the head, her grandmother Marie, who was ninety-five and simple, Tom, Steve and Teddy and Emilia, who was thirteen, and very quiet and shy; then me, and then the kids, Virginia and Joe the twins, and Carol and Judith, the babies of the family, back around the table next to Mrs. N. John lit the lamps, and faint reflections of us all sprang to in the big west window.

Emilia and Mrs. N. brought out plate after plate, until the tabletop was nearly invisible under them. Tom and I kicked each other under the table. One plate was covered, and when John took off its top steam puffed up, fragrant with the smell of chicken bubbling in a red sauce. There was a cabbage salad in a large wooden bowl, and soup in a porcelain tureen. There were plates of bread and tortillas, and plates covered with sliced tomatoes and eggs. There were jugs of goat's milk and water.

All of the smells made me drunk, and I said, "Mrs. N. this is a feast, a banquet."

The Nicolins laughed at me, and Tom said, "He's right, Christy. The Irish would sing songs about this one." We passed the plates around following Mrs. Nicolin's orders, and when our plates were piled high we started eating, and it was quiet for a time, except for the clink of cutlery. Soon enough Marie wanted to talk to Tom, for she just picked at her food. Tom bolted his so quickly that he had time to talk between bites. Marie was pleased to see Tom, who was one of the few people outside the family she regularly recognized. "Thomas," she piped loudly, "seen any good movies lately?"

Virginia and Joe giggled. Tom leaned over and spoke directly into Marie's ear: "Not lately, Marie." Marie blinked wisely and nodded.

"But Tom, Gran's wrong, Gran's wrong, there aren't no movies—"

"Aren't *any* movies," Mrs. N. said automatically.

"Aren't any movies."

"Well, Virginia—" Tom gobbled down some of the fish soup. "Here, try this."

"Yooks, no!"

"Marie was talking about the old time."

"She gets the old time mixed up with now."

"Yes, that's true."

"What?" Marie cried, sensing the talk concerned her.

"Nothing, Marie," Tom said in her ear.

"Why does she do that, Tom?"

"Virginia," Mrs. N. warned.

"It's okay, Christy. You see, Virginia, that's an easy thing for us old folks to do, mixing things up like that. I do it all the time."

"You do not, but why?"

"We've got so much old time in our heads, you see. It crowds into the now and we mix it up." He swallowed some more chicken, licking the sauce out of his moustache luxuriously. "Here, try this; chicken's a special treat cooked in this wonderful way your mother cooks it."

"Yooks, no."

"Virginia."

"Maw-ummmmmmm."

"Eat your food," John growled, looking up from his plate. I saw Steve wince a little. He hadn't said a word since we came inside, even when his mother talked directly at him. It made me a little apprehensive, but to tell the truth I was distracted by the food. There were so many different flavors, aromas, textures; each forkful of food had a different taste to it. I was getting full, but I couldn't stop. John began to slow down, and talked to no one in particular about the warm current that had hit the coast with the previous day's rain. Tom was still tossing it down, and Virginia said "No one's going to steal your plate, Tom," and the kids laughed. "Have some more chicken," Mrs. N. urged me, "have more milk." "Twist my arm," I replied. Little Carol started to cry, and Emilia got up to sit by her and spoon some soup into her mouth, or try to. It was getting pretty noisy, and Marie noticed and cried, "Turn on the tee vee!" which she knew would get her a laugh. Meanwhile Steve continued to eat silently, and I saw John notice it.

Over the remains of the meal we talked and nibbled equally. When Carol was calmed Emilia got up and started taking out dishes to the kitchen. "It's your night too," Mrs. N. reminded Steve. Without a word he got up and carried plates away. When the table was almost cleared they brought out berries and another jug of milk. Tom kicked me, and flapped his eyebrows like wings. "Looks wonderful, Christy," he said piously.

After we had feasted on berries and milk the kids were allowed to take Gran and scamper off, and John and Mrs. N., Steve and Emilia and Tom and I sat back in our chairs, shifting them around to face the window. John got a bottle of brandy from a cabinet, and we contemplated our reflections as we sipped. We made a funny picture. Steve wasn't talking tonight, and Emilia never talked, so the conversation was left to Tom and John, mostly, with an occasional word from Mrs. N. or me. John speculated some more about the current. "Seems warm currents bring colder clouds. Cold rain, and sometimes snow, when the water is forty degrees warmer than that. Now why should that be?"

None of us ventured a theory. Mrs. N. began to knit, and Emilia wordlessly moved over to hold the yarn. Suddenly John knocked back the rest of his brandy.

"So what do you think these southerners want?" he asked Tom.

The old man sipped his brandy. "I don't know, John. I guess I'll find out when I go down there."

"Maybe they just want to see something new," Steve said darkly.

"Maybe," Tom replied. "Or it could be they want to see what they can do. Or trade with us, or go farther north. I don't know. They're not saying, at least not up here they're not saying. That's why I want to go down there and talk to this mayor."

John shook his head. "I'm still not sure you should go."

The corners of Steve's mouth went white. Tom said casually, "Can't do any harm, and in fact we need to do it, to know what's going on. Speaking of that, I'll need to take a couple people along with me, and I figure the young ones are easiest spared, so I wondered if Steve could be one of them. He's the kind I need along—"

"Steve?" John glared at the old man. "No." He glanced at Steve, looked back at Tom. "No, he's needed here, you know that."

"You could spare me for a week," Steve burst out. "I'm not needed here all that much. I'd work double time when I got back, please—"

"*No,*" John said in his on-the-water voice. In the next room the sounds of the kids playing abruptly died. Steve had stood up, and now he jerked toward his father, who was still leaning back in his chair; Steve's hands were balled into fists, and his face was twisted up. "Steve," Mrs. Nicolin said quietly. John shifted in his chair to better stare up at Steve.

"By the time you get back the warm current will be gone. I need you here now. Fishing is your job, and it's the most important job in this valley. You can go south some other time, in the winter maybe when we aren't going out."

"I can pay someone to fill in for me," Steve said desperately. But John just shook his head, the grim set of his mouth shifting to an angry down-curve. I shrank in my chair. So often it came to this between them; they got right to the breaking point so fast that it seemed certain they would snap through one day. For a moment I was sure of it; Steve's hands clenched, John was ready to launch himself. . . . But once again Steve deferred. He turned on his heel and ran out the dining room. We heard the kitchen door slam.

Mrs. Nicolin got up and refilled John's glass. "Are you sure we couldn't get Addison Shanks to fill in for the week?"

"No, Christy. His work is here, he's got to learn that. People depend on that." He glanced at Tom, drank deeply, said in an annoyed voice, "You know I need him here, Tom. What are you doing coming down here and giving him ideas like that?"

Tom said mildly, "I thought you might be able to spare him."

"No," John said for the last time, putting his bulk into it. "I'm not gaming out there, Tom—"

"I know that." Tom sipped his brandy. I imitated Emilia and pretended I wasn't there, staring at the portrait of us all on the black glass of the window. We were a pretty unhappy looking group. Steve was long gone, on the beach, I figured. I thought about how he felt at that moment, and the fine meal in my stomach turned lumpy. Mrs. Nicolin, face tight with distress, tried to refill our glasses. I shook my head, and Tom covered his glass with his hand.

He said, "Well, I guess Hank and I'll get going, then." We stood. "Wonderful meal, Christy. Thanks, John. I'm sorry I brought all that up."

John grunted and waved a hand, lost in his thoughts. We all stood looking at him, a big man brooding in his chair, staring at his own colorless image, surrounded by all his goods and possessions. "No matter," he said, as if releasing us. "I can see what caused you to do it. Come tell me what it's like down there when you get back."

"We will." Tom thanked Mrs. N. again and we backed out the door. She followed us out. On the doorstep she said, "You should have known, Tom."

"I know. Good night, Christy."

We walked up the river path full of food, glum and heavy-footed. Tom muttered under his breath and took swings at branches near the path. "Should've known . . . nothing else possible . . . impossible to change . . . set like a wedge. . . ." He raised his voice. "History is a wedge in a crack, boy, and we're the wood. We're the wood right under the thin edge of the wedge, you understand, boy?"

"No."

"Ah . . ." He started muttering again, sounding disgusted.

"I do understand that John Nicolin is a mean old son of a bitch—"

"Quiet," Tom snapped. "A wedge in a crack," he went on. Suddenly he stopped and grabbed my arm, swung me around violently. "See over there?" he cried, pointing across the river at the other bank.

"Yeah," I protested, peering into the dark.

"Right there. The Nicolins had just moved here, just John and Christy and John Junior and Steve. Steve was just a babe, John Junior about six. They came in from the back country. One day John was helping with the first bridge, in the start of winter. John Junior was playing on the bank, on an overhang, and the overhang fell in the river." His voice was harsh. "Fell *plop* right in the river, you understand? River full of the night's rain. Right in front of John. He dove in and swam downstream all the way out into the sea. Swam nearly an hour, and never saw the kid at all. Never saw him again. Understand?"

"Yeah," I said, uneasy at the strain in his voice. We started walking again. "That still doesn't mean he needs Steve for fishing, because he surely doesn't—"

"Shut up," he said. After a few steps he said quietly, as if talking to himself, "And then we went through that winter like rats. We ate anything we could find."

"I've heard about those times," I said, irritated that he kept going back to the past. That was all we heard about: the God-damned past. The explanation for everything that happened. A man could behave like a tyrant to his son, and what was his excuse? History.

"That doesn't mean you know what it was like," he told me, irritated himself. Watching him in the dark I saw the marks of the past on him: the scars, the caved-in side of his face where he had no teeth left, his bent back. He reminded me of one of the trees high on the hills above us, gnarled by the constant onshore

winds, riven by lightning. "Boy, we were hungry. People died because we didn't
have food enough in the winters. Here was this valley soaked with rain and
growing trees like weeds, and we couldn't grow enough food from it to stay
alive. All we could do was hunker down in the snow—snow here, damn it—and
eat every little hibernating creature we could find. We were just like wolves, no
better. You won't know times like those. We didn't even know what day of the
year it was! It took Rafe and me four years to figure out what the date was." He
paused to collect himself and remember his point. "Anyway, we could see the
fish in the river, and we did our best to get them into the fire. Got some rods and
lines and hooks out of Orange County, tackle from fishing stores that should
have been good stuff." He snorted, spat at the river. "Fishing with that stupid
sport gear that broke every third fish, broke every time you used it . . . it was a
damned shame. John Nicolin saw that and he started asking questions. Why
weren't we using nets? No nets, we said. Why weren't we fishing the ocean? No
boats, we said. He looked at us like we were fools. Some of us got mad and said
how are we going to find nets? Where?

"Well, Nicolin had the answer. He went up into Clemente and looked, for
God's sake." He laughed, a quick shout of delight. "He found some commercial fishing warehouses. The third one we walked into was a warehouse full of
nets. Steel cables, heavy nylon—it was great. And that was just the start. We
found the boatyards in Orange County and we hauled their boats right down
the freeway."

"What about the scavengers?"

"There weren't many scavengers then, and there wasn't much fight in the
ones that were there."

Now there I knew he was lying. He was leaving himself out of the story, as
he always did. Almost everything I knew of Tom's history I had heard from
someone else. And I had a lot of stories about him; as the oldest man in the
valley, legends naturally collected around him. I had heard how he had led
those foraging raids into Orange County, guiding John Nicolin and the others
through his old neighborhoods and beyond. He had been death on scavengers in those days, they said. If ever they were hard pressed by scavengers Tom
had disappeared into the ruins, and pretty soon there weren't any scavengers
around to bother them. It was Tom, in fact, who introduced Rafael to guns.
And the tales of Tom's endurance—why, they were so numerous and outlandish that I didn't know what to think. He must have done some of those things
to get such a reputation, but which ones? Had he gone for a week without sleep
during the forced march from Riverside, or eaten the bark from trees when
they were holed up in Tustin, surrounded? Or walked through fire and held his
breath under water for a half hour? Whatever he had done, I was sure he had
run ragged every man in the valley, old as he was. I had heard Rafael declare

that the old man must have been radiated on the day, and mutated so that he was destined never to die, like the wandering Jew.

"Anyway," Tom was saying to me now, "John Nicolin did or directed everything that had to do with fishing, and doing it was what brought the people in this valley together. The second winter after he arrived was the first one no one died from hunger. Boy, you don't know what that means. There's been hard times since, but none to match those before Nicolin arrived. I admire him. So if he's got fish on the brain, if he won't let his son leave it for a week or even a day, then that's too bad. That's the way he is."

"But it doesn't matter how well fed he is, if he makes his son hate him."

"That's not his intention. I know he doesn't intend that. Remember John Junior. Could be, even if John himself doesn't know it, he just wants to keep Steve where he can see him. To try and keep him safe. So that even the fishing is just a cover. I don't know."

I shook my head. It still wasn't fair. A wedge in a crack. I understood a little better what Tom meant, but it seemed to me then that we were the wedges, stuck so far in history that we couldn't move but one way when we were struck by events. How I wished we could be clear and free to move where we would!

We had walked to my home. Firelight shone through the cracks around the door. "Steve'll make it another time," said Tom. "But us—we'll be off to San Diego on the next cloudy night."

"Yeah." Right then I couldn't rouse much enthusiasm for it. Tom hit my shoulder and was off through the trees.

"Be ready!" he called as he disappeared in the forest gloom.

The next cloudy night didn't come for a while. For once the warm current brought clear skies with it, and I spent my evenings impatiently cursing the stars. During the days I kept fishing. Steve was ordered by John to stay on the net boats, so off in my rowboat I wasn't faced with him hour after hour, but I did feel lonesome, and odd—as if I was betraying him. When we did work together, unloading fish or rolling nets, he just talked fishing, not meeting my eye, and I couldn't find anything to say. I felt tremendously relieved when three days after the dinner he laughed and said, "Just when you don't want clear days they come blaring down. Come on, let's use this one for what it was meant to be used for." Fishing was done, and with the hours of day left we walked out the wide beach to the rivermouth, where waves were slowly changing from blue lines to white lines. Gabby and Mando and Del joined us with the fins, and we waded out over the coarse tan sand of the shallows into the break. The water was as warm as it ever got. We took a fin each and swam out through the soup to the clear water outside the waves' breaking point. Out there the water was like blue glass; I could see the sand on the bottom. It was a pleasure just to tread water out there, to let the swells wash over my head and to look back at the tan cliffs and the green forest, edged by the sky and the ocean under my chin. I drifted back in and rode the waves with the others, happy they didn't resent me, too much, for getting the chance to go to San Diego.

When we got back on the beach, the others said goodbye to me, and left in a group. I sat in the sand, feeling strange.

A figure appeared walking down the riverside, in the narrow gap in the cliffs where the river rolled through to the sea. When it got closer I saw that it was Melissa Shanks. I stood and waved; she saw me and made her way around the pools on the beach to me.

"Hello, Henry," she said. "Have you been out bodysurfing?"

"Yeah. What brings you down here?"

"Oh, I was looking for clams up on the flats." It never occurred to me that she didn't have any rake or bucket with her. "Henry, I hear you're going down to San Diego with Tom?"

I nodded. Her eyes got wide with excitement.

"You must be thrilled," she said. "When are you going?"

"The next cloudy night. Seems like the weather doesn't want me to go."

She laughed, and leaned over to kiss my cheek. When I raised my eyebrows she kissed me again, and I turned and kissed back.

"I can't believe you're going," she said dreamily, between kisses. "It's just so—well, you're the best man to do it."

I began to feel better about this trip of mine.

"How many of you are going?"

"Just me and Tom."

"But what about those San Diegans?"

"Oh they're going too. They're taking us down."

"Just those two who came up here?"

"No, they have a whole crew of men waiting down the freeway where they stopped fixing up the tracks." I explained to her how the San Diegans ran their operation. "So we have to go on a cloudy night, so the Japs won't see us."

"My God." She shivered. "It sounds dangerous."

"Oh no, I don't think so." I kissed her again, rolling her back onto the sand, and we kissed for so long that I had her half out of her clothes. Suddenly she looked around and laughed.

"Not here on the beach," she said. "Why, anyone on the cliff could see us."

"No they couldn't."

"Oh yes they could, you know they could. Tell you what." She sat up and re-arranged her blue cotton shirt. I looked through her black hair to the late afternoon sun, and felt a surge of happiness pulse through me. "When you get back from San Diego, maybe we could go up Swing Canyon and take some swings."

Swing Canyon was a place where lovers went; I nodded eagerly, and reached for her, but she stood up.

"I have to be off now, really, my pa is going to be wondering where I got to." She kissed her forefinger and put it to my lips, skipped off with a laugh. I watched her cross the wide beach, then stood up myself. I shook myself, laughed out loud. I looked out to sea; were those clouds, out there?

Just after sunset my question was answered. Clouds streamed in like broken waves, and the sky was blue-gray and starless when it got dark. I took my coat off its hook and got a thick sweater from our clothes bag, chattering with Pa. Late that night Tom rapped at the door. I was off to San Diego.

part two

...SAN DIEGO

... 6

Out by the big eucalyptus Jennings and Lee stood waiting. We went to the freeway and headed south. Soon we passed the steep bank at the back of Concrete Bay, and were out of the valley and onto the Pendleton shore. The freeway was in pretty good shape down here; the surface was cracked, but it was clear of trees and shrubs, except for an occasional line of them filling a big crack like a fence. Most of the way the road was a light slash through dark forest. The level country it crossed was a narrow strip between steep hills and the sea cliff, cut often by deep ravines. Usually the freeway spanned these ravines, but twice it fell into them, and we were forced to descend their sides and cross the creeks at their bottoms on big blocks of concrete. Lee led the way over these breaks without a word. He was anxious to be in San Diego, it seemed.

A short distance beyond the second break in the freeway Lee stopped. I looked past him and saw a cluster of ruined buildings in the trees. Lee raised his hands to his mouth and made a passable imitation of a gull cry three times in a row, then three again, and from the buildings a shrill whistle replied. We approached the largest of the buildings, and were met halfway there by a group of men. They led us into the building, where a small fire gave off lots of smoke. The men from San Diego—seven of them—surveyed Tom and me.

"You sure took your time to get two specimens no better than these," a short man with a large belly said. He barked a laugh, but his little reddened eyes didn't look amused.

"Ain't San Onofre serious about talking to the Mayor?" the man next to him said. It was the first time I had ever heard *San* put in front of Onofre.

"Now enough of that," Jennings said. "This here is Tom Barnard, one of the oldest living Americans—"

"Granted," said the short man.

"*And* one of Onofre's leaders. And this boy here is his most able assistant."

Tom didn't even flinch during all this; he stared calmly at the short man, head tilted to the side like he was contemplating a new sort of bug. Lee hadn't stopped to listen. He was gathering rope under one arm, and he only paused to look up and say, "Get that fire out and get on the cars. I want to be in San Diego by sunup."

The men got their gear together and doused the fire, and we left the building and the freeway, striking out behind Lee in the direction of the ocean. We had only walked twenty or thirty paces when Lee stopped and lit a lantern.

In the gleam I saw their train: a platform on metal wheels, with a long bar set on a block in the middle of it. The men threw their stuff on the train. Behind the first I saw a second one. Approaching it I stepped over the rails. They were just like the rails that crossed our valley—bumpy and corroded, with spongy beams set every few feet under them. Tom and I stood watching as sledgehammers and axes, bundles of rope and bags of clanking metal stakes were stowed on the two platforms.

Quickly everything was aboard, and we climbed on the front train behind Lee and Jennings. Two of the men stood at the ends of the crossbar; one pulled on the high end, assisted by Lee, and with a crunch we were rolling over the rusty rails. When that end of the crossbar was low, the short man with the belly hauled down with all his weight on the other end. The two men traded pulls, and away we went, followed by the other car.

We rolled out of the copse of trees that had hidden the trains, onto a brush-covered plain. Here the hills lifted a few miles inland, rather than directly from the coast, and what trees there were grew mostly in the ravines. The rails ran just to the sea side of the freeway, and I could see the ocean from time to time when we topped a rise. We passed a headland that had taken Nicolin and me half a day to walk to; it was as far south as I had ever been. From there on I was in new territory.

The car's wheels ground over the tracks with a sound like a rasp on metal, and we picked up speed until we were going faster than a man could run. Rolling down a slope we moved even faster, and a cold wind struck me. Tom's beard was blowing back over his shoulders like a flag, and he grinned at me. "The only way to travel, eh?" I nodded. It felt like we were flying, no matter the crunch and rattle from below. "How fast are we going?" I asked.

Tom looked over the side, put his hand up to the wind. "About thirty miles an hour," he said. "Maybe thirty-five. It's been a good long while since I've gone this fast."

"Thirty miles an hour!" I cried.

The men laughed at me, but I didn't care. So far as I was concerned, they were the fools; we were going thirty miles an hour, and they sat there trying to avoid the wind!

"Want to pull?" Jennings said from the back end of the crossbar. At that the men laughed again.

"Do I!" I said. Jennings stepped aside and I took the T at the end of the pole on its upswing. When I pulled down on it I could feel the car surge forward, all out of proportion to the force I had exerted, and I whooped. I pulled hard, and saw the white grin of the man pulling across from me. He pulled just as hard, and we made that car fly down Pendleton like we were in a dream. All of a sudden I *knew* what it had been like to live in the old time, I *knew* that power they had wielded. All Tom's stories and all his books had told me of it, but now I felt it in my muscles and my skin, I could see it flying all by me, and it was exhilarating. We *pumped* that car down those tracks. Behind us the men on the following car hooted and hollered: "Hey! Who you got on the bar?" "We know it ain't Jennings doing that!" The men on both cars laughed at that. "Throw us a tow rope if you feel that good!"

"Slow it down some," Lee said after a while. "We got a ways to go, don't want to tire out those poor men back there."

So we slowed a bit. Still, when one of the men took my place, I was sweating from the effort, and standing there I chilled fast. I sat down and huddled in my coat. The land got hillier. On the up slopes we all had to get up and help pump the bar; on the downs we rolled so fast I wouldn't have wanted to stand.

We passed a bit of white cloth, hanging from a pole. Lee stood and pulled the brake lever, and we came to a halt blasting red sparks over the trackbed, with a screech that made me shudder, it hurt my ears so.

"Now comes the complicated part," Jennings said, and jumped off the car. In the sudden silence I could hear running water ahead of us. Tom and I got off the train and followed the rest of the men down the tracks. There in a dip lay a considerable stream, about half the width of our valley's river. Black posts stuck out of the surface in a double line, all the way across. Beams and planks connected some of the posts, and extended to the banks on either side, but there were big gaps as well.

"That's our foundation," Jennings said to Tom and me, while Lee directed the men on the bank. "The pilings are in good shape. We leveled them and brought up some beams that sit over the pilings. Then we set rail over the beams and roll the cars over, and haul the beams and rail to the other bank after us. It's a lot of work, but with the material hidden no one can tell we're crossing this bridge."

"Very ingenious," Tom said.

Three or four more lanterns had been lit, and their light was directed at the pilings by metal reflectors. The men hustled about in the dark, cursing at manzanita and brambles and pulling beams and rails out of the brush to the bank.

They hooked the beams to a length of rope they fished out of the shallows. This rope extended across the river under the water, where it was threaded through a large pulley and came back to our side. Men got out to the pilings on narrow planks, then fished up the beams and secured them atop the pilings. After that the rails.

"The first time they did this it must have been a lot of trouble," Tom said to me, crouched by my side with his hands around the lantern glass. "I guess it must hold those cars, but I sure wouldn't have wanted to be the first to take one across."

"They look like they know what they're doing," I said.

"Yeah. Tough work in the dark. Too bad they can't just build a bridge and leave it there."

"That's what I was thinking. I can't believe the . . ." I didn't know what to call them. "That they'd actually bomb a little bridge like this one."

"I know. But I don't think these folks are lying, or going to all this trouble for nothing. I guess whoever's up there is keeping the existing communities separated, like Jennings said. But I wasn't aware of it. It's a bad sign."

Jennings walked nonchalantly along one rail and jumped onto the bank to approach us. "Just about done," he announced. "You men should walk across now. We take the cars over as empty as we can get them, although it's just a precaution, you understand."

"That we do," said Tom. We crossed the downstream rail very carefully. The ties felt solid when I walked on them, but they were a touch warped, and the rail didn't lay directly on a few of them. I pointed this out to Jennings, who seemed very much at ease on the rail.

"It's true. We can't keep those beams flat. It makes for a little yaw when you cross, but nothing worse than that. At least not so far. We'll see if Lee has to go for a swim when he brings the first car over. I hope not—it's still a fair walk to San Diego."

On the south bank we gathered by the lanterns and the men holding them directed their light at the first car. Lee and another man cranked it slowly across. The rails squeaked and squealed as the car went over a tie; the rest of the time they were ominously silent. The car was an odd sight in the middle of the stream, hanging over both sides of the rails, a big black mass on two spindly strips, like a spider walking across its web strands. When they pumped it up the other bank the men said "All right," and "That was a good one."

They walked the equipment over, and pumped the second car across, and then pulled up and hauled the rails and beams to the south side. "Very ingenious," said Tom. "Very dangerous, very well done." Soon the platforms of the two cars were stacked with equipment again. We got on the front one with the other men, and were off rolling. "The next one's a lot easier," Jennings told us as we pumped up the slope and away.

I volunteered to pump again. This time I pulled at the front end, and watched the hills course away from us with the wind at my back. Once again I felt exuberant at the speed of our grinding flight over the land, and I laughed aloud.

"This kid pumps like a good resistance man," Jennings said. I didn't know what he meant, but the other men on the car agreed with him, those who bothered to speak, anyway.

But quickly I got tired and was relieved by the short man with the belly, who gave me a friendly slap on the shoulder and sent me to the rear of the platform. I sat down under my blanket, and after a while I drowsed off, still half aware of the train, the wind, the men's low voices.

I woke when the car stopped. "We at the next river?"

"No," Tom said quietly. "Look there." He pointed out to sea.

A completely hidden moon was making the clouds glow, and under them the ocean's surface was a patchy gray. I saw what Tom was pointing at: a dim red light in the middle of a black lump. A ship. A big ship—a huge ship, so big that for a second I thought it was just offshore, when actually it was halfway between the cliffs and the cloud-fuzzed horizon. It was so difficult to reconcile its distance from us and its immense size that I felt I could be dreaming.

"Kill the lanterns," Lee said.

The lanterns were put out. No one spoke. The giant ship ghosted north and its movement was as wrong as its size and position. It was fast, very fast, and was soon just a shape to the north.

"They don't come so close to the land in inhabited areas," Jennings told us in a voice filled with bravado. "That was a rare sighting."

Presently we started up again, and passing another white flag by the track-bed, we came to the banks of another river. This one was wider than the first, but the pilings extended right up both banks, and there was a platform across most of it. The San Diegans went to work laying track over the rickety platform, and Tom and I stayed on the car by the lanterns. It had gotten colder through the night, and we were tucked under blankets and breathing little plumes of frost. Eventually we got up to help carry equipment over. When the cars were across the river, and the bridge pulled apart, I got between two stacks of rope, out of the wind, and fell asleep.

Intermittent rough spots in the track woke me, and I cursed myself for missing part of my trip. I would poke my head up to look around, but it was still dark, and I was still tired, and I would fall asleep again. The last time I woke it was getting light, and all the men were standing to help pump us over a steep rise. I forced myself to get up, resolved to stay awake, and helped pump when a spot opened.

We were among ruins. Not ruins like in Orange County, where tangles of wood and concrete marked crushed buildings in the forest—rather there were blank foundations among the trees, and restored houses or larger buildings here and there. Cleaned up ruins. The short man pointed out the area where he lived and we passed inland of it. The bluffs we were traveling over alternated with marshes that opened onto the beach, so our tracks rose and fell regularly. We crossed the marshes on giant causeways, with tunnels under them to let the marsh's rivers reach the sea. But then we came on a marsh that didn't have a causeway. Or if it had, once upon a time, it was long gone. We were separated from the bluff to the south by a wide river, snaking through a flat expanse of reeds. It broke through the beach dunes to the sea in three places.

The San Diegans stopped the cars to look. "San Elijo," Jennings said to Tom and me. The sun was poking through clouds, and in the dawn air hundreds of birds were flapping out of the reeds and skimming the brassy bands of the meandering river. Their cries floated over the sound of the surf breaking on the beach.

Tom said, "How do you cross it? Pretty long bridge to build."

Jennings chuckled. "We go around it. We've set rails on the roads permanently. Down here *they*"—thrusting a thumb skyward—"don't seem to mind."

So we rode the tracks around the north side of the marsh, and crossed the river back in the hills where it was no more than a deep creek, on a permanent bridge like ours back home.

"Have you been able to determine how far away from San Diego you can build without disturbing them?" Tom asked as we crossed this bridge.

Jennings said, "Lee has a theory that the limits to what we can do are based on the old counties. Isn't that what you said, Lee?"

"Yes," Lee said.

"Me, I think I agree with the Mayor," Jennings went on. "He says there's no rhyme or reason to what they do. He gets really upset. We're like flies to the gods, he says."

"'Like flies to wanton boys are we to the gods,'" Tom corrected.

"Exactly. Madmen, looking down on us."

Lee shook his head. "There's more to it than that. It's a question how much they see, but their reaction is governed by rules. I imagine it's a charter from the United Nations or some such thing, telling the Japs out there what to do. In fact—" But there he stopped himself.

"No question they've got great cameras," Jennings said. "The question is how much they notice. We've made changes on that rail line north that can't be hid. That will be a good test of their attention, if you ask me."

We were rolling through a thick forest of torrey pine. The sun lanced the shadows and sparked the dew. The air warmed and I felt drowsy again, despite my fascination with the new country we were passing through. Among the trees were groups of houses from the old time, many of them restored and occupied; smoke rose from many a chimney. When I saw this I nudged Tom, powerfully disturbed. These San Diegans were nothing else but scavengers! Tom saw what I meant, but he just shook his head briefly at me. It wasn't the time to discuss it.

The tracks led to a village somewhat like ours, except there were more houses, and they were placed closer together, and many of them had been built in the old time. The screech of our brakes sent chickens cackling and dogs howling. Several men and women emerged from a big house across the clearing from the tracks. The San Diegans jumped off the cars and greeted the locals. In the light of day they looked filthy and red-eyed, but no one seemed to mind.

"Welcome to San Diego!" Jennings said to us as he helped Tom off the car. "Or to University City, to be more exact. Care to join us for breakfast?"

We agreed heartily to that. We were introduced to the group who had come from the big house to greet us, and followed them into it.

Inside the front door was an entryway two stories tall, carpeted red, with red and gold wallpaper on the walls, and a glass candle holder hanging from the ceiling. The staircase against one wall was carpeted as well, and it had a bannister of carved and varnished oak. Wide-eyed, I said, "Is this the Mayor's house?"

The San Diegans erupted with laughter. I felt my cheeks burn. Jennings put his arm around my shoulders with a whoop. "You've proved yourself tonight, Henry my boy. We aren't laughing *at* you; it's just . . . well, when you see the Mayor's place, you'll understand why. This is my house. Come on in and clean up and meet the wife, and we'll have a good meal to celebrate your arrival."

...7

After breakfast Tom and I slept for most of the day, on couches in the Jenningses' front room. Late in the day Jennings bustled in and woke us, saying, "I've been to talk to the Mayor—he's invited you to a dinner, and he doesn't like to be kept waiting."

"Be quiet and let them get ready," Jennings's wife said as she looked over his shoulder at us. She looked remarkably like him, short, thick, and cheerful. "When you're ready I'll show you to the bathroom." Tom and I followed her to it, and relieved ourselves in a working water toilet. When we were done Jennings hustled us outside. Lee and the short man were already on one of the train cars. We joined them, and they pumped us south. Apparently in the light of day the tubby man felt more sociable, and he introduced himself as Abe Tonklin.

We rattled over tracks laid on the cracked concrete of another freeway, under a canopy of torrey pine and eucalyptus, redwood and oak. The car crunched swiftly through alternating shadows and slanted beams of sunlight, and now and then we passed a big clearing in the forest, packed with crops, usually corn.

Over the roar of wheel on rail Jennings shouted, "We're almost there." We topped a rise and below us was a narrow lake, stretching right to left in front of us. It was as if a marsh similar to the ones to the north had flooded. Scattered on the lake's surface were towering buildings, *skyscrapers,* at least a dozen of them. One of them, to the left, was a giant circular wall. And in the middle of the lake stood a piece of freeway, up on concrete pilings above the water. A white house stood on this platform. Flying above this house I could make out a little American flag, snapping in the breeze. I looked at Tom, my mouth hanging open in amazement. Tom's eyes were big. I took in the sight again. Flanked by forested hills, lit by the low sun, the long lake and its fantastic collection of drowned and ruined giants was the most impressive remnant of the old time

I had ever seen. They were so big! Once again I had that feeling—like a hand squeezing my heart—that I *knew* what it had been like.

"Now *that's* the Mayor's house," Jennings said.

"By God, it's Mission Valley," Tom said.

"That's right," Jennings replied, as proudly as if he'd made it himself. Tom laughed. The tracks came to an end, and Lee braked the car with the usual nerve-jangling screech. We got off and followed the San Diegans down the freeway. It led right into the lake and disappeared. The piece of freeway standing on stilts in the lake's center was on a line with it, and in a notch of the hills forming the opposite shore I saw the gray concrete rising out of the lake again. All at once I understood that the section of freeway on stilts in the lake was all that was left of a bridge that had spanned the whole valley. Rather than have their road dip into the valley and rise again, they had placed it on towers for well over a mile, from hillside to hillside—just to avoid a drop and rise for their cars! I was stunned; I stared at it; I couldn't get a grasp on the sort of thinking that would even imagine such a bridge.

"You okay?" Lee asked me.

"Huh? Yeah sure. Just looking at the lake."

"Quite a sight. Maybe we can take a sail around it in the morning." This was as friendly as Lee had been to me, and I saw that he appreciated my astonishment.

Where the road plunged into the lake a large floating dock moored a score of rowboats and small catboats. Lee and Abe led us to one of the larger rowboats. We got in, and Abe rowed us toward the freeway island. As we got closer Jennings answered Tom's questions: "The rains washed mountains of dirt down to the rivermouth, which was bracketed by a pair of long jetties and crossed by several roads—just generally obstructed. So the dirt stuck there and formed a plug. A big dam. What? There's still a channel through to the ocean, but it's on top of the plug, so we got the lake back here. It's well above sea level. Runs all the way to El Cajon."

Tom laughed. "Ha! We always said a good rain would flood this valley, but *this*. . . . What about the overpass out here?"

"The first floods were pretty violent, they say, and the sides of the hills got ripped away, so the towers holding the road fell. Only the center ones held. We blasted the wreckage hanging from the center section so it would look cleaner."

"Sure."

As we rowed under it I could see the broken end of the freeway. Rusted metal rods stuck out from pocked concrete. The platform was about fifteen feet thick, and its bottom was twenty feet or so above the lake. The platform had been part of an intersection, and narrow ramps branched from the main north-south fragment to descend to the valley floor. Now these curving side roads served as convenient boat ramps for us. We glided to the eastern ramp, and were moored by a few men who were there to greet us. We stepped from the boat onto the concrete ramp. From the dwellings above we heard laughter and voices, and a tinkling of crockery.

"We're late," Lee said. "Let's go." As we ascended the ramp I noticed that it tilted side to side, as well as up. Tom told me, when I mentioned it, that this had been done to keep the cars coming down the ramp at high speed from skidding off the side. I looked over the edge to the water below and thought that the old Americans must have been fools.

The big house stood at the north end of the platform, and a cluster of smaller buildings, each about the size of my home, were arranged in a horseshoe at the south end. Half of the big house was only one story tall, and on the roof of this part, facing us, was a porch with a blue railing. Over the railing leaned several men, watching us. Jennings waved to them as we approached. I walked next to Tom, suddenly nervous.

Lee and Jennings led Tom and me into the big house. Once inside Jennings took a comb from a pocket and ran it through his hair. Lee grinned sardonically at this grooming, and pushed past Jennings to lead us up a broad staircase. On the upper floor we walked down a dim hallway to large glass doors that opened onto the roof porch.

Out there the Mayor stood in a group of men by the railing, watching us approach. He was a big man, tall, wide-shouldered, deep-chested. His forearms were thick with muscle, and under his plaid wool pants I could see his thighs were the same. One of his men helped him to shrug into a plain blue coat. His head looked too small for his body. "Jennings, who are these men?" he said in a high, scratchy voice. Underneath his black moustache was a small mouth, a weak chin. But as he adjusted his collar he looked us over with sharp, pale blue eyes.

Jennings introduced Tom and me.

"Timothy Danforth," the Mayor said in reply. "Mayor of this fine town." There was a little American flag in the lapel of his jacket. He shook hands with each of us; when I shook I squeezed as hard as I could, but I might as well have been squeezing rock. He could have squashed my hand like bread dough. As Tom said later, his handshake alone could have made him mayor. He said to Tom, "I am told you are not the elected leader of San Onofre?"

"Onofre doesn't have an elected leader," Tom said.

"But you hold some sort of authority?" the Mayor suggested.

Tom shrugged and walked past him to the porch rail. "Nice view you've got here," he said, looking west, where the sun had been halved by the darkening hills. I was shocked at Tom's rudeness; I wanted to speak up and tell the Mayor that Tom had as much authority as anyone in Onofre. But I kept my mouth shut. Tom kept looking at the sunset. The Mayor watched him out of narrowed eyes.

"Always good to meet another neighbor," the Mayor said, in a hearty voice. "We'll celebrate with a meal out here, if you like. It should be a warm enough evening." He smiled and his moustache waggled. "Tell me, are you one who lived in the old time?" His tone seemed to say, are you one of those who used to live in Paradise?

"How did you guess?" Tom said.

The dozen men on the porch laughed, but Danforth just stared at Tom. "It's an honor to meet you, sir. There aren't many of you left, especially in such good health. You're an inspiration to all of us."

Tom lifted his bushy eyebrows. "Really?"

"An inspiration," the Mayor repeated firmly. "A monument, so to speak. A reminder of what we're striving for in these most difficult of times. I find that old timers like you understand better what we're striving for."

"Which is?" said Tom.

Luckily, or perhaps deliberately, the Mayor didn't hear Tom's question. "Well, come sit down," he said, as if we had been refusing to. There were several round tables on the porch, among small trees in big buckets. As we sat around one next to the rail Danforth's little eyes peered at Tom. Tom innocently stared at the flag, which ruffled limply from a pole sticking out of the roof.

Twenty-five or thirty tables were set up on the freeway below, and more boats were arriving in the gloom of the early evening. The hills to the south were a brilliant green at their very tops, but that was the last of the light. From somewhere in the house a generator started to hum, and electric lights snapped on all over the island. The little buildings at the south end, the freeway railings, the rooms of the house behind us: all blazed with a sizzly white light. Girls my age or younger moved around the porch, bringing plates and silverware out from inside. One of the girls set my plate before me and gave me a smile. Her hair shone gold under the glare of the lights. Men and women appeared at the top of the east ramp, dressed like scavengers in bright coats and colorful dresses, but I didn't care. In San Diego things were obviously not the same. Down here they combined the best of scavenger and newtowner, I thought. One of the brighter lights shone on the flag, and everyone on the island stood at attention as the limp folds of red, white, and blue were lowered. Tom and I stood with them, and I felt a peculiar glow flushing my face and the chinks of my spine.

Around our table were Tom and me, Jennings, Lee, the Mayor, and three of his men, who were quickly introduced to us. Ben was the only name I remembered. Jennings told the Mayor about their trip north, describing the two bridges and all the major breaks in the track. He made the repair work sound difficult, and I guessed that they had come home behind schedule. Or maybe Jennings just exaggerated out of habit.

"What's the shortest time it would take you to train up to Onofre?" the Mayor asked Lee. Tom and I nudged each other: he knew which of his men to ask when he wanted a straight answer.

Lee cleared his throat. "Last night it took about eight hours, from our stopping point up there to University City. That's about as fast as it could be done, unless we left the bridges up."

"We can't do that." Danforth's face was grim.

"I guess not. Anyway, another fifteen minutes to Onofre. The track's in good shape to there."

"And beyond as well," Jennings added, which made Tom look up. The Mayor scowled. "Let's talk about that after dinner," he said.

After girls had set the tables, with plates and glasses and cloth napkins and silverware that looked like real silver, they brought out big glass bowls filled with salads made of lettuce and shrimp. Tom examined the shrimp with interest, forking one to get it closer to his eyes. "Where do you get these?" he inquired.

The Mayor laughed. "Wait till after the grace, and Ben here will tell you."

All the serving girls came out and stood still, and the Mayor stood and walked to the rail, so he could be seen from below. He had a limp, I noticed; his left foot wouldn't bend. We all bowed our heads. The Mayor declaimed the prayer: "Dear Lord, we eat this food you have provided us in order to make us strong in the service of you and of the United States of America. Amen." Everyone joined in on the amen, which covered the little sounds Tom was making beside me. I ribbed him hard.

We started in on the salad. From below voices chimed with the sounds of clinking dishes. Between bites Ben said to Tom, "We get the shrimp from the south."

"I thought the border was closed."

"Oh, it is. Definitely. Not the old border, though. Tijuana is no more than a battleground for rats and cats. About five miles south of that is the new border. It's made of barbed wire fences, and a bulldozed strip on each side of it three hundred yards wide. And guard towers, and lights at night. I've never heard of a single person that got over it." As he took a bite the other men at the table nodded their agreement with this. "There's a jetty where the fence hits the beach, too, and beyond that guard boats. But they're Mexican guard boats, see. The Japanese have the coast right down to the border, but beyond that the Mexicans take over. They don't do too good a job."

"Neither do the Japs," Danforth said.

"True. Anyway, the Mexican guard boats are there, but it's easy to get past them, and once past them the fishing boats will sell you anything they have or can get. We're just another customer as far as they're concerned. Except they know they have us over a barrel, so they squeeze us every trade. But we get what we want."

"Which is shrimp?" said Tom, surprised. His salad was gone.

"Sure. Don't you like it?"

"What do the Mexicans want?"

"Gun parts, mostly. Souvenirs. Junk."

"Mexicans love junk," Danforth said, and his men laughed. "But we'll sell them something different someday. Put them back where they belong, like it used to be." He had been watching Tom wolf his food; now that Tom was done, he said, "Did you live around here in the old time?"

"Up in Orange County, mostly. I came down here to school."

"Changed, hasn't it?"

"Sure." Tom was looking around for the next course. "Everything's changed." He was still being rude, apparently on purpose; I couldn't figure out what he was up to.

"I imagine Orange County was pretty built up in the old time."

"About like San Diego. Or a little more so."

The Mayor breathed a whistle, looking impressed.

When everyone had finished the salads the bowls were taken away, and replaced with pots of soup, plates of meat, stacks of bread, dishes of vegetables, pyramids of fruit. The plates just kept on coming, giving me chance after chance to smile at the blond girl: chicken and rabbit, pork pie and frog legs, lamb and turkey, fish and beef, abalone in big slabs—plate after plate after plate was set down, and the covered ones were opened for our inspection. By the time the girls were done, there was a feast on those tables that made Mrs. Nicolin's dinner look like the ones Pa and me ate every night. Nearly overwhelmed, I tried to decide where to start. It was hard. I had a little clam chowder while I thought it over.

"You know," said Danforth after we were well into it, "the Japanese are landing up there in your old home territory, these days."

"That so?" Tom said, shoveling abalone onto his plate. The amount of food on the table didn't seem to have impressed him. I knew he was interested in this stuff about the Japanese, but he refused to show it.

"You haven't seen any of them in Onofre? Or any signs?"

Tom appeared reluctant to take his attention from his food, and he did no more than shake his head as he chewed, and then give the Mayor a quick glance.

"They're interested in looking at the ruins of old America," the Mayor said.

"They?" Tom mumbled, his mouth full.

"Mostly Japanese, although there are other nationalities too. But the

Japanese, who were given the charter to guard our west coast, make up most of them."

"Who guards the other coasts?" Tom said, as if testing how much they claimed to know.

"Canada was assigned the east coast, the Mexicans the Gulf Coast."

"They're supposed to be neutral powers," Ben added. "Although in the world today the very idea of a neutral power is a joke."

The Mayor went on: "Japanese own the offshore islands here, and Hawaii. It's easiest for the rich Japanese to get to Hawaii, and then here, but we're told tourists of all nationalities want to try it."

"How do you know all this?" Tom said, barely able to disguise his interest.

Proudly Danforth said, "We've sent men to Catalina to spy it out."

Tom couldn't help himself, no matter how much he ate: "So what happened? Have we been quarantined?"

With a disgusted stab of his fork the Mayor said, "The Russians did it. So we've been told. Of course it's obvious. Who else was going to come up with two thousand neutron bombs? Most countries couldn't even afford the vans those things were hidden in when they went off."

Tom squinted, and I thought I knew why; this was the same explanation he had given us in his story Johnny Pinecone, which I was pretty sure he had made up. It was odd.

"That was how they got us," the Mayor said. "Didn't you know? They hid the bombs in Chevy vans, drove the vans into the centers of the two thousand largest cities, and parked them there. Then the bombs all went off at once. No warning. You know, no missiles coming or anything."

Tom nodded, as if a mystery had finally been cleared for him.

"After the day," Ben went on, as it seemed the Mayor was too upset to go on, "the U.N. reconvened in Geneva. Everyone was terrified of Russia, especially the nations with nuclear weapons, naturally. Russia suggested we be made off limits for a century, to avoid any conflict over us. A world preserve, they said. Clearly punitive, but who was going to argue? So here we are."

"Interesting," Tom said. "But I've heard a lot of speculation in the last fifty years." He started forking again. "Seems to me we're like the Japanese themselves were after Hiroshima. They didn't even know what hit them, did you know that? They thought maybe we had dropped manganese on the electric train tracks, and started a fire. Pitiful. And we're no better."

"What's Hiroshima?" the Mayor asked.

Tom didn't reply. Ben shook his head at Tom's doubts. "We've had men on Catalina for months at a time. And—well, I'll send you over to Wentworth's tomorrow. He'll tell you. We know what happened, more or less."

"Enough history," said the Mayor. "What's important is the here and now.

The Japanese in Avalon are getting corrupt. Rich Japanese want to visit America and do some sight-seeing. It's the latest adventure. They come to Avalon and contact people who will take them to the mainland. Those people, some of them Americans, sail them in past the coastal patrol at night, into Newport Beach or Dana Point. We've heard there are hundreds of them in Hawaii waiting to do it."

"That's what you said." Tom shrugged.

An exasperated scowl appeared on the Mayor's face and was gone. As dishes were cleared from the tables he stood up and leaned over the rail. "Tell the band to play!" he called down. The people below shouted to him, and he limped past us into the house. Over the railing I saw the big white-clothed tables below, piled with food and crockery. From above the San Diegans looked wonderfully groomed, their hair neatly cut and combed, their shirts and dresses bright and clean. Again I saw them as scavengers. From down the freeway a bit a small brass band started to play some stodgy polkas, and the Mayor appeared, moving from table to table. He knew everyone down there. As the people below finished their meals they got up and walked in front of the band to dance. All around us the water and the shores of the lake were dark: we were an island of light, propped up over the gloom. Below they were having a good time, but with the Mayor gone, the group on the porch looked bored.

Then Danforth reappeared between the tall glass doors, and laughed at the sight of us. "All done stuffing yourselves? Why don't you get down there and dance? This is a celebration! Get down there and mingle with the folks, and Ben and I will talk further with our guests from the north."

Happily the men and women seated around our tables stood and filed into the house. Jennings and Lee went with them, and only Ben stayed upstairs with the Mayor to talk with us.

"I have an excellent bottle of tequila in my study," Danforth said to us. "Let's go in there and give some a try."

We followed him in, down a hall to a wood-paneled room that was dominated by a large desk. Drapes covered a window, and bookcases covered the wall behind the desk. We sat in plush armchairs that were arranged in a half-circle facing the desk, and Tom tilted his head to the side in an attempt to read the book titles. Danforth got a long slim bottle from a shelf jammed with bottles, and poured us each a glass of tequila. He paced behind the desk, looking down at the carpet. He switched on a lamp that glared off the surface of the desk, lighting his face from below. It was quiet, no sound from the party outside. Solemnly he proposed a toast: "To the friendship of our two communities."

Tom lifted his glass and drank.

I tried a few sips of the tequila. It was harsh. My stomach felt like I'd put an iron ball in it, I'd eaten so much. I balanced the glass on the arm of my chair and sat back, ready to watch Tom and the Mayor go at it again—though what kind of contest it was, I couldn't figure.

The Mayor had a thoughtful, brooding expression. He continued to pace back and forth. He lifted his glass and looked through it at Tom. "So what do you think?"

"Of what?" Tom said.

"Of the world situation?"

Tom shrugged. "I just heard about it. You folks know a lot more than we did. If it's all true. We know there are Orientals out there on Catalina. Their bodies wash up on our beach occasionally. Beyond that, all we've heard is swap meet talk, and that changes every month."

"You've had Japanese bodies washing up?" Danforth asked.

"We call them Chinese."

The Mayor shook his head. "Japanese."

"So that coast guard is shooting up some of the illegal landing parties?" Tom ventured.

Again the Mayor shook his head. "The coast guard is paid off. It wasn't them." He took a sip from his glass. "It was us."

"How's that?"

"It was us!" the Mayor said, suddenly loud. He limped to the window, fiddled with the drapes. "We sail up off Newport and Dana Point, on foggy nights or nights when we've been tipped off that they're coming, and we ambush them. Kill as many as we can."

Tom looked at the glass in his hand. "Why?" he said finally.

"*Why?*" The Mayor's chin melted into his neck. "You're an old timer—you ask me why?"

"Sure."

"Because we aren't a zoo here, that's why!" He began to pace again, bobbing around behind his desk, around and behind our chairs, behind the desk again. Without warning he slammed his right palm onto the desktop, *smack!* I jumped in my chair. "They blew our country to pieces," he said in a strangled furious voice. "They killed it." He cleared his throat. "There's nothing we can do about that now. But they can't come sight-seeing in the ruins. No. Not while there are Americans left alive. We aren't animals in a cage to be looked at. We'll make them learn that if they set foot on our soil, they're dead." He took up the tequila bottle and refilled his glass. "When word gets around that no one ever comes back from a visit to America, they'll stop coming. There won't be any more customers for that scum north of you." He drank hastily. "Did you know there are scavengers in Orange County arranging to give guided tours to the Japs?"

"I'm not surprised," Tom said.

"Well I am. Those people are scum. They are traitors to the United States." He said it like a death sentence. "If every American joined the resistance, no one could land on our soil. We'd be left alone, and the rebuilding could get on. But we all have to be part of the resistance."

"I didn't know there was a resistance," Tom said mildly.

Bang! The Mayor's hand hit the desk again. He leaned over it and cried, "That's what we brought you here to tell you about!" He straightened up, sat down in his chair, held his forehead in his hand. Suddenly it seemed hushed and quiet again. "Tell him, Ben."

Ben leaned forward in his chair enthusiastically. "When we got to the Salton Sea we learned about it. The American resistance. Although usually they just called it the resistance. The headquarters are in Salt Lake City, and there are military centers in the old Strategic Air Command quarters under Cheyenne, Wyoming, and under Mount Rushmore."

"Under Mount Rushmore?" Tom said.

Head still cradled in one hand, face shadowed, the Mayor peered at him. "That's right. That's where the secret military headquarters of the United States always was."

"I didn't know," Tom said, eyebrows gently arched.

Ben went on. "There are organizations all across the country, but it's all one group really, and the goal is the same. To rebuild America." He rolled the phrase over his tongue.

"To rebuild America," breathed the Mayor. I felt that flush in my face and spine begin again. By God, they were in contact with the east coast! New York, Virginia, Massachusetts, England. . . . The Mayor reached for his glass and sipped; Ben jerked down two swallows as if it were a toast, and Tom and I likewise drank. For a moment there seemed a shared feeling in the room. I could feel the alcohol going to my head, along with the news of the resistance, this dream of Nicolin's and mine come to life. It made a heady mixture. Danforth stood again and looked at the framed map on the side wall of the study. Passionately he said, "To make America great again, to make it what it was before the war, the best nation on Earth. That's our goal." He pointed a finger through the shadows at Tom. "We'd be back to that already if we had retaliated against the Russians. If President Eliot—traitor, coward!—hadn't refused to defend us. But we'll still do it. We'll work hard, we'll pray hard, we'll hide our weapons from the satellites. They're inventing new ones in Salt Lake and Cheyenne, we're told. And one day . . . one day we'll spring out on the world again like a tiger. A tiger from the depths of the pit." His voice shifted to a scratchy mutter I couldn't make out. He was half turned away from us, and he went on like that for a while, talking to himself in a voice that moaned and sighed. The lamp on his desk flickered, flickered again. Ben jerked out of his chair and went to a corner to get a kerosene lamp.

With a tap of the knuckles on the desk the Mayor raised his voice again, sounding relaxed and reasonable. "That's what I wanted to talk to you about, Barnard. The largest resistance group on this coast is centered around Santa Barbara, we've heard. We met some of them out at the Salton Sea. We need to connect with them, and present a unified opposition to the Japanese on Catalina and the Santa Barbara islands. The first part of that task is to rid Orange County and Los Angeles of all Japanese tourists, and the traitors who guide them. So we need you. We need Onofre to join the resistance."

"I can't speak for them," Tom said. I bit my lip and stayed silent. Tom was right; it would have to be voted. Tom waved a hand. "It sounds . . . well, I don't know if we'll want in or not."

"You've got to want in," the Mayor said fiercely, fist held over the desk. "This is more important than what you want. You tell them they can make this country what it used to be. They can help. But we all have to work together. The day will come. Another Pax Americana, cars and airplanes, rockets to the moon, telephones. A unified country." Suddenly, without anger or whispery passion, he said, "You go back up there and tell your valley that they join the resistance or they oppose it."

"Not a very neighborly way of putting it," Tom observed, his eyes narrowed.

"Put it any way you please! Just tell them."

"I'll tell them. But they'll want to know just exactly what you want of them. And I can't guarantee what they'll say to it."

"No one's asking you to guarantee anything. They'll know what's right." The Mayor took a long look at Tom, his little eyes bright. "I would have thought an old timer like you would be hopping with joy to hear of the resistance."

"I don't hop much these days," Tom said. "Bad knees."

The Mayor circled the desk and bent over Tom's chair, looked at Tom. With both hands he trapped one of Tom's. "Don't lose your feel for America, old man," he said hoarsely. "It's the best part of you. It's what kept you alive for so long, whether you know it or not. You've got to fight to keep that feeling, or you're doomed."

Tom pulled his hand away. The Mayor straightened up and limped back around the desk. "Well, Ben! These gentlemen deserve to enjoy a little of the partying outside before they retire, don't you agree?" Ben nodded and smiled at us. "I know you men had a hard night last night," Danforth said, "but I hope you'll have enough energy to join the folks outside for at least a short while."

We agreed that we did.

"Before we go back out, then, let me show you a little secret." We stood and followed him out of the room. He bobbed down the hallway to another door, and pulled a key from his vest. "In here is the key to a whole new world." He unlocked the door, and we followed him into the room, which contained nothing but machine parts, scattered over three tables. On the biggest table was a metal box as big as a boat locker, covered with knobs and dials and gauges, with wires trailing out of it from two openings.

"Short wave radio?" Tom said.

"Exactly," said Ben, beaming with approval at Tom's good guess.

"We've got a man coming from the Salton Sea to fix this thing," the Mayor whispered. "And when we do that, we'll be in touch with the whole country. Every part of the resistance. It will be the start of a new age."

So we stood there and stared at it for a while, and then tiptoed out of the room. When the Mayor was done locking the door we went outside onto the freeway, where the band was still playing. Instantly the Mayor was surrounded by young women who wanted a dance with him. Tom wandered off toward the west railing, and I went for the drink table. The man behind the table recognized me; he had helped dock our boat when we arrived at the island. "Drink's on the house," he declared, and poured me a cup of tequila punch. I took it and walked in circles around the dance floor. The women dancing with the Mayor held close to him and danced in slow circles. I was feeling the drink. The music, the electric lights glaring off the concrete, the bright rugs thrown here and there, the cool breeze, the night sky, the eerie ruined skyscrapers rising blackly from the murk around us—the incredible news of the American resistance—it all combined to put me in a blaze. I was on the edge of a new world, truly. I twisted through the crowd to Tom, who was leaning against the fat railing, looking down at the water. "Tom, isn't it grand? Isn't it wonderful?"

"Let me think, boy," he said quietly.

So I walked back over to the band, subdued for a moment. But it didn't last. The girl dancing with the Mayor was the blond who had served our table at the feast. When she gave way to another girl I hurried out among the dancers and swept her into a hug.

"Dance with me too," I asked her. "I'm from the north."

"I know," she said, and laughed. "You sure aren't one of the boys from around here."

"From the icy north," I said as I awkwardly swept her into the polka. It made me a little dizzy. "From over glaciers and crevasses and great expanses of snow have I come to your fair civilized town."

"What?"

"Here from the barbarous north, to see your Mayor, the prophet of a new age."

"He is like a prophet, isn't he? Just like from church. My father says he's made San Diego what it is."

"I believe it. Did he make a lot of changes when he took office?"

"Oh, he's been mayor since before I can remember. Since I was two, I think Daddy said."

"Long time ago."

"Fourteen years . . ."

I kissed her briefly, and we danced three or four songs, until my dizziness returned and I had trouble with my bearings. She accompanied me to the tables, and we sat and talked. I chattered on like the most extravagant liar in California; Nicolin himself couldn't have beat me that night, and the girl laughed and laughed. Later on Jennings and Tom came by, and I was sorry to see them. Jennings said he was taking us to our night's lodgings on the other end of the platform. Reluctantly I said good night to the girl, and followed them drunkenly down the freeway south, singing to myself, "Oomp-pah-pah," and greeting most of the people we passed. Jennings installed us in one of the bungalows at the south end of the platform, and I chattered at the silent Tom for two or three minutes before I passed out. "A new age, Tom, I'm telling you. A new world."

...8

Shotgun blasts woke us up the next morning. Jumping up to look out the door of our little bungalow, we discovered that the Mayor and several of his men were taking target practice, shooting at plates that one of them was throwing out over the lake. The man threw—the plate arched out—the shooter aimed—*bam!*—a flat sound like two wet planks slapping together. About one in every three plates burst into white splinters. The rest clipped the sparkling surface of the lake and disappeared. Tom shook his head disdainfully as he regarded this exercise. "They must have found a lot of ammunition somewhere," he said. Jennings saw us in our doorway and came over and led us to one of the tables set outside the big house. There in the tangy clouds of gunpowder smoke we had a breakfast of bread and milk. Between the bangs of the gun I could hear the American flag snapping smartly in the fresh morning breeze. Every time a plate exploded the men hooted and talked it over. The Mayor was a good shot; he seldom missed, which may have been the result of taking his turn often. The rest of his men might as well have been dumping those plates into the lake by the boxful.

When we were done eating the Mayor gave his shotgun to one of the men around him, and clumped over to us. He looked a bit smaller in the sunlight than he had under the lanterns and electric lights.

"I'm going to send you back to Jennings's house by way of La Jolla, so you can talk to Wentworth."

"Who's he?" Tom asked, without any pretense of politeness.

"He's our bookmaker. He can tell you more about the situation Ben and I described to you last night. After you've talked to him, Jennings and Lee and their crew will take you back north on the train." He sat down across from us and leaned his thick forearms on the table. "When you get there, you tell your folk just what I said last night."

"Let me understand you clearly," Tom said. "You want us to join this resistance effort you've heard of."

"That we're part of. That's right."

"Which means what, in actual terms?"

Danforth stared steadily at Tom's face. "Every town in the resistance has to do its share. That's the only way we'll achieve victory. Of course we've got a much larger population down here, and we'll be providing most of the manpower on this coast, I'm sure. But we need to get through your valley on the tracks, for one thing. And you folks could make raids up the coast a lot easier than we can, living where you do. Or we could base our raids in your river, depending on how we decide to work it. See, there is no set way, you should understand that. But we need you to sign up."

"What if we don't want to?"

The Mayor's jaw tightened. He let Tom's question hang in the air for a while, and the men around us (target practice being over for the moment) grew silent. "I can't figure you, old man," Danforth complained. "You just take my message to the people in your valley."

"I'll tell them what you've told me, and we'll let you know our decision."

"Good enough. I'll be seeing you again." He pushed back his chair, stood up, and limped into the gleaming white house.

"I think he's done talking to you," Jennings said after another long silence. "We can be off." He led us back to our bungalow, and when Tom had gotten his shoulder bag we walked down the tilted ramp to the boats. Lee and Abe were waiting on the floating dock, and we all got in a boat and cut over the water to the lake's north shore. It was a fine day, sky free of clouds and not much wind. We climbed up to a different train than the one we had arrived on, set on different tracks, ones that took us west along the shore of the lake. "Quite a terminal you have there," Tom remarked, breaking his silence. Jennings began to describe every mile of the rail system, but since none of the names he mentioned meant anything to me I stopped listening and kept a lookout for the sea. We came to a big marsh just when I expected to spot it, and turned north to skirt the marsh's edge. A heavily forested hill marked the northern end of the marsh, and we clattered along on a freeway that snaked through a crease to the east of the hill. Lee braked the car—I had learned to stick my fingers in my ears when he did that. "We have to walk to La Jolla," Jennings said. "No tracks from here."

"Nor roads neither," Lee added.

We slid off the side of the handcar, and started up a trail that was the only passage through thick forest. It was more like what Tom called a jungle: ferns and creepers and vines wove the densely set trees together, and every lichen-stained branch was locked in a struggle for sunlight with ten other branches. Knots of torrey pine competed with trees I'd never seen before. There was a damp smell to the spongy trail, and fungus or bright green ferns grew on every log that had fallen across our path. Behind me Tom muttered as he walked, thumping his shoulder bag against his side. "Mount Soledad just another wet north face now. All the houses washed down. All fall down, all fall down." Lee, striding ahead of me, turned and gave Tom a funny look. I knew just what the look meant: it was hard to believe Tom had been alive when these ruins had stood whole. Tom cursed as he kicked a root and mumbled on, unaware of Lee's glance. "Flood and mud, rain and pain, lightning blast and fire burn, all fall down. And all that terrible construction. Ah ha, there's a foundation. Was that one Tudor? Chinese? Hacienda? California *ranch?*" "What's that?" Jennings called back, thinking he had heard a question. But Tom talked on: "This town was everything but itself. Nothing but money. Paper houses; this hill sure looks better with all that shit washed away. I wish they could see it now, hee hee."

On the ocean side of the hill it was a different story. Where the hillside leveled off, forming a point that thrust out from the coast on either side, all the trees had been cleared away. In this clearing a few old buildings were surrounded by wooden houses. The new houses had been put together with fragments of the old, so that some had massive roof beams, others wide chimneys, others orange tile roofs. Most of the houses had been painted white, and the old concrete had been painted pale shades of blue or yellow or orange. As we descended the west side of the hill we caught sight of the clearing through the leaves, and the little village in it shone against the backdrop of the dark blue ocean. We came out of the overhanging branches of the forest, and the trail widened into a straight street paved with thick grass.

"Paint," Tom observed. "What a good idea. But all the paint I've seen lately has been hard as rock."

"Wentworth has a way to liquefy it," Jennings said. "Same way he liquefies old ink, he tells me."

"Who is this Wentworth?" I said.

"Come and find out," said Jennings in reply.

At the far end of the street of grass, just above a small cove, was a low building made of tan blocks of stone. A wall made of the same blocks surrounded the place, and torrey pines stood against the wall. We walked through a big wooden gate that had a tiger carved into it, a green tiger. Jennings looked in the open door of the building inside the gate, and waved us in.

The first room had big glass windows in one wall, and with its door open it was as sunny as the courtyard. A half dozen kids and three or four adults were at work on low tables, kneading a pure white dough that by its smell could not be bread. A man with black-rimmed spectacles and a salt-and-pepper beard looked up from a table where he was giving instructions to the workers, and walked over to us.

"Jennings, Lee," he said, wiping his hands dry on a cloth tied around his waist. "What brings you here today?"

"Douglas, this here is Tom Barnard, a . . . an elder of Onofre Valley, up the coast. We brought him down on the new tracks. Tom, this is Douglas Wentworth, San Diego's bookmaker."

"Bookmaker," Tom repeated. He shook Wentworth's hand. "I'm happy to meet a bookmaker, sir."

"You take an interest in books?"

"I surely do. I was a lawyer once, and had to read the worst kind of books. Now I'm free to read what I like, when I can find it."

"You have an extensive collection?" Wentworth asked, knocking his glasses up his nose with a finger to see Tom better.

"No sir. Fifty volumes or so, but I keep trading them with our neighbors for others."

"Ah. And you, young man—do you read?" His eyes were the size of eggs behind his spectacles, and they held my gaze with ease.

"Yes, sir. Tom taught me how, and now that I can I enjoy it more than almost anything."

Mr. Wentworth smiled briefly. "It's refreshing to hear that San Onofre is a literate community. Perhaps you'd like to take a tour of our establishment? I can take a few moments from the work here, and we do have a modest printing arrangement that might be of interest."

"We'd be delighted," Tom said.

"Lee and I will go get some lunch," Jennings said. "Back shortly."

"We'll wait for you," Tom said. "Thanks for bringing us here."

"Thank the Mayor."

"Keep kneading until you get a perfect consistency," Wentworth was saying to his students, "then begin to roll out the water. I'll be back before the pressing."

He led us to another room with good windows, one filled with small metal boxes set on tables. A woman was turning a handle on the side of one of these machines, rotating a drum on which a piece of print-covered paper was clamped. More pages covered by print were ejected from the bottom of the box.

"Mimeograph!" Tom cried.

The woman working the machine jerked at Tom's shout, and glared at him.

"Indeed," said Wentworth. "We are a modest operation, as I said. Mimeographing is our principal form of printing here. Not the most elegant method, or the most long-lasting, but the machines are reliable, and besides, they're almost all we've got."

"I think it's beautiful," Tom said, taking up a page to read it.

"It suffices."

"Pretty color ink, too," I put in; the ink was a bluish purple, and the page was thick with it.

Wentworth let out a short, sharp laugh. "Ha! Do you think so? I would prefer black, myself, but we must work with what we have. Now over here is our true pride. A hand letter press." He gestured at a contraption of bars holding a big screw, which took up most of the far wall.

"Is that what that is," Tom said. "I've never seen one."

"This is what we do our fine work on. But there isn't enough paper, and none of us knew, at first, how to set type. So it goes very slowly. We have had some successes, however. Following Gutenberg, here is our first one." He hauled a big leather-bound book off the shelf beside the machine. "King James version, of course, although if I could have found a Jerusalem, it would have been a difficult choice."

"Wonderful!" Tom said, taking the book. "That's a lot of typesetting."

"Ha!" Wentworth took the book back from Tom. "Indeed. And all for the sake of a book we already have. That's not really the point, is it."

"You print new books?"

"That occupies at least half our time, and is the part I'm most interested in, I confess. We publish instruction manuals, almanacs, travel journals, reminiscences. . . ." He looked at Tom, his eyeballs swimming in the glass of his spectacles. "As a matter of fact, we invite all survivors of the war to write their story down and submit it to us. We're almost certain to print it up. As our contribution to historical record."

Tom raised his eyebrows, but said nothing.

"You ought to do it," I urged him. "You'd be perfect for it, all those stories you've got about the old time."

"Ah, a storyteller?" said Wentworth. "Then indeed you should. My feeling is, the more accounts we have of that period, the better."

"No thank you," Tom said.

I shook my head, perplexed once again that such a talky old man would so stubbornly refuse to discuss his own life story—which is all some people can be gotten to talk about.

"Consider it further," Wentworth said. "I think I could guarantee the readership of most of the San Diego residents. The literate residents, I mean to say. And since the Salton Sea people have contacted us—"

"They contacted you?" Tom interrupted.

"Yes. Two years ago a party arrived, and since then your guides Lee and Jennings, very industrious men, have supervised the reconstruction of a rail line out there. We've shipped books to them, and they tell us they've sent them even farther east. So distribution of your work, though uncertain, could very well span the continent."

"You agree that communication extends that far?"

Wentworth shrugged. "We see through a glass darkly, as you know. I have in my possession a book printed in Boston, rather well done. Beyond that, I cannot say. I have no reason to disbelieve their claims. In any case, a book by you might just as easily reach Boston as that book reached me."

"I'll think about it," Tom said, but in a tone that I knew meant he was just killing the subject.

"Do it, Tom," I objected.

He just looked at the big press.

"Come see what we have printed so far," Wentworth added by way of encouragement, and led us out of the printing room to a corner room, again a chamber bright with sun, its windows overlooking the point break below. Tall bookcases alternated with tall windows, and held books old and new.

"Our library," said Wentworth. "Not a lending library, unfortunately," he added, interpreting perfectly the greedy smacking of Tom's lips. "This case contains the works printed here." Tom began to examine the shelves of the bookcase Wentworth indicated. Most of the books on them were big folders, filled with mimeographed pages; one shelf held leather-bound books the size of the old ones.

Wentworth and I watched Tom pull out book after book. "*Practical Uses of the Timing Device From Westinghouse Washer-Dryers,* by Bill Dangerfield," Tom read aloud, and laughed.

"It looks like your friend might take a while," Wentworth said to me. "Would you like to see our gallery of illustrations?"

What I really wanted to do was look at the books along with Tom, but I saw Wentworth was being polite so I said yes sir. We went back into the hall. Before a long window made of several large panes of glass the hall widened, and against the wall opposite the window were pictures of all sorts of animals, drawn in bold strokes of black ink.

"These are the originals of illustrations for a book describing all the animals seen in the back country of San Diego."

I must have looked surprised, for the pictures included some animals I had seen only in Tom's tatty encyclopedia: monkeys, antelopes, elephants. "There were very extensive zoos in San Diego before the war. We assume that all the animals in the main zoo were killed in the downtown blast, but there was an annex to the zoo in the hills, and those animals escaped, or were freed. Those who survived the subsequent climatic changes have prospered. I myself have seen bears and wildebeest, baboons and reindeer."

"I like the tiger here," I said.

"I did that one myself, thanks. That was quite an encounter. Shall I tell you about it?"

"Sure."

We sat down in wicker chairs placed before the windows.

"We were on a trek beyond Mount Laguna, a considerable peak twenty miles inland. The snowpack lies heavy on it nearly all the year round, and in the spring the streams in the surrounding hills gush with the melt. Our expedition was dogged by bad luck every step of the way. The radio equipment we had been told of was demolished. The library of Western literature I had hoped to relocate was nowhere to be found. One of the members of our expedition broke an ankle in the ruins of Julian. Lastly, worst of all, on our return we were discovered by the Cuyamaca Indians. These Indians are exceedingly jealous of their territory, and parties traveling in the area have reported fierce attacks at night, when the Indians are least afraid of firearms. All in all, it was a bad day's march, our injured friend between us in a sling, and Cuyamucans on horseback observing us from every open hilltop.

"As nightfall approached I struck out ahead of my party to scout possible camps. I found nothing very suitable for night defense, and as it was getting near sundown I retraced my path. When I got to the small clearing where I had left my friends, however, they were not there.

"While I was pursuing my friends the sun went down, and as you know the forest begins immediately upon that departure to get very dark. I came to a steep creek; I had no idea where my party had gotten to. I looked at the creek, momentarily at a loss. Staring through the dusk at the tumbling water I became aware of the presence of another pair of eyes, across the creek from me. They were huge eyes, the color of topazes."

"What are topazes?" I asked.

"Yellow diamonds, I should have said. As I met the gaze of those unblinking eyes, the tiger who owned them stalked out of a clump of torrey pine to the bank of the stream directly across from me."

"You're kidding!" I exclaimed.

"No. He was a fully grown Bengal tiger, at least eight feet long, and four feet high at the shoulders. In the dim light of that glade his winter fur seemed green to me, a dull green banded by dark stripes.

"He appeared from the clump so suddenly that at first I was merely appalled at the catastrophic proportions my bad luck had reached. I was sure I was living out the last moments of my existence, and yet I could not move, or even take my eyes from the unblinking gaze of that beautiful but most deadly beast. I have no notion of exactly how long we stood there staring at each other. I know it was one of the central minutes of my life.

"Then the tiger stepped over the creek with a fluid little jump, as easy as you would step over that crack in the floor. I braced myself as he approached—he lifted a paw as wide as my thigh, and pressed it down on my left shoulder—right here. He sniffed me, so close I could see the crystalline coloring of his irises, and smell blood on his muzzle. Then he took his paw from me and with a nudge of his massive head pushed me to my right, upstream. I stumbled, caught my balance. The tiger padded past me, turned to look, as if to see if I were following. I heard a rasp from its chest—if it was a purr, it was to a cat's purr as thunder is to a doorslam. I followed it. My astonishment had gone outside itself, and prevented all other thought. I kept my hand on the tiger's shoulder, where I could feel the big muscles bunch and give as it walked, and I stayed at its side as it wound between trees on a path of its own. Every minute or two it would turn its head to look into my eyes, and each time I was mesmerized anew by its calm gaze.

"Much later the moon rose, and still we walked through the forest together. Then I heard gunshots ahead, and the beast's purring stopped, its shoulder muscles tensed. In a clearing illumined by moonlight I made out several horses, and around them men—Indians, I guessed, for my party had no horses with it. More gunshots sounded from trees on the other side of the clearing, and I surmised that my friends were there, for just as we had no horses, the Cuyamaca Indians had no guns. The tiger shrugged off my hand with a twitch of his fur, a twitch that no doubt usually removed flies, and strode ahead of me, down toward the clearing."

"Hey!" Tom cried, hurrying around the corner of the hallway. He held one of the books printed on the hand letter press firmly before him, and gestured with it at Wentworth.

"Which one have you found?" Wentworth inquired. He didn't seem disturbed by the interruption of his story, but I was squirming.

"*An American Around the World*," Tom read. "*Being an Account of a Circumnavigation of the Globe in the Years 2030 to 2039. By Glen Baum.*"

Wentworth uttered his sharp, spontaneous laugh. "Very good. You have found the masterpiece of our line, I believe. Besides being an intrepid adventurer, Glen can tell a tale."

"But is it true? An American went around the world and returned just eight years ago?" Put that way, I understood why Tom was so flabbergasted—I had been stuck with the tiger in the back country—and I got out of my chair to have a look at this book. Sure enough, there it was: *An American Around the World*, right there on the cover.

Wentworth was smiling at Tom. "Glen sailed to Catalina in 2030, that is certain. And he reappeared in San Diego one night in the fall of 2039." His egg eyes flickered and something passed between the two men that I didn't catch, for Tom laughed out loud. "The rest you have between those covers."

"I had no idea this kind of stuff was still being written," Tom said. "How wonderful."

"It is, isn't it."

"Where is this Glen Baum now?"

"He took off for the Salton Sea last fall. Before he left he told me the title of his next book: *Overland to Boston.* I expect it will be as interesting as the one you hold." He stood up. Down the hall I could hear Jennings, joking with the woman in the mimeograph room. Wentworth led us back into the library.

"So what happened to you and the tiger?" I asked.

But he was rooting in a box on the bottom shelf of one case. "We have a lot of copies of that book. Take one with you back to San Onofre, courtesy of the Green Tiger Press." He offered one of the leather-bound books to Tom.

Tom said, "Thank you sir. This means a lot to me."

"Always glad to get new readers, I assure you."

"I'll make all my students read it," said Tom, grinning as if he'd just been handed a block of silver.

"You won't have to make us," I said. "But what about the tiger that time—"

Jennings and Lee entered the room. "Lunch time," Jennings cried. Apparently it was the habit in San Diego to eat a meal in the middle of the day. "Have a good tour?" Tom and I told him that we had, and showed him our book.

"Another thing," Wentworth said, groping in a different box. "Here is a blank book, in case you decide to write that memoir." He riffled the pages of a bound book, showing them to be blank. "Give it back to us full, and we will set about the task of reproducing it."

"Oh, I couldn't," said Tom. "You've given us enough already."

"Please, take it." Wentworth held it out to him. "We have plenty of these. No obligation to write—but if you decide to, then the materials will be at hand."

"Well, thanks," Tom said. After a moment's hesitation he put the two volumes in his shoulder bag.

"Shall we have lunch out on their lawn?" Jennings asked, holding aloft a long loaf of bread.

"I must return to my class," Wentworth said. "But feel free to enjoy the courtyard." And to Tom, as he led us to the door: "Remember what I said about that memoir, sir."

"I will. You're doing great work here."

"Thank you. Keep teaching people to read, or it will all go to naught. Now I must get back. Goodbye, thank you for visiting, goodbye." He turned and went into the front room, where his students were still kneading the paper pulp.

After lunch in the sun-filled salt air of the courtyard, we hiked back over Mount Soledad to the tracks, and pumped the car northward up and down steep hills. A mile or so up the tracks Tom had Lee apply the brakes. "Mind if we go out to the cliffs for a look around?"

Jennings looked doubtful, and I said, "Tom, we can look off cliffs when we get home."

"Not like these." Tom looked at Jennings. "I want to show him."

"Sure," Jennings said. "I told the wife we'd be back for supper, but she won't have that ready till after dark anyway."

So we got off the car again, and made our way westward to the coast, through a dense forest of torrey pine and brambles. Pretty soon we came upon an outcropping of tall stone crags. When we got in among them I saw they were concrete. They were buildings. The walls that remained—some of them as high as our beach cliff—were surrounded by piles of concrete rubble. Blocks as big as my house rose out of the ferns and brambles. Jennings was talking a streak about the place, and Tom held me by the arm and told the two San Diegans to go on ahead of us to the cliff. "He's got it all wrong," he said sourly when Jennings was out of earshot.

After they were gone I wandered in the ruins. A bomb had gone off nearby, I reckoned; the north side of every standing wall was black, and as soft and crumbly as sandstone. In the rubble and weeds I saw shards of glass, angled bits of metal both rusty and shiny, strips of plastic, a ribcage from a skeleton, melted glass tubes, metal boxes. Rafael would have loved it. But after a time I felt oppressed, like I had in San Clemente. This was no different from that: the ruins of the old time, the signs of a giant past now shattered, a past so big that not all our efforts would ever get us back to it, or anything like it. Ruins like these told us how little our lives were, and I hated them.

I saw Tom in the outbreak of concrete crags to the north, wandering aimlessly from ruin to ruin, tripping over blocks and then staring down at them like they'd jumped into his path. He was tugging on his beard as if he wanted to pull it out. Unaware of my presence, he was talking to himself, uttering short violent phrases that all ended with a sharp tug on the beard. As I got closer I saw that all the thousand lines in his face drooped down. I'd never seen him look so desolate.

"What was this place, Tom?"

I thought he wouldn't answer. He looked away, pulled his beard. "It was a school. My school."

One time a couple of summers before, we had all gathered under the torrey pine in Tom's junkyard, Steve and Kathryn, Gabby and Mando and Kristen, Del and little Teddy Nicolin, all talking at once under sunny skies, we were, and fighting over who got to read *Tom Sawyer* next, and plotting to tickle Kristen till she cried, and the old man sitting with his back against the treetrunk, laughing and laughing. "All right, shut up you kids, shut up now, school's in session."

I let Tom be and walked west across the faint remains of a road, into trees where little tangles of rotted beams marked the sites of old buildings. Buildings you could believe people had once put up, had once inhabited. I sat at the edge of a canyon that dropped to the sea. I could tell that the cliffs were going to be big ones, because I was still far above the water, and the canyon was short. The sun got lower. I wished I was home.

Tom walked through the trees a distance away, looking for me. I stood and called out, walked over to him. "Let's go out to the cliff and find those guys," he said. He still looked low, and I fell in beside him without a word. "Here, around this way," he said, and led me to the south rim of the canyon.

The trees gave way to shrubs, then to knee high weeds, and then we were on the cliff's edge. Far below lay the ocean, flat and silvery. The horizon was really out there—it must have been a hundred miles away. So much water! A stiff wind hit me in the face as I looked down the pocked tan cliff, which fell down and down in nearly vertical ravines, to a very broad beach, strewn with seaweed. Jennings and Lee were a few hundred yards along the cliff edge, just tiny figures on top of that cliff, throwing rocks down at the beach, though they hit the middle of the cliff instead. Looking at the rocks fall I suddenly knew what the gulls saw, and I felt I was soaring in the sky, high above the world.

To the left, La Jolla stuck out into the sea, blocking the view farther south. To the north the cliff curved away, until in the distance little cliffs alternated with blank bluish spots, which were marshes. The tiny cliffs and marshes extended in a curve all the way up to the green hills of Pendleton, and up there where the hills met the sea and sky was our valley, our home. It was hard to believe I could see that far. The waves below broke in long curves, leaving their white tracery on the water with just a whisper. Tom was sitting down, his feet swinging over the edge. "The beach is at least twice as wide," he said. Talking to himself. "They shouldn't let the world change so much in one life. It's too hard." I moved to get out of earshot, so he could talk without being overheard. But he looked up at me; he was talking to me: "I spent hours down there when time could have stopped, and I wouldn't have minded."

I didn't know what to say to him. The setting sun lit the cliffs. Our shadows stretched far across the field behind us, and the wind was cold. The world seemed a big place, a big, windy, dusky place. Uneasily I paced up and down the cliff edge. The old man stayed where he sat. The sun sank into the water, drowning bit by bit, paring away until only the emerald wink of the green flash was left. The wind picked up. Jennings and Lee came along the cliff toward us, tiny figures waving their arms.

"Better be getting back," Jennings called when they got closer. "Elma will be having dinner on the table."

"Give the old man a minute more," I said.

"She'll be mad if dinner has to wait too long," Jennings said more quietly. But Lee said "Let him be," and Jennings stood quietly, looking down at the tapestry left by broken waves.

Eventually Tom stirred, walked down to us as if he'd just woken up. The evening star glowed like a lantern in the ocean sky.

"Thanks for bringing us out here," Tom said.

"Our pleasure," Jennings replied. "But we'd better head back now. It's going to be a hell of a walk through those ruins in the dark."

"We'll skirt them to the south," Lee said, "down that road that . . ." He sucked in his breath hard.

"What's wrong?" Jennings exclaimed.

Lee pointed north, toward Pendleton.

We all looked, saw nothing but the dark curve of the coast, the first faint stars above—

A white streak fell out of the sky, plunged into the hills far to the north and disappeared.

"Oh no," Jennings whispered.

Another streak from the sky. It fell just like a shooting star, except it didn't slow down or break into pieces; it fell in a straight line, like lightning set against a straightedge, taking no more than three blinks of the eye from the time it appeared high above to the time it silently disappeared into the coastline.

"Pendleton," Lee said. "They're busting up our track." He began to curse in a heavy, furious low voice.

"Shit!" Jennings shouted. "*Shit!* God damn those people, God *damn* them. Why can't they leave us alone—"

Three more streaks fell from the sky, one after another, landing farther and farther north, defining the curve of the coast. I closed my eyes and red bars swam around in the black. I opened them to see another streak burst into the world up there and plummet down onto the land.

"Where are they coming from?" I asked, and was surprised to hear my voice shake. I was afraid, I think, that they would be bombs like those that had fallen on the day.

"Airplane," Jennings said grimly. "Or satellite, or Catalina, or halfway around the world. How would we know?"

"They're hitting all over Pendleton," Lee said.

"They've stopped," Tom pointed out. In the dark I couldn't read his expression, but his voice was calm. We watched the sky for another one. Nothing.

"Let's go," Lee finally croaked. Slowly we crossed the weed field on the edge of the cliff in single file. Then into the forest. Halfway back to the train Jennings, walking ahead of me, said, "The Mayor ain't going to like this one little bit."

...9

Jennings was right: the Mayor didn't like it. He went north himself to inspect the damage, and when he returned to Jennings's home leading his little crew, he told us how much he didn't like it. "The rails where those bombs hit are melted," he shouted, stretching the seams of a tight blue coat to pound on the dining table. Limping around the room, pausing to shout in the impassive faces of Lee and Jennings, waving his fists overhead as he cursed the Japanese: he was in a state. I stayed behind Tom and kept quiet. "Puddles of iron! And the dirt around it like black brick. Trees burnt to a crisp." He stumped over to Lee and waved a finger in Lee's face. "You men must have left some sign that you were working on those tracks, something that could be seen in the satellite pictures. I hold you responsible for that."

Lee stood with his mouth clamped tight, staring angrily past the Mayor. I noticed that a couple of the Mayor's men (Ben for one) looked pleased at Lee's chastisement, and gave each other sneering glances.

Jennings, bold in his own home, stepped up to protest. "Most of that line goes through forest, Mayor, and can't be seen from above. You saw that. In the open patches we didn't touch a thing, even if we had to work the cars through brush. And the bridges look exactly like they did before. Not a thing had been changed except the track, and we *had* to change that to make it passable. There was nothing else that could be seen from above."

Jennings went on like that for a while, and when he had convinced the Mayor, the Mayor got even angrier. "Spies," he hissed. "Someone in Onofre must have told the scavengers in Orange County, and they told the Japs." He tested the strength of Jennings's table again, *wham*. "We can't have that. That sort of thing *has to be stopped*."

"How do you know the spies aren't here in San Diego?" Tom asked.

Danforth and Ben and the rest of the Mayor's men glared at Tom. Even Jennings and Lee looked shocked.

"There are no spies in San Diego," Danforth said, his chin tucked into his neck. His voice made me feel like I did when the brake was pulled on the train. "Jennings, you get hold of Thompson and have him sail you and Lee and these two up the coast. Get off at Onofre with them, and hike back down the tracks and survey the damage. I want to know how long it's going to take to get that route open again."

"Melted track will be hard," Jennings replied. "We'll have to replace it like we did on the Salton Sea line, and it'll be impossible to do without leaving signs. Maybe we could follow three ninety-five up to Riverside, then turn back to the coast—"

Wham. "I want the coastal tracks working. You get Thompson and do as I tell you."

"Yes sir."

The Mayor and his men left, without any kind of farewell to Tom and me. Jennings sighed, and made an apologetic face at his wife, who was in the entrance to the kitchen looking discouraged. "Lee, I wish you'd talk back to him sometimes. He just gets madder when you don't answer like that." But Lee was still angry, and he said no more to Jennings than he had to Danforth. Tom jerked his head and I followed him out of the room. "Looks like it's back by sea," he said with a shrug.

The next day a heavy wall of clouds moved onshore, so we pumped a handcar over steep hills back to the coast, and north to the Del Mar River. From the south side of the marsh we could see the hundred wandering channels that the river made in the grass and cattails, iron bands through solid green. The main channel of the river snaked back on itself in big S's, and there against the bank, curving with it, was a long wooden dock. We rolled faster down the tracks, which led us all the way to the sea beach before making a half-circle and coming back to the dock.

There a couple of men were working on a big sloop moored at the dock. The sloop was a long one, nearly thirty feet I reckoned, wide-beamed and shallow-keeled, with canvas decking before the mast, and open plank seats aft of it. As we walked onto the dock a whiff of fish reminded me of home.

"Looks like we'll be sailing in a storm," I observed, for the wind was picking up, and the clouds clearly held rain.

"That's the way we want it," said Jennings.

"Too much of a storm and we'll be in trouble."

"Maybe. But we've got anchorages up the coast, and Thompson has done this a thousand times. In fact it should be easier than usual, with no Jap landing parties to intercept. You'll be home almost as fast as if we'd gone by train."

"Let's be under way," a man hallooed from the sloop. "Tide's turning!"

Jennings introduced us to the speaker, who turned out to be Thompson, and to his two sailors, Handy and Gilmour. We stepped down into the sloop. Tom and I sat on the plank just aft of the mast. Jennings and Lee sat down on the plank aft of ours. The men on the dock unmoored us and pushed us into the stream. The sailors rowed lazily, keeping us pointed downstream and letting the current do the work. A dinghy tied to the stern of the sloop weaved behind us. We looped through the marsh, and scores of ducks paddled into the reeds as we passed. The river poured over a shallow break in the beach. We spilled over this bar and the rowers pulled like madmen to get us through the violent soup and over some waves. When we were outside the break they shipped the oars and pulled up the two sails. Thompson trimmed the sails from his seat at the tiller, and we heeled over and sailed up the coast, paralleling the swells so that we rolled heavily. The wind was from the southwest, so we clipped along at speed.

We stayed about a mile offshore, and before darkness fell we had a fine view of the beach cliffs and the forested hills behind them. But soon the sun must have set, for the murk turned to night darkness, and the black bulk of the land was scarcely visible. Over the hissing of our wake and the creaks of the boom rubbing the mast, Jennings told Thompson and Handy and Gilmour the story of how we had seen the bombing of the railroad tracks. Tom and I sat against the mast, huddled in every stitch of clothing we had. The swells riding under us smoked a little, and the clouds got lower and lower, till we sailed through a narrow layer of clear windy air, sandwiched between thick slices of water and cloud. Tom dozed from time to time, head lolling.

After a couple hours I stretched out on a pile of rope between two planks, and tried to imitate Tom and get some sleep. But I couldn't. I lay on my back and watched the gray sail, almost the color of the clouds above it. I listened to the voices of Jennings and the others in the stern, without making out half of what they said. I shut my eyes, and thought about things we had seen on our journey south: the Mayor pounding Jennings's table till the salt shaker bounced, the dial and gauge-filled front of the broken radio in the Mayor's house, the face of the pretty girl I had danced with. We were in a new world now, I thought. We were in a world where Americans could freely pursue their destiny, or fight for it when they were opposed. A world altogether different from our little valley's world, with its ignorance of anything beyond the swap meets. Nicolin would be ecstatic to hear of it, and to read the book Wentworth had given us—to learn how an American had traveled all over the world . . . to join the resistance with the rest of the valley, and fight our hidden enemies on Catalina. . . . Oh, I'd have news for the gang, all right, and tales to tell that would make their eyes bug. How would I describe the Mayor's island house, so unlike anything known in Onofre? All those electric lights, reflected in that black lake with all its ruined towers . . .

I must have succeeded in falling asleep for a while, because when I opened my eyes again we were sailing in fog. Sometimes there was clear air for a man's height above the water, other times the cloud came right down and mixed with the smoking surface of the water. I stuck my hand over the side and found that the water was warmer than the air. I burrowed my cold feet into the pile of rope I'd been lying on. Tom still sat beside me, awake now.

"How do they know where we are?" I asked, sucking salt off my chilled fingers.

"Jennings says that Thompson stays close enough to shore to hear the waves break." I cocked an ear landward and heard a faint crack and rumble.

"Big swell."

"Yeah. He says the sound changes when we pass a rivermouth, and Thompson knows which rivermouth is which."

"He must come up this way a lot to be able to do that."

"True."

"Let's hope he doesn't lose track and run us onto the Pulgas River delta."

"We're past that, he says. I believe we're ten or fifteen miles down from Onofre."

So I had slept for a while, which was a blessing. The men aft were still talking quietly among themselves, all of them awake and leaning back against the gunwales, their coats buttoned up and their necks wrapped in wool scarves. We sailed into a white patch, and Thompson, alert at the tiller, steered us seaward. I couldn't fall asleep again, and for a long time everything remained the same: the fog, the hiss of the swells sliding under the boat, the creaking of the boom, the cold. The wind blew in fits and starts, and I could hear Thompson and Lee discussing the possibility of running in to one of the rivermouths and spending the coming day there. "Hard to do," Thompson said in an unconcerned way. "Damned hard to do with this fog, and the wind dying down. And the swell is picking up, whoah, see what I mean? These'll make pretty damn big waves, I'd say." The mast creaked as if in agreement, and the way the steep and smoking swells lifted and dropped, lifted and dropped, without us ever being able to properly see them, made them seem especially big. Swell after swell lifted the boat and slid away from it, and the rhythm of it almost had me asleep again, when Tom sat up suddenly.

"What's that noise?" he said sharply.

I didn't hear anything unusual, but Thompson nodded. "Japanese cruiser. Getting closer."

Long moments passed while the rest of us heard the low muffled grumble of an engine. Thompson put the tiller over—

A curling white wave washed over the bow and stopped us dead. The main-sail flapped and then backed. Foaming water dripped over the canvas decking into my lap; Tom snatched up his shoulder bag to keep it from getting soaked. A cone of white light appeared in the fog. Our boat rocked at the bottom of this blinding cone, and one edge of the lit fog revealed the bulk of a tall ship, a black shape rumbling beside us, hardly seeming to move with the swell. My heart raced as I took all this in; I braced myself against Tom, looking at him fearfully. We were caught!

"Radar," Tom whispered.

"Put down your sail," a voice shouted. *"Everyone stand with hands on head."* The voice was loud, and had a metallic ring to it that made me cringe with fear. *"You are under arrest."*

I looked aft. Lee, all glare and black shadow in the searchlight's powerful whiteness, was aiming a rifle at the top of the cone. *Crack!* The light above us burst and went dark in a tinkling of glass. Immediately the stern of our boat was spitting fire, for every man back there was shooting up at the Japanese ship. Tom pulled me down, the gunfire was a continuous banging, overwhelmed by a great BOOM, and suddenly the front of the sloop was gone. Broken planks and cold seawater poured up the boat over us. "Help!" I cried, freeing my feet from the tangle of rope. I was making my way over the canted gunwale when the mast fell on me.

The next thing I knew, searchlights were breaking inside my eyelids. I was choking on seawater. Rough hands pulled me up, hurting my armpits. Being hauled up metal steps banged my knees. Choking and gasping, I vomited water onto a metal deck. Someone wrapped me in a coarse dry blanket.

I was on the Japanese ship.

When I realized this—it was the first thought I had, as I regained conscious-ness and saw the studded gray metal decking under my nose—I struggled to escape the hands holding me. Nothing doing. Hands restrained me, voices spoke nonsense at me: *mishi kawa tonatu ka*, and the like. "Help!" I cried. But my head was clearing, and I knew there was no help for me. The suddenness of it all kept me from feeling it. I shivered and choked as if I'd been walloped in the stomach, but the real extent of the disaster was just sinking in as the Japa-nese sailors began to strip my wet clothes from me and wrap me in blankets. One was pulling my shirt sleeve down my arm; I twisted my hand out of it and fisted him in the nose. He squawked with surprise. I took a good swing and caught another one on the side of the head, and then started kicking wildly. I got some of them pretty good. They ganged up on me and carried me through a doorway into a glass-walled room at the back of the bow deck. Put me down on a bench that followed the curve of the hull.

Up in the bow I could see sailors still searching the water, shining a new searchlight this way and that, and shouting into an amplifying box. Two of them stood behind a giant gun on a thick stand—no doubt the gun that had demolished our sloop. The ship vibrated with the hum of engines, but we drifted over the swells, going nowhere. At our height above the water the fog was impenetrable. They had little motor dinghies down there searching, puttering about in the murk, but I could tell by their voices that they weren't finding anything.

They had killed Tom. The thought made me cry, and once I started I sobbed and sobbed. All those years he had survived everything, every danger imaginable—only to get drowned by a miserable shore patrol. And all so fast.

After what seemed a long time, the men searching the water quit. I had pretty well recovered my wits, and some of my warmth, for the blankets were thick. I felt cold inside, though. I was going to make these men pay for killing Tom. Tom hadn't seemed too sure about the American resistance, but I was definitely part of it now, I thought to myself—starting right then and there, and for the rest of my life. In my cold heart I made a vow.

A door in the back wall of the glassed in room opened, and through it walked the captain of the ship. Or maybe he wasn't, but there were gold tags on the shoulders of his new brown coat, and the coat had gold buttons. His face looked like the faces of the bodies that washed up on our beach. Japanese, I had learned to call him. Two more officers, wearing brown suits without the gold shoulder tags or the buttons, stood behind him, their faces like masks.

Murderers, all of them. I stared fiercely at the captain, and he looked back, his eyes expressionless. The room pitched gently, and fog pressed against the dripping salt-encrusted windows, fog that looked red because of the little red light set over the door.

"How do you feel?" the captain said in English that was clear, but lilting in a way I'd never heard before.

I stared at him.

"Have you recovered from the blow to your head?"

I stared at him some more.

After a time he nodded. I've seen his face more than once since then, in dreams: his eyes dark brown, almost black; deep lines in his skin, extending from the outside corners of his eyes in fans around the side of his head; black hair cut so close to his scalp that it had the texture of a brush. His lips were thin and brown, and now they were turned down with displeasure. He looked devilish, taken all together, and I struggled to look unconcerned as I stared at him, because he scared me.

"You appear to have recovered." One of his officers gave him a thin board, to which sheets of paper were clipped. He took a pencil from the clip. "Tell me, young sir, what is your name?"

"Henry. Henry Aaron Fletcher."

"Where do you come from?"

"America," I said, and glared at each of them in turn. "The United States of America."

The captain glanced at his officers. "Good show," he said to me.

A gang of regular sailors in blue coats came in from the bow and jabbered at him. He sent them back to the bow, and turned to me again.

"Do you come from San Diego? San Clemente? Newport Beach?" I didn't answer, and he continued: "San Pedro? Santa Barbara?"

"That's way north," I said scornfully. Shouldn't have spoken, I thought. But I wanted to tear into him so bad I was shaking—shaking with fright, too—and I couldn't help talking.

"So it is. But there is no habitation directly onshore, so you must come from north or south."

"How do you know there isn't a habitation onshore?"

He smiled just like we do, though the results were ugly. "We have observed your coastline."

"Spies," I said. "Sneaking spies. You should be ashamed. You're a sailor. Don't you feel ashamed for attacking unarmed sailors on a foggy night and killing them all—sailors who weren't doing you any harm?"

The captain pursed his lips as if he'd bitten into something sour. "You were hardly unarmed. We took quite a few shots from you, and one of our men was hurt."

"Good."

"Not good." He shook his head. "Besides—I suspect your companions may have swimmed to shore. Otherwise we would have found them."

I remembered the dinghy we had been pulling, and thought a prayer.

"I must have an answer, please. You come from San Diego?"

I shook my head. "Newport Beach."

"Ah." He wrote on his paper. "But you were returning from San Diego?"

As long as I lied, it was okay to tell him things. "We were on our way to San Clemente and missed it in the fog."

"Missed San Clemente? Come now, we are several miles south of that town."

"I told you, we missed it."

"But you had been headed north for some time."

"We knew we had gone too far, and we were headed back. It's hard to tell where you are in the fog."

"In that case, why were you at sea?"

"Why do you think?"

"Ah—to avoid our patrols, you mean. Yet we don't interfere with coastal traffic. What was your business in San Clemente?"

I thought fast, looking down so the captain wouldn't see me doing it. "Well . . . we were taking some Japanese down there to hike in and look at the old mission."

"Japanese don't land on the mainland," the captain said sharply.

So I had startled him! "Of course they do," I said. "You say that because it's your job to see that they don't. But they do it all the time, and you know it."

He stared at me, then conferred with his officers in Japanese. For the first time I noticed I was hearing someone talk in a foreign tongue. It was peculiar. It sounded like they were repeating four or five sounds over and over again, too fast to actually be saying anything. But obviously they were, for the officers gestured and nodded agreement, the captain gave orders, all in a rapid gibberish. More than their skin or their eyelids, their meaningless speech brought it to me that I was dealing with men from the other side of the world—men a lot different from me than the San Diegans had been. When the captain turned and spoke to me in English it sounded unreal, as if he were just making sounds he didn't understand.

Scribbling on the page clipped to the board, he said, "How old are you?"

"I don't know. My pa can't remember."

"Your mother can't remember?"

"My father."

This struck him as odd, I could see. "No one else knows?"

"Tom guesses I'm sixteen or seventeen."

"How many people were on your boat?"

"Ten."

"How many people live in your community?"

"Sixty."

"Sixty people in Newport Beach?" he said, surprised.

"Hundred and sixty, I mean."

"How many people live in your house or dwelling?"

"Ten."

His nose wrinkled, and he lowered the board. "Can you describe the Japanese you met in Newport Beach?"

"They looked just like you," I said truculently.

He pursed his lips. "And they were with you tonight on the boat we sank?"

"That's right. And they came over here on a ship as big as this one, so why didn't you stop *them*? Isn't that your job?"

He waved a hand impatiently. "Not all landings can be stopped."

"Especially when you're paid not to try, eh?"

He pursed his lips again into that bad-taste look.

Shaking more and more, I cried, "You say you're here to guard the coast, but all you really do is bomb our tracks and kill us when we're just sailing—when we're just sailing home—" and all of a sudden I was crying again, bawling and crying. I couldn't help it. I was cold, and Tom was dead, and my head hurt, and I couldn't stand up to this stranger and his questions any longer.

"Your head is still painful?" I was holding my head between my arms. "Here, stretch out on this bench and rest. We need to get you to hospital." His hands took me by the shoulders, and helped me lie out against the curving metal of the ship's tall gunwale. The officers lifted my legs up and wrapped them in the blankets, moving the clipboard from where the captain had put it down. I was too dispirited to kick them. The captain's hands were small and strong; they reminded me of Carmen Eggloff's hands, strangely enough, and I was about to burst into sobs again, when I noticed the ring on the captain's left ring finger. It was a big darkened gold ring that held a cut red jewel in the top of it. Letters were carved into the gold around the jewel, curving around the stone so they were hard to read. But the hand wearing the ring stilled for a moment right before my nose, and I could make out the words. *Anaheim High School 1976.*

I jerked back and bumped my head against the gunwale. "Be peaceful, young sir. Don't agitate yourself. We'll talk further of these things in Avalon."

He was wearing an American ring. A class ring, like those the scavengers wore during the evenings at the swap meets, to show which of the ruins they came from. I quivered in the scratchy blankets as I thought about what that meant. If the captain of the ship assigned to keep foreigners from coming to our coast was himself visiting Orange County—visiting it regularly, and wearing a ring that a scavenger must have given him—then no one was guarding the coast in earnest. It was all a sham, this quarantine—a sham that had gotten Tom killed. Tears pooled in my eyes, and I squeezed them back, furious at the injustice, the corruption of it—furious and confused. It seemed just moments ago I had been dozing, eyes shut, in the San Diegans' sloop. And now—what had he said?—"We'll talk further of these things in Avalon."

I sat up.. They were taking me to Catalina to be questioned. Tortured, maybe. Thrown in prison, or made a slave—kept away from Onofre for the rest of my life. The more I thought of it the more frightened I became. Up to that point I hadn't stopped to think what they were going to do with me—I was confused, and that's a fact—but now it was obvious I should have; they weren't going to take me up the Onofre river and drop me off. They were going to take me with them. The idea made my heart thump so hard I thought my ribs would burst. My breathing was so quick and choppy I thought I might faint. Catalina! I would never see home again! Though it was selfish of me, I felt worse about that than I had about Tom's death.

The captain and his officers stood under the little red light over the door in the back wall. Salt crusts marred the dim red reflections of them in the big windows. The reflection of the captain's face was looking at me, which meant, I decided, he was watching my reflection. He was keeping an eye on me.

Out on the bow deck a couple of sailors still stood by the searchlight. It looked like they were fixing it. Otherwise, the deck was empty. Fog swept over us, cold and white. The ship vibrated ever so slightly, but we still hadn't gone anywhere.

They had taken every stitch of clothing off of me, to get me dry. All the better.

The captain walked back to me. "Are you feeling better?"

"Yes. I'm getting sleepy, though."

"Ah. We will take you into one of the berths."

"No! Not yet. I'd be sick if I had to move. I just want to rest here a minute more." I slumped down and did my best to look exhausted.

The captain watched me. "You said something about tracks being bombed?"

"Who, me? I never said anything about tracks."

He nodded doubtfully.

"Why do you do it?" I asked despite myself. "Why do you come halfway around the world to patrol here?"

"We have been given the responsibility by the United Nations. I don't believe you would understand all the details of the matter."

So it was true, what they had told us in San Diego. Part of it, anyway. "I know about the United Nations," I said. "But there isn't a person from America there to tell our side. Everything they do is illegal." I spoke drowsily, to put him off his guard. I shouldn't have spoken at all, but my curiosity got the better of me.

"They're all we've got, young sir. Without them, perhaps war and devastation would come to us all."

"So you hurt us to help yourselves."

"Perhaps." He stared at me, as if surprised I could argue at all. "But it may be that it is the best policy for you as well."

"It isn't. I live there. I know. You are holding us back."

He nodded briefly. "But from what? That is the part that you have not experienced, my brave young friend."

I feigned sleep, and he walked back to his officers under the red light. He said something to them and they laughed.

Up and down the room pitched, up and down, up and down, smooth and gentle. I jumped out of the blankets and ran toward the open doorway to the bow. The captain had been watching for me to make such a move: "Ha!" He yelled, leaping after me. But he had miscalculated. I just caught the astonished look on his face as I flashed out the door ahead of him—I was too fast for him. Once outside I raced for the gunwale, and dove past the startled sailors into the fog.

After a long fall my arms and face smacked the sea, and my body walloped them home. When I felt the water's chill I thought *Oh no.* The air had been knocked out of me, and ten feet under I had to breathe. When I popped back to the surface to suck in air a swelltop rolled over me and I breathed water instead. I was certain my hacking and gasping would give me away to the Japanese, who shouted after me. Undoubtedly they were lowering boats to search for me. The water was freezing, it made my whole body cry out for air.

I struck out swimming away from the shouts and the dim glow of the searchlight, and was rammed by an approaching swell. Damned if I hadn't jumped off the seaward side of the ship. I would have to swim around it. And I had been sure I was leaping off the landward side. How had I gotten so turned around? My confidence in my sense of direction disappeared, and for a minute I panicked, afraid I wouldn't be able to find my way to shore. I sure wasn't going to see it. But the swell was a reliable guide, as I quickly realized when it shoved me time after time in the same direction. It was coming a bit out of the south, I had noted in the sloop, and I only had to swim in with it, maybe angling a bit to the right as it propelled me, and I would be on the straightest course to shore.

So that was all right. But the cold shocked me. The water might still have been from that warm current we had enjoyed the previous week, but now, with the storm wind whipping across the surface and chilling my head and arms, it didn't feel warm in any way. I almost shouted to the Japanese to come to my rescue. But I didn't do it. I didn't want to face the captain again. I could imagine his face as I explained, yes sir, I *did* want to escape, but you see, the water was too cold. It wouldn't do. If they were to haul me out, that was fine—part of me hoped they would, and soon, too. But if they didn't, I was stuck with it.

To combat the cold I swam as hard as I could, trusting that I was around the bow of the ship and putting distance between us. It would be a nasty shock to clang into its hull unexpectedly, and it still seemed possible, because in the fog

I couldn't see ten feet. As swell after swell passed under me, however, it became less likely. Too bad, part of me thought. You're in for it now. The rest of me got down to the business of getting to shore, the sooner the better. I settled into a rhythm and began working.

Only once did I see or hear the ship again, and it was soon after I had made the final decision to swim for it. Usually the fog does not convey sound better than the open air, no matter what some folks would have you believe. It tends to dampen sound as it limits sight, though not as drastically. But it is funny stuff, and sometimes, fishing in a fog bank, Steve and I have heard the voices of other fishermen talking in low tones and sounding as if they were about to collide with us, when they were half a mile away. Tom could never explain it, nor Rafael neither.

It happened again on this night. The voices were behind me, and far enough above me that I guessed they came from the ship. I groaned, thinking that I had been confused in my swimming, and that I was still in the vicinity of the ship; but then a cold swirl of wind caught their voices midsentence, and blew them away for good. It was just me and the fog and the ocean, and the cold.

I only know three ways to swim. Or call it four. Crawl, backstroke, side-stroke, and a frog kick. Crawl was the fastest by far, and did the most to keep me warm, so I put my face in the brine—which scared me somehow, but keeping my head up was too tiring—and swam for it. I could feel the swells pick me up feet first, give a welcome shove, and pass under, leaving me floundering in the trough. Other than that, all I felt was the wind cutting into my arms as I stroked. That got so bad that I switched to the frog kick just to keep my arms under water. The water was still cold, but I had gotten used to it a little, and it was better than my wet arms in the wind. Working hard was the best solution, so after a few frog strokes I went back to the crawl and swam hard. When I got tired or my arms got too cold, I switched to frog kick or sidestroke, and let kicking and the swell carry me along. It was a matter of shifting the discomforts from spot to spot, and then bearing them for as long as I could.

The thing about swimming is it leaves you a lot of time to think. In fact there's little else to do but think, unlike when hiking through the woods, for instance, when there are rocks to look out for, and the path of least effort to be found. In the sea all paths are the same, and at night in the fog there's not much to look at. This is what I could see: the black swells rising and sinking under me; the white fog, which was becoming low clouds again as the wind unfortunately picked up; and my own body. And even these things were only visible when I had my head up and my eyes open, which wasn't very often. So I had nothing to do but worry about my swimming. Mostly I swam with my head in the brine and my eyes closed, feeling my muscles tire and my joints ache with cold, and though my thoughts raced wildly they never got too far from this vital feeling, which determined the stroke I used from moment to moment.

Kicking hard on my back warmed my feet some, and they needed it. I could barely feel them. But kicking was slow, and effortful too. I sure wished I had a pair of Tom's fins at that moment, the ones he lent us to body surf with. I loved those fins—old blue or green or black things that made us walk like ducks and swim like dolphins. What I wouldn't have done for a pair of them right then and there! It almost made me cry to think of them. And once they occurred to me I couldn't get them out of my mind. Now to my little assortment of thoughts was added, if only I had those fins.

I flopped back on my stomach and started the crawl again. The backs of my upper arms were getting stiff and sore. I wondered how long I had been at it, and how much longer I had to go. I tried to calculate the distance. Say the ship had been a mile offshore. That would be about half the length of our valley's beach. If I had started swimming at Basilone Hill, then by this time I'd be about to . . . well, I couldn't say. There was no way to tell. I was sure I had swum a good distance, though, from the way my arms hurt.

Stroke, stroke, stroke, stroke, stroke. Sometimes it was easy to blank the mind and just swim. I changed strokes at the count of a hundred; hundred after hundred slipped by. A lot of time passed. When I did the frog kick I noticed that the fog was lifting, becoming the low cloud bank that had rushed overhead when we were sailing north in the sloop. Perhaps that meant I was getting close to land. The clouds were very white against the black sea; probably the moon was now up. The surface of the water was a rolling obsidian plain. Swirling into it were little flurries of snow, flying forward over me as much as they were falling. When they hit the water they disappeared instantly, without a splash. The sight of them made me feel the cold more than ever, and again I almost started to cry, but couldn't spare the effort. I was crying miserable, though. If only I had those fins.

I put my head down and doggedly crawled along, ordering myself to think of something besides the cold. All the times I had looked out over a peaceful warm sea, for instance. I recalled a time when Steve and Tom and I were lazing up at Tom's place, looking for Catalina. "I wonder what it would look like if the water was gone," Steve had said. Tom had jumped on the notion with glee. "Why, we'd think we were on a giant mountain. Offshore here would be a plain tilted down and away from us, cut by canyons so deep we wouldn't be able to see the bottom of them. Then the plain would drop away so steeply we wouldn't be able to see the lowlands beyond. That's the continental shelf I've told you about. The lowland would rise again to foothills around Catalina and San Clemente islands, which would be big mountains like ours." On he had rambled, pulling up imaginary hipboots to lead us on an exploration of the new land, through mud and muck that was covered with clumps of seaweed and surprised-looking fish, in search of wrecked ships and their open treasure chests. . . .

It was the wrong time to remember that discussion. When I thought of how much water was underneath me, how far away the bottom was, I got scared and pulled my feet closer to the surface. All those fish, too—the ocean was teeming with fish, as I well knew, and some of them had sharp teeth and voracious appetites. And none of them went to bed at night. One of those ugly ones with its mouth crammed with teeth could swim up and bite me that very moment! Or I might blunder into a whole school of them, and feel their slick finny bodies colliding with mine—the sandy leather of a shark, or the spikes of a scorpion fish. . . . But worse than the fish was just being out there at all, with *all* that water below, down and down and colder and darker, all the way to the slimy bottom so far below. I thrashed with panic for a while, terrified at the thought of where I was, of how deep the sea was.

But several rushes of panic passed, and I was still there. There was nothing I could do to change things. And more and more as time passed the real danger, the cold, reasserted itself and made me forget my fears of the imagination. It couldn't be escaped, I couldn't swim hard enough now to ward it off, and the water felt icy, no longer any refuge from the snowy wind. The cold would kill me soon. I could feel that in my muscles. It was more frightening than the size of the sea by far.

My thoughts seemed to chill, becoming slothful and stupid. My arms hurt so I could barely move them. Backstroke was hard, crawl was hard, frog stroke was hard. Floating was hard. If only I had those fins. Such a long way to the bottom. My arms were as heavy as ironwood branches, and my stomach muscles wanted a rest. If they cramped I would drown. Yet I had no choice but to keep them tensed, and go on swimming. I put my numbed face in the water and plowed along in a painful crawl, trying to hurry.

There was a rhythm I could keep to if I could ignore the pain, and grimly I stuck to it. My sense of time left me. So did the notion of a destination. It was not so much a matter of getting somewhere, as it was avoiding death then and there. Left arm, right arm, breath; left arm, right arm, breath. And so on. Each motion a struggle against the cold. The few times I bothered to look up, nothing had changed: low white clouds, flakes of snow swirling ahead and disappearing into the sea with a faint *ssss, ssss, ssss.* I couldn't feel my hands and feet, and the cold moved up my limbs and made them less and less obedient to my commands. I was getting too cold to swim.

The time came when it seemed I would have to give up. All my fine stories for the gang were going to go to waste, told only to myself in a last rush of thought on the way to the bottom. A waste, but there it was. I couldn't swim any more. If only I had those fins. Still, each time I thought to myself, Hanker, this is it, time to sink—I found the energy to slap along a few strokes more. It felt like swimming in cold butter. I couldn't go on. Again I decided to give up, and again I found a few more kicks in me. I imagine that most of the people who drown at sea never do decide to give up; their bodies stop obeying, and that makes the decision for them.

On my back I could frog kick, and flap my arms at my sides. It was the only way left to me, so I kept at it, anxious to postpone the moment of letting go, though I knew it wasn't far away. The thought of it was terrifying, sickening. Like nothing else I'd ever felt. Being taken to Catalina was nothing compared to it, and now I knew for sure I had made a fatal mistake by jumping overboard. Swells swept up out of the dark, becoming visible as they lifted me. Maybe they could do the work for me, if I could stay afloat. I didn't want to die. I wasn't willing to quit. But I was too cold, too weak. On my back like I was, I had to work to avoid swallowing water when the crests of the swells passed over me, for one mouthful would have sunk me as fast as a hundred pounds of iron. Only dimly, at first, did I notice that the swells were getting taller. That's all I need, I thought. A bigger swell, how wonderful. Still—didn't that mean something? I was too cold, I wasn't thinking anymore in the way that we usually think, silently talking to ourselves. I had only the simplest sort of thoughts: sensations, a repeated refusal to sink, instructions to my feeble limbs.

Cold fingers brushed my back and legs, and I squealed.

Seaweed, slick and leafy. I struggled around the floating clump, granted a bit of strength by the scare. Then on top of a swell I heard it. *p-KKkkkkkkk* . . . *p-KKkkkkkkkk*. Waves breaking. I had made it.

Suddenly I had some energy. I couldn't believe I hadn't heard the sound of the waves before, it was so plain. At the crest of the next swell I looked landward, and sure enough there it was, a black mass big and solid under the clouds. "Yeah!" I said aloud. "Yeah!"

I ran into another clump of seaweed, but I didn't care. Disentangling myself from it I crested another swell, and from there the clear sound of the breaking waves told me my troubles weren't over. Even from behind, the long irregular *crack* of the waves falling was loud. And following the crack was a low roaring *krrkrrkrrkrrkrrkrrkrrkrr*, that faded away just enough to make the next break noticeable. All the sounds joined together in a fierce trembling boom; it was hard to believe I hadn't heard it earlier. Too tired.

I swam on, and now at the crests of the swells I could see the waves breaking ahead of me. As each wave broke, water sucked over the back of it like it was the edge of the world; white water exploded into the fog, and the whole churning mass tumbled in to the beach. There was going to be a problem getting to shore.

The swells kept pushing me in until one larger than the rest picked me up and carried me along with it, getting steeper and steeper as it went along. I was caught under the crest, and slowly it dawned on me that it was going to pitch over and throw me with it. I took a deep breath and plunged into the wave, felt it pulling me up as I struggled through the thick lip and out the back side. Even so I was almost taken over the back of the break into the churning soup. The next swell was nearly as big, and I had to swim as fast as I could back out to sea to get over it before it broke. I breasted its top while it stood vertical, and looked back down at the foam-streaked water some fifteen feet below. Had that black area down there been rock? Was there a reef under me?

Whimpering miserably I swam out a good distance, so I wouldn't get caught inside by a wave bigger than the two that had almost drowned me. The idea of a reef was horrifying. I was too tired for such a thing, I wanted to swim straight in to the beach. It was so close. It was possible that what I had seen was a patch of black water in the foam, but I couldn't be sure, and if I was wrong I would pay for it with my life. I treaded water for a time and studied the waves as they broke and sucked water over behind them. The place where they consistently broke first marked the shallowest water, and if there were rocks they probably were there. So I swam parallel to the beach a ways, to the spot where the waves consistently broke last. The cold was in my thoughts again, and my fear grew. I decided to start in.

I attended to the swells, because if a wave broke before it reached me, it would roll me under and never let me up. No, I needed to catch a wave and ride it in, just like we did for fun in the waves off Onofre. If I caught one right, I might take it all the way onto the sand. That was what I wanted. I needed a big wave—not too big, though: medium big. Waves usually came in sets of threes, a big one followed by two littler ones, but floating over them in the dark I couldn't get any sense of that. Looking back and forth I accidentally swallowed a mouthful of water, and it almost sent me to the bottom. I saw I couldn't afford to be picky, and I struck out backstroking, determined to catch the very next wave. If I ran into rocks that would be it, but I didn't have a choice. I had to take the chance.

As a swell picked me up I suddenly didn't feel tired at all, though I still couldn't swim well. I turned on my stomach as the wave tilted my feet up, and swam for it. What I would have given for a pair of Tom's fins, kicking as I was to match the growing speed of the wave! But I caught it anyway, just, and felt it pick me up and carry me along. I was high on the steep face as it pitched over, so that I dropped through the air and smacked my chest into the water. If it had been reef that would have been the end of me, but it wasn't, and I skidded over the water at the front edge of the broken wave, my head alone out of the white water, barreling over the suds at a tremendous speed.

The wave petered out too soon, however, and left me gasping in the soup. I stood and felt for the bottom—no bottom—sank, and hit sand with my feet almost immediately. I pushed back to the surface and saw another wave steaming in. Rolling myself into a ball I let the wave tumble me shoreward—a standard body surfing trick, but one inappropriate to my weakness. I barely struggled back to the surface when my forward motion stopped. But now I could stand, heaving, on good smooth sand! Walking cramped my legs and I collapsed. All of the water that had been pushed onto the beach by the last few waves chose that moment to sluice back down, and I knelt and clawed the coarse flowing sand as the torrent rushed over me. Then it was past, and I hobbled out of the water.

As soon as I got up the steep wash and beyond the high water mark, I fell down. The beach was covered with a gritty layer of melting hail. My stomach muscles relaxed at last, and I started to throw up. I had swallowed more water than I knew, and it took a while to get it all out. I didn't mind. It was the most triumphant retching I ever did.

I had made it. All well and good. But there was no chance to celebrate, because now there was a new set of problems. The snowing had stopped for a moment, but there was still a wind which cut me most distinctly. I crawled up the beach to the cliff backing it. Narrow beach, cliff three times my height—it could have been anywhere on the Pendleton shore. At the base of the cliff there was less wind, and I hunkered down behind a sandstone boulder, among other clumps of fallen cliff. I started wiping myself dry with my fingers, and while doing that looked around.

Out to sea moonlit clouds obscured the view. The beach stretched away in both directions, covered by black blobs of seaweed. I was beginning to shiver. One of the blobs of seaweed had a more regular shape than the rest. Standing up to look at it better I felt the onshore wind blow right through me. Still, that clump of weed—I stumbled around my boulder and walked toward it, being careful not to hurry and fall.

A break I had not noticed in the cliff was the mouth of a deep ravine, spilling its creek onto the beach to cut through the sand to the sea. I sat and slid down the sloping sand to the creek, stopping to drink some of its water—I was thirsty, strangely enough. When I stood again it was a struggle to make my way up the three foot embankment on the other side; I kept slipping, and finally, cursing and sniffling, I had to crawl up it and then stand.

Back on the plateau of the beach I could see the black blob clearly, and my suspicion was confirmed. It was a boat, pulled almost to the cliff. "Oh, yes," I said. It was farther away than it looked, but at last I staggered to its side and sat in the lee of it. Held the gunwale with my numb hands.

There were two oars in it and nothing else, so there was no way to be positive, but I was sure it was the dinghy we had been trailing behind our sloop. They had made it to shore! Tom was (most likely) alive!

I, on the other hand, was nearly dead. Presumably my companions were somewhere in the area—up the ravine was a good guess—but I couldn't follow them. I was too weak and cold to stand. In fact my head banged the dinghy's side while I was just sitting there. I knew I was in bad shape. I didn't want to die after taking the trouble to swim all that way, so I got to my knees. Too bad they hadn't left something in the boat besides the oars. Since they hadn't . . . I considered it at a snail's pace, as if very drunk. "Should get out of the wind, yeah." I crawled to a big clump of seaweed and pulled off the top layers. They were all tangled and didn't want to come. I got angry—"Stupid seaweed, let loose!"—blubbering like that until I got to the middle of the clump, which was still dry. Dryness felt like warmth. I pulled as many of the black leafy strands as I could carry out of the clump, and staggered back to the boat with them. Dropped the weed.

I pushed at the side of the dinghy. It might as well have been set in stone. I groaned. Pushing on the gunwale I could rock it a bit. "Turn over, boat." I was amazed and frightened by my lack of strength; normally I could have flipped that dinghy with one hand. Now it became the great struggle of my life to overturn the damn thing. I got out the oars, slid one under the keel, lifted the wide end, and balanced it on the handle end of the other one, which had its wide end jammed in the sand. That tilted the boat, and on the other side I stepped on the low gunwale and pulled at the high one, all at once and with all my might. The boat flipped and I had to fall away from it flat on my face to avoid being crushed.

I spit out sand and regained my feet. Carried a sandstone clod to the bow. Lifting the bow was not that hard, and I rolled the clod under it to keep it up. If I had had the sense to put the seaweed in the boat I would have been set, but at this point I wasn't thinking that far in advance. The seaweed just fit under the gap, and I stuffed it under, strand after strand, until all that I had dragged over with me was under the boat. Getting myself under was more difficult—I scraped my back, and finally pushed up with my head until the bow was lifted far enough to get my butt in.

Once under the boat I was tempted to just lie there, because I was beat. But I was still shivering like a dog, so I felt around in the blackness and pulled all the seaweed together. It made a pretty thick mat, and when I had crawled on it there was still a lot of weed left to pull over me, in a sort of blanket. I pulled the sandstone clod under the boat with me and was out of the wind, in a dry bed.

I started to shiver in a serious way. I shivered so hard my jaw hurt, and the seaweed around me cracked and rustled. Yet I didn't feel any warmer for it. Flurries of rain or slushy snow hit the bottom of the boat, and I was pleased with myself for being sheltered. But I couldn't stop shivering. I twisted around, put my hands in my armpits, gathered seaweed closer to me—anything to get warmer. It was a fight.

There passed one of those long hours that you seldom hear about when people are telling their tales—a cold, fearful time, spent entirely in the effort to warm up. It went on and on and on, and eventually I did warm a little. I was not toasty, you understand, but after the cold sea and the open windy beach, my bed of dry seaweed under the boat felt pretty good. I wanted to stay there forever, just huddle up and fall asleep and never have to move again.

But another part of me knew I should locate Tom and the San Diegans before they got out of my reach. I figured they would be waiting out the night in some sort of shelter, like I was, and that they would take off in the morning. Pushing up the bow of the dinghy I saw a thin slice of the dawn: sand, broken cliff bottom, dark cloud. The darkest and most miserable day ever. The wind whistled over the boat, but I decided it was time to find them, before they took off and left me.

Getting out from under the boat was easier than slipping beneath it had been; I lifted the bow, setting the sandstone block under it, and slithered through the gap. Returning to the wind was a shock. All my precious warmth was blown away in an instant. In the dawn I could see down the beach much farther than before. It was bare and empty, a desolate gray reach. Moving the boat to one side exposed the seaweed, and I tied strands of it around me and looped them over my shoulders until I was fairly well covered by the crackly black leaves. It was better wind protection than I would have guessed, and far better than nothing at all.

The ravine had cut a V in the cliff almost to the level of the beach, so that I could walk right up it, in the streambed to avoid brush. I was beyond caring what might happen to my feet in the creekbed, and luckily the bottom was rounded stones.

After climbing a short rapids I found myself among trees, and the brush became less dense. The ravine took a sharp bend to the right, then bent back again; after that the air was almost still. Overhead the treetops swayed and their needles whistled. Flurries of snow drifted among them, blurring their sharp black lines. I groaned at the sight and hiked on.

Short waterfalls fell when the ravine got steeper, and to ascend them I had to climb through mesquite, ignoring my skin's suffering and losing my seaweed coat strand by strand. I was so weak that when I came to the third of these tiny cliffs I didn't think I could make it. I climbed on hands and knees, crawling right up the creek itself to avoid the brush to either side. That was stupid, maybe, because I started shivering again, but at that point I wasn't going to win any prizes for thinking. I'm not sure there was any other way to get up the cliff anyway. Near the top I slipped and fell right under the water—I almost drowned in a knee-deep creek, after surviving the deep sea. But I managed to pull my head out, and to make it up the cliff. Once on top I was almost too tired to walk. If only I had Tom's fins, I thought. When I realized what I had thought I choked out a laugh. I waded the pool at the top of the little falls and continued on beside the stream, hunched over and trailing seaweed behind me, snuffling and moaning, sure I was about to die of the cold.

That was the state I was in when I stumbled into their camp. I rounded a thicket and almost walked into the fire, blink-brilliant yellow among all the grays and blacks.

"Hey!" someone cried, and suddenly several men were on their feet. Lee had a hatchet cocked at his ear.

"Here you are," I said.

"Henry!"

"Jesus—"

"What the hell—"

"*Henry!* Henry Fletcher, by God!" That was Tom's voice. I located him. Right in front of me.

"Tom," I said. Arms held me. "Glad to see you."

"You're glad to see *me?*" He was hugging me. Lee pulled him away to get a wool coat around me. Tom laughed, a cracked joyous laugh. "Henry, Henry! Hank, boy, are you okay?"

"Cold."

Jennings was throwing wood on the fire, grinning and talking to me or someone else, I couldn't tell. Lee pulled Tom off me and adjusted the coat. The fire began to smoke, and I coughed and almost fell.

Lee took me under the arms and put me by the fire. The others stared at me. They had a little lean-to made of cut branches. In front of it the fire blazed, big enough to burn damp wood.

"Henry—did you *swim* to shore?"

I nodded.

"Jesus, Henry, we rowed around out there for the longest time, but we never saw you! You must have swum right by us somehow."

I shook my head, but Lee said, "Shut up, now, and start rubbing his legs. This boy could die right here if we don't get him warm, can't you see how blue he is? And he can't talk. Lay him down here by the fire. He can tell us what happened later."

They laid me down at the open edge of the shelter, next to the fire. Pulled my seaweed from me and dried me with shirts. I was all sandy and I could tell the drying was scraping me, but I didn't feel it much. I was relieved, very relieved. I could relax at last. The fire felt like an opened oven. The heat struck me in pulses, wave after wave of it washing over me, slowly penetrating me. I'd never felt anything so wonderful. I held my hand just over some side flames, and Tom pulled it up a bit and held it there for me. Lee wrapped a thick wool blanket around my legs when they were fully dry.

"W-where'd you get all the c-clothes?" I managed to say.

"We had quite a bit of stuff in the dinghy," Jennings replied.

Tom put my arm back at my side and lifted the other one. "Boy, you don't know how happy I am to see you."

"No lie," Jennings said. "You should have seen him moaning. He sounded terrible."

"I felt terrible, I mean to tell you. But now I feel just fine. You have no *idea* how glad I am to see you, boy! I haven't been this happy in as long as I can re-member."

"Too bad we missed you in the dark," Jennings said. "You could have rowed in with the rest of us and saved a lot of trouble, I bet. We had lots of room." Thompson and the rest laughed hard at that.

"I got picked up by the Japanese," I said.

"What's this?" cried Jennings.

I told them as best I could about the captain and his questioning. "Then he said we were going to Catalina, so I jumped over the side."

"You jumped over the side?"

"Yes."

"And swam in?"

"Yes."

"Whoah! Did you see the dinghy on the beach?" "How did you get in with the swell breaking so high?"

I sorted the questions with difficulty. "Swam in. Saw the boat on the beach, and rested under it. I figured you must be up here." I looked at the men curi-ously. "How'd you get the boat in?"

Jennings took over, naturally. "When the sloop went down we all stepped in the dinghy, all except Lee who fell overboard. So we didn't even get wet. We rowed off a ways and pulled Lee out of the drink and waited for you. But we couldn't find you, and Thompson said he saw you go down under the mast. So we figured you'd drowned, and rowed ashore."

"How'd you get the boat in?" I asked again.

"Well, that was Thompson's doing. With all of us in that little boat we had about an inch clearance, so when he found where that little creek was pouring out and breaking the swell a bit, he booted Lee and me overboard, and we had to swim in. That was something, I tell you—although I guess you'd know. Any-way they caught one of the smaller waves and rode it right onto the beach. A nicer piece of seamanship you'll never see."

Thompson grinned. "Lucky we caught that wave right, actually."

"So except for Lee, and me at the end there, we didn't even get wet! But you, boy. That must have been one hell of a swim."

"Long way," I agreed. I lay on my side, curled so that all of me was equally close to the fire. I could feel the wool gathering all the heat and holding it around me, and I was happy—content to listen to the men's voices, without bothering any longer to decipher what they were saying.

Several times through that day Tom roused me to see if I was doing all right, and when I mumbled something he would let me go to sleep again. The first time I woke on my own, my right arm had gone to sleep, and I needed to shift on my bed of boughs. Shaking my arm awake I felt twinges all up and down it. Both arms were sore. I shifted onto an elbow and looked around. It was near dark. Wet snow was gusting down, filtering through the branches around us. The men were under the lean-to behind me, lying down or sitting on branches Lee had cut for the night's fire. Lee was scraping his hatchet's edge with a whetstone; he saw I was awake, and tossed another branch on the blaze. Thompson and his men were asleep. My back was cold. I rolled so it faced the fire, and felt the heat finger me. Tom and Jennings stared into the flames.

Our camp was in a little bend in the creek, in a hollow created where a big tree had fallen and torn out its roots. Beside our lean-to the roots still poked at the sky, adding to our shelter. The trees around the fallen one were tall enough to stick above the ravine, and their tops bobbed and swayed. I turned to the fire and nestled down again. The stream gurgled, the fire snapped and hissed, the treetops hooted as loudly as their broken voices would let them. I fell asleep.

The next time I woke it was night. The snow appeared to have stopped. We got the fire roaring, and stood and stretched around it. The last loaf of bread was pulled out of Thompson's pack, and divided among the seven of us. Kathryn's bread never tasted any better than this damp stale stuff. Tom pulled some sticks of dried fish from his shoulder bag and passed them around, and Lee handed us each his cup after he had heated some water in it. Noticing Tom's bag when he reached in it I said, "Did you save those books Wentworth gave you?"

"Yes. They never even got wet."

"Good."

Over the ravine the wind was strengthening, and I could make out low clouds racing overhead. The San Diegans discussed their plans, dragging it out to pass the time. They decided that unless the storm got worse or went away altogether, they would abandon the dinghy and hike down the rail line. They had food cached along the way, and seemed to feel there would be no trouble returning overland. Tom and I could come with them, or head north; Onofre, Lee assured us, was just a few miles away. Tom nodded at that. "We'll head home."

Silence fell. Jennings asked me to describe the Japanese captain again, and I told them everything I could remember. When I mentioned the captain's ring the San Diegans were disgusted, and in a way pleased. It was another sign of corruption. Tom frowned, as if he didn't like me giving them any more signs like that. The San Diegans began to tell us tales of the life on Catalina. I was interested, but couldn't keep awake. I sat down and nodded off.

Despite the cold and wet, I slept for several hours. I came to about midnight, however, and quickly found I had slept my fill. I took a branch from beneath me and laid it on the fire. We had a good bed of coals by that time, and the branch caught fire almost immediately. By its light I could see the other men, lying back in the lean-to or on their sides across the fire from me. To my surprise, firelight glinted off their eyes. Every one of them was awake, waiting for day to arrive. My feet were cold, I was stiff and sore all over, and there wasn't a chance I was going to fall asleep again. The hours passed ever so slowly—cramped, stiff, hungry, boring, miserable hours—another of those stretches that are skipped over when tales are told, although if mine is any example, a good part of every adventure is spent in just such a way, waiting in great discomfort to be able to do something else. Lee tossed another branch on the fire beside mine, and we watched it give off steam until flames appeared and got a purchase on it.

A lot of branches turned to ash before the ghostly light of a storm dawn slowly created distances between all the black shapes in the ravine. It was snowing again, fitfully. I could see, looking at the whiskery lined faces of the men, that they were as stiff and cold and hungry as I was. Lee rose and went to cut some more firewood. The rest of the men stood up as well, and walked away to take a leak or stretch out sore muscles.

When Lee came back, he threw the wood he had gathered on the coals, and cursed at the smoke. "We might as well get going," he croaked. "Weather isn't going to get any better for a good while, I don't believe. And I don't want to spend another day waiting it out."

Thompson and the sailors weren't so sure, I could tell. Jennings said to them, "When we get to Ten Post River there's a box of food and clothing. We can put up a shelter like this one here if we need to, and we'll have some food."

"How far away is that?" Thompson asked.

"Five miles, maybe."

"Pretty far in this weather."

"Yeah, but we can do it. And these two can be back up in Onofre by mid-day."

Thompson agreed to the plan, and without further ado we got ready to leave. Jennings laughed at my woeful face and gave me his underpants, thick white things that hung past my knees, and were still a trifle damp. "With these and that coat you should be okay."

"Thanks, Mr. Jennings."

"Say nothing of it. We're the ones who got you dumped in the drink. You've had a wild one, I'd say."

"It's not over yet," Tom said, looking up at the flying snow.

We hiked up the ravine until it was only a dip in the plain of the forest, and then stopped. Water dripped from the branches around us, and the wind swirled. Fearfully I felt the cold climb past my numb bare feet and up my legs; I'd had enough of that.

We said a hasty farewell to the San Diegans. "We'll be back to Onofre soon, so I can collect my clothes," Jennings told me.

"And the Mayor will want to hear from you," Lee said to Tom.

We promised to be ready for them, and after some awkward shuffling of the feet they were off through the trees. Tom and I turned and walked north. Soon we came upon the torn remains of a narrow asphalt road, and Tom declared we should follow it.

"Shouldn't we go up to the freeway?"

"Too exposed. The wind will be howling in the open stretches."

"I know, but there are open stretches here too. And it would be easier walking."

"Maybe so. Your feet, eh? But it's too cold up there. Besides, this road has a whole string of little cinderblock restrooms from when it was a beach park. We can stop in them if we have to, and I've got a couple of them stocked with wood."

"Okay."

The road was just patches of asphalt on the forest floor, broken pretty regularly by little ravines. We made slow going of it, and soon I couldn't feel my feet at all. Walking seemed exceptionally hard work. Tom kept on my windward side, and occasionally held me up with his right arm. I lost track of our surroundings until we came to a long stretch of treeless land, covered with waist-high brush that flailed in the wind. Here we could see far out to sea, and the wind struck us full force.

"Tom, I'm cold."

"I know. There's one of the old restrooms ahead; we'll stop there. See it?"

But when we got there we found that the opposite side of it was smashed, and the roof was gone. It was filling with slush.

"Damn," said Tom. "Must be the next one."

On we went. I couldn't seem to shiver. "Tengo sueño," I muttered. "Ten-go suen-yo." The cold: I know I've mentioned it many times. But not enough to indicate its power, its deadly influence—the way it hurts even when you're numb, and the way that the pain saps your strength, and the way that a part of your mind stays awake, scared to death that other parts are as asleep as your fingers. . . .

"Henry!"

". . . What."

"Here comes the next one. Put your arm around me. Henry! Put your arm around me. Like so." He held me up, and we stumbled toward the next little block pile—the only building from the old time I had ever seen that was smaller than my home.

"That's it," Tom assured me. "We'll just pop in there and get warmed up, and then take off again. It can't blow this hard all day. We're not more than two miles from home, I'd guess, but this wind is too much. We've got to take shelter."

The shrubs bounced against the ground again and again, and upslope the trees howled. Snow obscured the view to sea, it kept striking me in the eyes. We reached the block building, and Tom looked in the open doorway warily. "Oh good," he said. "This is the one. And no beasties in it either."

He pulled me inside, helped me sit down against one block wall. The doorway was on the inland side, so the wind shelter was complete. That in itself was a blessing. But in the corner across from me was a big pile of branches, wood long dead and perfectly dry. Tom leaped to the pile with cries of self-congratulation, and began shifting it into the doorway. When he had it all arranged to his satisfaction he dug around in his shoulder bag and pulled out a lighter. He snapped it; as if he had said a magic spell a tall flame stood off the end of it. Behind the little orange flame his face gleamed, a grin splitting it in two, showing his half-dozen remaining teeth. His eyes were wide open so that the whites showed over the iris. His hand shook, and he laughed like an animal. He flicked the flame off and on twice, then crouched down and applied it to the smaller branches and twigs at the bottom of his pile. In hardly any time at all the whole pile was blazing. The air in the little room cooked. I held my feet in my hands, and shifted across the floor to put them closer to the flames. Tom saw me move on my own and he hopped around the fire cheerfully.

"Now if we had food we'd be set. A castle wouldn't beat it. My own *house* wouldn't beat it. Man, look at that wind. Tearing it up. But the snow seems to be stopping. When we get nice and warm we should probably make a quick run for home and get a meal, eh? Specially if it stops snowing."

From inside our tiny fortress the roar of the wind was loud. I got warm enough to start shivering again, and my feet pricked and burned. Tom put more wood on. "Whoo-eee! Look at that wind. Boy, this is it. This is *it,* you understand me?"

"Uh." I thought I did understand him, but this wasn't *it* for me. *It* was treading water at night outside a giant swell breaking, not knowing whether there was rocks between me and the shore. I'd had my fill of *it*.

We got warm enough to take off our clothes and scorch a little water out of them. Then Tom urged me to get ready to leave. "It ain't snowing, and the day won't last forever." I was ravenous so I agreed with him, though I was unhappy to leave our shelter. In what sounded like a lull in the wind we left our blockhouse and hurried along the asphalt road. The wind instantly cooled our clothes back down, as I knew it would, and I could feel how wet my coat and pants were. The clouds galloped overhead, but for the moment the snow had stopped.

"Snow in July," Tom muttered with a curse. He took the windward side again and matched me step for step. Both of us had our faces turned away from the wind. "This area never used to get snow. Never. Barely got rain. And the ocean temperature bouncing around like that. Crazy. Something severely screwed up with the world's weather, Hank, I tell you that with the utmost certainty. I wonder if we've kicked off another ice age. Boy, wouldn't that teach them? Sure would teach them, damn it. If they did it with the war, serves them right and amen to that. If we kicked it off before they got us, then that would be funny. Posthumous revenge, right Henry? Eh?" On and on he puffed with his nonsense, trying to distract me. "You learnt a passage once that fits our situation here, didn't you Hank? Didn't I assign you something like this? Tom's a-cold, boy you said it. Freezing! I never did learn it by memory myself. Blow, winds! Hail, hurricanoes! Something like that. Surely good casting, if I say so myself . . ." and so on, until the cold got to him too, and he put his head down and his arm around my waist and we trudged it out. It seemed to go on forever. Once I glanced up, and saw the sea as green as the forest, gray clouds massed over it, whitecaps breaking out everywhere on its surface, so that it was almost as white as it was green. Then I put my head down again.

Finally Tom said, "There's my house ridge up there. We've almost made it."

"Good."

Then we were back among trees, and crossing that ridge. Past Concrete Bay and up to the freeway. It was snowing again and we could hardly see any distance at all. Trees appeared like ghosts out of the falling slush. I wanted to hurry but my feet were gone again and I kept stumbling on things. If it weren't for the old man I would have fallen a dozen times.

"Let's go to my house," I said. "Can't climb to yours."

"Sure. Your pa will want to see you anyway."

Even the valley seemed to stretch out, and it took hard walking to cross it. We weaved past the big eucalypus at the corner, up to my door. White slush slid down the roof as we pounded the door and burst in like long lost voyagers.

Pa had been asleep. Looking surprised he gave me a hug, tugged his moustache. "You look terrible," he said. "What happened to your clothes?" Tom and
I laughed. I put my feet right on the stove and felt the skin scorch. Tom was
talking fast as Jennings, and laughing every other sentence. I ransacked the
shelves and threw Tom a half loaf of bread, saving a chunk for myself. "Got
anything else?" Tom inquired, mouth full. Pa got out some jerky for us, and we
wolfed it down. We ate every scrap of food in the place, and stoked up the fire
in the stove higher than it had been since my ma died. "I didn't know *what* I
was going to tell you," Tom was saying. "He was gone for good!" Pa's eyes were
wide. I took out the wash bucket and washed myself with a rag, getting all the
sand out of my crotch and armpits. My feet burned something fierce. We both
kept telling Pa our story, confusing him no end. Finally we both shut up at the
same time.

"Sounds like you had a time," Pa said.

"Yes," Tom said. He jammed a last chunk of bread in his mouth, nodded,
swallowed. "That was something."

part three

...THE WORLD

... 11

After Tom went home I slept like a dead man for the rest of the day and all that night. When I woke up the next morning Pa heard me moan and stopped sewing. "Want me to get the water this morning?"

"No, I'll do it. I'm sore is all." My arms were blocks of wood, and my legs scissors, and scratches and scrapes and bruises hurt with every breath. But I had an urge to get out and look around.

When I started down the path, buckets jerking on my poor arms, the sunlight stung my eyes. There were still some clouds but mostly it was sunny, everything steaming. I creaked down the path staring at our valley. It makes the shape of a cupped hand filled with trees. Down in the crease of the palm is the river winding to the sea, and the fields of corn and barley and potatoes. The heel of the hand is Basilone Hill, and up there is the Costas' place, and Addison's tower, and Rafael's rambling house and workshop. On the other side are the spiny fingers of Tom's ridge. All of the oldest houses were eccentric, I saw; I had never thought of it that way before, but it was so. Rafael's place was like an X written on a W. Doc Costa had made his house of oil drums, and it whistled in the least little breeze; he said it didn't bother him, but I thought it might be the reason Mando scared so easily. The Nicolins had their big old-time house on the beach cliff, and the Eggloffs had their home burrowed into the hillside where thumb and finger would meet, if you were still thinking of the valley as a cupped hand; they lived like weasels in there, and by the graveyard too, but they claimed to have Doc all beat as far as warmth in the winter and cool in the summer were concerned. And then there was Tom, up on his ridge where he was bound to get frozen by storms and baked by the sun, but did he care? No—he wanted to see. So did Addison Shanks, apparently, high on Basilone Hill in a house built around an old electric tower; but maybe he was there because it was close to San Clemente, where he could conduct his dealings with no one the wiser. The newer houses were all down in the valley next to the fields, convenient to the river, and everybody had helped build them, so that they looked pretty much the same: square boxes, steel struts at the corners, old wood for walls, wood or sheet metal or tiles on the roofs. The same design twice as long and you had the bathhouse.

When I got to the river I sat gingerly. It all looked so familiar and yet so strange. Before my trip south, Onofre was just home, a natural place, and the houses, the bridge and the paths, the fields and the latrines, they were all just as much a part of it as the cliffs and the river and the trees. But now I saw it all in a new way. The path went where it did because there had been agreement that this was the best way to the river from the meadows. People's thinking made that path. I looked at the bridge—rough planks on steel struts, spanning the gap between the stone bases on each bank. People I knew had thought that bridge, and built it. And the same was true of every structure in the valley. I tried to look at the bridge in the old way, as part of things as they were, but it didn't work. When you've changed you can't go back. Nothing looks the same ever again.

Walking back from the river, arms aching with the weight of the full buckets, I was grabbed roughly from behind. "Ow!"

"You're back!" It was Nicolin, teeth bared in a grin. "Where you been hiding?"

"I just got back last night," I protested.

He took one of my buckets. "Well, tell me about it."

We walked up the path. "Man, you're all dinged up!" Steve said. "You're hobbling!" I nodded and told him about the train ride south, and the Mayor's dinner. Nicolin squinted as he imagined the Mayor's island house, but I thought, he's not getting it right. There was nothing I could do about it by talking, either. When I told him about the trip home, my swim and all, he put his bucket down in Pa's garden and took me by the shoulders to shake me, laughing at the clouds. "Jumped overboard! And in a storm! Good work, Henry. Good work."

"Hard work," I said, rubbing my arm as he danced around the bucket. But I was pleased.

He stopped dancing and pursed his lips. "So these Japanese are landing in Orange County?"

I nodded.

"And the Mayor of San Diego wants us to help put a stop to it?"

"Right again. But Tom doesn't seem real fond of the idea."

There were snails on the cabbage, and I stooped to kill them off. Down close I could see the damage pests had done to every head. I sighed, thinking of the salads at the Mayor's dinner.

"I *knew* those scavengers were up to no good," Nicolin said. "But helping the Japanese, that's despicable. We'll make them pay for it. And we'll be the American resistance!" He swung a fist at the sky.

"Part of it, anyway."

The idea took him into regions of his own, and he wandered the garden insensible to me. I yanked some weeds and inspected the rest of the cabbages. Gave it up as a bad job.

The next morning Steve dropped by to walk with me down to the river-mouth. The men there stopped launching the boats long enough to greet me and ask some questions. When John walked by we all shut up and looked busy until he passed. Eventually we got the boats off, and getting them outside the swell took all our attention. The men were impressed that I'd managed to swim in through such a swell at night, and to tell the truth, so was I. In fact I was scared all over again. Far to the south the long curving lines of the swell swept toward the land, crashed over, tumbled whitely to shore. For a display of raw power there was nothing to match it. I was lucky to be alive!

Rafael wanted to hear everything about the Japanese, so all the time we were getting the nets out I talked, and he questioned me, and I had a good time. John rowed by and ordered Steve to get out and do the rod fishing—told me to stay with the nets. Steve got in the dinghy and rowed off south, with a resentful glance over his shoulder at us.

And then it was fishing again. The boats tossed hard in the swell, the spray gleamed in the sun, the green hills bounced. We cast the nets (my arms complaining with every pull or throw), and rowed them into circles and drew them up again heavy with fish. I rowed, pulled on nets, whacked fish, caught my balance on the gunwale, talked, kneaded my arms, and, looking up once at the familiar sight of the valley from the sea, I figured my adventure had ended. Despite all I was sorry about that.

When the fishing was done and the boats on the flat, Steve and I found the whole gang waiting for us on the top of the cliff. Kathryn hugged me and Del and Gabby and Mando slapped my sore back, and oohed and aahed over my cuts and bruises. Kristen and Rebel joined us from the bread ovens, and they all demanded that I tell my story to them. So I sat and began to tell it.

This was the third time I'd told the tale in two days, and I had latched on to certain turns of phrase that seemed to tell it best. But it was also the third time that Nicolin had heard it, and I could tell by the tightness in the corner of his mouth, and the way he looked off into the trees, that he was getting tired of it. He recognized all my phrases, and it slowed me down. I found new ways to describe what had happened, but that didn't make much difference. I found myself passing over events as fast as I could, and Gab and Del jumped in to pepper me with questions about the details. I answered the questions, and I could see that Nicolin was listening, but he kept looking into the trees. Even though I was just telling the facts I began to feel like I was bragging. Kathryn braided her disobedient hair and encouraged me with an exclamation here and there; she saw what was going on, and I caught her giving Steve a hard look. We got back on the subject of San Diego, and I told them about La Jolla, thinking that Nicolin hadn't yet heard about that part of the trip. I described the ruined school, and the place where they printed books, and sure enough Nicolin's mouth relaxed and he looked at me.

". . . And then after he'd shown us the whole place he gave Tom a couple of books, a blank one to write in, and another one they just printed, called"—I hesitated for effect—"*An American Around the World*."

"What's this?" Steve said. "A book?"

"An American around the world," Mando said, savoring the words.

I told them what I knew. "This guy sailed to Catalina, and from there he went all the way around the world, back to San Diego."

"How?" Steve asked.

"I don't know. That's what the book tells, and I haven't read it. We didn't have time."

Said Steve, "Why didn't you tell me about this book before?"

I shrugged.

"Do you think Tom is done reading it yet?" Mando asked.

"I wouldn't be surprised. He reads fast."

Nicolin stood up. "Henry, you know I've already heard about your swim, so you'll excuse me if I go pry that book out of the old man's hands for us."

"Stephen," Kathryn said impatiently, but I cut her off, saying, "Sure."

"I got to read that book. If I get hold of it we can read it together in the morning."

"By that time you'll be done with it," Gabby said.

"Steve," Kathryn said again, but he was already on his way and he waved her off without looking back.

We all sat there and watched him hurry up to the freeway. I went on with my story, but even though Steve had been putting a crimp in my style, it wasn't as much fun.

It was near sunset when I finished. Gabby and Del took off. Mando and Kristen followed; at the freeway Mando sidled up to Kristen and took her hand. I raised my eyebrows, and seeing it Kathryn laughed.

"Yeah something's going on there."

"Must have happened while I was gone."

"Earlier, I think, but they're bolder now."

"Anything else happen?"

She shook her head.

"What was Steve like?"

"Not good. It bothered him. Things were tight between him and John. Those two . . ."

"I know."

"I was hoping he would calm down when you got back."

"Maybe he will."

She shook her head, and I guessed she was right. "Those San Diegans will be coming this way again, right? And that book. I don't know what will happen when he reads that." She looked afraid, and it surprised me. I couldn't remember ever seeing Kathryn look afraid.

"Just a book," I said weakly.

She shook her head and gave me a sharp look. "He'll end up wanting to go around the damn world, I know it."

"I don't think he could."

"Wanting is enough." She sounded so bitter and low that I wanted to ask her what was going on. Surely it was more than the book. But I hesitated. It was none of my business, no matter how well I knew them and no matter how curious I was. "We'd best be home," she said. Sun slipping under the hills. I followed her to the river path, watching her back and her wild hair. Across the bridge she put her arm around my shoulders and gave me a squeeze that hurt me. "I'm glad you didn't drown out there."

"Me too."

She laughed and took off. Once again I wondered what went on between her and Steve—what their talk was like, and all. It was like anything else: I was most curious about the things I couldn't know. Even if one of them were willing to tell me about it, they couldn't—there wasn't the time for it, nor the honesty.

That night Nicolin came by fuming. "He wouldn't give me the book! Can you believe it? He says come back tomorrow."

"At least he's going to let us read it."

"Well of course! He sure better! I'd punch him if he didn't and take it away from him! I can't wait to read it, can you?"

"I want to bad," I admitted.

"Do you suppose the author went to England? That would tell us more about the east coast; I hope he did." And we discussed possible routes and travel problems, without a fact to base our speculation on, until Pa kicked us out of the house, saying it was his bedtime. Under the big eucalyptus tree we agreed to go up to Tom's next day after fishing, and beat the book out of him if we had to; we were determined to dent our ignorance of the world, and this book seemed like it could do it.

By the time we got up to Tom's place the following day, Mando and Kristen and Rebel were already there. "Give it over," Nicolin said as we burst in the door.

"Ho ho," Tom said, tilting his head and staring at Steve. "I was thinking I might give it to someone else first."

"If you do I'll just have to take it away from them."

"Well, I don't know," Tom drawled. "By rights Hank here should get first crack at it. He saw it first, you know."

This was touching a sore spot; Nicolin scowled. He was dead serious, but Tom met his black gaze blinking like a lamb.

"Ha," Tom said. "Well, listen here, Steve Nicolin. I got to go and work the hives for a while. I'll lend you the book, but since these others want to read it too, you read a chapter or three aloud before you go. In fact, read until I get back, and we'll talk about our lending agreement then."

"Deal," Nicolin said. "Give it over."

Tom went into his bedroom and reappeared with the book in hand. Nicolin pounced on him and they yelled and pounded each others' shoulders until Nicolin had it. Tom gathered his beekeeping gear, saying, "You be careful of those pages now," and "Don't bend the back too hard," and the like.

When he was gone Steve sat by the window. "Okay, I'm gonna read. Sit down and be quiet."

We sat, and he read.

AN AMERICAN AROUND THE WORLD

Being an Account of a Circumnavigation of the Globe in the Years 2030 to 2039, by GLEN BAUM.

I was born in La Jolla, son of a ruined country, and I grew up in ignorance of the world and its ways; but I knew it was out there, and that I was being kept from it. On the night of my twenty-third birthday I stood on the peak of Mount Soledad and looked out at the ocean's wide waste. On the horizon to the west faint lights blinked like red stars, clustered on the black lump in the blackness that was San Clemente Island. Under those red pricks of light strode the never-seen foreigners whose job it was to guard me from the world, as if my country were a prison. Suddenly I found the situation intolerable, and I resolved then and there, kicking the rocks of the summit into a cairn as a seal of my pledge, that I would escape the constraints put upon me, and wander the globe to see what I would. I would discover what the world was really like; see what changes had occurred since the great devastation of my country; then return and tell my countrymen what I had seen.

After some weeks of thought and preparation I stood on the stub of Scripps pier with my tearful mother and a few friends. The little sloop that had been my father's bobbed impatiently over the waves. I kissed my mother good-bye, promising to return within four years if it was within my power, and climbed down the pier's ladder into my craft. It was just after sunset. With some trepidation I cast off and sailed into the night.

It was a clear night, the Santa Ana wind blowing mildly from starboard, and I made good time northwest. My plan was to sail to Catalina rather than San Clemente Island, for Catalina was rumored to have ten times as many foreigners as San Clemente. In my boat I carried a good thick coat, and a pack filled with bread and my mother's cheese; nothing else I could obtain in La Jolla would have been any use to me. I crossed the channel in ten hours, on the same reach the entire way.

To the east black was turning blue by the time I approached the steep side of Catalina Island. Its black hills were starred by lights red and white and yellow and blue. I sailed around the southern end of the island, planning to land on a likely looking beach and walk to Avalon. Unfortunately for my plan, the west side of Catalina appeared to be very sheer, beachless rock cliffs, unlike any similar stretch of the San Diego coast; and it was now that time of the dawn when everything is distinguishable but the colors of things. Through that gray world I coasted (in the island's lee the wind was slack) when to my surprise a sail was hauled up on a mast I hadn't seen before, against the cliff. Immediately I tried to veer back out to sea, but the boat tacked slowly out ahead of me and intercepted my course. I was contemplating steering into the cliff and taking my chances there, when I saw that the only person aboard the other boat was a blackhaired girl. She put her boat on a parallel course after crossing ahead of me, and brought her boat next to mine, staring all the while at me.

"Who are you?" she called.

"A fisherman from Avalon."

She shook her head. "Who are you?"

After a moment's indecision I chose boldness and cried, "I come from the mainland, travelling to Avalon and the world!"

She gestured for me to pull down my sail; I did, she did likewise, and our boats came together. Though her skin was white, her features were Oriental. I asked her if there was a beach I could land on. She said there was, but that they were patrolled, like all the island's shore, by guards who either saw your papers or took you to jail.

I had not foreseen this difficulty, and was at a loss. I watched the water lap between our boats, and then said to the girl, "Will you help me?"

"Yes," she replied. "And my father will get you papers. Here, get in my boat; we must leave yours behind."

Reluctantly I clambered over the gunwales, pack in hand. My father's boat bucked emptily. Before we cast off from it, I took a hatchet from the bottom of the girl's boat, reached over and knocked a hole in the bottom of mine. Surreptitiously I wiped a tear from my eye as I watched it founder.

When we rounded the southern point and approached Avalon the girl—her name was Hadaka—instructed me to get under the fish in the bottom of her

boat. She had been night fishing, and had a collection on her keel that I was unhappy to associate with—eels, squid, sand sharks, rockfish, octopus, all thrown
together. But I did as she said. I lay smothering, still as the dead fish over me, as
she stopped to be questioned in Japanese at the entrance to Avalon harbor; and
I sailed into Avalon with an octopus on my face.

When Hadaka had docked the boat I quickly jumped up and acted as her
assistant. "Leave the fish," she said when they were covered. "Quick, up to my
house." We walked up a steep street past markets just opening. I felt conspicu-
ous, for my smell if for no other reason, but no one paid any untoward attention
to us, and high on the hill surrounding the town we slipped through a gate and
were in her family's little yard garden. To the east the sun cracked the floor of
America and shone on us. I had left my country behind; I was on foreign soil for
the first time in my life.

"Well, that's Chapter One," Steve said. "He's on Catalina!"

"Read some more!" Mando cried. "Keep going!"

"No more," Tom said from the door. "It's late, and I need some peace and
quiet." He coughed, and put his bee gear down in a corner. He waved us out:
"Nicolin, you can keep the book for as long as it takes you to read it—"

"*Yow!*"

"Wait a minute! For as long as it takes you to read it aloud to the others
here."

"Yeah!" said Mando as he hungrily eyed the book.

"That would be fun," Kristen said, glancing at Mando.

"Okay," Steve agreed. "I like it that way anyway."

"Well then, get home to supper. All of you!" Tom shooed us out the door
with some dire warnings to Steve about what would happen if the book should
come to harm. Steve laughed and led us down the ridge path, holding the book
up triumphantly. I looked out in the direction of Catalina with whetted curiosity, but clouds obscured it from view. Americans were on that island! How I
longed to travel there myself. My battered toe thumped a rock and with a howl I
returned my attention to the ground beneath me. Down where the trail divided
we stopped and agreed to meet the following afternoon to read some more.

"Let's meet at the ovens," Kristen said. "Kathryn wants to do a full batch
tomorrow."

"After the fishing." Steve nodded, and skipped down the beach path, swinging the book overhead.

But the next day after fishing he wasn't so cheerful. John was on him for something or other, and when we got the boats pulled out of the river Steve was

ordered to help sort and clean the fish. He stood still as a rock staring at his pa, until I sort of nudged him and got him to walk away. "I'll tell them you'll be late," I said, and beat it up the cliff before he took his frustration out on me with more than a glare.

Up at the ovens Kathryn had the girls at work: Kristen and Rebel were pumping the bellows, all flushed with the effort, their hair streaked with flour. Kathryn and Carmen Eggloff were shaping the tortillas and loaves and arranging them on the trays. The air above the brick ovens shimmered with heat. Around behind the corner of the Marianis' house Mrs. M. was helping some of the other girls knead barley dough. Kathryn stopped bossing Kristen and Rebel long enough to greet me. "Go ahead and sit down," she said when I told them Steve would be late. "Mando and Del aren't here yet anyway."

"Men are always late," Mrs. M. said around the corner. It was her great pleasure to hang out with the girls and gossip. "Henry, where's your friend Melissa?" she asked, hoping to embarrass me.

"Haven't seen her since I got back," I replied easily. Then Mando and Del arrived, and then Steve. He swung Kathryn off the ground with a hug, and dusted the flour off his hands.

"Katie you're a mess!" he cried.

"And you smell like fish!" she cried back.

"Do not. All right, it's time for Chapter Two of this fine book."

"Not until we get these trays into the ovens," Kathryn said. "You can help."

"Hey, I finished my day's work."

"Get over there and help," Kathryn commanded. Steve shambled over, and we all got up to get the trays in.

"Pretty tough boss," Steve scoffed.

"You shut up and watch what you're doing," Kathryn said.

When we got the trays in we all sat, and Steve pulled the book from his coat pocket, and started the story again.

Chapter II. The International Island.

Between two rosebushes thick with yellow blooms stood a tall white woman holding a pair of garden shears. Though they did not look much alike, she was Hadaka's mother. When she saw me she snapped the shears angrily.

"Who is this?" she cried, and Hadaka hung her head. "Have you brought home another one, foolish girl?"

"So that's how she gets her boyfriends," Rebel interjected, to hoots from the girls. "Not a bad method!"

"That's what you call fishing for men all right," Carmen said.

"Quiet!" Steve ordered, and went on.

"I saw him sailing to the forbidden shore, mother, and I knew he came from the mainland—"

"Quiet! I've heard it all before."

I put in, "I am deeply grateful to your daughter and yourself for saving my life."

"This only encourages your father," Hadaka's mother fumed. Then to me: "They wouldn't have killed you unless you tried to escape."

"See," Kathryn said to me, "they might have killed you when you jumped off their ship. You were in a more dangerous position than you've let on."

I began "Umm, well—"

"Stow it," said Steve. He was tired of hearing about my adventure, that was sure. Mando added, *"Please."* Mando was desperate to hear the story; he really loved it. Steve nodded approvingly and started again.

Her shears snipped the air. "Come in and get yourself cleaned up." She wrinkled her nose as I passed her, and beslimed and bewhiskered as I was I could hardly blame her; I felt like a barbarian. Inside their tile-walled bathing room I washed under a shower that provided water from freezing to boiling, depending on the bather's desire. Mrs. Nisha (for such, I found, was their family name) brought me some clothes and showed me how to use a buzzing shaver. When all was done I stood before a perfect mirror in gray pants and a bright blue shirt, a cosmopolitan.

When he arrived home Hadaka's father was less upset by my presence than his wife had been. Mr. Nisha looked me up and down and shook my hand, invited me in harsh English to sit with the family. He was Japanese, as I may not have said, and he looked much like Hadaka, although his skin was dark. He was a good deal shorter than Mrs. Nisha.

"Must procure you papers," he said after Hadaka told him the story of my arrival. "I get you papers, you work for me a little while. Is it a deal?"

"It's a deal."

He asked a hundred questions, and after that a hundred more. I told him everything about me, including my plans. It seemed I had been even luckier than I yet knew, having Hadaka intercept me, for Mr. Nisha was a worker in the Japanese government of the Channel Islands, in the department supervising the Americans living there. In this work he had met Mrs. Nisha, who had crossed the channel as I had some twenty years before. Mr. Nisha also had a hand in a dozen other activities at least, and most of them were illegal, although it took me a week or two to realize this fully. But from that very night I saw that he was quite an entrepreneur, and I took pains to let him know I would serve him in any way I could. When he was done questioning me all three of them showed me to a cot in their garden shed, and I retired in good spirits.

Within the week I had papers proving I had been born on Catalina and had spent my life there, serving the Japanese. After that I could leave the Nishas' house freely, and Mr. Nisha put me to work fishing with Hadaka and weeding their garden. Later, after this trial period was done, he had me exchange heavy brown packages with strangers on the streets of Avalon, or escort Japanese from the airport on the backside of the island into town, without of course subjecting them to the inconveniences of the various checkpoints.

It should not be imagined that these and the other clandestine activities Mr. Nisha assigned to me were at all unusual in Avalon. It was a town teeming with representatives of every race and creed and nation, and as the United Nations had declared that the island was to be used by the Japanese only, and only for the purpose of quarantining the American coast, it was obvious that many visitors were there illegally. But officials like Mr. Nisha existed in great numbers, at all levels, both on Catalina and in the Hawaiian Islands, which served as the entry point to western America. Almost everyone in town had papers authorizing their presence, and it was impossible to tell whose were forged or bought; but wandering the streets I saw people dressed in all manner of clothing, with features Oriental, or Mexican, or with skin as black as the night sky; and I knew something was amiss in the Japanese administration.

I was happy to try conversing with any or all of these foreigners, employing my few words of Japanese, and listening to some peculiar versions of English. The only persons I was wary of talking to were those who looked American, and I noticed that they were not anxious to talk with me either. Chances were too good that they were refugees as I was, employed in some desperate enterprise to stay in Avalon; it was rumored that quite a few worked for the police. In the face of such dangers it seemed best to ignore any fellow feeling.

The old part of Avalon stood much as it had in the previous time, I was told: small whitewashed houses covering the hillsides that fell into the little bay that served as the harbor. Jetties had been built to enlarge the harbor, and new construction spilled over the hills to the north and west, hundreds of buildings in the Japanese style, with thick beams and thin walls, and peaky tile roofs. The whole of the island had new concrete roads, lined with low stone walls that divided the grounds of parklike estates, on which were giant mansions that the Japanese called *dachas*. Here officials of the U.N. and the Japanese administration made their homes. The dachas on the west side of the island were smaller; the really big ones faced the mainland, as the view of America was greatly prized. The biggest dachas of all, I heard, were on the east side of San Clemente Island; it was their lights I had seen on the night I decided to circumnavigate the globe.

A few weeks passed. I travelled in a car over the white roads, drove once and nearly crashed into a wall; when one drives there is a gale created merely by one's passage over the road, and everything moves a bit too fast for the reflexes.

"Isn't that what you said you felt when you were on the trains?" Rebel interrupted to ask me.

"That's true," I said. "You go so fast that you're ripping through the air. I'm glad we didn't have to drive that train; we would've crashed a hundred times."

"Quiet!" Mando exclaimed, and Steve nodded and went on, too absorbed in the story to even look up from the page.

I saw the giant flying machines, *jets,* land at the airport like pelicans, and take off with roars that almost burst the ears. All the while I pursued various tasks for the gain of Mr. Nisha. When I had fully obtained his trust, he asked me if I would guide a night expedition to San Diego, consisting of five Japanese businessmen who were visiting Catalina expressly for that purpose. I was extremely reluctant to return to the mainland, but Mr. Nisha proposed to split the fee he charged for such a trip with me, and it was enormous. I weighed the advantages and disadvantages, and agreed to it.

So one night I found myself motorboating back to San Diego, giving instructions to the pilot, Ao, the only other person aboard who spoke English. Ao knew where the coast patrol ships were to be that night, and assured me there would be no interference from them. I directed him to a landing site on the inside of Point Loma, took them up to the ruins of the little lighthouse, and walked them through the lined-up white crosses of the naval cemetery—a cemetery so vast it might have been thought to hold all of the dead from the great devastation. At dawn we hid in one of the abandoned houses, and all that day the five businessmen clicked their huge cameras at the spiky downtown skyline, and the blasted harbor. That night we returned to Avalon, and I felt reasonably happy about it all.

I led four more expeditions to San Diego after that, and they were all simple and lucrative but for the last, in which I was convinced against my better judgment to lead the boat up the mouth of the Mission River at night. My readers in San Diego will know that the mouth of the Mission is congested with debris, runs over an old pair of jetties and a road or two, changes every spring, and is in general one of the most turbulent, weird, and dangerous rivermouths anywhere. On this particular night the ocean was as flat as a table, but it had rained hard the day before, and the runoff swirled over the concrete blocks in the rivermouth as over waterfalls. One of our customers fell overboard under the weight of his camera (they have cameras that photograph at night), and I dove in after him. It took a lot of effort from myself and Ao to reunite us all, and escape to sea. In a sailboat we would have drowned, and I was used to sailboats.

After that I was not so pleased with the notion of guiding further expeditions. And I had accumulated, through Mr. Nisha's generosity, a good quantity of money. Two nights after the disaster trip, there was a big party at one of the plush dachas high on the east flank of the island, and the man whose life I had saved offered, in his dozen words of English, to hire me as a servant and take me with him to Japan. Apparently Ao had told him of my aspiration to travel, and he hoped to repay me for saving his life.

I took Hadaka out into the shaped shrubbery of the garden, and we sat over a lighted fountain that gurgled onto the terrace below. We looked at the dark bulk of the continent, and I told her of my opportunity. With a sisterly kiss (we had shared kisses of a different nature once or twice

"I'll bet they had!" Rebel crowed, and the girls laughed. Kathryn imitated Steve's reading voice:

"And I prepared to tell my dear mother back home that her grandchildren would be one-quarter Japanese. . . ."

"No interruptions!" Steve shouted, but we were in stitches now. "I'm going to go right on!" He read,

(we had shared kisses of a different nature once or twice, but I did not feel an attraction strong enough to risk Mr. Nisha's anger)

"Oooh, coward!" Kristen cried. "What a chicken!"

"Now wait a minute," said Steve. "This guy has a goal in mind; he wants to get around the world. He can't just stop on Catalina. You gals never think of anything but the romance part of the story. Quiet up now or I'll stop reading."

"Pleeeeeeease," Mando begged them. "I want to know what happens."

Hadaka informed me that it would be best for all if I took the chance and departed; though the Nishas had not made me aware of it, my staying with them was not entirely safe, as my papers could be proved counterfeit, which would immerse Mr. Nisha in all kinds of trouble. It occurred to me that this was why he had shared so much of the profit of our mainland trips with me—so I could eventually leave. I decided that they were a most generous family, and that I had been exceedingly lucky to fall in with them.

I went back inside the dacha, therefore, and avoiding the naked American girls who pressed drinks and cigarettes on everybody, I told my benefactor Mr. Tasumi that I would take up his offer. Soon afterward I bade a sad farewell to my Catalina family. When I had left my mother and friends in San Diego, I could truthfully say to them that I would try to return; but what could I say to the Nishas? I kissed mother and daughter, hugged Mr. Nisha, and in a genuine conflict of feelings was driven to the airport, there to embark on a seven-thousand-mile flight over the great Pacific Ocean.

"That's Chapter Two," Steve said, closing the book. "He's on his way."

"Oh read some more," Mando said.

"Not now." He gave a sour glance at the women, who were getting the trays out of the ovens. "It's about time for supper, I guess." Standing up, he shook his head at me and Mando. "These gals sure are hard on a story," he complained.

"Oh come on," Kathryn said. "What's the fun of reading it together if we can't talk about it?"

"You don't take it seriously."

"What does that mean? Maybe we don't take it *too* seriously."

"I'm off home," Steve said, sulking. "You coming, Hank?"

"I'm going back to my place. I'll see you in the morning."

"Tom wants a town meeting at the church tomorrow night," Carmen told us. "Did you know?"

None of us did, and we agreed to try to get together before the meeting, and read another chapter.

"What's the meeting about?" Steve asked.

"San Diego," said Carmen.

Steve stopped walking away.

"Tom'll bring up the question of helping the San Diegans fight the Japanese," I said. "I told you about that."

"I'll be there," Steve assured us sternly, and with that he was off. I helped Kathryn scrape the new loaves off the trays, and took one home to Pa, gnawing at one end of it and wondering how many days it would take to fly across the sea.

... 12

Usually our big meetings were held in Carmen's church, but this time she and Tom had been nagging every person in the valley to come—Tom had even gone into the back country to roust Odd Roger—so the church, which was a narrow barnlike building in the Eggloffs' pasture, wasn't going to be quite big enough, so we were meeting at the bathhouse. Pa and I got there early and helped Tom start the fire. As I carried in wood I had to dodge Odd Roger, who was inspecting the floor and walls for grubs, one of his favorite foods. Tom shook his head as he eyed Roger. "I don't know if it was worth the trouble dragging him here." Tom seemed less excited about the meeting than I'd expected him to be, and unusually quiet. I myself was really hopping around; tonight we were going to join the resistance, and become part of America again.

Outside the evening sky was streaked with mare's tail clouds still catching some light, and a stiff wind blew onshore. People talked and laughed as they approached the bathhouse, and I saw lanterns sparking through the trees. Across the Simpsons' potato patch their dogs were begging with pathetic howls to join us. Steve and all his brothers and sisters arrived, and we sat down on the tarps. "So I saw that the shark had his big mouth open and was about to swallow me," Steve was telling them, "and I stuck my oar between his jaws so he couldn't bite me." Then John and Mrs. Nicolin rounded the bend in the river path, and their kids got inside quick. Marvin and Jo Hamish ambled across the bridge, Jo in a white shift that billowed away from her quickening belly. Then people were coming from everywhere, descending on the bathhouse from every direction. Rafael and Mando and Doc came down the hill across the river, and behind them were Add and Melissa Shanks. I waved at Melissa and she waved back. A bit later Carmen and Nat Eggloff trooped out of the woods, carrying a heavy lantern between them and arguing, while Manuel Reyes and his family hurried behind them to stay in the lantern light. When the Marianis arrived I thought we might have more than a capacity crowd. But it was cold outside, so Rafael took over and sat everyone down: the men against the walls, the little kids in their mothers' laps, our gang in one of the empty bathing tubs. When we were done the whole population of the valley was packed in like fish in a box. Lanterns were hung on the walls and some big logs in the fire caught, and the room blazed like it never did during baths.

Tom moved about the room slowly, talking with folks he hadn't seen in a while. He called the meeting to order as he went, but the visiting continued despite his announcements, and others had begun to circulate and argue behind him. Lots of people had nothing but questions, however, and when Marvin said to Tom, "So what's this all about?" the room grew quieter.

"All right," Tom said hoarsely. He told them about our trip to San Diego. I looked around at all the faces. It seemed like a long time since Lee and Jennings had walked into this same room to tell us of their new train line. So much had happened to me since that it didn't seem possible a couple weeks could hold it all. I was a different person than the one who had listened to Lee and Jennings, but I didn't know how. It was just a feeling, a discomfort—an ignorance—as if I had to learn everything over again.

The way Tom told it, the San Diegans kept looking like fools or wastrels, little better than scavengers. So I interrupted him from time to time to add my opinion, and tell them about the electric batteries and generators, and the broken radio, and the bookmaker, and Mayor Danforth. We were arguing in front of everybody, but I thought they needed to know my side, because Tom was against the southerners. He disagreed with me sharply when I went on about the Mayor. "He lives in style, Henry, because he's got a gang of men doing nothing but help him run things, that's all. That's what gives him the power to send men off east to contact other towns."

"Maybe so," I said. "But tell them what they found out east."

Tom nodded and addressed the others. "He claims that his men have been as far as Utah, and that all the inland towns are banded together in a thing called the American resistance. The resistance, they say, wants to unify America again."

That hushed everyone. From the wall near the door John Nicolin broke the silence. "So?"

"So," Tom continued, "he wants us to do our part in this great plan, by helping the San Diegans fight the Japanese on Catalina." He told them about our conference with the Mayor. "Now we know why dead Orientals have been washing onto our beach. But apparently they haven't stopped trying to land, and now the San Diegans want our help getting rid of them for good."

"What exactly do they mean by help?" asked Mrs. Mariani.

"Well . . ." Tom hesitated, and Doc cut in:

"It means they'd want our rivermouth as an anchorage to base attacks from."

At the same time Recovery Simpson said, "It means we'd finally have the guns to do something about being guarded like we are."

Both of these opinions got a response, and the discussion split into a lot of little arguments. I kept my mouth shut, and tried to listen and find out who was thinking what. I saw that even a group as small as ours could be divided. Recovery Simpson and old man Mendez led the families who worked in the back country, hunting or trapping or sheep herding. Then there were the farmers; everyone did a little of that, but Kathryn directed the women who grew the big crops. Nicolin's fishing operation was the third big group, including all the Nicolins, the Hamishes, Rafael and me; and lastly there were the folks who didn't fit into any one group, like Tom, and Doc, and my pa, and Addison, and Odd Roger. These groupings were false, in that everyone did a bit of everything. But I noticed something: the hunters, whose work was already like fighting, were going for the resistance, while the farmers, who needed things to be the same from year to year (and who were mostly women anyway), were going against it. That made sense to me, and I bet to myself that the way Nicolin went would decide the issue; but around me I also saw that there were as many exceptions to my pattern as there were examples, and I lost the feeling that I understood what was happening.

Doc was one of the first to defy my expectations. Here he was as old as Tom, almost, and always arguing at the ancients' table at the swap meet that America had been betrayed by those who wouldn't fight. It seemed obvious to me that he would be disagreeing with Tom again and arguing for joining the San Diegans in their fight. But here he stood saying, "Bigger towns eat the littler ones around them. Henry just told you there's hundreds of people down there—"

"But we're not just the next canyon over," Steve objected. "There's miles between us and them. And we *should* be fighting the Japanese. Every town should be part of the resistance, otherwise it's hopeless." He was vehement, and several people nodded. Steve had a presence all right. His voice turned people's ears.

"Miles aren't going to matter if the train works," Doc answered. So he was against joining. Shaken, I was about to ask him how he could drop all his swap meet talk just when the chance for action had arrived, when Tom said real loudly, "Hey? Let's go it one at a time now."

Rafael jumped in the gap. "We should fight the Japanese every chance we get. They're hemming us in. And they're not only keeping us from the world, they're keeping us from each other, by bombing bridges."

"We only have the San Diegans' word for those attacks," Doc said. "How do we know they're telling the truth?"

"Of course they're telling the truth," Mando said indignantly. He waved a fist at his pa: "Henry and Tom *saw* the bombs hit the tracks."

"That may be so," Doc admitted. "But it doesn't mean everything else they said is true. Could be they want us scared and looking for help. That Mayor of San Diego will start thinking he's Mayor of Onofre the moment we join him."

"But what could he do to us?" Recovery said. "It just means we'll be dealing with one more town, like with the towns that come to the swap meet."

Doc said, "Exactly not! San Diego's a lot bigger than us, and they don't just want to trade. They've got a lot of guns."

"They're not going to shoot us," Recovery said. "Besides, they're fifty miles away."

"I agree with Simpson," old man Mendez said. "An alliance like this is part of knitting things up again. Those folks don't want anything we have, and they couldn't do anything to us if they did. They just want help in a fight that's our fight too, whether we join it or not."

"That's what I say," Rafael added firmly. "They're holding us down, those Japanese! We've got to fight them just to stand up."

Steve and I nodded our heads like puppets in a swap meet show. I hadn't known Rafe felt so strongly about our situation. Steve was twitching like a cat as he nerved himself to stand up and pitch in with those who wanted to fight. But before he did his father stepped out from the wall and spoke.

"We should be working. We should be gathering food and preserving it, building more shelter and improving what we got, getting more clothes and medicines from the meets. Getting more boats and gear. Making it all work. That's your job, Rafe. Not trying to fight people out there who have a million times the power we do. That's a dream. If we do anything in the way of fighting it should be right here in this valley, and for this valley. Not for anybody else. Not for those clowns down south, and sure not for any idea like *America*." He said it like the ugliest sort of curse, and glared at Tom. "America's dead. This valley is the biggest country we're going to have in our lives, and it's what we should be working for, keeping everyone in it alive and healthy. That's what we should be doing, I say."

The bathhouse was quiet. John was against it. Also Tom, and Doc. But Rafael rose to speak again. "Our valley isn't big enough to think that way, John. All the people we trade with depend on us, and we depend on them. We're all country-men. And we're all being held down by the guards on Catalina. You can't deny that, and you got to agree that working for us in this valley means being free to develop when we can. The way it is, we don't have that."

John just shook his head. Beside me Steve hissed. He was near boiling over—his hands were clenched into white fists as he tried to hold himself in. This was nothing new. Steve always disagreed with his father at meetings. But

John wouldn't abide Steve crossing him in public, so Steve always had to stay shut up. The usual meeting ended with Steve bursting with indignation and resentful anger. I don't know that this meeting would have been any different, but for Mando speaking up earlier, and arguing with Doc. Steve had noted that; and could he stand by silent, not daring to do what little Armando Costa had? No. And then I had been arguing with Tom all night. There were too many fires under Steve at once, and all of a sudden he popped up, face flushed and fists trembling at his sides. He looked from person to person, at anybody but his pa.

"We're all Americans no matter what valley we come from," he said rapidly. "We can't help it and we can't deny it. We were beat in a war and we're still paying for it in every way, but some day we'll be free again." John stared at him fiercely, but Steve refused to back down. "When we get there it'll be because people fought every chance they could."

He plopped back down on the tub edge, and only then did he look across the room at John, challenging him to reply. But John wasn't going to reply; he didn't deign to argue with his son in public. He just stared at him, his color high. There was an uncomfortable pause as everyone saw what was happening.

Tom saw it too, and said, "What about you, Addison?"

Add was against the wall, Melissa seated at his feet; he stroked Melissa's glossy hair from time to time, and watched the rest of us as we argued. Now Melissa looked down, her lower lip between her teeth. If it were true that Add dealt with scavengers, then he would likely have problems if we joined raids in Orange County. But he shrugged as if it didn't matter to him. "I don't care one way or the other."

"Pinché!" old Mendez said. "You must have some opinion."

"No," drawled Add, "I don't."

"That helps a lot," said Mendez. Gabby looked surprised to see his father speak; old Mendez was a silent man.

"Yeah, Add, what did you come for, anyway?" Marvin said.

"Wait a minute." It was my pa, scrambling to his feet. "Ain't a crime to come here without an opinion. That's why we talk."

Addison gave Pa a polite nod. That was just like Pa; the only time he spoke was to defend silence.

Doc and Rafael ignored Pa and went at it again, getting heated. There were arguments breaking out all over, so they could say angry things without embarrassing the other. "You're always wanting to play with those guns of yours," Doc said scornfully. Eyes flashing under his thick black brows, Rafael came back: "When you're the only medical care in the valley, we ain't doing so well you must admit." No one who heard them liked such talk, and I waved a hand between them and said, "Let's not get personal, eh?"

"Oh we're just talking about our *lives* is all," Rafe snapped sarcastically. "We wouldn't want to get *personal* about it. But I tell you, the doctor here is going to kiss snake's butt if he thinks I mess with guns just for the fun of it."

"But you guys are friends—"

"Hey!" Tom cried, sounding weary. "We haven't heard from everyone yet."

"What about Henry?" Kathryn said. "He went to San Diego too, so he's seen them. What do you think we should do?" She gave me a look that was asking for something, but I couldn't tell what it was, so I said what I was thinking and hoped it would do.

"We should join the San Diegans," I said. "If we feel like they're trying to make us part of San Diego, we can destroy the tracks and be rid of them. If we don't, we'll be part of the country again, and we'll learn a lot more about what's going on inland."

"I learn all I want to know at the swap meet," Doc said. "And wrecking the tracks isn't going to stop them coming in boats. If there's a thousand of them, as they say, and we number, what, sixty?—and most of them kids?—then they can pretty much do what they want with this valley."

"They can whether we agree or not," Recovery said. "And if we go along with them now, maybe we can get what we want out of it."

John Nicolin looked especially disgusted at that sentiment, but before he could speak I said, "Doc, I don't understand you. At the swap meets you're always grousing for a chance to get back at them for bombing us. Now here we have the chance, and you—"

"We *don't* have the chance," Doc insisted. "Not a thing's changed—"

"Enough!" Tom said. "We've heard all that before. Carmen, it's your turn."

In her preaching voice Carmen said, "Nat and I have talked a lot about this one, and we don't agree, but my thoughts are clear on the matter. This fight the San Diegans want us to join is useless. Killing visitors from Catalina doesn't do a thing to make us free. I'm not against fighting if it would do some good, but this is just murder. Murder is never the means to any good end, so I'm against joining them." She nodded emphatically and looked to the old man. "Tom? You haven't told us your opinion yet."

"The hell he hasn't," I said, annoyed at Carmen for sounding so preacherly and commonsensical, when it was just her opinion. But she gave me a look and I shut up.

Tom roused himself from his fireside torpor. "What I don't like about this Danforth is that he tried to make us join him whether we want to or not."

"How?" Rafael challenged.

"He said, we're either with them or against them. I take that as a threat."

"But what could they do to us if we didn't join?" Rafe said. "Bring an army up here and point guns at us?"

"I don't know. They do have a lot of guns. And the men to point them."

Rafael snorted. "So you're against helping them."

"I guess so," Tom said slowly, as if uncertain himself what he thought. "I guess I'd like to have the choice of working with them or not, depending on what they had in mind. Case by case, so to speak. So that we're not just a distant section of San Diego, doing what they tell us."

"The point is, they can't *make us* do what they say," Recovery said. "It's just an alliance, an agreement on common goals."

"You hope," said John Nicolin.

Recovery started to argue with John, and Rafael was still pressing Tom, so the discussion broke up again, and pretty soon every adult in the room was arguing, and most of the kids too. Fingers were waved under noses, curses flew even around Carmen, Kathryn had Steve by the front of the shirt as she made a point. It sounded like we were evenly split, too, so that neither side could win by volume. But I could see that we joiners were in trouble. The old man, John Nicolin, Doc Costa, and Carmen Eggloff—all four of them were against, and that was the story right there. Rafael and Recovery and old Mendez had a voice in things, but they didn't wield the same sort of influence that those four did. John and Doc circulated around the room conferring on the sly with Pa and Manuel, Kathryn and Mrs. Mariani; and I knew which way things were shifting for the vote.

At the height of the arguing Odd Roger stood and waved his arms with an absurd gleam of comprehension in his eye. "Kill every scavenger on the land, kill them! Scavenger poisons the water, breaks the snares, eats the dead. Unless the corruption be cut from the body the body dies! I say kill them all!"

"All right, Roger," Tom said, taking his arm and leading him to his corner. When he returned to the hearth Tom shouted the arguments down, vexed at last. "Shut up! Nobody's saying anything new. I propose we have the vote. Any objections?"

There were plenty of those, but after a lot of bickering over the wording of the proposition we were ready.

"All those in favor of joining San Diego and the American resistance to fight the Japanese, raise their hands."

Rafael, the Simpsons, the Mendezes, Marvin and Jo Hamish, Steve, Mando, Nat Eggloff, Pa and me: we raised our hands and helped Gabby's little brothers and sisters to raise theirs. Sixteen of us.

"Now all those against?"

Tom, Doc Costa, Carmen; the Marianis, the Shankses, the Reyes; and John Nicolin went down the line of his family, pulling up the arms of Teddy and Emilia, Virginia and Joe, Carol and Judith, and even Marie, as if she were one of the kids, which in mental power she was. Little Joe stood at attention, hand high, black hair falling over his face, belly sticking out under a snot-smeared shirt. Mrs. N. sighed to see that shirt. "Oh man," Rafael complained; but that was the rule. Everyone voted. So there were twenty-three against. But among the adults it was a lot closer, and in the strained silence after Carmen finished counting there were some hard stares exchanged. It was like nothing I had ever seen. A coming fight can feel good, at the swap meet when facing off with a scavenger gang; but in the valley, with no one there but friends and neighbors, it felt bad. Everyone was affected the same way; and no one thought of a way to patch it up.

"Okay," Tom said. "When they show up again I'll tell Lee and Jennings we aren't going to help them."

"Individuals are free to do what they want," Addison Shanks said out of the blue, as if he were stating a general principle.

"Sure," Tom said, looking at Add curiously. "As always. We aren't making any alliance with them, that's all."

"That's fine," Add said, and left, leading Melissa out.

"It's not fine by me," Rafael declared, looking around at us, but especially at John. "It's wrong. They're holding us down, do you understand? The rest of the world is getting along, making good progress with the help of machines, and medicines for the sick, and all of that. They blasted that away from us, and now they're keeping it away from us. It isn't right." His voice was bitter, not really Rafael's voice at all. "We should be fighting them."

"Are you saying you aren't going to go along with the rest of us?" John asked.

Rafael gave him an angry look. "You know me better than that. I go with the vote. Not that I could do much by myself anyway. But I think it's wrong. We can't hide in this valley like weasels forever, not sitting right across from Catalina like we do." He took in a big breath and let it out. "Well, shit. I don't guess we can vote it away anyway." He threaded his way through the folks and left.

The meeting was done. I crossed the bathhouse with Steve and Gabby. Steve was doing his best to avoid his pa. In all the milling around we saw Del gesture at us, and with a nod to Mando and Kathryn we followed them out.

Without a word we trailed up the river path, following someone else's lanterns. Then over the bridge, to the big boulders at the bottom of the barley field. In the blustery dark my companions were no more than shapes. Across the river lanterns blinked through the trees, stitching the trails that our neighbors were taking home.

"Can you believe it?" Gabby said.

"Rafael was right," Nicolin said bitterly. "What will they think of us in San Diego, and across the country, when they hear about this?"

"It's over now," said Kathryn, trying to soothe him.

"Over for you," Steve said. "It turned out the way you wanted. But for us—"

"For everyone," Kathryn insisted. "It's over for everyone."

But Steve wouldn't have it. "You'd like that to be true, but it isn't. It won't ever be over."

"What do you mean?" Kathryn said. "The vote was taken."

"And you were mighty happy with the results, weren't you," Steve accused her.

"I've had enough of this for one night," Kathryn said. "I'm going home."

"Why don't you go ahead and do that," Nicolin said. Kathryn glared at him. I was glad I wasn't Steve at that moment. Without a word she was off toward the bridge. "You don't run this valley!" Steve shouted after her, his voice hoarse with tension. "You never will!" I could just make out Kathryn as she crossed the bridge.

"I don't know why she was being such a bitch tonight," Steve whined.

After a long silence, Mando said, "We should have voted yes."

Del laughed. "We did, there weren't enough of us."

"I mean everybody."

"We should have joined," Nicolin shouted to the barley.

"So?" Gabby said—ready as always to egg Steve on. "What are you going to do about it?"

Across the river dogs yapped. I saw the moon through the scudding clouds. Behind me barley rustled, and I shivered in the wind. Something in the shifting shadows made me remember my desperate hike up the ravine to find Tom and the San Diegans, and the fear came on me again, rustling through me like the wind. It's so easy to forget what fear feels like. Steve was pacing around the boulders like a wolf caught in a snare. He said, "We could join them ourselves."

"What?" Gab said eagerly.

"Just us. You heard what Add said at the end there. Individuals are free to do as they like. And Tom agreed. We could approach them after Tom tells them no, and tell them we'd be willing to work with them."

"But how?" Mando asked.

"What kind of help do they want from us, hey? No one in there could say, but I know. Guides into Orange County, that's what. We can do better at that than anyone in Onofre."

"I don't know about that," Del said.

"We can do it as well as anybody!" Steve revised, for it was true that his pa and some others had spent a good bit of time up north in years past. "So why shouldn't we if we want to?"

Fearfully I said, "Maybe we should just go along with the vote."

"Fuck that!" Steve cried furiously. "What's with you, Henry? Afraid to fight the Japanese, now? Shit, you go off to San Diego and now you tell us what to do, is that it?"

"No!" I protested.

"You scared of them now, now that you've had your great voyage and seen them up close?"

"No." I was shocked by Nicolin's anger, too confused to think how to defend myself. "I want to fight," I said weakly. "That's what I said in the meeting."

"The meeting doesn't mean shit. Are you with us or not?"

"I'm with you," I said. "I didn't say I wasn't!"

"Well?"

"Well . . . we could ask Jennings if he wants some guides, I guess. I never thought of it."

"*I* thought of it," Steve said. "And that's what we're going to do."

"After they talk to Tom," Gabby said, clearing things up, pushing Steve on.

"Right. After. Henry and I will do it. Right Henry?"

"Sure," I said, jumping at his voice's prod. "Sure."

"I'm for it," Del said.

"Me too," cried Mando. "I want to too. I've been in Orange County as much as any of you."

"You're in it too," Steve assured him.

"And me," Gabby said.

"And you, Henry?" Steve pressed. "You're with us too?"

Around us nothing but shadows, windblown in the darkness. The moon slid into a cloud crease and I could see the pale blobs of my friends' faces, like clumps of dough watching me. We put our right hands together above the central boulder, and I could feel their calloused fingers tangle with mine.

"I'm with you," I said.

...13

The next time I saw the old man I gave him hell, because it was very possible that if he had come out on the side of the resistance the vote would have been different. And if the valley had voted to join the resistance, then Steve wouldn't have come up with his plan to join the San Diegans secretly, and I wouldn't have caved in and gone along with it. To avoid admitting to myself that I had caved in to Steve, I decided his plan was a good one. So in a way it was all the old man's fault. It was too bad we had to sneak off to help the San Diegans, but we had to be part of the resistance. I remembered staring at the metal deck of the Japanese ship, crying because I thought Tom and the others were dead, and vowing to fight the Japanese forever. And it was no thanks to them that Tom had survived, either. He just as well could have died, and so could have I. I told Tom as much as I stood berating him for his vote in the meeting. "And any time we go out there, the same thing could happen," I concluded, shaking a finger under his nose.

"Any time we sail out on a foggy night and shoot guns at them, you mean," he said, through a mouth jammed with honeycomb. We were out in his yard, sweltering under high filmy clouds, and he was scorching the slats of several boxlike supers from an unsuccessful hive. Hive stands and smokers and supers lay strewn about us on the weeds. "It may be that the jays ate every bee in this hive," he mumbled. "This one scrub jay was popping down ten at a meal. I set one of Rafael's mousetraps on top of the post he was landing on, and when he landed the trap knocked him about fifteen feet. Was he mad! He cursed me in every language known to jays."

"Ah shit," I said, yanking some of his long white hair out of the corner of his mouth. "All our lives you've been telling us about America. How great it was. Now we've got a chance to fight for it, and you vote against the idea. I don't get it. It's contrary to everything you've taught us."

"Is not. America was great in the way that whales are great, see what I mean?"

"No."

"You've gotten remarkably dense lately, you know that? I mean, America was huge, it was a giant. It swam through the seas eating up all the littler countries—drinking them up as it went along. We were eating up the world, boy, and that's why the world rose up and put an end to us. So I'm not contradicting myself. America was great like a whale—it was giant and majestic, but it stank and was a killer. Lots of fish died to make it so big. Haven't I always taught you that?"

"No."

"The hell I haven't! What about all those arguments at the swap meet with Doc and Leonard and George?"

"There you're different, but just to rile Doc and Leonard. Here at home you always make America sound like God's own country. Besides, right in the here and now there's no doubt we're being held down, just like Rafe said. We have to fight them, Tom, you know that."

He shook his head, and sucked in his cheek on the caved-in side of his mouth, so that from my angle it looked like he only had half a face. "Carmen hit the nail hardest, as usual. Did you listen to her? I didn't think so. Her point was, murdering those dumb tourists doesn't do a thing to change the structure of the situation. Catalina will still be Japanese, satellites will still be watching us, we'll still be inside a quarantine. Even the tourists won't stop coming. They'll just be better armed, and more likely to hurt us."

"If the Japanese are really trying to keep people away, we could kill all the visitors who sneak in."

"Maybe so, but the structure remains."

"But it's a start. Anything as big as this can't be done all at once, and the start will always look small. Why, if you'd been around during the Revolution, you'd have been against ever starting it. 'Killing a few redcoats won't change the *structure*,' you'd have said."

"No I wouldn't, because it wasn't the same structure. We aren't being occupied, we're being quarantined. If we joined San Diego in this fight the only result would be that we'd be part of San Diego. Doc was right just like Carmen was."

I thought I had him on the run, and I said, "The same objection could have been made in the Revolution. People from Pennsylvania or wherever could have said, if we join the fight we'll become part of New York. But since they were part of the same country, they worked together."

"Boy, it's a false analogy, like historical analogies always are. Just 'cause I taught you your history don't mean you understand it. In the Revolution the

British had men and guns, and we had men and guns. Now we still have men and guns like in 1776, but the enemy has satellites, intercontinental missiles, ships that could shell us from Hawaii, laser beams and atom bombs and who knows what all. Think about it logically for a bit. A tiger and a titmouse would make a better fight."

"Well, I don't know," I grumbled, feeling the weight of his argument. I wandered through the dismantled hives, the sundials and rain barrels and junk, to regroup. Below us the valley was a patchwork, the fields like gold handkerchiefs dropped on the forest, with gliding patches of sunlight making even larger fields of brilliant green. "I still say that every revolution starts small. If you had voted for the resistance, we could have thought of something. As it is, you've put me in a tough spot."

"How so?" he asked, looking up from the supers.

I realized I'd said too much. "Oh, in our talk, you know," I floundered. Then I hit on something: "Since we aren't going to help the resistance, I'll be the only one of the gang who got to go to San Diego. Steve and Gabby and Del don't like that much."

"They'll get there some day," he said. I breathed a sigh of relief to have him off track. But I felt bad to keep something from him, and I saw I would be lying to him regularly. His arguments had a sense that couldn't be denied, even though I was sure his conclusions were wrong. Because I wanted his conclusions to be wrong.

"You got your lesson ready?" he asked. "Other than the history of the United States?"

"Some of it."

"You're getting to be as bad as Nicolin."

"I am not."

"Let's hear it then. 'I know you. Where's the king?'"

I called the page up before my mind's eye, and against a fuzzy gray mental field appeared the yellow crumbly page, with the rounded black marks that meant so much. I spoke the lines as I saw them.

"'Contending with the fretful elements;
Bids the wind blow the earth into the sea,
Or swell the curled waters 'bove the main,
That things might change or cease; tears his white hair,
Which the impetuous blasts, with eyeless rage,
Catch in their fury and make nothing of;
Strives in his little world of man to outscorn
To to-and-fro-conflicting wind and rain.
This night, wherein the cub-drawn bear would crouch,

The lion and the belly-pinched wolf
Keep their fur dry, unbonnetted he runs,
And bids what will take all.'"

"Very good!" Tom cried. "That was our night, all right. 'All-shaking thunder, strike flat the thick rotundity of the world, crack nature's molds, all germens spill at once that make ingrateful man.'"

"Wow, you memorized two whole lines," I said.

"Oh hush. I'll give you lines from *Lear*. You listen to this.

"*'The weight of this sad time we must obey;*
Speak what we feel, not what we ought to say.
The oldest hath borne most; we that are young,
Shall never see so much, nor live so long.'"

"*We* that are young?" I inquired.

"Hush! O sharper than a serpent's tooth indeed. The oldest hath borne most, no lie." He shook his head. "But listen, ungrateful wretch, I gave you those lines to help you to remember our trip back up here in that storm. The way you've been carrying on up here since then, it's like you've already forgotten it—"

"No I haven't."

"—Or you haven't been able to believe in it, or fit it into your life. But it happened."

"I know that."

Those liquid brown eyes looked at me hard. Quietly he said, "You know that it happened. Now you have to go on from there. You have to learn from it, or it might as well not have happened."

I didn't follow him, but all of a sudden he was scraping the super resting on his knees. And saying, "I hear they're reading that book we brought back, down at the Marianis'—how come you're not down there?"

"What?" I cried. "Why didn't you tell me?"

"They weren't going to start until the bread was done. Besides, it was time for your lesson."

"But they would have finished baking midafternoon!" I said.

"Isn't that what time it is?" he asked, looking at the sky briefly.

"I'm gone," I said, snatching a dripping honeycomb from the flat behind him.

"Hey!"

"See you later." Off I ran down the ridge trail, through the woods on a shortcut of my own to the Mariani herb garden. There they were all out on the grass between the ovens and the river: Steve, Kathryn, Kristen, Mrs. Mariani, Rebel,

Mando, Rafael, and Carmen. Steve was reading, and the others barely glanced at me as I sat down, huffing like a dog. "He's in Russia," Mando whispered. "Well shit!" I said. "How'd he get there?" Steve never looked up from the page, but kept on reading, from about here as I recall:

"In the first year after the war they were very open with the U.N., to show they had nothing to do with the attack. They gave the U.N. a list of all the Americans in Russia, and after that the U.N. was adamant about knowing where we were and what was happening to us. If it weren't for that I wouldn't be speaking English. They would have assimilated us. Or killed us."

Johnson's tone made me look more closely at the heavily clad, harmless-looking Russians who were crowded in with us. Some of them glanced at us furtively when they heard our foreign speech; most slumped in their seats and slept, or stared dully out the compartment window. The smell of tobacco smoke was powerful, masking to a certain extent other smells: sweat, cheese, the raw alcohol odor of the drink *vodka*. Outside the huge gray city of Vladivostok was replaced by rolling forest, mile after mile of it. The train rolled along the tracks at a tremendous clip, and we crossed scores of miles every hour; still, Johnson assured me that our journey would take many days.

We had done little more than shake hands before walking under the eyes of the train guards. Now I asked him about himself; where he lived, what his history had been, what his occupation was.

"I'm a meteorologist," he said. Seeing my look, he explained, "I study the weather. Or rather, I did study it. Now I watch a Doppler screen used to predict weather and give severe storm warnings. One of the last fruits of American science, the Doppler systems, as a matter of fact. But they're old now, and it's a minor position really."

Naturally I was interested in this. I asked him if he could tell me why the weather had become so much colder on the California coast since the war. This was several hours into our trip, and the Russians around us filled the compartment with an air of utter boredom; at the prospect of talking about his specialty, Johnson's face brightened somewhat.

"It's a complicated question. It's generally agreed that the war did alter the world's weather, but how it effected the change is still debated. It's estimated that three thousand neutron bombs exploded on the continental United States that day in 1984. Not much long-term radiation was released, luckily for you, but a lot of turbulence was generated in the stratosphere—the highest levels of air—and apparently the jet stream altered its course for good. You know about the jet stream?"

I indicated that I did not. "I have flown on a jet, however."

He shook his head. "At the upper levels of the air the wind is constant, and strong. Big rivers of wind. In the northern hemisphere the jet stream circles around west to east, and zigzags up and down as it goes around the world, about four or five zigs and zags for every trip around." He made a ball of his fist and traced the course of the jet stream with a finger of his other hand. "It varies a little every time, of course, but before the war there was one anchor point, which was your Rocky Mountains. The jet stream invariably curved north around the Rockies, and then back south across the United States, like this." He pointed out the knuckle that had become the Rockies. "Since the war, that anchoring point has been gone. The jet stream has cut loose, and now it wanders— sometimes it's sweeping straight down from Alaska to Mexico, which is why you in California get Arctic weather occasionally."

"So that's it," I said.

"That's part of it," he corrected me. "Weather is such a complex organism, you can never point to any single thing and say, that's it. The jet stream is on the loose, but tropical storm systems are changed as well—and which caused which? Or are they causally related? No one can say. The Pacific high, for instance— this would affect you in southern California—there was a high pressure system, very stable, that sat off the west coast of North America. In the summer it would shift north and sit off California, keeping the jet stream pushed north; in the winter it would descend to an area below Baja California. Now it doesn't move north in the summer anymore, and so you aren't protected by it. That's another big factor: but again, cause or effect? And then there's the dust thrown into the stratosphere by the bombs and the fires, dropping world temperatures by a couple of degrees—and the permanent snowpack that resulted in the Sierra Nevada and the Rockies, generating glaciers that reflect the sunlight and cool things even more ... and the shifting of Pacific currents ... lots of changes." Johnson's expression was a curious mixture of gloom and fascination.

"It sounds as if California's weather has changed most of all," I said.

"Oh no," Johnson said. "California has been strongly affected, no doubt about it—like moving fifteen degrees of latitude north—but a few other parts of the world have been just as strongly affected, or even more so. Lots of rain in northern Chile!—and my, is that washing sand off the Andes into the sea. Tropical heat in Europe during the summer, drought during the monsoon—oh, I could go on and on. It has caused more human misery than you can imagine."

"Don't be so sure."

"Ah. Yes. Well, it isn't only the Russians' gray empire that has made the world such a sad place since the war; the weather has had a large part in it. Happily Russia itself has not gone unaffected."

"How so?"

He shook his head, and wouldn't elaborate.

Two days later—still in Siberia, despite our speed—I saw what he meant.

We spent the morning out in the corridor of our car, exhibiting our travel-ling papers to a trio of suspicious conductors. The fact that I spoke not a word of Russian was a real stumbling block to their acceptance of us, and I chattered at them in Japanese and fake Japanese in a nervous attempt to assure them I was from Tokyo as my papers declared me to be, hoping they would not know how unlikely that was. Luckily our papers were authentic, and they left satisfied.

When they were gone Johnson was too upset to return to our compartment. "It's those stupid busybodies in there who got the conductors on us. They heard us speaking a foreign language and that was enough. That's the Russians for you all over. Let's stay out here."

We were still out in the corridor, leaning against the windows, when the train came to a halt, out in the middle of the endless Siberian forest, with not a sign of civilization in sight. Tree-covered hills extended away in every direction for as far as the eye could see; we crossed a rolling green plain, under a low blue hemisphere filled with even lower clouds. I stopped my description of California, which Johnson could not get enough of, and we leaned out the window looking toward the front of the train. To the west the clouds, which had been low and dark, were now a solid black line. When Johnson saw this he leaned far out of the window, saying, "Hold my legs. Hold me in by the legs." When he slid back in there was a fierce grin on his usually dour face. Leaning close to me he whis-pered, "Tornado."

Within a few minutes conductors arrived in our car and instructed every-one to get off.

"Won't do a bit of good," Johnson declared. "In fact, I'd rather be on the train." Nevertheless we joined the crowd before the door.

"Why do they do it, then?" I asked, trying to keep an eye on the clouds to the west.

"Oh, once a whole train got picked up and flung all over the countryside. Killed everyone on it. But if you'd been standing right next to it you'd have been just as dead."

This was not very reassuring to me. "These tornadoes are common, then?"

Johnson nodded with grim satisfaction. "That's the weather change in Rus-sia I mentioned. Warmer midcontinent, but they get tornadoes now. Before the war ninety-five percent of the world's tornadoes occurred in the United States."

"I didn't know that."

"It's true. They were the result of a combination of local weather conditions, and the specific geography of the Rockies, the Great Plains, and the Gulf of Mexico—or so they deduced, tornadoes being another meteorological mystery. But now they're common in Siberia." Our fellow travellers were staring at us, and Johnson waited to continue until we were off the train. "And they're big. Big like Siberia is big. Several towns have been torn off the map by them."

The conductors herded us to a clearing beside the track, at the very end of the train. Black clouds covered the sky, and a cold wind made a ripping sound in the trees. The wind grew stronger in a matter of minutes; leaves and small branches flew almost horizontally through the air above us, and by drawing just a few feet apart from the rest of the passengers, we could talk without being overheard; indeed, we could barely hear ourselves.

"Karymskoye is just ahead, I think," Johnson said. "Hopefully the tornado will hit it."

"You hope it will?" I said in surprise, thinking I had misunderstood, for to tell the truth Johnson's English was accented somewhat.

"Yes," he hissed, his face close to mine. In the muted green light he suddenly looked wild, fanatical. "It's retribution, don't you see? It's the Earth's revenge on Russia."

"But I thought it was South Africa that set the bombs."

"South Africa," he said angrily, and grabbed me by the arm. "But where did they *get* the bombs? Three thousand neutron bombs? South Africa, Argentina, Vietnam, Iran—it doesn't matter who actually put them in the United States and set them off, I doubt we'll ever know for sure—perhaps they all did—but it was Russia that made them, Russia that arranged for their use, Russia that profited most from them. The whole world knows it, and sees how these monstrous tornadoes plague them. It's *retribution,* I tell you. Look at their faces! They all know it, every single one of them. It's the Earth's punishment. *Look! There it is.*"

I looked in the direction he was pointing and saw that the black cloud to the west now sank to the earth at a certain point, in a broad, swirling black funnel of cloud. The wind howled around us, tearing at my hair, and yet I could still hear a low grinding noise, a vibration in the ground, as if a train many times larger than ours was speeding along distant tracks.

"It's coming this way," Johnson shouted in my ear. "Look how thick it is!" On his bearded, craggy face was an expression of religious rapture.

The tornado now slimmed to a black column, spinning furiously on itself. At its base I could make out whole trees flying away from it, scores of them. The bass roar of it grew; some of the Russians in the clearing fell to the ground, others knelt and prayed, raising twisted faces to the black sky; Johnson waved a fist at them, shouting soundlessly in the roar, his face contorted. The twister must have struck Karymskoye, because the flying trees were replaced by debris, pieces of a city reduced to rubble in an instant. Johnson danced a little tilted jig, leaning into the wind.

I myself kept an eye on the unearthly storm. It was moving from left to right ahead of us, approaching at an angle. The condensed spinning column was so solidly black that it might have been a tower of whirling coal. The bottom of this tower bounced off the ground from time to time; it touched down on a hill past the stricken town, blasted trees away from it, bounced into the air almost up to the black cloud above it, extended and touched down again, moved on. To my relief it appeared that it would pass to the north of us by three or four miles. When I was sure of that, some of Johnson's strange elation spilled into me. I had just seen a town destroyed. But Russia was responsible for my country's destruction—thousands of towns—so Johnson had said, and I believed him. That made this storm retribution, even revenge. I shouted at the top of my lungs, felt the sound get torn away and carried off. I screamed again. I had not known how much I would welcome a blow struck against the murderers of my country—how much I needed it. Johnson pounded my shoulder and wiped tears from his eyes, we staggered against the wind across the clearing and into some trees, where we could scream and point and shout curses too terrible to be heard, lamentations too awful to be thought. Our country was dead, and this poor exile my guide felt it as powerfully as I did. I put my arm around him and felt that I held up a countryman, a brother. "Yes," he hissed again and again. "Yes, yes, yes." Within twenty minutes the tornado bounced back up into the cloud for good, and we were left in a stiff cold wind to compose ourselves. Johnson wiped his eyes. "I hope it didn't tear up much track," he said in his slightly guttural accent, "or we'll be here a week."

A shadow fell across the book, and Steve stopped reading. We all looked up. John Nicolin stood there, hands on hips.

"I need your help replacing that bad keel," he said to Steve.

Steve was still in the forests of Siberia, I could tell by the distant focus of his eyes. He said, "I can't, I'm reading—"

John snatched the book from him and closed it, *thud*. Steve jerked up, then stopped himself. They glared at each other. Steve's face got redder and redder. I held my breath, disoriented by the abrupt removal from the story.

John dropped the book on the grass. "You can waste your time any way you want when I don't need your help. But when I need it, you give it, understand?"

"Yes," said Steve. He was looking down at the book now. He stretched to pick it back up, and John walked away. Steve kept inspecting the book for grass stains, avoiding our gazes. I wished I wasn't there to see it. I knew how Steve felt about having such scenes observed. And here were Kathryn, Mando, Kathryn's mother and sister and the others. . . . I watched John's wide back disappear down the river path and cursed him in my thoughts. There was no call for that sort of showing it over Steve. That was pure meanness. No past could excuse it. I was glad he wasn't my father.

"Well, so much for reading," Steve said in his joking tone, or close to it. "But how about that tornado, eh?"

"I got to get home to supper anyway," Mando said. "But I sure want to hear what happens next."

"We'll make sure you're at the next reading," Kathryn said, when it became clear that Steve wasn't going to respond. Mando said goodbye to Kristen and scampered off toward the bridge. Kathryn stood up. "I'd best see to the tortillas," she said. She bent over to kiss Steve's head. "Don't look so glum, everybody's got to work sometime."

Steve gave her a bitter glance and didn't reply. The others wandered off with Kathryn, and I stood up. "I'm off too, I guess."

"Yeah. Listen Hank, you're still seeing Melissa, aren't you?"

"Now and then."

He eyed me. "But you make good use of the time, I bet."

I shrugged.

"The thing is," he went on, "if we offer to guide these San Diegans into Orange County, we've got to know more than how to follow the freeway north. Anyone can figure that out. They might not want to have anything to do with us if that's all we can offer them. But if we knew where the Japanese were going to land, and when, they'd be bound to take us along, don't you see."

"Maybe."

"Sure they would! What do you mean maybe?"

"Okay, but so what?"

"Well, since you're friends with Melissa, why don't you ask Addison if he could help us out like that?"

"What? Oh, man—I barely know Add. And his business in Orange County is his own, no one ever asks him anything about that."

"Well," Steve said, looking at the ground despondently, "it sure would help us out."

I winced to hear him sound like that. We looked at the ground for a while. Steve thwacked the book against his thigh. "Wouldn't hurt to try, would it?" he pleaded. "If he doesn't want to tell us something like that, he can just say so."

"Yeah," I said doubtfully.

"Give it a try, okay?" He still wasn't looking me in the eye. "I really want to do something up north—fight 'em, you know?"

I wondered who he really wanted to fight, the Japanese or his pa. There he stood, looking down, frowning, hangdog, still smarting from his pa's lording it. I hated to see him look that way.

"I'll ask Add and see what he says," I said, letting my reluctance sound clear in my voice.

He ignored my tone. "All right!" He gave me a brief smile. "If he tells us something, we'll be guiding the San Diegans for sure."

It felt odd to receive gratitude from Steve. I hadn't seen it much. Before, what we had done for each other was part of being friends—brothers. Before . . . oh, it was all changed now, changed past repair. Before when I disagreed with him, it was no big deal; we argued it out, and whatever the result it was no challenge to his leadership of the gang. But now if I argued with him in front of the group, he wouldn't abide it, he'd get furious. Now questioning him was questioning his leadership, and all because I had been to San Diego and he hadn't. I was beginning to wish I'd never taken that stupid trip.

And now, to add to the mess, I was the one who was friendly with Melissa and Addison Shanks, so just when he least wanted to, Steve had to ask me to act, while he stood on the sidelines again and watched; and he had to be grateful in the bargain! And me—I couldn't argue with him without endangering our friendship. I had to go along with his every plan, even the ones I didn't like. And now I had to go at his request and do something he would have loved to do himself, that I had no taste for. Things were out of my control. Or so it felt: we lie to ourselves a lot with that one.

All of this occurred to me in a single snap of understanding—one of those moments when a lot of things I'd seen but not comprehended came together. It had happened to me more and more that summer, but it still took me aback. I blinked and glanced at Steve again in a quick evaluation. "You'd better get down there and help your pa," I said.

"Yeah yeah," he said, pissed again. "Back to the pit. All right, see you soon, okay buddy?"

"See you," I replied, and walked up to the river path. When I got home I realized I hadn't seen a thing.

... 14

I was out in Pa's garden one clear evening when I saw a bonfire at Tom's place, blinking yellow in the dusk. I stuck my head in the door—"Off to Tom's," I said to Pa—and was gone.

Up on the ridge I ran into Rafael and Addison and Melissa standing in the trail and drinking a jar of something. Tom's bonfires drew people. Steve and Emilia and Teddy Nicolin were already in the yard, tossing wood on the blaze. Tom led Mando and Recovery out of his house, coughing and laughing. The Simpson kids were popping around the junk in the yard, trying to scare each other. "Rebel! Deliverance! Charity! Get your asses out of there!" Recovery shouted. We greeted each other and arranged the stumps and chairs a comfortable distance from the fire, and cheered a little when John and Mrs. Nicolin showed up with a bottle of apple brandy and a big chunk of butter wrapped in paper. By the time Carmen and Nat and the Marianis showed up the party was in full swing. No one referred to the meeting, of course, but looking around I couldn't help thinking of it. This party was the antidote. The idea of our gang bucking the vote made me uneasy, and I tried to forget it, but Steve kept jerking his head in Melissa's direction, already impatient for me to work on the Shankses.

Melissa was gulling with the Mariani girls, so I took my cup of hot buttered brandy and sucked on it cautiously before the fire. Mando was trying to make tripods of branches over the hottest part of the fire, playing with it (he learned that from me). Fire dazzles the mind into a curious sort of peace. Yellow transparent banners, flicking up from wood and vanishing: what is that stuff, anyway? I asked Tom for an explanation, but what he said came down to this: if things got hot enough they burned; and burning was the transformation of wood to smoke and ash by way of flame. Rafael choked on his brandy laughing when Tom finished.

"Very enlightening," I hooted, and dodged Tom's blows. "That's the lamest—hooo, heee—the lamest explanation you've ever made!"

"Wha—what about lightning?" Raphael cackled.

"What about why dolphins are warm-blooded?" Steve put in. Tom waved us off like mosquitoes and went for more brandy, and we kept laughing.

But Tom knew why fire so captured the eye. For millions of years, he said, humans had lived even more humbly than we did. Right on the edge of existence, for literally millions of years. He swore to that length of time, and made me try to imagine that many generations, which of course I couldn't. I mean, think about it. Anyway, back at the beginning fire only appeared to humans as lightning and forest infernos, and they scorched a path from the eye to the brain. "Then when Prometheus gave us control of fire—" Tom said.

"Who's this Prometheus?"

"Prometheus is the name for the part of our brains that contains the knowledge of fire. The brain has growths like tubers or boles on a tree, where knowledge of certain subjects accumulate. As the sight of fire caused this particular bole to evolve it got bigger, until it was named Prometheus and the human animal was in control of fire." So, he went on, for generation after generation to a number beyond counting men had sat around fires and watched them. To these ice-bitten ancestors fire meant warmth; to them, who bolted the flesh of smaller creatures every third day or so, it meant food. Between the eye and Prometheus grew a path of nerves like a freeway, and fire became a sight to turn the head and make one rapt. In the last century of the old time, civilized humanity had lost its dependence on simple fires, but that was no more than a blink of the eye in the span of human time. Now the blink was over, and we stared at fires hypnotized again.

"Let's have a story," Rebel Simpson said.

"Yes, tell us one, Tom," Mando said.

"Tell us Johnny Pinecone," Rebel pleaded. "I want to hear Johnny Pinecone."

I nodded at that. It was one of my favorite things, to hear how in the last seconds of the old time Johnny had stumbled on one of the hidden atom bombs in the back of a Chevy van, and had thrown himself on it like a Marine on a grenade, to use Tom's expression, hoping to protect his fellow citizens from the blast—how he had survived in the bubble of still air at ground zero, but been blown miles high and rearranged by cosmic rays, so that when he floated down like a eucalyptus leaf he was loony as Roger, and immortal as well. And how he had hiked up into the San Bernardino Mountains and up San Gorgonio, and gathered pinecones and taken them back to the coastal plains, planting them on every new riverbank "to put a cloak of green over our poor land's blasted nakedness"—back and forth, back and forth for year after year after year, until the trees sprang up and blanketed the countryside, and Johnny sat down under a redwood growing like Jack's beanstalk and fell asleep, where he snores to this day, waiting for the time when he's needed again.

It was a fine story. But others objected that Tom had told it last season. "Don't you know more than three stories, Tom?" Steve ragged him. "Why don't you ever tell us a new one? Why don't you ever tell us a story about the old time?"

Tom gave him his mock glare and hacked. Rafael and Recovery chimed in with Steve. "Give us one about you in the old time." I sucked brandy and watched him closely. Would he do it this time? He looked a touch worn and out of sorts. He glanced at me, and I think he recalled our argument after the meeting, when I told him how great he always made America seem to us.

"Okay," he decided. "I'll give you a story of the old time. But I warn you, nothing fancy. This is just something that happened."

We settled in to listen.

"Well," he said, "back in the old time I owned a car. God's truth. And at the time of this story I was driving that car from New York to here. A drive like that would take about a week. I was near the end of the trip, on Highway Forty in New Mexico. It was about sunset, and a storm was coming. Big black clouds rolling over desert floor littered with mesas. Nothing but shrubs and the two lines of the road. That's ghost country out there, dead Indians everywhere looking at you.

"First thing that happened was two sunbeams broke over the top of the clouds, like beacons fanning out to left and right of me.

"Second thing, my old Cortina puffed over a big rise and a sign on top said *Continental Divide*. I should have known. Just beyond it there was a hitchhiker by the side of the road.

"Now at that time I was a lawyer, and I valued my solitude. For a whole week I didn't have to talk, and I liked that. Even though I owned a car I had hitchhiked in my time, and I had known the hitchhiker's despair, made of a whole bunch of little disappointments in humanity, slowly adding up. And it was about to rain, too. But I still didn't want to pick this guy up, so as I drove by I was kind of looking off to the left so I wouldn't have to meet his eye. But that would have been cowardice. So at the last second I looked at him. And when I recognized him I had to put the car on the shoulder and skid over the gravel to a halt.

"That hitchhiker was me. He was me myself."

"Oh you liar," Rebel said.

"I'm not lying. That's what it was like in the old time. I tell you, stranger things than that happened every day. So let me get on with it.

"Anyway. We both knew it, this guy and me. We weren't just lookalikes, like the ones friends tell you about and then you meet them and they don't look anything like you. This guy was the one I saw in the mirror every morning when I shaved. He was even wearing an old windbreaker of mine.

"I got out of the car, and we stared at each other. 'So who are you?' he said, in a voice I recognized from tape recordings of myself.

"'Tom Barnard,' I said.

"'Me too,' says he.

"We stared at each other.

"Now as I said, at this time I was a lawyer, working winters in New York City. So I was a pretty slight little guy, with a bit of a gut. The other Tom Barnard had been doing physical work, I could tell; he was tough and fit, with a beard starting and weathered skin.

"'Well—do you want a ride?' I said. What else could I say? He nodded a bit uncertainly, picked up his backpack, and walked to my car. 'So the Cortina is still hanging in there,' he said. We got in. And the two of us sitting there, side by side in the car, made me feel so strange I could hardly start the engine. Why, he had a scar on his arm where I once fell out of a tree! It was too uncanny. But I took off down the road anyway.

"Well, sitting there silent gave us both the willies, and we started to talk. Sure enough, we were the same Tom Barnard. Born in the same year to the same parents. By comparing pasts all through the years we quickly found the time we had separated or broken in two or whatever. One September five years before, I had gone back to New York City, and he had gone to Alaska.

"'You went back to the firm?' he asked. With a wince I nodded. I had thought of going to Alaska, I remembered, after my work with the Navajo Council was done, but it hadn't seemed practical. And after much deliberation I had returned to New York. After a while we pinned down the moment exactly: the morning I left for New York, driving before sunrise, there was a moment getting on Highway Forty when I couldn't remember if the onramp was a simple left turn, or a cloverleaf circle to the right; and while I was still thinking about it I came to, already on the freeway headed east. The same thing had happened to my double, only he had gone west. 'I always knew this car was magical,' he said. 'There's two of it, too—but I sold mine in Seattle.'

"Well—there we were. The storm crashed over us, and we drove through little flurries of rain. Wind pushed the car around. After a time we got over our amazement, and we talked and talked. I told him what I had done in the last five years—mostly lawyering—and he shook his head like I was crazy. He told me what he had done, and it sounded great. Fishing in Alaska, mapping rivers in the Yukon, collecting animal skeletons for the fish and game service—hard work, out in the world. How his stories made me laugh! And from him I heard my laugh like other people heard it, and it only made me laugh the harder. What a crazy howl! Has it ever occurred to you that other people see you in the same way you see them, as a collection of appearances and habits and actions and words—that they never get to see your thoughts, to know how wonderful you really are? So that you seem as strange to them as they all appear to you? Well, that night I got to look at myself from the outside, and he sure was an odd guy.

"But the life he had lived! As we drove on, it gave me a sinking feeling in my stomach. He had lived a life very close to the one I had imagined living, there every winter in my little New York apartment. My life there—well, it was just sitting in boxes, one after the next, and watching people talk or talking myself. That was my life. But this Tom! He had gone and done what I wanted to do. And he didn't know what the rest of his life was going to be like, laid out for him like the road in front of us. I realized that I loved my cross-country drives because I *crossed country*—that during the times when I wished that I could turn the car around in New Mexico and head back to New York, there to turn and come west again, and keep on like that, as if the Cortina was on a pendulum hanging from the North Pole—it was because I wanted to stay in the country, to be out in it. I began to feel the emptiness of my life, the emptiness I had felt when I looked in the shaving mirror in my apartment in New York, looking at the lines under my eyes and thinking I could have lived a different life, I could have made it better.

"I got feeling so low that eventually I suggested to my double that maybe I was no more than a bad dream he was having. It seemed to make sense. He had made the strong choice, I the weak—didn't it make sense that I was no more than a ghost come to haunt him, a vision of what would have happened if he had made the mistake of returning to New York?

"'I don't think so,' he answered. 'It's likelier I'm a dream of yours, that you stopped and picked up along the way. You'd have to be a hell of a dream to ferry me all the way across New Mexico, after all. No, we're both here all right.' He punched me lightly in the arm, and the spot he hit got very warm.

"'I guess we're both here,' I admitted. 'But how?'

"'There was too much of us for any one body to hold!' he said. 'That was why we had trouble sleeping.'

"'I still get insomnia,' I said. And I knew why—I had lived my life wrong, I had chosen to live in boxes.

"'Me too,' he said, surprising me. 'Maybe from sleeping on the ground so much. But maybe from living such a life as mine.' For a moment he looked as discouraged as I felt. He said, 'I don't feel like I'm doing anything real, 'cause no one else does. I'm against the grain, I guess. It can cut into your sleep all right.'

"So he had his troubles too. But they sounded like nothing compared to mine. He was healthier and happier than I, surely.

"The storm picked up and I put on the windshield wipers, adding their squeak to the hum of the engine and the hiss of the wet tires. Our headlights lit up gusts of rain, and on the other road trucks trailing long plumes of spray roared by, going east. We put Beethoven's Third on the tape deck; the second movement was up, sounding like noises made by the storm. We sat and listened to it, and talked about when we were a kid. 'Do you remember this?' 'Oh, yeah.' 'Do you remember that?' 'Oh man, I never wanted anyone else to find out about *that*.' And so on. It was pretty friendly, but it wasn't comfortable. We couldn't talk about our different lives anymore, because there was something wrong there, a tension, a disagreement even though neither of us was satisfied.

"It was starting to rain harder, and the car was buffeted hard by wind. Very little was visible outside the cones of light from the headlights—the black mass of the earth, the black clouds above. The march from the second movement, music grander than you folks can imagine, poured out of the speakers, matching the storm stroke for stroke. And we talked and laughed, and we howled, overwhelmed by all that was happening—because the two of us being there meant we were special, you see. It meant we were magical.

"But right in the middle of our howling the Cortina sputtered, at the top of another rise. I pressed on the gas, but the engine died. I coasted onto the shoulder and tried to start it. No luck. 'Sounds like water in the distributor,' my double said. 'Didn't you ever get that fixed?'

"I admitted I hadn't. After some discussion we decided to try and dry it off. That wasn't going to be easy, but it beat sitting in the car all night. We got out our ponchos, and luckily the rain diminished to a steady falling mist. By the time I got my poncho on, my companion had the hood up and was leaning over the engine. He had a small flashlight in one hand, and was pulling at the distributor with the other. I reached in and three Barnard hands went to work on it, taking the distributor cap off, pulling it apart, drying it, getting everything back together dry. My double ran to get a plastic bag while I hunched over the engine, feeling its warmth, my poncho extended like a cape. My double returned—we were working at emergency speed, you understand—and he leaned over the engine, and then all four of our hands were working on the distributor with uncanny coordination. When we were done clamping it down he dashed to the driver's seat and started the engine. It caught and ran, and he revved it. We had fixed it! As I closed the hood my double got out of the car grinning. 'All right!' he cried, and slapped my hand, and suddenly he leaped up and spun in the air, howling the Navajo chant we had learned as a boy—and there I was spinning with him, swirling my poncho out like a Hopi dancing cape, screaming my lungs out. Oh it was a strange thing, the two of us dancing in front of that car, on that high ridge, hollering and spinning and stomping in puddles, and I felt—oh there isn't the *word* for the way I felt at that moment, truly.

"The rain had stopped. On the horizon to the south little lines of lightning flashed from low clouds into the earth. We stood side by side and watched them, two or three every second. No thunder.

"'My life feels just like this,' one of us said, but I wasn't sure who. And my right arm was hot, where it touched his left arm. I looked at it—

"And saw our arms met to enter a single hand. We were becoming one again. But it was a left hand—his hand. Then I noticed our legs came down to the same boot, a right boot. My foot.

"On the forearm wavering between us I could make out the reddish tissue connecting our arms, like burn-scar tissue. And I could feel the hot pulling and plucking. We were melting together! Already we shared part of the upper arm, and soon we would be joined at the shoulder like Siamese twins, and I felt the same burning in my right leg, oh, our time was up! First arms and legs, then torso then *heads!*

"I looked in his face and saw my mirror image, twisted with horror. I thought, that's what I look like, that's who I am, our time is over. Our eyes met.

"'*Pull,*' he said.

"We pulled. He grabbed the fender with his right hand, and I stepped out with my left foot, trying for traction in the muddy gravel. I leaned out and pulled like I had never pulled before. That forearm stuck out between us like a claw. We gasped and grunted and pulled, and the scar tissue above the elbow burned, and stretched, and gave us back a little of our arms. It was as painful as if I held on to something and deliberately tried to pull my arm off. But it was working. We both had elbows of our own now.

"'Hold on tight,' I gasped, and dove for the road! Boom! *Rip!*—an instant of agony, and I crashed onto wet asphalt. I pushed myself up with both hands. My feet were both there, I shook my right hand violently, grabbed my right boot. I was whole again.

"I looked at my double. He was leaning against the car, holding his left forearm in his right hand, shaking. Seeing it I felt my own trembling. He was staring at me with a furious expression, and for a second I thought he would attack me. For a second I had a vision, and saw him leap on me and pummel me, fists sinking into me and never coming out, so that we struggled and bit and kicked and melded into each other with every blow, until we became a single figure hitting itself, prone on the gravel, jerking and twitching.

"But that was just a vision I had. In actuality, he shook his head hard, his lip curled into a bitter look.

"'I'd better go,' he said.

"Said I, 'I think you better.' As I got to my feet he walked to the passenger door, and got his backpack out. He pulled his poncho off to get the pack on his back.

"'Back to home for you, eh Thomas?' he said. There was contempt in his voice, and suddenly I was angry.

"'And you can hit the road again,' I said. 'And I'm glad to see you go. You had me feeling like my whole life was a mistake, like you did it right and I did it wrong. But I'm not doing it wrong! I'm living with people the way a human being should, and you're just taking the escape, wandering the road. You'll burn out quick enough.'

"He glared at me, and said, 'You've got me wrong, brother. I'm trying to live my life the best I know how. And I'm not going to burn out, ever.' He put his poncho back on. 'You take the name,' he said. 'I don't know if we live in the same world or not, but someone might notice. So you keep the name. I have the feeling you're the real Tom Barnard, anyway.'

"So we had traded curses.

"He looked at me one last time. 'Good luck,' he said. Then he walked away from the road, up the ridge. Through the mist, under that poncho, he looked inhuman. But I knew who he was. And as I watched him fade into the dark my spirit sank, and I was filled with despair. That was my own self disappearing there; I was watching my own true self walk away in the rain. No one should have to watch that.

"When I couldn't see him anymore I drove off in a panic. Creaks in the car made me jump, and I was too scared to look around and see what it was. I drove faster and faster, and prayed the distributor would stay dry. The valleys of east Arizona rolled on and on, and for the first time, I think, I realized how gigantic the country really was. I couldn't stop thinking of what had happened. Things we had said seemed to ring aloud in the air. I wished that we had had more time—that we had parted friends—that we had allowed the joining to take place! Why were we so afraid of wholeness? But I was afraid; the fear of that union washed over me, and I drove ever faster, as if he might be running down the highway after me, wet and exhausted, miles behind."

Tom coughed a few times, and stared into the fire, remembering it. We watched him open mouthed.

"Did you ever see him again?" Rebel asked anxiously. That broke the spell and most of us laughed, including Tom. But then he frowned at her and nodded.

"Yes, I did see him again. And more than that."

We settled back; the older folks, who had heard this story before, I guessed, looked surprised.

"It was several years later when I next saw him; you'll know what year I mean. I was still a lawyer, older and slouchier and tubbier than ever. That was life in the old time—the years in the boxes took it out of you fast." At that point Tom looked at me, as if to make sure I was listening. "It was a stupid life really, and that's why I can't see it when people talk about fighting to get back to that. People back then struggled at jobs in boxes so they could rent boxes and visit other boxes, and they spent their whole lives running in boxes like rats. I was doing it myself, and it made no sense.

"Part of me knew that it made no sense, and I fought back in a weak sort of way. At this time I was out west doing that again, hiking a little. I decided to hike to the top of Mount Whitney, the tallest mountain in the United States. Weak as I was it was a killer task just to get up that ten mile trail, but after a couple days' hard work I made it. Mount Whitney. Right before sunset, this was—again—so that I was the only person on the peak, which was rare.

"So I was walking around the top, which was broad, nearly an acre. The trail goes up the south ridge, which is nice and gradual. But the eastern face is almost sheer, and looking down it into the shadows made me feel funny. Then I noticed a climber. He was coming up that sheer face alone, up one of the cracks in the face. Old John Muir had climbed the peak alone like that, but he was crazy for risks, and few climbers since had exposed themselves to such danger. It made me dizzy to look at this guy's exposure, but I watched all the same, naturally. As he got higher he kept looking up, and at one point he saw me and waved. And I felt funny. The closer he got the more familiar he looked. And then I recognized him. It was my double, in climbing gear and full beard, looking as strong an animal as you could ask for. And there on that granite face!

"Well, I thought about hightailing it down the trail, but at one point when he looked up at me, I saw that he recognized me too, and I realized we would have to say hello. Or something. So I waited.

"It seemed to go on forever, the last part of that climb, and him in mortal danger the whole time. But when he crawled onto the top, the sun was still over that distant western horizon, out over the Pacific way out there in the haze. He stood up and walked toward me. A few feet away he stopped and we stared at each other wordlessly, in an amber glow of light like you only get in the Sierras at dusk. There didn't seem anything to say, and it was like we were frozen.

"And then it happened." Here Tom's voice got hoarse and harsh, and he leaned forward in his chair and stared into the fire refusing to look at any of us. He hacked three or four coughs and spoke rapidly: "The sun was about half an orange ball lying out on the horizon, and—and one bloomed beside it, and then a whole bunch of others, up and down the California coast. Fifty suns all strung out and glowing for sunset. The mushroom balls as tall as us, and then taller. Little haloes of smoke around each column. It was the day, folks. It was the end.

"I saw what it was, and then I knew what it was; I turned to look at my double, and saw he was crying. He moved to my side and we held hands. So simple. We melted together as easy as that—as easy as agreeing to. When we were done, I was up there all alone. I remembered both of my pasts, and felt my brother's strength. The mushroom clouds blew toward me, coming on a cold wind. Oh I felt all alone, believe me, shivering and watching that horrible sight—but I felt, well . . . healed somehow, and . . . Oh, I don't know. I don't know. I got down off of there somehow."

He leaned back and almost rocked too far in his chair. We all took a deep breath.

Tom stood and prodded the fire with a stick. "You see, you couldn't live a whole life in the old time," he said, his voice relaxed again, even peevish. "It's only now that we're out by a fire, in the world—"

"No morals if you please," Rafael said. "You've told us enough of those lately, thank you." John Nicolin nodded at that.

The old man blinked. "Well, okay. Stories shouldn't have morals anyway. Let's get some more wood on that fire! This story's over, and I need something to drink."

With a cough he went to get the drink himself, and released us. Some stood and threw wood on the fire, others asked Mrs. N. if there was more butter—all a bit subdued, but satisfied. "How the old man talks," Steve said. Then he took my arm and indicated Melissa, over on the other side of the fire. I shrugged him off, but after a bit I walked around the fire and joined her. She put her arm around me. Feeling that small hand over my hip made the rum in me jump. We wandered out in the junk of the yard, and kissed hungrily. I was always surprised at how easy it was with Melissa. "Welcome home," she said. "You still haven't told me about your trip—I've heard it all second hand! Will you come over to my house later and tell me about it? Daddy will be there of course, but maybe he'll go to bed."

I agreed quickly, thinking more about her kisses than the information I was supposed to get from Add. But when it occurred to me (while nuzzling Melissa's neck, so beautiful in the firelight), I was pretty pleased with myself. It was going to be easier than I thought. "Let's see if there's more brandy," I said.

A while later we had found the drink and downed it, and Addison had found us. "Let's be off," he said to Melissa gruffly.

"It's early yet," she said. "Can we bring Henry with us? I want to hear about his trip, and show him our house."

"Sure," Add said indifferently. I waved goodbye to Steve and Kathryn behind Melissa's back, and felt pretty slick when I saw Steve's startled expression. The three of us took off down the ridge trail. Add led Melissa and me across the valley without a word or a look back, so he didn't see Melissa's arm around my waist, nor her hand in my pocket. The pocket had a hole convenient to her, but I was none too comfortable with Add right in front of us, and I didn't respond except with a kiss on the bridge, where I could trust my footing. Stumbling along the path up Basilone I could feel the brandy in my blood, and Melissa's fingers groping in my pants. Whew! But at the same time I was thinking, how am I going to ask Add about the scavengers and the Japanese? The liquor sloshed my thoughts when I considered it, but it was more than the drink. There wasn't a good way, that was all there was to it. I would have to cast without bait and hope for the best.

The Shanks house was one of the old ones, built by Add before hardly anybody lived in Onofre. He had used an electric wire tower as the framework of the place, so it was small but tall, and strong as a tree. The shingled walls sloped inward slightly, and the four metal struts of the tower protruded from the corners of the roof, meeting in a tangle of metal far above it.

"Come on in," Add said hospitably, and took a key from his pocket to unlock the door. Once inside he struck a match and lit a lantern, and the smell of burnt whale oil filled the room. Boxes and tools were stacked against the walls, but there wasn't any furniture. "We live upstairs," Melissa said as Add led us up a steep plank staircase in one corner. She giggled and pushed my butt as she followed me up, and I almost banged into one of the thick metal struts of the old electric tower.

Nobody from Onofre Valley had ever been on the second floor, as far as I knew. But it was nothing special: kitchen in one corner, blond wood tables, an old couch and some chairs. Scavenger stuff all. A stairway leading to a trapdoor indicated another floor above. Add set the lantern on the stove, and commenced opening windows and throwing back the shutters guarding them. There were a lot of shutters. When he was done we had a view in all four directions: dark treetops, every way. "You've got a lot of windows," I said, brandywise. Add nodded. "Have a seat," he said.

"I'm going to change clothes," Melissa said, and went up the stairway to the floor above.

I sat in one of the big upholstered chairs. "Where'd you get all this glass?" I asked, hoping that would be a start on my ultimate subject. But Add knew that I knew where glass came from, and he gave me a crooked smile.

"Oh around. Here, have another glass of brandy. I've got better than the Nicolins'."

I was fine already, but I took a glass from him.

"Here, sit on the couch," Add said, and took back the glass while I moved. "It's got the better view. If the air's clear you'll see Catalina. If not, then the great sea. Getting to be your second home, I hear."

"My last home, almost."

He laughed. "So I hear. Well." He sipped from his glass. "Quite a pleasant evening. I like Tom's stories."

"So do I." We both drank again, and for a moment it looked like we had run out of things to say. Luckily Melissa came back down the stairs, in a white house dress that pinched her breasts together. Smiling at us, she got a glass of brandy for herself, and sat right beside me on the couch, pressing against my arm and leg. It made me nervous, but Add gave us his crooked smile and nodded, seeming satisfied with how cozy we were. He leaned back and balanced his glass on the worn arm of his chair.

"Good brandy, isn't it?" Melissa said. I agreed that it was.

"We traded two dozen crabs for it. We only trade for the best available."

"I wish we were going to be trading with San Diego," Add said peevishly. "Was San Diego as big as Tom said it is?"

"Sure," I said. "Maybe bigger."

Melissa rested her head on my shoulder. "Did you like it down there?"

"I guess so. It was quite a trip, I'll say that."

They began to ask me about the details of it. How many little towns were there? Were there railroad tracks to all of them? Was the Mayor popular? When I told them about the Mayor's morning target practice they laughed. "And he does that every morning?" Add asked, rising to get us refills.

"So they said."

"That must mean they have a lot of ammunition," he said to himself in the kitchen. "Hey, this bottle's polished."

"You bet they do," I said. It seemed like there would be a way to get the conversation over to the scavengers pretty soon, so I relaxed and began to enjoy getting there. "They've got all those naval warehouses down there, and the Mayor has had every one of them explored."

"Uh huh. One moment; I have to go downstairs and get another bottle."

The second his head disappeared down the stairs Melissa and I kissed. I could taste the brandy on her tongue. I put my hand on her knee and she tugged her dress up so I was holding her bare thigh. More kissing, and my breath got short. I kept pushing the dress higher and higher, until I found she wasn't wearing anything under it. Blood knocked in my ears with the shock of the discovery. Her belly pulsed in and out and she rocked over my hand, pushing down on it. We kissed harder, her hand squeezed my cock through my pants, and my breath left me entirely, whoosh!

Thump, thump, answered Add's boots on the ladder, and Melissa twisted aside and threw her dress down. Fine for her, but I had a hard-on bulging my pants, and Melissa gave it a last malicious squeeze to make it harder still, giggling at my expression of dismay. I drank my brandy and scrunched around in the corner of the couch. By the time Add had gotten in the room and broken the seal on the new bottle I was presentable, although my heart was still pounding double time.

We drank some more. Melissa left her hand on my knee. Add got up and wandered the dimly lit room, peering out the windows and opening first one and then another, adjusting the circulation, he said. The liquor was clobbering me.

"Doesn't lightning ever hit your house?" I asked.

"Sure," they both said, and laughed. Add went on: "Sometimes it'll hit and a whole wall of shingles will pop off. Later when I check them they're all singed."

"My hair stands on end," said Melissa.

"Aren't you afraid of being electrocuted?" I asked, patiently rolling out the last word.

"No, no," Add said. "We're pretty well grounded here."

"What's that mean?"

"It means the lightning runs down the corner poles into the ground. I had Rafe out to look at the place, and he said we're in no danger. I like to remember that when the lightning hits and the whole house shakes, and blue sparks are bouncing around like hummingbirds."

"It's exciting," Melissa said. "I like it."

Add continued to play with the windows. When he was looking away Melissa took my hand and put it in her lap, trapping it between her legs. When he turned our way she released it and I yanked back upright. It was driving me wild. It got to where I didn't wait for her to take my hand, but plunged for her whenever I could. We drank some more. Finally the windows were adjusted to Add's satisfaction, and he stood over the side of the couch, looking down at me as if he knew what we had been up to.

"So what do you think that Mayor of San Diego is really after?" he said.

"I don't know," said I. I was in a daze—impatient to get back under Melissa's dress, but very aware of Add standing right over me.

"Does he want to be king of this whole coastline?"

"I don't think so. He wants the Japanese off the mainland, that's all."

"Ah. That's what you said before, in the meeting. I don't know if I believe it."

"Why not?"

"There's no sense to it. How many men does he have working for him, did you say?"

"I don't think I said. I never really knew, exactly."

"Do they have any radio gear?"

"Yes, how did you guess? They've got a big radio, but it doesn't work yet."

"No?"

"Not yet, but they said they were planning to get a man over from the Salton Sea to fix it."

"Who said this, now?"

"The folks in San Diego. The Mayor."

"Well what do you know."

With all these questions I judged that it was a perfect time for some questions of my own. "Add, where *did* you get all this glass from?"

"Why, at the swap meets, mostly." He was looking at Melissa, now—they exchanged a glance I didn't understand.

"From the scavengers?"

"Sure. They're the ones selling glass, aren't they?"

I decided to tack a little closer to the wind. "Do you ever trade directly with the scavengers, Add? I mean, outside the swap meets?"

"Why no. Why do you ask?" He was still grinning his crooked grin, but his eyes got watchful. The grin left.

"No reason," I said, feeling all of a sudden like he could see through my eyes and read what I was thinking. "I was wondering, that's all."

"Nope," he said decisively. "I never deal with the zopilotes, no matter what you hear. I trap crabs under Trestles, so I'm up there a lot, but that's the extent of it."

"They lie about us," Melissa said tragically.

"No matter," Add said, the grin back in place. "Everyone collects stories of one sort or another, I reckon."

"True," I said. And it was true; everyone who didn't live right on the valley floor, where their lives were under constant examination, had stories told about them. I could see how rumors would grow especially fast around Addison, him being such a private man. It really wasn't fair to him. I didn't know what to say. Obviously Steve was going to have to find some other way to get information for the San Diegans. I blinked and breathed deep and regular, trying to control the effects of the brandy. Add had never lit more than the one lantern, and even though the single flame was reflected in five or six windows, the room danced with shadows. There were a couple more swallows of the amber liquor in my glass, but I resolved to pass on them. Addison moved away from the couch, and Melissa sat up. Add went to the kitchen corner and consulted a large sand clock.

"It's been fun, but it's getting late. Melissa, you and I ought to be abed. We've got lots of work to do in the morning."

"Okay, Daddy."

"You walk Henry down and say good night to him real quick. Henry, come back and give us a visit sometime soon." I got to my feet, unsteady but eager, and Add shook my hand, squeezing hard and grinning at me. "Careful walking home."

"Sure. Thanks for the brandy." I followed Melissa down the ladder to the ground floor and out into the night. We kissed. I leaned back against the sloping wall of their house to keep myself upright, one leg thrust between Melissa's as she pressed against me. It reminded me of the first time we fooled around at the swap meet, only this time I was drunker. Melissa rubbed up and down my thigh, and let me feel her some more as she kissed my neck and breathed *umm, umm*. Then:

"He's waiting. I'd better go upstairs."

"Oh."

"Good night, Henry."

A peck on the nose and she was gone. I shoved off from the wall and staggered across the little clearing into the woods. There were foundations out there from the old time, concrete slabs I stumbled over. I sat down for a bit, looking back through the trees at the Shankses' tower. There was a silhouette in front of the lights in the living room. I tasted the finger that had been feeling Melissa. The blood rushed to my head. It seemed a terrible amount of trouble to stand again, so I sat awhile and recalled the feel of her. I could see her, too—the silhouette was her—moving about the kitchen part of the upper room. Cleaning, I guessed. I don't know how much time passed, but suddenly their kitchen lantern went dark, then reappeared—once, twice, three and then four times. That seemed a little odd.

Off to my right I heard a twig snap. I knew instantly it was people, walking over another foundation. I crawled silently between two large trees and listened. Around to the north of the house there were people, at least two of them, not doing a very good job of moving through the woods quietly. Valley people would never have made such noise. And there was no reason for any of them to be there anyway. All this occurred to me rapidly, no matter that I was drunk. Without thinking about it I found myself flat on my stomach behind a tree, where I could see the Shankses' door. Sure enough, shadows on the other side of the little clearing resolved into moving shapes, then into people, three of them. They walked right up to the door, said something up at the second story.

It was Melissa who let them in. While they were still on the first floor I slipped through the trees quiet as owlflight, and hauled ass over to the wall of their house. Only then did I wonder if I really wanted to be there. Drunk indeed.

From the ground I could hear their voices, but I couldn't make out enough of what they were saying to make sense of it. I remembered seeing blocks of wood nailed to the side of the house next to the door, making a ladder to the roof. I shifted along the wall to them, and step by step I ascended the blocks, taking a minute for each block so they wouldn't creak. When my head was under one of the windows I stopped and listened.

"They've got a radio," Addison said. "He says it isn't working yet, but they have someone from the Salton Sea coming to try and fix it."

"That's probably Gonzalez," said a nasal high voice.

A deeper voice added: "Danforth is always bragging he's got equipment right on the edge of working, but it doesn't always happen. Did he describe the radio's condition?"

"No," Add said. "He doesn't know enough to judge it, anyway."

They had been pumping me! Here I had gone up there thinking to pump them, and they had been pumping me instead. My face burned. What was worse, Melissa had no doubt arranged with Add to come on to me after I had gotten good and drunk, to distract my attention from the questions! Now that was ugly.

And then Melissa said scornfully, "He doesn't know any more than the rest of those farmers."

"He knows books," Add corrected her. "And he was digging around trying to find out something, I don't know what. Glass? Or Orange, more likely. He may have just been curious. Anyway he's not as ignorant as most of them."

"Oh, he's all right," Melissa said. "Can't hold his liquor, though."

One of the scavengers was moving about the room, and I could make out the bulk of him as he passed above me. I pressed into the wall and tried to look like a shingle. If they caught me . . . well, I could beat any of them through the woods at night. Unless I fell. I was in no shape for running, and suddenly I was scared, like I should have been all along.

They continued to discuss the San Diegans, and Addison and Melissa told them everything I had said. I was surprised at how much I had told them; I didn't even remember some of it. They had pumped me good. And I hadn't learned a thing from them. I felt like a fool.

But now I was getting back at them. And despite what she had done and what she was saying, part of me wanted to get up Melissa's dress again.

"Our island friends were planning to bring over people and goods soon," the nasal one said. "We need to know how much Danforth knows, and what he could do about it if he did know anything. Maybe we should move the landing."

"They don't know anything," Add said. "And Danforth is nothing but talk. If they could touch Dana Point they wouldn't be asking the Onofre folks for help."

"They may just want a good harbor up the coast here," the man above me said. He was facing my way. "Las Pulgas has got too many sandbars, and it's too far away."

"Maybe. But from the sound of it they're nothing to worry about."

The nasal one seemed to agree: "Danforth doesn't trust his best man, from what I hear—he can't be much of a leader."

They discussed Danforth and his men in some detail, and on my wooden step I trembled. To know so much they must have spies everywhere! We were ignorant simpletons, compared to such a network.

"We should be off," said the nasal guy. "I want to be in Dana Point at three." He went on, but the moment he mentioned leaving I started inching down the blocks, shifting my weight ever so slowly, and praying that the man above me was looking into the room. I was stuck against the house; no matter which way I left, there was a good chance someone would see me. The shortest gap was to the west, so I went to that side of the building and waited. Had they started downstairs? I guessed that they had, and stole off into the trees. Foxes couldn't have crossed that ground as fast as I did.

Sure enough, the scavengers quickly appeared at the front door, and I saw Melissa in the doorway waving goodbye, still in her white dress. I was tempted to approach the house again and spy on the two of them, but I didn't want to press my luck. As long as they didn't know I had overheard their meeting with the scavengers, I had turned the tables on them. That felt good. I started off for the river, walking slowly and quietly. In the end I had gotten more information than they had, and they still thought I was a dimwit; that might give me an advantage later. I wanted fiercely to get back at them. If only the scavengers had said exactly *when* the Japanese landing was going to be. . . . But I knew it was to be soon, and at Dana Point, and that was something substantial to tell Steve. Would I have a story for him! He would be envious again, I judged with drunken clarity. But I didn't care. I would get the Shankses—show Steve what I could do—whip the Japanese—get Melissa's dress off—triumph every which way—

A tree creaked and I jumped. I started paying attention to my progress through the forest. It took a long time to get home, and then a long time to get to sleep. Such a night! I recalled hanging on the wall of the Shankses' house. Why, I had done it again. That Melissa, though—she had hurt my feelings. But all in all I felt good. Escaping the Japanese ship, foxing scavengers and their spies . . . smart work all round. . . . After more of this drunken fuddle I fell asleep. That night I dreamt there were two of me, chased by two of the Japanese captain, and in a house over the river that didn't exist two Kathryns rescued us.

...15

W ell, Henry," Steve said when I told him about my night (juicing it up a little, and leaving out the part where Add and Melissa had pumped me for everything I knew), "we're going to have to know *when* they're going to land at Dana Point, or we don't have anything. Think you can find out?"

"Now how am I going to do that?" I demanded. "Add isn't going to tell me a thing. Why don't you find that out?"

He looked offended. "You're the one who knows Melissa and Add."

"Like I said, that's no help."

"Well—maybe we could spy on them again," he suggested dubiously.

"Maybe we could."

We went back to fishing. Sun smashing the water and breaking white on every swell. Steve started speculating about how we might spy on Add, and planning what he would say to Lee and Jennings. He had worked out everything he was going to say to them to convince them to let us guide them into Orange. As we rowed back to the rivermouth I spoke for the first time since telling him my story: "You can put all that good planning to work—that's Jennings on the beach talking to your pa."

"It is?"

"Yep. Don't you recognize him?" Even with his face smaller than my little fingernail I knew him. At the sight of him all my San Diego trip came back to me, as something that had really happened to me. It made me shiver. There was no sight of Lee. Jennings was talking as usual. Now that I could see him in the flesh our whole plan seemed foolish. "Steve, I still don't think dealing with the San Diegans on our own is a good idea. What'll the rest of the valley say when they find out?"

"They won't find out. Come on, Henry, don't fade on me now. You're my best friend, aren't you?"

"Yeah. But that don't mean—"

"It means you've got to help me with this. If you don't help I can't do it."

"Well . . . shit."

"We've got to hear what they're saying there." He rowed like he was in a race to the flats. As we grounded on the sand I said, "How will we get close enough to hear?"

We jumped out and lifted the boat up the flat. "Walk the fish past them and listen while you're near. I'll follow you, and we'll piece together what we heard."

"That won't be easy."

"Shit, we know what Pa is saying. Just do it!"

I picked up a pair of rock bass by the gills and trundled slowly to the cleaning tables, walking right behind Jennings. He turned and said, "Why hello, Henry! Looks like you made it home safe enough."

"Yes sir, Mr. Jennings. Where's Mr. Lee?"

His eyes narrowed. "He's not with us this time. He sends his regards." The two men with Jennings (one had been on my train) smirked.

"I see." That was too bad, I thought.

"We went up to see your friend Tom, but he was in bed sick. He told us to come and talk to Mr. Nicolin here."

"Which is what we're doing now," John said, "so clear out, Hank."

"Sick?" I said.

"Get going!" John said.

Jennings said, "Talk to you later, friend."

I carried the bass up to the cleaning tables and said hello to the girls. Walking back to the boat I passed Steve, then heard John say, "You got no call to be pressing on this, Mister. We don't want any part of it."

"All well and good," Jennings said, "but we need to use the tracks, and they run right across your valley."

"There are tracks back in the hills. Use those."

"Mayor doesn't want that."

And then I was out of earshot. It was tough hearing their voices with the gulls stooping us and screeching over the offal. I picked up a bonita and another bass and hurried back. Steve was just past them.

"Barnard wouldn't talk to me," Jennings said. "Is that because he wants us to work together?"

"Tom voted against helping you along with the majority of the people here, so that's that."

Over at the cleaning tables Mrs. Nicolin said, "Why is that man arguing with John?"

"He wants us to let them use the train tracks in the valley, and all that."

"But they're ruined, especially at the river."

"Yeah. Say, is the old man sick?"

"So I hear. You should go up and see."

"Is he bad?"

"I don't know. But when the old get sick . . ."

Steve nudged me from behind, and I turned to walk back.

"The Mayor ain't going to like this," Jennings was saying. "No one down our way is. Americans got to stick together in these times, don't you understand that? Henry! Did you know your trip to San Diego has gone to naught?"

"Um—"

"You know what's going on here?"

John waved a hand at me angrily. "You kids clear out," he ordered.

Steve heard that over the crying gulls, and he led me up the cliff path. From the top we looked back at the river flat; Jennings was still talking. John stood there with his arms across his chest. Pretty soon he was going to grab Jennings and throw him in the river.

"That guy is a fool," Steve said.

I shook my head. "I don't think so. The old man is sick, did you know that?"

"Yeah." He didn't sound interested.

"Why didn't you tell me?"

He didn't reply.

"I'm going to go see how he's doing." He had been coughing a lot when he told his story. And even back at the meeting he had seemed listless and hacky. All I remembered about my mother's death was that she had coughed a lot.

"Not yet," Steve said. "When that guy gives up on Pa we can catch him alone and tell him our plan."

"Jennings," I said sharply. "His name is Jennings. You'd better know that when you talk to him."

Steve looked me up and down. "I knew it."

I walked down the path a ways, angry. Down by the tables John walked away from the San Diego men, brushing by one of them with his shoulder. He turned to say something, and then the San Diegans were left to look at each other. Jennings spoke and they started up the cliff trail. "Let's get out of sight," Steve said.

We hid in the trees south of the Nicolins' yard. Soon Jennings and his two men appeared over the cliff edge and started our way. "Okay, let's go," I said. Steve shook his head. "We'll follow them," he said.

"They might not like that."

"We have to talk to them where no one will see us."

"Okay, but don't surprise them."

When they were in the trees to the south we took off in pursuit, stopping every few trees to peer ahead, like bandits in a story.

"There they are," Steve said, flushed with excitement. Their dark coats flashed through the trees ahead of us, and I could hear snatches of Jennings's voice, carrying on as usual.

Steve nodded. "In these woods is as good a place as any."

"Uh huh."

"Well, let's stop them."

"Fine," I said. "I'm not holding you back."

Once again he gave me the eye. He stepped out from behind a tree. "Hey, stop! Stop up there!"

Suddenly the forest was silent, and the San Diegans were nowhere to be seen.

"Mr. Jennings!" I called. "It's me, Henry! We need to talk to you."

Jennings stepped out from behind a eucalyptus, putting a pistol back in a coat pocket. "Well, why didn't you say so?" he said irritably. "You shouldn't be surprising people in the woods."

"Sorry," I said, giving Steve a look. He was flushed red.

"What do you want?" Jennings said impatiently. His two men appeared behind him.

"We want to talk with you," Steve said.

"I heard that. So speak up; what do you want?"

After a pause Steve said, "We want to join the resistance. Not everyone in the valley is against helping you. In fact, it was a damn close vote. If some of us were to help you, the rest of the valley might come along, eventually."

One of Jennings's men snickered, but Jennings silenced him with a gesture. "That's a good thought, friend, but what we really need is access through your valley to the north, and I don't think you can give us that."

"No, we can't. But we can guide you when you're up in Orange, and that's more important. If that goes right, like I said, the rest of the valley will probably join in later."

I stared at Steve in dismay, but Jennings wasn't looking at me.

"We know scavengers who are on our side," Steve went on. "We can find out from them when the Japanese will be landing, and where."

"Who can tell you that?" Jennings asked skeptically.

"People we know," Steve replied. Seeing the doubtful look on Jennings's face he said, "There are scavengers up there who know about the scavengers dealing with the Japanese, and they don't like it. There's not much they can do about it, but they can tell us, and then we'll do something about it, right? We've been up there a lot, we know the lay of the land and everything."

Jennings said, "We could use information like that."

"Well, we can do it."

"Good. That's good." Slowly he said, "We might make arrangements for getting information from you now and then."

"We want to do more than that," Steve said flatly. "We can guide you up to whatever spot the Japanese are landing at, no matter where it is. There aren't any of you know the ruins like we do. We've been up there at night a whole bunch of times. If you're going up there on a raid, you'll need to have someone who knows the land, to get you there and back fast."

Jennings's face wasn't much at concealing his thoughts, and now he looked interested.

"We want to go up there with you and fight them," Steve said more vehemently. "We're like the Mayor—we want the Japanese too scared to come ashore ever again. You provide the men and guns, and four or five of us will guide you up there and fight with you. And we'll tell you when the landings are going to happen."

"That's quite a proposal," Jennings drawled, looking at me.

"We're young, but that doesn't matter," Steve insisted. "We can fight—we'd ambush them good."

"That's what we do," Jennings said harshly. "We ambush and kill them. We're talking about killing men."

"I know that." Steve looked offended. "Those Japanese are invaders. They're taking advantage of our weakness. Killing them is defending the country."

"True enough," Jennings agreed. "Still . . . that man down there wouldn't appreciate us dealing with you behind his back, would he. I don't know if we should do that."

"He'll never hear of it. There's just a few of us, and none of us will say a word. We go up into the ruins at night a lot—they'll think we're doing that again when we go with you. Besides, if things go well, they'll have to join us."

Jennings shifted his gaze to me. "Is that so, Henry?"

"Sure is, Mr. Jennings." I went right along with it. "We could guide you up there and no one would be the wiser."

"Maybe," Jennings said. "Maybe." He glanced back at his men, then stared at me. "Do you know right now when a landing party is coming in?"

"Soon," Steve said. "We know one is coming in soon. We already know where, and we'll find out exactly when in the next few days, I'd guess."

"All right. Tell you what. If you hear of a landing, you come tell us at the weigh station where we stopped working the tracks. We'll have men there. I'll go back south and talk to the Mayor, and if he agrees to the idea, which maybe he will, then we'll bring men up and be ready to move. We got the tracks working again, did I tell you that, Henry? It was tough, but we did it. Anyway, you know where those buildings are, the weigh station."

"We all know that," Steve said.

"Fine, fine. Now listen: when you get word of a Jap landing, hustle to the station and tell us, and we'll see what we can do about it. We'll leave it at that for now."

"We have to go along on the raid," Steve insisted.

"Sure, didn't I say that? You'll be our guides. All this depends on the Mayor, you understand, but as I said, I think he'll want to do it. He wants to hit those Japs any way he can."

"So do we," Steve insisted.

"Oh, I believe you. Now, we'd better be off."

"When can we check with you and see what the Mayor said?"

"Oh—a week, say. But get down there sooner if you hear word."

Nicolin nodded, and Jennings pointed his men south.

"Good talking with you, friends. Good to know that someone in this valley is an American."

"That we are. We'll see you soon."

"Goodbye," I added.

We watched them slip through the trees in the forest. Then Steve struck me on the arm.

"We did it! They're going for it, Henry, they're going to do it."

"Looks like it," I said. "But what was that you said about how we'll know when the landing will come in a few days? You lied to them! There's no way we can be sure when we'll find that out, if we ever do at all!"

"Ah come on, Henry. You could see I had to tell them something. You pretend to object to all this, but you like it as much as I do. You're good at it! You're the fastest thinking, fastest running resistance man around, and the cleverest in figuring these kinds of things out. You'll be able to find out that landing date if you want to."

"I suppose I can," I said, pleased despite myself.

"Sure you can."

"Well . . . let's get back before anyone notices we're missing."

He laughed. "See? You are good at this, Henry, I swear you are."

"Uh huh."

And the thing is, I thought he was right. I was the one who had kept Jennings and his men from shooting us by mistake, back there. And every time I was in a spot, the right things seemed to happen to get me out of it. I began to feel that these things didn't just happen to me, but that I was doing them. I *made* them turn out right. I could make sure that we joined the resistance, and fought the Japanese, without breaking the vote or getting the rest of the valley angry at us. I really thought I could do it.

Then I remembered the old man, and all my feeling of power vanished. We were still in the forest between the Nicolins' and Concrete Bay; if I headed inland I would soon run onto Tom's ridge.

"I'm going up to see how the old man is doing," I said.

"I've got to get back to the pit," Steve said. "But I'll—wait a minute!"

But I was already off, making my way through the trees inland.

... 16

The old man's yard always looked untended, with weeds growing over the collapsing fence and junk scattered everywhere. But now as I climbed the ridge path apprehension made me see it all again: the small weatherbeaten house with its big front window reflecting the sky; the weeds; the gnarled trees on the ridge tossing in the wind. If the house's owner had been dead and buried ten years, it would all look as it did now.

Kathryn appeared in the window, and I tried to change my thoughts. Kathryn saw me and waved, and I lifted my head in hello. She opened the door as I walked into the yard, and met me in the doorway.

Casually I said, "So how's he doing? What's wrong with him?"

"He's asleep now. I don't think he slept much last night, he was coughing so bad."

"I remember he coughed some when he told us that story."

"It's worse now. He's all congested."

I studied Kathryn's face, saw the well-known pattern of freckles shifted by lines of concern. She reached out to hold my arm. I hugged her and she put her head to my shoulder. It scared me. If Kathryn was scared, I was terrified. I tried to reassure her with my hug, but I was trembling.

"Who's that out there?" Tom called from the bedroom. "I'm not sleeping, who's there?"

Then he coughed. It was a deep, wet, hacking sound, like he was choosing voluntarily to put a lot of force behind it.

"It's me, Tom," I said when he was done. I went to the door of his room. None of us had ever been welcome in there. I looked in. "I heard you were sick."

"I am." He was sitting up in bed, leaning against the wall behind it. Hair and beard were tangled and damp, face sweaty and pale. He eyed me without moving his head. "Come on in."

I walked into the room for the first time. It was filled with books, like the storeroom down the hall. There was a table and chair, and tacked to the wall under the one small window, a collection of curled photographs.

I said, "I guess you must have caught a cold on our trip back."

"Seems to me it should've been you who got it. You got the coldest."

"We all got cold." I remembered how he had walked on the seaward side of me to break the wind. The times he had held me up as we walked. I looked at the photographs, heard Kathryn move things around in the big room.

"What's she doing out there?" Tom asked. "Hey, girl! Quit that!" He started to cough again.

When he was done my heart was pounding. "Maybe you shouldn't shout," I said.

"Yeah."

Lamely I added, "It's rotten to have a cold in the summer."

"Yeah. Sure is."

Kathryn stood in the doorway.

"Where's your sister?" Tom said. "She was just here."

"She had to go do some things," said Kathryn.

"Anybody home?" came a voice from the door.

"That must be her now," Kathryn said. But it had been Doc's voice.

"Uh oh," said Tom. "You didn't."

"I did," Kathryn said apologetically.

Doc barged into the room, black bag in hand, Kristen on his heels.

"What are you doing here?" Tom said. "I don't want you fussing with me." He shifted in his bed until he was against the side wall.

Doc approached him with a fierce grin.

"Leave me alone, I'm telling you—"

"Shut up and lie flat," Doc said. He put his bag on the bed, and pulled his stethoscope from it.

"Ernest, you don't need to do this. I've just got a cold."

"Shut up," Doc said angrily. "Do as I say, or I'll make you swallow this." He held up the stethoscope.

"You couldn't make me blink." But he lay flat, and let Doc take his pulse, and listen to his chest with the stethoscope. He kept complaining, but Doc stuck a thermometer in his mouth, which shut him up, or at least made him incomprehensible. Then Doc went back to listening.

After a bit he removed the thermometer from Tom's mouth and examined it. "Breathe deep," he ordered, listening again to Tom's chest.

Tom breathed once or twice, caught—held his breath till he turned pink—then coughed, long and hard.

"Tom," Doc said, "you're coming to my house for a visit to the hospital."

Tom shook his head.

"Don't even try to argue with me," Doc warned. "It's the hospital for you, boy."

"No way," Tom said, and cleared his throat. "I'm staying here."

"God damn it," Doc said. He was genuinely angry. "It's likely you have pneumonia. If you don't come with me I'm going to have to move over here. Now what's Mando going to think of that?"

"Mando would love it."

"But I wouldn't." And Tom caught the look on Doc's face. It was probably true that Doc could have moved to Tom's easier than Tom could move to Doc's. But Doc's place was the hospital. Doc didn't do much serious doctoring anymore—I mean he did what he could, but that wasn't much. Breaks, cuts, births—he was good at those. His father, a doctor gone crazy for doctoring, had made sure of that when Doc was young, teaching him everything he knew with fanatic insistence. But now Doc was responsible for his best friend, who was seriously ill—and maybe moving Tom to the hospital was a way to say to himself that he could do something about it. I could see Tom figuring this out as he looked at Doc—figuring it out more slowly than he usually would have, I thought. "Pneumonia, eh?" he said.

"That's right." Doc turned to us. "You all go outside for a bit."

Kathryn and Kristen and I went out and stood in the yard, amid all the rusty machine parts. Kristen told us how she had located Doc. Kathryn and I stared out at the ocean, silently sharing our distress. Clouds were rolling in. It happened so often like that—a sunny day, blanketed by mid-afternoon by clouds. Wind whipped the weeds, and our hair.

Doc looked out the door. "We need some help in here," he said. We went inside. "Kathryn, get some of his clothes together, a few shirts he can wear in bed, you know. Henry, he wants to get some books together; go find out which ones he wants."

I went back in the bedroom and found Tom standing before the photographs tacked to the wall, holding one flat with a finger. "Oh, sorry," I said. "Which books do you want to take?"

He turned and walked slowly to the bed. "I'll show you." We went to the storeroom, and he looked around at the books stacked in the gloom. A pile near the door contained every book he wanted. He handed them to me from a crouch. *Great Expectations* was the only title I noticed. When my arms were full he stopped. He picked up one more.

"Here. I want you to take this one."

He held out the book that Wentworth had given us, the one with blank pages.

"What am I going to do with this?"

He tried to put it in my arms with the rest, but there wasn't room.

"Wait—I thought you were going to write your stories in that."

"I want you to do it."

"But I don't know the stories!"

"Yes you do."

"No I don't. Besides, I don't know how to write."

"The hell you don't! I taught you myself, by God."

"Yeah, but not for books. I don't know how to write books."

"It's easy. You just keep going till the pages are full." He forced the book under my arm.

"Tom," I protested, "no. You're supposed to do it."

"I can't. I've tried. You'll see the pages ripped out of the front. But I can't."

"I don't believe it. Why, the story you told the other night—"

"Not the same. Believe me." He looked desolate. We stood there looking at the blank book in my arms, both of us upset. "The stories I've got you wouldn't want written down."

"Oh Tom."

Doc came in the room. "Henry, you aren't going to be able to carry those books. Give them to Kristen; she's got a bag."

"Why, what am I carrying?"

"You and I are carrying Tom here, young man, can't you figure that out? Does he look like someone ready to walk across the valley?"

I thought Tom would hit him for that, but he didn't. He just looked morose and tired, and said, "I wasn't aware you owned a stretcher, Ernest."

"I don't. We'll use one of your chairs."

"Ah. Well, that sounds like hard work." He walked into the big room. "This one by the window is the lightest." He carried it out of the house himself, then sat in it.

"Put those books in Kristen's bag," said Doc.

"Ooof," Kristen said as I piled them in. I went to help Kathryn find Tom's shirts. Curiously I checked the photograph Tom had been looking at; it was a woman's face. Kathryn lifted an armful of clothes, and we went outside. The old man was staring at the sea. It was getting blustery, and whitecaps were starting to appear.

"Ready?" Doc asked.

Tom nodded, not looking at us. Doc and I got on either side of him and lifted the chair by its arms and bottom. Tom craned around to look back at his house as we stepped slowly down the ridge trail. Mouth turned down he said, "I am the last American."

"The hell you are," I said. And he chuckled.

It was tricky getting down the ridge path, but on the valley floor he seemed heavier. "Change places with me," Kathryn said to Doc. We put the chair down;

Tom sat there with his eyes closed and never said a word. So strange, to have the old man quiet! Though the wind was brisk, there was sweat beading on his forehead.

Kathryn and I lifted him. She was a lot stronger than Doc, so I had less to carry. Into the forest shade we went.

"Am I heavy?" Tom asked. He opened his eyes and looked up at Kathryn. Her thick freckled arms came together at the elbows, pinning her breasts together in front of his face. He mimicked a bite at them.

She laughed. "No more than a chairful of rocks," she said.

At the bridge we stopped for a rest, and watched the clouds roll over us, talking as if we were on a normal outing. On the bank upstream a group of kids splashed in the water; they stopped to watch us as we got across the bridge. Tom stared mournfully at the naked brats as they pointed and shrieked. Kathryn saw the look on his face and she squinted at me unhappily. Fat gray clouds lowered over us. I tried to find a way to distract Tom.

"I still don't see what I'm going to do with that blank book," I said. "You better keep it, Tom, you might want to do some writing in it up at Doc's."

"Nope. It's yours."

"But—but what am I going to do with it?"

"Write in it. That's why I'm giving it to you. Write your own story in it."

"But I don't have a story."

"Sure you do. 'An American at Home.'"

"But that's nothing. Besides, I wouldn't know how."

"Just do it. Write the way you talk. Tell the truth."

"What truth?"

After a long pause, he said, "You'll figure that out. That's what the book is for."

He lost me there, but by that time we were working our way up the path to the Costas', and were almost to the little cleared terrace in the hillside that it sat on. I looked at Kathryn and she thanked me for distracting him with a quick smile. We hefted him up the last steps.

The Costas' house gleamed black against the trees and clouds. Mando came out and greeted us. "How are you, Tom?" he said brightly. Without answering Tom tried to stand up and walk through the door into their house. He couldn't do it, and Kathryn and I carried him in. Mando led us to the corner room that they called the hospital. Its two outer walls were oil drums; there were two beds, a stove, an overhead trap door to let sun and air in, and a smooth wood floor. We put Tom on the corner bed. He lay there with a faint frown turning his mouth. We went into the kitchen and let Doc look at him.

"He's real sick, huh?" said Mando.

"Your dad says it's pneumonia," Kathryn said.

"I'm glad he's here, then. Have a seat, Henry, you look bushed."

"I am." While I sat Mando got us cups of water. Then he got out some of his animal drawings to show Kristen.

"Did you really see that bear, Armando?"

"Yes, I sure did—Del can tell you, he was with me."

Kathryn jerked her head at the door. "Let's go outside," she said to me.

We sat on the cut log bench in the Costas' garden. Kathryn heaved a sigh. For a long time we sat together without saying a word.

Mando and Kristen came out. "Pa says we should find Steve, and get him to come up and read from that book," Mando said. "He said Tom would like that."

"Sounds like a good idea," Kathryn said.

"I think he'll be at his house," I told them. "Or down the cliff right by the house, you know the place."

"Yeah. We'll try there." They walked on down the path, hand in hand. We watched them till they were out of sight, then sat silently again.

Abruptly Kathryn slapped at a fly. "He's too old for this."

"Well, he's gotten sick before." But I could tell this time was different.

She didn't answer. Her wild hair lifted and fell in the nippy onshore wind.

"I think of him as ageless," I said. "Old, but—you know—unchanging."

"I know."

"It scares me when he gets sick like this!"

"I know."

"At his age. Why, he's ancient."

"Over a hundred." Kathryn shook her head. "Incredible."

"I wonder why we get old at all. Sometimes it doesn't seem natural."

I felt her shrug more than saw it. "That's life."

Which wasn't much of an answer. The deeper the question the shallower the answer, until the deepest questions have no answers at all. Why are things the way they are, Kath? A sigh, arms touching, curled hairs floating across my face, the wind, the clouds overhead. What more answer than that? I felt choked, as if oceans of clouds filled my chest. A strand of Kathryn's hair rolled up and down my nose, and I watched it fiercely, noted its every kink and curl, every streak of red in the brown, as a way to hold myself all in. As a way to grab the world to me, to hold it against me so it couldn't slip away.

Time passed and that was that. Kathryn said, "Steve is so tense these days I'm afraid he's going to break. Like a twenty-pound bowstring on a sixty-pound bow. Fighting with his pa. And all that shit about the resistance. If I don't agree with every word he says, he starts a fight with me. I'm getting so sick of it."

I didn't know what to say.

"Couldn't you talk to him about it, Henry? Couldn't you discourage him about this resistance thing somehow?"

I shook my head. "Since I got back, he won't let me argue with him."

"Yeah, I've seen that. But in some other way. Even if you're for the resistance yourself, you know there's no reason to go crazy over it."

I nodded.

"Something other than arguing with him. You're good with words, Henry, you could find some way to dampen his enthusiasm for all that."

"I guess." What about my enthusiasm, I wanted to say; but looking at her I couldn't. Didn't I have doubts, anyway?

"Please, Henry." She put her hand on my arm again. "It's only making him unhappy, and me miserable. If I knew you were working on him to calm him down, I'd feel better."

"Oh Kath, I don't know." But her hand tightened around my upper arm, and her eyes were damp. With her hand touching me I felt connected with all this world that rushed over us, so chill and so beautiful. "I'll talk to him," I said. "I'll do my best."

"Thank you. Thank you. He listens to you more than anybody else."

That surprised me. "I'd think he'd listen to you most."

She pursed her lips, and her hand returned to her lap. "We aren't getting along, like I said. Because of all this."

"Ah." And I had agreed to help her there—I would always agree to help her if she asked, I realized—at the same time that I was conspiring with Steve in every spare moment to take the San Diegans into Orange County! What was I doing? When I thought about what I had just done I felt sick. All my connection with the green and white and the salt and the trees' voices disappeared, and I almost said to Kathryn I can't do it, I'm with Steve on this. But I didn't. I felt a knot tie inside me.

Steve appeared on the path below with Gabby, carrying the book in one hand and waving with the other. Gabby had to jog to keep up with him.

"Halloo!" he cried cheerfully. "Ahoy up there!"

We stood and met them at the Costas' door.

"So Doc brought him here, eh?" Steve said.

"He thinks he has pneumonia," said Kathryn.

Steve winced and shook his head. "Let's go keep him company, then."

Once inside I began to lose the knot, and when Steve and Tom went into their usual act I laughed with the others.

"What are you doing in the hospital, you old layabout? Have you bit any nurses yet?"

"Only to discourage them when they're washing my body," Tom said with a faint smile.

"Sure, sure. And is the food terrible? And the what d'you call thems, the bedpans is it?"

"Watch it, boy, or I'll turn a bedpan over your head. Bedpan indeed—"

And by the time they were done tussling and pounding each other, Steve had Tom up in his bed and leaning back against the oildrums. The rest of us crowded into the hospital and sat on the other bed, or the floor, and laughed like we were at one of Tom's bonfire parties. Steve could do that for us. Even Kathryn was laughing. Only Doc stayed serious through it all, his eye on Tom. Over here Tom was his responsibility, and already you could see the strain on him. I don't think Doc liked being our doctor. He'd rather have stuck to gardening. But even though he had trained Kathryn to assist him, and swore she knew everything he did, only he was trusted with the care of our sick. He was the one with the knowledge from the old time. But he didn't like it.

Mando was wild about *An American Around the World*, even worse than Steve, and now he clamored for it. Steve sat on the bed at Tom's feet, and Kathryn sat on the floor beside his legs. Gabby and Doc and I sat on chairs brought in from the kitchen, and Mando and Kristen took the empty bed, holding hands again.

The first chapter Steve read was Chapter Sixteen, "A Vengeance Symbolic Is Better Than None." By this time Baum was in Moscow, and on the day of the big May parade, when all the tyrants of the Kremlin came out to review Russia's military might, Baum smuggled a packet of fireworks—the strongest explosives he could get his hands on—into a trash can in Red Square. At the best part of the parade the fireworks went off, spewing red, white, and blue sparks, and sending the entire government under their chairs. This prank, a tiny echo of what Russia had done to America, gave Baum as much pleasure as the tornado had. But he also had to hightail it out of the capital, as the search for the culprit was intense. The things he had to do in the next chapter to make it to Istanbul would have tired a horse. It was one adventure after another. Doc rolled his eyes and actually began to chuckle in some places, like when Baum stole a hydrofoil boat in the Crimea, and piloted it over the Black Sea pursued by gunboats. Baum was in mortal danger, but Doc kept on giggling.

"Why are you laughing?" Steve stopped to demand of Doc, annoyed that his reading of Baum's desperate last-chance flight into the Bosporus had been marred.

"Oh no reason," Doc was quick to say. "It's just his style. He's so cool when he tells about it all, you know."

But in the next chapter, "Sunken Venice," Doc laughed again. Steve scowled and stopped reading.

"Now wait a minute," Doc said, anticipating Steve's censure. "He's saying the water level is thirty feet higher there than it used to be. But anyone can see right out here that the water level is the same as ever. In fact it may be lower."

"It's the same," Tom said, smiling at the exchange.

"Okay, but if so, it should be the same in Venice."

"Maybe things are different there," Mando said indignantly.

Doc cracked up again. "All the oceans are connected," he told Mando. "It's all one ocean, with one sea level."

"You're saying this Glen Baum is a liar," Kathryn said with interest. She didn't look at all displeased by the idea, and I knew why. "The whole book is made up!"

"It is not!" Steve cried angrily, and Mando echoed him.

Doc waved a hand. "I'm not saying that. I don't know what all is true in there. Maybe a few stretchers, to liven things up."

"He says Venice sank," Steve said coldly, and read the passage again. "The islands sank, and they had to build shacks on the roofs to stay above the water. So the sea level didn't have to rise." He looked peevishly at Doc. "It sounds likely to me."

"Could be," Doc said with a straight face. Steve's jaw was tight, his face flushed.

"Let's go on reading," I said. "I want to know what happens."

Steve read again, his voice harsh and rapid. Baum's adventures picked up their pace. He was in as much danger as ever, but somehow it wasn't the same. In the chapter called "Far Tortuga," when he parachuted from a falling plane into the Caribbean, with several others who then inflated a raft, Doc left the hospital and went into the kitchen, his face averted to conceal a grin from Steve and Mando. The men on the inflatable raft, by the way, perished one by one, victims of thirst and giant turtle attacks, until only Baum was left to land on the jungle beach in Central America. It should have been pretty dramatic, and sad, but when Baum met up with a jungle headhunter Tom went "heee, heee, heee," from his bed, and we could hear Doc busting up in the kitchen, and Kathryn started laughing too, and Steve slammed the book shut and nearly stomped on Kathryn as he stood up.

"I won't read for you folks anymore," he cried. "You've got no respect for literature!"

Which made Tom laugh so hard he started to cough again. So Doc came in and kicked us all out, and the reading session was done.

But we came back the next night, and Steve agreed sullenly to read again. Soon enough An American Around the World was done, which was probably just as well, and we went on to Great Expectations, and took the parts to read in Much Ado About Nothing, and tried some other books as well. It was all good fun. But Tom kept coughing, and he got quieter, and thinner, and paler. The days passed in a slow sameness, and I didn't feel like joining in the joking on the boats, or memorizing my readings, or even reading them. Nothing seemed interesting or good to me, and Tom got sicker as day followed day, until on some evenings I couldn't bear to look at him, lying on his back hardly aware of us, and each day I woke up with that knot over my stomach, afraid that it might be the last day he could hold on to this life.

... 17

Mornings I got up at dawn before the boats went out, and went up to check on him. Most mornings he was asleep. The nights were hard, Doc said. He got sicker, right up to the edge of death—I had to admit it—and there he hovered, refusing to pass on. One morning he was half awake and his bloodshot eyes stared at me defiantly. Don't write me off yet, they said. He hadn't slept that night, Mando told me. Now he didn't feel up to talking. He just stared. I pressed his hand—his skin was damp, his hand limp and fleshless—then left, shaking my head at his tenacity. Living a hundred years wasn't enough for him. He wanted to live forever. That look in his eyes told me, and I smiled a little, hoping he could do it. But the visit scared me. I hustled down the hill to the boats as if I was running from the death itself.

Another morning I noticed it was aging Doc to care for him. Doc was over seventy himself; in most towns he would have been the oldest one. Pretty soon he might be ours. One morning after a hard night I sat with Mando and Doc at the kitchen table. They'd been up through the small hours trying to ease Tom's coughing, which had lost power but was more constant. All Doc's wrinkles were red and deep, and there were rings under his eyes. Mando let his head rest on the table, mouth open like a fish's. I got up and stoked their fire, got some water on, made them some tea and hot cereal. "You're going to miss the boat," Doc said, but smiled his thanks with one corner of his mouth. His hand trembled his tea mug. Mando roused at the smell of corn and scraped his face off the table. We laughed at him and ate. I trudged down the hill with the knot over my stomach.

That was Saturday. Sunday I went to church. There were people there who (like me) hardly ever went to church: Rafael, Gabby, Kathryn, and hiding at the back, Steve. Carmen knew why we were there, and at the end of her final prayer she said, "And Lord, please return our Tom to health." Her voice had such power and calmness, to hear it was like being held. Her voice knew everything would be right. The amens were loud, and we walked out of the church like one big family.

That was Sunday morning, though. The rest of the week the tension made folks irritable. Mando took the short end of Doc's temper; he didn't much care what books I read from, or even whether we read at all. "Armando!" I said. "You of all people have *got* to want to read." "Just leave me be," he said blearily. Around the ovens the women talked in quiet voices. No boisterous tattling, no shrieks of laughter tearing the air. No old man jokes on the boats. I went out to help the Mendezes gather wood, and Gabby and I nearly got in a fight trying to decide how to carry a fallen eucalyptus tree to the two-man saw. Later that day I passed Mrs. Mariani and Mrs. Nicolin, arguing heatedly at the latrine door. No one would have believed me if I had told them about that. I hurried down the path unhappily.

One day at the rivermouth it got worse. They were pulling the boats onto the flat when I arrived—I was spending a week helping the Mendezes, and only came down to help clean up. I joined those moving fish from the boats to the cleaning tables. Steve was over with Marvin, pulling the nets out of the boats and washing them in the shallows, then rolling them up. Usually Marvin did this by himself; John saw Steve and called, "Steve, get over and help Henry!"

Steve didn't even look up. On his knees on the hard sand of the flat, he tugged at the stiff wire rope at the top of the net. Answer him! I thought. John walked over and looked down at him.

"Go over and help get the fish out," he ordered.

"I'm folding this net," Steve said without looking up.

"Stop it, and get over to the fish."

"And just leave the net here, eh?" Steve said sarcastically. "Just let me be."

John grabbed him just under the armpit and yanked him to his feet. With a stifled cry Steve twisted and jerked out of John's grasp, staggering back into the shallows. He pulled up and charged John, who walked straight at him and shoved him back into the shallows again. Steve stood and pulled back a fist, and was about to swing when Marvin jumped between them. "For God's sake!" Marvin cried, shouldering John back a step. "Stop this, will you?"

Steve didn't appear to hear him. He was rounding Marvin when I seized his right wrist in both hands and dragged him away, falling in the shallows to duck a left cross. If Rafael hadn't wrapped Steve in a bearhug he would have pounded me and gone after John again; his eyes were wild, they didn't recognize any of us. Rafael carried him down the beach a few steps and let him loose with a shove.

Every man and woman on the beach had stopped what they were doing. They watched now with faces grim, or expressionless, or secretly pleased, or openly amused. Slowly I stood up.

"You two are making it hard to work in peace around here," Rafael said. "Why don't you keep your family matters to yourself."

"Shut up," John snapped. He surveyed us and with a chopping motion of his hand said, "Get back to work."

"Come on," I said to Steve, pulling him up the flat and away from the boats. He shrugged free of me impatiently. We stumbled over the net where it had all started. "Come on, Steve, let's get out of here." He allowed me to pull him away. John didn't look at us. I led him up the riverbank. I was shaken, and glad that Marvin had had the wit to jump between them. If he hadn't been so quick . . . well, it didn't bear thinking about.

Steve was still breathing heavily, as if he had just bodysurfed every wave of a big set. Between his clenched teeth he was cursing, repeating the words in an incoherent string. We took the river path to the broken end of the freeway, sat under a torrey pine that hung over the river. Going for cover, like coyotes after a scrap with a badger.

For a while we just sat. I swept pine needles into stacks, and then scraped through the dirt to concrete. Steve's breathing slowed to normal.

"He's trying to make me fight him," he said. "I know he is."

I doubted it, but I said, "I don't know. If he is, you shouldn't rise to it."

"How am I supposed to do that?" he demanded.

"Well, I don't know. Just avoid him, and do what he says—"

"Oh sure," he cried, twisting to his feet. He leaned over and bawled at me, "Just keep on crawling around on my belly eating shit! That's a real help! Don't you try to tell me what to do with my life, Mister Henry Big Man. You're just like all the rest! And don't you get in my way again when I go after him, or I'll bust your face instead of his!" He stalked down the freeway, cut into the potato patch and disappeared.

I let out a deep breath, relieved that he hadn't hit me right then and there.

Kathryn had said that Steve listened to me more than to anybody else. Maybe that meant he didn't listen to anybody anymore. Or maybe Kathryn was wrong. Or maybe I had said the wrong thing—or said it in the wrong way. I didn't know. It took me a long time to get up the spirit to stand and walk on.

One day I took off up the river path, past the gardens and the ovens and the women washing clothes at the bridge bend, on up to where the hills closed together and the forest grew right down into the water on both banks. Here the path disappeared and everyone had to make their own way. I moved back into the trees and sat down, leaned back against the trunk of a big pine.

Wandering into the forest, to sit and be with it, was something I had done for a long time. It started when my mother died, when I imagined I could hear her voice in the trees outside our house. That was dumb, and soon I stopped. But now I was doing it again. With Tom sick there was no one I could talk to, no one who didn't want something from me. It made me lonely. So when I felt that way I went out into the woods and sat. Nothing could touch me there, and eventually the knot would leave my stomach.

This was a particularly good spot. Around me trees clustered, big torrey pines surrounded by littler daughter trees. The ground was padded with needles, the trunk bowed at just the right angle for a backrest, and the curly branches above blocked most of the sun, but not all of it. Patches of light swam over my patched blue jeans, and shadow needles fenced with the brown needles under me. A pinecone jabbed me. I scrunched against the flaky bark of my backrest. Rolling on it, I turned and picked some of the dried crumbly gum out of a deep crack. Pressed it between my fingers until the still-liquid center burst out of the crust. Pine sap. Now my fingers would be sticky and pick up all sorts of dirt, so that dark marks would appear on my hands and fingers. But the smell of it was so piney. That smell and the smells of sea salt, and dirt, and wood smoke, and fish, made up the odor of the valley. Wind raked through the needles and a few of them dropped on me, each fivesome of needles wrapped together by a little bark nub at their bottoms. They pulled apart with a click.

Ants crawled over me and I brushed them away. I closed my eyes and the wind touched my cheek, it breathed through all the needles on all the branches of all the trees, and said *oh, mmmmmmm*. Have you heard the sound of wind in pine trees—I mean really listened to it, as to the voice of a friend? There's nothing so soothing. It put me in a trance more like sleep than anything else, though I still heard. Each buffet or slacking shifted the hum or whoosh or roar of it; sometimes it was like the sound of a big waterfall around the bend, other times like the waves on the beach—still again, like a thousand folk in the far distance, singing *oh* as deep and wild as they could. Occasional bird calls tweeted through the sound, but mostly it was all that could be heard. The wind, the wind, *oh*. It was enough to fill the ear forever. I didn't want to hear any other voice.

But voices I heard—human voices, coming through the trees by the river. Annoyed, I rolled on my side to see if I could see who was talking. They weren't visible. I considered calling out, but I didn't feel obliged to them; they were invading my spot, after all. I couldn't blame them too much, it was a small valley and there weren't that many places to go if you wanted to get away from folks. But it was my bad luck that they'd come to this one. I laid back against my tree and hoped they would go away. They didn't. Branches snapped off to my left, and then the voices took up again, close enough so that I could make out the words—just a few trees over, in fact. That was Steve talking, and then Kathryn answered him. I sat up frowning.

Steve said, "Everybody in this valley is telling me what to do."

"Everybody?"

"Yes! You know what I mean. Jesus, you're getting to be just like everybody else."

"Everybody?"

Just that one word and I knew Kathryn was mad.

"Everybody," Steve repeated, more sad than angry. "Steve, get down there and catch fish. Steve, don't go into Orange County. Don't go north, don't go south, don't go east, don't row too far out to sea. Don't leave Onofre, and don't do anything."

"*I* was just saying you shouldn't deal with those San Diegans behind the backs of the people here. Who knows what those folks really want." After a pause she added, "Henry's trying to tell you the same thing."

"Henry, shit. He gets to go south, and when he comes back he's Henry Big Man, telling me what to do like everyone else."

"He is not telling you what to do. He's telling you what he thinks. Since when can't he do that?"

"Oh, I don't know. . . . It ain't Henry."

I scrunched down behind my tree uncomfortably. It was a bad sign, them talking of me; they'd sense me by the way my name sounded to them, and search around and see me, and I'd look like I was spying when I had only been trying to get some peace. I didn't want to hear all this, I didn't want to know about it. Well . . . that wasn't strictly true. Anyway I didn't move.

"What is it, then?" Kathryn asked, resigned and a little fearful.

"It's . . . it's living this little life in this little valley. Under Pa's thumb, stuck forever. I can't abide it."

"I didn't know life here was that bad for you."

"Ah come on, Kath. It isn't you."

"No?"

"No! You're the best part of my life here, I keep telling you that. But don't you see, I can't be trapped here all my life, working for my dad. That wouldn't be a life at all. The whole world is out there! And who's keeping me from it? The Japanese are. And here we have folks who want to fight the Japanese, and we're not helping them. It makes me sick. So I've got to do it, I've got to help them, can't you see that? Maybe it'll take all my life to make us free again, maybe it'll take longer, but at least I'll be doing something more with my life than gathering the food for my face."

A scrub jay flashed blue as it landed in the branch above me, and informed Steve and Kathryn of my presence. They weren't listening.

"Is that all the life here is to you?" Kathryn asked.

"No, shit, aren't you listening?" Annoyance laced his voice.

"Yes. I'm listening. And I hear that life in this valley doesn't satisfy you. That includes me."

"I *told* you that isn't true."

"You can't *tell* something away, Steve Nicolin. You can't act one way for months and months and then say, no it isn't that way, and make the months and what you did in them go away. It doesn't work like that."

I'd never heard her voice sound like it did. Mad—I'd heard it mad more times than I'd care to count. Now that angry tone was all beaten down flat. I hated to hear her voice sound like that. I didn't want to hear it—any of it—and suddenly that overcame my curiosity, and my feeling that it was my place. I started crawling away through the trees, feeling like a fool. What if they saw me now, lifting over a fallen branch to avoid making a sound? I swore in my thoughts over and over. When I got out of the sound of their voices (still arguing) I stood and walked away, discouragement dogging every step. Steve and Kathryn fighting—what else could go wrong?

Beyond the neck at the end of the valley, the river widens and meanders a bit, knocking through meadows in big loops. It's easier to travel in this back canyon by canoe, and after walking a ways I sat down again and watched the river pour into a pool and then out again. Fish tucked under the overhanging bank. The wind still soughed in the trees, but I couldn't get back my peace no matter how hard I listened. The knot in my stomach was back. Sometimes the harder you try the less it will go away. After a while I decided to check the snares that the Simpsons had set up on the edge of the one oxbow meadow, to give me something to do.

One of the snares had a weasel caught in it. It had been going after a rabbit, dead in the same snare, and now its long wiry body was all tangled in the laces. It tugged at them one last time as I approached; squeaked, and baring its teeth in a fierce grin, glared at me murderously, hatefully—even after I broke its neck with a quick step. Or so it seemed. I freed the two little beasts and set the snare again, and set off home with them both in one hand, held by the tails. I couldn't shake that weasel's last look.

Back in the neck I walked along the river, remembering a time when the old man had tried to detach a wild beehive from a short eucalyptus tree up against the south hillside. He had gotten stung and dropped the shirt wrapping the hive, and the furious bees had chased us right into the river. "It's all your fault," he had sputtered as we swam to the other side.

Sun going down. Another day passed, nothing changed. I followed a bend to the narrows where the river breaks over a couple knee-high falls, and came upon Kathryn sitting alone on the bank, tossing twigs on the water and watching them swirl downstream.

"Kath!" I called.

She looked up. "Hank," she said. "What are you doing here?" She glanced downstream, perhaps looking for Steve.

"I was just hiking up canyon," I said. I held up the two dead animals. "Checking a couple of the Simpsons' snares for them. What about you?"

"Nothing. Just sitting."

I approached her. "You look kind of down."

She looked surprised. "Do I?"

I felt disgusted with myself for pretending I could read her that well. "A little."

"Well. I guess that's right." She tossed another stick in.

I sat down beside her. "You're sitting in a wet spot," I said indignantly.

"Yeah."

"No big deal, I guess."

She was looking down, or out at the river, but I saw that her eyes were red. "So what's wrong?" I asked. Once again I felt sick at my duplicity. Where had I learned this sort of thing, what book of Tom's had taught me?

A few sticks rode over the falls and out of sight before she answered. "Same old thing," she said. "Me and Steve, Steve and me." Suddenly she faced me. "Oh," she said, her voice wild, "you've got to get Steve to stop with that plan to help the San Diegans. He's doing it to cross John, and the way they're getting along, when John finds out about it there'll be hell to pay. He'll never forgive him. . . . I don't know what will happen."

"All right," I said, my hand on her shoulder. "I'll try. I'll do my best. Don't cry." It scared me to see her cry. Like an idiot I had thought it impossible. Desperately I said, "Look, Kathryn. You know there isn't much I can do, the way he is these days. He almost hit me for grabbing him when he went after his dad the other day."

"I know." She shifted onto her hands and knees, leaned out over the water and ducked her head in it. The wet spot on the wide seat of her pants stuck into the air. After a good long time she came up blowing and huffing, and shook her head like a dog, spraying water over me and the river.

"Hey!" I cried. While she was under I had wanted to say, look, I can't help you, I'm with Steve on this one . . . but looking at her face to face, I didn't. I couldn't. The truth was, I couldn't do anything: no matter what I chose to do, I would be betraying someone.

"Let's go to my house," she said. "I'm hungry, and Mom made a berry pie."

"Okay," said I, wiping my face off. "You don't have to ask me twice when it comes to berry pie."

"I never noticed," she said, and ducked the scoop of water I sent her way.

We stood. Walked down the riverbank until the trail appeared—first as a trampled-down line in the weeds and shrubs, then as scuffed dirt and displaced rocks, then as trenches through the loam that became little creeks after a rain. New paths appeared beside these as they became too wet or deep or rocky. It reminded me of something Tom had said before we went to San Diego, about how we were all wedges stuck in cracks. But it wasn't like that, I saw; we weren't that tightly bound. It was more like being on trails, on a network of trails like the one crossing the bog beside the river here. . . . "Choosing your way is easy when you're on trails," I said, more to myself than to Kathryn.

She cocked her head. "Doing what people have done before, you mean."

"Yes, exactly. A lot of people have gone that way, and they find the best route. But out in the woods . . ."

She nodded. "We're all in the woods now." A kingfisher flashed over a snag. "I don't know why." Shadows from the trees across the river stretched over the rippled water and striped our bank. In the still of a side pool a trout broke the surface, and ripples grew away in perfect circles from the spot—why couldn't the heart grow as fast? I wanted to know . . . I wanted to know what I was doing.

The more I feel the more I see. That evening I saw everything with a crispness that startled me; leaves all had knife edges, colors were as rich as a scavenger's swap meet outfit. . . . But I only felt fuzzy things, oceans of clouds in my chest, the knot in my stomach. Too mixed to sort out and name. The river at dusk; the long stride of this woman my friend; the prospect of berry pie, making my mouth water; against these, the idea of a free land. Nicolin's plots. The old man, across the shadowed stream in a bed. I couldn't find the words to name all that, and I walked beside Kathryn without saying a thing, all the way downriver to her family's home.

Inside it was warm (Rafael had put pipes underneath their place to convey heat from the bread ovens), lamps were lit, the pies were on the table steaming. The women chattered. I ate my piece of pie and forgot everything else. Purple berries, sweet summer taste. When I left, Kathryn said, "You'll help?"

"I'll try." In the dark she couldn't see my face. So she didn't know that on the way home, at the same time I was thinking of arguments to get Steve to abandon his plan, I was also trying to figure out a way to get the landing date out of Add. Maybe I could spy on him every night until I heard him say it. . . .

I kept thinking about it, but no good trick to fool the date from Addison came to me. The next time I fished with Steve, it got to be a problem I couldn't sidestep.

"They're down at the station ruins," Steve said as we rowed out of earshot of the other boats. "I went down there and they were setting up what looked like a permanent camp in the ruins. Jennings was in charge."

"So they're here, eh? How many of them?"

"Fifteen or twenty. Jennings asked where you were. And he wanted to know when the Japanese were landing. When and where. I told him we knew where, and would find out when real soon."

"Why'd you tell him that?" I demanded. "I mean, first of all, the Japanese may not be landing soon at all."

"But you said you heard those scavengers say they would!"

"I know, but who's to say they were right?"

"Well, shit," he said, and tossed his lure into the channel. I stared at the steep back wall of Concrete Bay unhappily. "If you go at it that way, we can never really be sure of anything, can we. But if these scavengers told Add that much, it means Add is in on it, so he'll know when they're going to land. I told Jennings what we told him before, that we'd find that out for him."

"What *you* told him before," I corrected.

"You were in on it too," he said crossly. "Don't try and pretend you weren't."

I slung my lure out the opposite side from Steve's, and let the line run out. I said, "I was in on it, but that doesn't mean I'm sure it's a good idea. Look, Steve, if we get caught helping these folks after the vote went against it, what are people going to say? How are we going to justify it?"

"I don't care what people say." A fish took his lure, and he hauled the thing up viciously. "That's if they do find out. They can't keep us from doing what we want, especially when we're fighting for their lives, the cowards." He gaffed the bonita like it was one of the cowards he had in mind, pulled it into the boat, and whacked it on the head. It flopped weakly and gave up the ghost. "What is this, are you backing out on me now? Now that we got the San Diegans up here waiting for us?"

"No. I'm not backing out. I just don't know if we're doing the right thing."

"We *are* doing the right thing, and you know it. Remember all those things you said at the meeting! You were the best one there—what you said was right, every bit of it. And you know it. Let's get back to the matter at hand, here. We've got to get that date out of Add, and you're the one who knows the Shankses. You've got to go up there and get to Melissa somehow, that's all there is to it."

"Umph." Now it was getting to be very inconvenient that I hadn't told Steve the whole truth about how much Melissa and Add had fooled me. . . . I felt a bite, but I pulled too hard and the fish didn't take. "I guess." I couldn't admit that I'd lied to make myself look good.

"You've *got* to."

"All right all right!" I exclaimed. "Let me be, will you? I don't notice you suggesting any smart schemes for getting him to tell us if he don't feel like it. Just lay off!"

So we fished in silence, and looked after our lines. Onshore bobbed the green hillsides.

Steve changed the subject. "I hope we try whaling again this winter, I think we could make a go of it if we harpooned a small whale. From more than one boat, maybe."

"You can leave me out of that one, thanks," I said shortly.

He shook his head. "I don't know what's got into you, Hanker. Ever since you got back—"

"Nothing's gotten into me." Bitterly I added, "I could say the same about you."

"How come? Because I think we should try whaling again?"

"No, for God's sake." The only time we had tried to kill one of the gray whales in their migration down the coast, we had gone out in the fishing boats and harpooned one. It was an excellent throw by Rafael, using a harpoon of his own manufacture. Then we stood in the boats and watched all of the line attached to the diving whale fly out of the boat, until it was gone. Our mistake was tying the end of the line to an eye in the bow; that whale pulled the boat right down from under us. The bow was yanked under the surface and *slurp* it was gone. We ended up fishing men out of that cold water rather than whale. And the line had torn across Manuel's forearm, so that he almost bled to death. John had declared that whales were too big for our boats, and as I had been in the boat next to the one that went under, I definitely agreed with him.

But that wasn't what I was thinking about. "You're pushing things," I said slowly, "till your pa isn't going to take it. I don't know what you think'll happen—"

"You don't know what I think at all," he interrupted me, in a way that made it clear he didn't want me to pursue the matter. His mouth was tight, and I knew he could explode. Dogs get that look from time to time: nudge me once more, the look says, and I'll bite your foot off. A fish took my hook, so I could drop the matter easily enough, and I did. But obviously I was on to something. Maybe he thought John would kick him out of the valley, so he'd be free of it all. . . .

It was a big rock bass, and it took me a lot of time and effort to get it in the boat. "See, this fish is no longer than my arm, and I could barely get it in. Those whales are twice as long as this *boat*."

"They catch them up in San Clemente," Steve said. "They make a lot of silver off them at the meets, too. Why, one whale is how many jars of oil, did Tom say?"

"I don't know."

"You do too! What's this *I don't know.* I tell you. This whole valley is going to the dogs."

"No lie," I said grimly. Nicolin snorted, and we went back to fishing. After we got several more aboard he started again.

"Maybe we could poison the harpoons. Or, you know, harpoon a whale twice, from two boats."

"We'd get all tangled. The boats would be pulled together and crushed."

"What about poison, then."

"It would be better to put three boats' worth of line on the end of one harpoon, so we could let the whale run as far down as it liked."

"Now see, there you're talking." He was pleased. "Or how about this, we could have the harpoon at the end of a line that extended right back to the beach—held up by little floats or something. And then when the harpoon struck, the playing of the thing would be from the beach. Eventually we could just haul it right into the rivermouth."

"The harpoon would have to be pretty well fixed."

"Well of course. That would be true no matter what you did."

"I guess. But it's also a hell of a lot of line you're talking about. Usually those things are a mile or so offshore, aren't they?"

"Yeah. . . ." After some pondering, he said, "I wonder how those folks in San Clemente *do* catch them monsters."

"You got me. They sure aren't telling."

"I wouldn't either, if I was them."

"What's this? I thought you were telling me all the towns have to stick together, we're all one country and all that."

He nodded. "That's true. You've said so yourself. But until everyone agrees to it, you got to protect your advantages."

That seemed to have some application to me, but I couldn't figure out exactly what it was. Anyway, I had made the mistake of bringing the subject back to the situation, and as we rowed our full boat back to the rivermouth, Steve pressed me one more time.

"Remember, now, we've promised Jennings. And you *know* you want to go up there and fight those Japs. Remember what they did to you and Tom and the rest of you out there in that storm?"

"Yeah," I said. Well, Kathryn, I thought, I tried. But I knew better than that. Nicolin was right. I wanted those Japanese out of our ocean.

We negotiated the mouth break, and coasted in on the gentle waves that the high tide was shoving up the throat of the river. "So, get up there and see what you can do with Melissa. She's got a feeling for you, she'll do what you want."

"Umph."

"Maybe she'll ask Add for you."

"I doubt it."

"Still, you've got to start somewhere. And I'll see if I can't think of something myself. Maybe we could eavesdrop on them like you did last time."

I laughed. "It might come to that," I agreed. "I've thought of that myself."

"Okay, but do what else you can first, all right?"

"All right. I'll give her a try."

I spent a couple of days thinking about it, trying to figure something out—living with the knot over my stomach, so that it was hard to sleep. One morning before dawn I gave up trying and walked over the dew-soaked bridge to the Costas'. Doc was up, sitting at the kitchen table drinking tea and staring at the wall. I tapped at the window and he let me in. "He's asleep now," he said with relief. I nodded and sat down with him. "He's getting weaker," he said, looking into his tea. "I don't know. . . . Too bad you guys had such miserable weather coming back from San Diego. You're young and can take it, but Tom . . . Tom acts like he's young when he shouldn't. Maybe this will teach him to be more careful, to take better care of himself. If he lives."

"You should remember the same thing yourself," I said. "You look awful tired."

He nodded.

"If the train tracks had been left alone we would have come back easy as you please," I went on. "Those bastards . . ."

Looking up at me Doc said, "He may die, you know."

"I know."

He drank some tea. The kitchen began to get lighter with the dawn. "Maybe I'll go to bed now."

"Do it. I'll stick around till Mando gets up, and keep an eye on things."

"Thanks, Henry." He shoved the chair back. Lifted himself up. Stood and collected himself. Stepped into his room.

So I hiked onto Basilone Ridge that afternoon, to see if I could find Melissa at their house. Through woods and over the cracked greeny concrete of the old foundations. When I walked into the clearing around their tower I saw Addison, at leisure on his roof, smoking a pipe and kicking his heels against the side of the house, thump-thump, thump-thump. When he saw me he stopped kicking, and didn't smile or nod. Uncomfortable under his stare, I approached. "Is Melissa home?" I called.

"No. She's in the valley."

"No I'm not," Melissa called, emerging into the clearing from the north side—the side away from the valley. "I'm home!"

Add took the pipe from his mouth. "So you are."

"What's up, Henry?" Melissa said to me with a smile. She was wearing baggy burlap pants, and a sleeveless blue shirt. "Want to go for a hike up the ridge?"

"That's just what I was going to ask you."

"Daddy, I'm going with Henry, I'll be back before dark."

"If I'm not here," Add said, "I'll be home for supper."

"Oh yeah." They exchanged a look. "I'll keep it hot for you."

Melissa took my hand. "Come on, Henry." With a tug we were off into the forest above their house.

As she led the way uphill, dancing and dodging between the trees, she threw questions back my way. "What have you been doing, Henry? I haven't seen you very much. Have you been back to San Diego? Don't you want to go see all that again?"

Remembering what she had said to the scavengers that night, I could hardly keep from smiling. Not that I was amused. But it was so transparent what she was doing, pumping me for information once more. I lied with every answer I gave. "Yes, I've been down to San Diego again, on my own. It's a secret. I met a whole . . ." I was going to say a whole army of Americans, but I didn't want to show I knew what she was up to. ". . . a whole bunch of people."

"Is that right?" she exclaimed. "Why, when was that?" She was quite the spy. But at the same time, she was so lithe and springy slinking through the trees, and shafts of sunlight caught and broke blue in her black hair, and I wouldn't have minded having my hands all tangled up in that hair, spy or not.

Farther up the ridge the trees gave way to mesquite and a few stubborn junipers. We followed a little trickle ravine up to the ridge proper, and stood on it in the wind. The ridge edge was sandstone perfectly divided, like the back of a fish. We walked along that division, commenting on the views out to sea, and up San Mateo Valley. "Swing Canyon is just over that spur," I said, pointing a little ahead of us.

"Is it?" Melissa said. "You want to go there?"

"Yes."

"Let's." We kissed to mark the decision, and I felt a pang; why couldn't she be like one of the other girls, like the Marianis or the Simpsons?

We continued along the ridge. Melissa kept asking questions, and I kept on lying as I answered her. After Cuchillo, the peak of Basilone Ridge, several spurs headed down from the main ridge into the valley. The steep box canyon formed by the first two of these spurs was Swing Canyon; from our vantage we could look right down it, and see where its small stream made the final fall into one of Kathryn's fields. We slid on our butts down the steep walls at the top of the canyon, and then stepped carefully through thick low mesquite. All the while she questioned me. I was amazed at how obvious she was; but I suppose if I hadn't known what she was up to, I wouldn't have noticed. It was just like plain curiosity, or almost. Reflecting on this, I decided I could be more bold in my own questions to her. I knew more than she did. A bit more bold in every way: helping her down a vertical break, I used her crotch as a handhold and lifted her down; she held one knee wide so it would work, and giggled as she twisted free on landing. With a kiss we headed down again.

"Have you ever heard about the Japanese that come over from Catalina to look at what's left in Orange County?" I asked.

"I've heard it happens," she said brightly. "But nothing more than that. Tell me about it."

"I sure would like to see one of those landings," I said. "You know, when the Japanese ship picked me out of the water, I talked with the captain for a while, and I saw he was wearing one of the high school rings that the scavengers sell!"

"Is that right," she said, astonished. You're overdoing it, I wanted to say.

"Yeah! The captain of the ship! I figure all those Japanese coast guard captains must be bribed to let through tourists on certain nights. I'd love to go up there and spy on one of those landings, just to see if I could recognize my captain again."

"But why?" Melissa asked. "Do you want to shoot him?"

"No, no. Of course not. I want to know if I'm right about him or not. You know, whether he helps the landings like I think he does." It didn't sound very convincing to me (and I shouldn't have said the word *spy*), but it was the best I could think of.

"I doubt you'll ever find out," Melissa said reasonably. "But good luck at it. I wish there was some way I could help, but I wouldn't like going up there."

"Well," I said, "maybe you could help anyway."

We were down to the sink at the very head of the box canyon, and I stopped the conversation to give her a long kiss. After that we walked to the swing tree, near the spring that starts the canyon's stream. The spring made a little pool before tumbling over a sandstone rib down the canyon, and beside the pool was a flat spot, protected by a ring of sycamore trees. It was a favored spot for lovers. Melissa took my hand and led me right to it, so I guessed she was as familiar with it as I was. We sat in the gloom and kissed, then laid on the leaf and needle bed and kissed some more. We pressed against each other, rolled aimlessly over the crackling leaves. I nudged my fingers under the tie of her burlap pants, and slid them down her belly, into tightly curled hair . . . she held my hard-on through jeans, and squeezed hard, and we kissed, and kissed, and our breath got short and jerky. I was excited, but . . . I couldn't forget about everything else and just feel her. The other times I had lain with a girl—with Melissa before, or

Rebel Simpson the previous year, or that Valerie from Trabuco, who had made several swap meet nights so interesting—I would get started and my brain would melt into my skin, so that I never thought a thing and when we were done it was like coming to. This time, at the same moment I was feeling her and kissing her neck and shoulders I was wondering how I could make my desire to see the Japanese landings sound convincing, even essential; how I could ask her again to ask Addison. It was strange.

"Maybe you *can* help," I said between kisses, as if it had just occurred to me. My hand was still in her pants, and I nudged her with a finger.

"How so?" she asked, squirming.

"Couldn't your dad talk to some of his contacts about it? I mean, I know he doesn't have many contacts up there, but you said he has one or two—"

"I did not," she said sharply, and pulled back from me. My hand slid out from her pants and it groped over the leaves for her; *no, no,* it said. . . . "I never told you anything of the sort! Daddy does his own work, like we told you before." She sat up. "Besides, why should you want to go up there? I don't get it. Is that why you were up talking to him today?"

"No, of course not. I wanted to see you," I said with conviction.

"So you could ask me to ask him," she said, not impressed.

I shuffled to her side and nuzzled her hair and neck. "See, the thing is," I said indistinctly, "if I don't see that Japanese captain again, I'm going to be afraid of him for the rest of my life. He's giving me nightmares and all. And I know Add could help me to find one of those landings."

"He could not," she said, irritated. I tried to put my hand back down her pants to distract her, but she seized it and pushed it away. "Don't," she said coldly. "See? You did get me up here to ask me to pester my dad. Listen—I don't want you bothering him about Orange County or the Japanese or any of that, you hear? Don't ask him nothing and don't get him mixed up in anything you do." She brushed leaves out of her hair, crawled away from me to the edge of the pool. "He's got enough trouble in your damn valley without you trying to give him more." She cupped some water and drank, brushed her hair back with angry slaps.

I stood up unsteadily, and walked over to the swing tree. She had made me feel awful guilty and calculating; and she looked beautiful, kneeling there by the dark pool; but still! All that holy innocent routine, after the way she had talked to the scavengers that night—after she and Add had welcomed them into their house, to tell them what they had learned by spying on our "damn valley" and its most foolish citizen Henry Aaron Fletcher . . . it made me grind my teeth.

The swing tree grows out of the rib that holds the pool in. Long ago someone had tied a thick piece of rope to one of the upper branches, and the rope was used to swing out over the steep canyon below. Angrily I grabbed the rope by the knots at its loose end, and walked back from the drop-off. Taking a good hold above the knot, I ran across the clearing at an angle away from the tree, and swung out into space. It had been a long time. Swinging around in the shadows felt good. I could see the canyon wall opposite, still catching some sun, and below me, treetops in shadow. I spun slowly, looking back to locate the tree's thick trunk. I missed it by a good margin on landing. One time Gabby had taken a swing while drunk, and had come right into the tree, back first, hitting a little broken-off nub of a branch. That had taken the color out of him.

"Don't you talk to us about that stuff anymore, are you listening to me, Henry?"

"I'm listening."

"I like you fine, but I won't abide any talk about Daddy dealing with those folks up there. We get enough grief about that as it is, and for no good reason at all. There's no cause for it." She sounded so sorrowful and put upon, I wanted to yell down at her, you get grief for it because you're a pair of scavengers, you bitch! I've seen you spy for them! But I clamped my jaws together and said "Yeah," and started another swing. "I hear you," I said bitterly to the air. She didn't reply. The rope creaked loudly. I tapped my feet together, spinning nice and slow. When I came in I went out again, and then again. For a moment I felt how wonderful it was to swing, and I wished I could swing out there forever, spinning slowly at the rope's end, free of the earth and with no worries but clearing the tree, with nothing to think about but the air rushing by me, and the shadowed trees spinning around me, and the dark green pool below to one side. Surely the knot in my stomach would leave me then. When I landed I almost smashed face first into the treetrunk. That was just the way of it: spend your time in wishing and a tree smacks your face for you.

Melissa was crouched by the pool, holding her hair back with a hand, leaning over to drink directly from the spring. "I'm leaving," I said harshly.

"I need help getting up the ridge." She didn't look at me.

I considered telling her she could go down the canyon and around the valley and not need any help, but I thought better of it.

We didn't have much to say on the way back. It was hard work climbing up the final walls of the box canyon, and we both got dirty. Melissa refused to let me help her except when she couldn't get up without it, perhaps remembering the handhold I had used on the way down. The more I thought about the way she had worked on me, the angrier I got. And to think I had still wanted her. Why, I was a fool—and the Shankses were no better than thieves. Scavengers. Spies. Zopilotes! Not only that, but there was no way I was going to be able to get the information I needed out of them.

We walked down the Basilone slope a few trees apart. "I don't need your help anymore," Melissa said coldly. "You can go back to your valley where you belong."

Without a word I turned and cut across the slope down toward the valley, and heard her laugh. Seething, I stopped behind a tree and waited a while; then I continued on toward the Shankses', and circled around so that I came on it from the north, moving from tree to tree with great caution. From the notch of a split pine I could see their weird house perfectly. Addison was by the door, in earnest conference with Melissa. She pointed south to the valley, laughing, and Add nodded. He had on his long, greasy brown coat (a good match for his hair), and when he was done questioning Melissa, he opened the door and sent her inside with a slap on the butt. Then he was off into the woods, passing just a few trees from me as he headed north. I waited, and then followed him. There was a bit of a trail through the trees—made by Add himself, no doubt, in his many trips north—and I hustled along it tippytoe, watching for twigs on the ground, and Addison ahead. When I saw him again I dodged out of the trail and hid behind a spruce, breathing hard. I stuck my head around the tree and saw that he was still walking away from me; hopping around the trunk I highstepped through the trees, landing on the balls of my feet, on dirt or pine needles, and twisting my legs like I was dancing to avoid twigs or leaves that might snap under me. At the end of each crazy run I fetched up against a tree, and glanced around it to relocate Add. So far, so good; he didn't seem to have the slightest notion he was being followed. Time after time I checked to make sure his back was to me, and waited until he was obscured by the trees in between us, so I couldn't be sure which direction he was going in; then I leaped from cover and darted in whatever zigzag through the woods I thought would be the quietest. After several more batlike runs, I began to enjoy it. It wasn't that I was just losing my fear, either—I was positively enjoying it. After all the shit that Add and Melissa had pulled on me, it was a real pleasure to be tricking him—to be better at his business than he was.

There was pleasure in flitting through the woods like that, as well. It was like trailing an animal, only now it was possible in a way that chasing an animal wouldn't have been. Any animal in its senses would have been aware of me in an instant, and I never would have seen it again, nor known where it had gone to. A human, however, was very trackable. I could even choose which side of him I planned to come up on, and then cross over and trail him from the other side. Like it was a kind of hide and seek. Only now it was a game with some real stakes.

About halfway across San Mateo Valley I realized I was going to have a problem following him across the San Mateo River. The freeway was the only bridge, and it was as exposed as any bridge could be. I reckoned I would have to wait a long time after Add crossed it, and then hurry over, get back in the trees, and hope I could hustle ahead and relocate him.

I was still figuring all of this out when Add reached the bank of the San Mateo, considerably downriver from the freeway. I ducked behind yet another tree, a eucalyptus that was a bit too narrow for my purposes, and wondered what he was up to. He started looking all around, including back in my direction, and I crouched down and kept my head behind the trunk, so that I couldn't see him anymore. The scruffy bark of the eucalyptus oozed gum; breathing hard, I stared at it, afraid to poke my head out again. Had he heard me? At the thought my pulse went woodpecker, and suddenly trailing a man didn't seem pure fun after all. I lay flat, careful not to make a sound in all the eucalyptus crap behind me, and, holding my breath, I slowly stuck one eye's worth of face around the trunk.

No Add. I stuck both eyes around and still didn't see him. I scrambled to my feet again, and then I heard the sound of a motor, out on the river. Add came into sight again, still on the bank, looking seaward, waving a hand. I stayed put. Add never looked around again, and soon I caught sight, between the trees, of a little boat with three men in it. There weren't any oars; there was a motor, mounted on the aft. The man in the middle was Japanese. The one in the bow stood as they approached the bank, and he leaped to shore and helped Add secure the boat with a line around a tree.

While the other men clambered out of the boat, I crawled catlike from tree to tree, and finally slithered over a thick mat of eucalyptus leaves and pine needles, to a thick torrey pine only three or four trees from them. Under its low branches, and behind its trunk, I was sure they'd never see me.

The Japanese man—who looked somewhat like my captain, but was shorter—reached back into the boat and pulled out a white cloth bag, tied at the top. He handed it to Add. They asked Add some questions, and Add answered them. I could hear their voices, especially the Japanese man's—but I couldn't make out what they were saying. I drew in breath between my teeth, and cursed horribly in my mind. I really was very close to them—I couldn't risk going any closer, and that was that. But except for an occasional word they said, like "how" or "you," I could only get the tone of their voices. I was as close to them as I had been to Steve and Kathryn, when I overheard that conversation— but here the speakers were on a riverbank, and though the river didn't seem very noisy, it was just noisy enough. You can't eavesdrop on a riverbank, I was learning; and so all my chasing and stalking was going to go to waste. Here was Add talking with a Japanese, probably discussing exactly the stuff I wanted to know; and here was I, just where I wanted to be, no more than four boat lengths away. And it wasn't going to do me a bit of good.

Occasionally one of the two scavengers (scavengers I assumed they were, though they dressed like country folk) would laugh and kid Addison in a louder voice, so that I heard whole sentences. "Easy to fool fools," one of them said. Add laughed at that. "This'll all come back to us in a month or two," the other said, pointing at Add's bag. "Back to our whores, anyway!" the first one crowed. The Japanese man watched each of them in turn as they spoke, and never smiled at their jests. He asked a few more questions of Add, and Add answered them or so I assumed; with his back to me I could hardly hear Add at all.

And then, right before my eyes, the three men got back in the boat. Add untied the line and threw it to them, pushed off, and watched as they drifted downstream. They were out of my sight immediately, but I heard the motor start again. And that was it. I hadn't learned a thing I didn't know before.

Add watched them for only a moment or two, and then hiked right past me. I lay without moving for a bit, got up and headed after him. I actually pounded some of the trees I passed with my clenched fist. And Add was nowhere to be seen. I slowed down, so angry and frustrated that I didn't know if I wanted to hunt him down. What was the point? But the alternative—hiking back to Onofre alone—was somehow even worse. I started ranging forward in big diagonals, dancing between the trees again in my silent run.

I never even saw him until he had slammed into me with his shoulder and knocked me to the ground. He pulled a knife from his belt and came after me, nearly falling on me. I rolled and kicked the forearm above the knife, twisted and kicked his knee, scrambled to my feet, dodged and struck my clasped hands into his neck, as fast as I could move. He crashed into a tree, lay stunned against it; I quick snatched the bag from his left hand, leaping back to avoid a swing of the knife. I held the heavy little bag up like a club and retreated rapidly.

"Stay right there or I'll run and you'll never see this bag again," I rattled off. Thinking just ahead of my words, I said "I'm faster than you, and you won't catch me. Nobody catches me in the woods." And I laughed triumphantly at the look on his face, because it was true and he knew it. Nobody's quicker than I am, and beating Add and his knife around in the trees, faster than I could think, faster than I could plan my moves, made me *feel* it. Add knew it too. Finally, finally, I had Addison Shanks where I wanted him.

With his free hand he rubbed his neck, glaring at me with the same hateful expression I had seen in the eyes of that snared weasel. "What do you want?" he said.

"I don't want much. I don't want this here bag, though it feels like quite a bit of silver, and maybe stuff more important than that, eh?" I might not have guessed the contents right, but one thing was sure—he wanted the bag. He looked at it, shifted forward, and I took three steps back and to the right, along an opening in the trees. "I reckon Tom and John and Rafael and the others would be mighty interested to see this bag, and hear what I have to tell about it."

"What do you want?" he grated.

I stared back into his hating gaze. "I don't like how you've been using me," I said. The knife in his hand jerked, and I thought, don't tell him how much you know. "I want to see one of those Japanese landings in Orange County. I know they're doing it, and I know that you're in on them. I want to know when and where the next one lands."

He looked puzzled, and let the knife drop a hand's breadth. Then he grinned, his eyes still hating me, and I flinched. "You're with the other kids, aren't you. Young Nicolin and Mendez and the rest."

"Just me."

"Been spying on me, have you? And John Nicolin doesn't know about it, I bet. No."

I raised the bag. "Tell me when and where, Add, or I'm back to the valley with this, and you'll never be able to set foot there again."

"The hell I won't."

"Want to try it?"

A snarl curled his lips. I stood my ground. I watched him think it over. Then he grinned again, in a way I didn't understand. At the time I thought he was like that weasel, giving one last fierce grin of rage as it was killed.

"They're landing at Dana Point, this Friday night. Midnight."

I threw the bag at him and ran.

At first I ran like a hunted deer, leaping big falls of wood and crashing through smaller ones in my new luxury of sound, scared that I might have thrown Add a gun, or that he would turn out to be a knife thrower, and put that thick blade in my back. But after crossing most of San Mateo Valley I knew I was safe, and I ran for joy. Triumphantly I danced between trees, leaped over bushes where I could have run around them. I ran to the freeway, and sprinted down it at full speed. I don't think I've ever run faster in my life, or enjoyed it more. "Friday night!" I crowed at the sky, and flew down that road like a car, the knot in my stomach gone at last.

... 18

But the knot didn't stay away for long. I ran into the valley straight to the Nico- lins', only to be told by Mrs. N. that Steve was out somewhere with Kathryn. I thanked her and left, uneasy already. Were they arguing again? Making up? Was Kathryn talking him out of all this? I checked a few of our regular hang- outs, none too anxious to find Kathryn, but compelled by a desire to see Steve immediately. No sign of them anywhere. No way of guessing where they were or what they were doing. Climbing back down Swing Canyon I realized I didn't understand the two of them anymore, if I ever had. Where do you go after a fight like the one I had overheard? The private lives of couples—there's few things more private than that. Nobody but the two know what's going on be- tween them, even if they talk about it with others. And if they don't then it's a complete mystery, hidden from the world.

So that was Wednesday evening. I went back to the Nicolins' twice that night, but no one showed up. And the longer I waited to tell Steve, the more uneasy I got about it. What would Kathryn say when she learned my part in this? She would think I had lied to her, betrayed her trust. On the other hand, if I didn't tell Steve about the landing, and let it pass—and if he ever found out what I had done—well, that didn't bear thinking about. I'd lose my best friend at that very moment.

After my second visit to the Nicolins' I went home and went to bed. It had been such a day I thought I would have trouble falling asleep, but after a few minutes I was out. A couple of hours later I woke up, though, and for the rest of the night I tossed and turned, listened to the wind, considered what I should do.

Just after dawn I woke with the knot in my stomach, and trying to get back to sleep only made it worse. I faintly remembered a dream that was so awful I made no attempt to recall it more clearly—something about being chased—but a few moments later I wasn't even sure of that. Stepping outside for my morn- ing pee I discovered a Santa Ana wind—the desert wind that pours over the hills and pushes all the clouds out to sea. Santa Anas strike three or four times a year, and change our weather completely. This one was picking up even as I watched, twisting the trees all backward to their natural onshore bent. Soon pine branches would be snapping off and gliding seaward.

The empty water bucket gave me a shock when I picked it up. Static electricity, Tom called it, but try as he would he couldn't make me understand it. Something about millions of tiny fires rushing around, and all the wires strung between towers like the Shankses' place had carried this electricity around, and it had powered all the automatic machines of the old time. All that power from little snaps like the one I had felt.

Walking to the river everything was packed with color, as if static electricity might be something that made things brighter. The hair on my arms stood away from my skin, and I could feel the roots in my scalp as the wind pulled my hair this way and that. Static electricity—maybe it gathered over the stomach. At the river I stepped in to my knees, ducked my head under, sloshed water down my throat and back up, hoping the electricity might catch to the water and leave with it. It didn't work.

Wide awake now. Cat's paws fanned across the river's surface, one after another, helping it down to sea. Already the air was warm and dry; it felt like it would be burning soon. The sky was a bright pale blue. I drank half a bucket of water, threw rocks at a fallen tree stuck against the other bank. What to do? Gulls wheeled and flapped overhead, complaining at how hard they had to work in this backward wind. I walked home and ate a loaf of bread with Pa.

"What you doing today?" he asked.

"Checking snares. That's what old Mendez told me, anyway."

"That should make a good break from the fishing."

"Yeah."

Pa looked at me and wrinkled his nose. "You sure aren't talking much these days."

I nodded, too distracted to pay much attention to him.

"You don't want to get so's people can't talk to you," he went on.

"I'm not. I'd better be off, though."

I went to the river again, thinking to get up to the snares eventually. Sat down on one of the tiny bluffs that overhang the bank. Downriver the women appeared one by one, the Mariani clan and the rest of them, out while the Santa Ana was blowing to bathe and wash clothes and sheets and blankets and towels and anything else they could haul to the water. The air was a bit hotter every minute. The women got out the soap and stripped down, moved into the shallows at the bend with washboards and baskets of clothes and linens, and went to work, chattering and laughing, diving out into the mainstream to paddle around a bit and get the soap off them. The morning sun gleamed on their wet bodies and slicked-down hair, and I could have stayed longer to watch them, such sleek white creatures they were; like a pod of dolphins, tits swinging together as clothes were scrubbed over washboards, mouths open to laugh and grin at the sky. But they had seen me sitting upriver, and pretty soon if I stayed they would be throwing rocks, and lifting their legs to embarrass me, and calling out jokes. And besides I had other things on my mind anyway, so with a last glance I turned and walked upriver, forgot about the women, and began to worry again.

I could not tell him. I could say, Steve, I didn't find anything out and I don't know how I could, and left it at that. And Friday night would come and go and they would never know the difference. And everything would go on as before. Walking the river path this occurred to me, and as I hiked from snare to snare I considered it. In some ways it appealed to me.

But I remembered my fight with Add; how I'd knocked him against a tree when he held the knife and I didn't. And after clearing a rabbit out of a snare and resetting it, I remembered my escape from the Japanese, my swim to shore, my struggle up that ravine. It seemed like a great adventure to me now. I remembered climbing up the side of the Shankses' house to hear the conversation with the scavengers, and my silent bat-runs after Addison through the woods. I had enjoyed that more than anything that had ever happened in Onofre. I'd never felt such power. It seemed to me more than ever that these things were not just happening to me, but that I was *doing* them, that I was choosing to do certain things and then I was going out and doing them. And now I had the chance to do something better than anything so far, to fight for my lost country. This land I walked over was ours, it was all we had. They had to stay off it or suffer for it. We weren't a freak show, a bigger version of those little ones that visited the swap meets sometimes, exhibiting pathetic cripples, both animal and human. We were a country, a living country, living communities on living land, and they had to leave us alone.

So when I returned to the valley through the neck, I dropped off three rabbits and continued downriver to the Nicolins'. Steve was out front, shouting furiously at his mother in the doorway. Something about John again, I gathered, something he had said or done to enrage Steve. I winced and waited until he was done shouting. As he stalked toward the cliffs I approached him.

"What's up?" he said as he saw me.

"I know the date!" I cried. His face lit up. I told him all about it. When I was done I felt a certain chill, and I thought, well, you told him. I had never really decided to; the act itself was the decision.

"That's great," he kept saying, "that's great. Now we've got them! Why didn't you tell me?"

"I just did," I said, annoyed. "I just found out yesterday."

He slapped me on the back. "Let's go tell the San Diegans. We don't have much time—a day, whoo! They might need to get more men from south or something."

But now that I had told him, I was more uncertain than before that it was the right thing to do. I shrugged and said, "You go on down and tell them, and I'll tell Gabby and Del and Mando if I see them."

"Well"—he cocked his head at me curiously—"sure. If that's what you want."

"I've done my share," I said defensively. "We shouldn't both go down there; it might draw attention to us."

"I guess you're right."

"Come by tonight and tell me what they said."

"I will."

When he came by that night the wind was blowing harder than ever. The big eucalyptus's branches creaked against each other, and its leaves clicked down on us. The pines hummed their deepest chord.

"Guess who was at their camp?" Steve demanded, all charged up and even bouncing on his feet. "Guess!"

"I don't know. Lee?"

"No, the Mayor!"

"Is that right? What's he doing up here?"

"He's here to fight the Japs, of course. He was really happy when I told him we could lead them to a landing. He shook my hand and we drank some whiskey and everything."

"I bet. Did you tell him where it was?"

"Course not! Do you take me for a fool? I said we weren't getting the final word till tomorrow, and that we'd tell them when we were up there ourselves with them. That way they'll have to take us, see? In fact—I told them that only you know where they're landing, and that you wouldn't tell anyone."

"Oh, fine. Why would I do that?"

"Because you're a suspicious kind of guy, naturally, and you don't want the Japanese to find out somehow that we know. That's what I told them."

That suggested something to me that I hadn't thought of before, believe it or not: the Japanese could find out we knew from Add. The landing might not take place after all. Another possibility occurred to me: Add could have lied to me about the date. But I didn't say anything about that. I didn't want to bring up any problems. All I said was, "They must think we're crazy."

"Not at all, why should they? The Mayor was real pleased with us."

"I bet he was. How many men were with him?"

"Fifteen, maybe twenty."

"Was Jennings one of them?"

"Sure. Listen, did you tell Del and Gabby and Mando?"

"What about Lee? Was Lee with them?"

"I didn't see him. What about our gang?"

I was worried about Lee. I didn't understand or like the way he had disappeared from the group. "I told Gabby and Del," I said after a while. "Del's going over to Talega Canyon with his pa Friday, so he can't come."

"And Gabby?"

"He's coming."

"Good. Henry, this is it! We're part of the resistance!"

The hot push of the Santa Ana burned in my nose, and I felt the static electricity all through me. "True," I said.

Steve stared at me through the darkness. "You aren't scared, are you?"

"No! I am a bit tired, I think. I'd better get some sleep."

"Good idea. You're going to need it tomorrow." With a slap to the arm he was off into the trees. I went back inside, where Pa was sewing.

I didn't get much sleep that night. And the next day was the longest one I could remember. The Santa Ana blew strong all day; the land was drying out and heating up, and it got so hot that just to move was enough to break a sweat. I checked snares in the back country all day—not an animal in any of them. After I forced down the usual fish and bread I got so fidgety that I just had to do something. I said to Pa, "I'm going up to see the old man, and then we're going to work on the treehouse, so I'll be home late."

"Okay."

Outside it was twilight. The river was a silver sheen lighter than the trees on the other bank. I crossed the bridge and went up to the Costas'. From their vantage I could see the whole valley forest bouncing in the gloom.

Mando met me outside the door. "Gabby told me about it and I'm going, you hear?"

"Sure," I said.

"If you try to go without me, I'll tell everyone about it."

"Whoah, now. No need for threats, Armando, you're going with us."

"Oh." He looked down. "I didn't know. I wasn't sure."

"Why?"

"I thought Steve might not want me to go."

"Well, why don't you go down and talk to him. I bet he's still at his house."

"I don't know if I should. Pa's asleep, and I'm supposed to keep an eye on Tom."

"I'll do that, that's what I came here for. You go tell Steve you're coming. Tell him I'll be up here till we leave."

"Okay." Off he went, running down the path.

"Don't threaten him!" I shouted at his back, but the wind tore my words off toward Catalina, and he didn't hear me. I went inside. The Santa Ana was catching around the sides of the house, whistling in all the oil drums, so that the house said *Whoooo, whoooo, whooooo.* I looked in the hospital, where a lamp burned. Tom was flat on his back, head propped up on a pillow. He opened his eyes and looked at me.

"Henry," he said. "Good."

It was stuffy in the room; Doc's sun heating worked too well during these hot days, and if the vents were opened the wind would have torn through and made a shambles. I sat in the bedside chair.

Tom's beard and hair were tangled together, and all the gray and white curls looked waxy. They framed his face. I stared at that face like I'd never seen it before. Time puts so many marks on a face: wrinkles, blotches, sags and folds; the bend in his nose, the scar breaking up one eyebrow, the caved-in cheek where those teeth were missing. . . . He looked old and sick, and I thought, He's going to die. Maybe I was really looking at him for once. We assume that we know what our familiars look like, so that when we see them we're not really looking, just glancing and remembering. Now I was looking. Old man. He pushed up onto his elbows. "Put the pillow so I can sit up." His voice was only half as loud as usual. I moved the pillow and he pulled himself back to it. When we were done he was sitting upright, his back against the pillow, his head against the concave end of an oil drum. He pulled his shirt around so it was straight on his chest.

The one lamp that was lit flickered as a draft plunged down one of the partially opened roof vents. The yellow glow that filled the room dimmed. I stood and leaned over to give the flame a little more wick. The wind bent at an especially noisy angle around the corner of the house.

"Santa Ana, eh?" Tom said.

"Yeah. A strong one, too. And hot."

"I noticed."

"I bet. This place is like an oven. I'm sure glad I don't live in the desert if it's like this all the time."

"Used to be. But the wind isn't hot because of the desert. It gets compressed coming over the mountains, and that heats it up. Compression heats things."

"Ah." I started to describe the effect of the Santa Ana on the trees, that were so used to the onshore wind; but he knew about Santa Anas. I fell silent. We sat there a while. There was no rush to fill silences between us. All the hours we'd spent sitting together, talking or not talking, it didn't matter. Thinking about all those hours made me sad. I thought, You can't die yet, I'm not done learning from you. Who's gonna tell me what to read?

This time Tom made an effort to rouse things. "Have you gotten started on filling that book I gave you?"

"Oh, Tom, I don't know how to do such a thing. I haven't even opened it."

"I was serious about that," he said, giving me the eye. Even in that wasted visage the eye had its old severity.

"I know you were. But what am I going to write? I don't even know how to spell."

"Spelling," he said scornfully. "Spelling doesn't matter. The six signatures of Shakespeare we have are spelled four different ways. You remember that when you worry about spelling. And grammar doesn't matter either. You just write it down like you would talk it. Understand?"

"But Tom—"

"Don't but me, boy. I didn't spend all that time teaching you to read and write for nothing."

"I know. But I don't have any stories to write, Tom. You're the one with the stories. Like that one when you met yourself, remember?"

He looked confused.

"The one where you picked yourself up hitchhiking," I prompted him.

"Oh yeah," he said slowly, looking off through the wall.

"Did that really happen to you, Tom?"

The wind. Only his eyes moved, sliding over to look at me. "Yes."

Again the wind, whistling its amazement, *whooooooo!* Tom was quiet for a long time; he started and blinked and I realized he had lost track of what we were saying.

"That was an awful long time ago for you to remember it all so clearly," I said. "What you said and all. There's no way I could do that. I can't even re-member what I said last week. That's another reason I couldn't write that book."

"You write it," he commanded me. "Everything comes back when you write it down. Press the memory."

He fell silent, and we listened to the wind's howls. A branch thumped the wall. He clutched at the sheet covering his legs, clutched and twisted it. It had a frayed edge.

"You hurting?" I asked.

"No." Still he kneaded it, and looked at the wall across from me. He sighed a few times. "You think I'm pretty old, don't you boy." His voice was weak.

I stared at him. "You are pretty old."

"Yes. Lived a full life in the old time, was forty-five on the day—that makes me a hundred and eight years old now, is that right?"

"Sure, that's right. You know it best."

"And I look that old too, God knows." He took a deep breath, held it, let it go. I noticed that he hadn't coughed since I had arrived, and thought that the dry wind might be a help to him. I was about to remark on that when he said, "But what if I wasn't?"

"What?"

"What if I wasn't that old?"

"I don't understand."

He sighed, shifted around under the sheet. Closed his eyes for a time, so that I thought he might have fallen asleep. Opened them again.

"What I mean is . . . is that I've been stretching my age a bit."

"But—how can that be?"

He shifted his gaze and stared at me, his brown eyes shiny and pleading. "I was eighteen when the bombs went off, Henry. I tell you true for the very first time. Got to while I have the chance. I was going to go to that ruined school on the cliffs that we saw down south. I went for a trip in the Sierra the summer before and that's when it happened. When I was eighteen. So now I'm . . . now I'm . . ." He blinked several times in succession, shook his head.

"Eighty-one," I said.

"Eighty-one," he repeated dreamily. "Old enough, and that's the truth! But I only grew up in the old time. None of that other stuff. I wanted to tell you that before I go."

I stared at him, got up and walked around the room, and ended up at the foot of the bed where I stared at him some more. I couldn't seem to get him in focus. He stopped meeting my eye and looked uncomfortably at his mottled hands.

"I just thought you should know what I've been doing," he said apologetically.

"Which is what?" I asked.

"You don't know? No. Well . . . having someone around who lived in the old time, who knew it well—it's important."

"But if you weren't really there!"

"Make it up. Oh, I was there. I lived in the old time. Not for long, and without understanding it at the time, but I was there. I've not been lying outright. Just stretching."

"But why?" I cried.

For the longest time he was silent, and the wind howled my distress for me.

"I don't know how to put it," he said wearily. "To hold on to our past? To keep our spirits up? Like that book does. Can't be sure if he did it or not. Could be a Glen Baum did go around the world. Could be Wentworth wrote it right there in his workshop. Doesn't matter—it's happened now because of the book. An American around the world. We needed it even if it was a lie, understand?"

I shook my head, unable to speak. He sighed, looked away, bonged his head lightly on the oil drum. A million thoughts jammed in my mind, and yet I said something I hadn't thought. "So you didn't meet your double after all."

"No. Made it up. Made a lot of things up."

"But why, Tom? *Why?*" I started walking around the room again so he wouldn't see me cry.

He didn't answer me. I thought of all the times that Steve had called him a liar, and how often I had defended him. Ever since he had shown us the picture of the Earth taken from the moon, I had believed all his stories. I had decided he was telling the truth.

In a voice I could barely make out he said, "Sit down, boy. Sit down here." I sat in my chair. "Now listen. I came down and saw it, see? I was in the mountains, like I said. That part of the story was true. All the lies were true. In the mountains on a hike to myself. I didn't even know the bombs went off, can you believe it?" He shook his head like he couldn't believe it yet. Suddenly I realized he was telling me what he had never told anyone. "It was a fine day, I hiked over Pinchot Pass, but that night smoke blotted the stars. I didn't know but I knew. And I came down and saw it. Every person in Owens Valley was crazy, and the first one I met told me why, and that moment—oh Hank, thank God you won't ever have to live that moment. I went crazy like the rest of them. I was just older than you and all of them were dead, everyone I knew. I was mad with grief and my heart broke and it never did get mended. Hearts don't mend."

He swallowed hard. "Now I see why I don't talk about it." He bonged the oil drum with his head. In a fierce whisper he said, "But I got to, I got to, I got to," banging his head lightly, bong, bong, bong.

"Stop it, Tom." I put my hand behind his head. His hair was damp. "You don't have to."

"Got to," he whispered. I leaned forward to hear him. "At first I didn't believe it. But the Greyhound wasn't running and I knew. It took me a work of walking and hitching rides with madmen to get home, but when I came down Five it was still burning, the whole city. I knew it was true then and I was afraid of the radiation so I didn't go on to see my home. Up into the mountains looting and scavenging for food. How long I don't know, lost my mind and only really remember flashes. Killing. I came to in a cabin in the mountains and knew I would have to see it to believe they were all dead. My family. I didn't care about the radiation anymore, don't think I even remembered it. So I went back to Orange County, and there, oh!" he exclaimed; his hand was clutching at the sheet over and over. I held it. It was feverish.

"I can't tell that," he whispered. "It was evil. I ran and came here. Empty hills. I was sure the whole world was destroyed, world of insects and people dying on the beaches. When I hoped, I thought it might be just us and Russia, Europe and China. That the other countries would get help to us eventually." He squeezed my hand hard. "But no one knew. No one knew anything but what they could see. I saw empty hills. That was all I knew. Marines had kept them clear. I saw I could live in these hills without going mad, if I could avoid getting

killed by someone or starving. It could be done. See up to that point I didn't
know if it could be done. But here was the valley and I knew it could be done.
And I never set foot in Orange County again."

I squeezed his hand. I knew he had been up there since.

As if to contradict me he said, "Never, not to this day." He tugged my hand
and whispered rapidly, "It's evil, evil. You've seen them at the swap meets, scavengers, there's something wrong with them, something burst inside—there's
something wrong in their eyes, you can see it's driven them crazy to live up
there. And no surprise. You got to stay out of that place, Henry. I know you've
been up there at night. But listen to me, now, don't go up there, it's bad, *bad*."
He was leaning off the pillow toward me, both hands on my side of the bed
to prop himself up, his face intense and sweaty. "Promise me you won't go up
there, boy."

"Ah Tom—"

"You can't go up there," he said desperately. "Tell me you won't."

"Tom, I mean sometime I'm gonna have to—"

"No! What for? You get what you need from scavengers, that's what they're
for, please, Henry, promise me. There's evil up there so bad it can't be spoken of,
please, I'm asking you not to go up there—"

"All right!" I said. "I won't go up there. I promise." I had to say it to calm
him down. But the knot tightened across my stomach until I had to hold my left
arm over my ribs, and I knew I had done wrong. Again.

He collapsed back against the pillow, *bong*. "Good. Save you from that. But
not me."

I felt so awful I tried to change the subject. "But I guess it didn't harm you,
not in the long run. I mean here you are."

"Neutron bombs. Short term radiation. So I guess. I don't know. Something
like that. The earth will revenge us, but that's no solace. Their suffering won't
pay ours, nothing will ever, we were murdered." He squeezed my hand so hard
my knuckles hurt. He sucked in air. "The ones left were so hungry, we fought
and finished the murder off for them, that was the worst of it. So crazy. In the
year after more people died than had been killed by the bombs, and more and
more till it looked like every last one of us would die. Stupid Americans. So
far from the earth that we couldn't figure out how to live off it. Or those who
could were swamped by those who couldn't. Until there were so few left there
was no need to fight anymore, no one to fight. I saw Death walk down the road.
I waved to him and walked on by. Then out of the sky the storms. There was a
winter that lasted ten years, good limerick. But the suffering was too much. I
live to show what a person can bear and die not, good poem, remember it? Did
I give you that one? It got so when you saw a face that wasn't insane you wanted
to hug them right then and there. So when we settled here . . . it was a start.

Weren't more than a dozen of us. Every day a struggle. Food, we're slaves to it, boy. Grew up and didn't learn a thing about it. In that America was evil. The world was starving and we ate like pigs, people died of hunger and we ate their dead bodies and licked our chops. It's true what I say to Doc and George, we were a monster and we were eating up the world and they had reasons to do it to us, but still we didn't deserve it. We were a good country."

"Please, Tom. You're going to hurt yourself going on like this." He was sweating and I was scared. But he took a few deep breaths and went on, squeezing my hand and ordering me with his eyes to let him talk, to let him speak at last.

"We were free then. Not really, but it was the best we could do. We were trying. Nobody else did it better. It was the best country in history," he said grimly, like he had to convince me or die. "That's not saying much, but still, with all the flaws and stupidities, we were still the focus of the world, and they killed us for it. Killed the best country ever, it was suicide. Genocide, the murder of a whole people. That had happened before, we did it ourselves to the Indians. Maybe that's why it happened to us. I keep coming on reasons but they're not enough. We were wrong in a million ways, but we didn't deserve it."

"Calm down, Tom, please calm down."

"They'll suffer for it," he whispered. "Tornadoes, yes, and earthquakes and floods and fires, and murder. See I went back. I had to see. And it was all smoking and blasted flat. Home. And just a few blocks away it still stood, blasted flat all around it but not it, ground zero is a still spot. It really was the magic kingdom when I was a child." Now his whispering got so rapid and desperate I could barely hear him, and what he said made no sense, and I held his forearm with both hands as he went on. "Main Street was all full of trash, dead people here and there, ruins, the smell of death. Around the corner the steamboat used to come, one time when I was a little boy my folks took me and as the steamboat rounded the corner we could hear that horn cutting across the water like Gabriel's last call and the whole crowd knew it was him in an instant, Satchmo it was, Henry, Satchmo playing louder than the steamboat whistle, but now the lake was chock with corpses. I went to talk with Abraham Lincoln, looked in his sad eyes and told him they killed his country like they killed him but he knew already. Till every lash is paid with the sword. He called it all right. Went through the castle to the giant teacups, big blowsy woman and two men, laughing drunk trying to get the teacups to spin, she let a big green bottle go smash and in that instant I knew it was all true, and the man, he took his knife, *ohhhh—*"

"Please, Tom."

"But I survived! Ran from evil I don't know where, came to in the valley. I learned what I had to. Didn't learn a damned thing before. Schoolbook rubbish. I was lucky to live, he fell in the torrent and maybe I could have. Or the time they took her, but no Troy for us. Tiger justice, we're Greek now boy, it's as hard for us as it was for them, Death sitting there all the time, every day, skull in the sun, no wonder the tragedies, we were one of their plays, they killed us for pride, blasted us to desolation struggling in the dirt. Oh Henry, can you see why I did it, why I lied to you, it was to tell you. To make us Greek ghosts, pure and simple, so we can say we're still people, Henry, *Henry*—"

"Yes, Tom. Tom! Calm down, please." I was holding him by the shoulders, leaning over him. Twisting he started to speak again and I put my hand over his mouth, clamped it there. He struggled to breathe and I let my hand off him. "You're wearing yourself out," I told him. The lamp sputtered. Our shadows wavered against the black circles of the wall, the wind shrieked around the corner. "You're working yourself up too much. Listen to me now, lie down here. Please. Doc would be furious at us if he came in. You haven't got the strength for this."

"Do too," he whispered.

"Good, good. Simmer down some though, simmer down, simmer down."

He seemed to hear me, finally. He leaned back. I wiped the sweat from my forehead, and sat down again. I felt like I had been running for miles. "Jesus, Tom."

"Okay," he said. "I'll keep it down. But you got to know."

"I know you survived. Now we're past that, and that's all I need to know. I don't want to know any more," I said, and I meant it.

He shook his head. "You got to." He relaxed back into the pillow. *Bong, bong, bong, bong, bong, bong.*

"Stop that, Tom."

He stopped. The wind picked up again, filling the silence. *Whoooo, whooooo.*

"I'll be quiet," he said, the strain gone from his voice. "Wouldn't want Doc mad at me."

"No you wouldn't," I said. I was still scared; my heart still pumped hard. "Besides, you've got to save what energy you've got."

He shook his head. "I'm tired." The wind howled like it wanted to pick us up and knock us down. The old man eyed me. "You won't go up there, will you? You promised."

"Ah, Tom," I said. "Some time I may have to, you know that."

He slumped down onto the pillow, stared at the ceiling.

After a time he spoke, very calmly. "When you learn things so important you want to teach them, it always seems possible. Everything seems so clear. The images are there, even sometimes the words. But it doesn't work. You can't teach what the world has taught you. All the tricks of rhetoric, the force of personality—none of it's enough. Nothing works. So I've failed. It can't be done. What I ended up teaching you was exactly backward to what I was trying, I guess. But there's no help for it. I was trying to do the impossible, and so I got . . . confused."

He slid down the pillow until he was flat on his back. It looked like he would fall asleep right then, for his eyes were closed and he was breathing deep, in the way of an exhausted man. Then one brown eye opened and stared at me. "You'll be taught by something strong as this wind, boy. It will pick you up and throw you down."

part four

...ORANGE COUNTY

...19

Outside it was dark, and the wind howled. I stood at the log bench in the garden and felt the wind tear at me. To the west the ridge cut the last blue before night's black. It all looked different, as if I had walked out of the drum house into another time. I tried to collect myself.

"Ready?" Steve said sharply, and I jumped. He and Mando and Gabby were behind me. Impossible in the wind to hear anybody come up on you.

"Very funny," I said.

"Let's go."

Mando said, "I have to make sure Pa's awake to look after Tom."

"Tom's up," I said. "He can call your pa if he wants him. If you wake him up, what will you tell him you're going to do?"

In the dark Mando's blurred, uneasy face.

"Let's go," Steve insisted. "If you want to come along, that is."

Without a word Mando took off down the trail, back into the valley. We followed him. In the woods the wind became no more than a gust here and there. Trees creaked, moaned, hummed. Over Basilone we hiked, steering clear of the Shankses' house. Through overgrown foundations to the freeway, where we picked up the pace. Quickly enough we were in San Mateo Valley, and past the spot where I had confronted Add. Steve stopped, and we waited for him to decide what to do.

He said, "We're supposed to meet them where the freeway crosses the river."

"We'd best keep going, then," Gabby said. "It's ahead a bit."

"I know, but . . . seems to me we shouldn't walk right down there. That doesn't seem like the right way to do it."

"Let's get down there," I put in. "They might be waiting, and we've got a long way to go."

"Okay. . . ."

We walked close together so we could hear each other in the wind. A ball of tumbleweed bounced across the freeway and Mando shied. Steve and Gabby laughed. Mando pressed on ahead. We followed him to the San Mateo River. Nobody was there.

"They'll see us and let us know where they are," I guessed. "They need us, and they know we'll be on the freeway. They can hide."

"That's true," said Steve. "Maybe we should cross—"

A bright light flashed on us from below the freeway's shoulder, and a voice from the trees said "Don't move!"

We squinted into the glare. It reminded me of the Japanese surprising us in the fog at sea, and my heart hammered like it wanted to bound off by itself.

"It's us!" Steve called. Gabby snickered. "From Onofre."

The light went out, leaving me blind. Under the sound of the wind, some rustling.

"Good." A shape loomed on the sea side of the freeway. "Get on down here."

We felt our way down the slope, bumping together in a clump. There were a lot of men around us. When we got to the bottom of the slope we stood in bushes that came to our waists. A dozen or more men surrounded us. One of them bent over and opened the shade on a gas lantern. Standing in one dim beam in front of the lantern was Timothy Danforth, Mayor of San Diego. His trousers were muddy.

"Four of you, are there?" he said in his loud bray. His voice brought back every detail of my night at his house on the freeway island, and it was Nicolin who answered, "Yes, sir."

More men joined us, dark shapes coming up from the river. "That's all of you?" the Mayor said.

"Yes, sir," Steve said.

"That's all right. Jennings, get these men guns."

One of the men, looking like Jennings now that he had been named, crouched over a large canvas bag on the ground.

"Is Lee here?" I asked.

"Lee doesn't like this sort of thing," Danforth said. "He's no good at it, either. Why do you want to know?"

"He's someone I know."

"You know me, right? And Jennings here?"

"Sure. I was just wondering, that's all."

Jennings gave a pistol to each of us. Mine was big, and heavy. I crouched and looked at it in the lantern's light, holding it in both hands. Black metal business end, black plastic handle. It was the first time I had held a gun outside a swap meet. Jennings handed me a leather pouch filled with bullets, and kneeled beside me. "Here's the safety catch; you have to push it to here before it will shoot. Here's how you reload." He spun the cylinder to show me where the bullets fit in. The others were getting instructions around me. I straightened and blinked to help my night sight return, hefting the pistol in my hand. "You got a pocket it'll fit in?"

"I don't think so."

"All right, men!" If it weren't for the wind, the Mayor's voice would be heard all the way back in Onofre, it seemed. He limped over to me, and I had to look up at him. His hair danced over his shadowed face. "Tell us where they're landing, and we'll be off."

Steve said, "We can't tell you till we're up there."

"None of that!" said the Mayor. Steve looked at me. The Mayor went on: "We've got to know how far away they're landing, so we can decide whether or not to take the boats." So, I thought, they had boated up the coast to get past Onofre. "You men have got guns, and you're part of the raid. I understand your caution, but we're all on the same side here. I give you my word. So let's have it."

The circle of men stood around us silently.

"They're landing at Dana Point," I said.

There it was. If they wanted to leave us now, there was nothing we could do about it. We stood watching the Mayor. No one spoke, and I could feel Nicolin's accusing gaze, but I kept staring into the underlit face of the Mayor, who looked back at me without expression.

"Do you know what time they're landing?"

"Midnight, I heard."

"And who'd you hear from?"

"Scavengers who don't like the Japanese."

Another silence followed that. Danforth looked over at a man I recognized—Ben, his assistant.

"We'd better get going," Danforth said after this silent conference. "We'll go on foot."

Steve said, "It'll take a couple hours to walk to Dana Point."

Danforth nodded. "Is the freeway the best route?"

"Up to the middle of San Clemente it is. After that there's a coastal road that's faster, and less exposed to scavengers." Now that he was sure we were going, Steve's voice was filled with excitement.

"We don't have to worry about scavengers tonight," Danforth said. "They wouldn't attack a party this size."

We climbed back up the shoulder into the hot dry blast of the wind. Like me, Mando carried a gun in his hand; Steve and Gab had room in their coat pockets for theirs. When we were all on the freeway the San Diegans started north, and we followed. A few men disappeared ahead and behind us. They had all sorts of guns with them: rifles, pistols as long as my forearm, little fat guns on tripods.

Trees swayed on each side of the road, and branches tumbled through the air like injured night birds. The stars winked brightly in the cloudless black sky, and by their light I could see a fair amount: shapes in the forest, the whitish slash of the freeway stretching ahead through the trees, the occasional scout jogging back down the road to report to the Mayor. The four of us kept right behind Danforth, and listened silently as he discussed things and gave orders in a voice calculated to warn every scavenger in Orange County. Walking down the middle of the road, we topped the rise where brick walls tumbled into the freeway, climbed over them, and were in San Clemente.

"I expect the wind will slow them coming in," Danforth remarked to Ben, unaware of the boundary we had crossed, the boundary I had promised Tom I would never cross. "I wonder how much they had to pay those patrols to let them through. What do you think the going price is for a trip to the mainland, eh? Do you think they tell them it could cost their lives?"

Up and down over the hills. Trees bounded in place under the wind, and the wires still in the air swung like jumpropes. Eventually we came to the road Nicolin had mentioned, that led through San Clemente to Dana Point. Once off the freeway and down in the rubble-filled streets I was obsessed by thoughts of ambush. Branches flew overhead, planks slapped each other, tumbleweed ran at us or away, and every time I clicked over the safety of my pistol, ready to dive for cover and shoot. The Mayor highstepped over the junk in the middle of the street easy as you please. "That's our point man," he shouted to us, aiming with his pistol at a silhouette dodging through the street ahead. "There's tails a block behind us, too." He gave us the whole strategy of our positions in the street, which seemed like accidents of the moment. The men all had their rifles at the ready, and they were spread out well. "No wreckrats are going to give us trouble tonight, I don't believe." He kicked a brick in the road and stumbled. "*Damn* this road!" It was the third time he had nearly fallen. In all the rubbish it was necessary to watch every step, but he was above that sort of thing. "Doesn't the freeway go right to Dana Point?" he asked Steve. "The maps showed that it did."

"It turns inland about a mile from the harbor," Steve said, his voice raised to carry over the clatter the wind was making.

"That's good enough," Danforth declared. "I don't like the footing in this junk." He called to the forward scouts in a voice that made me wince. "Back to the freeway," he told them. "We need to hurry more than we need to hide." We turned up a street headed inland, and intersected the freeway. Once on the freeway again we marched at good speed north, all the way through San Clemente to the big marsh that separates San Clemente from Dana Point.

From the south side of the marsh we could see Dana Point clearly. It was a curve of bluffs, not tall like the cliffs down in San Diego, but tall for our part of the coast, and sticking out into the sea. Now it was a dark mass against the stars, not a light on it anywhere. Underneath the sheer part of the bluff was a marsh and strip of water bounded by a rock jetty. Once or twice when fishing to the north we had taken refuge behind the jetty in storms. The jetty was invisible from where we stood, but Steve described it in as much detail as he could.

"So they'll probably land there," the Mayor concluded.

"Yes sir."

"What about this marsh? It looks like a good-sized river. Is there a place where we can cross?"

"The beach road has held," Steve said. "It's a high bridge, so none of it's ever been washed out." He said this as proudly as if he were the bridge builder. "I've been across it."

"Excellent, excellent. Let's get over it, then."

The road leading from the freeway to the bridge was gone, however, and we were forced to descend a ravine, cross the creek at its bottom, and climb the other side. My pistol was getting to be quite an irritation in all this climbing, and I could see Mando felt the same. Danforth's exhortations kept us hurrying. Once on the beach road we hurried over it to the mouth of the estuary. As Steve had said, the bridge was still there. In a low voice Gabby asked me, "How does he know all this?" but all I could do was shrug and shake my head. Nicolin had made night treks on his own, I knew that—and now I knew that he had come all the way up here, on his own, and had never told me.

Out on the bridge we caught the full brunt of the wind for the first time since we had entered San Clemente. It peeled over the bridge with a force that made us stagger. The waves below burst off the bridge pilings and rebounded into the channel, to be carried out to sea slapping and hissing. Quickly we got over the bridge and under the bluffs of Dana Point, out of the wind's full power.

Tucked under the bluffs was the marshy flat that had once been the harbor. Only the channel directly behind the rock jetty was free of the sand and scrub that had drifted in and covered the rest of the little bay. We struggled through nettles and man-high brush to the beach facing the jetty, less than a stone's throw away from it. Swells broke on the line of rocks, giving it a white edging and making it visible in the starlight. Weak remnants of the swell washed up the pebbly beach. The jetty ended almost directly across from us; we stood at the entrance of what remained of the harbor.

"If they land here, they'll have to get through this marsh," Jennings said to the Mayor.

"You think they'll sail in there, then?" the Mayor said, pointing up the channel to where it ended against the curve of the bluff.

"Maybe, but when the swell is small like it is tonight, I don't see why they wouldn't avoid all this and sail over to the beach back there." Jennings pointed back the way we had come, at the wide beach stretching from the harbor south to the bridge.

"But what if we go there and they land here?" said Ben.

"Even if they do land somewhere in here," Jennings said, "they'll have to go by us if they're going to go up the valley to see the mission."

"Like you think they are," Danforth said.

"Don't you agree?"

"Maybe."

Jennings said, "Well either way, if we're over there we'll have them. They'll come by us wherever they land—they won't be going up those cliffs." He waved at the north end of the channel. "If we stay here and they land on that beach, they'll be able to run inland. We want to trap them against water."

"That's true," Ben said.

Danforth nodded. "Let's get back there, then." Everyone heard him, of course, and we tramped back through the thick shrubs cursing and struggling. Back on the road that led to the bridge, the Mayor called us together.

"We've got to be well hidden, because the scavengers might come to greet these people, and they'll be coming from behind us. So I want us all in buildings or among trees. We're assuming they're going to land at this beach here, but it's a good long stretch, so we may have to move after we sight them. If there's a group on the beach to greet them, we'll be able to adjust sooner, but we'll have to be quiet about it." He led us from the road onto the beach. "Don't walk where fresh tracks will show! Now. Main force, over here behind this wall." Several men followed his pointing finger, and walked over to a low tumbled-down wall of broken brick. "Get tucked in there good." He walked south down the beach. "Another group in that clump of trees. That will make a good crossfire. And you Onofre men . . ." He came back north, passed the first wall, came to a pile of cement blocks. "In here. See, this was a latrine. Clear some of these out and hunker down in here. If they try slipping around into that harbor swamp, you'll be here to stop them."

Mando and I put down our guns, and we climbed into the blocks and weeds and tossed some blocks out to make more room for us.

"That's good," Danforth said. "We don't want to make too much of a disturbance, they may have landed around here before, in which case we don't want to change anything. Get in that, let's see how well hidden you are." We climbed over the junk in the doorway and stood inside. Two of the walls didn't meet anymore, and we had a good view through the crack of the beach and the water. "Good. One of you stay where you can see down the beach."

"We can see through this break," Steve said, looking through the crack.

"Okay. That might be a good slot for shooting through, too. Stay out of sight, remember. They'll have night glasses, and they'll have a good look around before they land."

The rest of the San Diegans had disappeared in their various blinds. The Mayor looked around and saw they had dispersed; he checked the watch on his wrist and said, "Okay. It's still a couple hours before midnight, but the scavengers may come earlier to greet them, and they may land early anyway. When you see them come in, stay down. Don't even release the safeties of your guns until we fire on them, understand? That's very important. When we fire is your signal to fire too. Don't waste bullets. Lastly, if anything happens and we get separated in the fighting, we'll all meet on the bridge we crossed, and go back through San Clemente together. You know where I mean?"

"Sure," Steve said. "The bridge."

"Good men. I'm going to join the main group. Keep quiet, and keep one man looking hard." He shook each of our hands in turn, leaning into the latrine to do it. Once again he crushed my hand. "One more thing—we'll hold our fire until they're all on the beach. Remember that. Okay? Okay, then"—clenching a fist and swinging it overhead—"now's our chance to get them!" Then he was off, limping across the soft sand to the broken wall down the beach.

No one in sight. Steve stood at the big crack facing the water and said, "I'll take the first lookout."

We each slid into the best seat we could make, and began to wait. Gabby settled down on a pile of cement blocks. Mando and I got as comfortable as we could, sitting on each side of him. There was nothing to do but listen to the wind batter the ruins. Once I stood and looked over Steve's shoulder at the slice of the sea visible through the crack. Waves broke and sluiced up and down the beach; the offshore wind threw back a little spray, in white arcs barely lit by the starry sky. Whitecaps flecked the surface farther out to sea. Nothing else. I sat back down. Counted the bullets in my leather pouch. There were twelve of them. The gun was loaded, so theoretically I could kill eighteen Japanese. I wondered how many there would be. With my fingernails I could pluck the loaded bullets from their chambers and slip them back in, so I figured reloading wouldn't be a problem. Mando saw me and began fiddling with his gun, too.

"Do you think these things shoot straight?" he said.

"If you're close enough," said Gabby.

We waited some more. Leaning back against the cement wall I even dozed a bit, but I had one of those waking dreams, a quick vision of a green bottle tumbling my way, and I jerked awake again, my heart pumping. Still, nothing was happening, and I almost drifted off again, thinking in a disconnected dreamy way about the bricks of the latrine. Who had made such once-perfect bricks?

"I wish they'd get here," Mando said.

"Shh," Steve said. "Don't talk. It's getting close to time."

If they come at all, I thought. Overhead the stars flickered in the velvet black sky. I shifted to the other side of my butt. We waited. Off on the bluffs a pair of coyotes matched yowls. A lot of time passed, heartbeat by heartbeat, breath by breath.

Steve jerked and reached a hand back to snap in our faces. He leaned over, hissed "scavengers" in a whisper. We jumped to our feet and looked through the crack, peering around Steve.

Dark. Then against the white gleam of the shorebreak I made out figures moving down the beach. They stopped for a while near the wall where the San Diegans were hidden, then moved north, until they were between us and the water. Their voices were almost loud enough to be understood. They clumped together and then moved south again, stopping before they had come even with the San Diegans. One of them leaned down and struck a lighter near the sand, and by its tiny flame several pants legs were illuminated. They were dressed in their finery: in the little circle of light were flashes of gold, ruby, sky-blue cloth. The man with the lighter lit five or six lanterns and left them on the sand with several dark bags and a couple of boxes. One of the lanterns had green glass. Another scavenger took that one and a clear one, went to the water and swung them overhead, crossing them once or twice. By the lanterns' light we could make out parts of the whole crew, silver flashing from their ears and hands, wrists and waists. Several more appeared, carrying dry brush and some bigger branches, and with difficulty they started a fire. Once it was going the kindling burst into flame, and the bigger pieces crackled and spit burning pitch into the sand. Now in the bouncing light they were all clearly visible: fifteen of them, I counted, dressed in yellow and red and purple and blue and green, and weighted down with rings and necklaces of silver and copper.

"I don't see any boat out there," Steve whispered. "You'd think if they were signaling we could make out the boat."

"Too dark," Mando whispered. "And the fire cuts what we can see."

"Shh," Steve hissed.

"Look," said Gabby in an urgent whisper. He pointed past Steve's shoulder, but already I saw what he meant: there was a dark bulk rising out of the water, just off the end of the jetty. Waves rolled over this dark shape, defining it.

"It's coming up from under the water!" Gabby said tightly. "It didn't sail in at all."

"Get down," Steve said, and we crouched at his sides. "That's a submarine."

The man on the beach waved one lantern overhead now, the green one. Their fire gusted in the wind and the bright light bounced off yellow coats, emerald pants.

"So that's how they get past the coast guard," Gabby said.

"They go under them," Steve agreed.

"Do you think the San Diegans see it?" Mando said.

"Shh," Steve hissed again.

One of the submarine's lights came on, illuminating a narrow black deck. Figures came out of a hatch onto this deck, and in the water beside it they inflated big rafts. Others piled out of the submarine into the rafts. The scavengers' firelight reflected off the oars as the rafts were rowed to the beach. Two scavengers welcomed the raft by wading into the water up to their waists, and pulling it up the beach beyond the white wavefoam. Several men jumped out of the raft, and a couple more of them lifted packages and wooden boxes out of it. Scavengers handed them jars of amber liquid that glistened in the firelight, and as the Japanese visitors drank we could just hear the scavengers' greetings, raucous and jovial. The Japanese all looked very round, as if they were wearing two coats each. One of them looked just like my captain.

I pulled back from the crack. "We'll be too far from them when the ambush starts," I told Steve.

"No we won't. Look, here's another raft full of them."

I said, "We should get out of this latrine and get in the trees behind. Once they figure out where the firing is coming from, we'll be stuck here."

"They won't figure it out—how are they going to do that in the dark?"

"I don't know. We should be out of here."

One more raft rowed to shore, pulled up the beach. The thick Japanese men stepped out, looked around. The light on the submarine went out, but its dark bulk remained. Boxes were lifted out of the last raft, and some of the scavengers gathered around the boxes as they were pried open. One in a scarlet coat held up a rifle from a box for his fellows to see.

Crack! crack! crack! The San Diegans opened fire. Shot after shot rang out. From my crouch, looking past Steve's leg, I could see only the response of our victims on the beach: They fell to the sand, the lanterns were out in an instant, the fire knocked to sparks. From then on I couldn't see much, but already spits of flame showed they were firing back. I aimed to fire, and at the same moment there was a flat *whoosh*-BOOM, and we were in a cloud of oily gas, coughing and choking, gasping, crying—my eyes burned so badly I couldn't think of anything else—I feared the gas was eating them out of my head. As the wind swept the cloud out to sea there was another boom, and another, and the popping sound of our ambush was overwhelmed by tremendous long bursts of gunfire spraying off the beach. Through eyes burning with tears all I saw was the whitish flame spurting from the Japanese guns. I coughed and spit, feeling sick, raised my gun to shoot it for the first time (Steve was already shooting). I pulled the trigger and my gun went click, click, click.

A searchlight speared the darkness, originating on the submarine and lighting somewhere south of us, near the wall hiding the San Diegans. The whole area down there exploded. Gunfire boomed in the street behind us, and another cloud of poison gas mushroomed over the beach. The Japanese and the scavengers trapped on the beach stood and marched toward us through the gas, wearing helmets and firing machine guns. Blocks of our latrine fell on us. "Let's get out of here!" Steve cried. We leaped over the latrine's back wall and ran for the trees backing the beach. Once on the trash-blocked street flanking the strand, we ran—hopped, rather—struggled over piles of soggy wood and old brick, tripped and fell, got up again. My nose was streaming snot from the poison gas; I threw away my pistol. In an eyeblink the whole area was bright as day, bright with a harsh blue glare, the shadows solid as rocks. In the sky over us a flare was sputtering light, revealing the tiny parachute holding it up. The whole unit quickly tumbled off to sea, lighting the harbor so that for an instant between trees I could see the submarine, and men on it firing a mounted gun at us.

"The bridge!" Steve was shouting. "The bridge!" I read his lips more than heard him. It was astounding how loud the gunfire was, I wanted to collapse and clamp my hands over my ears. We scrambled over rubbish, fallen trees, driftwood from storm tides; Mando caught his foot and we pulled him loose. Bullets whanged over us, tearing the air *zip, zip,* and I ran hunched down so far my back hurt. Another flare burst into life, higher and farther inland. It floated over us like a falling star, making our way plain but also showing us to everyone so we had to crawl, foot by foot. Rips of machine gun fire came from the sea side of us, and behind us were explosions at frequent intervals: with a blinding flash and a *crack* to break the ears a building down the street fell. We got up from a tangle of planks and ran again, crouched over. Another flare lit the sky above. We fell and waited for the wind to take it to sea. A wrecked building up the hill exploded, then a trio of redwood trees were knocked apart. The flare blew away and we stumbled through the shadows for a good way before another flare burst into life, and we lay flat in a copse of eucalyptus.

"Do you think—" Gabby gasped. "Did the San Diegans get away?" No one answered. Mando was still carrying his pistol. We were just a ways from the bridge, and I wanted to get over it before the submarine blasted it into the river. Dana Point still rang with gunfire, it sounded like a real battle was going on, but they could have been fighting shadows. I wasn't sure the San Diegans would have run like we had. We got up again and scurried over the trash in the streets. A waft of the poison gas. Another fire sparked, but this one plunged fizzing into the marsh. I fell and cut my hand and elbow and knee. We made it to the bridge.

No one was there. "We've got to wait for them!" Steve shouted.

"Get across," I said.

"They won't know we're here! They'll wait here—"

"They will not," Gabby said bitterly. "They're over it and long gone. They told us to wait here so we'd slow down the Japs."

Steve stared at Gab open-mouthed. Another flare burst right above us and I crouched by the rail. Looking between the concrete rail posts I saw several of the flares tailing out to sea, making a ragged string that fell closer to the water, until the ones farthest out lit patches of water. The latest one sailed offshore and over the submarine.

"Go before they put up another one," Gabby said furiously. He stood and ran across the bridge without waiting for us to agree. We followed him, but another flare sparked the sky, lighting the bridge in ghastly detail. There was nothing to do but keep running, and run we did, because the submarine was shooting at us. The railing clanged and the air ripped like stiff cloth, like the first tearing sound of thunder. We got to the far side of the bridge and threw ourselves flat behind a stretch of canted asphalt. The submarine pummeled the bridge. From the hills inland a siren howled, low at first and then rising fast. Scavengers, sounding the alarm. But who were they fighting? Darkness, distant explosions, siren howls. The submarine stopped firing but my head rang so I couldn't hear. Little bangs slapped ahead of us in San Clemente. Steve put his face to my ear. "Go back through streets—" and something I didn't catch. The shooting to the south meant the San Diegans were already down there, I decided, and I cursed them for leaving us. We ran again, but the submarine must have seen us through its night glasses, because it fired again. Down we went. Crawled and hopped, ran doubled over through the ruins on the coastal road. The submarine stayed in the rivermouth, pounding away. We got off the coastal road, back against a low cliff, through trees and on another road. Into the wreck of San Clemente, the maze of trash. Mando was falling behind, limping. I thought it was his foot. "Hurry up!" Steve screamed.

Mando shook his head, limped to us. "Can't," he said. "They shot me."

We stopped and sat him down in the dirt. He was crying, he had his left hand up to his right shoulder. I lifted his hand away and felt the blood run over mine.

"Why didn't you tell us?" Steve cried.

"It just happened," Gabby said roughly, and pushed me away. He put his arm around Mando's. "Come on, we got to get him back as quick as we can."

By the distant light of the last flare I could make out Mando's face. He was staring at me as if he had something to tell me. "Help me *carry* him," Gabby rasped. I could feel the blood soaking the back of his shirt. Steve picked up his pistol and we were off. We could only take several steps at a time before some beam or collapsed wall stopped us. "We've got to stop him bleeding," I finally dared to say. It was running inside my sleeve and down my arm. We put him down and I ripped my shirt into strips. It was hard getting the compress tight over the bullet hole. By accident I brushed the wound with my fingers: a little tear under the shoulderblade, on his right side. It wasn't bleeding fast. Mando still stared at my face with a look I couldn't read. He didn't speak. "We'll have you home in a jiffy," I said hoarsely. I stood up too fast and staggered, but Steve helped us get him up, and we were off again.

The center of San Clemente is one big ruin, no plan or pattern to it, no clear way through. Gabby and I carried Mando between us and struggled along, while Steve ranged forward pistol in hand to find the best way. Sirens cut through the wind's shrieking from time to time, and we had to hide more than once to avoid roving bands of scavengers. Gunshots echoed in the clogged streets. I had no idea who was firing at who. We hiked into dead ends more than once. Steve yelled instructions back to us but sometimes Gabby and I just picked the easiest way; this caused Steve to yell more, in a high desperate shout. Calls came from behind us and Gabby and I lowered Mando to the ground, stuck in the middle of the street. Three scavengers approached us, guns in hand. Steve ran up and fired, *crack crack crack crack!* All the scavengers went down. "Come on," Steve screamed. We picked Mando up and staggered on. Dead ends made us backtrack and after a long time trying to find a way we caught up to Steve sitting in the road, houses collapsed all around us, wind and gunfire beyond, no way forward—our way blocked by a giant mare's nest of bones.

"I don't know where we are," Steve cried. "I can't find a way." I prodded him to take my side carrying Mando, grabbed his gun and ran across the street. Through trees I saw the ocean, the only mark we really needed when it came down to it. "This way!" I called, and hopped over a beam, dragged it out of their path, ran down and got another fix on the sea, picked a road, did what I could to clear it. That went on and on, till it seemed like San Clemente had stretched out all the way down Pendleton. And scavengers on the prowl, setting off their sirens and guns, howling with glee at the hunt. They put us to ground more than once; I didn't dare shoot at them because I wasn't sure how many they were or how many bullets were left in Steve's gun, if any.

While we cowered in the dark of our cover I did what I could for Mando. His breath was choked. "How are you, Mando?" No answer. Steve cursed and cursed. I nodded to Gabby and we got Mando up again. I left Steve to carry him and went out scouting. Scavengers gone, at least out of sight, that was all I wanted. I set to finding a way again.

Somehow we got to the southern end of San Clemente, down in the forest below the freeway. Scavengers were roaming the freeway; we heard their shouts and occasionally I saw their shapes. The only way across San Mateo River was the freeway. We were trapped. Sirens mocked us, gunshots might have marked a skirmish with the San Diegans, although I suspected Gabby was right and they were long gone, on their boats and under way. They wouldn't be back to help us. Gabby had Mando resting on his lap. Mando's breath gurgled in his throat. "We got to get him home," Gab said, looking at me.

I took the bullets from my pocket and tried to fit them into Steve's gun.

"Where's your gun?" Steve said.

The bullets didn't fit. I cursed and threw the pouch at the freeway. In the dirt we sat on was a rock I could just fit my hand around. I hefted it and started for the freeway. I don't know what I had in mind. "Bring him up close to the road and be ready to move him across San Mateo fast," I told them. "You *go* when I tell you to." But a series of explosions blasted the freeway above us, and when they ended (burnt powder smell blown by) it was quiet. Not a scavenger to be heard. The silence was broken by the sound of a vehicle coming up the freeway from the south. A little *whirrr*. I crawled up the shoulder of the road to take a look at it. I jumped out of the road to wave at him. "Rafael! Rafael! Over here!" I screamed, the words tearing out of me like no others ever had.

Rafael rolled up to me. "Christ, Hank, I almost shot you dead there!" He was in the little golf cart that sat in his front yard, the one he swore he could make work if he ever found the batteries.

"Never mind that," I said. "Mando's hurt. He's been shot." Gabby and Steve appeared, carrying Mando between them.

Rafael sucked air between his teeth. "Put him in back."

Scattered shots rang out from up the freeway, and one spanged off the concrete near us. Rafael reached into his cart and pulled out a metal tube, held by struts at an angle on a flat base. He put it on the road and dropped a hand-sized bomb or grenade (it looked like a firecracker) in it. *Thonk*, the tube said hollowly, and a few seconds later there was an explosion just off the freeway, about where the shots had come from. While Gabby and Steve got Mando in the cart Rafael kept dropping grenades in, thonk, BOOM, thonk, BOOM, and pretty soon no one was firing at us. With a final burst of three he jumped in the cart and we were off.

"When we go uphill, get out and push," Rafael said. "This thing won't carry all of us. Nicolin, take this and keep an eye out to the rear." He handed Steve a rifle. "How about more bullets," Steve said. Rafael gestured at the floor beside him. "In the box there." We hit the steep hill at the very south end of San Clemente, and pushed the cart up it at a slow run. Sirens wailed off the hills; I could make out three different ones, wavering at different levels as the wind tore at their sound. We made the rise and rolled into the San Mateo Valley. I cradled Mando's head and told him we were close to home. There were faint shouts behind us, but now we were moving faster than men on foot could. We reached the rise to Basilone Ridge and Rafael said, "Push again." He was calm, but when he looked at me his eye was hard. When we reached the top of Basilone rise Steve cried wildly, "I'm going back to make them pay!" and he was off in the dark, back up the freeway to the north, rifle in hand. "Wait!" I shouted, but Rafael struck my arm.

"Let him go." For the first time he sounded angry. He drove the cart to his house and jumped out, ran inside and came back out with a stretcher. We got Mando on it. His eyes were still open, but he didn't hear me. Blood trickled from the corner of his mouth. Gabby was huffing beside the stretcher as Rafael and I carried him. We struck out through the forest, traversing the side of Cuchillo to get to the Costas' as fast as possible. I stumbled and Gabby took over my end. We got to the Costas' place. Wind whistled over the oil drums; there was no way they could have heard us approach. Rafael propped the stretcher against his thigh, banged the door like he was out to break it. *Wham. Wham.*

"Get out here, Ernest," he said, still banging the door. "Get out here and doctor your boy."

... 20

It must have been something Doc had imagined many times before, the moment when they came to the door and it was his own son hurt. When he pulled the door away from Rafael's banging he didn't say a word to us; he came out and picked Mando up off the stretcher and carried him through the kitchen into the hospital without a glance or a question.

We followed him. In the hospital he laid Mando on the second bed, a small one, and pulled it out from the wall. At the scraping Tom snorted, rolled over. One of his closed eyes opened a crack, and when he caught sight of us he sat up, ground his knuckles in his eyes, surveyed the scene wordlessly. Doc used scissors to cut off Mando's coat and shirt, gesturing for Gabby to pull off his pants. Mando coughed, gargled, breathed fast and shallow. Under the bright lamps Rafael carried in from the kitchen his body looked pale and mottled. Below his armpit was that little tear, surrounded by a bruise. I sat on my heels against the wall, knees in my armpits, arms wrapped around my legs, looking away from Tom. Doc looked at no one but Mando. "Get Kathryn here," he said. Gabby glanced at me, hurried out.

Tom said, "How is he?"

Doc felt Mando's ribs carefully, tapped his chest, took his pulse at wrist and neck. He muttered, more to himself than Tom, "Middle caliber nicked the lung. Pneumothorax . . . hemothorax. . . ." Like a spell. He cleaned the blood from Mando's ribs with a wet cloth. Mando choked and Doc adjusted his head, reached in his mouth and pulled his tongue around. A plastic thing from the supply shelf behind Doc served to clamp the tongue in place. Plastic vise on the side of Mando's face, stretching his mouth open. The wind picked up, *wheeeeee*.

"Where's Nicolin?" Tom asked me.

I kept my eyes on the floor. Rafael answered from the kitchen:

"He stayed north to fire some rounds at the scavengers."

Tom was shifting around against his back wall, and he coughed. "Quit moving," Doc said. A flying branch knocked the house sharply. Mando's

breathing was rapid, harsh, shallow. Doc tilted his face to the side and wiped
bright blood from his mouth. Doc's own mouth was a tight lipless line. Bright
blood on cloth. Under me the floor, the grainy smooth boards of the floor.
Knots raised above the worn surface, cracks, splinters all shiny and distinct
in the lamplight, scrubbing sand in the corners against the walls. The bedpost
closest to me was shimmed. The sheets were so old that each thread of the fabric stood out; needlework in the patches. I stared at the floor. My breath hurt
so it might have been me shot. Kathryn's legs walked into the room, bending
down the floorboards a bit. Gabby's legs followed.

"I need help," Doc said.

"I'm ready," said Kathryn.

"We need to get a tube between these ribs and drain the blood and air in the
chest cavity. Get a clean jar from the kitchen and put a couple inches of water in
it." She left, came back. Their feet faced each other under Mando's bed. "I'm afraid
air's getting in and not getting out. Tension pneumothorax. Here, put down the
tube and tape, and hold him steady. I'm going to make the incision here."

Muffled coughs from the old man. A quick glance: Kathryn's back, in sweatshirt and string-tie pants; the old man, watching them with an unflinching gaze.
Down on the floor went the jar, clear plastic tube stuck in the water at the bottom
of it. Suddenly the water bubbled. Blood ran down the sides of the tube and stained
the water. More bubbles. The old man's steady gaze: I wrapped my arms over my
stomach and looked up. Kathryn's back blocked my view of Mando. Elbows busy
as she pulled tape from a roll and applied it to Mando, where I couldn't see.

She looked at me over her shoulder. "Where's Steve?"

"Up north."

She grimaced, turned to the work at hand.

Tom coughed again, lightly but several times. Doc looked at him. "You lie
back down," he said harshly.

"I'm okay, Ernest. Don't mind me."

Doc was already back at it. He leaned over Mando with a desperate look in his
eye. "We need oxygen." He tapped Mando's chest and the sound was flat. Mando's breathing was faster. "Got to stop the bleeding," Doc said. The wind gusted
till I couldn't make out their voices over the house whistling. "Use the wound
to put in another tube. . . ." Tom asked Gabby what had happened, and Gab explained in a sentence or two. Tom didn't comment on it. The wind dropped again
and I could hear the snip of Doc's scissors. He wiped sweat from his forehead.

"Hold it. Okay, get the other end in the jar, and give me the tape quick."

"Tape."

Something in the way she said it made Doc look at Tom with a bitter smile.
Tom smiled back but then he looked away. I felt a hand on my shoulder and
looked up to see Rafael.

"Come on out to the kitchen like Gabby is now, Henry. You can't do anything in here."

I shook my head.

"Come on, Henry."

I shrugged off his hand and buried my face in the crook of my arm. When Rafael was gone I looked up again. Tom was chewing on a curl of his hair, watching them intently. Kathryn put her head to Mando's chest. "His heart sounds distant."

Mando jerked on the bed. His feet were blue. "And his veins," Doc said, voice dry as the wind. "Tamponade, ohhh . . ." He drew back, his fist clenched up by his neck. "I can't help that. I haven't got the needles."

Mando stopped breathing. "No," Doc said, and with Kathryn's help he shifted Mando from his side to his back. "Hold the tubes," he said, and put his mouth and hands to Mando's mouth. He breathed in, holding Mando's nostrils shut, then straightened up and pressed hard on Mando's chest. Mando's body spasmed. "Henry, come hold his legs," Kathryn said sharply. I got up stiffly and held Mando by the shins, felt them twitch, struggle, tense up, slacken. Go slack. Doc breathed into him, breathed into him, pushed his chest till the pushes were nearly blows. Blood ran down the tubes. Doc stopped. We stared at him: eyes closed, mouth open. No breath. Kathryn held his wrist, feeling for a pulse. Gabby and Rafael were in the doorway. Finally Kathryn reached across Mando and put her hand on Doc's arm; we had all been standing there a long time. Doc put his elbows on the bed, lowered his ear onto Mando's chest. His head rolled till it was his forehead resting on Mando. "He's gone," he whispered. Mando's calves were still in my hands, the very muscles that had just been twitching. I let go, scared to be touching him. But it was Mando, it was Armando Costa. His face was white. It looked like the face of a sick brother of Mando's.

Kathryn got out a sheet from the cupboard against the wall and spread it over him, pushing Doc gently away so she could do it. Her sweatshirt was sweaty, bloodstained. She covered Mando's face. I recalled the expression his face had had when I was carrying him through San Clemente. Even that was preferable to this. Kathryn rounded the bed and pulled Doc to the door.

"Let's get him buried," Doc said intently. "Let's do it now, come on." Kathryn and Rafael tried to calm him but he was insistent. "I want it over with. Get the stretcher and let's get him down to the graveyard. I want it over with."

Tom coughed harshly. "Please, Ernest. Wait until morning at least, man. You've got to wait until daylight. Got to get Carmen, and dig the grave—"

"We can do that tonight!" Doc cried petulantly. "I want it over with."

"Sure we can. But it's late. By the time we're done it will be day. Then we can carry him over and bury him with people there. Wait for the day, please."

Doc rubbed his face in both hands. "All right. Let's go dig the grave."

Rafael held him back. "Gabby and I will do that," he said. "Why don't you stay here."

Doc shook his head. "I want to do it."

Rafael looked to Tom, then said, "All right. Come on with us, then."

He and Gabby got Doc into his coat and shoes, and bumped through the doorway after him. I offered to go but they saw I was useless and told me to stay. From the front door I watched them walk down the path to the river. Pre-dawn twilight, Gabby and Rafael on each side of Doc, holding him. Three little figures under the trees. When they were out of sight I turned around. Kathryn was at the kitchen table, crying. I went outside and sat in the garden.

The wind was dying down a bit with the coming of day. It only hit in gusts. The light grew till I could make out gray branches waving. Under the pale sky all distances seemed equal. Leaves fluttered and hung still, fluttered again, in waves that swelled across the treetops out to sea. The dome of the sky grew lighter and taller. Grays took on color, and then the sun, leaf green and blinding, cracked the horizon.

I sat in the dirt. My knee, elbow, and hands throbbed where I had cut them falling. It was impossible that Mando was dead, and that reassured me for long stretches of time. Then my hands felt his calves go slack. Or I heard Kathryn inside, clearing up, and I knew that impossible or not, it was real. But it wasn't a thought I could grasp for long.

The sun was more than a hand's breadth over the hills when Doc and Gabby came back up the path, Marvin and Nat Eggloff behind them. Rafael was down the river path, pounding on doors and waking folks up. Gabby fairly staggered up the last part of the path. His eyes were ringed red, and he was dirty, as were Doc and Nat. Doc looked up from the path at his house, stopped and waited. Marvin nodded to me and they went inside. I heard them talking with Kathryn. Then she started yelling at the old man. "Lie down! Don't be a fool! We got enough burials today!" Tom must have said his goodbyes to Mando inside. They came out with Mando on Rafael's stretcher, wrapped in the sheet. Unsteadily I stood. Everyone took a stretcher pole in hand, three on a side. We carried him down to the river, across the bridge. Sun brutal off the water. We took the river path through the trees. People given the news by Rafael caught up with us, family by family, looked shocked, or tearful, or withdrawn. Once looking back I saw John Nicolin leading all the rest of the Nicolins bar Marie and the babies, his face puffy with displeasure. My pa came to my side and put his arm around my shoulder. When he saw my face he squeezed my shoulders hard. For once he didn't look stupid to me. He still had that vague look of someone who doesn't quite get it. But he knew. Suffering you don't have to be smart to understand. With the knowledge in his eyes was mild reproach, and I couldn't look at him.

Back in the neck of the valley we were in the shade. Carmen met us outside her home and led us to the graveyard. She was wearing her preaching robe and carrying the Bible. In the graveyard was a new hole in the ground, a mound of fresh earth on one side of it, Mando's mother Elizabeth's grave on the other. We laid the stretcher on her grave and all the people trailing us circled around. Most of the valley's people were there. Nat and Rafael lifted Mando's body and the sheet into a coffin twice Mando's size. Nat held the lid in place while Rafael nailed it down. Whap, whap, whap, whap. Doc watched the nails being driven home with a desolate look. Both his wife and Mando had been so much younger than him, their years didn't add up to half his.

When the coffin was nailed shut John stepped forward and helped them arrange the ropes under the coffin. He and Rafael and Nat and my pa picked up the ropes and lifted the coffin over the hole. They lowered it to John's curt, quiet instructions. When it was settled in the hole they pulled the ropes up. John gathered them and gave them to Nat, his jaw muscles so tight it looked like he had pebbles in his mouth.

Carmen stepped to the edge of the grave. She read some from the Bible. I watched a sunbeam lancing through the trees. She told us to pray, and in the prayer she said something about Mando, about how good he had been. I opened my eyes and Gabby was staring at me from across the grave, accusing, terrified. I squeezed my eyes shut again. "Into Thy hands we commend his spirit." She took a clod of dirt and held it over the grave; held a tiny silver cross over it with the other hand. She dropped them both in. Rafael and John shoveled the damp earth into the hole, it made the hollow sound. Mando was still down there and I almost cried out for them to stop it, to get him out. Then I thought, it could have been me in that grave, and an awful terror filled me. The bullet that struck Mando had been one of swarms of them; that one or any of the others could have hit me, could have killed me. It was the most frightening thought I had ever had in my life—the terror filled me entirely. Gabby kneeled beside Rafael and pushed dirt in with his two hands. Doc twisted away, and Kathryn and Mrs. Nicolin led him back toward the Eggloffs'. But all I did was stand and watch; and I'm ashamed to write it, but I became glad. I was glad it wasn't me down there. I was so glad to be there alive and seeing it all, I thought thank God it wasn't me! Thank God it was Mando got killed, and *not me*. Thank God! Thank God!

Sometimes after a funeral quite a wake would develop at the Eggloffs', but not this morning. This morning everyone went home. Pa led me down the river path. I was so tired my feet didn't make it over bumps. Without Pa I would have fallen more than once. "What happened?" Pa asked, reproachful again. "Why'd you go up there?" There were people strung along the trail, shaking their heads, talking, looking back at us.

When we got home I tried to explain to Pa what had happened, but I couldn't do it. The look in his eye stopped me. I lay down on my bed and slept. I would say I slept like a dead man, but it isn't so.

Sleep doesn't knit the raveled sleeve of care, no matter what Macbeth said (or hoped). He was wrong that time as he was so often. Sleep is just time out. You can do all the knitting you like in dreams, but when you call time in it unravels in an instant and you're back where you started. No sleep or dream was going to knit back the last day for me; it was unraveled for good.

Nevertheless, I slept all through that day and evening, and when Pa's voice, or his sewing machine, or a dog's bark pulled me halfway out of slumber, I knew I didn't want to wake even though I didn't quite remember why, and I worked at returning to sleep until I slid back down the slope to dreams again. I slept through most of the evening, struggling harder and harder to hold on to it as the hours passed.

But you can't sleep forever. What broke my last hold on an uneasy half-sleep was the *w-whoo, w-whoo* of the canyon owl—Nicolin's signal, repeated insistently. Nicolin was out there, under the eucalyptus no doubt, calling me. I sat up, looked out the door; saw him, a shadow against the treetrunk. Pa was sewing. I got my shoes on. "I'm going out." Pa looked at me again with his puzzled reproach, his slight hint of condemnation. I was still wearing the torn clothes I had had on the night before. They stank with fear. I was ravenous, and paused to break off half a loaf of bread on my way out. I approached Steve chewing a big lump. We stood together silently under the tree. He had a full bag over his shoulder.

When the bread was done I said, "Where you been?"

"I was in Clemente till late this afternoon. God what a day! I found the scavengers that had been chasing us, and sniped at them till they didn't know *who* was after them. Got some too—they thought a whole gang was after them. Then I went back up to Dana Point, but by that time they had all gotten away. So—"

"Mando's dead."

". . . I know."

"Who told you?"

"My sister. I snuck in to get some of my stuff, and she caught me just as I was leaving. She told me."

We stood there for a long time. Steve took in a deep breath and let it out. "So, I reckon I got to leave."

"What do you mean?"

". . . Come give me some help." My night vision was coming in, and with the exhausted sound of his voice I could suddenly see his face, dirty, scratched, desperate. "Please."

"How?"

He took off toward the river.

We went to the Marianis', stood by the ovens. Steve made his owl call. We waited a long time. Steve tapped his fist against the side of the oven. Even I, with nothing at stake, felt nervous. That led me back to all that had happened the night before.

The door opened and Kathryn slipped out, in the same pants she had worn the night before, but a different sweatshirt. Steve's fingernails scraped the brick. She knew where he would be, and walked straight to us.

"So you came back." She stared at him, head cocked to one side.

Steve shook his head. "Just to say goodbye." He cleared his throat. "I—I killed some scavengers up there. They'll be out to get back at us. If you tell them at the swap meet that I did it and took off, that it was all my doing, maybe it will all stop there."

Kathryn stared at him.

"I can't stay after what's happened," Steve said.

"You could."

"I can't."

The way he said that, I knew he was leaving. Kathryn knew it too. She folded her arms over her chest and hugged herself as if she were cold. She looked over at me and I looked down. "Let us talk awhile, Henry."

I nodded and wandered to the river. The water clicked over snags like black glass. I wondered what he was saying to her, what she was saying to him. Would she try to change his mind when she knew he wouldn't?

I was glad I didn't know. It hurt to think of it. I saw Doc's face as he watched his son, the living part of his wife, lowered into the ground beside her. Helpless to stop myself I thought what if the old man dies tonight, right up there at Doc's place? What about Doc then? . . . What about Tom?

I sat and held my head but it didn't stop me thinking. Sometimes it would be such a blessing to turn all the thinking off. I stood and tossed rocks in the water. I sat down again when the rocks were gone, and wished I could throw away thoughts as easily, or the deeds of the past.

Steve appeared and stood looking over the river. I stood up.

"Let's get going," he said thickly. He walked down the river path toward the sea, cut into the forest. There was no talk between us, just the silent walking together, side by side, and briefly I recalled how it had felt for so long, for all our lives, when we had hiked together silently in the woods at night like brothers.

He went down the cliff path without looking at it, going from foothold to foothold with careless mastery. The moon was nearly on the water. I descended the obscure cliff more slowly. Once on the sand I followed him to the boats.

A couple of the fishing boats had sockets on the keel where you could step a small mast and spread a sail. Nicolin went to one of those. Without a word we took bow and stern and skewed the boat from side to side in the sand. Normally four or five men push a boat into the water, but that's just for convenience; Steve and I got it moving pretty easily. When it was across the tidal flat and in the shallows we stopped. Nicolin climbed in to step the mast, and I held the hull steady on the sand bottom.

I said, "You're going to sail to Catalina, like the guy who wrote that book."

"That's right."

"You know that book is a bunch of lies."

He never stopped unfurling the sail. "I don't care. If the book is a lie then I'll make it true."

"They aren't the kind of lies you can make true."

"How do you know?"

I did know, but I couldn't say. The mast was stepped and he started jamming the cotter pin through the socket. I didn't want to just come out and ask him to stay. "I thought you were going to spend your life fighting for America."

He stopped working. "Don't think I'm not," he said bitterly. "You saw what happened when we tried to fight here. There's not a thing we can do. The place where something can be done is Catalina. I bet there's a lot of Americans already there who think the same."

I could see he would have an answer to everything. I shifted the boat's stern, got ready to push.

"I'm positive the resistance is strongest over there," he said. "Don't you think so? I mean—aren't you coming with me?"

"No."

"But you should. You'll regret it if you don't. This is a little out-of-the-way valley here. That's the *world* out there, Henry!" He waved a hand westward.

"No." I leaned over the stern. "Come on, do you want help with this boat or not?"

He pursed his lips, shrugged. His shoulders drooped when the shrug was done, and I saw how tired he was. It would be a long sail. But I wasn't going to go, and I wasn't going to explain. He hadn't expected me to say yes anyway, had he?

He roused himself, got out of the boat to push. Quickly it floated clear of the sand. We stared at each other from across the boat, and he stuck out his hand. We shook. I couldn't think of anything to say. He leaped in and got the oars out while I held the stern. I shoved it into the current and he started rowing. With the crescent moon behind him I couldn't make out his features, and we didn't say a word. He rowed over a swell coming upriver. Soon he'd be out where what was left of the Santa Ana would clear the cliff and catch his sail.

"Good luck!" I cried.

He rowed on.

The next swell hid the boat from me for a moment. I walked out of the river, feeling chill. From the beach I watched him clear the rivermouth. The sail, a faint patch against the black, flapped and filled. Soon he was beyond the break. From there he wouldn't hear me unless I shouted. "Do some good for us over there," I said, but I was talking to myself.

I climbed the cliff path, water dripping from my pants. By the time I got to the top I was warmer. I walked along the cliff. It was a cloudless night again, and the setting moon shone across the water, marking the distance to the horizon. It was a night to make you see how vast the world was: the ocean, the spangled sky, the cliff, the valley, and the hills behind, they were all so huge I might as well have been an ant. Out there under a pale handkerchief patch was another ant, in an ant's boat.

On the horizon I could see it: dark mass of the sea below, dark sky above, and between them the black bulk of Catalina, bejeweled with white points of light both fixed and moving, and red lights to mark the highest peaks, and a few yellow and green lights here and there. It was like a bright constellation, the finest constellation, always on the verge of setting. For years I had considered it the prettiest sight I had ever seen. There was a cluster of light on the water at the south end that was invisible from the cliff—the foreigners' port—it could be seen from the height of Tom's house on a night like this, but I had no desire to go up there and see it. The dim patch of Nicolin's sail moved out of the narrow path of moonlight on the water and disappeared. He was one of the shadows among the few moony glitters on the black sea, but strain my eyes as I might I couldn't tell which one he was. For all I could tell the ocean had swallowed him. But I knew it hadn't. The little boat was still out there somewhere, sailing west to Avalon.

I stayed on the cliff looking out to sea for a long time. Then I couldn't stand it, and took off into the forest. Leaves clacked and pine needles quivered as I trudged under the trees. The valley never seemed so big and empty as it did then. In a clearing I looked back; the lights of Catalina blinked and danced, but I turned and walked on. I didn't give a damn if I never saw Catalina again.

... 21

The forest at night is a funny place. The trees get bigger, and they seem to come alive, as though during the day they were asleep or gone from their bodies, and only at night do they animate themselves and live, perhaps even pulling up their roots and walking the valley floors. If you're out there you can sometimes almost catch them at it, just beyond the corner of your eye. Of course on a moonless night it only takes a little wind to imagine such things. Branches dip to tousle the hair, and the falling-water sounds of the leaves are like soft voices calling in the distance. Two holes make eyes, a trail blaze is a smiling mouth, branches are arms, leaves hands. Easy. Still I think it may be true that they are a type of nocturnal animal. They are alive, after all. We tend to forget that. In the spring they sprout joyously, in the summer they bask in the sun, in the winter they suffer bare and cold. Just like us. Except they sleep during the day and come awake at night. So if you want to have much to do with them, night is the time to be out among them.

The different trees wake up in different ways, and they treat you differently. Eucalyptus trees are friendly and talkative. Their branches tend to grow across each other, and in a wind they creak constantly. And their hanging leaves twirl and clack together, making the falling-water sound, a rising and falling voice. The eucalyptus has a great voice. But you wouldn't want to touch one, or give it a hug, unless you could see it and avoid the gum. The bark is smooth and cool, fragrant like the rest of the tree with that sharp dusty smell, but it doesn't grow as fast as the wood inside it, I guess, and there are a lot of breaks in it as a result, cracks that split it completely. These cracks leak gum like a dog slobbers, and in the dark you can't keep from getting your hands and arms in it, and coming away all sticky.

Pine trees are more forbidding speakers. In a breeze their quiet *whoooos* are fey, and the wild *ohhhhhhhs* they utter when the wind is up can raise the hair on the back of your neck. But pines feel good to the touch, and you can look at their black silhouettes against the sky forever. Torrey pines have the longest needles, and their little branches are all curly. And the rough, brittle bark feels wonderful against the skin, it's like a giant cat's tongue. Redwood bark is even better, all split and hairy; you can put your fingers in cracks around the sides and hold on for dear life. It's like hugging a bear, or holding on to your ma and crying into her hair. Good friends, pine trees, though you have to ignore their stern voice and touch them to find that out.

Of course there are real living things in the forest at night, mobile things I mean, animals like us. A whole bunch of them, in fact: coyotes and weasels and skunks and raccoons and deer, and cats and rabbits and possums and bears and who knows what all. But damned if you'd know it by just walking around. Even a lone human sitting in the forest for hours might not catch sight of a single creature—much less a human who is crashing around hugging trees and such. Someone like that isn't going to see a single animal, or even hear one except for frogs. Frogs don't scare easily, they've got the river to hop in and they don't care. You have to come close to stepping on them before they'll shut up, much less move. All the others, though, they hear you coming or smell you way off, and they get out of the way and you never know they've been there, except if you chance to hear a rustle off in the distance. Of course a big cat might decide to eat you, but you hope they'd be wary enough to stay out of the valley. Generally they avoid crowds, and in the fall they're not very hungry. So . . . if you walk about you don't see a creature anywhere, which is funny because you know they're around you, getting a drink, chomping on sprouts or dead prey, hunting for or hiding from each other.

But I forgot about the birds. Occasionally you'll see the quick black shape of an owl, flying without a sound. It's uncanny how complete their silence is. Or higher, geese or herons migrating, their heads poked ahead on those long necks, flying in V's that flow in and out of shape.

That night I saw a flock of geese flying south. Two pairs of wide V's, passing over the valley in the hour before dawn, when the sky was blueing and I could see them quite clearly. Slow, steady wing strokes, and quite a conversation going on up there in that honk and squawk language. . . .

Of course they aren't part of the forest proper, but you can see them while in the forest. And I did see them that night. I slept earlier against a redwood, and then for a while curled between two gnarly roots. Mostly, though, I walked around. I had spent a lot of time in the forest, day and night, without paying the least attention to it. But this night I studied tree after tree, hung out with them and really got to know them well, touched them, climbed a couple.

Where the creek from Swing Canyon meets the river is a little meadow that always has a lot of animal tracks in it. I wandered that way when I woke up and saw the geese overhead, in hope of seeing some furry brothers taking a drink.

Sure enough, after I lay in the ferns behind a fungus-riddled log for a while, watching a spider weave her morning web, a family of deer came down and drank. Buck, doe, fawn. The buck looked around and sniffed; he knew I was there, but he didn't care about it, which showed good judgment. When they were done drinking they pushed off, across the meadow and out of sight.

I clambered up stiffly, went down to the creek and drank myself. My pants were still damp and my legs were cold, and I was stiff, and dirty, and cut up, and hungry, and dog tired, but mainly I felt all right. I walked down the west riverbank empty as an empty bowl. I wasn't going to start crying again, no matter whether I thought of Mando and Steve or not. I could think of them and not feel much of anything. It was done, and I was empty.

But then I rounded the bend above the bridge, and caught sight of a figure downriver on the same bank, at the foot of the cornfields. This was still early morning, when the whole world was nothing but shades of gray—a thousand shades of gray, but not a hint of color. Dew soaked every gray leaf and sprig and fern on the ground, a sign that the Santa Ana was ending.

The figure downstream was a woman. If a person is visible we know their sex, no matter how distant they are—I'm not sure how we tell sometimes, but we do. And the dark gray shade of this woman's hair would be brown in the sun, brown with a bit of red in it. Already in this world of grays I could see that touch of red. Kathryn it was, standing at the foot of her fields. From the knee down her pants were darker—wet, then, which meant she had been out walking for a while. Maybe she had been out all night too, yet another animal I had not seen. Her back was to me. I would have gone to her, but something held me. There are times when a back a hundred yards away is as expressive as our faces. She began walking downstream, toward the bridge. At the end of the field she suddenly swung to her right and gave a fearsome kick to the last corn-stalk. She wears big boots and the stalk shuddered and stayed tilted over. That didn't satisfy her. She got set and kicked it again and again, till it was flattened. The scene blurred before me and I stumbled away through the woods, all our catastrophes made real again.

I took to spending a lot of time on the beach. I couldn't stand to be with people. One day I tried to rejoin the fishing, but that was no good; they were too hard. Another time I wandered by the ovens, but I left; poor Kristen had a look that pierced me. Even eating with Pa made me feel bad. Everyone's eyes questioned me, or condemned me, or watched me when they didn't think I was going to notice: they tried to console me, or act like nothing was different, which was a lie. I didn't want any part of them. The beach was a good place to get away. Our beach is so wide from cliff to water, and so long from the coarse sand at the rivermouth to the jumbled white boulders of Concrete Bay, that you can wander on it for days. Long furrows from old high tides, filled with brackish water; tangled driftwood, including old logs with their octopus roots sticking up; sandflea-infested seaweed, like mounds of black compost; shells whole and broken; sand crabs and the telltale bubbles they leave in the wet sand; the little round white sandpipers with their backwards knees, charging up and down the shingle together to avoid the soup; all of these were worth investigating for hours and days. So I wandered up and down the beach and investigated them, and was miserable, or empty.

Because I could have not told them. In fact I could have refused to have anything to do with the whole plan right from the start. That is what I should have done. But even after I went along with it, I could have kept to myself what I had found out about the landing, and none of it would ever have happened. I had even considered it, and came close to doing it. But I hadn't. I had made my decision, and everything that had happened—Mando's death, Steve's flight—all followed from that. So it was my fault. I was to blame for one friend's running away, and another's death. And for who knows how many other deaths that had come that night, of people who were strangers to me, but who no doubt had families and friends grieving for them like we grieved for Mando. All of it came from my thinking; from my decision. I would have given anything to change that decision. But there's nothing as unchangeable as the past. Striding up the river path to home I recalled what the old man had said there, about how we were wedged in a crack by history, so our choices were squeezed down; but now I knew that compared to the way the past is wedged in there, the present is as free as the open air. In the present you have choices, but in the past you only did one thing; regret it with all your power, it won't change.

If I had been smarter, Mando wouldn't have died. Not only smarter—more honest. I had lied to and betrayed Kathryn, Tom, Pa—the whole valley, because of the vote. Everybody but Steve, and he was on Catalina. What a fool I had been! Here I thought I had been so clever, getting the time and place out of Add, and leading the San Diegans up to the ambush.

But it was us who had been ambushed. As soon as I thought of it that way it was obvious. Those folks hadn't just been defending themselves on the spur of the moment—they were ready for us. And who else would have warned them but Addison Shanks? He knew we knew about the landing, and all he had had to do was tell the scavengers we knew, and they could prepare for us. Ambush us.

Once I thought of it, it was as obvious as the sun in the sky, but it really hadn't occurred to me until then, walking up the river path and brooding over it. They had ambushed the ambushers.

And the San Diegans had set us farther north than them so that if anything went wrong, we would be the last over the bridge and would take up the attention of the enemy while the San Diegans escaped. Thrown in the road to trip the pursuit.

We had been twice betrayed. And I had been an incredible fool.

And my foolishness had cost Mando his life. I wished fiercely, now that the funeral was well past, that I had died and not him. But I knew that wishing was like throwing rocks at the moon; so I was safe to wish.

Wandering the beach and thinking about it a couple days later, I got curious and went up Basilone to the Shankses'. I didn't have anything in mind to say to them, but I wanted to see them. If I saw their faces I would know if I was right or not about Add warning the scavengers, and then I could be shut of them for good.

Their house was burned down. Nobody was around. I stepped across the charred boards that were all that was left of the south wall, and kicked around in the piles of charcoal for a bit. Dust and ash puffed away from my boot. They were long gone. I stood in the middle of what had been their storage room, and looked at the black lumps on the ground. Nothing metal. It looked like they had emptied the place of valuables before they fired it. They must have had help moving north. After what I had caught Add doing, as soon as they heard of my survival they must have decided to move north and join the scavengers completely. And of course Addison wouldn't leave us such a house.

The north wall was still there, black planks eaten through and ready to fall; the rest of the wood was ash, or ends and lumps scattered about. The old metal poles of the electric tower were visible again, rising up soot-black to the metal platform that had once held the wires. I felt as empty as always. It had been a good house. They weren't good people, but it had been a good house. And somehow, standing in the charred ruins of it, I couldn't bring up any feeling against Add and Melissa, although I could have easily moments before. It couldn't have been any fun to fire a good home like this and flee. And were they really that bad? Working with scavengers, so what. We all traded with them some way or other. Even helping the Japanese to land, was that surely so bad? Glen Baum had done it in that book of his, if he had done any of it, and no one called him traitor. Add and Melissa just wanted something different than I did. In ways they were better than I was. At least they kept their promises; they had their loyalties intact.

I dogged back into the valley, lower than ever. Stopped at Doc's: Tom sick, asleep and looking like death; Doc hollow-eyed at the kitchen table, alone, staring at the wall. I hustled down to the river, crossed the bridge, stopped at the bathhouse latrine to relieve myself. I walked out as John Nicolin walked in. He glared at me, brushed by me without a word.

So I went to the beach. And the next day I went back. I was getting to know the troops of little sandpipers: the one with one leg, the black one, the broken-beaked one. The tide moved in, drowning the flies' dining table. It moved back out, exposing the wet seaweed again. Gulls wheeled and shrieked. Once a pelican landed on the wet strand and stood there looking about aloofly. The shorebreak was big that day, however, and he was slow to get out from under a thick rushing lip; it thumped down on him and he tumbled, long wings and beak and neck and legs thrashing around in a tangled somersault. I laughed as he struggled up, all wet and bedraggled and huffy, but he walked funny as he ran to take off and glide down the beach, and my laughter caught in my throat.

The clouds came back. A gray wall sat on the horizon, and pieces of it broke loose and were carried onshore by the wind. The wind had backed at last. The Santa Ana had held the clouds out to sea for over a week, and now they were coming back to claim their territory. At first there were just a few of them, loose-knit and transparent except at their centers. Clouds beget clouds, though, and through the afternoon they came in darker and lower, until the whole wall picked up and advanced from the horizon, turning dark blue and covering the sky like a blanket. The air got cold, the gulls disappeared, the onshore wind picked up. The clouds grew top heavy, spat lightning onto the sea and then the land. I sat on a worn gray log and watched the first raindrops pock the sand. The iron surface of the ocean lost its sheen as the rain hit it. I pulled my coat around me and stubbornly sat there. The rain turned to hail. Hail fell until there was a layer of clear grains on top of the tawny ones: a beach of sand overlaid by a beach of glass.

I walked down the beach, climbed the cliff path. The hail turned back to rain. Hands in pockets I strode the river path, and let the rain strike me in the face. It ran down inside my coat, and I didn't care. I stayed out and walked through clearings and treeless patches on purpose, and it gave me pleasure because it was such a stupid thing to do.

I kept on up the valley until I stood at the edge of the little clearing occupied by the graveyard. Rain poured on it from low clouds just overhead, and in the dim light trees dripped and the ground splashed. I crossed the little section near the river where all the Japanese who had washed ashore had been buried. Their wooden crosses said *Unknown Chinese, Died 2045,* or whatever the date happened to be. Nat did a nice job carving letters and numbers.

Out in the clearing proper were our people. I squished from grave to grave, contemplating the names. Vincent Mariani, 1992–2038. A cancer got him. I remembered him playing hide and seek with Kathryn and Steve and me, when Kristen was a baby. Arnold Kalinski, 1970–2026. He had come to the valley with a disease, Tom said; Doc had been afraid we all would catch it, but we didn't. Jane Howard Fletcher, 2002–2030. My mother. Pneumonia. I pulled out some weeds from around the base of the cross, moved on. John Manley Morris, 1975–2029; Eveline Morris, 1989–2033. Cancer for him; she died of an infected cut in the palm of her hand. John Nicolin, Junior, 2016–2022. Fell in the river. Matthew Hamish, 2034. Malformed. Francesca Hamish, 2044. Same. And Jo pregnant again. Geoffrey Jones, 1995–2040; Ann Jones, died 2040. They both died when their house burned. Endeavor Simpson, 2039. Malformed. Elizabeth Costa, 2000–2035. Some disease, Doc never figured out what. Armando Thomas Costa, 2033–2047.

There were more, but I stopped my progress and stood at the foot of Mando's grave, looking at all the crosses. Even the Bible says something about men living their three score and ten, and that was ever so long ago. And here we were, cut short like frogs in a frost.

...22

B ut the old man lived.

I hardly believed it. I think everybody was surprised, even Tom. I know Doc was: "I couldn't believe it," he told me happily when I went up to see them on a cloudy morning. "I had to rub my eyes and pinch myself. I got up yesterday and there he was sitting at the kitchen table whining where's my breakfast, where's my breakfast. Of course his lungs had been clearing all week, but I wasn't sure that was going to be enough, to tell you the truth. But there he was bitching at me."

"In fact," Tom called from the bedroom, "where's the tea? Don't you respect a poor patient's requests anymore?"

"If you want it hot you'll shut up and *be* patient," Doc shouted back, rolling his eyes at me. "How about some bread with it?"

"Of course."

I went into the hospital and there he was sitting up in his bed, blinking like a bird. Shyly I said, "How are you?"

"Hungry."

"That's a good sign," Doc said from behind me. "Return of appetite, very good sign."

"Unless you got a cook like I do," said Tom.

Doc snorted. "Don't let him fool you, he's been bolting it in his usual style. Obviously he loves it. Pretty soon he'll want to stay here just for the food."

"When the eagle grins I will."

"So ungrateful!" Doc exclaimed. "And here I had to shove the food right down his face for the longest time. It got so I felt like a mama bird, I should have digested it all first for him I guess—"

"Oh that would have helped," Tom crowed, "eating vomit, yuck! Take this away, I've lost my appetite for good." He slurped the tea, cursed its heat.

"Well it was hard to get him to eat, I'll tell you. But now look at him go."

Doc watched with satisfaction as Tom tossed down chunks of bread in his old starved manner. When he was done he smiled his gap-toothed smile. His poor gums had taken a beating in his illness, but his eyes watched me with their old clear brown gaze. I felt my face stretched into a smile.

"Ah yes," Tom said. "There's nothing like a mutated freak immune system, I'll testify. I'm tough as a tiger. So tough! However, you'll excuse me if I take a little nap." He coughed once or twice, slid down under the covers and was out like one of his lighters snapping off.

So that was good. Tom stayed at Doc's for another couple of weeks, mostly to keep Doc company, I believe, as he was getting stronger by the day, and he surely wasn't fond of the hospital. And one day Rebel knocked on the door and asked me if I wanted to help move Tom and his stuff back to his house. I said sure, and we walked across the bridge talking. The sun was playing hide and seek among tall clouds, and coming down the path from Doc's were Kathryn and Gabby, Kristen and Del and Doc, laughing as Tom cavorted at the head of the parade. "Join the crowd," Tom called to us. "The young and the old, a natural alliance for a party, you bet." Kathryn gave me Tom's books, heavy in a burlap sack, and I threatened to throw them off the bridge as we crossed. Tom swung at me with his walking stick. We made a fine promenade up the other slope of the valley. I had never allowed myself to imagine this day; but there it was.

Once up to his house the old man got positively boisterous. With a dramatic flourish he kicked the door, but it stayed shut. "Great latch, see that?" He puffed at the dust on the table and chairs until the air was thick with it. There was a puddle on the floor, marking a new leak in the roof. Tom pulled his mouth down into a pouting frown. "This place has been poorly tended, very poorly tended. You maintenance crews are fired."

"Ho ho," said Kathryn, "now you're going to have to hire us back at wages to get any help." We opened all the windows and let the breeze draft through. Gabby and Del yanked some weeds, and Tom and Doc and I walked up the ridge trail to look at the beehives. Tom cursed at the sight, but they weren't that bad off. We cleaned up for a bit and went back down to the house on Doc's orders. Smoke billowed from the stove chimney, the big front window was scrubbed clean, and Gabby was balanced on the roof with hammer and nails and shingles, hunting for that leak and shouting for instructions from below. When we went in Kathryn was on a stool, thumping the underside of the roof with a broom. "That's it," Tom said, "bust that leak right out of there." Kathryn took a swing at him with the broom, overbalanced and leaped off the falling stool. Kristen dodged her with a yelp and quit dusting, Rebel took the kettle off the stove, and we gathered in the living room for some of Tom's pungent tea:

"Cheers," Tom said, holding his steaming mug high, and we raised ours and said back cheers, cheers.

That evening when I came home Pa said that John Nicolin had come by to ask why I wasn't fishing anymore. My share of the fish was our main source of food, and Pa was upset. So I started fishing again the next day, and after that I went fishing day in and day out, when the weather allowed. On the boats it was obvious the year was getting on. The sun cut across the sky lower and lower, and a cold current came in and stayed. Often in the afternoons dark clouds rolled off the sea over us. Wet hands stung with cold, and hauling net made them raw; teeth chattered, skin prickled with goosebumps. Hoarse shouts concerning the fishing were the only words exchanged, as men conserved their energy. The lack of small talk was fine by me. Winds chased us as we rowed back in the premature dusk. Under blue clouds the cliffs were brown, the hillsides were the green-black of the darkest pines, and the ocean was like iron. In all that gloom the yellow bonfires on the river flat blazed like beacons, it was a pleasure to round the bend in the river and see them. After getting the boats up against the cliff I huddled with the rest of the men around these fires until I was warm enough to go home. As the men warmed up, hands practically in the flames, the usual talk spilled out, but I never joined in. Even though I was happy the old man was well and home, the truth was that it didn't do much to cheer me. I felt bad a lot of the time, and empty always. When I was out fishing, struggling to make cold disobedient fingers hold on to the nets, I'd think of some crack Steve would have made in the situation, and I longed to hear him say it. And when the fishing was done, there was no gang up on the cliff waiting for me to join them. To avoid climbing the cliff and feeling their absence I often walked around the point of the cliff to the sea beach, and wandered that familiar expanse. The next day I'd take a deep breath, push myself into my boots and go fishing again. But I was just going through the motions.

It wasn't that the men on the boats were unfriendly, either. On the contrary—Marvin kept giving me the best of the fish to take home, and Rafael talked to me more than he ever had, joshing about the fish, describing his latest projects (which were interesting, I had to admit), inviting me by to see them. . . . They were all like that, even John from time to time. But none of it meant anything to me. My heart felt like my fingers did when the fishing was done, cold and disobedient, numb even next to the fire.

Somehow Tom figured this out. Maybe Rafael told him, maybe he saw it himself. One day after the fishing I pushed up the cliff path, feeling like I weighed as much as three of me, and there was Tom on the top.

I said, "You're getting around pretty well these days."

He ignored that and shook a knobby finger at me. "What's eating you, boy?"

I cringed. "Nothing, what do you mean?" I looked down at my bag of fish, but he grabbed my arm and pulled it.

"What's troubling you?"

"Ah, Tom." What could I say? He knew what it was. I said, "You know what it is. I gave you my word I wouldn't go up there, and I did."

"Ah, the hell with that."

"But look what happened! You were right. If I hadn't gone up there, none of it would have happened."

"How do you figure? They just would have gone without you."

I shook my head. "No. I could have stopped it." I explained to him what had happened, what my part had been—every bit of it. He nodded as I got each sentence out.

When I was done, he said, "Well, that's too bad." I was shivering, and he started up the river path with me. "But it's easy to be wise afterwards. Hindsight et cetera. You had no way of knowing what would happen."

"But I did! You told me. Besides, I felt it coming."

"Well, but listen, boy—" I looked at him, and he stopped talking. He frowned, and nodded once to acknowledge that it was right for me to reject such easy denials of my responsibility. We walked for a bit and then he snapped his fingers. "Have you started writing that book yet?"

"Oh for God's sake, Tom."

He shoved me in the chest, hard, so that I staggered out of the path and had to catch my footing. "Hey!"

"This time you might try listening to me."

That stung. I was round-eyed as he went on. "I don't know how much longer I can take this sniveling of yours. Mando's dead and you're partly to blame, yes. But it's going to fester in you not doing you a bit of good until you write it down, like I told you to."

"Ah, Tom—"

And he charged me, shoved me again! It was the kind of thing he used to indulge in only with Steve, and at the same time I was getting ready to punch him I was flattered. "Listen to me for once!" he cried, and suddenly I realized he was upset.

"I do listen to you. You know that."

"Well then do as I say. You write down your story. Everything you remember. The writing it down will make you understand it. And when you're done you'll have Mando's story down too. It's the best you can do for him now, do you see?"

I nodded, my throat tight. I cleared it. "I'll try."

"Don't try, just do it." I hopped away so he couldn't shove me again. "Ha! That's right—do it or face a beating. It's your assignment. You don't get any more schooling till you're done." He shook his fist at me, his arm a bundle of ligaments under skin, skinny as a rope. I almost had to laugh.

So I thought about it. I got the book down from the shelf, where it had been propping up a whetstone holder with only two legs. I looked through the blank pages. There were a lot of them. It was clear that I would never be able to fill all those pages. For one thing, it would take too long.

But I kept thinking about it. The emptiness still afflicted me. And as the days got shorter the nights in our shack got longer, and I found those memories were always in my mind. And the old man had been awful vehement about it. . . .

Before I even lifted a pencil, however, Kathryn declared it was time to harvest the corn. When she decided it was time, all of us who worked for her worked dawn to dusk, every day. Right after sunup I was out there with the others slashing at stalks with a scythe, then carrying stalks to the wains, pulling them over the bridge to the barrows and warehouses behind the Marianis', stripping off the leaves, pulling off the husked ears.

The bad summer storms made it a poor harvest. Soon we were done and it was time for the potatoes. Kathryn and I worked together on those. We hadn't spent much time together since the night at Doc's, and at first I was uncomfortable, but she didn't seem to blame me for anything. We just worked, and talked potatoes. Working with Kathryn was exhausting. In the mornings it seemed all right, because she worked so hard that she did more than her share, but the trouble was she kept going at that pace all day, so I got hooked into doing more than a day's work every day no matter how much I let her go at it. And harvesting potatoes is dirty, backbreaking labor, any way you do it.

When the harvesting was done we celebrated with a little drinking at the bathhouse. No one got overjoyed, because it was a bad harvest, but at least it was in. Kathryn sat beside me in the chairs on the bathhouse lawn to watch the sunset, and Rebel and Kristen joined us. At the other end of the yard Del and Gabby tossed a football back and forth. The flames of a bonfire were scarcely visible against the salmon sky. Rebel was upset about the potato harvest, even crying a little, and Kathryn talked a lot to cheer her up. "Pests are something you have to live with. Next year we'll try some of that stuff I got from the scavengers. Don't worry, it takes a long time to learn farming. It ain't like those spuds are your children, you know." Kristen smiled at that, the first smile I had seen from her since Mando died.

"Nobody will go hungry," I said.

"But I'm sick of fish already," Rebel said. The girls laughed at her.

"You couldn't tell by the way you eat them," Kristen said.

Kathryn sipped her brandy lazily. "What you been up to lately, Hank?"

"I've been writing in that book Tom gave me," I lied, to see how it sounded.

"Oh yeah? Are you writing about the valley?"

"Sure."

She raised her eyebrows. "About—"

"Yeah."

"Hmph." She stared into the fire. "Well, good. Maybe something good will come of this summer after all. But writing a whole book? It must be really hard."

"Oh it is," I assured her. "It's almost impossible, to tell you the truth. But I'm keeping at it."

All three of the girls looked impressed.

So I thought about it some more. I took the book off the shelf again, and kept it on the little stand beside my bed, next to the lamp and the cup and the book of Shakespeare's plays Tom had given me as a Christmas present. And I thought about it. When it had all begun, so long ago . . . those meetings with the gang, planning the summer. It wouldn't actually be grave-robbing, Steve had said, and I had snapped awake. . . .

So I started writing.

It was slow work. I didn't know what to say. Every night I quit for good. But the next night, or the one after, I would begin again. It's astonishing how much the memory will surrender when you squeeze it. Some nights when I finished writing I'd come to, surprised to be in our shack, sweat pouring down my ribs, my hand stiff, my fingers sore, my heart pounding with the emotions of time past. And away from the work, out on the boats heaving over the wild swells, I found myself thinking of what had happened, of ways to say it. I knew I was going to finish that book no matter what it took from me. I was hooked.

The evenings of the autumn took on a pattern. When the fish were on the tables I climbed the cliff. No gang to meet me. Steadfastly I ignored the ghost gathering and hiked home. There Pa greased the skillet and fried up some fish and onions, while I lit the lamp and set the table, and we made the usual small talk about what had happened during the day. When the fish was ready we sat down and Pa said grace, and we ate the fish and bread or potatoes. Afterwards we washed up and put things away and drank the rest of the dinner water, and brushed our teeth with scavenged toothbrushes. Then Pa sat at the sewing table, and I sat at the dinner table, and he stitched together clothes while I stitched together words, until we agreed it was time for bed.

I don't know how many nights went by like that. On rainy days it was the same, only all day long. Once a week or so I went up to Tom's. Since I promised I was writing he had relented and agreed to give me more lessons. He had me in

Othello, and I was pretty sure I knew why. I thought I had things to regret, but Othello! He was the only man in Shakespeare more fool than I.

> "... *O fool! fool! fool!*
> *When you shall these unlucky deeds relate,*
> *Speak of me as I am. Nothing extenuate,*
> *Nor set down aught in malice. Then must you speak*
> *Of one that lov'd not wisely, but too well;*
> *Of one not easily jealous, but, being wrought,*
> *Perplex'd in the extreme; of one whose hand*
> *(Like the base Indian) threw a pearl away*
> *Richer than all his tribe; of one whose subdu'd eyes,*
> *Albeit unused to the melting mood,*
> *Drop tears as fast as the Arabian's trees*
> *Their med'cinable gum. Set you down this ..."*

"So they had eucalyptus trees in Arabia," I remarked to Tom when I was done, and he laughed. And when upon leaving I demanded more pencils, he cackled and scrounged them up for me.

The days passed. The further I got in the story of the summer, the further away it was in time, and the less I understood it. Perplex'd in the extreme. One day it was raining and Pa and I both worked through the afternoon. We tried keeping the door open for light, but it was too cold even with the stove going, and rain kept blowing in when the wind shifted. We had to close it and light the lamps. Pa bent over the coat he was making. His hands moved as quickly as fingers snapping as he punched the holes, and yet the holes were perfectly spaced, in a line that could have been drawn by a straightedge. He slipped a thimble on his middle finger and stitched. Poke and pull, poke and pull ... cross-stitches appeared in perfect X's, the thread tugged so that the tension on it was constant. ... I had never paid such close attention to his sewing. His calloused fingers clicked along as nimbly as dancers. It was as if Pa's fingers were smarter than he was, I thought; and I felt bad for thinking it. Besides, it was wrong. Pa told his fingers what to do. They wouldn't do it alone. It was truer to say something like, Pa's sewing was the way in which he was smart. And in that way he was very smart indeed. I liked that way of saying it, and scribbled it down. Stitching thoughts. Meanwhile his deft fingers plied the needle, and it kept slipping through the pieces of cloth, pursing them together, pulling the thread taut, turning, piercing again. Pa sighed. "I don't see as well as I used to. I wish it were a sunny day. How I miss the summer."

I clicked my tongue. It was annoying to be sitting in a dark box in the middle of the day, using up good lamp oil. In fact it was worse than annoying. I felt my spirits plunge as I took stock of the bare insides of our shack. "Shit," I muttered with disgust.

"What's that?"

"I said, *shit.*"

"Why?"

"Ah. . . ." How could I explain it to him, without making him feel bad too? He accepted our degraded conditions without a thought, always had. I shook my head. He peered at me curiously.

Suddenly I had an idea. I jerked in my chair. "What?" said Pa, watching me.

"I got an idea." I got my boots on, put on my coat.

"It's raining pretty hard," Pa said dubiously.

"I won't go far."

"Okay. Be careful?"

I turned from the open door. "Yeah I will. I'll be back soon, keep sewing."

I crossed the bridge and went up Basilone to the Shankses', and kicked around in the piles of burnt wood. Sure enough, buried in soggy ash inside the north wall was a rectangular piece of glass, as wide as my outstretched arms, and nearly that tall. One of their many windows. A corner of it was very wavy near the bottom, and a little pocked—it looked like it had melted some in the fire—but I didn't care. I crowed at the sky, licked down raindrops, and very carefully returned to the valley, window held before me, dripping. Like a car's windshield maybe. I stopped and knocked on the door of Rafael's shop. He was at home, black with grease and hammering like Vulcan. "Rafe, will you help me put this window in the side of our place?"

"Sure," he said, and looked out at the rain. "You want to do it now?"

"Well . . ."

"Let's wait for a good day. We'll have to be tramping in and out a lot."

Reluctantly I agreed.

"I always wondered why you didn't put a window in that place," he remarked.

"Never had any glass!" I said happily, and was off. And two days later we had a window in our south wall, and the light streamed in over everything, turning every dust mote to silver. There was a lot of dust, too.

We even had good windowsills, thanks to Rafael. He peered at the wavy part of the bottom. "Yep, almost melted this one down, looks like." He nodded his approval and left, toting his tools over his shoulder, whistling. Pa and I hopped around the house, cleaning up and staring out, going outside to stare in.

"This is wonderful," Pa said with a blissful smile. "Henry, that was one great idea you had. I can always count on you for the good ideas."

We shook on it. I felt the strength in his right hand, and it sent a glow right through me. You got to have your father's approval. I kept pumping his hand up and down till he started to laugh.

It made me think of Steve. He never had that approval, never would have had it. It must have been like walking around with a thorn in your shoe. I feel it in my mind's foot, Horatio. I began to think that I understood him more, at the same time I felt like I was losing him—the real, immediate Steve, I mean. I could only recall his face well in dreams, when it came back to me perfectly. And it was hard to get him down right in the book; the way he could make you laugh, make you sure you were really living. I sat down to work on it, under the light of our new window. "I'll have to sew us some good curtains," Pa said, eyeing the window thoughtfully, measuring it in his mind.

A while after that I joined the small group going to the last swap meet of the year. Winter swap meets weren't much like the summer ones; there were fewer people there, and less stuff being traded. This time it was drizzling steadily, and everyone there was anxious to get their trading done and go home. Debates over prices quickly turned into arguments, and sometimes fights. The sheriffs had their hands full. Time after time I heard one of them bellowing, "Just make your deal and move on! Come on, what's the fuss!"

I hurried from canopy to canopy, and in the shelter from the rain did my best to trade for some cloth or old clothing for Pa. All I had to offer were some abalone and a couple of baskets, and it was tough trading.

One of the scavenger camps had gotten a fire going by pouring some gas over the wet wood, and a lot of folks congregated under the canopy. I joined them, and after a bit I finally found a scavenger woman willing to trade a pile of ragged clothing for what I had.

After we had counted it out piece for piece she said, "I hear you Onofreans really did it to that crew from down south."

"What's this?" I said, jerking slightly.

She laughed, revealing a mouthful of busted brown stumps, and drank from a jar. "Don't play simpleton with me, grubber."

"I'm not," I said. She offered me the jar but I shook my head. "What's this we're supposed to have done to the San Diegans?"

"Ha! Supposed to done. See how that washes with them when they come asking why you killed their mayor."

I felt the cold of that dim afternoon shiver into me, and I went from a crouch to sitting on my butt. I took the jar from her and drank some sour corn mash. "Come on, tell me what you've heard," I said.

"Well," she said, happy to gossip, "the back country folks say you all took that mayor and his men right up into a Jap ambush."

I nodded so she'd go on.

"Ah ha! Now he fesses up. So most of them were killed, including that mayor. And they're pretty hot about it. If they weren't fighting among themselves so hard to see who takes his place, they'd likely be on you pretty hard. But every man in San Diego wants to be mayor now, or so the back country folk say, and I believe them. Apparently things down there are wild these days."

I took another gulp of her terrible liquor. It went to my stomach like a big lead sinker. Around us drizzle misted down through the trees, and bigger drops fell from the edge of the canopy.

"Say, grubber, you okay?"

"Yeah yeah." I bundled up the rags, thanked her and left, in a hurry to get back to Onofre and give Tom the news.

Another rainy afternoon I sat in Rafael's workshop, relaxing. I had told Tom what I had heard at the swap meet, and he had told John Nicolin and Rafael, and none of them had seemed overly concerned, which was a relief to me. Now the matter was out of my hands, and I was just passing the time. Kristen and Rebel sat crosslegged before Rafael's set of double windows, making baskets and gossiping. Rafael sat on a short stool and tinkered with a battery. Tools and machine parts littered the stained floor, and around us stood products of Rafael's invention and industry: pipes to carry a stove's heat to another room, a small kiln, an electric generator connected to a bicycle on blocks, and so on.

"The fluids go bad," Rafael said, answering a question of mine. "All the batteries that were full on the day are long gone. But lucky for us, there were some sitting empty in warehouses. There's no use for them, so it's easy to trade for one. Some scavengers I know use batteries, and they'll bring the acids to the meet if I ask them. Only a few people want them, so I get a good deal."

"And that's how you got your cart out there running?"

"That's right. No use for it, though. Not usually."

We sat quiet for a while, remembering. "So you heard us that night?" I asked.

"Not at first. I was on Basilone and I saw the lights. Then I heard the shooting."

After a bit I shook my head to clear it, and changed the subject. "What about a radio, Rafe? Have you ever tried to repair one of those?"

"No."

"How come?"

"I don't know. They're too complicated, I guess. And the scavengers ask a lot for them, and they always look an awful wreck."

"So does most of the stuff you bring back."

"I guess."

I said, "You could read how they work in a manual, couldn't you?"

"I don't read much, Hank, you know that."

"But we could help you read. I'd read, and you could figure out what it meant."

"Maybe so. But we'd have to have a radio, and lots of parts, and I still wouldn't be sure I could do anything with them."

"But you would be up for trying?"

"Oh sure, sure." He laughed. "You run across a silver mine out there on that beach of yours?"

I blushed. "Nah."

Under the window Kristen and Rebel worked. The baskets they were weaving were made of old brown torrey pine needles, soaked in water so they were flexible again. Rebel took a needle and carefully bunched together the five individual slices of it, so that they made a neat cylinder. Then she curled the needle till it made a flat little wheel, and knotted several pieces of fishing line to it, splaying them out like spokes. Another pine needle was neatened up and tied around the outside of the first one. The first several needles were tied outside the ones before them, to make a flat bottom. It took two needles to make it around the circumference, then three. After that the nubs were set directly on top of each other, and the sides of the basket began to appear.

I picked up a finished basket and inspected it while Rebel continued to whip the line around the needles. The basket was solid. Each needle looked like a miniature piece of rope, the five splits fit together so well. The four rows of nubs studding the sides of this particular basket rose in S shapes, showing just how much the basket bulged out and then back in. Such patience, arranging all the needles! Such skill, whipping all of them into place! I whapped the basket on the floor and it rebounded nicely, showing its flex and strength. Watching Rebel coax the line between two needles and through a complicated little loop of line waiting for it, it occurred to me that I had a task somewhat like hers. When I penciled in my book, I tied together words like she tied together pine needles, hoping to make a certain shape with them. Briefly I wished I could make a book as neat and solid and beautiful as the basket Rebel wove. But it was beyond hope.

Rebel looked up and saw me watching her and laughed. "Why are you watching me?"

"It looks hard."

"No. Maybe the first time, but after that—no."

Another day the clouds would have given us a few hours for fishing, but the seas were running so high it was impossible to get the boats out. When I was done writing I walked to the cliffs, and there was the old man, sitting on a shelf under the cliff's lip, where he was protected from the wind.

"Hey!" I greeted him. "What you doing down here?"

"Looking at the waves, of course, like any other sensible person."

"So you think it takes sense to come down here and gawk at waves, eh?" I sat beside him.

"Sense or sensibility, yuk yuk."

"I don't get it."

"Never mind. Look at that one!"

The swells were surging up from the south, breaking in giant walls that extended from one end of the beach to the other. The swells were visible far out to sea; I could pick one out halfway to the horizon and follow it all the way in. Near the end they built up taller and taller, until they were gray cliffs rushing in to meet our tan one. A man standing at the foamy foot of one of those giants would have looked like a doll. When the towering top of a wave pitched out and the whole thing rolled over behind it, spray exploded in the air higher than the wave had stood, with a crack and a boom that distinctly vibrated the cliff under us. The tortured water dashed over itself in a boiling race to the beach. There floods of white water swept up the sand, then sucked back to crash into the next advance. Only a strip of sand against the cliff was left dry; it would have been worth your life to walk the beach that day. Tom and I sat in a haze of white salt mist, and we had to talk over the explosive roar of the surf. "Look at that one!" Tom shouted again and again. "Look at that one! That one must be thirty-five feet tall, I swear."

Out beyond the swells the ocean stretched to the haze-fuzzed horizon. A low sheet of bumpy white and gray clouds covered the sky, barely clearing the hills behind us. Breaks in the clouds were marked by bright patches in the leaden surface of the water, like the trail of a drunken scavenger with a hole in his pocket, scattering silver coins from here to the edge of the world. There was something about it all—the presence of that expanse of water, the size of it, the power of the waves—that made me stand back up and pace the cliff behind Tom's back—stop and stare as a particularly monstrous sea cliff collapsed— shake my head in wonder or dismay, pace and turn again, slapping my thighs and trying to think of a way to say it, to Tom or anybody. I failed. The world pours in and overflows the heart till speech is useless, and that's a fact. I wish I could speak better. I started to say things—spoke syllables and choked off the words—strode back and forth, getting more and more agitated as I tried to think exactly what it was I felt, and how I could then say that.

It was impossible, and if I had really held out for precision I reckon I would have stood there staring at those sea avalanches all day, mute and amazed. But my mind shifted to another mystery. I slapped my hand to my thigh and Tom glanced at me curiously. I blurted out, "Tom, why *did* you tell us all those lies about America?"

He cleared his throat. "Harumph-hmm. Who says I lied?"

I stood before him and stared.

"All right." He patted the sand beside him, but I refused to sit. "It was part of your history lessons. If your generation forgets the history of this country you'll have no direction. You'll have nothing to work back to. See, there was a lot about the old time we need to remember, that we have to get back."

"You made it seem like it was the golden age. Like we're just existing in the ruins."

"Well . . . in a lot of ways that's true. It's best to know it—"

I snapped my fingers at him. "But no! No! You also said the old time was awful. That we live better lives now than they ever did. That was what you *said*, when you argued with Doc and Leonard at the meets, and sometimes when you talked with us too. You told us that."

"Well," he admitted uneasily, "there's truth to that too. I was trying to tell you the way it was. I didn't lie—not much, I mean, and not about important things. Just once in a while to give you an idea what it was really like, what it felt like."

"But you told us two different things," I said. "Two contradictory things. Onofre was primitive and degraded, but we weren't to want for the old time to come back either, because it was evil. We didn't have anything left that was ours, that we could be proud of. You confused us!"

Abruptly he looked past me to the sea. "All right," he said. "Maybe I did. Maybe I made a mistake." His voice grew querulous: "I ain't some kind of great wise man, boy. I'm just another fool like you."

Awkwardly I turned and paced around a bit more. He didn't have any good reason for lying to us like he did. He had done it for fun. To make the stories sound better. To entertain himself.

I went over and plopped down beside him. We watched the sandbars plow a few more swells to mush. It looked like the ocean wanted to wash the whole valley away. Tom threw a few pebbles down at the beach. Gloomily he sighed.

"You know where I'd like to be when I die?" he said.

"No."

"I'd like to be on top of Mount Whitney."

"What?"

"Yeah. When I feel the end coming I'd like to hike inland and up Three-Ninety-Five, and then up to the top of Mount Whitney. It's just a walk to the top, but it's the tallest mountain in the United States. The continental states, excuse me. There's a little stone hut up there, and I could stay in that and watch the world till the end. Like the old Indians did."

"Sounds like a nice way to go." I didn't know what else to say. I looked at him—really looked at him, I mean. It was funny, but now that I knew he was eighty and not a hundred and five, he looked older. Of course his illness had wasted him some. But I think it was mainly because living a hundred and five years was in the nature of a miracle, which could be extended indefinitely, while eighty was just old. He was an old man, a strange old man, that was all, and now I could see it. I was more impressed he had made it to eighty than I ever used to be that he had made it to one hundred and five. And that felt right.

So he was old, he would die soon. Or make his try for Whitney. One day I would go up the hill and the house would be empty. Maybe there would be a note on the table saying "Gone to Whitney." More likely not. But I would know. I would have to imagine his progress from there. Would he even make it forty miles north, to his birthplace in Orange?

"You can't take off at this time of year," I said. "There'll be snow and ice and all. You'll have to wait."

"I'm not in any rush."

We laughed, and the moment passed. I began thinking about our own disastrous trip into Orange County. "I can't believe we did something that stupid," I said, voice shaking with anger and distress.

"It was stupid," he agreed. "You kids had the excuse of youth and bad teaching, but the Mayor and his men, why they were damned fools."

"But we can't give up," I said, pounding the sandstone, "we can't just roll over and lie there like we're dead."

"That's true." He considered it. "And maybe securing the land from intrusion is the first step."

I shook my head. "It can't be done. Not with what they have and what we have."

"Well? I thought you said we don't want to play possum?"

"No, right." I pulled my feet up from the cliffside so I could squat and rock back and forth. "I'm saying we've got to figure out some other way to resist, some way that will work. We either do something that works, or wait until we can. None of this shit in between. What I was thinking of was that all the towns that come to the swap meet, if they worked together, might be able to sail over and *surprise* Catalina. Take it over for a time."

Tom whistled his weak, toothless whistle.

"For a while, I mean," I said. The idea had come to me recently, and I was excited by it. "With the radio equipment there we could tell the whole world we're here, and we don't like being quarantined."

"You think big."

"But it's not impossible. Not someday, anyway, when we know more about Catalina."

"It might not make any difference, you know. Broadcasting to the world, I mean. The world might be one big Finland now, and if it is, all they're going to be able to do is say, we hear you brother. We're in the same boat. And then the Russians would sweep down on us."

"But it's worth a try," I insisted. "Like you say, we don't really know what's going on in the world. And we won't until we try something like this."

He shook his head, looked at me. "That would cost a lot of lives, you know. Lives like Mando's—people who could have lived their full span to make things better in our new towns."

"Their full spans," I said scornfully. But he had jolted me, nevertheless. He had reminded me how grand military plans like mine translated into chaos and pain and meaningless death. So in an instant I was all uncertain again, and my bold idea struck me as stupidity compounded by size. Tom must have read this on my face, because he chuckled, and put his arm around my shoulders.

"Don't fret about it, Henry. We're Americans; it ain't been clear what we're supposed to do for a long, long time."

One more white sea cliff smashed to spray and charged toward us. One more plan crumbled and swept away. "I guess not," I said morosely. "Not since Shakespeare's time, eh?"

"Harumph-*hmm!*" He cleared his throat two or three more times, let his arm fall, shuffled down the cliff away from me a bit. "Um, by the way," he said, looking anxiously at me, "while we're on the subject of history lessons, and, um, lies, I should make a correction. Well! Um . . . Shakespeare wasn't an American."

"Oh no," I breathed. "You're kidding."

"No. Um—"

"But what about England?"

"Well, it wasn't the leader of the first thirteen states."

"But you showed me on a map!"

"That was Martha's Vineyard, I'm afraid."

I felt my mouth hanging open, and I snapped it shut. Tom was kicking his heels uncomfortably. He looked about as unhappy as I had ever seen him, and he wouldn't meet my eye. Gazing beyond me he gestured, with an expression of relief.

"Looks like John, doesn't it?"

I looked. Along the cliff edge above Concrete Bay I spotted a squat figure striding, hands in pockets. It was John Nicolin all right. He walked fast in our direction, looking out to sea. On the days when we were kept from going out, when he wasn't fixing the boats he was on the cliffs, most of the time, and never more than when the weather was good and we were kept in by the swell. Then he seemed particularly affronted, and he paced the cliff grimly watching the waves, acting irritable with anyone unfortunate enough to have business with him. The swell was going to keep us off the water for two days at least, maybe four, but he stared at the steaming white walls as if searching for a seam or a riptide that might offer a way outside. As he approached us his pantlegs flapped and his salt-and-pepper locks blew back over his shoulder like a mane. When he looked our way and noticed us he hesitated, then kept coming at his usual pace. Tom raised a hand and waved, so he was obliged to acknowledge us.

When he stopped several feet away, hands still in pockets, we all nodded and mumbled hellos. He came a few steps closer. "Glad to see you're doing better," he said to Tom in an offhand way.

"Thanks. I'm feeling fine. Good to be up and around." Tom seemed as uncomfortable as John. "Magnificent day, ain't it?"

John shrugged. "I don't like the swell."

A long pause. John shuffled one foot, as if he might be about to walk on. "I haven't seen you in the last couple days," Tom said. "I went by your house to say hello, and Mrs. N. said you were gone."

"That's right," John said. He crouched beside us, elbow on knee. "I wanted to talk to you about that. Henry, you too. I went down to take a look at those railroad tracks the San Diegans have been using."

Tom's scraggly eyebrows climbed his forehead. "How come?"

"Well, from what Gabby Mendez says, it appears they used our boys as a cover for their retreat after the ambush. And now it turns out that mayor got killed. I went and asked some of my Pendleton friends about it, and they say it's true. They say there's a real fight going on right now down there, between three or four groups who want the power that the mayor had. That in itself sounds bad, and if the wrong group ends up on top, we could be in trouble. So Rafe and I were thinking that the railroad tracks should be wrecked for good. I went down to look at that first river crossing, and it's pretty clear Rafe could destroy the pilings with the explosives he's got. And he says he can blast the track every hundred yards or so, easy."

"Wow," said Tom.

John nodded. "It's drastic, but I think it's the right move. If you ask me, those folks down there are crazy. Anyway, I wanted to know what you thought of the idea. I was going to just get Rafe and go do it, but . . ."

Tom cleared his throat, said, "You don't want to call a meeting about it?"

"I guess. But first I want to know what some of you think."

"I think it's a good idea," Tom said. "If they think we were in on the ambush, and if that patriot crowd gets control . . . yeah, it's a good idea."

John nodded, looking satisfied. "And you, Henry?"

That took me aback. "I guess. We might want that track working for us someday. But we've got to worry about keeping them at a distance first. So I'm for it."

"Good," said John. "We should probably try to talk with them at the swap meet, if we get a chance. And warn the others about them, too."

"Wait a bit, here," Tom said. "You still have to get a meeting together, and get the vote. If we start deciding things like the boys here did, we'll end up like the San Diegans."

"True," John said.

I felt myself blushing. John glanced at me and said, "I'm not blaming you."

I scratched the sandstone with a pebble. "You should. I'm as much to blame as anyone."

"No." He straightened up, chewed his lower lip. "That was Steve's plan; I can see his mark on it everywhere." His voice tensed, pitched higher. "That boy wanted everything his way right from the start. Right out of his ma. How he cried if we didn't jump to his wishes!" He shrugged it off, looked at me sullenly. "I suppose you think I'm to blame. That I drove him off."

I shook my head, though part of me had been thinking that. And it was true, in a way. But not entirely. I couldn't make it clear, even to myself.

John shifted his gaze to Tom, but Tom only shrugged. "I don't know, John, I really don't. People are what they are, eh? Who made Henry here want to read books? None of us. And who made Kathryn want to grow corn and make bread? None of us. And who made Steve want to see the world out there? No one. They were born with it."

"Mm," John said, mouth tight. He wasn't convinced, even if it absolved him, even if he had been saying the same thing a second ago. John was always going to believe his own actions had effects. And with his own son, who'd spent a lifetime in his care . . . I could read his face thinking of that as clear as you can read the face of a babe. A wave of pain crossed his features, and he shook himself, and with a somber click of tongue against teeth reminded himself that we were here. He closed up. "Well, it's past," he said. "I'm not much of a one for philosophy, you know that."

So the matter was closed. I thought about how this conversation would have taken place at the ovens among the women: the chewing over every detail of event and motivation, the arguing it out, the crying and all; and I almost laughed. We men were a pretty tight-lipped crowd when it came to important things. John was walking in a circle like I had earlier, and quickly his nervous striding got to us, so that Tom and I stood to stretch out. Pretty soon the three of us were meandering in place like gulls, hands in pockets, observing the swells and pointing out to each other any particularly big ones.

Looking back at the valley, now filled with trees yellow among the evergreens,

I stopped pacing and said, "What we need is a radio. Like the one we saw in San Diego. A working radio. Those things can hear other radios from hundreds of miles away, right?"

Tom said, "Some of them can, yes." He and John stopped walking to listen to me.

"If we had one of them we could listen to the Japanese ships. Even if we didn't understand them we'd know they were there. And we could listen to Catalina, maybe, and maybe other parts of the country, other towns."

"The big radios will receive and transmit halfway around the world," Tom commented.

"Or a long way, anyway," I corrected him. He grinned. "It would give us ears, don't you see, and after that we could begin to figure out what's going on out there."

"I would love to have something like that," John admitted. "I don't know how we'd get one, though," he added dubiously.

"I talked to Rafael about it," I said. "He told me that the scavengers have radios and radio parts at the swap meets all the time. He doesn't know anything about radios right now, but he does think he can generate the power to run one."

"He does?" Tom said.

"Yeah. He's been working on batteries a lot. I told him we'd get him a radio manual and help him read it, and give him stuff to trade for radio parts at the swap meets this summer, and he was all excited by the idea."

John and Tom looked at each other, sharing something I couldn't read. John nodded. "We should do that. We can't trade fish for this kind of stuff, of course, but we can find something—shellfish, maybe, or those baskets."

Another huge set rolled in, washing all the way to the base of the cliff, and our attention was forced back to the waves. "Those must be thirty-five feet high at least," Tom repeated.

"You think so?" said John. "I thought this cliff was only forty feet."

"Forty feet above the beach, but those wave troughs are lower. And the crests are nearly as high as we are!" It was true.

John said that he wanted to get the boats out on days like this.

"So you *were* thinking about that when you walked down here," I said.

"Sure. See, follow the river current at high tide—"

"No way!" Tom cried.

"Look at the turbulance in the rivermouth," I pointed out. "Even those broken waves must be ten or fifteen feet tall."

"You'd be capsized and drowned by the first wave that hit you," Tom said.

"Hmm," said John reluctantly—with perhaps a gleam of humor in his eye. "You may be right."

We meandered around our shelf again, talked about currents and the possibility of a mild winter. Out to sea shafts of light still speared through the clouds to gild the lined ocean surface. Tom pointed out at them. "What you should try doing is fishing the whales again. They're due through soon."

John and I groaned.

"No, really, you guys gave up on that one too fast. You either harpooned an extra tough one, or Rafael didn't put the harpoon in a place that would do the beast much harm."

John said, "Easy to say, but he's never going to be able to place the harpoon right where he wants to."

"No, that's not what I'm saying, it's just that most of the time a harpoon will do them more damage, and they won't be able to dive so deep."

"If that's true," I said, "and if we added more rope to the end of the line—"

"There's not room for it in our boats," John told me.

But I was remembering the time Steve and I had discussed it. "We could tie the bottom end to line that runs over to a tub in another boat, and have twice as much."

"That's true," John said, cocking his head.

"If we were to get into the whale business we could really make a killing at the swap meet," said Tom. "We'd have oil to spare, and animal feed, and tons of meat."

"If we could keep it from going bad," John said. But he liked the idea; what was it but fishing, after all? "Could you really get the line set so that it went from boat to boat?"

"Easy!" Tom said. He knelt and picked up a pebble to draw in the dirt. He started to scratch a plan, and John crouched at his side. I looked out at the horizon, and this is what I saw: three sunbeams standing like thick white pillars, slanting each its own way, measuring the distance between the gray clouds and the gray sea.

... chapter the last

As the year fell away to its death the storms came more frequently, until every week or so one barreled in over the whitecaps and thrashed us, leaving the valley tattered and the sea a foamy pale brown from all the dirt sluiced into it. When we did get the boats out the fishing was miserably cold, and we didn't catch much. Most days I spent at the table under the window, where I read or wrote or watched black clouds bluster in. The clouds were the vanguard; after them a smack of the wind's hand, and maybe a low rumble of thunder, announced the arrival of the storm. Raindrops slid down the windowpane in a thousand tributaries that met and divided again as they wandered down the glass. The roof ticked or tapped or drummed under the onslaught. Behind me Pa labored away on his new sewing machine, and its *rn, rn, rn rn rnnnn!* rebuked my idleness, sometimes so successfully that I buckled down and wrote a sentence or two. But it was hard going, and there were lots of hours when I was content to chew my pencils and think about it, and watch it rain.

The first storm of December, it snowed. It was a real pleasure to sit in our warm house and look out the window at the flakes drifting silently through the trees. Pa looked over my shoulder. "It's going to be a hard winter." I didn't agree. We had enough food, even if it was fish, and more firewood was being dried in the bathhouse every day. After all the rain I was happy to see snow just for the way it looked as it fell, so slow it didn't seem real. Then to run outside, and hop white drifts, and slap snowballs together to throw at neighbors. . . . I loved the snow. The day after those storms the sun came out under a high pale, and the snow melted before midday. But the next storm brought more snow, and colder air, and a thicker tail of high clouds, and it was four days before the harsh sun came out and the white dusting melted and ran into the river. That got to be the pattern: valley first white-green under black skies, then black-green under white skies. Week by week it got colder.

Week by week my story got harder to write. I got lost in it—I stopped believing it—I wrote chapters and had to take a walk over the soggy leaf carpets in the woods, distressed and angry at myself. Still, I wrote it. The solstice passed, and Christmas passed, and New Year's passed, and I went to all the parties, but it was like I was in fog, and afterward I couldn't remember who I had talked to or what I had said. The book was the only thing for me—and yet it was so hard! Sometimes I wore out pencils faster biting than writing.

But the day came when the tale was on the page, pretty much. All the action done, Mando and Steve gone. I stopped then, and took one still day to read what I had said. It made me so mad I damn near burned the thing. Here all those things had *happened,* they had changed us for life, and yet the sorry string of words sitting on the table didn't hold even a fraction of the way it had looked, the way I *felt* about it.

I went out for a walk to try and recover. A few tall white clouds sailed above like galleons, but mostly it was a sunny day, and dead still, though the air had a bite to it. Wet snow lay on everything. Cakes of it were balanced on every branch, dripping and sparking the various colors of the rainbow. On the ground the snow melted to big clear grains that beaded the white blanket. Suncones melted through to tufts of grass, and snowbridges over the streams filling the paths collapsed, leaving dirty chunks of ice in the mud, and snow hummocks to each side, black with pine needles. I walked between these hummocks and over the remaining bridges (the ones in shadow) to the cliffs, thumping my boots in puddles and knocking snowcakes on branches into spray.

Out on the cliff overlooking the river I sat down. No swell whatsoever: tiny waves lapped the strand as if the whole ocean was shifting a hand's breadth up and down. There wasn't any snow left on the beach, but it was wet and bedraggled, with blue-and-white puddles dotting it everywhere. The scattered galleon clouds didn't hinder the sun much, but gave its light a tint so that the long stretch of cliff was the color of ironwood bark. No swell, still air, the ocean like a plate of blue glass, the galleons hovering over it, holding their positions.

I noticed something I had never seen before. On the flat blue sea were perfect reflections of the tall clouds, clearly shaped so you could tell they were upside down. It looked like they were floating underwater, in a dark blue sky. "Will you look at that," I said, and stood. Ever so slowly the clouds drifted onshore over the valley, and their upside-down twins disappeared under the beach. I stayed and watched that all afternoon, feeling like oceans of clouds were filling me.

In the winter the scavengers hole up in some of the big, shattered old houses—a dozen or more of them to a house, like dens of foxes. At night they use the neighboring houses for firewood, and light big bonfires in the front yards, and they drink and dance to old music, and fight and howl and throw jewelry at the stars and into the snow. A solitary man, gliding over the drifts on long snowshoes, can move amongst these bright noisy settlements without trouble. He can crouch out in the trees like a wolf, and watch them cavort in their colored down jackets for as long as he likes. Their summer haunts are open to his inspection. And there are books up there, yes, lots of books. The scavengers like the little fat one with the orange sun on the cover, but many more lie unattended in the ruins—whole libraries, sometimes. A man can load himself down till his snowshoes sink knee-deep, and then go back to his own country, a scavenger of a different sort.

At the end of January a particularly violent storm undermined the side of the Mendezes' garden shed (they called it a barn), and as soon as the rain stopped all the immediate neighbors—the Marianis, the Simpsons, and Pa and I, with Rafael called in for advice—got out to give them a hand in shoring up that wall. The Mendez garden was as cold and muddy as the ocean floor, and there wasn't a patch of solid ground to set beams on, to prop up the wall while we worked under it. Eventually Rafael got us to tie the shed to the big oak on the other side of it. "I hope the framing was nailed together good," Rafael joked when we were back under the sagging wall. Kathryn and I worked one side, Gabby and Del dug out the other, and we practically drowned in mud. By the time we got beams set crosswise under the wall for foundations, all four families were ready for the bathhouse. Rafael had gone before us, so when we got there the fire was blazing and the water steamed. We stripped and hopped in the dirt bath and hooted with glee.

"My suggestion is you leave that rope there," Rafael said to old Mendez. "That way you'll never have to find out if those beams will hold it up or not." Mendez wasn't amused.

I rolled over into the clean bath and floated with him and Mrs. Mariani and the others. Kathryn and I sat on one of the wood islands and talked. She asked me if I was still writing. I told her I was nearly done, but that I'd stopped because it was so bad.

"You're no judge of that," she said. "Just finish it."

"I suppose I will."

We talked about the storms, the snow, the condition of the fields (they were under tarps or cover crops for the winter), the swells battering the beach, food. "I wonder how Doc is doing," I said.

"Tom goes up there a lot. They're getting to be like brothers."

"Good."

Kathryn shook her head. "Even so—Doc's busted, you know." She looked at me. "He won't last long."

"Ah." I didn't know what to say. After a long pause looking at the swirling water, I said, "Do you ever think about Steve?"

"Sure." She eyed me. "Don't you?"

"Yeah. But I have to, with this book."

She shrugged. "You would book or not, if you're like me. But it's past, Henry. That's all it is—the past."

I told her about the day when the sea had been so glassy that it mirrored the clouds, and she sat back and laughed. "It sounds wonderful."

"I don't know when I've ever seen anything so pretty."

She reached over and ran a finger down the backside of my arm. I arched my eyebrows, slipped off the seat to otter into her. She caught me by the hair. "Henry," she laughed, and held my head under, giving me more immediate matters to think about, like drowning. I came up spluttering. She laughed again and gestured at the friends around us. "Well?" I said, and went under for a submerged approach, but she stood and sloshed away, leading me to the wall seats where the others were. After that we talked with Gabby and Kristen, and later old Mendez, who thanked us for our help with his barn.

But when Rafael declared the day's allotment of wood was burned, and we got out of the baths and dried off, and dressed, I looked around the room, and there was Kathryn looking at me from the door. I followed her out. The evening air chilled my head and hands instantly. There was Kathryn, on the path between two trees. I caught up with her and took her in a hug. We kissed. There are kisses that have a whole future in them; I learned that then. When we were done her mother and sisters were chattering out the bathhouse door. I let her go. She looked surprised, thoughtful, pleased. If it had been summer—but it was winter, there was snow everywhere. And summer was coming. She smiled at me, and with a touch walked off to join them, looking back once to meet my gaze. When she was out of sight I walked home through the dusk with a whole new idea in mind.

Some afternoons I just sat before the window and looked at the book—left it closed, in the middle of the table, and stared at it. One of these times the snowflakes were drifting down through the trees as slowly as tufts of dandelion, and every branch and needle was tipped with new white. Into this vision tramped a figure on snowshoes, wearing furs. He had a pole in each hand to help his balance, and as he brushed between trees he sent little avalanches onto his head and down his back. The old man, out trapping, I thought. But he hiked right up to the window and waved.

I slipped on my shoes and went outside. It was cold. "Henry!" Tom called.

"What's up?" I said as I rounded our house.

"I was out checking my traps, and I ran into Neville Cranston, an old friend of mine. He summers in San Diego and winters in Hemet, and he was on his way over to Hemet, because he got a late start this year."

"That's too bad," I said politely.

"No, listen! He just left San Diego, didn't you hear me? And you know what he told me? He told me that the new mayor down there is Frederick Lee!"

"Say what?"

The new mayor of San Diego is *Lee*. Neville said that Lee was always in trouble with that Danforth, because he wouldn't go along with any of Danforth's war plans, you know."

"So that's why we stopped seeing him."

"Exactly. Well, apparently there were a lot of people down there who were behind Lee, but there wasn't anything they could do about it while Danforth and his men had all the guns. Neville said this whole fall has been a dog fight down there, but a couple months ago Lee's supporters forced an election, and Lee won."

"Well, what do you know." We stared at each other. "That's good news, isn't it."

He nodded. "You bet it's good news."

"Too bad we blew up those train tracks."

"I don't know if I'd go *that* far, but it is good news, no doubt about it. Well"— he waved one of his poles overhead—"lousy weather to be standing around chattering in. I'm off." And with a little whistle he snowshoed off through the trees, leaving a trail of deep tracks. And I knew I could finish.

The book lay on the table. One night (February the 23rd) the full moon was up. I went to bed without looking at the book, but I couldn't sleep. I kept thinking of it, and talking to the pages in my mind. I heard a voice inside me that said it all far better than I ever could: this voice rattled off long imaginary passages, telling it all in the greatest detail and with the utmost eloquence, bringing it back just as lived. I heard the rhythms of it as sure as the rhythms of Pa's snores, and it put an ache in me it was so beautiful. I thought, It's some poet's ghost come to visit me.

Eventually it drove me to get up and finish the thing off. Our house was cold, the fire in the stove was down to filmy gray coals. I put on pants and socks, and a thick shirt and a blanket over my shoulders. Moonlight poured in the window like a silver bar, turning all the bare wood furnishings into almost living things. It was a light so strong I could write by it. I sat at the table under the window and wrote as fast as my hand would move, though what I wrote was nothing like the voice I had heard when I was lying down. Not a chance.

Most of the night passed. My left hand got sore and crampy from writing, and I was restless. The moon was dipping into the trees, obscuring my light. I decided to go for a walk. I put on my boots and my heavy coat, and shoved the book and some pencils in the coat's big pocket.

Outside it was colder yet. The dew on the grass sparkled where moonlight fell on it. On the river path I stopped to look back up the valley, which receded through the thick air in patchy blacks and whites. There wasn't a trace of wind, and it was so still and quiet that I could hear the snow melting everywhere around me, dripping and plopping and filling my ears with a liquid music, a forest water choir accompanying me as I slushed down the path, hands in my big coat pockets. River black between salt-and-pepper trees.

On the cliff path I had to step careful, because the steps were half slush. Down on the beach the crack of each little wave break was clear and distinct. The salt spray in the air glowed, and because of it and the moon hardly a star was visible; just a fuzzy black sky, white around the moon. I walked out to the point beside the rivermouth, where a sand hill had built up, cut away on both sides by river and ocean. On the point where these two little sand cliffs met I sat down, being careful not to collapse the whole thing. I took out the book and opened it; and here I sit at this very moment, caught up at last, scribbling in it by the light of the fat old moon.

Now I know this is the part of the story where the author winds it all up in a fine flourish that tells what it all meant, but luckily there are only a couple of pages left in this book, so there isn't room. I'm glad. It's a good thing I took the trouble to copy out those chapters of *An American Around the World* so that it turned out this way. The old man told me that when I was done writing I would understand what happened, but he was wrong again, the old liar. Here I've taken the trouble to write it all down, and now I'm done and I don't have a dog's idea what it meant. Except that almost everything I know is wrong, especially the stuff I learned from Tom. I'm going to have to go through everything I know and try to figure out where he lied and where he told the truth. I've been doing that already with the books I've found, and with books he doesn't know I borrowed from him, and I've found out a lot of things already. I've found out that the American Empire never included Europe, like he said it did—that they never did bury their dead in suits of gold armor—that we weren't the first and only nation to go into space—that we didn't make cars that flew and floated over water—and that there never were any dragons—I don't think, although a bird guide might not be where they were mentioned. All lies—those and a hundred more facts Tom told me. All lies.

I'll tell you what I do know: the tide is out, and the waves roll up the rivermouth. At first it looks like each wave is pushing the whole flow of the river inland, because all the visible movement is in that direction. Little trailers of the wave roll up the bank, break over the hard sand and add their bit to the flat's stippled crosshatching. For a time it looks like the wave will push upriver all the way around the first bend. But underneath its white jumble the river has been flowing out to sea all the while, and finally the wave stalls on top of this surge, breaks into a confused chop, and suddenly the entire disturbance is being borne out to sea—until it's swept under the next incoming wave, and the movement turns upriver again. Each wave is a different size, and meets a different resistance, and as a result there is an infinite variety of rippling, breaking, chopping, gliding. . . . The pattern is never once the same. Do you see what I mean? Do you understand me, Steve Nicolin? You rather be holding on to what can be made to last than out hunting the new. But good luck to you, brother. Do some good for us out there.

As for me: the moon lays a mirrorflake road to the horizon. The snow on the beach melted yesterday, but it might as well be a beach of snow the way it looks in this light, against the edge of the black sea. Above the cliffs stand the dark hillsides of the valley, cupped, tilted to pour into the ocean. Onofre. This damp last page is nearly full. And my hand is getting cold—it's getting so stiff I can't make the letters, these words are all big and scrawling, taking up the last of the space, thank God. Oh be done with it. There's an owl, flitting over the river. I'll stay right here and fill another book.

the gold coast

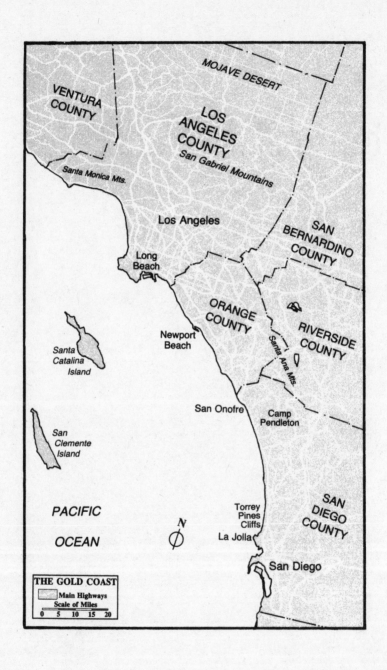

VENTURA COUNTY

MOJAVE DESERT

LOS ANGELES COUNTY

San Gabriel Mountains

Santa Monica Mts.

Los Angeles

Long Beach

SAN BERNARDINO COUNTY

Santa Catalina Island

Newport Beach

ORANGE COUNTY

Santa Ana Mts.

RIVERSIDE COUNTY

San Clemente Island

San Onofre

Camp Pendleton

PACIFIC

OCEAN

N

Torrey Pines Cliffs

La Jolla

SAN DIEGO COUNTY

San Diego

THE GOLD COAST
Main Highways
Scale of Miles
0   5   10   15   20

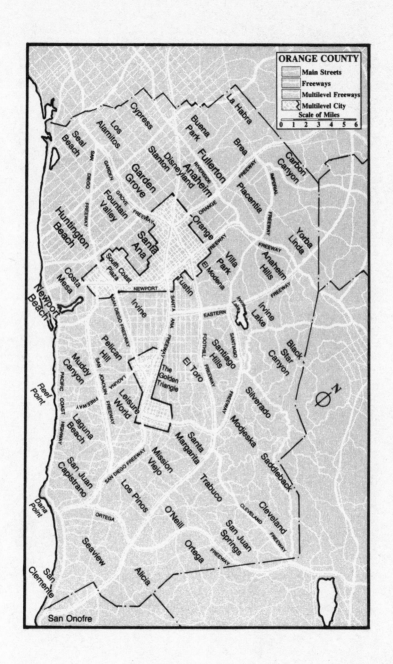

ORANGE COUNTY

Main Streets
Freeways
Multilevel Freeways
Multilevel City

Scale of Miles
0 1 2 3 4 5 6

La Habra

Cypress

Seal Beach

Los Alamitos

Buena Park

Brea

Carbon Canyon

Stanton

Disneyland

Fullerton

Anaheim

Placentia

Garden Grove

Fountain Valley

Orange

Yorba Linda

Huntington Beach

Santa Ana

Villa Park

El Modena

Anaheim Hills

Costa Mesa

South Coast Plaza

Tustin

Irvine Lake

Newport Beach

NEWPORT

Irvine

Eastern

Black Star Canyon

Pelican Hill

Santiago Hills

Reef Point

Muddy Canyon

The Golden Triangle

El Toro

Silverado

Laguna Beach

Leisure World

Modjeska

Saddleback

Santa Margarita

Dana Point

San Juan Capistrano

Mission Viejo

Trabuco

Cleveland

Los Pinos

O'Neill

San Juan Springs

ORTEGA

Ortega

Seaview

Alicia

San Clemente

San Onofre

N

... 1

Beep beep!
  Honk honk.

Jim McPherson sticks his head out the window of his car, shouts at a Mini-honda whose program has just automatically slotted it onto the onramp ahead of him. "You cut me off!" The man in the Minihonda stares back at him, look-ing puzzled. Jim's ancient Volvo swerves sharply up the curving track and sud-denly Jim's hanging halfway out the window and teetering, face inches from the concrete of the freeway. Abe Bernard grabs his belt and pulls him back in, whew!

Night in Orange County, here, and the four friends are cruising in autopia. Stars of their high school state championship wrestling team, ten years past that glory, they roll over the seats of the Volvo and try to pin Tashi Nakamura, to keep him away from the eyedropper of Sandy Chapman's latest concoction. Tash was their heavyweight and the only one still in good shape, and they can't do it; Tash surges up through their arms and seizes the eyedropper, all the while singing along with one of Jim's old CDs: "*Some*body give me a *cheese-*burger!" The onramp bends up, curves more sharply, the contacts squeak over the power-and-guidance electromagnetic track in the center of the lane, they're all thrown into a heap on the backseat. "Uh-oh, I think I dropped the dropper." "Say, we're on the freeway now, aren't we? Shouldn't someone be watching?"

Instantly Abe squirms into the driver's seat. He has a look around. Every-thing's on track. Cars, following their programs north, hum over the eight brassy bands marking the center of each lane. River of red taillights ahead, white headlights behind, some cars rolling over the S-curved lane-change tracks, left to right, right to left, their yellow turnsignal indicators blinking the rhythm of the great plunge forward, click click click, click click click. All's well on the Newport Freeway tonight. "Find that eyedropper?" says Abe, a certain edge in his voice.

"Yeah, here."

The northbound lanes swoop up as they cross the great sprawl of the intersection with the San Diego, Del Mar, Costa Mesa, and San Joaquin freeways. Twenty-four monster concrete ribbons pretzel together in a Gordian knot three hundred feet high and a mile in diameter—a monument to autopia—and they go right through the middle of it, like bugs through the heart of a giant. Then Jim's old buzzbox hums up a grade and suddenly it's like they're in a landing pattern for John Wayne International Airport over to their right, because the northbound Newport is on the highest of the stacked freeway levels, and they are a hundred feet above mother Earth. Nighttime OC, for miles in every direction. Imagine.

The great gridwork of light.

Tungsten, neon, sodium, mercury, halogen, xenon.

At groundlevel, square grids of orange sodium streetlights.

All kinds of things burn.

Mercury vapor lamps: blue crystals over the freeways, the condos, the parking lots.

Eyezapping xenon, glaring on the malls, the stadium, Disneyland.

Great halogen lighthouse beams from the airport, snapping around the night sky.

An ambulance light, pulsing red below.

Ceaseless succession, redgreenyellow, redgreenyellow.

Headlights and taillights, red and white blood cells, pushed through a leukemic body of light.

There's a brake light in your brain.

A billion lights. (Ten million people.) How many kilowatts per hour?

Grid laid over grid, from the mountains to the sea. A billion lights.

Ah yes: Orange County.

Jim blinks a big wash of Sandy's latest out of his eye, watches patterns pulse. All at once, in a satori illumination, he can see the pattern all the other patterns make: the layers of OC's lighting, decade on decade, generation on generation. In fact certain grids are lifting off and pivoting ninety degrees, to match the metapattern of the perceived whole. "I'd call this one Pattern Perception."

"Okay," Sandy says. "I can see that."

"You could take aspirin and see that from up here," Abe objects.

"That's true. I can see that too."

"Ought to call it Agreeability," says Tashi.

"That's true. I can see that."

"We're at the center of the world," Jim announces. Abe and Tashi start looking around like they missed the marker—should be a plaque or something, right? "Orange County is the end of history, its purest product. Civilization kept moving west for thousands of years, in a sunset tropism, until they came to the edge here on the Pacific and they couldn't go any farther. And so they stopped here and *did it*. And by that time they were in the great late surge of corporate capitalism, so that everything here is purely organized, to buy and sell, buy and sell, every little piece of us."

"Fucking Marxist Commie."

"They must have liked lights."

Jim shakes them off, waxes nostalgic. Mentioning history reminds him of the night's mission. "It didn't used to be this way!"

"You're kidding," says Tashi. He and Abe share grins: Jim can be funnier than the video.

"No, I'm not kidding. This whole basin was covered with orange groves, over two hundred square miles of them. There were more oranges then than there are lights now."

"Hard To Believe," his friends chorus together.

"But true! OC was one big orchard." Jim sighs.

Abe and Tash and Sandy eye each other. "That's a lot of trees," Abe says solemnly, and Tash stifles a laugh. Sandy doesn't bother; he goes into the famous Chapman laughing fit: "*Ah*, hahahahahaha— *Ah*, hahahahahaha."

"Say, don't you want to get off here?" Tash asks.

"Oh yeah!" Jim cries.

Abe ticks over the lane-change switch and they swerve into the right lane, then spiral down the offramp two levels to Chapman Avenue, eastbound. Sandy's street. Only two levels here, and eastbound is the upper. In El Modena even that ends and they're back on ground level, in two-way traffic. "What now, Professor?"

"Park in the mall," Jim says.

Abe parks them. Jim consults his map for the last time. He is tense with excitement; this is a new idea, this mission, a sort of personal archaeology. Years of reading his local history books have given him an uncontrollable urge to recover something—to see, to touch, to *fondle* some relic of the past. And tonight's the night.

They are parked in front of the El Torito restaurant at the end of the Hewes Mall. "This El Terriblo incorporates the oldest building in the area," Jim explains. "It was a Quaker church, built in 1887. They put a big bell in the tower, but it was too heavy and during the next Santa Ana wind the whole building fell over. So they built it again. Anyway, you can't tell now, the restaurant is built over it and they use the old room as a casino. But it gives me a coordinate point, see, on the old maps. And exactly a hundred and forty yards west of here, on the other side of the street, is the site of El Modena Elementary School, built in 1905."

"I missed that," says Tash.

"It's gone now. Razed in the 1960s. But my mom's great-uncle went there as a child, and he told me about it. And I looked it all up. There were two wooden buildings with a dirt yard in between. When they demolished the buildings they filled the cellars below with the debris, then covered it all in concrete. I've got the location of those buildings pegged exactly, and the west one is directly under the Fluffy Donuts Video Palace and its parking lot."

"You mean," says Abe, "we can just bust through the parking lot surface there—"

"Yeah, that's why I wanted you to bring some of your tools—"

"Bust through the concrete surface there, and dig through three or four feet of fill, and get down to the—get down to the *debris* of El Modena Elementary School, 1905 to 1960 A.D.?"

"That's right!"

"Well, shoot," Abe says. "What're we *waiting* for?"

"*Ahhh,* hahahahahahahaha . . ."

Out of the car, grab up packs of equipment, walk down Chapman. Faces stare from passing cars at the sight of people walking. Jim is getting excited. "There was a foundation stone, too, with the date carved on it. If we could find that . . ."

At Fluffy's people dressed in the bright spectrum-bend primaries fashionable this year are downing incandescent green and purple and yellow donuts, then setting out into the holo reality of what appears to be African savanna. The four friends skirt the building and enter a small dark parking lot, bounded by Fluffy's, a supermarket wall on one side, a movie complex wall on the other, and an apartment complex wall at the back. The glow of OC, reflected off low clouds, gives them all the light they need. Jim points out the chalkmarks he made during his reconnaissance trip, there on oil-splotched old concrete just behind the wall of Fluffy's. "Should be right under here."

Abe and Tash take off the backpacks and get out Abe's freeway rescue tools. Abe shakes his head at the sight of them. "I really shouldn't have taken these, we always have spares but you never know. . . ." He picks up an oscilloscopic saw, Tash a needlejack, and they crack the surface and chop a hole fairly quickly. It's noisy work, but the ambient white noise of the city covers most of the sound. They put on work gloves and start pulling up broken blocks of concrete. The blocks are only about four inches thick, so there isn't much problem. Stuck to the undersides of the pieces are inch-thick crusts of old asphalt. "They just poured it right over the old surface," Jim says. "Great stratification at this site."

Soon there's a square hole about four feet on a side, there in the parking lot.

"They're going to think someone was trying to break in and steal the secret donut formulas," says Tash. He and Sandy sing the Fluffy advertisement in a soft falsetto:

All sugar lovers in the know
Love what we leave in that round hole. . . .

"Well, Jim?" Tash inquires. "I don't see any El Modena Elementary School. Looks like dirt to me."

"Of course. That's the fill. We've got to clear it out."

Sandy hands Jim a short-handled aluminum shovel. "Your turn."

So Jim goes to work.

He is not strong; he was the flyweight on their wrestling team, in the 123-pound class despite medium height, and he relied more on speed than brute force, even when Coach "Mad Dog" Beagle had them lifting weights four hours every day.

Nor is he skillful; every stab and scoop of the shovel yields only a handful of dirt. Disgusted with these results, he puts one foot forward, takes the shovel in both hands, raises it far overhead, brings it down in a vicious strike—only to be jerked to a halt by Tashi's big hand grabbing the stock in midair. "Goddamn, Jim, you were just about to amputate your own foot! Watch what you're doing, will you?"

"*Ahh*, hahahahahahaha . . ."

But he is enthusiastic. And eventually the hole is about two feet deep, and Jim is having serious trouble keeping dirt from his side walls from sliding down to the bottom of the hole. Abe takes over and makes better progress. An hour or so after the start of the operation, he drives the shovel down and there is a wooden *thunk*. "Oh ho! Yo ho ho, in fact! Buried treasure."

Abe clears dirt away from a big beam of wood. It's solid hardwood, dry and unrotted. Next to it they find a dressed stone block, one side beveled and fluted.

"All right!" Jim exclaims. "This is it! This is the kind of foundation stone that's supposed to have the date on it."

Abe scrapes the stone's side clear of dirt. No date. "Might be on the other side. . . ."

"Gee, Abe," says Tash, nudging Sandy with an elbow. "How much do you think that stone weighs?"

Abe gives it a kick. "I don't know. Maybe a ton."

"Ah, come on!" says Jim.

"Yeah, okay . . . maybe only seven, eight hundred pounds."

"*Ah*, hahahahahahaha."

"How about a piece of this beam for a souvenir," Abe suggests to Jim. "Just a starter, of course." He takes the oscilloscopic saw and neatly slices off a trian-gular section that looks like a wooden prism, or an antique ruler. He hands it up to Jim. "Don't touch the black side for a minute or two."

Jim regards it dubiously. So this is the past. . . .

"Whoops!" says Sandy, who has ESP in these matters. He looks around the corner and out to the street. "Police." He has an escape route already planned, and without a pause he is gone down an alley between the supermarket and the ap wall, into the applex. Sandy can't afford even casual conversations with the police, much less an arrest for violating a parking lot surface.

The others snatch up Abe's tools and follow Sandy, just as a cosmic white light xenon beam snaps into existence and torches the parking lot with its glare. Amped-up voices of authority command them to stop, but they're already into the warren of the applex, as safe as roaches under the refrigerator. Except this time the police are in after them, can't let these hoodlums be tearing up the parking lots of OC, and it's chase time, the four friends dodging in irregular dispersal from the closetlike courtyards to second- and third-story walkways, dumpster nooks, doorway niches . . . The applex is typical L-5 architecture, dominant form of the twenty-first century, but it's smaller than most OC ap-plex mazes, and there just aren't as many good spots to scurry into. Crossing one twelve-by-twelve courtyard Jim stumbles over a kid's robot and drops his archaeological find, it clatters away and he's hopping around trying to locate it when Sandy runs into him and drags him off into a nearby elevator nook. Just in time, because a policeman wearing a helmet with an IRHUD happens by and well, who knows but what he can see the heat of their footprints right there on the ground!

Maybe so. He's paused in the courtyard. Sandy and Jim, praying that their shoe soles have been thick enough, crouch in the dark elevator doorway and watch the policeman's headlamps swing around the minicourtyard.

For a moment the beam of light illuminates the fragment of wood, there under a dead bush.

"Now, that's a piece of wood," Sandy whispers in Jim's ear. "And that"—gesturing after the departing policeman—"is a night in jail. You have to weigh your priorities, Jim. You've got to *think* before you act. . . ."

They recover the piece of wood and sneak off in the other direction. By this time Jim is hopelessly disoriented, but part of Sandy's ESP is a perfect internal compass, and he leads them east, then back down through the applex's laundry/recreation/administration building, with its wall of five hundred mailboxes, and out to Chapman Avenue again.

The copcar is still parked in front of Fluffy's. Ah ha, there's Abe and Tash, up ahead of them. After them and across the street to Jim's car. "What hap-pened to you guys?" Tash asks.

"I dropped the piece of wood," Jim says. "Had some trouble finding it."

"I hope you were successful," Abe chides him, "or we're sending you back for it!"

"No, here it is! See?"

His friends laugh loud and long. All's well that ends well. They jump in the car, click on the motor, slide back onto the track, and roll out onto Chapman. Abe says, "Let's get this precious fragment to the museum and track down to Sandy's to see how the party's going."

"*Ah*, hahaha. No party tonight, boys."

"That's what you think."

... 2

The next morning Dennis McPherson, Jim's father, takes United's commuter flight from LAX to National Airport in Washington, D.C. He wakes as the Boeing 7X7 drops back into the atmosphere, shuffles the papers on his lap back into his briefcase. They haven't helped him. Of course he's napped for most of the short flight, but even if he had been reading them they wouldn't have helped. He's here, first, to meet with Air Force Colonel T. D. Eaton, to confer on the progress of the Ball Lightning program, one of the big contracts currently in development at McPherson's company, Laguna Space Research. It's not McPherson's program, however, and he doesn't know how to explain the delays that have plagued it. His old friend Dan Houston should be fielding this one, but Houston is down at White Sands, trying to get a successful trial out of Ball Lightning's acquisition/pointing/tracking satellite. And McPherson has other errands to run in Washington, so he's been stuck with this one too. Great.

The other purpose for this visit is a conference with Major Tom Feldkirk, from the Air Force's Electronic Systems Division. Feldkirk requested the conference without giving a reason for it, which is worrying. LSR has several contracts with the Electronic Systems Division, and the problem to be discussed could be in one of a number of areas.

Because the truth of the matter is, LSR is struggling these days. Too many proposals have been lost, and too many of the contracts won have gone into delays and overruns. The Air Force is coming down on such problems harder than ever, and whatever Feldkirk wants to discuss, it isn't likely to be good.

The plane floats down the Potomac River basin and lands. Time to get to his hotel.

He goes onto automatic pilot. So many repetitions. . . . He's become chief errand boy at LSR for this kind of thing, sent to Washington about twenty times a year to put out one fire after another. (Off the plane, into the terminal. He's refined his luggage to a single flight bag, and goes straight out to the taxi line.) From all these more-or-less diplomatic assignments you might guess he was a hail-fellow-well-met kind of guy, someone who could pal around with the flyboys and drink away their objections. Not so: Dennis McPherson is a reserved man, with a contained manner that can make people nervous. (Into a taxi, off to the Crystal City Hyatt Regency. Traffic bumpertobumper on George Washington Parkway lower level.) He can handle his end of dinner talk as well as the next man; he just isn't into a bonhomie that in this context has to be transparent and false always, and therefore offputting. This is big business, after all, the biggest business: defense. Why even pretend that your favorite buddy is some Air Force jock you have to deal with?

Into the Crystal City Hyatt Regency, a big irregular space filled with mirrors, escalators, cascading fountains of water and light, walls of glossy greenery, hanging elevators, overhanging balconies. He threads the maze without a thought and checks in, goes up to his room. Into the chrome-and-white-tile bathroom, to stare into the darkened mirror, perhaps clean up a bit before the day's work.

Pink freckled skin. He needs a shave. Strawberry-blond hair, as Lucy always calls it, receding from a round Irish forehead. Cold blue eyes and deep vertical creases between his eyebrows; he's a stocky stubborn figure, one of those smoldering Irish who don't say much, and now he looks harried, tired, annoyed. It's going to be a tough day.

Strange how it's come to this. McPherson began as an engineer—damn it, he *is* an engineer. He has a degree in aerospace engineering from Cal Tech, and even though he's hopelessly off the edge these days, he can still follow it when his design people describe things. And McPherson can see the larger patterns, where engineering touches both invention and administration. But management itself? . . . Other program managers got there on leadership, they know how to coax or bully extra results out of their teams. McPherson's boss Stewart Lemon is a perfect example of this type, the Dynamic Leader of the business schools. McPherson leaves that kind of Napoleonic style to others, and in fact he despises it in Lemon. For his part, he just figures out what has to be done, and lays it out. Low-keyed approach. (Shower, shave.) No, it's not leadership that got him out of engineering and into administration.

How did it happen, then? He's never been too sure. (Into the day's clothes: colorless conservative dress, appropriate for Pentagon dealings.) He can explain technical matters to people who don't know enough to fully understand them. Administrators in LSR's parent company, Pentagon people, congressional aides . . . people who need to have a clear idea of technical problems before they can make their own decisions. McPherson can do that. He's not sure why, but it happens. He tries to explain, and they usually get it. Strange. His wife Lucy would laugh, perhaps angrily; she considers him awful at "communicating."

But that's what's gotten him where he is, and really it's not funny; it means that he has somehow strayed out of the line of work where he might have enjoyed himself, been comfortable.

Half an hour to kill. He turns on the video wall's news program. The war in Arabia is heating up; Bahrain is embroiled now, with U.S. Marines fighting the insurgents, which shows it's serious. They're finding the Hewlett-Packard IRHUD helmets are giving them a big advantage in night fighting, but the insurgents have some old Norwegian Kongsberg Vaapenfabrikk Penguin missiles that are wreaking havoc on the U.S. fleet offshore, all the aluminum in those old destroyers melting like plastic. And some Hughes Mavericks left over from the war in Thailand, still doing yeoman service in the desert hills . . . seems like most of the forty odd wars currently being fought are employing obsolete equipment, and the results, for democratic forces, are a real mess.

McPherson wanders past the bold rainbow of the immense bedspread to the window of his room. There before him stands the Hughes Tower, a hotel/restaurant/office complex, one of Crystal City's newest. Crystal City is getting bigger every year, the defense industry towers looking like an architectural rendering of their business, steel and glass ICBMs densepacked and pointed at the sky. All the money that leaves the Pentagon is funneled through these towers, through the crystal city of weapons procurement.

It's time to get over to the Pentagon. McPherson feels himself coming out of automatic pilot. Tuesday morning, Crystal City, USA: time to go offtrack, onto manual, into action.

Short taxi ride to the Pentagon. Into the security complex, out with his lapel badge. A lieutenant picks him up and they drive down the endless giant white corridors in a cart, dodging all the motor and foot traffic. They might as well be on a street. McPherson always gets a kick out of this blatant attempt to impress people. And it works, too, sure. The Pentagon may be old, but it's still immense. Seems to him that the latest reorganization has taken notice of current fashion; service and division markers are painted in bright spectrum-bend colors that pulsate under the xenon bulbs, against all the white walls.

He meets Colonel Eaton at the Air Force's SD Battle Management Division office, and Eaton takes him into one of the center courtyard commissaries. They talk over a lunch of croissants and salad. McPherson outlines some of the problems that Houston's team is having with the boost-phase interceptor.

Ball Lightning: the job is to detect and track as many as ten thousand Soviet ICBMs, launched simultaneously; then aim ground-based free-electron laser beams, bounce them off mirrors in space, and destroy the ICBMs while they're still in boost phase. It's a tough job, and McPherson is glad it isn't exactly his. But now he has to take Colonel Eaton's grilling about it, which is informed and relentless. The test results in your proposal, Eaton says, indicated that you could solve the problems you're telling me about. That's why you have the contract. Get it together, and soon. Or it's a Big Hacksaw for you.

McPherson cringes at the reference to the Hacksaw disaster, a gun program axed by the DOD for incompetence; it was the beginning of the end for Danforth Aerospace, which is now just a name in the corporate history books. That kind of thing could still happen; a big program could go bad so disastrously that it got the axe and brought its whole company down. . . .

So. Great lunch. McPherson tries to remember what he ate as he makes notes of the conversation, in the LSR offices on the top floor they rent in the Aerojet Tower. Apparently it didn't agree with him. Salad? No matter. He spends the rest of the afternoon on the phone to OC, and then to White Sands, to tell Dan Houston that the heat is on. Dan knows that already, and in an anxious, almost frightened voice, he asks for help. McPherson agrees to do what he can. "But it's not my program, Dan. Lemon may not give me the time to do anything. Besides, I'm not sure what I can do."

That evening Major Tom Feldkirk comes by and picks him up, and they track over the river into Georgetown.

Feldkirk is around forty-five, ex-flyer, wears his black hair longer than they'd like it back on base, in a swoop over his forehead and well down his back. He's dressed casually, sport shirt, slacks, loafers. McPherson has dealt with him twice before, likes him all right. They park in an underground lot, walk up onto a brick sidewalk and into the usual Georgetown crowd. They could be two lawyers, two congressmen, two of any part of Washington's success structure. They discuss Georgetown, the fashionable bars, the crowds. McPherson is familiar with the area by this time, and can mention favorite restaurants and the like.

"Have you been to Buddha In The Refrigerator?" Feldkirk asks.

McPherson laughs. "No."

"Let's try it, then. It's not nearly so bad as it sounds."

He leads them down M Street, then up one of the little sidestreets, where it looks like it could be 1880, if you ignored the tracks out on the cobblestone street. Or thought of them as streetcar tracks. McPherson has a brief vision of monorailed antique street cars, then reins in his thoughts. This is business, here. . . .

Inside, the restaurant looks Indian. Cloth prints of Buddha and various Hindu deities hang on the walls: six-armed, elephant-headed, outlandish stuff. McPherson's a bit worried, he prefers not to eat food he doesn't recognize, but then the menu turns out to have twenty pages, and you can order anything you can think of, but with every meal you'll get some fine Buddhist vegetables. That's okay. He orders salmon fillet. Feldkirk orders some kind of Asian soup. He was stationed on Guam for several years, and developed a taste for the food. They discuss the Pacific situation for a bit. "The Soviets have got the choke points," says Feldkirk, "but now we're stationed outside them all, so it doesn't really matter."

"Leaves Japan and Korea kind of hanging."

"True. But with the Japanese arming themselves so well, they can take the front line of their own defense. We can cover them from behind. It's not a bad situation."

"And Korea?"

"Well! . . ."

Their meals are served, and as they eat they discuss the Redskins and the Rams, then technical aspects of the war in Burma. McPherson begins to enjoy himself a bit. He likes this man, he can get along with him, he's sort of a kindred spirit. Feldkirk talks ruefully about his two sons, both now at Annapolis. "I took them sailing a lot when we were on Guam, but I never thought it would lead to this." McPherson laughs at his expression. Still, Annapolis is awfully hard to get into. "And your kids?" Feldkirk asks.

"Just one. He's still hanging out in Orange County, teaching night classes and working in a real estate office part-time." McPherson shakes his head. "He's a strange one. A brain without a program." And Feldkirk laughs.

Then the meals are done, they're lingering over drinks and cheesecake, watching Washington's finest chattering around them. Feldkirk leans back in his chair. "You're probably wondering what I've got in mind for tonight."

McPherson lifts his eyebrows: here it comes. "Sure," he says with a smile.

"Well, we have an idea for a system that I want to discuss with you. You see, the RX-16 is almost operational now."

"Is it?" The RX-16 is Northrop's RPV, a remotely piloted vehicle, which in certain quarters of the Electronic Systems Division is all the rage now: a robot jet craft with classified speeds, perhaps up to Mach 7, and capable of turns and rolls that would kill a pilot. Made of kevlar and other lightweight stealth materials, it has the radar signature of a bee. It's one of Northrop's most successful recent contracts, and McPherson was in fact aware it is about to go into production, but he didn't want to say so.

"Yeah. Great plane." Feldkirk looks wistful. "I bet it would be a real kick to fly one. But the time for manned fighter planes has passed, it looks like. Anyway, we've got some ideas for the use of this RX-16 in the European theater."

Use against the threat of the Warsaw Pact invasion, then, the Big Contingency that has stimulated so much of the conventional weapons upgrade spiral between the superpowers. McPherson nods. "Yeah?"

"Well, here's what we're thinking. The RX is ready, and for some time to come we think it'll be a good deal faster and more maneuverable than anything that the Soviets will have. Now if the tanks ever roll, we'd like to be able to use the RXs against them, because if we can do that, it might turn into a shooting gallery situation. We have in mind flying the RXs straight down at full speed from sixty thousand feet to terrain-following level, having them make covert runs down there, finding a dozen tanks and clotheslining the Harris Stalker Nine missiles to them, then popping out and up. And turning around for other runs, until the missiles and fuel run out."

"Stuka pilots would recognize the flight pattern," McPherson remarks, thinking about it. "So you need a navigation system for the terrain following." Tree-top contouring at a mile a second or more. . . .

"That's right."

"And covert, you say." Which means they don't want the plane sending out investigating signals that can be picked up by enemy detection systems. This contradicts the desire for tight navigation and makes things tough.

"That's right." The standard device for locating targets, Feldkirk goes on, a YAG laser operating at the 1.06 micron wavelength, won't do anymore. The new window for targeting lasers is from about eight to fourteen microns, which fits between the upper and lower ends of the Soviets' latest radar systems. "This means a CO-two laser, probably."

But CO_2 lasers don't penetrate cloud anywhere near as well as those using yttrium/aluminum/garnet. "You want it all-weather?" McPherson asks.

"No, just under the weather, day and night."

So they weren't concerned about fog, for instance. McPherson suddenly imagines the Soviet tanks waiting for fog to start World War Three. . . .

"How much weight?"

"We'd like it under five hundred pounds, if you've got it in a single pod. Maybe seven fifty if you put it in two wing pods. We can work that out later."

McPherson lets out a breath. That's a constraint for you. "And how much power can the plane give the system?"

"Maybe ten KVA. Ten point five, tops."

Another constraint. McPherson thinks about it, putting all the factors together in his mind. The components of such a system exist; it's a matter of putting them together, making them work on this new robot jet.

"Sounds interesting," he says at last. "I think we could make a proposal, given that my boss likes the idea, of course."

Feldkirk is shaking his head; a small smile makes him look boyish. "We aren't going to put out an RFP on this one."

"Ah!"

The meeting suddenly makes sense.

Legally, the Pentagon is obliged to offer all their programs for open bidding by contractors. This means publishing a Request For Proposal in *Commerce Business Daily*, which outlines the specifications for what they want. The problem with the system, of course, is that Soviet intelligence can buy *Commerce Business Daily* and get an excellent idea of the capabilities of the American military. In this case, they would know to close the window in their radar systems. "And," Feldkirk says, "if they know they have to speed up their antiaircraft response, and can do it, then we're no longer in the air. So we've decided to go superblack with this one, and deal with the company we judge would do the job best."

Illegal, of course. Technically. But the Pentagon is also charged with defending the country. Even Congress recognizes that some programs have to be kept secret. In fact, black programs are an acknowledged part of the system, and a few members of the Armed Services Committees hear about them regularly. A superblack program, however . . . that's between the Pentagon and the chosen contractor only.

So, LSR has a contract. Other defense contractors won't complain about it even if they do hear rumors, because they've all got secret programs of their own.

Feldkirk continues justifying the decision to make the program superblack. "We figure we've got other ways to keep the Soviets from rolling, for now. We don't need to make this public, to scare them. So while they're ignorant of it, we've got a safeguard—if the tanks do roll, they're goners. Ducks on the pond, as obsolete as aircraft carriers. Meanwhile, the government can get serious about the negotiations to get battlefield nukes off the front line. That should help reconcile the Soviets to our space installations, and it eases the use-'em-or-lose-'em situation with the artillery nukes in Turkey, Saudi Arabia, Thailand, all the rest. Nobody's ever liked those, but we're still living with them. This way, we might be able to end that risk—we just won't need battlefield nukes anymore to do the job, and that's the bottom line."

McPherson nods. "That would be good all right." He doesn't like to reflect on how fully American strategy is entangled in nuclear weapons; the situation repels him. It just isn't smart defense. "I'll have to consult back at the office, you know."

"Of course."

"But, truthfully, I can't imagine we'll turn it down."

"No."

So Feldkirk raises his glass, and they toast the deal.

And the next day McPherson gives Stewart Lemon a call, first thing.

"Yeah, Mac?"

"It's about my conference with Major Feldkirk at ESD."

"Yeah? What'd he want?"

"We've been offered a superblack."

...3

McPherson's boss, Stewart Lemon, stands in his office before his big seaside window, looking out at the Pacific. It's near the end of the day, and the low sun turns Catalina apricot, gilds the sails of the boats as they glide back in to Dana Point and Newport Beach harbors. His office is on the top floor of LSR's tower, on the coastal cliff between Corona del Mar and Laguna, overlooking Reef Point. Lemon often calls his window view the finest in Orange County, and since it includes no land but the distant bulk of Catalina, it may well be true.

Dennis McPherson is on his way up to give him the details of the meeting with Feldkirk, and Lemon, considering the meeting, sighs. Getting one's employees to put their maximum effort into the work is an art form; one has to alter one's methods for every personality under one's command. McPherson has been working for Lemon for a long time, and Lemon has found that the man works best when driven. Make him angry, fill him with resentment, and he flies into his work with a furious energy that is fairly productive, no doubt about it. But how tiresome the relationship has become! The mutual dislike has really become quite real. Lemon watches the contained insolence, the arrogance of this uncultured engineer, with an irritation that barely holds on to its amusement. Really, the man is too much. It's gotten to be almost a pleasure to bully him.

Ramona buzzes to tell him McPherson is there. Lemon begins to pace back and forth before the window, nine steps turn, nine steps turn. In McPherson comes, looking tired.

"So, Mac!" He gestures him to a chair, continues to pace in a leisurely way, staring out the window as much as he can. "You got us a superblack program, eh?"

"I was told to pass along the offer, that's right."

"Fine, fine. Tell me about it."

McPherson describes the system Feldkirk has requested. "Most of the components of the system are fairly straightforward, it'll only be a matter of linking them in a management program and fitting them into a small enough package. But the sensing systems, covert terrain ranger and target detector both—there could be some dangers there. The CO-two laser Feldkirk has suggested is only lab-tested so far. So—"

"But it's a superblack, right? It's only between the Air Force and us."

"That's right. But—"

"Every method has its drawbacks. That doesn't mean we don't go for it. In fact, we can't very well refuse the offer of a superblack—we might never get another one. And the Pentagon knows it's a high-risk program, that's why they've done it this way. And it's always the high-risk projects that bring in the highest profits. What's your schedule looking like, Mac?"

"Well—"

"You're clear enough. I'll assign the Canadair contract to Bailey, and you'll be clear to go at this thing. Listen here, Mac." Time to stick in a needle or two. "Twice in a row now you've been manager of proposals that lost. They were too expensive, too elaborate, and you almost missed the deadline for turning them in, both times. It's important to beat the schedule deadline by a couple of weeks, to show the Air Force we're on top of things. Now here you've got a superblack program, and there isn't a schedule per se. But with something outside normal channels like this, the trick is to get it done fast, while all conditions still obtain. You get me?"

McPherson is staring out the window, not looking at Lemon. The corners of his mouth are tight. Lemon almost smiles. McPherson no doubt still believes his losing proposals were the best made, but the truth is you can't afford to be a perfectionist in this business. Projects have to be cost-effective, and that requires a certain realism. Well, that's Lemon's contribution. That's what's gotten him where he is. And this time he's going to have to ride herd a little more closely than before.

He stops his pacing and points at McPherson, surprising him. "You're in charge of this one because I think the Pentagon people want it that way. But I want this done *quickly*. Do you understand?"

"Yes."

The clamming up does absolutely nothing to hide the anger and contempt in McPherson's eyes; he's as easy to read as a freeway exit sign. TURN OFF HERE, OVER THIS CLIFF. Now he will go back down there and work himself sick to get the program done quickly, to jam it back down Lemon's throat. Fine. It's that kind of work that makes Lemon's division one of the most productive at LSR, despite the myriad technical difficulties they encounter. The job gets done.

"Let me know when you've got a preliminary proposal worked up. You'll fly out and present it to them as soon as it's done."

"The targeting system and the management program may take a while—"

"Fine. I'm not denying there are problems to be solved, there always are, aren't there? I just want them dealt with as soon as possible." A bit of dictatorial irritation: "No more getting bogged down! No more excuses and delays! I'm tired of that kind of thing!"

McPherson leaves with his jaw clamped so hard that he can barely mumble his good-byes. Lemon can't help but laugh, though there is a part of him that is genuinely angry as well. Arrogant bastard. It's funny what it takes to get some men to give it their all.

Next comes Dan Houston, the last conference of Lemon's day. They do this a lot. Dan is a completely different situation from McPherson: more limited technically, but infinitely better with people. He and Lemon have been friends since they both began working for Martin Marietta, years before. The same headhunter lured them to LSR, bringing Lemon in at the higher position, a distance Lemon has only extended through the years. But Houston doesn't be-grudge it, he isn't envious. Lemon can charm him. In fact, if Lemon were to come down hard on Dan it would only hurt his feelings, make him sullen and slow him down. It's necessary to coddle him a bit, to pull rather than push. And the truth is, Lemon likes the man. Houston admires him, they have a good time together sailing, playing racketball, going out with their allies Dawn and Elsa. They're friends.

So he sits down when Houston comes in, and they look out the window and critique the tacking of the boats clawing back from the south toward Newport. They laugh at some really bad luffs. Then Lemon asks him what the latest is with the Ball Lightning project. Houston starts bitching about it again.

It's one of their three biggest contracts, and inwardly Lemon seethes; they can't afford for it to get bogged down too much. But he nods sympathetically. "No one's solved the dwell time problem," he says, thinking aloud to himself. "The power requirements are just too much. The Air Force can't expect magic."

"The problem is, they thought we had it solved when they gave us the con-tract."

"I know." Of course he knows. Who better? It was Lemon who okayed the inclusion of those Huntsville test results. Dan can be kind of a fool. . . . "Listen, have you gotten McPherson's input on this?"

"Well, I've asked him for it. He doesn't like it much."

"I know." Lemon shakes his head. "But Dennis is kind of a prima donna." Got to play this carefully, as Dan and McPherson are also friends. "A little bit, anyway. Get him to talk to your design team, and the programmers. See what he can suggest. He'll be busy with a new proposal of his own, but I'll tell him to take time for this. You can't spend the whole of every day working on one project, after all."

"No, that's true. Lot of waiting to be done." Dan sounds satisfied; he'd like the help. And McPherson has a certain flair for the technical problems, no doubt about it.

Not only that, but this way Lemon can begin to tie McPherson into the Ball Lightning program, and all its troubles. Lemon is just annoyed enough with McPherson to enjoy the idea of this move. He'll really have the man under some screws, and who knows, McPherson might just troubleshoot Ball Lightning as well, even if he does dislike the program. Excellent.

They chat a bit longer, discussing in great detail the rigging of a ketch running down to Dana Point. Beautiful yacht. Then Lemon wants to go home. "I'm doing *navarin du mouton* tonight, and it's a slow cooker." Houston dismissed, Lemon's off to his car in the executives' lot. The Mercedes-Benz door slams with a heavy, satisfying *clunk*. He clicks in a CD of Schumann's Rhenish Symphony, lights a cigar of Cuban tobacco lightly laced with a mild dose of MDMA, and tracks south on the coast highway toward Laguna Beach.

It's been a good day, and they've needed one. LSR is a division of Argo AG/ Blessman Enterprises, one of the world's corporate giants; Lemon's boss, Donald Hereford, president of LSR, is based in New York because he is also a vice-president at A/BE as well. Fascinating man, but he hasn't been pleased with LSR's record in the past year or two. News of this new superblack should take some heat off concerning the Ball Lightning problems and the recent string of lost bids. And that's good. Lemon shifts over to the fast track, lets the Mercedes out.

He decides to dice two cloves of garlic rather than one into the *navarin du mouton*, and maybe throw in a basil leaf or two. It was a little bland the last time he made it. He hopes Elsa managed to find some good lamb. If she bothered to leave the house at all.

...4

Dennis McPherson leaves LSR some time after Lemon and tracks home. Up Muddy Canyon Parkway past Signal Hill, through the Irvine condos to Jeffrey, turn left on Irvine, right on Eveningside, left on Morningside, up to the last house on the left, now a duplex; the McPhersons own the street half of the house, along with the carport and garage. As he tracks into the driveway and under the carport Dennis sees Jim's shabby little Volvo out on the street. Here for another free meal. Dennis isn't in the mood for any more irritants at the end of this long day, and he sighs.

He enters the house to find Jim and Lucy arguing over something, as usual. "But Mom, the World Bank only lends them money if they grow cash crops that the bank approves of, and so then they don't do subsistence farming and they can't feed themselves, and then the cash crops market disappears, and so they have to buy their food from the World Bank, or beg for it, and they end up owned by the bank!" "Well, I don't know," Lucy says, "don't you think they're just trying to help? It's a generous thing to give." "But Mom, don't you see the principle of the thing?" "Well, I don't know. The bank lends that money with hardly any interest at all—it really is almost like giving, don't you think?" "Of course not!"

Dennis goes back to the bedroom to change clothes. He doesn't even want to have the day's debate clarified. Jim and Lucy argue like that constantly, Lucy from the Christian viewpoint and Jim from the pseudo-socialist, both mixing large matters of philosophy with questions of daily life, and making a mash of everything. Lord. It's just theoretical for the two of them, like debaters going at it to keep in practice; just one more part of their constant talk. But Dennis hates arguments, to him they're no more than verbal fights that can make you furious and upset you for days after. He gets his fill of that kind of thing at work.

They're still at it when Dennis comes back out to read the daily news on the

video wall, WAR IN BURMA SPILLS INTO BANGLADESH. "Stop that," he says to
them.

They eye each other, Jim amused, Lucy frustrated. "Dennis," she complains,
"we're just talking."

"Talk, then. No bickering."

"But we weren't!" Still, Lucy gives up on it and goes to prepare dinner, telling Jim about members of her church, with Jim asking highly informed questions about people he hasn't seen in ten years. Dennis scans the news and turns
the wall off; tomorrow the headlines'll say the same thing, artfully altered to
appear original. WAR SPILLS INTO (pick country)—

They sit down to dinner, Lucy says grace, they eat. Afterward Jim says,
"Dad, um, sorry to mention it, but the old car is tending to shift lanes to the
right whether I want it to or not. I've done what I could to check the program,
but . . . I didn't find anything."

"The problem won't be in the program."

"Oh. Ah. Well, um . . . could you take a look at it?"

The visit is explained. Irritated, Dennis gets up and goes outside without a
word. The thing is, he's over a barrel; the freeways are in fact dangerous, and
if he refuses to fix Jim's car and tries to make him learn to do a little work of
his own, then next thing he knows he'll get a call from the CHP to tell him the
fool's car has failed and he's dead inside, and then Dennis will have to wish that
he'd done the damn repair. So he drives the thing into the garage and goes at it,
unscrewing the box over the switcher mechanism by the light of a big lamp set
next to him on the floor.

Jim follows him into the garage and sits on the floor to watch. Dennis slides
back and forth on the floor-sled, putting all the screws in one spot, testing the
magnetic function of all the points in the switcher . . . ah. Two are dead, two
more barely functional, and commands are being transferred right on through
to the right-turn points, which explains the problem. Small moment of satisfaction as he solves the little mystery, which wasn't, after all, so mysterious.
Anyone could have found it. Which returns him to his irritation with Jim.
There he sits, spaced out in his own thoughts, not learning a thing about the
machine he relies on utterly to be able to lead his life. Dennis sighs heavily. As
he replaces the points with spares of his own (and they're expensive) he says,
"Are you doing anything about getting a full-time job?"

"Yeah, I've been looking."

Sure. Besides, what kind of job is he fit to apply for? Here he's been going
to college for years, and so far as Dennis can tell, he isn't qualified to do anything. Clerk work, a little marginal night school teaching . . . can that really be
it? Dennis gives a screw a hard twist. What can Jim do? Well . . . he can read
books. Yes, he can read books like nobody's business. But Dennis can read a

book too, and he didn't go to college for six years to learn how. And meanwhile, here he is out on his back after an eleven-hour day, fixing the kid's car!

Time to make him help. "Look here, take that point and reach down from above and insert it into this slot here," pointing up with the screwdriver.

"Sure, Dad." And Jim moves around the motor compartment, blocking the floor lamp's light, and leans down into it, the point between his fingers. "There we go—oops!"

"What'd you do?"

"Dropped it. But I can see where it went—down between the motor and the distributor—just a sec—" And he's leaning down, stretched out over the motor, blocking Dennis's light.

"What're you doing?"

"Just about—uh-oh—"

Jim falls into the motor compartment. His weight sinks the front end of the car abruptly and Dennis, flat on his back underneath it, is almost crushed by the underbody.

"Hey! For God's sake!"

It's a good thing the car has decent shocks—put in by Dennis himself last year—otherwise he would have been pancaked. Very carefully he tries to roll from beneath the car, but the edge of the body hits his ribs and . . . well, he can't scrape under it. "Get your feet back on the ground and take your weight off the car!"

"I, um, I can't. Seem to have my hand—stuck under this thing here."

"What *thing here*."

"I guess it's the distributor. I've got the point, but—"

"If you drop the point, can you get your hand free?"

"Um . . . no. Won't go either way."

Dennis sighs, shifts sideways until he tilts off the floor-sled, it bangs up against the car bottom and he slides down onto the garage floor, smacking the back of his head. A slow, awkward shimmy past the track pickups, which are pressed against the ground, and he's out from under the car.

He stands, rubs the back of his head, looks at the waving legs emerging from under the hood of the car. It looks like the kid just up and dived headfirst into the thing. In fact that's probably pretty close to what he did. Dennis takes a flashlight and directs its beam into the motor compartment; Jim's head is twisted down and sideways against his chest.

"Hi," Jim says.

Dennis points the flashlight at the end of Jim's arm, where it disappears under the distributor. "You say you've let go of the point?"

"Yeah."

Sounds like he's had a clamp put on his throat. Dennis leans in, reaches down to the distributor, pulls the clips away and lifts the distributor cap. "Try now."

Jim gives a sudden jerk up, his hand comes free and his head snaps back up into the hood of the car, knocking it off its cheap metal stand so that the hood comes down with a clang, just missing Dennis's fingers and Jim's neck. "Ow! Oops."

Dennis looks over the frames of his garage glasses at Jim. He reopens the hood. He replaces the distributor cap. "Where did you say that point was?"

"I've got it," Jim says, rubbing his head with one hand. With the other he holds the point out proudly.

Dennis finishes the job himself. As he screws the box back on he gives all the screws a really hard final twist; if Jim ever tries to get them loose (fat chance) he'll know who screwed them in last.

"So how's your work going?" Jim asks brightly, to fill the silence.

"Okay."

Dennis finishes, closes up. "I'm going to have to be in Washington most of next week," he tells his son. "Might be good if you came up an evening or two and had dinner here."

"Okay, I'll do that."

Dennis puts the tools back in the tool chest.

"Well, I'm off now, I guess."

"Say good-bye to your mom, first."

"Oh yeah."

Dennis follows him back in the house, shaking his head a little. Legs waving about in the air . . . kind of like a bug turned on its back.

Inside Jim says his farewells to Lucy.

"How come we haven't seen Sheila lately?" Lucy asks him.

"Oh, I don't know. We haven't been going out that much, these last weeks."

"That's too bad. I like her."

"Me too. We've just both been busy."

"Well, you should call her."

"Yeah, I will."

"And you should give your uncle Tom a call too. Have you done that lately?"

"No, but I will, I promise. Okay, I'm off. Thanks for the help, Dad."

Dennis can see him forgetting the promises to call even as he walks out of the door. "See you. Be careful," he says. Try not to get stuck in your car's motor compartment. As the door slams shut Dennis laughs, very shortly.

... 5

Jim tracks away angry. He forgets instantly about calling Sheila, about calling Uncle Tom; he's too absorbed in his own feelings. Long minutes alone on the freeway, so much of life spent this way; thinking angrily, sifting and rearranging events until it's all his father's fault, until he's angry only at Dennis and not at himself. That look over the glasses, after he managed to extricate himself from his damned car! Humiliating.

He parks in South Coast Plaza's subterranean garage, takes the elevator up to the top of the mall, south end; some of the most expensive apartments in OC are up here. Through one soundproofed door comes the thump of percussion and a tiny wash of voices. In Jim goes.

Sandy and Angela's ap consists of six big rooms, set like boxcars one after the next. Window walls in each face southwest; it's a heliotropic home. Outside these windows a balcony extends the whole length of the ap. The balcony and all the rooms but the bedroom are filled with people, maybe sixty of them. It's the nightly party, no one is too excited. Sandy's not there yet. Jim walks into the kitchen, the first room. There are houseplants everywhere, giant ones in giant glazed pots. They look so healthy they might be plastic; people say Angela has a polymer thumb.

Jim sees no one he particularly wants to talk to, and continues through the kitchen to the balcony. He leans on the chest-high railing and looks down at the lightshow of coastal OC, pulsing at the speed of a rapid heartbeat. That's his town.

Jim's depressed. He's a part-time word processor for a title and real estate company, a part-time night school teacher at Trabuco Junior College. His father thinks he's a failure; his friends think he's a fool. This last has been his angle, of course, he's cultivated it because laughs are at a premium among his friends, and they're all comedians; the fool routine keeps Jim from being nothing more than part of the laughtrack. But it can get old, old, old. How much nicer it would be to be . . . well, something else.

Sandy shows up, three hours late to his own party. SOP. "Hell*ooo!*" he shouts, and Angela Mendez his ally comes over to give him a kiss. He moves on, his pale freckled skin flushed with excitement. "Hey, hello! Why are you just *sitting* there?" He goes to the music wall, cranks the volume up to say a hundred thirty decibels, Laura's Big Tits singing "Want Becomes Need" over thick percussion that sounds like twenty spastics in a room full of snare drums. "*Yeah!*" Sandy pulls some girls off the long beige couch in the video room, starts them dancing around the screens hanging from the ceiling, he won't be satisfied until everyone is dancing for at least one number, this is understood and everyone gets up and starts to bounce, happy at the action. Sandy flies from dancer to dancer, shoves his face right in theirs, psycho grin pulsating, pale blue eyes popping like they might fall out and bob at the end of springs any second now: "You look too *normal*! Try *this*!" And they're holding eyedroppers full of Sandy's latest, Social Affability, Apprehension of Beauty, Get Wired, who knows what the little label will say this time, but it's sure to be fun. Sandy's the best drug designer in OC—famous, really. And he doesn't disdain the old-fashioned highs either. Angela is mixing pitchers of margaritas in the kitchen, Sandy is stopping at certain broad-leafed houseplants and pulling giant spliffs from hiding places, lighting them with a magnum blowtorch, throwing them at people, shouting, "*Smoke this!*" Jim, looking in from the balcony, can only laugh. There is a Sandy who is subtle, thoughtful, quick-witted, a culturevulture in Jim's own league; but that isn't him in there, putting the jumper cables to his own party. Time for a different act: Wired Host. Is there an eyedropper with that on the label?

Jim goes to work on an eyedropper called Pattern Perception (so his name has been chosen!), with a couple whose names he can almost remember. Blink, blink. Are those stars or streetlights? "I'm fourth-generation OC," he tells them apropos of nothing. "I have it in my genes, this place, I have a race memory of what it used to be like when the orange groves were here."

"Uh-huh."

"Nowadays we'd have a hard time living that slowly though, don't you think?"

"Uh-huh."

There's something lacking in this conversation. Jim is about to ask his companions if they have brains at home they can plug in but forgot to bring, or if they have to pretend like this *all* the time, when Tashi interrupts. "Hey McPherson," he says from the French doors to the game room. "Come take up the paddle."

Of course this is Jim the Fool they're requesting. His ping-pong style is a bit unorthodox, call it clumsy in fact; but that's okay. Any request is better than none.

Arthur Bastanchury is just finishing off Humphrey Riggs, and Humphrey, Jim's boss at the real estate office, hands over the sweaty paddle to Jim with a muttered curse. Jim's up against the Ping-Pong King.

Arthur Bastanchury, the Ping-Pong King, is about six feet two, eyes of blue, dark-haired and wide-shouldered. Women like him. He's also a dedicated anti-war activist and underground newspaper publisher, which Jim admires, as Jim has socialist ideas himself. And an all-round Good Guy. Yes, Arthur, in Jim's opinion, is someone to reckon with.

They take a long warm-up, and Jim discovers he has blinked the wrong amount of Pattern Perception. He can see the cat's cradle in time that he and Arthur are creating, but only well after the fact, and the contrail-like after-images of the white ball are distracting. It looks like trouble for McPherson.

They start and it turns out to be even worse than he expected. Jim's got quick hands, but he is awkward, there's no denying it. And his fine-tuning is badly out of order. Giving up, more or less, he decides to go recklessly on the attack, thinking Let's get this fucking pinko, which is funny since he actually agrees completely with what he knows of Arthur's political views. But now it's useful to go into a redkiller mindset.

Also useful not to care about appearances; Arthur is a power player with a monster slam, and Jim has to make some, well, funny moves—twists and contortions, dives into the walls and such. . . . In fact, Angela hears he's playing and comes in to move her plants out of danger. Fine, more room to maneuver.

Still, Jim is losing badly when he tries a vicious topspin and smacks himself right in the forehead with the edge of his paddle. General laughter accompanies this move; but actually, after the pain recedes and the black lights leave his vision, the blow seems to have stimulated something inside Jim's brain. Synapses are knocked into new arrangements, new axons sprout immediately, the whole game suddenly becomes *very clear.* He can see two or three hits ahead of time where the ball is *destined* to go.

Jim rises to a new level, a pure overcompetency, his backhand slam begins to work, any opportunity on that side and a snap of the wrist sends over a crosscourt shot angled so sharply that people sitting right at netside take it in the face. Alternate those with down-the-line backhands, tailing away. These slaps plus the bold, not to say idiotic, dives into the wall to retrieve slams when on defense, reverse the game's momentum. He takes his last serves and wins going away, 21–17.

"Two out of three," Arthur says, not amused.

But it's a mistake to go for a rematch when Jim is on like this. So much of ping-pong is just the confidence to hit the thing as hard as possible, after all.

Second game Jim feels the power flow through him, and there's nothing Arthur can do about it.

Jim can even take the luxury of noticing that the video room next door is filling up with spectators. Sandy has turned on the game room cameras, and the watchers are treated to eight shots of live action, all played out on the big screenwall and the various free screens hanging from silver springs that extend down from the ceiling: Jim and Arthur, flying around from every angle. The game room clears out, in fact, as people go into the video room to observe the spectacle, and the two players have room to really go at it.

But Arthur's out of luck tonight, Jim's getting a sort of . . . *uncanny* ability here, premonitions so strong that he has to hold back on his swing to allow Arthur time to hit it to the preordained spots. What a joy, this silly table game.

Second game, 21–13. Arthur tosses his paddle on the table. "Whew!" He grins, gracious in defeat: "You're hot tonight, Jim Dandy. Time for those margaritas."

Jim starts to wind down. He looks around; Tashi and Abe weren't even in the game room or the video room. Too bad they missed it, Jim likes his friends to see him being more than just The Fool. Oh well. The act is its own reward, right?

Sometimes Jim has a hard time convincing himself of this.

"Nice game," says a voice behind him. He turns; it's Virginia Novello.

Adrenaline makes a little comeback. Virginia, Arthur Bastanchury's ally until just a couple months ago, is Jim's idea of female perfection. Standing right there in front of him.

Long straight thick blond hair,
Bleached by sun but still full of red and yellow.
Yes, they sell that hair color, and call it California Gold.
She's a touch under medium height.
It's the body women go to the spa to work for.
Virginia goes there herself.
Sleeveless blouse, embroidered white on white, scoop neck.
Muscular biceps, little toy triceps,
Perfectly defined under smooth tanned skin. Whoah.
Aesthetic standards change over time, but why?
The California Model's features: small fine nose, curvy mouth, wide-set blue
    eyes.
This is the Look, in the society of the Look:
Freckles on cheeks, under a sunburn that might start peeling right now.
That brake light in your brain. . . .

Well, it's worth a little adrenaline, Jim thinks. Of course everyone is beautiful these days, we're in California after all, but for Jim, Virginia Novello is *it*.

And here she is talking to him. She has before, of course, a bit remotely perhaps, and in the context of Arthurness, but now . . . Jim offers her his new margarita and she takes a sip. Arm muscles slide and bunch under tan skin, silky hairs on forearm gleam in the light. Her white blouse is a nice change from all the spectrum-slide primaries in the room. These are fabrics that are colored in a very narrow band of the spectrum, say fifteen hertz, so that you can, for instance, just begin to see a blue blouse shade into violet, or yellow into green, across the whole of the piece of cloth. It's a great look, and very popular because of that, but still, a change is nice. Kind of bold.

"Ping-pong is funny," Jim says. "It really varies from day to day how much you can count on your game working. You know?"

"I think most sports are like that. The edge comes rarely. Maybe it goes beyond sports, eh?"

Jim nods, regarding her. Her smile, seldom seen, small and controlled, is actually quite nice. He doesn't know much about her, despite the admiration from a distance. Business executive of some sort? Funny match with Arthur's political activism. Maybe that's why they broke up. Let's not worry about it.

They go out on the balcony, and Jim asks her about her work. She helps to administer Fashion Island, the old mall above Newport Beach. So she's working for the management company hired by the Irvine Corporation, which owns the land. The old rancho dismemberment wealth, extending two hundred years into time . . . although Irvine's only a name now, the family long out of it. Jim talks about this aspect of the land ownership of OC, and Virginia listens, interested and inquisitive. "It's funny, you never think about how things got this way," she says brightly.

Well. Jim does. But he passes on that. He tells her about the recent archaeological dig under Fluffy Donuts, making himself the butt of the jokes, and she laughs. The Fool, after all, can be a useful role, as he already knows. Especially after a show of competence at the ping-pong table; then it can be mistaken for modesty. They watch cars track over the freeways. Leaning over the red geraniums that line the balcony's top, their arms brush together. It's accidental and means nothing, sure.

"Do you surf?" Virginia asks.

"No. Tash tried to teach me, but the moment I stand the board flies away and I fall down."

She laughs. "You've got to just commit and jump up without thinking about balance. I bet I could teach you."

"Really? I'd love it." No lie. Virginia at the beach? What an image. "Tash just always says, like I've done it on purpose, 'Don't *fall*, Jim.'"

She laughs again.

Now, at this time Jim is in alliance with Sheila Mayer. As his mom would be quick to point out. They've been allied for almost four months now, and it's been a pretty good four months, too. But Jim has been taking it for granted for some time; the thrill is gone, and Sheila is a Lagunatic and doesn't get up to central OC more than twice a week, and Jim has been entertaining himself pretty frequently with other women he's met at Sandy's. All his friends therefore know about it, and he's come to consider himself a free man, though Sheila might be surprised to hear it. But there's not been a really comfortable time to discuss it with her, yet. He will soon. Meanwhile he fancies that his infidelities make him a little less The Fool in the eyes of his friends, a little more The Man of the World.

And at the moment he isn't thinking about any of that anyway. He's forgotten Sheila, in fact, and if he's thinking about friends, it's only a vague underfeeling that he would be *really* impressive if allied with Virginia Novello.

They talk for quite some time about the relative values of surfing and bodysurfing, and other philosophical issues of that sort. They go in and sit down on one of the long beige couches and drink more margaritas. They talk about Jim's work, people they know in common, music groups they like. The party is getting emptier, only the old regulars left, Sandy and Angela's actual friends. Sandy drops by and crouches at their feet to chat for a while. "Did Jim tell you about our attack on the parking lot?"

"Yeah, I want to see this piece of ancient wood you liberated."

"Did you bring it, Jim?"

"I'm having it made into the handle of my ping-pong paddle." They laugh; he made a joke, apparently! This must really be his night.

Tashi's ally Erica stands over Sandy, grabs him by his long red ponytail and pulls. "Sandy, are you going to open the sauna and jacuzzi tonight?"

"Yeah, haven't I already? Man, what time is it? One?" The psycho grin grows impossibly wide, Sandy goggles at Erica with his lecher leer. "Come on along while I turn on the heat, you can test it out for me."

"Test what out for you?"

Arms around each other they walk toward the sauna and jacuzzi room at the end of the ap, calling for Tash and Angela.

"Want to jacuzzi?" Virginia asks Jim.

"Sure," he says coolly.

They follow Sandy and Erica and Tash and Angela and Rose and Gabriela and Humphrey and one or two others down the hall and into the jacuzzi room. Sandy snaps on light, water heater, sauna heater, water jets. The room is hot, humid, filled with Angela's most tropical houseplants, hanging in a network of macramé. Redwood decking, redwood walls, domed skylight, big blue ceramic tile jacuzzi bath: yes, Sandy and Angela live a good life. They go into the changing rooms and strip.

Of course they do this often at Sandy's place, social nudity is casual and no big deal at all. That's why Jim's left eye has gotten stuck looking straight into his nose, from trying to watch both Virginia and Erica undress at the same time. Surreptitious knuckle in there to free the poor thing, for more looking you bet; video saturation has trained Jim, like everyone else, to a fine appreciation of the female image. Now when arms are crossed and those blouses come over those heads in a single fluid motion, breasts falling free, hair shaken out all over shoulders, the men exhale a happy connoisseur's sigh. No doubt the women get a little peak in the readout too, moment of pseudotaboo exhibitionism here, quite a thrill just to Take It All Off in Front of Everybody, whoah, besides here's all these wrestler/surfer muscles everywhere. . . . But it's a casual scene, sure, of course, obviously.

Naked, they go out into the jacuzzi room and step into the bath. Rose and Gabriela, long-time allies, duck each other under the hot water. Steam and laughter fill the room. Debbie Riggs, Humphrey's sister, comes in to find out what the noise is all about. The water's too hot for Virginia and she sits dripping on the decking beside Jim. They all talk.

> Bodies. Wet skin over muscles. We all know the shapes.
> Ruddy light breaks in wet curls of hair.
> Wrestlers' bodies, swimmers' bodies, surfers' bodies, spa bodies.
> Tall breasts, full from the collarbones down.
> Cocks float in the bubbles, snaking here and there, hello? hello?
> Hello?
> Curled pubic hair: equilateral eye magnets.
> Blink blink, blink blink, blink blink (in the brain).

Virginia leans forward over powerful thighs to check one manicured and painted toenail. She's gone for the muscly look, especially in arms and legs, although her lats show a lot of rowing and her abdominals a lot of sit-ups. It's a nicely balanced look, refreshing after some of the other women's extremism: Rose, for instance, who has left her upper body childlike while her bottom and legs are immensely strong, or Gabriela, who has bench presser's pecs and campily big breasts over boyish hips and long slim legs . . . both just going with their original forms, both bizarrely attractive in their own ways; but there's something to be said for moderation, the standard proportions taken to their perfect end point.

Virginia gets back in the water, she and Jim are pressed together flank to flank. Bubbles cover the scene below. Passing an eyedropper their fingers touch and it seems to complete a circuit of some sort. Slick bodies are everywhere, sliding together like a pod of dolphins. Across from them Angela, who has an angelic body, hormonic aid making it lusher than standard but who's complaining, stands, legs apart, arms overhead to hold the eyedropper to upturned face: a vision. The *image*. . . .

A breast shoves into his arm. "I live in SCP north," Virginia says suddenly, under the crowd noise. "Want to come over?"

Jim, master of wit as always, says "Twist my arm."

... 6

Their wet hair cools in the breeze blowing scrap paper around the parking garage. A two-minute drive to the north side of South Coast Plaza, where there is a set of condos that match the aps Sandy and Angela live in. Up to Virginia's place, inside, a laughing race to the bedroom.

Virginia flips on the lights, turns on the video system. Eight little cameras mounted high on the walls track them with IR sensors, and two big sets of screens on the side walls show Virginia undressing, from both front and back. Jim finds the images arousing indeed, and by the time he gets his pants off half the screens show him with a hard-on waving about wandlike; Virginia cracks up and pulls him by it onto the bed. They maneuver into positions where they can both see a wall of screens. Images of Virginia—

Smooth curve of thigh; it's spent a lot of time on the bike machines.
Blond wash of hair above.
Black pubic hair below, shaved to an arrow pointing down and in.
Blink! Blink!
Swinging breasts (the Image).
Lats, standing out from rib cage—

—pierce him utterly. She straddles him, slides onto him. Ah: the vital connection. She's on top and she plays at holding down his wrists, so that her biceps bulge and her face is in exquisite profile as she looks to the screens to her left, and her breasts . . . well, it's almost enough to distract Jim from the screens, but on the wall he's looking at there is a view from above his head, so he can still see breasts falling from taut pectorals, while the screen next to it has the reverse angle, and shows the obscene, pornographic, not to say anatomically improbable image of his cock sliding in and out of her: concealed by the big muscles of her bottom, revealed pink and wet, concealed—

The screens flicker and go blank. Glassy gray-green nothingness.

Virginia jumps off Jim. "What the fuck!" Angrily she punches the buttons of the control panel over by the light switches. "It's *on!*" But no pictures. The cameras are not following her as she moves, either. "Well, what the hell!" She's flushed with exertion, exasperation, she tries the buttons again, hitting them hard. "The damn thing must be broken!" Something in her tone of voice makes Jim start to go limp, despite the way she looks standing there. Besides, he's distracted himself. What happened to them? "Can you fix it?" she asks.

"Well . . ." Dubiously Jim rolls off the gel bed and looks at the control panel. Everything appears to be in order there. . . . He looks up at all the cameras; cables still extend from them into the walls. "I don't *think* so. . . ."

"Shit." She sits on the bed, bounces beautifully.

"Well, but . . ." Jim gestures at the bed. "We've still got the major piece of equipment."

Her mouth purses into a moue of irritation. She glances up, flips his deflated cock against his leg. "Oh yeah?" She laughs.

Now Jim, who is beginning to get a bit concerned, cannot afford a decent bedroom video system himself, and his little set is always breaking down. So he's used to ad-libbing in difficult situations like these. He takes a look in the bathroom. "Ah ha!" There's a free-standing full-length mirror in the great skylighted expanse of the bathroom, and full of hope he pulls it out into the bedroom. Virginia is draped out on the bed like a centerfold, looking for eye-droppers in the bedside table drawer. "Here we have it," says Jim. "Early version of the system."

She laughs, gives him directions as he positions the mirror. "Down a little. There, that's good." Quickly they are back at it, across the bed so they can both look to the side and see the mirror, where their twins thrash away. It's discon-certing to have the twins looking back at them, but interesting too, and Jim can't help grinning lasciviously at himself. The image itself is different also, the video's softness and depth of field replaced by a hard, silvered, glossy materi-ality, as if they've got a window here and are spying on a couple in some more glassy world.

When they're done, Jim drawls "Pret-ty kink-y." And can't help laughing.

Virginia isn't amused. "I'll have to get the repairmen by to fix it, and I hate that. It's always, 'Excuse me, ma'am, but we need a test of some kind to see if the system's working.'"

Jim laughs. "You should tell them to fuck themselves, make that the test."

Virginia scowls. "They probably would, the perverts."

Well, okay. Now that they're done, Virginia gets restless. Appears she still wants to party some more. Jim's agreeable, whatever this beautiful new friend likes is fine by him. He likes to party too. So soon they're up, dressed, back to Sandy's.

...7

On the way up to Sandy's they run into Arthur Bastanchury, who is returning to the party's end carrying a big over-the-shoulder bag. Jim is uncomfortable, here he's just gone to bed with Arthur's ex-ally and who knows what's still going on between them, really. But both Virginia and Arthur are cool, and after they go inside and sit in the video room and chat for a while about what's on the screens, Jim relaxes too. We're in the postmodern world, he reminds himself, alliances are no more than that: every person is a sovereign entity, free to do what they want. No reason to feel any unease.

Sandy and Angela, Tashi and Erica come out of the jacuzzi room wrapped in big thick white towels, steaming faintly. They go on into the kitchen to rustle up a late-night snack. Arthur puts his bag on the floor and opens it, begins to arrange things inside. "So are you coming with me?" he shouts into the kitchen.

"Not tonight," Sandy calls back in. "I'm beat." No word from the others. Arthur makes a face. "Ginny?"

Virginia shakes her head. "'Fraid not, Art. I told you before, I think it's a waste of time."

Arthur looks disgusted with her, and abruptly she gets up and walks into the kitchen, where their friends are laughing over something Sandy has done or said. Ruefully Arthur shakes his head: he's going to have to go it alone again, the expression says.

"What's a waste of time?" Jim asks.

Arthur pins him with a challenging stare. "Trying to make a difference in this world. Virginia thinks that trying to make a difference is a waste of time. I suppose you think the same. You all do. A lot of talk about how bad things are, how we have to change things—but when it comes to a question of action, it turns out to be nothing but talk."

"Don't be so sure!"

"No?" Arthur's tone is careless, his grin sardonic; he looks down to arrange the papers in his bag. Offended, Jim rises to it.

"No! Why don't you tell me what you have in mind?"

"I've got some posters in here. I'm going to do an information blitz in the mall. Here—" He pulls one out, hands it up to Jim without looking at him.

From one angle it's a holo of a wave at the Pipeline, a perfect tube about to eat some ecstatic goofy-footed surfer. Shift the poster just a bit, though, and it becomes a holo of a dead American soldier, perhaps taken in Indonesia. The legs are gone. Under this apparition bold letters proclaim:

DO YOU WANT TO DIE?
Open Wars in Indonesia, Egypt, Bahrain, and Thailand.
Covert Wars in Pakistan, Turkey, South Korea, and Belgium.
There Are American Soldiers in Every One.
350 of Them Die EVERY DAY.
THE DRAFT IS BACK. YOU COULD BE NEXT.

Jim rubs his chin. Arthur laughs at him. "So?" he taunts. "Want to come with me and put these up?"

"Sure," Jim says, just to shut off that contemptuous look. "Why not?"

"It could land you in jail, that's why not."

"Freedom of speech, right?"

"They have ways around that. Littering. Defacement. These things have to be lased off, they have molecular-ceramics bonds on the back."

"Hmph. Well, so what? Are you planning to get caught?"

Arthur laughs. "No." He stares at Jim, a curious look in his eye. Despite the events of the night—Jim's ping-pong victory, his jump in bed with Arthur's ex-ally . . . or perhaps because of them, somehow . . . Arthur seems to have some curious kind of moral high ground, from which he speaks down to Jim. Jim doesn't understand this; he only feels it.

"Come on, then." Arthur's up and off to the door. Jim follows him out and just has time to register the scowl on Virginia's face, there in the kitchen. Oops.

"Let's start at the north end and work our way back here," says Arthur as they descend to the ground floor of the mall. They get on the empty people mover and track through the complex to South Coast Village, buried under the northward expansion of the mall proper. "Good enough. Let's keep it fast, say twenty minutes total. But casual. Watch out for the mall police."

They start down the wide concourse of the mall. Escalators in mirrors branch off to a score of other floors, some real, some not. "Put the posters up then rub this rod over them. That activates the bond."

Jim puts one small poster up, on the window of a Pizza City. This one's a holo of a naked girl standing in knee-deep tropical surf; the shift of angle and it's another blood-soaked fallen soldier, with the words "THE DEFENSE DEPT. RUNS THIS COUNTRY—RESIST" underneath. "Whoah. This might spoil a few dinners."

By now it's nearly four A.M., although it's impossible to tell inside the mall, which is as timeless as a casino. The big department stores are closed, but everywhere else the windows and mirrors and tile walls gleam with a jumpy neon insistence:

Lights! Camera! Action!

Long central atrium, five stories tall.

Plastic trees, colored light fountains. Reflected

Images. Game parlors, snack bars, video bars: all open, all pulsing.

Hey, guess what! I'm hungry.

The South Coast carousel is spinning. All its animals have riders.

Glazed eye. Clashing music spheres. Blinks.

Gangs in the restroom niches, in closed shop entries.

Into an expresso bar. Hanging out.

Shopping.

On Main Street.

You live here.

Jim and Arthur slap their posters on walls, windows, doors. "The mortuary is really hopping tonight," Arthur says.

Jim laughs. He hates malls himself, though he spends as much time in them as anyone. "So why do you poster a place like this? Isn't it a waste of molecular ceramics?"

"Mostly, sure. But the draft has gotten teeth since the Gingrich Act was re-enacted, and a lot of people in here are bait. They don't know it because they don't read newsheets. In fact when you get right down to it they don't know a fucking thing."

"The sleepwalkers."

"Yeah." Arthur gestures at a group lidded almost beyond the point of walking. "Sleepwalkers, exactly. How do you reach people like that? I published a newsheet for a while."

"I know. I liked it."

"Yeah, but you *read*. You're in a tiny minority. Especially in OC. So I decided to move into media where I can reach more people. We make videos that do really well, because they're sex comedies for the most part. The newsheet equipment has been converted to poster work."

"I've seen the ones on Indonesia that Sandy has in his study. They're beautiful."

Arthur waves a hand, annoyed. "That's irrelevant. You culturevultures are all alike. It's all aesthetics for you. I don't suppose you really believe in anything at all. It's just whatever attracts the eye."

Without replying Jim goes into the McDonald's, puts up a poster over the menu. On the one hand he feels a little put upon, it's a bit unfair to attack him while he's right here risking jail to put up these stupid posters, isn't it? At the same time, there's a part of him that feels Arthur is probably right. It's true, isn't it? Jim has despised the ruling forces in America for as long as he has been aware of them; but he's never done anything about it, except complain. His efforts have all gone to creating an aesthetic life, one concentrating on the past. King of the culturevultures. Yes, Arthur has a certain point.

When they rendezvous outside Jack-in-the-Box, where Arthur has been at work, Jim says, "So why do you do all this, Arthur?"

"Well just look at it!" Arthur bursts out. "Look at these sleepwalkers, zombieing around in some kind of L-5 toybox. . . . I mean, this is our country! This is it, from sea to shining sea, some kind of brain mortuary! While the rest of the world is a real mortuary. The world is falling apart and we devote ourselves to making weapons so we can take more of it over!"

"I know."

"That's right, you know! So why do you ask?"

"Well, I guess I meant, do you really think this kind of thing"—swinging his poster bag—"will make any difference?"

Arthur shrugs, grimaces. "How do I know? I feel like I have to do something. Maybe it just helps me. But you have to do *something*. I mean, what the hell do you do? You type a word-cruncher for a real estate office, you teach technoprose to technocrats. Isn't that right?"

Almost against his will, Jim nods. It's true.

"You don't give a shit about your jobs. So you drift along being ace culturevulture and wondering what it's all about." The grimace intensifies. "Don't you believe in *anything*?"

"Yeah!" Feeble show of defiance. Actually, he's always thought he should be more political. It would be more consistent with his hatred for the wars being waged, for the weapons being made (his father's work, yes!)—for the way things are.

"I've heard you talk about the way OC used to be," Arthur says. They spot a mall cop and stand watching the keno results appear in the Las Vegas window, green numbers embedded in glass. When the cop has passed Arthur covers the numbers with another dead soldier. "Some of what you say is important. The attempts to make collective existences out here, Anaheim, Fountain Valley,

Lancaster—it's important to remember those, even if they did fail. But most of that citrus utopia bit is bullshit. It was always agribiz in California, the Spanish land grants were grabbed up in parcels so big that it was a perfect location for corporate agriculture, it was practically the start of it. Those groves you lament were picked by migrant laborers who worked like dogs, and lived like it was the worst part of the Middle Ages."

"I never denied it," Jim protests. "I know all about that."

"So what's with this nostalgia?" Arthur demands. "Aren't you just wishing you could have been one of the privileged landowners, back in the good old days? Shit, you sound like some White Russian in Paris!"

"No, no," Jim says weakly. They plaster restroom doors and walls with posters, approach the May Company at the south end of the mall. "There were some serious attempts to make cooperative agricultural communities, here. A lot of them had to do with the orange groves. We have to remember them, or, or their efforts were wasted!"

"Their efforts *were* wasted." Arthur slaps up a poster. "We'd better get out of here, the cops are bound to have seen some of these by now." He pokes Jim in the arm with a hard finger. "Their efforts were wasted because no one followed up on them. Even this kind of thing is trivial, it's preaching to the deaf, making faces at the blind. What's needed is something more active, some kind of *real resistance*. Do you understand?"

"Well, yeah. I do." Although actually Jim isn't too clear on what Arthur means. But he is convinced that Arthur is right, whatever he means. Jim's an agreeable guy, his friends convince him of things all the time. And Arthur's arguments have a particular force for him, because they express what Jim has always felt he should believe. He knows better than anyone that there is something vital missing from his life, he wants some kind of larger purpose. And he would love to fight back against the mass culture he finds himself in; he knows it wasn't always like this.

"So you mean you *are* doing something more active?" he asks.

Arthur glances at him mysteriously. "That's right. Me and the people I work with."

"So what the hell!" Jim cries, irritated at Arthur's dismissals, his secretive righteousness. "I *want* to resist, but what can I do? I mean, I might be interested in helping you, but how can I tell when all you're doing is spouting off! What do you *do*?"

Arthur gives him the eye, looks at him hard and long. "We sabotage weapons manufacturers."

...8

The bones of whales lie scattered in the hills.

For millions of years it was a shallow ocean. Water creatures lived in forests of seaweed, and when the creatures and the forests died their bodies settled to the bottom and turned to mud, then stone. We stand on them.

Overhead the sun coursed, hundreds of millions of times. Underneath tectonic plates floated on the mantle, bumped together: pieces of a jigsaw puzzle, trying to find their proper places, always failing.

Where two pieces rubbed edges, the earth twisted, folded, buckled over. That happened here five million years ago. Mountains reared up, spewing lava and ash. Rain washed dirt into the shallow sea, filling it. Eventually it came to look like what we know: a chain of sandstone mountains, a broad coastal plain, a big estuary, an endless sandy beach.

And so a hundred thousand years ago, on a continent free of human beings, this land became home to fantastic creatures. The Imperial mammoth, fifteen feet tall at the shoulder; the American mastodon, almost that tall; giant camels and giant bison; an early horse; ground sloths eighteen feet high; tapirs; bears, lions, saber-toothed tigers, dire wolves; a vulture with a twelve-foot wingspan. Their skeletons too can be found in the hills, and the bluffs above the estuary.

But time passed, and species died. It rained less and less. The plain was crossed by one river, our Santa Ana River, which was older even than the mountains, cutting through them as they rose. This river fell out of the mountains to the estuary of our Newport Bay.

Around this big salt marsh grew the salt-tolerant plants, arrowgrass, pickleweed, sea lavender, salt grass. Upstream, along the fresh river, trees grew: cottonwood, willow, sycamore, elderberry, toyon, mulefat; and up in the hills, white alder and maple. Out on the plains grew perennial bunchgrasses, needlegrass, and wildflowers; also sagebrush and mustard; and up in the hills, chaparral and manzanita. In low spots on the plain there were freshwater marshes, *home to cattails, sedges, duckweed, and water hemlock; and there were vernal pools, drying every spring to become flower-filled meadows. The foothills and the slopes of the mountains were covered by live oak forests, the oaks protecting grassy understories, and mixing with walnut, coffeeberry, redberry, and bush lupines; and above them, higher on the mountains, were knobcone pines and Tecate cypress. All these plants grew wildly, constrained only by their genes, their neighbors, the weather. . . . Evolving to fill every niche in conditions, they grew and died and grew.*

Offshore, among the myriad fish, our cousins lived: whales, dolphins, porpoises, sea lions, sea otters, seals. Around the marshes, in the reeds, our brothers lived: coyotes, weasels, raccoons, badgers, rats. On the plains our sisters lived: deer, elk, foxes, wildcats, jackrabbits, mice. In the hills our parents lived: mountain lions, grizzly bears, black bears, gray wolves, bighorn sheep. . . . There were a hundred and fifty different species of mammals living here, once upon a time; and snakes, lizards, insects, spiders—all of them were here.

This warm dry basin, between the sea and sky, was—and not so long ago— crawling with life. Teeming with all manner of life, saturated with the vigor of a complete ecology. Animals everywhere—in the grasslands, and the tidal marshes, and the sagebrush flats, and the oak forests of the foothills—animals everywhere. Animals everywhere! Animals everywhere. Animals . . . everywhere.

And the birds! In the skies there were birds of every kind. Gulls, pelicans, cranes, herons, egrets, ducks, geese, swans, starlings, pheasants, partridge, quail, finches, grouse, blackbirds, roadrunners, jays, swallows, doves, larks, falcons, hawks, eagles, and condors, the biggest birds in the world. Birds beyond counting, birds such that even as late as the 1920s, a man in Orange County could say this: "They came by the thousands, I am a little reluctant about saying how many, but I can only say we measured them by acres and not by numbers. In the fall of the year the ground would be white with wild geese."

I can only say we measured them by acres and not by numbers.

The ground white with wild geese.

...9

Abe Bernard guns his GM freeway rescue truck down the fast track, scattering the cars ahead with the power of the truck's sound and light show. "Get out of the way!" he shouts, his swarthy hatchet face twisted with anger. He and his partner Xavier have just been tapped out a few moments before, and he is still a bit jacked on the initial adrenaline surge. The driver of a passing car flips them off; Xavier says "Fuck you too, buddy," and Abe laughs shortly. Stupid fools, when they've crashed he hopes they lie there in the metal remembering how often they obstructed rescue teams, realizing that other fools are doing it that very moment as the trucks try to get to them. . . . Another recalcitrant driver ahead, Abe turns up the siren to its full howl, the music of his work: "Get—out—of the *way!*"

They're into the permanent traffic snarl where Laguna Canyon Highway meets the Coast Highway, pretty beach park to the right, century-long volleyball games still going, sun glancing off the sea in a million spearpoints. Abe keeps the siren on and they push cautiously through a red light, up the Canyon Highway. Beside him Xavier is on the box trying to get some more information on the accident, but Abe can't hear much through the siren and the radio crackle.

The oceanbound lanes across from them are bumpertobumper and crawling, and without a doubt it's worse on the far side of the accident, everyone overriding their carbrains to slow down and stare over into the other lane, bloodlust curiosity surging. . . . But going upcanyon they can still move; they haven't reached the accident's backup yet.

"Indications seem to be that the track has once again been left behind, causing two cars to occupy the same space at the same time," Xavier says in his rapid on-the-job patter. "We suspect lane changing is perhaps the culprit. My, look at the traffic ahead."

"I know." They've reached the backup. Ahead of them the brake light symphony is blinking, redred, redred, redred redred redred. Overrides everywhere, nowhere for people to go, impossible for the computers to clear things up when the lanes clog this badly, it's time to take the old Chevy supertruck offtrack, yes this baby has an *internal combustion engine* under its big hood. "Independent lo-co*motion*," Xavier sings as Abe turns the key and revs the engine, 1056 horsepower, atavistic Formula One adrenaline rush here as he steers them off the magnetic track into the narrow gap between fast-track cars and the center divider, roaring along in vibratory petrol power, let the poor saps breathe a bit of that carbon monoxide ambrosia, nostalgic whiff of last century's power smog as they zroom by almost taking off door handles, sideview mirrors, sure why not clip a few to give them a story to tell about this ten-millionth traffic jam of their OC condo lives? Abe still gets a bit buzzed putting the antique skills to work, firing by all the cars; he's just short of his first anniversary on the job. He cools it, drives closer to the center divider, still just manages to squeeze the gap left by some Cadillac monster, fiberglass body a replica of the 1992 cow, "Sure buddy, *I'm* the one in a *car*, here, a big fucking *truck* in fact and I'll shave your whole plastic side off if you don't get *over.*"

They barrel up the curves of the canyon road past traffic stopped dead on the tracks, past the condos covering the hills on both sides, ersatz Mediterranean minivillas in standard OC style—these carefully named Seaview Clifftops because they're the first homes upcanyon without the slightest chance of a glimpse of the ocean. Vroom, vroom, vroom, past the complex's too-small-to-be-used park, where as Jim tells it a hippo that escaped from Lion Country Safari settled down to establish a little hippo's empire in a pond, until they darted him to crane him out and killed him with too much tranquilizer, the idiots. And just past that heraldic fragment of OC natural history they accelerate over chewed asphalt covered with trash and chips of broken headlight plastic, around a corner and into the *sota*, the scene of the accident. One Chippie-mobile there off the tracks, its rooflight doing a strobe over the scene, red eye winking over and over.

Abe puts the truck in neutral and turns on the exterior power system, and they jump out and run to the scene. CHP are out on the tracks doing what they do best, setting out flares. Fast lane is a mess. As they approach Abe feels the sick horror and helplessness that anyone would feel, *oh my God no*, then he passes through the membrane as always and the professional takes over, the structural analyst trying to comprehend a certain configuration, and the best way to extricate the organic components of it from the inorganic.... And the horrified helpless witness is left up in a back corner of the mind, staring over the shoulder of the other guy, storing up images for dreams.

This time one of the lane-changing tracks appears to have malfunctioned. It's rare, but it happens. Working correctly, the computer controlling the magnetic track takes a request from an approaching car, slows cars in the adjacent lane to make a gap, slots the car onto the lane-change track and into a quick S-curve onto the track of the desired lane, fitting it neatly into the flow of traffic. No room for human error, and really it's thousands of times safer than letting drivers do it. But the one in ten million has come up once again, and the cause of accident is *sits*, something in the silicon; a car in the middle lane was tracked directly into the side of another in the fast lane, knocking it off its guidance system and into the center divider, while the first car spun and was plowed into by a follow-up car. All at around sixty-five mph. One more follow-up crunched mildly into the mess. The driver of that one, saved by the power of electromagnetic brakes, is out and babbling to the Chippies with the usual edge of hysteria. Abe and Xavier hop around the three main participants. The car against the center divider has a single occupant, crushed between dash, door, and divider. Chest cavity caved and blood-soaked, neck apparently broken. On to the impacting car, a couple in the front seat, driver unconscious and bleeding from the head, woman trapped underneath him and dash, bleeding heavily from the neck but apparently still conscious, eyes fluttering. Main follow-up with heavily starred windshield, not wearing those seat belts were you, two people already dragged out and on the ground, heads bloody.

"Those two in the middle car," Xavier pants as they run for the truck. "Yeah," says Abe. "The one on the divider is dots." Meaning dead on the spot. Xavier grabs his medic pack and hauls back to the car. Abe brings the truck down the shoulder as close to the middle car as he can get. Then he's out and pulling the cutters from the truckside, yanking on the power cord, hands shoved down into the sleeves, it's waldo time here and novice expert cutter Abe Bernard now has all the power of modern robotics in his hands. He starts snipping the flimsy steel of the car's sidewall as if it were chocolate. There's no resistance to the sheers at all. Water streams out over the metal under the cutters, spraying over Xavier who is crawling around just beyond the reach of Abe's work, squeezing into the new hole to do his medic routine. Xavier did two tours on Java with the Army and is very good indeed. At this point they could sure use another man or two, but budgets are tight everywhere, lot of rescue trucks to be kept manned and ready for tap-out, and budgets are tight, budgets are tight!

The horrified witness in the back of Abe's mind watches him snip steel as if he is cutting origami, with Xavier and the woman passenger just beyond the end of the blades, and wonders if he really knows how to do this. But the thought never reaches the part of Abe's mind that's at work. A Chippie comes over to help, pulls the wet steel back with his gloved hands, Abe keeps cutting, they make a good new door approximately where the old one used to be, and Xavier's got some compress kits plastered on the woman and is busy injecting her with various antishock superdrugs and a lot of new plasma/blood. Then it's time to get her into the inflatable conformable braces, neck and spine held firm and they reach in and everyone takes a hold, carefully here, breath held, warm flesh squeezed between the fingers, blood trickling over the back of the hand, they lift her out, oops her hand is caught, Abe snips the folded section of dash and she's free. Onto a stretcher, off to the ambulance room in the back of the truck. They run back and extricate the man, who may or may not be living, his head looks bad indeed but they stretcher him and run him into the gutbucket, lay him next to the woman. "Shit I've got to confirm the guy in the lead car," Abe remembers, grabs Xavier's steth and runs back. He has to break a window and lean in to get the steth on the driver's neck. Readout shows flat and he's back to the truck. A private gutbucket has showed to pick up the two from the follow-up car, Abe gives them a quick thumbs-up and guides the cutters as they're reeled back on board and jumps in the driver's seat, seat belt on yes, off they go. These old gasoline hogs can really accelerate.

Xavier sticks his head out the window that connects the cab to their rolling ER. "Going to the Lagunatic Asylum?"

"No, the canyon is so fucked up, I figure UCI is faster." Xavier nods.

"How are they?"

"The guy's dead. He was dots, I imagine. The woman's still going, but she's lost a lot of blood and her heart's hurting. I got her patched and plugged in and she's drinking plasma, but her pulse be weak still. She could use a proper heart machine." Xavier's black face is shiny with sweat, he's looking uptrack anxiously, he wants them to go faster. Abe guns it, they rocket around the last curve onto the Laguna Freeway link between 405 and 5, left on 405 onramp and up the San Diego Freeway, not ontrack but on the shoulder beside it, flying past the tracked cars on their left, pushing 100, 105, quickly to the University Drive offramp and onto the meandering boulevard, here's where the driving gets tricky, don't want to pull a Fred Spaulding here, Fred who put a rescue truck into an overpass pylon and killed everyone aboard except the crash victim in back, who died two days later in the hospital.

Headlights, taillights, don't you dare make that left turn in front of me there isn't time *screech,* he puts the siren on full volume and the howl fills everything, throat sinuses cranium, they reach the campus and go down to California Avenue, hang a mean left and fire up the hill to the ER driveway and up to the ambulance doors. By the time he's out and to the back of the truck Xavier and an ER nurse are rolling the woman through swinging doors and inside.

Abe sits on the loading dock, quivering a bit. A couple more ER nurses come out and he gets up, helps them get the dead driver onto a gurney. Inside. Back onto the rubber edge of the loading dock.

Xavier comes back out, sits heavily beside him. "They're working on it." All those years of medic work, the two tours in Indonesia and all, and still Xavier gets into it, every run. He lights a cigarette, hands trembling, takes a deep drag. Abe watches, feeling that he is just as bad as Xavier, though he tries not to care at all. Don't get into a savior complex! as the unit counselor would say. He looks at his watch: 7:30. Two hours since they got the call. Hard to believe; it feels longer, shorter—like six hours have banged by in fifteen minutes. That's rescue work for you. "Hey, we were off half an hour ago," he remembers. "Our shift is over."

"Good."

Time passes.

A doctor bumps out the swinging doors. "Bad luck this time, boys," he says cheerily. "Both dead on arrival, I'm afraid." Briefly he puts his hands on their shoulders, goes back inside.

For a while they just sit there.

"Shit," says Xavier, flicking his cigarette into the darkness. In the dim light Abe can just see the look on his face.

"Hey, X, we did what we could."

"The woman was *not* DOA! They let her go inside!"

"Next time, X. Next time."

Xavier shakes his head, stands up. "We're off, hey?"

"Yeah."

"Let's get out of here then."

Silently they roll. Abe puts them back on track, enters the program that will take the truck to MacArthur and the Del Mar Freeway, then up the Newport to Dyer. Everything seems empty, quiet. They track into the Fire and Rescue station, park the truck among a few dozen others, go inside, file reports, clock out, walk to their own cars in the employee lot. Abe approaches his car feeling the familiar drained emptiness. Every time he reaches for his own keys in this lot it's the same. "Catch you later, X," he calls at the dark figure across the lot.

"Doubtless. When we on again?"

"Saturday."

"See you then."

Xavier backs out, off to the depths of lower Santa Ana, and some life Abe can barely imagine: X has a wife, four kids, ten thousand in-laws and dependents . . . a life out of his grandfather's generation, as full of melodrama as any video soap. And X, supporting the whole show, is right on the edge. He's going to crack soon, Abe thinks. After all these years.

He gets back onto the Newport Freeway, great aorta of all the OC lives. River of red fireflies, bearing him on. He punches the program for South Coast Plaza south, sits back. Clicks in a CD, need something loud, fast, aggressive . . . Three Spoons and a Stupid Fork, yeah, powering out their classic album *Get the Fuck Off My Beach.*

What would your carbrain say if it could talk?
Would it say Jump In? Would it say Get Out and Walk?
    (You are a carbrain
    You're firmly on track
    You're given your directions
    And you don't talk back)
You are a carbrain
And your car is going to crash!
On the cellular level
Everything'll go smash!
    (And you'll be inside
    You'll be taken for a ride)

Abe sings along at the top of his lungs, tracks into SCP, finds parking almost directly below Sandy's place, takes the elevator up, pops on in. Blast of light, loud music, it's the Tustin Tragedy on the CD here, singing "Happy Days" in Indonesian gamelan style, punctuated by machine-gun fire. The rhythms perk Abe up immediately, and Erica gives him a peck on the cheek. "Tashi was looking for you." Good. Sandy barges around a corner, "Abra*ham*, you look wilted, you just got off work, right?" The Sandy grin, an eyedropper appears in his fingers and it's head back, lids pulled open, drip drip drip. Abe offers it back to Sandy; "Polish it, there's more." Drip, drip, drip, his spinal cord is suddenly snapping off big bursts of excess electricity and he wanders into the next room, they're dancing there and he feels great shocks of energy coursing up his spine and out his fingertips, he dances hard, leaping for the ceiling, shaking it all out, now that feels good. He tilts his head back, "Yow! Yow! Yoweeee!" Coyote time at Sandy's place, traditional high point of the parties, everyone just hauls back and lets loose, they must be audible all the way to Huntington Beach. Great.

Feeling much better, he goes out onto the balcony. Still no sight of Tash, though the balcony's his spot; Tash never goes indoors when he can help it. Even lives on a roof, in a tent. Abe loves it; Tash, his closest friend, is like a cold salt splash of the Pacific.

Instead he encounters Jim. Jim's a good friend too, no doubt about it. But sometimes . . . Jim's so earnest, so unworldly; Abe has to be in the right mood to really enjoy Jim's intense meaningfulness. Or whatever it is. Not now. "Hey there, bro," Abe says, "Howzit." Pretty lidded, he is.

"Good. Hey, you worked today, huh? How'd it go?"

Ah, Jimbo. Just what he doesn't want to talk about. "Fine." Jim cares, and that's nice, but Abe wants some distraction, here, preferably Tash, or one of his young women friends . . . a little chat and he's off.

Still no Tash on the balcony. To his surprise, he runs into Lillian Keilbacher instead. "Hello, Lillian! I didn't know you knew Sandy!"

"I didn't, till tonight." She looks thrilled to have been introduced, which is funny since Sandy knows everyone.

Lillian is maybe eighteen, a fresh-faced cute kid, blond and suntanned, a lively innocent interest in things. . . . Her mother and Jim's mother and Abe's mother are stalwarts of the tiny church they all attended as kids; the mothers are still into it, Abe and Jim have fallen away like the rest of civilization, Lillian . . . perhaps in that transition zone, who knows. Shit, Abe thinks guiltily, she shouldn't be at a party like this! But that almost makes him laugh. Who is he, anyway? He realizes he's holding the eyedropper sort of hidden, and thinks he's probably insulting her by being condescending to her youth. Besides, they lid out in second grade these days. He offers it to her. "No thanks," she says, "it just makes me dizzy."

He laughs. "Good for you." He lids a drip, laughs again. "Shit, what are you doing here? Last I saw you you were about thirteen, weren't you?"

"Probably. But, you know, it doesn't last."

He cracks up. "No, I guess not."

"I probably know more than you think I do."

Utterly transparent come-on in her eyes as she sidles up to him, so girlish that he wonders if it's actually a sophisticated come-on in clever disguise. He laughs and sees she's hurt, instant contraction back into herself as when you touch a sea anemone, ah, clearly she knows just as little as he suspected she did, maybe less. A girl, really. "You shouldn't be here," he says.

"Don't you worry about me." She sniffs disdainfully. "We're leaving soon to go to my friend Marsha's to spend the night anyway."

Jesus. "Good, good. How are your folks?"

"Fine, really."

"Say hello to them for me." Lillian agrees and with a last winsome over-the-shoulder smile she's off with her buddies. Abe remembers the girlish come-on and cracks up. Maybe she had in mind a first kiss from this handsome dashing old acquaintance, an older man no lie. A nice kid, truly; Sandy's seems definitely the wrong place for her, and he's glad to see her and her young friends giggling together out the door, the brave exploration into the den of sin completed.

He's even gladder half an hour later when Tash is pulled dripping from the jacuzzi, naked and totally lidded. Giggling young women, friends of Angela's that Sandy calls the Tustin Trollops, maneuver Tashi onto the surfboard surrogate and urge him to ride some video waves for them, which he does with a perfect stoned grace, unaware of anything but the video wave, a Pipeline beauty twenty feet tall and stretching off into eternity. "Whoah," says Tash from deep in his own tube. Erica, Tash's ally, watches him with a look of sharp disapproval; Abe laughs at her.

Jim says "Hey, with his arms out like that he looks just like the statue of Poseidon in the Athens museum, here wait a second." He goes to the video console and starts typing at the computer, and suddenly the wave is replaced by the motionless image of a statue: tall darkened-bronze bearded man, arms up to throw a javelin, eyes empty holes in the metal. Tash looks up, takes the pose instantly, and it brings down the house. "He does look just like him!" everyone exclaims. Jim, laughing, says, "Even the eyes are the same!" Tash growls in mock anger, without breaking the pose.

Abe laughs loud enough to draw the attention of a couple of the Tustin Trollops. Mary and Inez come over and join him on the couch; they're part of Abe's little fan club, and their lithe bodies press against his warmly, their fingers tangle in his black curls. Ah, yes, the blisses of unallied freedom. . . .

He's putting his arm around Inez when something—the give of soft flesh?—causes the image of the injured woman to strike him. Pulled from the wreck, bent, patched, braced, bloody—Fuck. Tension twists his stomach and he hugs Inez to him violently, clamping his eyes shut; his face contorts back to a mask of normality. "Where's that eyedropper I had with me?"

... 10

Dennis McPherson walks into his office one morning, just a mail visit before he runs over to White Sands, New Mexico, to oversee a test of the RPV system, now called Stormbee. He finds a note commanding him to go up and see Lemon.

His pulse goes up as the elevator rises. It's only been a week since Lemon flared into one of his tantrums, pounding his desk and going scarlet in the face and shouting right at McPherson. "You're too slow to do your job! You're a god-damned nitpicking perfectionist, and I won't abide it! I don't allow dawdlers on my team! This is a war like any other! You seize the offensive when the chance comes, and go all the way with it! I want to see that proposal for Stormbee *yesterday*!" And so on. Lemon likes to burst all constraints occasionally, everyone working for him agrees about that. This doesn't make McPherson like it any better. Lemon's been out of engineering so long that little matters like *weight* or *voltage* or *performance reliability* don't mean anything to him anymore. Those are things for others to worry about. For him it's *cost-effectiveness*, *schedules*, the team's *momentum*, its *look*. He's the team's fearless leader, the little führer of his little tin reich. If the project were perpetual motion he'd still be screaming about schedules, costs, PR . . .

This morning he's Mr. Charm again, ushering McPherson in, calling him "Mac," sitting casually on the edge of his desk. Doesn't he realize that the charmer routine means nothing when combined with the tantrums? Worse than that—the two-facedness turns him into a slimy hypocrite, a manic-depressive, an actor. It would be easier to take if he just did the screaming tyrant thing all the time, really it would.

"So, how's Stormbee coming along, Mac?"

"We've manufactured a prototype pod that is within the specs set by Feldkirk. The lab tests went okay and we're scheduled to test it on one of Northrop's RPVs out at White Sands this afternoon. If those go well we can either run it through some envelope testing or give it to the Air Force and let them go at it."

"We'll give it to the Air Force. The sooner the better." Of course. "They'll be testing it anyway."

That's true, but it would be a lot safer for LSR if they found out about any performance problems before they let the Air Force see it. McPherson doesn't say this, although he should. This abrogation of his responsibility to the program irritates him, but he's sick of the tantrums.

Lemon is going on as if the matter is settled. That's the trouble with super-black programs; the contractor tends to do less testing than any competition for a white program could possibly get away with. And yet there's no good reason for it; they don't have a deadline. Feldkirk just said they should get back to him as soon as they could. So the haste is just Lemon's obsession; he's weakening the strength of their proposal by a completely irrational sense that they have to hurry. . . .

"We're going as fast as we can," McPherson allows himself to say. It's risking another outburst, but to hell with it.

"Oh I know you are, I know." A dangerous gleam appears in Lemon's eye, he's about to press home the point of how he knows—because he's the boss here, he's in charge, he knows all. But McPherson deadpans his way through the moment, passes through unscathed. Lemon trots out some more of his führer encouragements, then says, "Okay, get yourself out to White Sands," with a very good imitation of a smile. McPherson doesn't attempt to reciprocate.

He tracks to San Clemente and takes the superconductor to El Paso. Fired like a bullet in an electromagnetic gun.

It's been a tough couple of months, getting this test prepared. Every weekday he's gone into the office at six A.M., made a list of the day's activities that is sometimes forty items long, and gone at it until early evening, or even later than that. At first he had to deal with all of the tasks concerned with designing the Stormbee system: talking with the engineers and programmers, making suggestions, giving commands, coordinating their efforts, making decisions . . . It's good work at that point, responding to the technical challenge and dealing with the problems presented by them. And his design crew is a good group, resourceful, hardworking, quirky; he has to ride herd on the efforts of this disparate bunch, and it's interesting.

Then they got into the production and components testing phase, and the debugging of the programming. That was frustrating as always; it's beyond his technical competence to contribute much in the way of specifics at that point, and all he could do was orchestrate the tests and keep everyone working at them. It's a bit too much like Lemon's role at that point, not that he'd ever go about it in the same style.

Then it was time for the big components' tests. And now, time for the first test of the entire system.

The train arrives inside the hour, and from the tube station at El Paso the LSR helicopter lofts him over to White Sands Missile Range, the testing grounds that a consortium of defense companies leases from the government.

As he gets out of the helicopter McPherson reaches in his coat pocket for the sunglasses he brought with him. It really is uncanny how white the sand in this area is: a strange geological feature, for sure. Not that anyone actually visits the little national park on the edge of the testing grounds.

McPherson is carted to the LSR building on the range, and several of the engineers there greet him. "It's ready to go," says Will Hamilton, LSR's on-site testing chief. "We've got Runway Able for noon and one, and the RPV is fueled and prepped."

"Great," says McPherson, checking his watch. "That's half an hour?"

"Right."

They have coffee and some croissants in the cafe, then take the elevator up six floors to the observation deck on the roof. Cameras and computers will be monitoring all aspects of the test, but everyone still wants to see the thing actually happen. Now they stand on a broad concrete deck, looking out over the waves of pure white dunes, extending to the horizons like an ocean that has been frozen and then had everything but pure salt bleached away. Such a weird landscape! McPherson enjoys the sight of it immensely.

Over to the north are the runways that the companies all share, crossing each other like an X over an H, their smudged concrete looking messy in the surrounding pureness. Compounds for Aerodyne, Hughes, SDR, Lockheed, Williams, Ford Aerospace, Raytheon, Parnell, and RWD lie scattered around in the dunes, like blocks dropped by a giant child. There's a great plume of smoke out to the east, lofting some thirty thousand feet into the sky; someone's test has succeeded, or failed, it's hard to tell, although there's an oiliness to the plume that suggests failure. "RWD was trying out the new treetop stealth bomber's guidance system," Hamilton informs McPherson. "They say it didn't see a little hill over that way."

"Too bad."

"The pilot was automatically ejected no more than a second before impact, and he survived. Only broken legs and ribs."

"That's good."

"RPVs are the coming thing, there's no doubt about it. Everything moves too fast for pilots to be useful! They're just up there at risk, and it costs ten times as much to make a plane that will accommodate them, even though they can't do anything anymore."

McPherson squints. "As long as all the automatic systems work."

Hamilton laughs. "Like ours, you mean. Well, we'll find out real soon now." He gestures to the west. "The target tanks are out there on the horizon. We've followed your instructions, so they're equipped with the Soviets' Badger anti-aircraft systems, and surrounded by Armadillo SAM installations. Those should give the plane a run for its money."

McPherson nods. The six tanks on the western horizon, also under remote control, are little black frogs trundling south in a diagonal pattern, churning up sugary clouds of sand. "It's a fair test."

They wait, and to pass the time they talk some more about the test, saying things they both already know. But that's all right. Everyone gets a little nervous when the time comes to see if all their efforts will actually amount to anything. Will the numbers translate into reality successfully? The talk is reassuring.

The deck intercom crackles as they're patched into air control for the runways. A hangar north of the runway has opened, and out of it rolls a long black jet with a narrow fuselage.

Below the fuselage are two pods.
They're as big as the fuselage itself: one black, one white.
Sensors. You can close your eyes, it won't matter.
Under each delta wing, flanking the turbines: arrays of little fletched missiles.
The front of the fuselage comes to a long point, like a narwhale's.
The rear flares out into stabilizers almost as big as the wings.
Under the fuselage, a small cylindrical rocket booster.
Understand: it doesn't look like a plane anymore.
And those brake lights, winking in the axons . . .

Altogether it's a weird contraption, appearing mole blind and not at all aerodynamic. There's something eerie about the way it rolls to the end of the runway, turns, fires up the jets, and shoots down the runway and up into the dark blue sky. Who's minding the store? Hamilton is grinning at the sight, and McPherson can feel that he is too. There's something awfully . . . ingenious about the thing. It really is quite a machine.

The intercom has been giving takeoff specs and such; now, as the RPV's rocket booster cuts in and it recedes to nothing but a flame dot in the sky, they listen. "Test vehicle three three five now approaching seventy thousand feet. Test program three three five beginning T minus ten seconds. Test program beginning now."

Ten of the dozen men on the deck start the stopwatch functions of their wristwatches. Some of them have binoculars around their necks, but there won't be a chance to use them until after the test strike is made; there's nothing to be seen in the sky, it's a clean, dark blue, darker than any sky ever seen in OC. Nothing in it. McPherson finds that he's not breathing regularly, and he concentrates on hitting a steady rhythm. Scanning the sky, in the area where the RPV was last seen, probably not where it will reappear, look around more . . . his eyesight is remarkably sharp, and unfocusing his attention so that he sees all the expanse of blue above him, he notices a tiny flaw, there far to the north.

"Up there," he says quickly, and points. The chip of light moves overhead and then quicker than any of them can really follow it the black thing darts down zips over the *boom* white dunes and the tanks become orange blooms of fire as the thing turns up and fires back into the stratosphere like a rocket. Mach 7, really too fast for the eye to see: the whole pass has taken less than three seconds. The tanks are black clouds of smoke, *BoomBoom B-B-B-B-BOOOOM!* The sound finally reaches them. Empty blue sky, white dunes marred by six pillars of oily flame, off there on the horizon. Every tank gone.

They were shouting when the booms hit. Now they're shaking hands and laughing, all talking at once. No matter how many tests they've witnessed, the extreme speed of this craft, and the tremendous volume and power of the explosions, inevitably impresses them. It's a physical, sensory shock, for one thing, and then conceptually it's exhilarating to think that their calculations, their work, can result in such an awesome display. Hamilton is grinning broadly. "Those Badgers and Armadillos didn't even have time to register incoming, I'll bet! The data will show how far they got."

"And the pods all worked," McPherson says. That was the crucial test, the one of the target designation and tracking. With all those things functioning, they've fulfilled the specs. The fact that the Soviets' best field SAM system isn't fast enough to stop the Stormbee is just gravy, confirmation that the Air Force has asked for the right things. The main fact is, they have a system that works.

They spend the next few hours going over the data that the test generated. It all looks very good indeed. They pop the cork on a bottle of champagne and click plastic cups together before McPherson gets on the helicopter with the data, to return to El Paso and OC.

Flying over the magnets in the soundless, vibrationless calm of the tube train, McPherson can't help but feel a little glow of accomplishment. He ignores the printouts in his lap and looks around the plush car of the train. Businessmen in the big seats are hidden behind opened copies of *The Wall Street Journal.* With no windows and no vibration and no noise, it's difficult to believe that they are moving at Mach 2. The world has become an incredible place. . . .

When he returns it'll be time for the painful task of writing up the description of the system, in proposal form. Several hundred pages it will run to, not as much as a bid proposal, it's true, but still, it will be his job to oversee and edit the ungodly number of descriptions, charts, diagrams and such. Not fun.

Still. Being at that stage means a lot; it means they have a working system, within the size and power specs given. It's more than a lot of LSR's programs can say, at the moment. McPherson thinks of Ball Lightning briefly, shoves the thought away. This is one of the rare times that a program director can say, The work is done, and it's a success. He hasn't been given all that many commands like this one, and it means a lot.

The image of the test comes back to him. That inhumanly swift stoop, attack, disappearance; the quick, precise, and total destruction of the six lumbering tanks; it really was quite extraordinary, both physically and intellectually.

And remembering it, McPherson suddenly sees the larger picture, the meaning of the event. It's as if he just stood back from a video screen, after months of examining each dot. Now the image is revealed. This system, this RPV with its Stormbee eyes, its armament of smart missiles, its speed, its radar invisibility, its cheapness and lack of a human pilot put at risk—this system is the kind of pinpoint weapon that can really and truly change the nature of warfare. If the Soviets roll out of Eastern Europe with their giant Warsaw Pact army—for that matter, if any army starts an invasion anywhere—then these pilotless drones can drop out of space and fire their missiles before any defensive system can find them or respond, and for each run a half dozen tanks or vehicles are gone. And quick as you can say wow the invading force is gone with it.

The net result of that, given that this technology is pretty much out there for anyone to develop—LSR is not a superinventor after all, nobody is—the net result is that when every country has systems like this one, then *no one will be able to invade another country.* It just won't be possible.

Oh, of course there will still be wars—he is not so idealistic as to think that pinpoint weapons systems will end war as an institution—but any major invasion force is doomed to a swift surgical destruction. So really, large-scale invasions become out of the question, which severely curtails how big a war can get.

And all this without having to use the threat of nuclear weapons. For a hundred years now, almost, NATO has used nuclear weapons as the ultimate stopper to any Warsaw Pact invasion. Battlefield nukes in artillery shells, nuclear submarines in the Baltic and Med, the illegal intermediate-range "messenger missiles" hidden in West Germany, ready to make a demonstration pop if the tanks roll. . . . It's one of the most dangerous situations in the world, because if one nuke goes off, there's no telling where it will stop. Most likely it won't stop until everyone's dead. And even if it does stop, Europe's cities will be wiped out. And all to resist tanks!

But now, now, with Stormbee . . . They can take the nuclear weapons out of there, and still have a completely secure defense against a conventional invasion. The cities and their populations won't have to go up with the invaders; nothing will be needed but a precise, limited, one could even say humane, response. If you invade us, your invading force will be picked off, by unstoppable robot snipers. Swift, surgical destruction for any invading force; and the war wiped out with it. War—major wars of invasion, anyway—made impossible! My God! It's quite a thought! A weapon that will *make antagonists talk*—without the horrific threat of mutual assured destruction. In fact, with weapons like these, it really makes perfect sense to dismantle all the megatonnage, to get rid of the nuclear horror. . . . Can it really be true? Have we reached that point in history where technology finally will make war obsolete, and nuclear weapons unnecessary?

Yes, it seems it can be true: he has seen the leading edge of that truth, just barely seen it as it swooped down over the white sands of the desert like a Mach 7 mirage, a peripheral vision, that very day. It actually looks as if his work, the sweat of his brow, might help to lift from the world the hundred-year-long nightmare threat of nuclear annihilation. Might even help to lift the thousand-year-long threat of major, catastrophic war. It's . . . well, it's work you can take pride in.

And hurtling back over the surface of the desert, McPherson suddenly feels that pride more strongly than he ever has in his entire life, something like a radiant glow, a sun in his chest. It really is something.

... 11

In his dream Jim walks over a hillside covered with ruins. Below the hill spreads a black lake. The ruins are nothing but low stone walls, and the land is empty. Jim wanders among the walls searching for something, but as always he can't quite remember what it is he seeks. He comes across a piece of violet glass from a stained-glass window, but he knows that isn't what he is after. Something like a ghost bulges out of the top of the hill to tell him everything—

He wakes in his little apartment in Foothill, the sun beaming through the window. He groans, rolls onto the floor. Hangover here. What were they lidding last night? Groggily he looks around. His room is a mess, bedding and clothing scattered everywhere, as if a rainbow collapsed and landed in his bedroom.

Three walls of the room are covered with big Thomas Brothers maps of Orange County: one from the 1930s (faint tracing of roads), one from 1990 (north half of county gridded with interlocking towns, southern half, the hills and the Irvine and O'Neill ranches, still almost empty), one the very latest edition (the whole county gridded and overgridded). Kind of like keeping X-rays of a cancer on your walls, Jim has thought more than once. Surrealty tumor.

Stagger to the bathroom. Standing at the toilet he stares at a badly framed print of an old orange crate label. The bathroom walls are covered by these:

Three friars, taste-testing oranges by the white mission. Behind them green
    groves, and blue snow-topped mountains in the distance.
Portola, standing with Spanish flag unfurled, silent, on a peak in Placentia.
Two peacocks in front of a Disneyland castle: "California Dream."
Little bungalow in the neat green rows of a grove in bloom.
Beautiful Mexican woman, holding a basket of oranges. Behind her green groves,
    and blue mountains in the distance.
You have never lived here.

The labels, from the first half of the twentieth century, are the work of printer Max Schmidt and artists Archie Vazquez and Othello Michetti, among others. The intensely rich, exotic colors are the result of a process called zincography. Taken together, Jim believes, these labels make up Orange County's first and only utopia, a collective vision of Mediterranean warmth and ease astonishing in its art deco vividness. Ah, what a life! Jim tries to imagine the effect on the poor farmers of the Midwest, coming in to the general store from the isolated wheat farm, the Depression, the subzero temperatures, the dustbowls—and there among the necessary goods in their drab boxes and tins, these fantasies in stunning orange, cobalt, green, white! No wonder OC is so crowded. These labels must have given those farmers a powerful urge to Go West. And in those days they really could move to the land pictured on the boxes (sort of). For Jim it's out of reach. He lives here, but is infinitely further away.

The utopias of the past are always a little sad. Jim steps into pants, pulls on a shirt, pads through his ap and looks out the front door.

Sunny day. Overhead looms the freeway, with its supporting pylons coming down in backyards or on streetcorners. Kind of a big concrete *thing*, squatting up there in the sky, crossing it side to side. The Foothill Freeway, in fact, extended into southern OC around the turn of the century. The land it needed to cross was by then completely covered by suburbia, and homeowners objected strenuously to having their houses bought up and torn down. The solution? Make the new freeway a viaduct, part of the elevated autopian network being built over the most congested parts of the Newport and Santa Ana freeways. Values for the homes below the flying concrete would plummet, of course, but they would still be there, right?

Now it's a perfect place for white-collar poor folk like Jim to live, in apartmentalized old suburban homes. The cars above aren't even that loud anymore. And the shade of the freeway can be pretty welcome on those hot summer days, as the real estate agents are quick to remind you.

Jim goes back inside, feeling blah. Hung over, confused. While he eats his cereal and milk he thinks about Arthur Bastanchury. Good old Basque name, from shepherds who came to OC when James Irvine used his land to raise sheep. Arthur still looks a little Basque: dark complexion, light eyes, square jaw. And they have a good long tradition of active resistance back home in Spain. Not to mention terrorism. Jim doesn't want to have anything to do with terrorism. But if there's something else that can be done—some other way . . . He sighs, eats his cereal, stares at his living room. His living room stares back at him.

Books everywhere. The OC historians, Friis, Meadows, Starr et al.
Volumes of poetry. Novels. Stacks and stacks, anything anywhere.

In the corner under the window, the Zen center: mat, incense, candle.
CD disks all over an old console, on a bookcase of bricks and boards.
The desk is buried in paper. The couch is tattered, bamboo and vinyl.
Paper everywhere. Newspapers, mail, scraps.
A poem is a grocery list.
We eat our culture every day.
How does it taste to you?
Oops! Someone's forgotten to do the dishes.
No one minds a little dust, either.

"We believe that the truly staggering amounts of money and human effort (which is what money stands for, remember) that are being invested in armaments represent the greatest danger of our time," Arthur said to Jim later on the night of their poster blitz. "Nothing that we've tried in the legal channels of American politics has ever slowed the military-industrial complex down. They're the biggest power in the country, and nothing can stop them. We wanted to stay nonviolent, but it was clear we had to act, to go outside politics. The technology was available to attack the products without attacking the producers, and we decided to use it."

"How can you be sure you won't hurt anybody?" Jim asked uneasily. "I mean, it always starts this way, right? You don't want to be violent, but then you get frustrated, maybe careless, and pretty soon you fall over the line into terrorism. I don't want to have anything to do with that."

"There's a big difference between terrorism and sabotage," Arthur said sharply. "We use methods that harm plastics, programs, and various composite construction materials, without endangering people. Then we select what we think are the most destabilizing weapons programs, and by God we take it to them. Maybe later I can go into more detail. But we're patient, you see. We aren't going to start escalating just because we don't get results right away. It might take twenty years, forty years, and we know that. And we are absolutely committed to making sure people aren't physically hurt. It's vital to us, you see. If we don't hold to that we become just another part of the war machine, a stimulus to the security police industry or whatever."

Jim nodded, interested. It made sense.

Now, eating his breakfast, he is less certain about it all. On the poster-blitz night he told Arthur he was interested in helping, and Arthur said he would get back to him. That was what, a week ago? Two weeks? Hard to say. Would Arthur bring the matter up again? Jim doesn't know, but he isn't easy about it.

Upset, he decides to meditate. He sits in his Zen corner and lights a stick of incense. Preparation for *zazen*; empty the mind. No thoughts, just openness. Watch sunlight pierce the sweet rising smoke.

The no-thoughts part is hard, damned hard. Concentrate on breathing. In, out, in, out, in, out, yeah there he was doing it! Oops. Spoiled it. Start over. Must have gotten off five or ten seconds, though. Pretty good. Shh! Try again. In, out, in, out, in, out, wonder who the Dodgers are playing today *oops*, in, out, in, out, pretty smoke curl *shh!*, in, what's that out there? Ah, hell. Don't think, don't think, okay I'm not thinking, I'm not thinking, I'm not thinking, hey look at that I'm not thinking! . . . Oh. Well. In? Out?

It's useless. Jim McPherson must be the most wired Zen Buddhist in history. How can he actually stop thinking? Impossible. It doesn't even happen in his sleep!

Well, he did it for about fifteen seconds there. Better than some mornings. He gets up, feeling depressed. Mornings are typically low for him, must be low blood sugar or the lack of the various drugs that are usually in him. But this one's a special bummer. He's pretty confused, pretty depressed.

Might as well go with the flow of it. Jim puts on his "Supertragic Symphony," a concoction of his own made up of the four saddest movements of symphonic music that he knows of. He's recorded them in the sequence he thinks most effective. First comes the funeral march from Beethoven's Third Symphony, grand and stirring in its resistance to fate, full of active grief as an opening movement should be. Second movement is the second movement of Beethoven's Seventh Symphony, the stately solemn tune that Bruno Walter discovered could be made into a dirge, if you ignored Beethoven's instruction to play it allegretto and went to adagio. Heavy, solemn, moody, rhythmic.

The third movement is the third movement from Brahms's Third Symphony, sweet and melancholy, the essence of October, all the sadness of all the autumns of all time wrapped up in a tuneful *tristesse* that owes its melodic structure to the previous movement from Beethoven's Seventh. Jim likes this fact, which he discovered on his own; it makes it look like the "Supertragic Symphony" was meant to be.

Then the finale is the last movement of Tchaikovsky's *Pathetique*, no fooling around here, all the stops pulled, time to just bawl your guts out! Despair, sorrow, grief, all of czarist Russia's racking misery, Tchaikovsky's personal troubles, all condensed into one final awful *moan*. The ultimate bummer.

What a symphony! Of course there's a problem with the shifting key signatures, but Jim doesn't give a damn about key signatures. Ignore them and he can gather up all of his downer feelings and sing them out, conduct them too, wandering around the ap trying feebly to clean up a bit, collapsing in chairs, crawling blackly over the floors as he waves an imaginary baton, getting lower and lower. Man, he's *low*. He's so low he's getting high off it! And when it's all over he feels drained. Catharsis has taken place. Everything's a lot better.

He even feels in the mood to write a poem. Jim is a poet, he *is* a poet, he is he is he is.

He finds it hard going, however, because the piles of poetry collections on his bookcases and around his junk-jammed desk contain so many master-pieces that he can't stand it. Every tap at the old computer keyboard is mocked by the volumes behind and around him, Shakespeare, Shelley, Stevens, Snyder, shit! It's impossible to write any more poetry in this day and age. The best poets of his time make Jim laugh with scorn, though he imitates them slavishly in his own attempts. Postmodernism, moldering in its second half century—what does it amount to but squirming? You have to do something new, but there's nothing new left to do. Serious trouble, that. Jim solves the problem by writ-ing postmodern poems that he hopes to make post-postmodern by scrambling with some random program. The problem with this solution is that postmod-ern poetry already reads as if the lines have been scrambled by a random pro-gram, so the effects of Jim's ultraradical experimentation are difficult to notice.

But it's time to try again. A half hour's staring at the blank screen, a half hour's typing. He reads the result.

Rent an apartment.
There are orange trees growing under the floor.
Two rooms and a bath, windows, a door.
The freeway is your roof. What shade.
The motorized landscape: autopia, the best ride.
Magnetism is invisible, but we believe in it anyway.
Step up the pylon ladder in the evening sun.
Lie on the tracks to catch a tan.
They truck the sand in for all our beaches.
Do you know how to swim? No. Just rest.
Eat an orange, up there. Read a book.
Commuters running over you take a brief look.

Okay, now run this through a randomizer, the lucky one that seems to have such a good eye for rhythm. Result?

The freeway is your roof. What shade.
Eat an orange, up there. Read a book.
The motorized landscape: autopia, the best ride.
Rent an apartment.
Lie on the tracks to catch a tan.
Two rooms and a bath, windows, a door.
Magnetism is invisible, but we believe in it anyway.

They truck the sand in for all our beaches.
Commuters running over you take a brief look.
Do you know how to swim? No. Just rest.
There are orange trees growing under the floor.
Step up the pylon ladder in the evening sun.

There, pretty neat, eh? Jim reads the new version aloud. Well . . . He tries another variation and suddenly all three versions look stupid. He just can't get past the notion that if you can let your computer scramble the lines of a poem, and in doing so come up with a poem that's better, or at least just as good, then there must be a certain deficiency in the poem. In, for instance, its sequentiality. He thinks of Shakespeare's sonnets, Shelley's "Julian and Maddalo." Is he really performing the same activity they did? "Rent an apartment"?

Ach. It's a ridiculous effort. The truth is, Arthur was right. He doesn't have any work that means anything to him. And in fact he's almost late for this meaningless work, the one that brings in the money. That isn't good. He throws on shoes, brushes his teeth and hair, runs out to his car and hits the program for the First American Title Insurance and Real Estate Company, on East Fifth Street in Santa Ana. Oldest title company in Orange County, still going strong, and when Jim arrives at his desk there and boots up he finds that there's the usual immense amount of work waiting to be typed in and processed. Transfers, notices, assessments, the barrage of legal screenwork needed to make sales, move land in and out of escrow. Jim is the lowliest sort of clerk, a part-time typist, really. The three-hour shift is exhausting, even though he does the work on automatic pilot, and spends his time thinking about the recent conversation with Arthur. Everyone's typing away at their screens, absorbed in the worlds of their tasks, oblivious to the office and the people working around them. Jim doesn't even recognize anyone; there are so many people on the short shifts, and Jim has so few hours, that few of his colleagues ever become familiar. And none of them are here today.

It gets so depressing that he goes in to visit Humphrey, who is sort of his boss, in that Humphrey makes use of the services of Jim's pool. Humphrey is the rising young star of the real estate division, which Jim finds disgusting. But they're friends, so what can he say?

"Hi, Hump. How's it going."

"Real good, Jim! How about you?"

"Okay. What's got you so happy?"

"Well, you know how I managed to grab one of the last pieces of Cleveland when the government sold it."

"Yeah, I know." This, to Jim, is one of the great disasters of the last twenty years: the federal government's decision, under immense pressure from the southern California real estate lobby and the OC Board of Supervisors, to break up the Cleveland National Forest, on the border of Orange and Riverside counties, and sell it for private development. A good way to help pay the interest on the gargantuan national debt, and there wasn't really any forest out there anyway, just dirt hills surrounded by a bunch of communities that desperately needed the land, right? Right. And so, with the encouragement of a real estate developer become Secretary of the Interior, Congress passed a law, unnoticed in a larger package, and the last empty land in OC was divided into five hundred lots and sold at public auction. For a whole lot of money. A good move, politically. Popular all over the state.

"Well," Humphrey says, "it looks like the financing package is coming together for the office tower we want to build there. Ambank is showing serious interest, and that will seal things if they go for it."

"But Humphrey!" Jim protests. "The occupancy rate out in Santiago office buildings is only about thirty percent! You tried to get people to commit to this complex and you couldn't find anybody!"

"True, but I got a lot of written assurances that people would consider moving in if the building were there, especially when we promised them free rent for five years. The notes have convinced most of the finance packagers that it's viable."

"But it isn't! You know that it isn't! You'll build another forty-story tower out there, and it'll stand there empty!"

"Nah." Humphrey shakes his head. "Once it's there it'll fill up. It'll just take a while. The thing is, Jim, if you get the land and the money together at the same time, it's time to build! Occupancy will take care of itself. The thing is, we need the final go-ahead from Ambank, and they're so damn slow that we might lose the commitment of the other financiers before they get around to approving it."

"If you build and no one occupies the space then Ambank is going to end up holding the bills! I can see why they might hesitate!"

But Humphrey doesn't want to think about that, and he's got a meeting with the company president in a half hour, so he shoos Jim out of his office.

Jim goes back to his console, picks up the phone, and calls Arthur. "Listen, I'm really interested in what we talked about the other night. I want—"

"Let's not talk about it now," Arthur says quickly. "Next time I see you. Best to talk in person, you know. But that's good. That's real good."

Back to work, fuming at Humphrey, at his job, at the greedy and stupid government, from the local board of supervisors up to Congress and this foul administration. Shift over, three more hours sacrificed to the great money god. He's on the wheel of economic birth and death, and running like a rat in it. He shuts down and prepares to leave. Scheduled for dinner at the folks' tonight—

Oh shit! He's forgotten to visit Uncle Tom! That won't go over at all with Mom. God. What a day this is turning out to be. What time is it, four? And they have afternoon visiting hours. Mom's sure to ask. There's no good way out of it. The best course is to track down there real quick and drop in on Tom real briefly before going up for dinner. Oh, man.

On the track down 405 to Seizure World he clicks on the radio, they're playing The Pudknockers' latest and he blasts himself with a full hundred and twenty decibels of volume, singing along as loud as he can:

I'm swimming in the amniotic fluid of love
Swimming like a finger to the end of the glove
When I reach the top I'm going to dive right in
I'm the sperm in the egg—did I lose? did I win?

Seizure World spreads over the Laguna Hills, from El Toro to Mission Viejo: "Rossmoor Leisure World," a condomundo for the elderly that used to be only for the richest of the old. Now it's got its ritzy sections and its slums and its mental hospitals just like any other "town" in OC, and overpopulation sure, there's more old folks now than ever before, an immense percentage of the population is over seventy, and two or three percent are over a hundred, and they have to go somewhere, right? So there are half a million of them densepacked here.

Jim parks, gets out. Now this place: this is depression. He hates Seizure World with a passion. Uncle Tom does too, he's pretty sure. But with emphysema, and relying completely on Social Security, the old guy doesn't have much choice. These subsidized aps are as cheap as you can get, and only the old can get them. So here Tom is, in a condomundo that looks like all the rest, except everything is smaller and dingier, closer to dissolution. No pretending here, no Mediterranean fake front on the tenement reality. This is an old folks' home.

And Tom lives in the mental ward of it—though usually he is lucid enough. Most days he lies fairly calmly, working to breathe. Then every once in a while he loses it, and has to be watched or he'll attack people—nurses, anyone. This has been the pattern for the last decade or so, anyway. He's over a hundred.

Jim can't really bear to think about it for too long, so he doesn't. When he's out in OC it never occurs to him to think of Uncle Tom and how he lives. But during these infrequent visits it's shoved in his face.

Up the wheelchair ramp to the check-in desk. The nurse has a permanent sour expression, a bitchy voice. "Visiting hours end in forty-five minutes."

Don't worry.

Down the dark hallway, which smells of antiseptic. Wheelchair cases bang into the walls like bumper cars, the old wrecks in them drooling, staring at nothing, drugged out. A young nurse pushes one chair case down the hall, blinking rapidly, just about to cry. Yes, we're in the nursing home again. ("Did I lose? did I win?")

Tom's got a room just bigger than his bed, with a south-facing window that he treasures. Jim knocks, enters. Tom's lying there staring out at the sky, in a trance.

Wrinkled plaid flannel pajamas.

Three-day stubble of white beard.

Do you live here?

Clear plastic tube, from nostrils to tank under bed. Oxygen.

Bald, freckled pate. Ten thousand wrinkles. A turtle's head.

Slowly it turns, and the dull brown eyes regard him, focus, blink rapidly, as the mind behind them pulls back into the room from wherever it was voyaging. Jim swallows, uncomfortable as always. "Hi, Uncle Tom."

Tom's laugh is a sound like plastic crackling. "Don't call me that. Makes me feel like Simon Legree is about to come in. And whip me." Again the laugh; he's waking up. The bitter, sardonic gleam returns to his glance, and he shifts up in the bed. "Maybe that's appropriate. You call me Uncle Tom, I call you Nigger Jim. Two slaves talking."

Jim smiles effortlessly. "I guess that's right."

"Is it? So what brings you here? Lucy not coming this week?"

"Well, ah . . ."

"That's all right. I wouldn't come here myself if I could help it." The plastic cracks. "Tell me what you've been up to. How are your classes?"

"Fine. Well—teaching people to write is hard. They don't read much, so of course they don't have much idea how to write."

"It's always been like that."

"I bet it's worse now."

"No takers there."

Tom watches him. Suddenly Jim remembers his archaeological expedition. "Hey! I went and dug up a piece of El Modena Elementary School. Shoot, I forgot to bring it." He tells Tom the story, and Tom chuckles with his alarming laugh.

"You probably got some construction material from the donut place. But it was a nice idea. El Modena Elementary School. What a thought. It was old when I went there. They closed it as soon as La Veta was finished. Two long wooden buildings, two stories high with a cellar under each. Big bell in one. The high school got the bell later and the principal, who had been principal of the elementary school years before. Went crazy at the dedication. Had a nervous breakdown right in front of us. Big dirt lot between the two buildings. They were firetraps, we had fire drills almost every day. I played a lot of ball on that lot. Once I singled and stretched it to two, they overthrew and I took third, overthrew again and I went home. They made a play on me there, and I was safe but Mr. Beauchamp called me out. Because he didn't like me hot-dogging like that. He was a bastard. We used to bail out of swings at the top of the swing. Go flying. I can't believe we didn't break limbs regularly, but we didn't."

Tom sighs, looking out the window as if it gives a prospect onto the previous century. He recounts his past with a wandering, feverish bitterness, as if angry that it's all so far gone. Jim finds it both interesting and depressing at once.

"There were a couple of girls that hung together, everyone hounded them without mercy. Called them Popeye and Mabusa, meaning Medusa I suppose. Although it amazes me that any kid there knew that much. They were retarded, see, and looked bad. Popeye all shriveled, Mabusa big and ugly, Mongoloid. Boys used to hunt for them at recess, to make fun of them." Tom shakes his head, staring out the window again. "I had a game of my own that I played on the teacher who was recess monitor, a kind of hide-and-seek. Psychological warfare, really. I used the cellars to get from one side of the yard to the other to pop out and surprise her. The monitor would see me here, then there—it drove her nuts. One time I was doing that, and I found Popeye and Mabusa down there in the cellar hiding, huddled together. . . ." He blinks.

"Kids are cruel," Jim says.

"And they stay that way! They stay that way." Coppery bitterness burrs Tom's voice. "The nurses here call us O's and Q's. O's have their mouths hanging open. Q's have their mouths hanging open with their tongues stuck out. Funny, eh?" He shakes his head. "People are cruel."

Jim grits his teeth. "Maybe that's why you became a public defender, eh?" Seeing two retarded kids, huddled together in a cellar: can that shape a life?

"Maybe it was." The little room is taking on a coppery light, the air has a coppery taste. "Maybe it was."

"So what was it like, being a public defender?"

"What do you mean? It was the kind of work that tears your heart out. Poor people get arrested for crimes. Most crimes are committed by really poor people, they're desperate. It's just like you'd expect. And they're entitled to representation even though they can't afford it. So a judge would appoint one of us. Endless case loads, every kind of thing you can imagine, but a lot of repetition. Good training, right. But . . . I don't know. Someone's got to do that work. This isn't a just society and that was one way to resist it, do you understand me boy?"

Jim nods, startled by this intersection with his own recent thoughts. So the old man had tried to resist!

"But in the end it doesn't matter. Most of your clients hate you because you're just part of the system that's snared them. And a good percentage are guilty as charged. And the case loads . . ." The plastic cracking, it really seems like something in him must be breaking. "In the end it doesn't make any difference. Someone else would have done it, yes they would! Just as well. I should have been a tax lawyer, investment counselor. Then I'd have enough money now to be in some villa somewhere. Private nurse and secretary. . . ."

Jim shivers. Tom knows just exactly what he's living in, he's perfectly aware of it. Who better? It's despair making all those Q's and O's, in this old folks' mental ward. . . .

"But you did some good! I'm sure you did." Doubtfully: "You saved some people from jail who were grateful for it. . . ."

"Maybe." *Crack crack crack.* "I remember . . . I got this one Russian immigrant who could barely speak English. He'd only been in the country a month or two. He was lonely and went into one of the porno theaters in Santa Ana. The police were trying to close those places down at the time. They made a sweep and arrested everyone they could catch. So they got this Russian and he was charged with public indecency. Because they said he was masturbating in there. If you can believe that. When I first saw him he was really scared. I mean he was used to the Soviet system where if you're arrested then you're a goner. Guilty as charged. And he didn't understand the charges and I mean he was *scared.* So I took it to trial and just massacred the assistant D.A.'s case, which was bullshit to begin with. I mean how can you prove something like that? So the judge dismissed it. And the look on that Russian's face when they let him out . . ." *Crack! Crack!* "Oh, that might have been worth a few days in this hole, I guess. A few days."

"So . . ." Jim is thinking of his own problems, his own choices. "So what would you do today, Tom? I mean, if you wanted to resist the injustices, the people who run it all . . . what would you do?"

"I don't know. Nothing seems to work. I guess I would teach. Except that's useless too. Write, maybe. Or practice law at a higher level. Affect the laws themselves somehow. That's where it all rests, boy. This whole edifice of privilege and exploitation. It's all firmly grounded in the law of the land. That's what's got to change."

"But how? Would you resist actively? Like . . . go out at night and sabotage a space weapons factory, or something like that?"

Tom stares out the window bright-eyed. As often happens, his bitterness has galvanized him, made him seem younger. "Sure. If I could do it without hurting anybody. Or getting hurt myself." *Crack!* "A liberal to the end. I guess that's always been my problem. But yeah, why not? It would take a lot of that kind of thing. But they should be stopped somehow. They're sucking the world dry to fuel their games."

Jim nods, thinking it over.

They talk about Jim's parents, a natural enough association, although neither of them mentions Dennis's occupation. Jim talks a bit about his work and friends, until Tom's eyes begin to blur. He's getting tired: slumping down, speech coming with an ugly hiss of breath. Jim sees again that the mind, that sharp-edged bitter quick mind, is trapped in an old wreck of a body that is just barely kept going by constant infusion of oxygen, of drugs. A body that poisons its mind occasionally, blunts all its edges . . . One gnarled hand creeps over the bedsheet after the other, like a pair of crabs; spotted, fleshless, the joints so swollen that the fingers will never straighten again. . . . That has to hurt! It all does. He must live with pain every day, just as a part of living.

Jim can't really imagine that, and the thought doesn't stay with him long. Too hard. It's getting time to go, it really is.

"Tell me one last Orange County story, Tom. Then I've got to go."

Tom stares through him, without recognition: Jim shivers.

The focus returns, Tom stares out the window at the sky. "Before they built Dana Point harbor, there was a beautiful beach down there under the bluff. Not many people went there. The only way down was a rickety old wood staircase built against the bluff. Every year steps came out and it got chancier to go down it. But we did. The thing was to go after a big storm had hit the coast. The beach was all fresh, sand torn out and flushed and thrown back in. And in the sand were tiny bits of colored stones. Gem sand, we called it. It was really an extraordinary thing. I don't know if they really were tiny bits of sapphires, rubies, emeralds—but they looked like it, and that's what we called them. Not driftglass, no, real stones. Walking along the beach real slow, you'd see a blink of colored light, green, red, blue—perfectly intense and clear against the wet sand. You could collect a little handful in a day, and if you kept them in a jar of water . . . I had one at home. Wonder what happened to that. What happens to all the things you own? The people you know? I'm sure I never would have thrown that out. . . ."

And Tom falls off into reverie, then into an uneasy sleep, tossing so that the oxygen tube presses against his neck. Jim, who has heard about the gem sand before, arranges the tube and the sheets as best he can, and leaves. He feels sad. There was a place here, once. And a person, with a whole life. Now hanging on past all sense. This awful condomundo—a jail for the old, a kind of concentration camp! It really is depressing. He's got to come by more often. Tom needs the company. And he's a historical resource, he really is.

But tracking up 5, Jim begins to forget about this. The truth is, the overall experience is just too unpleasant for him. He can't stand it. And so he forgets his visits there, and avoids the place.

On to dinner at the folks'. Then his class! It really is turning out to be a hell of a long day.

... 13

After Jim leaves, Old Tom continues the conversation in his head.

I played in the orange groves as a child, he tells Jim. When you lived on a street plunging into a grove that extended away in every direction, then you could go out any time you liked. Mid-afternoon when everything was hot and lazy was a good time. It was always sunny.

They cleared the ground around the trees, nothing but dirt. Around each tree was a circular irrigation moat maybe thirty feet across, which made the groves look strange. As did the symmetrical planting. Every tree was in a perfect rank, a perfect file, and two perfect diagonals, for as far as you could see. The trees were symmetrical too, something like the shape of an olive, made of small green leaves on small twisted branches.

There were almost always oranges on the trees, they blossomed and grew twice a year and the growing took up most of the time. Oranges first green and small, then through an odd transition of mixed green and yellow, to orange, darkening always as they ripened—until if not picked they would darken to a browny orange and then go brown and dry and small and hard, and then whitish brown and then earth again. But most of them were picked.

We used to throw them at each other. Like snowballs already formed and ready to go. Old ones were squishy and smelled bad, whole new ones were hard and hurt a little. We fought wars, boys throwing oranges back and forth and it was kind of like German dodgeball at school. Getting hit was no big deal, except perhaps when you had to explain it to your mother. During the fights itself it was kind of funny. I wonder if any of those young friends ended up in Vietnam? If so, they were poorly trained for it.

We took bows and arrows out into the groves to shoot the jackrabbits we often saw bounding away from us. They could really run. We never even came close to them, happily, so we shot at oranges on trees instead. Perfect targets, quite difficult to hit and a wonderful triumph if you did, the oranges burst open and flew off or hung there punctured, it was great.

We ate the oranges too, choosing only the very best. The green and slightly acrid sweat that comes out of their skin as you peel them, the white pulpy inside of the peels, the sharp and fragrant smell, the wedges of inner fruit, perfectly rounded crescent wedges . . . odd things. Their taste never seemed quite real.

I spent a lot of time out there in the groves, wandering in the hot dusty silence with my bow and arrow in hand, talking to myself. It was a very private world.

But when they started to tear the groves down I don't remember we ever cared all that much. No one could imagine that *all* the groves would be torn down. We played in the craters, and the piles of wood left when the trees were chopped up, and it was different, interesting. And the construction sites— new foundations, framing thrown up in hours—made great playgrounds. We swung from rafters and tested if newly poured concrete would melt if you held a candle under it, and jumped from new roofs down into piles of sand, and once Robert Keller stepped on a nail sticking up through a board. Fun.

And then when the houses were built, fences put up, roads all in—well—it was a different place. Then it wasn't so much fun. But by then we weren't kids anymore either, and we didn't care.

... 14

When Stewart Lemon hears the bad news—direct from LSR president Donald Hereford in New York—he can scarcely believe it. All of his premonitions have come true in the worst way. While on the phone with Hereford he has to keep cool, take it calmly, make assurances that it's all still under control, the contract virtually in the bag. In fact, Hereford's brusque, icy questioning frightens him considerably. So that when the call is done and Lemon is alone, he gets so angry, so frightened, that he locks his office, shuts down all the systems, and runs amok—kicks the desk and chairs, throws the paperweights against the wall, punches the soft backing of his swivel chair until he's thoroughly killed it.

Breathing heavily, he surveys the room, then very carefully puts everything back in order. He's still angry, but physically he feels less like he's going to explode. His health really can't take the pressures of this job, he thinks; it's a race between ulcers and heart attack, and both contestants are picking up the pace as they near the finish line. . . . He swallows a Tagamet and a Minipress, hits the intercom button, says to Ramona in his calmest voice, "Is McPherson back from White Sands yet?"

"Let me check. . . ." Ramona knows perfectly well that this dead-calm voice means he is furious. All the better, he likes people to know when he's mad. She gets back to him quickly: "Yes, he's just in."

"Get him up here now."

Actually it takes more like fifteen minutes for McPherson to show up. He looks annoyed in his usual minimalist way, mouth drawn tight, eyes staring an accusation. *He's* angry? Lemon stands up the moment he walks in, feels the pressure in him rising again.

Nearly shouting, he says, "I asked you to hurry on the Stormbee program, didn't I! And you gave me that what's-the-big-hurry look, there's no deadline, and now I'll *tell* you what the big hurry was, goddamn it!"

McPherson flinches under this immediate onslaught, then clams up completely. No expression on his face at all. Lemon hates this robot response, and he sets about cracking it open: "They've made your superblack program white, do you understand? If we'd gotten the proposal to the Pentagon when I wanted to they wouldn't have been able to do this, but *you* had to hold on to it! And now it's a white program and the RFP is out there for everyone to go after!"

That got him all right. McPherson has visibly paled, his mouth is nothing but a tight white line across his face. "When did you hear?" he manages to say, jaw bunching and unbunching.

"Just now! I'm not as slow as you are, I just got the call from New York. From Hereford himself."

"But—" The man is really in shock, or else he wouldn't deign to ask Lemon questions like this: "What happened? Why?"

"Why? I'll tell you why! You were too fucking slow, that's why!" Lemon pounds his desk hard. "Let me try to explain the Air Force to you again, McPherson. They like results! They don't have the patience of a hummingbird, and when they ask for something they want it now! If they don't get it they go somewhere else. So you didn't produce as fast as they wanted! It's been four months, for Christ's sake! Four months! And so now the RFP for the Stormbee contract is coming out this Friday in *Commercial Business Daily*, and after that we're just one of any number of bidders. If the Pentagon had already gotten our proposal and accepted it this couldn't have happened, but as it is now, we're fucked! We're back to square one!"

Lemon has worked himself into a therapeutic frenzy with this outburst, and he can see McPherson is infuriated too, the man's lips are going to fuse if he doesn't watch out. If he were a normal kind of guy they'd shout it out, get it all off their chests and be able to go out afterward and drink it off and plan some strategy, the hard words forgotten as things spoken in the heat of anger. But McPherson? No, no, he just holds it all in with an almost frightening compression, till it metamorphoses into a hate for Lemon that Lemon can see just as sure as he can see the man's face. And it makes Lemon mad. He hates that closemouthed supercilious style, it angers him personally and it *loses them business*. Disgusted, he waves the man away. He can't stand to look at him. "Get out of here, McPherson. Get out of my sight."

"I take it we'll be making a bid?"

"*Yes!* For Christ's sake, do you think I'm going to let all that work go to waste? You get this thing whipped into proper proposal shape and do it *fast*. Was the test at White Sands successful?"

"Yes."

"Good! You get this proposal into the selection board first. With the head start we've had we should be able to make the strongest bid by a good margin."

"Yeah."

"You bet, *yeah*. I'll tell you this, McPherson—your ass is on the line, this time. After all the stunts you've pulled—you'd better win this one. You'd better."

Stiffly the man nods, stomps out. Goddamned robot. Lemon can't believe he's got such a tight-ass robot working for him still. It just isn't his style, he can't work with a man like that. Well—this is McPherson's last chance, he has tinkered around in perfectionist dilettante style one time too many. Vengefully Lemon hits the intercom and tells Ramona to send a memo: "To Dennis McPherson. Tell him that along with program management for the Stormbee *proposal*, I want him co-directing the Ball Lightning program with Dan Houston. Tell him Houston remains head, but he is to render all assistance asked of him."

That'll give the bastard something to think about.

... 15

So Jim tracks up to his parents' home that evening, to join them for dinner. Up the knob of Red Hill, the first rise off the big flat plain of the OC basin, a sort of lookout point sticking out from the hills behind it. Jim's books say there was a mine there in the 1920s, the Red Hill mercury mine, with tailings that could be found decades later. And the soil of the hill had a reddish cast, because of the high amount of cinnabar in it.

Home is the same. Dennis is back from work, out in the garage working on his car's motor, which is already in perfect factory condition. He doesn't reply to Jim's hello, and Jim goes on into their section of the house. Lucy is making dinner; happily she greets him, and he sits down comfortably at the kitchen table. Quickly enough he's up on the latest developments at the little church: the minister still has some problem related to the death of his wife, the new vicar continues to vex the veteran membership, Lillian Keilbacher has started work as Lucy's assistant in the minister's office.

Then he hears about Lucy's friends, and then Dennis's work. This is the only way that Jim ever hears about his father's work, perhaps because Dennis assumes, correctly, that Jim is a pacifist bleeding-heart pseudoradical who wouldn't approve of any of it. So Dennis never speaks of it to Jim. Apparently he's almost as bad with Lucy; her account is fragmented and incomplete, consisting mostly of her own judgments and opinions, generated by the minute bits of evidence Dennis mutters when he arrives home, disgruntled and close-mouthed. "He hates this Lemon he's working for," Lucy opines, shaking her head in disapproval. It's not Christian, it's not good for his health, it's not good for his career. "He should try to like him more. It's not as if the man is the devil or something like that. He probably has troubles of his own."

"I don't know," Jim says. "Some people can be pretty awful to work for."

"It's what you make of it that counts." Sigh. "Dennis should have a hobby, something to take his mind off work."

"He's got the car, right? That's a hobby."

"Well, yes but it's just more of the same, isn't it. Trying to get some machine to work."

Jim has begun a radically censored account of his week, when Dennis comes in and washes up for dinner. Lucy sets out the salad and casserole and they sit down; she says grace and they eat. Dennis eats in silence, gets up and goes back out to continue his work.

Lucy gets up and goes to the sink. "So how is Sheila?" she asks.

"Well, um . . ." Jim fumbles, feeling sudden guilt. He hasn't even thought of Sheila for a long time. "Actually, we aren't seeing each other as much these days."

A quick *tkh* of disapproval. Lucy doesn't like it. Jim gets up to help clean the table. Of course she's ambivalent about it; Sheila wasn't a Christian, and she'd really like Jim to settle down with a Christian girl, even get married—in fact she knows some candidates down at the church. On the other hand, she met Sheila many times and liked her, and the real and actual always count more for Lucy than the theoretical. "What's wrong?" she complains.

"Well . . . we're just not on the same track." It's a phrase of Lucy's.

She shakes her head. "She's nice. I like her. You should call her and talk to her. You've got to communicate." This is a sacred tenet with Lucy: talking will cure everything. Jim supposes she believes it because Dennis doesn't talk much. If he did, she'd know better that the tenet wasn't true.

"Yeah, I'll call her." And really he should. Have to tell her that he's, um, seeing other people. A difficult call at best. And so a part of him is already busy forgetting the resolution. Sheila will get the idea. "I will."

"Did you go see Tom?"

"Yeah."

"How was he?"

"Same as always."

She sighs. "He should be living here."

Jim shakes his head. "I don't know where you'd put him. Or how you'd take care of him, either."

"I know." There's a slight quiver at Lucy's jaw, and suddenly Jim perceives that she's upset. He doesn't have the faintest idea why. "But it isn't right."

Maybe that's it. "I'll go down there more often." This too he instantly begins to forget.

"Dennis has got to go to Washington again this week."

"He's been going a lot this year."

"Yes." She's still upset, throwing dishes into the dishwasher almost blindly. Jim doesn't want to ask her why, she'll start crying and he doesn't want to deal with it. He ignores the signs and tells her cheerily of his week, his classes and what he's been reading, while she pulls it together. Is she angry at Dennis about something? he wonders. He can't tell; there's lots he doesn't know or understand about his parents' relationship. He's more comfortable with it that way.

Dishes finished, the talk continues desultorily. Jim's mind wanders to his various problems and he doesn't catch one of his mom's questions. "What's that?"

"Jim. You don't *listen*." A cardinal sin, in this household where it happens so often. . . .

"Sorry." But at the same time he's glancing at a newsheet headline that's grabbed his eye. "I can't believe this famine in India."

"Why, what's it say?"

"Same old thing. Third major famine of the year in Asia, kills another million. And look at this! Fight in Mozambique killed a hundred!" From their kitchen window they can see the two giant hangars down at El Toro Marine Base, the helicopters rising and dropping like bees around a hive.

"They should learn to talk."

Jim nods, absorbed in the details of the second article. When he's done he says, "I'm off. Gotta go teach my class."

"Good. Don't forget about visiting Tom more often, now." She is serious, scolding, insistent: still upset about something.

"I won't, but remember I just saw him today. I'll go again next Thursday."

"Tuesday would be better."

Jim goes out to the garage. He doesn't notice the intensity of Dennis's silence, hasn't noticed the tension in him all evening long. Dennis is quiet a lot; and Jim hasn't really been paying attention.

He clears his throat; Dennis looks up from a bundle of colored wires running over the motor block of his car. "Um, Dad, my car's having some power troubles going uptrack."

Dennis pokes his glasses up his nose, glares at Jim. "How does it start?" he asks after a long pause.

"Not so well."

"Have you cleaned the track contacts lately?"

"Um . . ."

Angrily Dennis grabs up some tools, rags, leads Jim out to his car. It looks shabby and unkempt under the streetlight. Dennis pulls up the hood wordlessly, reaches down to shift the contact rod up into maintenance position. His back says he's sick of doing work on Jim's car.

"Look at these brushes, they're caked!" A black paste of oily scum adheres to the contacts where they come closest to the road and the track. "Here, you clean them."

Jim starts on it, fumbles with a screwdriver, gouges the side of one brush, propels a gob of the pasty black goo right past Dennis's eye.

Dennis elbows him aside. "Watch out, you're wrecking them. Watch how I do it."

Jim watches, bored. Dennis's hands move surely, economically. He gets every brush coppery clean, factory perfect. "I suppose you'll just let all this go to hell again," Dennis says bitterly as he finishes, gesturing at the car's motor.

"No," Jim protests. But he knows that after years of negligence and ineptitude with his car, there's nothing he can do now to convince Dennis that he is really interested. It is interesting, of course, in a theoretical way; forces of entropy, resistance to it, a great metaphor for society, etc. But ten seconds after the hood is down the actual physical details fade for Jim, the words turn back into jargon and he's as ignorant as he was when the lesson started. His memory is retentive, so maybe he truly isn't interested.

"Have you done anything about getting another job?" Dennis demands.

"Yeah, I've been looking."

Disgust twists Dennis's features. "You know I'm still making the insurance payments on this car?" he says as he gathers his tools. "Do you remember that?"

"Yeah, I remember!" Jim squirms at this accusation, feeling the shame of it. Still supported by his parents: he can't even make his own way in the world. He can see Dennis's contempt and it makes him defensive, then angry. "I appreciate it, but I'll take them over starting with the next one." As if Dennis has been keeping him from paying on his own.

The pretense makes Dennis angry too. "You will not," he snaps. "It's illegal to be without that insurance, and you can't afford it. If I gave it to you and you let it lapse and then got in an accident, then I'd be the one ended up paying the bills, wouldn't I?"

Stung that his father would imagine him capable of that, Jim scowls at the ground. "I wouldn't let it lapse!"

"I'm not so sure about that."

Jim turns and walks off across the lawn, circling. He's ashamed, hurt, furiously angry. There's nothing he can say. If he starts to cry in front of his father he'll . . . "I don't do things like that! I keep my commitments!" he shouts.

"The hell you do," Dennis says. "You don't even support yourself! Isn't that a commitment? Why don't you get a job where you can afford all your own expenses? Or why don't you budget what you make to pay for them? Are you going to tell me you don't spend any of what you make on entertaining yourself?"

"No!"

"So here you are twenty-seven years old and I'm still paying your bills!"

"I don't want you paying for them! I'm sick of that!"

"*You're* sick of it! Fine, I won't. That's it for that. But you'd better find your-self a decent job."

"I'm *looking*! At least the jobs I have are decent work!"

For a second it almost looks like Dennis is going to hit him; he even shifts all the tools to his left hand, instantly, without thinking. . . . Then he freezes, snarls, turns away and walks into the house. Jim runs to his car, jumps in, tracks off cursing wildly, blindly.

... 16

Inside the house Dennis hears Jim's old car click over the street track and hum away. It almost makes him laugh. When he was a kid, sons angry at their fathers could rev a car up to seven thousand RPM and burn rubber in a roaring, screeching departure; now all they can do is go hum, hum.

"Is that Jim?" says Lucy. "He didn't come in to say goodbye."

Damn. Dennis goes to sit before the video wall without a word.

"I wish you two wouldn't argue," Lucy says in a small, determined voice. "There aren't that many jobs to be had, you know. Half the kids Jim's age are unemployed."

"The hell they are." Dennis is angrier than ever. Now the kid's gotten Lucy upset too, and *he* doesn't like arguing with his son and having him tear off with that look of hurt resentment on his face: who would? But what can you do? And after a day like he's had . . . Remembering it just makes him feel worse. After a successful test like the one at White Sands, having the program jerked back out to the uncertainties of open competition . . . Lemon's fierce tongue-lashing . . . hell. An awful day. "I don't want to talk about it."

After a while he gets up from his chair, turns off the video; he's been blind to it, hasn't seen a thing. He goes to the sliding glass door, stares through his reflection at the lights of the condos of Citrus Heights, the pulsing head- and taillights of the Foothill Freeway viaduct, standing above the flats of Tustin. People everywhere. He'd like to go outside, into the house's little backyard, but it belongs to the Aurelianos who own the other side of the house. They wouldn't mind, but Dennis does.

He thinks of their land, up on the northern California coast near Eureka. Beautiful windswept pines, on a rocky hillside falling down into a wild sea. Ten years ago they bought five acres as an investment, and Dennis had even thought to retire up there, and build a home on the land. "Sometimes I'd like to just throw it in, move up to our land and get to work up there," he says aloud.

To build something with your own hands, something physical that you could see taking shape, day by day . . . it's work he could love, work in stark contrast to the abstract, piecemeal, and endlessly delayed tasks he performs for LSR.

"Uh-huh," Lucy says carefully.

It's the tone of voice she uses when she wants to humor him, but doesn't agree with whatever point he's making. As Dennis well knows, Lucy hates the idea of moving north; it would mean leaving all her friends, the church, her job . . . Dennis frowns. He knows it's just a dream, anyway.

"Do you think the trees have grown back yet?" Lucy asks.

Just a year after they bought their land a forest fire burned over several hundred acres in the Eureka area, including everything they bought. They tracked up on vacation to have a look; the ground was black. It looked awful. But the locals told them it would all recover in just a few years. . . .

"I don't know," Dennis says, irritated. He suspects the fire did not bother Lucy all that much, as it made it impossible for them to move up there for a good long while. "I'll bet it has, though. The new trees will be small, but they'll be there. The land recovers fast from something like that—it's part of the natural cycle."

"Except they found out some kids set the fire, didn't they?"

Dennis doesn't reply to that. After a minute or two he sighs, answers what he takes to be Lucy's real point: "Well, we can't go up there anyway."

His black mood condenses to a big lump in his stomach. That bastard Lemon. He feels bad; certainly he transferred some of his anger at Lemon onto his idiot son, who surely deserved it, but still . . . that look on his face . . .

What a day.

"Did Jim say he was looking for a job?"

"I don't want to talk about it."

... 17

Tashi Nakamura gets to Jim's writing class just before starting time. Tashi's interest in writing is minimal, but Jim's classes depend on enrollment for survival, and this semester it looked like there might not be enough students to keep the class going. So Tashi decided to sign up. It was a typical Tashi act; he has a streak of generosity that few know about, because of his shyness and poverty.

Jim arrives ten minutes late, just as his students are packing up to leave. Instantly Tashi can see that Jim is upset about something; he's flushed, his mouth is a tight line, he slams his daypack down on his desktop and glares at it. Stands there pulling himself together.

After a while he takes a deep breath, begins the night's lecture in a monotone. His explanations of comma use, shaky at the best of times, are now almost incoherent. In the middle of them he stops, veers off into one of his historical jags. "So the Irvine Ranch, which began as the county's only force for conservation, ended up by selling out to a corporation that leased all its land to developers, who made it into a replica of the northern half of the county, ignoring all the lessons they should have learned and grading the hills with a complete disregard for the land. In fact our fine college is part of that heritage. And this development came at the time when the ballistic defense was being put into orbit, so the arms industry expanded into this new land and increased a hold on the county that was already completely dominant!"

Jim's other students blink at him, completely unimpressed. In fact they're looking rather mutinous. Most have taken the class to get by the minimal writing test necessary to graduate Trabuco, and they are impatient with Jim's digressions. Learning to write is hard enough as it is. One of the more aggressive men breaks into Jim's monologue to complain. "Listen here, Mr. McPherson, I still don't have the slightest idea when to use 'that' or 'which,' or which one goes with commas or how to use the commas." Really disgusted about it, too.

Jim, flustered and still really upset about something, Tash can't guess what, tries to return to the dropped explanation. He makes a hash of it. The students are looking openly rebellious. Rules of punctuation are not Jim's forté anyway; he's more an inspirational teacher than a technical one. But it's a student body looking for rules and regulations, and they are getting angry at him as he flounders.

"The example you used with me," Tash says in an ominously silent pause, "is definition versus added information. You use 'that' to help define, like in, 'On the day that it rained.' And there's never a comma there. 'Which' is for additional information—'Last Friday, which was rainy, turned out well.' And there you use commas to bracket the interjected phrase." Several students are nodding, and a relieved Jim is quickly writing examples on the blackboard, *screech!* Wow, got to watch that chalk, Jimbo. He's definitely not all there tonight. What's the problem? "That's how you put it when I asked you last week," Tash adds, and begins scribbling the examples in his own notebook.

Then when class is over, Jim packs up swiftly and is out the door and gone before Tash even has time to stand. Too upset to talk about it? Now that *is* unusual.

Tash shakes his head as he leaves the concrete bunkers above the Arroyo Trabuco condos. Too bad. Well, maybe he'll find out about it later, after Jim's had a chance to calm down. Meanwhile he can't worry about it; he's got to get ready to go surfing.

Yes, it is just after ten P.M., and Tashi Nakamura is going to go home and eat and do a little carbrain repair, and then drive down to Newport Beach and go surfing. This is his latest innovation; after all, the waves are jammed with hordes of surfers by day, and so—think about it—if you want to avoid them, there's no choice but to surf at night.

All his friends laughed themselves silly at this idea. It had the trademark Tashi characteristics, following a solution out to a logical but crazy end; Tashi, Jim said, just didn't believe in *reductio ad absurdum*. And they laughed themselves sick. *Ahhh, hahahaha.*

But did they ever try it? No, people tend to judge new ideas without actually testing them, and so they remain on track all their lives, a part of the great machine. That's fine with Tash, because among other things, it means he can have the nighttime waves all to himself.

The trick is to do it when there is a full moon, like tonight. So at 3:30 A.M. Tash parks in Newport Beach, walks down the dark, quiet street, surfboard under his arm. Curious how unanimously diurnal people are. Between the fashionable beachfront condos, with their walls of dark glass facing the sea. Onto the broad expanse of sand, milky in the moonlight, lifeguard stands looming on the bright surface like ritual statuary.

Stone groins extend into the water every four blocks; they're there to help keep the trucked-in sand on the beach. Just off their sea ends waves break, faint white in the darkness. That's another trick to night surfing: find a regular point break with a clear orienting marker. Each groin starts a left break when there's a south swell, as there is tonight; and they're easy to see. Perfect.

Tashi waxes his board, steps down to the water. He arrived in his wetsuit, so sweat reduces by a fraction the room for seawater. Still, wading in and strapping the board's leash onto his ankle, the soup surges up his legs and gives him the familiar shock. Cold! Lovely salt stimulation. He shoves the board into a broken wave, jumps chest first onto it and paddles out, puffing walruslike at the rush of chill water down the wetsuit's neck. Pull of the backwash, the rise into a wave almost breaking, slap of water into his face, the clean cold salt taste of it; he takes in a big mouthful of ocean, sloshes it around in his mouth till the taste fills him. Swallows some to get it down his throat. He's back in Mother Ocean, the original medium, the evolutionary home of the ancient ancestor species that he now feels cheering wildly, down there in his brainstem. Yeah!

Outside the break, paddling with smooth lazy strokes. Pretty much directly out from the 44th Street groin, his favorite. Newport Beach now seems a long strip of white sand backed by hundreds of toy blocks. As usual there's no wind, and the water is perfectly glassy, like dawn glass only better. A liquid heavier than water.

Seeing the waves. It is a bit of a problem, naturally. But the moon's millions of squiggled reflections rise and fall on the swells outside, making a pattern. And close up the black wall of a wave is hard to miss. It's a good sharp left tonight, lips pitching out and dropping over with clean reports as they hit.

Tashi digs the board in, paddles to match the speed of a point about to break, pushes up and stands in one fluid thoughtless motion. Now he's propelled along without further effort, it's merely a matter of balancing his weight in a way that will keep him moving ahead of the break. There's a kind of religious rapture in feeling this movement: as the universe is an interlocking network of wave motions, hitting the stride of this particular wave seems to click him into the universal rhythm. Nothing but gravitational effects, slinging him along. Tuning fork buzzing, after a tap of God's fingernail.

A wall in the wave that Tash doesn't see knocks him over, however, and it's underwater night soup time, an eerie experience of cold wet zero-gee tumbling, up to the roiling moonwhite surface, where a million bubbles are hissing out their lives and popping a fine salt rain into the air just above the water. Tug on leash, grab board, get on, paddle hard to get over the next wave before it breaks. Success, barely. Back over to the point off the groin. Try another one.

It's a pas de deux with Mother Ocean at her most girlish and playful. Quickly Tashi gets into a rhythm, the interval between crests is known to his body more than his eyes, and sometimes he takes off on a wave without even looking at it. He wonders if the blind could surf, concludes it would be possible.

Well. Of course waves are variable; like snowflakes, there are no two the same. And in the dark they bring a lot of surprises, sudden wall-offs, unexpected bowls, backwash ripples, and so forth, which catch Tash off guard and knock him down. No big deal, it's interesting, a challenge. But the neat thing is that about the time he is getting tired of the unexpected variable dumping him, the stars in the east dim, and the sky grows blue. The water is quick to soak up the sky's color, as always. Tash finds himself skimming over a velvet blue like the sky in Jim's orange crate posters, a pure, intense, glossy, rich, *blue* blue. Wow. And he can see a lot more of the wave's surface. It's so glassy that he looks at one smooth wall about to crunch him and decides he must need a haircut: wild-haired guy grinning back at him like an Oriental Neptune, surfing inside the wave like the dolphins do. Who knows, maybe it was Neptune.

The best part of the day. A renewable miracle: always so astonishing, this power of the ocean to resist humans. Here he lives in one of the most densely populated places in the world, and all he has to do is swim a hundred yards offshore and he's in a pure wilderness, the city nothing but a peculiar backdrop. Wildlife refuge, and him the wildlife.

Not only that, but the tide is going out and the waves are getting hollower and hollower, little four-foot tubes tossed into existence for the five seconds necessary to stall back into them, so that he can clip along in a spinning blue cylinder that provides swirling floor walls and roof, with a waterfall fringe at the open end, leading back out into the world. Might as well be in a different dimension when you're in the tube, it is such a wonderful feeling. Tubed, man! How tubular!

Ah, but good times are like tubes, here briefly and then gone forever. There's enough light now for anyone to surf; and within half an hour or so, just about anyone is surfing.

Little clumps of bright wetsuits up and down off each groin.
Scattered surfers between the clumps, hoping for anomalous waves.
Spectrum bands, magenta, green, orange, yellow, violet, pink:
Solids and stripes: wetsuits and boards.
Rising and falling.
The concept of play is either bourgeois or primitive, but does that matter?
Looks like a child's plastic bead necklace, thrown on the water.
The glassy blue water, the waves.

The real problem is that most of the occupants of these colorful wetsuits are assholes. They average about thirteen years old, and ruder little tykes couldn't be imagined. Densepacking at the takeoff point is intense, and the young surf-nazis have dealt with the problem by forming gangs and taking off in groups. If two gangs take off on one wave, it's war. People are pushed off, fights are started. They think this is funny, surfing at its finest.

Tash just continues to do his thing, ignoring the crowd. Aside from a lot of violent threats he is rarely bothered. The truth is, the surfnazis think he is a kind of killer kung-fu character, Bruce Lee crossed with Gerry Lopez, and they leave him alone. But this time one of the more hostile kids deliberately drops in ahead of Tash, shouting "Get the fuck off, Grandpa!" and trying to drive him back into the break. Tash makes his normal bottom turn, comes up and is surprised when he knocks the kid off the wave.

As Tash paddles back out his harasser steams over toward him shrieking abuse and calling on his buddies to help beat up this intruder. Tash just sits up on his board and stares the kid down. Calling him names won't do any good; these poor masochistic sleepwalkers like to be called nazis, in fact it's a compliment among them: "Hey, fucker," one will say to another after a good ride. "That's real nazi."

So Tash just looks at the kid. The rest of the gang hangs back. Tash allows himself a little theatrics, says to the enraged surfer in a tiny horror-video whisper, "Don't cut me off again, my child. . . ."

That not only infuriates the young nazi, it gives him the creeps. Tash paddles back out to the point, chuckling.

But here he is chuckling over terror tactics, when just an hour ago he was involuntarily grinning at the sweet dark face of nature itself, as it rushed up to embrace him. Now it's mallsprawl on the water, surfing another video game. Tash rides a few more waves, and no one actively bothers him, but the mood is gone.

So he paddles out of the new machine, walks up the beach. Sits down to dry off, warm up.

Watches sand grains roll down the side of a hole his toe is making.

The sun gets higher, people begin to populate the beach. By the time he picks his way across the expanse of sand it is dotted with hundreds of figures on towels.

Let's spend a day at the beach!
Talk. Smell of oil, try this coconut!
Here I'll put it on you. Coconut is popular this month.
Thirty tunes clash in the baked shimmery air.
Lifeguard stands are open. Green flags on top.
Lifeguards in red trunks, burnt noses, aren't they cute?
Pastel colors of the old beachfront condos. Neon rainbow overlay.

You don't know how to make a book.
A seabreeze flutters the flags.
White sand, colored towels. See it!
Girls with lustrous dark skin, lying on their backs.
Bright patches of the cache-sexe:
Colors repeat the wetsuit array.
Your head aches when you think about it!
Oiled legs, arms, breasts,
Backbone lifting to a round bottom.
Skin poked out by shoulderblades.
Silky blond hairs, swirled in oil on inner thigh.
The erotic beach. Beautiful animals.

Tash observes the sunbathers with the sort of godlike detachment that a morning of surfing can bring. What is the cosmos for, after all? If the highest response to the universe is an ecstatic melding with it, then surfing is the best way to spend your time. Nothing else puts you in such a vibrant contact with the rhythm and balance of the cosmic pulse. No wonder the godlike detachment afterward. And seen from that vantage, lying flaked on the beach looks lame indeed. Minds turned off, or tuned to trivia (their selves). Surfing calls for so much more grace, commitment, attention.

Or it can, anyway. Tash recalls the surfnazis. It depends on what you make of it. Maybe there are people out there in the prone zone turning the activity into a deep sunworshiping contemplation? . . . No. They lie there chattering. Divorced from it all. No land, seasons, fellow animals, work, religion, art, community, home, world. . . . Hmm, quite a list. No wonder the erotic beach, the alliance merry-go-round. All they have left.

Oh well. Nothing to be done. Time to go home.

Tashi's home is a tent, set on the roof of one of the big condotowers in the Newport Town Center. The roof used to be a patio, but was closed when a resident fell over the too low railing to her death. Soon afterward Tashi saved the building manager from a bad mugging in Westminster Mall, and over drinks the manager told Tash about the roof, and later allowed him to move up there, with the understanding that Tash would never allow anyone to fall over the side. Tashi sewed a big tent, with three large rooms in it, and that has been his home ever since. In the concrete block that holds the elevator there is a small bathroom that still functions, and all in all it couldn't be nicer.

Tashi's friends tend to giggle about the arrangement, but Tash doesn't mind. His home is part of his larger theory, which goes like so: The less you are plugged into the machine, the less it controls you. Money is the great plug, of course; need money, need job. Since most jobs are part of the machine, it follows that you should lead a life with no need for money. No easy task, of course, but one can approximate, do what is possible. The roof is a fine solution to the major money problem, and it even helps with the other major need: he has vegetables growing in long boxes, most of them set in rows next to the railing, to provide a margin of safety. Neat. And he's out in the weather; has a view of the ocean, a great blue plain to the southwest; and above him, the ever-changing skyscapes. Yes, it's a fine home.

He washes down his wetsuit, showers. As he's finishing up in the bathroom the elevator door opens. Sandy and Tash's ally Erica Palme emerge. "In here!" he calls as they pass the bathroom headed for the tent. They look in. "We've brought some lunch along," Erica says.

"Good."

Sandy starts laughing. "*Ah*, hahahaha— Tashi! What are you *doing*?"

"Well—" He's about to brush his teeth, actually. It's obvious. "I'm brushing my teeth."

"But why are you tearing up the toothpaste tube?"

"Well, it's about out. I was just getting the last of it."

"You're tearing open a toothpaste tube to get out the last of the toothpaste?"

"Sure. Look how much was left in there."

Sandy looks. "Uh-huh. Yeah, that's right. You should be able to brush several teeth with that."

"Hmph! Oll sh' oo!" Tashi brushes triumphantly. Sandy cracks up while Erica drags him off to the tent.

Once inside they go to work on the bags from Jack-in-the-Box. Tashi finishes well ahead of the others, starts to work on a broken carbrain. He buys the little computers from car yards, fixes them, and sells them to underground repair shops. Another part of OC's black economy. Income from this alone is almost enough to pay the bills, although it's only one of many activities that Tashi pursues, in a deliberately diffuse way.

Erica watches this work with a sour expression that makes Tash a little uncomfortable. A vice-president in the administration of Hewes Mall, she never seemed to mind Tashi's semi-indigence before; but lately that appears to be changing. Tashi doesn't know why.

Sandy notices Erica's stare and Tashi's discomfort under it, and says, "Last week I made a connection with my supplier at Monsanto San Gabriel, and I was tracking back home with about three gallons of MDMA on the passenger seat, when I ran into a Highway Patrol spot-check point—"

"Jesus, Sandy!" Erica purses her mouth.

"I know. It was one of those mechanical checks, to make sure all my track points were functional, which they were. But meanwhile one of the Chippies walks over to me and looks in, right at the container. He says, 'What's that?'"

"Sandy!" Erica cries, scolding him for getting into such a situation.

"Well, what could I do? I told him it was olive oil."

"You're kidding!"

"No, I said I worked for a Greek restaurant in Laguna and that this was a whole lot of olive oil. And there was so much of it there, he couldn't imagine that it would be anything illegal! So he just nodded and let me go."

"Sandy, sometimes I can't believe you."

Tash agrees. "You should be more careful. What if he had asked to taste it?"

After Sandy and Erica have left to get back to work, Tash operates on a circuit board and shakes his head, recalling Sandy's tale. Sandy's dealing is getting a little crazier all the time. For a while there he was talking about making a bundle, investing it, and retiring. He might have, too; but then his father's liver failed after a lifetime of abuse, and since then Sandy has been paying for regeneration treatments in Dallas, Mexico City, Toronto, Miami Beach. . . . Radically expensive stuff, and Sandy's been pushing hard for almost a year now, about to untrack under the stresses of his schedule. Only his closest friends know why; everyone else assumes it's just Sandy's manic personality, magnified by the effects of his products. Well, that might be part of it, actually. A tough situation.

Tash sighs. Sandy, Jim. Abe too. Everyone in the machine. Even if you aren't you are.

... 18

After a morning's work at the church, Lucy McPherson tracks under the Newport Freeway and into the depths of Santa Ana. Poor city. More than half of it is under the upper level of the freeway triangle, and the ground level, under a sky of concrete, has inevitably gone to slums. Lucy looks nervously through the windshield at the shadowy, paper-filled streets; she doesn't much trust the people who live down here.

She certainly doesn't approve of the woman she's been called to help. Her name is Anastasia, she's about twenty years old, Mexican-American, and she has two small children, although she's never been married. She lives in a run-down old applex under the upper mall at Tustin and 4th.

There's a sidewalk that crosses a dirty astroturf lawn to the front door of the beige stucco building; some fierce and unkempt young men are sitting on the lawn on both sides of the sidewalk. Lucy grits her teeth, leaves her car and walks past them, enters the smelly, olive-green hallway of the complex. Walking down it she can barely see a thing. Knock on the battered door.

"Hello, Anastasia!" Lucy's social mask is solid, and she projects all the sympathetic friendliness she can muster, which is a very considerable amount indeed. Although she can't help but note the dirty dishes stacked in the sink, the heaps of soiled laundry on the bed filling the bedroom nook. Anastasia's hair is oily and uncombed, and apparently the babe has scratched her cheek.

"Lucy, thank God you're here. I gotta go out and get some groceries or we'll starve! Baby's asleep and Ralph's watching TV. I'll just be a few minutes."

"Okay," Lucy says, but adds firmly, "I absolutely have to leave before eleven, I've got business I can't miss."

"Okay, sure. That won't be a problem." Out the door flies Anastasia, without brushing her hair.

Lucy hopes she'll come back on time; once she was stuck here for an entire day, and it's made her distrustful. In fact she didn't mention that her crucial business was a meeting with Reverend Strong, for fear that Anastasia wouldn't consider it important enough to return. She heaves a deep sigh. Some of these good works are really a pain.

Dishes washed, some of the laundry washed in the sink and hung up over the shower curtain rod to dry—not a laundromat within two miles, Anastasia has said—and Lucy sits down with Ralph, a passive six-year-old. She tries to teach him to read, using the only book in the house, a *Reader's Digest Condensed Books for Children*. Ralph stumbles over the first sentence and turns the page to the scratch-'n'-sniff pads that illustrate, or enscentify, the story. As usual, she ends up reading to him. How do you teach someone to read? She points to each word as she reads it. They go through the alphabet letter by letter. Ralph gets bored and cries to have the video wall put back on. Lucy, irritated, resists. Ralph screams.

Lucy thinks, I'm too old for this. Is this really the Lord's work? Baby-sitting? Does Anastasia regard it as such? Quite a few of Lucy's friends feel that they're being taken advantage of in this program of theirs, aiding young women who appear to be joining the church only to get free help. Well, if it's true, Lucy thinks, it still represents a chance to change people's minds, over time, perhaps. And if not . . . well . . .

> God does not expect us
> To cause the seed to sprout—
> He just said to plant it,
> And plant it all about.

She can talk to Anastasia about coming to Bible class when she returns. Speaking of which—it's 11:30. Lucy begins to get annoyed. By noon she's really angry.

Anastasia returns at 12:20, just as Lucy has settled down for an all-day rip-off. Stiffly Lucy reminds Anastasia that she had an appointment at eleven. Anastasia, already upset at something else, begins to cry. They put the meager supply of groceries into the filthy refrigerator: tortillas, soy hamburger, beans, Coke. Pampers into the bathroom. Anastasia has no money left, the utilities bill is overdue, Ralph has outgrown his shoes . . . Lucy gives her fifty dollars, they end up both in tears as she leaves.

Tracking away she can barely see. She just isn't a social worker, she hasn't got the mentality, the ability to distance herself. The people she helps become like family, and it's painful and frightening to see what sordid lives some people lead in this day and age. And so few of them Christian. No help for them from anywhere, not even faith in God. Reverend Strong has clipped a newspaper article that says that only 2 percent of Orange County residents are churchgoing

Christians anymore, and he's stuck it to the office bulletin board as a sort of challenge; but Lucy has to sit at her desk and look at it all day as she works, and given everything else she has to face, she finds it depressing indeed.

Reverend Strong is finishing lunch at the vicarage when she arrives, and he understands about her missing the meeting. "I figured it was Anastasia," he says with a cynical laugh. Lucy isn't yet to the point where she finds it funny. They go into the office and discuss the various works at hand.

Reverend Strong is a nice enough man, but sadly—tragically—his wife was killed in a bomb explosion while they were on a mission to Panama, and Lucy feels that the experience gave him a secret dislike for the poor. He tries to control it, but he can't, not really. And so he is surprisingly, almost shockingly, cynical about most of their good works programs, and he is prone to oblique and confused outbursts in his sermons, against sloth, ambition, political struggle. It leaves most of the congregation confused, but Lucy is sure she understands what is going on. It's the explanation for his frequent return to the parable of the talents. Some people are given only one talent, and instead of working with it they try to steal from the man given the ten talents. . . . Really, the more he harps on it, the more Lucy begins to wonder if the parable of the talents wasn't a bit of a mistake on God's part. In any case, she has the constant problem of getting the reverend's approval for the works that the church obviously has to undertake, in the poorer parts of the community. . . .

These days Reverend Strong says he is worrying intensely about the theological issues raised in the doctrinal negotiations with the Roman Catholics that have been going on for a year at the Vatican. He doesn't want to be bothered with practical problems concerning community work; he has to think about abstract theology, it takes up all his mental energy. This is what he tells Lucy over their late lunch.

Lucy ends up suggesting solutions to their most pressing problem—fundraising—and absentmindedly he agrees to them. So, she thinks angrily: time for another futile, pathetic garage sale . . . because who cares if we don't have enough money to help out our poor neighbors? They don't deserve it anyway! They were only given their one talent. . . .

The afternoon goes to helping Helena, and to calling all the local newsheets to announce the garage sale, and to visiting four families in El Modena with care packages, and to teaching Lillian Keilbacher how to assist in the office, keeping the records. That last part is actually fun. Lillian, her friend Emma's daughter, is now being paid as a part-time assistant, which means she goes at it harder than most of the young people. Lucy really enjoys her company, especially after Anastasia, who must be just a year or two older.

"Lucy, I just hit the command key to get the mailing list and everything disappeared!"

"Uh-oh." They sit down looking at the computer screen, which stays stubbornly blank no matter what they try. "You sure you only hit the command key?"

"Well that's what I thought, but I must be wrong." Lillian is cross-eyed with consternation. Then the screen beeps for their attention and starts displaying a brightly colored sequence of graphs and figures.

"Wow!" They laugh at the extravagance of it. "Do you think this disk is damaged?" Lillian asks.

"I hope so. It's either that or the computer is haunted."

Lillian laughs. "Maybe we can get the reverend to, you know, cure it."

"Exorcise it, sure."

It's fun. A nice girl, Lucy says to herself after Lillian leaves; and that's her highest praise.

Office in order and closed, home to start dinner. Lucy chats on the phone with her friend Valerie while she chops up potatoes for a new casserole she's trying. Into the microwave.

Then Jim comes by. He looks messy, tired.

"You aren't going to teach looking like that, are you?"

He looks affronted. "Looking like what?"

"Those clothes, Jim. You look like you came out of lower Santa Ana."

"Now, Mom, don't be prejudiced."

"I am *not* being prejudiced." As if she were some bigoted recluse! When was the last time he was in lower Santa Ana? It's too much. But he doesn't understand, he's giving her the what-did-I-say-now look that she also gets from Dennis. They look surprisingly alike sometimes. Usually the wrong times. Lucy sniffs hard and collects herself while tending the microwave. "Anyway, you should try to look better. It would make you a better teacher."

"I look like what I look like, Mom."

"Nonsense. It's all under your control. And it sends out signals about what you think of the people you're with. And of yourself, of course."

"Semiotics of clothing, eh Mom?"

"I don't know. Semiotics?"

"What you were saying about signals."

"Well, yes then. Go look in the mirror."

"In a bit."

"Are you staying for dinner?"

"No. Just dropped by to see if any mail's come for me."

Great. "No, nothing's here." And off he goes, hurrying a bit to make sure he's gone by the time Dennis gets home.

This worries Lucy greatly, this growing rift between Dennis and Jim. She knows very well that it's bad for both of them. Both of them need to have each other's respect to be fully happy, that's only natural. And when there are so many other forces in action to make them unhappy, it becomes more important than ever. It's support, mutual support, in a crucial area . . . Thinking these thoughts Lucy picks up the phone and calls Jim as he tracks east on the Garden Grove Freeway. "Listen, Jim, can you come to dinner tomorrow night? We haven't been seeing you often enough recently." Not at all, in fact, since he and Dennis had that fight out in the driveway. They haven't seen each other even once since then, and it's been over a week, and Lucy can feel the resentment and anger growing on both sides.

Jim says, "I don't know, Mom."

Annoyance and concern clash in her. "You don't just come by here and check for mail," she snaps. "We're more than a post office box. You come by and eat a meal with your father soon, do you understand me?"

"All right," he says, voice sharp. "But not tomorrow. Besides, I don't see what good it'll do—he'll just think it's another way that he's supporting me." And he hangs up.

Only minutes later Dennis stalks in, in a foul mood indeed. Lucy decides that he needs distraction from work thoughts, and she risks rebuff to tell him about Anastasia and Lillian. Dennis grunts his way through dinner. She tries another tack. Get him to talk it out, not bottle things up. "What did you do today?"

"Talked with Lemon."

Ah. That explains it. Really, this Lemon must be quite unpleasant, though Lucy has a hard time imagining it, given the charming man she has met at LSR parties. "What about?"

But Dennis doesn't want to go into it, and he retires to the video room table to get out the briefcase and pore over papers. Lucy cleans up, sits down to rest her feet. She's teaching the Bible class tomorrow morning and they're doing a chapter of Galatians that is problematic indeed. Paul is an ambiguous writer, when you read him closely; conflicting desires in him, some selfless and some not, make for a somewhat incoherent output. She reads over the teacher's manual again and worries about the class. She finds herself nodding off. Time for bed already; the evenings always disappear. Dennis is out there staring at nothing, head tilted at an angle. Probably thinking of their plot of land up near Eureka, dreaming of an escape. Lucy shudders at the thought; she didn't like that desolate coastline, its immense distance from her friends, family, work, the world. In fact she has wondered guiltily if the fire that burned the land was somehow an unwanted response to prayer, God granting her least worthy desire as a peculiar kind of lesson or warning to her. . . .

They retire. Another day done. Sleepy prayers. She's got to get Jim back up here. Work on that some more tomorrow. Important. After class. Or the session with Lillian. Or . . .

... 19

That Saturday morning the same old party is beginning at the spa when Sandy gets sick of it. It's sunny outside and the spa with its plants, mirrors, spectrum slide walls, clanking Nautilus machinery, gym shorts, leotards, and the sweet smell of clean sweat, just isn't big enough to do the day justice. *"Ahhh-hhhh! Boring!!!!"* He lets the lat pull go and its weights crash down, then he fires off into the mall and comes back with softballs, bats, and a dozen gloves. "Let's *go*! Play *ball*!" He dragoons the whole crowd and they're off.

It takes them a while to think of a park big enough to play softball in, but Abe does and they track south and east to Ortega, where a large grass park surrounded by eucalyptus trees lies empty. Perfect. There's even a backstop. They split into teams, lid some eyedroppers, and start up a game.

None of them have played since junior high school at best, and the first innings are chaotic. Sandy plays shortstop and does pretty well with the grounders, until one bad hop jumps up and smacks him right on the forehead. He grabs the ball in midair and throws out the speedy Abe by a step. His forehead has a red bruise that shows the ball's stitching perfectly; it looks like some of the surgical work on Frankenstein's monster. When Sandy's told this he starts acting the part, which makes for somewhat stiff shortstopping.

Tashi has apparently lidded some Apprehension of Beauty; he watches everything with the dazed wonder of a four-year-old, including, when he comes to bat, the first two pitches from Arthur. Openmouthed awe, bat forgotten—what an arc! Sandy runs up and reminds him of his purpose there, mimes a hit. Tashi nods. "I know—I was just getting the trajectory down." Next pitch he hits one so far over Humphrey's head in left field that by the time Humphrey even touches the ball Tashi has crossed the plate and sat down, looking more dazed than before. "Home run, huh? Beautiful."

Third out and Jim takes left field in a state of rapture. "I love softball!" "Jim, you never play." "I know, but I love it." Trotting out onto that pure green diamond time disappears, all the adult concerns of life disappear, and Jim feels like an eight-year-old.

Unfortunately for his team he also plays like an eight-year-old. Arthur is up, and he hits a fly ball toward Jim. The moment it's hit Jim begins to run forward, because after all the ball is in front of him, right? But while running in a little basic trajectory analysis shows him that in fact the ball is destined to fly far over his head. He tries reversing direction instantaneously and falls on his ass. Scrambles up, oh shoot there goes the ball, running desperately backwards trying to look over his shoulder for the ball, left shoulder, right shoulder, how do you decide? Now the ball's falling, awful acceleration as it does, Jim running full tilt makes a great leap, the ball hits his outstretched glove then bounces off and out, *no*, an inch more of leather and it would have been an unbelievable catch! He falls, runs to the ball, throws it wildly past Sandy as cut-off man, watches Angela recover it and fire it in sidearm as Arthur cruises across the plate. Damn! Virginia, on deck, is laughing hard. Jim throws his glove down, shrugs ruefully at his grinning teammates. "Hit another one out here!"

"I'll be trying," Virginia calls back.

More hits, more alarming misjudgments, awkward scrambles after the ball, wild throws back in. It's fun.

Next time at bat Tashi hits one even farther than the first time. Home run again. For his subsequent at-bat the outfielders have dropped back until they're standing in the eucalyptus trees, and Tash laughs so hard he can barely stand. "I couldn't hit it that far no matter what!" "Sure, sure. Go ahead and swing."

Moving the outfielders so far back does create some monster gaps up the alleys, and Tash proceeds to hit a screaming line drive that stays eight feet off the ground for about two hundred feet, then skips off the grass and rolls forever. Another homer. And the time after that he does it again. Four for four, all homers. Tash just stands there, mouth hanging open. "Four homers, right? Three? Four? Beautiful."

It's a different story in the field. Playing center, Tash catches a medium-deep fly and sees Debbie tag from third for home. Really a good chance to nail her at the plate, so Tash rears back and puts everything he's got into the throw. Unfortunately his release is a little premature. The ball is still rising as it rockets forty feet over the backstop and into the trees. Who knows where it'll land. Tash stands in center inspecting his right hand. Everyone sits down they're laughing so hard. Then they can't find the ball. Sandy declares the game over and they sit down in the hazy sun to eat Whoppers and fries and drink Coke and Buds. "Do you think it achieved orbit?" "Great game."

Great day. Jim sits on the grass and flirts with Rose and Gabriela, who have singled him out for the afternoon. They only pick on guys they can trust not to take them seriously, it's a sign they feel comfortable and friendly with you, and so of course Jim enjoys that part of it; also he can't help fantasizing that they really are serious this time. That would be a night to remember: what the screens would show!

Jim doesn't really notice Virginia, sitting on the other side of him. And unfortunately she appears to be peeved about something; she knocks his hands away from her when he does turn to her, snaps at him. "What's the problem?" he says, irritated.

She just snarls. And she won't confess to any reason for being disgruntled, which annoys Jim no end. He can't figure it out. He has to suffer the *sotto voce* lash of her sharp tongue, even while they're both being very hearty and friendly with everyone else. Great. Jim hates this kind of thing, but Virginia knows that and so she pours it on.

Finally Jim asks her to come along with him for a short walk, and they go off into the eucalyptus trees.

"Listen, what the hell are you so upset about?"

"Who's upset?"

"Oh come on, don't give me that. Why don't you tell me? It's stupid to be bitching at me when I don't even know what for."

"You don't, do you."

"*No!*"

"That's just like you, Jim. Off in your own little dreamworld, completely unaware of what's going on around you. People don't mean a damn thing to you. I could be dying and you wouldn't even notice."

"Dying! What do you mean, dying?"

Virginia just grimaces with disgust, turns to walk away. Jim grabs her by the wrist to pull her back around, and furiously she swings her arm free. "Leave me alone! You don't have the slightest idea what's going on!"

"You're right I don't! But I do know that I hang out with you by choice—I don't have to. If it's going to be like this—"

"Leave me alone! Just leave me alone!" And she storms off, back to the others out in the sun.

Well. So much for that alliance. Jim doesn't understand why it's ended, or why it began, but . . . Oh well. Confused, frustrated, angry, he walks back out onto the playing field. Beyond the seated group of friends, Virginia is conferring with Arthur; then, to Jim's relief, she walks off with Inez and they track away.

But the feelings generated by the fight don't go away; the real world has intruded back into Jim's afternoon, and anger makes the Whopper lie heavy on his stomach. Virginia's bad mood adds to the other more serious bummers of the last couple of days, forms a fierce brew, a desire to strike back somehow. . . .

When Arthur stands to leave Jim approaches him. "Arthur. You talked about real resistance work. Something more serious than the postering."

Arthur stops and stares at him. "That's right. And you called the other day. I was wondering if you'd ever do anything more."

Jim nods. "I had to think about it. But I want to do something. I want to help."

"There's something coming up," Arthur acknowledges. "It's a lot more serious, this time."

"What you mentioned before. Sabotaging weapons plants?"

Arthur looks at him even longer. "That's right."

"Which one?"

"I'd rather not say, till the time comes." And Arthur's look becomes sharp indeed. They both know what this means: Jim has to commit himself to sabotaging any of the defense corporations in OC, including, presumably, Laguna Space Research. His father's company.

"All right," Jim says. "No one will get hurt?"

"No one in the plants. *We* could get hurt—they've got some tough security on those places. It's dangerous, I want you to know that."

"Okay, but no one inside."

"No. That's the ethic. If you do it any other way, you just become another part of the war."

Jim nods. "When?"

Arthur looks around to make sure they are still quite alone. "Tonight."

The Whopper does a little backstroke in Jim's stomach.

But this is his chance. His chance to make some meaning out of his life, to strike back against . . . everything. Against individuals, of course—his father, Virginia, Humphrey, his students—but he doesn't think of them, not consciously. He's thinking of the evil direction his country has taken for so long, in spite of all his protests, all his votes, all his deepest beliefs. Ignoring the world's need, profiting from its misery, fomenting fear in order to sell more arms, to take over more accounts, to own more, to make more money . . . it really is the American way. And so there's no choice but action, now, some real and tangible form of *resistance*.

"Okay," Jim says.

... 20

So that very night Jim finds himself tracking with Arthur through the network of little streets on the east side of the City Mall, in Garden Grove. They
turn down Lewis Street, which is a tunnellike alley through the underlevel,
walled on both sides by warehouse loading docks, all of them closed in the late
evening. Arthur turns his headlights off and on three times as they turn into
a ten-car parking lot between two warehouses. Parked in this cubbyhole is a
station wagon. Four men standing by it, a black a white and two Latinos, jump
to the back of the station wagon as Arthur and Jim slide into the lot. They lift
out some small but apparently heavy plastic boxes, put them in the backseat
of Arthur's car. With a few muttered words and a quick wave he's out into the
alley again, tracking toward the freeway.

"That's the usual method," he says matter-of-factly. "The idea is to keep hold
of this stuff for as short a time as possible. No one has it for more than a couple
of hours, and it's constantly on the move."

And no more than an hour after that, Jim finds himself crawling on his belly
up the dry bed of the Santa Ana River, scraping over sand, gravel, rocks, plastic
shards, styrofoam fragments, bits of metal, and pools of mud. He's dressed in a
head-to-foot commando suit Arthur has provided out of one of the four boxes.
This suit, as Arthur explained, is completely covert. It holds Jim's body heat in,
so that he gives out no IR signal; one layer is made of filaboy-37, Dow Chemical
and Plessey's latest stealth material, a honeycomb-structured synthetic resin
whose irregular molecules not only distort but "eat" radar waves; and it's a flat
bland color called chameleon, very difficult to see.

Jim peers out through eyepieces that have some kind of head's-up display,
green and violet visuals from covert low-frequency sensors giving him a fairly
good view of the night world, though the colors are out of a bad drug hallucination. And he can't see Arthur at all. The suit's sauna effect is intense, he's
soaked with sweat.

They get up to climb the east side of the riverbed. Jim is cooking. The world looks as if it's under very turbid green and violet water. "Thus they crossed the Lake of Fire . . ." Oh, it is weird, weird.

Here on the Newport Beach side, occupying the site of an old oil field now gone dry, is the physical plant of Parnell Airspace Corporation: fully lit (each light a white-green magnesium flare in Jim's bizarre field of vision), surrounded by a high fence that is electrically defended so conspicuously that the barbed wire on top can only be for decoration, or nostalgia—a symbol, like the mark of a brand over a modern cattle factory.

Jim bumps into Arthur, crouches beside him, puts down the box that he's been carrying or pushing along with him. It's heavy. The buildings of the Parnell complex are still some three or four hundred yards away, dark masses on a green plain of concrete, which is dotted here and there by lavender cars.

Arthur crawls up to the fence and gently hangs on it what looks like a tennis racket without a handle. The frame adheres to the fence, and the wire mesh of the fence caught inside the frame falls away. The frame is now giving out the proper response to the fence's sensors, convincing them that no hole exists—so Arthur has explained to Jim as they prepared for their raid.

"Where do you get all this stuff?" Jim asked at the time.

"We have our suppliers," Arthur said. "This is the crucial item here, the solvent missile. . . ."

Now he shuffles back to Jim and they quickly set up a missile launcher, with the missile already in it. They nail the base of it into the ground. It's got a covert laser targeter, and all in all it's the latest in microarmament: it looks like a Fourth of July skyrocket, or a kid's toy. When they fire it, it will shoot through the new hole in the fence and behave like a little cruise missile, following its laser clothesline into the door of Parnell's physical plant; impact will penetrate the door and release a gas containing degrading enzymes and chemical solvents, mostly a potent mix called Styx-90, another Dow product; and all the plastic, filaboy, reinforced carbon, graphite, epoxy resin, and kevlar reached by the gas will be reduced to dust, or screwed up in some less dramatic way. And Parnell, primary contractor for the third layer of the ballistic missile defense architecture, currently trying to make satellite mirror stations covert or semicovert, will have the bulk of its ground stock handed to it on a plate. Turned into dust and odd lumps on the floor.

Aiming the device is simple though a bit risky, as it makes them semicovert for that instant that the laser targeting is happening. Arthur does it, and they crawl down the fence fifty yards and repeat the whole operation, aiming at another building's door.

Now comes the hard part. The missiles have secondary manual starters, in case radio signals happen to be jammed or responded to with some kind of return fire. Arthur has judged either possibility to be all too likely, so they are using the manual starters, which are buttons at the end of cords connected to the minimissiles. The cords are about a hundred yards long. So Jim crawls backwards through the sage and the trash as far away as the cord lets him, and Arthur does the same from the first missile. They angle toward each other, but Jim can't see Arthur when he comes to the end of his cord. In the suits they're completely invisible to each other.

Arthur has anticipated this difficulty, however. He's given Jim one end of an ordinary length of string, and now Jim feels three tugs on it. They're ready to go. When he gets three more hard tugs he pushes the button on the firing cord, drops both cord and string, and starts running.

It really is a very simple business.

Hitting the button is like turning on all the alarm systems in the world at once; there's a wail of sirens and glare of supplementary floodlights back on the Parnell lot. There's no way of knowing exactly what the missiles did—not a chance of hearing any small crunches that they might have made on impact— but judging by the response, *something* sure happened.

Jim finds himself flying down the riverbed, crouched over so far that he's in danger of smacking his nose with his knees, and leading Arthur by a good distance. They reach Arthur's car, which he parked in the rivermouth beach parking lot; they jump in and track out of there, toward Newport Beach. The commando suits are stripped off in a panic hurry. They track into traffic, Arthur gets in the slow lane and tosses the suits out the window when they pass over Balboa Marina. Off the bridge and into the water. At that point they become two citizens out on the road, nothing to connect them to the buildings full of weapons-become-slag back on the old oil field.

They both smell strongly of sweat, it's like the spa's weight room in Arthur's car. The towels Arthur brought along are damp before they're through drying off, and they struggle back into street clothes still sticky and hot. Jim's hands shake, he can hardly button the buttons on his shirt. He feels a little sick.

Arthur laughs. "Well, that's that. Intelligence estimates we got about ninety million dollars of space weaponry. They'll find the missile stands, but that won't tell them anything." Suffused with energy that is still welling up in him, he sticks his head out the window, shouts "Keep—the sky—*clean*!"

Jim laughs wildly, and the fight-or-flight adrenaline of their run downriver courses through him—one of the most powerful drugs he's ever felt. The best stimulant in the world. "That was great. *Great*. I actually—did something."

He stops, thinks about that. "I've actually done something. You know"—he hesitates, it sounds silly—"I feel like this is the first time in my life that I've actually *done* something."

Arthur nods, stares at him with raptor intensity. "I know just what you mean when you say that. And that's what resistance can do for you. You feel you're in a system so big and so well entrenched that nothing at all could bring it down. Certainly nothing you can do individually will make the slightest bit of difference. But if you hold to that conviction and do nothing, then it's self-fulfilling—you create the very condition you perceive.

"But take that very first step!" He laughs wildly. "Take that first step, perform an act of resistance of even the smallest kind, and suddenly your perception changes. Reality changes. You see it can be done. It might take time, but—" He laughs again. "Yeah! You bet it can be done! Let's go celebrate your first act." He hits the dashboard, hard. "Here's to resistance!"

"To resistance."

...21

They lived here for over seven thousand years, and the only sign they left behind were some piles of shells around the shores of Newport Bay.

This is all we know of them, or think we know:

They came down from the plains east of the Sierra Nevada, wandering members of the Shoshonean tribes, setting up camps and then wandering farther to trade and gather food. When they reached the sea, they stopped and set up camp for good.

They had many languages.

They were what we call hunter-gatherers, and did no cultivating, kept no animals. The men made weapons and hunted with bows and arrows. The women gathered berries and edible roots, and made thistle sage into a porridge; but acorns and pine nuts were their staples. They had to leech the tannin out of their acorn flour, and used a fairly complex set of drains and pits to do it. I wonder who invented the method, and what exactly they thought they were doing, changing this white powder from inedible poison to the daily bread. No doubt it was a sacred act. Everything they did was a sacred act.

They lived in small villages, their dwellings set in circles. In the gentle climate they had little need for protection from the weather, and they slept out except when it rained. Then they slept in simple homes made of willow frames and cattail thatch. The women wore rabbit-pelt skirts, the men animal pelts thrown over the shoulder, the children nothing. Fur cloaks were worn in the winter for warmth.

They traded with tribes from every direction. Obsidian and salt were obtained from the people in the desert. Branch coral came up from Baja. The pelts of sea mammals came from the Channel Island people, who paddled over from the islands ten to a canoe.

They smoked tobacco, and carved stone figures of birds and whales and fish.

The political system was like this: most of the people in a village were family. A headman guided the village with the permission of everyone in it. They changed the headman occasionally.

Sometimes they fought wars, but mostly they were at peace.

They made some of the finest baskets in America, weaving intricate symbolic patterns into them.

They spent part of every day in a sweathouse, pouring water over hot coals and talking in the steam.

In the centers of the villages, they built circular chambers of willow and cattail and brush. The tribes to the north called this sacred sweathouse a yoba, the southern tribes called it a wankech. Here they held their major religious ceremony, the toloache ritual, where the young men drank a jimsonweed liquid, and saw visions, and were initiated as adults. Each sacred chamber held an image of their most important god, Chinigchinich, the one who had named things. The complete skin of a coyote or wildcat was removed from a body, then filled with arrows, feathers, deer horns, lions' claws, beaks and talons of hawks, and sewn back up, so that it resembled the live animal, except that arrows came out of its mouth, and it wore a feather skirt. During the toloache ritual Chinigchinich spoke to the participants through this image, telling them the secret names of all things, which revealed their innermost identities, and gave humans power over them. And so the young became adults.

This is what we know of them; and we know that their village life went on, year after year, generation after generation, existing in an unobtrusive balance with the land, using all of its many resources, considering every rock and tree and animal a sacred being—for seven thousand years. For seven thousand years!

See them, in your mind's eye, if you can, living out their lives on that basin crowded with life. Doing the day's work in the steady sun. Visiting the neighboring village. Courting. Sitting around a fire at dusk. See it.

And then a band of men came by, looking kind of like crabs, wearing shells that they could take off. They could kill from a distance with a noise. They didn't know any of the languages, but had one of their own. History began.

When these soldiers left, the Franciscans stayed. After Junipero Serra founded San Juan Capistrano, in 1776, and went on up "El Camino Real" to found the rest of the missions, a Fray Gerónimo Boscana stayed behind to help run the mission, and convert the locals to Christianity. Those around the mission were called Juaneños, after the mission; those farther north were called Gabrielinos, after the mission at San Gabriel. Fray Boscana wrote, "I consider these Indians in their endowments like the soul of an infant."

And so he put them to good Christian work, cultivating the land and building the mission. Within fifty years all of them were dead. And all that went away.

... 22

For Abe as for most people, the weeks fly by in a haze of undifferentiated activity. He can never believe it as he tears the month past off the calendar: whatever happened to that one? His shifts on the job all blur together, especially since he deliberately tries to forget most of them. He couldn't tell you a thing about his mad drive from Laguna Canyon Road up to UCI hospital: did they lose the victim that time? Was he working with Xavier? He has no idea, and what was it, one, two months ago? No one can tell; no one is operating on that kind of long-term time scale anymore. Lucky if you can remember what happened day before yesterday.

Somewhere inside him, of course, it is all remembered: every crash, every drive, every expression flitting over X's face as he sweats it out with the victims in the gutbucket. But the recollection mechanism is firmly turned off. As far as Abe knows in his waking hours, it's completely gone. Two months ago? Gone! It's present tense for Abe, the here and now his only reality, the moment and the only moment. This may account for the fact that he very seldom has an ally. He doesn't think about it. Alliance? With Inez, right? Or was it Debbie. He'll find out tonight at Sandy's party.

Tonight he's working with Xavier again, as usual. As long as one of them doesn't trade around off days to extend a vacation (which happens fairly frequently) they're a team. They like that. It gives the job some continuity, makes it a little more like ordinary jobs.

The radio crackles, X picks it up. "We hear you, All-Seeing One."

They're tapped out. Code nine, pile-up, five to eight cars, Foothill Freeway just west of the Eastern Freeway, still up on the viaduct. They're on the Santa Ana Freeway in Tustin, they gun up the Eastern and then up onto the Foothill. The tracks are stacked, Abe drives them on the really narrow viaduct shoulder toward a seemingly airborne forest of flashing reds and blues, three CHPs and another rescue truck already on the scene. Abe and Xavier jump out. The other rescue pair is engaged at the front of the pile-up, so they go to work on the rear end. "X, see if you can get another truck or two here fast."

Third car in has been accordioned to a pancake of metal and glass no more than ten feet thick, and driver and passenger are still in it, both unconscious. Viciously Abe pulls over his primary cutter from the truck, goes to work on the passenger side. The passenger, an older woman, is dots. "A definitive case of the dots," as X mutters while crawling over her toward the driver. "Real chicken pox." Driver, an older man, is thrashing around suddenly. Abe leaps over to his side of the car, X is slapping on the drug patches and trying to assess the damage. "Here, Abe, chop a hole for me to get in th'other side." Screech of metal cut like paper, waldo Superman yanks the roof up and X slithers in, cursing at a sharp edge that catches at his crotch. He flops over the front seat and goes at the driver, Abe continues to widen the door, snip snip snip, Chippie puts a halogen floodlight on them and it's all overexposed, howl of approaching sirens, it's loud out here on the freeway but Abe doesn't hear a thing, it's only stubborn metal here. He chops away the whole side of the car, looks up to see the hundred cars passing slowly, vampire eyes feasting on the sight.

"Abe! *Abe!*" X is hanging down underneath the steering wheel. Abe leans in. "Look man, he's caught here, the driveshaft wall has snapped over and crushed the right ankle."

Abe can see that.

"Cut that loose, will you?"

Abe goes to work on it.

"Not so close!"

"Well shit, how else can I get that sheet turned back?"

"Work higher around it, man this guy's gonna bleed to death from his fucking foot! Can't get the patch all the way around—"

Snip. Crrk. Crrk. Crrk. Snip.

"The driveshaft and the motor are pressing down on that wall, I'll have to get the crane on it and yank it up—"

"No time for that! Okay—I got a tourniquet on the calf. That foot is almost torn off anyway, and he gonna die if we don't get him out of here right fast, so listen here Abe, take those snips and cut his foot clear—"

"What?"

"You heard me, amputate right here. I'll get him to the car. Do what I say, man, I'm the medic here!"

Abe set the edges of the cutter blades against a bloodied black sock, resists an urge to look away. Just like scissors. "That's it, right there." He squeezes the master handles together gently. "Quick now." There's no resistance at all to the flesh. Only a little resistance, a slight crunch, as the blades cut through the bone. The footless driver sighs. X slaps a fix on the stump, hands flying, breath *whoosh*ing in and out of him as he wiggles around, lifts the driver out, they pull him free of the dash and get him on a street gurney. "Cut that foot free and bring it along," X says as he runs the gurney to the truck.

"Fuck." Abe attacks the motor from the front, puts the snips to it and presses together hard as he can; it takes all of his and the teleoperator's strength to cut the driveshaft in half, but that done he can sink the cutter into the motor and pull it forward by main strength. Then he can get a grip on the driveshaft wall, a tricky maneuver, but he does it and bends the wall back, runs around to the driver's door, reaches in, yep, there, he can reach in and grab the thing, shoe all full of blood, and here he is running back to the truck with a foot and ankle in his hand. Part of him can't believe it's happening. He throws it in back on the bed with its owner, X looks up from his man, "Let's get this guy to an ER fast." Abe is in the driver's seat, seat belt on, off he goes, Mission Viejo's got a little hospital with a good ER to handle all their swimming casualties, no track now, it's full speed ahead and X's sweaty face in the window. "I got him stabilized, I think. He's looking good."

"Will they be able to graft that foot back on?"

"Yeah, sure. It's a clean cut. They could graft your head back on these days." He laughs. "You shoulda seen the look on your face when you tossed it in to me."

"Shit."

"Ha, ha! That's nothing. On Java once I was carrying a whole *leg* out, hip down, and damned if it didn't keep *kicking* me."

"Shit."

"You didn't feel anything twitching or anything? Ha, ha. . . ."

"Please, X."

Abe flies down La Paz and up the tortured curving streets that are supposed to make old Mission Viejo somehow different. To the hospital, onto the ER dock, wheel the guy and his foot inside. Whew. They sit on the dock.

X gets up and gets towels and water bottle from the ambulance compartment. They towel off their faces, drink deeply. Abe feels the shakes begin to hit. The kinetic memory of the amputation returns, that crunch when the waldo suddenly overcame the bone's resistance. "Man," he says. X laughs softly.

Brrk! Crrk! "Truck five twenty-two, code six, a two car head-on where the Coast Highway meets Five in Capistrano Beach—"

Tapped out again. Reflexively they're up. Xavier yells in to the ER nurses, Abe gets the truck started. X jumps in. Seat belts on. "Man they're densepacked tonight."

"Drive, road pilot, drive this baby."

... 23

Dennis McPherson reads of the sabotage at Parnell on the morning wall news, shoots air between his teeth. A bad business. There have been several attacks by saboteurs on defense contractors recently, and it's hard to tell who's behind them. It's beginning to look like more than intercompany rivalries. Every company's security division, including LSR's, is involved in some questionable activities, usually concerned with getting their hands on classified military documents or the plans of other companies; this McPherson is aware of, as is everybody. And in isolated cases a zealous or desperate security team may have gotten out of hand and done some mischief to a rival. It's happened, sure, and in recent years, with the Pentagon's budget leveling off a little, the competition has become more and more unscrupulous. But mostly it's been confined to intelligence and minor-league tampering. This widespread sabotage appears to be something new. The work of the Soviets, perhaps, or of some Third World power; or of homegrown refusniks.

Dennis laughs without humor to read that the composite-compound solvents used in the attack were mostly Styx-90, made by Dow. Parnell is owned by Dow. And he laughs again when it occurs to him that these companies, whose main business it is to defend America from ICBM attack, cannot even effectively protect themselves from little field cruisers. Who anymore can possibly believe in Fortress America?

Certainly not the security men at the gate of the LSR complex. They look distinctly unhappy as they check to see if McPherson is the correct occupant of his car. They're there to defend against industrial espionage, not guerrilla attack. They've got an impossible job.

And the people inside?

For the last several weeks McPherson has been whipping the informal Stormbee proposal into formal shape. Going from superblack to white. There are advantages to a white program that McPherson appreciates. Everything's on the table, the specs are there in the RFP and can't be changed by some clown in the Air Force who happens to come up with a new idea. And they're forced by the intense competition to do a thorough job, including tests that are run until every part of the system has been proved to work, under all kinds of circumstances. And that's good in the long run, as far as McPherson is concerned. He's been out to White Sands seven times in the last month, working on further tests of the system, and in the tests they discovered, for instance, that if the target tanks were grouped in a mass the laser target designator tended to fix only on the tanks on the perimeter, leaving those in the middle alone. Some work by the programmers and the problem was solved, but if they hadn't even known about it? Yes, this is the way McPherson likes to work. "Let's get it right," he tells his crew almost every day. In fact his programmers call him LGIR behind his back, pronounced "Elgir," which has led certain music-minded programmers to speak of cello concertos, or to whistle "Pomp and Circumstance" to indicate the boss's arrival on the scene. . . .

So, McPherson sits down at his desk and looks at the list of Things To Do that he left the night before. He adds several items that have occurred to him over the night, and on the drive in.

9:00 meet Don F. re Strmbee prop printing
see Lonnie on CO_2 laser problems
work Strmb prop introduction
1:30 meeting software group re guidance
call Dahlvin on Strmb power
work Strmb prop
4:00 meet Dan Houston on Ball Lightning

He lifts the phone, punches the button for Don Freiburg. The day begins.

Becoming a white program means that the Stormbee proposal is now part of the mainstream of public military procurement in America. This is a vastly complicated process that contains hundreds of variables, and very few people, if any, understand all the facets of it. Certainly McPherson does not; he concentrates on the part of the process that is important to his work, just as everyone else does. Thus he is an expert in the Air Force's aerospace technology procurement, and knows little or nothing about other areas. Just learning his own little area is difficult enough.

It begins within the Air Force itself, like so: One of the operating commands, say the Strategic Defense Phase One Group (SDPOG), makes a Statement of Operational Need (SON) with a Mission Element Need Analysis (MENA) to the United States Air Force Headquarters (HQ USAF). If HQ USAF decides that the SON represents a major program, they make a Justification for Major Systems New Start (JMSNS), which is reviewed by the Requirements Assessment Group (RAG), and this review is then submitted to the Secretary of the Air Force (SAF). If SAF decides that the JMSNS represents an Air Force Designated Acquisition Program (AFDAP), he approves the JMSNS, and it becomes an AFJMSNS. The SAF then submits the AFJMSNS as part of the next Air Force Program Objectives Memorandum (POM) to the Secretary of Defense (SECDEF). If the SECDEF approves the POM, and thus the AFJMSNS, the HQ USAF prepares and issues a Program Management Directive (PMD), and Planning, Programming and Budgeting System (PPBS) action is taken. The Concept Exploration Phase (CEP) has begun. In this phase the various Preliminary System Operational Concepts (PSOCs) are explored, and altogether they constitute the Phase Review Package (PRP). From the PRP a System Concept Paper (SCP) is prepared by HQ USAF, and it is again reviewed by the RAG, and by the Air Force Systems Acquisition Review Council (AFSARC), after which it is submitted to the SAF. If the SAF approves the SCP, it is reviewed by the Defense Systems Acquisition Review Council (DSARC), which recommends it to the SECDEF. If the SECDEF approves the SCP—a Milestone I decision—then HQ USAF issues another PMD and the program enters the Validation and Demonstration Phase (VDP).

All clear? Well, it's at that point that the program first connects with private industry. If the SAF and the SECDEF have agreed that the program must remain top secret, then the program becomes a superblack program and a single contractor or two is contacted by Air Force personnel directly in the Pentagon. At least usually. There are also the ordinary black programs, which are given directly to contractors like the superblacks; a few people in Congress are told about these as well, so they can think that they are in on all the Pentagon's secrets.

But by far the majority of the programs are so-called white programs, and these require more complicated procedures. During the VDP, HQ USAF begins floating draft Requests For Proposals (RFPs) and Requests For Information (RFIs) to relevant defense contractors, asking for comments. The interested companies respond with technical suggestions based on their evaluations of the RFP, and these become part of the Decision Coordination Process (DCP). Eventually HQ USAF issues a final RFP, which is usually published in *Commerce Business Daily*. At this point there has already been an important tactical struggle between the interested contractors, as each attempted to get things written into the RFP that only they were competent to do. But now the RFP is out there for anyone to respond to, and the race is on.

Typically companies have ninety days to submit proposals to the Program

Manager (PM), who is an Air Force colonel or brigadier general. After submission, the proposal evaluation process begins. Part of it is conducted by the
Air Force Test and Evaluation Center (AFTEC), which is part of the Air Force
Systems Command (AFSC) based at Andrews AFB; part of it is conducted out
of HQ USAF in the Pentagon, or under the PM. From these units and others
a Source Selection Evaluation Board (SSEB) is convened, under the command
of a Source Selection Authority (SSA), who is usually but not always the PM.
The various proposers are brought in and grilled over every detail of their proposals, and when that six-week process is over, the SSEB makes its evaluation,
which is then summarized by the SSA, who uses his summary to justify his decision to the people above him. The decision to award the program to a bidder
(or to award it to two bidders in a competitive development, or in a so-called
leader-follower arrangement) is thus ultimately the SSA's decision, but he usually follows the recommendations of the SSEB, and he also has to secure the
approval of his superiors, up to the SAF or even the SECDEF.

All clear?

But meanwhile, at this point, all Dennis McPherson has to worry about is
putting together a proposal that will stand up under the technical testing and
budgetary demands that the SSEB will soon be making. Not too many days
left; and so it is nearer five-thirty than four when he finally gets free for the
first conference with Dan Houston about the Ball Lightning program, which
Lemon has vengefully commanded him to work on, in his "spare time" from
the Stormbee proposal.

McPherson can still remember perfectly the mistake that got him stuck
with this. He was down in LSR's executive restaurant, walking in with Art
Wong, and in response to something Art said, without pausing to think (or
look around), he said, "I'm damned glad I don't have the job you guys do. The
whole ballistic defense program is nothing but a black hole for money and effort if you ask me." And then he turned around and there was Stewart Lemon,
standing right there and glaring at him.

And so now he's assigned to Ball Lightning. Lemon never forgets.

Dan is ready to quit for the day, and he's about to go with some of his crew
to the El Torito just down the road. He wants McPherson to come along and
join them for margaritas, and McPherson hides his irritation and agrees to it.
On the short drive over he calls Lucy to let her know he'll be home late, and
then ascends the office complex's maze of exterior staircases to the restaurant
on the top floor. Fine view of the Muddy Canyon condos, and in the other
direction, the sea.

Dan and Art Wong and Jerry Heimat are already there at a window table, and the pitcher of margaritas is on its way. McPherson sits and starts in on the chips and salsa with them. They're talking shop. Executives at Grumman and Teledyne have been indicted for taking kickbacks from subcontractors. "That's why they call the Grumman SAM the 'Kicker,' I guess," says Dan. This gets them on the topic of missiles, and as the pitcher of margaritas arrives and is quickly disposed of, they discuss the latest performances in the war in Indonesia. It seems a General Dynamic antitank missile has gotten nicknamed "the Boomerang" for persistent problems with guidance software or vane hinges, no one is quite sure yet. But they just keep on flying in curved trajectories, a weird problem indeed. No one wants to use these devices, but they're ordered to anyway because the Marines have huge quantities of them and won't acknowledge that the problems have gotten above an acceptable percentage. So soldiers in the field have taken to firing their GDs ninety degrees off to the side of the target tanks . . . or so the gossip mill says. No doubt it's a pack of lies, but no one likes GD so it makes for a good story.

"Did you hear about Johnson at Loral?" asks Art. "He's in charge of the fourth-tier ICBM program, shooting down leakers. So, one day he gets a directive from SDC, and it says, Please assume that you will have to deal with twenty percent *more than* the total amount estimated to be launched in a full-scale attack!" They all laugh. "He almost has a heart attack, this is a couple of orders of magnitude more incoming than he thought the system was going to have to deal with, and all his software is shit out of luck. The whole system is overwhelmed. So he calls the Pentagon just before his ticker says good-bye, and finds out that whoever wrote 'twenty percent *more than*' should have written 'twenty percent *of*'. . . ."

"He's still got trouble," Dan says when they stop laughing. "They can't even knock down one incoming with more than fifty percent reliability, so they're going to have to at least double the number of smart rocks, and the Pentagon is already threatening to dump him." This reminds Dan of his own troubles, and with a grim smile he downs the rest of his margarita.

Art and Jerry, aware of their boss's moods, sense this change of humor. And this is supposed to be a conference between the two managers. So they chat for a while longer, and finish their drinks, and then they're up and off. Dan and Dennis are left there to talk things over.

"So," Dan says, smiling the same unhumorous smile. "Lemon has stuck you into the Ball Lightning program, eh?"

"That's right."

"Worse luck for you." Dan signals to a passing waitress for another pitcher. "He's running scared, I'll tell you that. Hereford is calling from New York and putting the pressure on, and right now he's feeling it but good, because we are stuck." He shakes his head miserably. "Stuck." "Stuck."

"Tell me about it."

Dan gets out a pen, draws a circle on the yellow paper tablecloth. "The real problem," he complains, "is that the first tier has been given an impossible job. Strategic Defense Command has said that seventy percent of all Soviet ICBMs sent up in a full attack are to be destroyed in the boost phase. We won a development contract using that figure as the baseline goal. But it can't be done."

"You think not?" McPherson suspects that Dan may just be making excuses for his program's problems. He sips his drink. "Why?"

Houston grimaces. "The necessary dwell time is just too long, Mac. Too long." He sighs. "It's always been the toughest requirement in the whole system's architecture, if you ask me. The Soviets have got their fast-burn boosters down to sixty seconds, so most of their ICBMs will only be in boost phase for that minute, and half that time they'll be in the atmosphere where the lasers won't do much. So for our purposes we're talking about a window of thirty seconds."

He scribbles down the figures on the tablecloth as he talks, nervously, without looking at them, as if they are his signature or some other deeply, even obsessively memorized sign. $t_B = 30$.

"Now, during that time we've got to locate the ICBMs, track them, and get the mirrors into the correct alignment to bounce the lasers. Art's team has got that down to around ten seconds, which is an incredible technical feat, by the way." He nods mulishly, writes $t_T = 10$. "And then there's the dwell time, the time the beam has to be fixed on the missile to destroy it." He writes $t_D =$, hesitates, leaves the other side of the equation blank.

"You told the Air Force we could pulse a large burst of energy, right?" McPherson asks. "So the damage is done by a shock wave breaking the skin of the missile?"

Dan nods. "That's right."

"So dwell time should be short."

"That's right! That's right. Dwell time should be on the order of two seconds. That means that each laser station can destroy N missiles, where," and he writes:

$$N = \frac{t_B}{t_D + t_T}$$

"However," Dan continues carefully, looking down on the simple equation, one of the basic Field-Spergels that he has to juggle every day, "dwell time in fact depends on the hardness of the missile, the distance to the target, the brightness of the laser beam, and the angle of the incidence between the beam and the surface of the missile." He writes down H, B, R, and 0, and then, obsessively, writes down this equation too, another Field-Spergel:

$$t_D = \frac{4\partial^2 HR^2}{\pi PD^2 \cos 0}$$

"And we've been getting figures for hardness of about forty kilojoules per square centimeter." He writes $H = 40$ KJcm^2. "Our lasers have twenty-five megawatts of power hitting ten-meter-diameter mirrors at wavelength two point seven nanometers, so even with the best angle of incidence possible, dwell time is," and he writes, very carefully:

$$t_D = 53 \; seconds.$$

"What?" says McPherson. "What happened to this pulse shock wave?"

Dan shakes his head. "Won't work. The missiles are too hard. We've got to burn them out, just like I used to say we'd have to, back before we got this development contract. The mirrors are up there and they won't be getting any bigger, the power pulse is already incredible when you think that over a hundred and fifty laser stations will have to be supplied all at once, and we can't change the wavelength of the lasers without replacing the entire systems. And that's the whole ball game."

"But that means that dwell time is longer than boost time!"

"That's right. Each laser can bring down about eight-tenths of a missile. And there's a hundred and fifty laser stations, and about ten thousand missiles."

McPherson feels himself gaping. He takes the pen from Houston, starts writing on the tablecloth himself. He surveys the figures. Takes another drink.

"So," he says, "how did we get this development contract, then?"

Dan shakes his head. Now he's looking out the window at the sea.

Slowly he says, "We got the contract for Ball Lightning by proving we could destroy a stationary hardened target in ground tests, with the sudden pulse shock wave. They gave us the contract on that basis, and we were put in competition with Boeing who got the same contract, and after three years we have to show we can do it in boost phase, in real-time tests. It's getting close to time for the head-to-head tests. The winner gets a twenty-billion-dollar project, just for starters, and the loser is out a few hundred million in proposal and development costs. Maybe it'll get a follower's subcontract with the winner, but that won't amount to much."

McPherson nods impatiently. "But if we could do it on the ground?"

Dan polishes off another glass in one swallow. "You want another pitcher?"

"No."

He pours foam and ice into his glass. "The problem," he says carefully, "is that the test wasn't real. It was a strapped chicken."

"*What?*" McPherson sits up so fast his knee knocks the table and almost tips his glass over. "What's this?"

But it's clear what Dan means. The test results didn't mean what LSR said they did.

"Why?"

Dan shrugs. "We were out of time. And we thought we had the problem licked. We thought we could send a beam so bright that it would create a shock wave in even the hardened skins, the calculations made it look like all we needed was a little more power and the brightness would be there. So we simulated what would happen when we did solve the problems, and figured we could validate the tests retroactively, after we had the contract. But we've never been able to." He stares at the table, unable to meet McPherson's gaze.

"For God's sake," Dennis says. He can't get over it.

"It's not like no one has ever done it before," Dan says defensively.

"Uhn."

In fact, as they both know, the strategic defense program has a long history of such meaningless tests, beginning under its first R&D PM. They blew up Sidewinder missiles with lasers, when Sidewinders were designed to seek out energy sources and therefore were targets that would latch on to the beams destroying them. They sent electron beams through rarefied gases, and claimed that the beams would work in the very different environments of vacuum or atmosphere. They bounced lasers off space targets and claimed progress, when astronomy rangers had done the same for decades. And they set target missiles on the ground, and strained them with guy wires so that they would burst apart when heated by lasers, in the famous "strapped chicken" tests. Yes, there's a history of PR tests that goes right back to the beginning of the whole concept. You could say the ballistic missile defense system was founded on them.

But now—now the system is being produced and deployed. It's the real thing now, sold to the nation and in the sky, and with a strapped chicken in their part of the system, they're in serious trouble. The Pentagon is not as lenient with private contractors as they were with their own research program, needless to say. The company could even be liable to prosecution, though it seldom comes to that. It doesn't have to to ruin the company, though.

And here Lemon has put him into this program! McPherson already knew that Lemon gave him the task out of malice; it complicated his primary work quite a bit; but this! This! It goes beyond malice.

"Does Lemon know?"

". . . No."

But McPherson can see in Dan's face that he's lying, trying to cover for his boss, his friend. Amazing. And there's no way Dennis can call Dan on it, not now. "My God." He stops a waitress and orders another pitcher of margaritas.

They sit in silence until the new pitcher arrives. They fill up. "So what do you think we should do?" Dan says hesitantly. There's a certain desperation in his voice; and he's drinking the margaritas as fast as he can.

"How the hell should I know?" Dennis snaps. The question makes him suddenly furious. "You've got Art and Jerry's people working on the pulse problem?"

"Yeah. No go so far, though."

McPherson takes a deep breath. "Would more power help?"

"Sure, but where will we get it?"

"I don't know. I suppose . . ." He is thinking to himself now. "I suppose the best thing to do is try jamming all the power we do have into as short a burst as we can manage. And focus it to as small a space." He sighs, picks up the pen and starts scribbling formulas. The two of them bend their heads over the table.

... 24

—RRKK!—"Slightly radioactive still. On the foreign front the score is still in our favor in Burma—as for Belgium, I don't want to talk about it, all right? Now let's put an ear to the new hit by our favorite group The Pudknockers, 'Why My Java Is Red White and Green'—"

Sandy Chapman turns off the radio. Groan, moan. Stiffness in the joints, he feels like an old man. Sunlight streams into the plant-filled, glass-walled bedroom; it's warm, humid, smells like a greenhouse. Sandy manages to lever himself into a seated position. Angela is long gone, off to work in the physical therapy rooms at St. Joseph's Hospital.

All the glossy green leaves blur. Bit of fuzz vision, too much eyedropping yesterday as usual, leads to a sort of eyeball hangover, as if he'd been teargassed or had his corneas sandblasted or something. He's used to it. He gets up, pads off to the bathroom. The face in the mirror looks wasted. Dark circles under bright red eyes, stubble, mouth caked white, long red hair broken out of pony-tail, looking electrocuted. Yes, it's morning time. Ick.

In the kitchen he starts the coffee machine, sits staring out at the San Diego Freeway until it's ready. Back to the bedroom, where he sits on the floor among the plants. Eyedrop a little Apprehension of Beauty . . . ah. That's better. Just the lubrication feels good. He sips coffee, relaxes, thinking nothing: no worries, no plans. Odors of coffee, hot plants, wet soil. "Hey this is why my Java is red white and green," he sings, "the blood in the jungle, the smoke white machine. . . ." This is the sole moment of peace in his day, waxy leaves around him glowing translucent green in the mote-filled sunny air, everything visible, a world of light and color. . . .

Need another cup of coffee. Fifteen minutes later the thought occurs to him again, and he stands. Oops got up too fast. Through warm patches to the kitchen. Ah, feeling much better now. Sensuousness of feet on warm tile, taste of coffee cutting through fuzz in mouth, video of Angela getting undressed last night, running on the kitchen screens. Ready to get a start on the day's business. A day in the life, sure enough.

But first he stops to call his father, down at the experimental clinic in Miami Beach. They talk on the video link for twenty minutes or so: George seems good today, hearty and cheerful despite the pallor and the IV lines. Sandy finds it reassuring, sort of.

Then he's dressed, alert, out the door to work like any other businessman.

Sandy begins his day on time. And while he's only depending on himself, he stays on schedule. He tracks to a rundown area of the underlevel of Santa Ana, a mile or so north of South Coast Plaza, and unlocks the door to the warehouse he rents, after turning off all the alarms. Inside is his laboratory.

Today he starts with cytotoxicity assays, one of the most crucial parts of his work. Anyone can make drugs, after all; the trick is finding out if they'll kill you or not without testing them personally. Or giving them to rats. Sandy doesn't like killing rats. So he likes these assays.

Since the cornea's epithelium will be the first place the drugs hit, epithelial cells get the first tests. A couple of days ago Sandy joined the crowd of biochem techs at the slaughterhouse and bought a package of cow eyeballs; now he takes them from the fridge and uses a device called a rubber policeman to scrape the epithelial cells off the basement membrane. Tapped into a petri dish with some growth medium, and a carefully measured dose of the drug in question—a new one, a variant of 3,4,5 trimethoxyamphetamine that he's calling the Visionary—these cells will either proliferate or die or struggle somewhere in between, and staining them at the end of a week will tell the tale.

That assay set up, Sandy moves on to trickier stuff. The new drug's effect on lymphocytes has to be checked as well, because blood will be carrying it a lot of the time. So Sandy begins a chromium release assay, injecting chromium 51 into lymphocytes, then centrifuging them so only the cells remain. At that point all the chromium in the mix is within the cells. Then the Visionary is added—in doses ranging from femtomolars up through picomolars, nanomolars, micromolars—and it all goes into a growth medium that should keep lymphocytes happy. But with the drug in there who knows. In any case dying or dead cells will release the chromium, and after another centrifuging, the free chromium found will be a good measure of the drug's toxicity.

Later more tests of stationary cells and organ cells, particularly bone marrow cells, will be necessary. And eventually, after a lot of hours in the lab, Sandy will have a good idea of the Visionary's toxicity. Neat. As for long-term negative effects of the new drug, well, that's not so clear. That's not in the guarantee. That's not something he likes to think about, and neither does anybody else. None of these new drugs are well understood on the long-term level. But if there are problems down the road, they will no doubt come up with something, like they did for the various viral killers. Make the body into a micro-battlefield and win it all: the brain can finally prove it is smarter than viruses. Who knows what demon will fall next?

So, not to worry about long-term physical effects. As for the new drugs' effects on the mind, well, it isn't so cut and dried, but he does have a collection of cross spiders, building their webs under the influence of the new products. The particular nature of the altered state induced by the drug can be partially predicted by the computer's Witt analysis of the webs. Amazing but true. More precise knowledge in this area will come after some extensive field testing; he has a lot of volunteers.

The fact is, he buys his drugs in an advanced state, so the molecular engineering he does to make his new products is nothing really supercomplex, though he has a reputation for genius that he does nothing to try to dispel. Actually, he has got a talent for pharmacometrics—taking the basic drugs from the companies and then guessing, with the aid of a structure/activity relationships program pirated from Upjohn, which alterations in chemical structure will shift the psychoactive properties of the drugs in an interesting way. Pharmacometrics is really quite an art, still, even with the program's indispensable aid: structure/activity relationships is a big and complex field, and no one knows it all. So to that extent he is a kind of artist.

Into the second hour of work. Sandy moves among the various endomorphins and alkaloids and solutions on the shelves in their bottles and flasks, and the reference texts and papers that spill over one big bookcase, and the bulks of the secondhand centrifuges, refrigerators, the g.c./mass spec . . . It would be easy to impress any visitors allowed to drop by. For a few minutes he attacks again the problem of the synergistic self-assembly effects of La Morpholide 15 and an enkephalin introduced into the brain at the same time—a sophisticated problem in pharmacokinetics, sure, and interesting as hell, but a little bit much for this morning. Easier to return to the final plans for fitting 5-HIAA to the serotoninergic neurons, which he's already almost mastered. Should be a nice hallucinogen, that.

So it's a fascinating couple of hours in the lab, as always. But he's supposed to meet one of his suppliers, Charles, at noon, and looking up at the clock he finds he'd better hurry. Sure enough, he shows up at Charles's place in Santa Ana at 12:05. Nothing to complain about, right?

However, the inevitable process of getting behind schedule begins immediately, with Charles inviting him in to share an eyedropper, followed by a close discussion of Charles's difficulties in life. So the simple pickup of a liter of Sandoz DMT takes him until 1:30.

He then heads to the first of his distributors, in Garden Grove, and discovers no one home. Twenty minutes of waiting and they show up, and it's the same program there; only really need to lay twenty eyedroppers on them and collect the money for them, could take five minutes, right? But no. Got to blink another eyedropper of Social Affability, light up a Sandy spliff, and socialize for a bit. That's sales for you, it's a social job and you can't escape that. Not many people realize how full Sandy's schedule of deliveries actually is, and of course he doesn't want to make too big a point of saying so. It's a test of his diplomacy to get out in under an hour; so now it's almost three. He hurries up to Stanton to make a drop at June's, then tracks at street level to La Palma to meet Sidney, hits the freeway to get back to Tustin and the Tunaville drug retailers' weekly meeting, down to Costa Mesa to see Arnie Kalish, on to Garden Grove to see those Vietnamese guys in Little Saigon . . . until he's over three hours behind schedule and losing ground fast, with a dozen more people who want to see him before dinner. Whew.

Luckily this happens every day, and so everyone expects Sandy to be late. It's an OC legend; stories abound of Sandy showing up for lunches at dinner, for dinners at midnight, for parties the next day . . . By this time it would no doubt actually shock people if he showed up on time. But, he thinks, it's never my fault!

So he works his way along, tracking like a maniac to sit through one glacial transaction after another. It's a bit of an effort, when he's tired or depressed, living up to the task of being Sandy Chapman; he's expected to show up at a friend/client's house and galvanize the day, burst in with manic energy and his crazy man's grin, discuss all the latest developments in music, movies, sports, whatever, shifting registers from full-blown culturevulturehood to astonishing mallworld ignorance . . . pull out yet another eyedropper, of Affability or Funny Bone or California Mello or the Buzz, whatever seems to be called for at the moment, eyes bugging out with manic glee as he holds up the dropper and pulls his face under it. . . . He's used to operating rationally under the weight of monumental highs; in fact it's just everyday reality for him, stonedness, it's a handicap he barely notices anymore. His tolerance level is so high that he only really notices the effect of that first drip of Apprehension of Beauty at the beginning of each day. So he lids with whatever household he has reoriented to party mode, smokes dope with them, inhales capsules of snapper, giggles at them as they exhibit the first signs of brain damage, fills them full of that comic spirit that is surely the main thing he is selling. It's quite a performance, though he seldom feels it as such. Method acting.

Long after sundown he finishes making his last delivery, some five hours late. On the way home he stops and buys the ten-trillionth Big Mac fries and a Coke, eats while tracking home. Reaches home, but it's no rest for the weary; the party there is in dormant mode and reflexively he sparkplugs it, gets it on-track and rolling. Then into his bedroom, to check on phone messages.

The answering machine can barely hold all the messages that have been left, and Sandy sits on the bed buzzing like a vibrator, watching the surfing on the wall screens and listening to them. One catches his wandering attention and he repeats it from the start:

"Hey, Sandy. Tompkins here. We're having a small party tonight at my place and we'd like to see you, if you can make it. We want to introduce you to a friend from Hawaii who has a proposal, too. It'll go late so don't worry about when you arrive. Hope this reaches you in time—later—"

Sandy goes out to the game room. Jim is absorbed in the hanging video screens, and Sandy checks them out. Collage city. "What's on, Jim Dandy?"

Jim gestures at one flickering black-and-white square. "Best *Hamlet* ever filmed. Christopher Plummer as the Dane, shot by the BBC at Elsinore years ago."

"I like the old Russian one, myself. His father's ghost, ten stories tall—how could you beat it?"

"That's a nice touch, all right." Jim seems a bit down. He and Virginia looked to be in a heated discussion when Sandy walked in, and Sandy guesses they have been arguing again. Those two are not exactly the greatest alliance ever made; in fact they both keep saying it's over, although it seems to be having a long ending. "Do you think you can drag yourself away from the Bard for a jaunt to La Jolla? My big-time friends have invited us to a party at their place."

"Sure, I've got this at home."

Sandy collects Arthur, Abe, Tashi. "Let's see if we can get Humphrey to drive," he says with his wicked grin.

They laugh; Humphrey keeps his electric bill down by driving as little as possible. He's an almanac of all the shortest distances, he can give you the least expensive route between any two points in OC faster than the carbrains can. They approach him in a gang, Sandy says, "Humphrey, you've got a nice big car, give us a ride down to La Jolla and I'll get you into a party there you won't forget."

"Ah, gee, what's wrong with this one? Can't ask for more, can you?"

"Of course you can! Come on, Humphrey...." Sandy waves a fresh eye-dropper of the Buzz, Humphrey's favorite, in front of his eyes.

"Can't leave your own party," Humphrey starts to say, but founders in the face of the statement's absurdity. Sandy steers him to the door, stopping for a quick kiss and an explanation for Angela. Remembering Jim and Virginia, he runs back in and kisses her again. "I love you." Then they're out, followed by Arthur, Abe, Tashi, and Jim, who elbow each other and snicker as they all clump down the rarely used stairwell. "Think Humph's got the coin slots installed on his car doors yet?" Abe asks under his breath, and they giggle. "Taxi meter," Tashi suggests. "Better profit potential."

"Subtler," Arthur adds.

Humphrey, next flight down, says to Sandy, "Maybe we can all go shares on the mileage, huh?" The four above them nearly explode holding the laughs in, and when Sandy says, "Sure thing, Humphrey, and maybe we should figure out the wear on the tires, too," they experience catastrophic failure and burst like balloons. The stairwell echoes with howls. Tashi collapses on the banister, Abe and Arthur and Jim crumple to the landing and take the next flight down on hands and knees. Humphrey and Sandy observe this descent, Humphrey perplexed, Sandy grinning the maniac's grin. "You men are stoned." Which lays them out flat. Maybe they are.

They scrape themselves off the floor in the parking lot and get in Humphrey's car, carefully inspecting the door handles and the car's interior. "What are you guys looking for?" Humphrey asks.

"Nothing, nothing. Can we go now? Are we gone yet?"

They're gone. Off to San Diego.

On the track down 405 they sit in the three rows of seats in Humphrey's car and talk. Sandy, slumped in the front passenger seat, just smiles; he looks zoned, as if he's catching some rest before he dives back into it in La Jolla.

Humphrey tells them about a trip he and Sandy and some others took to Disneyland. "We had been in the line for Mr. Toad's Wild Ride for about forty-five minutes when Chapman went nuts. You could see it happen—we were all standing there just waiting, you know, hanging out and moving with the line, and suddenly his eyes bug out past his nose and he gets that happy look he gets when he's got an idea." The others laugh, "Yeah, yeah, show us the look, Sandy," and half-asleep Sandy shows them a perfect simulacrum of it. "So he says real slow, 'You know, guys, this ride only lasts about two minutes. Two minutes at the most. And we'll have been in line for it an hour. That's a thirty-to-one ratio of wait to ride. And the ride is just a fast trackcar going through holograms in the dark. I wonder . . . do you think . . . could it be . . . that this is the *worst* ratio in Disneyland?' And he gets the insanity look again and says, 'I wonder, I just wonder . . . which one of us can rack up the *worst* ratio for the whole day?' And we all see instantly we've got a new game, a contest, you know, and the whole day is transformed, because it's a miserable day at Disneyland, totally densepacked, and there's some real potential here for racking up some fantastic scores! So we call it Negative Disneyland and agree to add points for stupidest rides combined with the worst ratios."

The four in back can't believe it. "You've got to be kidding."

"No, no! It's the only way to go there! Because with Sandy's idea we weren't fighting the situation anymore, you know? We were running around finding the longest lines we could, stepping through our paces like we were on the ride itself, and timing everything on our watches, and every time we turned another corner in the line we'd see Sandy standing there up ahead of us towering over the kids, eyes bugged out and grinning his grin, just digging these monster delays to get on Dumbo the Elephant, Storybook Canal, Casey Junior, the Submarine . . ."

Sandy's smile turns blissful. "It was a stroke of genius," he mutters. "I'll never do it any other way, ever again."

"So who won?" Jim asks.

"Oh Sandy, of course. He totaled five and a half hours of waiting for eighteen minutes of ride!"

"I can beat that," Tashi says promptly. "Hell, I've beaten that trying *positive* Disneyland!" Sandy denies it and they make a bet for next time.

They leave OC and track through the immense nuclear facility at San Onofre, eighteen concrete spheres crowding the narrow valley like buboes bumping out of an armpit, powerlines extending off on ranked towers to every point of the compass, glary halogen and xenon and mercury vapor lamps peppering spheres, towers, support buildings. "Camp Pendleton," Jim announces, and they all pitch in together: "Protecting California's Precious Resources!" Or so the neon sign says. The motto is a joke; aside from the nuclear plant, the Marines have contracted with the towns of south OC to take all their sewage into a gigantic treatment facility, which covers the hills south of San Onofre. Concrete tanks and bunkers resemble an oil refinery, and altogether it's as extensive as the power plant north of it. Then comes the land they've leased for the desalination plant that provides OC with much of its water; that means another immense complex of bunkers and tubes, nearly indistinguishable from the nuclear facility, and a whole stretch of the coast blasted by salt mounds and various processing tanks.

After that they're into the supercamp for Marine recruits, then into Oceanside, and the precious resource is passed. Past Oceanside it's like OC on a rollercoaster, same condomundo and mallsprawl and autopia, broken up only by some small dead marshes in the low parts of the rollercoaster ride. Yes, San Diego, along with Riverside and Los Angeles and Ventura and Santa Barbara, is nothing more than an extension of OC. . . .

They get off on La Jolla Village Drive and track west, around the megaversity to La Jolla Farms Road. Here they are stopped at the security gate, Sandy calls his friends, and they're in. La Jolla Mansion Road, it should be called; they track slowly by a long series of multimillion-dollar homes, all single-family dwellings. Abe, who lives in an annex of his parents' house on Saddleback Mountain, isn't impressed, but the rest of them stare. Humphrey goes into his real estate mode and estimates values and mortgage payments and the like in religious tones.

Sandy's friends' house is near the end of the road, on the ocean side, therefore on the crumbling edge of Torrey Pines Cliff. They find parking with difficulty, go to the door and are only let in after Sandy's friend Bob Tompkins

comes and okays them. Bob is fortyish, tanned, golden-haired, perfectly fea-
tured, expensively dressed. He shakes all their hands, ushers them in, introduces them to his partner Raymond. Raymond is if anything even more perfect
than Bob; his jawline could open letters. Perhaps they got their start in mod-
eling.

But now the two are partners in major minor drug dealing, and this is sort
of a party for field reps. Sandy recognizes quite a few people he knows. He starts
pingponging among them, and rather than follow him his OC friends grab
drinks and go out onto the cliff-edge lawn, which is on three terraced levels
some three or four hundred feet over the black sea. They've got a perfect view
of the hilly curve of La Jolla jutting into the dark water, its sparkling skyscraper
hotels reflecting like fire off the bay in between; and to the north stretches the
whole curve of the southern California coast, a white pulsing mass of light.
Major light show, here.

It's a class-A party. Among the guests on the lawn are some Lagunatics they
know, and happily they fall to drinking and talking and dancing.

Jim notices Arthur disappearing down the wooden staircase that leads
down to the beach below, following—was that Raymond? Arthur was caustic
indeed about the mansions on this road, so seeing him with Raymond is a bit
of a surprise to Jim.

This turns some key in Jim's sense of curiosity. Ever since their raid on Parnell Jim has been asking Arthur questions, and Arthur has been putting him
off. It's better if Jim doesn't know too much, he says. Jim is up on the theory
of revolutionary cells, sure, but it seems to him to be going too far not even to
know the name of the group he's part of. Sure the cause is just, but still . . . And
Arthur—well, who knows exactly why he came along tonight? It isn't something he'd ordinarily do. And once he said he got his equipment from "the
south" . . . could be that Raymond used drug smuggling as a cover . . . well, that
would be crazy, but . . .

Jim's curiosity is aroused. He wanders down the wooden steps of the staircase, into the dark.

The stairs switch back from platform to platform down the steep sandstone
cliff: thick planks are nailed into parallel four-by-fours that are bolted to telephone poles driven into the cliff face, and the whole structure is painted some
bright color, yellow or pink or orange, hard to tell in the dark. Spectrum band,
no doubt. Iceplant and some bushy trees have been planted all around the staircase in semisuccessful efforts to stop the erosion of the cliff. Through one thick
clump of trees the stairway proceeds in a groomed tunnel of foliage, and beyond that, on the next platform, Jim sees two dark figures standing. Above
them stereo speakers facing westward challenge the even roar of the surf with
the majestic end of *The Firebird Suite*, cranked to high volume.

Curious, and pitched to a bolder level by the music. Jim slips off the staircase into the iceplant. Ho, it's steeper than it looks! But he can hold his footing, and very slowly he descends through the bushy trees. Any noise he is making is overwhelmed by waves below and music above, which has segued from the *Firebird* to "Siberian Khantru," brilliant lead guitar piercing the night and leading the supple bass on a madcap ramble. Fantastic. The last knot of trees overhanging the stairway is just above the platform, fine, Jim wiggles his way down through the low branches, slips on iceplant and jerks to a halt jammed down into the fork of two thick branches. Ribs a little compressed. Hmmm. Seems he might be a little stuck, here. On the other hand, he's just above the platform, and the two figures, seated on the rail looking down at the faint white-on-black tapestry of breaking waves, are just within earshot. Wouldn't want to be much closer, in fact. Jim gives up struggling to escape, accepts the salt wetness of his perch, concentrates on listening.

Arthur seems to be making a report, although the booming of the surf makes it difficult to hear everything. "What it comes . . . the campaign has got its own momentum . . . supply material and give . . . do a one-night . . . bigger operation than there really is."

"Do any of your" *krkrkrkrkrkrkrkrrr* asks Raymond.

". . . assume, well, whatever. They don't *know* anything."

"So you guess."

"I'm pretty sure."

"And you think a concerted action could bring in the people we're trying to find?"

"Makes sense, doesn't it? They" *krkrkrkrkrkrkrrrr*

"Possibly. Possibly." Raymond jumps down and stalks the deck of the platform nervously, looking right up at the clump of trees that holds Jim. "If that happens, we might have a hard time finding out about it. Being sure."

Arthur's back is now to Jim, and Jim can't hear his voice at all. But he can hear Raymond's reply:

"That'd be one way to find out, sure. But it would be dangerous, I mean some of you might just disappear."

Jim feels his throat and stomach take a big swallow. Disappear?

His paranoia quotient soars into the megapynchons, his understanding of his sabotage adventure with Arthur trapdoors out from under him, leaving him hanging like, well, yes, like a man stuck in a tree on the side of a cliff. His ribs begin to complain vociferously. But he definitely doesn't want to move until Arthur and Raymond leave.

Relief for his ribs, and frustration for his mounting curiosity, arrive in the form of night beach partyers climbing back up the stairs. Raymond greets them cheerily, and he and Arthur ascend with them. Soon Jim is alone with

Torrey Pines Cliff, in his tree. He'd love to take time and think over what he's just heard, sort it out some, but his ribs protest at the idea and he tries to extricate himself. Arms up, hands on branches to each side, push out. This frees him to fall down the iceplant slope, he lets the branches go when his arms begin to snap out of their sockets, and one branch clips him in the ear as he slides by, heading down here uh-oh, turn into the iceplant and clutch, feet digging, thump, thump, thump! Stopped, thank God. Below him it gets markedly steeper, in fact kind of vertical. All alarms go off in the McPherson body, he convinces one hand to declutch with great difficulty, resets it a foot over toward the stairway. Footwork is trickier, need knobs or clumps of iceplant, the usual spread of the stuff is damned slippery, not that he's complaining; without it he would be one with the sandstone blocks on the beach, still a couple hundred feet below. Carefully he makes ten or twelve heartstopping handhold transfers, and traverses to the stairway. Leeches onto it, heaves up and over the banister. A group descending the stairs catches him in the final act of rolling over the banister to safety, and they laugh at his evident inebriation. "Fell off, hey? Come on down with us and swim it off."

"Is he sober enough to swim?"

"Sure, a blast of ocean water will do him good."

Jim agrees in as calm a voice as he can muster. It'll be a good way to wash some of the dirt and crushed iceplant off of his hands and face. They descend to the beach, strip, walk to the water. The white, almost phosphorescent rush of broken waves over Jim's ankles feels good. It's cold but not anywhere near as bad as he expected. He runs into the water, dives into the chill salt waves. A great rush, cleansing and refreshing. Broken waves tumble him about and he lets them. Maybe Tashi has something in this night surfing idea. Jim does a little desultory bodysurfing in the shore break.

While he's at it he tumbles into a young lady from the group; she squeaks, clings to him, her body incredibly warm in the ocean chill. Legs wrapped around his middle, arms around his neck, a quick kiss, whoah! Then a wave knocks them apart and she's off, he can't find her.

He swims around in an unsuccessful search, chills down, walks out of the water and up the beach. Major refreshment. Remarkably warm out. Beautiful naked women emerge from the surf and walk up to him, give him one of their towels, towel-dry before him. Dryads would they be, or Nereids?

Some quality of the encounter in the dark sea has quickened something in him; it's not the same as his usual lust, not at all. The others dress, he dresses. Up the stairway, back to the party. No time to sort it out; but some part of him remembers. . . .

Up top people are dancing in three rooms. Tashi and Abe are in one, doing the beach boy bounce, dance considered as a helix of pogo hops. "Been swimming?" Abe asks, panting. "Yeah. Plus a small mystical experience." And a big mysterious conversation. Jim joins in the dance. It's The Wind'n'Sea Surf Killers, singing their latest hit "Dance Till Your Feet Are Bloody Stumps." Perfect.

And so the party progresses as parties do. Jim never manages to identify his oceanic love. Along about three he finds himself very tired, and unenthusiastic at the prospect of any chemical reascendance. No. He sits in a fine leather chair in the front room, where he can see the entryway. Lot of people in and out. Humphrey and Tash come sit with him and they talk about San Diego. Humphrey enjoys it because of all the deals down in Tijuana. "Of course," Abe cries as he joins them and sits on the floor. "You should see Humphrey in Tijuana! He grinds those shopkeepers like you can't believe! 'Two hundred pesos, shit, you must be joking! I'll give you ten!'" The others laugh as Abe catches Humphrey's tone of indignation and pleasure exactly. Humphrey nods, grinning. "Sure."

"Man, those poor people open up on a Saturday morning and see Humphrey coming in first thing in the day, and it's like *disaster* for them, they know they're going to end up selling half their stock for a couple handfuls of pesos."

"Rather see an armed robber come in the door," Tash adds.

"Better deal—"

"Less pain—"

"*Safer*—"

Arthur shows up. They sit and wait for Sandy. Quietly Jim watches Arthur, who seems the same as always. No clues there.

... 26

Sandy, however, has only just now been able to get off with Bob Tompkins for a little conference. They retire to Bob's bedroom with a friend of Bob's that Sandy hasn't met yet, and sit on a gigantic circular bed.

Eight video cameras:
Two walls of screens show them sitting cross-legged, from eight angles.
Life in the kaleidoscope: which image is you?
Bedspread of green silks. Wallpaper bronze flake. Carpet silver gray.
Oak dressers, topped by a collection of ornate hookahs:
Ceramic jars, copper bowls, woven tubes,
Six speakers play soft zither music.
A poem is a list of Things To Do.
Have you done them yet?

"This is Manfred," Bob says to Sandy. "Manfred, Sandy."

Manfred nods, his eyes bright and very dilated. "Good to meet you." They shake hands across the green silk.

"Well, let's try out some of my latest while we talk about Manfred's proposition." Bob puts a big round wooden platter on the middle of the bed, between the three of them. He gets a smallish hookah from the collection, puts it on the platter, sits down, fills one part of the multichambered bowl with a black tarry substance. There are three tubes coming out of the bulbous ceramic base of the pipe, and they each take one and breathe in as Bob waves the flame of a lighter over the bowl. The moment the smoke hits his throat Sandy begins coughing his lungs out. The other two are coughing too, more moderately but only just. On the wall screens it looks like a whole gang of men have just been teargassed in a bordello.

"Gee," Sandy chokes out. "Great."

The other two wheeze their laughter. "Just wait a couple of minutes," Bob advises. He and Manfred take another hit, and Sandy tries, but only starts coughing again. Still, the pattern of the bedspread has lifted off the bed and begun to rotate clockwise as it becomes ever more elaborate; and the bronze flake wallpaper is glittering darkly, breaking up the subdued lamplight from the dresser into a trillion meaningful fragments. Strangely beautiful, this chamber. "A great reckoning in a little room," Sandy mutters. He puts his thumb over the soapstone mouthpiece of his tube while the other two smoke on. Advanced-lane opium smokers, here. Pretty primitive stuff, opium—noisy as hell, kind of a sledgehammer effect to the body. Sandy finds himself thinking he can do better than this in his lab. Still, as a sort of archaeological experiment . . . Jim should be in on this, didn't the Chinese who built the California railroads use this stuff? No wonder there are no more railroads.

When Manfred and Bob are done smoking, they sit back and talk. The talk flows in unexpected channels, they laugh a lot.

Finally Manfred tells Sandy their proposition. "We've got a very illegal drug from Hong Kong, by way of Guam and Hawaii. The amounts are fairly large, and the DEA has got a spike into the source, so it all added up to trying a different channel for getting it in."

"What is it?" Sandy asks bluntly.

"It's called the Rhinoceros. The tricky thing about sexual arousal is that you have to be stimulated and relaxed in the right degrees of both, and in the right synergy. Two systems are involved and both have to be squeezed just right. So we've got a couple of compounds, one called Eyebeep and the other a modified endomorphin imitant. They self-assemble in the limbic region."

"An aphrodisiac?" Sandy says stupidly.

"That's right. A real aphrodisiac. I've tried it, and, well . . ." Manfred giggles. "I don't want to talk about it. But it works."

"Wow."

"We're sailing it over from Hawaii, that's our new route. Our idea is to make a brief rendezvous with a small boat that will come out from Newport and meet us behind San Clemente Island. Then the small boat will bring it on in. I realize it's a risk for the last carrier, but if you were willing to do it, I'd be willing to pay you for that risk, in cash and in a part of the cargo."

Sandy nods noncommittally. "How much?"

"Say, twenty thousand dollars and six liters of Rhino."

Sandy frowns. Is there really going to be a demand for six liters of some strange new aphrodisiac? Well . . . sure. Especially if it works. OC's new favorite, no doubt.

Still, the plan goes against Sandy's working principle, which demands a constant low profile and labor-intensive work in small quantities. "And what percentage of the total does that represent?"

They begin to dicker over amounts. It goes on slowly, genially, as a kind of theoretical discussion of how much such a service *would* be worth if one were to contemplate it. A lot of joking from Bob, which the other two appreciate. This is the strange heart of drug dealing; Sandy has not only to come to a financial agreement with Manfred, but also to reach a certain very high level of trust with him. They both have to feel this trust. No contract will be signed at the end of their dealing, and no enforcement agency will come to one's aid if the other breaks their verbal agreement. In this sense drug dealers must be much more honest than businessmen or lawyers, for instance, who have contracts and the law to fall back on. Dealers have only each other, and so it's crucial to establish that they're dealing with someone they can trust to stick to their word. This, in a subculture of people that includes a small but significant number of con artists whose very art consists in appearing trustworthy when they are not. One has to learn how to distinguish between the false and the real, by an intuitive judgment of character, by probing at the other in the midst of the joking around: asking a sudden sharp question, making a quick gesture of friendliness, making an outright, even rude, challenge, and so on; then watching the responses to these various maneuvers, looking for any minute signs of bad faith. Judging behavior for what it reveals of the deeper nature inside.

All this subtle business taking place, of course, under a staggering opium high; but they're all used to that kind of handicap, it can be factored in easily. Eventually Sandy gets a secure feeling that he is talking to a good guy, who is acting in good faith. Manfred, he can tell, is coming to a similar conclusion, and as they are both pleased the meeting becomes even friendlier—a real friendliness, as opposed to the automatic social imitation of it that they began the meeting with.

Still, the basic nature of the deal is not something Sandy likes, and he stops short of agreeing to do it. "I don't know, Manfred," he says eventually. "I don't usually go in for this kind of thing, as Bob probably told you. For me, in my situation you know, the risks are too high to justify it."

Manfred just grins. "It's always the high-risk projects that bring in the highest profits, man. Think about it."

Then Manfred gets up to go to the bathroom.

"So what does Raymond think of this?" Sandy asks Bob. "How come he isn't doing the pickup himself?" For Raymond has done a whole lot of major drug smuggling from offshore in his time, and claims to enjoy it.

Bob makes a face. "Raymond is really involved in some other things right now. You know, he's an idealist. He's always been an idealist. Not that it keeps him from going after the bucks, of course, but still it's there. I don't know if you ever heard about this, but a year or so ago some of Ray's friends in Venezuela were killed by some remotely piloted vehicles that the Venezuelan drug police had bought from our Army. They were good friends, and it really made Ray mad. He couldn't really declare war on the U.S. Army, but he's done the next best thing, and declared war on the people who made the robot planes." He laughs. "At the same time keeping an eye out for profits!" He laughs harder, then looks at Sandy closely. "Don't tell anyone else about this, okay?" Sandy nods; he and Bob have done a lot of business together over the years, and it's gone on as long as it has because they both know they form a closed circuit, as far as information goes, including gossip. And Bob appreciates it, because he does love to gossip, even— or especially—about his ally Raymond. "He's been importing these little missile systems that can be used perfectly for sabotaging military production plants."

"Ah, yes," Sandy says carefully. "I believe I've read about the results of all that."

"Sure. But Raymond doesn't just do it for the idea. He's also finding people who want these things done more than he does!"

Sandy opens his eyes wide to show how dubious he is about this.

"I know!" Bob replies. "It's a tricky area. But so far it's been working really well. There are customers out there, if you can find them. But it's murky water, I'll tell you. Almost as bad as the drug scene. And now he thinks he's been noticed by another group who are into the same thing."

"Uh-oh."

"I know. So he's all wrapped up in that now, trying to find out who exactly is out there, and whether he can come to terms with them."

"Sounds dangerous," Sandy says.

Bob shrugs. "Everything's dangerous. But anyway, you can see why Ray isn't interested in this smuggling deal. His mind is occupied with other things these days."

"You bet."

Manfred comes back from the bathroom. They try a few more puffs of the harsh black smoke, talk some more. Manfred presses Sandy to commit himself to the aphrodisiac smuggling enterprise, and carefully, ever so diplomatically, Sandy refuses to make the commitment. What he has just heard from Bob isn't any encouragement. "I'm going to have to think about it, Manfred. It's really far out of my usual line."

Manfred accepts this with grace: "I still hope you'll go for it, man. Think about it some more and then let me know—we've still got a week or so."

Sandy looks at his watch, rises. "I've got a working day tomorrow, starts in about four hours actually. I should get back home." Farewells all around and he's off, into the living room where Tashi, Jim, Humphrey, Abe, and Arthur are sitting around talking to people. "Let's go home."

... 27

Tracking back north Jim dozes. He's sitting in the middle seat, leaning against the right window. Arthur is beside him, Abe and Tash behind him in the backseat. Jim finds it difficult to joke around with Arthur; easier to doze. The act of falling asleep often brings hypnagogic visions to him, and the sensation of falling down a black cliff jerks him awake. "Whoah!" Arthur and Raymond, on the cliffside platform. Snatches of a conversation. Warm body in the ocean's chill. It's been a strange night.

Out the window is the single stretch of southern California's coast left undeveloped: the center of U.S. Marine Camp Joseph H. Pendleton. Dark hills, a narrow coastal plain cut by dry ravines, covered with dark brush. Grass gray in the moonlight. Something about it is so quiet, so empty, so pure.... My God, he thinks. The land. A pang of loss pierces him: this land that they live on, under its caking of concrete and steel and light—it was a beautiful place, once. And now there's no way back.

For a moment, as they track up the coast and out of the untouched hills, into the weird cancerous megastructures of the desalination plant and the sewage plant and the nuclear facility, Jim dreams of a cataclysm that could bring this overlit America to ruin, and leave behind only the land, the land, the land . . . and perhaps—perhaps—a few survivors, left to settle the hard new forests of a cold wet new world, in tiny Hannibal, Missouris, that they would inhabit like foxes, like deer, like real human beings. . . .

They track on into the condomundo hills of San Clemente, and the absurdity of his vision, combined with its impossibility, and its cruelty, and its poignant appeal, drive Jim ever deeper into depression. There is no way back; because there is no way back. History is a one-way street. It's only forward, into catastrophe, or the track-and-mall inferno, or . . . or nothing. Nothing Jim can imagine, anyway. But no matter what, there is no going back.

Humphrey gets them up the empty freeway to Sandy's place, and they all get out to go to their own cars. Humphrey says, "Listen, the odometer shows about a hundred and forty miles, divide it among the six of us and it'll be really cheap—"

"*Really* cheap," say Tashi and Abe together.

"Yeah, so let me just figure it out here and we can even up before you guys forget."

"Figure it out and bill me," Sandy says, walking off toward the elevator. Even Sandy seems a little weary. "We will recompense you *fully*." Arthur's off without a word. Tashi and Abe are emptying their pockets and giving Humphrey their change, "Sure that covers wear on the brake pads, Humph?" "Don't forget oil, Bogie, that big hog of yours just *sucks* the oil." "No lie."

"Yeah, yeah," Humphrey says seriously, collecting their coins. "I took all that into my calculations." He drives off without a blink at Tash and Abe's gibing, perfectly unaware of it. Jim laughs to see it. The guy is so perfectly unself-conscious! And of his chief characteristic!

As he walks to his car Jim marvels over it. And tracking home he wonders if everyone is, perhaps, unaware of the principle aspect of their personality, which looms too large for them to see. Yeah, it's probably true. And if so, then what part of his own character doesn't he see? What aspect of him do Tash and Abe giggle over, behind his back or even right in front of him, because he doesn't even realize it's there to be made fun of?

It comes to him in a flash: he's got no sense of humor at all!

Hmm. Is that right? Well, it certainly is true that he has about the same amount of wit as a refrigerator. His carbrain would be quicker with repartee, if it only had a speaker. Yes, it's true. Jim has never really thought of it this way before, but many's the time when he's recalled a funny conversation, Abe and Sandy and Tash jamming on one comic riff or another, and a great line to throw into the hilarious sequence will come to him!—only a week or so too late. A bit slow in that department, you could say.

Of course his friends are perfectly aware of this; now Jim sees it clearly. They'll get on a jag and everyone'll be laughing hard and Sandy will get that gleam in his eye and demand swiftly of Jim, "What do *you* say about that, Jimbo?" and Jim will conquer his giggling and puff and wheeze and blow out all his mental circuits trying to think of just one of the kind of witticisms that are flying out of his friends as natural as thoughts, and finally he'll say something like, "Well . . . *yeah!*" and his three friends will collapse, howling like banshees. Leaving Jim grinning foolishly, only dimly aware that in a gang of wits a dorker can be more valuable than another quick tongue.

What joy it would be to convulse the crowd with an ad-libbed one-liner, tossed into a long sequence of them! But it's not something Jim, Mr. Slow, has ever managed. He's just a convulsee, a one-man audience, the great laugher;

when they get Jim going they can drive him right to the floor with laughing, he gasps and chuckles and screams and beats the floor, stomach muscles cramping, Sandy and Tash and Abe standing over him giggling, extemporizing one comic theme or another, Sandy saying "Should we kill him right now? Should we asphyxiate him right here on the spot?"

Sigh. It's been a long night. Partying can be damned hard work. And rather disturbing as well.

Mr. Dull walks in the door of his little ap just before dawn. In the gray light it looks messy, stupid. Books in the city built tomorrow. Sigh. Go to sleep.

... 28

But he hasn't been sleeping for long when he wakes to the sound of Virginia Novello coming in the door.

"What are you doing, still sleeping?"

"Yeah." Didn't she give her key to his place back to him last week? Throw it at him, in fact?

"Christ, this place is a mess. You are so lazy." She sits on the bed hard, rolls him over.

"Hi," he says fuzzily.

Kiss on the forehead. "Hello, lover."

And suddenly he is in the world of sex. Virginia gets up, turns on his bedroom video, undresses, climbs into the rumpled bed with him. He watches the screens goggle-eyed.

"Want me to cook you some breakfast?" she says when they're done.

"Sure."

Jim rolls over and begins to wonder what Virginia is doing there. Officially they broke up their alliance at the famous softball game, but since then they have gotten together pretty frequently, for no real reason that Jim can see. Except for some easy sex, and perhaps a stimulating fight or two. . . . He gets up, feeling uneasy, and goes to the bathroom.

From the shower he can just hear her voice, raised to carry over the sound of the freeway. "You really should try to keep your kitchen cleaner. What a mess!" After a bit: "So where were you last night?"

"San Diego."

"I know. But I don't know why you didn't ask me along."

"Um," Jim says, drying off. "Couldn't find you at Sandy's, you know—"

"Bullshit, I was there the whole time!" She appears in the bathroom doorway, potholder on one hand clenched like a boxing glove. Jim pulls up his shorts more quickly than usual.

"The truth is," she says sadly, "you'd rather be away from me than with me."

Sigh. "Come on, Virginia, don't be ridiculous please? I just woke up."

"Lazy bastard."

Sigh. From endearment, to complaint, to recrimination: it's a familiar pattern with Virginia. "Give me a break?"

"Why should I, after you skipped off my track last night?"

"I just went with the guys to another party. You and I didn't have anything on last night."

"Well whose fault was that?"

"Not mine."

"Oh yeah? You *wanted* to go off with your friends that you're so queer for. Sandy, Tashi, Abe, you'd rather do *anything* with them than *something* with me."

"Ah come on."

"Come on where? Admit it, you and those guys—"

"We're friends, Virginia. Can you understand that? Friendship?"

"*Friends*. Your friends are all heroes to you."

"Don't be silly." Actually that may be true, sure; Jim's best friends are heroes to him, each in his different way. "Besides, what's wrong with liking your friends?"

"It's more than that with you, Jim, you're weird about it. You idolize them and try to model your life on theirs, and you aren't up to it. I mean none of you even have jobs."

Jim has gotten used to Virginia's logic, and now he just follows wherever it leads. "Abe has a job. We all have jobs."

"Oh, *grow up*! Will you grow up? Ever?"

"I don't know—"

"You don't know!"

"I don't know what you mean, I was going to say. Let me finish what I'm saying, all right?"

"Are you finished?"

"Yeah, I'm finished."

Jim stalks past her to the kitchen, disgusted by the stupidity of their debate. Scrambled eggs have gone black in the pan. "Shit."

"Now look what you made me do," Virginia cries, rushing past him and putting the pan under the faucet.

"Me? Get serious!"

"I am serious, Jim McPherson. You don't have a real job and you don't have a real future. Your little jobs are just part-time excuses for work. You laze around all day writing stupid poems, while I work and make the money we use to go out, when you can be dragged away from your friends to go!"

Part of Jim is thinking, Fine, if that's what you think then leave, quit bothering me. This alliance is over anyway! Another part is remembering the good times they've had, with their friends, out together, talking, in bed. And that part hurts.

Jim shakes his head. "Let me make some breakfast," he says. Why does she even bother, he thinks, if she feels this way about him? Why did she come by? Why doesn't she make it easy for him and leave for good? He doesn't have the courage to tell her to leave him alone; she would crucify him with how cruel he was being to her. Besides, is he sure that's what he wants? She's smart, beautiful, rich—everything he desires in an ally, in theory. When she sloshes across the jacuzzi with everyone watching her, to sit on his lap with that perfect rounded bottom, he thinks that it's worth all the fights, right? That's right. Jim likes that. He wants that.

Ach. Just another tricky day with Virginia Novello. How long have they been doing this? One month, two? Three? And it's been like this from the start. It's gotten so he can cook and eat and carry on a fight and at the same time be considering what else he should read before tackling his next poem. Sure, why not? Everyone can run parallel programs these days.

But this time he really loses his temper. They aren't allies anymore, they're ex-allies, there's no reason he has to stand for this kind of thing! He tells her that in a near shout and then storms out the front door.

Oops. He's on his street; he's just stormed out of his own ap. Bit of a mistake. He had thought, momentarily, that he was at Virginia's. Now he's in kind of an embarrassing position, isn't he. What to do?

He drives around the block, returns, looks in his window surreptitiously. Yes, she's gone. Whew. Got to remember where he is a little more securely.

Well, enough of that. The day can begin.

But when he sits down to write, a knot in his stomach forms that won't go away: he keeps reimagining the argument in versions that leave Virginia repentant, then naked in bed; or else crushed by his bitter dismissal, and gone for good. And yet those and all the other self-justifying scenarios leave him feeling as sick as the reality has. He doesn't write a single word, all day; and everything he tries to read is dreadfully boring.

He turns on the video and replays the tape of this morning's session in bed. Watches it morosely, getting aroused and disgusted in equal measure.

He's twenty-seven years old. He hasn't learned anything yet.

Stewart Lemon wakes early and pads out to his sunlit kitchen. His house is on Chillon Way in the Top of the World complex in Laguna Beach, and from the kitchen windows there's a fine view out to sea. Lemon goes to the breadbox on top of the orange ceramic countertop, and judges that the sourdough bread there is stale enough to make good French toast. He puts a pan on the stove and whips up the egg and milk. A little more cinnamon than usual, today. Slice the bread, soak it, throw it in the pan. Sweet cinnamon smell as it sizzles away. Shafts of sunlight cutting in the windows, one of them lighting the Kandinsky in the hall. Lemon likes the Kandinsky better than their little Picasso, and has hung it where he can see it often. It soothes the spirit. A beautiful morning.

Still, Stewart Lemon is not at peace. Things are not going well at LSR these days, and Donald Hereford, the company's president and an ever-growing power at Argo/Blessman, is really putting the heat on. Ball Lightning is in trouble and about to go into a showdown with Boeing, one of the giants. That's enough cause for worry right there, but in addition to that Hereford is demanding a yearly growth rate of several percent, and the only chance that that will happen this year lies with the Stormbee proposal, another project in trouble. If both of these were to go down, LSR would not only not show any growth, it would without a doubt be a loss for Argo/Blessman for the year. And probably longer. And Hereford, and the people above him, aren't the kind that will stand for that very long. They might sell LSR, they might send in a new team to take it over and turn it around; either way, Lemon would be in big trouble. A whole career . . . and at a time when it seems everyone else in the defense industry is prospering! It's maddening.

And worrying, to the point that Lemon barely tastes his French toast. He leaves the dishes for Elsa—give her at least that to do—goes in and dresses. "I'm off," he says brusquely to the sleeping form, still in her bed. Elsa just mutters something from a dream, rolls over. She hasn't spoken to him for . . . Lemon's mouth tightens. He leaves the house and tries to forget about it.

Into the Mercedes. A Vivaldi oboe concerto for the ride along the coast to work. In his mind are mixed images of Elsa in bed, the Ball Lightning proposal, Hereford watching him over the video from his desk in the World Trade Center. Dan Houston's hangdog look, the Ball Lightning figures. Ach—the pressures on the executives are always the most extreme: but it's what he's trained for, what he's always wanted. . . .

First meeting of the day is with Dennis McPherson, to go over the numbers for the Stormbee proposal. The proposals are due in just over a week, and McPherson is still dawdling; it's time to get serious. Time to decide the amount for the bid, the money total, the number of dollars. This is probably the crux of the whole process, the moment when they will either win or lose.

"All right, Mac," Lemon begins impatiently. Might as well settle immediately into their usual dialectic, Lemon sarcastic and oppressive, McPherson stiff and steaming. "I've looked over the numbers you've sent up, and my judgment is that the final total is considerably too high. The Air Force just doesn't want to pay this much for unmanned systems, they still have a strong prejudice against planes without pilots and they're only going for this stuff because the technology makes it inevitable. But we've got to play to that, or we're going to be left out."

McPherson shrugs. "We've kept everything down as much as we could."

Lemon stares at him. "All right. Pull your chair over to the desk here, and let's go into it line by line."

Micromanagement. Lemon grits his teeth.

McPherson's people have got all the figures printed out in a sheaf of graph-filled sheets. First comes the full-scale engineering development costs. Prime mission equipment, $189 million. Training, less than a million, as always. Flight test support equipment, $10 million. System test and evaluation, $25 million. System project management, $63 million. Data, $18 million. Total, $305 million.

Lemon presses McPherson on the prime mission equipment figures, running through the subtotals and pointing items out. "Why should it take that much? I've done a rough estimate using prices of the components we're buying from other companies, and it shouldn't be more than one thirty."

McPherson points to the breakdown sheet, which has all the components priced exactly. "The CO-two laser is being modified to match the specs in the RFP. We can't buy that off the shelf. Then the pods have to be assembled, which is accounted for in this category. The robotics for that are going to be expensive."

"I know, I know. But do we have to use Zenith chips, for example? Texas Instruments are a quarter the cost, and there's nine million right there."

"We need Zenith chips because there's a complete reliance on them for the whole system to work. As a criticality they get top priority."

Lemon shakes his head. Texas Instruments chips are just as good, in his estimation, but there's no denying the industry thinks otherwise. "Let's go on and come back to this."

They go on to production readiness. Here the figures are less firm, as it is a step beyond the FSED. Still, McPherson's team has worked up the totals. Each category—the same group of them as for the FSED—has a few pages of explanations. Total, $154 million. They go over it line by line, Lemon objecting to equipment decisions, estimates of LSR's labor costs, everything he can think of. McPherson stubbornly defends every single estimate, and Lemon gets irritated. The figures can't possibly be that firm. McPherson just doesn't think about money; it isn't a factor for him.

An hour later they move on to the estimate sheet for production lot one, which would consist of eighty-eight units. Prime mission equipment, $251 million, system test and evaluation $2 million (it had better be working by then!), system project management, $30 million, data, $30 million. Total, $313 million. Lemon is fierce in his denunciation of the management and data costs. Here he knows more than McPherson, he's got the authority to bend these figures down. McPherson shrugs.

So, the complete bid comes to $772 million dollars. "You've got to get that down!" Lemon orders. "I don't have exact figures on the bids of McDonnell/Douglas or Parnell, but the feelers are out and it's looking like the low seven hundreds will be common."

McPherson just shakes his head. "We've cut it to the bone. You've just seen that." He looks tired; it's been a long onslaught. "If we try to slash numbers, the Air Force will just go over the proposal and bump them back up in their MPCs." Members of the SSEB will do Most Probable Cost estimates on all the bids, and depending on whether they're feeling friendly or not, the results can be devastating. "If they bump them up far enough we'll look like monkeys."

Lemon stands, irritated anew. "You don't have to teach me my job, Mac."

"I'm not." He must be tired, to speak out like this! "You asked me how much the system will cost. I've told you. I'm not telling you how much our bid should be. That's your decision. You can order us to make the system cheaper by downgrading the product, or you can keep the system the same and adjust the bid anyway. That's your decision. But you can't get me to tell you this system as designed will cost less than it does, because I won't do it. My job is to tell you how much this system costs. I've done that. You can take it from there."

So he has finally gotten McPherson to speak up! But it doesn't make him any less angry, as he always imagined it would. In fact, he's stung to the point that he forgets his persona. "Take that stuff and leave," he says violently, and abruptly he goes to the window so that McPherson won't see his face. Something—something in what McPherson has just said, perhaps—has given Lemon a fright, somehow, and it's made him unaccountably furious. "Get out of here!"

McPherson leaves. Lemon heaves a sigh of relief, sits down and regains control of himself. That arrogant son of a bitch has put him on the spot again. The bid is too high, the system over-designed. But he can't change that without endangering the bid from the technical point of view. You've got to balance quality and cost, but how to do that with a man like McPherson designing the thing? The man is crazy!

When he's completely calm again he calls Hereford on the video link.

Hereford comes onscreen; he's at his desk, before the window. Behind him is a fine view of New York harbor. They express pleasure at each other's views, the usual opening between them.

Lemon hesitates, clears his throat nervously. He's more than a little in awe of Donald Hereford, and he can't help it. Lemon has driven himself all his life, and he's risen at LSR very quickly indeed—about as fast as one can, he thinks. And yet Hereford is about his age, perhaps even a year or two younger, and there he is high in the complex power structure of Argo/Blessman, one of the biggest corporations in the world, sixtieth in the Fortune 500 the year before. . . . Lemon can't really imagine how the man did it. Especially since he is by no means a monomaniac; on the contrary, he is very urbane, very cultured; he has Manhattan's cultural world, perhaps the richest anywhere, at his fingertips, as he proves every time Lemon comes for a visit. Small galleries, the Met, theater on Broadway and off, the Philharmonic, dance . . . it's admirable. In fact, Lemon finds it incredibly impressive.

So he gives the facts to Hereford in as casual and efficient a tone as he can muster. Hereford pulls at his lean jaw, scratches his silver hair, straightens a five-hundred-dollar tie. His face remains impassive. "This man McPherson is good, you say?"

"Yes. But he's a bit of a perfectionist, and in the art of presenting a proposal, balancing all the factors involved . . . well, he's still an engineer at heart."

Hereford nods briefly, his aquiline nose wrinkling. "I understand. In fact, I was wondering why you described him as good, when his previous two proposals lost."

Yes, yes; Lemon is perfectly aware of Hereford's powerfully retentive memory, thanks. He shrugs, scrambling mentally, says, "I meant from the engineering standpoint, of course."

Hereford looks down at Manhattan. Finally he speaks. "Cut everything by five percent, and the management and data costs by ten. Any more than that and the MPCs are likely to be embarrassing. But that'll bring it down into the range of the other bids, right?"

"I think so, yes."

"Good. When's the proposal due?"

"A week from today."

"Talk to me then. I've got to go now." And the video screen goes blank.

...30

Abe and Xavier are driving back from Buena Park Hospital after working a nasty head-on in Brea, and Abe can feel that Xavier has about gone over the redline. The torque has been too heavy for too long, all the parts are fatigued to shear points, Abe can hear the gears grinding within and it sounds like all the teeth are about to strip out and fly away.... The truth is that they're both stressed, to the burnout point and beyond. Making up for clumps of vacation time in the past, setting up clumps of vacation time in the future, filling in for other friends on the squad: one way or another they have arranged for too many hours on in the last month, and the effects are showing.

So they get a call from the radio dispatcher and they both groan and then just stare at the thing. Tapped out again. Slowly, very slowly, Xavier presses the transmit button. "What do you want."

They're directed to a side street near Brookhurst and Garden Grove Avenues, in Garden Grove. "How could anybody get up enough speed in that neighborhood to make more than a fender-bender?" Xavier wonders.

"The call was not too coherent, I'm told," says the voice of the dispatcher. "No idea of the code or anything. There might even have been a relevant address—1246 Emerson."

"Sure this one isn't a police matter?"

"Said rescue squad."

Xavier clicks off. "Don't kill us getting there. This one has got to be bullshit somehow."

So Abe drives then to Brookhurst and Garden Grove, and they find no sign of a wreck. They see only:

A Jeans Down discount clothing store.
A Seedy audio outlet, a See-All Video Rental.
The Gay/Lesbian Adult Video Theater, A Kentucky Colonel's.

Your dingy apartment complex. You live there.

A retail furniture warehouse outlet.

A robotics and camera discount repair shop.

Two used-car lots. A Pizza Hut.

Yes, despite theory, the monad still exists.

Here you are, right?

A coin and map store. A dance hall.

The parking lot fronting all these establishments. The cars.

Billboards, traffic signals, street lights, street signs,

Telephone wires scoring the sour milk sky,

and so on, out to where parallax brings the tracks and the two sides of the long straight boulevard together. In short, the OC commercial street, which one can see repeated a hundred times anywhere in the county. But no sign of an accident.

"Well?" says Abe.

"Let's try the address they gave us."

"But,"—they track around to Emerson Street backing Garden Grove Avenue—"it's just the back lot for the furniture outlet, isn't it?"

"Yeah, but observe, there's maybe some aps tucked on top of it there. A look is in order."

Abe shakes his head. "Looks suspiciously like police work to me."

They get out of the truck and walk up the outside of the building on concrete stairs that rise above an alley between buildings. The alley is filled with gray metal trash dumpsters and flattened cardboard boxes of immense size. At the top of the stairs is a wooden door that's been kicked open a lot, once painted an orange that's faded to dusty yellow. Xavier raises a fist to knock and there's a sudden yelping, like a dog in pain. They look at each other. Xavier knocks.

"Keep out! Ah, God—get the fuck out of here!" It's a woman's voice, hoarse and wild.

"Hmm," says Xavier. Then he calls out: "Rescue squad, ma'am!"

"Oh! Oh, you! Help! Help!"

Xavier shrugs, tries to open the door. It's locked. "Your door is locked!"

"Don't bust it! He'll evict me—ahh! Ahh! *Help!*"

"Well, come open up, then!"

"Can't!"

"Well." Xavier looks at the door, jiggles the knob. Nothing doing.

"Help, damn you!"

"We're trying, lady! It'd be easier if you hadn't locked your door!" X looks around. "Here, Abe, the kitchen window is just over the rail, and it's open. It looks like you'd just about fit in."

Abe looks at the little window dubiously. "It's too small. Besides, it's hanging out over the alley!"

"No it's not. Give it a try, I'll hold on to you."

So Abe climbs over the flimsy black-iron railing, reaches inside and finds nothing to hold on to except the sink faucet. The window really is too small. But . . . he steps onto the railing and squirms inside. Powerful stench of garbage left under the sink too long. His shoulders just make it through, then it's a matter of twisting over the sink and pulling his legs in. X gives him a final shove that catapults him onto a dirty kitchen floor. "Hey!"

"Help! Oh—oh—help!"

Abe gets to his feet and rushes into the little living room/bedroom of the ap. A black-haired woman in a sweat-soaked long T-shirt is on her back on the floor. And unless she's unfashionably fat—nope—pregnant woman here, gone into labor. Abe rushes to the door. "Hey!" the woman shouts. "Over here!"

"I know!"

He unlocks the door and Xavier hurries in. The woman jerks back awkwardly against an old green vinyl couch. "Hey! Who are you!"

"Rescue squad." Xavier kneels beside her, holds her wrist and moves her hand off her belly. "Relax, lady—"

"Relax! Are you kidding? What took you so long? Ahh! ahh!" Her face is dripping with sweat, she rolls her head from side to side. "I wanted an ambulance!"

"We are the ambulance, lady. Try to relax." Xavier checks her out. "Hey, how long have you been in labor?"

"Couple hours. I guess."

"Say, you're making awfully fast progress."

"You're telling me! Listen who the fuck are you?"

"Rescue squad."

"I don't want some spade playing around down there while I'm trying to—ahh!—have a baby!"

Xavier frowns at her. "I'll try to refrain from molesting you till you're done, all right? It's a little too crowded in there to rape you just now."

The woman takes a weak swing at him. "Get away from me! Leave me alone! Ah, God!"

"We're the rescue squad, ma'am," Abe tries to explain.

"Will you cut that *ma'am* shit! All I need is the ambulance!"

"We can do that too," Xavier says. "Abe, run down quick and get the stretcher. I think we've got time to get her over to St. Joe's."

Abe runs down and grabs the furled stretcher, carries it back upstairs. Back in the ap Xavier and the woman are arguing loudly. "They can't hold your kid hostage, woman! If you can't pay, you can't pay! You're going too fast here, and it's pretty sure to rip you up some. You'd best be in the hospital!"

The woman is hit by a severe contraction and can't reply. Abe can see she wants to reply, her eyes are fixed on Xavier's and she's glaring fiercely, shaking her head. "Don't—want—to go!"

"That's tough. We're not allowed to just let you bleed to death, are we."

Abe finishes getting the stretcher unfurled and set up. As they lift the woman onto it she arches, sobbing with pain. "Try to push in a rhythm, will you?" Xavier says. "Don't you know anything about how to do this?"

"Fuck you!" the woman cries, trying again to hit him. "Goddamned molesters! I didn't even know—ahh!—didn't know I was pregnant until two months ago."

"Great. Here, Abe, hold her shoulders up for her. Push, woman, push!"

"No!" But push she does, an awful straining effort, the veins and tendons in her neck standing out like pencils under the skin. Abe finds that he's a little freaked, here; paramedics are supposed to run into this situation all the time, but it's a first for him, and the way that she's writhing under his hands is disconcerting indeed. He isn't so sure he doesn't prefer them a little more comatose.

They're about to pick up the stretcher when the contractions begin again, and Xavier stops to check her out once more. "Oops, top of its head is showing here, I don't think we've got time anymore. Push, woman."

"Can't—"

"Yes, you can, here when I press on your belly. Legs up, hands down here. A big push, hold it, let off. Rest for a bit. Now again."

"X, have you done this before?" Abe asks.

"Sure."

"Are you going to do an, an episiotomy?"

"Are you kidding? This kid's doing it himself."

"Great!" the woman cries in a break between pushes. "Just what I want to hear! What kind of medic are you?"

"Army. Here, pay attention to what you're doing."

"As if I've—got any choice!"

The woman gasps, bears down again. She's gasping for more air. Abe had no idea they had to work so hard at it. He jumps up and gets a grayed towel from the bathroom, wipes off her face. Her belly heaves again, she squeaks, teeth clamped, eyes squeezed shut so hard the lids are white in a bright red face. "Breathe in, push on the exhale," Xavier says softly. "Okay, push. Push."

"Fuck off."

Suddenly Abe notices that the light has dimmed; there's a big crowd of neighbors in the doorway! The woman notices them and curses between gasps. "Hey, get out of here!" Abe says. "Unless you're a doctor or a midwife, go wait outside! And close the door!" He gets up and chases them off, having trouble with the smallest kids, who are fast. Mostly kids and teenagers, looking in round-eyed with curiosity.

"Push! Push, yeah! Here we go, head's out. Now push those shoulders out right quick." Xavier's hands are busy at the woman's crotch, Abe glances and sees a wet blood-and-mucus-streaked baby, rubbery-looking red in X's black hands, just about clear of her, sliding out the last part of the way. Amazing. Xavier starts working on the umbilical cord and the placenta. He flicks the infant on the side and it wails. "Here, Abe, take it." Abe crouches and is handed a baby. Wet, warm, sticky. It hardly weighs a thing, and its whole head fits in one hand easily.

"A little hemorrhaging," Xavier remarks, frowning.

"Hey—when do I push!"

"You're done, lady. The kid is born."

"What? Why didn't you tell me!" The woman takes a weak swing at the air. "What kind of doctor are you, anyway? Hey! Boy or girl?"

"Umm . . ." Abe checks. "Boy, I think."

"You *think*?" the woman demands. She and Xavier laugh. "What you got here, spade, some kind of medical student or something?"

"Come on," Xavier says. "We've still got to get to the hospital. Lady, can you hold the kid on top of you while we carry you downstairs?"

She nods, and they arrange the little creature on the wet T-shirt, in her arms. It makes quite a picture—messy, but . . . good.

As they maneuver her down the stairs, however, shooing the neighborhood kids ahead of them, the woman fades a little. She lets the kid slip off to the side; they have to drop the stretcher and grab the baby fast before it goes over the railing and into the dumpsters. Thump, thump, the stretcher and the woman land half on Xavier, who almost falls down the stairs; he has to sit fast to avoid it. "Lady, what are you *doing*?"

"Who are you guys anyway! Trying to kill me! Give me my kid back!"

"Try holding on to it this time, okay?" X is disgusted. "Little tip for mothers, I give to you free—don't drop your kid into trashbins when you can help it."

They make it down the stairs and to the truck. Xavier jumps in back with her, Abe drives them off toward St. Joe's.

Xavier calls out from the ambulance chamber. "Make it snappy, Abe, I can't really get the compresses up where the bleeding is."

"You damn well better not try!" Abe hears the woman say sharply. "It was one of your spade brothers knocked me up in the first place."

"Uh-huh. You just relax, lady, and shut up if you can. I'll keep a hold on myself."

X sticks his head through the window, into the cab beside Abe. "Ungrateful bitch."

"So you've done deliveries before?" Abe asks.

"Yeah, couldn't you tell? That was the real midwife touch, there."

"I see. Was this one unusual?"

"Awful fast."

"That's what you think!" the woman cries from the back.

"Quiet, lady. Save your strength."

Abe says, "I didn't know it was such hard work. I mean I'd heard, but I'd never seen it."

"No? Man, you are a rookie. Yeah, it wipes them out. Brains have gotten bigger a lot faster than cunts, and that makes it dangerous. You got two healthy people there and they can still both die on you. In fact, step on it, will you?"

When they get to St. Joe's, and get the woman and her child onto a gurney at the ER entrance, she gets sentimental and starts to cry. "I really appreciate it—I was really scared. I'm sorry I said all those things about you. You aren't really a spade."

"Well," X says, compressing his lips to keep a straight face.

"What's your names? Abe? Okay. Xavier? Xavier? How do you spell that? Okay. I'm gonna name him William Xavier Abraham Jeffers, I really am. I really am. . . ."

She's wheeled away. They wash up in the ER men's room, then go back to the waiting room.

A doctor comes out in a few minutes and tells them that the woman is fine, the baby is fine, there are no problems. No problems at all.

Back out in the truck. Abe has kind of an unreal feeling. They're both grinning like fools. "So," Abe says. "William Xavier Abraham Jeffers, eh?"

"Got any cigars?" X asks.

And they both start to laugh. They laugh, they shake hands, they pound each other on the arm, they laugh. "Could you believe it when the whole neighborhood came in to watch?" "Or when the kid fell off into the trashbins!" "Hey, aren't we about done for the night? Let's go get a drink."

So they go to celebrate at the Boathouse in lower Santa Ana, on Fourth Street. One of X's regular hangouts. They drink a lot of beer. Abe relaxes, feeling good to be a part of X's off-work life, to be accepted in this black bar, if only for a little bit, as a friend of X's. Xavier tells their story to the guys and the whole place howls, immediately sets to retelling the story with a million elaborations. "Why you ain't no spade after all! *Heeee,* heee heeee *heeeee* . . ."

Abe and Xavier get drunk. Abe watches X's laughing face, and feels his own grin. He hasn't seen X this relaxed in . . . well, whenever. Abe squeezes his eyes shut, trying to hold on to the moment, the smell of smoke and sweat, the rowdy voices of X's friends, the look on X's face. Hold, time. Stop.

... 31

But time, of course, does not stop. And eventually they take the truck back to headquarters, and Xavier goes home.

Abe tracks to Sandy's place, still feeling high. Into the endless party, and for once he's in sync with the prevailing mood. There's been a headline in the *Los Angeles Times* that morning:

DEA DECLARES ORANGE COUNTY "DRUG CAPITAL OF THE WORLD"

and Sandy has therefore declared the day a local holiday. He and Angela have gone all out to decorate the ap, with balloons, ribbons, confetti, streamers, noisemakers, and big strips of paper that have the headline reproduced on them in various spectrum bends. Samples of every recreational drug known to science are on hand and in action, Sandy is in the kitchen singing along with the blender as it grinds up quantities of ice cream, chocolate sauce, milk, and, well, Abe isn't too sure what else, but he has his suspicions. "Rnn rnn rnn, rnn rnn rnn!" Sandy sings, and grabs the blender from its base. He pours the frothy milkshakes into tall plastic glasses, handing them to whoever gets a hand out first, "Hey, drink this! Try this!" His pupils are flinching just inside the blue rims of the irises as he sees Abe and hands him a glass. Cold in the hand. Sandy uses the blender itself to clink a toast. "To the day's work!" with that Sandy grin blazing at San Onofre–level megawatts. Now how did he know that his toast would be appropriate on this night of all nights? Another drug mystery. Abe drinks deep. No taste but chocolate, though it's maybe a bit chunky. What might it be? He'll soon find out. Best to establish a transitional period by lidding as much as possible.

A lot of people are already pretty stoned, they've got eyes like black holes and their mouths are stretched wide like they're trying to do imitations of Sandy's ordinary smile, they're grinding their teeth and giggling a little and staring around like the walls have sprouted fantastic morphological formulations out of the usual condo cottage cheese ceilings, say, is that, could that be a, a stalactite there? Abe can only laugh. But Sandy splutters with dismay. "No zoning out here, this is a celebration, get on your feet!" People stare at him like he's maybe part of the ceiling's deformations. "Uh-oh. Jim! Jim! Jim—put something inspiring on the CD."

Happily Jim hurries to the collection of tattered old CDs, bought in boxfuls by Sandy and Angela at swap meets, no idea what's in the boxes, a perfect situation for Jim, who is in heaven bopping from box to box and rooting around. Abe laughs again, lidding from an eyedropper of the Buzz and feeling his spine begin to radiate energy. Jim, King of the Culturevultures. Hopping birdlike box to box, talking as fast as he can to people who clearly aren't understanding a word he says. Head still as a bird's, snapping instantaneously from position to position just like a finch's, except that now Abe sees a kind of after-image of Jim, trailing behind him. A hallucinogen, eh? Fine by Abe. He can't help laughing at his good friend Jim, who would no doubt look for the perfect music till dawn; but Sandy returns and grabs him by the elbow. "Now, huh? Desperate need for music *now*!"

Jim nods, his face suddenly twisted with nervousness. They're really going to play his choice? What if he has gone off on some spiral of reasoning that has led him to a completely stupid choice, he can't be at all sure that he hasn't! Abe can read all this perfectly in Jim's comically exaggerated expression of alarm, and he starts laughing hysterically. Jim trails Sandy to the CD player changing his mind, trying to get more time to think it over, but Sandy beats him away with one arm while inserting the CD with the other, and suddenly the speakers are roaring out some big symphonic fanfare. What's this?

"'Pomp and Circumstance'!" Jim shouts at Sandy and Abe, scowling with desperate uncertainty. Sandy grins, nods, turns the volume up so that the people on Catalina can enjoy it too. Then the march begins and Sandy highsteps around the rooms of the ap, leaning over to scream in the face of anyone who has remained sitting. Soon everyone's up and marching like toy soldiers with scrambled circuits, banging into walls and knocking over plants and each other. Abe marches behind Jim and feels the dust in the blood begin to fly in him, the dumb old march has somehow acquired this immense *majesty*, now everyone's out on the balcony, marching: twenty drum majors, a can-can line over by the railing, goose-steppers trying some kick-boxing. . . . Abe jumps up and down in place, feeling the glory of pure Being surge all through him. Incredible rush of exhilaration, face to the stars, it's clear tonight and up there on the fuzzy black vault of the night are the big fast satellites, the solar panels in their polar orbits, the microwave transmitters, the ballistic missile mirrors to the north—all the new artificial constellations, swimming around up there and nearly blocking out the little old twinkly stars. And planes falling onto John Wayne Airport like space stations landing, like fireflies in formation: what an amazing sky! Abe leans all the way back and howls. Coyote's entrance, here, the others take it up, and they howl and yip at the blinking night sky.

Angela, always first in these things, pulls off her blouse and throws it on the floor of the balcony, in the middle of the marchers. Bra next. Can she get her jeans off while doing the can-can? In a manner of speaking. Howls scale the sky. Clothes begin to fly onto the pile, a flurry of shirts, pants, blouses, silk underwear, boxer shorts. Quickly they're a ring of naked dancers, as in some pagan rite of spring, they can all feel it and for once it has that quality of primitive sensuousness, no all-American tits-n-ass consciousness in Abe tonight, it's just the clean joy of having a body, of being able to dance, of Being and Becoming. The way the pink of skin jumps out of the night's smeary darkness is just part of the joy of it. Freckled Sandy tosses all the couch cushions in the ap onto the big pile of clothing, and then he dives on, swims into the pile, ah-ha, a pile-on here. Naked Humphrey is dancing wallet in hand, can't just throw *that* in a pile of other people's clothes, right? Abe starts howling again, laughing and howling, he can't get over how good everything feels, how happy every face looks to him, there's Jim happy, Sandy happy, Angela happy, Tashi and Erica happy, Humphrey happy, all of them dancing in a circle and howling at the sky, Abe dives into the great mass of clothes and people and cushions, clean laundry smell, he's buried, he's coming up for air, coming up to be born, like the baby he helped bring into the world just hours before—born out of their clothes, naked, shocked at the pure glossy presence of things, their sensuous reality, their there-ness. For the second time that night Abe Bernard squeezes shut his eyes and wills the moment to stop, to stop while he and all his friends are happy, to stop, stop, stop, stop, stop.

... 32

... In the 1790s the area still belonged mostly to the Indians, now called Gabri-elinos. The Spanish rarely ventured away from San Juan Capistrano and the El Camino Real, and they avoided the swamps and marshes above Newport Bay, because these were difficult to traverse on foot or horseback.

But during those years the bay had some visitors. A party of French-American colonists, en route to Oregon by way of the long trip around Cape Horn, sailed into the bay and wintered there. The next year a small group re-turned from Oregon, and they lived on the mesa above Newport Bay for nearly twenty years. These were the first non-Indian residents of the area.

History doesn't tell us much more about these French-Americans than that. But we can deduce a fair amount about the lives they must have led. They were from Quebec, they were used to the wilderness, and they knew the crafts nec-essary for survival in it. They must have been fishermen, and perhaps they did some farming as well. We don't know if they were literate, but they easily could have been; they may have had some books along with them, a Bible perhaps.

They must have had contact with the Indians who lived on the bay; perhaps they learned where to dig for clams, where to set snares, from Indian friends. There was an Indian village on Newport Mesa, called Genga; they must have spent some time there, learned a bit of the Gabrielino language. The Spanish called the bay Bolsa de Gengara, after this village; what did these French call it? If we knew what the Indians called it, perhaps we could guess.

At that time, in the same years that the French Revolution and Napoleon were causing such upheavals in Europe, Newport Bay did not look like it does now. The Santa Ana River, which ran all year around, drained into the vast marshes at the upper end of the bay; these marshes extended all the way in to Santa Ana and Tustin. And the upper section of Newport Bay was open to the sea. Balboa Peninsula did not then exist; it was created by flooding of the Santa Ana River in 1861. The river itself did not swing into its new delta at 56th Street until the 1920s, in another great flood.

Ocean, estuary, marsh, grasslands, hillsides; it was a land of great variety, teeming with life. And this little group of French-Americans—how many were there?—lived in the midst of this wilderness, with their Indian neighbors, in peace, for over twenty years.

What must their lives have been like? They must have made their own clothes, shoes, boats, homes. Children must have been born to them, raised until they were perhaps twenty years old. Perhaps some of them died there. Their days must have been spent hunting, farming, fishing, exploring, making, talking—speaking French, and Gabrielino.

Why did they leave? Where did they go, when they left? Did they return to Oregon, to Quebec, to France? Were they in Paris when the Napoleonic wars ended, when the train tracks were laid? Did they ever think back to the twenty years they had spent on the California coast, isolated from all the world?

Perhaps they never left. Perhaps they stayed on the shores of the primeval bay, in a little bubble of history between the dream time of the Indians and the modern world, until they were exterminated with the rest of the Gabrielinos when the Europeans came up from Mexico—killed by people who couldn't tell them from Indians anymore.

...33

Next time Arthur comes by, Jim decides to take the direct approach.

"We have another strike planned," says Arthur.

And Jim replies, "Listen, Arthur, I want to know more about who you are, who we are. Who exactly we're working for and what the long-range goals are! I mean, the way it is now, I don't really know."

Arthur stares at him, and Jim swallows nervously, thinking that he may have gone too far somehow. But then Arthur laughs. "Does it really matter? I mean, do you want a name? An organization to pledge allegiance to?"

Jim shrugs, and Arthur laughs again. "Kind of old-fashioned, right? The truth is that it's more complicated than you probably think, in that there is more than one so-called group doing all this. In fact, we're stimulating a lot of the action indirectly. It's getting so that half of the attacks you hear about are not actually our doing. And it seems to be snowballing."

"But what about us, Arthur. *You.* Who supplies you, who are you working for?"

Arthur regards him seriously. "I don't want to give you anybody's name, Jim. If you can't work with me on that basis, you can't. I'm a socialist and a pacifist. Admittedly my pacifism has changed in nature since I've decided to join the resistance against the weapons industry. But like I told you, the methods I tried before—talking to people, writing, lobbying, joining protests and sit-ins—none of them had any tangible impact. So, while I was doing that I met all sorts of socialists. You wouldn't think any existed anymore in America."

"I would," Jim says.

Arthur shrugs. "Maybe. It's almost a lost concept, that individuals shouldn't be able to profit from common property such as land or water. But some of us still believe in it and work for it. There could be a combination of the best of both systems—a democratic socialism, that gave individuals the necessary freedoms and only prohibited the grossest sorts of profiteering. Everyone has a right to adequate food, water, shelter, and clothing!" Frustration twists Arthur's face into the intense mask Jim remembers from their poster raid on SCP. "It's not that radical a vision—it could be achieved by votes, by an evolutionary shift in the law of the land. It doesn't have to be accomplished by violent revolution! But . . ."

"But it doesn't happen," Jim prompts him.

"That's right. It doesn't happen. But do you know what to do about it? No. None of us do. But now, after everything else, I'm convinced that unless the plan includes active, physical resistance, it isn't going to work. It's like the defense industry is the British before the revolution—they control us in the same way—and we're the small landowners in Virginia and Massachusetts, determined to take our lives into our own hands again. *We* being a group of Americans who are determined to fight the military-industrial complex on every front. There are lobbying groups in Washington, there are newsheets and videos and posters, and now there's an active arm, dedicated to physical resistance that hurts nothing but weaponry. Since there's so much public about this group, it's absolutely necessary to keep the active arm of it secret. So. I know a couple of people—just a couple—who supply me with the equipment, and the intelligence necessary to carry out the operations. That's all I really know. We don't have a name. But you can tell by the public statements, really, who we're a part of."

Jim nods.

Arthur watches him closely. "So. Is it okay?"

"Yeah," Jim says, convinced. "Yeah, it is. I was worried by how little I really knew. But I understand, now."

"Just think of it as you and me," Arthur suggests. "A personal campaign. That's what it all comes down to in the end, anyway. Not the name of the organization that you belong to. Just people doing what they believe in."

"True."

And so that night they track into the warren of streets behind the City Mall, to the little parking lot between the warehouses at Lewis and Greentree. There they flash their headlights three times and meet the same four men and their station wagon full of boxes, and the four men help them load the boxes into Arthur's car. Their leader pulls Arthur aside for a brief muttered conversation.

And then they track into the Anaheim Hills, putting on another pair of stealth suits as they take the Newport and Riverside freeways north. Once off the freeway they track up to the edge of a tiny park in an applex, one dotted with long-neglected slides and swings and benches. They crawl to the edge of the park, where a small slope of grass overlooks the Santa Ana Canyon. Below them and across the freeway-filled gorge, on a knoll, sprawls the big manufacturing plant of Northrop. And in the northeast corner of the expanse of buildings, all lit by blazing xenon lights, with a perimeter fence that is swept by roving searchlights, are the three long warehouselike buildings that hold the production facilities for the third tier, midcourse layer of the ballistic missile defense—that is to say, space-based chemical lasers, which will be transported to Vandenberg and hauled up into orbit. The "High Fire" system.

Quickly they hammer four little missile stands into the grass, and Arthur aims them at four doors in these buildings. This is the dangerous moment, the semicovert moment, and if the defenses are sensitive enough . . .

Arthur, Jim has time to think, is connected up with some excellent intelligence sources: he knows the right buildings, the correct doors, he knows the buildings will be empty, the night security forces elsewhere in the complex . . . Such information must be top secret in the companies involved, so that the espionage involved in getting hold of it must be sophisticated indeed.

Missiles set and targeted, they trail the ignition cords across the tiny park, back toward Arthur's car. Buttons pushed, run to the car, track away, tear the suits off, dump them down a storm drain. No sign at all of pursuit; in fact, they can't even tell what the missiles might have done, because they're on the other side of the hill now, getting onto the Riverside Freeway with all the rest of the cars. They never even heard a siren this time, because the little condo park was over a mile from the Northrop complex. It really is *very simple*. But one can assume that the little missiles have followed the laser light directly to their targets, and have dissolved the materials in the plant susceptible to the solvents in the payloads. . . .

Despite the ease of the attack, Jim's heart is racing, and he and Arthur shake hands and pound the dash with the same sharp exhilaration that they felt in the first raid against Parnell. Jim becomes more certain than ever that he is only really alive, really living a meaningful life, when he is doing this work. "Here's to resistance!" he cries again. He has a slogan now.

... 34

In the month after LSR submits its bid for the Stormbee program, Dennis McPherson flies to Dayton four times to meet various members or subcommittees of the Source Selection Evaluation Board. The questions are tough and exacting, and each session drains McPherson completely. But so far as he can tell, they are faring well. Except for a whole day's worth of questions concerning the laser system's abilities in bad weather, the so-called blind let-down issue, he has satisfactory answers for all of their technical questions, and these in turn justify the estimated costs of the system. As for blind let-down, well, there's nothing much they can do about that. The RFP asked for a covert system, so they're stuck with the CO_2 laser's inability to see well through clouds. McPherson tries not to worry about it; he figures that the SSEB is merely trying to find out which of the bidders' proposed systems will deal with this handicap the best.

So. Four intense grillings, each with its ritual humiliations, the various reminders that the Air Force is in control here, it's the biggest buyer's market of all history and so everyone gathering around to sell has to do a little submission routine, rolling on their backs and exposing throat and belly like dogs . . . at least in certain ritual moments, as when beginning or ending presentations, or answering irrelevant, insolent questions, or greeting members of the board at the occasional lunch or cocktail party on the base. McPherson goes through all that grimly and concentrates on the actual sessions, on clear concise answers to the questions asked. It really is wearing.

But eventually the time runs out, and the SSEB has to stop and make its report, and the Source Selection Authority—General Jack James, a serious aloof man—has to stop and make his decision, and this decision has to be reviewed by HQ USAF, and then it finally comes time for the Air Force to award the contract for Stormbee. Somewhere in there the decision has been made. One company will have its bid chosen and will be in charge of a $750 million system, the other four competitors will be sent home to try again, each some several million dollars out of pocket as a result of their attempt.

Because of McPherson's reports on the grillings, and the original choice of LSR by the Air Force back when the program was superblack, Lemon is confident that their bid is going to be the one chosen. All the Dayton questions indicate a strong interest in the problems of development and deployment, and Lemon thinks the proposal is so strong that no weaknesses have been found. Donald Hereford, in New York, appears convinced by Lemon, and on his orders a big contingent of LSR people travel to Crystal City for the Air Force's announcement of the award. Hereford himself comes down, with a small crew of underlings. The night before the announcement they have a party in the restaurant above the LSR offices in the Aerojet Tower, and the mood is celebratory. The rumor, spreading industrywide, is that LSR has indeed nailed the contract.

McPherson is politely cheerful at the party, but as for the rumor, he's trying to wait and see. He's too nervous to make any assumptions. This is his program, after all. And rumors are worthless. Still, it's impossible not to be infected by the mood a little bit, to allow hope to break out of its hard tight bud. . . .

The next day, in one of the Pentagon's giant white meeting rooms, McPherson feels talons of nervousness digging into him. A whole lot of people fill the room, including big groups from all five bidders: Aeritalia, Fairchild, McDonnell/Douglas, Parnell, and LSR, each team gathered in knots around the room. McPherson eyes the other companies' teams curiously. Jocularity with the rest of his own group is a tough bit of acting, and it's doubtful that he really pulls it off. Really all he wants is to sit.

It's actually a relief to see the Air Force colonel come into the room and stride to the flag-bedecked podium at the front. Video lights snap on and a microphone in the cluster of them at the podium begins to hum. It's another big media conference, the Pentagon's idea of high entertainment. And everyone else seems to agree. Several cameras are trained on the speaker, and McPherson recognizes many of the trade reporters, from *Aviation Week and Space Technology, National Defense, SDI Today, Military Space, L-5 Newsletter, The Highest Frontier, Electronic Defense,* and so on; ID badges also announce reporters from *The Wall Street Journal,* AP, UPI, *Science News, Science, Time,* and many newspapers. This is big news, and the Pentagon has been canny about turning the award ceremonies into PR events for itself. The colonel who will be their master of ceremonies is obviously an experienced PR man: a handsome flyboy, McPherson thinks sourly, about to award the contract that will make pilots obsolete.

For the sake of the reporters and cameras, they first have to endure a glowing description of the Stormbee system and its tremendous importance for American security. Also its great size and monetary worth, of course. Tension among the competitors present reduces them all to a state of sullen, tight attentiveness. Nearly seventy minds are thinking, Get to it, you bastard, get to it. But it's part of the ritual, one of the reminders of who is boss in this game. . . .

For a moment McPherson is distracted by these thoughts, and then he hears: "We're pleased to announce that the contract for the Stormbee system has been awarded to Parnell Aviation Incorporated. Their winning bid totaled six hundred ninety-nine million dollars. Details of the decision process are available in the document that will now be distributed."

McPherson's stomach has closed down to a singularity. Lemon is red-faced with anger, and something in his expression ignites fury in McPherson more than the announcement itself did. He snatches one of the booklets being passed around, reads the basic information page feverishly. When he finishes he is so surprised that he stops and goes back to read it more slowly, blinking in disbelief.

Apparently they're using a YAG laser system, in a two-pod configuration. And $669 million! It's impossible! It's instantly clear that Parnell has made a lower bid than they can possibly stick to. And the Air Force has let the fraud pass. Has, in fact, colluded in it. The room is filling with incredulous or angry voices, enough to overwhelm the happy chatter of the Parnell team, as more and more people get the gist of the booklet. Reporters are scurrying around, surrounding the Parnell group, faces bright under the video lights—disembodied pink faces, smiles, eyes—

Something snaps in McPherson. He stands, speech spills out of him. "By God, they've rigged it! We've got the best proposal in there, and they've given it to one that's an obvious lie!"

Lemon and the rest of the Laguna Hills folks are staring at him in amazement. They've never in their lives heard such an outburst from Dennis McPherson, and they're really taken aback. Art Wong's mouth hangs open.

Donald Hereford, silver-haired and calm, just looks at McPherson impassively. "You think their bid is unrealistically low?"

"It's impossibly low! I can't imagine the MPC evaluations letting this crap pass! And the proposal itself—look how they've ignored the specs in the RFP—two pods, YAG laser, eleven point eight KVA, why the planes won't have the power to run these rigs!" Heart racing, face flushed hot, McPherson slams the booklet down on the back of a chair. "We've been screwed!"

Hereford nods once, no expression on his face at all. "You're certain our proposal is superior to this?"

"Yes," McPherson grates out. *"We had a better proposal."*

Hereford's mouth tightens. After a moment he says, "If we let them do it this time, they'll feel free to do it again. The whole bid process will unhinge."

He looks at Lemon. "We'll file a protest."

The possibility hadn't even occurred to McPherson. His eyes fix on Hereford. A protest! . . .

Lemon starts to say something: "But—"

Hereford cuts him off with a hand motion, a quick chop. Perhaps he's angry too? Impossible to tell. "Contact our law firm here in Washington, and start giving them all the particulars. We need to hurry. If there are irregularities in their compliance with the RFP, then we may be able to get a court injunction to halt the award immediately."

Court injunction.

McPherson's stomach begins to return to him, a little at a time. They have recourse to some legal action, apparently. It's a new area for him, he doesn't know much about it.

Lemon is swallowing, nodding. "Okay. We'll do it." He looks confused.

McPherson forces down a few deep breaths, thinking *court injunction, court injunction*. Meanwhile, across the room, the Parnell people are still in paroxysms of joy, the dishonest bastards. They know better than anyone else that they can't possibly build the Stormbee system for only $699 million. It's just a ploy to get the bid; later they can get into the matter of some unfortunate "cost overruns." It can only be a deliberate plan on their part, a deliberate lie. That's the competition, the people he has to put his own work up against: cheaters and liars. With the Air Force going along with them all the way, completely a part of it, of the cheating and lying. In control of it, in fact. Feeling physically ill, McPherson sits down heavily and stares through the booklet, seeing nothing at all.

... 35

Sandy Chapman is in the middle of an ordinary business day, snorting Poly-morpheus and listening to The Underachievers with his friend and client John Sturmond, watching the hang-gliding championships at Victoria Falls on John's wall video and talking about the commercial possibilities of a small-scale aural hallucinogen. Suddenly John's ally Vikki Gale bursts in, all upset. "We've been ripped off!"

Turns out that she and John fronted nearly a liter of the Buzz to a retailer of theirs named Adam, who has now disappeared from the face of OC. No chance of finding him, or collecting the bill, which means they are out some ten thousand dollars. Gone like a dollar bill dropped in the street, and with no lost and found. And no police to call. It's gone. The price you pay for bad character judgment.

Vikki is collapsed on the couch crying, John is up striding around, shouting, "Fuck! Fuck! Fuck! I knew I shouldn't have trusted that guy!"

Heavy gloom ensues. Sandy sighs, roots around in his Adidas bag and pulls out a large eyedropper of California Mello. "Here," he says. "There's only one solution to a situation like this, and that's to get as stoned as you can."

So they start lidding. "Think of it as an event," Sandy drones. "An experience. I mean, how often does it happen? It's great, in a way. Teaches you some about the realms of experience and emotion."

"For sure," Vikki says.

"I'm with you there," says John.

"Besides, I fronted you, and okayed the front to this thief Adam, so I'll halve the loss with you. We'll just have to sell more and make it back."

"For sure."

"That's really tubular of you, man. Absolutely *untold*."

They lid some Funny Bone. Now the whole thing strikes them funny, but they're too mellow to laugh.

"It's a high-risk industry." Giggles.

"Investment portfolio just walked off on us." Chuckles.

"We've been completely fucked."

But beneath all that, under the attempt to take the bummer in style, Sandy is thinking furiously. He had expected to be paid several thousand by John and Vikki, which apparently they thought they were going to get from the absent Adam. So much for that.

But he needs that several thousand to buy the supplies for the next shipment from Charles, who works C.O.D. only. Without the several thousand, he is into a serious cash-flow problem, especially given the giant bills from the medical center in Miami. He starts doing some serious accounting in his head, where all the books are anyway, at the same time holding down his part of the conversation with John and Vikki.

Somewhere in that conversation John says something that Sandy finds particularly interesting, and after he's done with his calculations—which remain disheartening—he tries to track back to it.

"What did you say a second ago?"

"Huh?" John says. "What?"

"I say, say what? What did you say? Say it again?"

"Oh man, you're asking a lot! What were we talking about?"

"Um, dangerous work, something about chancy occupations like ours, and you said something about aerospace plants?"

"Oh yeah! That's right. This guy I know, Larry, he's working for a friend in San Diego who does industrial espionage. He slips into offices as a repairman or janitor and rips off paperwork and disks. Now that's already chancy enough, but he tells me that it's escalated into sabotage recently."

"Yeah, yeah, I've read about some of that I guess," Sandy says. This is connecting up with something he heard . . . when was that? "Do you know the friend?"

"Larry didn't mention the name. But they're hiring out to people that want the work done, apparently, and Larry is freaked. Even though the pay is good he's not too comfortable with the way things are trending."

"He's doing the actual sabotage himself?"

"Some of it. And then he's got people working for him too. Like your friend Bastanchury."

"Arthur's one?"

Dispassionately Sandy considers it. Up until this point he hadn't placed the earlier conversation he remembers having on this topic, but now with the mention of Arthur the party on Torrey Pines Cliffs comes back to him, the opium conference with Bob Tompkins. What was it Bob had been saying? Whew. There is this problem with drug taking at Sandy's level: functioning in the present is possible, just barely, with the most intense concentration; but the past . . . the past tends to disappear. A lot of tracks branch back up into the hippocampus there, and he doesn't seem to have much of a program for navigating them.

Well, he couldn't give a word-for-word transcript, but finally he does recall the gist of it. Something about Raymond taking revenge against the military, which is a funny idea on the face of it, although it's developing disturbing aspects. Instinctively he is curious. He wants to know what is going on. Partly this is because it is going on in his territory, the black economy of OC, and it's important for him to know as much as he can about the territory. Then partly it's because he has the feeling that the whole affair might have something to do with his friends, through Arthur. Jim hangs out with Arthur a lot these days, and probably he doesn't know what Arthur's gotten himself into. . . .

For the moment, however, he's distracted by the memory of Raymond and Bob Tompkins. That was the night that Bob's friend Manfred made the proposal concerning the aphrodisiac coming in from Hawaii, that's right. A little smuggling for twenty thousand and a lot of aphrodisiac, which no doubt there would be a good demand for. Of course it goes against Sandy's usual operating principle, but in a situation like this one . . . necessity makes its own principles. Now when was that conference? Just a week or so ago, wasn't it? So there might still be time. . . .

Vikki starts crying again. She was the one who first met this disappearing Adam, and introduced him to John and Sandy, and so she feels responsible. "Let's lid some more," John suggests morosely.

Without a word, Sandy shifts back into support mode, pulls another eyedropper from his bag. Impassively he watches his friends blink Mello into their tears. We use drugs as a weapon, he thinks suddenly; a weapon to kill pain, to kill boredom. The thought shocks him a little, and he forgets it.

After cheering them up again he makes his way out. He types in the program for his next appointment, and sits in the driver's seat watching the cars tracking around him. Ten thousand dollars. John and Vikki won't be able to repay him for months and months, if ever, so essentially the loss is entirely his. Ach. Thieves, frauds, con men, do they ever think how their victims feel? He redoes the accounting, confirms the results; he is in a bad cash crunch.

Bleakly he picks up the car's phone, calls Bob Tompkins. "Bob? Sandy here . . . I'm calling about your friend Manfred . . ."

So he agrees to do it. Bob says he has a few days before the transfer is to take place. The boat is all ready, in a slip in Newport harbor. Fine.

Once or twice during the next couple days Sandy remembers to ask casually about the industrial sabotage thing. It turns out that there are a whole lot of rumors about sabotage attacks on defense contractors—that they're being made by members of the black economy's extended family. But the rumors tend to contradict each other. No one but John Sturmond has heard Arthur's name connected with it. Eveline Evans believes that the security chief at Parnell is behind it all, and that it's all a manifestation of an intercorporations war. But Eveline is a big fan of intercorporate espionage videos, so Sandy is suspicious. This is a problem; filtering through rumors to real information is not an easy task. But Sandy keeps at it, when he remembers.

One night around 2:00 A.M. he's talking with Oscar Baldarramma, a friend and a big distributor of the lab equipment and tissue cultures Sandy needs for his work. They're out on Sandy's balcony, near the end of the nightly party. And Oscar says, "I hear that Aerojet is going to get hit tonight by those saboteurs."

"Is that right? How do you know?"

"Ah, Raymond himself was up here last night, and he let it slip."

"Not very good security."

"No, but Raymond likes to show off."

"Yeah, that's what Bob says. Is that all Raymond's doing this stuff for, though?"

"'Course not. He's doing it for money, just like he does everything. There's lots of people happy to pay to see some of these companies suffer a setback or two."

"Yeah." And Sandy is thinking of Arthur, who left the party a couple hours before, after turning down an eyedropper of the Buzz, which surprised Sandy. And, for that matter, what happened to Jim?

... 36

Hurrying to his night class Jim stops at Burger King for a quick hamburger-friesandcoke. He picks up the little free paper, the *Register*, and scans it briefly. Among the personals and real estate ads that constitute the bulk of the paper is a small OC news section; the headline reads, AEROJET NORTH LATEST VICTIM OF SABOTAGE. Yes, that's Jim and Arthur's work again. Jim reads the details with interest, because just as at Northrop and Parnell, they never got to see the effects of their action. Appears the ballistic missile defense software program has taken a serious blow, according to the Aerojet PR people. Fantastic, Jim thinks. He throws the paper in the trash on the way out, feeling that he is becoming a part of history. He is now an actor on the stage of the world.

Thus it's difficult to concentrate on the grammatical problems of his little class. Tonight one of his students hands in a gem: "We can take it for granite that the red gorillas will destroy Western civilization if they can." Jim shudders to think of the student's conception of the wars in Indonesia and Burma: Marines being hunted down by giant crimson apes . . . And take it for granite! It's perfect, really; the way the student has heard the phrase even makes sense, as metaphor. Solid as granite. Jim likes it. But it's one more sign among many others that his students don't read. Thus writing is completely foreign to them, a different language. And it's impossible to teach a language in one short semester. They've all got an impossible task. Why even try?

Class over, Jim collects the papers on the table. Turns off the room's light, walks into the hall. The door to the room across from his is open, which is unusual. Inside it a black-haired woman is lecturing vigorously.

Wild black frizzed-out mane, flying behind her.
She's big: tall, bulky, big-boned.
Army fatigue pants, frumpy wool sweater rucked up over the arms.
Boots.

Working at an easel: ah. An artist. That explains it, right?
Wrong. Brake light. A poem is a list of
Things To Do.

Jim moves to one side of the doorway, to try and see what's on the easel. Black lines. She sketches with careless boldness, sometimes looking at the class while she does it. "Try that," she commands. Try drawing while looking the other way?

While they try she comes to the door. "You lost?"

"No! No, I just finished teaching across the hall here." Though, still, I may be lost.... "I was just watching."

"Come in if you're going to watch."

Jim hesitates, but she's back at the easel, and just to disappear seems impolite. So he slips in and sits at a desk by the door. Why not?

The students are at tables, desks, easels, drawing away. The teacher's sketch is a landscape, in an Oriental style: mountain peaks piled on each other, disappearing in cloudbanks and reappearing. At the bottom, tiny pine trees, a stream, a teahouse, a group of fat monks laughing at a bird. It's like the illustrations in one of his books on Zen. He's given up on Zen as hopelessly apolitical, but still, the art has something.... The teacher looks at the clock, says, "We're going overtime. Time to stop." While the students pack up, she says, "You practice the strokes until you can do them without thinking, so that it's your head painting. That takes a long time. And all that time you've got to practice seeing too. It's a matter of vision as much as technique. Using the white spaces, for instance. Once you've learned washes, it's entirely a matter of vision." She walks among them. "We sleepwalk our way through most of this life, and it won't do. It won't do. You've got to throw your mind into your eyes and see. Always be watching." She takes her paintbox to a sink in the corner, where some others are washing brushes. "When it becomes a habit you begin to see the world as a great sequence of paintings, and the technique you know will help get some of them onto a surface. Tonight when you walk out the door, remember what I've said, and wake up! Okay, see you Thursday."

The students leave, talking in small groups. Jim sits and watches her. She tosses her equipment into a large briefcase, almost a suitcase. Snaps it shut. "Well?" she says to Jim.

"I'm learning how to see."

She wrinkles her nose. "Watch out you don't break something."

Jim hesitates. "Want to get something at the Coffee Hut?"

She looks away from him uncomfortably. He thinks she's shy, and almost smiles; would her students believe it possible? "All right." She pulls the suitcase off the table and barges out the door.

Jim follows. They exchange names. Hers is Hana Steentoft. She lives up in Modjeska Canyon, not all that far from the college. "And you're an artist?" Jim asks.

"Yes." She's amused for some reason.

They enter Trabuco J.C.'s pathetic attempt at a coffee house in the Bohemian style: plastic wood ceiling beams, dimmed lighting, old posters of European castles, a wall of automatic food and drink dispensers. Nothing can hide the fact that Trabuco is a commuter's junior college. The place is empty. They sit in the corner opposite the janitor washing the imitation wood floor.

"Do you paint in the style you were teaching tonight?"

"No. I mean it's a tool, a stylistic resource. I love the look of some dynasties, and Ming Dynasty painting is perfect for some of what I do, but . . . you teach writing? It's like if you taught a class in sonnet writing, and I asked you if you wrote sonnets. You probably don't, but you might use what you learned from sonnets in other poems."

Jim nods. "So you sell your paintings?"

"Sure. Can't live on what they pay us here, can you." She laughs.

Jim doesn't reply to that one. "So who are your customers?"

"Individuals, mostly. A group in the canyons, and in Laguna. And then some banks. Murals for their offices." She changes the subject. "And what do you write?"

"Ah—poetry, mostly. But I'm teaching bonehead English."

"You don't like it?"

"Oh, it's all right, it's all right." He regrets calling it that.

She chugs down most of her beer. They talk about teaching. Then about painting. Jim knows the Impressionists, and the usual culturevulture selection of others. They share an enthusiasm for Pisarro. Hana talks about Cassatt, then about Bonnard, her special hero. "Even now we haven't fully understood aspects of his work. That coloration that at first looks so bizarre, and then when you look closer at the real world you see it there, kind of underneath the surface of things."

"Even those white shadows in that one painting?"

She laughs. "*Cabinet de Toilette*? Well—I don't know. That was for the composition, I guess. Haven't seen any white shadows, myself. But maybe Bonnard did, I wouldn't doubt it. He was a genius."

They talk about genius in art, what it consists of and how those without it can best learn from it. Jim, who will concede in an instant that he is no artistic genius, and only hope that he is not pressed further to concede that he is in fact no artist at all, notices that Hana never makes any of these concessions. She makes no claims, either. This is intriguing. They continue to share enthusiasms, they find themselves interrupting each other to elaborate on the other's remarks. Jim is intrigued, attracted.

"But you can't just mean that paying closer attention to what you see is all of it, can you?" Jim asks, referring to her lecture to her class. "I mean, that's just like getting a good focus on a camera, or a telescope—"

"No no," she says. "We don't see like cameras at all. That's part of what makes photographs so interesting. But focusing your eyesight and your vision aren't the same thing, you see. Focusing your vision means a change in the way you pay attention to things. A clarification of your aesthetic sense, and of your moral sense as well."

"Vision as moral act?"

She nods vigorously.

"Now *that's* not postmodernism."

"No, it isn't. But now we're leaving postmodernism, right? Changing it. It's a good time for artists. You can take advantage of the open space left by the death of postmodernism, and the absence of any replacement. Help to shape what comes next, maybe. I like being a part of that."

Jim laughs. "You're ambitious!"

"Sure." She looks at him briefly; mostly she watches the table when she talks. "Everyone's ambitious, don't you think?"

"No."

"But you—aren't you?"

"Ah." Jim laughs again, uncomfortable. "Yeah, I guess so." Of course he is! But if he says so, doesn't it underline his lack of accomplishment, his lack of effort? It isn't something that he likes to talk about.

She nods, watching the table again. "Everyone is, I think. If they can't admit it, they're scared somehow."

A bit of mind-reading, there! And Jim hears himself say. "Yeah, it scares me, actually."

"Sure. But you admitted it anyway, didn't you."

"I guess so." Jim grins. "I'd like to see some of your work."

"Sure. And maybe I can read some of yours."

Stab of fear. "It's terrible."

She smiles at the table. "That's what they all say. Uh-oh, look. They're closing the place."

"Of course, it's eleven!" They laugh.

They gather their things and leave. As they walk under the light in the entryway Jim notices how wild looking she is. Hair unbrushed, sweater poorly knitted, she really is strange looking. Couldn't be more out of fashion if she tried. Jim supposes that's the point, but still . . .

"We should do this again," he says. She's looking off at the ground, maybe checking out the way ground bulbs underlight the shrubbery edging the quad. It is a weird effect. Ha—here's Jim seeing things, all of a sudden.

"Sure," she says indifferently. "Our classes end the same time."

He walks her to her car. "Thursday, then?"

"Sure. Or whenever."

"Okay. See you." Jim gets in his car and drives off, thinking of things they have talked about. Is he really ambitious? And if so, for what? You want to make a difference, he thinks. You want to change America! In the writing, in the resistance work, in the teaching, in everything you do! To change America, whoah—you can't get much more grandiose than that. Remarkable, then, how lazy he is, and what a huge gap there is between his desires and his achievements! Big sigh. But there, look at that string of headlights snaking along the shore of Rattlesnake Reservoir, reflected in the black water as a whole curved sequence of squiggly S-blurs . . .

It's a question of vision.

...37

ennis McPherson is not surprised to find that Lemon is furious about all aspects of the Stormbee decision, including the protest. Since the protest was Hereford's idea, stimulated by McPherson's outburst and made before the whole traveling crew of the company, it makes Lemon look like he is not crucial to the policy-making process of LSR, and he can't stand it. So with his most malicious smile he gives McPherson the job of representing LSR in the long and involved matter of the appeal. He guesses that McPherson will hate it, and he is right. Now McPherson has two main tasks: flying to Washington and talking to their law firm, appearing before committees and making depositions and the like; and helping Dan Houston, back in Laguna, with the disaster that Ball Lightning is about to become. Great. McPherson can feel his stomach shrinking, a little more every day.

So he's off to Crystal City again. In for consultation with LSR's law firm, Hunt Stanford and Goldman Incorporated. One of the most prosperous firms in the city, which is saying a lot.

It's Goldman who has been put in charge of their case; Louis Goldman, who is fortyish, balding, handsome, and a very snappy dresser. McPherson, who for years has believed lawyers to be one of the principal groups of parasites in the country, along with advertisers and stockbrokers, was at first quite stiff with the East Coast smoothie. But it turns out that Goldman is a nice guy, very sharp, and someone who takes his job seriously, and McPherson has grown to respect and then like him. For a lawyer he isn't bad.

Tonight they're having dinner up in Crystal City's finest restaurant, a rotating thing on the roof of the forty-story Hilton. Planes landing at National Airport cruise down the Potomac River basin, already below them: a strange sight.

McPherson asks about the appeal and Goldman makes a little flow chart on a napkin. "The whole history of the project prior to the Air Force's RFP is out, of course," he says. "No one wants these superblack programs acknowledged in public, and there's nothing written down concerning it anyway, so for our purposes it's irrelevant."

McPherson nods. "I understand that. But the RFP as published matched the specs they gave us for the superblack program, so any deviation from that—"

"Sure. That could be grounds for a successful challenge. Let's see if I've got the main points as you see them. Air Force asked you for a covert guidance system for a remotely piloted aircraft that could be dropped from low orbit, to underweather but without blind let-down, where it would be navigated at treetop level. Then it was to locate enemy military vehicles and lock on air-to-surface missiles it would be carrying."

"That's what they wanted."

"And they wanted it in one pod, preferably, and it was to use less than eleven KVA."

"Right. And yet they chose a system that uses two pods, and although Parnell claims they only need eleven point five KVA, they appear to be lying, according to our calculations of the needs of their system. The Air Force should have been able to see that too."

Goldman jots down these points on a pad he's put by his dessert plate. No napkin for this stuff. "And they've got a radar system, you say?"

"Right. See, the RFP repeats the original request that the system be covert, that it doesn't give itself away by its outgoing signals. Parnell has ignored that feature of the RFP and put in a radar system. So they won't be covert, but it does mean that they'll be able to do a blind let-down. And now the Air Force is listing that capability as a plus for Parnell, even though it's not asked for in the RFP." McPherson shakes his head, disgusted.

"It's a good point. And there are other discrepancies?"

"That's the main one, but there's others." They go over them, and Goldman fills out his list. The Air Force has listed Parnell's accelerated schedule as an advantage, then given them a contract with a relaxed schedule. And the Air Force's most probable cost estimates of the LSR and Parnell proposals consistently upped LSR's figures, while leaving Parnell's alone, or even lowering them. Then the lower cost of the Parnell system, as determined by the Air Force, was listed as a plus for them.

"It's pretty clear from all this that the Air Force wanted Parnell, no matter what the proposals were like," Goldman remarks. "Do you have any idea why that might be?"

"None." McPherson's anger over the matter is getting its edge back. "None whatsoever."

"Hmm." Goldman taps his pen against a tooth. "I've got some of my moles looking into the matter, actually. Don't tell anyone that. But if we can figure out their motive for doing this, and find any way of proving it, that would be a big help to the appeal."

"I believe it." They order brandies and sit back as the table is cleared. "So where do we go from here?" McPherson asks.

Back to the flow chart on the napkin. "Two approaches initially, see? First, we've petitioned the courts in the District to make an injunction halting the award of the contract until an investigation by the General Accounting Office is made. At the same time we've asked the GAO to make the investigation. Results so far have been fifty-fifty. The GAO has agreed to investigate, and that's very good. They're an arm of Congress, you know, and one of the most impartial bodies in Washington. One of the only real watchdogs left. They'll go after it full force, and I think we can count on a good effort from them."

Goldman swirls his brandy, takes a sip. "The other front has brought some bad news, I'm afraid. In the long run it could be pretty serious."

"How so?" McPherson feels the familiar tightening in the stomach.

"Well, you make a request for an injunction to the judiciary system, and in the District of Columbia it goes to the federal court system and is given to one of four appellate courts, each with a different presiding judge. It's not a regional thing, so someone in the system makes a decision and sends your request to one court or another. Mostly it's a random process, as far as we can tell, but it doesn't have to be. And in this case, our request for an injunction has been given to court four, Judge Andrew H. Tobiason presiding."

Another sip of brandy. Goldman seems to have the habit of courtroom timing: a little dramatic pause, here. "So?" McPherson says.

"Well, you see," says Goldman, "Judge Andrew H. Tobiason is also Air Force Colonel Andy Tobiason, retired."

Stomach implosion. A peculiar sensation. "Hell," says McPherson weakly, "how could that be?"

"The Air Force has its own lawyers, and many of them work in the District of Columbia. When they retire, some are made judges here. Tobiason is one. Giving him this particular case is probably a bit of mischief worked by the Air Force. A few phone calls, you know. Anyway, Tobiason has refused to make the injunction; he's decided the contract is to be carried out as awarded, until the GAO finishes its investigation and its report is conveyed to him." Goldman smiles a wry smile. "So, we've got a bit of an uphill battle. But we've also got a lot of ammunition, so . . . well, we'll see how it goes."

Still, he can't deny it's bad news. McPherson sits back, drains the brandy snifter. A terrible singer is moaning ballads over bad piano work, in the center of the revolving restaurant. Their table's window is now facing out over the lit sprawl of Washington, D.C. The dark Mall is a strip across the lights, the

Washington Monument white with its blinking red light on top, the Capitol like an architect's model, same for the Lincoln Monument there in the trees . . . all far, far below them. Washington has kept its maximum height law for buildings, and everything over there is under ten stories, and far below them. And of course height means the same thing it always has; the isobars for altitude and prosperity, that is to say altitude and power, are an almost perfect match in every city on earth. Height = power. So that here in Crystal City they look down on the capital of the nation like gods looking down on the mortals. And it isn't just a coincidence, McPherson thinks; it's a symbol, it says something very real about the power relationship of the two areas, the massive Pentagon and its lofty crowd of luxury-hotel sycophants densepacked around it—looking across the river and down, on the lowly government of the people. . . .

"The Air Force has a lot of power in this town," Goldman says, as if reading his mind. "But there's a lot of power in other places as well. So much power here! And it's scattered pretty well. Could be better, but there are some checks and balances still. All kinds of checks and balances. We'll get our chance to manipulate them."

To be sociable McPherson agrees. And they talk in an amiable way for another hour. He enjoys it, really. Still, on his way back to his hotel room, his mood is black. A retired Air Force colonel for a judge! For Christ's sake!

A well-dressed woman gets into the elevator with him. Perfume, bright lipstick, glossy hair, backless yellow dress. And alone, at this hour. McPherson's eyes widen as it occurs to him that she is probably one of the Crystal City prostitutes, off to fulfill a contract of her own. Stiffly McPherson returns her smile as she gets off. Just another military town.

...38

Now Jim looks forward to seeing Hana Steentoft, but he certainly can't count on it happening; she doesn't seem quite as interested in getting together. Some nights she's gone before Jim dismisses his class. Other nights she has work to do; "Sorry," she says diffidently, looking at the ground. "Got to be done." Then again there are the nights when she nods and looks up briefly to smile, and they're off to the pathetic Coffee Hut, to talk and talk and talk.

One night she says, "They've given me a studio on campus. I've got to work in a while, but do you want to come see it first?"

"Sure do."

They walk over dark paths, between concrete buildings lit from below. Sometimes they get wedge views of the great lightshow of southern OC. Nobody else is on campus; it's like a big video set, the filming completed. One of the concrete blocks holds Hana's studio, and she lets them in. Lights on, powerful glare, xenon/neon mix.

Piled against the walls are rows of canvases. Jim looks through one stack while Hana goes to work mixing some paints, in a harsh glare of light. The canvases are landscapes, faintly Chinese in style, but done in glossy blues and greens, with an overlay of dull gold for pagoda roofs, streams, pinecones, snowy mountaintops in the distance.

The results are . . . odd. No, Jim is not immediately bowled over, he does not suffer a mystical experience looking at them. That isn't the way it works. First he has to get used to their strangeness, try to understand what's going on in them. . . . One looks totally abstract, great stuff, then Jim realizes he's got it upside down. Oops. Real art lover here. Reversed, it's still interesting, and now he understands to look at them as abstract patterns as well as mountains, forests, streams, fields. "Whoah. They're wonderful, Hana. But what about—well, what about Orange County?"

She laughs. "I knew you'd ask that. Try the stack in the corner. The short one." Laughter. "It's harder, of course."

Well. Jim finds it extremely interesting. Because she's used the same technique, but reversed the ratios of the colors. Here the paintings are mostly gold: gold darkened, whitened, bronzed, left itself, but all arranged in overlapping blocks, squares tumbled one on the next in true condomundo style. And then here and there are moldlike blotches of blue or green or blue-green, trees, empty hillside (with gold construction machinery), parks, the dry streambeds, a strip of sea in the distance, holding the gold bar of Catalina. "Whoah." One has an elevated freeway, a fat gold band across a green sky, bronzed mallsprawl off to the side. Like his place, under the freeway! "Wow, Hana." Another abstract pattern, Newport harbor, with the complex bay blue-green, boats and peninsula gold blocks. "So how much do you charge for these?"

"More than you can afford, Mr. Teacher."

"Sandy could afford it. Bet he'd like one of these in his bedroom."

"Uh-huh."

Jim watches her mixing a couple of gold paints together in blue bowls, the paint sloshing bright and metallic in the light, Hana's tangled black hair falling down over her face and almost into the bowl. It's a picture in itself. Some unidentifiable feeling, stirring in him. . . .

As she mixes paints he talks about his friends. Here's Tashi writing tales of his surfing with a clarity and vividness that put Jim's work to shame. "Because he isn't trying for art," Hana says, and smiles at a bowl. "It's a valuable state of mind."

Jim nods. And he goes on to talk about Tashi's great refusal, his secret generosity; about Sandy's galvanic, enormous energy, his complex dealing exploits, his legendary lateness. And about Abe. Jim describes Abe's haggard face as he comes into the party after a night's work, transformed by an act of will into the funtime mask, full of harsh laughter. And the way he holds himself at a distance from Jim now, mocking Jim's lack of any useful skills, teaming with Tash or Sandy in a sort of exclusion of Jim; this combined with flashes of the old sympathy and closeness that existed between them. "Sometimes I'll be talking and Abe will give me a look like an arrow and throw back his head and laugh, and all of a sudden I realize how little any of us know what our friends are, what they're thinking of us."

Hana nods, looking straight at him for once. She smiles. "You love your friends."

"Yeah? Well, sure." Jim laughs.

"Here, I'm ready to work. Get out of that light, okay? Sit down, or feel free to track or whatever."

"I'll look at the other ones here." He studies painting after painting, watching her as well. She has the canvas flat on a low table, and is seated next to it, bent over and dabbing at it with a tiny brush. Face lost in black hair. Still bulky body, hand moving deftly, tiny motions . . . it must take her hours to do one painting, and here there are, what, sixty of them? "Whoah."

After a while he just sits by one stack and watches her. She doesn't notice. Every once in a while she heaves a big breath, like a sigh. Then she's almost holding it. Cheynes-Stokes breathing, Jim thinks. She's at altitude. Once he comes to and realizes he's been watching her still form without thought, for— he doesn't know how long. Like the meditation he can never do! Except he's about to fall asleep. "Hey, I'm going to track." "All right. See you later?" "You bet."

On the drive home he can hear a poem rolling around in his mind, a great long thing filled with gold freeways and green skies, a bulky figure perched over a low table. But at home, staring at the computer screen, he only hears fragments, jumbled together; the images won't be fixed by words, and he only stares until finally he goes to bed and falls into an uneasy insomniac's slumber. He dreams again that he is walking around a hilltop in ruins, the low walls broken and tumbled down, the land empty out to the horizon . . . and the thing rises up out of the hill to tell him whatever it is it has to say, he can't understand it. And he looks up and sees a gold freeway in a green sky.

...39

Sandy manages to talk Tash into accompanying him on his sailing trip to rendezvous with the incoming shipment of Rhinoceros. As always it's the personal plea rather than financial arguments that convince Tash.

Soon after that Sandy is visited by Bob Tompkins, who gives him the latest information on the smugglers, and the keys to the boat moored in Newport harbor. When that business is done they retire to Sandy and Angela's balcony for a drink. Angela comes out and joins them.

"So how's Raymond doing?" Sandy asks casually when they are suitably relaxed.

"Oh, okay."

"Is he still involved with this thing in OC, the defense industry vendetta?"

"Yeah, yeah. More than ever."

"So he has people up here that he's recruited, then?"

"Hired, to be exact. Sure. You don't think Raymond would do all this by himself?"

Sandy hesitates, trying to figure out an unobtrusive opening; Angela takes the direct approach. "We think some of our friends might be working for him, and we're worried that they'll get in trouble."

Bob frowns. "Well...I don't know what to say, Angela. Raymond's going about it with his usual security measures, though. He swears it's all going very quietly."

"Rumors are flying up here," Sandy says.

"Yeah?" Bob frowns again. "Well, I'll tell Raymond about that. I think it'd be nice if he stopped, myself, but I don't know if he will."

Sandy looks at Angela, and they let the conversation drift to other topics. Afterward, thinking about it, Sandy decides he didn't really find out much. But he might have sent some useful news up the line to Raymond.

The next afternoon Sandy goes down with Tash to the upper bay. They've got all the keys they need: one for the marina parking lot, one for the marina, one for the cage around the boat's slip, one to turn off the boat's alarm system, three to get into the boat, and one to unlock the beam and the rigging.

It's a thirty-three-foot catamaran, big-hulled and slow as cats go, named *Pride of Topeka*. Solid teak paneling, dark blue hull and decking, rainbow sails, little auxiliary engines in each hull. They get it out of the slip and putter down the waterways of Newport harbor.

Past five thousand small boats.
Past Balboa Pavilion, and the ferry kept running for tourists.
Past the house split in two by feuding brothers. That's History.
Past the buoy marking where John Wayne moored his yacht.
Past the Coast Guard station (look innocent).
Past the palm trees arched over Pirate's Cove. That's your childhood.

And out between the jetties. They're caught in the five-mile-per-hour traffic jam of the busiest harbor on earth. Might as well be on the freeway. To their left over the jetty is Corona del Mar, where Duke Kahanamoko introduced surfing to California. To their right over the longer jetty is the Wedge, famous body-surfing break. "I wonder where they got the boulders for the jetties," Sandy says. "They sure aren't local."

"Ask Jim."

"Remember when we were kids and we used to run out to the end?"

"Yeah." They look at the metal tower at the end of the Corona del Mar jetty, the green light blinking on its top. Once it was one of their magic destinations. "We were crazy to run over those boulders."

"I know!" Sandy laughs. "Just one slip and it's all over! I wouldn't do it now."

"No. We're a lot more sensible now."

"*Ahhh*, hahaha. Speaking of which, it's time for an eyedropper, eh?"

"Let's get the sails up first so we don't forget how."

They put up the mainsail, the boat heels over, they sail south.

Engines off. White wake spreading behind.
Sun on water. Wind pushing onshore.
The sail bellies
Full.

Sandy takes a big breath, lets it out. "Yes, yes, yes. Free at last. Let's celebrate with that eyedropper."

"Really change the routine."

After a few blinks Sandy sighs. "This is the only way to travel. They should flood the streets, give everyone a little Hobie cat."

"Good idea."

They're headed for the backside of San Clemente Island, some sixty miles off the north San Diego coast. It's owned by the government, inhabited only by goats, and used by the Navy and the Marines to practice amphibious landings, helicopter attacks, parachuting, precision bombing, that sort of thing. Sandy and Tash are scheduled to rendezvous sometime the next day or night with the boat from Hawaii, off the west side of the island.

They sail in a comfortable silence, broken only occasionally by stretches of talk. It's an old friendship, there's no pressure to make conversation.

That's the sort of companionship that brings people out; even the quiet ones talk, given this kind of silence. And suddenly Tash is talking about Erica. He's worried. As Erica rises ever higher in the management of Hewes Mall, her complaints about her layabout ally and his eccentric life-style become sharper. And no one can get sharper than Erica Palme when she wants to be.

Sandy questions Tash about it. What does she want? A businessman partner, kids, a respectable alliance in the condomundos of south OC?

Tash can only blink into an eyedropper and declare "I don't know."

Sandy doubts this; he suspects Tash knows but doesn't want to know. If Sandy's guesses are correct, then Tash'll have to make changes he doesn't want to make, to keep the ally he wants to keep. Classic problem.

Sandy has the solidest of allies in Angela; she's biochemically optimistic, as he's joked more than once, she appears to have equal amounts of Funny Bone, Apprehension of Beauty, the Buzz, and California Mello running in her veins. If he could get his clients to Angela's ordinary everyday mental state, he'd be rich. Sandy treasures her, in fact they're really old-fashioned that way; they're in love, they've been allies for almost ten years. Some kind of miracle, for sure. And the more Sandy hears from all his friends, the more he sees of their shaky, patched-up, provisional alliances, the luckier he feels.

So he can only sympathize with Tash concerning his problem; he can't really claim to offer any help out of his own experience. It's a difficult situation, no doubt about it; it is, in fact, a dilemma. Choosing either course of action means painful consequences. Change to suit Erica, remain the same and lose her; what will Tash do?

As night falls they talk less and less. Events from their childhood, events from the world news. Among the blurry stars overhead the swift satellites and the big mirrors slowly move, north, south, east, west, like stars cast loose and spinning off on crazy courses of their own. "Death From the Stars." "No lie." Sandy shivers in the wind, watching them. He pulls out soggy Togo's sandwiches and they eat. Afterward Sandy feels a bit queasy. "Marijuana reduces nausea, right?"

"So they say."

"Time to test it out."

It works only indifferently.

To their left OC bounces up and down.

The coast an unbroken bar of light.

The hills behind bumpy loafs of light.

Lights stationary, lights crawling about.

A flat hive of light, squashed between black sea and black sky.

The living body of light.

A galaxy seen edge-on.

Sandy retires to the cabin in the left hull, leaving the first watch to Tashi. He wakes to find Tashi drowsing over the tiller in gray predawn.

"Why didn't you wake me?"

"Fell asleep."

"I take it they didn't show."

"That's right."

"Tonight, then. Hopefully."

Tashi retires to his cabin in the right hull. Sandy has the dawn to himself. Gentle offshore breeze blowing. Tash had the tiller and sail set perfectly, even in his sleep. Sandy can see Catalina to the north behind him, and San Clemente Island poking up over the horizon to the south, perhaps another ten or fifteen miles ahead.

The stars and satellites wink out. Color comes to sea and sky. The sun rises over the mountains behind San Diego. Morning at sea. Sandy thinks about his usual schedule and feels blessed. Hiss and slap of water under the hulls. So peaceful. Maybe it's true, what Jim always says; there was a better way of life, once, a calmer way. Not in OC, of course. OC sprang Athena-like, full blown from the forehead of Zeus Los Angeles. But somewhere, somewhere.

Midmorning Tash comes up, they eat oranges and make cheese sandwiches. They sail around San Clemente Island just to pass the day. It's strange: scrub-covered, except where erosion has ripped out raw dirt watersheds, the hills are everywhere littered with wrecked amphibious landers, tanks, helicopters, troop carriers. And the west side, the side away from the mainland, is heavily pocked with bomb craters. Top of one hill gone. Another is covered by a mass of concrete, from which springs scores of radar masts and other protuberances.

"Is it really a good idea to pick up sixty liters of illegal aphrodisiac right under the Navy's nose?" Tash inquires.

"Purloined letter principle. They'll never expect it."

"They won't have to! Those surveillance arrays up there will probably analyze the goods by molecular weight. And hear our conversations."

"So let's not talk about it."

Their instructions are to lay to, four miles directly west of the southernmost tip of the island. They do some compass work and establish triangulated landmarks that will keep them near the spot after dark.

The southwest end of the island is benched in a series of primordial beaches that terrace the hills a hundred feet high or more. They can see some goats on one terrace. "Those must be the most paranoid goats on earth," Tash remarks. "Can you imagine their lives? Just peacefully eating sage, when suddenly wham bang, they're being strafed and bombed again."

Sandy can't help but laugh. "Horrible! Can you imagine their world view? I mean, how do they explain it to each other?"

"With difficulty."

"Like flies to small boys are we to the gods, or something like that."

"I wonder if they have a civil defense program."

"Something about as good as ours, no doubt. 'Hey, here they come! Run like hell!'" They laugh. "Like flies to small boys . . . how does that go?"

"Need Jim here."

Sandy nods. "He'd enjoy this, those benches and all."

"Should have brought him instead of me."

"He's got class tonight."

"So do I!"

"Yeah, but you don't have to teach it."

"Not most nights, anyway." They laugh. "Hey, did you know he's seeing a woman who teaches across the hall from us?"

"Good for him. Beats suffering with Virginia."

"No lie. . . . I wonder what ever happened with Sheila. I liked her."

"Me too. But Jim is . . ."

"An idiot?"

"*Ah*, hahahahaha. No, no, you know what I mean. Anyway, maybe with this teacher."

"Yeah."

After dark the island gets more active. As they eat more sandwiches they hear roars, clanking, grinding, the soft feathery whirr of combat helicopters. All without a single light anywhere, except for one red on-and-off to mark the high point of the island. Once or twice Tash spots the bulk of a helicopter against the stars. Then *swu*BAM, BOOM, and the island is momentarily lit by a ball of orange fire blackened with the dirt it's thrown up. Both of them jump convulsively. "Damn!"

Tash laughs. "Let's hope none of those things' heat-seeking targeters lock on to us."

"Tash, don't say that!"

"They're like clotheslines, tied from firing platform down to the target, which is located by its heat. Infrared system. Then you clip a bomb on the clothesline, and down it slides."

The island elaborates: *whoosh*BOOM.

"Lucky we don't have any heat here."

"Just us."

"Well hey! Maybe we ought to go in the cabins?"

"Nah. These are the best fireworks we'll ever see, unless they draft us. Every burst probably costs a hundred thousand dollars."

"Man, that's a lot of money!"

"No lie."

The battle exercises go on for an hour, until their ears begin to hurt. When it ends Sandy retires again. "Wake me this time."

Tashi does, at 3:00 A.M. They appear to be at the same heading off the island. All is dark and calm, there's hardly a breeze. Up and down on a deep ground-swell. Salt air fills Sandy to the brim; he's suddenly happy.

Tash is in no hurry to retire. "Do you ever think about leaving OC?" he asks.

"Ah, yes, I suppose so. Sometimes." Actually it has never occurred to Sandy; he never has time to think about that kind of thing. "Santa Cruz, maybe."

"That's just OC north."

"What isn't?"

"I was thinking of Alaska."

"Wow. I don't know, man. Those winters. The people I've talked to from up there say it's a manic-depressive life, manic in the summer and depressed in the winters, with the winters twice as long. Doesn't sound like such a deal to me."

"Yeah, I know. But it'd be a challenge. And it'll always stay empty, because of those winters. And it means I could get out into the real world every day, you know?"

There's a strain in Tashi's voice, a kind of poignant longing that Sandy hasn't heard before. He thinks, When you're on the horns of a dilemma, you do your best to find a third way. But he doesn't say this. "That would be something, wouldn't it. Surfing might be a problem, though."

Tash laughs. "No more so than here. The crowd scene is too much."

"Even at night?"

"Nah, but look around—can you see the waves? It beats war with nazis, but still, it's not the same."

"Alaska, then. Hmm. Sounds like a possibility. Maybe you can grow pot for me."

"Maybe."

"Speaking of which . . ." They rock on the water. Tash falls asleep. Sandy keeps a hand on the tiller, worrying about his friend. Maybe he'll mention it to Jim. Maybe Jim will think of something to say to Tashi. So many troubles, these days . . . alliances going bad left and right . . . things falling apart. What to do, what to do?

In the predawn he starts awake, then falls into a doze. He's half-awake, now, watching gray swells surge up and down under his fingertips, up and down, up and down, up and down. There's a light mist smoking off the swell tops, liquid turning to gas. There is a lovely glassy sheen to the water's surface, it's so smooth, so smooth. Maybe he's dreaming. The terraced benches of the island are obscured by mist, the gray hills rise out of it as on the first day, an unreal solidity intruding into a liquid world. Everything seems surreal, dreamlike, mesmerizing.

Suddenly there's a creak, and a forty-foot yacht has hove to alongside them. Three men jump down onto the deck of the cat, frightening Sandy. The thumps and the sudden tilt of the deck wake Tash, and he appears out of his cabin to stand beside Sandy. Sandy still feels like he's in a dream, he's too groggy to move. The three strangers form a chain and small metal drums are hefted over the water onto the cat's middeck, behind the mast.

While they're at it, right in the middle of their operation, there's a deep *crump* from the island, followed by a huge sonic boom. BOOOOMM!!!! Whoah!

That'll wake you up. Tash stares out to sea. "Look there, quick," he says urgently, and points. Sandy looks. A black dot, just over the water out on the horizon, skimming in over the mist . . . it's moving fast and jinking from side to side as it approaches, *zoom* past the two boats faster than Sandy can turn his head, and *crump* into the island. BOOOM! a racking sonic boom, like the fabric of the world has been ripped. And another dot has appeared out there. . . .

Bizarrely, the strangers from the yacht have continued to sling the drums over onto their deck, not missing a stroke, completely ignoring the missiles screaming overhead. When there's twelve drums on board they stop. One man comes back to them. "Here." A card is put in his hand, the man hops up to the deck of the yacht. It pulls away, all its sails angel-wing white over the mist. Around the southern tip of the island, and gone.

Sandy and Tash are still staring at each other, wordless and bleary-eyed. Here comes another skittering black dot, another *crump*, another shattering roar. "What *are* they?" Sandy cries.

"Cruise missiles. Look how fast and low they fly! Here comes another one—"

Skimming black dot. One every couple minutes. Each sonic boom smacks their nerves, makes them jump. Finally Tash stops waiting for them to cease. He checks the drums on the middeck, returns. "I guess we're the proud owners of twelve drums of aphrodisiac," he says. BOOM! The mast is quivering in the blasts of air. "Let us get the fuck out of here."

...40

Late that afternoon they are approaching Dana Point harbor, under the fine rugged bluff of Dana Point. This is where Bob Tompkins asked them to bring the boat. But then Tash spots two Coast Guard cutters, lying off the jetty. They appear, through binoculars, to be stopping boats and boarding them. "Sandy, I don't think we should try to go in past those two, not with this cargo."

"I agree. Let's change course now before it gets too obvious we're avoiding them."

They tack and begin a long northwesterly reach to Newport, using the auxiliary engines to gain speed. Sandy will just have to call Tompkins and tell him the goods are elsewhere. Tompkins won't be overjoyed, but that's life. No way they can risk a search by the Coast Guard, and it looks like that's what they're doing. Could they be searching for Sandy and Tash's cargo? Sandy doesn't like to think such obviously paranoid thoughts, but it's hard to avoid them with what they've got aboard.

An hour later Tashi climbs the minimal mast halyards, with some difficulty, for a look north using the binoculars. "Shit," he says. "Look here, Sandy, let's cut back toward Reef Point."

"Why?"

"There's Coast Guard off Newport too! And they're stopping boats."

"You're kidding."

"I wouldn't kid you about something like that. There's a lot of them, in fact, and I think—I think—yeah, a couple of them are coming this way. Making a sweep of the coast, maybe."

"So, you're thinking of dropping the stuff off?"

"Right. And we'd better be quick about it—it looks to me like they're only stopping cats of about our size."

"Damn! I wonder if they've been tipped off?"

"Maybe so. Let's get the drums back on deck."

Tashi descends and they quickly lift the metal drums out of the cabins. The cat is slower in the water with the drums aboard, but the effect is least when they're clumped right behind the mast, so that's where they put them.

Tashi takes the tiller and brings them in past the reefs of Reef Point, a beachless point on the continuous fifty-foot bluff that makes up the old "Irvine coast," from Corona del Mar to Laguna. The top of the bluff in this area is occupied by a big industrial complex; just to its right are the condos of Muddy Canyon.

Tash motors them further in, out of view of the buildings on the bluff above them. "That's where Jim's dad works," Tashi says as he luffs to a stop in waist-deep water, just outside the shorebreak. Happily it's a day without surf. "That's Laguna Space Research, right above us." He tosses the boat's little anchor over the side. "Hurry up, Sandy, those cutters were coming south pretty fast."

He jumps overboard and Sandy picks up the drums and hands them down to him. Both of them handle the drums as if they were empty; adrenaline is about to replace their blood entirely. Tash takes the drums onto one shoulder and runs them up the mussel-and-seaweed-crusted boulders at the base of the sand-stone bluff. He puts them into gaps between boulders, roots around like a mad dog to find small loose boulders to place over them. Sandy jumps in and rushes from boat to shore with the drums, huffing and puffing, splashing in the small shore-break, skidding around on the slick rock bottom in search for better footing. They both are panting in great gasps as the sprint exertions catch up with them.

Then all the drums are hidden and they're back on the boat and motoring offshore. No sight of other boats. Ten minutes, perhaps, for the whole operation, although it felt like an hour. Whew.

They motor west until they can circle around and approach Newport again, from out to sea. Sure enough, off Newport harbor they're stopped by a Coast Guard cutter, and searched very closely indeed. It's a first for both of them, although it resembles police searches of their cars on land. Sandy has thrown all the eyedroppers overboard, and he is polite and cooperative with the Guardsmen. Tash is grumpy and rude; they're doing good detainee/bad detainee, just out of habit.

Search done, the Guardsmen let them go impassively. They motor on into the harbor, subdued until they get into the slip and are off the boat, onto the strangely steady, solid decking. Back to the parking lot and Sandy's car, away from the scene of the crime, so to speak. Now, no matter what happens to the Rhinoceros, they are safe.

"Pretty nerve-racking," Tash says mildly.

"Yeah." Despite his relief, Sandy is still worried. "I don't know what Bob is going to say about this." Actually, he does know; Bob will be furious. For a while, anyway.

"Well hey, it looks to me like they had a pretty bad information leak."

"Maybe. Still, to put the stuff right under LSR. They're sure to have security of some kind. I suspect I am going to be status but not gratis with the San Diego boys."

"To hell with them."

"Easy for you to say."

And there won't be any payment without the goods delivered. Sigh. "Well. We'd better go get stoned and think it over."

"No lie."

...41

Sandy decides that the best thing to do is return immediately to Reef Point and recover the drums, and he calls Bob Tompkins to explain about the delay, also to complain about the apparent information leak. But Tompkins is in Washington to do some lobbying, and that same afternoon Sandy is visited by a worried-looking Tashi. "Did you see the news?" Tashi asks.

"No, what's up? San Clemente Island blown to smithereens?"

Jim looks up from Sandy's computer. "Where'd that word come from?"

"Ignore him," says Sandy. "He's testing my new drug, Verbality."

"Verbosity, more like. Here, check out the news." Tash clicks on the main wall screen and taps in the command for the *Los Angeles Times*. When it appears he runs through it until he reaches the first page of the Orange County section. The screen fills with a picture of what appears to be a twentieth-century newspaper page, a formatting gimmick that has gotten the *Times* a lot of subscriptions down at Seizure World. "Top right."

Sandy reads aloud. "LSR Announces Increased Security For Laguna Hills Plant, oh man, because of recent spate of sabotage attacks, defense contractors in OC, perimeter now patrolled, blah blah blah so what," so Tashi cuts in and reads a sentence near the bottom of the article: "The new measures will include cliff patrols and boat patrols in the ocean directly off LSR's seacliff location. 'Any sea craft coming within a mile of us is going to be under intense surveillance,' says LSR's new security director Armando Perez."

"They must be joking," Sandy says weakly.

"I don't think so."

"It's illegal!" Panic seeping in everywhere. . . .

"I doubt it."

Jim looks up. "What could be the difficulty that is encumbering and freighting your voices with the sounds of *sturm und drang,* my brethren?"

"Scrap that new drug," Tashi suggests.

"I will. The difficulty," Sandy explains to Jim, "is that we have stashed twelve big drums of an illegal new aphrodisiac at the bottom of a bluff now under the intense scrutiny of a trigger-happy private security army!"

"Zounds! Jeepers!"

"Shut up." Sandy rereads the article, turns it off. The initial shock over, he is again thinking furiously. "I've got an idea."

"What's that?"

"Let's go to Europe."

"Taking the constructive approach, I see."

"No, let's go!" Jim says. "Semester break frees me after Wednesday's class! On the other hand"—crestfallen—"I am a trifle short of funds."

"I'll loan it to you," Sandy says darkly. "High interest." Actually, he's short of funds himself. But there's always Angela's emergency account. And this is an emergency; he needs to be out of town when Bob gets this news, to give him time to adjust to it. Bob's like that; he has two- or three-day fits of anger, then collects himself and returns to cool rationality. The important thing is to be out of reach during those first two or three days, so that nothing irrevocable can happen. "Bob's in Washington for a couple days, so I'll leave a message on his answering machine outlining the situation. By the time we get back, he'll have had time to cool down."

"And you'll have time to think of something," Tash says.

"Right. You coming, Tash?"

"Don't know."

The news spreads quickly: they're going to Europe. Jim asks Humphrey for time off work, and Humphrey agrees to it, as long as he can come along. Angela agrees to the use of her emergency account, takes her vacation time, and is coming too. Abe can't get the time off. Tashi is thinking of splurging for it, but Erica's angry about it—"*I've* got to work, of course"—and he decides against going.

Humphrey takes over arrangements for the trip and finds them a low-budget red-eye no-frills popper that will put them in Stockholm two hours after departure. After they arrive they'll decide where to go; this is Sandy's decree.

Following his last class on Wednesday, Jim tells Hana that he's off to Europe with friends. "Sounds like fun," she remarks, and wishes him bon voyage. They make arrangements to meet again when the next semester begins, and happily Jim goes back home to pack.

"Off to the Old World!" he says to his ap. "I'll be walking waist deep in history wherever we go!" And as he packs he sings along with Radio Caracas, playing the latest by the Pentagon Mothers:

We only want to take you to the thick of the fray!
World War Three? It isn't just on its way!
You're in it, you're a part of it, you win every day!
So come on everybody, let's all stand up and say:
Mutual Assured Stupiditee-uh-eeeeeeeee!

... 42

On the next trip to Washington Dennis McPherson is taken by Louis Goldman to a restaurant in the "old" section of Alexandria, Virginia. Here prerevolutionary brick is shored up by hidden steel, and the old dock warehouses are filled with boutiques, ice-cream shops, souvenir stands, and restaurants. Business is great. The seafood in the restaurant Goldman has chosen is superb, and they eat scallops and lobster and enjoy a couple bottles of gewürztraminer before getting down to it.

Plates cleared, glasses refilled, Goldman sits back in his chair and closes his eyes for a moment. McPherson, getting to know his man, takes a deep breath and readies himself.

"We've found out some things about the decision-making process in your case," Goldman says slowly. "It's a typical Pentagon procurement story, in that it has all the trappings of an objective rational process, but is at the same time fairly easy to manipulate to whatever ends are desired. In your case, it turns out that the Source Selection Evaluation Board made its usual detailed report on all the bids, and that report was characterized as thorough and accurate by our information source. And it favored LSR."

"It favored us?"

"That's what our source told us. It favored LSR, and this report was sent up to the Source Selection Authority without any tampering. So far so good. But the SSA takes the report and summarizes it to use when he justifies his decision to the people above him. And here's where it got interesting. The SSA was a four-star general, General Jack James, from Air Force Systems Command at Andrews. Know him?"

"No. I mean I've met him, but I don't know him."

"Well, he's your man. When he summarized the SSEB's report, he skewed the results so sharply that they came out favoring Parnell where they had originally favored you. He's the one that introduced the concern for blind let-down that's not in the RFP, and he's the one who oversaw the most probable cost evaluations, to the extent of fixing some numbers himself. And then he made the decision, too."

Remarkable how this Goldman can spoil a good dinner. "Can we prove this?" McPherson asks.

"Oh no. All this was given to us by an insider who would never admit to talking with us. We're just seeking to understand what happened, to find an entry point, you know. And some of this information, conveyed privately to the investigators at the GAO, might help them aim their inquiries. So we've told them what we know. That's how these legal battles with the Pentagon go. A lot of it consists of subterranean skirmishes that are never revealed or acknowledged to be happening. You can bet the Air Force lawyers are doing the same kind of work."

This news sends a little chill through McPherson. "So," he says, "we've got a General James who didn't want us to get the contract. Why?"

"I don't know. I was hoping you could tell me. We're still trying to find out, but I doubt we will any time soon. Certainly not before the GAO releases their report. It's due out soon, and from what we hear it's going to be very favorable to us."

"Is that right?" After all he has heard so far, McPherson is surprised by this. But Goldman nods.

All of a sudden the possibility of getting these men—James, Feldkirk, the whole Air Force—Parnell—the possibility of taking their corrupt, fraudulent, cheating decision and stuffing it back down their throats and *choking* them on it—the possibility of forcing them to acknowledge that they have some accountability to the *rules*—oh it rises in McPherson like a great draft of clean fresh air; he almost laughs aloud. "And if it is favorable to us?"

"Well, if their report is stated in strong enough terms, Judge Tobiason won't be able to ignore it, no matter what his personal biases are. He'll be forced to declare the contract improperly awarded, and to call for a new process under the Defense Procurement statutes of 2019. They'd have to repeat the bidding process, this time adhering very closely to the RFP, because the courts would be overseeing it."

"Wow." McPherson sips his drink. "That might really happen?"

Goldman grins at his skepticism. "That's right." He raises his glass, and they toast the idea.

So McPherson returns to California feeling as optimistic about the whole matter as he has since the proposal went from superblack to white.

Back at the office, however, he has to turn immediately to the problem of Ball Lightning. Things are as bad as ever on that front. McPherson's role has been deliberately left vague by Lemon, as part of the punishment; he is to "assist"

Dan Houston, whatever that means, Dan Houston who has had less time with the company and is clearly not competent to do the job. Galling. Exactly what Lemon had in mind.

But worse than that are the problems with the program itself. The Soviets' new countermeasure for their slow-burning boosters, introducing modest fluctuations in their propulsion—called "jinking"—has made LSR's trajectory analysis software obsolete, and so their easiest targets have become difficult. Really, offensive countermeasures to the boost-phase defenses are so easy and cheap that McPherson is close to convinced that their free-electron laser system is more or less useless. They'd have better luck throwing stones. (In fact there's a good rival program at TRW pursuing a form of this very idea.) But the Air Force is unlikely to be happy to discover this, some thirty billion dollars into the project, with test results in their files that show the thing is feasible. Strapped chicken results.

Dan Houston, bowed down by all these hard facts, has already given up. He still comes into the office, but he's not really thinking anymore. He's useless. One day McPherson can barely keep from shouting at the man.

That afternoon, after Dan has gone home early, his assistant Art Wong talks to McPherson about him. "You know," Art says, hesitant under McPherson's sharp gaze, "Dan's having quite a bit of trouble at home."

"What's this?"

"Well, he made some bad investments in real estate, and he's pretty far in debt. I guess he might lose the condo. And—well—his ally has left. She took the kids and moved up to LA. I guess she said he was drinking too much. Which is probably true. And spending too much time at work—you know he never came home in the evenings when he first started on this program. He really put in the long hours trying to get it to work, after we won the bid."

"I'll bet." Considering the tests that won it. Ah, Dan . . .

"So . . . well, it's been pretty hard on him. I don't think . . ." Art Wong doesn't know what else to say.

"All right, Art," McPherson says wearily. "Thanks for telling me."

Poor Dan.

That night at the dinner table Dennis watches Lucy bustle around the kitchen telling him about the day's events at the church, which as usual he is tuning out entirely; and he thinks about Dan. McPherson has spent much of his life—too much of it—at work. On the weekends, in the evenings . . . But he can see, just by looking at her, that it has never even occurred to Lucy to leave him because of that, no matter how sick of it she may have gotten. It just isn't something she would do. He can rely on that, whether he deserves it or not. As she passes his chair he reaches out impulsively and gives her a rough hug. Surprised, she laughs. Who knows what this Dennis McPherson will do next, eh?

No one. Not even him. He gives her a wry grin, shakes his head at her inquiries, eats his dinner.

And at work he tries to treat Dan with a little more sympathy, tries to lay the eye on him a little less often. Still, one day he can hardly contain himself. Dan is moaning again about the impossibility of their task, and says in a low voice, as if he has a good but slightly dangerous idea, "You know, Dennis, the system makes a perfectly fine weapon for fixed ground targets like missile silos. We've worked up its power so much for the rapidly moving targets that stationary ones wouldn't stand a chance. Missile silos hit before they launch, you know."

"Not our job, Dan." Strategy. . . .

"Or even cities. You know, just the threat of a firestorm retaliation for any attack—who could ignore that?"

"That's just MAD all over again, Dan," McPherson snaps. He tries to control himself. "It wasn't what they bought this system for, so really, it's irrelevant. We just have to try to track and hold the boosters long enough to cook them, that's all there is to it. We've done everything possible to the power plant—let's work on tracking and on phased-array to increase the brightness of the beam, and just admit to the Air Force that the kill process will take longer than expected. Call it a boost phase/post–boost phase defense."

Dan shrugs. "Okay. But the truth is that every defense system we've got works even better at suppressing defenses. Or at offense."

"Just don't think about that," McPherson says. "Strategy isn't our area."

And they get back to it. Software design, a swamp with no bottom or border. With the deadline closing in on them.

Dennis is in Laguna when he gets the next call from Louis Goldman. "The GAO report is out."

"And?" Heartbeat accelerating at an accelerating rate, not good for him. . . .

"Well, it concludes that there were irregularities, and recommends the contract be bid on again."

"Great!"

"Well, true. But it's not really as gung-ho as I expected, frankly. The word is that the Air Force really put the arm on the GAO in the last couple of weeks, and they managed to flatten the tone of the report considerably."

"Now how the hell can they do that?" McPherson demands. "I mean, what sort of power could the Air Force have over the GAO? Isn't GAO part of Congress? They can't possibly threaten them, can they?"

"Well, it's not a matter of threatening physical violence, of course. But you know, these people have got to work with each other in case after case. So if the Air Force cares enough, they can say, Listen, you lay off us on this or we'll never cooperate with you again—we'll make sure any dealings you have with us are pure torture for you, and you won't be able to fully function in this realm anymore. So, the folks at GAO have to look beyond this particular case, and they're realists, they say, this one is top priority for them, but not for us. And so the report gets laundered a little. No lies, just deemphasizing."

McPherson doesn't know what to say to this. Disgust makes him too bitter to think.

"But listen," Goldman goes on, "it isn't as bad as I'm making it sound. In the main the GAO stuck to their guns, and after all they did recommend a new bidding process. Now we'll just have to wait and see what Judge Tobiason decides in the case."

"When will that take place?"

"Looks like about three weeks, judging by his published schedule."

"I'll come out for it."

"Good, I'll see you then."

Thus McPherson is in a foul mood, apprehensive and angry and hopeful all at once, when Dan Houston comes by at the end of the day and asks him to come along to El Torito for some drinks.

"Not tonight, Dan."

But Dan is insistent. "I've really got to talk to you, Mac."

Sigh. The man's hurting, that's clear. "All right. Just one pitcher, though."

They track over and take their usual table, order the usual pitcher of margaritas, start drinking. Dan downs his first in two swallows, starts on a second. "This whole BM defense," he complains. "We can barely make these systems work, and when we do they work just as well against defensive systems, so in essence they're another offense. And meanwhile we aren't even paying attention to cruise missiles or sub attack, so as for a real umbrella, well that isn't even what we're trying for!"

McPherson nods, depressed. He's felt that way about strategic defense for years. In fact that was his big mistake, accidentally letting Lemon know how he felt. And his dislike for the concept springs from exactly the reasons Dan is speaking of; every aspect of it has spiraled off into absurdity. "You'd think the original system architects would have thought of these kinds of things," he says.

Dan nods vehemently and puts down his margarita to point, spilling some ice over the salt on the rim. "That's right! Those bastards . . ." He shakes his head, is already drunk enough to keep going: "They just saw their chance and took it. During their careers they could make it big designing these programs and selling them to the Air Force, making it all look easy! Because for them it meant bucks! It meant they had it made. And it's only after it was put in space and began to come on line that the next generation of engineers had to make the system work. And that's us! We're the ones paying for their fat careers."

"Well, whatever," McPherson says, uncomfortable with Dan's raw bitterness. There is a sort of team code in the defense industry, and really, you don't say things like this. "We're stuck with it, anyway, so we might as well make the best of it."

Here he is, sounding like Lucy. And Dan, drunk and miserable, far past the code, will have none of it: "Make the best of it! How can we make the best of it? Even if we could get it to work, all the Soviets have to do is put a bucket of nails in orbit and wham, ten of our mirrors are gone. Talk about cost-effective at the margin! A ten-penny nail will take out a billion-dollar mirror! Ha! ha! So we defend those mirrors by claiming that we will start a nuclear war with anyone who attacks them, so it comes right back to MAD to defend the very system that was supposed to get us away from all that."

"Yeah, yeah. I know." McPherson can feel the margaritas fuzzing his brain, and Dan has had about twice as many as he has. Dan's getting sloppy drunk here, McPherson can see it. So he tries to prevent Dan from ordering another pitcher, but Dan shoves his hand away angrily and orders another anyway. Nothing McPherson can do about it. He feels depression growing in him, settling into a knot around the tequila in his stomach. This is a waste of his time. And Dan, well, Dan . . .

Dan mutters on while waiting for the next drink to arrive. "Soviets get their own BMD and we don't like it, no no no, even though the whole strategy demands parity. All sorts of regional wars start so our hard guys can express their displeasure without setting off the big one. Boom, bam, hook to the jaw, jab in the eye, *Bulletin of Atomic Scientists* sets the war clock at one second to midnight—one second to midnight, man, set there for twenty years! And, and the Soviets' beam systems could be trained on American cities, burn us to toast in five minutes, and we could do the same to them like I was saying today but we all ignore that, that's not real no no no, we pretend they're defensive systems only and we work on knocking each other's stuff down before the other side does, so we can MIRV each other right into the ground—"

"All right, all right," McPherson says irritably. "It's complicated, sure. No one ever said it wasn't complicated."

A tortilla chip snaps in Dan's fingers. "I'm not saying it's just complicated, Mac! I'm saying it's crazy! And the people who designed this architecture, they knew it was crazy and they went ahead and did it anyway. They went along with it because it was good for them. The whole industry loved it because it was new business just when the nukes were topping out. And the physicists went along with it because it made them important again, like during the Manhattan Project. And the Air Force went along with it because it made them more important than ever. And the government went along with it because the economy was looking bad at the end of the century. Need a boost—military spending—it's been the method of choice ever since World War Two got them out of the Great Depression. Hard times? Start a war! Or pump money into weapons whether there's a war or not. It's like we use weapons as a drug, snort some up and stimulate the old economy. Best upper known to man."

"Okay, Dan, okay. But calm down, will you? Calm down, calm down. There's nothing we can do about that now."

Dan stares out the window. The next pitcher arrives and he fills his new glass, spilling over the edge so all the big grains of salt run in yellow-white streams down onto the paper tablecloth. He drinks, elbows on the table, leaning forward. He stares down into the empty glass. "It's a hell of a business."

McPherson sighs heavily; he hates a maudlin drunk, and he's about to physically stop Dan from refilling his glass yet again when Dan looks up at him; and those red-rimmed eyes, so full of pain, pierce McPherson and hold him in place.

"A hell of a business," Dan repeats soddenly. "You spend your whole life working on *proposals*. Bids, for Christ's sake. It isn't even work that is ever going to see the light. The Pentagon just sets companies at each other's throats. Group bids, one-on-one competitions, leader-follower bids. Kind of like cockfighting. I wonder if they bet on us."

"Stimulates fast development," McPherson says shortly. There's no sense talking about this kind of thing. . . .

"Yeah, sure, but the waste! The waste, man, the waste. For each project five or six companies work up separate proposals. That's six times as much work as they would need to do if they were all working together in coordination, like parts of a team. And it's hard work, too! It eats people's lives."

Now Dan gets an expression on his face that McPherson can't bear to watch; he's thinking of his ally Dawn now, sure. McPherson looks around for the waitress, signals for their check.

"All their lives used up in meeting deadlines for these proposals. And for five out of every six of them it's work wasted. Nothing gained out of that work, nothing made from it. Nothing *made* from it, Mac. Whole careers. Whole lives."

"That's the way it is," McPherson says, signing the check.

Dan stares at him dully. "It's the American way, eh Mac?"

"That's right. The American way. Come on, Dan, let's get you home."

And then Dan slips in the attempt to stand, and knocks the pitcher off the table. McPherson has to hold him up by the arm, guide him between tables as he staggers. My God, a sloppy drunk; McPherson, red-faced with embarrassment, avoids the eyes of the other customers as they watch him help Dan out.

He gets Dan into his car, fastens his seat belt around him, reaches across his slumped body to punch the car's program for home. "There you are, Dan," he says, irritation and pity mixing about equally in him. "Get yourself home."

"What home."

...43

... *Under the Spanish and then the Mexicans, Orange County was a land of ranchos. To the north were Ranchos Los Coyotes, Los Alamitos, Los Bolsas, La Habra, Los Cerritos, Cañon de Santa Ana, and Santiago de Santa Ana. Midcounty were Ranchos Bolsa Chica, Trabuco, Cañada de Los Alisos, and San Joaquín. In the south were Ranchos Niguel, Misión Vieja, Boca de La Playa, and Lomas de Santiago.*

To give an idea of their size: Rancho San Joaquín was made up of two parts; first Rancho Ciénega de las Ranas, "Swamp of the Frogs," which extended from Newport Bay to Red Hill—second Rancho Bolsa de San Joaquín, which contained much of the land that later became the Irvine Ranch. Say 140,000 acres.

These huge land grants were surveyed on horseback, with lengths of rope about a hundred yards long. They used landmarks like patches of cactus, or the skull of a steer. More precise than that they didn't need to be; the land remained open, and cattle roamed over it freely.

In the spring, after the calving, the roundups took place. Horsemen, reputed to be among the best who ever lived, and including among them a good number of the rapidly disappearing Indians, rounded up the cattle and led them to the branding stations, several for each rancho, as they were all so large. The stations became festival centers, with tables set out and decorated, and great feasts of meat, beans, tortillas, and spicy sauces spread out on them. After the new calves were branded, and strays sent back to their correct ranchos, the celebrating began. The most important events were the horse races; many took place over a nine-mile course.

Other games were more bloody: trying to grab the head from a rooster buried to the neck, while galloping by it at full speed, for instance. Or the various forms of bull-baiting.

Then in the evenings there were dances, using forms invented at San Juan Capistrano, which throughout this period remained the biggest settlement in the area.

Houses were one story, adobe, with simple furnishings made in the area. Clothing fashions were those of Europe some fifty to eighty years before, transformed by local manufacture and custom. There was no glass. They were rich only in cattle, and in open land.

It was a life lived so far away from the rest of the world that it might as well have been alone on the planet: backed by empty mountains and desert, facing an empty sea.

When Jedediah Smith traveled overland from Missouri in 1826, the Mexican governor of California tried to kick him out of the state. But ten years later, when other Americans arrived to trade, they were welcomed. They brought with them various goods of modern Europe, and took away tallow and hides.

Some of the Americans who came to trade liked the look of the land, and stayed. They were welcomed in this as well. Learn Spanish, become a Catholic, marry a local girl, buy some land: more than one American and Englishman did just that, and became respected members of the community. Don Abel Stearns and Don John Forster (known better as "San Juan Capistrano" for his obsession with the old mission, which he bought after its secularization) did even better than that, and became rich.

All the Americans who came in contact with the Californians, even the most anti-Papist among them, came away impressed by their honesty, dignity, generosity, hospitality. When Edward Vischer visited Don Tomás Yorba, head of the most distinguished family in the area, he complimented Don Tomás on a horse that the don rode while seeing Vischer off his rancho; and as Vischer boarded his ship in San Diego the horse was ridden up to the dock and given to him, along with a message from Don Tomás asking him "to accept his beautiful bay as a present and a remembrance of California."

Cut off from the world, existing in the slow rhythms of cattle raising, the ranchos of Orange County gave their people a slow, pastoral, feudal life, dreamlike in its disconnection from Europe, from history, from time. For four generations the cycle of ranch existence made its simple round, from branding to branding. Little changed, and the dominant realities were the adobe homes, the hot sun in the clear blue sky, the beautiful horses, the cattle out on the open hillsides, on the great broad coastal plain. The few foreigners who arrived to stay were welcomed, taken in; the traders brought glass. They didn't make any difference to the Californians.

But then the United States declared war on Mexico, and conquered California along with the rest of the great Southwest. And then gold was discovered in the Sierra Nevada, and Americans flocked to San Francisco, crazed by a gold rush that has never stopped. History returned.

The cattle of the south were driven north to feed these people, and Los Angeles grew on the business. As Americans poured into southern California, the immensity of the Spanish and Mexican land grants gained immediate attention; they were rich prizes to be captured. The Treaty of Guadalupe Hidalgo, which ended the Mexican War, guaranteed the property rights of Mexican citizens in California; but that was just a treaty. Like the treaties the United States made with the Indian tribes, it didn't mean a thing. Two years later Congress passed a law that forced the rancheros to prove their titles, and the hunt was on.

The old rancheros were asked to provide documentation that there had never been any need for, in earlier times, and court cases concerning the ownership of the land took up to twenty years to settle. The rancheros' only assets were their land and their cattle, and most of the cattle died in the great drought of 1863–64. To pay their lawyers and their debts, in the fight for their land, the rancheros had to sell parcels of it off. And so win or lose the court fights, they lost the land.

By the 1870s all the land was owned by Americans, and was being rapidly subdivided to sell to the waves of new settlers.

And so all that—the cattle roaming the open land, the horsemen rounding them up, the adobe homes, the huge ranchos, and the archaic, provincial dignity of the lives of the people on them—all that went away.

...44

They land in Stockholm after a two-hour flight over the North Pole—just enough time to catch the in-flight movie *Star Virgin*. Once in the city they quickly decide that the Great Stagemaster in the Sky has shifted San Diego east and north to give them a surprise. Everyone speaks English, even. They eat at a McDonald's to confirm the impression and hold a conference in Sandy and Angela's hotel room to decide what to do next. Jim is for going north to the Arctic Circle and above, but no one else has much enthusiasm for the idea. "You can get reindeer steaks at Trader Joe's," Sandy tells him, "and snow on Mount Baldy. Midnight sun in the tanning parlor. No, I want to see someplace *different*."

"Well shoot," Humphrey says, "why don't we just go visit the Disneyland near Paris? That's bound to be different! We can walk around and note all the differences between it and the original Disneyland."

"The real Disneyland."

"The true Disneyland."

"The one and only and forevermore always the *best* Disneyland!"

Sandy nods. "Not a bad idea. But I've got a better one. We'll fly to Moscow."

"Moscow?"

"That's right. Get behind that Iron Curtain and see how the Russkies really live. It's bound to be different."

"It would be a challenge to the businessman," Humphrey says dreamily. "I'd have to do some shopping first."

Jim is in favor of the idea, he wants to see this Great Adversary that America has worked so hard to create and support. Angela is up for it.

So they go to Moscow. Well, sure. It reminds Humphrey of Toronto, his childhood home. Streets are clean. A lot of well-dressed people are out walking. Little untracked gas-engine cars roar about on the streets, which the travelers find delightfully quaint and noisy. At their hotel, recommended by the

Intourist Bureau at the airport, they ask where they can rent a car and are told they cannot. "We'll see about that," Humphrey declares darkly. His eyes gleam crazily. "Time for some private sector enterprise." He has smuggled a number of videocassettes in, and as soon as they've unpacked in their rooms he stuffs several in his jacket and goes out to flag a taxi. Half an hour later he is back, pockets crammed with rubles. "No problem. Asked my driver if he knew any-one interested, and of course he was. The cab drivers are the big black market dealers here. The bellboy wants some too."

He looks affronted as Jim and Sandy and Angela laugh themselves silly. "Well, it's not so funny. We've got a serious problem here, in that they won't let you exchange rubles for real money. So this is like Monopoly money, you know?"

Sandy's eyes light up. "So while we're playing the game we might as well move to Boardwalk, is that it?"

"Well, yeah, I guess so." This is against Humphrey's grain entirely, but he can't figure out why he should object.

"What's the most expensive hotel in town?" Sandy asks.

They end up just behind Red Square in an immense old hotel called the Rijeka, and take up a suite on the top floor. Their window view of Red Square, filtered though it is, is impressive. "What a set, eh?" Sandy orders champagne and caviar from room service, and when it arrives Humphrey goes to work on the hotel employees, who speak excellent English. It's actually a disadvantage for the employees in this case, as it allows Humphrey to work them over more completely. When they leave the gang is many rubles richer, and Humphrey marches about the room ecstatically quoting long extempore passages from *Acres of Diamonds* in between attacks on the caviar, waving fistfuls of rubles in each hand.

They leave the hotel and go touristing, all ready to explore Red Square and say hello to Lenin and infiltrate the Kremlin and buy out GUM and do all the other great American-in-Moscow activities. In GUM they stand in a basement sale with hundreds of Russian women, and shout to each other across the crowds; they're a head and more taller than any of the locals there. Funny. The clothes on sale are remarkably gauche and Angela falls in love with several outfits. Back out-side Humphrey flags a taxi and they sing "America the Beautiful" over Sandy's McCarthyite rap, "Better dead—than red, yeah better dead—than red."

They instruct their stoical driver to take them into the residential areas of the city, where great applexes are grouped around green parks. Up on a hill they figure they're in Party territory, everything's upscale as always in the hill districts of a city. And in fact they reach one cul-de-sac with a view over much of Moscow, and stare about them amazed. Sandy sputters: "Why it's—it's—it's *condomundo*! It's just like—*just like*—" and they all pitch in:

"Orange County!"

Total collapse. They must return immediately to the hotel and order more champagne. OC has conquered the world. "James Utt would be proud," Jim says solemnly.

As soon as they can spend all Humphrey's rubles they're gone. "We still haven't seen anything *different*," Sandy complains.

"The Pyramids," Jim suggests. "See how it all began."

They fly to Cairo. The airport is in a desert of pure sand, even the Mojave can't compare to it. At the baggage collection they're met by an enterprising "agent of Egyptian tourist police" who is happy to offer them all of his private tourist firm's tours. He is smooth, but hasn't reckoned on Humphrey, who takes note of the many rival agencies in a long string of booths next to the agent's, and uses that fact to grind the man until he's sweating. Sandy, Angela, and Jim just keep standing up and sitting back down on Humphrey's orders, depending on how the negotiations are going. In the end they have a free ride to a big hotel on the Nile offering half-price rooms, and transport to Giza for quarterprice tours and free tickets to the sound and light show here. The agent is punch-drunk by the time they leave, he looks like he's been mugged.

Cairo turns out to be the same color as the desert. The buildings, the trees, the billboards, even the sky, all are the same dust color. The Nile Hilton, across the river, has been painted turquoise to combat the monochrome, but the turquoise has turned sand-colored as well. Only the old snake river itself achieves a certain dusty dark blue.

When they leave the funky old freeway and hit the streets they see that the city is terrifically densepacked. Most of the buildings are tenements. Every street is stopped up by cars and pedestrians; they can't believe how many people are actually *walking*. Their hotel, old and dusty, is a welcome refuge. They chatter with excitement as they unpack and wait for the tour guide and driver to arrive and take them to Giza. Humphrey goes down to investigate currency exchange rates and comes back excited; there's an official rate, a tourist rate, various black market rates, and some theft rates, designed to tempt greedy people into exposing lots of cash. With some manipulation of this market Humphrey figures he can generate hundreds of Egyptian pounds, and he is about to start with the hotel staff when their guide arrives. Off they go to the Pyramids of Giza.

The Pyramids are to the west, in a morass of hotels and shops. When they get out of their car they are inundated by street merchants and the guide can't beat them away, especially with Humphrey asking about wholesale deals and the like. They dismiss their guide for saying "Thegreatandancientpyramidsof-Giza" once too often, and walk up to the broad stone deck between pyramids one and two.

"Gee, they're not all that big, are they?" says Humphrey. "Our office building is bigger."

"You have to remember they were built by hand," Jim objects, resisting a certain disappointment that he too feels.

Sandy sees a chance to kid him a bit and chimes in with Humphrey. "Man they're nowhere near as big as South Coast Plaza. They're not even as big as Irvine City Hall."

"Kind of like the Matterhorn at Disneyland," Humphrey says. "Only not as pretty."

Jim is outraged. He gets even more distressed when he finds out no one is allowed to climb the Pyramids anymore. "I can't believe it!"

"Unacceptable," Sandy agrees. "Let's try the backside." They find guards on all sides of it, however. Jim is distraught. Their affronted guide retrieves them; it's time for the sound and light show, apparently a major spectacle. Sunset arrives, and with it busloads of tourists to see the show.

Tonight's show is in English, unfortunately. Between great sweeps of movie soundtrack romanticism a booming voice cracks out of twenty hidden speakers with a pomposity utterly unballasted by factual content. "THE PYRAMIDS . . . HAVE CONQUERED . . . TIME." The laser lights playing across the Pyramids and the Sphinx use the latest in pop concert technology and aesthetics, including a star cathedral effect, some satellite beaming down thick cylinders of light, yellow, green, blue, red, bathing the whole area in a lased glow. Amazing display. "Never let them tell you there haven't been useful spin-offs from the space defense technology," Sandy growls.

The booming voice carries on, more fatuous by the second. Angela leans over Sandy to whisper heavily to them all, "I am the Great and Powerful Wizard of Oz," and with the vocal style of the narrator pegged they can't restrain themselves, they get more hysterical at every sentence, and they're attracting a lot of irritated looks from the reverent tourists seated around them. Well, to be obnoxious is un-Californian, so they sit up rigidly and nod their heads in approval at each new absurdity, only giggling in little pressure breakthroughs. But on the drive back they simply roll on the seats and howl. Their guide is mystified.

But that night—that night, after the others have retired—that night, Jim McPherson wanders down to the hotel bar. He feels unsettled, dissatisfied. They aren't doing the Old World justice, he knows that. Going to see the Pyramids turned into bad pop video; that isn't the way to do it.

The hotel bar is closed. The clerk recommends McDonald's, then when she better understands Jim's desires, the Cairo Sheraton, just a few blocks away. It's simple to get there, she says, and Jim walks out into the dry, warm night air without a map.

There's a desert wind blowing. Smell of dust, static cling. Neon scrawls of Arabic script flicker over green pools of light that spill out into the dark streets. A few pedestrians, hardly any cars. From one shop comes the pungent smell of roasting spiced lamb, from another the quarter-tone ululations of a radio singer. Men in caftans are out doing the night business. Hardly anyone glances at Jim, he feels curiously accepted, part of the scene. It's peaceful in a way, the bustle is half-paced and relaxed. Men sit in open cafes over games that look a bit like dominos, smoking from giant hookahs whose bowls seem to contain chunks of glowing red charcoal. What are they smoking? Sandy would want to inquire, analyze a chunk for chemical clues; Humphrey would want to buy a bushel just in case. Jim just looks and passes on, feeling a ghost. The wailing music is eerie. Arab voices in the street are musical too, especially when relaxed like this. A cab driver plays the fanfare from "Finlandia" on his horn; all the cabbies here use that rhythm.

It occurs to Jim that he should have reached the Sheraton by now. It's on the Nile and shouldn't be that hard to find. But where, exactly, is the Nile? He turns toward it and walks on. Auto mechanics work on a car jacked up right in the street. Policemen stay in pairs, carry submachine guns. Jim seems to have gotten into a poorer neighborhood, somehow. Has he gotten his orientation off by ninety degrees, perhaps? He turns again.

The neighborhood gets poorer yet. Down one alley he can see the tower of the Sheraton, so he is no longer lost and all at once he pays real attention to what lies around him.

The street is flanked by four-story concrete tenements.
Doors are open to the night breeze.
Inside, oil lamps flicker over mattresses on the floor.
A stove.
Each family or clan has one room.
Ten faces in a doorway, eyes bright.
Other families sleep on the sidewalks outside.
Their clothing is sand-colored. A torn caftan hood.
You live here, too.
A man in a cardboard box lifts a little girl for Jim's inspection.

Jim retreats. He thinks again, returns, hands the man a five-pound note. Five pounds. And he retreats. Off into the narrow alleys, he's lost sight of the Sheraton and can't recall where it was. Arms are extended out of piles of darkness, the cupped palms light in the gloom, the eyeballs part of the walls. It's all palpably real, and he is there, he is right there in it. He picks up the pace, hurries past with his head held up, past the hands, all the hands.

He makes it to the Sheraton. But past the guards, in the big lobby, which could be the lobby of any luxury hotel anywhere, he experiences a shiver of revulsion. The opulence is dropped on the neighborhood like a spaceship on an anthill. "There are people out there," he says to no one. With a shock he recalls the title of Fugard's play: *People Are Living There*. So that's what he meant. . . .

He leaves, forces himself to return to the street of beggars. He forces himself to look at the people there. This, he thinks. This man, this woman, this infant. This is the world. This is the real world. He scuffs hard at the sidewalk, feels his breath go ragged. He doesn't know what he's feeling; he's never felt it before. He just watches.

Faces in the open doors, people sitting on the floor. Looking back at him.

This moment seems never to end—this moment does not end—but has its existence afterward inside Jim, in a little pattern of neurons, synapses, axons. Strange how that works.

Next morning he says, "Let's leave. I don't like it here."

...45

So they fly to Crete, another of Jim's ideas. "We'll give you one more chance, Jimbo. ..." They land at Heraklion, eat at Jack-in-the-Box, rent a Nissan at the Avis counter. Off to Knossos, a gaily painted reconstruction of a Minoan palace. It's quite crowded, and just the slightest bit reminiscent of the Pyramids.

Jim is disappointed, frustrated. "Damn it," he says, "give me that map."

Sandy hands him the Avis map of the island. Minoan ruins are marked by a double axe, Greek ruins by a broken column. Jim looks for broken columns, understanding already that on this island Minoan ruins are first-class ruins, Greek ruins are second-class ruins. Find one away from towns, at the end of a secondary road, on the sea if possible. "Whoah." Several fit all the criteria. His mood lifts a bit. He picks one at random. "Humphrey, drive us to the very end of the island."

"Right ho. Gas is expensive here, remember."

"Drive!"

"Right ho. Where are we headed?"

"Itanos."

Sandy laughs. "World famous, eh Jim?"

"Exactly not. The Pyramids are world famous. Knossos is world famous. Red Square is world famous."

"Point taken. Itanos it is. What's there?"

"I don't have the slightest idea."

So they drive east, along the northern coast of Crete.

It strikes them all at the same time that the land looks just like southern California—to the extent that they know what southern California looks like, that is. Like the middle section of Camp Pendleton. Rocky dry scrubland, rising out of a fine blue sea. Dry riverbeds. Bare bouldery hilltops. Some tall mountains inland. "The first wave of American settlers always called southern

California Mediterranean, when they tried to tell the people back east what it was like," Jim says slowly, staring out the window. "You can see why."

It's the same land, the same landscape; but look how the Greeks have used theirs.

Scrub hills.

Scattered villages. Concrete blocks, whitewashed. Flowers.

Untidy places, but not poor; Jim's ap is smaller than any home here.

Olive groves cover the gentler hills.

Gnarled old trees, crooked arms, silver-green fingers.

The road is spotted with black oily circles: crushed olives.

Do you live here?

Blue-domed, whitewashed church, there on the hilltop. Inconvenient!

An orange grove. . . .

"This is how it looked," Jim says quietly. And his friends listen to him, they stare out the windows.

They stop in at a village store and buy yogurt, feta cheese, bread, olives, oranges, a salami, retsina, and ouzo, from a very friendly woman who has not a single word of English. After Egypt's ceaseless venality her friendliness pleases them no end.

Late in the day they drive down one last blacktop ribbon of road, which follows a dry streambed to the sea.

Scrub hills flank them on both sides.

Hills breaking off in the dark blue sea.

A beach, divided into two by a knoll sitting in a small bay.

The knoll is covered with ruins.

The landscape is empty, abandoned. Nothing but the ruins, the scrub.

"My God!" Jim jumps out of the car. His recurrent dream, walking about in some great ruin of the past—ever since the effort to find El Modena Elementary School, it's been haunting him. On waking he always scoffed. No site exists without fences, ticket booths, information plaques, guides, visiting hours, lines, roped-off areas, snack bars, hordes of tourists milling around and wondering what the fuss was about; isn't that right?

But here they are. He pushes through shrubs, climbs a tumble of broken blocks, stands in the shattered entrance of an ancient church. Cruciform floor plan, altar against the back wall, which is dug into the knoll. Columns rolled against the walls.

The others appear. "Look," Jim says. "The church is probably Byzantine, but when they built it they used the materials at hand. The columns are probably Roman, maybe Greek. The big blocks in the walls that are all spongy, those are probably Minoan. Cut two thousand years before the church was built."

Sandy nods, grinning. "And look at the stone in the doorway. They had a locking post on the door, and as it swung open it scraped this curve here. Perfect semicircle." He laughs the Sandy laugh, a stutter of pure delight.

Humphrey and Angela walk to the north side of the knoll, investigating what looks like a small fortress, its walls intact. "Well preserved," Sandy remarks. "It's probably Venetian," Jim says. "A thousand years newer than the church."

"Man, I can't really grasp these time scales, Jimbo."

"Neither can I."

On the beach below them are a pair of decrepit boats, pulled onto the sand. One appears to have an outboard motor under a tarp. From their vantage on the knoll they can see far out to sea, and back inland. Emptiness everywhere; the land deserted, the Aegean a blank plate.

"Let's camp here tonight," Jim suggests. "Two can sleep in the car, and two on our beach towels in the sand. We can eat the rest of the lunch food."

It's late and they've spent the day traveling; they all like the plan.

The sun nears the hills to the west as they bring the food up to the ruined church. The slightly hazy evening light brings out the orange in the rock, and the entire knoll turns deep apricot. Frilly pink herringbone clouds are pasted to the sky. The fallen blocks on the church entryway make perfect stools, tables, backrests.

They eat. The food and drink have vivid tastes. There's a group of goats on the hillside to the south of them. Sandy holds his hand up to the light, framing a pair of black rams. "Back in the Bronze Age."

After dinner they sit back and watch the florid twilight clouds as the light leaks away from the land. An abandoned, still, dusky landscape. "Tell us about this place, Jim," Angela says.

"Well, the back of the map has a few sentences about it, and that's all I know, really. It began as a Minoan town, around 2500 B.C. Then it was occupied by the Greeks, the Romans, and the Byzantines. Under the Greeks it was an independent city-state and coined its own money. It was abandoned around either 900 A.D. or 1500 A.D., because of earthquakes."

"Only six hundred years' difference," Sandy says. "My Lord, the time scales!"

"Immense," Jim says. "We can't imagine them. Especially not Californians."

Sandy takes this as a challenge. "Can too!"

"Cannot!"

"Can too!"

About five reps of that, and Sandy says, "Okay, try this. We'll go backwards from now, generation by generation. Thirty-three years per generation. You tell us what they were doing, I'll keep count."

"Okay, let's try it."

"Last generation?"

"Part of Greece."

Sandy makes a mark in the dirt between flagstones. "Before that?"

"Same."

Five generations go by like that. Jim has his eyes squeezed shut, he's concentrating, trying to recall Cretan history from the guidebooks, his history texts back home. "Okay, this guy saw Crete deeded over from Turkey to Greece. Before him, under the Turks."

"And his parents?"

"Under the Turks." They repeat these two sentences over and over, slowly, as if completing some ritual, so that Jim can keep track of the years. Sixteen times! "That's one big Thanksgiving," Humphrey mutters.

"What's that?"

"Lot of Turkey."

Then Jim says, "Okay. Now the Venetians."

So the response changes. "And their parents?" "Venetian." Ten times. At which point Jim adds, "We've just now reached the end of Itanos, by the way. The end of this city."

They laugh at that. And move to the Byzantines. Seven times Jim answers with that. Then: "The Arabs. Saracen Arabs, from Spain. Bloody times." Four generations under the Arabs. Then it's back to the Byzantines, to the times when the church before them was functioning, holding services, having its doorsill scraped by the door's locking post, again and again. Fifteen times Jim answers "Byzantine," eyes screwed shut.

"And their parents?"

"In Itanos. Independent city-state, Greek in nature."

"Call it Itanos. And their parents?"

"Itanos."

Twenty-six times they repeat the litany, Sandy keeping the pace slow and measured. At this point none of them can really believe it.

"Dorian Greeks." After a few more: "Mycenaean Greeks. Time of the Trojan War."

"So this generation could have gone to Troy?"

"Yes." And on it goes, for eight generations. Sandy's shifting to get fresh dirt to scratch. Then: "Earthquakes brought down the Minoan palaces for the last time. This generation felt them."

"Minoan! And their parents?"

"Minoan." And here they fall into a slow singsong, they know they've caught the rhythm of something deep, something fundamental. Forty times Sandy asks "And their parents?" and Jim answers "Minoan," until their voices creak with the repetition.

And finally Jim opens his eyes, looks around as if seeing it all for the first time. "This generation, it was a group of friends, and they came here in boats. There was nothing here. They were fishermen, and stopped here on fishing trips. This hill was probably fifty feet inland, behind a wide beach. Their homes down near the palace at Zakros were getting crowded, they probably lived with their parents, and they were always up here fishing anyway, so they decided to take the wives and kids and move up here together. A group of friends, they all knew each other, they were having a good time all on their own, with their kids, and this whole valley for the taking. They built lean-tos at first, then started cutting the soft stone." Jim runs his hand over the porous Minoan block he is leaning against. Looks at Sandy curiously. "Well?"

Sandy nods, says softly, "So we can imagine it."

"I guess so."

Sandy counts his marks. "A hundred thirty-seven generations."

They sit. The moon rises. Low broken clouds scud in from the west, fly under the moon, dash its light here and there. Broken walls, tumbled blocks. A history as long as that; and now the land, empty again.

Except headlights appear on the road inland. Their beams lance far over the dark land, fan across it as they turn onto the side road to Itanos. The group falls silent. The headlights go right down to the beach below them. Car doors slam, cheery Greek voices chatter. A Coleman lantern is lit; its harsh glow washes the beach, and the Greeks go to work on the two old boats. "Fishermen!" Sandy whispers.

After leisurely preparations the boats are launched, their motors started. What a racket! They putter out of the bay and to sea, lanterns hung from their bows. After a time they're only stars on the water's flat surface, far out to sea. "Night fishing," Jim says. "Octopus and squid."

Sandy and Angela find a spot to lie down and sleep. Humphrey returns to the car. Jim climbs to the top of the knoll and watches the boats at sea, the moon and its flying clouds, the rough town map below him, defined by its tumbledown walls. Again he's filled with some feeling he can't name, some complex of feelings. "The land," he says, speaking to the Aegean. "It's not abandoned after all. Fishing, goat keeping, some kind of agriculture on the other side of the valley. Empty-looking, but used as much as scrubland can be. After all these many years." He tries to imagine the amount of human suffering contained in a hundred and thirty-seven generations, the disappointments, illnesses, deaths. Generation after generation into dust. Or the myriad joys: how many festivals, parties, weddings, love trysts, in this little city-state? How often had someone sat on this knoll through a moony night, watching clouds scud by and thinking about the world? Oh, it makes him shiver to think of it! It's a hilltop filled with spirits, and they're all inside him.

He tries to imagine someone sitting on top of Saddleback, to look across the empty plain of OC. Ah, impossible. Unimaginable.

How could history have coursed so differently for these two dry coasts? It's as if they're not part of the same history, they are separated by such a great chasm; how to make any mental juncture? Are they different planets, somehow? It is too strange, too strange. Something has gone wrong back home in his country.

He sits there through the night, dozing once, waking to the boats puttering back in, dozing again. He dreams of rams and fallen walls, of his father and licorice sticks, of a bright lantern under a cloudy moon.

He wakes to a dawn as pink as the sunset was orange, a woven texture of cloud over him. Pink on blue. In the bay below Angela is swimming lazily. She stands on the smooth pebble bottom and walks out of the water, wet, sleek, supple. It's the dawn of the world.

A little later a pickup truck drives slowly down the road, honking its horn. A horde of sheep and goats come tumbling out of the hills at this signal, *baa*ing and clanging their bells. Feeding time! Far up the valley someone is burning trash.

Well, Angela has to be back to work in a couple of days, and so they have to start back home. Reluctantly they pack up. Jim takes a last walk over the site. He surveys the scene from his hilltop. Something about this place . . . "They're part of the land, it's not abandoned. The story's not over here. It'll go on as long as anything else." Humphrey honks. Time to go. "Ah, California. . . ."

...46

... The first wave of American settlers trickled in by wagon from New Mexico, or came around the Horn in ships, or rode down from San Francisco after trying their luck in the gold rush. There weren't very many of them. The first new town, Anaheim, was begun by a small group of Germans determined to grow grapes for wine. They arrived from San Francisco in 1859, and there were only a hundred or two of them. The town was platted in the middle of open cattle range, and so they put up a willow pole fence that took root and became a living wall of trees, a rectangle with four gates in it, one on each side. They dug a ditch five miles long to obtain water from the Santa Ana River. And they grew grapes.

The other towns followed quickly after the partitioning of the great ranchos. When the ranchos were broken up and sold off, the new owners made advertisements to sell the land, and started towns from scratch.

Some of the landowners were interested in the new ideas of social organization circulating at the time, and several of the towns began as utopian efforts in communalism: the Germans in Anaheim were a cooperative, the Quakers helped to found El Modena on Society principles, Garden Grove began as a temperance community, and Westminster was a religious commune. Later the Polish group led by the Modjeskas settled in Anaheim and began a separate little utopia, although it fell apart almost at once. El Toro was founded by some English, who made it another outpost of the Empire, celebrating Queen Victoria's birthday and forming the first polo team in America: the British notion of utopia.

When the Southern Pacific Railroad extended from Los Angeles to Anaheim, a boom began that lasted through the 1870s. Santa Ana was founded, with lots sold at twenty to forty dollars apiece, when they weren't given away. Two years later there were fifty houses erected in the town. East of Santa Ana, Tustin was founded by Columbus Tustin, and the rivalry between the two new villages for the spur rail line from Anaheim was intense. When Santa Ana won the spur,

Tustin was destined to remain a village for many years, while Santa Ana went on to become the county seat.

Orange was founded by Andrew Glassell and Alfred Chapman, two lawyers who were active in the rancho-partitioning lawsuits, thus becoming rich in both land and money. The town began with sixty ten-acre lots, surrounding a forty-acre townsite.

Southwest of these towns, on the coast, the lumbermen James and Robert McFadden built a landing that became an important point for shipping. The wharf was known as McFadden's Landing, and the town that grew around it was called Newport. The McFaddens had bought the land from the state for a dollar an acre.

Soon towns had sprung up everywhere across the county. In Laguna Beach because of the pretty bay. In El Modena because there was good land for vineyards, and the water from Santiago Creek. In Fullerton because the train line passed that way. And so on. Developers bought pieces of the ranchos, set out some streets, held a big party and brought out some of the crowds arriving in Los Angeles for a free lunch and a sales pitch. Sometimes it worked, sometimes it didn't. Towns like Yorba, Hewes Park, McPherson, Fairview, Olinda, Saint James, Atwood, Carlton, Catalina-on-the-Main, and Smeltzer, didn't last much longer than their opening days. Others, like Buena Park, Capistrano Beach, Villa Park, Placentia, Huntington Beach, Corona del Mar, and Costa Mesa, survived and grew.

In 1887 this growth was accelerated when the Santa Fe Railroad completed a line across the continent to Los Angeles and immediately began a rate war with the Southern Pacific, which had been the only line. Fares that had been $125 from Omaha plunged to a rate war special of $1 before leveling off at around $25 for a year or two. The trickle of settlers became a small flood, and sixty towns were founded in forty years.

The only area of Orange County that did not experience this blossoming of towns was the great landholding of James Irvine. Irvine came penniless from England to San Francisco during the gold rush, and engaged in land speculation in the city until he was rich. Then he and his partners moved to southern California, and they bought the entirety of the old Ranchos San Joaquín and Lomas de Santiago, which meant that, after Irvine bought out his partners, he owned one-fifth of all the land in Orange County, in a broad band that extended from the ocean far into the Santa Ana Mountains. His land crossed all the possible train routes from Los Angeles to San Diego, and he was powerful enough to hold off the Southern Pacific Railroad, which could be said of no one else in the state; his ranchers fought off forced efforts by the Southern Pacific construction crews to push a line through, and he granted permission of passage to the Santa Fe Railroad just so he could balk Southern Pacific for good.

The Irvine land itself was kept free of new towns, and after a decade or two of sheep ranching it was cultivated, in hay, wheat, oats, alfalfa, barley, and lima beans, and much later in orange groves. For a hundred years the marked distinction between the heavily developed northwestern half of Orange County, and the nearly empty southeastern half, was due to the 172 square miles of the Irvine Ranch, and Irvine and his heirs' policy of keeping the land free.

In 1889 the county of Orange was carved out of Los Angeles County. With the help of some money slipped to legislators in Sacramento, the border was set at Coyote Creek rather than the San Gabriel River, so that when it came time to choose the county seat, Santa Ana was more central and was chosen over Anaheim. Anaheim's citizens were very upset.

So the little towns grew, and the farms around them. Despite all the feverish land speculation and real estate development going on, the actual number of people involved was not great. The largest towns, Santa Ana and Anaheim, had populations of only a few thousand, and the newer towns were much smaller than that. Between each town were miles of open land, covered by farmland or the old range, head high in mustard. The roads were few, the little rail systems even fewer. Under the constant sun there was an ease to life that drew people from the east, but in small waves that grew very slowly in size. Publicists based in Los Angeles trumpeted the virtues of southern California; it was America's own Mediterranean, the golden land by the sea. The new orange groves contributed to that image, and orange growing was sold as a middle-class agriculture, more socially and aesthetically pleasing than the giant isolated wheat and corn farms of the Midwest. And perhaps it was so, at first; though many a man found himself working his grove and another job as well, to pay the grove off.

An American life of Mediterranean ease: perhaps. Perhaps. But there were disasters, too. There were floods; once it rained every day for a month, and the entire plain, from the mountains to the sea, was covered with water. All the new adobe buildings of Anaheim were melted back to mud. And once there was an outbreak of smallpox that finished off the last of the Indians at San Juan Capistrano, which remained as a silent remnant of the mission past. And the crops failed often; brought in from afar and usually planted in monocultural style, the grapes, the walnuts, and even the oranges suffered from blights that killed thousands and thousands of plants.

But by and large it was a peaceful life here, at the Victorian end of the frontier. Under the hot sun Americans from the East arrived and started up new lives, and most were happy with the results. The years passed and new settlers kept arriving and starting little towns; but it was a big land and they were accommodated without much change or sign of their arrival; they disappeared into the groves, and life went on.

The new century arrived, and the sun-drenched life by the sea fell into a pattern that it seemed would never end. In 1905 the young Walter Johnson, pitching for Fullerton High School, struck out all twenty-seven batters in a game with Santa Ana High. In 1911 Barney Oldfield raced his car with a plane, and won. In 1912 Glenn Martin flew a plane he had built himself from Newport to Catalina, the longest flight over water ever. In fact you could say that Martin began the aeronautics industry in Orange County, by building a plane in a barn. But no one could guess what would come of that kind of ingenuity, that pleasure taken in the possibilities of the mechanical. At that time it, like life itself, seemed a marvelous game, played in the midst of a prosperous, sunny peace.

And all that—and all that—and all of that—

All that went away.

Back in OC Jim can't shake a feeling of uneasiness. It's as if somewhere the program and the magnetic field keeping him on his particular track have been disarranged, fallen into some awful loop that keeps repeating over and over.

And in fact he falls into the habit of tracking about for several hours each day, all his free time spent in a big circle pattern on the freeways, Newport to Riverside to San Gabriel to San Diego to Santa Ana to Trabuco to Garden Grove to Newport, and so on. While he stares out the window looking down at his hometown. Around and around the freeways he goes, stuck in a loop program that resembles a debugging search pattern caught by a bug itself. Software going bad.

Once he stops to cruise through South Coast Plaza.

Twelve department stores: Bullock's, Penney, Saks, Sears, KlothesAG, J. Magnin's, I. Magnin's, Ward's, Palazzo, Robinson's, Buffum's, Neiman-Marcus.

Three hundred smaller shops, restaurants, video theaters, game parlors, galleries ...

A poem is a laundry list.

You wear your culture all over you.

Chrome, and thick pile carpets.

Mirrors everywhere, replicating the displays to infinity.

Is that an eye I see in there?

Escalators, elevators, half-floors of glass, fountains.

Lots of plants. Most are real, from the tropics. Hothouse blooms.

Spectrum bends, rack after rack after (mirrored) rack.

Entering Bullock's, Magnin's, Saks: thirteen counters of perfume each.

Perfume! Earrings, scarves, necklaces, nylons, stationery, chrome columns,
    blouse racks, sportswear, shoes—
You complete the list (every day).

Jim walks through this place untracked, his uneasiness bouncing back from
every mirror, every glossy leaf and fabric. The memory of his night in Egypt
is overlaid on his sight like the head's-up display of a fighter pilot's helmet. IR
images in a faint green wash: of beggars in Cairo, too poor even to live in the
jammed miserable tenements around them. How many people could live in
a structure like SCP? The luxury surrounding him, he thinks, is a deliberate,
bald-faced denial of the reality of the world. A group hallucination shared by
everyone in America.

Jim wanders this maze, past the sleepwalkers and the security police, until
he has to sit down. Disoriented, dizzy, he might even be sick. Some mall kids
hanging out by the video rental window stare at him curiously, suspecting an
OD. They're right about that, Jim thinks dully. I have ODed on South Coast
Plaza. The kids stand there hoping for some theatrics. Jim disappoints them by
getting up and walking out under his own power. His damaged autopilot gets
him through the maze of escalators and entry levels to the parking lot, to his
car.

He calls Arthur. "Please, Arthur, give me some work. Is anything ready to go?"

"Yeah, as a matter of fact there is. Can you do it tonight?"

"Yes." And Jim feels immense relief that he can *act* on this feeling of revulsion.

That night he joins Arthur enthusiastically as they stay up all night to arrange a successful strike against Airspace Technology Corporation, which
makes parts for the orbiting nuclear reactors that provide the old space-based
chemical lasers with their power. Off to the rendezvous at Lewis and Greentree,
in the little warehouse parking lot; the same men load the boxes into Arthur's
car; and they're off to San Juan Hot Springs Industrial Park. Despite security
precautions that include fence-top heat-seeking missiles, the strike succeeds;
in Airspace Tech's main production plant, all that was composite has fallen
apart. . . .

But the next morning, back in his ap, exhausted to emptiness, Jim has to
admit that the operation hasn't changed all that much for him. He's still sitting
in his little ap under the freeway looking around. Nothing in it soothes him.
He's heard his music too often. He's read all the books. The orange crate labels
mock him. He's looked at the maps till he knows them by heart, he's seen all
the videos, he's scanned every program in the history of the world. His home is
a trap, the complex and massively articulated trap of his self. He has to escape;

he looks around the dusty disorderly room, with its treasured shaft of nine A.M. sunlight, and wonders how he ever stood it.

The phone rings. It's Hana. "How are you?" she says.

"Okay! Hey, I'm glad you called! You want to come down to my place for dinner tonight?"

"Sure."

And the flood of relief that fills him has other components in it he can't tag so readily; it's the kind of pleasure he gets when Tash or Abe give him a call to arrange something, the sense that one of his good friends reciprocates his regard, and will actually take the trouble to initiate a get-together, something that is usually left for Jim to do.

So he goes out and buys spaghetti and the materials for the sauce and a salad. A bottle of Chianti. Back home for some hapless, hopeless attempts to clean the place, or at least order it a little.

Hana shows up around seven.

"I'm really glad you called," Jim says, stirring the spaghetti sauce vigorously.

"Well, it's been a while." She's sitting at the kitchen table, staring past him at the floor, throwing her sentences out casually. Attack of shyness, it seems. Her black hair as tangled as ever.

"I—I think I'm losing it, somehow," Jim says, surprising them both. "This trip, it just reinforced everything I was feeling before!" And it all spills out of him in a rush, Hana glancing up now and then as he rattles on about Cairo and Crete and California. He mixes his account of them so that it must be impossible for her to figure out which place he's talking about, but she doesn't interrupt until a desperate edge tears his voice. Then she stands, briefly, puts a hand to his arm. This is so unlike her that Jim is struck dumb.

"I know what you mean," she says. "But look. Your dinner's almost ready, and you shouldn't eat when you're upset."

"I'd starve if I didn't."

But he pours the spaghetti into the colander with a wry grin, feeling a bit more relaxed already. There's something new floating in the steam between them, and he likes it. As they sit down to eat he goes and puts on one of his amalgamations of classical music, and they eat.

"What's the music?" Hana asks after a while.

"I've taken all the slow movements from Beethoven's five late string quartets, and also the slow movement from the *Hammerklavier* Sonata as the center-piece. It has a very serene effect—"

"Wait a minute. You mean all these movements come from different quartets?"

"Yeah, but they're unified by a similar style and—"

She is laughing fit to burst. "What a terrible idea! Ha, ha, ha, ha! . . . Why did you do that?"

"Well." Jim thinks. "I found when I put on the late quartets I was usually doing it to hear the slow movements. It's for a mood I have that I like to, I don't know. Soundtrack, or reinforce, or transform into something higher."

"You've got to be kidding, Jim! You know perfectly well Beethoven would cringe at the very idea." She laughs at him. "Each quartet is a whole experience, right? You're cutting out all the other parts of them! Come on. Go put on one of them complete. Choose the one you like best."

"Well, that's not so easy," Jim says as he goes to the old CD console. "It's odd. Sullivan says in his book on Beethoven that opus 131 is by far the greatest of them, with its seven movements and the spacy opener and so on."

"Why should that matter to you?"

"What Sullivan says? Well, I don't know . . . I guess I get a lot of my ideas out of books. And Sullivan's is one of the best biographies in the world."

"And so you accepted his judgment."

"That's right. At first, anyway. But finally I admitted to myself that I prefer opus 132. Beethoven wrote it after recovering from a serious illness, and the slow movement is a thanksgiving."

"Okay, but let's hear the whole thing."

Jim sticks in the CD of the LaSalle Quartet performance, and they listen to it as they finish dinner. "How you could pass on this part?" Hana says during the final movement.

"I don't know."

After dinner she wanders his ap and looks at things. She inspects the framed orange crate labels with her nose about an inch from their surfaces. "These are really nice." In his bedroom she stops and laughs. "These maps! They're great! Where did you get them?"

Jim explains, happy to talk about them. Hana admires the Thomas Brothers' solution to the four-color map problem. Then she notices the video cameras in the corners where walls meet ceiling; she wrinkles her nose, shudders. Back into the living room, where she goes over the bookcase volume by volume, and they talk about the books, and all manner of things.

She notices the computer on Jim's battered old sixth-grade desk, and the piles of printout beside it. "So is this the poetry, then? Do I get to read some?"

"Oh no, no," Jim says, rushing to the desk as if to hide the stuff. "I mean, not yet, anyway. I haven't got any of it in final form, and, well, you know. . . ."

Hana frowns, shrugs.

They sit on the bamboo-and-vinyl couch and talk about other matters. Then suddenly she's standing and looking at the floor. "Time to go, I have to work tomorrow." And she's off. Jim walks her to her car.

Back in his ap he looks around, sighs. There at the desk, all those feeble half-poems lying there, broken-backed and abandoned. . . . He compares his work habits to Hana's and he is ashamed of his laziness, his lack of discipline, his amateurishness. Waiting for inspiration—such nonsense. It really is stupid. He doesn't even like to think about his poetry anymore. He's an activist in the re-sistance, it's time for praxis now rather than words, and he only writes when he has the time, the inclination. It's different for him now.

But he doesn't really believe that. He knows it's laziness. And Hana—how is he ever going to show her any of his work? It just isn't good enough; he doesn't want her put off by his lack of talent. He's ashamed of it. He identifies the feel-ing and that makes him feel even worse. Isn't this his work, his real work?

...48

The pace never slackens for Lucy McPherson; on the contrary, it seems there's a little more to do every day. One morning she wakes up alone. Dennis is off in Washington and Lucy's been up later than usual the night before watching the video, and now she's slept right through her alarm. Late from the word go. She hustles out without breakfast, down to the church, gets the office opened and starts the day's opening round of calls. The organizational routine ticks off fairly well. The fund-raising is more problematic. Then it's down to Leisure World for a too-brief visit with Tom. Tom looks worse than usual, complains of coming down with a cold. He listens to Lucy's associational rattle of news with his eyes, nodding occasionally.

"How's Jim?" he says.

"Okay, I guess. I haven't seen him much in the last month. He and Dennis . . ." She sighs. "Hasn't he been down to see you?"

"Not for a while."

"I'll tell him to come."

Tom smiles, eyes closed. He looks so old today, Lucy thinks. "Don't pester the boy, Lucy. I think he's having a hard time."

"Well, there's no reason for it. And no reason he can't come down here once in a while."

Tom shakes his head, smiles again. "I do enjoy it."

Then it's back on the freeway, to an early lunch with her study group. And back to the office, back to the fund-raising. Lillian comes in at two and they work together at it. Lucy was flagging, but now she picks up; it's more fun with Lillian there, someone to talk to.

"Well, he did it again," Lillian says after looking around conspiratorially.

"Reverend Strong?"

"Yep. Right at the end of class." Lillian is in the church's little confirmation class, which the reverend teaches on Thursday evenings.

"Better the end than the beginning."

Lillian laughs. "Less people listening, I know. But still, it isn't fair! It isn't the poor people's fault if they're poor, is it?"

"I don't think so," Lucy says slowly. She remembers Anastasia; got to visit her again next week. "Sometimes, though, you wonder. . . . Well, you can see where Reverend Strong gets his ideas."

Lillian nods. The lesson last week was based on the parable of the prodigal son. Why, the reverend demanded, should God value the prodigal son more than the one who had been faithful all along? This was clearly unfair, and the reverend spent over half an hour discussing the problems in the Greek text and the likelihood of a mistranslation from the original Armenian dialect. "So that by the end of it," Lillian says with a laugh, "he was basically saying that the Bible had got it backwards!"

"You're kidding."

"No. He said that it was the elder son who would always be God's favorite, for never having strayed away. The ones who stray can't be trusted, he said. You can forgive them but you can't trust them."

Lucy shakes her head. The parables—some of them are just too ambiguous. The prodigal son story never seemed quite fair to the elder son, it's true, and as for the parable of the talents . . . well, the way the reverend can *use* these stories! She finds it hard to think about them. And these are New Testament stories, too, the ones she has really committed herself to. The story of Job, and God and Satan betting over him—of Abraham and Isaac, and the faked sacrifice— she doesn't even try to understand those anymore. But Christ's parables . . . she's obliged to acknowledge the authority of them. Still, when the reverend can take the parable of the talents and use it to prove that the poor in OC are poor because it was meant to be . . . and imply that the church shouldn't waste its time trying to help them! Well, that was the reverend's fault, but the parable sure gave him room to run with it.

So Lucy and Lillian discuss strategies for getting around the reverend's biases. The programs that are already under way are the obvious channels to work through; keep the momentum going with those, and the fact that the reverend will never start another won't really matter. It's a question of fund-raising, of getting volunteer help, of going out there and working. Between them they should be able to do it.

There's only one problem; they need a new fund-raiser with all its funds tagged for the neighborhood poverty program, or it won't survive. It's the kind of thing Reverend Strong is sure to deny approval for. "I've got a plan," Lucy says. "See, it's me that the reverend is beginning to associate with these pro- grams, and now it's getting so that every time I suggest something he turns it down. So what we should do, I think, is present the mail campaign idea as yours—something that you and the other people in the confirmation class thought up."

"Sure!" Lillian says, pleased at the subterfuge. "In fact I can suggest it to the class, and then we can tell the reverend about it together!"

Lucy nods. "That should work."

They discuss the upcoming garage sale. "I'll try again to get Jim to come and help," Lucy says, mostly to herself.

Lillian cocks her head curiously. "Do Jim or Mr. McPherson ever come to church anymore?"

Lucy shakes her head, coloring a little. "I tell them they should, but they don't listen to me. Dennis thinks he's too busy, I guess, and Jim has all sorts of reasons why it isn't a good idea. If he came and heard a sermon like the reverend's last one he'd go crazy. Even though he sounds like the reverend himself sometimes. But he just doesn't understand that the church isn't the individual people and their weaknesses. And it isn't the history, either. It's faith. And I guess he doesn't have that, at least right now." She sighs. "I feel sorry for him. I suppose I'll talk to him again."

"Maybe you can talk to them both together."

"Just getting them together would be the problem."

"Why's that?"

Lucy sighs. She doesn't like to talk about it, but . . . she's noticed already that what she says to Lillian stays with Lillian; even Emma doesn't hear it. And she needs to talk with *someone*. "Well, they're not getting along. Dennis is tired of Jim not working in a better job, and Jim is mad at Dennis because of it. Or something like that. Anyway, they've had a couple of arguments, and now Jim isn't coming around anymore."

"They need to talk to each other," Lillian says.

"Exactly! That's just what I say."

A small smile from Lillian, but Lucy doesn't notice it. Lillian says, "If I were you I'd try to get them together and talking again."

"I have been, but it just isn't working."

"You have to keep trying, Lucy."

Lucy nods. "You're right. I will."

And that night she tries, to the extent she can with Dennis back in Washington. Well, it's simple enough; she needs to get Jim up to dinner some time when Dennis is home. She gives Jim a call. "Hi, Jim? Mom here."

"Oh hi, Mom."

"How was the trip to Europe?"

"It was really interesting." He tells her briefly about it.

"It sounds like you had a good time. Listen, Jim, how about coming up for dinner next week? Dad will be back home then."

"Oh."

"Jim. Dad hasn't seen you for over two months, isn't that right? And it isn't right. He needs you just as much as you need him."

"Mom . . ."

"Don't Mom me. All these silly arguments, you should have more faith."

"What?"

"You'll come next week?"

"What?"

"I said, you'll come up next week for dinner?"

"I'll try, Mom. I'll think about it. But he's just going to think I'm leeching dinner from you guys again."

"Don't be ridiculous, Jim."

"I'm not!"

"You are. You're both too stubborn for your own good, and you're just hurting yourself by it. You come up here, you understand?"

"All right, Mom, don't get upset, okay? I'll . . . I'll try."

"Good."

They hang up. Lucy goes out to the video room, into the chair. The cat sits on her lap while she reads from next week's lesson. Paul's letter to the Ephesians, the verses swimming into double focus as she tries to stay awake and concentrate on them. On the screen a hot-air balloon is floating over a snowy peak, in a dark blue sky. The verses are floating about, big and black on the white page . . . She jerks to, finds it's after midnight. She's been sleeping in the chair, the Bible open on her lap. She lifts the cat off, gets up stiffly to go to bed.

...49

Hana's too busy to see Jim for several nights running, and he goes down to Sandy's party depressed. She's working, he's not. What must she think of him?

At Sandy's he stands leaning against the balcony wall, watching cars flow through the great interchange pretzel of the five freeways. Something to stare at for hours.

Suddenly there's Humphrey's younger sister Debbie Riggs, standing beside him and elbowing his arm to get his attention. "Oh hi, Debbie! How are you?" He hasn't seen her in a while. They're good friends, they've known each other since junior high; in years past she's been sort of a sister to him, he thinks.

"I'm fine, Jimbo. You?"

"Okay, okay. Pretty good, really."

They chat for a bit about what they've been up to. Same things. But there's something bugging her. Debbie is one of the most straightforward people that Jim knows; if she's irritated with you she just comes right out with it.

And she's a good friend of Sheila Mayer's.

So without too much delay it bursts out of her. "Jim, just what did you think you were doing about Sheila? I mean, you guys were allies for over four months, and then one day, wham, not a visit not a call! What kind of behavior is that?"

"Well," Jim says uncomfortably. "I tried to call—"

"Bullshit! Bullshit! If you want to call someone you can get through to them, you know that. You can leave a message! There's no way you tried to call her." She points a finger at him accusatively and anger makes her voice harsh: "You screwed her, Jim! You fucked her over!"

Jim hangs his head. "I know."

"You don't know! I visited her after you suddenly disappeared out of her life, and I found her sitting in her living room, putting together one of Humphrey's jigsaw puzzles, one of those ten-thousand-piece ones. That's all she would do!

And when she was done with that one she went out and bought some more, and she came back home and that's all she did was sit there in her living room and put together those stupid fucking jigsaw puzzles, for a whole month!"

Eyes flashing, face flushed, relentlessly she holds Jim's gaze: "And you did that to her, Jim! You did that to her."

Long pause.

Jim's throat is constricted shut. He can't take his eyes from Debbie. He nods jerkily. The corners of his mouth are tight. "I know," he gets out.

She sees that he has gotten it, that he sees the image of Sheila at that coffee table, understands what it means. Her expression shifts, then; he can see that she's still his friend, even when she's furious with him. Somehow that makes the anger more impossible to deny. And even though he's gotten it, Debbie is so angry that that isn't, at the moment, quite enough. Perhaps she has thought it would mean more to her. Jim can see her remembering the sight herself; her friend studiously sifting through the pieces, focusing on them, not letting her attention stray anywhere else; suddenly Debbie's blinking rapidly, and abruptly she turns and walks off. And he sees the image better than ever; it's burned into him by Debbie Riggs's distress.

"Oh, man," he says. He turns and leans on the balcony rail. Headlights and taillights swim through the night. He feels like he's swallowed one of the flower pots by his elbow: giant weight in his stomach, tasting like dirt.

Jigsaw puzzles.

Why did he do it?

For Virginia Novello. But what about Sheila? Well, Jim didn't think of her. He didn't really believe that he mattered enough that anyone would care about him. Or he didn't really believe in the reality of other people's feelings. Of Sheila Mayer's feelings. Because they got in the way of what he wanted to do.

He sees these reasons clearly for the first time, and disgust washes over him in a great wave.

Suddenly he sees himself from the outside, he escapes the viewpoint of consciousness and there's Jim McPherson, no longer the invisible center of the universe, but one of a group of friends and acquaintances. A physical person out there just like everyone else, to be interacted with, to be judged! It's a dizzying, almost nauseating experience, a physical shock. Out of body, look back, there's this skinny intense guy, a hollow man with nothing inside to define him by— defined by his fashionable ally and his fashionable beliefs and his fashionable clothes and his fashionable habits, so that the people who care about him— Sheila—

Empty staring at a jigsaw puzzle. Concentrate on it. The headlights all blur out.

...50

Stewart Lemon's sitting at his desk, in a reverie. It's been another miserable morning, Elsa keeping up the silent treatment and walking around the house mute, like a naked zombie . . . how long has it been since she stopped speaking? Lemon sits and dreams of leaving her for his secretary, starting a new alliance, free of such a long history of pain. But if he leaves he'll lose the house. And doesn't Ramona have an ally? Ah, it's a fantasy; looked at realistically it falls apart. So that means he has to continue with Elsa. . . .

Ramona buzzes. Donald Hereford is in Los Angeles on Argo/Blessman business, and has decided to drop on down for a visit. He'll be here in half an hour.

Lemon groans. What a day! It's always tense for him when Hereford comes by, especially lately. Given the various troubles LSR is having, the visits can only be in the nature of judgments—check-ups to see whether Argo/Blessman's aerospace subsidiary is worth keeping. . . . This is even more true when there is no specific reason for the visit, as in this case.

So as much as he tries to compose himself, he is nervous as Hereford arrives. He leads him into his office and they sit down. Hereford looks at the ocean as he listens to Lemon go over the latest on the various LSR projects of note.

"How's the appeal of the Stormbee decision coming?"

"The court rules on it end of this week or the beginning of next. Did you see the GAO report?" Hereford shakes his head briefly. Lemon describes the report. "It's pretty favorable," he concludes, "but our lawyers can't tell if it will be enough to sway Judge Tobiason. They think it should, but given Tobiason's background they aren't making any promises."

"No." Hereford sighs. "I wonder about that case."

"Whether it was . . ." Lemon was going to say, "a good idea to protest the decision," when he recalls that it was Hereford's idea.

Hereford looks up at him from under mildly raised eyebrows, and laughs.

"A good idea? I think so. We had to show the Air Force that they can't just flaunt the rules and walk over us. But we've done that, now, I think. They've had to kowtow to the GAO pretty seriously. So that whatever Tobiason says, we may have accomplished our goals in the matter."

"But—winning the contract?"

"Do you think the Air Force would ever allow that, now?"

Lemon considers it in silence.

Hereford says, "Tell me all the latest about the Ball Lightning program."

Now it's Lemon's turn to sigh. In a matter-of-fact voice he describes the latest round of troubles the program has been experiencing. "McPherson has put them onto tracking the ICBMs longer, in a phased array, so that their defenses can be overcome, and it looks as promising as anything we've tried. But the Air Force specs don't really allow for anything more than the first two minutes after launch, so we don't know what they'll make of this."

"You have asked them?"

"Not yet."

Hereford frowns. "Now the Air Force already has test results that show we could do it in the two minutes, right?"

"Under certain special circumstances, yes."

"Which are?"

"Well, a stationary target, mainly. . . ."

Slowly and patiently Hereford drags the whole story out of Lemon. He gets Lemon to admit that the early test results reported by Dan Houston's team could be interpreted as fraudulent if the Air Force wanted to get hard about it. And since LSR has gotten hard in the Stormbee matter. . . .

Lemon, squirming in his seat, gets the strong impression that Hereford already knew all these details, that he has been making him go through them again just to bake him a little. Lemon tries to relax.

"McPherson's involved with this one too?"

"I assigned him to it to help Houston out. McPherson is a good trouble-shooter." And troublemaker, he thinks. Don't the two always go together?

Hereford nods. "I want to see the on-site facilities for the Ball Lightning program." He stands. Lemon gets to his feet, surprised. They walk to the elevator, take it down to the ground floor and leave the executive building. Over to the engineer's offices, and the big building housing the labs and the assembly plant. It's your typical Irvine Triangle industrial architecture: two stories high and a couple hundred yards to a side, the walls made of immense squares of coppery mirrored glass, reflecting the obligatory lawns and cypress trees.

They enter and Lemon leads Hereford, by request, through all the labs and assembly rooms that have any part in the Ball Lightning program. Hereford doesn't really look at any single one very closely, but he seems interested in determining their locations in the building, strangely enough. When he's done doing that, he wants to survey the grounds outside the plant: the picnic benches in the small groves of cypress, the high security fence surrounding the property . . . it's strange. Lemon's beginning to get a headache thinking about it, out in the bright sun, coffee wearing off, stomach growling. . . . Finally Hereford nods. "Let's go have some lunch."

Orange County just can't provide the kind of culinary sophistication that Manhattan boasts, which is galling to Lemon when he has to try to impress Hereford. He takes him down to Dana Point, and they eat at the Charthouse over the harbor. Hereford concentrates on the salad bar, eats with obvious relish. "They still can't do this properly in New York, I'm not sure why." A couple of young women in bathing suits sit at the next table, and Lemon says, "Yes, there are certain advantages to living in California." Hereford smiles briefly.

When they're done eating Hereford asks, "So what do you make of this rash of sabotages against defense contractors in this area?"

Ah ha. Here might be the explanation for the inspection of the grounds. Lemon says, "Our security thinks it's a local group of refusniks, and they're working with the police on it. Apparently they won't attack any place where there are people working, because they don't want to kill or injure anyone. So we've taken the precaution of having several night watchmen in the plant, as well as people patrolling the perimeter of the grounds, and the beach below us. And we announced the fact at a press conference—it was pretty well reported."

Hereford is disturbed by this. "You mean you're assuming these saboteurs won't make a mistake, or change their policy? If it is indeed their policy?"

"Well . . ."

Hereford shakes his head. "Get all the night watchmen out of the building."

"But—"

"You heard me. The risk is too great. I don't like the idea of using people's lives as a shield, not when we're dealing with an unknown enemy." He pauses, purses his lips. "The truth is, we've got reason to believe that the sabotage out here is backed by a very large, very professional group."

Lemon raises his eyebrows in unconscious imitation of Hereford. "Not the Soviets!"

"No no. Not directly, anyway. The truth is it may be one of our competitors, providing the money, anyway."

Lemon's eyebrows shoot up for real. "Which one?"

"We're not sure. We've penetrated the organization on a lower level, and naturally the links between levels are well concealed."

"I suppose it would have to be one of the companies that hasn't been hit."

"Not necessarily."

Now, this statement turns certain tumblers in Lemon's mind. He's silent for a time as he considers the implications of what Hereford has said. A company attacks others to harm their work and eventually damage their reputation for efficiency with the Air Force. Then it attacks itself to keep suspicion away from it. And, at the same time, it could use the attack on itself to get rid of something potentially damaging in and of itself. Sure, it makes sense.

But say another company learned it was going to be attacked; and say, it had something, say it had a program that was in really serious trouble for one reason or another. . . .

"Should we increase our security on the perimeter?" Lemon asks, testing his hypothesis.

"No reason to." Around Hereford's eyes there is an amused crinkle; perhaps he thinks that Lemon is dense, perhaps he is amused that Lemon has finally gotten it; no way of telling. "We've done what we can, I think. Our insurance is in good shape, and all we can do is hope for the best."

"And . . . and get the night watchmen out of there."

"Exactly."

"Do you . . . do you have any information that indicates we might become . . ."

"A target?" Hereford shrugs. This goes too far, it shouldn't be talked about. "Nothing definite enough to go to the police with." But his eyes, Lemon thinks, his eyes; they look through the map of the Caribbean on their table, and they know. They know.

Lemon sits back in his seat, sips at his Pinot blanc. He's been let in on it, really. If he's smart enough to put it together, then he's in the know. Maybe he had to be. Still, it's a good sign.

And this means that maybe, just maybe, something will happen soon that will get him off the hook with the Ball Lightning program. Get LSR off the hook as well. And insurance . . . incredible. He swallows the wine.

...51

Back at work in the First American Title Insurance and Real Estate Company, back at work in his night classes, Jim finds he cannot keep Sheila Mayer and her jigsaw puzzles from his mind. Now it's the principal element of the uneasiness that oppresses him. And he can't escape it.

Hana is still working hard, she has no time. Hana is working, he is not.

Finally, impelled to it, he sits at his computer and stares at the screen. He's got to work, to really work, he's *got to.* Tonight it's as much an escape from his life, from his uneasiness, as anything else. But any motive will do at this point.

He thinks about his poetry. He considers the poetry of his time. The thing is, he doesn't like the poetry of his time. Flashy, deliberately ignorant, concerned only with surfaces, with the look, the great California image, reflected in mirrors a million times. . . . It's postmodernism, the tired end of postmodernism, which makes utterly useless all his culturevulturing, because for postmodernism there is no past. Any mall zombie can write postmodern literature, and in fact as far as Jim can tell from the video interviews, that's who is writing it. No, no, no. He refuses. He can't do that anymore.

And yet this is his time, his moment; what else can he write about but now? He lives in a postmodern world, there is no way out of that.

Two of the writers most important to Jim wrote about this matter of one's subject. Albert Camus, and then Athol Fugard, echoing Camus—both said that it was one's job to be a *witness* to one's times. That was the writer's crucial, central function. Camus and the Second World War, then the subjugation of Algeria—Fugard and apartheid in South Africa: they lived in miserable times, in some ways, but by God it gave them something to write about! They had something to witness!

While Jim—Jim lives in the richest country of all time, what's happening man, nothing's happening man. . . . Jack-in-the-Box is faster than McDonald's!

My Lord, what a place to have to be a witness to.

But how did it get this way?

Hmm. Jim mulls that over. It isn't really clear, yet; but something in that question seems to suggest a possible avenue of action for him. An approach.

But that brings up a second problem: it's all been done before.

It's like when his English teacher at Cal State Fullerton told the class to go out and write a poem about autumn. Great, Jim thought at the time. First of all, we live in Orange County—what is autumn to us? Football season. Wetsuits for surfing. Like that. He's read that Brahms's Third Symphony is autumnal, he's read that the rhythms of the Book of Psalms are autumnal—okay, so what's autumn? Brahms's Third Symphony! The Book of Psalms! That's the kind of circles you run in, when the natural world is gone. Okay, take those fragments and try to make something of it.

> I listen to Brahms
> And watch the Rams
> I read from Psalms
> We are only lambs
> Putting on our wetsuits
> To surf the autumn waves.

Hey, pretty good! But then the professor gets out "To Autumn" by John Keats, and reads it aloud. Oh. Well. Take your poem and eat it. In fact scratch that topic entirely, it's been done before to perfection. Well fine! Ain't no such topic in OC anyway!

The trouble is that if you start that process you quickly find that every topic in the world goes out the window the same way. It's either been covered to the max by the great writers of the past, or else it doesn't exist in OC. Usually both.

Be a witness to what you see. Be a witness to the life you live. To the lives we live.

And why, why, why? How did it get this way?

Back to that again. All right. Make that the orientation point, Jim thinks, the organizing principle, the Newport Freeway of your writing method. He thinks of *In the American Grain*, by William Carlos Williams. Williams's book is a collection of prose meditations on various figures of American history, explaining it all with that fine poet's eye and tongue. Of course Jim can't duplicate that book: he doesn't have any more writing ability than Williams had in his little fingernail. Every time WCW cut his fingernails, Jim thinks, he lopped off ten times more talent than I will ever have, and wrapped it in newspaper and tossed it in the wastebasket. He giggles at the thought. Somehow it makes him feel freer.

Duplication isn't the problem, anyway. It's OC Jim is concerned with, Orange County, the ultimate expression of the American Dream. And there aren't any great individuals in OC's history, that's part of what OC means, what it is. So he couldn't follow Williams's program even if he wanted to.

But it gives him a clue. Collectively they made this place. And so it has a history. And tracing this history might help to explain it, which is more important to Jim, now, than just witnessing. How it got to its present state: "The Sleepwalkers and How We Came to Be." He laughs again.

If he did something like that, if he made that his orienting point, then all his books, his culturevulturing, his obsession with the past—all that could be put to use. He recalls Walter Jackson Bate's beautiful biography of Samuel Johnson, the point in it where Bate speaks of Johnson's ultimate test for literature, the most important question: Can it be turned to use? When you read a book, and go back out into the world: *can it be turned to use?*

How did it get this way?

Well, it's a starting point. A Newport Freeway. You can get anywhere from the Newport Freeway. . . .

How did it happen?

It was World War Two that began the change, World War Two that set the pattern.

After Pearl Harbor the two thousand Orange County citizens of Japanese origin were gathered up and relocated in a shabby desert camp in Poston, Arizona. And people poured west to wage war. President Roosevelt called for the construction of fifty thousand planes a year, and the little airplane factories in Los Angeles and Orange had room to grow, they had empty farmland around them, every one. Thus the aeronautics industry in southern California had its start.

And the soldiers and sailors came west. They saw Orange County, and it looked just like the labels on the orange crates back home: the broad flat plain, covered with orange trees in their symmetrical rows; long lines of towering eucalyptus trees breaking the land into immense squares; the bare foothills behind, and the snowy mountains behind them; the wide, sandy, empty beaches down at Newport and Corona del Mar; the little bungalows tucked in their gardens, under the grapevine bowers, nestled each in an orange grove all its own.

There were only a hundred and thirty thousand people in all the county, lost in the millions of trees. City boys from the East, farmers from the cold Midwest and the poor South, all children of the Depression—they came out and saw the dream, the Mediterranean vision of a rich and easeful agricultural life, under an eternal sun. They went to the beach on Christmas day. They laughed punch-drunk in warm salt waves. They drove old Fords down the country roads, flashing through the ranked shadows of the eucalyptus trees, drinking beer and laughing with local girls and breathing in the thick scent of the orange blossoms, in the bright sun of February. And they said: When this war is over. I'm coming back here to make my home.

There was land, empty farmland, that the military could use. And people were happy to see the military there, it meant good business. Patriotism, good business: the equation took root in Orange County, beginning with this war. The Santa Ana City Council, for instance, rented four hundred acres of the Berry ranch, for $6,386 a year, then turned around and rented the land to the War Department for a dollar a year, inviting the department to use the land for whatever they liked. It was patriotic, it was good business. The War Department made the ranch into the Santa Ana Army Air Base, and through the war 110,000 men trained there. They saw the land.

Next to the air base was established the Army Air Forces Flying Training Command, the "University of the Air." Sixty-six thousand pilots got their wings there. They all saw the land.

The Navy established one U.S. Naval Air Station at Los Alamitos, and another in Tustin, to house its blimps. It dredged the harbor at Seal Beach, and relocated two thousand residents, and established the U.S. Naval Ammunition and Net Depot, at a cost of $17 million—all of it paid to the local construction industry.

Groves in El Toro were torn out to make room for the U.S. Marine Corps Air Station, El Toro, one of the biggest in the country.

Orange County Airport became the Santa Ana Army Airdrome. Irvine Park became Camp George E. Rathke, infantry training center. And through all of these military bases poured the men, and the money.

So much of the population was directed to the war effort that not enough were left over to farm. Mexican braceros were brought in to pick the oranges. German POWs were brought in to pick the oranges. A group of Jamaicans were brought in to pick the oranges. ("These Negroes have Oxford accents!" a resident said.)

But the soldiers, the sailors, the fliers, the airplane factory workers, they all served the war. Orange County became part of a war machine; and this military-industrial infrastructure was built, and left in place, and it provided work for the thousands of men who returned after the war, with their new families; they came, and bought houses built by the construction industry that had been so well primed by military construction, and they went to work. In the 1950s the Santa Ana Freeway was extended down into Orange County from Los Angeles, and then you could work in LA but live in Orange County; like the coming of the railroad, like all the other improvements in the efficiency of transportation, it fueled the boom, and the military-industrial machine grew again. And so the machine served the Korean War, and the Cold War, and the Vietnam War, and the Cold War, and the Central American War, and the Cold War, and the African War, and the Cold War, and the

Indonesian War, and the Cold War, and the Space War . . . a war machine, ever growing.

And none of that ever went away.

... 53

Sandy's return from Europe is a bit hectic. His answering machine goes on for two and a half hours, at a minute maximum per message. It seems that half the messages are from Bob Tompkins, too. So he calls Bob. "Hi, Bob, Sandy here."

"Ah, Sandy! You're back!"

"Yeah, I decided to, to—"

"To let things cool down a little, eh Sandy? Well, it worked."

Bob laughs, and Sandy nods to himself. It did indeed work. Talking to Bob on the day he got the news would have been blistering.

"You shouldn't worry so much about things, Sandy. I mean when I first got your message I was upset, sure, but it didn't take me a week to get over it, for Christ's sake! I mean when you've got the Coast Guard breathing down your neck, what else can you do? You could have dumped those barrels over the side, right? So just the fact that we might be able to recover them is a big plus. Listen, if you can liberate that stuff, there'll be a bonus in it for you, for duty above and beyond the call."

"That's great, Bob, I'm glad you feel that way about it. But there's a certain problem with where we stashed the stuff. We just picked the nearest isolated spot on the coast, you know, and dumped them in a bunch of boulders. But then we noticed that the buildings for Laguna Space Research were on the top of the bluff above us. And they've just announced an increase in security around their facility, because of the recent sabotages. Including a watch against boats landing."

"Ah ha. That is a problem. So . . . this company is a defense contractor, then?"

"Yeah."

"I see." Long pause. "Okay, well listen Sandy, we'll have to figure something out to help you, then. I'll get back to you on this, okay? Meanwhile just let it ride."

Fine with Sandy. He's free to concentrate on some heavy-duty dealing. He's got quite a bit of ground to make up, and so for the next few days he goes into overdrive, working sixteen, sometimes eighteen hours each day, to the point where he has to put some serious effort into supply as well as sales. Angela, who sees the need, is doing overtime herself taking care of him and the ap and their meals and the nightly party, which has regained its momentum in the days since their return. The constant running around in traffic, keeping track of handshake deals, doing the bookkeeping in the head, all over a ground base of massive drug intake, is exhausting in the extreme. In fact he's finding it hard to come home at night and really enjoy the party.

"Wow, burnout," he says to Angela.

"Why don't you take tomorrow night off. In the long run it'll help you keep this pace."

"Good idea."

So the next night he comes home early, around eleven, and corrals Abe, Tashi, and Jim. "Hey you guys, let's cruise."

The others like the idea. They get in Sandy's big car and track onto Newport Freeway north. Sandy programs a loop into the car: Newport Freeway north, Riverside west, Orange south, Garden Grove east, and then north on the Newport again: it's upper level all the way in each of these directions, so that it's like going for a little plane ride on autopia, with the great lightshow and all the other cars and their passengers for entertainment.

They started doing this together on the wrestling team, when they first got driver's licenses. Starving and thirsty high school kids, trying to make weight, or celebrating the end of the weekly necessity to make weight by pigging out. . . . Tonight there's a strongly nostalgic feeling about it; they're cruising the freeways, a basic OC activity. How could they have lost the habit?

Sandy is driving, Abe's in the front passenger seat, Jim is behind Abe, Tash behind Sandy. The first order of business is to deploy a few eyedroppers, in fact there's a sort of synergistic capacity upgrade when these four get together like this, and they really drown their eyes, according to long-standing tradition.

"Nothing like coming down to the old club and settling in," Jim says blissfully. "The lightshow is good tonight, isn't it? Look there, you can see in the pattern of the streetlights, the original plattings for the first towns in the area. See the really tight squares of streetlights are the oldest towns, when the platting was into really small blocks. There's Fullerton . . . there's Anaheim, the oldest . . . pretty soon we'll see Orange . . . and in between the pattern stretches way out, see? Longer blocks and twisty housing tracts."

"Yeah, I see it!" Sandy says, surprised. "I never noticed that before, but it's there."

"Yep," Jim says, proudly. He goes rattling on about real estate history, which his employer First American Title Insurance and Real Estate has all the records for; then about First American and Humphrey's attempt to build his office building on the land of the dismembered Cleveland National Forest; then about a new computer system that the company has installed in the offices, very advanced, "I mean you really can talk to it, not just simple commands but really complicated stuff, it's like the real beginning of the man-computer interface, and it's really going to mean a lot for," and then suddenly all three of his friends have turned to stare Jim in the face.

He comes to a halt and Sandy giggles. Abe, shaking his head, says in a pitying, exasperated voice: "Jim, no one gives a fuck about computers."

"Ah. Yes. Well. You know." And Jim starts to giggle himself. Must have been an eyedropper of Funny Bone, that last unmarked one.

Abe is pointing down at the Orange Mall. "Sandy, did you ever tell these guys about the time we were in the parking garage there?"

"No, don't think I did," Sandy says, grinning.

Abe turns to the two in the backseat. "We were leaving the mall and driving out of the big parking garage they have, you know, the thirty-story one, and we're following the arrows down the ramps from floor to floor, and it's not a simple spiral staircase situation at all, they've got it screwed up and you have to go to successive corners of each floor to get down, or something like that. So here we are following the arrows down, and Sandy's eyes do their bug-out-of-his-head thing, you know?"

Tashi and Jim nod, imitating the look in tandem.

"Exactly." Abe laughs. "And he says, 'You know, Abraham, if it weren't for these arrows . . .' and I say uh-huh, yeah, what? And he says, 'Stop the car! Wait a minute! Stop the car, I forgot something!' So I sit there while he goes back in the mall, and then he comes running back out with two big cans of paint—one can white, one a gray the color of the garage floors. And two brushes. 'We'll start at the bottom,' he says, 'and no one will ever escape.'"

"*Ahhh*, hahaha."

"The labyrinth without the thread," Jim says.

"You aren't kidding! I mean, think about it! So we drive around and at every arrow Sandy jumps out and quick paints over the old one and puts a new one down, pointing in a new direction—not necessarily the opposite direction, just a new one. And finally we reach the top floor. Already we can hear the honking and the cursing and all from the floors below. And then Sandy turns to me with this puzzled expression, and says, 'Hey, Abe—how are we going to get out of here?'"

Sandy's manic laugh dominates the rest.

They're tracking south on the Orange Freeway, coming to the giant interchange with the Santa Ana and the Garden Grove freeways—another immense pretzel of concrete ribbons flying through the air, lightly buttressed on concrete pillars. Their change to the Garden Grove east will take them right through the middle of the knot. Great views over Santa Ana to the south, then Orange to the north; just names in the continuum of the lightshow, but given what Jim has said about the pattern of the streetlights, interesting to observe.

Tashi rises up like he's achieved enlightenment, and speaks the message from the cosmos: "There are only four streets in OC."

"What?" cries Abe. "Look around you, man!"

"Platonic forms," Jim says, understanding. "Ideal types."

"Only four." Tash nods. "First there's the freeways."

"Okay. I'll grant you that."

"Then there's the commercial streets, big ones with parking lots flanking them and all the businesses behind the parking lots, or on them. Like Tustin Avenue, right down there." He points north.

"Or Chapman." "Or Bristol." "Or Garbage Grove Boulevard." "Or Beach." "Or First." "Or MacArthur." "Or Westminster." "Or Katella." "Or Harbor." "Or Brookhurst."

"Yeah yeah yeah!" Tashi interrupts them. "Point proven! There are many commercial streets in OC. But they all are one."

"I wonder," Sandy says dreamily, "if you blindfolded someone and spun them around to disorient them, then took off the blindfold somewhere on one of the commercial streets, how long it would take them to identify it?"

"Forever," Tash opines. "They're indistinguishable. I think they made a one-mile unit and then just reproduced it five hundred times."

"It would be a challenge," Sandy muses. "A sort of game."

"Not tonight," Abe says.

"No?"

"No."

"The third kind of street," Tashi forges on, "is the residential street, class A. The suburban streets of the housing tracts. Please don't start naming examples, there are ten zillion."

"I like the cute curly ones in Mission Viejo," Sandy says.

"Or the old cul-de-sac exclusive models," Jim adds.

"And the fourth type?" says Abe.

"Residential street, class B. The urban ap streets, like down there in Santa Ana."

"A lot of that's original platting," Jim says. "Now it's as close to slums as we've got."

"As close to slums?" Abe repeats. "Man, they're there."

"I guess you're right."

"There's a fifth kind of street," Sandy announces.

"You think so?" Tash asks, interested.

"Yeah. I guess you could call it the street-freeway. It's a street, but there's nothing facing it at all—it's backed by housing-development walls, mostly, and there's no shops, no pedestrians—"

"Well, none of them have pedestrians."

"True, but I mean even less than usual. They're just avenues for tracking fast where there aren't freeways."

"Negative numbers of pedestrians?"

"Yeah, we use those a lot," Abe says. "Like Fairhaven, or Olive, or Edinger."

"Exactly," Sandy says.

"Okay," Tash agrees. "We'll make it five. There are five streets in OC."

"Do you think it's because of zoning laws?" Jim asks. "I mean, why is that?"

"More use habits than zoning, I'd bet," Tash says. "Stores like to be together, housing developments are built in group lots, that kind of thing."

"Each street has a history," Jim says, staring out the window with his mouth hanging open. "My God!"

"Better get writing, Jim. . . ."

"Speaking of streets and history," Sandy says, "I was driving east on the Garden Grove on a really clear morning a few weeks ago, first morning of a Santa Ana wind, you know? You could see Baldy and Arrowhead and everything. And the sun was just up, and I looked north to where the old Orange Plaza used to be—a little west of that, I'd guess. And I couldn't believe my eyes! I mean, down there I suddenly saw this street that I'd never seen before, and it had really tall skinny palm trees on one side of it, and the street surface was like white concrete, wider than usual, and the houses on each side were solo houses with yards, little bungalows with enclosed porches and grass lawns, and sidewalks and *everything*! I mean it was like one of those old photos from the 1930s or something!"

Jim is bouncing in his seat with excitement, leaning over into the front. "Where, where, where, where!"

"Well, that's the thing—I don't know! I was so surprised that I got off at the next exit and tracked on over to take a look for it. I thought you'd be interested, and I even thought I might want to buy a house there if I could, it looked so . . . So I tracked around for about a half hour looking for it, and I couldn't find it! Couldn't even find the palm trees! Since then every time I drive that stretch I look for it, but it just *isn't there*."

"Whoah."

"Heavy."

"I know. I figure it had something to do with the light or something. Or maybe a time warp. . . ."

"Oh, man." Jim hops up and down on his seat, thinking about it. "I want to find that."

They track some more. In the cars around them other people live their lives. Occasionally they track by freeway parties, several cars hooked together, people passing things between them, music all the same from every car.

"Let's fuel up," Tashi says. "I'm hungry."

"Let's swing into one of the drive-thrus," Sandy says, "so we don't have to leave the loop. Which shall it be?"

"Jack-in-the-Box," says Abe.

"McDonald's," says Jim.

"Burger King," says Tashi.

"Which one?" Sandy shouts as they pass one of the drive-thru complex off-ramps. The others all shout their choices and Tash reaches over Sandy's shoulder for the steering switch. Abe and Jim grab his arm and try to move it, and the struggle begins. Shouts, curses, wrestling holds, karate chops: finally Sandy cries, "Taste test! Taste test!" The others subside. "We'll try all of them."

And so he gets off at the Lincoln exit in Orange and they drive-thru the Burger King and the Jack's, stopping briefly to order pay and collect from the little windows on the upper level; then around the bend to the Kraemer exit in Placentia, for Jim's Big Macs.

"See, look. The Burger King Whopper has indisputably got the best meat. Check it out."

"Isn't that some kind of bug there, Tash?"

"No! Let's look at yours if you dare, you know they make those Big Macs out of petroleum byproducts."

"They do not! In fact they won the slander case in court on that!"

"Lawyers. Look at that meat, it's sludge!"

"Well, it's better than the double Jack Abe's got, anyway."

"Sure, but that's saying nothing."

"Hey," says Abe. "The Jack's are adequate, and look here at the malt and fries you get at Jack's. Both absolutely unmatchable. Burger King malts are made of air, and McDonald's malts are made of styrofoam. You only get a real ice-cream malt at Jack's."

"Malt? Malt? You don't even know what malt tastes like! There hasn't been malt in this country since before the millennium! Those are shakes, and the McShake is just fine. Orange-flavored, even."

"Come on, Jim, we're trying to eat here. Don't make me puke."

"And the McFries are also the best. Those Jackfries, you could inject drugs with those things."

"Ho, Mr. Get Tough! Your fries are actually shot puts in disguise! Get serious!"

"I am serious! Here, Sandy, you be judge. Eat this, here."

"No, Sandy, mine first! Eat this!"

"Mmff mmff mmff."

"See, he likes mine better!"

"No, he just said Burger Whop, didn't you hear him?"

Sandy swallows. "They taste the same."

"What kind of a judge are you?"

Abe says, "Best malt—"

"Shake! Shake! No such thing as malt! Mythical substance!"

"Best malt, best fries, perfectly standard burger."

"In other words the burger is disgusting," Tashi says. "There's no fighting it, the basis of the American body is the hamburger, the rest is just frills. And Burger King has the best burger by miles. And so there you have it."

"All right," Sandy says. "Tashi, give me the patty out of yours."

"What? No way!"

"Yeah, come on. There's only half left anyway, right? Give it to me. Now Abe, give me the bun with the secret sauce. Not the other one, that's blank! *Ahhh*, hahahahahahaha, what a burger, Jesus, give me the secret sauce. Jim, hand over that smidgin of lettuce, right, okay, and the ketchup in its convenient poison-proofed pill-sized container. Fine, fine. Abe, hand over the malt. Yeah, you win! Hand it over. The fries, hmm, well, let's just mess them all together here, on the seat here, that's okay. Where'd that ketchup go? Slip down the straw, did it? Squirt it on there, Abe, and watch out you don't get it all on one fry. Right. There we have it, bros. Le Grand Compromis, the greatest American meal of all time! Fantastic! Dig in!"

"Whoah."

"Think I've lost my appetite, here. . . ."

When they're done eating, Sandy takes over the controls and turns them back toward home. It's late, he's got another full day tomorrow.

They track down the Newport Freeway, on the underlevel, the adscreens hanging from the underside of the upper level, flashing over them is a colorful subliminal parade of words, images, images, words. BUY! NEW! LOOK! NOW! SPECTAC! They slump back in their seats, watch the lights streak in the car windows.

No one speaks. It's late, they're tired. There's a feeling in the car that is somehow . . . elegiac. They've just performed one of their rituals, an old, central ritual that seems to have been a part of their lives always. How many nights have they cruised autopia and talked, and eaten a meal, and looked at the world? A thousand? Two thousand? This is how they were friends together. And yet this night it feels, somehow, as if this may have been the last time they will perform this particular ritual. Nothing lasts forever. Centrifugal forces are tugging on all their lives, on their collective life; they feel it, they know that the time is coming when this long childhood of their life will have to end. Nothing lasts forever. And this feeling lies as heavy in the car as the smell of French fries. . . .

Sandy punches a button and his window slides down. "An eyedropper for the road?"

After they enter SCP's parking garage and Abe and Tash have walked off to their cars, Sandy gestures Jim back to him. Scratching his head sleepily, he says, "Jim, have you seen much of Arthur lately?"

"Oh, a little. Once since we got back, I guess."

Sandy considers what line of questioning would be best. "Do you know if he's involved in anything, you know, anything more serious than those posters he puts up?"

Jim blushes. "Well, you know. I'm not really sure. . . ."

So Arthur is involved. And Jim knows about it. Meaning that Jim may be involved, too. Possibly. Probably. It's hard for Sandy to imagine Jim taking part in sabotage actions against local industrial plants, but who can say? He is one to follow an idea.

And now it's Sandy's turn to consider how much he can say. Jim is one of his best friends, no doubt about it, but Bob Tompkins is a major business partner, and by extension he has to be careful of Raymond's interests too. It's a delicate question, and he's tired. There doesn't seem to be any pressing hurry in the matter; and it would be better, actually, if he had more of substance to tell Jim, if he decides to speak to him. He's certain now that Arthur Bastanchury is working for Raymond, and pretty sure that Jim is working with Arthur. The question is, does Raymond work for anyone? That's the important thing, and until he learns more about it there's no use in upsetting Jim, he judges. Truth is, he's too tired to think about it much right now.

He pats Jim's arm. "Arthur should be careful," he says wearily, and turns to go to the elevator. "And you too," he says over his shoulder, catching a surprised look on Jim's face. He gets in the elevator. Three A.M. If he gets up at seven, he can reach his dad before lunch in Miami.

... 54

Jim gets several days in a row at the office of First American Title Insurance and Real Estate Company, which is good for his bank account if not for his disposition. On one of these days Humphrey comes in grinning triumphantly. "We're doing it, Jimbo. We're building the Pourva Tower. Ambank approved the loan package, and the last papers were signed today. All we have to do is reconfirm the other financiers within the next few days, so it's just a matter of doing the computer work quickly, before anyone cools off."

"Humphrey, you still don't have any occupants for this building."

"Well, we've got all those interested parties. Besides, it doesn't matter! We'll get them when the building is there!"

"Humphrey! What's the occupancy rate for new office buildings in OC? Twenty percent?"

"I don't know, something like that. But it's bound to change, so much business is moving in here."

"I don't see why you say that. The place is saturated."

"No way, Jim. There's no such thing."

"Aggh . . ." Nothing he can say to that. "I still think it's stupid."

"Listen, Jim, the rule is, when you have the money and you have the land, you build! It's not easy getting the two together at the same time. As you know from how this one's gone. But we've done it! Besides, this one will do well—we'll even be able to advertise that it has a filtered view of the ocean."

"Filtered by the whole bulk of the Santa Ana Mountains, eh Hump?"

"No! You can see down over Robinson Rancho, a little bit of it anyway."

"Yeah, yeah. Build another empty tower."

"Don't worry about that, Jim. Our only problem is to make sure everything moves along as fast as possible."

Jim goes home from his clerking in a foul mood. The phone rings and he grabs it up. "What!"

"Hello, Jim?"

"Ah, Hana! Hey, how are you?"

"Something wrong?"

"No, no, I always answer the phone like that after a day at the office. Sorry."
She laughs. "You'd better come up here for dinner then."

"You bet! What should I bring?"

And so an hour later he's tracking into the hills, out the Garden Grove Freeway, across to Irvine Park and the Santiago Freeway, and then up narrow, deep Modjeska Canyon. Hana lives beyond the Tucker Bird Sanctuary, up a narrow side canyon, in a converted garage at the end of a gravel drive, in a grove of big old eucalyptus trees. The main house is a small whitewashed colonial-style cottage; its general modesty doesn't hide the fact of the secluded, wooded yard, the exclusiveness of it all. Hana's landlord is rich. And Hana?

Her garage has been turned into a painter's studio, mostly. The main room fills most of the place, and it's stacked with canvases and materials like her studio at Trabuco J.C. Kitchen and bathroom have been partitioned off in one corner, and a bedroom not much bigger than the bathroom is in the other corner. "I like it," Jim says. "It reminds me of my place, only nicer." Hana laughs. "You don't have any of your paintings up."

"God no. I like to be able to relax. I mean, imagine sitting around looking at your mistakes all the time."

"Hmm. They all have mistakes?"

"Sure."

She's staring past him at the floor, throwing her sentences out casually. Attack of shyness, it seems, Jim follows her into the kitchen, and helps her take hamburgers out to a hibachi on the gravel drive.

They barbecue the meat and eat the hamburgers out on the driveway, sitting in low lawn chairs. They talk about the coming semester and their classes. About Hana's painting. Jim's work at the office. It's very relaxed, though Hana's eyes look anywhere but at Jim.

After dinner they sit and look up at the sky. There are even some stars. The eucalyptus leaves click together like plastic coins. It's a warm evening, there's a touch of Santa Ana wind blowing, even.

Hana suggests a walk up the canyon. They take the dinner materials inside, and then walk up the narrow, dark road.

"Do you know much about the Modjeskas?" Hana asks as they walk.

"A little. Helena Modjeska was a Polish actress. Her real name was something longer, and very Polish. She married a count, and their salon in Warsaw was very fashionable. The salon members got the idea of starting a utopia in southern California. This was in the 1870s. And they did it! The colony was down near Anaheim, which was also a utopian project started by a group of

Germans. The Modjeskas' thing fell apart when none of them wanted to do farm work, and the Modjeskas moved to San Francisco, where she took up acting again. She became very famous there, and the count was her business manager, and they did well. Then in the late 1880s they returned, and bought the place up here. They called it Arden."

"*As You Like It*. What a nice idea."

"Yeah. This time it was a life of leisure—no farming. They had vineyards and orange groves and flower gardens, and a big shady lawn, and a pond out front with swans in it. During the days they rode horses around their land, and in the evenings Helena gave readings from her various roles."

"Very idyllic."

"True. It seems unreal, now. Although it's funny, up here I can imagine it happening. There's this feeling of being completely cut off from the world."

"I know. That's one of the things I like best about living up here."

"I believe it. It's amazing you can get that feeling anywhere in OC."

"Yeah, well, you should see Santiago Freeway at rush hour. Bumper to bumper."

"Of course. But here, and now . . ."

She nods, touches his upper arm. "Here, follow this trail. This little side canyon is pretty long and deep, and there's a way up to a lookout point over Riverside."

They hike through trees, up a steep-sided narrow canyon, one without a road at its bottom. Hana leads the way. Jim can hardly believe it; they're out in the bush! No condos! Can it be real?

The canyon's sandstone walls steepen until they're in a sort of roofless hallway, moving single file up a steep trail through the brush and trees. There's a stale, damp smell in the air, as if the sun seldom reaches the canyon's bottom. Then the walls lay back, and the canyon opens up into a small amphitheater filled with live oak. They turn back and up, and climb the walls they had previously been under, until they're on a ridge; there's a view back down to the scattered lights in Modjeska Canyon. And off to the east, as Hana said, there is a long fuzzy band of light, just visible: the Highway 15 corridor, in Riverside County.

"Whoah. You can really see a long way. Do you come up here often?"

He thinks he sees a small smile, but in the dark he can't be sure. "No. Not often. Look here." She walks to a big oak. "This tree's called the Swing Tree. Someone's tied a rope on that big upper branch, out away from the trunk. You take it"—she grabs the thick rope with both hands, just above a knot at the end of it—"and walk back uphill with it—and then—"

She runs down the hill, swings off into the space above the canyon, makes a slow turn, flies back in and runs to a halt.

"Whoah! Let me try that!"

"Sure. There are two ways to go—you can run straight out and come straight back in, or you can take off angling out away from the tree, and that'll put you in a circle and land you on the other side of the trunk. You have to be sure to go hard that way, though, to get around the trunk all the way."

"I see. Believe I'll go straight out, this time."

"Good idea."

He seizes the rope, runs outward, flies off into space. It's slow, dark. Air hoots in his ears. He feels a little point of something like weightlessness, or weight coming back, at the outer limit of his ride—hung out there for a moment—then it's around and back in, whoah, got to run quick on touchdown. "Great! Fantastic! I want to do it again."

"Well then we'll just have to take turns. My turn now." She takes off with a quick sprint. Dark shape floating out there, hair flying wild against the stars— creak of rope against branch, up above—flying woman coming in from deep space, right at him—"Whoah!" He catches her up and they collide into a hug.

"Oops. Sorry. Took off at an angle, I guess."

He flies again. It's funny how simple all the real pleasures are (did he think that?). It's a long rope, the flights last a long time. Don't try to figure out how long, Jim thinks. It doesn't matter. Avoid timing, distance records, etcetera. . . .

After a few straight in-and-out runs, Hana takes the rope and runs out to the left, swings free of the ground, curves out, then left to right across the sky, spinning slowly, until she comes back in to the right side of the trunk. Round the horn. It looks lovely. "Let me try that!"

"Okay. Take off hard."

He does, but leaves the ground before he gets that last push-off step in. Oh well. Flying, here, spinning in a great circle, long seconds of a deep dream-flying calm. Coming back in he turns to face landward and notes that the tree trunk is going to—oops—

He just manages to turn sideways as he crashes into the tree. He tumbles to the ground, stunned.

He's lying in leaves. Hana has rushed over and is crouched over him. "Jim! Are you okay?"

He pulls her down and kisses her, surprising them both.

"Well, I guess you are."

"Not sure, though. Here—" He kisses her again. Actually, about half his body is sore indeed. Right ear, shoulder, ribs, butt, thigh, all of them are pounding. He ignores them all, pulls Hana onto him. The kiss extends off into a long sequence. Her hands are running over him very gently, making sure he's still all there. He reciprocates, and their kisses get a lot more passionate. Time out to breathe.

They're in a great drift of leaves, between two big roots that run over the hard ground. Leaves, whatnot—it's probably better not to investigate too closely. The leaves are dusty, dry, crunchy under them. They're lying side by side now, and clothes are giving way. In the dark Jim can just barely see her face against his, nothing more. The lack of visual stimulation, of the image, is disorienting. But that look on her face—all shyness gone, that small inward smile . . . his heart thumps, his skin is flushed or somehow made more sensitive, he can feel better, the rough uneven ground under his good side, his bad side throbbing in the cool air, crackling leaves, her hands on him, their mouths, whoah—when has a mere kiss ever felt like this? And it's Hana Steentoft, his friend, here; the distance gone, the inwardness turned out onto him, the friendship suddenly blooming like a Japanese paper flower hitting a bowl of water. It's exciting! They make love, and that's more exciting yet. Jim's body goes into a kind of shell-shocked mode: such a sequence of intense sensation! He mentions it to her at a certain still interval and she laughs. "Better watch it, you're going to be wanting to crash every time before you make it."

"Kinky indeed. Can you imagine it? Getting intimate—oh, excuse me—"

"Stand up and run straight into the wall—"

"There, okay, I'm ready now. . . ."

When their giggling subsides, Jim says, "I'll only do it with you. You'll understand."

"You'll only do it with me?" Quick grin, mischievous movement against him—"Yes"—and they are back in the world of sex, a duet collaborating in the most fascinating variations on a theme: the kinetic melody with its intense blisses, accompanied by crackling leaves and the odd squeak, hum, moan, grunt, whoah, exhalation, endearment, giggle, and a whole lot of heavy breathing. It's incredible fun.

... 55

They sleep together cuddled like spoons. In the morning Jim wakes to find Hana already at work, painting at a table in the main room. She's put on a bulky sweater and army fatigues. He watches her, noticing the brusque concentration, the tangled hair, the tree-trunk legs. The indirection that is not really shyness, but some unnamed cousin to shyness. She gets up and walks into the kitchen, passes a mirror without even noticing it. He gets up to run give her a hug. She laughs at him.

"So," she says after breakfast. "When do I get to read something of yours?"

"Oh, well." He panics. "I really don't have anything ready right now."

And he cringes a little to see the quick grimace on her face. She thinks he's being stupid. Wonders if he isn't just lying about his poetry, a bogus artist trying to impress her, with nothing behind it. He can see all that in the quick flow of expression in her face, which is just as quickly suppressed. No, no! But he really is scared; his poetry is so trivial, and there is so little of it, he's sure her estimation of him will drop radically when she reads it. So he doesn't want her to. But that desire in itself gives it all away. She might even be imagining it's worse than it really is. Jim sighs, confused. Hana lets the matter slide.

He fills in as he so often does, by telling tall tales of his friends' exploits. Tashi and the night surfing. Humphrey's empty tower. That kind of thing.

After a while Hana looks at the floor. "And when am I going to meet these amazing friends of yours?"

Jim gulps. It's the same question, isn't it: do I get to be part of your life? And by God, he wants her to be; he's forgotten whatever reservations he might have had about her. What were they about, her clothes, her *look*? Absurd. "There's a party at Abe's house tonight. His parents are going on vacation and he has the house to himself. Want to come?"

"Yes." She smiles, looks up at him.

Jim smiles too. Although he's remembering that Virginia will probably be there. As well as two dozen other perfect examples of the Modern California Woman. But he doesn't care, he tells himself. He doesn't care at all.

However, when he tracks by that evening to pick her up, she's wearing the very same army surplus pants, with their Jackson Pollock paint spray all over them. And yet another bulky brown-on-brown wool sweater. Jim winces. Then he notices that she has washed and brushed her hair, and it's drying still, curling in a way he thinks stunning. Anyway who cares about this stuff? He doesn't care about it. He doesn't care at all. He shakes it off, they get in his battered old car and drive.

Abe lives in an annex of his parents' house up on Saddleback Mountain, on the Santiago Peak side, just below the peak, overlooking all of OC and beyond. It's the most exclusive neighborhood of all, in accordance with Humphrey's law, height = money. Switchbacking up the steep residential road they pass mansion after mansion, most hidden from the road by a botanical garden's variety of trees and lawns, all as exotic and glossy as houseplants. But some are right out there for people to see:

Mirrored boxes that resemble the industrial complexes in Irvine,
Pagodas, chateaux,
Complicated wooden-box structures à la Frank Lloyd Wright,
Or the Greene brothers' Gamble house in Pasadena, (Cardboard shacks in a
    field of mud!)
Mission-style monsters of whitewash and orange tile roofs,
Circus tent shapes of glass and steel that imitate
The dominant mall designs down on the floodplain. . . .
You live here, sure. There's no doubt of it.

They track slowly and enjoy eyeballing the passing parade of architectural extravagance, making fun of most of the homes, ogling lustfully the few that strike them as tasteful, livable places. And marveling always that these are single-family dwellings, and not disguised duplexes, triplexes, aps, or condos. It's really hard to believe. "Like seeing an extinct animal," Jim says.

"Dinosaurs, grazing in your backyard."

Abe's parents, the Bernards, live on the outside of one of the hairpin turns near the top of the road, on a little deck of land all their own. The home is a multilevel sprawl, made entirely of wood; a Japanese garden out front has bonsai pines overhanging moss lawns, big odd-shaped boulders, and a small pool with a bridge over it. They've arrived early, so there's still parking on the street in front of the house. They get out, walk up and over the pool. "Just like the Modjeskas," Hana says softly. "All they need are swans."

As they approach the massive oak front doors, Abe and his father open them and walk out. Dr. Francis Bernard is a well-known logician who holds patents on some important computer software; he's also been a diplomat and social activist. He is one of the calmest people Jim has ever met; very quiet, and not much like Abe, except for the sharp dark face, the black hair. Jim introduces Hana to them. Mrs. Bernard left for Maui a couple weeks before, and Abe and his father have been living together alone since that time; now Dr. Bernard is off to the airport, headed for Maui himself. The two of them shake hands. Abe says, "Well, brother . . ."

"Brother," scoffs Dr. Bernard, obviously pleased. "See you in a month." And with a quiet good-bye he's off, into the garage.

"Come on in," Abe says, glancing at Hana curiously.

They enter the house and follow Abe through a succession of rooms, to a kind of enclosed porch or pavilion, overlooking the terraced yard that stands high above OC. Below them spreads the whole lightshow, just sparking up to full power in the hazy dusk. A plain of light.

Hana notices the view and goes out on the terrace to have a look. Abe and Jim retire to the porch kitchen and work up a chili con queso dip in a big crockpot. Jim tells Abe about the things that impressed him during the trip to Europe, making each event into something profoundly significant, as he so often does with Abe. Abe responds with his sharp, interested questions, attentive to moods and significances himself. And then there is his sudden laugh, transforming something Jim has been solemn about to high comedy; supplying the wit but acting as if it were Jim's. At times like this it's hard to imagine Abe as the unresponsive and scornful friend that Jim often feels him to be; now Jim too is a "brother." Is this a matter of mood, or is it just that whomever Abe fixes his full attention on becomes "brother" for that period of attention—which can be distracted, or missing from the start?

No way of knowing. Abe is the most inscrutable of Jim's friends, that's all there is to it. Visiting him up in this mansion Jim is reminded of Shelley's visits to Byron. It's gross flattery to compare himself to Shelley, he knows that, but there is something in the thought of the poor and idealistic poet visiting his rich, worldly, complex, and powerful friend that reminds him of this feeling, up here on the very roof of OC.

So when Hana comes back inside and sits on a stool beside him, Jim watches with as much pleasure as apprehension the process of these two friends getting acquainted. Hana is plopped on a stool, the wind has pushed her hair into its usual disorder, and as Dennis would say, she looks like something the cat dragged in. But Abe clearly enjoys talking to her; she's got a quick wit and can keep up with him. In that realm they're both far beyond Jim, who only laughs and cuts chilis for the dip. Abe, curious as always about people's work and their livelihoods, questions Hana closely about how the art business is carried on, and Jim learns things he didn't know before.

"And you?" Hana says. "Jim says you're a paramedic?"

Abruptly Abe laughs, elbows Jim. "Telling her about us, eh?"

Jim grins. "All lies, too."

Abe nods at Hana. "Yeah, I work for the OC Freeway Rescue squads."

"That must be hard work sometimes."

Jim winces a little inside; when he says things along these lines Abe tends to scowl at him or ignore him. But now he says, "Sure, sometimes. It's up and down. You get callused to the bad parts, though, and the good parts stay good always."

Hana nods. She's eyeing Abe closely, and he is inspecting the chili con queso; and she says, "So you two were on the wrestling team, hey? How long have you known each other?" Abe grins at Jim. "From the beginning."

Then Sandy and Angela come in from the yard entrance, and it's time for more introductions. With Sandy there the tempo jumps and pretty quickly they're jabbering away like they're old friends who haven't seen each other in a year. Hana chatters as much as any of them, chiefly to Abe but increasingly with Sandy and Angela. Angela, bless her heart, couldn't be friendlier. And then the crowd begins to arrive, Humphrey and his sometime ally Melina, Rose and Gabriela, Arthur, Tashi and Erica, Inez, John and Vikki, and so on; the party begins in earnest, people swirl in the slow ocean current patterns of parties everywhere. Hana stays on her stool and forms a sort of island around which one current swells; people stop in this eddy to talk to her. She asks a lot of questions, tries to sort out who's who, laughs. She's a hit. Jim, coming back to her after many small forays out into the currents, is pleased to see Hana and Abe engage in a long conversation, and Sandy join it; then Hana and Angela have a talk that leaves them laughing a lot, and even though Jim suspects that he is the subject of the laughter, he is pleased. All going so well.

Then Virginia arrives. When Jim sees her, blond mane breaking light in the hallway, his heart races. He moves to Hana and Angela and disrupts their conversation with some false heartiness, feeling nervous indeed. Virginia is quick to spot them, and she hurries over, smiling a bright smile full of malice. "Well hello, James. I haven't seen you in a while!"

"No."

"Aren't you going to introduce me to your new friend?"

"Oh, yeah. Virginia Novello, this is Hana Steentoft."

"Hello, Hana." Virginia extends a hand, and in her direct gaze there is a smiling, straightforward contempt. She's judged this dowdy newcomer in a single glance, and wants Jim to know it. Angrily, fearfully, Jim looks sideways at

Hana; she is gazing past Virginia, at the floor, indifferent to her, waiting for her to go. Virginia has been dismissed. Virginia smiles at Jim with open hostility, walks off without saying anything more.

Afterward, on the way home, Hana refuses to go to Jim's place. "Let's go to mine."

So they do. As they track she says, "That's one expensively dressed crowd of women you hang out with."

"Ah, yeah." Jim isn't listening, he's pleased at the whole evening, and at a final small gathering with Abe and Sandy and Angela. "They really go overboard into the whole thing. I'm so glad you don't care about any of that."

"Don't be stupid, Jim."

"Huh?"

"I said, don't be stupid."

"Huh?"

"Of course I care! What do you think I am?"

She's angry with him, he's just heard it. "Ah."

And suddenly he gets it: no one can escape. You can pretend not to care about the image, but that's as far as the culture will let you get. Inside you have to feel it; you can fight it but it'll always be there, the contemptuous dismissal of you by the Virginia Novellos of the world. . . . No doubt Hana saw that look and was perfectly aware of it, all the rest of the evening. And she did look different from the rest of the women there; how could anyone forget that in such a crowd of them? And now he had implied that she was so far out of the norm that she wouldn't have the common human response, wouldn't even notice, wouldn't even care.

He's a fool, he thinks. Such a fool. . . . What to say? "Sorry, Hana. I think you're beau—"

"Quiet, Jim. Just shut up about it, okay?"

"Okay."

He drives her to her home in an awkward, ominous silence.

...56

The time comes for Judge Andrew H. Tobiason of the Fourth Court of Appeals of the District of Columbia to make his judgment in the case of Laguna Space Research versus the United States Air Force. Dennis McPherson is there in the courtroom with Louis Goldman, seated just behind the plaintiff's bench that is occupied by three of Goldman's colleagues from his firm. On the other side are the Air Force lawyers, and McPherson is unpleasantly surprised to see behind them Major Tom Feldkirk, the man who got him into this in the first place. Feldkirk sits at attention and stares straight ahead at nothing.

Behind the parties in the case, the rather formal and imposing neoclassical room is filled with reporters. McPherson recognizes one of the main feature writers from *Aviation Week*, in a big crowd of others from the aerospace press. It's hard for McPherson to remember that much of this is taking place in public; it seems to him a very private thing. And yet here they are in front of everybody, part of tomorrow's business page without a doubt, if not the front pages. Newsheets and magazines everywhere, filled with LSR vs. USAF! It's too strange.

And it's too fast. McPherson has barely gotten seated, and used to the room and the seashell roar of its muttering crowd, when the judge comes in his side door and everyone stands. He's barely down again when the sergeant-at-arms or some official of the court like that declares, "Laguna Space Research versus United States Air Force, Case 2294875, blah blah blah blah . . ." McPherson stops listening to the announcement and stares curiously at Feldkirk, whose gaze never leaves the judge. If only he could stand up and say across the room, "What about the time you gave us this program as our own project, Feldkirk? Why don't you tell the judge about that?"

Well. No use getting angry. The judge no doubt knows about that anyway. And now he's saying something—McPherson bears down, focuses his attention, tries to ignore the feeling that he's caught in a trap he doesn't understand.

Judge Tobiason is saying, in a quick, clipped voice, "So in the interests of national security, I am letting the contract stand as awarded."

Goldman makes a quick tick with his teeth. The gavel falls. Case closed, court dismissed. The seashell mutters rise to a loud chatter, filling the room like the real sound of the ocean. McPherson stands with Goldman, they walk down the crowded central aisle.

By chance McPherson comes face to face with Tom Feldkirk. Feldkirk stares right through him, without even a blink, and marches out with the other Air Force people there. No looking back.

He's sitting in a car with Goldman. Goldman, he realizes, is angry; he's saying, "That bastard, that bastard. The case was clear." McPherson remembers the feeling he had at the ceremony where the contract was awarded; this is nothing like that for him, but for Goldman . . .

"We can pursue this," Goldman says, looking at McPherson and striking the steering switch. "The GAO's report has got the House Appropriations Committee interested, and several aides to members of the House Armed Services Committee are up in arms about it. We can make a formal request for a congressional investigation, and if some representatives are open to the idea then they could sic the Procurements Branch of the Office of Technology Assessment on them, as well as light a fire under the GAO. It could work."

McPherson, momentarily exhausted at the complexity of it all, only says "I'm sure we'll want to try it." Then he takes a deep breath, lets it out. "Let's go get a drink."

"Good idea."

They go up to a restaurant in Georgetown and sit at a tiny table placed under the street window. Window shoppers check them out to see if they are mannequins. They down one drink in silence. Goldman describes again the plan to influence the committees in Congress, and it sounds good.

After a while Goldman changes the subject. "I can tell you what went on behind the scenes at the Air Force. We finally got the whole story."

Curious despite his lassitude, McPherson nods. "Tell me."

Goldman settles back in his seat, closes his eyes briefly. He is getting over his anger at the judge's contempt for the rule of law, he's convinced they can win in Congress, and he's seduced by the gossip value of the story he's ferreted out: McPherson can read all that clearly. He's getting to know this man. "Okay, it started as far as you knew when Major Feldkirk came to you with a super-black program."

"Right." The cold bastard.

"But the truth is, that was part of a story that has been going on for years. Your Major Feldkirk works for Colonel T. D. Eaton, head of the Electrical Systems Division at the Pentagon—and Eaton works for General George Stanwyck, a three-star general also based in the Pentagon, and responsible for much of the ballistic missile defense. Now, your superblack program was presented to the Secretary of the Air Force as part of a campaign to pull the power of weapons procurement a little closer to the chest, so to speak—back completely in the Pentagon's power. Official reasoning for that was that procurement is in terrific disarray, because so many ballistic missile defense programs are getting into serious cost overruns, or deep technical trouble."

"I'm aware of that," McPherson says bleakly.

"The fact is, the whole procurement system is so badly screwed up that Congress is about to intervene again, which is one reason we have a very good chance there."

"That's the official reason, you said? And the unofficial?"

"That's where it gets interesting. Stanwyck, okay, he's in the Pentagon. Three-star general. And General Jack James, out at Air Force Systems Command at Andrews Air Force Base, is a four-star general. And they know each other."

Goldman looks at the palm of one hand, shakes his head. "It's curious how these things last. They went to the Air Force Academy together, you see. They started the same year, they were classmates. And you know how the officers are graduated from the military academies in ranked order? Well, those two were the competition for number one. In the last year it got pretty intense."

"You're kidding me," McPherson exclaims. "In *school*?"

"I know. It's sort of unbelievable what's behind these kind of conflicts, but several sources have confirmed this. I guess the whole thing was well-known in Boulder at the time. No one knows exactly how the rivalry started—some talk about a practical joke, others a disagreement over a woman cadet, but no one really knows—it's just one of those things that got rolling and kept going. I personally think it was probably just the number one thing, the competition for that. And James ended up first in the class, with Stanwyck second.

"Ever since then James has always done just that little bit better in terms of promotion. But recently Stanwyck got assigned to the Pentagon. And since then he's been a big force in the development of remotely piloted vehicles for combat missions. As you probably know, most of the Air Force brass has a strong bias against unpiloted vehicles, no matter how much sense they make in terms of current weapons technology."

"Sure. If all combat planes become remotely piloted, it'll be cheaper and fewer people will be killed, but where's the glory?"

"Exactly. If it happens, the whole Air Force becomes nothing but air traffic controllers, and they can't stand it. No more flying aces, no more right stuff, the whole tradition down the tubes. So it's obvious why they're so opposed to it. James among them, since he was a big flyer, one of the so-called flying colonels when they were choosing the design for the second generation ATF. But Stanwyck, now, he's been on the ground for a long time. And he'd like nothing more than to ground the flyboys too, and have James know it was all his doing. Thus all James's fault.

"Not only that, but Stanwyck is part of the Pentagon group that is trying to centralize all the armed forces, which would weaken the autonomy of the Air Force, and indirectly strip Air Force Systems Command, out at Andrews, of any real independent power at all."

McPherson shakes his head. "So we were pawns in a battle between two parts of the Air Force? It wasn't even interservice?"

Goldman pauses to consider it. "Basically true. But it was the program that was the pawn, though. And from what we now know, I suspect it was a pawn that Stanwyck intended to sacrifice all along. Because"—he stops to sip at his drink—"it was Stanwyck himself who told James of the existence of the Storm-bee program. This was after you had been working on your superblack proposal for some time, see, *after* Stanwyck had made sure, by the use of in-house spies, or inquiries from Feldkirk or whatever, that you had a good, workable system. Only at that point, when the superblack mechanism was already rolling to award LSR the contract, did Stanwyck tell James about it, supposedly in the course of answering a request for information. But I think it was planned. I think that that was the shoving of the pawn out into an exposed position, to set up the sacrifice."

"You mean Stanwyck wanted the program taken away and turned white?"

"Well, think about what had to happen as a result. James gets mad as hell, and because he's a four-star general he has the authority to make it a white program, and take over the administration of the bidding process. At that point, you people at LSR are doomed, because no matter what the various other bids look like, James is bound and determined that LSR is not going to win this contract, because you are the company that Stanwyck chose. At the same time, as Stanwyck well knows, LSR has a damn good system worked up. So . . . do you see?"

"He set James up to initiate cheating in the evaluation process," McPherson says. He feels a certain theoretical pleasure in understanding at the same time that disgust is twisting his stomach again. "If it happened, and we protested successfully, then James loses power."

"He might even lose his job! They might force him to retire, no doubt about it. At this point James has his back to the wall, and that's a fact."

"So Stanwyck's gambit worked. The pawn was taken, but the king is in trouble."

"Yes." Goldman nods precisely. "And as you might guess, it's people in Stan-wyck's command at the Pentagon who have leaked a fair amount of the material used by us and the GAO. Now, Judge Tobiason is either on James's side, or he isn't aware of the conflict and is only protecting the Air Force. Or else he disapproves of the fight and only wants to stop it. Impossible to tell. We don't really know. It doesn't really matter, now that that stage of the battle is over."

"And where did you get this information about Stanwyck and James?"

"From James's subordinates. He isn't much liked, and the story is widespread at Andrews. And from Stanwyck's people, who want it known."

"Hmph."

They order another round, then talk about tactics in the campaign to get Congress to act. Goldman is enthusiastic about this in a way McPherson hasn't seen before; apparently Goldman wrote off their chances in court ever since Tobiason was appointed judge in the case, so that this is the point where he can really work with some hope of success.

But McPherson finds himself very tired of the matter. The truth is, the day has seen the end of one of their last chances. Once a pawn has been sacrificed successfully and taken off the board, what real chance is there for it to petition its way back on, to protest the way it was used, to redress its grievances?

Well, Goldman thinks their chances are pretty good. It isn't exactly chess, after all. Much more ambiguous and uncertain. But McPherson goes back to the Crystal City Hyatt Regency feeling depressed, and more than a little drunk.

Out one of the great mirror-windowed walls of the Hyatt stands the Pentagon Annex, a massive concrete bunker defended against all the world. Impenetrable. Who could really believe it could be defeated?

He gets lost on the way to his room, has to consult three bad maps and walk half a mile of halls to find it. When he does there's nothing there but the bed, the video, a window facing the inky Potomac. Can he stand to turn the video on?

No. He sits on the bed. Tomorrow he can fly home. Be back with Lucy. Only fourteen hours to get through till then.

Some two hours later, just as he is falling asleep watching the dead video screen, the phone rings. He leaps up as if shot. Answers it.

"Dennis? Tom Feldkirk here. I—I just wanted to tell you that I'm sorry about what's happened in this case. I didn't have any part in it and didn't have any way to change things. And I want you to know I don't like what's happened one bit." The man's voice is strained to the point of shaking. "I'm damned sorry, Dennis. It isn't how I meant it to happen."

McPherson sits dully with phone to ear. He thinks of the stories Goldman told him that evening. It's possible, even likely, that Feldkirk wasn't aware of how the superblack program would be used by Stanwyck. He probably found out after it was too late to do anything about it. Another pawn in the game. Otherwise why even call?

"Dennis?"

"That's all right, Tom. It wasn't your fault. Maybe next time it'll go better."

"I hope so. I hope so."

Awkward good-bye. McPherson hangs up, looks at his watch.

Only twelve hours to go.

... 57

In 1940 the population was 130,000. By 1980 it was 2,000,000.

At that point the northwestern half of the county was saturated. La Habra, Brea, Yorba Linda, Placentia, Fullerton, Buena Park, La Mirada, Cerritos, La Palma, Cypress, Stanton, Anaheim, Orange, Villa Park, El Modena, Santa Ana, Garden Grove, Westminster, Fountain Valley, Los Alamitos, Seal Beach, Huntington Beach. Newport Beach, Costa Mesa, Corona del Mar, Irvine, Tustin: all of these cities had grown, merged, melted together, until the idea that twenty-seven cities existed on the land was just a fiction of administration, a collection of unnoticed street signs, announcing borders that only the maps knew. It was one city.

This new megacity, "Orange County North," had as its transport system the freeways. The private car was the only way; the little train system of the early days had been pulled out, like the more extensive electric rail network in Los Angeles, to make more room for cars. In the end there were no trains, no buses, no trams, no subways. People had to drive cars to work, to get food, to do all the chores, to play—to do anything.

So after the completion of the Santa Ana Freeway in the late 1950s, the others quickly followed. The Newport and Riverside freeways bisected the county into its northwest and southeast halves; the San Diego Freeway followed the coast, extended the Santa Ana Freeway south to San Diego; the Garden Grove, Orange, and San Gabriel freeways added ribbing to the system, so that one could get to within a few miles of anywhere in Orange County North that one wanted to go, all on the freeways.

Soon the northwestern half was saturated, every acre of land bought, covered with concrete, built on, filled up. Nothing left but the dry bed of the Santa Ana River, and even that was banked and paved.

Then the Irvine Ranch was bought by a development company. For years the county government had taxed the ranch as hard as it could, trying to force it out *of agriculture, into more tract housing. Now they got their wish. The new owners made a general plan that was (at first) unusually slow and thoughtful by Orange County standards; the University of California was given ten thousand acres, a town was built around it, a development schedule was worked up for the rest of the land. But the wedge was knocked into the southeast half of the county, and the pressure for growth drove it ever harder.*

Meanwhile, in the northwest half the congestion grew with an intensity that the spread to the southeast couldn't help; in fact, given the thousands of new users that the southward expansion gave to the freeway system, it only made things worse. The old Santa Ana Freeway, three lanes in each direction, was clogged every day; the same was true of the Newport Freeway, and to a lesser extent of all the freeways. And yet there was no room left to widen them. What to do?

In the 1980s a plan was put forth to build an elevated second story for the Santa Ana Freeway, between Buena Park and Tustin; and in the 1990s, with the prospect of the county's population doubling again in ten years, the Board of Supervisors acted on it. Eight new lanes were put up on an elevated viaduct, set on massive pylons thirty-seven feet above the old freeway; they were opened to southbound traffic in 1998. Three years later the same was done for the Newport and Garden Grove freeways, and in the triangle of the elevated freeways, three miles on each side, the elevated lanes were joined by elevated gas stations and convenience stops and restaurants and movie theaters and all the rest. It was the beginning of the "second story" of the city.

The next generation of freeways were the Foothill, Eastern, and San Joaquin, all designed to ease the access to the southern half of the county. When those were in it made sense to connect the ends of the Garden Grove and Foothill freeways, which were only a few miles from each other; and so they were spliced by a great viaduct above Cowan and Lemon Heights, leaving the homes below devalued but intact. Then the new Santiago and Cleveland freeways were built in the same way, flying through the sky on great pylons, above the new condos springing up everywhere in the back hills, in what used to be Irvine Ranch, Mission Viejo Ranch, O'Neill Ranch—now the new towns of Santiago, Silverado, Trabuco, Seaview Terrace, San Juan Springs, Los Pinos, O'Neill, Ortega, Saddleback, Alicia, and so on and so on. And as the land was subdivided, platted, developed, covered with concrete, built up, the freeway system grew with it. When the national push for the electromagnetic road track system began, the freeways of Orange County were in place and ready for it; it only took five years to make the change, and work created by this transformation helped head off the recession of the Boring Twenties before it plunged into outright worldwide depression. A new transport system, a new boom; always the case in Orange County, as in all the American West.

So the southeast half of Orange County, when the flood burst over the Irvine

Ranch and the development began, grew even faster than the northwest half had, fifty years before. In thirty quick years it became indistinguishable from the rest of the megacity. The only land left was the Cleveland National Forest. The real estate companies hungrily eyed this empty, dry, hilly land; what condos could be put up there, what luxury homes, on the high slopes of old Saddleback Mountain! And it only took a sympathetic administration in Washington to begin the dismemberment of this insignificant little national forest. Not even any forest there! Why worry about it! The county was crowded, they needed that 66,000 acres for more homes, more jobs, more profits, more cars, more money, more weapons, more drugs, more real estate, more freeways! And so that land was sold too.

And none of that ever went away.

... 58

Abe and Xavier have been sitting around headquarters for a good half of their shift, a rare event indeed. They've been playing video football, pumping weights, napping, and playing more football. Xavier is killer at the game, he plays for money at the Boathouse, and he hits the keys of his control board like a typist going at two hundred words a minute, so that all eleven of his men play like inspired all-stars. On offense Abe is constantly being tackled for a loss, sacked, intercepted, or having his punts blocked, and once on defense he gets steamrolled every way possible. In the latest game the stat board shows him with minus 389 yards rushing, in a game he is losing 98–7. And he got the seven by screaming, *"Look out!"* just after beginning a play, actually fooling Xavier into glancing around while he tossed a successful bomb.

So Abe quits.

"No, Abe, no! I'll play with my eyes shut, I swear!"

"No way."

And Abe is napping again when the alarm goes, a high, not-so-loud ringing that squeezes every adrenal gland in his body. He's up and out and fastening his seat belt before he's even awake, and only as they zip out onto Edinger and into traffic does his heart rate sink back to a halfway reasonable patter. Another year off his life, no doubt; firemen and paramedics have a really high heart attack rate, as a result of the damage caused by these sudden leaps of adrenal acceleration. "Where'm I going?"

"Proceed northward on the Newport until encountering the Garbage Grove Freeway, west to the Orange Freeway, north to Nutwood, and over to State. We have been called to render assistance at a car crash."

"You're kidding."

Abe notices that Xavier's hand is clamped on the radio microphone so tight that the yellowy palm is almost completely white. And the joky rapid-fire patter has an edge in it, it always did of course, but now it burrs X's voice to the point where the dispatcher asks him to repeat things sometimes. Xavier needs a long vacation, no doubt about it. Or a change of work. He's burning out, Abe can see it happening shift by shift. But with his own family, and the dependency of what sounds like a good chunk of Santa Ana's populace, he can't afford to quit or to take a long break. Pretty obviously he won't stop until it's him that breaks.

Abe concentrates on driving. Traffic is bad where the Garden Grove Freeway bleeds into the Orange and Santa Ana, in the giant multilevel concrete ramp pretzel, every ramp stopped up entirely, it's offtrack time again, the song of the sirens howling up and down, power sensation as the truck leaps under his foot, the tracked cars on his right flying by in a blur of color, one long rainbow bar of neon metal flowing by, whoops there's a car offtrack right in their path blocking it entirely, heavy brakes. "Shit! What's that doing there!"

"Get back ontrack."

"I'm trying, man, can't just drive over these civilians you know." Abe puts on flasher, blinkers, the truck is strobing light at a score of frequencies, should hypnotize the car drivers if nothing else. No break in the traffic appears.

"They think we a Christmas tree," X says angrily, and leans far out of his window to wave futilely at the passing stream. "Just edge over into them, man."

Abe takes a deep breath, eases in the clutch, steers right. Xavier shouts abuse at the cars in the fast lane, and finally says to Abe, "Go for it," and blindly Abe floors it and steers over into the lane, expecting a crunch from the side any second. As soon as he gets past the stalled car on the shoulder he veers back onto the concrete shoulder and guns it, fishtailing almost into the rail. Xavier is waving thanks to the driver who gave them the gap. They're up to speed again. "We got a dangerous job," Xavier says heavily as he settles back into his seat. "Opportunities for impaction while attempting to reach our designated destination are numerous indeed."

Abe sings the last line of their "Ode to Fred Spaulding":

And he never, exceeded, the speed, limit—againnnn!

Xavier joins in and they cackle wildly as they trundle at eighty miles an hour up the freeway shoulder. Abe's hands clamp the steering wheel, Xavier's palm is white-person white on the mike.

X says, "Have you heard the latest Fred Spaulding joke? Fred sees the overpass pylon coming at them, he shouts back into the ambulance compartment, 'Tell the victim we'll have him there in a second!'"

Abe laughs. "That's like the one where he asks the victim what's the definition of bad luck."

"Ha! Yeah. Or where he asks him to explain double-in-demnity insurance."

"Ha! ha! Or the one where he says, 'Have you got insurance?' and the victim says, 'No!' and Fred says, 'Don't worry about it!'"

Xavier is helpless at this, he puts his forehead on the dash and giggles away. When he's done he says, "Wish I didn't believe in insurance. You wouldn't believe how much I pay every month."

"It's a good bet, remember that."

"That's right. You die young, the insurance company says, 'You win!'" He laughs again, and Abe is cheered to see it. Abe adds:

"And if you lose the bet, you're still alive."

"Exactly."

They reach Nutwood, turn off the freeway and head west to College Avenue, shooting through the shops and restaurants and laundromats and bookstores that serve Cal State Fullerton. Crowds watch them pass, cars skitter over to the slow track or slide into empty parking slots, giving Abe little scares each time they hesitate and almost scatter into his path. Familiar surge of power as they part traffic likes Moses at the Red Sea. Up ahead traffic is dense, stopped, the brake lights go off in his brain, Chippie car lights rolling red and blue in the intersection. "We need the cutters," Xavier reports from the radio. "Code six."

Abe sucks down air, he's breathing rapidly. He drives onto a sidewalk to make half a block, thumps back over the curb and crawls by cars to the *sota*.

They're there. Three-car job. Sits, something in the silicon. Or maybe this was a combination of silicon breakdown and human error. College had a green light, cars were pouring through, apparently; a truck fired through its red light on Nutwood and broadsided a left-lane car that was caught against the car in the right lane, the three of them skidding over into a traffic light and a power pole, knocking the poles flat over. Both the cars are crunched, especially the middle one, which is a pancake. And the truck driver isn't too well off either, no seat belt natch.

Abe is out of the truck and on the move, dragging his cutters over to the cars, where Chippies are gesturing violently for him. Someone's caught in the middle car, and with all the sparks from the power lines, they fear electrocution for those inside.

There are two people in the front seat of the sandwiched car. Abe ignores the driver as she appears dots, sets to work on the roof of the car to get to the passenger. Again he's at work, cutting with a delicate touch as the snips shear the steel with great creaks and crunches, metallic shrieks covering repeated moans from the girl in the passenger seat. Xavier slithers in from above and is quickly at work, giving a rapid sequence of very exact commands to Abe above, "Cut another foot and a half back on the midline and pull it up. Farther. Okay, take that sidewall out of the rear door, we can get her out here." Stretcher set, for a teenager in yellow blouse and pants, all stained blood red in an alarmingly bright pattern. Xavier and the Chippies run her to the truck and Abe works his way into the smashed car to check on getting the driver out. In the right rear door, lean over the blood-soaked seatback—

It's Lillian Keilbacher. Face white, lips cut, blond hair thrown back. It's definitely her. Her chest—crushed. She's dead. Dots, no doubt about it. That's Lillian, right there. Her body.

Abe backs out of the car. He notes that the car was a new Toyota Banshee, a little sport model popular among kids. Seems he's gone deaf; he sees the turmoil of spectators and cars around them, but can't hear a thing. He remembers Xavier, sweating, talking in a near hysteria about the time he turned over a dead kid in a car and saw, just for a moment, his son's face. He makes a move toward the car, thinking to check the girl's ID. But no, it's her. It's her. Carefully he walks to the curb and sits on it.

"Abe! Where—Abe! What are you doing, man?" Xavier is crouched at his side, hand on his shoulder. "What's wrong?"

Abe looks at him, croaks, "I know her. The driver. Friend of the family. Lillian, Lillian Keilbacher."

"Oh, man. . . ." Xavier's face scowls with distress; Abe can't stand to look at him. "We got to go anyway, the other one's still alive. Come on, bro. I'll drive, you can work in back."

Abe is qualified to do the medic work, but when they reach the truck he can't face it. He balks at the rear door. "No, man. I'll drive."

"You sure you can?"

"I'll drive!"

"Okay. Be careful. Let's go to Anaheim Hospital."

Abe gets in. Seat belt on. He drives. He's a blank; he finds himself at the freeway exit leading to Anaheim Memorial and he can't remember a single thought from the drive, or the drive itself. Xavier pops his head through the window. "This one looks like she'll pull through. Here, make a left here, man, ER is at the side."

"I know."

Xavier falls silent. Wordlessly they sit as Abe drives them to the ER ramp. He sits and listens while Xavier and the nurses get Lillian's friend inside. Memory brings up to him the image of Lillian's dead face rolling toward him, looking through him. His diaphragm's all knotted, he's not breathing well. He blanks again.

Xavier opens the driver's door. "Come on, Abe, slide over. I'll drive for a while."

Abe slides over. Xavier puts them on the track to the street. He glances at Abe, starts to say something, stops.

Abe swallows. He thinks of Mrs. Keilbacher, his favorite among all his mother's friends. Suddenly he realizes she'll have to be told. He imagines the phone call from a stranger, this is the Fullerton police, is this Mrs. Martin Keilbacher? At the thought his jaw clamps until he can feel all his teeth. No one should ever have to get a call like that. Better to hear it from—well, anybody. Any other way has to be better. He takes a deep breath. "Listen, X, drive me up onto Red Hill. I got to tell her folks, I guess." As he says this he begins to tremble.

"Oh, man—"

"Someone's got to tell them, and I think this would be better. Don't you?"

"I don't know. —We're still on duty, you know."

"I know. But they're almost on the route back to the station."

Xavier sighs. "Tell me the way."

As they turn up the tree-lined, steep street that the Keilbachers live on, Abe begins shaking in earnest. "This one on the left."

Xavier stops the truck. Abe looks past the white fence and the tiny yard, to their window of the duplex. A light is on. He gets out, closes the truck door quietly. Walks around the hood. Come on, he thinks, open the door and come out, ask me what's wrong, don't make me come knock on your door like this!

He knocks on the door, hard. Rings the bell. Stands there.

No answer.

No one's home.

"Shit." He's upset; he knows he should feel relieved, but he doesn't, not at all. He walks around the duplex, looks in the kitchen window. Dark. Light left on in the living room while they're out, SOP. Xavier is leaning his head out the window. Abe returns to the truck. "No one's home!"

"It's all right, Abe. You did what you could. Get back in here."

Abe stands, irresolute. Can't leave a note in the door about this! And the two of them are still on duty. But still, still . . . he can't rid himself of the idea that he should tell them. He climbs back in the truck, and as he sits he has an idea. "Jim's folks live up here too, and his mom is a good friend of theirs. Drive me by there and I'll tell her and she can take over here, we can get back to the station. They go to church together and everything."

Xavier nods patiently, starts up the truck. He follows Abe's directions and drives them past house after house. Then they are at Jim's parents' duplex, well remembered by Abe from years past, looking just the same to him. Drapes are closed, but lights are on inside.

Abe jumps out and walks to the kitchen door, which is the one the family always uses. Rings the bell.

The door opens on a chain, and Lucy McPherson looks out suspiciously. "Abe! What are you doing here?"

At the question Abe loses the feeling that it made sense to come to her. Lucy closes the door to undo the chain, opens it fully. She looks at him curiously, not getting it. "It's good to see you! Here, come in—"

Abe waves a hand quickly. Lucy squints at him. She's nice, Abe thinks, he can remember a hundred kindnesses from her when he was the new kid in Jim's group. But in recent years he's noticed a distance in her, a certain reserve behind her cheery politeness that seems to indicate disapproval . . . as if she perhaps thought Abe was responsible for whatever changes in Jim she doesn't like. It has irked him, and a couple times he found himself wanting to say, Yes, yes, I personally have corrupted your innocent son, sure.

Random thoughts, flashing through Abe's confusion as he sees that tiny squint of suspicion or distrust. "I—I'm sorry, Mrs. McPherson." Say it. "I've got bad news," and he sees her eyes open wide with fear, he puts a hand forward quickly: "No, not about Jim—it's about Lillian Keilbacher. I just came from their house, and there's no one home to tell! You know, you know I'm a paramedic."

Lucy nods, eyes shining.

"Well," Abe says helplessly, "I just found Lillian in a car crash we were called to. And she was dead, she'd been killed."

Lucy's hand flies to her mouth, she turns to one side as if bracing for a blow. It's as bad as Mrs. Keilbacher. No, it's not.

"My Lord. . . ." She reaches out hesitantly, touches Abe's arm. "How awful. Do you want to come in and sit down?"

That's almost too much. Abe can't take it, and he backs up a step, shakes his head. "No, no," he says, choking up. "I'm still on call, got to go back to work. But I thought . . . someone they knew should tell them."

She nods, looking at him with a worried expression. "I agree. I'll go get the Reverend Strong, and we'll try to find them."

Abe nods dumbly. He looks up into her eyes, shrugs. For a moment they share something, some closeness he can't define. "I'm sorry," he says.

"I'm glad you came here," she says firmly. And she walks him back to the truck. Something in the kindness of those words, and in the fact that his task is done, breaks the restraints in Abe, he can feel the shock of it again: and he shakes hard all the way back to the station, while X drives grimly, muttering "Oh, man . . . oh, man . . ."

Back at the station they collapse on the couch. The football game mocks them.

After a while Xavier says slowly, "You know, Abe, I don't think we're cut out for this job."

Abe drinks his coffee as if it were whiskey. "No one is."

"But some more than others. And not us. You've got to be stupid to do this job right. No, not stupid exactly. It takes smarts to do it right. But . . ." He shakes his head.

"You've got to be a robot," Abe says dully. "But I'll be damned if I'll become a robot for the sake of some job." He drinks again.

"Well . . ." X can only shake his head. "That was bad luck, tonight. Damned bad luck."

"A new definition." But neither of them even cracks a smile.

For a long time they just sit there on the couch, side by side, staring at the floor.

Xavier nudges him. "More coffee?"

... 59

Lucy returns to the duplex and wanders the rooms aimlessly. Dennis is due back from Washington late that night. Jim's got class. Briefly she cries. "Oh, Lillian—"

Then she goes to put on her shoes. "Got to get organized, here." She calls the Keilbachers. No answer. She's got her sweater on, ready to go—but where? She calls the church. Reverend's out on call, she gets his answering machine. Everyone's gone! What is this? Vicar Sebastian, ineffectual as always, answers his phone and is reduced to speechlessness by Lucy's news. He and Lillian were good friends, it may be he even had a crush on her. So he's no help. Lucy finally says she'll come pick him up. He agrees. Then she calls Helena, who thank the Lord is home, and tells her the bad news. Helena can't believe it. She agrees to meet Lucy at the church.

Lucy drives to the church without seeing a thing. She just had lunch with Emma Keilbacher that day, and Emma didn't mention any plans to go out that evening, did she? So hard to remember at a time like this. And she just worked with Lillian yesterday—

She forbids herself to think along those lines, and collects herself before going in to the church offices. Helena is already there, bless her. The vicar, pale and red-eyed, slows them for a prayer that Lucy has no patience for. They've got to find Emma and Martin.

So they get into Lucy's car, and she drives to the Keilbachers' house. Still no one home.

"I suppose they could have gone out to eat when Martin came home. . . ."

"They usually just go to Marie Callender's during the week."

"Yeah, that's right." Between them Lucy and Helena know every restaurant that Emma and Martin might frequent. So Lucy drives them to Marie Callender's, but they're not there.

"Where next?"

They try the El Torito on Chapman. No luck there. They track to Three Crowns, and then Charlie's; the Keilbachers are nowhere to be seen.

They return to the house. No luck. It's really very frustrating.

After that it's a matter of friends they might be visiting. Vicar Sebastian feels telephoning around is a bad idea, so there follows a nightmarish interval of visits to all the friends of the Keilbachers they know: finding they aren't there, pausing to give the friends the news, driving on.

Lucy begins to feel more and more strongly that they should *find* them, it strikes her as terrible, somehow, that so many people should know and Emma and Martin still be unaware. They're all getting frustrated, vexed, upset; it's hard to agree on what to try next.

"Do you suppose they already heard from the police?" Sebastian asks.

Lucy shakes her head. "Abe came straight to me, there wouldn't have been time, I don't think."

They track all the way to Seal Beach where the Jansens moved, then into Irvine, back to the house, over to the church, then to the Cinema 12 theaters down in Tustin. . . . No luck, they just aren't to be found.

"Where *are* they?" Lucy demands angrily. Helena and the vicar, cowed by Lucy's determination to find them, are out of ideas.

Defeated, Lucy can only drive back to their house, frustrated and mystified. Where in the world are they?

She parks on the street in front of the Keilbachers' duplex. The three of them sit in the car and wait.

There isn't much to say. The whole neighborhood is still. The streetlight overhead flickers. Street, gutter, curb, grass, sidewalk, grass, driveways, houses, they're all flickering too, leeched of color by the mercury vapor's blue glow: a gray world, flickering a little. It's strange: like holding watch for some mysterious organization, or performing a new ritual that they don't fully understand. So strange, Lucy thinks, the things life leads you into doing.

Headlights appear at the bottom of the street, and Lucy's heart jumps in her, like a small child trapped inside, trying to escape. The car approaches slowly. Turns into the Keilbachers' driveway.

"Oh, my God," says Helena, and begins to cry.

The vicar begins to cry.

"Now wait a minute," Lucy says harshly as she opens the door and begins to get out of the car. "We're doing God's work here—we're his messengers, and it's God speaking now, not us," and sure enough it must be true, because here's Lucy McPherson crossing the lawn toward the surprised Keilbachers, Lucy who gets teary if she's told the story of someone's suffering or sacrifice, Lucy who waters up if you look at her sideways—here she is just as calm as can be, as she stands before Emma and Martin and gives them the news—as steady as a doctor, as they help Emma off the lawn and inside. And all through that long horrible night, as Emma is racked with hysterical grief, and Martin sits on the back porch staring at little handprints in the concrete, at nothing, it's Lucy that they turn to to make coffee, to fix soup, to hold Emma, to deal with the police, and with the mortuary, and with all the business that the others cannot face, shaken as they are; it's Lucy they turn to.

... 60

When Dennis arrives home from Washington, very late that night, exhausted and depressed, he finds an empty house. And no note. At first he's angry, then worried; and he can't think what to do about it. It's completely unlike Lucy, he can't think of a possible explanation where she could be at three in the morning. Has she left him, like Dan Houston's wife? A moment of panic spikes into him at the thought; then he shakes his head, clearing it of such nonsense. Lucy wouldn't do it.

Has something happened to her? An hour passes and the fear grows in him, then almost two hours pass, and it's just occurred to him that he could call the reverend, rather than the police, when she pulls into the driveway. He hurries out to greet her, relieved and angry.

"Where have you been!"

She tells him.

"Ah," he says stiffly, and puts his arms around her. Holds her.

He's too tired for this, he thinks. Too tired.

They stand there. He's awfully tired. He remembers a game he played with his brother when they were boys, during the marathon driving tours his parents took them on. At night in the motel rooms they took a deck of cards and divided it, and made card houses on the floor, in opposite corners of the room. Card fortresses would be a better name for them. Then they took a plastic spoon from McDonald's, and used it as a projectile—bent it back like a catapult arm with their thumbs and fingers, and let fly. The spoon took the most hilarious knuckleball flights across the room, and mostly missed. They laughed. . . .

And when the spoon hit the card houses, it was so *interesting*; it didn't matter whose was hit, it was just fun to see what happened. They noted that the card houses acted in one of two ways when struck by a direct hit. *Thwap!* They either collapsed instantly, the cards scattering, or else they resisted, settled down a little, and somehow in the hunkering down lost little or none of their structural integrity, their ability to hold up. Perhaps curiosity about that made Dennis an engineer.

Random images, in the exhausted mind. Where did that come from, he thinks. Ah. We're the card house now. There's never a situation where one card is threatened, the others left in peace; they're all threatened together and at once. All in a permanent crisis. How long has it been going on? Spoons flying from every direction. And the house of cards either holds or flies apart.

He's too tired for this, too depressed; there's no comfort in him to give. Lucy begins to sob in earnest. He tries to remember the Keilbacher girl; he only saw her a few times, flitting in and out. Blond hair. A lively kid. Nice. Easier to imagine Martin and Emma. Ach. Bad luck. Terrible luck. Worse by far than having Judge Andrew Tobiason turn down a protest despite the evidence; worse than anything possible in all that world of corruption and graft. Ach, it's bad everywhere. Spoons from every direction. He'll have to check out Jim's car, make sure it's all right. He doesn't know what to say. Lucy always wants something said, words, words, but he doesn't have any. Are there any words for this? No. Some strange stubbornness, of an interlocking placement, holds certain card houses up, under a fluky barrage of blows. . . . He hugs her harder, holds them up.

... 61

Jim hears about it the next day, from Lucy. "It was Abe who was the paramedic called to the accident."

"Oh, no. You're kidding."

"No, and he drove by to tell the Keilbachers, but they weren't home, so he came by to tell me. He looked bad."

"I bet."

Jim tries to get Abe on the phone, but Abe's parents are still on vacation and there's no answer up at the house; the answering machine is off.

He goes to the funeral the next morning, and stands at the back of the chapel at Fairhaven Cemetery. Watches the ceremony dully. He knew Lillian Keilbacher mostly in churches, he thinks. There was a time in high school when he was volunteered by Lucy to help build the Bible school on the back of the church lot; the church was too poor to hire a real construction crew, and the work was all volunteer, led by two churchgoing carpenters who seemed to get a kick out of it all, though it went awfully slowly. Every day that Jim was there he saw a skinny blond girl with braces who had the biggest, most enthusiastic hammer swing you could imagine. The carpenters used to go pale as they watched, but she was surprisingly accurate. That was Lillian. Jim can see perfectly the delighted brace-bright grin of the girl as she knocked a nail all the way in to the wood with one immense swing, Don the head carpenter clutching his heart and spluttering with laughter. . . .

They move outside into a shaft of sun. The cemetery is under the upper level of the Freeway Triangle, a concrete sky like low threatening clouds, but there is a big skylight gap overhead to let a little sunlight down. They walk slowly behind a hearse as it navigates the complex street plan of the city of the dead. Population over 200,000. Again Jim walks behind, watching the little crowd of people around the Keilbachers, the way they hold together. There is a feeling in their church community, standing on its little island of belief in the flood of twenty-first-century America, a feeling of solidarity that Jim has never experienced again since he stopped going. The camaraderie, the joy they shared, building that little Bible school! And it turned out solid, too, it's still there. Yes, there's no doubt Lucy is on to something with her involvement in the church. . . . But his faith. He has no faith. And it can't be faked. And without faith. . . .

Beyond the last row of graves is an orange grove, standing under a big skylight. The procession is in shade now, under the concrete underside of the Triangle, and the wide shaft of light falling on the green-and-orange trees is thick with dust, very bright. The trees are almost spheres, sitting on the ground: green spheres, dotted with many bright orange spheres. It's the last orange grove in all of Orange County. It belongs to the cemetery, and is slowly being taken out to make room for the dead.

The ceremony at graveside is short. No sign of Abe, Jim notes. He excuses himself to a disapproving Lucy, and slips off; the idea of a wake is too much.

He tracks up Saddleback Mountain, listening to Beethoven's *Hammerklavier Sonata*. There's no one home at Abe's place.

He follows the road up to the lookout parking lot on Santiago Peak, the easternmost of Saddleback's two. The western one, Modjeska Peak, is a few feet lower. He gets out of the car, walks to the stone wall on the parking lot's edge, looks down at Orange County.

There spread below him is his hometown. During the daytime it's a hazy jumble of buildings and flying freeway viaducts, no pattern visible. Even the upper level in the Freeway Triangle, which dominates the central plain, is hard to pick out. It's as if they brought cement trucks with their big cylindrical barrels up to this peak, and let loose a flood of concrete lava that covered the entire plain. Western civilization's last city.

Jim recalls the view from the hilltop in Itanos.

His thoughts are scattered, he can't make them cohere. Things are changing in him, the old channels of thought are breaking up and disappearing, with nothing new to take their place. He feels incoherent.

Depressed, he drives back down the mountain. He feels he should locate Abe, so he goes to Sandy's. Abe is not there, and neither is Sandy. Angela has heard of the accident, and she takes Jim out to the balcony, talks to him about other things. Jim sits there dully, touched by Angela's concern. She really is a wonderful person, one of his best friends, the sister his family didn't provide.

Now she stares at the palms of her hands, looking troubled. "Everything seems to be going wrong," she says. "Have you heard that Erica has broken off the alliance with Tashi?"

"No—what?"

"Yeah. She did it at last. She's stopped coming by here, too. I guess she decided on a total change." Angela isn't bitter, but she does sound sad. They sit on the balcony, looking at each other. The hum of the freeway wafts over them.

"It's no big surprise," Angela says. "Erica's been unhappy now for a long time."

"I know. . . . I wonder how Tash is taking it."

"It's so hard to tell with Tash. I'm sure he's upset, but he doesn't say much."

He does to Jim, though. Sometimes. "I should go see him. My God, everyone! . . ."

"I know."

The doorbell rings, and through the houseplants comes Virginia. "Hello, Jim." Quick kiss on the cheek. "I heard about your friend. I'm really sorry."

Jim nods, touched by her concern. Seems everyone pulls together at times like these.

Virginia looks lovely in the hazy afternoon light, hair banded white gold, flashing with an almost painful brightness. It's all part of the pattern, Jim sees. This is what it means to have friends, to be part of a functioning community. And that's what they are; another island poking out of the concrete. . . .

"Let me take you out to dinner," Virginia says, and gratefully Jim agrees. Angela sees them off with determined cheerfulness. They take Jim's car and track down to the Hungry Crab in Newport Beach.

Since they haven't talked in a while, there is a fair amount to say; and as they work their way through two bottles of wine and a crab feast, they get more and more festive. Jim can even describe the various comedies of the European jaunt; their fighting is past, they're beyond that, into a more mature stage of their relationship. Jim watches Virginia laugh, and the sight of her is more intoxicating than the wine: perfect glossy hair like a cap of jewels, deep beach tan, snub nose, freckles, wide white smile, a perfect match for the decor, perfect, perfect, perfect.

So he is quite drunk, both with wine and with his proximity to this beautiful animal, when they pay the bill and leave. Out into the salt cool of a Newport Beach evening, lurching together, holding hands, laughing at a pair of goggle-eyed sunburnt tourists—thoroughly enjoying themselves as they approach a group of students walking their way.

Then Jim sees Hana Steentoft in the group, head down in characteristic pose. As the group passes them she looks up at him, looks down again. The group walks by and into the Crab.

Jim has stopped, and at some point jerked his hand free of Virginia's. Now as he looks back at the restaurant the old sardonic smile is on her face. She says, "Ashamed to be seen with me, eh?"

"No, no."

"Sure."

Jim doesn't know what to say, he can't concentrate on Virginia right now, he doesn't care what Virginia thinks or feels. All he wants to do is rush into the Crab and try to explain things to Hana. It's like a nightmare: somehow trapped in an old disaster alliance, which poisons the new relationship—he's had nightmares just like this! How could it be happening?

But it is happening, and here he is, standing on the sidewalk with a furious Virginia Novello. Abandoning her in Newport Beach and running in to throw himself at Hana's feet in a group of friends is just too melodramatic for Jim, too extreme, he can't see himself doing it.

So he stays to face Virginia's wrath.

"You really are rude, you know that, Jim?"

"Come on, Virginia. Give me a break."

How easily they fall back into it. All the variations on a theme: It's all your fault. No it's not; I'm not conceding a thing to you; it's all your fault. Back and forth, back and forth. You're a bad person. No I'm not, I'm a good person. You're a bad person. There are a lot of ways to say these things, and Jim and Virginia rehearse the whole repertory on the way home, the little moment of camaraderie completely and utterly forgotten.

Their favorite coda, as Jim tracks into South Coast Plaza and stops the car: "I don't want to ever see you again!" Virginia shouts.

"Good!" Jim shouts back. "You won't!"

And Virginia slams the door and runs off.

Jim takes a deep sigh, puts his forehead down on the steering switch. How many people can he hurt at once? This day . . .

He sits for several minutes, head miserably on the dash, worrying about Hana. He's got to do something, or he'll . . . he doesn't know what. Abe. Can't find Abe. Tashi! Man, it's hitting everywhere at once, as if the whole island is threatened by flood. All falling apart! He tracks down Bristol, heading toward Tashi's place.

... 62

Up on Tashi's roof it's quiet and dark. The tent is lit on one side by the dull glow of a lamp inside. On the other side of the roof, among the vegetable trays, there's a dim glow of hibachi coals. Tashi, a big bulk in the darkness, sits in a little folding beach chair beside the fire. A sweet soy smell of teriyaki sauce rises from the meat on the fire. "Hey, Jim."

"Hey, Tash." Jim picks up a folded beach chair from beside the tent wall and unfolds it. Sits.

Tash leans forward to flip over one of his infamous turkey burgers, and the grease flares on the coals for a moment, lighting Tashi's face. He looks as impassive as ever, picking up a water bottle, spraying out the flames. In the renewed dark he squeezes a little of his homemade teriyaki on the turkey burgers, and they hiss and steam aromatically.

"I heard about Erica."

"Hmm."

"She just left?"

". . . It was a little more complicated than that. But that's what it comes down to." Tash leans forward again, slides the spatula under the burger and checks it out. Puts it into a sandwich already prepared. Eats.

"Damn." Jim finds himself furious with Erica. "She just . . . did it?"

"Umph."

"Unbelievable." To leave someone like Tash! "Stupid woman. Man, it's such a dumb thing to do!"

Tash swallows. "Erica doesn't think so."

Jim clicks his tongue, irritated. Tash seems so even-headed about the whole thing, as if he has judged the matter and found he is perhaps in agreement with Erica. . . .

Tash finishes eating. "Let's get stoned."

They get out a full container of California Mello, and lid the whole thing, back and forth, back and forth, until the tears are running down Jim's face, and his corneas feel like thick slabs of glass. White-orange clouds, heavily underlit by the city, roll slowly inland. Slowly, very slowly, Jim's anger subsides. It's still there, but it's been muted, banked like the coals in the hibachi to a small, melancholy feeling of betrayal. That's life. People betray you, betray your friends. He recalls the look on Debbie Riggs's face as she yelled at him. He himself has betrayed more people than have ever betrayed him, and the realization dampens his anger even more. He was shifting onto Erica what he felt toward himself. . . .

"Angela called," Tash says. "She said you went to dinner with Virginia?"

"Yeah. Damn it."

Tash chuckles. "How is she?"

"Feeling enormous amounts of righteous indignation, I would guess, this very moment."

"Virginia nirvana, eh?"

Jim laughs. They can insult each other's ex-allies, and cheer each other up. Very sensible. The Mello continues to kick in and he sees how silly his thoughts are. He's blasted into a calm almost beyond speech.

"Whoah."

"No lie."

"Heavy."

"Untold."

They chuckle, but only in a very mellow way.

Much cloud gazing later, Jim says, "So what will you do?"

"Who knows." After a long silence: "I don't think I can go on living this way, though. It's too much work. I've been thinking about moving." And suddenly Jim can hear pain in Tashi's voice, he understands that the stoic mask is a mask and nothing more. Of course the man is hurt. Emotions punch their way through the fog of the Mello, and Jim regrets the anesthetizing. He feels, all of a sudden, overwhelmingly helpless. There's nothing he can do to help, not a thing.

"Where to?"

"Don't know. Far away."

"Oh, man."

They sit together in silence, and watch a whole lot of orange clouds float inland.

...63

When Jim tracks home later that night, he is feeling about as low as he can remember feeling. He's below music, he doesn't even try it. Just the sounds of the freeway as he types in the program for home and tracks along, slumped back in his seat. Even in the middle of the night the lightshow is pinballing all over the basin, a clutch of silent helicopters hovering over the Marine Station like flying saucers, jets booming down onto John Wayne, the flying freeways almost at capacity. . . .

Again home strikes him as an empty shell, a dirty little studio under a freeway, filled with futile paper and plastic attempts to stave off reality. Which isn't such a bad idea. He goes to the videotapes, sees the stack of them that Virginia and he made on their bedroom systems, when they were first going out. Perversely he feels a strong desire to look at one. Virginia undressing, in the casual routine of taking off clothes, with the thoughtlessness of untying shoelaces. Standing naked before a tall complex of mirrors, brushing her hair and watching the infinity of images of herself. . . .

"No!" The repugnance at his desire rises faster than the desire itself, a new feeling in Jim. If he becomes captive to her video image tonight, just hours after their last fight, how much easier will it be in the weeks and months to come? It'll be so easy just to concentrate on the image . . . and he'll be in thrall to it, having an affair with a video lady, like so many other men in America.

Fearfully he grabs up the stack of cassettes. "I'm pulling out for good," he shouts at the video, and laughs crazily. He pulls an eyedropper of Buzz from his bookshelf and lids drops until he's blind. Instant hum in all his nervous system, replacing lust. Like the buzz in the telephone wires, or the freeway magnetic tracks, a sort of drunkenness of the nerves, which makes him want to get really drunk. He goes to the fridge, pops a Bud, downs it. Downs another one.

Back to the cassettes. "I live a life of symbolic gestures, and not much more," he tells the room. "But when it's all you've got . . ."

There are nine cassettes of Virginia and him, the labels penciled over, sometimes in Virginia's hand: US, *IN BED*. Should he save just one? "No, no, no." He throws them all in his daypack, goes outside.

It's a warm night. Overhead the freeway hums, right in phase with Jim's nerves. He can see the sides of the cars in the fast lane zoom by, one headlight each. One of the freeway's great concrete pylons thrusts out of the sidewalk just three houses down. The maintenance men's ladder starts ten feet up, but the neighborhood kids have tied a nylon rope ladder to it. With some difficulty, aware of his buzz, his drunkenness, Jim gets the daypack on his back and ascends the ladder. When his head is at the level of the freeway he stops. Buzz of cars passing, lightshow of headlights strobing by, zoom zoom zoom zoom. Funny to think that only the little units extending down from the front axle, not quite touching the shiny strip of the track, are guiding the cars, and keeping them from running into each other, or over the rail above Jim's head, down onto the houses below. Magnetism, what is it, anyway? Jim shakes his head, confused. Concentrates on the task at hand. Left arm wrapped over a step of the ladder, he frees the daypack from his right arm and twists it around to unzip it. Out comes a cassette. All the cars' tires run over approximately the same part of the freeway; they've made two black bands on the freeway's white concrete, a couple feet to left and right of the track, and almost two feet wide themselves. He's not too far from the nearer one.

He slides a cassette over the concrete, and it stops right in the black band. The next car to pass crunches it to smithereens. Loops of tape blow off to the side.

"Yeah! Good shot!" Jim continues to cheer himself on as cassette after cassette skids onto the tire track of the fast lane, and is reduced to plastic fragments and streamers of tape.

The last one, however, goes too far, landing between the tire marks and the guidance track. Without pausing to think about it Jim climbs onto the freeway, catching the daypack on the rail and practically pulling himself off into space. Oops. During one of the rare gaps in traffic he runs out into the fast lane, recovers the cassette, trips and staggers, puts the cassette on the tire marks, scrambles desperately back to the ladder.

A big car crunches the cassette under its wheels.

Carefully, awkwardly, Jim descends. Safe on the ground again, he sucks in a deep breath. "Probably should have kept just one." He laughs. "No backsliding now, boy! You're free whether you like it or not." Overhead, long tangles of videotape float across the sky.

...64

No sooner has Jim returned to his ap, which, to tell the truth, looks just as dreary and lifeless as before, than there's a sharp knock at the door. He opens it.

"Abe! What are you doing here?"

Abe smiles lopsidedly.

Stupid question. Abe's eyes have a drawn, tired, defiant look, and Jim understands: he's here for the company. For help. Jim can hardly believe it. Abe's never come to Jim's place before, except once or twice to pick him up. Given their homes it makes sense to go up Saddleback and hang out there, on the roof of OC, if hanging out is what they're going to do.

"I'm here to get wasted," Abe says harshly, and laughs.

"What, Sandy's not home?"

"That's right." Again the abrupt laugh. But then Abe's direct gaze catches Jim's eye, admitting that there's more to it than that. Abe steps in, looks around. Jim sees it through Abe's eyes.

"Let's go outside," he says, "and sit on the curb. I'm sick of this place."

Seated on the curb, next to the fire hydrant at the corner, feet crossed in the gutter, they can look up at the freeway overhead and see the roofs of the cars in the fast lane, see the fans of light from the headlights, sweeping by. Two men sitting on a curb.

Abe pulls out one of Sandy's monster spliffs and lights it. They pass it back and forth, expelling great clouds of smoke into the empty street. A passing car tracks through the cloud and scatters it. "Quit passing so quickly," Abe says at one point. "Take two hits, then pass it. Don't you even know how to smoke a joint?"

"No."

They sit silently. Nothing to say? Not exactly. Jim supposes that his value in times like these is his willingness to start conversations, to talk about things that matter.

"So," he says, coughing on a deep hit. "You were the paramedics called to Lillian's crash, huh?"

"Yeah."

"You and Xavier?"

"Yeah."

Long pause.

"How's he doing?"

A shrug. "I don't know. Same as ever. Falling apart, hanging on. I guess it's a permanent condition for X."

"Sounds tough."

Abe purses his mouth. "Impossible. I can't do it, anyway."

He starts fidgeting in typical Abe fashion, finally getting up to squat on his hams, balancing over his feet with armpits on knees, in the aboriginal crouch that is a favorite with him, because then even sitting takes nervous energy. "Have I changed much this last year, that you can tell?"

"Everyone changes."

Abe gives him a sidelong glance, laughs sharply. "Even you?"

"Maybe," Jim says, thinking of the last month. "Maybe, at last."

Abe accepts that. "Yeah. Well, I'm wondering. I mean, I've been getting like X, all this last year. I'm wondering if I can keep going. You know . . ."

His voice tightens, he's looking down in the gutter now. "X told me that once when he was losing it bad he couldn't stand any of the crashes with kids in them. Because once he looked in this backseat and found a body and said to himself, What the hell is this black kid doing with these white folks, and he turned it over and it had one of his kids' faces. And he sort of fainted on his feet, and when he came to it was some white kid he'd never seen."

"My God."

"I know. You can see why X worries me. But—but"—Abe is still resolutely looking in the gutter—"when I saw it was Lillian, I stepped away and all of a sudden remembered X's story and I thought I had gone crazy, that it wasn't her and I had hallucinated it. And then when I was sure it was Lillian, I mean really sure . . . I was almost glad!"

"I understand."

"No you don't!"

Abe jumps up, paces back and forth in front of Jim, out in the street. He hands Jim the forgotten spliff: "You don't understand! You think you do because you read so fucking much, but you never really do any of it so you don't really know!"

Jim looks at Abe calmly. "That's probably true."

Abe grimaces, shakes his head a few times. "Ah, no. That's bullshit. Everyone knows, as long as they're not sleepwalkers. But shit. I would rather have had Lillian Keilbacher dead than have gone crazy for even one minute!"

"Just at that moment, you mean. It's a natural reaction, you were shocked out of your mind. You can think anything at times like that."

"Uhn." Abe isn't satisfied by that. But he sits down on the curb again, takes the spliff.

"Most people would have just freaked on the spot."

Abe shakes his head, taking a hit. "Not so."

"Well, not many would try to go tell the family like you did."

"Uhn."

They smoke a while in silence.

Jim takes a deep breath; he's used to the Bernards' Saddleback house becoming a brooding, Byronic place, overhanging the world; but it appears Abe can confer the atmosphere wherever he goes, if his immense nervous energy is spinning him in the right way, in the right mode . . . so that Jim's streetcorner curb under its sodium vapor light now swirls with heraldic significance, it looks like an Edward Hopper painting, the bungalow aps lined out side by side, the minilawns, empty sidewalks, fire hydrant, orange glare of light, giant pylons and the great strip of freeway banding the white-orange sky—all external signs of a dark, deep moodiness.

Abe holds the spliff between thumb and forefinger, speaks to it softly. "It's getting so that anytime I can hear that *sound*"—glancing up briefly at the freeway—"or, or anytime I see a stream of headlights flowing red white, I hear the snips ripping through the metal. I hear the cutting hidden in the rest of the sound, sometimes I even hear some poor torn-up bastard moaning—just in the freeway sounds!"

He's squishing the spliff flat, and suddenly he hands it back to Jim.

"And following taillights is like blood over exposed bone, red on white, you know the headlights, so bright coming at you . . . I mean I really see that."

His voice is going away, Jim can barely hear his words. "The way the cars crumple and shear, and the blood—there's a lot of it in a body. And their faces always look so—like Lillian's face, it was so . . ." He's shaking now, his whole body is racked with shaking, his face is contorted in the mask that faces go to when crying is stopped short no matter the cost to the muscles. Abruptly he stands again.

As if on a string Jim stands too. Tentatively he puts a hand to his friend's shoulder. "It's your work, Abe. It's hard work, but it's good work, I mean we need it. It's what you want to do—"

"It's *not* what I want to do! I don't want to do it anymore! Man, haven't you been listening?" He jerks away from Jim, turns and paces around him like a predatory animal. "Pay attention, will you?" he almost shouts. "I'm going crazy out there, I tell you, I can't even do my job anymore!"

"Yes you can—"

"I cannot! How do you know? Don't tell me what I can or can't do out there—so fucking glib—" He reaches up and takes a wild swing at Jim's up-raised hand, hits it away, swings again and backhands Jim on the chest, for an instant he looks like he's going to beat Jim up, and appalled Jim holds his arms up across his chest to take the blows—

Abe stops himself, shudders, twists away, takes off rapidly down the street; turns, wavers indecisively, plops down on the curb and leans over the gutter, face between his knees, buried in his hands. And there he rocks back and forth, back and forth.

Jim, frightened, his throat crimped tight at the sudden exposure to so much pain, stands there helplessly. He doesn't know what to do, doesn't have any idea what Abe might *want* him to do.

After a long while he walks down the street, and sits down next to Abe, whose rocking gets slower and slower as his shaking subsides. They both just sit there.

The forgotten roach, black with oil, is still pressed between Jim's thumb and forefinger; he pulls a lighter from his shirt pocket, torches the roach's ashy end, sucks on it till it blooms smoke. He takes a hit so big that he can't contain it, and coughs hard. Abe has his elbows on his knees now, and he's staring silently out at the street. His face is all streaked. Jim offers him the roach. He takes it, puffs on it, passes it back, all without a word. A final paroxysm shudders through his flesh, and then he's still.

After a while he looks at Jim with a wry grimace. "See what I mean?"

Jim nods. He's at a loss for words. Without premeditation he says, "Yeah, man. You're fucking nuts."

Abe laughs shortly. Sniffs.

They finish the roach in silence. They sit on the curb and watch the traffic hum by overhead.

Abe sighs. "I never thought it would get this hard."

... 65

Abe leaves. Shaken to the core, Jim finds himself prowling his ap restlessly. Nothing in it offers the slightest consolation. What a day it's been. . . .

The longer he stays in the ap, the more intense becomes his helpless, miserable nervousness. He can't think what to do. What time is it, anyway? Three A.M. The dead hour. Nothing to do, no one to turn to—the friends he might have looked to for help are looking to him, and he isn't up to it.

There isn't a chance of sleeping. The malignancy of thought, vision and memory, all drugged, speeded up, spiked by fear, makes sleep out of the question. The day keeps recurring in his mental theater in a scramble of images, each worse than the last, the sum making him sick with a synergistic toxicity. He recalls Hana's face, as she saw him and Virginia stagger out of the Hungry Crab together. No great scowl of anguish or despair, no nothing that melodramatic; just a quick snap of shock, of surprise, and then an instantly averted gaze, a disengagement, a refusal to look at him. Goddamn it!

He gives up on any attempt to get hold of himself, and calls Hana's number, without a thought in his head as to what he's going to say. At the sound of the ring he panics, his pulse shoots up, he'd hang up if he weren't sure that Hana would know it was him waking her and then failing to hold together the nerve to speak to her, and with that prospect before him he holds on, through ring after ring. . . .

Nobody home.

...66

Nobody home.

How did it happen?

At first it was a result of the tracts, the freeways, the cars. If you lived in a new suburb, then you had to drive to do your shopping. How much easier to park in one place, and do all your shopping in one location!

So the malls began. At first they were just shopping centers. A big asphalt parking lot, surrounded on two or three sides by stores; there were scores of them, as in most of the rest of America.

Then they became complexes of parking lots mixed with islands of stores, as in Fashion Square, the oldest shopping center in the county. They were popular. They did great at Christmastime. In effect they became the functional equivalent of villages, places where you could walk to everything you needed—villages tucked like islands into the multilayered texture of autopia. Once you parked at a shopping center, you could return to a life on foot. And at that idea the body, the brainstem, said Yeah.

South Coast Plaza was one of the first to go beyond this idea, to complete the square of stores and roof it, putting the parking lot on the outside. Call it a mall. An air-conditioned island village—except, of course, that all the villagers were visitors.

When South Coast Plaza opened in 1967 it was a giant success, and the Segerstrom family, heirs to the lima bean king C. J. Segerstrom, kept building on their land until they had the mall of malls, the equivalent of several fifty-story buildings spread out over a thousand acres, all of it enclosed. A sort of spaceship village grounded on the border between Santa Ana and Costa Mesa.

They made a lot of money.

Other malls sprang up, like daughter mushrooms in a ring around SCP. They all grew, enclosing more space, allowing more consumers to spend their time indoors. Westminster Mall, Huntington Center, Fashion Island, the Orange

Mall, Buena Park Center, the City, Anaheim Plaza, Brea Mall, Laguna Hills Mall, Orange Fair Center, Cerritos Center, Honer Plaza, La Habra Fashion Square, Tustin Mall, Mission Viejo Fair, Trabuco Marketplace, the Mission Mall, Canyon Center, all were in place and flourishing by the end of the century, growing by accretion, taking up the surrounding neighborhoods, adding stores, restaurants, banks, gyms, boutiques, hairdressers, aps, condos. Yes, you could live in a mall if you wanted to. A lot of people did.

By 2020 their number had doubled again, and many square miles of Orange County were roofed and air-conditioned. When the Cleveland National Forest was developed there was room for a big one; Silverado Mall rivaled SCP for floorspace, and in 2027 it became the biggest mall of all—a sign that the back country had arrived at last.

The malls merged perfectly with the new elevated freeway system, and midcounty it was often possible to take an offramp directly into a parking garage, from which one could take an escalator through the maze of a mall's outer perimeter, and return to your ap, or go to dinner, or continue your shopping, without ever coming within thirty feet of the buried ground. Everything you needed to do, you could do in a mall.

You could live your life indoors.

And none of that, of course, ever went away.

... 67

Dennis gets a call from Washington, D.C. "Dennis? It's Louis Goldman. I wanted to tell you about the latest developments in the Stormbee case. It's looking very hopeful, I think."

"Yeah?"

"We've been pursuing several avenues here, and a couple are really moving for us. We've been in contact with Elisha Francisco, the aide to Senator George Forrester. Forrester is head of the Senate Budget Committee, and he's on the Armed Services Committee, and he's been in a kind of a feud with the Air Force for about four years. So his office is always receptive to ammunition for this feud, and when I gave Francisco the facts of our case he jumped on the matter instantly."

"And what can they do?" McPherson asks cautiously.

"They can do a lot! Essentially the GAO, the Congress's watchdog, was steamrolled in our case, and Congress is touchy about being ignored like that. Senator Forrester has already asked the Procurements Branch of the Office of Technology Assessment for an independent report on the matter. That should be really interesting, because the OTA is as far out of the pressure points as you can be in this town. Procurements Branch at OTA has the reputation of being the most impartial assessment group that you can bring to bear on the military. Anyone in Congress can ask them for a report, and no one else has any leverage on them at all, so they pride themselves on giving a completely unbiased spread of the pros and cons, on *anything*. Nerve gas, biological warfare, persuasion technology, you name it, they'll give you a report on it that sticks to technological efficiency and only that."

"So we might see the report that the GAO should have made?"

"That's right. And Forrester will hammer the Air Force with it, too, you can bet on that."

"Can he get the Stormbee decision thrown out, then?"

"Well, not all by himself. There's no mechanism for it, see. The best that could happen is that the Secretary of the Air Force would knuckle under to Congress's prodding, but that isn't too likely, no matter how much Forrester hammers them. However, if there were another appeal by LSR moving forward at the same time as this—if we appeal the decision to a higher court, and all this other stuff is breaking in Congress, then a new judge will almost certainly overturn Tobiason's decision, and you'll be back in business."

"You think so?"

"I'm sure of it. So we're sending a letter to you and to Argo/Blessman advising you to authorize us to initiate an appeal, but I wanted to tell you about it since you're the liaison, so you can do what needs to be done at your end."

"Yeah, sure. I'll get right on it. So—so, you think we have a chance with this?"

"It's better than that, Dennis. Senator Forrester is one of the most powerful people in Washington, and he's a good man, as straight as they come. He doesn't like what he's heard about this, and he's not one to forget. I think it's our turn at last."

"Great."

McPherson writes a memo to Lemon immediately after the phone call, outlining what he has learned and suggesting immediate approval of the appeal.

As he writes down the facts, his hopes come flooding back. It seems to him, all of a sudden, that the system might really work after all. The network of checks and balances is almost suffocating in its intricacy—it is perhaps too intricate; but what that means in the end is that power is spread out everywhere, and no one part of the network can cheat another, without the balance of the whole being upset. When that happens the other parts of the network will step in, because their own power is threatened if any other part gains too much; they'll fly in with a check like a hockey defenseman's, and the balance will be restored. The Air Force tried to assert that it was above the system, outside the network; now the rest of the network is going to drag them back into it. It's the American way, stumbling forward in its usual clumsy, inefficient style—maddening to watch, but ultimately fair.

So, feeling better about that, he spends the rest of the day working on the Ball Lightning program. And here too he sees signs of some progress, signs that they might possibly reach the deadline with a workable system. The programmers have come to him chattering with excitement about a program that will successfully latch the beams from several lasers to a missile, in a phased array; this vastly increases the intensity of the beam, so that the shock pulse will work again. They also believe they can track the missiles past the boost phase, by extrapolating their courses very precisely. Combine that with the shorter dwell time offered by the phased array and . . . they might just be able to knock down the percentage specified by the Air Force. It could happen. Even though it may take them into the post–boost phase a bit.

Spurred by the possibility, McPherson wheedles, coaxes, and bullies Dan Houston into reactivating his brain and doing his share of the work; it will take a push effort by everyone to get the job done in time, a sort of phased array of effort. And Houston is a mess. He's never mentioned to Dennis the evening at El Torito when Dennis had to help him down to his car; but now it's clear to Dennis that that was not a particularly unusual evening. Dan is drinking heavily every day; he needs a haircut, sometimes he needs a shave, his clothes look slept in; really, he's the stereotype of the man whose ally has left him, whose life is falling apart. Sometimes Dennis wants to snap at him, say, "Come off it, Dan, you're living a video script!"

But then it occurs to him that Houston's pain is real enough, and that this is the only way he knows how to express it, if he is consciously living the role. And if not, it's just what happens when you don't care anymore, when you've lost hope, when you've started drinking hard.

So McPherson takes him out to lunch, and listens to his whole sad story, which he is now willing to talk about openly—"The truth is, Mac, Dawn has moved up to her folks'." "Oh, really?"—and Dennis gives him a pep talk, and talks to him in intense detail about what needs to be done by Houston and Houston's part of the team, and he even refuses to allow Houston to order another pitcher of margaritas, though that only gets him a look of dull resentment. "Do it after work if you have to, Dan," McPherson snaps, irritated with him. Stewart Lemon tactics? Well, whatever it takes; they don't have much time left.

And the fact is, Houston puts in a better afternoon's effort than he has in weeks and weeks. By God, McPherson thinks, looking over his list of Things To Do before he goes home—we might pull it off after all.

Jim sleeps on his living room couch through the day, curled on his side around a tensely knotted stomach. He wakes often, each time more exhausted than the last. Every time he gains enough autonomy to pull himself upright, he calls Hana. No answer, no answering machine. More uneasy, unrestful sleep. His dreams are sickening, the problems in them more outlandishly insoluble than ever before. In the last of them he dreams he and all his friends have been captured by the Russians and held in the Kremlin. He tries to escape through a pinball machine, but the glass top slides back too quickly and cuts off his head. He has to climb back out and go through the ordeal of finding his head without the help of his eyes, then place the head back on his neck and balance it there very carefully. No one will believe he is walking around with his head chopped off. Premier Kerens, in a uniform with lots of medals, is flanked by Debbie and Angela and Gabriela, all wearing nothing but underwear bottoms. "Okay," the premier says, holding up a device like an artificial hand that will cut out hearts. "You choose which one goes first."

He wakes up sweating, his stomach clenched as if by cramp.

About two P.M. he tries Hana again, and she answers.

"Hello?"

"Ah? Oh! Hana! It's Jim. I've . . . been trying to get hold of you."

"Have you."

"Yeah, but you weren't home. Listen, ah, Hana—"

"Jim, I don't feel like talking to you right now."

"No, Hana, no—I'm sorry!"

But she's hung up.

"Shit!" He slams down the phone so hard it almost cracks. After a moment he dials the number again. Busy signal, hateful sound. She's left the phone off the cradle. No chance for contact. It's so stupid! "Oh, man."

He wants to go up there, beg her forgiveness. Then he gets angry at the unfairness of it, he wants her to beg his forgiveness, for being so unreasonable. "Come on! I was just having dinner with a friend! After the funeral of another friend!" But that isn't exactly true. He pulls his big Mexican cookbook from the shelf and furiously slams it to the floor, kicks it across the kitchen. Very satisfying, until the moment he stops.

An hour later, angrier than ever, he calls up Arthur. "Arthur, have you got anything ready to go?"

"Well—come on over and we'll talk about it."

Jim tracks over to Arthur's place in Fountain Valley. Arthur's face is flushed, he is in a strong field of excitement, he takes Jim's upper arm in a tight grip and grins. "Okay, Jim, we're on for another strike, but this one's a little different. The target is Laguna Space Research." His straightforward blue gaze asks the obvious question.

Jim says, "What about the night watchmen they made the announcement about?"

"They've been taken out of the plants and are out on the perimeter."

"Why?" Jim doesn't understand.

Arthur shrugs. "We're not sure. Someone bombed a computer company's plant up in Silicon Valley, and a janitor inside was killed. Not our doing, but LSR doesn't know that. So they're going to automatic defenses and a perimeter watch. It's going to be a little more dangerous. We've got them all running scared. But this time—well, I wasn't going to call you, because it was LSR."

Jim nods. "I appreciate it. But it's the ballistic missile defense system we're going after, right?"

"Right. LSR has the lion's share of the boost-phase defense, Ball Lightning as they call it. A successful strike against it could be devastating." Arthur's excitement is evident in the tightness of his grip on Jim's arm.

"I want to do it," Jim says.

It's the only avenue of action left to him, and he can't stand not to act; the tension in him would drive him mad. "My father's in another program, this won't have anything to do with him. Besides, it has to be done. It has to be done if anything is ever going to change!"

Arthur nods, still looking at him closely. "Good man. It'll be easier with your help, I'll admit that."

Gently Jim shifts his arm out of Arthur's grip. Arthur looks at his hand, surprised. "I'm wired," he confesses. "It's tomorrow night, see. Tomorrow night, and I thought I was doing it on my own."

"Same procedure?"

"Yeah, everything'll go just the same. Should be simple, as long as we keep a good distance away and under cover, and . . ."

Jim listens to Arthur absently, distracted by his own anger, by everything else. He thought the commitment to action would release some of the tension in him; instead he is more tense than ever, he almost needs to bend over, give in to the contraction of the stomach muscles. Laguna Space Research . . . Well, do it! None of these companies should be exempt! Something has to be done!

It's time to act, at last.

... 69

Sandy hears about the planned attack on LSR from Bob Tompkins, who gives him a call that afternoon. "Good news, Sandy. Raymond is going to give us a hand in the matter of the lost laundry. Our guardian angel is going to have some trouble tomorrow night, at about midnight. One of those accidents that have been happening lately, you know."

"One of Arthur's ventures?" Sandy asks.

Brief silence at the other end. "Yeah, but let's not talk about it in too much detail now. The point is, when the accident happens our guardian angels will have their hands full, and it'll be on the side opposite our little aquatic problem, so we think surveillance there will be temporarily abandoned. If you're ready out there, you'll be able to rescue the laundry you had to put on hold."

"I don't know, Bob." Sandy is frowning to himself. "I don't like the sound of it, to tell you the truth."

"We need that laundry, Sandy. And since you put it there, you'll have the easiest time finding it again."

"I still don't like it."

"Come on, Sandy. We didn't make the mess. In fact, we're the ones making you the opportunity to get out of it gracefully. Solvently. Just go for a little night boating, cruise in to your beach, collect the laundry, and return. There won't be a problem tomorrow night, and all will be well."

Sandy recognizes the threat behind the pleasantry, and in some ways it does sound like a very easy out of a sticky dilemma, which up to this point has only offered him the choice of either big debt, or the permanent loss of his Blacks Cliffs friends (at best). And it does sound like it will go. . . .

"Okay," he says unwillingly. "I'll do it. I'll need some help, though. My assistant from last time probably won't be interested."

"We'll send someone, along with the keys to a motorboat based in Dana Point. In fact I may come myself."

"That would be good. What time does this happen?"

"Tomorrow, midnight."

"All right. And you'll show when?"

"I'll give you a call tomorrow morning. Me or a friend will meet you in Dana Point in the evening."

"All right."

"Tubular, man. See you then."

Sandy calls Tash and asks for his help, but as he expected, Tash refuses to have anything to do with it. "It's stupid, Sandy. You should pass on the whole thing."

"Can't afford to."

This gives Tashi pause, but in the end he still refuses.

Sandy hangs up, sighs, checks his watch. He's already late for half a dozen appointments, and he's still got twenty calls to make. In fact he's going to have to pinball around all day and tomorrow morning to get ready for this rescue operation. No rest for the weary. He lids some Buzz and Pattern Perception, starts tapping out a phone number.

As the line rings he thinks about it.

Now he knows that Jim is working with Arthur, and Arthur is working for Raymond, and that Raymond is pursuing a private vendetta for private purposes—and perhaps making a profit on the side, or so it appears. The shape of the whole setup is clear to him.

But now—now he's in a situation where he can't do anything with what he knows. All his detective work was done with the idea that he could tell Jim something Jim didn't know, help him out, perhaps warn him away from trouble. Tell him what was really going on, so that he wouldn't continue thinking he was part of some idealistic resistance to the war machine, or whatever he is thinking—so he could get out of it before something went wrong.

Now Sandy can't do anything of the kind. In fact he has to hope that Jim does a good job of it. "Come through for me, Jimbo. . . ."

... 70

Lemon gets a call from Donald Hereford in New York. It looks like a sunny evening in Manhattan.

Hereford gets right to the point: "Have you gotten all of the night watchmen out of the plant out there?"

"Yes, we did that right after you visited. But listen, the Ball Lightning team reports some significant breakthroughs, and I thought I should tell you about them—"

Hereford is shaking his head. "Just keep the situation in the plant stable, especially in the next few days."

Lemon nods stiffly, frustration tugging at the corners of his mouth. "Do you know . . ."

Hereford frowns. "We've found the source of the difficulty. He's doing it for hire."

"And he's been hired by?"

But that's going too far. Hereford looks out at New York's big harbor, says, "Let's not talk about this anymore now. Later we might be able to discuss it more fully."

"Okay."

He'll never find out anything more about this, Lemon realizes; it's happening on a level he isn't on, it's above him. Part of him is galled by the realization; part of him is happy not to know, not to be involved. Leave this sort of thing to others!

Hereford is about to switch off when Lemon remembers something else. "Oh, listen, we've gotten a request from our legal representative in Washington, to file an appeal in the Stormbee decision." He describes the situation in detail. "So, it sounds like another appeal and we'll really have a good chance of success."

Hereford frowns. "Let me get back to you on that," he says, and the screen goes blank.

...71

The next day, after a productive morning and a busy lunch conferring with Dan Houston, Dennis gets a call from Lemon's secretary Ramona, instructing him to come up for a conference with the boss. McPherson needs to talk to him anyway, so he ignores his usual irritation at the peremptory summons and goes on up.

Lemon is standing in front of his window as usual, looking out at the sea. He seems on edge, ill at ease—at least to a certain minute extent. It's hard to tell, but McPherson has had to become an expert in reading the tiny signals that mark his boss's mercurial mood swings, and now, as he sits down on the hot seat and watches Lemon pacing, he senses something unusual, a tension beyond the usual manic energy.

At first he speaks only of the Ball Lightning program. He really grills McPherson about it, a cross-examination as intense as any Lemon has ever subjected him to, something reminiscent of an SSEB questioning back in Dayton. Lemon hasn't discussed technical matters in such detail as this in years; he's really done his homework.

But why? McPherson can't figure it out.

"What it comes down to," Lemon says heavily when he is done, "is that you've got a great idea for a phased array attack, which takes us far into the post–boost phase. But we can't meet the specs that we supposedly proved we could meet, in the initial proposal that won us the program."

"That's right," McPherson says. "It isn't physically possible."

"Not for you, you mean."

McPherson shrugs. He's so tired of Lemon he doesn't even care about hiding it anymore. "Not for me, right. I can't change the laws of physics. Maybe you can. But if you fake tests to try to bend the laws of physics, you always get caught at this point, don't you."

Lemon's eyes are just barely narrowed, a dangerous sign. "You're saying Houston faked the tests on the proposal?"

"We've just gone over all the data, right? We've known this ever since you put me on the program. What's the point of all this? Someone either concocted a good-looking test, with real but irrelevant results—and if that's faking the Air Force has been doing it for years—or else someone made a stupid mistake, and assumed the test proved the system would work in the real world, when it didn't."

Lemon nods slowly, as if satisfied with something. For a long time he stands staring out the window.

McPherson watches him; he's lost the drift of the meeting, he still doesn't know what Lemon wanted him here for. Confirmation that the Ball Lightning program is really and truly sunk? It isn't, if you stretch the definition of the boost phase, give the defense more time; but Lemon doesn't seem interested in that, he seems to think that the Air Force will reject the system if any spec is unfulfilled. And he may be right about that, but they have to try.

McPherson brings up the matter of Goldman's phone call and the Stormbee appeal.

Lemon nods. "I got your memo yesterday."

"We only need to give them an okay to initiate the appeal, and we're in business. It looks really promising, from Goldman's account."

Lemon turns his head to look at him. Face blank. No expression at all. Sunlight makes his left eye look like crystal.

Slowly he shakes his head. "We've gotten other instructions from Hereford. No appeal."

"What?"

"No appeal."

Even through his shock, McPherson can see that Lemon is not rubbing this one in in his usual style, taunting McPherson with it. In fact, he looks uncomfortable, depressed. But all this is just his continuous Lemon-watch, going on automatically under the shock of the news.

McPherson stands. "Just what the hell is going on? We've worked on this for a year now, and put some twenty million dollars into it, and we're right on the edge of winning the contract!"

Lemon puts a hand up. "I know," he says wearily. "Sit down, Mac."

When McPherson remains standing, Lemon sits himself, on the edge of his desk.

"It's a victory we can't afford to win."

"What?"

"That's Hereford's decision. And I suppose he's right, though I don't like it. Do you know what a Pyrrhic victory is, Mac?"

"Yes."

Lemon sighs heavily. "Sometimes it seems like all the victories are Pyrrhic, these days."

He gathers himself, looks at McPherson sharply. "It's like this. If we win this one—force the Air Force to take back their award, and win the contract ourselves—then we've got the Stormbee system, sure. But we've also embarrassed the Air Force in front of the whole industry, the whole country. And if we do that, then Stormbee is the last program we can ever expect to get from the Air Force again. Because they'll remember. They'll do their best to bankrupt us. Already they've got our balls in a vise with this Ball Lightning program going bad on us. That's bad enough, but beyond that—no more black programs, no more superblack programs, no more early warnings on RFPs, no more awards in close bidding competitions, consistent screwings on the MPCs—my God, they can do it to us! It's a buyer's market! There's only one buyer for space defense systems, and that's the United States Air Force. They've got the power."

Lemon's face twists bitterly as he acknowledges this. "I hate it, but that's the case. We've got to be agreeable, and stand up for our rights when we have to, but without really beating them, see. So Hereford is right, even though I hate to say it. We can't afford to win this one. So we're giving up. The law firm will be called off."

McPherson can barely think. But he remembers something: "What about the investigation in Congress?"

"That's their doing. We won't cooperate any further. It's belly-up time— bare the throat to the top dog, goddamn it." Lemon gets up, goes to the window. "I'm sorry, Mac. Go home, why don't you. Take the rest of the day off."

McPherson finds he is already standing. When did that happen? He's at the door when Lemon says, perhaps to himself, "That's the way the system works."

And then he's out in the hall. In the elevator. In his mouth is a coppery taste, as if he had thrown up, though he feels no nausea. The body's reaction to defeat is a bitterness at the back of the throat. The idea of being "bitter" is another concept taken directly from sensory experience. He knows he is bitter because his throat gags on a coppery taste roiling at the back of his mouth. He's in his office. The whole operation, so neat, so efficient, so *real* looking, is all a sham, a fake. The work done in this office might as well be replaced by the scripts of a video screenplay; it would all come to the same in the end. Engineering, he thinks, isn't real at all. Only the power struggles of certain people in Washington are real, and those battles are based on whims, personal ambitions, personal jealousies. And those battles make the rest of the world unreal. The walls around him might as well be cardboard (thwack! thwack!), the computers empty plastic shells—all parts of a video set, a backdrop to the great battles of the stars in the foreground. He's an extra in those battles, his little scene has been filmed—then the script rewritten, the scene tossed out. His work, tossed out.

He goes home.

...72

About the time Dennis is called into Lemon's office to hear the bad news, Jim gets a call from Lucy. "Are you coming up to dinner tonight like you said?"

Oh, man— "Did I say *tonight*?"

"I've made enough for three already. You said you would, and we haven't seen you in weeks."

Uh-oh. That tone in her voice, the ultimate Lucy danger signal. . . .

Very reluctantly Jim says, "Okay."

"And did you visit Uncle Tom like you said you would?"

"Oh, man. No. I forgot."

Now she really is upset. There's something wrong there, up at the folks'. "I didn't go this week because of the funeral," she says, voice strained, "and you didn't go last week when I thought you did—no one's been down there for almost three weeks. Oh, Jim, you get down there today and then you come to dinner, you hear me?"

"Yeah! I hear you." He doesn't want to cross her when she's in this temper, when her voice sounds like that. "I'm on my way. Sorry, I just forgot."

"You don't just forget things like that!"

"All right. I know. I'll see you for dinner."

"Okay."

So he's off to Seizure World, which in his mood is the last place in the world he wants to be, but there he is and in a black mood indeed he slams his car door and goes to the reception desk of the nursing home complex. "Here to see Tom Barnard."

He's sent along. In the hall outside Tom's room a nurse stops him. "Are you here to see Tom?" Accusation in her eyes. "I'm glad someone finally came. He's been having a hard time."

"What's this?" Jim says, alarmed.

Hard glance. "His respiration has gotten a lot worse. I thought he was going into a coma last week."

"What? Why wasn't his family told about it?"

The nurse shrugs, the gaze still hard. "They were."

"The hell they were! I'm his family, and I wasn't told."

Another shrug. "The front desk makes the calls. Don't you have an answering machine?"

"Yes, I do," Jim says sharply, and moves by her to Tom's door. He knocks, gets no answer, hesitates, enters.

Inside it's stuffy, the bedsheets are rumpled. Tom is flat on his back, his breath harsh and labored, his skin gray, his freckled bald pate yellowish.

His eyes slide over in his motionless head to look at Jim. At first there's no recognition, and this sends a stab of fear so far down into Jim that nothing else in the past miserable week bears any comparison to it. Then Tom blinks, he shifts awkwardly on his bed, says, "Jim. Hello." His voice is a dry rasp. "Here. Help me up."

"Oh, man, Tom, are you sure? I mean wouldn't it be better for you if you stayed flat, maybe?" Desperate fear that Tom will overexert himself somehow, die right here in front of him. . . .

"Help me up. I'm not a Q yet, no matter, evidence to the contrary." Tom tries pulling up onto his pillow himself, fails. "Help me, boy."

Jim holds his breath, helps Tom up so that his shoulders are on the pillow and his head leaning against the wall behind the bed. "Let me get the pillow behind your head."

"No. Bends my neck too far forward. Need all the airspace I can get."

"Ah. Okay."

They sit there and look at each other.

"I'm sorry I haven't been by in a while," Jim says. "I—well, I've been busy, Mom's been busy too. I was supposed to come last week but I forgot. I'm really sorry. The nurse says you haven't been feeling well."

"Got a cold. Almost killed me."

"I'm sorry."

"Not your fault. Stupid to die from a cold. So I didn't." Tom chuckles and it makes him cough, all of a sudden he's hacking for breath and Jim, heart pulsing right there in his fingertips, helps him back down onto the bed and turns up his oxygen flow to maximum. Slowly, painfully, Tom regains control of his breathing. He stares up at Jim and again his eyes don't register any recognition.

"It's Jim, Tom."

"How are you, Jim?"

"I'm fine, Tom, fine."

"Little trouble breathing. I'm okay now. The nurses never come when you ring. Once I was dreaming. I flailed out at something. And knocked this oxygen out of my nose. Pain woke me up, my nose was bleeding. Suffocating in here, regular air now and I suffocate. Can you imagine that? So I rang the bell. And they never came. Managed to pick the tube up. Stuck it in my mouth 'cause my nose. Bleeding. Stayed that way ringing the bell. Nurse came at seven when the new shift started. Graveyard shift sleeping. I did that myself, working at the Mobil station. Around three all the work done, no one awake. Whole town quiet and foggy, streetlights blinking red. I'd sleep by the heater under the cash register. Or walk around picking up cigarette butts off the asphalt."

"When was this, Tom?"

"But when I wake up it's only this room. Do you think they put me in prison for something? I do. Public defender for too long. I've seen too many jails. They all look like this. People are cruel, Jim. How can they do it? How?"

Tom stops, unable to catch his breath anymore, and for a while he only breathes, sucking the air in over and over. Jim holds on to his clammy palm. It seems he has a fever. He rocks his head back and forth restlessly, and when he talks again it's to other people, a whispered outrush of words punctuated by indrawn gasps, incoherent muttering that Jim can't make sense of. Jim can only hold his hand, and rock in the chair with him, feeling like a black iron weight will expand out of his stomach and fill him and topple him over.

The old man looks up at him with a wild expression. "Who are you?"

Jim swallows, looks at the ceiling, back at Tom. "Your great-nephew, Jim. Jim McPherson. Lucy's son."

"I remember. Sorry. They say the oxygen loss kills brain cells. According to my calculations, my brain is ten times gone." He wheezes once to indicate a laugh. "But I may be off by a magnitude." Wheezes again. He looks out the window. "It's hard to stay sane, alone with your thoughts."

"Or in any other situation, these days."

"That so? Sorry to hear you say that. Me—I try not to think too much anymore. Save what's left. Live in, I don't know. Memory. It's quite a power. What can explain it?"

Jim doesn't know what to say. Nothing explains the memory, as far as he knows. Nothing explains how a mind can cast back, through the years, live there, get lost there. . . .

"Tell me another story, Tom. Another story about Orange County."

Tom squeezes his eyes shut. Face a map of raw red wrinkles in gray skin.

"Ah, what haven't I told you, boy. It's all confused. When I first came to Orange County. The groves were still everywhere. I've told you that." He breathes in and out, in and out, in and out.

"Our first Christmas here there was a Santa Ana wind. And there was a row of big eucalyptus trees behind our house. Our street stuck right into a grove, the first thrust. And the trees squeaked when the Santa Ana blew. And leaves spinning down. Smelled of eucalyptus. And—ah. Oh. It was the night we were supposed to go Christmas caroling. My mom organized it. My mom was a lot like yours, Jim McPherson. Working for people. And mine was a music teacher. So all the kids were gathered, and a few of the parents, and we went around the neighborhood. Singing. Only half the houses in the development were finished. That wax is hot when it drips on your hand. And the wind kept blowing the candles out. It was all we could do to light them. Made shells of aluminum foil. And we sang at every house. Even the house of a Jewish family. My mom had some secular Christmas carol ready, I forget what it was. Funny idea. Where she found these things! But everyone came out and thanked us, and we had cookies and punch afterwards. Because everyone there had just moved out from the Midwest, you see? This was the way it was done. This is what you did to make a place a home. A neighborhood, by God. Because they didn't know! They thought they lived in a neighborhood still. They didn't know everyone would move, people be in and out and in and out—they didn't know they had just moved into a big motel. They thought they were in a neighborhood still. And so they tried. We all tried. My mother tried all her life."

"Mine too."

But Tom doesn't hear, he's off in a dark Santa Ana wind, muttering to himself, to his childhood friends, trying to recall the name of that carol, trying to keep the candles lit.

So they hold hands and look at the wall. And the old man falls asleep.

Jim frees his hand, stands, checks to see that the oxygen line is clear and the tank over half-full. He straightens the sheets the best he can. He looks at Tom's face and then finds he can't look anymore. In fact he has to sit down. He holds his head, squeezes hard, waits for the fit to pass. When it does he hurries out of the place and drives home to dinner.

...73

So Jim gets to his parents' home not long after Dennis does.

Dennis is out under their little carport, working on the motor of his car. "Hi, Dad." No answer. Jim's feeling too low for this sort of thing, and he goes into their portion of the house without another word.

Lucy asks about Tom.

"He's had a cold. He's not so well."

Hiss of breath, indrawn. Then she says, "Go out and talk to your father. He needs something to take his mind off work."

"I just said hello and he didn't say a thing."

"Get out there and talk to him!" Fiercely: "He needs to talk to you!"

"All right, all right." Jim sighs, feeling aggrieved, and goes back outside.

His father stands crouched over the motor compartment, head down under the hood, steadfastly ignoring Jim. Ignoring Jim and everything else, Jim thinks. A retreat into his own private world.

Jim approaches him. "What are you working on?"

"The car."

"I know that," Jim snaps.

Dennis glances up briefly at him, turns back to his task.

"Want some help?"

"No."

Jim grits his teeth. Too much has happened; he's lost all tolerance for this sort of treatment. "So what are you working on?" he insists, an edge in his voice.

Dennis doesn't look up this time. "Cleaning the switcher points."

Jim looks into the motor compartment, at Dennis's methodically working hands. "They're already clean."

Dennis doesn't reply.

"You're wasting your time."

Dennis looks at him balefully. "Maybe I ought to work on your car. I don't suppose that would be wasting my time."

"My car doesn't need work."

"Have you done any maintenance on it since I last looked at it?"

"No. I've been too busy."

"Too busy."

"That's right! I've been busy! It isn't just in the defense industry that people get busy, you know."

Dennis purses his mouth. "A lot of night classes, I suppose."

"That's right!" Angrily Jim walks up to the side of the car, so that only the motor compartment and the hood separate him from Dennis. "I've been busy going to the funerals of people we know, and trying to help my friends, and working in a real estate office, and teaching a night class. Teaching, that's right! It's the best thing I do—I teach people what they need to know to get by in the world! It's good work!"

Dennis's swift, smoldering glance shows he understands very clearly the implication of Jim's words. He looks back down at the motor, at his hands and their intensely controlled maneuvers. A minute passes as he finishes cleaning the points.

"So you don't think I do good work, is that it?" he says slowly.

"Dad, people are starving! Half the world is starving!" Jim is almost shaking now, the words burst out of him: "We don't need more bombs!"

Dennis picks up the point casing, places it over the points, takes up a wrench and begins to tighten one of the nuts that holds it to the sidewall.

"Is that all you think I do?" he asks quietly. "Make bombs?"

"Isn't that what you do?"

"No, it isn't. Mostly I make guidance systems."

"It's the same thing!"

"No. It isn't."

"Oh come on, Dad. It's all part of the same thing. Defense! Weapons systems!"

Dennis's jaw is bunched hard. He threads the second nut, begins to tighten it, all very methodically.

"You think we don't need such systems?"

"No, we don't!" Jim has lost all composure, all restraint. "We don't have the slightest need for them!"

"Do you watch the news?"

"Of course I watch the news. We're in several wars, there's a body count every day. And we provide the weapons for those wars. And for a lot of others too."

"So we need some weapons systems."

"To make wars!" Jim cries furiously.

"We don't start the wars by ourselves. We don't make all the weapons, and we don't start all the wars."

"I'm not so sure of that—it's great business!"

"Do you really think that's it?" Surely that nut is tight by now. "That there are people that cynical?"

"I suppose I do, yes. There are a lot of people who only really care about money, about profits."

Abruptly Dennis pulls the wrench off the nut.

"It's not that simple," he says down at the motor, almost as if to himself. "You want it to be that simple, but it isn't. A lot of the world would love to see this country go up in smoke. They work every day to make weapons better than ours. If we stopped—"

"If we stopped they would stop! But what would happen to profits then? The economy would be in terrible trouble. And so it goes on, new weapon after new weapon, for a hundred years!"

"A hundred years without another world war."

"All the little wars add up to a world war. And if they go nuclear it's the end, we'll all be killed! And you're a part of that!"

"Wrong!" *Bang* the wrench hits the underside of the hood as Dennis swings it up, points it at Jim. Behind the wrench Dennis's face is red with anger, he's leaning over the motor compartment, staring at Jim, his face an inch from the hood; and the wrench is shaking. "*You listen to what I do,* boy. I help to make systems for use in precision electronic warfare. And don't you look at me like they're all the same! If you can't tell the difference between electronic war and the mass nuclear destruction of the world, then you're too stupid to talk to!" *Bang* he hits the underside of the hood with the wrench. There's a hoarse edge in his voice that Jim has never heard before, and it cuts into Jim so sharply that he takes a step back.

"I can't do a thing about nuclear war, it's out of my hands. Hopefully one will never be fought. But conventional wars will be. And some of those wars could kick off a nuclear one. Easily! So it comes to this—if you can make conventional wars *too difficult to fight,* just on technical grounds alone, then by God you put an end to them! And that lessens the nuclear threat, the main way that we might fall into a nuclear war, in a really significant way!"

"But that's what they've always said, Dad!" Appalled by this argument, Jim's face twists: "Generation after generation—machine guns, tanks, planes, atomic bombs, now this—they were all supposed to make war impossible, but they don't! They just keep the cycle going!"

"Not impossible. You can't make war impossible, I didn't say that. Nothing can do that. But you can make it *damned* impractical. We're getting to the point where any invasion force can be electronically detected and electronically opposed, so quickly and accurately that the chances of a successful invasion are nil. Nil! So why ever try? *Can't you see?* It could come to a point where no one would try!"

"Maybe they'll just try with nuclear weapons, then! Be sure of it!"

Dennis waves the wrench dismissively, looks at it as if surprised at its presence, puts it down carefully on the top of the sidewall. "That would be crazy. It may happen, sure, but it would be crazy. Nuclear weapons are crazy, I don't have anything to do with them. The only work I do in that regard is to try and stop them. I wish they were gone, and maybe someday they will be, who knows. But to get rid of them we're going to have to have some other sort of deterrent, a less dangerous one. And that's what I work at—making the precise electronic weapons that are the only replacement for the nuclear deterrent. They're our only way out of that."

"There's no way out," Jim says, despair filling him.

"Maybe not. But I do what I can."

He looks away from Jim, down at the concrete of the driveway.

"But I can only do what I can," he says hoarsely. The corners of his mouth tighten bitterly. "I can't change the way the world is, and neither can you."

"But we can try! If everyone tried—"

"If pigs had wings, they'd fly. Be realistic."

"I *am* being realistic. It's a business, it's using up an immense amount of resources to no purpose. It's corrupt!"

Dennis looks down into the motor compartment, picks up the wrench, turns it over. Inspects it closely. His jaw muscles are bunching rhythmically, he looks like he's having trouble swallowing. Something Jim has said . . .

"Don't you try to tell me about corruption," he says in a low voice. "I know more than you'll ever imagine about that. But that's not the system."

"It is the system, precisely the system!"

Dennis only shakes his head, still staring at the wrench. "The system is there to be used for good or bad. And it's not all that bad. Not by itself."

"But it *is!*" Jim has the sinking feeling you get when you are losing an argument, the feeling that your opponent is using rational arguments while you are relying on the force of emotion; and as people usually do in that situation, Jim ups the emotional gain, goes right to the heart of his case: "Dad, the world is *starving.*"

"I *know* that," Dennis says very slowly, very patiently. "The world is on the brink of a catastrophic breakdown. You think I haven't *noticed*?"

He sighs, looks at the motor. "But I've become convinced . . . I think, now, that one of the strongest deterrents to that breakdown is the power of the

United States. We can scare a lot of wars away. But up till now most of our scare power has been nuclear, see, and using it would end us all. So little wars keep breaking out because the people who start them know that we won't destroy the whole world to stop them. So if... if we could make the deterrent more precise, see—a kind of unstoppable surgical strike that could focus all its destructiveness on invading armies, and only on them—then we could dismantle the nuclear threat. We wouldn't need it because we'd have the deterrent in another form, a safer form.

"So"—he looks up at Jim, looks him right in the eye—"so as far as I'm concerned, I'm doing the work that is most likely to free people from the threat of nuclear war. Now *what*"—voice straining—"what better work could there be?"

He looks away.

"It was a good program."

Jim doesn't know what to say to that. He can see the logic of the argument. And that fearful strain in his father's voice... His anger drains out of him, and he's amazed, even frightened, at what he has been saying. They've gone so far beyond the boundaries of their ordinary discourse, there doesn't seem any way back.

And suddenly he recalls his plans for the night: rendezvous with Arthur, assault on Laguna Space Research. He can't stand across from Dennis with that in his mind, it makes him sick with trembling.

Dennis leans against the car, face down, the averted expression as still as stone. He's lost in his own thoughts. His hands are methodically working with the wrench, loosening a nut on the next point casing. Jim tries to say something, and the words catch in his throat. What was it? He can't remember. The silence stretches out, and really there's nothing he can say. Nothing he can say.

"I—I'll go in and tell Mom you're about ready to eat?"

Dennis nods.

Unsteadily Jim walks inside. Lucy is chopping vegetables for the salad, over by the sink, in front of the kitchen window that has the view of the carport. Jim walks over and stands next to her. Through the window he can see Dennis's side and back.

Lucy sniffs, and Jim sees she is red-eyed. "So did he tell you what happened down at work?" she asks, chopping hard and erratically.

"No! What happened?"

"I saw you talking out there. You shouldn't argue with him on a day like today!" She goes to blow her nose.

"Why, what happened?"

"You know they lost that big proposal Dad was working on."

"Sort of, I guess. Weren't they appealing it?"

"Yes. And they were doing pretty well with that, too, until today." And Lucy tells him as much as she knows of it all, pieced together from Dennis's curt, bitter remarks.

"No!" Jim says more than once during the story. "No!"

"Yes. That's what he said." She puts a fist to her mouth. "I don't think I've ever seen him as down as this in my whole life."

"But—but he just stood out there . . . he just stood out there and defended the whole thing! All of it!"

Lucy nods, sniffs, starts chopping vegetables.

Stunned, Jim stares out the window at his father, who is meticulously tightening a nut, as if tamping down the last pieces of a puzzle.

"Mom, I've gotta go."

"What?"

He's already to the front door. Got to get away.

"Jim!"

But he's gone, out the door, almost running. For a moment he can't find his car key. Then he's found it, he's off and away. Tracking away at full speed.

Dennis will think he's left because of their argument. "No!" Jim can barely see the streets, he doesn't know what he's doing, he just tracks for home. Halfway there he goes to manual and tracks to the Newport Freeway. Southbound, under the great concrete ramp of the northbound lanes, in the murky light of the groundlevel world, in the thickets of halogen light. . . . He punches the dashboard, gets off at Edinger to turn back north, then returns to the southbound lanes. Where to go? Where can he go? What can he do? Can he go back up there to dinner with his parents? Eat a meal and then go blow up his father's company? For God's sake!—how could he have gotten to this point?

On he drives. He knows the defense industry is a malignancy making money in the service of death, in the face of suffering, he knows it has to be opposed in every way possible, he knows he is right. And yet still, still, still, still, still. That look on Dennis's face, as he stared down at the immaculate motor of his car. Lucy, looking out the window about to cut her thumb off. "It was a good program." His voice.

Mindlessly Jim tracks north on the San Diego Freeway. But what in the world is there for him in LA? He could drive all night, escape. . . . No. He turns east on the Garden Grove Freeway, south on the Newport. Back in the loop, going in circles. Triangles, actually. Furious at that he tracks south into Newport Beach, past the Hungry Crab which makes him feel sick, physically sick. He has fucked up every single aspect of his life, and he's still at it. Going for an utterly clean sweep.

At the very end of the Newport peninsula he gets out of his car, walks out to the jetty. The Wedge isn't breaking tonight, the waves slosh up and down the sand as if the Pacific were a lake.

Someone's got a fire going in a barbecue pit, and yellow light and shadows dance over the dark figures standing around it as the wind whips the flames here and there. It's too dark to walk very far over the giant boulders of the jetty. A part of him wonders why he would want to, anyway. The jetty ends, he would have to return to the world eventually, face up to it.

He returns to his car. For a long time he just sits in it, head on the steering switch. Familiar smell, familiar sight of the dusty cracked dash . . . sometimes it feels like this car is his only home. He's moved a dozen times in the last six years, trying to get more room, better sun, less rent, whatever. Only the car remains constant, and the hours spent in it each day. The real home, in autopia; so true. Too true.

Except for his parents' home. Helplessly Jim thinks of it. They moved into the little duplex when Jim was seven. He and his dad played catch in the driveway. One time Jim missed an easy throw and caught it in the eye. They threw balls onto the carport roof and Jim caught them as they rolled off. Dad set up a backboard. He painted an old bike he bought for Jim, painted it red and white. They all went for a trip together, to see the historical museum and the last acres of real orange grove (part of Fairview Cemetery, yes).

The junk of the past, the memory's strange detritus. Why should he remember what he does? And does any of it matter? In a world where the majority of all the people born will starve or be killed in wars, after living degraded lives in cardboard shacks, like animals, like rats struggling hour to hour, meal to meal—do his middle-class suburban Orange County memories matter at all? Should they matter?

It's ten P.M.; Jim has an appointment soon. He clicks the car on, puts it on the track to Arthur Bastanchury's ap.

...74

So Jim turns around and tracks back up the freeway. Somewhere over Costa Mesa he decides what to do. "Oh, man." He picks up his car's phone, calls Arthur. His heart stutters at the same frequency as the ringing phone: Br-r-r-r-r-r-ring! Br-r-r-r-r-r-ring!

"Hello?"

"Arthur. It's Jim. I can't make it to your house in time to leave for the rendezvous. I'll meet you there at the parking lot where we get the boxes."

Silence. Curtly Arthur says, "Okay. You know the time."

"Yeah. I'll be there then."

Back onto Newport Freeway, north to Garden Grove Freeway (typing instructions into his carbrain), out west and off at Haster, under the City Mall's upper level.

Dim world of old streets, gutters matted with trash.
Dead trees. Garbage Grove.
Old suburban houses, boarding a family per room.
The streetlights not broken are old halogen: orange gloom,
An orange glaze on it all.
A roofed world. The basement of California.
You've never lived here, have you.

Hyperventilating, Jim looks around him for once. Parking lots, laundromats, thrift shops: "You had to go to Cairo to see this!" he shouts, and for a moment his resolve is confused; he feels like invisible giants are aiming invisible giant firehoses at him, battering him this way and that in a game he knows nothing of; he can only hold to his plan, try not to think anymore. Stop thinking, stop thinking! It's time to act! Still his stomach twists, his heart stutters as he is buffeted about by contrary ideas, contrary certainties about what is right. . . .

Lewis Street is the same as always, a kind of tunnel alley behind the west side of the City Mall, both sides floor to ceiling with warehouses, truck-sized metal doors shut and padlocked for the night.

He reaches Greentree, which dead-ends into Lewis like one sewer pouring into another. The concrete roof overhead holds a few halogen bulbs, a few mercury vapor bulbs. No plan to it. Jim tracks forward slowly, enters the small parking lot set between warehouses, twenty slots set around two massive concrete pylons that support the upper levels of the mall. There's the same car as always, a blue station wagon, on a parking track at the back of the lot.

Jim turns into the lot, flicks his headlights on and off three times. He stops his car beside the station wagon, gets out.

Four men surround him, pinning him against his car. He's seen all of the faces before, and they recognize him too. "Where's Arthur?" the tallest black guy says.

"He'll be here in a few minutes," Jim says. "Meanwhile let's get the equipment into my car. We can't use Arthur's tonight, and as soon as he shows up he wants us out of here."

The man nods, and Jim swallows. No turning back.

He follows the four men to the back of the station wagon, and the hatchback is pulled up with an airy hiss. In the dark orange shadows Jim can just make out the six plastic boxes. He picks up one in his turn; it's heavier than he remembered. Steps awkwardly to his car. "Backseat," he says, and onto the shabby cracking vinyl they go, five in the backseat, one on the passenger seat.

Jim shuts the door of his car, checks his watch. It's ten till eleven. Arthur will be here soon. He leans in the driver's window and pushes the button that activates the program he typed in on the way up the freeway. The four men don't notice. Jim returns to the station wagon.

"Big load tonight," says the man who spoke before.

"Big job to do."

"Yeah?"

"You'll see it in the papers."

"I'm sure."

Jim paces around the two cars nervously. Twice he walks out to Lewis and looks up and down the long tunnel street. Several warehouses down, in a gap between buildings, there is an infrequently used entrance to the mall; Jim noticed it on one of their earlier runs. It looks almost like a service entrance, but it's not.

The four men are standing around the station wagon, watching him with boredom, amusement, whatever. Jim is thankful it makes sense to act nervously, because he's not sure he could stop it. In fact he feels like throwing up, his whole body is hammering with his pulse, he can't even breathe without a great effort. Still time to—

Headlights, approaching. Jim looks at his watch. It's time, it's time, adrenaline spikes up through him: "Hey!" he calls to the men. "Police coming!"

And his car jerks forward on its own, out of the parking lot and down Lewis to the south, accelerating as fast as it can. Jim takes off running north, toward the little back entrance to the mall.

Up the entrance steps, almost tripping; he's scared out of his mind! Into the mall maze, up to concourse level, then up a broad, gentle staircase to mezzanine; once there there are ten directions he can run in, and he takes off with only a single glance back.

Two of the men are chasing him.

Jim runs full speed through the crowd of shoppers, skipping and dodging desperately to avoid knots of people, open airshafts, planters, fountains, hall displays and food stands. Up a short escalator three steps at a time, around the big open space filled by the laser fountain. Looking down and across he can see his pursuers, already lost. Then one spots him and they're off running again. They're in a tough position, trying to chase someone in a mall; if Jim had more mall experience he'd lose them in a second. As it is he's lost himself. Floors and half floors, escalators and staircases extending everywhere in the broken, refracted space . . . shops are going out of business every day because shoppers can't ever find the same place twice; what chance for two men pursuing a panic-stricken, very mobile individual? It's a three-D maze, and Jim has only to run a random pattern, trending westward, and he's lost them.

Or so Jim thinks, fearfully, as he runs. But when he reaches the east side of the mall and flies through the entryway doors, damned if the two men aren't coming up an escalator back there, at full speed!

Outside, however, on the street bordering the parking lot, he sees his car, which has made it there on its own. Good programming. He runs out to where it sits by the curb, noticing only at the last second the three policemen approaching to inspect it.

Panic on top of panic; Jim's systems almost blow out at the sight, but his pursuers are in the parking lot now and there's no time to lose. Without thinking he runs up to the car and shouts at the policemen, "It's mine! They're robbing me, they dragged me out of the car and now they're chasing me!"

The three policemen regard him carefully, then look as he points at the two men, running across the parking lot. "That's them!"

The two men see what's happening, and quickly turn and run back inside. Perfect.

But there's Arthur and the other two suppliers, tracking up in Arthur's car, stuck in the traffic on the street. Jim says quickly, "There's the rest of them in that car there! Quick, right there! Yeah!"

And he points. And Arthur sees him pointing.

Arthur ignores the policemen flagging him down and shifts to the fast track. This gets the cops' attention, and two of them hustle off to their truck, parked behind Jim's car. The third appears to be staying behind, and he's looking into Jim's car curiously.

Jim says, "There's the others again, Officer!" and points at the east doors of the mall. While the policeman peers in that direction Jim yanks open his car's door, leaps in and jams the accelerator to the floor. The car jerks away over the right track, leaving the policeman shouting behind him.

Jim makes a sharp right on Chapman, because ahead of him on the City Avenue, the police truck is in hot pursuit of Arthur and his two companions. Arthur. . . .

Jim tracks onto the Santa Ana Freeway south. He's free of all pursuit, as far as he can tell. His reaction is to feel acutely sick to his stomach. He might even throw up in his car. And that look on Arthur's face, as he saw Jim pointing him out to the police . . . "No, no! That isn't what I meant! . . ."

Nothing for it now. Arthur will very likely be picked up, with the two suppliers. But will the police have any reason for holding them? Jim has no idea. He only knows he's in a car with six boxes of felony-level weaponry, and the police likely have his license plate number. And he's just betrayed a friend to the police, for no reason. No reason? My God, he can't tell! He has the feeling that he has, in fact, betrayed everyone he knows, in one way or another.

He checks the rearview mirror nervously, looking for CHP, local police, sheriffs, state troopers—who knows what they'll send after industrial saboteurs? He catches sight of his unshaven face, the expression of sick fear on it. And suddenly he's furious, he slams his fist against the dash, filled with disgust for himself. "Coward. Traitor. Fucking idiot!" Unleashed at last, all the directionless angers pour out at once, in fists flailing the dash, in incoherent, sobbing curses. "You know—you know—what should—be done—and you—can't—*do it*!"

All control gone, he remembers the cargo he has and tracks like a madman to South Coast Plaza. He jams to a halt in an open-air parking lot across from SCP's administrative tower, jumps out of his car, tears open the box on the passenger seat, pulls out a Harris Mosquito missile with its Styx-90 payload. There among scattered parked cars he glues the little missile base to the concrete and aims it at the dark windows of the tower. He sets the firing mechanism, clicks it on. The missile suddenly gives out a loud *whoosh* of flame and disappears. Up in the administrative tower a window breaks, and there's a tinkle of glass, a tinny little alarm sounding. Jim hoots, drives away.

Up into Santa Ana, to the office of First American Title Insurance and Real Estate. It's dark, no one is there. Another missile set in the parking lot, aimed at the main doors; it'll melt every computer in there, every file. He'll be out of a job! He laughs hysterically as he sets the mechanism and turns it on. This time the missile breaks a big plate-glass window, and the alarms are howlers.

In the distance there are sirens. What else can he knock out? The Orange County Board of Supervisors, yeah, the crowd that has systematically helped real estate developers to cut OC up, in over a hundred years of mismanagement and graft. Down under the Triangle to the old Santa Ana Civic Center. It's dark there too, he can set up his Mosquito without any danger. Click the firing mechanism over and the little skyrocketlike thing will fly in there and knock the whole corrupt administration of the county apart. So he does it and laughs like mad.

Who else? He can't think. Something has snapped in him, and he can't seem to think at all.

There's a closed Fluffy Donuts; why not?

Another real estate office; why not?

One of the Irvine military microchip factories; why not?

In fact, he's close to Laguna Space Research. And he's crazy enough with anger now to want to punish them for his betrayals, made for their sake. They deserve a warning shot, they should know how close they came to destruction. Give them a scare.

And then they'll know to look out, to be on guard.

As confused in his action as in his thinking, Jim gets lost in a Muddy Canyon condomundo, but when he comes out of it he's at an elementary school on the edge of a canyon, and across the canyon is LSR. He unboxes two Mosquitos and carries them out to a soccer field overlooking the canyon. Sets them up, aims them both for the big LAGUNA SPACE RESEARCH signs at the entrance to the plant. He clicks over the firing mechanism and hustles back to the car.

Just a couple left. He blasts two more dark real estate offices in Tustin.

Only the boxes left, now; he throws them out on the Santa Ana Freeway, watches traffic back up behind him. Back onto the streets in Tustin, his breath catching in his throat, in ragged, hysterical sobs. Redhill Mall mocks all his efforts, even when he gets out and throws stones at its windows. They're shatterproof and the stones bounce away. He can't make OC go away, not with his idiot vandalism, not even by going crazy. It's everywhere, it fills all realities, even the insane ones. Especially those. He can't escape.

He drives home, still mindless with rage and disgust. His ap maddens him, he rushes to the bookcase and pulls it over, watches it crunch the CD system under it. He kicks the books around, but they're too indestructible and he moves on to his computer. A hard left and the screen is cracked, maybe a knuckle too. "Stupid asshole." He goes and gets a frying pan to complete the job. Crack! Crack! Crack! On to the disks. Each one crunched is a couple thousand pages of his utterly useless writing gone for good—thank God! Drawers of printed copy, not that much of it, and it's easy to rip in fourths and scatter around like confetti. What else? CDs, he can frypan all his mix-and-match symphonies to plastic smithereens, reassemble the scattered pieces and finally get the random mishmash the method deserves. What else? A sketch of Hana's, ripped in half. Orange crate labels, smashed and torn apart. The room's beginning to look pretty good. What else?

Into the bedroom. First the video system, he can bring those cameras down and smash them to pieces. And the maps! He leaps up, catches the upper edge of one of the big Thomas Brothers maps, rips it down. It tears with a long, dry sound. The other maps come down as well, he ends up sitting in a pile of ripped map sections, tearing them into ever-smaller fragments, blinded by tears.

Suddenly he hears a car pull up and stop on the street out front. Right in front of his ap. Police? Arthur and his friends? Panic surges into Jim's mindless rage again, and he wiggles out the little bedroom window, across the yard filled with dumpsters. It occurs to him that Arthur and his friends might want to trash his ap in revenge for his betrayal, and at the thought he doubles over laughing. Won't they get a surprise? Meanwhile he continues through the applex, staggering, giggling madly, bent over the hard knot of his stomach. . . .

No problem losing pursuit in such a warren. The boxes we live in! he thinks. The boxes! Okay, he's out on Prospect, they'll never find him. Police cars are cruising, heading down toward Tustin and the scene of his attacks. Busy night, hey Officer? Jim feels an urge to run out into the street and shout "I did it! I did it!" He actually finds his feet on the track when fear jumps him and he hauls ass back into the dark between streetlights, shivering uncontrollably. Are those people on foot, back there? That's not normal, he has to run again. Can't go back for his car, no public transport, can't reach anywhere on foot. He laughs hard, tries hitchhiking. Turn right down Hewes. He gives up hitchhiking, no one ever picks up hitchhikers, and besides where is he going? He jogs down Hewes to 17th, gasping. Over into Tustin, onto Newport, then Redhill. A couple of times he stops to pick up good stones, and then throws them through the windows of real estate offices that he passes. He almost tries a bank but remembers all the alarms. By now he must have tripped off a score of lesser alarms, are the computers tracking his course this very moment, predicting the moves that he is helplessly jerking through?

People passing in cars stare at him: pedestrians are suspicious. He needs a car. Cut off from his car he is immobilized, helpless. Where can he go? Can he really be here, doing this? Is he really in this situation? He seizes an abandoned hubcap, frisbees it into the window of a Jack-in-the-Box. A beautiful flight, although the window only cracks. But it's like hitting a beehive; employees and customers pour out and in a second are after him. He takes off running into the applex behind him, threads his way silently through it. He stumbles over a bicycle, picks it up with every intention of stealing it and pedaling off, gives up and drops it when he sees the Mickey Mouse face, staring at him from between the handlebars.

Back on Redhill, farther south, he sees a bus. Incredible! He jumps on it, pays, and off they go. Only one other passenger, an old woman.

He stays on all the way to Fashion Island, trying vainly to catch proper hold of his breathing. The more time he has to think, the angrier he gets at himself. So that I'll go out and do something even stupider! he thinks. Which will make me angrier, which will make me do something even more stupid! . . . Hopping out at Fashion Island he goes immediately to a Japanese plastic bonsai garden with some real, and truly fine, rocks in it. Rocks like shot puts. After pulling some of the plastic trees apart he picks up these rocks, and has one big one in each hand as he approaches the Bullock's and I. Magnin's. Huge display windows, showing off rooms that could house a hundred poor people for five hundred years. All there to display rack after chrome rack of rainbow-colored clothes. He takes aim and is about to let fly with both of them at once, when there is a grunt of surprise from behind him, and he is grabbed up and lifted into the air.

He struggles like a berserker, swings the rocks back viciously, where they clack together and fall out of his hands; he kicks, wriggles, hisses—

"Hey, Jim, lay off! Relax!"

It's Tashi.

Jim relaxes. In fact, when Tashi lets him down and lets go of him, he almost falls. When he recovers from the little blackout he tries to pick up one of the rocks and heave it at the I. Magnin's, but Tashi stops him. Tash takes the two rocks, underhands them back into the shredded garden. "For Christ's sake, Jim! What in the world is wrong?"

Jim sits down and starts to shake. Tash crouches beside him. He can't seem to breathe right anymore. He's hurt something inside, every breath spikes pain through him. "I—I—" He can't talk.

Tash puts a hand on his shoulder. "Just relax. It's okay now." .

"It's not! It's not!" The hysteria floods back.... "It's not!"

"Okay, okay. Relax. Are you in trouble?"

Jim nods.

"Okay. Let's go up to my place, then, and get you out of sight. Come on." He helps him up.

They walk uphill, along the lit sidewalks through the dark of Newport Heights, and reach Tashi's tower. A police car hums by, and Jim cowers. Tash shakes his head: "What in the hell has happened?"

Up on Tashi's roof Jim manages to stutter out part of the story.

"Your breathing is all fucked up," Tash observes. "Here, lid some of this." He gets him to lid some California Mello. Then Tash stands in front of his big tent and thinks it over.

"Well," he says, "I was planning on taking a farewell trip anyway. And it sounds like you should get out of town for a while. Here, just sit down, Jim. Sit down! Now, I'm going to stuff another sleeping bag, and get you a pack packed. We'll have to buy more food in Lone Pine in the morning. You just sit there."

Jim sits there. It's possible he couldn't do anything else.

An hour later Tash has them packed. He puts one compact backpack over

Jim's shoulders, picks up another for himself, and they're off. They descend to Tashi's little car, get onto the freeway.

Jim, in the passenger seat, stares at the lightflood of red/white, white/red. Autopia courses by. Slowly, millimeter by millimeter, his stomach begins to unknot. His breathing gets better. Somewhere north of LA he jerks convulsively, shudders.

"My God, you won't believe what I did tonight."

"No lie."

Jim tries to tell it. Over and over Tashi exclaims "Why? But why?"

And over and over Jim says, "I don't know! I don't know."

When he finishes they are on an empty dark road, up on the high desert northeast of LA. Jim, shivering lightly, jerking upright from time to time, falls into a restless sleep.

... 76

(And meanwhile, out at sea, a small boat is drifting onshore, rising and falling on a small swell, coming ever closer to the short bluff at Reef Point. Then as it nears the reefs searchlights burst into being, their glare blinds everyone around, the black water sparkles, the heavy boom of a shot blasts the air, reverberates—

A warning shot only. But the two men obey the voice hammering over the loudspeakers, they stand hands overhead, eyes terrified, looking like the figures in the Goya sketch of insurgents executed by soldiers under a tree—)

When Jim wakes they are tracking through the Alabama Hills in the Owens Valley. The oldest rocks in North America look strange in this hour before dawn, rounded boulders piled on each other in weird, impossible formations. Beyond them the eastern escarpment of the Sierra Nevada rises like a black wall under the indigo sky. Tashi sits in the driver's seat listening to Japanese space music, a flute wandering over Oriental harp twanging; he looks awake, but lost in some inner realm.

In the roadside town of Independence, which looks like a museum of the previous century, Tashi rouses. "We need more food." They stop at an all-night place and buy some ramen, cheese, candy. Outside Tash goes to a phone box and closes himself in for a call. It really is like a museum. When he comes out he is nodding thoughtfully, a little smile on his face. "Let's go."

They turn west, up a road that heads straight into the mountains. "Here comes the tricky part," Tash says. "We only have a wilderness permit for one, so we'll have to take evasive action on the way in."

"You have to get a permit to go into the mountains?"

"Oh yeah. You can get them at Ticketron." Tash laughs at Jim's expression. "It's not a bad idea, actually. But sometimes it's not practical."

So they track up the immense slope of the range's eastern face, following a crease made over eons by a lively stream. Tashi's car slows on the steep road. They leave behind the shrubs and flowers of the Owens Valley, track up among pines. Their ears pop. They follow a series of bends in the road, lose sight of the valley below. The air rushing in Tashi's window gets cooler.

They come to a dirt road that forks down to the stream on their left. Tashi stops, drives the car off the track, hums down the dirt road on battery power. "Fishing spot," he says. "And still outside the park boundary."

They put the extra food in the backpacks, put the packs on, and walk up the asphalt road. It's getting light, the sky is sky blue and soon the sun will rise.

The road flattens and Jim sees a parking lot and some buildings, surrounded on three sides by steep mountain slopes. "Where do we go?"

"That's the ranger station. We're supposed to check in there, and real soon a couple of rangers will be out on the trails to make sure we have. There's another one stationed in Kearsarge Pass, which is the main pass here, right up on top." He points west. "So we're going north, and we'll get over the crest of the range on a cross-country pass I know."

"Okay." It sounds good to Jim; he doesn't know what a cross-country pass is.

They hike around the parking lot and into a forest of pines and firs. The ground is layered with fragrant brown needles. The sun is shining on the slopes above them, though they are still in shadow. They reach a fork in the trail and head up a canyon to the north.

They hike beside a stream that chuckles down drop after drop. "LA's water," Tashi says with a laugh. Scrub jays and finches flit around the junipers and the little scraps of meadow bordering the stream. Each turn of the trail brings a new prospect, a waterfall garden or jagged granite cliff. The sun rises over a shoulder to the east, and the air warms. Despite the rubbing of his boots against his heels, Jim feels a small trickle of calmness begin to pour into him and pool. The cool air is piney, the stream exquisite, the bare rock above grand.

They ascend into a small bowl where the stream becomes a little lake. Jim stands admiring it openmouthed. "It's beautiful. Are we staying here?"

"It's seven A.M., Jim!"

"Oh yeah."

They hike on, up a rocky trail that rises steeply to the east. It's hard work. Eventually they reach the rock-and-moss shore of another surrealistically perfect pond.

"Golden Trout Lake. Elevation ten thousand eight hundred feet."

Suddenly Jim understands that they're at the end of the trail, at the bottom of a bowl that has only one exit, which is the streambed they have just ascended. "So we're staying here?"

"Nope." Tash points above, to the west, where the crest of the Sierra Nevada looms over them. "Dragon Pass is up there. We go over that."

"But where's the trail?"

"It's a cross-country pass."

It all comes clear to Jim. "You mean this so-called pass of yours has no trail over it?"

"Right."

"Whoah. Oh, man. . . ."

They put on their packs, begin hiking up the slope. In the morning sun it gets hot. Jim suspects the tweaks from each heel indicate blisters. The straps of his pack cut into his shoulders. He follows Tashi up a twisting trough that Tash explains was once a glacier's bed. They are in the realm of rock now, rock shattered and shattered again, in places almost to gravel. Occasionally they stop to rest and look around. Back to the east they can see the Owens Valley, and the White Mountains beyond.

Then it's up again. Jim steps in Tashi's elongated footprints and avoids sliding back as far as Tash does. He concentrates on the work. How obvious that this endless upward struggle is the perfect analogy for life. Two steps up, one step back. Finding a best path, up through loose broken granite, stained in places by lichen of many colors, light green, yellow, red, black. The goal above seems close but never gets closer. Yes, it is a very pure, very stripped-down model of life—life reduced to stark, expansive significance. Higher and higher. The sky overhead is dark blue, the sun a blinding chip in it.

They keep climbing. The repetition of steps up, each with its small tweak from the heels, reduces Jim's mind to a little point, receiving only visual input and the kinetics of feeling. His thighs feel like rubber bands. Once it occurs to him that for the last half hour he has thought of nothing at all, except the rock under him. He grins; then he has to concentrate on a slippery section. Sweat gets in his eye. There's no wind, no sound except their shoes on the rock, their breaths in their throats.

"We're almost there," Tashi says. Jim looks up, surprised, and sees they are on the last slope below the ridge, the edge of the range with all its towers extending left to right above them, for as far as they can see. They're headed for a flat section between towers. "How do you feel?"

"Great," says Jim.

"Good man. The altitude bothers some people."

"I love it."

On they climb. Jim gets summit fever and hurries after Tashi until his breaths rasp in his throat. Tashi must have it too. Then they're on top of the ridge, on a very rough, broad saddle, made of big shards of pinkish granite. The ridge is a kind of road running north–south, punctuated frequently by big towers, serrated knife-edge sections, spur ridges running down to east, out to west. . . . To the west it's mountains for as far as they can see.

"My God," Jim says.

"Let's have lunch here." Tashi drops his pack, pulls off his shirt to dry the sweaty back of it in the sun. There is still no wind, not a cloud in the sky. "Perfect Sierra day."

They sit and eat. Under them the world turns. Sun warms them like lizards on rock. Jim cuts his thumb trying to slice cheese, and sucks the cut till it stops bleeding.

When they're done they put on the packs and start down the western side of the ridge. This side is steeper, but Tashi finds a steep chute of broken rock—

talus, he teaches Jim to call it—and very slowly they descend, holding on to the rock wall on the side of the chute, stepping on chunks that threaten to slide out from under them. In fact Jim sends one past the disgusted Tashi and sits down hard, bruising his butt. His toes blister in the descent. The chute opens up and the talus fans down a lessened slope to a small glacial pond, entirely rockbound: aquamarine around its perimeter, cobalt in its center.

They drink deeply from this lake when they finally reach it. It's mid- or late afternoon already. "Next lake down is a beauty," says Tash. "Bigger than this one, and surrounded by rock walls, except there's a couple of little lawns tucked right on the water. Great campsite."

"Good." Jim's tired.

The west side of the range has a great magic to it. On the east side they looked down into Owens Valley, and so back to the world Jim knows. Now that link is gone and he's in a new world, without connection to the one Tashi yanked him from. He can't characterize this landscape yet, it's too new, but there's something in its complexity, the anarchic profusion of forms, that is mesmerizing to watch. Nothing has been planned. Nevertheless it is all very complex. No two things are the same. And yet everything has an intense coherence.

Clouds loft over the great eastern range. They descend, crossing a very rough field of lichen-splotched boulders. Mosses fill cracks, mosses and then tiny shrubs. Cloud shadows rush over them. Jim wanders off parallel to Tashi so he can find his own route. For a long time they navigate the immensity of broken granite, each in his own world of thought and movement. Already it seems like they have been doing this for a long time. Nothing but this, for as long as the rock has rested here.

Late in the afternoon they come to the next lake, already deep in the shadow of the spur ridge circling it. Its smooth surface reflects the rock like a blue mirror.

"Whoah. Beautiful."

Tashi's eyes are narrowed.

"Uh-oh. We can't camp here—there's *people* over there!"

"Where?"

Tashi points. Jim sees two tiny red dots, all the way on the other side of the lake. Slightly larger dot of an orange tent. "So what? We'll never hear them, they won't bother us."

Tashi stares at Jim as if he has just proposed eating shit. "No way! Come on, let's follow the exit stream down toward Dragon Lake. There's bound to be a good campsite before that, and if not it's a fine lake."

Wearily Jim humps his pack and follows Tashi down the crease in the rib that holds the lake in, where water gurgles over flat yellow granite and carves a ravine in the slope falling off into a big basin.

They hike until sunset. The sky is still light, but the ground and the air around them are dim and shadowed. Alpine flowers gleam hallucinogenically from the black moss on the stream's flat banks. Gnarled junipers contort out of cracks in the rock. Each bend in the little stream reveals a miniature work of landscaping that makes Jim shake his head: above the velvet blue sky, below the dark rock world, with the stream a sky-colored band of lightness cutting through it. He's tired, footsore, he stumbles from time to time; but Tash is walking slowly, and it seems a shame to stop and end this endless display of mountain grandeur.

Finally Tash finds a flat sandy dip in a granite bench beside the stream, and he declares it camp. They drop their packs.

Four or five junipers.
To the west they can see a long way;
A fin of granite, poking up out of shadows.
"Fin Dome," Tashi says.
To the east the great crest of the ridge they crossed is glowing.
Vibrant apricot in the late sunset light.
Each rock picked out, illuminated.
Each moment, long and quiet.
The stream's small voice talks on and on.
Light blue water in the massy shadows.
Two tiny figures, walking aimlessly:
"Whoah. Whoah. Whoah."
Slowly the light leaks out of the air.
And you have always lived here.

"How about dinner?" says Tashi. And he sits by his pack.

"Sure. Are we going to build a fire? There's dead wood under these junipers."

"Let's just use the stove. There really isn't enough wood in the Sierras to justify making fires, at least at this altitude."

They cook Japanese noodles over a small gas stove. Somehow Jim manages to knock the pot over when cooking his, and when he grabs the pot to save his noodles from spilling, he burns the palm and fingers of his left hand. "Ah!" Sucks on them. "Oh well."

Tashi has brought a tent along, but it's such a fine night they decide to forgo it, and they lay their sleeping bags on groundpads spread in the sandy patches. They get in the bags and—ah!—lie down.

The moon, hidden by the ridge to the east, still lights the wild array of peaks surrounding them, providing a monochrome sense of distance, and an infinity of shadows. The stream is noisy. Stars are dumped all across the sky; Jim has never seen so many, didn't know so many existed. They outnumber the satellites and mirrors by a good deal.

Soon Tashi is asleep, breathing peacefully.

But Jim can't sleep.

He abandons the attempt, sits up with his bag pulled around his shoulders, and . . . watches. For a moment his past life, his life below, occurs to him; but his mind shies away from it. Up here his mind refuses to enter the mad realm of OC. He can't think of it.

Rocks. The dark masses of the junipers, black needles spiking against the stars. Moonlight on steep serrated slopes, revealing their shapes. Ah, Jim—Jim doesn't know what to think. His body is aching, stinging, and throbbing in a dozen places. All that seems part of mountains, one component of the scene. His senses hum, he's almost dizzy with the attempt to really take it in all at once: the music of falling water and wind in pine needles, the vast and amazingly complex vision of the stippled white granite in the foreground, the moonlit peaks at every distance. . . . He doesn't know what to think. There's no way he can take it all in, he only shivers at the attempt. There's too much.

But he has all night; he can watch, and listen, and watch some more. . . . He realizes with a flush in his nerve endings, with a strange, physical rapture, that this will be the longest night of his life. Each moment, long and quiet, spent discovering a world he never knew existed—a home. He had thought it a lost dream; but this is California too, just as real as the rock underneath his sore butt. He raps the granite with scraped knuckles. Soon the moon will rise over the range.

... 78

Stewart Lemon is visited by Donald Hereford, out from New York early on the morning after Jim's rampage. Hereford steps out of the helicopter that has brought him over from John Wayne, and walks out from under the spinning blades without even the suggestion of a stoop or a run. He looks over at the physical plant that he and Lemon inspected together not more than two weeks before.

"What happened?" he says to Lemon.

Lemon clears his throat. "An assault was made, I guess, but something went wrong with it. No one knows why. They got the sign at the entrance to the parking garage. And—and we caught a pair in a boat offshore, but they didn't have anything on them, so . . ."

Feeling silly, Lemon walks Hereford from the helipad around the physical plant to the car entrance to the complex. There six round metal poles stick out of two hardened puddles of blue plastic. They're the signs that used to announce LAGUNA SPACE RESEARCH to the cars passing by. Ludicrous.

Two FBI analysts are at work at the site, and they pause to speak briefly with Hereford and Lemon. "Appears it was a couple of the Mosquitoes that they've been using around here. Made by Harris, and carrying a load of Styx-ninety."

Hereford makes a *tkh* sound with tongue and roof of mouth, kneels to touch the deformed plastic. He leads Lemon away from the FBI agents, around the building and out in the open ground near the helipad.

"So." His mouth is a tight, grim line. "That's that."

"Maybe they'll try again?"

Brusque shake of the head.

Lemon feels his fear as a kind of tingling in his fingers.

"Couldn't we somehow . . . stimulate another attack?"

Hereford stares. "Stimulate? Or simulate?" He laughs shortly. "No. The point is, we've been warned. So now it's our responsibility to see it doesn't happen again. If it does, it will look like we let it. So."

Lemon swallows. "So what happens now?"

"It's already happening. I've given instructions for the Ball Lightning program to be moved to our Florida plant and given to a new team. The Air Force is going to descend on us next month no matter what we do, but hopefully we can indicate to them that we have already acknowledged the problem in the production schedule and taken steps to rectify it."

Lemon hopes that his face doesn't look as hot as it feels. "It's not just a problem in the production schedule—"

"I know that."

"The Air Force will know it too."

"I'm aware of that." Hereford's glance is very, very cold. "At this point I don't have a whole lot of options left, do I? Your team has given me a program that could very easily do a Big Hacksaw on us. In fact I would bet now that that's what will happen, no matter what I do. But I still have to take all the last twists I can. It's possible that the ballistic missile defense problems that everyone else is having will camouflage us. You never know."

"So what do I do with my team here?" Lemon demands.

"Fire them." Calmly Hereford looks at him. "Lay off the production unit. Shift the best engineers somewhere else, if there's room for them."

"And the executive team?"

Hereford's gaze never wavers. "Fire them. We're clearing house, remember? We have to make sure the Air Force sees that we're serious. Do the usual things, forced retirements, layoffs, whatever it takes. But do it."

"All right. All right." Lemon thinks fast. "McPherson's gone—he's been in charge of the technical side of Ball Lightning for the last few months, and anyway, after the Stormbee fiasco our Andrews friends will be happy to see him go, no doubt. But Dan Houston, now . . . Houston's a useful fellow. . . ."

In the face of Hereford's baleful stare Lemon can't continue. He begins to understand how Hereford got so high so fast. There's a ruthlessness there that Lemon has never even come close to. . . .

Finally Hereford says, "Houston too. All of them. And do it fast."

And then, as he turns to go back to the waiting helicopter: "You're lucky you aren't going with them."

Early that afternoon Dennis McPherson finds out that he is forcibly retired. Dismissed. Fired. The news comes in a freshly printed and stiffly worded letter from Lemon. He's given two months' notice, of course, but given his accumulated vacation time and sick leave—and since there's nothing left to work on, as someone else is overseeing the transfer of the Ball Lightning program to the Florida plant—which is a meaningless and in fact stupid maneuver, as far as McPherson can tell—well . . . Nothing to keep him here. Nothing at all.

He makes sure with a quick calculation of his vacation days on the desk calculator. Nope. In fact they owe him a few days. But after twenty-seven years of work here, what does it matter?

Numbly he orders up a box and packs his few personal possessions from the office into it. He gives the box to his secretary Karen to mail to him. She's been crying. He smiles briefly at her, too distracted by his own thoughts to respond adequately. She tells him that Dan Houston has been dismissed too. "Ach," he says. That on top of everything else; bad for Dan. "I think I'll go home now," he says to the office wall.

The quick, shocked automatism of his actions gives him one moment of satisfaction; he's on his way out when Lemon steps out of the elevator and says, "Dennis, let me talk to you," with that automatic boss-assumption in his hoarse voice, the assumption that people will always do as he says. And without a glance back McPherson keeps on walking, out the door and down the stairs to the parking garage.

Driving out he doesn't even notice the melted company sign at the entrance.

Automatic pilot home, as on so many other days of his life. It's impossible to believe this is the last one. Traffic is a lot better this time of day. The only real clog is at the Laguna Freeway-Santa Ana Freeway interchange. On the way up Redhill the streets look empty and wrongly lit, like a bad movie set of the city. Same with Morningside, and his house.

Lucy is out. At the church. Dennis sits down at the kitchen table. Funny how not once during the struggle for the Stormbee program did it occur to him that he was fighting for his job. He thought he was only fighting for the program. . . .

He sits at the kitchen table and looks dully at the salt and pepper shakers. He's numb; he even knows he's numb. But that's how he feels. Just go with your feelings, Lucy always says. Fine. Time to get behind some deep shock, here. Dive full into numbness.

It was nice the way he was able to walk out on Lemon at last. Just like he always wanted to. What could they possibly have in mind moving the Ball Lightning program to Florida? It'll just screw up the work they were doing on the phased array; and if they had gotten that working right—

But no. He laughs shortly. A habit of mind. Working on the problems at home, in reveries around this table.

What will he think about now?

He solves the problem by not thinking anything.

Lucy comes home. He tells her about it. She sits down abruptly.

He glances up from the table, gives her a look: well? That's that—nothing to be done. She reaches across the table and puts her hand on his. Amazing how extensive the private language of an old married couple can be.

"You'll get another job."

"Uhn." That hadn't occurred to him, but now he doubts it. It's not a track record that is likely to impress the defense industry too much.

Lucy hears the negative in his grunt and goes to the sink. Blows her nose. She's upset.

She comes back, says brightly, "We should go up to our land by Eureka. It would do you good to get away. And we haven't seen that land since the year it burned. Maybe it's time to build that cabin you talk about."

"The church?"

"I can get Helena to fill in for me. It would be fun to have a vacation." She is sincere about this; she loves to travel. "We might as well make what good we can out of the opportunity. Things will work out."

"I'll think about it." Meaning, don't pester me about it right now.

And so she doesn't. She begins making dinner. Dennis watches her work. Things will work out. Well, he's still got Lucy. That's not going to change. Poor Dan Houston. She's all sniffly. He almost grins; she hates the idea of that cabin on the coast of northern California, away from all her friends. It's always been his idea. Build a cabin all by himself, do it right. There must be churches up there, she'd have new friends inside a week. And he—well, it doesn't matter. He doesn't have any friends down here, does he? None to speak of, anyway—a colleague or two, most of them long gone to different companies, out of his life. "I should call Dan Houston." So it wouldn't make any difference, being up near

Eureka. He loved that tree-covered sweep of rocky coastline, its bare empty salt reaches.

"We could visit, anyway," he says. "It's too late in the year to start building. But we could pick the site, and look around a bit."

"That's right," Lucy says, looking steadfastly into the refrigerator. "We could make a real vacation of it. Drive up the coast all the way."

"Stop at Carmel, first night."

"I like that place."

"I know."

Fondness wells up in him like some sort of . . . like a spasm of grief. As he comes out of the numbness his feelings are jumbled. He doesn't know exactly what he feels. But there is this woman here, his wife, whom he can count on to always, always, always put the best face on things. No matter the effort it costs her. Always. He doesn't deserve her, he thinks. But there she is. He almost laughs.

She glances at him cautiously, smiles briefly. Maybe she can sense what he's feeling. She goes to work at the counter by the stove. A sort of artificial industriousness there, it reminds him of LSR. Ach, forget it. Forget it. Twenty-seven years.

As Lucy is serving the hot casserole, the phone rings.

She answers it, says hesitantly, "Yes, he's here."

She gives the phone to Dennis with a frightened look.

"Hello?"

"Dennis, this is Ernie Klusinski." One of Dennis's long-lost colleague friends, now working for Aerojet in La Habra.

"Oh hi, Ernie. How are you?" Unnatural heartiness to his voice, he can tell.

"Fine. Listen, Dennis, we've heard over here about what happened at LSR today, and I was wondering if you wanted to come up and have lunch with me and my boss Sonja Adding, to sort of talk things over. Look into possibilities, you know, and see if you're at all interested in what we're doing here." Pause. "If you're interested, of course."

"Oh I'm interested," Dennis says, thinking fast. "Yeah, that's real nice of you, Ernie, I appreciate it. Uh, one thing though"—he pauses, decides—"Lucy and I were thinking of taking a vacation up the coast. Given the opportunity, you know." Ernie laughs at this feeble jest. "So maybe we can do it when I get back?"

"Oh sure, sure! No problem with that. Just give me a ring when you get back, and we'll set it up. I've told Sonja about you, and she wants to meet you."

"Yeah. That'd be nice. Thanks, Ernie."

They hang up.

Still thinking hard, Dennis returns to the table. Stares at his plate, the casserole steaming gently.

"That was Ernie Klusinski?"

"Yeah, it was." It's been a strange day.

"And what did he want?"

Dennis gives her a lopsided grin. "He was head-hunting. Word has gotten around I was let go, and Ernie's boss is interested in talking to me. Maybe hiring me."

"But that's wonderful!"

"Maybe. Aerojet has got those ground-based lasers, phase six of the BMD— I'd hate to get mixed up in that again."

"Me too."

"It's a goddamned waste of time!" He shakes his head, returns to the topic at hand. "But they're big, they have a lot of things going. If I could get into the right department . . ."

"You can find that out when you talk to them."

"Yeah. But . . ." How to say it? He doesn't understand it himself. "I don't know . . . I don't know if I want to get back into it! It'll just be more of the same. More of the same."

He doesn't know what he feels. It's nice to be wanted, real nice. But at the same time he feels a kind of despair, he feels trapped—this is his life, his work, he'll never escape it. It'll never end.

"You can figure that out after you talk to them."

"Yeah. Oh. I told him we'd be off on vacation for a while."

"I heard that." Lucy smiles.

Dennis shrugs. "It would be good to see our property." He eats for a while, stops. Taps his fork on the table. "It's been a strange day."

That night they pack their suitcases and prepare the house, in a pre-trip ritual thirty years old. Dennis's thoughts are scattered and confused, his feelings slide about from disbelief to hurt to fury to numbness to bitter humor to a kind of breathless anticipation, a feeling of freedom. He doesn't have to take the job at Aerojet, if it comes to that. On the other hand he can. Nothing's certain anymore. Anything can happen. And he'll never have to deal with Ball Lightning again; he never has to listen to Stewart Lemon boss him around, ever again. Hard to believe.

"Well, I should call Dan Houston."

Reluctantly he does it, and is more relieved than anything else to get an answering machine. He leaves a short message suggesting that they get together when he returns, and hangs up thoughtfully. Poor Dan, where is he tonight?

Lucy calls up Jim. No answer. And his answering machine isn't turned on. "I'm worried about him," she says, nervously packing a suitcase.

"Leave a note on the kitchen screen. He'll see it when he comes over."

"Okay." She closes the suitcase. "I wish I knew . . . what was wrong with him."

"*He* doesn't even know what's wrong with him," Dennis says. He's still annoyed with Jim for leaving before dinner, the previous night. It hurt Lucy's feelings. And it was a stupid argument; Dennis is surprised he ever let himself say as much as he did, especially to someone who doesn't know enough to understand. Although he *should* understand! He should. Well—his son is a problem. A mystery. "Let's not worry about him tonight."

"All right."

Dennis loads the car trunk. As they go to bed Lucy says, "Do you think you'll take this other job?"

"We'll see when we get back."

And the next morning, at 5:00 A.M., their traditional hour of departure, they back out of the driveway and track down to the Santa Ana Freeway, and they turn north, and they leave Orange County.

...80

By the time Tashi and Jim return to Tashi's car, three days later, Jim is a wreck. He has several big blisters, three badly burned fingertips, a cut thumb, a bruised butt, a badly scratched leg, a knee locked stiff by some unfelt twist, a torn arch muscle in his left foot, deeply sun-cracked lips, and a radically sunburnt nose. He has also stabbed himself in the face with a tent pole, almost poking out his eye; and he tried to change the stove canister by candlelight, thereby briefly blowing himself up and melting off his eyelashes, his beard stubble, and the hair on his wrists.

So, Jim is no Boy Scout. But he is happy. Body a wreck, mind at ease. At least temporarily. He's discovered a new country, and it will always be there for him. Both physically, just up the freeway, and mentally, in a country in his mind, a place that he has discovered along with the mountains themselves. It will always be back there somewhere.

He moans as they reach the car and throw their packs in the back, he moans as Tashi drives the car up the dirt road to the track, and heads down; he moans as he sits in the passenger seat. But in truth, he feels fine. Even the prospect of returning to OC can't subdue him; he has new resources to deal with OC, and a new resolve.

"We should get Sandy to come up here with us," he says to Tashi. "I'm sure he'd love it too."

"He used to come up with me," Tash says. "Too busy now. And . . ." He makes a funny moue with his mouth. "We'll have to see how Sandy is doing when he gets back. He should be out on bail, I guess."

"What?"

"Well, see . . ." And Tashi tells him about the aphrodisiac run, the stashing of the goods at the bottom of the bluff below LSR. "So with LSR's security tightened, the drugs were stuck there, see. So, apparently the attack you guys were going to make on Laguna Space was supposed to serve as a distraction that would cover Sandy while he snuck in by sea and recovered the stash."

"*What?* Oh my God—"

"Calm down, calm down. He's all right. I called Angela the next morning when we stopped for food, to find out what had happened. Sandy was caught by LSR's security forces, and turned over to the police. No problem."

"No problem! Jesus!"

"No problem. Being nabbed by cops isn't the worst thing that could happen. I was worried that he might have gotten hurt. He easily could have been shot, you know."

That idea is enough to stun Jim into complete silence.

"It's okay," Tash says after a while.

"Jesus," says Jim. " I didn't know! I mean, why didn't Sandy tell me!"

"I don't know. But then what would you have done, anyway?"

Jim gulps, speechless.

"Since Sandy's okay, it's probably better you didn't know."

"Oh, man. . . . First Arthur, and now Sandy. . . ."

"Yeah." Tash laughs. "You changed a lot of people's plans, that night. But that's okay."

And they track on south. Jim's mind is filled again with OC problems, he can't escape them. That's what it means to go back; it'll be damned hard to keep even a shred of the calm he felt in the Sierras. He could lose that new country he discovered, and he knows it.

Tash, too, gets quieter as they approach home. On they drive, in silence.

In the evening they track over Cajon Pass and down through the condomundo hills to the great urban basin. LA, City of Light. The great interchange where 5 meets 101, 210, and 10 looks utterly unreal to them, a vision from another planet, one entirely covered by a city millions of years old.

Soon they're back in OC, where the vision at least has familiarity to temper their new astonishment. They know this alien landscape, it's their home. The home of their exile from the world they have so briefly visited.

Tashi drops Jim off at his ap.

"Thanks," Jim says. "That was . . ."

"That's okay." Tash rouses from the reverie he has been in throughout southern California. "It was fun." He sticks out a hand, unusual gesture for him, and Jim shakes it. "Come and see me."

"Of course!"

"Good-bye, then." Off he goes.

Jim's alone, on his street. He goes into his ap. It's a wreck too; he and his home are of a piece. Same as always. He observes the detritus of his hysteria, his madness, with a certain equanimity, tinged with . . . remorse, nostalgia; he can't tell. It's not a happy sight.

Over piles of junk, the trashed bookcase and the broken CDs and disks, to the bathroom. He strips. His dirty body is surely dinged up. He steps in the shower, turns it on hot. Pleasure and stinging pain mix in equal proportions, and he hops about singing:

Swimming in the amniotic fluid of love
Swimming like a finger to the end of the glove
When I reach the end I'm going to dive right in
I'm the sperm in the egg: did I lose? did I win?

Gingerly he dries off, gingerly he crawls into bed. Sheets are such a luxury. He's home again. He doesn't know what that means exactly, anymore. But here he is.

He spends the next day down at Trabuco Junior College, arranging next semester's classes, and then back home, cleaning up. A lot of his stuff has been wrecked beyond saving. He'll have to build up the music collection again from scratch. Same with the computer files. Well, he didn't lose much of value in the files anyway.

The wall maps, now; that's a real shame. He can't really afford to replace them. Carefully he takes the tatters off the walls, lays each map in turn facedown on the floor, tapes up all the rips, flattens them as best he can. Puts them back up.

Well, they look a little strange: rumpled, with tear marks evident. As if some paper earthquake has devastated the paper landscape, three times over no less, a recurrent disaster patched up again and again. Well . . . that sounds about right, actually. A map is the representation of a landscape, after all, and many landscapes, like OC's, are principally psychic. Besides, there isn't anything else he can do about it.

He then wanders the living room gathering the torn paper scattered around the desk. This heap of scraps represents the sum total of his writing efforts. Seeing them ripped apart, he feels bad. The stuff on OC's history didn't really deserve this. Well . . . it's all still here, in the pile somewhere. He begins to inspect each piece of paper, spreading them over the couch in a new order, until all the fragments have been reunited. He tapes the pages together as he did the maps. After that he reads them, throws away everything except the historical pieces. Other than those, he will start from scratch.

When he's done with that job he gets out the vacuum cleaner and sucks the dust up from everywhere the thing can reach. Sponge and cleanser, dust rag, paper towels and window cleaner, laundry whitener for spots on the walls . . . he goes at it furiously, as if he were on a hallucinogen and had conceived a distaste for clutter and dirt, seeing it in smaller and smaller quantities. Music from his little kitchen radio, luckily overlooked in the purge, helps to power him; the latest by Three Spoons and a Stupid Fork:

> You are a carbrain
> You're firmly on track
> You're given your directions
> And you don't talk back
> You're very simply programmed
> And you don't have much to say
> And you're gonna have a breakdown
> It'll happen some day.

"Well fuck you!" Jim sings at the radio, and continues the song on his own: "And after the breakdown, the carbrain can see, cleaning all his programs, so he can be free. . . ."

Yes, there must be an *order* established; nothing fetishistic, but just a certain pattern, symbolic of an internal coherence that is as yet undefined. He's struggling to find a new pattern, working with the same old materials. . . .

All his poor abused books are on the couch. Stupid to attack them like that. Luckily most were just thrown around. He props up the bookcase of bricks and boards, starts to reshelve them. Is the alphabet really a significant principle for ordering books? Let's try putting them back arbitrarily, and see what comes of it. Make a new order.

Finally he's done. The late afternoon sun ducks under the freeway, slants in the open window. Door open, shoo out all the dust motes with a cross breeze. The place actually looks neat! Jim carries the accumulated trash out to the dumpster, comes back. He carries out the busted-up bedroom video system, throws it away too. "Enough of the image." He comes back in and finds himself surprised. It's not a bad ap, at least at this time of the day, of the year.

He makes himself a dinner of scrambled eggs. Then he calls Hana. No answer, no answering machine. Damn. He calls his parents. Their answering machine is on, which surprises him. It's not a Friday evening; where are they? They usually only turn on the machine when they leave town.

There's nothing to do at home, so after a while he drives over to check it out.

No one home, that's right. A note from Lucy is on the kitchen screen.

"Jim—Dad's been laid off at work—we've gone up to Eureka to visit our place—please water plants in family room etc.—we'll be back in two weeks."

Laid off! But there's no lack of work at LSR!

Confused, Jim wanders his childhood home aimlessly. What could have happened?

It's odd, seeing the place this empty. As if all of them have gone for good.

Why did they fire him? "Bastards! I should have let them melt you down! I should have helped them do it!"

But if he had, then his father just as certainly would have been fired, wouldn't he? Jim can't see how the destruction of the plant in Laguna Hills would have made it any likelier that LSR would have kept his father on; in fact, the reverse seems more likely. He doesn't really know.

Jim stands in the hallway, where he can see every room of the little duplex, the rooms where so much of his life has been acted out. Now just empty little rooms, mocking him with their silence and stillness. "What happened?" He recalls Dennis's face as he looked over the opened motor compartment of the car, Dennis holding to his beliefs with a dogged tenacity. . . .

Jim leaves, feeling aimless and empty. I'm back, he thinks, I'm ready to start up in a new way. Begin a new life. But how? It's just the same old materials at hand. . . . How do you start a new life when everything else is the same?

...81

He tracks down to Sandy's, refusing even to look at South Coast Plaza.

Sandy's door opens and it's quiet inside. Angela's there. "Oh hi, Jim."

"Hi Angela. Is Sandy—is Sandy okay?"

"Oh yeah." Angela leads him into the kitchen, which seems odd, so quiet and empty. "He's fine. He's gone down to Miami to visit his father."

"I just heard from Tashi what happened the other night. We've been up in the mountains since then or I would've been by sooner. I'm really, really sorry—"

Angela puts a hand on his arm to stop him. "Don't worry about it, Jim. It wasn't your fault. Tash told me what you did, and to tell you the truth, I'm glad you did it. In fact I'm proud of you. Sandy's all right, after all. And he'll be back in a few days and everything will be back to normal."

"But I heard he got arrested?"

"It doesn't matter. They can't make any of the charges stick. Arrests by security cops don't mean much to the courts. Sandy and Bob said they were just boating out there, and there was nothing to indicate they weren't. Really, don't worry about it."

"Well . . ."

Angela sits him down, comforts him in typical Angela style: "Sandy wasn't even to shore when they caught him. It was pretty scary, he said, because they fired a warning shot to stop him, and then they had submachine guns aimed at him and all. And he spent a couple days in jail. But nothing's going to come of it, we hope. Sandy may have to quit dealing for a while. Maybe for good. That's my opinion." She smiles a little.

Jim asks about Arthur.

"He's disappeared. No one knows where he's gone or what's happened to him. I'm not sure I care, either." Apparently she blames Arthur for getting all of them involved with the sabotage/drug rescue attempt at LSR; although, Jim thinks, that's not exactly right. For a moment she looks bleak, and all of a sudden

Jim sees that her cheerfulness is forced. Optimism is not a biochemical accident, he thinks; it's a policy, you have to work at it. "That was damned stupid, what he was doing," she says, "and he was using you, too. You should have known better."

"I guess." They were being used to cover a drug run, after all; what can he say? And in the earlier attacks . . . was that all there was to it? "But . . . no, I think Arthur believed in what we were doing. I don't think he was doing it for money or whatever—he really wanted to make a change. I mean, we have to resist somehow! We can't just give in to the way things are, can we?"

"I don't know." Angela shrugs. "I mean we should try to change things, sure. But there must be ways that are less dangerous, less harmful."

Jim isn't so sure. And after they sit in silence for a while, thinking about it, he leaves.

On the freeway, feeling low. How could he have guessed that sabotaging the sabotage would get Sandy in such trouble? Not to mention Arthur! And what, in the end, did he and Arthur accomplish? Were they resisting the system, or only part of it?

He wonders if anything can ever be done purely or simply. Apparently not. Every action takes place in such a network of circumstances. . . . How to decide what to do? How to know how to act?

He drives by Arthur's ap in Fountain Valley. Into the complex, up black wood stairs with their beige stucco sidewalls, along the narrow corridor past ap after ap. Number 344 is Arthur's. No one answers his knock: it's empty. Jim stands before the window and looks at the sun-bleached drapes. That visionary tension in Arthur, the excitement of action . . . he had believed in what he was doing. No matter what the connection with Raymond was. Jim is certain of it. And he finds he is still in agreement with Arthur; something has to be done, there are forces in the country that have to be resisted. It's only a question of method. "I'm sorry, Arthur," he says aloud. "I hope you're okay. I hope you keep working at it. And I'll do the same."

Walking back to his car he adds, "Somehow." And realizes that keeping this promise will be one of the most difficult projects he will ever give himself. Since both Arthur and his father are "right"—and at one and the same time!—he is going to have to find his own way, somewhere between or outside them—find some way that cannot be co-opted into the great war machine, some way that will actually help to change the thinking of America.

It's late, but he decides to drive down to Tashi's place, to discuss things. He needs to talk.

He takes the elevator up the tower, steps out onto the roof.

It's empty. The tent is gone.

"What the hell?"

What is *happening*? he thinks. Where is everyone *going*? He walks around the rooftop as if its empty concrete can give a clue to Tashi's whereabouts. Even the vegetable tubs are gone.

Below him sparkle the lights of Newport Beach and Corona del Mar. Somewhere someone's playing a sax, or maybe it's just a recording. Sad hoarse sax notes, bending down through minor thirds. Jim stands on the edge of the roof, looking out over the freeways and condos to the black sea. Catalina looks like an overlit sea liner, cruising off on the black horizon. Tashi. . . .

After an insomniac night on the living room couch, Jim calls Abe. "Hey, Abe, what happened to Tashi?"

"He left for Alaska yesterday." Long pause. "Didn't he say good-bye to you?"

"No!" Jim remembers their parting after the drive back. "I suppose he thinks so. Damn."

"Maybe you were out when he called."

"Maybe."

"So how did you like the mountains?"

"They were great. I want to tell you about it—you going to be home today?"

"No, I'm going to work soon."

"Ah."

Long silence. Jim says, "How's Xavier?"

"Hanging in there." Another silence.

But maybe Abe hears something in it. "Tell you what, Jim, I'll call you tomorrow, see if you're still up for getting together. We've got to plan a celebration for when Sandy comes back, anyway. As long as nothing happens to his dad."

"Yeah, okay. Good. You do that. And good luck today."

"Thanks."

Jim tracks by First American Title Insurance and Real Estate Company, just because he can't think of anything to do and old habits are leading him around.

Humphrey is out front, looking morosely at the construction crew that is cleaning up the inside of the building. It's a mess in there—it resembles fire damage, although it isn't black. They've got most of it cleaned.

"They blew it away," Humphrey tells him. "Someone blasted it with a bomb filled with a solvent that dissolved everything in there. They got a whole bunch of real estate companies, the same night."

"Oh," Jim says awkwardly. "I hadn't heard. I was up in the mountains with Tashi."

"Yeah. They got all my files and everything else." He shakes his head bleakly. "Ambank has already pulled out of the Pourva Tower project because of the delays, they said. I just think they're scared, but whatever. It doesn't matter. The project is a goner."

"I'm sorry, Humph," Jim says. "Real sorry." And the part of him that would have been pleased at this unexpected turn—something good coming out of his madness, after all—has gone away. Seeing the expression on Humphrey's face it has vanished, at least for the moment, from existence. "I'm sorry."

"That's all right." Humphrey says, looking puzzled. "It wasn't your fault."

"Uh-huh. Still, you know. I'm sorry."

All these apologies. And he's going to have to give Sheila Mayer a call sometime, and apologize to her too. He groans at the thought. But he's going to have to do it.

So Jim spends the afternoon pacing his little living room. He stares at his books. He's much too restless to read. To be on his own, by himself—not today, though! Not today. He calls Hana again. No answer, no answering machine. "Come on, Hana, answer your phone!" But he can't even tell her that.

Okay. Here he is. He's alone, on his own, in his own home. What should he do? He thinks aloud: "When you change your life, when you're a carbrain suddenly free of the car, off the track, what do you do? You don't have the slightest idea. What do you do if you don't have a plan? You make a plan. You make the best plan you can."

Okay. He's wandering the living room, making a plan. He walks around aimlessly. He's lonely. He wants to be with his friends—the shields between him and his self, perhaps. But they're all gone now, scattered by some force that Jim feels, obscurely, that he initiated; his bad faith started it all. . . . But no, no. That's magical thinking. In reality he has had hardly any effect on anything. Or so it seems. But which is right? Did he really do it, did he really somehow scatter everyone away?

He doesn't know.

Okay. Enough agonizing over the past. Here he is. He's free, he and he only chooses what he will do What will he do?

He will pace. And mourn Tashi's departure. And rail bitterly against . . . himself. He can't escape the magical thinking, he knows that it has somehow been all his fault. He's lonely. Will he be able to adapt to this kind of solitude, does he have the self-reliance necessary?

But think of Tom's solitude. My God! Uncle Tom!

He should go see Tom.

He runs out to the car and tracks down to Seizure World.

On the way he feels foolish, he is sure it's obvious to everyone else on the freeway that he is doing something utterly bizarre in order to prove to himself that he is changing his life, when in reality it's all the same as before. But what else can he do? How else do it?

Then as he drives through the gates he becomes worried; Tom was awfully sick when he last dropped by, anything can happen when you're that old, and sick like he was. He runs from the parking lot to the front desk.

But Tom is still alive, and in fact he is doing much better, thanks. He's sitting up in his bed, looking out the window and reading a big book.

"How are you, boy?" He sounds much better, too.

"Fine, Tom. And you?"

"Much better, thanks. Healthier than in a long time."

"Good, good. Hey Tom, I went to the mountains!"

"Did you! The Sierras? Aren't they beautiful? Where'd you go?"

Jim tells him, and it turns out Tom has been in that region. They talk about it for half an hour.

"Tom," Jim says at last, "why didn't you tell me? Why didn't you tell me about it and make me go up there?"

"I did! Wait just a minute here! I told you all the time! But you thought it was stupid. Bucolic reactionary pastoral escapism, you called it. Mushrooms on the dead log of Nature, you said."

That was something Jim read once. "Damn my reading!"

Tom squints. "Actually, I'm reading a great book here. On early Orange County, the ranchero days. Like listen to this—when the rancheros wanted to get their cowhides from San Juan Capistrano to the Yankee trading ships off Dana Point, they took them to the top of Dana Point bluff, at low tide when the beach was really wide, and just tossed them over the side! Big cowhides thrown off a cliff like frisbees, flapping down through the air to land out there on the beach. Nice, eh?"

"Yes," Jim says. "It's a lovely image."

They talk a while longer about the book. Then a nurse comes by to shoo Jim away—visiting hours are over for a while.

"Jail's closed, boy. Come back when you can."

"I will, Tom. Soon."

Okay. That's one stop, one step. That's something that will become part of the new life. All his moaning about the death of community, when the materials for it lay all around him, available anytime he wanted to put the necessary work into it. . . . Ah, well.

Okay. What else? Restlessly Jim tracks home, starts pacing again. He tries calling Hana, gets no answer. And no machine. Damn it, she's got to be home sometime!

What to do. No question of sleep, it's early evening and again this isn't a night for it, he can tell. His head is too full. As a seasoned insomniac he knows there isn't a chance.

He stops by his desk. Everything neatly in place, the torn-up and taped-together OC pages on top at one corner. He picks them up, starts to read through them.

As he does, the actual words on the page disappear, and he sees not OC's past but the last few weeks. His own past. Each painful step on the path that got him here. Then he reads again; and the anguish of his own experience infuses the sentences, fills the county's short and depressing history of exploitation and loss. Dreams have ended before, here.

Okay. He's a poet, a writer. Therefore he writes. Therefore he sits down, takes up a sheet of paper, a ballpoint pen.

There's a moment in OC's past that he's avoided writing about, he never noticed it before and at first he thinks it's just a coincidence; but then, as he considers it, it seems to him that it has been more than that. It is, in fact, the central moment, the hinge point in the story when it changed for good. He's been afraid to write it down.

He chews the end of the pen to white plastic shards. Puts it to paper and writes. Time passes.

...82

This is the chapter I have not been able to write.

Through the 1950s and 1960s the groves were torn down at the rate of several acres every day. The orchard keepers and their trees had fought off a variety of blights in previous years—the cottony cushion scale, the black scale, the red scale, the "quick decline"—but they had never faced this sort of blight before, and the decline this time was quicker than ever. In these years they harvested not the fruit, but the trees.

This is how they did it.

Gangs of men came in with trucks and equipment. First they cut the trees down with chain saws. This was the simple part, the work of a minute. Thirty seconds, actually: one quick downward bite, the chain saw pulled out one quick upward bit.

The trees fall.

Chains and ropes are tossed over the fallen branches, and electric reels haul them over to big dumpsters. Men with smaller chain saws cut the fallen trees into parts, and the parts are fed into an automatic shredder that hums constantly, whines and shrieks when branches are fed into it. Wood chips are all that come out.

Leaves and broken oranges are scattered over the torn ground. There is a tangy, dusty citrus smell in the air; the dust that is part of the bark of these trees has been scattered to the sky.

The stumps are harder. A backhoelike tractor is brought to the stump. The ground around the stump is spaded, churned up, softened. Chains are secured around the trunk, right at ground level, or even beneath it, around the biggest root exposed. Then the tractor backs off, jerks. Gears grind, the diesel engine grunts and hums, black fumes shoot out the exhaust pipe at the sky. In jerks the stump heaves out of the ground. The root systems are not very big, nor do they extend very deeply. Still, when the whole thing is hauled away to the waiting dumpsters, there is a considerable crater left behind.

The eucalyptus trees are harder. Bringing the trees down is still relatively easy; several strokes of a giant chain saw, with ropes tied around the tree to bring it down in the desired direction. But then the trunk has to be sawed into big sections, like loggers' work, and the immense cylinders are lifted by bulldozers and small cranes onto the backs of waiting trucks. And the stumps are more stubborn; roots have to be cut away, some digging done, before the tractors can succeed in yanking them up. The eucalyptus have been planted so close together that the roots have intertwined, and it's safest to bring down only every third tree, then start on the ones left. The pungent dusty smell of the eucalyptus tends to overpower the citrus scent of the orange trees. The sap gums up the chain saws. It's hard work.

Across the grove, where the trees are already gone, and the craters bulldozed away, surveyors have set out stakes with red strips of plastic tied in bows around their tops. These guide the men at the cement mixers, the big trucks whose contents grumble as their barrels spin. They will be pouring foundations for the new tract houses before the last trees are pulled out.

Now it's the end of a short November day. Early 1960s. The sun is low, and the shadows of the remaining eucalyptus in the west wall—one in every three—fall across the remains of the grove. There are nothing but craters left, today; craters, and stacks of wood by the dumpsters. The backhoes and tractors and bulldozers are all in a yellow row, still as dinosaurs. Cars pass by. The men whose work is done for the day have congregated by the canteen truck, open on one side, displaying evening snacks of burritos and triangular sandwiches in clear plastic boxes. Some of the men have gotten bottles of beer out of their pickups, and the click pop hiss of bottles opening mingles with their quiet talk. Cars pass by. The distant hum of the Newport Freeway washes over them with the wind. Eucalyptus leaves fall from the trees still standing.

Out in the craters, far from the men at the canteen truck, some children are playing. Young boys, using the craters as fox-holes to play some simple war game. The craters are new, they're exciting, they show what orange roots look like, something the boys have always been curious about. Cars pass by. The shadows lengthen. One of the boys wanders off alone. Tire tracks in the torn dirt lead his gaze to one of the cement mixers, still emitting its slushy grumble. He sits down to look at it, openmouthed. Cars pass by. The other boys tire of their game and go home to dinner, each to his own house. The men around the trucks finish their beers and their stories, and they get into their pickup trucks—thunkl thunkl—and drive off. A couple of supervisors walk around the dirt lot, planning the next day's work. They stop by a stack of wood next to the shredder. It's quiet, you can hear the freeway in the distance. A single boy sits on a crater's edge, staring off at the distance. Cars pass by. Eucalyptus leaves spinnerdrift to the ground. The sun disappears. The day is done, and shadows are falling across our empty field.

... 83

When Jim is done, he types a fair copy into the computer. Prints it up. He sticks it in with the taped-up pages. No, those poor tape-up jobs won't do. He types them all into the computer again, filling them out, revising them. Then he prints up new copies of each. There we go. Orange County. He never was much of a one for titles. Call it *Torn Maps*, why not.

Much of the night has passed. Jim gets up stiffly, hobbles out to look around. Four A.M.; the freeway at its quietest. After a bit he goes back inside, and holds the newly printed pages in his hands. It's not a big book, nor a great one; but it's his. His, and the land's. And the people who lived here through all the years; it's theirs too, in a way. They all did their best to make a home of the place—those of them who weren't actively doing their best to parcel and sell it off, anyway. And even them . . . Jim laughs. Clearly he'll never be able to resolve his ambivalence regarding his hometown, and the generations who made it. Impossible to separate out the good from the bad, the heroic from the tawdry.

Okay, what next? Light-headed, Jim wanders his home again, the pages clutched in his hand. What should he do? He isn't sure. It's awful, having one's habits shattered, having to make one's life up from scratch; you have to invent it all moment to moment, and it's hard!

He eats some potato chips, cleans up the kitchen. He sits down at his little Formica kitchen table; and briefly, head down on his pages, he naps.

While he's asleep, crouched uncomfortably over the table, he dreams. There's an elevated freeway on the cliff by the edge of the sea, and in the cars tracking slowly along are all his friends and family. They have a map of Orange County, and they're tearing it into pieces. His father, Hana, Tom, Tashi, Abe, his mom, Sandy, and Angela . . . Jim, down on the beach, cries out at them to stop tearing the map; no one hears him. And the pieces of the map are jigsaw puzzle pieces, big as family-sized pizzas, pale pastel in color, and all his family take these pieces and spin them out into the air like frisbees, till they stall and tumble down onto a beach as wide as the world. And Jim runs to gather them up, hard work in the loose sand, which sparkles with gems; and then he's on the beach, trying to put together this big puzzle before the tide comes in—

He starts awake.

He gets up; he has a plan. He'll track up the Santiago Freeway to Modjeska Canyon and Hana's house, with his pages, and he'll sit down under the eucalyptus trees on the lawn outside her white garage, and he'll wait there till she comes out or comes home. And then he'll make her read the pages, make her see . . . whatever she'll see. And from there . . . well, whatever. That's as far as he can plan. That's his plan.

He goes to the bathroom, quick brushes his teeth and hair, pees, goes out to the car. It's still dark! Four-thirty A.M., oh well. No time like the present. And he gets in his car and tracks onto the freeway, in his haste punching the wrong program and getting on in the wrong direction. It takes a while to get turned around. The freeway is almost empty: tracks gleaming under the moon, the lightshow at its absolute minimum, a coolness to the humming air. He gets off the freeway onto Chapman Avenue, down the empty street under flashing yellow stoplights, past the dark parking lots and shopping centers and the dark Fluffy Donuts place that stands over the ruins of El Modena Elementary School, past the Quaker church and up into the dark hills. Then onto the Santiago Freeway, under the blue mercury vapor lights, the blue-white concrete flowing under him, the dark hillsides spangled with street-lights like stars, a smell of sage in the air rushing by the window. And he comes to Hana's exit and takes the offramp, down in a big concrete curve, down and down to the embrace of the hills, the touch of the earth. Any minute he'll be there.

ACKNOWLEDGMENTS

Some of my friends and family gave me a lot of help with various aspects of this book. I'd like to thank Terry Baier, Daryl Bonin, Brian Carlisle, Donald and Nancy Crosby, Patrick Delahunt, Robert Franko, Charles R. Ill, Beth Meacham, Lisa Nowell, Linda Rogas, and Victor Salerno.

A special thanks to Steve Bixler and Larry Huhn; and to my parents.

pacific edge

for my parents

... 1

Despair could never touch a morning like this.

The air was cool, and smelled of sage. It had the clarity that comes to southern California only after a Santa Ana wind has blown all haze and history out to sea—air like telescopic glass, so that the snowtopped San Gabriels seemed near enough to touch, though they were forty miles away. The flanks of the blue foothills revealed the etching of every ravine, and beneath the foothills, stretching to the sea, the broad coastal plain seemed nothing but treetops: groves of orange, avocado, lemon, olive; windbreaks of eucalyptus and palm; ornamentals of a thousand different varieties, both natural and genetically engineered. It was as if the whole plain were a garden run riot, with the dawn sun flushing the landscape every shade of green.

Overlooking all this was a man, walking down a hillside trail, stopping occasionally to take in the view. He had a loose gangly walk, and often skipped from one step to the next, as if playing a game. He was thirty-two but he looked like a boy, let loose in the hills with an eternal day before him.

He wore khaki work pants, a tank-top shirt, and filthy tennis shoes. His hands were large, scabbed and scarred; his arms were long. From time to time he interrupted his ramble to grasp an invisible baseball bat and swing it before him in a sharp half swing, crying, "Boom!" Doves still involved in their dawn courtship scattered before these homers, and the man laughed and skipped down the trail. His neck was red, his skin freckled, his eyes sleepy, his hair straw-colored and poking out everywhere. He had a long face with high pronounced cheekbones, and pale blue eyes. Trying to walk and look at Catalina at the same time, he tripped and had to make a quick downhill run to recover his balance. "Whoah!" he said. "Man! What a day!"

* * *

He dropped down the hillside into El Modena. His friends trickled out of the hills in ones and twos, on foot or bicycle, to converge at a torn-up intersection. They took up pick or shovel, jumped into the rough holes and went to work. Dirt flew into hoppers, picks hit stones with a *clink clink clink*, voices chattered with the week's gossip.

They were tearing out the street. It had been a large intersection: four-lane asphalt streets, white concrete curbs, big asphalt parking lots and gas stations on the corners, shopping centers behind. Now the buildings were gone and most of the asphalt too, hauled away to refineries in Long Beach; and they dug deeper.

His friends greeted him.

"Hey, Kevin, look what I found."

"Hi, Doris. Looks like a traffic light box."

"We already found one of those."

Kevin squatted by the box, checked it out. "Now we've got two. They probably left it down here when they installed a new one."

"What a waste."

From another crater Gabriela groaned. "No! No! Telephone lines, power cables, gas mains, PVC tubing, the traffic light network—and now another gas station tank!"

"Look, here's a buncha crushed beer cans," Hank said. "At least they did some things right."

As they dug they teased Kevin about that night's town council meeting, Kevin's first as a council member. "I still don't know how you let yourself get talked into it," Gabriela said. She worked construction with Kevin and Hank; young, tough and wild, she had a mouth, and often gave Kevin a hard time.

"They told me it would be fun."

Everyone laughed.

"They told him it would be fun! Here's a man who's been to hundreds of council meetings, but when Jean Aureliano tells him they're fun, Kevin Claiborne says, 'Oh, yeah, I guess they are!'"

"Well, maybe they will be."

They laughed again. Kevin just kept wielding his pick, grinning an embarrassed grin.

"They won't be," Doris said. She was the other Green on the council. Having served two terms she would be something like Kevin's advisor, a task she didn't appear to relish. They were housemates, and old friends, so she knew what she was getting into. She said to Gabriela, "Jean chose Kevin because she wanted somebody popular."

"That doesn't explain Kevin agreeing to it!"

Hank said, "The tree growing fastest is the one they cut first."

Gabriela laughed. "Try making sense, Hank, okay?"

The air warmed as the morning passed. They ran into a third traffic light box, and Doris scowled. "People were so wasteful."

Hank said, "Every culture is as wasteful as it can afford to be."

"Nah. It's just lousy values."

"What about the Scots?" Kevin asked. "People say they were really thrifty."

"But they were poor," Hank said. "They couldn't afford not to be thrifty. It proves my point."

Doris threw dirt into a hopper. "Thrift is a value independent of circumstances."

"You can see why they might leave stuff down here," Kevin said, tapping at the traffic boxes. "It's a bitch to tear up these streets, and with all the cars."

Doris shook her short black hair. "You're getting it backwards, Kev, just like Hank. It's the values you have that drive your actions, and not the reverse. If they had cared enough they would have cleared all this shit out of here and used it, just like us."

"I guess."

"It's like pedaling a bike. Values are the downstroke, actions are the upstroke. And it's the downstroke that moves things along."

"Well," Kevin said, wiping sweat from his brow and thinking about it. "If you've got toeclips on, you can get quite a bit of power on your upstroke. At least I do."

Gabriela glanced quickly at Hank. "Power on your upstroke, Kev? Really?"

"Yeah, you pull up on the toeclips. Don't you get some thrust that way?"

"Shit yeah, Kev, I get a lot of power on my upstroke."

"About how much would you say you get?" Hank asked.

Kevin said, "Well, when I'm clipped in tight I think I must get twenty percent or so."

Gabriela broke into wild cackles. "Ah, ha ha HA! This, ha!—this is the mind about to join the town council! I can't wait! I can't wait to see him get into some heavy debate with Alfredo! Fucking *toeclips*—he'll be talking TOECLIPS!"

"Well," Kevin said stubbornly, "don't you get power on your upstroke?"

"But twenty percent?" Hank asked, interested now. "Is that all the time, or just when you're resting your quads?"

Doris and Gabriela groaned. The two men fell into a technical discussion of the issue.

Gabriela said, "Kevin gets into it with Alfredo, he'll say toeclips! He'll say, 'Watch out, Fredo, or I'll poison your blood!'"

Doris chuckled, and from the depths of his discourse Kevin frowned.

Gabriela was referring to an incident from Kevin's grade school days, when he had been assigned with some others to debate the proposition, "The pen is mightier than the sword." Kevin had had to start the debate by arguing in favor of the proposition, and he had stood at the head of the class, blushing hot red, twisting his hands, rocking back and forth, biting his lips, blowing out every circuit—until finally he said, blinking doubtfully, "Well—if you had just the pen—and if you stuck someone—they might get blood poisoning from the ink!"

Heads to the desks, minutes of helpless howling, Mr. Freeman wiping the tears from his eyes—people falling out of their chairs! No one had ever forgotten it. In fact it sometimes seemed to Kevin that everyone he had ever known had been in that classroom that day, even people like Hank, who was ten years older than him, or Gabriela, who was ten years younger. Everybody! But it was just a story people told.

They dug deeper, ran into rounded sandstone boulders. Over the eons Santiago Creek had wandered over the alluvial slopes tailing out of the Santa Ana Mountains, and it seemed all of El Modena had been the streambed at one time or another, because they found these stones everywhere. The pace was casual; this was town work, and so was best regarded as a party, to avoid irritation at the inefficiency. In El Modena they were required to do ten hours a week of town work, and so there were opportunities for vast amounts of irritation. They had gotten good at taking it less than seriously.

Kevin said, "Hey, where's Ramona?"

Doris looked up. "Didn't you hear?"

"No, what?"

"She and Alfredo broke up."

This got the attention of everyone in earshot. Some stopped and came over to get the story. "He's moved out of the house, on to Redhill with his partners."

"You're kidding!"

"No. I guess they've been fighting a lot more lately. That's what everyone at their house says. Anyway, Ramona went for a walk this morning."

"But the game!" Kevin said.

Doris jabbed her shovel into dirt an inch from his toe. "Kevin, did it ever occur to you that there are more important things than softball?"

"Well sure," he said, looking dubious at the proposition.

"She said she'd be back in time for the game."

"Good," Kevin said, then saw her expression and added quickly, "Too bad, though. Really too bad. Quite a surprise, too."

He thought about Ramona Sanchez. Single for the first time since ninth grade, in fact.

Doris saw the look on his face and turned her back on him. Her stocky brown legs were dusty below green nylon shorts; her sleeveless tan shirt was sweaty and smudged. Straight black hair swung from side to side as she attacked the ground. "Help me with this rock," she said to Kevin sharply, back still to him. Uncertainly he helped her move yet another water-rounded blob of sandstone.

"Well, if it isn't the new council at work," said an amused baritone voice above them.

Kevin and Doris looked up to see Alfredo Blair himself, seated on his mountain bike. The bright titanium frame flashed in the sun. Without thinking Kevin said, "Speak of the devil."

"Well," Doris said, with a quick warning glance at Kevin, "if it isn't the new mayor at leisure."

Alfredo grinned rakishly. He was a big handsome man, black-haired, moustached, clear clean lines to his jaw, nose, forehead. It was hard to imagine that just the day before he had moved out of a fifteen-year relationship.

"Good luck in your game today," he said, in a tone that implied they would need it, even though they were only playing the lowly Oranges. Alfredo's team the Vanguards and their team the Lobos were perpetual rivals; before today this had always been a source of jokes, as Ramona was on the Lobos. Now Kevin wasn't sure what it was. Alfredo went on: "I'm looking forward to when we get to play you."

"We've got work to do, Alfredo," Doris said.

"Don't let me stop you. Town work benefits everyone." He laughed, biked off. "See you at the council meeting!" he yelled over his shoulder.

They went back to work.

"I hope when we play them we beat the shit out of them," Kevin said.

"You always hope that."

"True."

Kevin and Alfredo had grown up on the same street, and had shared many classes in school, including the class assigned to debate the proposition. So they were old friends, and Kevin had had many opportunities to watch Alfredo operate in the world, and he knew well that his old friend was a very admirable person—smart, friendly, popular, energetic, successful. Good at everything; everything came easily to him and everyone liked him.

But it was too nice a day to let the thought of Alfredo wreck it.

Besides, Alfredo and Ramona had broken up. Obscurely cheered by the thought, Kevin hauled a boulder up into a hopper.

When they stopped for lunch they were about eye-level with the old surface of the intersection, which was now a chaotic field of craters, pocked by trenches and treadmarks, with wheelbarrows and dumpsters all over. Kevin squinted at the sight and grinned. "This is gonna make one hell of a softball diamond."

After lunch the spring softball season began. Players biked into Santiago Park from all directions, bats over handlebars, and they fell collectively into time-honored patterns; for softball is a ritual activity, and the approach to ritual is also ritualized. Feet were shoved into stiff cleats, gloves were slipped on, and they walked out onto the green grass field and played catch in groups of two and three, the big balls floating back and forth, making a dreamy knitwork of white lines in the air.

The umpires were running their chalk wheelbarrows up the foul lines when Ramona Sanchez coasted to the third base side and dumped her bike. Long legs, wide shoulders, Hispanic coloring, black hair. . . . The rest of the Lobos greeted her happily, relieved to see her, and she smiled and said, "Hi, guys," in almost her usual way; but everyone could see she wasn't herself.

Ramona was one of those people who always have a bright smile and a cheery tone of voice. Doris for one found it exasperating. "She's a biological optimist," Doris would grouse, "it isn't even up to her. It's something in her blood chemistry."

"Wait a second," Hank would object, "you're the one always talking about values—shouldn't optimism be the result of will? I mean, *blood chemistry?*"

And Doris would reply that optimism might indeed be an act of will, but that good looks, intelligence, and great athletic skill no doubt helped to make it a rather small one; and these qualities were all biological, even if they weren't blood chemistry.

Anyway, the sight of Ramona on this day was a disturbing thing: an unhappy optimist. Even Kevin, who started to play catch with her with the full intention of behaving normally, thus giving her a break from unwanted sympathy, was unnerved by how subdued she seemed. He felt foolish trying to pretend all was well, and since she ignored his pretense he just caught and threw, warming her up.

Judging by the hard flat trajectory of her throws, she was considerably warm already. Ramona Sanchez had a good arm; in fact, she was a gun. Once Kevin had seen one of her rare wild throws knock a spoke cleanly out of the wheel of a parked bike, without moving the rest of the bike an inch. She regularly broke the leather ties in first basemen's gloves, and once or twice had broken fingers as well. Kevin had to pay close attention to avoid a similar fate, because the ball jumped across the space between them almost instantaneously. A real gun. And not in a good mood.

So they threw in silence, except for the leather smack of the glove. There was a certain companionableness about it, Kevin felt—a sort of solidarity expressed. Or so he hoped, since he couldn't think of anything to say. Then the umpires called for the start of the game, and he walked over and stood beside her as she sat and jammed on her cleats. She did it with such violence that it seemed artificial not to notice, so Kevin said, hesitantly, "I heard about you and Alfredo."

"Uh huh," she said, not impressed.

"I'm sorry."

Briefly she twisted her mouth down. That's how unhappy I would be if I let myself go, the look said. Then the stoic look returned and she shrugged, stood, bent over to stretch her legs. The backs of her thighs banded, muscles clearly visible under smooth brown skin.

They walked back to the bench, where their teammates were swinging bats. The team captains gave line-up cards to the scorer. All activity began to spiral down toward the ritual; more and more that was not part of it fell away and disappeared, until when one team took the field—first baseman rolling grounders to the infielders, pitcher taking practice tosses, outfielders throwing fly balls around—everything extraneous to the ritual was gone. Kevin, the first batter of the new year, walked up to the plate, adrenaline spiking through him. Players called out something encouraging to him or the pitcher, and the umpire cried "Play ball!"

And the batter stepped into the box, and the first pitch of the season rose into the air, and the shouts ("Get a hit!" "Start it off right!" "Hey batter, hey batter!") grew distant, faded until no one heard them, not even those who spoke. Time dilated and the big fat shiny new white ball hung up there at the top of its arc, became the center of all their worlds, the focus—until it crossed the plate, the batter swung, and the game began.

It was a great game as far as Kevin was concerned: the Lobos kept the lead throughout, but not by much. And Kevin was four for four, which would always be enough to make him happy.

In the field he settled down at third base to sharp attention on every pitch. Third base like a razor's edge, third base like a mongoose among snakes: this was how the announcer in his head had always put it, ever since childhood. Occasionally there was a sudden chance to act, but mostly it was settling down, paying attention, the same phrases said over and over. Playing as a kind of praying.

So he was lulled a bit, deep in the rhythms of what was essentially a very ordinary game, when suddenly things picked up. The Oranges scored four runs in their final at-bat, and now with two outs Santos Perez was coming to bat. Santos was a strong pull hitter, and as Donna prepared to pitch, Kevin settled into his cleat-scored position off third base, extra alert.

A short pitch dropped and Santos smashed a hot grounder to Kevin's left. Kevin dove instantly but the ball bounced past his glove, missing it by an inch. He hit the dirt cursing, and as he slid forward on chest and elbows he looked back, just in time to see the sprinting Ramona lunge out and snag the ball.

It was a tremendous backhand catch, but she had almost over-balanced to make it, and now she was running directly away from first base, very deep in the hole. There was no time to stop and set, and so she leaped in the air, spun to give the sidearm throw some momentum, and let it fly with a vicious flick of the wrist. The ball looped across the diamond and Jody caught it neatly on one hop at first base, just ahead of the racing Santos. Third out. Game over.

"Yeah!" Kevin cried, pushing up to his knees. "Wow!"

Everyone was cheering. Kevin looked back at Ramona. She had tumbled to the ground after the throw, and now she was sitting on the outfield grass, long, graceful, splay-legged, grinning, black hair in her eyes. And Kevin fell in love.

Of course that isn't *exactly* how it happened. That isn't the whole story. Kevin was a straightforward kind of guy, and crazy about softball, but still, he was not the kind of person who would fall in love on the strength of a good play at shortstop. No, this was something else, something that had been developing for years and years.

He had known Ramona Sanchez since she first arrived in El Modena, when they were both in third grade. They had been in the same classes in grade school—including, yes, the class with the famous debate—and had shared a lot of classes in junior high. And Kevin had always liked her. One day in sixth grade she had told him she was Roman Catholic, and he had told her that there were Greek Catholics too. She had denied it disdainfully, and so they had gone to look it up in the encyclopedia. They had failed to find a listing for "Greek

Catholic," which Kevin could not understand, as his grandfather Tom had certainly mentioned such a church. But having been proved right Ramona became sympathetic, and even scanned the index and found a listing for "Greek Orthodox Church," which seemed to explain things. After that they sat before the screen and read the entry, and scanned through other articles, talking about Greece, the travels they had made (Ramona had been to Mexico, Kevin had been to Death Valley), the possibilities of buying a Greek island and living on it, and so on.

After that Kevin had had a crush on Ramona, one that he never told anyone about—certainly not her. He was a shy boy, that's all there was to it. But the feeling persisted, and in junior high when it became the thing to have romantic friends, life was a dizzying polymorphous swirl of crushes and relationships, and everyone was absorbed in it. So over the course of junior high's three years, shy Kevin gradually and with difficulty worked himself up to the point of asking Ramona out to a school dance—to Homecoming, in fact, the big dance of the year. When he asked her, stammering with fright, she made him feel like she thought it was an excellent idea; but said she had already accepted an invitation, from Alfredo Blair.

The rest was history. Ramona and Alfredo had been a couple, aside from the brief breaks that stormy high school romances often have, from that Homecoming to the present day.

In later years, however, as El Modena High School's biology teacher, Ramona had developed the habit of taking her classes out to Kevin's construction sites, to learn some applied ecology—also carpentry, and a bit of architecture—all while helping him out a little. Kevin liked that, even though the students were only marginally more help than hassle. It was a friendly thing, something he and Ramona did to spend time together.

Still, she and Alfredo were partners. They never married, but always lived together. So Kevin had gotten used to thinking of Ramona as a friend only. A good friend, sort of like his sister Jill—only not like a sister, because there had always been an extra attraction. A shared attraction, it seemed. It wasn't all that important, but it gave their friendship a kind of thrill, a nice fullness—a kind of latent potential, perhaps, destined never to be fulfilled. Which made it romantic.

A lifelong thing, then. And before the softball game, while warming Ramona up, he had been conscious of seeing her in a way that he hadn't for years—seeing the perfect proportions of her back and legs, shoulders and bottom—the dramatic Hispanic coloring, the fine features that made her one of the town beauties—the grace of her strong overhand throw—her careless unselfconsciousness. Deep inside him memories had stirred, memories of feelings he would have said were long forgotten, for he never thought of his past much, and if asked would have assumed it had all slipped away. And yet there it was, stirring inside him, ready at a moment's notice to leap back out and take over his life.

So when he turned to look at her after her spectacular play, and saw her sprawled on the grass, long brown legs akimbo so that he was looking at the green crotch of her gym shorts, at a white strip of their underlining on the inside of one thigh—her weight on one straightened arm, white T-shirt molded against her almost flat chest—brushing hair out of black eyes, smiling for the first time that afternoon—it was as if all Kevin's life had been a wind-up, and this the throw. As if he had stepped into a dream in which all emotions were intensified. *Whoosh!* went the air out of his lungs. His heart thudded, the skin of his face flushed and tingled with the impact of it, with the *recognition* of it, and yes—it was love. No doubt about it.

To feel was to act for Kevin, and so as soon as they were done packing up equipment and changing shoes, he looked for Ramona. She had become unusually silent again, after the rush of congratulations for her game ender, and now she was biking off by herself. Kevin caught up with her on his little mountain bike, then matched her speed. "Are you going to the council meeting tonight?"

"I don't think so."

Not going to see Alfredo sworn in as mayor. It was definitely true, then. "Wow," he said.

"Well, you know—I just don't feel like being there and having lots of people assume we're still together, for photos maybe even. It would be awkward as hell."

"I can see that. So . . . What're you gonna do this afternoon?"

She hesitated. "I was thinking of going flying, actually. Work some of this out of my system."

"Ah."

She looked over at him. "Want to join me?"

Kevin's heart tocked at the back of his throat. His inclination was to say "Sure!" and he always followed his inclinations; thus it was a measure of his interest that he managed to say, "If you really feel like company? I know that sometimes I just like to get off by myself. . . ."

"Ah, well. I wouldn't mind the company. Might help."

"Usually does," Kevin said automatically, not paying attention to what he was saying, or how it failed to match with what he had just said before. He could feel his heart. He grinned. "Hey, that was a hell of a play you made there."

At a glider port on Fairhaven they untied the Sanchezes' two-person flyer, a Northrop Condor, and after hooking it to the take-off sling they strapped themselves in and clipped their feet into the pedals. Ramona freed the craft and with a jerk they were off, pedaling like mad. Ramona pulled back on the flaps, the sling uncoupled, they shot up like a pebble from a slingshot; then caught the breeze and rushed higher, like a kite pulled into the wind by an enthusiastic runner.

"Yow!" Kevin cried, and Ramona said, "Pedal harder!" and they both pumped away, leaning back and pushing the little plane up with every stroke. The huge prop whirred before them, but two-seaters were not quite as efficient as one-seaters; the extra muscle did not quite make up for the extra weight, and they had to grind at the tandem pedals as if racing to get the craft up to two hundred feet, where the afternoon sea breeze lifted them dizzily. Even a two-seater weighed less than thirty pounds, and gusts of the wind could toss them like a shuttlecock.

Ramona turned them into this breeze with a gull's swoop. The feel of it, the feel of flying! They relaxed the pace, settled into a long distance rhythm, swooped around the sky over Orange County. Hard work; it was one of the weird glories of their time, that the highest technologies were producing artifacts that demanded more intense physical labor than ever before—as in the case of human-powered flight, which required extreme effort from even the best endurance athletes. But once possible, who could resist it?

Not Ramona Sanchez; she pedaled along, smiling with contentment. She flew a lot. Often while working on roofs, absorbed in the labor, imagining the shape of the finished home and the lives it would contain, Kevin would hear a voice from above, and looking up he would see her in her little Hughes Dragonfly, making a cyclist's *whirr* and waving down like a sweaty air spirit. Now she said, "Let's go to Newport and take a look at the waves."

And so they soared and dipped in the onshore wind, like their condor namesake. From time to time Kevin glanced at Ramona's legs, working in tandem next to his. Her thighs were longer than his, her quads bigger and better defined: two hard muscles atop each leg, barely coming together in time to fit under the kneecap. They made her thighs look squared-off on top, an effect nicely balanced by long rounded curves beneath. And calf muscles out of an anatomical chart. The texture of her skin was very smooth, barely dusted by fine silky hair. . . .

Kevin shook his head, surprised by the dreamlike intensity of his vision, by how well he could *see* her. He glanced down at the Newport Freeway, crowded as usual. From above, the bike lanes were a motley collection of helmets, backs, and pumping legs, over spidery lines of metal and rubber. The cars' tracks gleamed like bands of silver embedded in the concrete, and cars hummed along them, blue roof red roof blue roof.

As they cut curves in the air Kevin saw buildings he had worked on at one time or another: a house reflecting sunlight from canopies of cloudgel and thermocrete; a garage renovated to a cottage; warehouses, offices, a bell tower, a pond house. . . . His work, tucked here and there in the trees. It was fun to see it, to point it out, to remember the challenge of the task met and dealt with, for better or worse.

Ramona laughed. "It must be nice to see your whole resumé like this."

"Yeah," he said, suddenly embarrassed. He had been rattling on.

She was looking at him.

Tall eucalyptus windbreaks cut the land into giant rectangles, as if the basin were a quilt of homes, orchards, green and yellow crops. Kevin's lungs filled with wind, he was buoyant at the sight of so much land, and all of it so familiar to him. The onshore breeze grew stronger over Costa Mesa, and they lofted toward the Irvine Hills. The big interchange of the San Diego and Newport freeways looked like a concrete pretzel. Beyond it there was a lot of water, reflecting the sunlight like scraps of mirror thrown on the land: streams, fish ponds, reservoirs, the marsh of Upper Newport Bay. It was low tide, and a lot of gray tidal flats were revealed, surrounded by reeds and clumps of trees. They could smell the salt stink of them on the wind, even up where they were. Thousands of ducks and geese bobbed on the water, making a beautiful speckled pattern.

"Migration again," Ramona said pensively. "Time for change."

"Headed north."

"The clouds are coming in faster than I thought they would." She pointed toward Newport Beach. The afternoon onshore wind was bringing in low ocean clouds, as often happened in spring. The torrey pines loved it, but it was no fun to fly in.

"Well, what with the council meeting it won't do me any harm to get back a little early," Kevin said.

Ramona shifted the controls and they made a wide turn over Irvine. The mirrored glass boxes in the industrial parks glinted in the sun like children's blocks, green and blue and copper. Kevin glanced at Ramona and saw she was blinking rapidly. Crying? Ah—he'd mentioned the council meeting. Damn! And they'd been having such fun! He was an idiot. Impulsively he touched the back of her hand, where it rested on the control stick. "Sorry," he said. "I forgot."

"Oh," she said, voice unsteady. "I know."

"So . . ." Kevin wanted to ask what had happened.

She grimaced at him, intending it to be a comic expression. "It's been pretty upsetting."

"I can imagine. You were together a long time."

"Fifteen years!" she said. "Nearly half my life!" She struck the stick angrily, and the Condor dipped left. Kevin winced.

"Maybe it was too long," she said. "I mean too long with nothing happening. And neither of us had any other partners before we got together."

Kevin almost brought up their talk over the encyclopedia in sixth grade, but decided not to. Perhaps as an example of a previous relationship it was not particularly robust.

"High school sweethearts," Ramona exclaimed. "It is a bad idea, just like everyone says. You have a lot of history together, sure, but you don't really know if the other person is the best partner you could have. And then one of you gets interested in finding out!" She slammed the frame above the controls, making Kevin and the plane jump.

"Uh huh," he said. She was angry about it, that was clear. And it was great that she was letting it out like this, telling Kevin what she felt. If only she wouldn't emphasize her points with those hard blows to the frame, so close to the controls.

Also there was hardly any resistance in his pedals. They were turning the same chain together, and she was pumping away furiously, more than enough for both of them. And they were shuddering through little sideslips every time she pounded a point home. Kevin swallowed, determined not to interrupt her thoughts with mundane worries.

"I mean you can't help but wonder!" she was saying, waving a hand. "I know Alfredo did. I'm not all that interesting, I suppose—"

"What?"

"Well, there's only a few things I really care about. And Alfredo is interested in *everything*." Bang. Right above the flaps. "There's so many things he's into that you can't even *believe it*." Bang! "And he was always so God-damned *busy!*" BANG BANG BANG!

"You have to be, to be a hundred," Kevin said, watching her hands and cringing. With the slips they were losing altitude, he noted. Even pumping as hard as she was.

"Yeah, sure you do. And he could be two hundreds! He could be a millionaire if they still had them, he really could! He's got just what it takes."

"Must take a lot of time, huh?"

"It takes your whole life!" WHAM.

Kevin pedaled hard, but he was just spinning around, as if his pedals weren't connected to a chain at all.

"At least that's what it felt like. And there we were not going anywhere, high school sweethearts at thirty-two. I don't care that much about marriage myself, but my parents and grandparents are Catholic, and so are Alfredo's, and you know how that is. Besides I was getting ready to have a family, you know every day I'm helping out with the kids in our house, and I thought why shouldn't one of these be ours?" Bang! "But Alfredo was not into it, oh no. I don't have time! he'd say. I'm not ready yet! And by the time he's ready, it'll be too late for me!" BANG! BANG! BANG!

"Uck," Kevin said, looking down at the treetops apprehensively. "It, uh, it wouldn't take that much time, would it? Not in your house."

"You'd be surprised. A lot of people are there to help, but still, you always end up with them. And Alfredo . . . well, we talked about it for years. But nothing ever changed, damn it! So I got pretty bitchy, I guess, and Alfredo spent more and more time away, you know. . . ." She began to blink rapidly, voice wobbling.

"Feedback loop," Kevin said, trying to stick to analysis. A relationship had feedback loops, like any other ecology—that's what Hank used to say. A movement in one direction or another could quickly spiral out of control. Kind of like a tailspin, now that Kevin thought about it. Harder than hell to re-stabilize after you fell into one of those. In fact people were killed all the time in crashes caused by them. Uncontrolled feedback loop. He tried to remember the few flying lessons he had taken. Mostly he was a grinder when he went flying. . . .

But it could work both ways, he thought as some resistance returned to his pedals. Upward spiral, a great flourishing of the spirit, everything feeding into it—

"A very bad feedback loop," Ramona said.

They pedaled on. Kevin pumped hard, kept his eye on the controls, on Ramona's vehement right fist. He found her story rather amazing in some respects. He didn't understand Alfredo. Imagine the chance to make love with this beautiful animal pumping away beside him, to watch her get fat with a child that was the combination of him and her. . . . He breathed erratically at the thought, suddenly aware of his own body, of his balls between his legs—

He banished the thought, looked down at Tustin. Close. "So," he said, thinking to go right at it. "You broke up."

"Yeah. I don't know, I was getting really angry, but I probably would have stuck it out. I never really thought about anything else. But Alfredo, he got mad at me too, and . . . and—"

She started to cry.

"Ah, Ramona," Kevin said. Wrong tack to take, there. The direct approach not always the best way. He pedaled hard, suddenly doing the work for both of them. Enormous resistance, she didn't seem to be pedaling at all now. Not a good moment to bother her, though. He gritted his teeth and began to pedal like a fiend. Their flyer dropped anyway, sideslipping a bit. Incredible resistance in the pedals. They were dropping toward the hills behind Tustin. Directly at them, in fact. Ramona's eyes were squeezed shut; she was too upset to notice anything. Kevin found his concern distracted. Fatal accidents in these things were not all that infrequent.

"I'm sorry," he panted, pumping violently. "But . . . uh . . ." He took a hand from the frame to pat her shoulder, briefly. "Maybe . . . um . . ."

"It's okay," she said, hands over her face, rubbing hard. "Sometimes I can't help it."

"Uh huh."

She looked up. "Shit, we're about to run into Redhill!"

"Um, yeah."

"Why didn't you say something!"

"Well . . ."

"Oh Kevin!"

She laughed, sniffed, reached over to peck his cheek. Then she started to pedal again, and turned them toward home.

Kevin's heart filled—with relief, certainly—but also with affection for her. It was a shame she had been hurt like that. Although he had no desire to see her and Alfredo achieve a reconciliation. None at all. He said, very cautiously, "Maybe it's better it happened now, if it was going to."

She nodded briefly.

They circled back in toward El Modena's little gliderport. A Dragonfly ahead of them dropped onto it, heavy as a bee in cold weather. Skillfully Ramona guided them in. The afternoon sun lit the treetops. Their shadow preceded them toward the grassy runway. They dropped to an elevation where the whole plain seemed nothing but treetops—all the streets and freeways obscured, most of the buildings screened. "I fly at this altitude a lot," Ramona said, "just to make it look like this."

"Good idea." Her small smile, the trees everywhere—Kevin felt like the breeze was cutting right through his chest. To think that Ramona Sanchez was a free woman! And sitting here beside him.

He couldn't look at her. She brought them down to the runway in a graceful swoop, and they pedaled hard as they landed, as gently as sitting on a couch. Quick roll to a stop. They unstrapped, stood unsteadily, flexed tired legs, walked the plane off the strip toward its berth.

"Whew," she said. "*Estoy cansada.*"

Kevin nodded. "Great flight, Ramona."

"Yeah?" And as they stored the plane in the gloomy hangar, she hugged him briefly and said, "You're a good friend, Kevin."

Which might have been a warning, but Kevin wasn't listening. He still felt the touch. "I want to be," he said, feeling his voice quiver. He didn't think it could be heard. "I want to be."

El Modena's town council had its chambers in the area's oldest building, the church on Chapman Avenue. Over the years this structure had reflected the town's fortunes like a totem. It had been built by Quakers in 1886, soon after they settled the area and cultivated it in raisin grapes. One Friend donated a big bell, which they put in a tower at the church's front end; but the bell's weight was too much for the framing, and in the first strong Santa Ana wind the whole building fell down, *boom!* In similar fashion grape blight destroyed the economy, so that the new town was virtually abandoned. So much for El Modena One. But they changed crops, and then rebuilt the church, in the first of a long sequence of resurrections; through the barrio and its hidden poverty (church closed), through suburbia and its erasure of history (church a restaurant)— through to the re-emergence of El Modena as a town with a destiny of its own, when the council bought the restaurant and converted it into a cramped and weird-looking city hall, suitable for renting on any party occasion. Thus it finally became the center of the community that its Quaker builders had hoped it would be nearly two centuries before.

Now the white courtyard walls were wrapped with colored streamers, and Japanese paper lanterns were hung in the courtyard's three big willows. The McElroy Mariachi Men strolled about playing their loose sweet music, and a long table was crowded with bottles of Al Shroeder's atrocious champagne.

Uneasily Kevin pedaled into the parking lot. As a contractor he had appeared before the council countless times, but walking into the yard as one of the council members was different. How in the hell had he got himself into it? Well, he was a Green, always had been. Renovate that sleazy old condo of a world! And this year they had needed to fill one of their two spots on the council, but most of the prominent party members were busy, or had served before, or were otherwise prevented from running. Suddenly—and Kevin didn't really know who had decided this, or how—they were all encouraging him to do it. He was well-known and well-liked, they told him, and he had done a lot of visible work in the community. Very visible, he said—I build houses. But in the end he was won over. Green council members voted all important issues as an expression of the group, so there wasn't that much to it. If there were things he didn't know, he could learn on the job. It wasn't that hard. Everyone should take their turn. It would be fun! He could consult when he needed to.

But (it occurred to him) he would most need to consult when he was actually up there behind the table—just when consulting was impossible! He brushed his hair with his fingers. Just like him, he thought morosely, to think of that only now. It was too late; the job was his. Time to learn.

Doris biked in with an older woman. "Kevin, this is Nadezhda Katayev, a friend of mine from Moscow. She was my boss when I did the exchange at their superconductor institute, and she's over here for a visit. She'll be staying with us."

Kevin shook hands with her, and they joined the crowd. Most of the people there were friends or acquaintances. People kidded him as usual; no one was taking the evening very seriously. He was handed a cup of champagne, and a group from the Lobos gathered to toast the day's game, and the political stardom of their teammates. Several cups of champagne later he felt better about everything.

Then Alfredo Blair entered the courtyard, in a swirl of friends and supporters and family. The McElroys tooted the opening bars of "Hail to the Chief," and Alfredo laughed, clearly having a fine time. Still, it was odd to see him at such an event without Ramona there, serving as the other pole of a powerful eye magnet. A sudden vision, of long legs pumping beside his, of her broad expressive face tearful with rage, pounding the ultralite's frame—

The party got louder, charged along. "There's a madman here," Doris observed, pointing to a stranger. They watched him: a huge man in a floppy black coat, who sidled from group to group with a strange rhinocerine grace, disrupting conversation after conversation. He spoke, people looked confused or shocked; he departed and barged in elsewhere, hair flying, champagne splashing out of his cup.

The mystery was solved when Alfredo introduced him. "Hey Oscar, come over here! Folks, this is our new town attorney, Oscar Baldarramma. You may have seen him in the interview process."

Kevin had not. Oscar Baldarramma approached. He was huge—taller than Kevin, and fat, and his bulk rode everywhere on him: his face was moonlike, his neck a tree trunk, and an immense barrel chest was more than matched by a round middle. His curly black hair was even more unruly than Kevin's, and he wore a dark suit some fifty years out of date. He himself looked to be around forty.

Now he nodded, creasing a multiple chin, and pursed thick, mobile lips. "Nice to meet the other rookie on the team," he said in a scratchy flat voice, as if making fun of the phrase.

Kevin nodded, at a loss for words. He had heard that the new town attorney was a hotshot from the Midwest, with several years of work for Chicago under his belt. And they needed a good lawyer, because El Modena like most towns was always getting sued. The old council had taken most of six months to replace the previous attorney. But then to choose this guy!

Oscar stepped toward Kevin, lowered his head, waggled his eyebrows portentiously. A bad mime couldn't have been more blatant: *Secrecy. Confidential Matter.* "I'm told you renovate old houses?"

"That's my job."

Oscar glanced around in spy movie style. "I've been permitted to lease an elderly house near the gliderport, and I wondered if you might be interested in rebuilding it for me."

Oh. "Well, I'd need to take a look at it first. But assuming we agree on everything, I could put you on our waiting list. It's short right now."

"I would be willing to wait."

It seemed a sign of good judgment to Kevin. "I'll drop by and look the place over, and give you an estimate."

"Of course," the big man whispered.

A tray was passed around and they all took paper cups of champagne. Oscar stared thoughtfully into his. "A local champagne, I take it."

"Yeah," Kevin said, "Al Shroeder makes it. He's got a big vineyard up on Cowan Heights."

"Cowan Heights."

Doris said sharply, "Just because it isn't from Napa or Sonoma doesn't mean it's terrible! I think it's pretty good!"

Oscar gazed at her. "And what is your profession, may I ask?"

"I'm a materials scientist."

"Then I defer to your judgment."

Kevin couldn't help laughing at the expression on Doris's face. "Al's champagne sucks," he said. "But he's got a good zinfandel—a lot better than this."

Oscar went slightly cross-eyed. "I will seek it out. A recommendation like that demands action!"

Kevin snorted, and Nadezhda grinned. But Doris looked more annoyed than ever, and she was about to let Oscar know it, Kevin could tell, when Jean Aureliano called for silence.

Time for business. Alfredo, who had already spent six years on the council, was sworn in as the new mayor, and Kevin was sworn in as new council member. Kevin had forgotten about that part, and he stumbled on his way to the circle of officials. "What a start!" someone yelled. Hot-faced, he put his hand on a Bible, repeated something the judge said.

And yet in the midst of the blur, a sudden sensation—he was part of government now. Just like sixth grade civics class said he would be.

They moved into the council chambers, and Alfredo sat at the centerpoint of the council's curved table. As mayor he was no more than first among equals, a council member from the town's most numerous party. He ran their meetings, but had one vote like the others.

On one side of him sat Kevin, Doris, and Matt Chung. On the other side were Hiroko Washington, Susan Mayer, and Jerry Geiger. Oscar and the town planner, Mary Davenport, sat at a table of their own, off to the side. Kevin could clearly see the faces of all the other members, and as Alfredo urged the spectators to get seated, he looked them over.

Kevin and Doris were Greens, Alfredo and Matt were Feds. The New Federalists had just outpolled the Greens as the town's most numerous party, for the first time in some years; so they had a bit of a new edge. Hiroko, Susan, and Jerry represented smaller local parties, and functioned as a kind of fluctuating middle, with Hiroko and Susan true moderates, and Jerry a kind of loose cannon, his voting record a model of inexplicable inconsistency. This made him quite popular with some Modeños, who had joined the Geiger Party to keep him on the council.

Alfredo smacked his palm against the table. "If we don't start soon we'll be up all night! Welcome to new member Kevin Claiborne. Let's get him right into it with the first item on the agenda—ah—the second. Welcoming him was the first. Okay, number two. Re-examining order to cut down the trees bordering Peters Canyon Reservoir. An injunction against complying with the order was issued, pending review by this council. And here we are. The request for the injunction was made by El Modena's Wilderness Party, represented tonight by Hu-nang Chu. Are you here, Hu-nang?"

An intense-looking woman stepped up to the witness's lectern. She told them forcefully that the trees around the reservoir were old and sacred, and that cutting them down was a wanton act of destruction. When she began to repeat herself Alfredo skillfully cut her off. "Mary, the order originated from your people—you want to comment first on this?"

The town planner cleared her throat. "The trees around the reservoir are cottonwoods and willows, both extremely hydrophilic species. Naturally their water comes out of the reservoir, and the plain fact is we can't afford it—we're losing approximately an acre foot a month. Council resolution two oh two two dash three instructs us to do everything possible to decrease dependency on OC Water District and the Municipal Water District. Expanding the reservoir helped, and we tried to clear the area of hydrophilic trees at the time of expansion, but the cottonwoods are especially quick to grow back. Willows, by the way, are not even native to the area. We propose to cut the trees down and replace them with scrub oaks and adapted desert grasses. We also plan to leave one big willow standing, near the dam."

"Comments?" Alfredo said.

Everyone on the council who cared to comment approved Mary's plan.

Jerry remarked it was nice to see El Modena cut down some trees for once. Alfredo asked for comments from the audience, and a few people came to the lectern to make a point, usually repeating an earlier statement, sometimes in an inebriated version. Alfredo cut those off and put it to a vote. The order to cut down the trees passed seven to zero.

"Unanimity!" Alfredo said cheerily. "A very nice omen for the future of this council. Sorry, Hu-nang, but the trees have a drinking problem. On to item number three: proposal to tighten the noise ordinance around the high school stadium, ha! Who's the courageous soul advocating this?"

And so the meeting rolled on, filling Wednesday night as so many meetings had before. A building permit battle that became a protest against town ownership of the land, a zoning boundary dispute, an ordinance banning skateboards on bike trails, a proposal to alter the investment patterns of the town funds . . . all the business of running a small town, churned out point by point in a public gathering. The work of running the world, repeated thousands of times all over the globe; you could say that this was where the real power lay.

But it didn't feel like that, this particular night in El Modena—not to Kevin. For him it was just work, and dull work at that. He felt like a judge with no precedent to guide him. Even when he did know of precedents, he discovered that they were seldom a close enough fit to the current situation to really provide much help. An important legal principle, he thought fuzzily, trying to shake off the effects of Al's champagne: precedent is useless. Often he decided to vote with Doris and figure out the whys and wherefores later. Happily there was no mechanism for asking them to justify their votes.

At about the fifth of these votes, he felt a strong sinking sensation—he was going to have to spend every Wednesday night for the next two years, doing just this! Listening very closely to a lot of matters that didn't interest him in the slightest! How in the *hell* had he gotten himself into it?

Out in the audience people were getting up and leaving. Doris's old boss Nadezhda stayed, watching curiously. Oscar and the council secretary took a lot of notes. The meeting droned on.

Kevin's concentration began to waver. The long day, the champagne. . . . It was nice and warm, and the voices were all so calm, so soothing. . . .

Sleepy, yes.

Very, very sleepy.

How embarrassing!

And yet intensely drowsy. *Completely* drowsy. At his first council meeting. But it was so nice and warm. . . .

Don't fall asleep! Oh my God.

He pinched himself desperately. Could people see it when you clamped down on a yawn? He had never been sure.

What were they talking about? He wasn't even sure which item on the agenda they were discussing. With an immense effort he tried to focus.

"Item twenty-seven," Alfredo said, and for a second Kevin feared Alfredo was going to look over at him with his raffish grin. But he only read on. A bunch of water bureaucracy details, including nominations by the city planning office of two new members for the watermaster. Kevin had never heard of either of them. Still befuddled, he shook his head. Watermaster. When he was a child he had been fascinated by the name. It had been disappointing to learn that it was not a single person, with magical powers at his command, but merely a name for a board, another agency in an endless system of agencies. In some basins they merely recorded, in others they set groundwater policy. Kevin wasn't sure what they did in their district. But something, he felt, was strange. Perhaps that he had not recognized the names. And then, over at the side table, Oscar had tilted his head slightly. He was still watching them with a poker face, but there was something different in his demeanor. It was as if a statue of the sleeping Buddha had barely cracked open an eye, and glanced out curiously.

"Who are they?" Kevin croaked. "I mean, who are these nominees?"

Alfredo handled the interruption like Ramona fielding a bad hop, graceful and smooth as ever. He described the two candidates. One was an associate of Matt's. The other was a member of the OC Water District's engineering board.

Kevin listened uncertainly. "What's their political affiliation?"

Alfredo shrugged. "I think they're Feds, but what's the big deal? It's not a political appointment."

"You must be kidding," Kevin said. Water, not political? Drowsiness gone, he glanced through the rest of the text of Item 27. Lots of detail. Ignoring Alfredo's request to explain himself, he read on. Approval of water production statements from the wells in the district, approval of annual report on groundwater conditions (good). Letter of thanks to OCWD for Crawford Canyon land donated to the town last year. Letter of inquiry sent by town planning board to get further information on the Metropolitan Water District's offer to supply client towns with more water—

Doris elbowed him in the ribs.

"What do you mean?" Alfredo repeated for the third time.

"Water is always political," Kevin said absently. "Tell me, do you always put so many things into one item on the agenda?"

"Sure," Alfredo said. "We group by topic."

But Oscar's head shifted a sixteenth of an inch to the left, a sixteenth of an inch to the right. Just like a Buddha statue coming alive.

If only he knew more about all this. . . . He chose at random. "What's this offer from MWD?"

Alfredo looked over the agenda. "Ah. That was something a few sessions ago. MWD has gotten their Colorado River allotment upped by court decision, and they'd like to sell that water before the Columbia River pipe is finished. The planning office has determined that if we do take more from MWD, we can avoid the penalties from OC Water District for overdrafting groundwater, and in the end it'll save us money. And MWD is desperate—when the Columbia pipe's done it'll be a real buyer's market. So in essence it's a buyer's market already."

"But we don't pump that much out of the groundwater here."

"No, but the pump taxes for overdrafting are severe. With the water from MWD we could replenish any overdraft ourselves, and avoid the tax."

Kevin shook his head, confused. "But extra MWD water would mean we would never overdraft."

"Exactly. That's the point. Anyway, it's just an inquiry letter for more information."

Kevin thought it over. In his work he had had to get water permits often, so he knew a little about it. Like many of the towns in southern California, they bought the bulk of their water from Los Angeles's Metropolitan Water District, which pumped it in from the Colorado River. But much more than that he didn't know, and this. . . .

"What information do we have now? Do they have a minimum sale figure?"

Alfredo asked Mary to read them the original letter from MWD, and she located it and read. Fifty acre feet a year minimum. Kevin said, "That's a lot more water than we need. What do you plan to do with it?"

"Well," Alfredo replied, "if there's any excess at first, we can sell it to the District watermaster."

If, Kevin thought. At first. Something strange here. . . .

Doris leaned forward in her seat. "So now we're going into the water business? What happened to the resolution to reduce dependency on MWD?"

"It's just a letter asking for more information," Alfredo said, almost irritably. "Water is a complex issue, and getting more expensive all the time. It's our job to try and get it as cheaply as we can." He glanced at Matt Chung, then down at his notes.

Kevin's fist clenched. They were up to something. He didn't know what it was, but suddenly he was sure of it. They had been trying to slip this by him, in his first council meeting, when he was disoriented, tired, a little drunk.

Alfredo was saying something about drought. "Don't you need an environmental impact statement for this kind of thing?" Kevin asked, cutting him off.

"For an inquiry letter?" Alfredo said, almost sarcastically.

"Okay, okay. But I've stood before this council trying to get permission to couple a greenhouse and a chicken coop, and I've had to make an EIS—so somewhere along the line we'd surely have to have one for a change like this!" Sudden spurt of anger, remembering the frustration of those many meetings.

Alfredo said, "It's just water."

"Fuck, you *must* be kidding!" Kevin said.

Doris jabbed him with an elbow, and he remembered where he was. Oops. He looked down at the table, blushing. There was some tittering out in the audience. Got to watch it here, not just a private citizen anymore.

Well. That had put a pause in the conversation. Kevin glanced at the other council members. Matt was frowning. The moderates looked concerned, confused. "Look," Kevin said. "I don't know who these nominees are, and I don't know any of the details about this offer from MWD. I can't approve item twenty-seven in such a state, and I'd like to move we postpone discussing it until next time."

"I second the motion," Doris said.

Alfredo looked like he was going to make some objection. But he only said, "In favor?"

Doris and Kevin raised their hands. Then Hiroko and Jerry did the same.

"Okay," Alfredo said, and shrugged. "That's it for tonight, then."

He closed the session without fuss, looked at Matt briefly as they stood.

They *had* hoped to slip something by, Kevin thought. But what? Anger flushed through him again: Alfredo was tricky. And all the more so because no one but Kevin seemed to recognize that in him.

Their new town attorney bulked before him. Buddha standing. "You'll come by to see my house?"

"Oh yeah," Kevin said, distracted.

Oscar gave him the address. "Perhaps you and Ms. Nakayama could come by for breakfast. You can see the house, and I might also be able to illuminate some aspects of tonight's agenda."

Kevin looked at him quickly. The man's big face was utterly blank; then his eyes fluttered up and down, wild as crows' wings. *Significance*. The moonlike face blanked out again.

"Okay," Kevin said. "We'll come by."

"I shall expect you promptly at your leisure."

Biking home in the night, the long meeting over. Kevin had had to take some tools over to Hank's, and Doris and Nadezhda had gone directly home, so now he was alone.

The cool rush of air, the bouncing headlamp, the occasional whirr of chain in derailleur. The smell everywhere of orange blossoms, cut with eucalyptus, underlaid by sage: the braided smell of El Modena. Funny that two of the three smells were immigrants, like all the rest of them. Together, the way they could fill him up. . . .

Freed of the night's responsibilities, and still a little drunk, Kevin felt the scent of the land fill him. Light as a balloon. Sudden joy in the cool spring night. God existed in every atom, as Hank was always saying, in every molecule, in every particulate jot of the material world, so that he was breathing God deep into himself with every fragrant breath. And sometimes it really felt that way, hammering nails into new framing, soaring in the sky, biking through night air, the black hills bulking around him. . . . He knew the configuration of every dark tree he passed, every turn in the path, and for a long moment rushing along he felt spread out in it all, interpenetrated, the smell of the plants part of him, his body a piece of the hills, and all of it cool with a holy tingling.

Kevin's thighs had stiffened up from the afternoon's flight, and feeling them, he saw Ramona's legs. Long muscles, smooth brown skin, the swirl of fine silky hair on inner thigh. Wham, wham, the frame of the ultralite shuddering under all that anger and pain. Still wrapped up with Alfredo, no doubt of that. Hmmm.

Long day. Four for four, boom, boom! His wrists remembered the hits, the solid vibrationless smack of a line drive. Thoughtlessly around the round-about, up Chapman. Overlying the physical memories of the day, the meeting. Oh, man—stuck on that damned council for two whole years! Anger coursed through him again, at Alfredo's subterfuge, his smoothness. Buddha standing, the weird mime faces of their new town attorney. Something going on. It was funny; he had caught that from right as near sleep as he could have been. He knew he was slow, his friends made fun of him about it; but he wasn't stupid, he wasn't. Look at his houses and see. Would he have noticed that crammed item on the agenda if he had been fully awake? Hard to say. Didn't matter. Pattern recognition. A kind of subconscious resistance. Intelligence as a sort of stubbornness, a refusal to be fooled. No more classrooms falling off their chairs.

He took the left to home, pumped up the little road. He lived in a big old converted apartment block, built originally in a horseshoe around a pool. He had done the conversion himself, and still liked it about the best of any of his work; big tented thing bursting with light, home to a whole clan. His housemates, the neighbors inside, the real family.

Last painful push on the thighs, short coast to the bike rack at the open end of the horseshoe. Upstairs Tomas's window was lit as always, he would be up there before his computer screen, working away. Figures crossed before the big kitchen windows, Donna and Cindy no doubt, talking and pounding the cervezas, watching the kids wash dishes.

The building sat in an avocado grove at the foot of Rattlesnake Hill, one of the last knobs of the Santa Ana Mountains before the long flat stretch to the sea. Dark bulk of the hill above, furry with scrub oak and sage. His home under the hill. His hill, the center of his life, his own great mound of sandstone and sage.

He slipped the front tire of his mountain bike into the rack. Turning toward the house he saw something and stopped. A motion.

Something out there in the grove. He squinted against the two big squares of kitchen light. Clatter of pots and voices. There it was; black shape, between trees, about mid-grove. It too was still, and he had the sudden feeling it was looking back at him. Tall and man-shaped, sort of. Too dark to really see it.

It moved. Shift to the side, then gone, off into the trees. No sound at all.

Kevin let out a breath. Little tingle up his spine, around the hair on the back of his neck. What the . . . ?

Long day. Nothing out there but night. He shook his head, went inside.

... 2

2 March 2012, 8 A.M. I decided that as a gesture to its spirit I would write my book outdoors. Unfortunately it's snowing today. The balcony above ours makes a sort of roof, however, so I am sticking to my resolve. Roll out computer stand, extension cords, chair. Sit bundled in down booties, bunting pants, down jacket, down hood. Plug in and pound away. The mind's finest hour. My hands are cold.

"Stark bewölkt, Schnee." We haven't seen the sun all year, even the Zürchers are moaning. Suddenly a dream comes back to me: Owens Valley in spring bloom.

Writing a utopia. Certainly it's a kind of compensation, a stab at succeeding where my real work has failed. Or at least an attempt to clarify my beliefs, my desires.

I remember in law school, thinking that the law determined the way the world was run, that if I learned it I could change things. Then the public defender's office, the case loads, the daily grind. The realization that nothing I did there would ever change things. And it wasn't much better at the CLE, or doing lawsuits for the Socialist Party, miserable remnant that it was. So many attacks from so many directions, we were lucky if we could hold on to the good that already existed. No chance to improve things. Nothing but a holding action. Really it was a relief when this post-doc of Pam's gave me the chance to quit.

Now I'll change the world in my mind.

Our balcony overlooks a small yard, surrounded by solid brick buildings. A massive linden dominates smaller trees and shrubs. Wet black branches thrust into a white sky. Below me are two evergreens, one something like a holly, the other something like a juniper; the birds are clustered in these, fluffed quivering feather-balls, infrequently cheeping. Between two buildings, a slice of Zürich: Grossmünster and Fraumünster and their copper-green spires, steely lake, big stone buildings of the university, the banks, the medieval town. Iron sound of a tram rolling downhill.

I'm writing a utopia in a country that runs as efficiently as Züri's blue trams, even though it has four languages, two religions, a nearly useless landscape. Conflicts that tear the rest of the world apart are solved here with the coolest kind of rationality, like engineers figuring out a problem in materials stress. How much torque can society take before it snaps, Dr. Science? Ask the Swiss.

Maybe they're too good at it. Refugees are pouring in, Ausländer nearly half the population they say, and so the National Action party has won some elections, become part of the ruling coalition. With a bullet. Return Switzerland to the Swiss! they cry. And in fact yesterday we got an einladung from the Fremdenkontrolle der Stadt Zürich. The Stranger Control. Time to renew our Ausländerausweise. It's down to every four months now. I wonder if they'll try to kick us out this time.

For now, all is calm. White flakes falling. I write in a kind of pocket utopia, a little island of calm in a maddened world. Perhaps it will help make my future seem more plausible to me—perhaps, remembering Switzerland, it will even seem possible.

But there's no such thing as a pocket utopia.

The next morning Nadezhda joined Kevin and Doris for the visit to Oscar Baldarramma. They biked over in heavy traffic (voices, squeaky brakes, whirring derailleurs) and coasted down Oscar's street, gliding through the spaced shadows of liquid amber trees, so that it seemed the morning blinked.

Oscar's house was flanked by lemon and avocado trees. Unharvested lemons lay rotting in the weeds, giving the air a sweet-sour scent. The house itself was an old stucco and wood suburban thing, roofed with concrete tiles. A separate garden and bike shed stood under an avocado tree at the back of the lot, and a bit of the house's roof extended before the shed: "Carport," Kevin said, eyeing it with interest. "Pretty rare."

Oscar greeted them in a Hawaiian shirt slashed with yellow and blue stripes, and purple shorts. He ignored Doris's exaggerated squint, and led them inside for a tour. It was a typical tract house, built in the 1950s. Doris remarked that it was a big place for one person, and Oscar promptly hunched over and took a long sideways step, waggling his eyebrows fiercely and brandishing an invisible cigar: "Always available for boarding!"

Kevin and Doris stared at him, and he straightened up. "Groucho Marx," he explained.

Kevin and Doris looked at each other. "I've heard the name," Doris said. Kevin nodded.

Oscar glanced at Nadezhda, who was grinning. His mouth made a little O. "In that case . . ." he murmured, and turned to show them the next room.

When the tour was finished Kevin asked what Oscar wanted done.

"The usual thing." Oscar waved a hand. "Big clear walls that make it impossible to tell if you're indoors or out, an atrium three stories tall, perhaps an aviary, solar air conditioning and refrigeration and waste disposal, some banana trees and cinnamon bushes, a staircase with gold bannisters, a library big enough to hold twenty thousand books, and a completely work-free food supply."

"You don't want to garden?" Doris asked.

"I detest gardening."

Doris rolled her eyes. "That's silly, Oscar."

Oscar nodded solemnly. "I'm a silly guy."

"Where will you get your vegetables?"

"I will buy them. You recall the method."

"Huh," Doris said, not amused.

They viewed the backyard in a frosty silence. Kevin tried to get Oscar to speak seriously about his desires, but had little success. Oscar spoke of libraries, wood paneling, fireplaces, comfortable little nooks where one could huddle on long winter nights. . . . Kevin tried to explain that winter nights in the region weren't all that long, or cold. That he tended to work in a style that left a lot of open space, making homes that functioned as nearly self-sufficient little farms. Oscar seemed agreeable, although he still spoke in the same way about what he wanted. Kevin scratched his head, squinted at him. Buddha, babbling.

Finally Nadezhda asked Oscar about the previous night's council meeting.

"Ah yes. Well—I'm not sure how much you know about the water situation here?"

She stood to attention, as if reciting a lesson. "The American West begins where the annual rainfall drops below ten inches."

"Exactly."

And therefore, Oscar went on, much of the United States was a desert civilization; and like all previous desert civilizations, it was in danger of foundering when its water systems began to clog. Currently some sixty million people lived in the American West, where the natural supplies of water might support two or three. But even the largest reservoirs silt up, and most of the West, existing not just on surface water, had mined its groundwater like oil—thousands of years of accumulated rainfall, pumped out of the ground in less than a century. The great aquifers were drying up, and the reservoirs were holding less each day; while drought, in their warming climate, was more and more common. So the search for water was becoming desperate.

The solution was on a truly gigantic scale, which pleased the Army Corps of

Engineers no end. Up in the Northwest, the Columbia River poured enormous amounts of water into the Pacific every year. Washington, Oregon, and Idaho squawked mightily, remembering how Owens Valley had withered when Los Angeles gained the rights to its water; but the Columbia carried more than a hundred times the water those states were ever expected to need, and their fellow states to the south were truly in need. The Corps of Engineers loved the idea: dams, reservoirs, pipelines, canals—a multi-billion-dollar system, rescuing the sand-choked civilizations of the south. Grand! Lovely! What could be nicer? "It's what we've done in California for years; instead of moving to where the water is, we move the water to where the people are."

Nadezhda nodded. "We have this tradition in my country too. There was a plan to turn the Volga River right around, the whole thing, and send it south for irrigation purposes. Only when it seemed that world weather patterns might be shifted was the plan abandoned." She smiled. "Or maybe it was just lack of funds. Anyway, in your situation, where water will soon be plentiful again, what did that item on last night's agenda mean?"

"I'm not sure, but there were two parts I found interesting. One, the inquiry to Los Angeles's Metropolitan Water District, which supplies most of our town's water from their Colorado River pipeline. Second, the nominations for the watermaster. On the one hand, it looks like an attempt to bring more water to El Modena; on the other, an attempt to control its use when it arrives. You see?"

His guests nodded. "And what about this offer from Los Angeles?" Nadezhda said.

A ghost of a smile crossed Oscar's face. "When the federal courts made the original apportionment of the Colorado River's water to the states bordering it, they accidentally used a flood year's estimate of the river's annual flow. Every year after that they came up short, and the states fought like dogs over what water there was. To solve the problem the court cut all the states' shares proportionally. But California—the MWD, to be precise—recently won back the rights to their original allotment."

"Why is that?"

"Well, first, because they had been using their rights the longest, and most fully, and that solidifies their claim. And secondly, it's felt that the Columbia pipeline will solve the competing states' problems, so they won't need the Colorado's water. So, the MWD has more water than they have had for years, and since these rights are made more secure by usage, they're anxious to have their new water bought up and used as quickly as possible. All of their clients in southern California are being offered more water. Most are refusing it, and so MWD is getting anxious."

"Why are most refusing it?"

"They have what they need. It's a method of growth control. If they don't have the water, they can't expand without special action. The Santa Barbara strategy, it's called."

"But your mayor wants this water."

"Apparently so."

"But *why?*" Kevin said.

Oscar pursed his lips. "Well, you know what *I* heard."

Suddenly he jerked to left and right, peering about in a gross caricature of a check for spies. Low conspirator's voice: "I was dining at Le Boulangerie soon after my arrival in town, when I heard voices from the next booth—"

"Eavesdropping!" Doris exclaimed.

"Yes." Oscar grimaced horribly at her. "I can't help myself. Forgive me. Please." Doris made a face.

Oscar went on: "Later I discovered the voices were those of your mayor, and someone named Ed. They were discussing a new complex, one which would combine labs with offices and shops. Novagene and Heartech were mentioned as potential tenants."

"Alfredo and Ed Macey run Heartech," Doris told him.

"Ah. Well."

"Did they say where they wanted to build?" Kevin asked.

"No, they didn't mention location—although Mr. Blair did say 'They want that view.' Perhaps that means in the hills somewhere. But if one were contemplating a new development of any size in El Modena, it would be necessary to have more water. And so last night when I saw item twenty-seven, I wondered if this might not be a small first step."

"The underhanded weasel!" Doris said.

"It all seemed fairly public to me," Oscar pointed out.

Doris glared at him. "I suppose you're going to claim a lawyerly neutrality in all this?"

Kevin winced. The truth was, Doris has a prejudice against lawyers. We're suffocating in lawyers, she would say, they're doing nothing but creating more excuses for themselves. We should make all of them train as ecologists before they're let into law school, give them some decent values.

They do take courses in ecology, Hank would tell her. It's part of their training.

Well they aren't learning it, Doris would say. Damned parasites!

Now, in Oscar's presence, she was icily discreet; she only used the adjective "lawyerly" with a little twist to it, and left it at that.

Though he certainly heard the inflection, Oscar eyed her impassively. "I am not a neutral man," he said, "in any sense of the word."

"Do you want to see this development stopped?"

"It is still only a matter of conjecture that one is proposed. I'd like to find out more about it."

"But if there is a large development, planned for the hills?"

"It depends—"

"It depends!"

"Yes. It depends on where it is. I wouldn't like to see any empty hilltops razed and built on. There are few of those left."

"Hardly any," Kevin said. "Really, to get a view over the plain in El Modena, there's only Rattlesnake Hill. . . ."

He and Doris stared at each other.

Oscar served them a sumptuous breakfast of French toast and sausages, but Kevin had little appetite for it. His hill, his sandstone refuge . . .

When they were done Nadezhda said, "Assuming that Rattlesnake Hill is Alfredo's target, what can you do to stop him?"

Oscar rose from his chair. "The law lies in our hands like a blackjack!" He took a few vicious swings at the air. "If we choose to use it."

"Champion shadow boxer, I see," Doris muttered.

Kevin said, "You bet we choose to use it!"

"The water problem has potential," Oscar said. "I'm no expert in it, but I do know California water law is a swamp. We could be the creature from the black lagoon." He limped around the kitchen to illustrate this strategy. "And I have a friend in Bishop we should talk to, her name's Sally Tallhawk and she teaches at the law school. She was on the State Water Resources Control Board until recently, and she knows more than anyone about the current state of water law. I'm going there soon—we could talk to her about it."

Nadezhda said, "We need to know more of the mayor's plans."

"I don't know how we'll get them."

"I do," Kevin said. "I'm just going to go up to Alfredo's place and ask him!"

"Direct," Oscar noted.

Doris said, "Alternatively, we could crawl under his windows and eavesdrop until we learn what we want to know."

Oscar blinked. "Nothing like a little confrontation," he said to Kevin.

"Doesn't Thomas Barnard live in this area?" Nadezhda asked.

"That's my grandfather," Kevin said, surprised. "He lives up in the hills."

"Perhaps he can help."

"Well, maybe. I mean, true, but . . ."

Kevin's grandfather had had an active career in law and politics, and had been a prominent figure in the economic reforms of the twenties and thirties.

"He was a good lawyer," Nadezhda said. "Powerful. He knew how to get things done."

"You're right." Kevin nodded. "It's a good idea, really. It's just that he's a sort of hermit, now. I haven't seen him myself in a long time."

Nadezhda shrugged. "We all get strange. I would like to see him anyway."

"You know him?"

"We met once, long ago."

So Kevin agreed, a bit apprehensively, to take her up to see him.

Before they left Oscar showed them his library, contained in scores of cardboard boxes; one whole room was full of them. Kevin glanced in a box and saw a biography of Lou Gehrig. "Hey Oscar, you ought to join our softball team!"

"No thank you. I detest softball."

Doris snorted. "What?" Kevin said. "But why?"

Oscar shifted into a martial arts stance. Low growl: "The world plays hardball, Claiborne."

The world plays hardball. Sure, and he could handle it. But not his hill, not Rattlesnake Hill!

It was not just that it stood behind his house, which was true, and important; but that it was his place. It was an insignificant little round top at the end of the El Modena hills, broken dirty sandstone covered with scrub, and a small grove of trees which had been planted by his grandfather's grade school class, many years before. It stood there, the only empty hilltop in the area, because it had been owned for decades by the Orange County Water District, who left it alone.

And no one seemed to go up there but him. Oh, occasionally he'd find an empty beer dumpie or the like, thrown away on the summit. But the hill was always empty when he was there—quiet except for insect creaks, hot, dusty, and somehow filled with a sunny, calm presence, as if inhabited by an old Indian hill spirit, small but powerful.

He went up there when he wanted to work outdoors. He took his sketchpad, up to his favorite spot on the western edge of the copse of trees, and he'd sit and look out over the plain and sketch rooms, plans, interiors, exteriors. He'd done that for most of his life, had done a fair amount of homework there in his schooldays. He had scrambled up the dry ravines on the western side, he had thrown rocks off the top, he had followed the track of an old dirt road that had once spiraled up it. He went there when he was feeling lazy, when he only wanted to sit in the sun and feel the earth turning under him. He went there with women friends, at night, when he was feeling romantic.

Now he went up there and sat in the dirt, in his spot. Midday, the air hot, filled with dust and sage oils. He brushed his hands over the soil, over the sharp-edged nondescript sandstone pebbles. Picked them up, rubbed them together in his hands. He couldn't seem to achieve his usual feeling of peace, however, his feeling of connection with the ground beneath him; and the ballooning sense of lightness, the kind of epiphany he had felt while bicycling home the other night, eluded him completely. He was too worried. He could only sit and touch the earth, and worry.

At work he thought about it, worried about it. He and Hank and Gabriela were busy finishing up two jobs, one down in Costa Mesa, and he worked on the trim and clean-up in a state of distraction. Could they really want to develop Rattlesnake Hill? "It's that view they're after." If they were going to build, they would need more water. If they were going to have a view, in El Modena . . . there really wasn't any other choice! Rattlesnake Hill. A place where—he realized this one morning, scraping caulking off of tile—where when you were there, you felt quite certain it would never change. And that was part of its appeal.

Usually when Kevin was working he was happy. He enjoyed most of the labor involved in construction, especially the carpentry. All of it, really. The direct continual results of his efforts, popping into existence before his eyes: framing, wiring, stucco, painting, tilework, trim, they all had their pleasures for him. And as he did the designs for their little team's work, he also had the architect's pleasure of seeing his ideas realized. With this Costa Mesa condo rehab, for instance, a lot of things had been uncertain: would you really be able to see the entire length of the structure, rooms opening on rooms? Would the atrium give enough light to that west wing? No way to be sure until it was done; and so the pleasure of work, bringing the vision into material being, finding out whether the calculations had been correct. Solving the mystery. Not much delayed gratification in construction. Immediate gratification, little problem after little problem, faced and solved, until the big problem was solved as well. And all through the process, the childlike joys of hammering, cutting, measuring. Bang bang bang, out in the sun and the wind, with clouds as his constant companions.

Usually. But this week he was too worried about the hill. Touch-up work, usually one of his favorite parts, seemed pale diversion, finicky and boring. He hardly even noticed it. And his town work was positively irritating. They would be digging out that street forever at their pace!

He had to get some answers. He had to go up and confront Alfredo, like he had said he would that morning at Oscar's. No way around it.

So one afternoon after town work he pedaled up into the hills, to the house on Redhill where a big group of Heartech people lived. Alfredo's new home.

The house was set on a terrace, cut high on the side of the hill above Tustin and Foothill. It was a huge white lump of Mission Revival, a style Kevin detested. To him the California Indians were noble savages, devastated by Junípero Serra's mission system. Thus Mission Revival, which every thirty years or so swept through southern California architecture in a great nostalgic wave, seemed to Kevin no more than a kind of homage to genocide. Any time he got the chance to renovate an example of the style he loved to obliterate it.

One small advantage to Mission Revival was it was always easy to find the front door—in this case a huge pair of oak monsters, standing in the center of a massive wall of whitewashed adobe, under a tile-roofed portico. Kevin stalked up the gravel drive and yanked on a thick rope bellpull.

Alfredo himself answered, dressed in shorts and a T-shirt. "Kevin, what a surprise. Come on in, man."

"I'd rather talk out here, if you don't mind. Do you have time?"

"Sure, sure." Alfredo stepped out, leaving the door open. "What is it?"

No really indirect approach to the issue had suggested itself to Kevin, and so he said, "Is it true that you and Ed and John are planning to build an industrial park on Rattlesnake Hill?"

Alfredo raised his eyebrows. Kevin had expected him to flinch, or in some other way look obviously guilty. The fact that he didn't made Kevin uneasy, nervous—a little bit guilty himself. Perhaps Oscar had misoverheard.

"Who told you that?"

"Never mind who—I just heard it. Is it true?"

Alfredo paused, shrugged. "There're always plans being talked around—"

Ah ha!

"—but I don't know of anything in particular. You would know if there was something up, being on the council."

Anger fired through Kevin, quick and hot. "So that's why you tried to slip that water stuff past us!"

Alfredo looked puzzled. "I didn't try to slip anything past anyone. Some business was taken care of—or we tried—in front of the whole council, in the ordinary course of a meeting. Right?"

"Well, yeah, that's right. But it was late, everyone was tired, I was new. No one was watching anymore. It was as close to slipping the thing under the door as you could get."

"A council meeting is a council meeting, Kevin. Things go on right till the last moment. You're going to have to get used to that." Alfredo looked amused at Kevin's naïveté. "If someone wanted to slip something by, it could have been shoved in among a bunch of other changes, it could have been done in the town planner's office and presented as boilerplate—"

"I guess you wish you had done it that way, now."

"Not at all. I'm just saying we didn't try to slip one by you." Alfredo spoke slowly, as if doing his best to explain a difficult matter to a child. He moved out onto the gravel drive.

"I think you did," Kevin said. "Obviously it isn't something you'd admit now. Anyway, what are you doing trying to turn some of our open land into a mall?"

"What mall? Look here, what are you talking about? We're making an inquiry about the extra water MWD is offering, because it makes sense, it saves us money. That's part of our job on the council. Now as to this other thing, if someone is exploring the possibilities of a multi-use center, what's the problem? Are you saying we shouldn't try to create jobs here in El Modena?"

"No!"

"Of course not. We need more jobs—El Modena is small, we don't generate much income. If some businesses moved here everyone would benefit. You might not need your share increased, but other people do."

"We already make enough from town shares."

"Is that the Green position?"

"Well..."

"I didn't think so. As I recall, you said increased efficiency would increase the shares."

"So it would!"

Alfredo walked further down the drive, to the low mounds of an extensive cactus garden. Standing there they had a view over all of Orange County's treetopped plain. "It gets to be a question of how we can become more efficient, doesn't it. I don't think we can do it without businesses to *be* efficient. But you—sometimes I think if you had your way you'd empty out the town and tear it down entirely." He gestured at the cacti. "Back to mustard fields and scrub hills, and maybe a couple of camps down on the creek."

"Come on," Kevin said scornfully. In fact, he had quite often daydreamed about just such a return to nature when tearing old structures down. But he knew it was just a fantasy, a wish to live the Indians' life, and he never mentioned it to others. It was disconcerting to hear Alfredo read his mind like that.

Alfredo saw his confusion. "You can only go so far with negative growth before it becomes harmful, Kevin. I realize there's a lot of momentum in your direction these days, and believe me, I think it's been a good thing. We needed it, and things are better now because of it. But any pendulum can swing too far, and you're one of those trying to hold it out there when it wants to swing back. Now that you're in a position of responsibility you've got to face it—the people who talked you into joining the council are extremists."

"We're talking about your company here," Kevin said feebly.

"We are? Well heck, say that we are. At Heartech we make cardiovascular equipment and blood substitutes and related material. It helps everyone, especially the regions still dealing with hepatitis and malaria. You were in Tanzania for your work abroad, you've got to know the kind of help it does!"

"I know, I know." Heartech was an important part of Orange County's booming medtech industry, doing state-of-the-art work. It was right at the legal limits on company size; most of its long-time workers were hundreds, which meant that the company paid an enormous amount of money into Tustin's town shares, which were then redistributed out among the town's citizens, as part of their personal income. And Heartech helped a lot of liaison companies in Africa and Indonesia as well. No doubt about it, it was a good company, and Alfredo believed in it passionately. "Listen," he said, "let's follow this through. Don't you think bio-technology is valuable work?"

"Of course," Kevin said. "I use it every day."

"And the medical aspects of it save lives every day."

"That's true. Sure."

"Now wouldn't it be a good thing if El Modena contributed to that?"

"Yeah, it would. That would be great."

Alfredo spread his hands, palms up.

They looked at cacti.

Kevin, beginning to feel the way he did when he rode the Mad Hatter's Teacups in Disneyland, tried to gather his thoughts. "Actually, it seems to me it isn't so important where it happens . . ." Ah yes: where. "I mean where exactly do you have in mind, Alfredo?"

"Where what? Sorry, I've lost track of what you're talking about."

"Well, if you're thinking of building in the hills. Are you?"

"If there were people thinking about a development in the El Modena Hills, it would be a matter of attracting the best tenants possible. Things like that are important when you're competing with places like Irvine."

So he was thinking of the hills! "You should be mayor of Irvine," Kevin said bitterly. "Irvine is just your style."

"You mean they make money there? They attract business, they have big town shares?"

"Yes."

"But that's what our town council is for, right? I mean, there are people in this town who could use it, even if you can't."

"I'm not against the town shares growing!"

"Good. I'm glad to hear it."

Kevin exhaled noisily, frustrated. Feeling completely dizzy, he said, "Well—still—"

"So we should do what we can, right?"

"Yeah, sure—"

"I think we're more in agreement than you realize, Kevin. You build things, I build things. It's really the same thing."

"Yeah, but, but if you're tearing up wilderness!"

"Don't worry about that. There isn't any wilderness in El Modena in the first place, so don't get too romantic about it. Besides, we'll all be working out anything that happens here in the next couple of years, so we'll bang out a consensus just like always. Don't let your friends make you too paranoid about it."

"My friends don't make me paranoid. You make me paranoid."

"I don't appreciate that, Kevin. And it won't help in the long run. Look, I build things to make money, and so do you. We're in the same business, aren't we? I mean, aren't you in the construction business?"

"Yeah!"

Alfredo smiled. "Well, there you have it. We'll work it out. Hey, I've got to get going—I've got a date—down in Irvine, in fact." He winked, went into the house.

Ka . . . CHUNK.

Kevin faced the door, and after a moment's thought he slammed his fist into his palm. "It's completely different!" he shouted. "I do renovation!" Or else we tear down a structure and put another one in its place. And it always fits the land better. It's entirely different!

But there was no one there to argue with.

He let out a long breath. "Shit."

What had happened? Well, maybe Alfredo and his partners were planning a development. Maybe they weren't. Maybe it was up in the hills. Maybe it wasn't. He had learned that much.

He pulled his bike from the rack, observed his hands shaking. Alfredo was too much for him; try as he might, Alfredo could run rings around him. Chagrined at the realization, he turned the bike and headed downhill.

He needed help. Doris, Oscar, Oscar's friend in Bishop; Jean and the Green party organization; Nadezhda. Perhaps even Ramona, somehow. He shied away from the thought—the implication that his dislike for Alfredo had nonpolitical components—it was a political matter, nothing more!

And Tom.

Once home he went looking for Nadezhda. "Do you still want to meet my grandfather?"

Kevin's grandfather lived in the back country, on a ridge in the broken hills north of Black Star Canyon. Kevin led Nadezhda and Doris up a poorly kept trail to his place, winding between sage and scrub oak and broken ribs of sandstone. Nadezhda was inquisitive about everything: plants, rocks, Tom's livelihood.

She had a beautiful low voice, and had learned her English in India, so that the musical lilt of the subcontinent filled all her sentences.

"Well, Tom takes his ten thousand and lets it go at that. He's got a garden and some chickens, and he does some trapping and beekeeping and I don't know what all. He really does keep to himself these days. Didn't used to be that way."

"I wonder what happened."

"Well, he retired. And then my grandma died, about ten years ago."

"Ten years."

A switchback, and Kevin looked down at her. Next to Doris she seemed slight as a bird, graceful, cool, fit. No wonder Doris admired her. Ex-head of the Soviet State Planning Commission, currently lecturer in history on a school freighter, which was up in Seattle—

"He can get ten thousand dollars a year without working?"

"At his age he can. You know about the income magnitude thing?"

"A legal floor and ceiling on personal income, yes?"

"Yeah. Tom takes the floor."

She laughed. "We have a similar system. Your grandfather was a big advocate of those laws when they were introduced. He must have had a plan."

"No doubt. In fact he told me that once, when I was a kid."

Hiking with Grandpa, up the back canyons. Up Harding Canyon to the little waterfall, bushwhacking up crazy steep slopes to the ridge of Saddleback, up the dirt road to the double summit. Birds, lizards, dusty plants, endless streams of talk. Stories. Sandstone. The overwhelming smell of sage.

They topped a rise, and saw Tom's house. It was a small weather-beaten cabin, perched on the ridge that boxed the little canyon they had ascended. A big front window looked down at them, reflecting clouds like a monocle. Walls of cracked shingle were faded to the color of sand. Weeds grew waist high in an abandoned garden, and sticking out of the weeds were broken beehive flats, rain barrels, mountain bikes rusted or disassembled, a couple of grandfather clocks broken open to the sky.

Kevin thought of homes as windows to the soul, and so Tom's place left him baffled. The way it fit the ridge, disappeared into the sandstone and sage, was nice. A good sign. But the disarray, the lack of care, the piles of refuse. It looked like the area around an animal's hole in the ground.

Nadezhda merely looked at the place, black eyes bright. They walked through a weedy garden to the front door, and Kevin knocked. No answer.

They stepped around back to the kitchen door, which was open. Looked in; no one there.

"Well, we might as well sit and wait a while," Kevin said. "I'll try calling him." He went to the other side of the ridge, put both hands to his mouth and let loose a piercing whistle.

There was a tall black walnut up the ridge, with a bench made of logs underneath it; Doris and Nadezhda sat there. Kevin wandered the yard, checking the little set of solar panels in back, the connections to the satellite dish. All in order. He pulled some weeds away from the overrun tomatoes and zucchini. Long black and orange bugs flew noisily away; other than that there was a complete, somehow audible silence. Ah: bees in the distance, defining the silence they buzzed in.

"Hey."

"Jesus, Grandpa!"

"What's happening, boy."

"You frightened me!"

"Apparently so."

He had come up the same trail they had. Bent over, humping some small iron traps and four dead rabbits. He'd been only feet from Kevin's back when he announced his presence, and not a sound of approach.

"Up here to weed?"

"Well, no. I brought Doris and a friend. We wanted to talk with you."

Tom just stared at him, bright-eyed. Stepped past and ducked into his cabin. Clatter of traps on the floor. When he re-emerged Doris and Nadezhda had come over from the bench and were standing beside Kevin. Tom stopped and stared at them. He was wearing pants worn to the color of the hillsides, and a blue T-shirt torn enough to reveal a bony white-haired chest. The hair edging his bald pate was a tangle, and his uncut beard was gray and white and brown and auburn, stained around his mouth. A dust-colored old man. He always looked like this, Kevin was used to it; it was, he had thought, a part of aging. But now Nadezhda stood before them neat as a bird after a bath, her silvery hair cut so that even when windblown it fell perfectly into place. One of her enamel earrings flashed turquoise and cream in the sun.

"Well?"

"Grandpa, this is a friend of Doris's—"

But Nadezhda stepped past him and extended a hand. "Nadezhda Katayev," she said. "We met a long time ago, at the Singapore Conference."

For an instant Tom's eyebrows shot up. Then he took her hand, dropped it. "You look much the same."

"And you too."

He smiled briefly, slipped past them with a neat, skittish movement. "Water," he said over his shoulder, and took off down a trail into a copse of live oak. His three guests looked at each other. Kevin shrugged, led the women down the trail. There in the shade Tom was attaching a pump handle to a skinny black pump, then pumping, slowly and steadily, his back to them. After quite a while water spurted from the pump into a tin trough, and through an open spigot into a five-gallon bucket. Kevin adjusted the bucket under the spigot, and then the three of them stood there and watched Tom pump. It was as if he were mute. Feeling uncomfortable, Kevin said, "We came up to talk to you about a problem we're having. You know I'm on the town council now?"

Tom nodded.

Kevin described what had happened so far, then said, "We don't really know for sure, but if Alfredo is interested in Rattlesnake Hill, it would be a disaster—there just aren't that many empty hills left."

Tom squinted, looked around briefly.

"I mean in El Modena, Tom! Overlooking the plain! You know what I mean. Shit, you planted the trees on top of Rattlesnake Hill, didn't you?"

"I helped."

"So don't you care what happens to it?"

"It's your backyard now."

"Yeah, but—"

"And you're on the council?"

"Yeah."

"Stop him, then. You know what to do, you don't need me."

"We do too! Man, when I talk to Alfredo I end up saying black is white!"

Tom shrugged, moved the full bucket from under the spigot and replaced it with an empty one. Stymied, Kevin moved the full bucket onto flat ground and sat beside it.

"You don't want to help?"

"I'm done with that stuff, Kevin. It's your job now." He said this with a friendly, birdlike glance.

Second bucket filled, Tom pulled out the pump handle and put it in a slot on the pump's side. He lifted the two buckets and started back toward the cabin.

"Here, let me take one of those."

"That's okay, thanks. I need the two for balance."

Following Tom up the trail to his cabin, Kevin looked at the old man's bowed back and shook his head, exasperated. This just was not the Grandpa he had grown up with. In those years there had been no more social animal than Tom Barnard; he was always talking, he organized camping trips for groups from town constantly, and he had taken his grandson up into the canyons and over the Santa Ana Mountains, and the San Jacintos, and back into Anza Borrego and Joshua Tree, and over to Catalina and down into Baja and up into the southern Sierras—and talking the whole way, for hours at a time every day, about everything you could possibly imagine! Much of Kevin's education—the parts he really remembered—had come from Tom on their hikes together, from asking questions and listening to Tom ramble. "I hated capitalism because it was a lie!" Tom would say, fording Harding Canyon stream with abandon. "It said that everyone exercising their self-interest would make a decent community! Such a lie!" Splash, splash! "It was government as protection agency, a belief system for the rich. Why, even when it seemed to work, where did it leave them? Holed up in mansions and crazy as loons."

"But some people like to be alone."

"Yeah, yeah. And self-interest exists, no one can say it doesn't—the governments that tried got in deep trouble, because that's a lie of a different kind. But to say self-interest is all that exists, or that it should be given free rein! My Lord. Believe that and nothing matters but money."

"But you changed that," Kevin would say, watching his footwork.

"Yes, we did. We gave self-interest some room to work in, but we limited it. Channeled it toward the common good. That's the job of the law, as we saw it then." He laughed. "Legislation is a revolutionary power, boy, though it's seldom seen as such. We used it for all it was worth, and most liked the results, except for some of the rich, who fought like wolverines to hold on to what they had. In fact that's a fight that's still going on. I don't think it will ever end."

Exactly! Kevin thought, watching his strangely silent grandfather toil up the trail. The fight will go on forever, and yet you've stepped out of it, left it to us. Well, maybe that was fair, maybe it was their turn. But he needed the old man's help!

He sighed. They got to the cabin and Tom ducked inside. One bucket of water went into a holding tank. The other was brought out into the sun, along with the four dead rabbits. Big knife, slab of wood, tub for the blood and guts. Great. Tom began the grisly task of skinning and cleaning the little beasts. Hardly any meat on them; hardly any meat on Tom. Kevin went around the side and fed the chickens. When he returned Tom was still at it. Doris and Nadezhda were seated on the ground under the kitchen window. Kevin didn't know what to say.

"This conference in Singapore you met at—what was it about?" Doris finally said, breaking a long silence.

"Conversion strategies," Nadezhda said.

"What's that?"

Nadezhda looked up at Tom. "Maybe you can explain it more clearly," she said. "My English is not so good to be explaining such a thing."

Tom glanced at her. "Uh huh." He went into the kitchen with the skinned rabbits; they heard a freezer door open and shut. He came back out and took the tub of entrails over the Emerson septic tank, dumped them in, shut the lid, and clamped it down.

Nadezhda shrugged at Doris, said, "We were finding ways to convert the military parts of the economy. The big countries had essentially war economies, and switching to a civilian economy without causing a depression was no easy thing. In fact, no one could afford to change. So strategies had to be conceived. We had a big crowd in Singapore, though some there opposed the idea. Do you remember General Larsen?" she said to Tom. "U.S. Air Force, head of strategic defense?"

"I think so," Tom said as he walked by her. He went out into his garden and started plucking tomatoes.

Nadezhda followed him. She picked up his basket, followed him around as he shifted. "I am thinking people like him made aerospace industries the hardest to change."

"Nah."

"You don't think so?"

"Nah."

"But why?"

Long silence.

Then Tom said, "Aerospace could be sicced on the energy problem. But who needs tanks? Who needs artillery shells?"

He lapsed back into silence, rooted under weeds in search of another tomato. He glanced at Nadezhda resentfully, as if she had tricked him into speaking. Which, Kevin thought, she had.

"Yes," Nadezhda said, "conventional weapons were hard. Remember those Swiss plans, for cars built like troop movers?" She laughed, a low clear chuckle, and even elbowed Tom in the arm. He smiled, nodded. She said, "What about those prefab schoolrooms, made by the helmet and armor plants!"

Tom smiled politely, got up and went into the kitchen.

Nadezhda followed him, talking, taking down a second cutting board and cutting tomatoes with him, going through his shelves to find spices to add to oil and vinegar. Talking all the while. Occasionally in passing she put a hand to his arm, or while cutting she would elbow him gently, as old friends might: "Do you remember? Don't you remember?"

"I remember," he said, with that small smile. He glanced at her.

"When the engineers got the idea of it," she said to Doris and Kevin, "their eyes lit up. It was the best problems they were ever having, you could hear it in their voices! Because everything helped, you see? With all that military work redirected to survival problems, conflicts caused by the problems were eased, which reduced the demand for weapons. So it was a feedback spiral, and once in it, things changed very quickly." She laughed again, suffused with nervous energy, doing her best, Kevin saw, to arc that energy into Tom; to charm him, cajole him—seduce him. . . .

Tom merely smiled that brief glancing smile, and offered them a lunch of tomato salad. "All there is." But he was watching her, out of the corner of his eye; it seemed to Kevin that he couldn't help it.

They ate in silence. Tom wandered off to the pump with his buckets. Nadezhda went with him, talking about people they had known in Singapore.

Doris and Kevin sat in the sun. They could hear voices down at the pump. At one point Nadezhda exclaimed "But we acted!" so sharply they could make it out.

Muttered response, no response.

When they returned she was laughing again, helping with one bucket and telling a story. Tom was as silent as before. He still seemed friendly—but re-mote, watching them as if from a distance. Glancing frequently at Nadezhda. He took one bucket down to the Emerson tank, began working there.

Eventually Kevin shrugged, and indicated to the women that he thought it was time to leave. Tom wandered back as they stood. "You sure you won't help us?" Kevin asked, catching Tom's gaze and holding it.

Tom smiled. "You get 'em this time," he said. And to Nadezhda: "Nice to see you again."

Nadezhda looked him in the eye. "It was my pleasure," she said. She smiled at him, and something in it was so appealing, so intimate, that Kevin looked away. He noticed Tom did the same. Then Nadezhda led them down the trail.

...3

23 March. *There is no such thing as a pocket utopia.*

Consider the French aristocracy before the revolution—well fed, well clothed, well housed, well educated—brilliant lives. One could say they lived in a little utopia of their own. But we don't say that, because we know their lives rested on a base of human misery, peasants toiling in ignorance and suffering. And we think of the French aristocracy as parasites, brutal, stupid, tyrannical.

But now the world is a single economy. Global village, made in Thailand! And we stand on little islands of luxury, while the rest—great oceans of abject misery, bitter war, endless hunger. We say, But they are none of our affair! We have our island.

The Swiss have theirs. Mountain island with its banks and its bomb shelters— as fast as some Swiss take refugees in, other Swiss kick others out. Schizoid response, like all the rest of us.

Spent the morning at the Fremdenkontrolle, one office of the police station on Gemeinderstrasse. Clean, hushed. Marble floors and desktops. Polite official. But, he explains slowly in high German so I will understand, the new laws. As you don't have a job. Tourist visa only. And as you have been here over a year already, this no longer possible is. No Ausweis. Yes, wife can stay till end of employment. Daughter too, yes.

But who'll take care of her? I wanted to shout. Of course that's part of the plan. Kick out one and the rest of the family will follow, even if they have work. Efficient.

So we sit at the kitchen table. Pam's post-doc has seven months to go. She needs to finish—even with it it'll be hard to find work in the States, with all regulatory agencies under a hiring freeze. She's thinking about that, I can see. Eight years' work, and for what. I'll have to take Liddy, too—Pam can't work and care for her both. We have a month to get out. Meaning six months apart. The post-docs from China have to do worse than that all the time. But with Liddy so young.

We can protest, I say. Pam shakes her head, mouth bitter. Picks up In'tl Her-

ald Tribune. *Southern Club defaulting on all debt. Prediction of twenty-five percent reduction in world population called optimistic by. Civil war in India, in Mexico, in. Deforestation in. World temperature up another degree Centigrade since. Species going extinct—*

I've already read it.

Pam throws the paper aside, looking beat. Never seen her so grim. Stands to wash dishes. I watch her back and can see she's crying. Six months.

We are the aristocracy of the world. But this time the revolution will bring down more than the aristocracy. Could be everything. Crumpled newspaper, compartmentalized disaster. Catastrophe by percentage points.

We can avoid it, I swear we can. Must concentrate on that to be able to continue.

When the heart dies, you can't even grieve.

Tom rolled out of bed feeling old. Antediluvian. Contemporary of the background radiation. Eighty-one years old, actually. Well-propped by geriatric drugs which he abused assiduously, but still. He groaned, limped to the bathroom. Came awake and the great solitude settled on him again.

Standing in the doorway, looking out at the sage sunlight and not seeing a thing. Depression is like that. Sleep disrupted, affect blocked, nothing left but wood under the skin and an urge to cry. The best pills could do was to take the last feeling away and make it all wood. Which was a relief, although depressing in its own way if you considered it.

It was this: when his wife died he had gone crazy. And while he was crazy, he had decided never to become sane again. What was the point? Nothing mattered anymore.

Say two strong trees grow together, in a spiraling of trunks. Say one of the trees dies and is cut away. Say the other is left twisted like a corkscrew, an oddity, always turning in an upward reach, stretch, search. Leafy branches bobbing, searching the air for something lost forever.

So the great solitude settled on him. No one to talk to, nothing interesting to do. Even the things he had enjoyed doing alone were not the same, because the solitude in them was not the same as the great solitude. The great solitude had seeped into everything, into the sage sunlight and the rustle of leaves, and it had become the condition of his madness, the definition of it, its heart.

He stood in the doorway, feeling it.

Only now he had been disturbed. A face from the past. Had he really lived that life? Sometimes it was flatly impossible to believe. Surely every morning he woke up an entirely new creature, oppressed by false visions of false pasts. The great solitude provided a continuity of sorts, but perhaps it was just that he had been condemned to wake up every morning in the body of yet another creature under its spell. The Tom Barnard who ran buffeted in the storms of his twenties. Later the canny lawyer chopping away at the law of the land, changing it, replacing it with laws more just, more beautiful. We can escape our memes just as we escaped our genes! they had all cried then. Perhaps they were wrong on both accounts, but the belief of the moment, of that particular incarnation . . .

A face from a previous incarnation. My name is Bridey Murphy, I can speak Gaelic, I knew a Russian beauty once with raven hair and a wit like the slicer for electron microscopes. Sure you did—Anastasia, right? And he's your grandson, too, the builder. Sure. A likely story. We can escape our genes, perhaps it was true. If he himself woke a new creature every morning, why expect his daughter's son to bear any resemblance to any incarnation along the way? We live with strangers. We live with disjunctures; he had never done any of it; just as likely to have been raising bees in some bombed-out forest, or lying flat on his back in an old folks' home, choking for breath. Incarnations too, no doubt, following other lines. That he had carved this line to this spot, that the world had spun along to this sage sunlight and the great solitude; impossible to believe. He would never become sane again.

But that face. That tough sharp voice, its undercurrent of scorn. He had liked her, in Singapore, he had thought her . . . attractive. Exotic. And once he and his young wife had climbed up through the cactus on the back side of Rattlesnake Hill, to watch a sunset and make love in a grove of trees they had helped to plant some incarnations before, in a dream of children. Sylphlike naked woman, standing between trees in the dusk. And jumping across time, a ghost of joy. Like an arrow into wood, *thunk*. Pale smooth skin, dark rough bark, and in that vision a sudden spark, the ghost of an epiphany.

They shouldn't be allowed to take that hill.

Bridey Murphy, the canny lawyer, stirring inside. "God damn it," he cried, "why didn't you leave me alone!"

He limped back inside and threw on his clothes. He looked at the cascading sheets on the bed and sat on it and cried. Then he laughed, sitting there on his bed. "Shit," he said, and put on his shoes.

So he came down out of the hills. Through trees, sunbeams breaking in leaves, scuffing the trail, watching for birds. At Black Star Canyon road he got on his little mountain bike and coasted down to Chapman. Coming through the cleft in the hills he looked to the right, up Crawford Canyon to Rattlesnake Hill. Scrub and cactus, a little grove of live oak, black walnut, and sycamore on its round peak. The rest of the hills in view were all built up, exotic trees towering over homes, sure. Height equals money equals power. A miracle any hill was left bare. But OC Water District had owned Rattlesnake Hill before El Modena incorporated, and they were tough. Toughest watermasters in California, and that was saying a lot. So they had kept it clear. But a year or two before, they had deeded it over to the town; they hadn't needed it to fulfill their task, and the task was all that mattered to them. So now El Modena owned it, and they would have to decide what it was for.

Farther down Chapman he passed Pedro Sanchez, Emilia Deutsch, Sylvia Waters, and John Smith. "Hey, Tom Barnard! Tom!" They all yelled at him. Old friends all. "Doesn't anything ever change down here?" he said to them, braking to a halt. Big smiles, awkward chat. No, nothing ever changed. Or so it seemed. Nothing but him. "I'm off to find Kevin." "They're playing a game," Pedro told him. "Down on Esplanade." Invitations to come over for dinner, cheery good-byes. He biked off, feeling strange. This had been his town, his community. Years and years.

Down on the Esplanade diamonds a softball game was in progress. The sight of it stopped him, and again the wood in him was pierced by ghost arrows. He had to stop.

There on a rise behind the Lobos dugout lolled Nadezhda Katayev and a tall fat man, laughing at something. He gulped, felt his pulse in him. Out of the habit of talking; a great wash of something like grief passed through him, lifted the wood, buoyed it up. Grief, or . . .

He pedaled down and joined them. The man was the new town attorney, named Oscar. They were deciding which movie star each ballplayer most resembled. Nadezhda said Ramona looked like Ingrid Bergman, Oscar said she looked like Belinda Brav.

"Nah she's prettier than that," Tom murmured, and felt a little creak of surprise when they laughed.

"What about me?" Oscar said to Nadezhda.

"Um . . . maybe Zero Mostel."

"You must have had quite an interesting career as a diplomat."

"What about Kevin?" Tom said.

"Norman Rockwell," Nadezhda decided. "Hay in his mouth."

"That's not a movie star."

"Same thing."

"A cross between Lyle Sims and Jim Nabors," Oscar said.

"No crosses allowed," Nadezhda ruled. "One of the Little Rascals, anyway."

Kevin came to bat, swung at the first pitch and hit a sharp line drive to the outfield. By the time they got the ball back in he was standing on third, with a grin splitting his face. You could see every tooth he had.

Nadezhda said, "He's like a little kid."

"Nine years old forever," Tom said, and cupped his hands to yell "Nice hit!" Automatic. Instinctual behavior. Couldn't stop it. So much for changing your memes.

Kevin saw him and laughed, waved. "Little Rascals for sure," Nadezhda said.

They watched the game. Oscar lay back on the grass, rubbing one pudgy hand over the cut blades, looking up at clouds. The sea-breeze kept them cool. Fran Kratovil biked by, and seeing Tom she stopped, came over with a look of pleased surprise, greeted him, chatted a while before taking off. Old friends. . . .

Kevin came to bat again, lined another sharp hit. "He's hitting well," Tom said.

"Hitting a thousand," Oscar said.

"Wow."

"Hitting a thousand?"

They explained the system.

"He has a beautiful swing," she noted.

"Yes," Tom said. "That's a buggy whip swing."

"Buggy whip?"

"Quick wrists," Oscar said. "Flat swing, high bat speed. It looks like the bat has to bend to catch up with the rest of the swing."

"But why a buggy whip?"

Silence. Hesitantly, Tom said, "A buggy whip was a flexible pole, with a switch at the end. So it makes sense—a quick bat would look more like that than like a bull whip, which was like a piece of rope. Funny—I don't suppose anyone has actually seen a buggy whip for years, but they still have that name for the swing."

The other team came to bat, and got a rally going. "Ducks on the pond!" someone yelled.

"*Ducks* on the *pond?*"

"Runners in scoring position," Oscar explained. "From hunting."

"Do hunters shoot ducks when they're still on the water?"

"Hmm," Tom said.

Oscar said, "Maybe it means that knocking the runners in is easier than shooting ducks in the air."

"I don't know," Tom said. "It's more a question of potential. RBI time, you know."

"RBI time!" someone in the dugout yelled.

Then Doris came blasting over a grassy rise and coasted down to them, skidding to a halt.

"Hey, hi, Tom." She was excited. "I went to the town offices and checked through the planner's files to see if there were any re-zoning proposals in the works, and there are! There's one for Rattlesnake Hill!"

"Do you remember what the change was?" Oscar asked.

Doris gave him a look. "Five point four to three point two."

The two men thought about it.

Nadezhda said, "Is that an important change?"

"Five point four is open space," Oscar replied. He had rolled onto his side, and was lying on the grass with his massive head propped on one hand. "Three point two is commercial. How much are they proposing to change?"

Doris glared at him, incensed at his evident lack of concern. "Three hundred and twenty acres! It's the whole Water District lot—land I thought we were going to add to Santiago Creek Park. And damned if they aren't trying to slip it by in a comprehensive zoning package."

"It's stupid for Alfredo to try to slip all this stuff by," Tom said, thinking about it. "There's no way it'll work for long."

Oscar agreed. For the zoning change alone there would certainly have to be an environmental impact statement, and a rubber stamp town vote at the least—perhaps a contested town vote; and much the same would be true of any increase in the amount of water bought from MWD.

"The smart way to do it," Tom said, "would be to explain what you had in mind for the hill, and once that was generally approved of, get the necessary legislation through for it."

"It's almost as if . . ." Oscar said.

"As if he needs to do it this way." Tom nodded. "That's something to look for. If you can find out why he's trying to do the groundwork first, you might have found something useful." He gazed mildly at Doris and Oscar. Oscar rolled back onto his back. Doris gave Oscar a disgusted look, and fired away on her mountain bike.

After the game Oscar returned to work, and Nadezhda asked Tom to show her the hill in question. They went by Kevin and Doris's house, where Nadezhda was staying, then through the back garden to the bottom slope of the hill. An avocado grove extended up it fifty yards or so. "This is it. Crawford Canyon down there to the left, Rattlesnake Hill above."

"I thought so. It really is right behind their house."

Working in the grove was Rafael Jones, another old friend. "Hey, Tom! Everything okay?"

"Everything's fine, Rafe."

"Man, I haven't seen you in years! What brings you down here?"

Tom pointed a thumb at Nadezhda, and the other two laughed. "Yeah," Rafael said, "she's shaking up our house too." He was part of Kevin and Doris's household, the senior member and the house farmer; he ran their groves, and the garden. Tom asked him about the avocados and they chatted briefly. Feeling exhausted at the effort, Tom pointed uphill. "We're off to the top."

"Okay. Good to see you again, Tom, real good. Come on down and have dinner with us sometime."

Tom nodded and led Nadezhda up a trail. The irrigated greens gave way abruptly to deer-colored browns. It was May, which in southern California was the equivalent of late summer. Time for golden hills. Hesitantly Tom explained; southern California spring-time, when things bloomed, occurred from November through February, corresponding to the rainy season. Summer's equivalent would be March through May; and the dry brown autumn was June through October. Leaving no good equivalent for winter proper, which was about right.

He really had forgotten how to talk.

Up the trail, wending between scrub oak, black sage, purple sage, matilija poppy, horehound, patches of prickly pear. The sharp smells of the hot shrubs filled the air, dominated by sage. The ground was a loose light-brown dirt, liberally mixed with sandstone pebbles. Tom stopped to search for fossils in the outcrops of sandstone, but didn't find any. They were there, he told Nadezhda. Shark teeth from giant extinct species, scores of mollusk-like things, and the teeth of a mammal called a desmostylian, which had no close relatives either living or extinct—kind of a cross between a hippo and a walrus. All kinds of fossils up here.

Occasionally they disturbed a pheasant, or a crowd of crows. From time to time they heard the rustling of some small animal getting out of their way. The sun beat on their necks.

First a flat ridge, then up to the hill's broad top. The wind struck them coolly. They walked to the little grove of black walnut and sycamore and live oak at the hill's highest point, and sat in the shade of a sycamore, among big brown leaves.

Nadezhda stretched out contentedly. Tom surveyed the scene. The coastal plain was hazy in the late afternoon light. There was Anaheim Stadium, the big hospital in Santa Ana, the Matterhorn at Disneyland. Other than that, treetops. Below them the houses and gardens of El Modena caught the light and basked in it, looking like the town's namesake in Tuscany.

He asked her about her home, ignoring the ghosts in the grove. (A young couple, in there laughing. Beyond them children, planting foot-high trees.)

She was from Sebastopol in the Crimea, but spoke of India as her home. After many years there, she had moved back to Moscow. "That was hard."

"India changed you?"

"India changes everyone who visits it, if they stay long enough, and if they stay open to it. So many people—I understood then how it would be possible to overrun the Earth, and soon. I was twenty-four when I first arrived. It gave me a sense of urgency."

"But then you went back to Moscow."

"Yes. Moscow is nothing compared to India, ah! And then my government was strange regarding India. Work there and when you came back you found no one was listening to you anymore. You were tainted, you see. Made untouchable." She laughed.

"You did a lot of good work anyway."

"I could have done more."

They sat and felt the sun. Nadezhda poked a twig through dead leaves. Tom watched her hands. Narrow, long-fingered. He felt thick, old, melancholy. Be here now, he thought, be here now. So hard. Nadezhda glanced at him. She mentioned Singapore, and it came back to him again, stronger than ever. She had been one of the leaders of the conference. They had had drinks together, walked the crowded, hot, color-filled streets of Singapore, arguing conversion strategies just as fast as they could talk. He described the memory as best he could, and she laughed. It was the same laugh. She had a kind of Asian face, hawk-nosed and imperious. Cossack blood. The steppes, Turkestan, the giant spaces of central Asia. Slender, fashionable, she had dressed in Singapore with liberal flourishes of Indian jewelry and clothing. Still did. Of course now she sailed with Indians again.

He asked about her life since then.

"It has not been so very interesting to tell. For many years I lived and worked in Moscow." Her first husband had been assigned to Kazakhstan and she had done regional economic studies, until he was killed in the riots of a brief local insurgency. Back to Moscow, then to India again, where she met her second husband, a Georgian working there. To Kiev, back to Moscow. Second husband died of a heart attack, while they were on vacation. Scuba diving in the Black Sea.

Children?

A son in Moscow, two daughters in Kiev. "And you?"

"My daughter and her husband, Kevin's folks, are in space, working on solar collectors. Have been for years. My son died when he was young, in a car
accident."

"Ah."

"Kevin's sister is in Bangladesh. Jill."

"I have five grandchildren now, and a sixth is coming in a month." She
laughed. "I don't see them enough."

Tom grunted. He hadn't seen Jill in a year, his daughter in five. People moved
around too much, and thought that TV phones made up for it. He looked up at
the sun, blinking through leaves. So she had had two husbands die on her. And
here she was laughing in the sunlight, making patterns with dead leaves and
twigs, like a girl. Life was strange.

Back down the hill, in the sunset's apricot light. Tuscany in California. Kevin
and Doris's house glowed in its garden, the clear panels and domes gleaming
like a lamp lighting the surrounding trees. They went inside and joined the
chaos of dinnertime. The kids dashed around shrieking. Sixteen people lived
in the building, and at dinner time it seemed most of them were kids. Actually
only five. Rafael and Andrea were clearly delighted to see him; they had worked
together on El Modena's town charter, and yet it had been years. . . . They embarrassed Tom by getting out the good china and trying to get the whole house
down to the table. Tomas, however, wouldn't leave his work screen. Tom knew
Yoshi and Bob, they had been teachers when Kevin was in school. And he was
acquainted with Sylvia and Sam, Donna and Cindy. But what a crowd! Even before the great solitude had descended, he couldn't have lived in such a constant
gathering. Of course it was a big place, and they seldom got together like this.
But still . . .

After dinner Tom poured cups of coffee for him and Nadezhda, and they
went out to the atrium, where chairs were set around the fishpond. Overhead
the skylight's cloudgel fluttered a bit in the breeze, and from the kitchen voices
chattered, dishes clattered. The atrium was dark and cool, the cloudgel clear
enough to reveal the stars. The open end of the old horseshoe shape of the
apartment complex gave them a view west, and they were just enough up the
side of the hill that the lights from the town bobbed below, like the lamps of
night fishermen on a sea. They sipped coffee.

Doris rushed in, slammed the door, stomped off to the kitchen. "Where's
my dinner?" she shouted.

About fifteen minutes later Kevin came in, looking pleased. He had been
flying with Ramona, he said, and they had gone out to dinner afterward.

Doris brought him right back to earth with her news of the zoning proposal. "It's definitely Rattlesnake Hill they're after."

"You're kidding," Kevin said feebly. He collapsed onto one of the atrium chairs. "That bastard."

"We're going to have a fight on our hands," Doris predicted grimly.

"We knew that already."

"It's worse now."

"Okay, okay, it's worse now. Great."

"I'm just trying to be realistic."

"I know, I know." They went into the kitchen still discussing it. "Who the fuck ate everything?" Doris roared.

Nadezhda laughed, said quietly to Tom, "Sometimes I am thinking perhaps my Doris would not be unhappy if those two got back together."

"*Back* together?"

"Oh yes. They have had their moments, you know."

"I didn't know."

"Nothing very much. And a long time ago. When they first moved into this house, apparently. They almost moved into a room together, but then they didn't. And then Doris came over to work for me for a time. She told me about it then, when she was really feeling it. Then when she returned things were not working out so much, I guess. But I think she is still a bit in love with him."

Tom considered it. "I guess I hadn't noticed." How could he, up in the hills? "She does watch him a lot."

"But then there is this Ramona."

"Yeah, that's what Kevin just said. But I thought she lived with Alfredo."

Nadezhda filled him in on the latest. Telling him about the affairs of his own townspeople, and with a buoyant, lively curiosity. With pleasure. And she made it all so . . . suddenly he wanted to feel like she did, he wanted that *engagement* with things.

"Ah," he said, confused at himself. Hawk-nosed Asian beauty, gossiping to him in the dark atrium. . . .

They sat and watched stars bouncing on the other side of the cloudgel. Time passed.

"Will you be staying here tonight?" she asked.

The house had several spare rooms, but Tom shook his head. "It's an easy ride home, and I prefer sleeping there."

"Of course. But if you'll excuse me, I think I will be going to bed."

"Sure, sure. Don't mind me. I'll be setting off in a while."

"Thanks for taking me up on the hill. It's a good place, it should be left alone."

"We'll see. I was glad to go up there again myself."

She walked up the stairs to the second floor, then around the inner balcony to the southeast curve of the horseshoe, where the best guestroom was. Tom watched her disappear, thinking nothing. Feelings fluttered into him like moths banging into a light. Creak of wood. So long since he had done any of this! It was strange, strange. Long ago it had been like this, as if he slept years every night, and woke up in a new world every morning. That voice, laughing on the streets of Singapore—was it really them? Had it happened to him? Impossible, really. It must be. And yet . . . a disjuncture, again—between what he felt to be true, and what he knew to be fact. All those incarnations made his life.

He stood slowly. Tired. It would be a long ride home, but suddenly he wanted to be there. Needed to be there.

The next couple of weeks were warm and humid, and there was a dull feeling of tension in the air, as if more and more static electricity were building, as if any day a Santa Ana wind would come pouring over the hills and blow them all into the sea.

Tom didn't come back down into town, and eventually Nadezhda got in the habit of going to see him. Sometimes he was there, sometimes he wasn't. When she found him at home they talked, in fits and starts; when he wasn't there she worked in his garden. Once she saw him slipping away as she hiked up the last stretch of trail, and realized he was having trouble adjusting to so much company. She stopped going, and spent her days with Doris or Kevin or Oscar, or Rafael and Andrea, or her other housemates. And then one evening Tom showed up at the house, to have a cup of coffee after dinner. Ready to talk for an hour or two, then slip away.

Kevin and Ramona fell into a pattern of a different sort; they got together in the late afternoon after work, every few days, to go flying, and then perhaps have dinner. While in the air they talked over the day's work, or something equally inconsequential. Out of nowhere, it seemed, Kevin had found an instinct for avoiding certain topics—for letting Ramona choose what to talk about, and then following along. It was a sort of tact he had never had; he hadn't cared enough, he hadn't been paying enough attention to the people he was with. But on these flights he was *really* paying attention, with the same dreamlike intensity he had felt on their first flight. Every excursion aloft was a whole and distinct adventure, the most important part of his day by far. Just to soar around the sky like that, to feel the wind lift them like a gull . . . to see the land, lying below like a gift on a plate!

And there was something wonderful about working so hard in tandem, harnessed to the same chain, legs pumping in the same rhythm. The physicality of it, the things they learned about each other's characters while at the edge of physical endurance—the constant reminder of their bodies, of their animal reality . . . add that to their softball games, and the swim workouts they sometimes joined in the mornings, and there wasn't much they didn't know about each other, as animals.

And so Kevin paid attention. And they pumped madly in the seats of the Ultralite, and soared through the air. And pointed out the sights below, and talked about nothing but the present moment. "Look at that flock of crows," Kevin would say, pointing at a cloud of black-dot birds below.

"Gangsters," Ramona would reply.

"No, no! I really like crows!" She would laugh. "I do, don't you? They're such powerful flyers, they don't look pretty but they do it with such efficiency."

"Fullbacks of the air."

"Exactly!" There were thousands of crows in Orange County, living in great flocks off the fruit of the groves. "I like their croaky voices and the sheen on their wings, and that smart look in their eye when they watch you"—he was discovering all this in himself only at the moment he spoke it, so that it felt marvelous to speak, to discover—"and the way they hop sideways all shaggy and awkward. I really love them!"

And Ramona would laugh harder at each declaration. And Kevin would never speak of other things, knowing it was what she wanted. And she would fly them around the sky, more graceful than the crows, as graceful as the gulls, and the sweat would dry white on their skins as they worked like dervishes in the sky. And Kevin's heart . . . well, it was full. Brimming. But he had an instinct, now, telling him what to do. Telling him to bide his time.

Thus the most important part of his life, these days, was taking place two or three hundred feet in the air. Of course he was concerned about the workings of the town council, and it took up a fair amount of time, but from week to week he didn't worry about it much. They were waiting for Alfredo to make his next move, and doing what they could to find out more about his intentions. Doris had a friend in the financial offices of her company, who had a friend in a similar job with Heartech, and she was digging carefully there to find out what the rumors were in Alfredo's base of operations. There were rumors of a move, in fact. Perhaps they could get more details out of this friend of a friend; Doris was excited by the possibility, and put a lot of work into it, talking, acting innocent and ignorant, asking questions over lunches.

Then the re-zoning proposal appeared on the agenda, and it included the re-zoning of the old OCWD tract. Doris and Kevin walked into the council meeting like hunters settling into a blind.

It was a much more modest affair than the inaugural meeting; the people who had to be there were there, and that was it. The long room was mostly empty and dark, with all the light and people crowded into the business end of things. Alfredo ran the meeting through its paces with his usual efficiency, only lightly peppering things with jokes and asides. Then he came to item twelve. "Okay, let's get to the big stuff—re-zoning proposals."

Petitioners in the audience laughed as if that were another of his jokes. Kevin hunched forward in his seat, put his elbows on the table.

Doris, seeing the way Kevin's hands were clenched, decided she had better do the talking. "What about this change for the Crawford Canyon lots, Alfredo?"

"They're the lots that OCWD used to own. And the land up above it, across from Orange Hill."

"That's called Rattlesnake Hill," she said sharply.

"Not on the maps."

"Why a zoning change? That land was supposed to be added to Santiago Park."

"No, nothing's been decided about that land, actually."

"If you go back to the minutes of the meeting where those Crawford Canyon condos were condemned, I think you'll find that was the plan."

"I don't recall what was discussed then, but nothing was ever done about it."

"Going from five point four to three point two is a big change," Jerry Geiger noted.

"It sure is!" Kevin said loudly. "It means you could do major commercial building. What's the story, Alfredo?"

"The planning commission wanted to be able to consider that land as a possibility for various projects, isn't that right, Mary?"

Mary looked down at her notes. "Three point two is a general purpose classification."

"Meaning you could do almost anything up there!" Kevin exclaimed.

He was losing his temper already. Doris scowled at him, tried to take back their side of the argument. "It's actually commercial zoning, isn't it, Mary?"

"It allows commercial development, yes, but doesn't mandate it—"

Face red with emotion, Kevin said, "That is the *last empty hill in El Modena!*"

"Well," Alfredo said calmly. "No need to get upset. I know it's more or less in your backyard, but still, for the good of the town—"

"Where I live has nothing to do with it!" Kevin exclaimed, sliding his chair back as if he might stand. "What the fuck does that have to do with anything?"

A shocked silence, a titter. Doris elbowed Kevin in the side and then stepped hard on his foot. He glanced at her, startled.

"Don't you need an EIS for a change like that?" she said quickly.

"Zoning changes in themselves don't require impact statements," Alfredo said.

"Oscar, is that right?" Doris asked.

Oscar nodded slowly, doing his sleeping Buddha routine. "They are not re-quired, but they can be requested."

"Well I request one!" Kevin said. "Anything could be done up there!"

"I second the request," Doris said. "Meanwhile, I want to have some things on record. Who made this re-zoning proposal, and why?"

An odd, expectant silence. Finally Alfredo said, gently, "As Kevin pointed out, this land includes one of the last empty hilltops in the area. As such, the land is extremely valuable. *Extremely* valuable. When we condemned those condos under the hill, I thought it was so we would be able to put the land to use that would better serve the whole town. That's what I said at the time. Now, if the land is made part of Santiago Park, that's nice for the park, and for the people living in the immediate area—"

Kevin's chair scraped the floor.

"We all live in the immediate area," Doris said, smacking her knee into Kevin's and wishing she had a cattle prod.

"Okay, okay," Alfredo said. "Some people are closer than others, but we're all in the neighorhood. And that's the point. That land is valuable to all of us, and Matt and I think all of us are concerned to see that it is used in the best way possible for the good of the town."

"Do you have a specific plan for it?" Jerry Geiger asked suddenly.

"Well, no. We only want the possibility to be there."

"Does this explain the request to buy more water from MWD?" Jerry asked, looking interested.

"Well, if we had the water . . ." Alfredo said, and Matt picked up the thought:

"If we had the water and the land was zoned for commercial use, then we could begin to look seriously at how to make use of the situation."

"You haven't looked seriously up till this point," Jerry said, sounding sardonic—though with Jerry it was hard to be sure.

"No, no. We've talked ideas, sure. But . . ."

Alfredo said, "Of course nothing can done unless the infrastructural pos-sibility is there. But that's what our job is, to make sure the possibilities are there."

"Possibilities for what?" Kevin said, his voice rising. Doris attempted to step on his foot again, but he moved it. "First you're thinking about upping the water from MWD, supposedly because it saves us money. Then we're given a zoning change with no explanation, and when we ask for an explanation we get vague statements about possibilities. I want to know what exactly you have in mind, Alfredo, and why you're going about all this in such an underhanded manner."

For a split second Alfredo glared at him. Then he turned away and said in a relaxed, humorous voice, "To repeat this proposal, made before the full council in the course of a normal council meeting, we are interested in re-zoning these lots so that we can then discuss using them in some way. Currently they are zoned five point four, which is open land and only open land—"

"That's what they should be zoned!" Kevin said, nearly shouting.

"That's your opinion, Kevin, but I don't believe it's generally shared, and I have the right to express my belief by proposing a change of this sort. Don't you agree?"

Kevin waved a hand in disgust. "You can propose all you want, but until you explain what you mean to do you haven't made a full proposal. You've only just tried to slip one by. The question is, what do you have in mind to do on that land? And you haven't answered it."

Doris tightened the corners of her mouth so she wouldn't smile. There was something to be said for the mad dog approach, after all. Kevin's bluntness had taken Alfredo aback, if only for a moment. He was searching for an answer, and everyone could see it.

Finally Alfredo said, "I haven't answered that question because there is no answer to it. We have no specific plans for that land. We only want to make it possible to think about it with some expectation that the thought could bear fruit. It's useless to think about it unless we zone the land in a way that would make development legal. That's what we're proposing to do."

"We want an EIS," Doris said. "It's obvious we'll need one, since as you say the re-zoning would mean a great deal for that land. Can we vote on that?"

They voted on it, and found they were unanimously in favor of an environmental impact statement on the proposed zoning change. "Of course," Alfredo said easily. "These are facts we need to know."

But the look he gave them as they got up at the end of the meeting, Doris thought, was not a friendly one. Not friendly at all. She couldn't help smiling back. They had gotten to him.

Not long after that the Lobos had their first game of the season with the Vanguards, and from the moment Kevin stepped into the batter's box and looked out at Alfredo standing on the pitcher's mound, he could see that Alfredo was going to pitch him tough. The council meetings, Kevin and Ramona's flights over the town—if Alfredo had not seen them himself, he had surely heard of them, and what did he think of that? Kevin had his suspicions. . . . Even the fact that Kevin was still batting a thousand, a perfect seventeen for seventeen—oh, yes. Alfredo had his reasons, all right.

And he was a good pitcher. Now softball is a hitter's game, and a pitcher isn't going to strike a batter out; but that doesn't mean there's nothing he can do but serve it up. If the pitcher hits the back of the square of carpet that marks the strike zone with a high-arced pitch, it becomes damned difficult to hit the ball hard. Alfredo was good at this kind of pitch. And he had honed the psychological factor, he had the look of a power pitcher, that Don Drysdale sneer of confident disdain, saying *you can't hit me*. This was a ludicrous look for a softball pitcher to have, given the nature of the game, but somehow on Alfredo it had its effect.

So he stared in at Kevin with that contemptuous grin, seeming both not to recognize him and to personally mark him out at the same time. Then he threw up a pitch so high that Kevin immediately decided not to swing at it.

Unfortunately it landed right in the middle of the carpet. Strike one. And in their league batters got only two strikes, so Kevin was only a pitch away from striking out.

Alfredo's sneer grew wider than ever, and his next pitch was ridiculously high. Kevin judged it would fall short, and held up. He was right by no more than an inch, whew! One and one.

Unfazed, Alfredo threw up another pitch just like the previous one, only a touch deeper, and with a sudden jolt of panic Kevin judged it would be a strike. He swung hard, and was more surprised than anyone when he saw the ball flying deep into right-center field, rocketed by the desperation of Kevin's swing. Whew! He ran to second and smiled at his teammates, who were cheering loudly from the dugout. Alfredo, of course, did not turn around to look at him. Kevin laughed at his back.

In subsequent innings Alfredo walked Kevin twice. He was ridden hard for this failure by Kevin's teammates, and he got noticeably sharper as he urged on his own teammates. Meanwhile the rest of the Lobos were hitting him unusually well also. So it was not a good game for Alfredo, and the Lobos were ahead 9–4 when the Vanguards came up for the last time. Alfredo himself led off, and hit a single up the middle. He stood on first shouting to his teammates, clapping with an excess of energy.

The next batter, Julie Hanson, hit a hard line drive over Kevin's head. Kevin went to cover third, and then he was in that weird moment when things were happening all around him and he was very much a part of it, but not doing a thing: watching Mike race over and cut the ball off, seeing Alfredo barrel around second on his way to third, seeing Mike throw the ball hard toward him. He straddled the base to take the throw on one bounce. The ball tailed off to the right and he jumped out to stop it, and at the same moment he caught it *boom!* Alfredo slammed into him, knocking him head over heels into foul territory.

Dazed, Kevin shook his head. He was on hands and knees. The ball was still in his glove. He looked over at Fred Spaulding, who had his thumb up in the out sign. People were converging on them from all directions, shouting loudly. Alfredo was standing on third base, yelling angrily himself—something about Fred's umpiring. A crowd was gathering, and someone helped Kevin to his feet.

He took the ball from his glove and walked over to Alfredo, who eyed him warily. Without planning to he flipped the ball against Alfredo's chest, where it thunked and fell to the ground. "You're out," he said harshly, hearing his voice in a way he usually didn't.

He turned to walk away, was suddenly jerked around by the arm. He saw it was Alfredo and instantly lashed out with a fist, hitting Alfredo under the ear at about the same time that Alfredo's right struck him in the mouth. He fell, and then he and Alfredo and several others were in a chaotic clump of wrestling bodies, Alfredo screaming abuse, Kevin cursing and trying to get an arm free to swing again, Fred shouting at them to stop it and Mike and Doris and Ramona doing the same, and there were hands all over him pulling him away, restraining him. He found himself held by a bunch of hands; he could have broken free of them, but they were friends' hands for the most part, recognizable as such by feel alone. Across a stretch of grass Alfredo was similarly held. Alfredo glared furiously across the gap, shouting something at Fred. Nothing anyone said was comprehensible, it was as if he stood under an invisible bell jar that cut off all meaning, but in the cacophony he suddenly heard Ramona shriek "*What do you think you're doing!*" He took his eyes from Alfredo for an instant, afraid she meant him. But Ramona was transfixing Alfredo with a fierce look, it was him she was yelling at. Kevin wondered where he'd hit him. His right knuckles were throbbing.

"Fuck that!" Alfredo was shouting at Fred, "Fuck that! He was in the baseline, what'm I supposed to do? It's perfectly legal, it happens all the time!"

This was true.

"He's the one that started something," Alfredo shouted. "What the fuck is this?"

"Oh shut up, Alfredo," Ramona interjected. "You know perfectly well you started it."

Alfredo spared only a second to glare at her, but it was a cold, cold glare. He turned back to Fred: "Well? Are you going to do your job?"

A bunch of people from both teams began shouting accusations again. Fred pulled a whistle from under his shirt and whistled them down. "Shut up! Shut up! Shut up! I'm going to stop the game and give you both defeats if you don't get back to your dugouts! Come on, this is stupid. Move it!" He walked over to the clump of Lobos holding Kevin, and said, "Kevin, you're out of the game. This whole thing is your fault."

Loud contradictions from Kevin's teammates.

"—when you're in the baseline!" Fred carried over them. "The runner has the right to the baseline, and fielders have no complaint if they get run into while standing in it. So there was no call to throw the ball at him. Go sit it out. There's only a couple outs to go anyway, and I want to get this game finished so the next one can begin! Move it!"

Kevin found himself being pulled back toward the dugout. He was sitting on the bench. His throat was sore—had he been shouting too? Must have been.

Ramona was sitting next to him, hand on his arm. Suddenly he was aware of that touch, of a strong hand, trembling slightly, supporting him. She was on his side. Publicly. He looked at her and raised his eyebrows.

She took her hand away, and now it was his body that was quivering. Perhaps it had been his all along.

"That bastard," she said, with feeling. She stared across at Alfredo, who stood in his dugout still shouting at Fred.

Kevin could only swallow and nod.

After the game—which the Lobos held on to win—Kevin walked away a bit dazed, and considerably embarrassed. To be kicked out of a softball game, my Lord. It happened occasionally, especially between certain rival teams who tended to drink beer during the game. But it was rare.

He heard Alfredo's voice all the way across the field, and turned to look for him, surprised by the intensity of his dislike. That little figure over on the hillside, surrounded by its friends . . . a bundling, a node of everything he despised. If only he could have gotten in one more punch, he would have flattened him—

"Hi, Kev."

He jumped, afraid his thoughts could be read on his face. "Hi, Ramona."

"Pretty exciting game."

"Yeah."

"Here, come with me. I have to teach the afternoon class, but it ends early and then we can go flying."

"Sure." Kevin had been planning to return to work too, but they were finishing the Campbell house, and Hank and Gabriela could take care of clean-up for the afternoon.

They biked over to the high school, and Kevin showered in the gym. The old room brought back a lot of memories. His mouth hurt, the upper lip was swelling on one side. He combed his hair, futile task, and went up to Ramona's class. She was already into a lecture, and Kevin said hi to the kids and sat in the back.

The lecture had to do with population biology, the basic equations that determined population flux in a contained environment. The equations were nonlinear, and gave a rough model for what could be seen in the outside world, populations of a given species rising and falling in a stable but unpredictable, non-repeating cycle. This concept was counter-intuitive and Ramona took a long time explaining it, using examples and moving into a conversational style, with lots of questions from the students.

Their lab took up the whole top floor of one building, and the afternoon light poured in all the western windows and shattered blue in Ramona's black hair. She brought Kevin into the discussion and he talked about the variety of biologic systems used in modern architecture, settling on the example of Chinese carp in an atrium pool. These fish were among the steadiest in terms of numbers, but the equations still held when describing fluctuations in their population, and they were put to immediate use in deciding the size of the pool, the number of fish to be harvested, and so on.

Still, the nonlinearity of the equations, the tendency for populations to suddenly jump up or down, confused some of the students. Kevin could understand this, as it always struck him as a mystery as well.

Ramona dragged out a Lorenz waterwheel to give them a concrete example. This was a simple waterwheel with twelve buckets around its rim, and it could turn in either direction. When the water was turned on from a hose hung above the wheel, the slowest stream of water wouldn't move the wheel at all; slowly the top bucket filled and then water dribbled over its side to the tub below. At a moderate flow the top bucket filled and tilted off to one side, and after that the wheel turned in a stately circle, buckets emptying on the bottom and partially filling under the hose. This was what they all expected, this was what common sense and experience from the outside world would suggest was normal. Thus it was even more of a surprise when Ramona turned up the water from the hose, and the wheel began to turn rapidly in one direction, slow down, speed up, *reverse direction*—

The class gasped at the first reversal, laughed, chattered. The wheel moved erratically, buckets sometimes filling to the brim, sometimes flashing under the hose. Chaotic movement, created by the simplest of inputs. Ramona moved from wheel to blackboard, working through the equations that described this oddity, which was actually quite common in nature. Then she set the students to exercises to demonstrate the issue for themselves, and they crowded around computer screens to see the results of their work in spectacularly colored displays.

Kevin sat at the back and watched her work. Despite her ease and laughter there was something objective, even formal in her manner. The kids were relaxed but respectful around her, and if they horsed around excessively a laser glance from her dark eyes would be enough to put them back to the task. Remembering their own days in high school—in the very same room—Kevin had to laugh: she had been a hell-raiser then. Maybe that was an advantage, now that it was her job to keep control. Station to station, running each student through the work, making sure they understood, moving on with instructions for further experiments on-screen. . . . It was clear she was a good teacher, and that was a pleasure to see. It was important for a teacher to have a certain distance, she should be liked and admired but also at a distance, a strong personality presenting a strong and coherent portrait of the world. This is the way the world is! the strong teacher says in every phrase and glance; not to downplay the complexity of the world, but to present a clear and distinct single view of it, which students could then work against in building their own views. It wasn't so important that the teacher present all sides of a case, or pretend to neutrality in controversial issues. Over the years the multiplicity of teachers that every student got would take care of that. What was more important was that a teacher advocate a vivid, powerful set of ideas, to be a force, to make an impact. Population biology was still a seething mass of theoretical controversy, for instance, but Ramona argued the case for her beliefs as firmly as if speaking to a dissertation committee judging her—outlining other opinions, but then countering them with the ones she believed in. And the students listened. Kevin too.

Then class was done, and they were out in the late afternoon's honey light. The color of high school swim team workouts. "Come on, we just have enough time to tour El Toro before dinner. I've got to make the meal tonight, you can help."

"Sure." They were going to have to gain altitude fast to catch up to Kevin.

Dear Claire:

I am here.

I arrived three weeks ago, and was offered my choice of housing: I could lease a small empty tract house, or I could take up residence in a large communal home which had some empty rooms. I went to visit the communal home, and found it occupied by a number of extraordinarily friendly, healthy, energetic, and beautiful people. Naturally I chose the small empty tract house. Note address below.

The town is indeed as arcadian as I thought when visiting for the interviews—idyllic or bucolic, depending on mood. Part of it lies just under foothills; then these same foothills form the middle of the town, geographically, though they are sparsely populated; and behind the foothills there is a section of high canyon within the town limits. Most of the town seems to consist of gardens, truck farms, nurseries—in any case, land in cultivation—except for that given over to bike paths, swimming pools, or sport fields. Orchards are popular. Although we are in Orange County, the trees seem mostly to be lemon, avocado, olive—I promise at first opportunity I will open the tree guide you gave me, and figure out which. I know you will want to know.

There is just as much sun as legends say, perhaps more. Three weeks of it and I feel a bit stunned. Imagine the effect of lifetimes of it, and you will more fully understand the local culture.

They bike to excess. In fact there is no public transport except for car rentals on the freeways, which are expensive. Motorbikes are even more expensive. Obviously the feeling is that your own legs should move you. People here have strong legs.

On the other hand they don't know who Groucho Marx is. And as far as I can determine, not only is there no live theater in El Modena—the whole county is bare of it! Yes, I'm in the Gobi. I'm in Nova Zemlya. I'm in—yes—*I'm in Orange County*. I'm in the land where culture consists of a vigorous swim workout, followed by a discussion of the usefulness of hand paddles.

I witnessed this very discussion the other day, when my new friend Kevin urged me to come by the pool. I dropped by and saw about thirty people, swimming back and forth. Back and forth, and back and forth. And so on. Very, very energetically. The exercise certainly creates some beautiful bodies—something I'd rather watch than have, as you know.

At one point Kevin leaped out salmonlike and invited me to join them. I explained that an allergy, alas, prevented me from doing so.

Oh too bad, he said. Allergic to chlorine?

To exertion.

Oh, wow—what a shame!

I suggested to him that they were wasting a fine energy source. Look, I said, if you were only to tie lines to your ankles, and have the lines wound on spools that offered a little resistance, then it might be possible to store some small fraction of the calories used to swim across the pool. One or more solar panels could be retired from service, the constellations made less cluttered. Kevin nodded thoughtfully. Good idea! he said. But he bogged down in design difficulties, and promised he would get back to me.

Kevin, by the way, is the builder I've hired to renovate my new domicile; he's a bioarchitect. Yes, the latest thing, it's my style now. In fact I saw several examples of Kevin's work before hiring him, and he is very good—a sort of poet of homes, with a talent for spacious, sculpted interior space. My hopes are high.

Having seen his work, it was at first disconcerting to meet Kevin himself, because in person he strikes one as a very ordinary carpenter: tall, lanky, loose in a way that makes you immediately confident that he can field grounders with the best of them. He grins a lot. In fact he wandered through my whole house grinning, on his first visit; but with a squint that could have indicated Deep Thought. I hope so. In any case, a new friend. He laughs at my extravagances, I at his, and in our mutual amazement we are both well entertained.

And actually Kevin is the emperor of intellect, compared to his partner

Hank. Hank is short and balding, with forearms as thick as his neck. He's in his mid-forties, though he looks older than that. Apparently he was once a student in the seminary of that Native American church down in New Mexico, and it shows. He is prone to sudden spells of gaping. He'll be working at a maniac's pace (the only one he has) when *bang* he'll stop whatever he is doing and stare open-mouthed at it, entranced. Say he is sawing a two-by-four when he's trans-fixed, perhaps by a knot in the wood. Seconds pass; a minute or two may pass. Then: We are whorls of pattern, he'll say in an awed tone, tossed out by the surging universe.

What's the matter, Hank? Gabriela will call from across the house. Find a bug?

Once when they were talking I heard him say, Hard to believe they've bro-ken up, I remember when those two was so close they would've held water.

Another time he was describing a fight Kevin and the town's mayor had on the softball diamond (a famous fight, this; these people gossip so much they make Chicago seem like a city of mutes—you won't believe that, but it's true), and he said, Alfredo was so worked up it's lucky he has two nostrils.

People are always dropping by to talk to him, I'm not sure why. As far as I can tell they seem in want of advice, although about what I couldn't guess. Hank is always happy to see them, and they chat as he works, or go out and sit in the driveway, sometimes for a good part of the day. Between that and the gaping I would say he is not the driving element in the team.

And the way their third partner Gabriela stares at him! He never ceases to amaze her. She's younger than the men are, hired straight out of school a year or two ago, to keep up their energy, Hank explained. She has a piercing eye, and a sharp tongue as well, and a wild laugh, usually inspired by her two partners. They can lay her flat on the floor.

It may be a while before work on my house is completed.

Other entertainment: I am joined here by a fellow exile, a Soviet woman named Nadezhda Katayev. She is here visiting an acquaintance of hers, one Doris Nakayama. Doris works in superconductors, and has perhaps been affected by too close contact with her materials. She is cool, tough, humorless; boggled by my bulk and confused by my speech. But she does have this friend Nadezhda, who, if she were not in her seventies and the spitting image of my grandmother, would soon be the object of my advances. Maybe she will be anyway. We loaf around town together like two aging diplomats, assigned to a backwater post in the twilight of our careers.

Our latest expedition was to a garden party. Ah yes, I thought: country culture. A pastoral Proustian affair, drinks in the topiary, flower-beds and hedges, perhaps even a maze. Nadezhda and I biked over together, me dressed in colonial whites, trundling along with other cyclists gazelling by me on both sides, and Nadezhda in a flower print dress which constantly threatened to get caught in the spokes of her bike.

We were greeted at the door of the Sanchez's big communal house by our hostess Ramona Sanchez, who was dressed in her usual outfit of gym shorts and a T-shirt, plus giant canvas gardening gloves. Yes, this was a garden party; meaning we all were supposed to go out and work in the garden.

So I spent the better part of an afternoon sitting in my whites on newly turned earth, making repartee with dissected worms and keeping close track of the progress of my blisters. The only consolations were the beer, Nadezhda's mordant commentary, muttered to me in delicious counterpoint to her polite public pronouncements, and the sight of Ramona Sanchez's long and leggy legs. Ramona is the town beauty; she looks like either Ingrid Bergman or Belinda Brav, depending on whether you take my word or Nadezhda's. Currently she is the focus of a great deal of gossip, as she recently broke up with her long-time mate Alfredo the mayor. My friend Kevin is interested in taking Alfredo's place, but then so am I—the difference being that Ramona appears to reciprocate some of Kevin's regard, while for me she has only a disinterested friendliness.

Though she did join me to weed for a half hour or so. I argued the civil rights of the poor decimated or bimated worms, writhing around us. Ramona assured me in her best biology teacher style that they were beneath pain, and that I would approve the sacrifice when I ate the food that resulted from it. A specialty of the area? I asked, squinting with trepidation. Luckily she only meant the salad.

Well, you get the idea. It really exists! Arcadia! Bucolica! Marx's "idiocy of rural life"! I don't think I truly believed it until now.

Not that the town is free of trouble! My daily workload reminds me constantly that in fact it exists entangled in intricate webs of law. Their system is a mix, combining a communalism of the Santa Rosa model—land and public utilities owned in common, residents required to do ten hours a week of town work, a couple of town-owned businesses in operation to use all the labor available, that sort of thing—with aspects of the new federal model: residents are taxed more and more heavily as they approach the personal income cap, and they can direct 60 percent of their taxes to whatever services they support the most. Businesses based in town are subject to the same sort of graduated system. I am familiar with much of this from my years in Bishop, which has a similar system. As usual in these set-ups, the town is fairly wealthy, even if it is avoided by businesses looking for the best break possible. From all the income generated, a town share is distributed back out to the citizens, which comes to about twice the national income floor. But people still complain that it isn't higher. Everyone wants to be a hundred. And here they believe that a properly run town could make everyone hit the cap as a matter of course. Thus there is the kind of intense involvement with town politics typical of these set-ups, government mixed with business mixed with life-styles, etc.

And so there is also the usual array of Machiavellian battles. Prominent among these at the moment is an attempt by the mayor to appropriate an empty hilltop for his own company's offices. He's got at least an even chance of succeeding, I'd say; he appears popular, and people want the town shares larger. Moving Heartech into town would certainly do that, as it's a very successful medtech company, right at the legal limit for company size.

The opposition to the mayor comes mainly from Kevin and his friends, and they are getting a quick education, with little or no help from the Green party brass, a fact I find faintly suspicious. Most recently they got the council to order an EIS for the zoning change that would make development possible, and they thought this was a big victory. You see what I mean about naïveté! Naturally the town planner, a functionary of the mayor's, went out and hired Higgins, Ramirez, and Bretner to do the EIS, so we'll get another LA Special in a few weeks from the infamous HRB, urging the creation of an environment by development as soon as possible. And my friends will learn that an EIS is just one more cannon on the battlefield, to be turned in different directions depending on who holds it. I'm going to take them up to Sally and let her educate them.

But enough for this time, or too much.

Do write again. I know it is a lost and dead form of communication, but surely we can say things in correspondence that calls would never allow. As for instance, I miss you. In fact I miss almost all of my life in Chicago, which has disappeared like a long vivid dream. "I feel as if great blocks of my life have broken off and fallen into the sea," isn't that how Durrell puts it in the *Quartet?* I suppose I should consider El Modena my Cycladean isle, removed from the Alexandrian complexities of Chi and my life there; here I can do my work in peace, far from the miseries of the entanglement with E, etc. And there's something to it. Waking every morning to yet another sunny day, I do feel a Grecian sense of light, of ease. It is no accident that the old real estate hucksters called this coast Mediterranean.

So, I will sit under my lemon trees, recover, write my reflections on a hillside Venus. Anxiously await your next. Thanks for sending the latest poems as well. You are as clear as Stevens; forge on with that encouragement in mind. Meanwhile I remain,

Your Oscar

...4

Light cracks on the black gloss of the canal, and a gondola oar squeaks under us. Standing on the moonlit bridge, laughing together, listening to the campanile strike midnight, I decide to change Kid Death's hair from black to red—"

Something like that. Ah yes—the vibrant author's journal in The Einstein Intersection, young mind speaking to young mind, brilliant flashes of light in the head. No doubt my image of Europe owes much to it. But what I've found . . . could half a century have changed that much? History, change—rate constants, sure. It feels so much as if things are accelerating. A wind blows through the fabric of time, things change faster than we can imagine. Punctuated equilibrium, without the equilibrium. Hey, Mr. Delany, here I am in Europe writing a book too! But yesterday I spent the morning at the Fremdenkontrolle, arguing in my atrocious German which always makes me feel brain-damaged, getting nowhere. They really are going to kick me out. And in the afternoon I did laundry, running around the building in the rain to the laundry room, Liddy howling upstairs at a banged knee. Last load dry and piled in the red basket, jogging round the front I caught my toe on a board covering the sidewalk next to some street work, fell and spilled clothes all over the mud of the torn-up street. I sat on the curb and almost cried. What happened, Mr. Delany? How come instead of wandering the night canals I'm dumping my laundry in the street? How come when I consider revisions it's not "change Kid Death's hair from black to red" but "throw out the first draft and start the whole thing over"?

And only two weeks before Liddy and I leave.

What a cheat utopias are, no wonder people hate them. Engineer some fresh start, an island, a new continent, dispossess them, give them a new planet sure! So they don't have to deal with our history. Ever since More they've been doing it: rupture, clean cut, fresh start.

So the utopias in books are pocket utopias too. Ahistorical, static, why should we read them? They don't speak to us trapped in this world as we are, we look at

*them in the same way we look at the pretty inside of a paperweight, snow drifting
down, so what? It may be nice but we're stuck here and no one's going to give us
a fresh start, we have to deal with history as it stands, no freer than a wedge in
a crack.*

Stuck in history like a wedge in a crack
With no way out and no way back—
Split the world!

*Must redefine utopia. It isn't the perfect end-product of our wishes, define
it so and it deserves the scorn of those who sneer when they hear the word. No.
Utopia is the process of making a better world, the name for one path history can
take, a dynamic, tumultuous, agonizing process, with no end. Struggle forever.*

Compare it to the present course of history. If you can.

One Saturday morning before dawn, Kevin, Doris, and Oscar biked down to
the Newport Freeway, shivering in chill wet air. They checked out a car from a
sleepy state worker and took off.

The freeway was dead at that hour, in all lanes. Quickly they hummed up
to the car's maximum speed, in this case about sixty miles an hour. "Another
piece of shit," Doris said. Kevin yawned; traveling in cars always made him
sleepy. Doris complained about the smell, opening the windows and cursing
the previous users.

"Spoken like a solid citizen," Oscar said.

She gave him an ugly look and stared out the window.

Hum of the motor, whirr of the tires, whoosh of the cool air. Finally Doris
rolled the windows up. Kevin fell asleep.

They took the Riverside Freeway up the Santa Ana Canyon, passing under
huge live oak trees on the big canyon floor. In Riverside they switched to highway 395 and headed north, up California's back side.

The sun rose as they traveled over the high desert north of Riverside. Long
shadows striped the bare harsh land. Here and there in the distance they spotted knots of date palms and cotton-woods. These oases marked the sites of new
villages, scattered in rings around the towns of Hisperia, Lancaster, Victor-
ville. None of these villages were big, but taken together they accounted for
a percentage of the diaspora out of the LA basin. You could say that "Greater
Los Angeles" now extended out across the Mojave, making possible a much
reduced density—even some open land—in the heart of the old monster itself.

Kevin woke up. "How do you know this Sally Tallhawk?" he asked Oscar.

"She was one of my teachers in law school."

"So you haven't seen her for a while?"

"Actually we get together pretty frequently. We have a good time."

"Uh huh. And she's on the state water board?"

"She was. She just left it. But she knows everyone on it, and she knows everything we might need to know about California water law. And it's the state laws that determine what the towns can or cannot do, when it comes to water usage."

"You aren't kidding—I hear that all the time when I try to get building permits."

"Well, you can see why it has to be that way—water is a regional concern. When towns had control over water there were some horrible local fights."

"Still are, as far as I can tell."

The country they were crossing got higher, wilder. To their left the Sierra Nevada's eastern escarpment jumped ten thousand feet into the sky. To their right lower ranges, the Slate and the Panamint, and then the White Mountains, rose burnt and bare. They passed Owens Lake, a sky-colored expanse with a crusty white border, and were in Owens Valley.

High and narrow, tucked between two of the tallest ranges on the continent, Owens Valley was a riot of spring color. Orchards made a patchwork of the valley floor (apples, almonds, cherries, pears), and many of the trees were in bloom, each branch thick with blossoms, every tree a hallucinatory burst of white or pink. Behind them stood wild slopes of granite and evergreen.

They passed Lone Pine, the largest town in the valley at almost a hundred thousand people. Beyond Lone Pine they tracked through the strange tortured shapes of the Alabama Hills, some of the oldest rock in North America. After Independence, another big town, they came to Bishop, the cultural center of the valley.

The main street of Bishop, which was simply highway 395 itself, formed the town's "historic district." Kevin laughed to see it: an old Western drive-thru town, composed of motels, Greyhound bus stations, drive-in food stops, steak restaurants, auto parts shops, hardware stores, pharmacies, the rest of the usual selection. Bishop clearly treasured it.

Away from Main Street the town had been transformed: sixty thousand people lived in some of the most elegant examples of the new architecture Kevin had ever seen, as well as some of the most bizarre. In the northwest quarter of town sprawled the University of California campus. After they dropped off their car at the depot, the three travelers walked over to it.

The land at the university had been donated partly by the city of Los Angeles, partly by the Bishop reservation of the Paiute and Shoshone Indians. The buildings imitated the local landscape: two rows of tall concrete buildings stood like mountain ranges, over low wooden structures tucked among a great number of pines. They found a map of the campus along one walkway, located Kroeber College and walked to it, passing groups of students sitting on the grass, eating lunch.

Before some low wooden offices Oscar stopped them and pointed to a woman sitting in the sun, eyes closed. "That's Sally Tallhawk."

She was in fact tall, but not particularly hawkish—she had the broad face of the Paiutes, with thick black eyebrows. She wore a long-sleeved shirt (sleeves rolled up onto big biceps), jeans, and running shoes. A small pair of gold-rimmed bifocals made her seem quite professorial.

She heard their approach, rose to greet them. "Hey, Rhino," she said to Oscar easily, and they shook hands left-handed. Oscar introduced Kevin and Doris, and she welcomed them to Bishop. Her voice was low and rapid. "Look here," she said, "I'm off to the mountains, I was just about to leave."

"But we came all this way to talk to you!" Oscar exclaimed. "And we have the festival games tomorrow night."

"It's just an overnighter I have in mind," she said. "I want to check snow levels in Dusy Basin. I can get you folks all the equipment you need from the department, and you can come along." Imperiously she quelled Oscar's protest: "I'm going up into the mountains, I say! If you want to talk to me you'll have to come along!"

So they did. An hour later they were at the trailhead at South Lake, putting packs on their backs. And then they were hiking, up onto the wild sides of California's great backbone. Kevin and Doris glanced at Oscar, then at each other. How would Oscar handle the hard work of hiking?

As it turned out he toiled upward without complaint, sweating, heaving for breath, rolling his eyes behind Tallhawk's back; but listening intently to her when she spoke. Occasionally he looked at Kevin and Doris, to make sure they could hear, to make sure they were enjoying themselves. They had never seen him so solicitous. The work itself didn't seem to bother him much at all. And yet Sally Tallhawk was leading them at a rapid pace.

After two or three hours they rose out of the pine forest, into a mixed zone where patches of dark green lodgepole pine stood here and there, among humps of bare dark red granite. They came to the shores of a long island-filled lake, and hiked around it. Snow patches dotted the north faces of the peaks that towered around them, and white reflections shimmered in the dark blue water.

"You see how much water pours down into Owens Valley," Tallhawk said, waving a wide hand, wiping sweat from one eye. "And yet under the old laws, all of it could be piped away to Los Angeles."

As they hiked she told the old story, of how the LA Department of Water and Power had obtained the water rights for all the streams falling out of the east side of the Sierra into Owens Valley—in effect draining the yearly snowfall of the watershed off to LA.

"Criminals," Doris said, disgusted. "Where were their values?"

"In growth," Oscar murmured.

There had been a man working for the Federal Bureau of Reclamation, Sally said, making a survey of the valley's water resources. At the same time he was being paid as a consultant by LA, and he passed along everything he learned to LA, so that they knew which streams to gain the rights to. And so Owens Valley was sucked dry, its farms and orchards destroyed. The farmers went out of business and LA bought up their land. Owens Lake dried up completely, and Mono Lake came close, and the groundwater level fell and fell, until even the desert plants began to die.

"I can't believe they could get away with it!" Doris said.

Tallhawk only laughed. "They ended up with the peculiar situation of a city in one county being the major landowner in another county. This was so disturbing that laws were passed in Sacramento to make any repetition of that kind of ownership impossible. But it was too late for Owens Valley."

Telling this story took a while. By the time Tallhawk was done they were above Long Lake, into wild, rocky territory, where the ponds were small, and bluer than seemed possible. Shadows were cast far to the left, toward a jagged skyline Sally identified as the Inconsolable Range. Oscar huffed and puffed, showing a surprising endurance. They were all in a rhythm, walking in a little line—a little line of tiny figures, hiking across a landscape of blasted stone, dwarfed by the huge bare mountains that now surrounded them on three sides.

The trail wound over a knob called Saddlerock, then turned left, up a monstrous trench in the Inconsolable Range. They were in shadow now, and the scattered junipers with their gnarled cinnamon branches and dusky green needles seemed like sentient things, huddled together to watch them pass.

They started up an endless series of switchbacks that ascended the right wall of the enormous trench, stomping through snow more and more often as they got higher. Tallhawk pounded up the trail at a steady pace, and they rose so quickly they could pop their ears. Eventually the trail was completely filled with snow, tromped down by previous hikers. At times they looked back down at the route they had taken, at a long string of lakes in late afternoon shadow; then the trail would switch back, and they stared directly across at the sharktooth edge of the Inconsolable Range, rising to the massive pyramid of Mount Agassiz. They were far above treeline now, it was nothing but rock and snow.

Finally they topped the right wall of the great trench, and the trail ran over the saddle of Bishop Pass. At the high point of the broad pass they walked by the King's Canyon park boundary sign, and into the Dusy Basin.

To their left the broad ridge curved up to the multiple peak of Agassiz, a wild broken wall of variegated granite. Here Mesozoic volcanic sediments had metamorphosed under the pressure of rising granitic masses called plutons, and all of that had folded together, light and dark rock mixing like the batter in a marble cake. They trod over shattered fields of dark Lamarck granodiorite, and then over bands of the lighter alaskite, which zigzagged up and striped the great wall of Agassiz, and provided the thunderbolts in Thunderbolt Peak. And as they hiked Tallhawk's voice babbled like the sound of a distant low brook, enumerating every stone, every alpine flower tucked in the granite cracks.

Not too long after they started down the other side of the pass, they came to the highest lake in Dusy Basin, which was unnamed. Its shores were fiercely rocky, but there was one tiny grassy spot suitable for a campsite, and they threw down their packs there. Sally and Doris began to put up the tents; Oscar flopped flat on his back, looking like a beached whale; Kevin got out the gas stove and cooking utensils, quick with hunger. They chattered as they worked, looking around them all the while. Oscar complained about Sally's idea of a pretty campsite and they all laughed, even him; the place was spectacular.

In the evening light the wild peaks glowed. Mount Agassiz, Thunderbolt Peak, Isosceles Peak, Columbine Peak, The Black Giant—each a complete masterpiece of form alone, each a perfect complement to the others. Huge boulders stood scattered on the undulating rock floor of Dusy Basin, and down at its bottom there was a narrow string of ponds and trees, still half-buried in snow. The sun lay just over the peaks to the west. The sky behind the mountains was twilight blue, and all the snow on the peaks was tinted a deep pink. Chaos generating order, order generating chaos; who could say which was which in such alpenglow?

As they made camp the conversation kept returning to water. Sally Tallhawk, it was clear, was obsessed with water. Specifically, with the water situation in California, a Gordian knot of law and practice that no one could ever cut apart. To learn the system, manipulate it, explain it—this was her passion.

In California water flows uphill toward money, she told them. This had been the primary truth of the system for decades. Most states used riparian water law, where landowners have the right to water on their land. That went back to English common law, and a landscape with lots of streams in it. But California and the other Hispanic states used parts of appropriative water law, which came from dry Mexico and Spain, and which recognized the rights of those who first made a beneficial, consumptive use of water—it didn't matter where their land was in relation to it. In this system, later owners of land couldn't build anything to impede the free passage of water to the original user. And so money—particularly old money—had its advantage.

"So that's how LA could take water from Owens Valley," Doris said.

The tents were up, sleeping bags out. They gathered around Kevin and the stove with the materials for dinner.

"Well, it's more complex than that. But essentially that's right."

But in the end, Tallhawk told them, the water loss did Owens Valley a kind of good. LA tried to compensate for its appropriation by making the valley into something like a nature preserve. And so the valley missed all the glories of twentieth century southern California civilization. Then, when water loss threatened the native desert plants of the valley, Inyo County sued LA, and the courts decided in Inyo's favor. This led to new laws being passed in Sacramento, laws that gave control of Inyo's water back to it. But by this time feelings about growth and development had changed, and the valley towns went about rebuilding according to their own sense of value. "The dry years saved us from a lot of crap."

Oscar said to Kevin and Doris, "You'll have to remember that if we lose this case."

Doris shook her head irritably. "It's not the same. We won't be able to go back from a situation like ours."

Tallhawk said, "You can never be sure of that. We're working now on the final arrangements for the removal of the Hetch Hetchy dam, for instance. That was the biggest defeat ever for the environmental movement in California, right back at its start—a valley described as a second Yosemite, drowned so San Francisco could have a convenient water supply. John Muir himself couldn't stop that one. But now we're making them store the water in a couple of catchments downstream, and when that's done they'll drain Hetch Hetchy and bring that valley back out into the light of day, after a century and a half. The ecologists say the valley floor will recover in fifty to a hundred years, faster if they truck some of the mud out into the San Joaquin as fertilizer. So you see—some disasters can be reversed."

"It would be better to avoid disaster in the first place," Kevin said.

"Undoubtedly," Tallhawk said. "I was just reminding you that there's not too many things that are irrevocable, when you're talking about the waterscape. Water flows forever, so there is a resilience there we can rely on."

"Glen Canyon next, eh?" Oscar said.

"My God, yes!" Tallhawk cried, and laughed.

The sun disappeared. It got cold fast. The sky turned a dark velvet blue that seemed to crackle where it met the glowing white snow ridges. Steam rose from the pot on the stove, and they could smell the stew.

"But in El Modena . . ." Kevin said.

"In El Modena, I don't know."

Then the stew bubbled over, and it was declared ready. They spooned it into cups and ate. Tallhawk had brought a bottle of red wine along, and they drank it gratefully.

"Can't we use water to stop Alfredo's plan?" Kevin asked as he finished eating.

"Maybe."

It was strange but true, she told them: Orange County had a lot of water. It was one of the best water districts in the state, in terms of groundwater conservation.

"What does that mean, exactly?" Kevin asked.

"Well, do you understand what groundwater is?"

"Water under the ground?"

"Yes, yes. But not in pools."

She stood, waved her arms at the scene, talking as she pulled her down jacket from her pack. Walked in circles around them, looking at the peaks.

Soil is permeable, she said, and the rock below soil is also permeable, right down to solid bedrock, which forms the bottom of groundwater basins. Water fills all the available space in permeable rock, percolating everywhere it can go. And it flows downhill as it does on the surface, not as quickly, but just as definitely. "Imagine Owens Valley is a big trench between the ranges, which it is. Filled almost halfway up with rock and soil eroded out of the mountains. The San Joaquin Valley is the same way, only much bigger. These are immense reservoirs of water, then, only the water level lies below the soil level, at least in most places. Geologists and hydrologists have charted these groundwater basins everywhere, and there are some *huge* ones in California.

"Now some are self-contained, they don't flow downstream. There's enormous amounts of water in these, but they're only replenished by rainfall, which is scarce out here. If you pump water you empty basins like those. The Ogdalilla basin under Oklahoma was one of those, and it was pumped dry like an oil field, which is why they're so desperate for the Columbia's water now.

"Anyway, you have to imagine this underground saturation, this underground movement." She stretched her arms forward and reached with her fingers, in a sort of unconscious groundwater dance. "The shapes of the basin bottoms sometimes bring the water closer to the surface—if there's an underground ridge of impermeable bedrock, and the groundwater is flowing downhill over this ridge, water gets pushed to the surface, in the very top of a giant slow-motion waterfall. That's how you get artesian wells."

Silence as she walked around the camp. Now it seemed they could hear the subterranean flow, murmuring beneath them, a deep bass to the wind's tremolo.

"And El Modena?" Kevin said.

"Well, when a groundwater basin drains into the sea, there's a strange situation; the water doesn't really drain very much, because there's water pressure on both sides. Fresh water forces itself out if there's flow coming in from upstream, but if not . . . well, the only thing that keeps sea water from reversing the flow and pushing into the ground under the land is the pressure of the fresh water, pouring down.

"Now Orange County's basin doesn't have a whole lot of water coming into it anymore. Riverside takes a lot before it reaches Orange County, as do all the other cities upstream. And agriculture in Orange County itself took a lot of water from the very start of settlement. They pumped more than was replenished, which was easy to do. But the pressure balance at the coastline was altered, and sea water began to leach inland. Wells near the coast turned salty. There's no way to stop that kind of intrusion except to keep the basin full, so that the pressure outward is maintained. So the Orange County Water District was formed, and their job was to keep the groundwater basin healthy, so all their wells wouldn't turn to salt. This was back in the 1920s. They were given the taxing and allocation powers necessary to do the job, and the right to sue cities upstream. And they went at it with a kind of religious fervor. They did it as well as any water district in California, despite all the stupidity going on above ground in that area. And so you have a healthy basin under you."

They had finished eating. They cleaned up the cups and the pot; their hands got wet, and quickly they got cold. They scrambled to get into the down jackets and bunting pants that Tallhawk's department had provided. Then they sat on their groundpads, sleeping bags bunched around them, making a circle around the stove, which served as their campfire. The great arc of peaks still glowed with some last remnant of light, under a dark sky. Sally pulled out a small bottle of brandy and passed it around, continued:

"It means that you live on an enormous pool of water, renewed all the time by OCWD. They buy water from us and from LA, and pour most of it right into the ground. Store it there. They keep the pressure regulated so very little of it is lost to the sea; there's a balance of pressures at the coastline. So the artesian wells that gave Fountain Valley its name will never come back, and no one there would want them to! But you have the water you need. It's strange, because it's a desert coastline with hardly any rainfall. But the OCWD planned for a population increase that other forces balked—the population increase never occurred, and so there's water to spare now. Strange but true."

"So water won't help us stop them?" Kevin said, disappointed.

"Not a pure scarcity. But Oscar says you have a resolution banning the further purchase of water from LA. You could try to stand on that."

"Like Santa Barbara?"

"Santa Barbara slowed development by turning off the tap, yes. But they're in a different situation—they stayed out of the California Water Project, and they don't buy water from LA, and they don't have much of a groundwater basin. So they're really limited, and they've made a conscious decision not to change that. It works well if you have those initial conditions. But Orange County doesn't. There's a lot of water that was brought into the area before these issues were raised, and that water is still available."

Kevin and Doris looked at each other glumly.

They listened to the wind, and watched the stars pop into existence in a rich blue sky. On such a fine night it was a shame to get into the tents, so they only shifted into their sleeping bags, and lay on the groundpads watching the sky. The snow patches scattered among the rocks shone as if lit from within. It seemed possible to feel them melt, then rush into the ground beneath them, to fall down the slope into Le Conte Canyon and seep a slow path to the sea, in invisible underground Columbias. Kevin felt a stirring in him, the full-lunged breathlessness that marked his love for El Modena's hills, extending outward to these great peaks. Interpenetration with the rock. He was melting like the snow, seeping into it. In every particulate jot of matter, spirit, dancing . . .

"So what do you suggest, Sally?" Doris finally said.

"We'd like our town to end up as nice as Bishop," Kevin added. "But with people like Alfredo running things . . ."

"But he's not really running things, right?"

"No, but he is powerful."

"You've got to expect a lot of resistance to what you're trying to do. Saving the land for its own sake goes against the grain of white American thought, and so it's a fight that'll never end. Why not grow if we can, why not change things completely? A lot of people will never understand the answer to that question, because to them a good life only means more things. They have no feeling for the land. We have an aesthetic of wilderness now, but it takes a certain kind of sensibility to feel it."

"So in our case . . ." Kevin prompted, feeling anxious.

"Well." Tallhawk stood up, reached for the nearly empty brandy bottle. "You could try endangered species. If there is any kind of endangered species inhabiting your hill, that would be enough. The Endangered Species Act is tough."

"I don't think Rattlesnake Hill is likely to have any," Doris said. "It's pretty ordinary."

"Well, look into it. They stopped a freeway down near your area because of a very ordinary-looking lizard that happens to be rare.

"Then the California Environmental Quality Act is a good chance. Under the terms of the act, environmental impact reports come early in the process, and once you have one, you can use it."

"But if it's not particularly favorable to us?" Oscar asked, sounding sleepy.

"You could consider going to the National Trust for Land, or the Nature Conservancy—they lend assistance to movements like yours, and they have the money to fight large developers. You could maybe convince them to bid against the development if it comes to that."

"The town itself owns all the land," Doris said.

"Sure. But these groups can help you with lobbying and campaigning when the issue comes to a vote, and they could even pay to lease it."

"That would be good."

"But there's nothing we could use to stop them before a referendum?" Kevin asked. "I'm just scared Alfredo would win. He's good at that."

"Well, the environmental stuff I mentioned. Or you could see if the hill has some unique water properties, like a spring."

"It doesn't," Kevin said.

"You could try drilling a spring on the sly."

She laughed at the long silence.

"Well it's a thought, right? Here, have some brandy. One swallow left each. You'll think of something. If not, let me know and we'll come down and threaten this guy. Maybe we can offer you a discount on Owens Valley water if you leave the hilltop alone. Inyo County influencing southern Californian politics, I like that!" She laughed. "Or find a sacred ancient Indian burial mound or the like. Except I don't think the Gabrielinos were into that kind of thing. Or if they were, we don't know about it."

Kevin shook his head. "The hillside is basically empty. I've been all over it. I've hung out on that hill ever since I was a kid, I've *crawled* all over it."

"Might be fossils," Oscar said.

"You'd have to make a world-class find," Tallhawk said. "El Modena tar pits. I'd try to rely on something a bit more solid if I were you."

They thought about it, listening to wind over rock, over snow. Listening to water seep into the ground.

"Ready for tomorrow's match?" Tallhawk asked Oscar.

Oscar was a Falstaffian mound, he looked like one of the boulders surrounding them. "I've never been readier," he muttered.

"Match?" Kevin said. "What's this? Going to be in a chess match, Oscar?" Tallhawk laughed.

"It is like chess," Oscar murmured, "only more intricate."

"Didn't you know the redneck festival starts tomorrow?" Tallhawk asked Kevin and Doris.

"No."

"Tomorrow is opening day for hunting season; in fact, we'll have to haul ass out of here to avoid getting shot by some fool. Bishop celebrates opening day with age-old customs. Jacked-up pick-up trucks painted in metallic colors, with gun racks in their back windows—fifty cases of whiskey, shipped in from Kentucky—tomorrow night'll be wild. That's one reason I wanted to come up here tonight. Get a last taste of quiet."

They lay stretched out in their bags.

Kevin listened to the wind, and looked around at the dark peaks poking into the night sky. Suddenly it was clear to him that Sally had had a reason to bring them up here to have this talk; that this place itself was part of the discourse, part of what she wanted to say. The university of the wilderness. The spine of California, the hidden source of the south's wealth. This hard wild place . . .

Around them the wind, spirit of the mountains, breathed. Water, the soul of the mountains, seeped downward. Rock, the body of the mountains, stood fast.

Held in a bowl like God's linked hands, they slept.

The next day they hiked back over the pass and down the trail, and drove a little gas car down to Tallhawk's house in Bishop to clean up.

As dusk fell they walked downtown, and found that Bishop had filled with people. It seemed like the entire population of eastern California must have been there, dressed in blue jeans, pendletons, cowboy boots, cowboy hats, camouflaged flak jackets, bright orange hunter's vests, square dancing dresses, rodeo chaps, bordello robes, cavalry uniforms, animal furs, southern belle ball gowns, Indian outfits—if it had ever been seen in the American West before, it was there now. Main Street was packed with pick-up trucks, all track-free, running on grain alcohol and making a terrific noise and stink. Their drivers revved engines constantly to protest the long periods of gridlock. "A traffic-jam parade," Oscar said.

They ate at a coffee shop called Huk Finns, then walked in a stream of people toward the Paiute reservation. Over the screech of pick-ups burning rubber they heard occasional gunshots, and the dark streets were illuminated by the glare of skyrockets bursting overhead. Oscar sang loudly: "Oh the rocket's red glare, the bombs bursting in air—"

"Where are we going?" Doris shouted at him.

"Bishop High School gymnasium," he replied.

Which was filling rapidly, with a rowdy, even crazed audience. Oscar led Kevin and Doris to a row of benches in the front of the upper deck. The basketball court below was filled with a large boxing ring. "Not boxing!" Doris said.

"Of course not," Oscar said, and walked off. Kevin and Doris stared at each other, nonplussed. They sat for nearly fifteen minutes, and nothing happened. Then into the ring stepped a woman wearing a tuxedo jacket over a black body suit and dark fishnet nylons, with high heels and a top hat. Tumultuous applause.

Inexpert spotlights bounced to left and right, finally settling on her. She lifted an absurdly large microphone and said, "ARE YOU READY?"

The crowd was ready. Doris stuck her fingers in her ears. People standing were shouted down, and the aisles filled. There were perhaps ten thousand people jammed into the place. "OKAY THEN! FIRST MATCH: BRIDE OF GERONIMO VERSUS THE RHINOCEROS!"

"I'll be damned," Kevin said, his words completely drowned by the uproar. The spots swung around drunkenly as their operators searched for the entering contestants. By the time they found them, they were almost to the dark green mat of the ring: two large figures in long capes, one scarlet, the other incandescent blue. The crowd roared, the two contestants shook their fists over their heads: Oscar and Sally Tallhawk, no doubt about it.

Quickly the two contestants were in the ring and mugging it up, bouncing against each other chest to chest. The Mistress of Ceremonies—also the referee—tried to separate them, at the same time holding her mike where it would catch their dire threats. Tallhawk snarled as she detailed the ravages Oscar would suffer: "I'm using your scalp as a floormop! Your skin will make good window squeegees! And I need some new dingleberries to hang from my rear-view mirror!"

The crowd roared.

Oscar puffed out his cheeks, mumbled "Prediction is always dangerous, but the Rhino is reasonably confident the match will ultimately be decided in his favor."

The crowd gave him an ovation.

The MC let them at it.

They circled each other, knocking hands aside and snarling. The Bride grabbed the Rhino's wrist and pulled, and the Rhino flew through space and hit the ring ropes, which were very elastic. The Rhino fell deep into them, rebounded back and was kicked in the chest—he staggered, the Bride took a flying leap across the ring and landed on his shoulders, bearing him to the mat. She got a knee across his throat and pounded her elbow into his face. When she stood and threw her arms overhead the crowd screamed "GERONIMA!" and the MC announced, "THE BIG G SEEMS TO HAVE LEVELED THE RHINO WITH HER FAMOUS BLUBBERHAWK FROM SPACE MOVE."

But the Rhino, twitching in agony on the mat, reached out a hand and jerked both of Geronima's feet from under her, felling her like a tree, allowing him to stagger up and away.

It happened several times: Bride of Geronimo used Rhino for a punching bag, but when Rhino was prostrate and the Bride reaping the crowd's approval, the Rhino would resuscitate, barely, and deliver a stinging riposte. Once he pulled the rope on one side and let it go, which caused the rope on the other side to snap Geronima in the back and bring her down. In revenge she grabbed a lightbulb from the top of one of the rope poles, broke it and ground it into the Rhino's face, until the MC knocked her away with the mike. The Rhino kept both hands to his face, grunting in agony as Geronima chased him about the ring. Clearly he was blind. It was a prime opportunity; Mrs. G. raced around the ring, revving up for truly impressive leaps off the corner poles, attempting her Blubberhawk from Space kill—but each time as she dropped from the air the Rhino would trip, or stagger, or hear something above, and neatly sidestep away, looking absurdly light-footed for all his bulk—and Geronima would land flat on her face. Time after time this happened, until Geronima was raving with frustration, and the crowd was in a frenzy. Then Rhino reached into his back pocket and smeared something over his face. "AH HA!" said the MC. "LOOKS LIKE HE'S USING SOME OF THAT NEW PLASTIC SKIN TO REPAIR HIS FACE—YES—SEE HOW FAST IT'S HEALED—WHY—LOOK AT THAT!— HE'S OKAY!"

Rhino dodged another leap and muttered into the mike. "MY ALMANAC INDICATES THAT THE TIDE MAY HAVE TURNED, MISSUS GEE." And then he was all over the ring, sidestepping, looking right and left in grossly exaggerated glances, then leaping forward to box the Bride's ears or twist her to the mat. Finally he got behind her and began bouncing her off his knee. "UH OH!" the MC cried. "IT'S RHINO'S ATOMIC DROP! NO ONE CAN TAKE THAT FOR LONG!"

And indeed Geronima collapsed to the mat, flat out. Rhino nodded shyly to the roaring crowd. The MC gave him a kiss, which gave him an idea—he tiptoed after her and took a tug at her tux, which came apart at the seams. Now the crowd really loved him.

But the MC was incensed, and turned to stalk him. He stumbled backwards across the ring, tried to wake Geronima, but to no avail. The Bride was out. The Rhino began to fly about the ring, thrown by a voluptuous woman in a fishnet body stocking, who paused only to continue in her role of commentator: "NOW I'M FINISHING THIS NOSEY RHINO OFF WITH A TRIPLE-SPIN KIDNEY HAMMER." Rhino tried desperately to escape the ring, grasping at spectators through the ropes with eyes bugged out; but he was pulled back in and pounded. The Bride even roused herself to join the final carnage, before collapsing again after a single chop from the MC, who wanted no help. In the end the MC stood alone over the two prone wrestlers, and when she had caught her breath and straightened her hair, and tried on the torn tux and tossed it away as a bad job, she calmly announced the next bout. "UGLY GEORGE

VERSUS MISTER CHICKENSHIT, COMING UP AS SOON AS WE GET THE LARD OFF THE CANVAS."

There were several more bouts scheduled, but Kevin and Doris left their seats and struggled through the crowd to an exit, then made their way down to the locker room doors on the ground floor. Oscar was just emerging, freshly showered and back in street clothes, blinking in a kind of Clark Kentish way. After signing autographs for a gang of youngsters he joined Kevin and Doris.

"That was great!" Kevin said, grinning at Oscar's owlish innocence.

Doris said, "Where's Sally?"

"Thank you," Oscar said to Kevin. "Sally has another match later in the evening. Would you care to join me for something to drink? I find I am thirsty—I could even use another dinner, to tell the truth. I have to eat lightly before a match."

"I believe it."

So they went back to Main Street and Huk Finns. Oscar ordered corned beef and hash, and poured whiskey over the hash, to Doris's horror. But she joined in as they drank most of a bottle.

Kevin couldn't stop grinning. "So Oscar, how'd you get into professional wrestling?"

"Just fell into it."

"No, really!"

"I liked the money. Sally was already doing it, and she thought I had the necessary . . . talent."

"Do you ever get hurt?" Doris asked.

"Certainly. We make mistakes all the time. Once I missed on the Atomic Drop and caught Sally on the tailbone, and a couple minutes later she popped me right on the nose. Bled all over. We both got miffed, and it turned into a serious fight for a while. But those look dull compared to the tandem stuff."

"You really ought to join our softball team," Kevin said. "Your footwork is great, you'd do fine!"

Oscar shook his head, mouth full.

They left a bit unsteady on their feet, but in high spirits. Main Street was not quite as crowded as before, but there were still hundreds of people wandering about. They were passing a loud group when a tall man stopped them. "Hey, ain't you the Rhino? Hey!" he bellowed to his companions. "This here's the Rhino, the guy who wrestles the Bride of Geronimo!"

"Fame," Doris said.

"Hey Rhino, let's try a takedown right here, whaddya say? I used to wrestle in high school, here, try some real wrestling moves."

He grabbed for Oscar's wrist, but Oscar's wrist had moved.

"What's a matter, Rhino? Chicken?"

"Drunk," Oscar said.

For answer the man drove his shoulder at Oscar's chest, and missed; turned with a roar and charged again. Oscar shuffled to one side, avoiding him in the dark. The man cannoned into Kevin.

"Hey, fuck you," Kevin said, and punched the man in the nose.

Immediately they were in a free-for-all, swinging away amid shrieks and curses. Chaos in the dark. People came running to watch or to join the melee, and it only stopped when a whole gang of police drove up and strode among them, blowing their whistles and poking with nightsticks anyone who continued to fight. Soon the fighters were lined up and wristbanded.

"Anyone with a wristband stopped again will go to jail," the officer in charge told them. "The bands will come off in a couple days. Now go home and sober up."

Oscar and Kevin and Doris started toward Tallhawk's house. "That was stupid," Doris told Kevin.

"I know."

She glanced around. "Those guys are following us."

"Let's lose them now," Oscar suggested, and took off running.

Their belligerents followed in noisy but fairly efficient pursuit. It took them several blocks of twisting, turning, and flat-out running to shake them.

When they were free of pursuit they stood on a street corner, gasping. "This sure is fun," Doris said acidly.

Oscar nodded. "I know. But now I'm lost." He shrugged. "Oh well."

It took them another hour to find Tallhawk's house, and by that time Oscar was dragging. "This is far more exercise than I like," he said as he opened the door of the darkened house. He entered a study with a long couch, collapsed on it. "It always happens like this when I visit Sally. She's a maniac, essentially. The guest room is down the hall."

Kevin went to the bathroom. When he returned to the guest room, he found that it had only one bed, and a rather narrow one at that.

Doris was undressing beside it. "It's okay," she said unsteadily. "We can both fit."

Kevin swayed for a moment. "Um," he said. "I don't know—there's another couch out there, I think—"

Then she pressed against him, hugging him. "Come on," she said in a muffled voice. "We've done this before."

Which was true. He had looked down onto that head of black hair, in embraces just like this. Although. . . . And besides, he. . . . Drunkenly he kissed the part, and the familiar scent of her hair filled him. He hugged back, too drunk to think past the moment. He gave in to it. They fell onto the bed.

The trip back was long, and hung over. Kevin was tired, bored with the end-less Mojave Desert, awkward and tongue-tied with his old friend Doris. Oscar slumped in his seat, a portrait of the sleeping Buddha. Doris sat looking out her window, thinking unreadable thoughts.

Images of Sally Tallhawk jumped Kevin as if out of ambush: striding around their campsite with the evening sun flush on her broad face, arms spread out as she talked in a low chant of water sluicing into the underworld, pooling, drawn inward, making its secret way to the sea. The ragged ridge of Thunderbolt Peak against a sky the color of the ocean, stripes of white rock like marble crisscross-ing the dark basalt, hypnagogic visions of her dancing by the lakeshore with its black wavelets, throwing Oscar out onto it where he skated as if on ice—

Jerking back awake. Trying to nod off again. The car's monotonous hum. Off to their right, the weird illuminated black surface of one of the microwave catchments, receivers like immense stereo speakers flat on their backs, soaking rays, the photon space music, the lased power sent down from the solar panels soaring in their orbits. They were almost done setting out that array of orbit-ing panels, his parents' work would be finished. What would they do then? Space junkies, would they ever come down? Visit El Modena? He missed them, needed to talk to them. Couldn't they give him advice, tell him what to do, make it all as simple as it once had been?

No. But he should give them a call anyway. And his sister Jill as well.

Then, home at the house—having said a very awkward "good night" to Doris, pretending that there was no reason he should not go to his own room just as he always did—the TV was blinking.

It was a message from Jill.

"All right!" he said as he saw her face. That sort of coincidence was always cropping up between them. He would think of her, she would call.

She looked like him, but only in a way; all his hayseed homeliness had been transformed into broad, wild good looks, in that peculiar way that happens in family resemblances, where minute shifts in feature can make all the differ-ence between plainness and beauty: big mobile mouth, upturned nose, freck-les, wide blue eyes with light eyelashes and eyebrows, and auburn hair turning burnt gold under the Asian sun.

Now her little image said in the familiar hoarse voice, "Well, I've been try-ing to get you for the last couple of days because I'm moving out of Dakka to learn some tropical disease technique at a hospital in Atgaon, up in the northeast near the Indian border—in fact I've already moved out there, I'm just back to pick up the last of my things and slog through the bureaucracy. You wouldn't believe what a mess that is, it makes California seem like a really regulation-free place. I hate doing these recordings, I wish I could get hold of you. Anyway, Atgaon's about as far away from Dakka as you can get and still be in Bangladesh, it takes all day to get there, on a new train built on a big causeway to keep it above the floodplain. It must go over a hundred bridges, it's a really wet country.

"Atgaon is a market town on the Tista River, which comes down from Sikkim. The hospital is the most important thing in town, it's associated with the Institute for the Study of Tropical Diseases, and getting to be one of the leaders in the area—like, this is the place they developed the once-a-year malaria pill. The whole thing was started by the Rajhasan Landless Cooperative Society, one of the land reform groups, which is pretty neat. They do tons of clinical work, and they have a bunch of good research projects. I'm going to work on one concerning hepatitis-B-two. Meanwhile I'm helping out in the emergency room and in clinic visits, so it's mostly busy, but I like it—the people are nice and I'm learning a lot.

"I'm living in a little bungalow of my own on the hospital grounds. It's pretty nice, but there are some surprises. Like my first day there I turned on the light and tossed my bag on the bed, and a gigantic centipede came clattering out at me! I took a broom and smacked the thing with the handle and cut it in half, and *both sides started to crawl away in different directions.* Can you believe it? I was freaked and put a bed post on one half of the thing in place, while I pulverized the other half with the broom handle. Then I did the same to the half under the post. What a *mess.* Later they told me to check out bedsheets and clothes before using them—I told them hey, I know!"

She grinned her sister grin, and Kevin laughed. "Oh, Jill—" he said. He wanted to talk, he needed to talk!

He stopped the tape, tried to put a call through to Bangladesh. It wouldn't go; she wasn't there in Dakka to answer.

Feeling odd, he started the tape again.

". . . Happy to know that there's a woman's softball league out here, can you believe it? Apparently there was an exchange program, nurses here went to Guam, and some from Guam came here, and the ones here started softball games, and when the nurses visiting Guam came back they were hooked on it too, so they kept it going. Now it's grown, they've got some fields and a five-village league and everything. I haven't seen Atgaon's field yet, but they say it's a good one. They're proud of having a woman's league, women in the rural areas are just getting out from under Islamic law, and now they're doing all kinds of work, and involved in the land reform, and infiltrating the bureaucracy too, which means in a few years they'll have taken over! And playing sports like this together, it's new for them and they love it. Team spirit and all that. The big sport around here is cricket, of course, and women are doing that too, but there's also this little softball league.

"Anyway, they figured since I was American I must play softball, and they got me out to play catch with them, and now I'm not only on a team but have been appointed head umpire for the season, because they were having trouble with their umpires taking sides. It's the last thing I would have expected when I came. But I guess I shouldn't be surprised, I mean you can go to the El Toro mela every summer, so why not softball over here? Everything everywhere, that's what it's coming to.

"Well, I'm going to get off, this is costing me fun times in Dakka. There aren't any phones like this in Atgaon—the hospital has a recorder but no transmitter, so I'll try to make some letters there, and send them when I can. Meanwhile you can send letters like this to me in Dakka, and I'll get to play them eventually. I hope you will, it's not as good as really talking but it's better than nothing. Say hi to everyone there, I love you."

The image flickered out.

Kevin sat in his dark room, staring at static on the screen. He could hear Tomas in the next room, tapping away at his computer's keyboard. He could go and talk to Tomas, who would take a break for something like that. Or he could go down to the kitchen, Donna and Cindy would be down there soaking it up and talking to people on TV. Or Sylvia and Sam. Friends were the real family, after all. Family were not actually family until they were friends too. And yet, and yet . . . his sister. Jill Claiborne. He wanted to talk to his sister.

... 5

May. Hard buds on the branches, vibrant green in the rain. Barely a day's sun all April. I can't remember.

Pam came home last night tired and footsore after running two experiments at once. She thinks she can finish the lab work early and do the writing up in the States. Shorten separation. So she's in Pamela Overdrive. I made dinner and she threw the paper down in disgust, told me about her day. "The probe compound and internal standards diffused out of the water sample into the headspace until an equilibrium between the liquid and gas phases was reached."

"Uh huh."

"And that depends on the water solubility and the volatility of the two compounds."

As she went on I stared at her. What Chemists Say To Spouses! What Spouses Understand. Blah blah blah, Tom, blah blah blah.

She saw the doggie look on my face, smiled. "So how'd the book go?"

"The same." It's not fair, really. I can't understand a word she says when she talks of her work, while for me, on this project at least, she is a crucial sounding board. "I'm thinking of alternating chapters of fiction with essay chapters which discuss the political and economic problems we need to solve."

"My God." Wrinkled nose, as if something gone bad in fridge.

"Hey, H.G. Wells did it."

"Which book?"

"Well—one of the major utopian novels."

"Still in print?"

"No."

"Libraries have it?"

"University libraries."

"So Wells's science fiction adventures are still in every library and bookstore, *while this major utopia with the essays is long gone, and you can't even remember the title?"*

I changed the subject.

Think I might pass on the essays.

Six months, four months. Three months? Go quickly, mysterious experiments. Go well. Please.

Kevin woke from a dream in which a huge bird was standing on the limpid water of a rapid stream, wings outstretched as it spun on the clear surface, keeping a precarious balance. Foggily he shook his head, grinned at himself. "Sally Tallhawk," he said, rolling out the syllables. The strategies she had listed while wandering around her sublime campsite filled his thoughts, and feeling charged with energy he decided to visit Jean Aureliano before work and confer.

Jean's office was on the saddle between Orange Hill and Chapman Hill. Kevin blasted up the trail in fifth gear and skidded into her little terrace. Her office was a low set of rooms built around a tiny central stone garden, with open walls and pagoda corners on the low roof. Kevin had done some work on it. When he walked into her office she looked up from the phone and smiled at him, gestured at him to take a seat. Instead he wandered around looking at the prints on the walls, Chinese landscape paintings in the Ming dynasty style, gold on green and blue. Jean spoke sharply, arguing with someone. She had iron gray hair, cut short in a cap over a solid, handsome head. Big-boned and heavyset, she moved like a dancer and had a black belt in karate. For many years now she had been the most powerful person in El Modena, and one of the most powerful in Orange County, and she still looked it. The smoldering glare of the Hispanic matriarch was currently fixed on whoever was on the other end of the line, and Kevin, glancing at her quickly, was glad it wasn't him.

"Damn it," she said, interrupting a tinny whine coming over the phone, "the whole Green alliance is breaking up on the shoals of extremists like you, we're in the modern world now—no, no, don't give me that, there's no going back, all this talk of water-shed sovereignty is so much nostalgia, it's no wonder there's shrieks of protest from all sides! You're tearing the party apart and losing us the mandate we've had! Politics is the art of the possible, Damaso, and if you set impossible goals then what kind of politician are you? It's stupid. What? . . . No. Wrong. Marx can be split into two parts, the historian and the prophet. As a historian he was great and we use his paradigm every day, I don't contest that, but as a prophet he was wrong from the start! By now anyone who calls themselves a Marxist in that sense has *elote* for brains. . . . Damaso, I can't believe you sometimes. *Los pobres*, come on, you think you help them with this balkanization?—*Chinga* yourself!" And then a long string of sulphurous Spanish.

Angrily she hit the phone, cutting off the connection. "What do you want?" she said to Kevin without looking up.

Nervously Kevin told her.

"Yes," she said. "Alfredo's great plan. From the crown of creation to the crown of the town. I've been keeping track of it and I think you and Doris are doing a good job."

"Thanks," Kevin said, "but we've been trying to do more. We talked to a water lawyer from UC Bishop—"

"Tallhawk?"

"Uh huh."

"Yeah, she's a good one. What did she say?"

"Well, she said we were unlikely to stop this development on the water issue alone."

Jean nodded. "But we've got resolution two-oh-two-two to hang onto, there."

"Yeah. But she gave us some suggestions for other avenues to take, and one of them was to use the various requirements of the California Environmental Quality Act. Oscar said you would know about that and how it was going—you could ask to see their EIS when it comes in."

"Yeah that's right, we'll do that. The problem is that they'll probably be able to minimize the environmental impact on that little hill, it barely touches Santiago Park, and with all the other hills already built up—" She made a quick gesture at her office.

"Wouldn't that be a point in our favor?"

"More likely a precedent. But we'll do what we can about it."

"Oscar said that if you mobilized the party machinery to fight the proposal . . ."

"Exactly. We should be able to crush it, and I'll certainly be trying, believe me." She stood up, strode around the office, flung open one sliding wall door, stepped half out onto the porch. "Of course if it comes to a referendum you can never be sure. It's just impossible to tell what the people in this town will vote for and what they won't. A lot of people would be happy if the town were making more money, and this would do that, so it's a dangerous thing to bring to a vote. What I'm saying is that it would be a lot safer if we could stop it in the council itself, right there at the zoning. So you and Doris have to keep at the moderates. We all do."

They discussed Hiroko Washington, Susan Mayer, and Jerry Geiger in turn; Jean knew them intimately from her years as mayor, and her assessment was that their chances of convincing the three were fairly good. None could be counted on for sure, but all were possibilities. "We only need to get two. Keep after it every way you can, and I'll be doing the same up here." There was a look on her face—determined, stubborn, ready to fight. As if she were going in for her black belt trial again.

Reassured, Kevin left her office and coasted down to work. He and Hank and Gabriela were beginning the renovation of Oscar's house, and the other two were already hard at it, tearing out interior walls. Oscar emerged from his library from time to time to watch them. "You look like you're having fun," he observed.

"This is the best part of carpentry!" Gabriela exclaimed as she hammered plaster away from studs, sending white dust flying. "Yar! Ah! Hack!"

"You're an anarchist, Gabriela."

"No, I'm a *nihilist*."

"I like it too," Hank said, eyeing a joint in exposed framing. He took an exploratory slam at it.

"Why is that?" Oscar asked.

Hank squinted, stilled. "Well . . . carpentry is so precise, you always have to be very careful and measured and controlled, and you're always having to juke with edges that don't quite meet and make everything look perfect—it's such a perfectionist thing, even if you're just covering up so it looks right even though it ain't—anyway . . ." He looked around as if tracking a bird that had flown into the room. "Anyway, so you get to the part of the job that is just destructive—"

"Yar!" Bang. "Ha!" Bang. "Hack hack hack!" BANG. BANG. BANG.

"I see," Oscar said.

"It's like how Russ and his vet friends are always going duck-hunting on the weekends. Same principle."

"Fucking schizophrenics," Gabriela said. "I went over there one time and they had some duck they had found while they were hunting, it had busted a wing or something so they brought it home so they could nurse it back to health, had it in a box right next to the bag of all the other ones they'd blasted to smithereens that same day."

"I understand," Oscar said. "No one breaks the law as happily as a lawyer."

"We want to wreck things," Gabriela said. "Soldiers know all about it. Generals, how do you think generals got to be generals? They just have more of it than the rest of us."

"Should call you General Gabby, eh?" Hank said.

"Generalissimo Gabrielosima," she growled, and took a vicious swing at a stud. BANG!

Around noon Oscar made them all sandwiches, and after lunch he followed Kevin around, poring over the plans Kevin had drawn up for the renovation, and asking him questions. Each answer spawned more questions, and in the days that followed Oscar asked more, until it became a regular cross-examination.

"What don't you like about these old places you work on?"

"Well, they're pretty poorly built. And, well, they're dead."

"Dead?"

"Yeah, they're just boxes. Inert. They don't do anything, except protect you from wind and rain. Hell, you can do that with a box."

"And you like the new houses because they're alive?"

"Yeah. And the whole system is so neat, so . . . ingenious. Like this cloud-gel." He pulled at a long roll of clear fabric, stretched it between his fists, let it contract. "You put panels of this stuff in the roof or walls, and if the temperature inside the room is low, then the cloudgel is clear, and sunlight is let in. At around seventy degrees it begins to cloud up, and at eighty it's white, and reflecting sun away. So it thermostats, just like clouds over the land. It's so *neat*."

"Spaceship technology, right?"

"Yeah. Apply it here, along with the other stuff, and you can make a really efficient little farm of a house. Stick in a nervous system of sensors for the house computer, run a tube down into the earth for cool air, use the sunlight for heat and to grow plants and fish, sling a couple of photovoltaic cells on the roof for power, put in an Emerson tank—you know, depending on how far you want to go with it, you can get it to provide most of your daily needs. In any case you're saving lots of money."

"But what about styling? How do you keep it from looking like a lab?"

"Easy! Lot of panels and open space, porches, atriums, French windows— you know, a lot of areas where it's hard to say if you're inside or out. That's what I like, anyway." He tapped one of the sketches scattered on the kitchen table. "There's this architect in Costa Mesa putting homes on water, they float on a little pond that stabilizes the temp and allows them to rotate the house in relation to the sun, and do a lot of aquaculture—"

"You row across to it?"

"Nah, there's a bridge."

"Maybe I want one of those."

"Please."

"But what about food? Why a farmhouse?"

"Why not? Don't you like food?"

"It's obvious I like food. But why grow it in my house? To me it seems no more than fashion."

"Of course it's a fashion. House styles always are. But it makes so much sense, given the materials at hand. Extra heat is going to be generated in the south-facing rooms, especially in this part of the country. And the house computer has the capacity for millions of times more work than you've given it so far. Why not put that heat and attention to work? See here, three small rooms on the south front, so you can vary temperatures and crops, and control infestations better."

"I want no bugs in my house."

"Nobody does, but that's greenhouses for you. Besides the computer is actually pretty good at controlling them. Then look, a pool in a central sky-lighted atrium. Panels adjustable so the skylight can be opened to make it a real atrium."

"I have no central atrium."

"Not yet, but look, we're just gonna knock a little hole in your ceiling here—"

"We're going to knock a giant fucking hole in your ceiling!" Gabriela said as she walked by. "Don't let him fool you. You ain't gonna have a roof any bigger'n a cat's forehead by the time we're done."

"Ignore her. See, cloudgel skylight over a pool."

"I don't know if I like the idea of water in my house."

"Well, it's a good idea, because it's so stable thermally. And you can grow fish and provide a good bit of your protein."

"I detest fishing."

"The computer does it. First thing you know they're fillets in your fridge. Chinese carp is the usual staple."

"I don't like the idea of eating my house guests."

From the next room: "He don't like the idea of a computer that can kill occupants!"

"Good point."

"You get used to it. Then here, we'll enclose the area under the old carport, make it a breakfast room and part of the greenhouse, keep that peach tree in one wall, it'll be great. I love that kind of room."

"Is that why you like this work? To create rooms like that?"

"I like making the whole house. Changing bad to good. Man, I go into some of those old condo complexes, and my God—six hundred square feet, little tiny white-walled rooms with cottage cheese ceilings, cheap carpet over plywood floors, no light—they were like rats in a cage! Little white prison cells, I can't believe people lived like that! I mean they were more prosperous than that, weren't they? Couldn't they have done better?"

Oscar shrugged. "I suppose they could have."

"But they didn't! Now I go into one of those places and blast some space and light into them, do the whole program and in the end you can house just about as many people, but the feel of living there is completely different."

Oscar said, "You have to believe that you can live in a more communal situation without going crazy. You have to be willing to share space."

"I always make sure everyone has a room of their own, that's important to me."

"But the rest of it—kitchens, living rooms, all that. Social organization has to change for you to be able to redo those big places."

"So it's like Doris says—it's a matter of values."

"Yes, I think that's right."

"Well, I like our values. Seeing homes as organisms—there's an elegance to that, and if you can still make it beautiful . . ."

"It's a work of art."

"Yes, but a work of art that you live in. If you live in a work of art, it does something to you. It . . ." Kevin shook his head, unable to express it. "It gives you a good feeling."

From the next room Gabriela hooted. "It *gives* you a good *feeling?*"

Oscar called to her, "The aestheticization of *la vie quotidienne!*"

"Oh, now I get it! Just what I was going to say!"

Hank appeared in the doorway, saw and two-by-four in his hands. "It's Chinese, really. Their little gardens, and the sliding panels and the indoor-outdoor, and the communal thing and the domestic life as art—they've been doing it for thousands of years."

"That's true," Kevin said. "I love Chinese landscaping."

But now Hank was entranced by the two-by-four in his hand. "Uh oh, I appear to have sawed this one a little sigogglin." He made a face, hitched up his pants, walked back out under the carport.

One time after the day's work they bought some dumpies of beer and went up onto Rattlesnake Hill to look for endangered species. This was Kevin's idea, and they gave him a hard time about it, but he held fast. "Look, it's one of the best ways to stop the whole thing dead in its tracks, all right? There were some horned lizards down in the Newport Hills stopped a whole freeway a few years back. So we should try it."

And so they did, hiking up from Kevin and Doris's, and stopping often to inspect plants along the way. Jody was their botanist, and she brought along Ramona for a back-up. It was a hot afternoon, and they stopped often to consult with the beer.

"What's this tree, I don't remember seeing a tree quite like that."

It was a short twisted thing, with smooth gray bark runnelled by vertical lines. Big shiny leaves hid clumps of berries. "That's a mulefat tree," Jody said.

"How the hell did a tree get a name like that?"

"Maybe it burns well."

"Did they burn mule fat?"

"I don't think so. Pass that dumpie over."

Kevin wandered around as the rest sat to observe the mulefat tree. "What about this?" he said, pointing to a shrub with threadlike needles bushing everywhere on it.

"Sage!" they all yelled at him. "Purple sage," Jody amended. "We'll also see black sage and regular gray sage."

"About as endangered as dirt," Hank said.

"Okay, okay. Come on, you guys, we've got the whole hill to go over."

So they got up and continued the search. Kevin led them, and Jody identified a lot of plants. Gabby and Hank and Oscar and Ramona drank a lot of beer. A shrubby tree with oval flat leaves was a laurel sumac. A shrub with long stiff needles poking in every direction was Spanish broom. "Make it bigger and it's a foxtail pine," Hank said. Ramona identified about half the plants they ran across: mantilija poppy with its tiny leaves; horehound, a plain shrub; periwinkle with its broad leaves and purple flowers, a fine ground cover on the hill's north side; a tree that looked like a torrey pine but was actually a Coulter pine; and on the crown of the hill, in the grove Tom had helped plant so long ago, a pair of fine black walnuts, with the bark looking broken, and the small green leaves in neat rows.

On the west side of the hill there were some steep ravines leading down into Crawford Canyon, and they clambered up and down, scrabbling for footholds in the loose sandstone and the sandy dirt. "What about this cactus?" Kevin said, pointing.

"Jesus, Kevin, that's prickly pear," Jody said. "You can get that stuff pickled down at the Mexican deli."

"That's it!" Gabriela cried. "Pickled cactus gets so popular that they're cutting it down everywhere to supply the market, and so suddenly it's endangered up here, yeah!"

"Ah shut up," Kevin said.

"Hey, here's some wildlife," Hank said from some distance away. He was on his hands and knees, his face inches from the dirt.

"Ants," Gabriela said as they walked over. "Chocolate covered ants get popular, and so suddenly—"

"No, it's a newt."

So it was; a small brown newt, crawling across an opening between sage bushes.

"It looks like rubber. Look how slow it moves."

"That's obviously a rare fake newt, put here to get Kevin's hopes up."

"It does look fake."

"They should be endangered, look how slow they are." The newt was moving each leg in turn, very slowly. Even blinking its little yellow eyes took time.

"The battery's running down."

"All right, all right," Kevin said, walking away angrily.

They followed him down the hill.

"That's all right, Kevin," Ramona said. "We've got a softball game tonight, remember?"

"True," Kevin said, perking up.

"Hey, are you still hitting a thousand?"

"Come on, Gabby, I don't want to talk about it."

"You are, you are! What is it, thirty for thirty?"

"Thirty-six for thirty-six," Ramona said. "But it is bad luck to talk about it."

"That's all right," Kevin said. "I'm not gonna mind when it ends anyway, it's making me nervous."

And this was true. Batting a thousand was not natural. Hit as well as possible, some line drives should still be caught. To keep firing them into empty places on the field was just plain weird, and Kevin was not comfortable with it. People were razzing him, too, both opponents and his own teammates. Mr. Thousand. Mr. Perfect. Heaven Kevin. It was embarrassing.

"Strike out on purpose, then," Hank suggested. "Get it over with. That's what I'd do."

"Damned if I will!"

They laughed at him.

Besides, each time he walked to the plate, that night or any other, and stood there half-swinging his bat, and the pitcher lofted up the ball, big and white and round against the black and the skittering moths, like a full moon falling out of the sky—then all thought would fly from his mind, he became an utter blank; and would come to standing on first or second or third, grinning and feeling the hit still in his hands and wrists. He couldn't stop it even if he wanted to.

Another day as they were finishing work Ramona cruised by and said to Kevin, "Want to go to the beach?"

His heartbeat tocked at the back of his throat. "Sure."

Biking down the Newport Freeway the wind cut through him, and with clear road ahead he shifted into high gear and started pumping hard. Ramona drafted him and after a while took the lead, and they zipped down the gentle slope of the coastal basin pumping so hard that they passed the cars in the next lane, and all for the fun of going fast. On the narrow streets of Costa Mesa and Newport Beach they had to slow and negotiate the traffic, following it out to the end of Balboa Peninsula. Here apartment blocks jumbled high on both sides of the street. Nothing could be done to reduce the population along such a fine beach, and besides the ocean-mad residents seemed to enjoy the crowd. Many of the old crackerbox apartments had been joined and reworked, and now big tentlike complexes quivered like flags in the wind, sheltering co-ops, tribes, big families, vacation groups, complete strangers—every social unit ever imagined was housed there, behind fabric walls bright with the traditional Newport Beach pastels.

They coasted to the end of the peninsula, under rows of palm trees. Scraps of green tossed overhead in the strong onshore breeze. They came to the Wedge and stopped. This was the world's most famous body surfing beach. Here waves from the west came in at an angle to the long jetty at the Newport Harbor channel, and as the waves approached the beach, masses of water built up against the rocks. Eventually these masses surged back out to sea in a huge backwash, a counterwave which crossed subsequent incoming swells at an angle, creating peaks, fast powerful cusps that moved across the waves very rapidly, often just at the point they were breaking. It was like something out of a physics class wave tank, and it was tremendously popular with body surfers, because the secondary wave could propel a body across the face of the primary wave with heartstopping speed. Add an element of danger—the water was often only three feet deep at the break, and tales of paralysis and death were common— and the result was a perfect adrenalin rush for the OC ocean maniac.

Today, however, the Pacific was pacific, almost lakelike, and the Wedge Effect was not working. This was fine with Ramona and Kevin, they were happy just to swim. Cool salt tang, the luxurious sensuality of immersion, flotation, the return to the sea. Kevin sharked over the rippled tawny sand on the bottom, looked up through silver bubbles at the surface, saw its rise and fall, its curious partial reflectivity, sky and sand both visible at once. Long graceful body in a dark red suit, swimming overhead with powerful strokes. Women are dolphins, he thought, and laughed a burst of silver at the sky. He ran out of air and shot to the surface, broke into blinding white air, eyes scored by salt and sun, delicious stinging. "Outside," Ramona called, but she was fooling; no waves of any size out there, only flat glary blue, all the way to the horizon. Nothing but shore break. They grunioned around in that for a long time, mindless, lifted up and down by the moon. After that their suits were full of sand, they had to swim out again to flush them clean.

Back on the beach. Sitting on sand, half dry. Salt crust on smooth brown skin. The smell of salt and seaweed, the cool wind.

"Want to walk out the jetty?"

Onto the mound of giant boulders, stepping carefully. Rough uneven surfaces of basalt and feldspar gleamed in the light, gray and black and white and red and brown. Between the rocks the swells rose and fell, sucking and slapping the barnacles.

"We used to come out here all the time when we were kids."

"Us too," Ramona said. "The whole house. Boulder ballet, we called it. Only on the other jetty, because my mom always took us to Corona del Mar." Newport Harbor's channel was flanked on both sides by jetties, the other one was some two hundred yards across the water.

"It was always the Wedge for us. There was something magical about walking out this jetty when I was a kid. A big adventure, like going to the end of the world."

They stepped and balanced, hopped and teetered. Occasionally they bumped together, arm to arm. Their skin was warm in the sun. They talked about this and that, and Kevin felt certain boundaries disappearing. Ramona was willing to talk about anything, now, about things beyond the present moment. Childhoods in El Modena and at the beach. The boats offshore. Their work. The people they knew. The huge rocks jumbled under them: "Where *did* they come from, anyway?" They didn't know. It didn't matter. What do you talk about when you're falling in love? It doesn't matter. All the questions are, Who are you? How do you think? Are you like me? Will you love me? And all the answers are, I am like this, like this, like this. I am like you. I like you.

"We used to race out to the end sometimes, running over these rocks! Crazy!"

"Yeah, we're a lot more sensible now," Ramona said, and grinned.

They came to the end, where the causeway of stone plunged into the sea. The horizon stood before them at eye level, a hazy white bar. Sunlight broke on the sea in a billion points, flickering like gold signal mirrors, sending a Morse of infinite complexity.

They sat on a flat boulder, side by side. Ramona leaned back on both hands, jacking her elbows forward. Muscley brown forearms bulged side to side, muscley brown biceps bulged front to back. Triceps stood out like the swells between the jetties.

"How's things at your house?"

"Okay," Kevin said. "Andrea's back is bothering her. Yoshi is sick of teaching English, Sylvia's worried that the kids have chicken pox. Donna and Cindy are still drinking too much, and Tomas still spends all his time at the screen. The usual lunacy. I bet Nadezhda thinks we're bedlam."

"She's nice."

"Yeah. But sometimes the house is just howling, and the look on her face . . ."

"It can't be any worse than India."

"Maybe. Maybe it bothers me more than her. I tell you, some nights when the kids are wild I wonder if living in small families isn't a good idea."

"Oh no," Ramona said. "Do you think so? I mean, they're so isolated."

"Quieter."

"Sure, but so what? I mean, you've always got your room. But if it were only you and a partner and kids! Try to imagine Rosa and Josh doing that! Rosa doesn't do a thing to take care of Doug and Ginger, she's always working or down here surfing. So those kids are there and they're really into being entertained constantly, and sometime I know Josh would just go crazy if he were in a little house all by himself. He almost does already."

"A lot of them did, I guess. Mothers."

"Yeah. But at our place Josh can get me or my mom to take the kids while he goes out to swim or something, and we can talk with him, and he tells us about it and feels better, and by the time Rosa's back he's having a good time and he doesn't care. Unless he's really pissed at her. But they manage. I don't think their marriage would survive if they lived by themselves."

Kevin nodded. "But what about other couples who're different? What you're saying is that marriages are less intense now because people tend to live in groups. But what about the really good marriages? Then reducing the intensity is just diffusing something good."

"Diffusing it, yeah, spreading it around. Maybe we need to have that kind of good diffused out. The couple won't suffer."

"No? Well. Maybe not." What about us, then? Kevin wanted to say. He had never even found someone he felt like trying with. And she and Alfredo, fifteen years? What went wrong? "But . . . something is gone, I think. Something I think I'd like."

Ramona frowned, considering it. They watched swells run up and down the seaweedy, mussel-crusted band of rock at sea level. Talked about other things. Felt light crash into their skin.

Ramona pointed north. "Couple of big ships coming."

"Oh, I love to watch those." He sat up, shaded his eyes with a hand. Two tall ships had risen over the horizon, converging on the harbor from slightly different angles, one from San Pedro, and the other rounding Catalina from the north. Both were combinations of square rigged and fore-and-aft rigged, the current favorite of ship designers. They resembled the giant barkentines built in the last years of sailing's classic age, only the fore-and-aft sails were rigid, and bulged around the masts in an airfoil shape. Each ship had five masts, and the one rounding Catalina had an isosceles mast for its foremast, two spars rising from the hull to meet overhead.

Suddenly all the yards on both ships bloomed white with sail, and the little bones of white water chewed by their sharp bows got larger. "Hey they're racing!" Kevin said. "They're racing!"

Ramona stood to watch. The onshore breeze was strengthening, and the two ships were on a reach across it, so their sails bulged toward shore. Stunsails bloomed to each side of the highest yards, and from a distance it seemed the ships flew over the water, gliding like pelicans. Working freighters only, so big they could never be really fast, but those stacks of white sail, full-bellied with the wind! Complex as jets, simple as kites, the two craft cut through the swells and converged on the harbor, on each other. It seemed possible the windward ship might try to steal the other's wind, and sure enough the leeward ship began to luff off a bit, toward the beach. Perhaps the pilot would have to try swinging behind the windward ship, to trade places and reverse the tactic; a dangerous maneuver, however, as they might never catch up. "Isosceles is trying to push them into the beach," Ramona observed.

"Yeah, they're caught inside. I say Isosceles has them."

"No, I say Leeward's closer, they'll slip right around the jetty here, we'll probably be able to step aboard."

"Bet."

"Okay."

On the end of the other jetty a group of kids were standing and shouting at the sight. The wind pushed at them, Kevin raised his arms to feel it. That something so free and wild should be harnessed to the will: the ancient elegance of it made him laugh.

"Go, Isosceles!" "Go, Leeward!" And they shouted and bumped shoulders like the kids on the other jetty. As the ships got closer they could see better how big they were. The channel couldn't take any larger, it looked as if the main-yards would stretch from one jetty to the other, great silver condor wings of alloy. The crews of the two ships were standing on the windward rails as ballast, and someone on each ship hurled amplified insults across the ever-narrowing gap of water between them. It really did look as though they would reach the channel mouth in a dead heat, in which case Isosceles would be forced to luff off, according to race protocol. Ramona was gleefully pointing this out to Kevin when a long silver spar telescoped out from the windward side of Isosceles's bow, and an immense rainbow-striped balloon spinnaker whooshed into existence like a parachute, dragging the whole great ship behind it. Swells exploded under the bow. "Coming through!" they heard the tinny loudspeaker from Isosceles cry, and with a faint Bronx cheer the Leeward sloughed off. Its stunsails rolled up into their spars, and the spars telescoped back in under the yards. Sail was taken in everywhere, without a single sailor aloft, and the ship settled down into the water like a motorboat with the throttle cut. When Isosceles turned into the channel entrance, to the cheers of spectators on both jetties, its sails too disappeared, rolling up with the faint hum of automated rigging and tackle blocks. Three of the five topsails and the isosceles top section served to propel it down the channel at a stately five miles an hour, and the bare spars stood high against the hills of Corona del Mar. Leeward followed it in, looking much the same. The crews waved back at them.

"They're so *beautiful*," Kevin said.

"I wonder if one of them is Nadezhda's ship," Ramona said. "It's due soon."

They sat down again, leaned back against the warm rock side by side, arms touching. A thick rain of light poured down on them, knitting tightly with the onshore wind. Photon by photon, striking and flaking off, filling the air so that everything—the sea, the tall ships, the stone of the jetties, the green light tower at the other jetty's end, the buoys clanging on the groundswell, the long sand reach of the beach, the lifeguard stands and their streaming flags, the pastel wrack of apartments, the palm fronds swaying over it all—everything floated in a white light, an aura of salt mist, ethereal in the photon rain. In every particulate jot of being . . . Kevin settled back like a sleepy cat. "What a day."

And Ramona leaned over, black hair blinding as a crow's wing, and kissed him.

Over the next weeks matters progressed on the Rattlesnake Hill issue, but slowly and amorphously, so that it was hard to keep a sense of what was happening. A letter came back from LA's Metropolitan Water District, outlining their offer of more water. What it came down to was a reduced rate if they purchased more. Mary and the town planner's office immediately made inquiries with the OCWD concerning sell-through rates. Clearly they were hoping that El Modena could buy the extra water from LA, and then give what they didn't use to OCWD by pouring it into the groundwater basin. This would get them credits from OCWD that they could use against pump taxes, and the net result might be a considerable savings, with a lot of water in reserve.

Oscar shook his head when he heard about it. "I believe I'd like to look into this one a little more," he murmured. First of all, he told Kevin, town resolution 2022 would have to be overthrown or some sort of special dispensation made, which would take council action or a town vote. And then the whole maneuver would tend to put the town in the water business, buying it here and selling it there, and the State Water Resources Control Board was likely to have some thoughts about that, no matter what the district watermaster said. If it came to a town vote that superficially looked like it was only about saving money, Oscar wanted to talk to Sally Tallhawk about her suggestion concerning Inyo County's water. Inyo now owned the water that used to belong to Los Angeles, and it was possible they could work out some kind of deal, and buy even cheaper water from Inyo than the MWD was offering, with some use stipulations included that would keep the water from fueling a big development. Certainly Inyo would appreciate the irony of altering the shape of development in southern California, after the years of manipulation they had suffered at the hands of LA.

So Oscar was busy. Kevin for his part dropped by to talk with Hiroko, Susan, and Jerry, to see what they were thinking about the matter. Jerry had let his law practice lapse so that he could help run a small computer firm located down on Santiago Creek where it crossed Tustin Avenue, and Kevin found him there one day, eating lunch by the creek. He was a burly man in his early sixties, who looked as calm and sensible as you could ever want, until you noticed a glint in his eye, the only indication of a secret sense of humor, a sort of anarchist's playfulness that the town had come to know all too well.

He shrugged when Kevin asked him about the hill matter. "Depends what it is. I need to see Alfredo's plans, what it would do for the town."

"Jerry, that's the last empty hill in the whole area! Why should he take that hill? I notice you're content to have your business down here on the flats."

Jerry swallowed a bit of sandwich. "Maybe I'm not content. Maybe I'd like to take some offices up there in Alfredo's complex."

"Ah, come on. Here you are down by the creek for lunch. I know you appreciate the way this town has been working, what it stands for. Why else would you be here?"

"I was born here."

"Yah, well . . ." Kevin sighed. Talking to Jerry was hard. "All the more reason you should want to protect it. It's a miracle the water district held on to that hill for so long, and now that we've got it, it would be a shame to make it look like all the rest of them. Think about it."

"I'll think about it." He swallowed. "Know what I heard?"

"What?"

"I heard Alfredo's being pressed into trying for this move. Needs to do it."

Kevin thought about that as he rode over to see Susan Mayer. Susan was chief scientist at the El Modena Chicken Farm, which supplied much of northern Orange County with chickens. Kevin found her out in the farm's lab, cursing a gc/mass spec: an athletic woman in her forties, one of the best swimmers in town. "I don't really have time to talk about it now, Kevin, but I assure you I know just what you're worried about. Alfredo is a nice man, and good for the town, but sometimes it seems like he should be in Irvine or Anaheim where the stakes are higher." She wouldn't say more than that. "Sorry, I've got to get to work on this, it looks like we might have an outbreak in one of the coops. We'll have to wait and see about the hill stuff until we know more anyway, right?"

Sigh. On to Hiroko, botanist and orchard farmer. Also a landscape gardener, and she was out on a job. Kevin found her and gave her a hand digging up a front yard, and they had a good long talk as they worked. Hiroko had been on the council on and off for about twenty years, and so nothing much in that area excited her anymore. But she seemed sympathetic, and skeptical about Alfredo and his big plans, as she put it. Kevin left her feeling good. If they could count on Hiroko, then it would only take one more to have a majority on the council. Susan and Jerry were both possibles, and so . . .

He told Doris what Jerry had said about Alfredo needing to make the move. "Hmm," Doris said. "Okay, I'll see if pretending I know that for sure will pull anything more out of John." She was working the hardest of them all, pumping her connections for more news from inside Heartech. Her friend John heard a lot in the financial office of her own firm, Avending, and his friend over in Heartech's offices knew even more. The next time she talked to him, she said something about Alfredo having to make a move. "Yeah, it's an outside thing," John said, "Ann's sure of it. They've always had a source of outside money, she says. That's why it's ballooned so fast."

Apparently Heartech's growth had been even more rapid than it appeared to the public. And some of that growth was being absorbed by a hidden backer, so that Heartech would remain within legal company size, and avoid any special audits from the IRS. Or so the rumors had it. "They're iceberging in the black, Ann says," John told Doris in a low voice.

"Unbelievable," Doris said. If it were true, then they would have the best weapon possible to stop any office-building by Heartech. Proving it, however . . . "But if they build this development they're going to come under the microscope! No way they can fund it themselves—they'll either have to apply for government help or have a partner."

"True," John said a week later. "And Doris—I'm sorry to tell you, but . . ."

Dear Claire:

. . . Yes, I went to Opening Day in Bishop, and provided the usual entertainment for the masses with Sally. Our match was witnessed by Kevin and Doris; the sturdy Doris was either appalled or disgusted, she couldn't decide which. She had little spare time to scorn the Grand Sport, however, as she and Kevin spent at least part of the weekend recomplicating an old relationship. They were lovers long ago, Nadezhda told me, and currently Doris seems both attracted to and exasperated by Kevin, while he, it seems to me, relies on her rather more than he realizes. They spent a night in Sally's guest room, and afterwards the currents swirling around under the surface of things would have spun a submarine. This, at the same time that Kevin is enthusiastically exploring the consequences of Ramona the Beauty's freedom. It's getting pretty complicated in Elmo. . . .

. . . Yes, Nadezhda is still here, though she won't be for long; her ship is in Newport Harbor, and in two or three weeks it will depart, taking her with it. That will be a sad day. We have done a lot together, and it has been a delight. Often she calls to ask if I want to cruise the town, and if I agree I am dragged all over Orange County in a kind of parody of an educational tour. She's like Ben Franklin on drugs. What are you doing here? Why are you doing it this way and not that? Is it really true that mustard grass was part of the original ground cover on this plain? Couldn't you use bigger cells? Aren't you thinking the mayor is pushing things too fast? Is it true what they say about Kevin and Ramona? She peppers them with questions till they reel, then bikes away muttering about slowness, ignorance, sleepwalking. What zombies, she'll mutter if they're unresponsive. What sheep! On the other hand, when she runs into people who know what they are doing and enjoy talking about it, she gets them going for hours, and bikes away glowing. Ah, what energy, what ingenuity, what boldness! she will cry, face flushed, eyes bright. And so the people here love her, while at the same time being slightly afraid of her. With her combination of fire and wisdom, of energy and experience, she seems like some higher life form, some next step in evolution. Old but young. Those geriatric drugs must really be something. Maybe I'd better start taking them now.

Certainly her presence has put the jumper cables to Tom Barnard, who was living a hermit's life in the hills before her arrival. Now he comes into town pretty regularly. Many people here know him, especially among the older generations, and Nadezhda has worked hard at getting him re-involved in their lives, in her usual energetic fashion. They're doing a lot of socializing together. Also, we've started to get him seriously involved in the struggle over the plans for Rattlesnake Hill.

Developments (so to speak) in the hill battle abound, as Kevin and Doris try to put Sally's suggestions into action. They may even drill a spring. This was Sally's suggestion, and I am sure she was joking, but she played it like a wooden Indian, and they took her seriously. Far be it from me to disabuse them, and explain that a drilled spring (or *well*, as we call it) will not stop development.

One night in the midst of this activity Doris came home from work slamming doors and snarling. I had just dropped by their house to talk to Kevin, and found no one home but the kids. I was the only adult there, an unusual situation that neither Doris nor I would have wanted, I am sure.

However, I asked what was wrong. She shouted her reply; a friend in the financial department of her company, Avending, had told her that Avending was negotiating with Heartech, the mayor's company, over plans to propose a new complex in El Modena. Here we had been wondering who Alfredo and his partners would get to join them in building this complex, and it was Doris's own company!

I tried to make a joke. At least she would be within walking distance of her job, I said. She gave me her Medusa imitation, a very convincing one.

I'm quitting, she said. I can't work there anymore.

Something in the way she said it made me feel mischievous. I wanted to push at this virtue of hers, see how far it extended. I said, first you ought to find out what you can about their plans.

She stared at me. Do you think so?

I nodded.

I'd need some help.

I'll help you, I said, surprising both of us.

So she called her friend in the financial office, and spoke urgently with him for nearly half an hour. And then I found myself accompanying Fierce Doris to her place of employment, Avending of Santa Ana.

It was a small complex of labs and offices near the freeway. Doris led us in past a security guard, explaining I was a friend.

Once in her lab I stared around me, amazed! It was the biggest surprise of a pretty surprising night; the office part of the lab was filled with sculpture! Small pieces, large pieces, abstracts, human and animal figures . . . made of metals, ceramics, materials I couldn't identify. What is this? I said.

You know, we develop materials here, she said. Superconductors and like that. These are throwaways from various experiments.

You mean they just come out like this? I said stupidly.

She laughed shortly.

You sculpt them, I said.

Yes, that's right. I'm going to have to get all these home. . . .

You could have knocked me over with a feather, or at least a pillow. Who knows what depths these southern tidepools conceal? Any step might plunge you overhead in the brine. . . .

Doris went to work on the computer, and soon the printer was ejecting page after page of records. We need to do the rest in John's office, she said. That's tricky—I'm in my lab all the time at night, but there's no reason to be in his office. You'll have to keep a lookout for security, and the cleaning robots.

We tiptoed down the corridor into her friend's office. Again the computer, the print out. I kept watch in the hall while Doris xeroxed pages from a file cabinet. She began to fill boxes.

A cleaning robot hummed down the hall toward us. Feverishly I disarranged an office between us and it, hoping to slow it down. I didn't get out in time, and it bumped into me coming in the doorway. "Excuse me," it said. "Cleaning."

"Quite all right. Could you please clean this office?"

"Excuse me. Cleaning." It entered the office and uttered a little click, no doubt dismayed at the mess I had just made. I dashed past it, back to Doris.

She was done xeroxing, and about two hours later she was done printing out. We carried box after box into the parking lot, finishing just ahead of the cleaning robot's entrance.

Outside we had a bicycle built for two, with a big trailer attached behind. We piled that trailer so high with boxes that when we got on the bike, it was as if it were set in cement. There we were, absconding with Avending's entire history, and we couldn't move an inch. Both of us jumped up and down on the pedals; no movement. What would security say when they saw us? Thieves, escaping at zero miles an hour.

I had to get off and apply the Atomic Drop to the trailer to get us started, and then run around and leap into my saddle, to hop furiously on a pedal that moved like an hour hand. Unfortunately the right turn we took onto the street killed our momentum. It was necessary to apply three Atomic Drops in succession to get us moving again. After that it was a matter of acceleration. Once we got up to about five miles an hour, we found we could maintain it pretty well.

The next day Doris quit her job. Now she is getting Tom to help her go through the records she stole. It is unclear whether they will be of use, but Tom thinks it is possible the two companies have illegal sources of capital, or will obtain them to help finance the complex. Worth looking for, he says. And something in the records made him suggest that Hong Kong might be implicated. So our raid is justified. Fierce Doris strikes again!

She gave me one of her sculptures, in thanks for my help. Big slabs of a blue-green ceramic alloy: a female figure, tossing aloft a bird, a raptor in its first downstroke. A wonderful sense of movement. We stared at it, both embarrassed to speechlessness.

Have you been sculpting long? I asked.

A few years.

What inspired you to begin?

Well—I was running experiments on certain materials under pressure, and when they came out of the kiln, they looked funny. I kept seeing things in them, you know, like you see shapes in clouds. So I started to help bring the shapes out.

I'll put this in my atrium when they're done working, I said.

. . . Work on my house continues apace. Right now it looks like the Parthenon: roofless and blown apart. They assure me it will begin to coalesce soon, and I hope so, because some strange things have happened when I am home alone, and perhaps when the house is finished they will stop happening.

. . . Of course I still feel disoriented—unprotected, in the midst of growing a new shell, of building a new life. But the old life in Chicago seems more and more like a dream to me—a very long and vivid dream, admittedly—but a dream still, and like a dream it is growing less intense and less easy to remember as I drift further away. Strange, this life, isn't it? We think, nothing could ever get more real than this! Then *this* becomes nothing more than a darting fragmentary complex of pure mentation, while a new reality, more real than ever! steps in to obscure all previous candidates. I never get used to it. Well—write soon, please—I miss you—xx oo—

Your Oscar

... 6

Been on plane four hours now. Liddy finally asleep. Tapping on lap keyboard. Might as well distract myself.

Strategies for changing history. Invent the history leading out of this world (please) into the world of the book. Causes of utopian process gaining upper hand.

Words scroll up and disappear forever, like days.

Lincoln not assassinated, no, no, we know it didn't happen that way, we know we can't take that road. Not useful. Someone appears to lead us, no! No Great Man theory here. No individual can save us. Together or not at all.

Together or nothing. Ah, Pamela—

Some group. In power or out. Act together. Say lawyers, the law? Still can't escape the feeling that there's where a difference could be made, despite my own experience. Remake the law of the land. Say a whole class of Harvard Law School, class of '12 goes out to fill posts of all kinds, government, World Bank, IMF, Pentagon. Save the twenty-first century. Plausible? No. A story. But at least it's possible, I mean we could do it! Nothing stopping us but inertia, ideology. Lack of imagination! Teachers, religious leaders . . . but there are few politically active people in any group. And to agree on a whole program of action, all of them. How implausible can something be before it's useless? It's conspiracy theory, really. We don't need that either.

History changed by a popular book, a utopia, everyone reads it and it has ideas, or vague pokes in the direction of ideas, it changes their thinking, everyone starts working for a better world—

Getting desperate. Marcuse: one of the worst signs of our danger is we can't imagine the route from here to utopia. No way to get there.

Take the first step and you're there. Process, dynamism, the way is the life. We must imagine the way. Our imagination is stronger than theirs! Take the first step and you're on the road.

And so? In my book?

Stare at empty screen. My daughter sighs in her sleep. Her sleeping face. It's a matter of touch, and if you can't touch the one you love—can't see her—

We're thirty-five thousand feet above the earth. People are watching a movie. The blue curve of the world, such a big place, so much bigger than we ever think, until something takes us. . . .

Words scroll up and disappear forever, like

The night of Hank's Mars party they rode into the hills in a big group, bike lamps bobbing like a string of fireflies. The Lobos formed the core of the party, then Oscar was along, and Tom and Nadezhda, weaving dangerously on a bicycle built for two. They came to the end of the paved road near Black Star Canyon and left the bikes behind. Hank's backpack clinked as he led them up the dark trail. Oscar stumbled in the forest twilight: "Humanity lands on the fabled red planet, and we celebrate this feat by wandering in the dark like savages. It's *2001* run backwards. Ow!"

The air was warm. The sage and low gnarled oaks covering the canyon walls clattered and shooshed in irregular gusts of wind. A Santa Ana wind was arriving, sweeping down from the north, compressing over the San Jacintos, warming and losing moisture until it burst out of the canyons hot and dry. "Santa Ana!" Tom said, sniffing. He explained to Nadezhda, touched the back of her hand and she jumped. "Static electricity. It's a good sign."

An electric shock with every touch.

After a half hour's climb they came to Black Star Hot Springs, a series of small pools in a narrow meadow. Sycamore, live oak, and black walnut stood crowded on the flat canyon floor, surrounding the pools. Near the largest pool was a small cabin and pavilion. Hank had rented it from the town for the night, and he unlocked the door and turned on a lamp inside. Yellow window squares illuminated the steam bubbling off the pool's surface. Stiff live oak leaves clacked together. Branch rubbed on branch, adding ghostly creaks to the susurrous of leaf sound.

"Yow—it's hot tonight."

The large pool was two down from the source of the spring. Concrete steps and an underwater concrete bench had been built into it, and the rest of the bottom was a hard gritty sandstone not much different from the concrete in texture. The pool was about twenty feet across, and varied between three and five feet in depth. In short, a perfect hot springs pool.

Hank, Jody, Mike, and Oscar put food and drink into the cabin's refrigerator. The rest shed their clothes and stepped into the pool. Abrupt splashes, squeals of pain, hoots of delight. The water was the temperature of a hot bath, deliciously warm once past the initial shock of it.

Oscar appeared at the pool's edge, a big white blob in the dim light. "Watch out," Kevin said. Oscar threw his massive head back; in the darkness he seemed three times the size of a man, broad-shouldered, barrel-chested, big-bellied, thick-legged. His friends stared despite themselves. Suddenly he crouched, threw his arms wide, mimed jumping out over them. Just the way he shifted on his feet and whipped his head around implied the whole action of running forward and leaping up, landing in a giant cannonball dive. "No, no! The pool! You'll crack the bottom!" He pawed the ground with a bare foot, shook his black curls ferociously, took a little run back, then forward to the pool's edge, then back again, arms outstretched like a surfer's, tilting with the absurd rhinocerine grace Kevin and Doris had seen in Bishop. Hank and Jody and Mike came out of the cabin to see what the ruckus was about, and with a last great wind-up Oscar took off, into the air like a great white whale, suspended in a ball several feet above them. Then KERPLOP, and an enormous splash.

Wild shrieks. "My God," said Gabriela, "the water's two feet lower."

"And just think if Oscar weren't in the pool."

Doris, laughing hard, said "Oscar, you have to stay in so we aren't beached."

"Glug," Oscar said, spurting water from his mouth like an Italian fountain, an immense Cupid.

"What's the flow rate of this spring?" Mike said. "Ten gallons a minute? We should be back to normal by morning."

"We'll have to pour some tequila in," Hank said solemnly, carrying out a big tray filled with bottles and glasses. "A sacrifice. Here, start working on these."

Jody passed around glasses, leaning out over the water.

"You look like a cocktail waitress, stop working so hard, we can get this stuff."

"Hank's bringing out the masks, then we're done."

Hank brought out a stack of papier-mâché masks he had made, animal faces of all kinds. "Great, Hank." "Yeah, I spent a couple months on these, every night." He gave them out, very particular about who got which one. Kevin was a horse, Ramona an eagle, Gabriela a rooster, Mike a fish; Tom was a turtle, Nadezhda a cat; Oscar was a frog, Doris a crow, Jody a tiger, and Hank himself was a coyote. All the masks had eyeholes, and mouths convenient for drinking. They walked around the pool inspecting each other and giggling. Masked heads, naked bodies: it was weird, bizarre, dangerous looking.

"Rabbit!"

They all joined in with the appropriate cry.

Jody stepped into the pool and whistled at its heat, her long body feline under the tiger mask. Hank hopped around handing people glasses, or bottles for those who needed them to be able to drink through their masks.

"This is Hank's own tequila," Tom told Nadezhda. "He grows the cactus in his garden and does all the extraction and fermentation and distillation himself." He took a gulp from his glass. "*Horrible* stuff. Here, Hank, give me some more of that."

"It tastes fine to me," Nadezhda said, then coughed hard.

Tom laughed. "Yeah, tequila is heavenly."

Hank stood at one end of the pool, looking perfectly natural, as if he always went naked and sported a coyote head. "Listen to the wind." He prowled around the pool's edge. Over the trickle of water they could hear the wind soughing, and suddenly the shape of the canyon was perfectly clear to them: the narrowing upstream, the headwall, the side canyons up above—all that, just in sound. Hank began humming, and some of them picked it up, the great "aum" shifting as different people joined in or stopped to breathe. Over this ground bass Hank muttered what sounded like random sentences, some intelligible, some not. "We come from the earth. We're part of the earth." Then a low breath chant, "Hi-ya *huh*, hi-ya *huh*, au-oom," and then more complex and various, a singsong poem in a language none of them knew, punctuated by exclamations. "We come from the earth like this water, pouring into the world. We are bubbles of earth. Bubbles of earth." Then another language, Sanskrit, Shoshone, only the shaman knew. He prowled around them like Coyote checking out a hen-house, growling. They could feel his physical authority; they stood in the pool milling around to face him, chanting too, getting louder until Coyote howled, and suddenly they were all baying at the moon, as loud as voices could ever be.

Hank hopped in the pool, hooted. "Man when you're wet that wind is cold!"

"Quick," Tom said, "more awful tequila."

"Good idea."

Jody went to get more from the cabin, and while she was there she pulled the cabin's TV onto the deck and turned it on, with the sound off. It seemed a kind of lamp, the faces and command centers mere colored forms. Jody dialed up music, Chinese harps and low flute tones, whistling over the sound of the wind. Overhead the stars blinked and shivered, brilliant in the so-black sky; the moon wouldn't rise for a hour or two. Just over the treetops one of the big orbiting solar collectors shone like a jewel, like a chip of the moon or a planet ten times bigger than Jupiter.

Ramona stood in the shallow end, a broad-shouldered eagle, collarbones prominent under sleek wet skin. "The water gets too hot, but with the wind it feels really cold when you get out. You can't get it right."

"Reminds me of Muir's night on Shasta," the turtle said. "He was tough, his father was a Calvinist minister and a cruel man, he beat Muir and worked him at the bottom of wells. So nothing in the Sierras ever bothered him. But one time he and a friend climbed Shasta and got caught in a storm up there at the top, a real bad blizzard. It should have killed them, but luckily Shasta was more active in those days, and there was still a hot spring pool in the summit caldera. Muir and his friend found this pool and jumped in, but the water in it was like a hundred and fifty degrees, and full of sulphur gas. So they couldn't stay in it, but when they got out they started to freeze instantly. It was scald or freeze, no middle ground. All they could do to survive was keep dipping in and out of the pool, lying in the shallows and rolling over all night long, one side in the water and the other in the wind, on and on until their senses were so blasted that they couldn't tell the hot from the cold. Afterwards Muir said it was the most uncomfortable night he had ever spent, which is saying a lot, because he was a wild man."

"Sounds like our Hank," the tiger said. "One time we were up in the Sierras and a lightning storm struck, and I turned around and there was Hank climbing a tall tree—I said what the hell are you doing? and he said he wanted to get a better look."

Said the rooster, "One time we went to Yosemite and climbed to the top of Yosemite Falls, and Hank, he walked right out knee deep to where he could look over the edge! Three thousand feet down!"

"Hey," Hank said, "how else you gonna see it?"

They laughed at him.

"It was October, I tell you, the water was low!"

"How about that time we were on top of that water tower on the Colorado and these crazies hauled up in a motor boat and ran up the tower and dove off into the river—must have been fifty or sixty feet! And soon as they were finished Hank just leaned out over, and kept on leaning till he dove in too! Sixty feet!"

"I woulda done it before," Coyote said, "but it didn't occur to me till I saw those guys do it."

The rooster crowed with laughter. "Once we were riding a ski lift at Big Bear and Hank says to me Don't this look like a great take-off point, Gabby? It'd be just like dropping in on a big wave, wouldn't it? And before I could say no it wouldn't be anything like dropping in on a big wave he had *hopped out of the fucking ski lift*, dropped and turned thirty feet through the air and hit the slope flying!"

"Actually, I cut my forehead on the front of my skis on that one," Hank said. "Don't know how."

"What about the time you took Damaso climbing in Joshua Tree—"

"Oh, that was a mistake," Coyote said. "He got freaked and came off when we were crossing Hairball Ledge, and fell so fast I had to grab him by his *hair* as he slid by. A hundred feet up and we're hanging there by two fingertips and Damaso's *hair*."

"I feel comfortable again," the eagle announced, head bobbing on the water's surface. "Or at least safer."

She floated over to the horse. Instantly Kevin felt a dizzying stallion's rush of blood coursing through his side as hers touched him. Knees, whole thighs; she stayed there, pressed against him. The blood poured through him, spurting out of his heart in great booms, flushing out every capillary in his skin, so that he had to take in a big shivery breath to contain all the tingling. The power of the touch. Their shoulders brushed, and her newly emergent wet flesh felt as warm as the water. Steam caught the rose light from the TV screen. They were showing a close-up of Mars. The horse considered the idea of an orgasm through his side.

Oscar and Doris, frog and crow, were discussing the most dangerous things they had ever done, in a facetious style so that they spoke only of accidents. Getting caught under a bronze mold, flying with Ramona, wrestling the Vancouver Virgins, trying to rescue a college paper from a burning apartment. . . . Their claims for their own stupidity were matched only by their claims for the other's. Hearing this from across the pool, the cat nudged the turtle and made a tiny gesture in their direction. The turtle shook his head, nodded with his round head toward the horse and the eagle. The cat shrugged.

"I think it's time," Coyote declared. "Isn't Mars getting closer?"

"Should I turn up the sound?"

"NO."

Flute and Chinese harp, and the wind in the trees, served them as soundtrack for humanity's first touch of another planet. So often delayed, so often screwed up, the journey was finally coming to its end—which was also a beginning, of something none of them could see, exactly, though they all knew it was important. A whole world, a whole history, implied in a single image. . . .

From orbit the expedition had dropped several robot landers, in Hellas Basin where they planned to touch down, and all of these robots were equipped with heat-seeking cameras, which were now trained on the manned lander as it descended. The directors of the TV program had any number of fine images to choose from, and often they split the screen to provide more than one. The view from the lander as Hellas, the biggest of all craters, got closer and more distinct, its floor a rock-strewn plain of reddish sand. Or the view from the ground, looking up into a dark pink sky, where there was an odd thing, a black dot in the middle of a white circle, growing larger. It resolved to the lander and its parachute, then bloomed with white light as retro-rockets fired. The view shifted to a shot from orbit, in super telephoto, the lander a white spot of thistledown, drifting onto a desert floor. Ah yes—images that would become part of history forever and ever, created in this very moment, in the knife-edge present that is all we ever inhabit. The TV seemed huge.

Coyote shaman started chanting again, and some of the other animals provided the purring background hum. Everything—the stars shivering overhead, the black leaves clicking in the black sky, the deep whoosh of the wind, the wet chuckle of water, the weird Chinese music, their voices, the taste of cactus, the extraordinary square of rich red color, over against the dark mass of the pavilion—all fused to a single whole, a unit of experience in which nothing could be removed. The turtle, pulling out of it for a moment, had to admire the shaman's strange sense of ritual, of place. How better to be part of this moment, one of humanity's greatest? Then the lander fell closer to the ground and their voices rose, they saw the sand on the desert floor kick up, as if in a wind like the one swirling their wet skin, and the turtle felt a surge of something he had almost forgotten. Grinning inside his mask, he howled and howled. They all were howling. The lander dropped lower, throwing out clouds and clouds of dust and red sand. They screamed at the stars as it touched down, jumping and cheering wildly. "Yaay! Yaay!"

There were people on Mars.

After that the action on screen returned to the business of astronauts and commentators. Hank ran to the cabin and came back with a couple of light beachballs that he threw in the pool. They batted the balls around in volleyball style, talked, drank, watched the continuing drama of the astronauts suiting up. "What will they say, you know, their first words?"

"If they say something stupid like on the moon, I'll throw up."

"How about, 'Well, here we are.'"

"Home at last."

"The Martians have landed."

"Take me to your leader."

"If we don't turn the sound up we'll never know."

"That would be an odd thing to say."

"We'll find out tomorrow, leave it down. We're doing better than they will anyway, you know astronauts."

A ball in the middle of the pool rolled over slowly on the water, pushed seemingly by the steam that curled off the surface in lazy arabesques. Foggy yellow light. Images of raised arms, flexing shoulders, breasts and pecs, animal faces. They glowed in the dark, their bodies looked like translucent pink skins containing some sort of flame.

They sat in a circle, silent, resting, feeling the water flow over them, the wind course through them. Muscles relaxed to mush in the warmth, and minds followed. The eagle crossed the pool to sit by the horse again, moving slowly, in a sort of dream dance that threw up a wake of steam streamers. A sudden flurry of sycamore leaves spiraled down onto the pond, alighting it seemed just a fraction of an inch over the water on each side of the eagle as she turned and sat. Powerful torso twisting, revealing wide rangy shoulders, lats bulging out from ribs, flat chest. Glowing pinkly in the dark. One leaf perched on the eagle head.

The conversation broke into pieces. Fish and rooster wandered off on their own, towels in hand. Tom and Nadezhda talked about the Mars landing, about people they had known who had been involved in the effort, many years before—part of conversation strategy, after all. Coyote and tiger got out of the pool, sat facing each other, hands twined, chanting in time to the music: Hank small and compact, a bundle of thick wire muscles—Jody tall and curvy, big muscles, lush breasts and bottom. Kevin and Ramona watched them, knees touching.

The frog and the crow sat across from each other at the narrow end of the pool, occasionally batting the ball back and forth across the water, to keep it from floating down the exit stream and away. They didn't have much to say. The crow, in fact, was covertly watching horse and eagle. And from across the pool, in the midst of her relaxed talk with Tom, Nadezhda watched them all.

"Look at my fingertips," the horse said. "They're really pruning up."

"Mine too," the eagle replied. "My whole skin is doing it, I think." She sat on the concrete rim of the pool. She took off her mask, shook her head. Water sprayed out from her in a yellow corona. Hank had accomplished his reversal; it seemed to Kevin that this exposure of the face was infinitely more revealing and intimate than bare bodies could ever be.

She looked at him and he couldn't breathe. "I'm overheating," she said.

He nodded.

"Want to go for a walk?"

"Sure," he replied, and the stallion inside reared for the sky. "Moon should be up soon. We could take the middle canyon up to the ridge, get a view."

"Whatever."

They got out of the pool, went to the cabin, dried and dressed. Returned to the pool. "We're going for a walk," Ramona said.

They took off up the poolside trail. Soon after they left, Doris sat up on the pool rim herself. Her rounded body looked small and plump after Ramona's ranginess. "It is getting hot," she said to no one in particular, in a strained voice. She stood with a neat motion. The frog watched her silently. She walked quickly to the cabin, started dressing.

The cat slid over to the frog. "Don't you think you should join her?" she said quietly.

"Oh, no," the frog said, looking down at the water. "I think if she wanted that she would have asked."

"Not necessarily. If she asked you in front of us, and you said no . . ."

"But I don't think so. She wants . . . well. I don't know." He turned to the rim, picked up a bottle, drained it empty. "Whew." He surged out of the pool, causing a sudden little tsunami. He padded over to the picnic table, drank from another bottle. Turning, he saw that Doris was gone.

He took off his frog mask, dressed. The pool seemed to pulse with a light from its bottom that filtered up through a tapestry of reddish steam. The ripples on the surface were . . . something. But Doris was gone. Oscar felt his diaphragm contract a bit, and the corners of his mouth tighten. Perhaps she had wanted him to ask to join her. Never know, now. Unless—

The wind coursing over his wet head felt cool and dry. Despite the evaporative cooling he could tell it was a hot wind. It felt good to be out in it. All his body felt cool, warm, relaxed, melted. And perhaps. Well, if he could find her. Sooner the better, as far as that went. Brusquely he pulled on his shoes, walked to the pool, crouched beside Nadezhda. "I think I'll go take a look for her," he said softly.

The cat nodded. "She went up that same trail, by the pools. I think she'll appreciate it."

Oscar nodded, straightened. The sycamore overhead had a fractal pattern of such complexity that it made him dizzy. So many branches, all of them waving against the stars, not in concert but each in a rhythm of its own, depending on how far from the trunk it was . . . another drink of tequila, sure. Looking down he saw the trail as clear as the yellow brick road. He lumbered off along it, into the forest.

Tom and Nadezhda sat beside each other, masks off. The wind felt good on Tom's face. Hank and Jody were still chanting, voices ordering the night's sound, and feeling it fill him Tom joined in, *Aum.* Under his feet the sandstone was both slick and gritty at once. Between the leaves the sky to the east had a faint white aureole—desert dust in the wind, and the moon about to rise. Hank and Jody stood, short man, tall woman, and walked across the pavilion hand in hand, stopping only to pick up a towel.

"Well," Tom said. "Here we are." He laughed. On the screen the lander stood on the red rocky plain of Hellas. "Such an alien little car."

"Is that what they'll say when they step out?"

He shook his head. "That's what I say here. And now."

Nadezhda nodded gravely. "But they should say that. Why don't you get us another bottle of the tequila. I'm developing a taste for it."

"Uh oh." He went and got a full bottle from the table. "I'm kind of drunk, myself."

"Me too. If that's what it is. You're right, it feels a little different. But I like it."

"You do now."

"That's what counts. You know, I'm getting colder rather than warmer. It's like a bath you've been in too long."

"We could move upstream to the next pool. It's hotter."

"Let's do that."

She stood and stepped into the stream bed, walked upstream with small, hesitant steps. Even in the dark her silvery white hair shone like a cap. Slender as she was, in the dark she almost looked like a young girl. Tom blinked, grasped the neck of the bottle more firmly, followed her.

Odd to have a stream's water be the warmest part of the surroundings. Nadezhda was just a shape now between trees, her hair the most visible part of her. Something in the sight gave Tom a quiver: naked woman walking up a streambed in the dark, between trees. Wisps of steam were just visible. Ferns on the bank curled in black nautilus patterns, like fossils held up on stems for their viewing.

When he came to the next pool Nadezhda was standing on its concrete bench, knee deep in water, waist deep in steam. The moon was coming up over the east wall of the canyon, and to his dark-adjusted eyes it was as bright as any streetlight. He almost wished it weren't there. But then his pupils shrank and again it seemed dim, dark even. Nadezhda watched him. "You're right," she said. "It is warmer."

"Good." They sat side by side on the edge of the pool, feet on the concrete bench below. They passed the slim bottle back and forth. The wind had almost dried their bodies, but after a bit it felt cool, and they lowered themselves into the water.

"I hope Oscar finds Doris."

"I guess."

"Well, he has to try." She laughed. "Pretty bodies."

"Yeah. Especially Ramona and Jody."

She elbowed him. "And Kevin and Hank!"

"Yeah, okay."

"And Gabby and Mike and Doris and Oscar!"

He laughed. "It's true."

She took a slug from the bottle, shifted closer to him. "Except, I don't know, I am thinking they are a little unformed. Like porcelain, or infants. To be really beautiful a body has to have a bit more to it. Their skin is too smooth. Beautiful skin has to have some pattern to it." She pinched together the skin of his upper arm. "Like that."

He laughed. "Yeah, they need some wrinkles, show some character!" He laughed again. Here I am, he thought; here I am.

"I have a lot of character," Nadezhda said, and giggled.

"Me too."

"And, and their hair is always just one color. No mix."

"Pied beauty. Give thanks to God for dappled things. . . ."

"Pied beauty, yes. On a chest with some heft to it." Her fingers traced lines over him.

Tom's hand found wet warm silt, beside the concrete rim of the pond; he picked some up, drew his initials on Nadezhda's chest. "Hmm, TB, looks good but subject to confusion." He changed the two letters to boxes.

Nadezhda got a handful, put stripes on his cheeks and forehead, around his eyes. "You look scary," she said. "Like one of the holy wanderers in India."

"Aaar." He worked on her face too, pulling it closer to his. Just two stripes on each cheek. "Spooky."

"I bet they don't know how to kiss, either," she said, and leaned into him.

When they stopped Tom laughed. "No," he said, "I bet they don't know that."

As they fell further into it, they kept drawing patterns on each other. "Bet they don't know this." "Or this." "Or—oh—this."

The moon was half full. Tom could see Nadezhda well indeed, her body all painted and pulsing, glowing pinkly, warm as the water under him. A muddy kiss of her breast. Taste of the earth. He was too bemused to hold a thought in his head, there was too much to take in. The wind in the trees, the flow of hot water over his legs, the half moon all marred, the perfect stars, the body sliding up and down between his hands. He held skin and felt it slide over ribs like slats in a fence.

They heard the distant yowl of coyotes, yipping in astounding glissandos that no dog could even approximate—crazily melodic, exultant, moonstruck. From the direction of the cabin they heard a single cry of release, and looking at each other they laughed, laughed at the way everything was falling together in a pattern beyond any calculation or hope of repetition: we do these things once, then they're gone! The distant coyotes kept howling and the wind picked up, swirled the branches overhead, and Nadezhda hugged him as they moved together.

When they returned to the world she laughed with her breath, shortly. "Our blessing on all of them."

Kevin and Ramona, horse and eagle, walked up the canyon past the spring and into the darkness of dense night forest. If there was a trail here they couldn't see it. Kevin smiled, enjoying the twisting between trees, the stepping over fronds and fallen logs. It felt good to be out of the water and into the wind— his body was overheated at the core, and his face kept sweating so that the hot wind seemed cool, refreshing, comfortable.

He stopped as the canyon bottom divided into two forks, and Ramona came up beside him. Pressed against him. He knew these canyons from boyhood, but in the uncertain light, distracted as he was, he found it hard to concentrate on what he knew, hard to remember any of that—it was just forest, night. Moon would be up soon, then he would remember. Meanwhile he chose the left fork and they continued on. Should eventually get them onto a ridge, and then he would know their location.

It was rougher up this side canyon, which rose like a broken staircase; there was a rock with a long oak bannister. They used their hands to pull themselves up. A final scramble brought them up the headwall of the canyon, and they stood on a broad ridge, sloping slowly up to the long crest of the range that led to Saddleback. Here the ground was dry and crumbled—a layer of dirt over the sandstone below. Dwarfish scrub oaks and gnarly sage bushes dotted the ridge irregularly, and in most places it was easy to walk between them.

To the east the horizon glowed, then broke to white. Moonrise. Immediately the stars dimmed, the sky became less purely black—it was a pastel black now. Shadows jumped into existence like solid ghosts, and everything on the ridge suddenly looked different. The half spheres of the sage bushes crouching on the earth like hiding animals, the wind-tossed scrub oaks crabbed and threatening.

When the moon—big and fat, its dark half just as visible as the bright half—when this ball, half light, half dark, was almost breaking free of the horizon, they saw movement in its face. "What?" Then Kevin saw that the movement was on a ridge to the east. Silhouetted against the moon, animals pointed their long thin muzzles at the sky. A few dream seconds of silence later they heard the cries.

Coyotes. "Hank gets around fast," Kevin whispered. The weirdness of the sound, the impossible slides up and down, the way the yips and barks and sliding yowls crossed over each other, making momentary harmonies and disharmonies that never once held still—all sent great shivers up Kevin's spine. The skin on his arms and back goose-pimpled. Thoughtlessly he drew Ramona to him (a little static shock). They embraced. This was something friends often did in their town, but Kevin and Ramona never had—given what was and what was not between them, it would have been too much. So this was the first time. They drew back to look at each other in the fey light, and even without color Kevin could see the perfect coloring of Ramona's face, the rich skin, raven hair—the whites of eyes and teeth . . . teeth that bit lower lip and then they were kissing. The coyotes' ecstacy yipped from inside them now, a complete interpenetration of inner and outer. Their first true kiss. Kevin's blood transmuted to something lighter, faster, hotter, freer—to wind. His blood turned to wind.

For Doris it was not like that. She left the hot springs angry and then morose, and paid little attention to where she was going. Upcanyon, yes, in the direction that Kevin and Ramona had gone. But she would never follow them. It would be stupid. And anyway impossible. But if only she could come upon Kevin and say to him—shout at him—*why?* Why her and not me? We've made love before, how many times? We've been good friends, we've lived in that house together for how many years? A long, long, long long time. And you never once looked at me like you do at her. We had fun, we laughed, we made love, we seemed to be enjoying ourselves, but still you were never all there, you never committed anything. You were never *passionate*. Wanting. It was just floating along for you, a friendship, "Damn you," she said aloud. In the noise of the wind, canyon soughing like a great broken flute, no one would ever hear her. They were in conspiracy together, she and the wind and the canyon, covering for each other, protecting each other. No one could hear. Unless she screamed. And she would never do that. "Not me, I'm not the kind to scream. Shout, maybe, or perhaps a sharp, staccato, cutting remark. A stiletto of a remark. But no histrionics from Doris Nakayama, no, of course not," voice rising with every word, till she let out a little shriek, *"Aah!"* Clapped her hand over her mouth, bit her fingers, laughed angrily. She sniffed and spit the snot out on the ground. Dashed tears from her cheeks. It felt good to stumble through the trees ranting and raving, crashing through brush when there was no obvious way. "Stupid fool, I mean just because she's tall and beautiful and smart and a good fucking shortstop. And she's sweet, sure, but when will she make you laugh? When will she make you think or teach you anything? Ah, fuck, you're two peas in a pod. A very boring pod. The two of you together have no more wit than a rock. So I suppose you'll never miss it, you bastard."

The canyon forked and Doris bludgeoned her way to the left, up a steep side canyon that gave her a lot of opportunity to work off steam. She attacked the boulders like personal enemies. Overheated from the damned hot springs. Muttering to herself she walked straight into the middle of a sage brush, and a whole flock of sleeping doves shot away, cooing and clucking and landing in a bush nearby together. Their liquid calls pursued her as she continued up the defile. She smelled of sage now, the very smell of these hills, of this wind, of Orange County itself. Before the people and the oranges and the eucalyptus and the labs it had smelled like this. She crushed a twig of it between her fingers, smelled it. Hank and his loony ceremony, she hummed the *Aum*, smelled the sage running all through her. They were more her hills than anyone else's.

She topped the headwall of the canyon just as the coyotes began their mad song, and so she had just turned up the ridge when she saw the figures above her. Frightened, she dropped behind a bush. They would think she had followed them. All thought of getting Kevin alone and lambasting him disappeared as she crouched to the ground. Finally she dared to move, to peer around the side of the hemispherical sage. And so she saw them embrace and kiss: silhouetted figures in the moonlight, like a silver on black nineteenth-century etching entitled "Love." Careless of noise she turned and ran back down the ridge, tore down into another canyon.

Ramona broke away from their kiss. "What was that?"

"Huh?"

"Didn't you hear it? And I saw something move, out of the corner of my eye. Back the way we came."

"Maybe another coyote."

"It was bigger than that."

"Hmm."

The shape Kevin had seen in the night, after his first council meeting. He had forgotten it, but now he remembered. And there were mountain lions in the Santa Ana Mountains again, it was said—Kevin had never seen one. It was unlikely one would have come so close to people, though—the areas they liked were higher, up on the back side of Saddleback. Well, he wouldn't mention the possibility, for fear it would spoil the mood.

"Do you think it could have been a mountain lion?" Ramona said matter-of-factly.

"Nah." He cleared his throat. "Or at least, it isn't very likely."

The coyotes' yipping seemed to assure them that it was, on the contrary, entirely possible.

"Let's go down the next canyon over," Ramona suggested.

Kevin nodded, and they walked the top of the ridge, winding between sage brushes. The rounded edge of the ridge curved in a big bow, until they had the moon at their backs. Their shadows stretched long before them, black and solid. The wind threw their hair across their faces. They stopped often to kiss, and each kiss was longer and more passionate, more a complete world in itself.

To their right, and so back in the general direction of the hot springs, they saw a rather shallow, wide canyon. "Look!" Ramona said, pointing down into it. At the first dip in the canyon floor there was a copse of big old sycamore trees. The biggest stood by itself, overlooking the canyon below, and there seemed to be a vine dropping from one high, thick branch. "It's the swing," she said. "It's Swing Canyon!"

"Sure enough!" Kevin said. "Hey, I know where we are now."

"Come on," she said, leading him down, looking over her shoulder with a girlish smile. "Let's go swing."

Down at the big tree they found the swing was the same as ever. It was not an ordinary swing, but a single thick rope, tied to a crook in a side branch, so that it hung well clear of the battered old trunk. The ground fell away in a smooth slope downcanyon, so it was possible to grasp the rope over a round knot and run down the slope, and when lifted off the ground one could put one's feet on a bar of wood holed and stuck above a knot at the bottom of the rope. And so one swung out into space in a long slow arc, above the brush-covered drop to the lower canyon.

They took turns doing this. Kevin rode into space feeling the mounting exhilaration of the kisses between rides, the rough contact of their bodies as they stopped each other, the windy joy of the rides themselves, out in the wind and the spinning moonlit shadows. At the end of each flight he felt lighter and lighter, as if casting off dross with each spin. He was escaping by degrees the pull of the earth. The wind was rushing downcanyon, so that each flight was pushed further out among the stars, and on the way back in he found he could face into the wind, spreadeagle his spirit and land light as a feather, to be caught in Ramona's strong arms. He felt they had joined the people on Mars, and flew in gravity two-fifths that of the world they had known.

"Here," Ramona said breathlessly at the end of one run. "We can do it together. Hold on from opposite sides, and run down and put our feet on each side of the bar." They kissed hard and their hands explored each other hungrily. "Do you think it'll work?" "Sure! I mean who knows? Let's try it."

"Okay." Kevin seized the rope. Ramona's hands closed just above his. They took off running. When the rope pulled them free of the earth their feet scrabbled for a hold on the bar, which teetered under them. Finally they balanced on it, and could take their weight off their arms. Standing together, face to face, flying through the night with the hot dry wind, they kissed long and hard, and their tongues spoke directly to each other in a language of touch so much more direct and powerful than the language of words that Kevin thought he might forget speech entirely. Ramona pulled away, laughed. They were spinning slowly. She pressed against him. "Do you remember when we were in third grade and we went behind the school and kissed?" she said in his ear. "No!" Kevin said, astonished. Had that really happened? She kissed his ear, thrust her tongue in it. That whole side of his body buzzed as if touched by some electricity of sex, he almost fell off. He held the big muscles of her bottom, larger than the full spread of his hand. She breathed in his ear, rubbed the hard band of her public bone over his thigh. They were spinning. The wind rushed by as they unzipped each other's pants. "I want to kiss you all over," Ramona said under her breath. She reached into his pants and squeezed him hard—Kevin gasped, the shock of it shot straight up his belly and spine, he very well might fall off, Ramona pulled her pants down and kicked them off into the night, pressed against him and they kissed, spinning. They had no weight at all, they were lofted like tufts of dandelion in the dry wind, spinning—

"Oh hey," Kevin said. "Here comes the ground." With a rush they were stumbling up the slope, hanging onto the rope to keep from falling over, sliding over the soft dirt, slewing to one side. They fell together, collapsed onto the ground, let the rope fall away. Seemed Ramona's pants were actually still on, his too, how had that happened? Mind getting ahead of the game. Exquisite delay to get them off, over her butt, down her long legs, shove them to one side. Undressing twice? he noted hazily. Very nice idea. One of the best parts, after all, unbutton each other's buttons, pull each other free of all that raiment, reveal the naked self inside. When we are naked we are still clothed inside, but the beautiful, physical, sexual thereness of the flesh, pulsing warmly under the fingers, bodies pressed together, seeking maximum contact, skin to skin, everything touching everything and all those cloth barriers gone—it's easy to be overwhelmed by that. And to be inside her, to be the male half of a new creature the two of them made, to have such a female half there all around him. . . .

He looked up and saw that the rope was swinging idly in the wind, that it had knocked down some of the periwinkle blooms that spiraled up the sycamore trunk. Petals and whole flowers floated down diagonally in the wind and were landing all around them, on his back, in Ramona's face (eyes closed, mouth open in a girlish O of surprise), petals like leaves falling around them, little fingers on his back, piling up, drifting against their sides until they moved in a mound of periwinkle blossoms, a blanket of them. He saw a pure black mountain lion pad by, purring its approval. It levitated with a casual leap into the lowest fork of their tree, where it sprawled over both sides of a big branch, legs all akimbo, perfectly relaxed, staring at them with big moon eyes, purring a purr as deep and rasping as waves breaking on shingle, purring a purr that enveloped them like the sound of the wind in the branches. Kevin felt it deep inside, vibrating both him and Ramona completely as they plunged toward oblivion, the universal now. They were spinning.

Oscar had lost the canyon trail immediately, almost falling in the little gurgling pool at the source of the spring; he had to sink to one knee abruptly to keep from pitching in. Spiraling blade fronds slapped him gently in the face. He stared transfixed at the roiled surface of the pool, which turned over itself as if a hose were spurting out water somewhere below the surface. So odd—here they were on a desert coastline, the mountains mostly bare and brown, and before his eyes water poured out of a hill. And steaming hot to boot. Where did it come from? Oh, he knew that. Law classes, surprising how much you had to understand for the law to make sense. And the way Sally taught that class, up in Dusy Basin and down on the campus; he felt he understood groundwater basins. He stood on the bony cracked hills, eons old, porous to water right down to the bedrock. So the ground beneath him was saturated, up to some level below him, a few feet, several hundred feet, depending on where he stood. Water down there slowly flowing, down its secret watersheds. A rib of bedrock, an underground upwelling. This was the top of one, pouring out a crack. A reservoir filled with stone. Underground waterfall. And hot because some cracks in deep bedrock were letting the earth's internal heat seep up. My God. Could it actually be that hot down there? Well, the crust was only a few miles thick, and after that it was a few *thousand* miles to the core. Essentially he was standing on a ball of molten lava, with something as thin as aluminum foil insulating him from it.

The spring water scalded his fingers, and hastily he pulled away. Uneasy at the heat, which seemed now to have a faint red glow to it, he stepped over the stream and upcanyon, aware suddenly of a Pellucidar below like the insides of a foundry, bright yellow spills of molten metal leaving intense afterimages in his sight. Except in reality the superheated rock below was under such gravitational pressure that it could be called neither a liquid or a solid, not if you wanted to be accurate. A slight variation, a bolide gravitational or magnetic, and the dark night might suddenly explode on him. Have to live with that.

The woods were dark. Black on black. Oscar blundered into branches that were like wooden arms trying to tackle him. He couldn't see well enough to move around out here, how did the others do it? The canyon floor was irregular and much of what he stepped on was soft. It made him squeamish and light-footed. Needed a flashlight. Definitely dark. Once a friend in Virginia had taken him out to see one of the caverns in the Shenandoah Mountains, and the guide there had shut down the light in one deep cavern, so they could see the purity of a complete lack of light. You couldn't see your hand right in front of your nose, nor distinguish any motions it made. It was simply a field of the richest, blackest black he had ever seen.

This wasn't like that. Overhead stars sparked between wind-tossed branches, and a single solar panel station blinked in the west like a streetlight seen from miles away. Presumably these were casting some light on the scene. How many candlepower was a star? Let's see, a lit candle some eight miles away is supposed to be visible. They did an experiment about that, in the early days, wandering out on a clear desert basin. One man tramped back and forth to find out at just what point he lost sight of the distant candle. Eight miles? Maybe it wasn't that far. What was stopping the light from being visible, anyway? What got in the way? Imagine that man out there wandering back and forth, a distant prick of light winking in and out of existence.

He could in fact see his hand in front of his face. Experiment proved this. Black octopuslike thing. But what stood before him, or at his feet: inky shapes on a field of sable velvet. It was possible to walk right into a tree. He proved that by experiment too. Subsequently he made his way with his hands stretched out before him, like a sleepwalker.

Nothing to see, but lots to hear. Airy voice of the wind scraping stone, hooting from time to time around sharp corners. The myriad shivery clicks of leaves overhead and around, a sound sometimes like water falling, but with the individual sounds sharper, more individualized—but so many of them. . . . The creaks of branches rubbing together, eucalyptus trees did that a lot, they were talkative trees. A scurrying underfoot that made him tread even more slowly, more lightly. Tiny creatures were rushing away as he approached, much as little people ran from city-stomping Godzillas in Japanese movies. And maybe some little guys with a superweapon like snake poison would try to bring him down. Necessary to move very slowly. Give them time to escape.

After a while he increased his pace again. Rattlers were likely to be asleep after all, and they were the only superpowers around. Maybe. Anyway he had to venture on. But it was probably best to give as much warning of his arrival as possible, so instead of trying to reduce the noise of his passage he increased it, swinging a stick around and hitting things with it. It also served as a blind man's cane, warning him of trees and the like. Best, clearly, to move by sense of sound and touch. He recalled an acquaintance's story, of walking by a lake at night in east Texas in early summer, stepping *squick, squick* at every step, as each step came down on one of millions of young frogs hopping about. Ick.

He came to the dim bulk of a canyon wall. So it was possible to see something. A bit confusing; apparently the canyon must fork here. He went right, and soon found himself struggling up through thickets of sage and other shrubs. One type was kind of a Spanish bayonet thing, a bunch of long, stiff, and very sharply pointed blades. Best to avoid. Really, this was stupid. What did he think he was doing? What did he expect to find? Surely no one else would have taken a route as crowded with vegetation as this. Bulldozer approach.

Still he struggled on through the tangled mass of branches. One advantage to hiking alone; you can do things so stupid that no two people together would ever carry on with it. Manzanita, or was it mesquite, anyway there was no way he could go through a nest of that stuff, no matter it was only thigh-high. Those branches were like steel. Go around. Keep going. Pure stubbornness, but after all he could turn around any time and get back to the hot springs easily, so why not? He could do this just for the fun of stupid stubbornness, mindless and pure. Holding to a course just because he was on one. Inertia. A gyroscope in the spirit, spinning madly. One time his friends had rated everyone in their group for strangeness, charm, and spin. One to ten. Oscar was the only one given tens in all categories. Nice friends. But his placid moon-faced bulk, spinning? They must have been seeing in to this gyroscope.

The bushwhacking got more fun. This was life, after all—bashing around in the dark, fighting through tangles of very tough clutching branches, sometimes knee-high, sometimes well overhead. Allegory, Everyman, bungle in the jungle.

The moon rose, and everything changed. Something like a thick translucent white syrup poured into the canyon, making the trees into distinct beings, the mesquite patches into densely textured surfaces, as in an arty black-and-white photo of the sea's surface, or snow on a forest, or something equally dappled. The droopy long leaves of eucalyptus trees swung in the wind, clattering lightly together. A spiky-barked, spiky-leaved, dusty little tree stood in his path like a growth seen through a microscope. Bacillus scrub-oakus. Oak, he has a heart of oak, Hank said when recommending Oscar be hired as town attorney. Should have known that any town that consulted someone like Hank when hiring an attorney was going to be seriously weird. Shadows moved and jumped, quivered and bobbed. He could see just enough to see that everything was moving. The wind didn't seem as strong, or as loud. Moonlight thick as gel. Sage smell.

The moon itself was an intense white, its violent history marked all over it. A rabbit stirring a bowl of rice, the Chinese saw. Nothing so simple as a face. Moonfaced, like Oscar. Sister moon. Just tilt your head to the right a bit and there it was, the rabbit's two long laid-back ears as clear as could be. Bowl of rice, well it certainly could have been a bowl of pudding, that was guesswork. But the rabbit was there, looking down at him.

There was a rustle underfoot, and in the distance the wind made a sound like crying souls. Not like the wind at all. Must have been coursing through a hole in the sandstone to create such an eerie sound. Just like a cry. Shadows moved suddenly to the left and in the sudden depth of the third dimension that the moon added to the world he thought he saw a bulk shift between trees. Yes, there it was, something fast and big—

It crashed downcanyon, charging sightlessly at him—

Oscar threw out his hands reflexively. "Hey!"

"Aaa!" it cried, leaping back.

"Doris!" Oscar exclaimed, reeling his mind back in. "Excuse me—"

"*What?—*"

"It's me!"

"Who?" The panic in her voice was shifting to anger.

"Oscar!" he said, and then, "You remember, I was down at the pools—"

"Don't joke with me!" There was a wild note in her voice. She wiped her face with a hand. Something more than embarrassment at being frightened by their sudden encounter. Words burst out of her: "What are you doing following me?"

"I'm not! I mean—I—" A number of alternative explanations jammed on his tongue, as he struggled for the right tack to take with her in this fierce mood. "I was just out for a walk. I figured if I ran into you I'd have some company—"

"I don't want company!" she cried. "I don't like you following me, leave me alone!"

And she rushed downcanyon, crashing through sagebrush almost as much as he had.

He stood there in the moony dark, stunned by the dislike in her voice. His heart tocked in his ears, seemed to pound in the earth beneath him. Intense hurt, mood plummeting like a bird hit by shot. Thump thump, thump thump, thump thump. Not fair. Really. A lifetime's defenses went into action. No schoolmate's taunt could touch him. "Well," he said absently, in a John Wayne voice. "Guess I'll hafta carry on up this here mountain all by m'self." Muttering with all the voices, the whole cast of an imaginary movie, moving up the scrub-filled canyon. "Terrible vines here, ain't they Cap'n." "Yes, son, but they help hide us from the Injuns. Those Paiutes find us and it would be blubberhawk from space time."

It got steeper, and he found himself on hands and knees, to get under the thickest part of the brush. Sometimes he crawled right on his belly, heedless of the dirt shoving under his shirt and belt. Clean dry dirt. Some dry leaves, not many. The smell of sage was so strong that he gasped. Must've dropped the spice rack, Cap'n.

At the end of his struggle he found himself beached on a broad ridge. The moon bathed it in light, and the monochrome landscape was revealed to the eye: bony gray hills rose in long broad waves to the mountains around the bulk of Saddleback. Black canyons dropped into the depths between them. The moon was surrounded with a talcum of white light which blotted out the stars. The wind was strong, a hot breath rushing over him. Occasional treetops stuck up in the air, like black gallows or the ruins of old houses. There, in the corner of his eye, a movement.

He spun to face it, saw nothing. But that hadn't been just a branch waving in the wind. Had Doris returned to stalk him? Pound on him some more? Or—an absurd little ray of hope—apologize to him for her rudeness? Sure. "Doris?" The hope died. Not likely at best. Besides, it had been—

And there it was again, a smooth shape flowing between two bushes. Shadow in the moon's twilight. An animal.

And in the distance, floating on the wind, a weird yipping bark, yodeling away. Like the cry he had heard before, only . . . wolves?

"Not possible, Jones," he whispered. "The timber wolf was driven into the Tetons in my granddad's time."

Still, he hurried up the ridge, as it seemed the easiest route. Possible to see farther, too. His ankle hurt. Up the ridge was a knob of hard sandstone boulders, thrusting up among the stars. Like a refuge. A lookout in every direction.

Getting there was a problem. He zigzagged between bushes and short trees, nearly fell off the ridge. A rose bush caught at his clothes, stabbed him, the roses were a bright light gray, most of the blooms just opening, branches extending all over like ropes. As he struggled out of them the blooms fanned open, dropped blown, their yellow quite clear and distinct even in this black-and-white world. Frightened, he hurried away and up the ridge. He tripped and fell to his knees. Two branches twined together, squeaked out the word "Beware! Bewaaare!" He broke them off—they were deadwood. They struggled for a minute in his hands before becoming a wooden broadsword, thick and solid. Behind him the black shadow slipped from bush to bush like quicksilver across glass. Its eyes were bright.

He stumbled into a cleared area of grass, saw that waist-high boulders had been placed in a circle on it. Maybe twenty of them, casting shadows blacker than themselves across the grass. One stone wobbled, rolled off. Wings dashed the air, dive-bombing him and flitting away. No sound to the wings at all. Owls were supposed to fly like that.

Suddenly the peak seemed a trap, a final aerie he couldn't escape from. A horror of sacrifice filled him, he turned off the ridge and down the head of a canyon. He ran under trees into sudden dark and fell. Cut, bruised, palm of hand burning. A tree stood over him triumphantly, its knobby arms waving in the attempt to free themselves from their paralysis and seize him. So many bony hands. Whaddyou get? bon-y fingers, he sang in his mind. He rolled in dried leaves and crunchy twigs. Dark. Ring of dimly glowing mushrooms, making a circle like the stone ring above. A rose bush wilted before him and the dread washed in again. He crashed away.

Now the canyon floor was fairly level. Eucalyptus trees filled the glade, and below it was as bare as a room. The trees dripped an herbicide that kept the area all to themselves. Easy walking. Suddenly low white shapes dashed about his knees, and he cried out in surprise. The shapes honked. They glowed like the mushrooms had. Ducks? Bigger, no, they were geese. Geese! He laughed, they scattered and scolded him with angry short honks. Nipped at his calves.

He allowed the little flock to guide him downcanyon. About ten of them, it seemed, scuttling about underfoot and honking impatiently. They guided him left, nipping. Up a gentle slope, side wall of the canyon nearly flat here, opening to the sky. Higher yet up the canyon's side, and the dark waving canyon bottom was filled with treetops. Ocean of round-topped waves. They came to a broad shelf, floored with silver sand. His breath was harsh in his throat. There was a yip and the geese all honked and gathered behind him, huddling there as if he would protect them. Low doggy shapes whipped around the shelf and stood—

long tails, foxlike. Fox and geese? The geese turned as one and hissed at one of the creatures. Coyote, sure. Bigger than a fox. Geese and coyote. The coyote moved like a sheepdog with a recalcitrant flock of sheep. Geese and sheep, similar creatures. No doubt geese were smarter.

Several more coyotes appeared out of the darkness, herded Oscar and the geese to the back wall of the shelf. Here the sand was thick and bright, mica chips flashing moonlight, the geese standing out like cottonballs, dashing about complaining. They nipped back at the coyotes if pushed too far, noisy as they clacked and honked and hissed, in a language very expressive, very emotive. Clear as could be what they meant. The coyotes' tongue, on the other hand, was utterly alien. Sliding yips, how did they do it? Vocal chords like a pedal steel guitar.

The geese settled down, began to peck in the sand. They groomed their feathers with their bills, their long necks stretching in impossible curves, loops. Grooming each other or the coyotes who sprawled among them, calm and watchful. Oscar sat down heavily, crossed his legs. A coyote still ambling around their beach-like extrusion plopped down behind him, lay on its side, its back pressing Oscar's. He found he was weeping, he couldn't see anything but dim white blobs in the darkness. The moon set and the geese themselves provided the light, glowing like little moons. The coyote braced against him sighed heavily, squeaked softly with contentment, like a dog. Comfortable. A few more coyotes heard the sound, padded over to join them. The wind filled Oscar's chest until he thought it might burst him, or waft him away like a balloon. His eyes felt dry and sandy, his nose was clogged. He breathed in and out through his mouth, trying to keep from overfilling. Furry warmth, the tickle of a tail flicking against his ankle. Contentment spilled through him, he was an artesian well of contentment. The down under the feathers of the geese; nothing softer. They buzzed through their bills when they were happy. He lay on his side, feeling a warm exhaustion wash down through him, groundwater, muscles melting. One night when he was five years old, the shadow of the tree outside his window had waved on the floor, and he had felt something like this—felt how big the world was, and how charged everything was with meaning. It made you breathe so deep, made your chest fill so full! In and out, in and out, in the rhythm of the sand underneath him. Geese slept with their heads under one wing.

When he woke it was not from sleep, but from a dream so vivid and real that it seemed opening his eyes was like disappearing, turning into a ghost. Stepping from some bright world into a dimmer one. He was lying on sand, his side was damp and stiff. The night's wandering stood clear in his memory, including the flock of white geese and their guardian coyotes. But now the sandy shelf was bare. Paw prints everywhere. He was alone.

He sat up, groaning. The sky was the gray of his pearl gray suit, and seemed low and cloudy, though a few stars pricked it to show that it was actually the clear dome of the sky, cloud-gray in this moment of the dawn. Everything was still monochrome, grays everywhere, a million shades of it. There were thorny weeds edging the patch of sand. Bird song started in the canyon below, and small birds here and there joined in.

Moaning and groaning he stood, hiked down from the shelf. How . . . He lost the thought. All the intense emotions of the night before had drained away. The wind still gusted, but not inside him. He was calm, emptied, drained. Trees stood around him like great silent saints. He walked downcanyon. Eventually he would come on something. At times he felt sure he was still dreaming, despite a stubbed toe. Warm dry air, even at dawn.

Far down the canyon, where it opened up and joined a bigger one, he came upon a big bare sycamore tree, filled with sleeping crows. A tree very old, very big, mostly dead, no leaves except on one live strip that twisted greenly off to the side; and entirely filled with still black birds.

"Now wait a minute." He pinched himself. Bit the skin between thumb and forefinger. Yes, he was awake. He certainly seemed awake. Mountain canyon at dawn, Santa Ana Mountains. Yes, he was awake! Anyway this happened a lot, even down in town. There were a lot of crows around, flocks of really big ones, like ravens it seemed to him. Loud birds, pests, little Mongols of the air, dominating wherever they wanted to. He had seen a flock descend on a tree before; in fact they had their favorites, which they stopped in ritually at the end of the day, when heading back up to their night haunts—up to here, in fact, for this particular horde. A whole flock perched up there silently, sleeping, filling every branch like black fruit, on twisting gray branches against the gray sky. The green of the live strip beginning to show.

He took a deep breath and shook his head, feeling strange. He knew he was awake, nearly sober, relatively sane; but the sight was so luminous, so heavy with some meaning he couldn't express. . . .

An idea struck him, and he walked under the tree. Standing foursquare he looked up; then threw his arms wide and shouted, "*Hey!*"

The tree exploded with birds! Flapping black wings, cawing wildly, crows burst away to every point of the compass, loose-winged, straggle-feathered, leaving black images of their powerful downstrokes against the delicate tracery of bare gray branches. Cawing, they regrouped in a swirl above the tree, then flew off to the west, a dancing irregular cloud of winged black dots. Oscar stood dazed, face to the sky, mouth hanging open.

...7

Last week a nightmare. Landed at Dulles and arrested in Immigration. On a list, accused of violating the Hayes-Green Act. Swiss gov't must have told them I was coming, flight number and everything. What do you mean? I shouted at officious official. I'm an American citizen! I haven't broken any laws! Such a release to be able to speak my mind in my native tongue—everything pent up from the past weeks spilled out in a rush, I was really furious and shouting at him, and it felt so good but it was a mistake as he took a dislike to me.

Against the law to advocate overthrowing US gov't.

What do you mean! I've never done anything of the kind!

Membership in California Lawyers for the Environment, right? Worked for American Socialist Legal Action Group, right?

So what? We never advocated anything but change!

Smirk of scorn, hatred. He knew he had me.

Got a lawyer but before he arrived they put me through physical and took blood sample. Told to stay in county. Next day told I tested positive for HIV virus. I'm sure this is a lie, Swiss test Ausländer every four months and no problem there, but told to remain county till follow-up tests analyzed. Possessions being held. Quarantine possible if results stay positive.

My lawyer says law is currently being challenged. Meanwhile I'm in a motel near his place. Called Pam and she suggested sending Liddy on to folks in OC so can deal better with things here. Put Liddy on plane this morning, poor girl crying for Pam, me too. Now two days to wait for test results.

Got to work. Got to. At local library, on an old manual typewriter. The book mocks: how can you, little worm crushed in gears, possibly aspire to me? Got to continue nevertheless. In a way it's all I have left.

The problem of an adequate history bothers me still. I mean not my personal troubles, but the depression, the wars, the AIDS plague. (Fear.) Every day everything a little worse. Twelve years past the millenium, maybe the apocalyptics *were just a bit early in their predictions, too tied to numbers. Maybe it just takes a while for the world to end.*

Sometimes I read what I've written sick with anger, for them it's all so easy. Oh to really be that narrator, to sit back and write with cool ironic detachment about individual characters and their little lives because those lives really mattered! Utopia is when our lives matter. I see him writing on a hilltop in an Orange County covered with trees, at a table under an olive tree, looking over a garden plain and the distant Pacific shining with sunlight, or on Mars, why not, chronicling how his new world was born out of the healthy fertility of the old earth mother, while I'm stuck here in 2012 with my wife an ocean to the east and my daughter a continent to the west, "enjoined not to leave the county" (the sheriff) and none of our lives matter a damn.

Days passed and Kevin never came down, never returned to feeling normal. Late that week, watching a news report on the Mars landing, it dawned on him that he was never going to feel *normal* again. This startled him, made him faintly uneasy.

Not that he wasn't happy. When he recalled the night in the hills with Ramona he got lighter, physically lighter, especially when working or swimming. Exhilaration resisted gravity as if it were a direct counterforce. "Walking on air"—this extravagant figure of speech was actually an accurate description of a lived reality. Amazing.

But it had been such a strange night. It felt like a dream, parts of it seemed to slip away each time he thought of other things, so that he didn't want to think of anything else, for fear the whole night might slip away. When he saw Ramona again, down at their streetwork, his heart skipped a beat, and shyly he looked down. Would she acknowledge it? Had it really happened?

Then when he looked up he saw that Ramona smile, a beacon of pleasure, black eyes looking right at him. She remembered too. If it was a dream, they had dreamed it together. Relief gave his exhilaration another lift, he slammed a pick into the broken asphalt and felt like he might be tossed aloft.

Now he was truly in love. And for the first time. Late bloomer indeed! Most of us first fall in love in our teens, it's part of the intensity of those years, falling for some schoolmate, not so much because of the qualities of the loved one but because of a powerful unspoken desire to be in love. It is part of the growth of the soul. And though the actual nature of the loved one is not crucially important, it would not be true to say that first love is thereby lessened, or less intensely felt. On the contrary—because of its newness, perhaps, it is often felt with particular strength. Most adults forget this in the flood of events that the rest of life pours over them, or perhaps they're disinclined to remember those years at all, filled as they were with foolishness, awkwardness, shame. Often enough first love was part of the awkwardness, inappropriately directed, poorly expressed, seldom reciprocated . . . we prefer not to remember. But remember with courage and you will feel again its biting power; few things since will have made you as joyfully, painfully alive.

Kevin Claiborne, however, had not fallen in love in adolescence—or, really, at any time thereafter. The desire never struck him, and no one he met inspired him to it. He had gone through life enjoying his sexual relationships, but something was missing, even if Kevin was only vaguely aware of it. Doris's angry attempts to tell him that, years before, had alerted him to the fact that there was something others felt which he did not. It was confusing, because he felt that he loved—loved Doris, his friends, his family, his housemates, his teammates. . . . Apparently it wasn't what she was talking about.

So the affair with Doris had ended almost as it began. And when Kevin felt romantic love for the first time, at the age of thirty-two, after years of work at home and abroad, after a thousand acquaintances and long years of experience with them, it was not because of the obscure adolescent desire to love *somebody*. Nor was it just forces in his own soul, though no doubt there was movement there too, as there always is, even if it is glacially slow. Instead it was a particular response, to Ramona Sanchez, his friend. She embodied what Kevin Claiborne loved most in women, he had known that for some time, somewhere in him. And when suddenly she became free and turned her attention to him— her affection to him—well, if Kevin's soul had been glacially slow, then it was now like a certain glacier in Alaska, which had crawled for centuries until one year it crashed down hundreds of yards, cutting off a whole bay.

It was a remarkable thing, this being in love. It changed everything. When he worked it was with an extra charge of satisfaction, feeling the sensual rush of the labor. At home he felt like a good housemate, a good friend. People relaxed around him, they felt they were having a good time, they could talk to him— they always could, but now he seemed to have more to give back. At the pool he swam like a champion, the water was like air and he flew through it, loving the exertion. And he was playing ball better than ever. The hitting streak extended without any worry, it was just something that happened. It wasn't very hard to hit a softball, after all. A smooth stroke, good timing, a line drive was almost inevitable. Was inevitable, apparently. He was 43 for 43 now, and everyone was calling him Mr. Thousand, making a terrible racket when he came to bat. He laughed, he didn't care, the streak didn't matter. And that made it easier.

And the time spent with Ramona. That morning in their torn-up street he understood what it would be like—she was there, he could look over at her whenever he wanted, and there she would be, graceful, strong, unselfconsciously beautiful—and when she looked at him, he knew just what it said. *I remember. I'm yours.*

My God. It was love.

For Doris, the days after their party were like a truly enormous hangover. She felt queasy, disoriented, dizzy, and very irritable. One night when Hank was over for dinner she said angrily to him, "God damn it, Hank, somehow you always get me to drink about ten times more of your damned tequila than I really want to! Why do you *do* that!"

"Well, you know," Hank said, looking sheepish. "I try to live by the old Greek rule, you know. Moderation in all things."

"Moderation in all things!" Doris shouted, disgusted.

The rest of the table hooted. "Moderation in all things," Rafael said, laughing. "Right, Hank, that's you to a T."

Nadezhda said, "I visited Rhodes once, where that saying was born. Cleobolus said it, around 650 B.C. The guide book I bought was a translation, and they had it 'Measure is in all the best.'"

Andrea smiled. "Doesn't have the same ring to it, does it."

"What the hell do you mean, Hank?" Doris demanded. "Just how does moderation in all things explain pounding twenty-five bottles of atrocious tequila?"

"Well, you know—if you say moderation in all things, then among all things you gotta include moderation itself, see what I mean? So you gotta go crazy once in a while, if you ask me."

Then Tom showed up, and after dinner he and Doris began poring over the records Doris had taken from Avending. At one point Tom shook his head. "First of all, a lot of this looks to be coded. It may just be a cipher, but if it's in cipher and coded too then we're shit out of luck."

Doris scowled.

"Besides," Tom went on, "even if we break the code—hell, even with the straight stuff—it won't make that much sense to me. I'm no financial records analyst, never have been."

"I thought you might be able to see at least some trends," Doris said.

"Well, maybe. But look, your friend John is not likely to have had access to Avending's most intimate secrets anyway, especially if they've been involved in some funny stuff. His clearance just wouldn't go that high."

"Well, shit," Doris said, "why did I bother to take this stuff in the first place!"

"Don't ask me."

Nadezhda said to Tom, "Don't you have any friends left in Washington who could be helping you with this kind of problem?"

Tom considered it. "Maybe. I'll have to make some calls. Here, while I'm doing that, sort this stuff into what's in English and what's coded. Where you can tell the difference."

"Actually John's clearance is pretty damn high," Doris said.

Tom just shook his head and got on the TV. For a while he talked to a small gray-haired black woman, leaning back in a rotating chair; then to a tall man with a shiny bald head; then to the blank screen, for three or four conversations. There was a lot of incidental chat as he renewed old acquaintances, caught up on news: "Nylphonia, it's me. Tom Barnard."

"I thought you were dead."

That sort of thing. Finally he got into a long conversation with a female voice and a blank screen, one punctuated several times by laughter. "That'll take hours," Tom said at one point. "We've got thousands of pages here."

"That's your problem," the voice said. "If you want us to help, you'll have to send it all along. Just stick them in front of the screen one at a time and I'll set my end to photo. I'm off to breakfast anyway, and I'll get back to you later when we've gone through them."

"You think it'll be worth it?"

"How do I know? But from what you've said, I think we'll be able to come up with something. That much data should reveal the shape of the company's financial relations, and if they're hiding things, that'll show in the shape of what they're not hiding. We'll show you."

"What about the coding?"

Laughter.

"Well, thanks, Em." Tom turned to Doris and Nadezhda. "Okay, we've got to put every one of these sheets of paper on the TV screen, and the better order they're in, the easier it'll be for my friends to analyze them."

So they set to work getting the data transferred. Kevin came in and took his turn. Each sheet sat on the screen for only a second before there was a beep from the phone. Even so it took them until well into the night to get everything photographed. "And to think most of this stuff is irrelevant," Doris said at one point.

"Worse for my friends than for us," Tom replied.

"Are we going to have to pay them for this?"

"You bet. But it's a whole network of friends we're plugging into, and some of them owe me. We'll figure something out after they've looked at this stuff."

"What exactly will they be looking for?" Kevin asked.

"Infractions of the laws governing company size, capital dispersion, and that sort of thing. Corporate law is a gigantic body of stuff, see, very complex. The main thrust of the twenty-forty international agreements was to cut down on the size of corporations, cut them down so far that only companies remain. It's actually anti-corporate law, I mean that's what we were doing for twenty-five years. We chopped up the corporations and left behind a teeming mass of small companies, and a bunch of associations and information networks—all well and good, but there are projects in this world that need a lot of capital to be carried off, and so mechanisms for that had to be instituted, new banking practices and company teamwork programs, and that's where you get the morass of law dealing with that. Alfredo's lawyers are undoubtedly playing all those angles and it may be that Avending has been brought in in a legal way, or it could be that there's an illegal corporate ownership aspect to things. There's no reason why they shouldn't have used legal methods, it's not that hard and a lot safer for their project. But they might be cutting corners—hell, it might have been forced on them, by someone with some leverage. The way Alfredo has introduced the zoning and water stuff . . ."

"It's sure that Alfredo and his Heartech partners got to be hundreds damned fast," Doris said.

"And live like more than hundreds," Kevin added.

"Do they? Well, it's worth looking into."

A few days later the environmental impact statement was filed by Higgins, Ramirez, and Bretner, and there it was in the town computer for anyone to call up and inspect. Kevin read it while eating lunch over at Oscar's house. By the time he was done reading, he had lost his appetite. Theatrically he cast a half-eaten sandwich onto the table. These days even getting angry felt sort of good. "What do they mean erosion on the western side? There's no erosion at all there!"

"Them ravines," Hank said. "Must be erosion, don't you think?"

"Yeah, but it's perfectly natural, I mean it isn't accelerated or anything. I know every inch of that hill and there's no unusual erosion at all there!"

Oscar came into the kitchen to make his own lunch. "Ah. HRB strikes again. Natural state equals erosion, litter, underuse. Sure." He read the TV screen while putting together a Reuben sandwich. "See the way alternative four is slanted. Construction of a commercial center, paths to the peak—this is probably the best description of what Alfredo has in mind that we've seen so far. Parking lot down at the head of Crawford Canyon. This will help stop erosion on the western slope, clean up the refuse on the peak, add sightly landscaping, and increase town awareness and enjoyment of the prospect."

"Shit," Kevin said.

"That's an LA Special all right. Hmm. Other alternatives are generally downplayed, I see. Hill turned into park, how can they downplay that? Ah. Would be a small addition to Santiago Park, which is already underutilized, and some seventeen percent of town property. Indeed."

"Shit!" Kevin said.

Oscar went back to his sandwich. Environmental impact statements had come a long way since the early days, he told Hank and Kevin. LA's Metropolitan Water Department had once submitted four unacceptable statements in a row, for instance, when attempting to finesse the fact that excessive mining of the groundwater in Owens Valley was going to destroy even the desert flora that had survived the earlier diversions of surface water. The obvious bias in those statements had been one factor in Inyo County's eventual victory over LA, in the Sacramento courts and legislature; and every agency forced to submit an EIS had learned a lesson from that. Alternative uses had to be described in detail. Obvious harmful effects could not be ignored. The appearance, at least, of a complete and balanced study had to be maintained. "The days of 'There is no environment here' are over. Consulting firms like HRB are extremely sophisticated—they make their reputations by writing statements that will stand up to challenges. Complete, but still getting the job done, you know—making whatever impression the agency that hired them wants."

"Well, shit!" Kevin said.

Gabriela, walking through the kitchen on her way to the roof, said "Time to poison his blood, hey Kev?"

That night Kevin made a chicken stroganoff dinner, while the others checked out the California Environmental Quality Act and the town charter, looking for ways to challenge the EIS.

"Look, the land belongs to us!" Kevin said from the kitchen.

Tom grinned. "El Modena has a population of about ten thousand, so we're three ten-thousandth owners."

"Not enough," Doris said.

"No. But it is true that essentially this is a battle for the opinion of the rest of the owners. The rest of the state and the nation and the world have a say as well, and we might be able to manipulate those forces to our purpose, but the main thing is convincing the people in town to agree with us. The rest of the world doesn't care that much about Rattlesnake Hill."

Oscar had dinner with them fairly often, as his kitchen was in an inconvenient state of renovation. One night he came in with the tiniest hint of a smile on his face, and seeing him, Kevin said "Hey, what's up?"

Oscar lifted an eyebrow. "Well, you know I have been making inquiries with the State Water Resources Control Board."

"Yeah, yeah?"

Oscar accepted a glass of water from Doris, sat heavily by the pool. Things were a mess in Sacramento, he told them, as usual. On the one hand, Inyo County's victory over the city of Los Angeles had had the statewide effect of making each county the master of its groundwater. But groundwater basins paid no heed to county lines, and so use of the groundwater in many cases had to be adjudicated by the courts. In many cases state control was stronger than ever. The waterscape was simply bigger than local governments could effectively manage. And so there was a mixed effect; some counties now had control over water that had previously been mined out from under them, while other counties were suddenly feeling pinched. Into that mix came the new source of water from the north, controlled by the state, and funneled through the canals of the old Central Water Project. Confusion, disarray—in other words, the typical California waterscape, in its general feel. But many of the particulars were new.

"So," Oscar said, "it has taken me a while to find out what the board would make of this proposal of Alfredo's, to buy water from the MWD and then sell whatever excess there might be to the OCWD. Because no one on the board is inclined to talk about hypothetical cases. They have enough real cases to keep them occupied, and hypothetical cases are usually too vague to make a judgment on. But one of the board members is a good friend of Sally's, they were on the board together. I finally got her cornered long enough to listen to me, and she prevaricated for a long time, but it comes down to this—they wouldn't allow it."

"Great!"

"How does she mean that?" Tom asked.

"Buying water and selling it, or using it for other water credits, is not something the board allows municipalities to do anymore—it's the state's prerogative."

"What about the MWD?"

"They've been turned into a kind of non-profit clearing house."

"You mean after all those years of manipulation and control and raking it in at the expense of Owens Valley and the rest of the south, LA is now collecting and distributing all that water as a non-profit operation?"

"That's right."

Tom laughed for a long time.

Oscar surged up out of his chair, went to the kitchen to refill his glass. "There's no swamp like water law," he muttered under the sound of Tom's laughter.

So Kevin was feeling good about things, and late one afternoon after a hard day's work at Oscar's place, he gave Ramona a call. "Want to go to the beach for sunset?"

"Sure."

It was that easy. "Hey, isn't your birthday sometime soon?"

She laughed. "Tomorrow, in fact."

"I thought so! We can celebrate, I'll take you to dinner at the Crab Cooker."

"It's a deal."

It seemed like his bike had a little hidden motor in it.

It was a fine evening at Newport Beach. They went to the long strand west of the 15th Street pier, walked behind the stone groins. The evening onshore wind was weak, a yellow haze lay in the air. The sun sank in an orange smear over Palos Verdes. The bluffs behind the coastal highway were dark and furry, and it seemed this beach was cut off from the world, a place of its own. Stars blurred in the salt air. They scuffed through the warm sand barefoot, arms around each other. Down the beach a fire licked over the edge of a concrete firepit, silhouetting children who held hot dogs out on coathangers bent straight. The twined scent of charred meat and lighter fluid wafted past, cutting through the cold wet smell of seaweed. Waves swept in at an angle, rushed whitely toward them, retreated hissing, left bubbling wet sand. We do this once, it never happens again.

At the Santa Ana River's mouth they stopped. A lifeguard stand stared blankly at the waves, which gleamed in the dark. They climbed the seven wooden steps which lifeguards could descend in a single leap. They sat on the damp painted plywood, watched waves, kissed until they were dizzy. Lay on the wood, on their sides, embracing and kissing until that was all that existed. How perfect the noise of surf was for making out; why should that be? A waft from the barbecue blew by. "Hungry?" "Yeah."

Biking lazily to the Crab Cooker, Kevin felt better than he could ever remember feeling. That happiness could be such a physical sensation! Ravenously he ate salad, bread, and crab legs. The white wine coursed through him like Hank's tequila. He was very aware of Ramona's hands, of the lips that had so recently been kissing his. She really was stunning.

They sat over coffee after dinner, talking about nothing much. They concentrated on what had been theirs together, laying out for their mutual inspection their long friendship, defining it, celebrating it.

Outside the night was cool. They biked in the slow lane of the Newport Freeway, taking almost an hour to get home. Without a word Ramona led the way down Fairhaven, past the gliderport to her house, a squarish old renovated apartment block. They rolled the bikes into the racks, and she led him by the hand into the building. Through the atrium and by the pool, up the stairs to the inner balcony, and around and up again, to her room. He had never been in it before. It was a big square room—big enough for two, of course—set above the rest of that wing of the house, so that there were windows on all four sides.

"Ooh, nice," he said, checking out the design. "Great idea." Big bed in one corner, desk in the other corner, shelves extending from the desk along walls on both sides, under the windows. Occasional gaps on the shelves were the only signs of the recently departed occupant. Kevin ignored them. One corner of the room was taken up with bathroom and closet nook. There were clothes on the floor, knick-knacks here and there, a general clutter. Music system on a lower shelf, but she didn't turn it on.

They sat on the floor, kissed. Soon they were stretched out beside each other, getting clothes off slowly. Making love.

Kevin drifted in and out. Sometimes his skin was his mind, and did all his thinking. Then something would happen, they would stop moving for a moment, perhaps, and he would see his fingers tangled in her black hair. Under her head the carpet was a light brown, the nap worn and frayed. She whispered something wordless, moved under him. This is Ramona, he thought, Ramona Sanchez. The surge of feeling for her was stronger than the physical pleasure pouring through his nerves, and the combination of the two was . . . he'd never felt anything like it. This was why sex was so . . . he lost the thought. If they kissed at the same time they moved together, he would burst. They were creeping across the carpet, soon their heads would bump the wall. Ramona made little squeaks at his every plunge into her, which made him want to move faster. Moving under him, tigerish . . . He held her in his arms, bumped the top of his head firmly against the wall, thump, thump, they were off into the last slide, breath quick and ragged and wordless, his mind saying Ramona, Ramona, Ramona.

Afterward he lay in her arms, warm except for where sweat dried on his back and legs. His face was buried in the fragrant hair behind her ear. I love you, I love you. The intensity of it shocked him. All his life, he thought, his happiness had been no more than animal contentment, like a cow in the sun. A carpenter roofing on a sunny day with a breeze, hitting good nails with a good hammer. Swinging the bat and barely feeling the ball when he struck it. Animal sensation, wonderful as far as it went. But now something in him had changed, and without being able to articulate it, he knew he would never be the same again. And he didn't want to be, either. Because he was lying on an old brown carpet next to his love, head against a wall, in an entirely new world.

"Let's go to bed," Ramona said. He sat back, watched her stand and walk to the bathroom. Such a strong body.

She returned, pulled him to his feet, led him to her bed. Pulled the covers down. They got in and drew a sheet over them. The ordinary reality of it, the sheer domesticity of it, filled Kevin up—the world sheered away and after a while they were making love again, using the springiness of the bed to rock into each other. Euphoria set every nerve singing, this was the best time yet.

Their night in the hills had been so strange, after all. Kevin had not known how to think of it. It could have been a stroke of magic, falling through his life just once—a result of Mars, Hank's tequila, the sage hills themselves, intoxicating the whole party. But tonight was an ordinary night, in Ramona's every-night bed, with white cotton sheets that made her body dark as molasses, that made everything more real. He was there and so was she, lying beside him, one long leg spreadeagled over his, the other disappearing under sheets. Really there.

Her breathing slowed. She was getting drowsy. "Remember Swing Tree?" she asked, voice sleepy.

"Yes?"

"That one swing—the long one?"

"I think we must have been out there an hour."

She laughed softly. "All night. It felt like we did everything in that one ride. I thought we had our clothes off and everything."

"Me too!"

"So wonderful. The long swing."

"Happy birthday," Kevin whispered after a while.

"Wonderful presents."

She fell asleep.

Kevin watched her. His eyes adjusted to the dark. Far away in the house a door closed, voices sounded. Someone up late.

Then it was quiet. Time passed. Kevin kept looking at her, soaking her in. He was lying on his left side, head propped on his left hand. Ramona lay on her back, head turned to the side, mouth open, looking girlish. Kevin closed his eyes, found he didn't want to. He wanted to look at her.

She had really powerful shoulders, you could see where her bullet throws came from. Funny how flat-chested she was. Dark nipples made little breast shapes of their own. He remembered her once, laughing resentfully and saying, Alfredo's always looking at women with tits. Still she looked so female. Small breasts drew attention to the greyhound proportions of torso, flanks, hips, bottom, legs. She was perfectly proportioned as she was.

Time passed, but Kevin didn't grow tired. In a way he wanted to wake her and make love again. Then again, just to lie against her side while she slept . . . a long quiver shook him, he thought it might wake her. No chance—she was out.

His hand fell asleep, and he lowered his head. Her hair spilled over the pillow, black shot silk against the white cotton. Perhaps he dozed for a while. He shifted and felt her, looked at her again. Occasionally he had seen love stories on TV. I adore you, I worship you. He had watched them thinking, how stories exaggerate. But they didn't—in fact they couldn't express it at all—poor stories, trying to match the intensity of the real! They never got it, they never could. *Adore*—it was all wrong, it didn't explain it at all, it was just a word, an attempt to get beyond *love*. He loved his sister, his parents, his friends. He needed another word for this, no doubt about it.

The room was lightening. Dawn on its way. No! he thought. Too fast! The slow increase of illumination brought the room's dimensions into focus, made everything a bit translucent, as if it were a world made entirely of gray glass. In this light Ramona glowed with a dark, sensuous presence. She stirred, spoke briefly. Talking in her sleep. Kevin stared at her, drank her in, the fine skin, the occasional freckle or mole shifting over ribs, the sleek curve of her flank and hip. Outside birds chirped.

And day came, too quickly. Because when the sun cracked over the hills and the little studio room was fully lit, Ramona shifted, rolled, sighed, woke up. The night was over.

They took turns in the bathroom, and when Kevin came out she had on gym shorts and a T-shirt. "Shower?" he said.

She shook her head. "Not yet. You go ahead, I'll start up some coffee."

So he showered, wishing she was under the crash of warm water with him. Why not?

Then later as he sat on the floor beside the coffee-maker, she quickly showered herself. What the hell, he thought. Hadn't it been an invitation? . . . Well, whatever. Maybe she liked to shower alone.

Then she was out, hair slicked back with a comb, towel around her neck, dressed again. They sat on the floor in the sun, drinking coffee from her little machine. She asked him what his plans were for the day. He told her a little about Oscar's house, the progress of the work there.

There was a knock at the door. She looked surprised. It was still a little before eight. She went to answer, coffee mug in hand. She opened the door.

"Happy birthday!" said a voice from the landing at the top of the stairs.

Alfredo.

"Thanks," Ramona said, and stepped outside. Closed the door behind her.

Kevin's diaphragm was in a hard knot under his ribs. He relaxed it, deliberately took a sip of coffee. He stared at the door. Well, Alfredo would have had to find out eventually. Hard way to do it, though. He could just hear their voices out there. Suddenly the door opened and he jumped. Ramona stuck her head in. "Just a sec, Kev. It's Alfredo."

"I know," Kevin said, but the door was closing. He could hear Alfredo's voice, sounding strained, upset. He was keeping it low, and so was she.

What were they saying? Curious, Kevin stood and approached the door. He still couldn't distinguish their words. Just tones: Alfredo upset, perhaps pleading. Certainly asking questions. Ramona flat, not saying much.

He wandered away from the door, feeling more and more uncomfortable. Fright and confidence both filled him, canceling each other out and leaving him nearly blank, except for a light oscillation, a confused feeling. A discomfort. This was strange, he thought. Very strange.

All the objects in the room had taken on a kind of lit *thereness,* as things will on a morning when you have had little or no sleep. There on her desk, a few books: dictionaries, *Webster's* and a yellow Spanish/English one. Several books in Spanish. A volume of the sonnets of Petrarch. He picked it up but couldn't concentrate enough to read even a line. Something by Ambrose Bierce. A sewing repair kit. Six or seven small seashells, with a few grains of sand scattered under them. A desk lamp with a long extendable metal arm. From this window one looked into the branches of the torrey pine in their atrium. What could they be saying?

After perhaps fifteen minutes Ramona opened the door and came in alone. She approached him directly, took his hand. Her expression was worried, guarded. "Listen, Kevin. Alfredo and I, we have a lot of things to talk about— things that never got said, that need to be said now. He's upset, and I need to explain to him about us." She squeezed his hand. "I don't want you to just be sitting around in here trapped by us going over a bunch of old stuff."

Kevin nodded. "I understand." No time to think.

"Why don't you go ahead and go to work, and I'll come over later."

"Okay," he said blankly.

She walked him to the door. Alfredo would see his damp hair and assume they had showered together. In any case he knew Kevin had spent the night. Good. Kevin stopped her before she opened the door, gave her a kiss. She was distracted. But she smiled at him, and the previous night returned in a rush. Then she opened the door, and Kevin stepped out.

Alfredo was standing at one side of the landing, leaning against the railing, looking down. Kevin paused at the head of the stairs and looked at him. Alfredo looked up, and Kevin nodded a hello. Alfredo nodded back very briefly, his face pinched and unhappy. His glance shifted away, to the open door and Ramona. Kevin walked down the stairs. When he looked up Alfredo was inside, the door was closed.

Kevin went to work on Oscar's place. He and Hank and Gabriela worked on the roof, pulling out the old cracked concrete tiles to clear the way for the clerestory windows that would stand on top of the south-facing rooms. All day he expected Ramona to come biking down the street from Prospect, any minute now, for minute after minute after minute. Long time. Memories of the previous night struck him so strongly that sometimes he forgot what he was doing and had to stop right in the middle of things, looking around to catch his balance. Sometimes this happened while he was working with Hank. "Shit, Kev, you're acting kinda like me today, what's the problem?"

"Nothing."

"You okay?"

"Yeah, yeah."

"Flashbacking, eh?"

"I guess so."

The only person who biked up to the house was Oscar himself, trundling home for lunch. He stared up at them for a while, then went inside and made lunch for everyone. After they ate he questioned them about the day's work, ascended a creaking ladder to take a look at it. Then he biked away, and they went back to work.

And still no Ramona. Well, perhaps she didn't know he was at Oscar's. No, she knew. It was odd. Then again didn't she have to teach today? Of course. So she couldn't come by till after three or four. And what time was it now?

And so the afternoon ticked along, inching through a dull haze of anxiety. What had Ramona and Alfredo said to each other? If . . . It must have been a shock to Alfredo, to find Kevin there. He couldn't have had any warning. Unless someone who had been up at the hot springs had mentioned something and news had spread, the way it tended to in El Modena. Still, there wouldn't have been any warning about last night, or this morning. But why had he come by to say happy birthday so damned early?

"You sure you're okay?" Hank asked as they put their tools in Oscar's garden shed.

"Yeah, yeah."

He biked home, ate a dinner he didn't notice. Afterwards he stood in the atrium for ten minutes fidgeting, then walked over to Ramona's house. He couldn't help it.

Hesitantly he knocked at the kitchen door, looked in. Pedro, Ramona's father, was in there washing dishes. "Come on in," Pedro said.

"Thanks. Is Ramona home?"

"I don't think so. She didn't eat here."

"Do you know where she is?"

"Nope. Actually I thought she was at your place. I haven't seen her today."

"Oh." Kevin shifted uncomfortably. Part of him wondered how much Pedro knew, but mostly he was thinking *where is she?* He found he couldn't talk very well. Pedro was shorter than Ramona but he had the same coloring, his black hair now sprinkled with white. A handsome man. The way he spoke reminded

Kevin of Ramona, obviously the daughter had imitated him in years past. Now there was just the same crease between his eyebrows, a mild frown of concern as he chatted.

"I guess I'll try back tomorrow," Kevin said. "Will you tell her I dropped by?"

"Sure. Do you want me to have her call you when she gets in?"

"Yeah," he said gratefully, "do that."

But that was a mistake, because he spent the evening waiting for the phone to ring. Well into the night, in fact. And it never rang.

The next day he worked in the morning, and then spent the afternoon up at Tom's, working on the pump, which had broken. While he was there Tom got a call, and spent half an hour inside.

When Tom came back down to the pump he said, "My friends think there may be an outside connection in the Heartech-Avending deal."

"What does that mean?"

"Means Avending or Heartech might have an illegal source of capital. It might be here or it might be in Hong Kong, they're getting signs of both."

"Hong Kong?"

"The Chinese are using Hong Kong to generate money—they overlook all kinds of black conglomerates there, even though they've agreed to the international protocols that should make the conglomerates illegal. Then the Chinese zap them for a good bit of whatever profit they make."

"So we might have something. That would be nice."

"Nice? If my friends can pin it down, that would do your job for you! What's bugging you, boy?"

"Nothing. I'm just wondering how it will all turn out, that's all. Say, where's Nadezhda?"

"She's down at her ship. They'll be leaving before too long—I guess they've got a delay. Waiting for some stuff from Minnesota."

Kevin listened to Tom talk about it for a while, but there was grit in his thinking, and he kept losing track of the conversation. Finally Tom said, "Go home, boy, you must be tired. Get some rest."

Then when he got home he found Ramona sitting in the kitchen, helping Denise and Jay with their homework. She looked up at him and smiled, and he felt a rush of relief so powerful that he had to sit. Until that moment he hadn't known how anxious he was.

Ramona set the kids to work on their own, led Kevin into the atrium. He caught her up in the dark and gave her a hug. She hugged back, but there was a stiffness in her spine, and she avoided his kiss. He pulled back frowning, the knot back in his stomach.

She laughed at his expression. "Don't worry!" she said, and leaned up to kiss him briefly.

"What happened? Where have you been? What did he want? Why didn't you call?"

Ramona laughed again, led him by the hand to poolside. They sat on the low chairs.

"Well, I've been talking to Alfredo," she said. "I guess that answers all your questions at once. He came over yesterday morning to talk about things, apparently. Then when he found you there and realized we had spent the night together, he—well, he fell apart. He needed to talk anyway, and the more that sank in, the more he needed to."

"About what?"

"About him and me. You know. What happened, what went wrong."

"Does he want you two to get back together?" Kevin asked, hearing the strain in his voice.

"Well." She looked away. "Maybe so. I'm not sure why, though, even after all the talking we did. I don't know."

"And you?" Kevin asked, pressing right to the point, too nervous to avoid it.

Ramona reached over, took his hand. "I . . . I don't know what I want, Kev."

He felt his diaphragm seizing up, getting tighter with every breath, every absence of breath. Oh my God, he thought. Oh my God.

"I mean," she said, "Alfredo and I were together for a long time. We went through a lot together. But a lot of it was bad. Really bad. And you and I—well, you know how I feel about you, Kev. I love you. And I love the way we are together. I haven't felt the way I have the last week in a long time."

I've never felt like I have in the last week! Kevin wanted to say, and he only just bit back the words, suddenly frightened of speech.

"Anyway," Ramona said, still squeezing his hand, "I don't know what to think. I don't know what I feel about things with Alfredo. He says he wants to get back together, but I don't know. . . ."

"Seeing us together," Kevin suggested.

"Yeah, I know. Believe me." And suddenly she was blinking rapidly, about to cry. What was this? Kevin's fright grew. "I don't know what to do," she exclaimed painfully. "I can't be sure about Alfredo, and I hate having anything happen between you and me, to get in the way when we were just beginning!"

Exactly, Kevin thought, squeezing her hand in turn. Don't let it! Should he say that, or would it just be more pressure? He shifted his chair closer to hers, tried to put an arm around her.

"But," she said, pulling herself together, putting a hand to his arm and forestalling him. "The fact is, it's happened. I can't just ignore it. I mean that's fifteen years of my life, there. I can't just tell him to leave me alone, not after all

that—especially—well, especially"—losing it again, voice getting desperate—
"especially when I don't know what I feel!" She turned to him beseechingly,
said, "Don't you *see?*"

"I see." He couldn't swallow well. His diaphragm was as hard as if a block of
wood had been inserted under his ribs. "But Ramona," he said, not able to stop
himself, "I love you."

"Ah," she said, as if he'd stuck her with a pin; and suddenly he was terrified.

She threw herself up out of her chair as if to run away, collapsed against
him as he stood, embraced him, head against his chest, breathing in convulsive
gasps, almost sobs. Kevin held her against him, feeling her warmth, frightened
in a way he had never been before. Another new feeling! It was as if he had
been exiled from a whole enormous world of emotion, and now he was in it—
but he wasn't sure he wanted to be, because this love that caused him to clutch
Ramona to him so tightly—this love made him so *vulnerable.* . . . If she left. He
couldn't think of it. Was this what it meant to be in love, to feel this horrible
fear?

"Come upstairs," he said into her hair.

"No," she said, muffled into his shirt. "No." She composed herself, sniffed
hard, pulled away from him, stood fully. Eye to eye she faced him, her wet eyes
unblinking, her gaze firm. "I'm not going to sleep with anybody for a while. It's
too . . . it's too much. I need to know what I think, what I want. I've got to have
some time to myself. Do you understand?"

"I understand," he said, barely able to form the words. Such fear . . .

"I do love you," she said, as if she had to convince him of it, as if he were
doubting her. Horrible!

"I know," he said weakly. He didn't know what to say. He was stunned. A
new world.

She was watching his face, nodding. "You should know," she said firmly.
Then, after a pause, "I'm going home now. I'll see you at the games and the
street work and all. Please. Don't worry."

He laughed briefly, weakly. "Don't worry."

"Please?"

He took a deep breath. "Oh, Ramona . . ." His voice was unsteady, his throat
suddenly clamped. "I won't be able to help it," he got out.

She sniffed, sighed. "I'm sorry. But I've got to have some time!" she cried
softly, and darted forward to peck him with a kiss, and was off, across the dark
atrium and out the door.

The following days were long. Kevin had never known this kind of tension, and
it disagreed with him. At times he found himself wishing that Ramona and

Alfredo had never broken up, that he had never thought of her as free, or gone up in the ultralite with her, or walked into the night hills with her, or spent the night in her room. Any of it. Better to leave him the way he had been before, happy in himself, in his own life! To have his happiness, even his ability to function, dependent on someone else . . . he hated it.

Two or three days passed, and he found out that Ramona had gone to San Diego to stay with friends. She left a short note on his house screen. Jody was substituting for her at school, and she expected to be away a week. Damn, he thought when he read the note. Why didn't you tell me? Why are you doing this? Make up your mind! Don't leave my whole life hanging like this!

Still, it was somewhat easier knowing that she wasn't in town. He couldn't see her, and didn't have to decide not to try. Alfredo couldn't see her either. He could try to pretend that everything was normal, go on with daily life.

That Wednesday's town council meeting, for instance. It was an ordinary agenda on the face of it, fire-fighting equipment expenditures, the fate of the old oak on Prospect and Fairhaven, the raccoon problem along Santiago Creek, permission for a convenience store, et cetera. Alfredo led them through these matters with his usual skill, but without aplomb. To Kevin he seemed distracted and remote, his face still pinched. He never looked Kevin in the eye, but addressed him while tapping a pencil on his notes, looking down at them. Kevin for his part tried to appear as relaxed as he could, joking a bit with witnesses and the like. But it was an effort, an act. In reality he felt as nervous as Alfredo looked.

He wondered how many people at the meeting knew what was going on. Certainly many in town knew he and Ramona had been getting close. Oscar, over at his table with his moonlike impassive face; he wouldn't be telling people about it. Nor Hank, nor Tom and Nadezhda. Jody? Gabriela or Mike? It would only take one leak for the story to spread everywhere, that was town life for you. Were some of the audience here tonight to see Alfredo and him pick at each other? Ach . . . no wonder Alfredo looked so guarded. Oh well. Not worth worrying about, not with the agenda in that department already full.

He remembered something Tom had said. "Every issue is related to this zoning change issue now, because you're on a council of seven, and your ability to act is determined by your working relationship with the other six members. Some will be your opponents no matter what, but others are in the middle, undecided. Those are the ones you have to cultivate. You have to back them on the things they care about most. That's the obvious angle. But then there's the unobtrusive stuff, following up their remarks with something that reinforces what they said—asking them questions to defer to their areas of expertise— that sort of thing. It has to be subtle—very, very, very subtle. And continuous. You have to *think,* Kev. Diplomacy is hard work."

So Kevin sucked on his coffee and worked. Hiroko Washington was impatient indeed with the witnesses who wanted the Santiago Creek raccoons left entirely alone. "Just where do you live? Do you have kids there?" she demanded of them. Jerry Geiger seemed down on the raccoon fans as well. It was doubtful Jerry could be influenced by anything, his memory was only one agenda item long, but still, both him and Hiroko . . .

"Have we got a population count on them?" Kevin asked the Fish and Game rep.

"No, not a recent one."

"Can you guess reliably from the data you have?"

"Well . . ."

"Aren't there maximum populations beyond which it's bad for them?"

"Sure."

"So we may be near that number, and killing some would be good for the remaining raccoons?"

"Sure."

"How long would it take to make a count?"

And so on. And once or twice he saw Hiroko nod vigorously, and it was she who moved that a new population count be made. And Jerry who seconded it.

Good. Diplomacy in action. One hand washes the other. Kevin pursed his lips, feeling cynical. But it was a cynical business, diplomacy. He was beginning to understand that.

And then they were on to the convenience store, and he lost his close focus on it, and it all seemed trivial. My God, is this what it meant to be a citizen in a democracy? Is this what he was actually spending the evenings of his only life doing? His whole existence stood in the balance, and they were arguing over whether or not to give permission to build a convenience store?

And so the tension came and went, obsession then distraction.

How slowly time passed. Hours dragged like whole afternoons. He had trouble sleeping, nights seemed unbearably long. So much of life was wasted lying down, comatose. Sometimes, unable to sleep, he hated the very idea of sleep, hated the way his body forced him to live.

At work he kept forgetting what the next task was supposed to be. The June overcast extended into July, clouds rolling in from the sea every day. And he found himself standing on Oscar's roof shivering, staring up at clouds, feeling stunned.

Hank and Gabby, who knew now what was going on, left him alone. Sometimes Hank brought along some dumpies of beer, and at the end of the day they sat down on stacks of two-by-eights and drank them, not saying much of anything. Then it was home for another long night.

Kevin took to spending a lot of time at the TV, talking with the house's sister families around the world, catching up on what they were all doing. Awful the way people tended to ignore these humans who appeared on their screens once a month, in a regular rotation. Oh sure, there were occasional conversations over meals, but often the people on both sides of the screens avoided the commitments these screen relationships represented. Still, it only took paying attention, an inquiry, a hello; the translating machines went to work and there he was in another place, involved in distant lives. He needed that now, so he turned up the sound, faced the screen, said Hi, asked how people were doing. The Indonesian couple had just had their third child and were facing killer taxes. The South African family was complaining about their government's bungling trade policies. The big Russian household near Moscow was building a new wing onto their complex, and they talked to Kevin for almost two hours about it. He promised to be there next month to check in on how they were doing.

And then every night the screen would go blank, and he'd be left with his own household, whatever members of it were at home. They were a distraction, though he would have preferred to talk to Tom. But Tom was usually out with Nadezhda. So he wished his sister would call. He would try calling her, but she was never in Dakka. He didn't want to talk about it with his parents. Jill, however . . . he wanted to talk to her, needed to. But she was never home. He could only leave messages.

Life on pause. His hitting streak, going beyond all laws of chance and good fortune, began to seem like a macabre joke. He hated it. And yet it seemed vitally important that he keep it going, as if when the streak broke, he would too. Then he went to bat afraid, aware of the overwhelming likelihood of making an out. In one game, in his first at-bat he nubbed one but managed to beat it out. The next time he took a pitch on a full count, and Fred Spaulding called it a ball despite the funny bounce to one side that it took. The third time up he nubbed another one, directly in front of the plate. He took off running to first base thinking it's over now, it's over. But, as they told him afterward, the Tigers' catcher, Joe Sampson, slipped on the strike carpet and fell face first into the grass, fingers just inches from the ball. And since the fielder had never touched the ball, it couldn't be scored an error. It was a hit, even though the ball had traveled less than four feet.

"Holy moly," Hank said afterwards. "That was the lamest two-for-two I ever expect to see in the life of the universe!"

Kevin could only hang his head and agree. The streak was a curse in disguise.

It was mocking him, it was out to drive him crazy. Better if it were ended. And nothing would be easier, actually. He could just go up to the plate and whiff at a couple and it would all be over, the pressure gone.

In the next game he decided to do it. He would commit streak suicide. So in his first at-bat he squeezed his eyes shut, waited, swung, missed. Everyone laughed. He gritted his teeth, feeling horrible. Next pitch he squeezed his eyes shut harder than before, groaned, swung the bat hard. *Thump.* He opened his eyes, astonished. The right fielder was going to field the ball on a hop. His team-mates were yelling at him to run. He jogged to first, feeling dazed, as if he had jumped off a building and a safety net had appeared from nowhere.

Of course he could keep his eyes open and miss for sure. But now he was scared to try.

When the inning was over he went to the dugout to get his glove, and Jody said, "Pressure getting to you, eh?"

"No!" Kevin cried.

Everyone laughed.

"Well, it's not!" Kevin insisted, feeling his face flush.

They laughed harder.

"That's all right," Jody said. "I'd be crazy by now. Why don't you just go up there next time and take two whiffs and get it over with?"

"No way!" Kevin cried, jumping away from her. Had she seen his eyes squeezed shut? Had all of them seen?

But they all were laughing cheerily. "That's the spirit," Stacey said, and slapped his shoulder in passing. They ran out onto the field chattering, Kevin's stress-out forgotten. But Kevin couldn't forget, couldn't loosen up. Here he was in a softball game, and his diaphragm was a block of wood inside him. He was falling apart.

The following week felt like either a month or a day, Kevin couldn't say which, but there he was in the council meeting again, so a week it was. Numbly he went through his paces, bored by the meeting, inattentive. It went smoothly, and near the end Matt Chung said, "We've got the information we need to proceed on the question of the proposal from the Metropolitan Water District, shall we use this time and go ahead on that? It'll be item two next week anyway."

No one objected, and so suddenly they were in the discussion. Should they buy the extra water from MWD or not?

Kevin tried to gather his thoughts.

While he was still at it Doris said, "Alfredo, what will we do with the extra water there will undoubtedly be?"

Alfredo explained again that it would be a smart move financially to pour it into the groundwater basin and get credits against their drafting from the OCWD.

Doris nodded. "Excuse me, Mr. Baldarramma, have you checked on the legality of such a move?"

Oscar nodded. "I have."

"And?"

"Wait a second," Alfredo interrupted, staring at Oscar. "Why did you do that?"

Oscar met his stare, said blandly, "As I understand it, my job as town attorney is to check the legal status of council actions."

"There's been no action on this yet."

"A proposal is an action."

"It is not! We've only just discussed this."

"Do you object to knowing the legal status of your suggestions?"

"Well no, of course not. I just think you're getting ahead of yourself here."

Oscar shrugged. "We can discuss my job description after the meeting, if you like. Meanwhile, would you like to hear the legal status of your suggestion concerning the use of this water?"

"Sure, of course."

Oscar moved a sheaf of paper in front of him, glanced at the members of the council. "Several years ago the State Water Resource Control Board responded to new laws passed by the California State Assembly by writing a new set of regulations governing water sales. The Revised California Water Code states that no California municipality can buy water and later sell it or use it as credit, unless said municipality has made the water available for consumption for the first time, and in that case, only for as long as is necessary to pay for the method of procurement. The right to buy and then sell water without using it is reserved to the state."

"So we couldn't sell any excess we had if we bought this water from MWD," Doris said quickly.

"That's right."

"So we'd have to use it all."

"Or give it to OCWD, yes."

A silence in the council chambers.

Doris pressed on. "So we don't need this water, and it won't save us money to buy it, because we can't resell it. And buying it would be breaking the council resolution of twenty twenty-two that ordered El Modena to do everything it could to reduce our water dependency on MWD. Look here, I move that we vote on this item, and turn it down. We simply don't need this water."

"Wait a second," Alfredo said. "The discussion isn't finished."

But the discussion was out of his hands, for the moment. Doris kept pressing, asked for a vote in every pause, inquired acidly whether there really was anything left to be said. Before too long Alfredo was forced to call for a vote. He and Matt voted to buy the water. The rest of the council voted against it.

Afterwards, walking over to the house to celebrate, the others were in fine spirits. "All right," Kevin said. At least something was going well. "That look on Alfredo's face when Oscar zapped him—ha." Fine. Fuck him.

In a deep voice Doris said, "'Do you object to knowing the legal status of your suggestions?'" She laughed out loud.

Tom was there at the house, sitting with Nadezhda and Rafael and Cindy and Donna by the pool. Kevin and Doris told him all about it. Kevin downed most of a dumpie of beer in one swallow. "So much for messing with our hill!" he said.

"Come on," Tom said. He laughed. "It only means they'll have to change their strategy."

"What do you mean?" Kevin said.

"They were trying to lay the groundwork for this development before they proposed it, to make things easier. Now that that's failed, they'll probably propose the development anyway, and try to convince the town it's a good thing. If they can do that then they can say, Hey, we need more water, we need different zoning. If the general concept has been approved then it'll happen."

"So," Kevin said, staring at the dumpie of beer.

"Hey, it's still a good thing." Tom slapped him on the arm. "Momentum, you know. But it's a battle won, not the war."

Four days later Kevin heard that Ramona was back in town. He heard it from Stacey down at the chickenhouse, accidentally, as Stacey was talking to Susan. That he had heard about it like that frightened him, and he jogged home with his package of breasts and thighs, desperately trying not to think about it. That she was back in El Modena and hadn't told him, hadn't come by his place first thing. . . .

He got home and called her up. Pedro answered, went to get her. She came on. "I hear you're back," Kevin said.

"Yeah, I just got in this morning." She smiled, as if there was nothing unusual happening. But it was just before sunset. Her eyes watched him guardedly. "Why don't you come over and we can talk."

He blanked the screen, rode over to her house.

She came out and met him in the yard, and they turned and walked down the path toward Santiago Creek. She was wearing jeans worn almost white, frayed at the cuffs. A white blouse with a scoop neck.

Suddenly she stopped him, faced him, took up his hands in hers, so that they hung between the two of them. Curious how held hands could make a barrier.

"Kevin—Alfredo and I are going to get back together. Stay together. He wants to, and I want to too."

Kevin disengaged his hands from hers. "But . . ." He didn't know what to say. Couldn't think. "But you broke up," he heard himself saying. "You gave it a try for years and years and it didn't work. Nothing's changed except you and I got started. We just started."

"I know," Ramona said. She bit her lip, looked down. "But . . ." She shook her head. "I don't want it to be like this." She looked off to one side. "But Alfredo came down to San Diego, and we talked about it for a long—"

"*What?*" Kevin said. "Alfredo came to San Diego?"

She looked up at him, eyes bright in the twilight. "Yes."

"But"—a twist in him, ribs pulled in—"Well shit! You said you were going to get away from us both and think about it and that's what I thought you were doing! And here you were off with him!"

"I meant to get away. But he followed me down there. He found out where I was staying and he went down there, and I told him to leave but he wouldn't, he refused to. He just stood out there on the lawn. He said he had to talk, and he wouldn't leave, all night long, and so we started to talk, and—"

Kevin took off walking, fast.

"Kevin!"

He ran. Around a corner he felt the muscles in his legs and he ran even harder. He sprinted as fast as he could for over a minute, right up Chapman and into the hills. On a sudden impulse, the instinct of an animal running for cover, he turned left and crashed up through the brush, onto Rattlesnake Hill.

He sat under the sycamores and black walnuts at the top.

Time passed.

He stared at the branches against the sky. He broke up leaves, stuck their stems in the earth. Occasionally he thought of crushing lines to say, in long imaginary arguments with Ramona. Mostly he was a blank.

Much later he tromped down through cool wet midnight air to his house, weary and heartsick. He was completely startled to find Ramona sitting on the ground outside the back door of the house, head on her knees.

She looked up at him. She had been crying.

"I don't want it to be this way," she said. "I love you, Kevin, don't you know that?"

"How can I know that? If you loved me you'd stay with me."

She pressed her hands to the sides of her head. "I . . . I hate not to, Kevin. But Alfredo and I have been together for so long. And now he's really unhappy, he really wants us to be together. And I've put so much work into making that relationship go, I've tried so hard. I can't just give all those years up, don't you see?"

"It doesn't make sense. You tried hard all those years, right, and it didn't work, you were both unhappy. Why should it work now? Nothing's different."

She shivered. "Things are different—"

"All that's different is you and I fell in love! And now Alfredo is jealous! He didn't want you, but now that I do. . . ."

She shook her head, hard. "It's more than that, Kevin. He was coming over on my birthday to say all the same things he said afterwards, and he didn't even know about us."

"So he says now."

"I believe him."

"So what was I, then? What about you, what do *you* want?"

She took a deep breath. "I want to try again with Alfredo. I do. I love him. Kevin. I've always loved him. It's part of my whole life. I want to make it work, so that all those years—that part of me—my whole life . . ." Her mouth twisted. "He's part of what I am."

"So I was just a, a, a kind of crowbar to get Alfredo's thinking straight!"

Tears welled up in her eyes, spilled down her cheeks. "Not fair! I didn't want this!"

Kevin felt a grim satisfaction, he wanted her unhappy, he wanted her as miserable as he was—

She stood. "I'm sorry. I can't take this." She started to walk away and he grasped her arm. She pulled free. "Please! I said I'm sorry, please don't torture me!"

"*Me* torture *you!*"

But she was the one running away now, her white shirt a blur in the darkness.

His satisfaction dissipated. For a while he felt bad. Surely she hadn't wanted things to come to this. She hadn't planned it.

Still, he got angrier and angrier at her. And Alfredo, going down to San Diego to find her! Fucking hypocrite, he hadn't cared for her when he had her, only when he didn't, only when it looked like he might lose her. Jealousy, nothing more; jealousy. So she was a *fool* to go back to him, and he got even angrier at her. She should have sent Alfredo away when he showed up in San Diego, if she wanted to be fair! Instead a talk with him, many talks, a reconciliation. A happy return to some San Diego bed.

He couldn't sleep that night. A dull ache filled him. Other than that he couldn't feel anything.

Two days later the Lobos had a game. Kevin showed up late. He coasted down to the field and dropped his bike. Ramona biked in right behind him, and everyone else was already paired off and warming up, so without a word they put on their cleats and walked out to the outfield, to throw a ball back and forth. All without a word.

And so it comes to this: out on the far edge of a busy softball diamond, two people play catch, in silence. A man and a woman. The evening sun casts long shadows away from them. The man throws the ball harder and harder with every throw, so that it looks like they're playing a game of Bullet. But the woman never says a word, or flinches, or steps back. She puts up her glove and catches each throw right in the pocket, on the thin leather over her palm. The ball smacks with a loud *pop* each time she catches it. Right on the palm. The man only throws the ball harder. The woman bites her lower lip. She throws the ball back almost as hard as it comes, with a smooth violent snap of the wrist. And the man only throws harder.

And so back and forth the white ball flies, straight and hard, like a little cannonball. *Smack. Smack. Smack. Smack. Smack.*

...8

In a camp in Virginia. Interned. Big mistake to antagonize that immigration officer. That a single official's enmity can result in this! But it's more than that, of course. A tidal wave of fear. Lawyer says private tests all negative, so this is just a ploy to hold me while they put together a case under the H-G Act. False positives. Meanwhile here in a kind of camp. Wooden dormitory barracks in rows, dead grass, dirt baseball diamonds, benches, fences. Barbed wire, yes. City of the dying. False positives, those bastards. Actually a lot of people here make the same claim. Some of them obviously wrong.

Summer in Virginia, hot, humid. Thunderstorms black with hail and lightning. The daily blitzkrieg of the news. War spilling into the Balkans like a bad summer re-run. TV apocalypse. Four planes blown up in transatlantic flights, and international flights soon to be severely curtailed. Pam will have to return by ship, if she can get home at all. World getting bigger as it falls apart. I can't write any more.

As Tom had predicted, Alfredo was now forced to go public with his plans for Rattlesnake Hill. He and Matt took time on the town talk TV channel in the dinner hour before the Wednesday night council meeting, and they announced their proposal, walking around a large architect's model of the hill after it had been built up according to their plans. The model was covered with little dark green trees, especially on top—the copse already there would be allowed to remain, at least in part. And the structures were low, built around the hilltop in a sort of crown, stepped in terracelike levels and in some places, apparently, built into the hillside. The buildings were of pale blond brick, and what was not building was lawn. It was a beautiful model, attractive as all miniatures are, ingenious, detailed, small.

Matt went through the town finances, comparing El Modena's shares to those of the surrounding towns and discussing the downturn they had taken in the last ten years. He went over charts showing how the new complex would contribute to the town income, and then moved on to show briefly where Heartech and Avending would get the financing to build the complex. Timetables were presented, the whole program.

Finally Alfredo came back on. "In the end it's your town, and it's your land, so you all have to make the decision. All we can do is make the proposal and see what you think, and that's what we're doing. We think it would be a real contribution to El Modena, the restaurants and shops and promenades up there would really make the hill used, and of course the restaurants and shops down below would benefit as well. We've made proposals on the council concerning zoning and water resources that would make the project feasible on the infrastructural level. The environmental impact report has been made, and it says pretty much what we're saying here, that the hill will be changed, sure, but not in a degrading way. Nearly a quarter of the town's land is parkland just like the hill, immediately behind it—we could easily afford that hill, and use its prominence in Orange County's geography to make a stronger profile for the town as a civic and financial unit."

"Fuck," Kevin said, watching his screen. "What babble!"

Tom laughed. "You're catching on, boy."

Alfredo and Matt ended by asking those watching to spread the word, because few townspeople would be watching, and to speak to their council members in favor of the proposal, if they were so inclined. More detailed messages and plans and updates and mailings were promised.

"Okay, it's in the open," Tom said. "Time to start asking the hard questions in the council. You can still stop the whole thing right in council if the zoning proposal doesn't pass. If people want it then they'd have to elect a new council, and at least you'd have bought some time."

"Yeah, but if people want it, the council will probably go for it."

"Maybe. Depends on the council members—they don't have to pay any attention to polls if they don't want to, it's representative government after all, at least in this part of things."

"Yeah, yeah."

Kevin could barely talk about it. The truth was, since his talk with Ramona he just didn't care very much, about the hill or anything. He was numb. No more new worlds of feeling; just withdrawn, in a shell, stunned. Numb.

One night Tom got a call from his old friend Emma. "Listen, Tom, we've caught a good lead in this Heartech case you've put us on. We haven't followed it all the way yet, but it's clear there's a really strong relationship between your company and the American Association for Medical Technology."

"What's that?"

"Well, basically they're an umbrella organization for all the old profit hospitals in the country, with a lot of connections in Hong Kong."

"Ah ha!" Tom sat up. "Sounds promising."

"Very. This AAMT has been implicated in a number of building programs back on the East Coast, and in essence what they're up to is trying to take over as much of the medical industry as they can."

"I see. Well—anything I can do?"

"No. I've passed it to Chris, and she's going to be going after it as part of her federal investigations, so it's coming along. But listen, I wanted to tell you—we broke cover to get the opening on this."

"They know they're being investigated?"

"Exactly. And if Hong Kong is part of it, that could be bad news. Some of those Hong Kong banks are rough."

"Okay, I'll keep my eyes open."

"You do that. I'll get back to you when I have more, and Chris may be contacting you directly."

"Good. Thanks, Em."

"My pleasure. Good to have you back on the map, Tom."

Doris was angry. Mostly she was angry at herself. No, that wasn't quite true. Mostly she was angry at Kevin. She watched his evident suffering in the affair with Ramona, and her heart filled with pity, anger, contempt. Stupid fool, to fall so hard for someone clearly in love with someone else! Kind of like Doris herself, in fact. Yes, she was angry at herself, for her own stupidity. Why care for an idiot?

Also she was angry at herself for being so rude to Oscar Baldarramma, that night in the hills. It had been a transference, and she knew it. He hadn't deserved it.

That was the important part. If people deserved it, Doris felt no compunction about being rude to them. That was the way she was. Her mother Ann had brought her up otherwise, teaching politeness as a cardinal virtue—just as Ann's mother had taught her, and her mother her, and so on and so forth back to the Nisei and Japan itself. But it hadn't taken with Doris, it went against the grain of her nature. Doris was not patient, she was not kind; she was sharp-tongued, and hard on people slower than she was. She had been hard on Kevin, perhaps—she had needled him, and he never appeared to mind, but who knew? No doubt she had hurt him. Yes, her mother's lessons still held, somewhere inside her—transformed to something like, People should not be subjected to anger they don't deserve. She had blown that one many a time. And never so spectacularly as with Oscar, up in the hills.

Which was galling. That night . . . two sights stuck in her mind, afterimages from looking into the sun of her own emotions. One, Kevin and Ramona, embracing on a moonlit ridge, kissing—okay, enough of that, nothing she could do about it. The other, though: Oscar's big round face, as she lashed out at him and ran. Shocked, baffled, hurt. She'd never seen him with an expression remotely like it. His face was usually a mask—over-solemn impassivity, grotesque mugging, all masks. What she had seen that night had been under the mask.

So, vastly irritated with herself and the apparently genetic imperative to be polite, she got on her bike after work one evening and rode over to Oscar's house. The front door was missing, as the whole southern exposure of the house was all torn up by Kevin's renovation. She went around to the side door, which led through a laundry room to the kitchen, and knocked.

Oscar opened the door. When he saw her his eyebrows drew together. Otherwise his face remained blank. The mask.

She saw the other face, moonstruck, distraught.

"Listen, Oscar, I'm really sorry about that night in the hills," she snapped. "I wasn't myself—"

Oscar raised a hand, stopping her. "Come in," he said. "I'm on the TV with my Armenian family."

She followed him in. On his TV screen was a courtyard, lit by some bare light bulbs hanging in a tree. A white table was crowded with bottles and glasses, and around it sat a gang of moustachioed men and black-haired women, all staring at the screen. Suddenly self-conscious, Doris said, "It must be the middle of the night there."

She heard her remarks spoken in the computer's Armenian. The crowd at the table laughed, and one said something. Oscar's TV then said, "In the summer we sleep in the day and live at night, to avoid the heat."

Doris nodded.

Oscar said, "It's been a pleasure as always, friends, but I should leave now. See you again next month."

And all the grinning faces on the screen said, "Good-bye, Oscar!" and waved. Oscar turned down the sound.

"I like that crowd," he said, moving off to the kitchen. "They're always inviting me to visit in person. If I did I'd have to stay a year to be sure I stayed in everyone's house."

Doris nodded. "I've got some families like that myself. The good ones make it worth the ones who never even look at the screen."

She decided to start again. "Listen, I'm really sorry about the other night—"

"I heard you the first time," he said brusquely. "Apology accepted. Really there's no need. I had a wonderful night, as it turned out."

"Really? Can't say I did. What happened to you?"

Oscar merely eyed her with his impassive stare. Ah ha, she thought. Maybe he is angry at me. Behind the mask.

She said, "Listen, can I take you out to dinner?"

"No." He blinked. "Not tonight anyway. I was just about to leave for the races."

"The races?"

"Yes. If you'd like to come along, perhaps afterwards we could get something. And there are hot dogs there."

"Hot dogs."

"Little beef sausages—"

"I know what hot dogs are," she snapped.

"Then you know enough to decide."

She didn't, actually, but she didn't want to give him the satisfaction of appearing curious. "Fine," she said. "Let's go."

He insisted they take a car, so they wouldn't be late. They tracked down to southern Irvine and parked at the edge of an almost full parking lot, next to a long stadium. Inside was a low rumbling.

"Sounds like a factory," Doris said. "What kind of racing is that?"

"Drag racing."

"*Cars?*"

"Exactly."

"But are they using gas?"

Roars from inside smothered Oscar's answer. Shit, Doris thought, he is mad at me. He's brought me here because he knows I won't like it. "Alcohol!" Oscar said in a sudden silence.

"Fueling cars or people?"

"Both."

"But they aren't even *going* anywhere!" Road races at least had destinations.

Oscar stared at her. "But they go nowhere so fast."

All right, Doris said to herself. Calm down. Don't let him get to you. If you walk away then he'll just think you're a stuffy moralistic bitch like he already does, and he'll have won. To hell with that. He wasn't going to win, not tonight.

Oscar bought tickets and they walked into the stadium. People were crammed into bleachers, shouting conversations and drinking beer from dumpies and paper cups. Peanuts were flying around. Lots of dirty blue jeans, and blue-jean vests or jackets. Black leather was popular. And a lot of people were fat. Or very solid. Maybe that's why Oscar liked it.

They sat in the top bleachers, on numbered spots. Oscar got beers from a vendor. Suddenly he stood and bellowed, in a great rising baritone:

Race-way!"

national,

In-ter-

County,

"Orange,

By the time he got to "In-ter-national," the whole crowd was bellowing along. Some kind of anthem. People turned to yell at Oscar, and one said bluntly "Who's that you got with you!" Oscar pointed down at Doris. "Dor-is Nak-ayama!" he roared, as if announcing a professional wrestler. "First timer!"

About thirty people yelled "Hi, Dor-is!"

She waved weakly.

Then cars rolled onto the long strip of blackened concrete below them. They were so loud that conversation was impossible. "Rail cars!" Oscar shouted in her ear. Immense thick back tires; long bodies, dominated by giant black and silver engines. Spindly rails extended forward to wheels that wouldn't have been out of place on a bicycle. Drivers were tucked down into a little slot behind the engine. They were big cars, something Doris realized when she saw the drivers' heads, little dot helmets. Even idling, the engines were loud, but when the drivers revved them they let out an explosive stutter of blasts, and almost clear flames burst from the big exhaust pipes on the sides. Bad vibrations in her stomach.

"Quarter miles," Oscar shouted. "Get up to two hundred miles an hour! Tremendous acceleration!"

His bleacher friends leaned in to shout more bits of information at her. Doris nodded rapidly, trying to look studious.

The two cars practiced starts, sending back wheels into smoking, screeching rotation, swerving alarmingly from side to side as the wheels caught at the concrete. The stink of burnt rubber joined the smell of incompletely burned grain alcohol.

"Burning rubber!" Oscar's friends shouted at her. "Heats the tires, and—" *blattt blattt screech!* "—traction!"

"Oscar's bike tires do that when he brakes," Doris shouted.

Laughter.

The two cars rumbled to the starting line, spitting fire. A pole with a vertical strip of lights separated them, and when the cars were set and roaring furi-ously, the lights lit in a quick sequence from top to bottom, and the cars leaped forward screeching, the crowd on its feet screaming, the cars flying over the blackened concrete toward the finish line in front of the grandstand. They flashed by and roared down the track, trailing little parachutes.

"They help them slow down," Oscar said, pointing.

"No, really?" Doris shouted loudly.

Two more cars trundled toward the starting line.

So the evening passed: an earsplitting race, an interval in which Oscar and his friends explained things to Doris, who made her commentary. The raw power of the cars was impressive, but still. "This is really silly!" Doris said at one point. Oscar smiled his little smile.

"Oscar should be driving one of those!" she said at another point.

"They'd never fit him in."

"Funny cars you could."

"You'd just need a bigger car," Doris said. "An Oscarmobile."

Oscar put his hands before him, drove pop-eyed, then cross-eyed.

"That's it," Doris said. "Most of those cars appear to need a bit more weight on the back wheels anyway, don't they?"

Immediately several of them began to explain to her that this wasn't neces-sarily true.

"It's a tough sport," Oscar said. "You have to change gears without using the clutch, and the timing of it has to be really fine. Then the cars tend to sideslip, so one has to concentrate on steering and changing gears at the same time."

"Two things at once?" Doris said.

"Hey, drag racing is a very stripped-down sport. But that means they really get to concentrate on things. Purify them, so to speak."

Then what looked like freeway cars appeared, lurching and spitting their way to the starting line. These were funny cars, fiberglass shells over huge en-gines. When two of them took off Doris finally got a good feeling for how fast these machines were. The two little blue things zipped by, moving four times as fast as she had ever seen a freeway car move. "My!"

They loved her for that little exclamation.

When the races were over the spectators stood and mingled, and Oscar became the center of a group. Doris was introduced to more names than she could remember. There was a ringing in her ears. Oscar joined a long discus-sion of various cars' chances in the championships next month. Some of his friends kidded him about the Oscarmobile, and Doris spent some time with a pencil sketching the design on a scrap of paper: rail car with a ballooning egg-shape at the rear end, between two widely separated wheels.

"The three-balled Penismobile, you should call it."

"That was my plan."

"Oh, so you and Oscar know each other pretty good, eh?"

"Not that good!"

Laughter.

Ordinary clothes, "Americana" outfits, blue jeans and cowboy boots, automotive types in one-piece mechanics' jumpers . . . Oscar's recreations seemed to involve costuming pretty often, Doris thought. Masks of all kinds. In fact some of the spectators called him "Rhino," so perhaps his worlds overlapped a bit. Professional wrestling, drag car racing—yes, it made sense. Stupid anachronistic nostalgia sports, basically. Oscar's kind of thing! She had to laugh.

As they left the stadium and returned to their car they passed a group wearing black leather or intricately patched blue-jean vests, grease-blackened cowboy boots, and so on. The women wore chains. Doris watched the group approach the part of the parking lot filled with motorbikes. Many of the men were fatter than Oscar, and their long hair and beards fell in greasy strands. Their arms were marked with black tattoos, although she noticed that spilled beer seemed to have washed most of one armful of tattoos away. The apparent leader of the group, a giant man with a long ponytail, pulled back a standard motorbike and unlocked it from the metal stand. He sat on the bike, dwarfing it; he had to draw up his legs so that his knees stuck out to the sides. His girlfriend squeezed on behind him, and the little frame sank almost to the ground. The back tire was squashed flat. The leader nodded at his followers, shouted something, kicked his bike's motor to life. The two-cylinder ten-horsepower engine sputtered, caught like a sewing machine. The whole gang started their bikes up, *rn rn rnn*, then puttered out of the parking lot together, riding down Sand Canyon Road at about five miles an hour.

"Who are they?" Doris asked.

"Hell's Angels."

"*The* Hell's Angels?"

"Yes," Oscar said, pursing his lips. "Current restrictions on motorcycle engine size have somewhat, uh . . ."

He snorted. Doris cracked up. Oscar tilted his head to the sky, laughed out loud. The two of them stood there and laughed themselves silly.

Tom and Nadezhda spent the days together, sometimes in El Modena talking to Tom's old friends in town. They went out to look at Susan Mayer's chicken ranch, and worked in the house's groves with Rafael and Andrea and Donna, and lunched at the city hall restaurant with Fran and Yoshi and Bob and a whole crew of people doing their week's work in the city offices. People seemed so pleased to see Tom, to talk with him. He understood that in isolating himself he had hurt their feelings, perhaps. Or damaged the fabric of the social world he had been part of, in the years before his withdrawal. Strange perception, to see yourself from the outside, as if you were just another person. The pleasure on Fran's face: "Oh, Tom, it's just so nice to be talking to you again!" Sounds of agreement from the others at that end of the table.

"And here I am trying to take him away," Nadezhda said.

Embarrassed, Tom told them about her proposal that he join her. But that was not the same thing as holing up in his cabin, apparently. They thought it was a wonderful idea. "You should do it, Tom!"

"Oh, I don't know."

One day he and Nadezhda cycled around Orange County together, using little mountain bikes with high handlebars and super-low gears to help them up the hills. Tom showed her the various haunts of his youth, now completely transformed, so that he spoke like an archeologist. They went down to Newport Harbor and looked around the ship. It really was a beautiful thing. Up close it seemed very large. It did not have exactly the classical shape of the old clipper ships, as its bow was broad, and the whole shape of the hull bulky, built for a large crew and maximum cargo space. But modern materials made it possible to carry a lot more sail, so that it had a clipper's speed. In many ways it looked very like paintings and photos of the sailing ships of the nineteenth century; then a gleam of titanium, or a computer console, or the airfoil shape of a spar, would transform the image, make it new and strange.

Again Nadezhda asked Tom to join them when they embarked, and he said "Show me more," looking and feeling dubious. "I'd be useless as a sailor," he said, looking up into the network of wire and xylon rigging.

"So am I, but that's not what we'd be here for. We'd be teachers." *Ganesh* was a campus of the University of Calcutta, offering degrees in marine biology, ecology, economics, and history. Most of the instructors were back in Calcutta, but there were several aboard in each discipline. Nadezhda was a Distinguished Guest Lecturer in the history department.

"I don't know if I'd want to teach," Tom said.

"Nonsense. You teach every day in El Modena."

"I don't know if I like that either."

She sighed. Tom looked down and massaged his neck, feeling dizzy. The geriatric drugs had that effect sometimes, especially when over-used. He stared at the control board for the rigging. Power winches, automatic controls, computer to determine the most efficient settings. He nodded, listening to Nadezhda's explanations, imagining small figures spidering out a spar to take in a reef in high seas. Sailing.

"Our captain can consistently beat the computer for speed."

"At any given moment, or over the course of a voyage?"

"Both."

"Good to hear about people like that. There are too few left."

"Not at sea."

Biking through the Irvine Hills, past the university and inland. Sun hot on his back, a breath of the Santa Ana wind again. Tom listed the reasons he couldn't leave, Nadezhda rebutted them. Kevin could tend the bees. The fight for Rattlesnake Hill was a screen fight for him, it could be done from the ship. The feeling he should stay was a kind of fear. They pedaled into a traffic circle and Tom said "Be careful, these circles are dangerous, a guy was killed in this one last month."

Nadezhda ignored him. "I want to have you along with me on this voyage."

"Well, I'd love to have you stay here, too."

She grimaced, and he laughed at her.

At the inland edge of Irvine he stopped, leaned the bike against the curb. "One time my wife and I flew in to visit my parents, and the freeways were jammed, so my dad drove us home by back roads, which at that time meant right through this area. I think he meant it to be a scenic drive, or else he wanted to tell me something. Because it just so happened that at that time this area was the interface between city and country. It had been orange groves and strawberry fields, broken up by eucalyptus windbreaks—now all that was being torn out and replaced by the worst kind of cheap-shot crackerjack condominiums. Everywhere we looked there were giant projects being thrown up, bulldozers in the streets, earthmovers, cranes, fields of raw dirt. Whole streets were closed down, we kept having to make detours. I remember feeling sick. I knew for certain that Orange County was doomed."

He laughed.

She said, "I guess we never know anything for certain."

"No."

They biked on, between industrial parks filled with long buildings covered in glass tinted blue, copper, bronze, gold, green, crystal. Topiary figures stood clustered on the grass around them.

"It looks like Disneyland," Nadezhda said.

He led her through residential neighborhoods where neat houses were painted in pastels and earth tones. "Irvine's neighborhood associations make the rules for how the individual homes look. To make it pretty. Like a museum exhibit or an architect's model, or like Disneyland, yes."

"You don't like it."

"No. It's nostalgia, denial, pretentiousness, I'm not sure which. Live in a bubble and pretend it's 1960!"

"I think you'd better board the *Ganesh* and get away from these irritating things."

He growled.

Further north the sky was filled with kites and tethered hot air balloons, straining seaward in the freshening Santa Ana wind. "Here's the antidote," Tom said, cheering up. "El Toro is a village of tree lovers. When the Santa Ana blows their kites fly right over Irvine."

They pedaled into a grove of immense genetically engineered sycamores. Tom stopped under one of these overarching trees and stared up through branches at the catwalks and small wooden rooms perched among them. "Hey, Hyung! Are you home?"

For answer a basket elevator controlled by big black iron counterweights descended. They climbed in and were lifted sixty feet into the air, to a landing where Hyung Nguyen greeted them. Hyung was around Nadezhda's age, and it turned out that they had once met at a conference in Ho Chi Minh City, some thirty-five years before. "Small world," Tom said happily. "I swear it's getting so everyone's met everyone."

Hyung nodded. "They say you know everyone alive through a linkage of five people or less."

They sat in the open air on Hyung's terrace, swaying ever so slightly with the massive branch supporting them, drinking green tea and talking. Hyung was El Toro's mayor, and had been instrumental in its city planning, and he loved to describe it: several thousand people, living in sycamores like squirrels and running a thriving gene tech complex. Nadezhda laughed to see it. "But it's Disneyland again, yes? The Swiss Family treehouse."

"Sure," Hyung said easily. "I grew up in Little Saigon, over in Garden Grove, and when we went to Disneyland it was the best day of the year for me. It really was the magic kingdom when I was a child. And the treehouse was always my favorite." He sang the simple accordion ditty that had been played over and over again in the park's concrete and plastic banyan tree, and Tom joined in. "I always wanted to hide one night when they closed the park, and spend the night in the treehouse."

"Me too!" Tom cried.

"And now I sleep in it every night. And all my neighbors too." Hyung grinned.

Nadezhda asked how it had come about, and Hyung explained the evolution: orange groves, Marine air base, government botanical research site, genetic engineering station—finally deeded over to El Toro, with part of the grove already in place. A group of people led by Hyung convinced the town to let them build in the trees, and this quickly became the town's mark. "The trees are our philosophy, our mode of being." Now there were imitations all over the country, even a worldwide association of tree towns.

"If you can do that here," Nadezhda said, "surely you can save one small hill in El Modena."

They explained the situation to Hyung, and he agreed: "Oh, hell yes, hell yes. It's not a matter of legal battles, it's simply a matter of winning the opinion of the town."

"I know," Tom said, "but there's the rub. Our mayor is proposing this thing, and he's popular. It might be he can get the majority in favor of it."

Hyung shrugged. "Then you're out of luck. But that's where the crux will lie. Not in the council or in the courts, but in the homes." He grinned. "Democracy is great when you're in the majority, eh?"

"But there are laws protecting the rights of the minority, there have to be. The minority, the land, animals—"

"Sure. But will they apply to an issue like this?"

Tom sucked air through his teeth, uncertain.

"You ought to start a big publicity campaign. Make the debate as public as possible, I think that always works best."

"Hmm."

Another grin. "Unless it backfires on you."

A phone rang and Hyung stepped down free-standing stairs to the window-filled room straddling the big branch below. Tom and Nadezhda looked around, feeling the breeze rock them. High above the ground, light scattering through green leaves, big trees filling the view in every direction, some in groves, others free-standing—wide open spaces for gardens and paths: a sensory delight. A childlike appeal, Nadezhda said. Surface ingenuity, structural clarity, intricate beauty.

"It's our genes," Tom replied. "For millions of years trees were our home, our refuge on savannahs filled with danger. So this love has been hardwired into our thinking by the growth of our brains themselves, it's in our deep structure and we can never lose it, never forget, no matter these eyeblinks in the city's grimy boxes. Maybe it's here we should move."

"Maybe."

Hyung hurried upstairs, looking worried. "Fire in the hills, Tom—east of here, moving fast. From the description it sounded near your place."

And in fact they could see white smoke, off over the hills, blown toward them in the Santa Ana wind.

Tom leaped to his feet. "We'd better go."

"I know. Here, take a car and come back for your bikes later. I called and they'll have one for you at the station." He punched a button on the elevator control panel, and great black weights swung into the sky.

A summer brushfire in the California foothills is a frightening sight. It is not just that all the hillside vegetation is tinder dry, but that so much of it is even more actively flammable than that, as the plants are filled with oils and resins to help enable them to survive the long dry seasons. When fire strikes, mesquite, manzanita, scrub oak, sage, and many other plants do not so much catch fire as explode. This is especially true when the wind is blowing; wind fans the flames with a rich dose of oxygen, and then throws the fire into new brush, which is often heated nearly to the point of combustion, and needs only a spark to burst violently into flame. In a strong wind it looks as if the hillsides have been drenched with gasoline.

Nadezhda and Tom rounded the last turn in the trail to Tom's place, following several people and a three-wheeled all-terrain vehicle piled with equipment. They caught sight of the fire. "Ach," Nadezhda said. The ravine-scored hillside east of Tom's cottage was black, and lightly smoking, and the irregular line that separated this new black from the ordinary olive gray hillside was an oily orange flickering, ranging from solid red to a transparent shimmering. White smoke poured up from this line of fire, obscuring the sun and filling the air downwind, filtering the light in an odd, ominous way. Occasionally fire leaped out of the burn line and jumped up the hill toward Tom's place, licks of flame rolling like tumbleweed, trees and shrubs going off suddenly, bang, bang, bang, like hundreds of individual cases of spontaneous combustion. It was loud, the noise an insistent, crackling roar.

Tom stood rigidly on the trail before Nadezhda, staring through the strange muted light, assessing the danger. "Damn," he said. Then: "The bees."

Hank ran by with some others. "Come on," he said, "can't fight a fire from a distance."

Kevin appeared shovel in hand, his face and arms streaked with black ash and brown dirt. "We got the beehives onto a cart and out of here. I don't know how many were smoked inside. Got the chickens out too. We've been watering your roof and they're cutting a break down this ridge, but I don't know if we're going to be able to save it or not, this wind is so fucked. You'd better get what you want out—" and he was off. Tom jogged up the trail to the cabin, and Nadezhda followed. The air was hot, thick with smoke and ash. It smelled of oils and burnt sage. Unburnt twigs and even branches blew by overhead. Just east of the cabin a big crowd of people worked with picks, shovels, axes, and wheelbarrows, widening an ancient overgrown firebreak. The cabin stood in a wide spot in this old break, and so theoretically it was well-placed, but the ridge was narrow, the terrain on both sides steep and rough, and Nadezhda saw immediately that the workers were having a hard time of it. A higher ridge immediately to the west offered a better chance, and in fact there were people up there too, and pick-up trucks.

Overhead a chopping sound blanketed the insistent whoosh and crackle of the fire, and four helicopters swept over the skyline onto them. Gabriela was shouting into a walkie-talkie, apparently directing the pilots. They clattered by in slow, low runs, dropping great trailing quantities of a white powder. One dropped water. Billows of smoke coursed up and out, were shredded in the wind. The helicopters hovered, turned, made another run. They disappeared over the skyline and the roar of the fire filled their ears again. In the ravine below them the fire appeared subdued, but on their side of the ravine shrubs and trees were still exploding, whooshing torchlike into flame as if part of a magician's act, adding deep booms to the roar.

On the break line almost everyone Nadezhda had met in El Modena was hacking away at the brush, dragging it down the ridge to the west. Axe blades flashed in the eerie light, looking dangerous. Two women aimed hoses, but there was little water pressure, and they couldn't spray far. They cast white fans of water over everything within reach, firefighters, the new dirt of the break, the brush being pulled away. Down below the house Kevin was at work with a pick, hacking at the base of a sage bush with great chopping swings, working right next to Alfredo, who was doing the same; they fell into a rhythm as if they had been a team for years, and struck as if burying the picks in each other's hearts. The sage bush rolled away, they ran to another one and began again.

Nadezhda shook herself, followed Tom to the cabin. Ramona was inside with all the other Sanchezes, her arms filled with clothing. "Tom, hey, get what you want right now!" It was stifling, and out the kitchen window Nadezhda saw a burning ember float by. Solar panels beyond the emptied beehives were buckling and drooping.

"Forget the clothes!" Tom said, and then shouted: "Photo albums!" He ran into a small room beside the bedroom.

"Get out of there!" someone outside the house shouted, voice amplified. "Time's up!" The megaphone made it a voice out of a dream, metallic and slow. "Everyone get out of the house and off the break! NOW!"

They had to pull Tom from the house, and he was yelling at them. A huge airy rumble filled the air, punctuated by innumerable small explosions. The whole hillside between ravine and ridge was catching fire. Hills in the distance appeared to float and then drop, tumbling in the superheated air. People streamed down the firebreak they had just made, and those who had been in the house joined them. Tom stumbled along looking at the ground, a photo album clutched to his chest. Alfredo and Kevin argued over a map, Kevin stabbing at it with a bloody finger, "That's a real firebreak right up there," pointing to the west. "It's the only thing this side of Peter's Canyon that'll do! Let's get everyone there and widen it, clear the backside, get the choppers to drop in front. We should be able to make a stand!"

"Maybe," Alfredo said, and shrugged. "Okay, let's do it." He shouted instructions as they hurried down the trail, and Gabriela stopped to talk into her walkie-talkie. White smoke diffused through the air made it hard to breathe, and the light was dim, colors filtered and grayish.

At the gouged trail's first drop-off there was a crush of people. They looked back, saw Tom's cabin sitting among flames, looking untouched and impervious; but the solar panels beyond had melted like syrup, and were oozing dense black smoke. All the weeds in the yard were aflame, and the grandfather clocks burned like men at the stake. As they watched the shingles on one corner of the roof caught fire, all at once as if a magician had snapped his fingers. Poof! One whole wall gone up like newspaper in the fireplace. Nadezhda held Tom by the arm, but he shrugged her off, staring back at the sight, clutching the album still. His wrinkled face was smeared with ash, his eyes red-rimmed with the smoke, his fringe of hair flying wildly, singed to curls in one spot by a passing ember. His mouth was in a tight disdainful knot. "It's only things," he said to Nadezhda hoarsely, angrily. "Only things." But then they passed a small knot of smoked bees lying on the dirt, and he hissed, looking anguished.

He insisted on helping at the firebreak to the west, and Nadezhda went along, packed into the back of a pick-up truck with a crowd of smoky, sweaty Modeños. She got the feeling they would have been joking and cursing with great vitality if it weren't for Tom among them. At the firebreak they leaped out and joined a big crowd already working there. This firebreak was on a long, level, broad ridge, and it had been recently cleared. They worked like madmen widening it, and all the while the line of rising smoke with the terrible orange base approached. The black behind the line seemed to extend all the way to the horizon, as if all the world had been burnt. Voices were cracked, hoarse, furious. Hills, ravines, canyons, all disappeared in the smoke. No colors but gray and brown and black left, except for that line of whitish orange.

Helicopters poured overhead in a regular parade, first civilian craft, then immense Marine and Coast Guard machines. When these arrived everyone cheered. Popping over the horizon like dragons out of a nightmare, fast as jets and only meters off the treetops, they bombed the fire relentlessly, great sheets of white powder trailing behind them. The powder must be heavy, Nadezhda thought at one point, not to be lofted like the ash and embers. She had a burn on her cheek, she didn't know where it had come from. She ran a wheelbarrow from workers to pick-up trucks, feeling a strange, stark happiness, pushing herself till

she choked on the gritty air. Once she was drenched by the spray from a helicopter's water drop. Little bulldozers arrived, looking like Moscow snowplows.
They widened the firebreak quickly, until it was an angry reddish strip nearly
thirty meters wide, extending along the ridge for a few kilometers. It looked
good, but with the wind gusting it was hard to tell if it would hold the fire or not.
Everything depended on the wind. If it slacked they would be okay. If it grew
stronger, Peter's Canyon was in trouble. If it stayed constant . . . they couldn't
be sure. They could only work harder. An hour or two passed as they tore fran-
tically at the vegetation, and watched the fire's inexorable final approach, and
cheered or at least nodded in approval at every pass of the helicopters.

At one point Kevin stopped beside Nadezhda. "I think the choppers might
do it," he said. "You should get some gloves on."

Nadezhda looked down the line of the break. Gabriela was driving a dozer,
shouting happily at a patch of mesquite she was demolishing. Ramona and
Hank were hosing down the newly cleared section of firebreak, following
a water truck. Alfredo was hacking away at a scrub oak with an axe. Stacey
and Jody were running brush to a pick-up, as Nadezhda had been until just
a moment before. Many others she had not met were among them performing similar tasks; there must have been a hundred people up there working at
this break, maybe two. Several had been injured and were being tended at an
ambulance truck. She walked over to look for Tom. "Is this your volunteer fire
department?" she asked a medic there.

"Our what? Oh. Well, no. This is our town. Whoever heard about it, you know."

She nodded.

The firebreak held.

Hank walked up to Tom and held his arm. "House burns, save the nails."

Just before sunset Hank and Kevin joined Alice Abresh, head of El Modena's
little volunteer fire department, and they drove one of the pick-up trucks back
around Black Star Canyon Road, to search for the origins of the fire. In a wind
like theirs such a search was relatively simple; find the burnt ground farthest
east, and have a look around.

This point turned out to be near the top of a small knoll, in the broken
canyony terrain east of Tom's place. From this hilltop scorched black trees extended in a fan shape to the west, off to the distant firebreak. They could see the
whole extent of the burn. "Some plants actually need that fire as part of their
cycle," Hank said.

"In the Sierra," Alice replied absently, looking around at the ground. She picked up some dirt, crumbled it between her fingers, smelled it. Put some in plastic bags. "Here they mostly just survive it. But they do that real well."

"Must be several hundred acres at least," Kevin said.

"You think so?"

"Smell this," Alice said to them. They smelled the clod of dirt. "This is right where the thing had to start, and it smells to me like kerosene."

They stared at each other.

"Maybe someone's campfire got away from them," Kevin said.

"Certainly a bad luck place for a fire as far as Tom's concerned," Hank said. "Right upwind of him."

Kevin shook his head. "I can't believe anyone would . . . do that."

"Probably not."

Alice shook her head. "Maybe it was an accident. We'll have to tell the cops about this, though."

That night Tom stayed at the house under Rattlesnake Hill, using a guest room just down from Nadezhda's. When they had seen that the second firebreak would hold, they had led him down to the house, but after a meal and a shower he had taken off again, and was gone all evening, no one knew where. People came by the house with food and clothes, but he wasn't there. The house residents thanked them.

Nadezhda glanced through the photo album he had saved. Many of the big pages were empty. Others had pictures of kids, Tom looking much younger, his wife. Not very many pictures had been left in the album.

Much later he returned, looking tired. He sat in a chair by the atrium pool. Nadezhda finished washing dishes and went out to sit by him.

The photo album was on the deck beside him. He gestured at it. "I took a lot out and tacked them to the walls, a long time ago. Never put them back in." He stared at it.

Nadezhda said, "I lost four shoeboxes of pictures once, I don't even know how or when. One time I went looking for them and they weren't there."

She got up and got a bottle of Scotch and two glasses from the kitchen. "Have a drink."

"Thanks, I will." He sighed. "What a day."

"It all happened so fast. I mean, this morning we were biking around and everything was normal."

"Yeah." He took a drink. "That's life."

They sat. He kicked the photo album. "Just things."

"Do you want to show them to me?"

"I guess so. You want to see them?"

"Yes."

He explained them to her one by one. The circumstances for most of them he remembered exactly. A few he was unsure about. "That's in the apartment, either in San Diego or Santa Cruz, they looked alike." A few times he stopped talking, just looked, then flipped the big pages over, the clear sheets that covered the photos flapping. Fairly quickly he was through to the last page, which was empty. He stared at it.

"Just things."

"Not exactly," Nadezhda said. "But close enough."

They clicked glasses, drank. Overhead stars came out. Somehow they still smelled of smoke. Slowly they finished the glasses, poured another round.

Tom roused himself. He drained his glass, looked over at her, smiled crookedly. "So when does this ship leave?"

It was strange, Kevin thought, that you could fight a fire, running around slashing brush with an axe until the air burned in your lungs like the fire itself, and yet never feel a thing. To not care, to watch your grandfather's house ignite, and note how much more smokily plastic burns than pine. . . .

Numb.

He spent a lot of time at work. Setting tile in Oscar's kitchen around the house computer terminal. Grout all over his hands. Getting into the detail work, the finishing, the touch-ups. You could lose yourself forever in that stuff, bearing down toward perfection far beyond what the eye would ever notice standing in the door. Or lost in the way it was all coming together. Oscar's house had been an ordinary tract house before, but now with the south rooms all made one, and clerestory windows installed at the top of their walls, they formed a long plant-filled light-charged chamber, against which the living rooms rested, behind walls that did not reach the ceiling. Thus the living rooms—kitchen, family room, reading room—were lit from behind with a warm green light, and had, Kevin thought, an appealing spaciousness. Some floors had been re-leveled, and the pool under the central skylight was surrounded by big ficus trees alternating with black water-filled pillars, giving the house a handsome central area, and the feeling Kevin always strove for, that one was somehow both outdoors and yet protected from the elements. He spent several hours walking through the house, doing touch-up, or sitting and trying to get a feel for how the rooms would look when finished and furnished. It was his usual habit near the end of a project, and comforting. Another job done, another space created and shaped. . . .

He never saw Ramona anymore, except at their games. She always greeted him with a smile both bright and wan at once, a smile that told him nothing, except perhaps that she was worried about him. So he didn't look. He avoided warming up with her so they wouldn't get into another session of Bullet. Once they were in a four-way warm-up, and lobbed it to each other carefully. She didn't talk to him as she used to, she spoke in stilted sentences even when cheering him on from the bench. Deliberate, self-conscious, completely unlike her. Oh well.

His perfect hitting continued, like a curse he could never escape. Solid line drives these days, slashed and sprayed all over the field. He didn't care anymore, that was the key. There's no pressure when you don't care.

Once he ran into her at Fran's bakery and she jumped as if frightened. God, he thought, spare me. To hell with her if she felt guilty about deserting him, and yet didn't act to change it.

If you don't act on it, it wasn't a true feeling. One of Hank's favorite sayings, the text for countless incoherent sermons. If the saying were true, and if Ramona was not acting, then . . . Oh well.

Work was the best thing. Get the breakfast room under the old carport as sunny and tree-filled as possible. Put the skylights in place, boxes into the roofing, bubbles of cloudgel onto the boxes, get the seal right, make it all so clean and perfect that someday when roofers came up here to repair something they'd see it and say, here was a carpenter. Wire in the homeostatic stuff, the nervous system of this rough beast. More kitchen tiles, a mosaic of sorts, the craft of the beautiful. Sawing wood, banging nails in the rhythm of six or seven hits, each a touch harder, the carpenter's unconscious percussion, the rhythm of his dreams, tap-tap-tap-tap-tap-TAP, tap-tap-tap-tap-tap-TAP. Rebuilding the northside roof and the porch extending out from it, in a flash he imagined falling off and his elbow hurt. Gabriela wore an elbow sleeve for tendonitis, carpenter's elbow, and she was the young one. They were all getting old. The master bedroom would be cool no matter what.

One day after work Hank pulled a six-pack from his bike box and plunked it down in front of Kevin, who was taking off his work boots. "Let's down this."

They had downed a couple of dumpies when Hank said, "So Ramona has gone back to Alfredo, they say."

"Yeah."

"Too bad."

Kevin nodded. Hank slurped sympathetically at the beer. Kevin couldn't help declaring that Ramona was now living a lie, that she and Alfredo couldn't be happy together, not really.

"Maybe so." Hank squinted. "Hard to tell. You never really can tell from the outside, can you."

"Guess not." Kevin studied his dumpie, which was empty. They opened two more.

"But ain't none of it cut in stone," Hank said. "Maybe it won't last between them, and could be you might pick up where you left off, after they figure it out. Partly it depends on how you act now, you know? I mean if you're friends you don't go around trying to make her feel bad. She's just trying to do what's right for her after all."

"Urgh."

"I mean if it's what you want, then you're gonna hafta work for it."

"I don't want to play an act, Hank."

"It ain't an act. Just working at it. That's what we all gotta do. If you really want to get what you want. It's scary because you might not get it, you're hanging your ass out there, sure, and in a way it's easier not to try at all. Safer. But if you really want it . . ."

"If you don't act on it, it wasn't a true feeling," Kevin said heavily, mocking him.

"Exactly, man! That's just what I say."

"Uh huh." And thus Alfredo had gone down to San Diego.

"Hey man, life's toof. I don't know if you'd ever noticed. Not only that, but it goes on like that for years and years. I mean even if you're right about them, it still might be years before they figure it out."

"Jeez, man, cheer me up why doncha."

"I am!"

"God, Hank. Just don't try to bum me out someday, okay? I'm not sure I could handle it."

Years and years. Years and years and years and years. Of his one and only life. God.

"Endure," Hank would say, standing on the roof and tapping himself in the head with his hammer. "En-doourrr."

Pound nails, set tile, paint trim, scrape windows, lay carpet, program thermostating, dawn to dusk, dawn to dusk. Swim four thousand yards every evening, music in the headphones drowning thought.

He didn't know how much he depended on work to kill time until it came his turn to watch the neighborhood kids for the day. This was a chore that came up every month or so, depending on work schedules and the like. Watching all the adults leave as he made breakfast, herding all the tykes over to the McDows' house, starting up the improvised games that usually came to him so easily . . . it was too slow to believe. There were six kids today, all between three and six. Wild child. Too much time to think. Around ten he rounded them up and they made a game out of walking down the paths to Oscar's house. It was empty— with Kevin gone, the others were off to start a new project in Villa Park. So he got the kids to carry tiles from the stacks in the drive back to the hoist. Fine, that made a good game. So did scraping putty off windows in the greenhouses. And so on. Surprising how easily it could be made into a child's game. He snorted. "I do kindergarten work."

Onshore clouds massed against the hills, darkened, and it started to rain. Rain! First a sprinkle, then the real thing. The kids shrieked and ran around in a panic of glee. It took a lot of herding to get them back home; Kevin wished he had a sheepdog. By the time they got there everyone around was out getting the raincatchers set, big reversed umbrellas popping up over every rainbarrel and cistern and pool and pond and reservoir. Some were automatic but most had to be cinched out. "All sails spread!" the kids cried. "All sails spread!" They got in the way trying to turn the cranks, until Kevin got out a long wide strip of rainbow plastic and unrolled it along a stretch of grass bordering the path. The rain spotted it with a million drops, each a perfect half sphere; shrieking louder than ever the kids ran down the little rise between houses and jumped onto the plastic and slid across it, on backs, bellies, knees, feet, whatever. Adults joined in when the raincatchers were set, or went inside to break out some dumpies, singing "Water." The usual rain party. Water falling free from the sky, a miracle on this desert shore.

So Kevin kept an eye on his kids, and organized a sliding contest, and took off on a few slides himself, and got a malfunctioning raincatcher to work, and caught a dumpie from Hank as Hank pedaled past in a wing of white spray, throwing beer and ice cream like bombs; and he sang "Water" like a prayer that he never had to think about. And all of that without the slightest flicker of feeling. It was raining! and here he was going through the motions, sliding down the plastic strip in a great spray, frictionless as in a dream, heading toward an invisible home plate after a slide that would have had to begin well behind third base, he's . . . safe! and feeling nothing at all. He sat on the grass soaked, in the rain, hollow as a gourd.

But that night, after an aimless walk on the hill, he came home and found the message light blinking on the TV. He flipped it on and there was Jill's face. "Hey!"

He turned it on, sat before it. "—having trouble getting hold of me, but I've been in Atgaon and up to Darjeeling. Anyway, I just got into Dakka tonight, and I can't sleep." Strange mix of expressions, between laughing and crying. "I umped a game this afternoon back in Atgaon, I have to tell you about it." Flushed cheeks, small glass of amber liquid on the table beside her. She stood suddenly and began to pace. "They have this women's softball league I told you about, and their diamond is back of the clinic. It's a funny one, there are trees in left field, and right in the middle of right center field there's a bench, and spectators sit there during the games." Laughter, brother and sister together, a world and several hours apart. "The infield is kind of muddy most of the time, and they have a permanent home plate, but it's usually so muddy there that you have to set a regular base about four feet in front of the home plate, and play with that as home. And that's what we did today."

She took a sip from the glass, blinked rapidly. "It was a big game—the local team, sponsored by the Rajhasan Landless Coop, was taking on a champion team from Saidpur, which is a big town. Landowners from Saidpur used to control all the local khas land, which is supposed to belong to the government. There's some resentment here still, so it's kind of a rivalry.

"The champions arrived, and they were big women, and they had uniforms. You know how unie teams always look like they really know how to play. I saw some of the local team looking at them and getting worried, and all in all it was a classic underdog-overdog situation.

"The locals were actually pretty good—they looked ragged, but they could play. And the unies could play too, they weren't just show. They had a big fat catcher who was what I would call neurotic, she would yell at the pitcher for anything. But even she could play ball.

"So they played the first few innings, and it was clear the unies had a lot of firepower. But the local team turned some great defensive plays. Their third baseman nabbed a couple of shots down the line, and she had a good arm, although she was so pumped up she kept almost throwing them away. But they got the outs. Their defense was keeping them in the game. They gave up a few runs, sure, but they got some, too—their center fielder came up with two women on base, and powdered a line drive that shot under the bench in right center, it scattered the spectators like a bomb!" She laughed. "Home run."

Another slug from the glass. "So that made it four to three in favor of the unies. A tight game, and it stayed that way right to the end. You know how it gets tense at the end of a close game. The crowd was going wild, and both teams were pumped up.

"So." She paused to take another sip. "Scotch," she said, shivering. "So it got to the bottom of the ninth, and the locals had their last chance. The first batter flew out, the second batter grounded out. And up to bat came that third baseman. Everyone was yelling at her, and I could see the whites of her eyes all the way around. But she stepped into the box and got set, and the pitcher threw a strike and that third baseman clobbered it! She hit a drive over the left fielder's head and out into the trees, it was *beautiful*. Everyone was screaming, and the third baseman rounded the bases as fast as she could, but the unies' left fielder ran around out there in the forest and located the ball faster than I would have thought possible, and threw between trees to the shortstop, who turned and fired a bullet over the catcher's head into the backstop, just as the third baseman crossed the plate!"

She stared into the screen, rolled her eyes. "However! In her excitement, the third baseman had run across the *old* home plate, the permanent one! Everyone there saw it, and as she ran toward her teammates they all rushed out at her, waving their arms and screaming no, wrong base, go back, and the crowd was screaming too, and it was so loud that she couldn't hear what they were saying, I guess—she knew something was wrong, but she didn't know what. Saidpur's big boss catcher was running around the backstop chasing down the ball, and when the third baseman saw that she knew the play was still going, so she just *flew* through the air back toward the plate, and slid on her face *right back onto the old home plate again.* And that big old catcher snatched up the ball and fell right on her."

Jill took a deep breath, had a drink of Scotch.

"So I called her out. I mean I had to, right? She never touched the home base we were playing with!

"So her whole team ran out and started yelling at me, and the crowd was yelling too, and I was pretty upset myself, but what could I do? All I could do was wander around shouting 'She's out! She didn't touch the God-damned home plate that we're playing with! Game's over! She's out! It's not my fault!' And they were all crying and screaming, and the poor coach was pleading with me, an old guy who used to live in Oakland who had taught them everything, 'It was a home run and you know it was a home run, ump, you saw it, those home plates are the same,' and so on and so forth, and all I could do was say nope, she's out, those are the rules, there's only one home base on the diamond and she didn't touch it, I'm sorry! We must have argued for twenty minutes, you can see I'm still hoarse. And all that time the unies were running around congratulating themselves as if they had really won the game, it was enough to make you sick. They really were sickening. But there was nothing I could do.

"Finally it was just me and the coach, standing out there near the pitcher's mound. I felt horrible, but what could I do? His team was sitting on the bench, crying. And that third baseman was long gone, she was nowhere to be seen. The coach shook his head and said that broke her heart. That broke her heart—"

And Kevin snapped off the TV and rushed out of the house into the night, shaking hard, crying and feeling stupid about it—but that drunken look of anguish on his sister's face! That third baseman! He was a third baseman too. That broke her heart. To step in the box under that kind of pressure, and make that kind of hit, something you could be proud of always, and then to have it change like that—Night, the rustle of eucalyptus leaves. When our accomplishments rebound on us, when the good and the bad are so tightly bound together—It wasn't fair, who could help but feel it? That broke her heart. That broke her heart.

And Kevin felt it.

...9

ight in the dormitory, in the heat and the dark. Sounds of breathing, hacking cough, nightmare whimpers, insomniac fear. Smell of sweat, faint reek, that they could do this to us. There's noise at the far end of the room, someone's got a fever. One of the signs. Bleeding gums, vomiting, high fever, lassitude, disorientation. All signs. Trying to be quiet. They're trying to talk him into calling the meds, going into the hospital. He doesn't want to go of course, who would? They don't come back. That there's a place makes people want to stay here. Smell of fear. He's really sick. They turn on the light in the bathroom to get a glow, and try to stay quiet and yet every man in the dorm is wide awake in his bed, listening. Meds are here. Kill all of them. Whispered conversation. Shifting him onto a stretcher, the sick man is crying, carried between beds and everyone is silent, no one knows what to say, then one shape rises up—"See you over there, Steve." Several people say this, and he's gone.

He took off into the hills. Up the faint track switchbacking up Rattlesnake Hill. Late sun pierced breaking clouds, pencil shafts of light fanned down over the treetopped plain. The eucalyptus grove on the lower south knob of the hill looked like a bedraggled park, the trees well-spaced, the ground beneath clear, as if goats were pastured there. Nothing but packed wet dirt and eucalyptus leaves. There were chemicals in those leaves that killed plants. Clever downunder trick. Stepping on soft green acorns and matted leaves. There are people like those trees, harmful to everything smaller around them, creating their own fine space. America. Alfredo. Tall, handsome, strong. But shallow roots. And fungicidal. Everything on this hill killed, so his space would be secure. So he would be a hundred. Where would he send his directable over-hundred? Defense, no doubt. Create more business for his medtech. Business development, sure.

Everyone was a kind of tree. Ramona a cypress. Doris an orange tree, no a lemon tree. Old Tom a gnarled Sierra juniper, hanging on despite the dead branches. Oscar, one of the El Toro sycamores. Hank a manzanita, nature's bonzai, a primal part of the hills. Kevin? A scrub oak. Strong limbed, always shedding, looks like it's falling apart.

Up the wet root-rimmed trail to the real peak, feeling his quads. Onto the broad top. Sit for hours. Watch the sunset. Watch the dark seep out of the earth. Watch the dark leak into the sky.

Back down the hill, through the avocado trees. He was too restless to go inside the house. He got on his bike and started to ride. The cool air of the night, the foothill roads.

Thoughtlessly he coasted down into the roundabout where Foothill met Newport, circling into it to head up Newport to Crawford Canyon Road; and there was Alfredo, biking through in the other direction. Alfredo looked up, saw Kevin, looked down again. But as they zipped by each other Kevin caught a glimpse of the expression on his face, and it was a mix, so much in it, but the dominant emotion was—triumph. Triumph, pure and simple, suppressed and then he was past.

And at that moment Kevin hated Alfredo Blair more than he had hated anything in his life.

He was astounded at the virulence of the feeling, its power to dominate his thoughts. He rode and rode but he couldn't think of anything else. If only he and Alfredo could get into another fight on the softball diamond, what he would *do* to him. It was an incredible stimulant, hatred—a poisonous amphetamine, sending him into long wrenching fantasies of justice, retribution, revenge. Revenge! Fierce fights, both verbal and physical, all complicated (even in fantasy) by Ramona's presence, which meant that Kevin could never be the aggressor. Unless he were to catch him out one night, alone—like tonight—crash bikes, leap on him, strangle him, leave him dead—so much for his look of triumph!

Then again it wasn't hard to imagine scenarios where he was defending himself, or Ramona, or the town, fighting to save them all from Alfredo's malignant, arrogant drive to power. Punching him in the face *hard*—the idea made him hunch over, in little paroxysms of hatred. Oh to do it, to do it, to do it! It really was astonishing.

At last, much later, he returned home. His legs were tired. He walked through the garden to the house—

And there in the grove, movement. That shape! Instantly Kevin thought of the patch of kerosene east of Tom's place—arsonist, voyeur, intruder in the night (maybe Alfredo, there to gloat, there to be killed)—"Hey!" he said sharply, and was off running, jumping over the tomatoes and into the grove, movement out there, black on black. Between the rows of misshapen avocado trees, fallen avos like ancient grenades black on the tilled dirt, movement, movement, nothing. A sound and he was off again, trying to pant silently as he followed the weak clicks of dry avo twigs breaking.

He turned and saw it again, fifteen trees down, dark shape, still and large. A tiny sound, giggle-chuckle, and his anger shifted, an electric quiver of fear ran up his spine; *what was it?* He ran for it and it slipped left, downhill. He turned at the tree, looked down an empty row.

No movement, no sound.

An empty still grove, black in the black. Kevin standing in it trembling, sweating, darting glances left and right.

One day he climbed the hill and there in the copse of trees were Tom and Nadezhda, sitting under the tallest sycamore.

They waved him over. "How's it going?" Tom said.

"Okay. And you?"

"Fine. Nadezhda's ship has gotten its cargo aboard, and they're under way soon. I think I'm going to go along."

"That's good, Tom." He smiled at them, feeling low. "I was hoping you'd do that."

"I'll just keep him one voyage," Nadezhda said.

Kevin waved a hand, sat before them.

They talked about the hill for a while. "You know I've been getting calls from my friends," Tom said. "About the information from Avending we sent them, and some other stuff. I think I know now why Alfredo has done all this."

"Really!" Kevin exclaimed. "And?"

"Well—it's a long story." Tom picked up a handful of leaves, began dropping them on the ground. "Heartech makes cardiac aids, right? Cardiac aids, artificial blood, all that kind of thing. Alfredo and Ed Macey started the company eight years ago, when they were finishing grad school at UCI. It was a way of marketing an improved heart valve they had invented. To start, they got a loan from the American Association for Medical Technology, which is one of the information associations that sprang up to fill the gap left in the thirties when the venture capital laws changed. In the years since, unfortunately, the AAMT has become the refuge for a lot of the greediest elements in American medicine. Bits of the old AMA, people from the profit hospitals, they all found their way

into this AAMT, and started building their power base again." Tom laughed
shortly. "There are people in this country, as soon as you set limits of any kind,
their only goal in life becomes to break them. Being a hundred isn't enough—
for a lot of them, the thrill is to have more power than they should. More than
allowed! They love that.

"But Alfredo isn't like that, as far as I can judge. He wanted to build medical devices, that's all. You remember how he used to talk about it when they
were beginning. And they got their start, fine. But like a lot of small companies
beginning, it got rough. It wasn't clear at first that their valve was an improve-
ment over the other models on the market, and they were struggling. It got
to the point where it looked like they would go under—and that's where the
AAMT stepped in again.

"They offered Alfredo and Ed another loan. This one would be illegal under
the new laws, but they said they believed in Heartech's product, they wanted
to help. The AAMT would start a black account for Heartech, and then they'd
have a place ever afterward where they could go for help, deposit funds they
didn't want to report—a whole program, a whole black bank. And Alfredo and
Ed—they could have tried to find some other way out, I guess, but they didn't.
They went for it."

Kevin whistled. "How did your friends find out about this?"

"First by looking into the AAMT's Hong Kong bank, which covers a lot of
this action. And my friends have a mole in the AAMT who hears a lot, and
from her the stories get to my friends.

"So." Tom spread his hands. "That was the start of it. Heartech got through
its hard year, began to prosper. Some excellent evaluations of the new valve
came in, and it became the standard for certain conditions, and then they expanded into other products. You know that part of the story. But all along,
they were getting more deeply involved with the black side of the AAMT, using
funds, and after they hit the size limits for a company of their kind, banking
funds as well. They're iceberging, it's called. Most of their overprofit is going to
taxes, but they're hiding a part of their operation in the AAMT in order to be
able to do even more."

"But why?" Nadezhda asked. "Why do that?"

Tom shrugged. "It's the same impulse that got Alfredo started, if you ask
me. He believes in this equipment, he knows it saves lives, he wants to do even
more of it. Save more lives, make more money—the two are all mixed up in his
business, and if you try to limit the latter in any way, it looks to him like you're
limiting the former."

Kevin said, "But he could have started up an association of his own, and
farmed some of the profit out to smaller companies, right? The procedures are
there!"

"Yeah, yeah, he could have. But he didn't. They took the easy way, and the upshot of it is, they're in the AAMT's pocket."

"A Faustian bargain," Nadezhda observed.

"That's right." Tom picked up more leaves. "And he should have known better, he really should have. He must have felt desperate, back there that first time. Or else he's one of those smart people who is also fundamentally a little stupid. Or he's simply drawn to the power."

"But are you saying that the AAMT is responsible for this development idea?" Kevin asked.

Tom nodded. "They've been using the little companies they've got in their pocket as fronts, and funding developments like this all over the country. In one small town outside Albany, New York, they were getting resistance, and so they bought its whole city council—contributed illegally to the campaigns of several New Fed candidates for the council, and when they won, it was shoved right through. So they got that one built. They've done it all over the country. Once the developments are in place, the AAMT can use them. They've got a lot of control over them, and they can use them to build medical centers, or labs that generate profits that can be slipped into the AAMT and used to generate more, and so on. They no doubt would tell you they're doing it for the good of the nation's health care services. And maybe there's some truth to that, but there's a lot of raw power drive in it too. Putting the complexes in prominent, attractive places—that's part of it too, and that's mostly the drive for power, if you ask me. Pretty places."

"So was this one their idea?"

"That's what my friends have been told. In fact they were told that Alfredo tried to resist it, at first."

"You're kidding!"

Tom shook his head. "Alfredo told them it was a bad idea, and he didn't want Heartech involved. But he's in their pocket, see? They've got the goods on him, they can twist him like a dishrag.

"Still, he squirmed around trying to fight it. He said, listen, the hill's protected, it's zoned open land, and besides the town doesn't have any water to spare. Tell you what—I'll try the zoning and water issues and see what happens. If they don't go, we can't build anyway. Because he was pretty sure they wouldn't go. That's why he started all this backwards, you see? And indeed the water thing didn't go. But he's simply in no position to make a deal. They've got him, and they said, Hey—propose it directly, and see how that goes. And so that's what he's doing now."

"How did your friends find *that* out?" Kevin said, amazed.

"Their mole in AAMT has seen this one up close, apparently. She knows for sure, I'm told."

"Well—" Confused, Kevin didn't know which of several things on his mind he wanted to say. "Well, hey—then we've got him, don't we. I mean, when this story gets out . . ."

Tom frowned. "It's a question of proving it. We'll need something other than just the story, because the mole isn't coming out for this particular case. So we'll need some kind of documentation to back the charge, or they'll deny it, and it'll look like a smear campaign."

"Will there be any documentation?"

"Not much. They don't write these kinds of arrangements down, they don't put them in computers. The black economy is a verbal game, by and large. But my friends are looking—following traces of the money, mostly. They seem confident they'll come up with something on the Hong Kong end of things. But they haven't yet."

The three of them sat for a while.

"Wow," Kevin said. "I just had no idea."

"Me neither."

Nadezhda said, "It makes sense, though. There wasn't much motive to go for this hill in particular."

"Oh, I don't know," Tom said. "I think maybe Alfredo likes the idea, now. Height equals power, after all, and he's fond enough of power. But it's true— now we've got more of the story, we can see he's . . . hoist on his own petard, to an extent."

"I had no idea."

"People's motives are mixed, Kevin."

"I guess." He sighed.

After a while he said, "In a way I wish you weren't leaving."

"I'm not going to stop working on it. Most of what I'm doing is by phone, and I'll keep doing that from the ship."

"Part of it's your presence," Kevin said.

Tom regarded him steadily. "If that's so, it's going to change. That part's up to you, now."

Kevin nodded.

"You'll do fine."

Kevin nodded again, feeling doubtful.

Time passed in silence.

Nadezhda asked him what was happening with Ramona.

Awkwardly, hesitantly, Kevin found himself telling the story. The whole story. The childhood stuff, the softball game, the ultraflight, the night in the hills, the birthday party, the following morning. The little that had happened since.

It felt good to tell it, in a way. Because it was *his story,* his and his alone, nobody else's. And in telling it he gained a sort of control over it, a control he had never had when it happened. That was the value of telling one's story, a value exactly the reverse of the value of the experience itself. What was valuable in the experience was that he had been out of control, living moment to moment with no plan, at the mercy of other people. What was valuable in the telling of the story was that he was in control, shaping the experience, deciding what it meant, putting other people in their proper place. The two values were complementary, they added up to something more than each alone could, something that . . . completed things.

So he told them his story, and they listened.

When he was done he sat crouched on the balls of his feet, feeling pensive.

Tom looked at him with his unblinking birdlike look. "Well, it ain't the worst thing that could happen."

"I know." But this is bad enough for me! he thought.

He recalled Tom's long years of silence, his retreat to the hills after Grandma died. Years and years. Sure, worse things could happen. But at least Tom had had his great love, had gotten to live it to its natural end, to live it out! Kevin's throat was tight.

"There is not much worse," Nadezhda said to Tom, rebuking him. Then to Kevin: "Time will make a difference. When enough time is passing—"

"I won't forget!" Kevin said.

"No. You never forget. But you change. You change even if you try not to."

Tom laughed, tugged at the white hair over one ear. "It's true. Time changes us in more ways than we can ever imagine. What happens in time . . . you become somebody else, do you understand?" His voice shook. "You don't forget, but how you feel about what you remember . . . that changes."

He stood up suddenly, walked to Kevin and slapped him on the shoulder. "But it could be worse! You could forget! And that would be worse."

He stood by Kevin's side. Nadezhda sat on the ground beyond them. For a long time the three of them rested there, silent, watching sunlight tumble down through clouds.

That night while they were making dinner Kevin said, "One thing that really bothers me is the way everyone in town seems to know about it. I hate people talking about me like that, about my private affairs."

"Hell, you can't ever escape that," Tom said. "People are talking about me and Nadezhda too, no doubt."

Donna and Cindy and Yoshi came into the kitchen. "The bad thing," Kevin said, "is that now when I fight Alfredo over the hill it looks like it's just because of Ramona."

"No it doesn't. Everyone knows you're against that development, and the Greens are too. This thing is only likely to get you sympathy votes. And you can use all the votes you can get."

As they ate Kevin brooded over Tom's departure. Mexico, Central America, across the Pacific to Manila, Hong Kong, Tokyo. Working the winds and currents as so many ships had before. Well, it sounded great. Good for Tom. But with Jill in Asia, his parents in space . . .

Hank would still be there. Gabby. The team. Yoshi, Cindy, Donna, the kids, the rest of the household. Doris would still be there. Doris.

Two days later Kevin was the only one who went down to Newport with Tom and Nadezhda to see them off. Everyone else was too busy, and said their good-byes that morning at the house, or over the phone. "Seem's like half the town is overseas," Jerry Geiger complained. "Don't stay away long."

They took a car to Balboa, and Kevin helped them get their baggage aboard. The ship seemed huge. Overhead the dense network of rigging looked like a cat's cradle in the sky. Gulls flashed across the sun in screeching clouds, mistaking them for a fishing trip. The pavilion behind the dock was crowded.

Eventually *Ganesh* was ready. Kevin hugged Nadezhda and Tom, and they said things, but in the confusion of shouts and horns he didn't really hear. Then he was on the dock with the other well-wishers, waving. Above him Tom and Nadezhda waved back. *Ganesh* swung away from the dock, then three topsails unfurled simultaneously, on the foremast, the second mast, and the mizzenmast. Slowly, as if drifting, the ship moved downchannel.

Feeling dissatisfied with this departure, Kevin jogged down the peninsula to the harbor entrance. He walked over the boulders of the Wedge's jetty, looking back to see if the ship had appeared.

Then it was there, among the palms at the channel turn. The wind was from the north, so they could sail out on a single reach. With only the topsails set its movement was slow and majestic. Kevin had time to get to the end of the jetty and sit on the flat rocks. He couldn't help recalling the last time he had been out there, with Ramona, watching the ships race in. Don't think of it. Don't think.

The topsails were set nearly fore-and-aft, emphasizing the elegant transfer of force that propelled the ship across the wind. Always beautiful to see a square-rigged ship set so. People on both jetties stood watching it pass.

Then it was even with him, and Kevin could make out figures on the deck. Suddenly he spotted Tom and Nadezhda, standing by the bowsprit. He stood and cupped his hands around his mouth. "Tom! TOM!" He wasn't sure they would be able to hear him; the ocean's ground bass ate all other sound. But Nadezhda spotted him and pointed. All three of them waved.

Ganesh swung to the south, the yards shifting in time with the movement, so that the topsails were square to what was now a following wind. And then all the sails on the ship unfurled at once, mainsails, topgallants, skysails, moonsails, stunsails, royals, jibs. It was as if some strange creature had just spread immense wings. Immediately it leaped forward in the water, crashing across the incoming swells and shooting broad fans of spray out to starboard. Kevin waved. The ship drew away from him and grew smaller, the centerpoint of a wide V of startling white wake. Maybe that was Tom and Nadezhda in the stern, waving. Maybe not. He waved back until he couldn't see the figures anymore.

Back in El Modena Kevin went to work campaigning against the Rattlesnake Hill development, just as Tom had suggested. He and Doris went down to the town's TV studio and made a spot to put on the town affairs show, going over their arguments one by one. They walked around an alternative model of the hill with the development on it, one that showed the roads necessary, and had the landscaping changed so the extent of the buildings was more visible. Oscar directed the spot, and added points to their argument, including a long section he had written himself on the water requirements of the new structure. Doris pointed at graphs of the costs involved and the expected returns, the possible population increase, the rise in the cost of housing in the town when people poured in. "We set the town's general policy over a long period of years, and it's been a consensus agreement about El Modena's character, its basic nature. If we approved this construction all that would change." Every graph made a different point, and Doris walked from each to each, leading the watchers through to her inescapable conclusion. Then Kevin showed videos he had made on the hill, at dawn, in a rain shower, looking down at the plain on the clear day, in the grove on the top, down among the sage and cacti, with the lizards and ants. Bird song at dawn accompanied these images, along with Kevin's laconic commentary, and an occasional cut shot of South Coast Plaza or other malls, with their crowds and concrete and the bright waxy greenery that looked plastic whether it was real or not.

It was a good spot, and the response to it was positive. Alfredo and Matt did a rebuttal show which concentrated on their economic arguments, but still it seemed to Kevin that they had won the first TV round, surely one of the crucial ones. Tom saw a tape on *Ganesh,* and in one of their frequent phone conversations nodded happily. "That will get you votes."

Then, at Tom's urging, Kevin went out door to door, stopping at all the big houses and talking to whoever was there for as long as their patience allowed. Four nights a week he made himself go out and do this, for two hours at a time. It was wearing work. When he got tired of it he thought of the hill at dawn, or of the expression on Alfredo's face that night on the bikes. Some people were friendly and expressed a lot of support for what he was doing; occasionally they even joined him for the rounds in their neighborhood. Then again other households couldn't be bothered. People told him right to his face that they thought he was being selfish, protecting his backyard while the town shares languished. Once someone accused him of going renegade against the Green party line. He denied it vehemently, but it left him thinking. Here was where the party organization could help—there should be lots of people out doing these visits, or making calls. He decided to go up and see Jean about it.

"Ah good," Jean said, looking up from the phone. "I'd been meaning to get you up here."

Kevin settled into the seat across from her.

She cut off the speaker on the phone: "Let me get back to you, Hyung, I've got someone here I need to talk to." She tapped the console and swung her chair around to face him.

"Listen, Kevin, I think it's time to slack off on this idea of Alfredo's. It's medical technology he wants to bring into town, not a weapons factory. It makes us look bad to oppose it."

"I don't care what it is," Kevin said, surprised. "The hill is wilderness and was slated to be made part of Saddleback Park, you know that."

"Right now it's zoned open space. Nothing ever happened with that park proposal."

"That's not my fault," Kevin said. "I wasn't on the council then."

"And I was, is that what you're saying?"

Kevin remained silent.

Jean swiveled in her chair, stood, walked to her window. "I think you should stop campaigning against this development, Kevin. You and Doris both."

"Why?" Kevin said, stunned.

"Because it's divisive. When you take an extreme position against a development like that, then it makes the whole Green party look like extremists, and we can't act on real issues."

"This is a real issue," he said sharply. She eyed him from the window. "I thought this was what the Green party was about—slowing growth, fighting for the land and for the way of life we've got here. It's the Green party that made this town the way it is!"

"Exactly." She looked out the window at the town. "But times are changing, Kevin, and having established the town's style, we have to see what we can do to maintain it. That means taking a central position in affairs—if we do that, all subsequent decisions will be made by us, see? You can't do that when you're at one extreme of community opinion."

"But this is exactly what we stand for!"

"I know that, Kevin. We still defend the land. But I think that land can be put to use, and it will actually be good for other land around the town."

She wouldn't say anything more. Finally Kevin left, frustrated to the point of fury.

"I just don't understand her!" he exclaimed when he described the meeting to Oscar. "What the hell does she mean, good for other land? She's just caving in!"

"No, she's not. I think she and Alfredo are working out a deal. I've been hearing rumors of it in the town offices. The work we've been doing has put pressure on Alfredo, and I think Jean feels it's a good time to get him to make concessions. The Greens lay off on Rattlesnake Hill, and in return Alfredo puts all the rest of the Green program through the council."

"You're kidding."

"No."

"Well why didn't she tell me that?"

"She probably figured you wouldn't go along with it."

"Well she's right, God damn it!"

He went back up to see Jean again. "What's this I hear about you making a deal with Alfredo?" he said angrily, the moment he walked into her office.

She stared at him coldly. "Sit down, Kevin. Calm down."

She went to the window again. She talked about the Greens' gradual loss of influence in the town. "Politics is the art of the possible," she said again at one point.

"The thing is"—finally getting to it—"we've taken a bunch of polls in town about this issue, and they show that if it comes to a town referendum, we're going to lose. Simple as that.

"Now that may change, but it's my judgment that it won't. Alfredo, though— he can't be as sure. It's a volatile situation."

And Alfredo knows things you don't, Kevin thought suddenly.

"So he's nervous, he's feeling vulnerable, and he's ready to deal. Right now. It's a matter of timing—we can get him to agree to do things now that he simply won't have to agree to later on. Now, this development could be good for the town, and it can be done in a way that won't harm the hill. At the same time, we can get Alfredo to agree to the back country plan and the big garden strip down by the freeway, and the road and path plan, and a population cap. He's willing to go along with all that. Do you see what I mean?"

Kevin stared at her. "I see that you're giving up," he said absently. His stomach was contracting to its little knot of wood again. Nothing but scattered images, phrases. He stood up, feeling detached. "We don't have to concede anything to him," he said. "We can fight every one of those issues on their own merits."

"I don't think so."

"I do!" Anger began to flood through him, gushing with every hard knock of his heart.

Jean gave him a cold stare. "Listen, Kevin, I head the party here, and I've talked with all the rest of the leadership—"

"I don't give a shit who you've talked to! I'm not giving Rattlesnake Hill away!"

"It's not giving it away," she snapped.

"I'm not trading it, either."

"You were elected to fill a Green slot, Kevin. You're a Green member of this council."

"Not anymore I'm not."

He walked out.

He went to see Oscar and told him what had happened. Was it legal for him to quit the Greens while he was holding a Green slot on the council?

Oscar thought about it. "I think so. The thing is, while you're the Green on the council, your policy is the Green policy. See what I mean? You don't really have to quit the party. You can just say, this is what Green policy is. People may disagree, you may get in trouble with the party, and not get picked to run again. But there's no legal problem."

"Good. I'm not running for re-election anyway."

But after that, the nightly house-to-house campaigning got more difficult. A lot of people didn't want to talk to him. A lot of those who did wanted to argue with him. Many made it clear they thought he was waging a personal war with Alfredo, and implied that they knew why.

One night after a particularly tough walk around he came home and the downstairs was empty, and he went up to his room. Ramona was with Alfredo and Tom was on his ship and Jill was in Bangladesh and his parents were in space, and thinking about it he began to quiver, and then to tremble, and then to shake hard.

Tomas appeared in his doorway. "Home late, I see."

"Tomas! What are you doing?"

"I'm taking a break."

"You're *taking* a *break?*"

"Yeah, sure. Come on, everyone's got to take a break sometime."

"I wish I had this on videotape, Tomas, we could use it to pry you away from your screen more often."

"Well I'm busy, you know that. But I've been finding I get a twitch in the corner of my right eye when I look at the screen for too long. Anyway, let's go down to the kitchen and see if Donna and Cindy have left any beers in the fridge."

"Sure." So they went down to the kitchen and talked, about Yoshi and Bob, Rafael and Andrea, Sylvia and Sam. About themselves. At one point Kevin thought, I'm catching up on the life of the guy who lives in the room right next to mine. Still, he appreciated it.

Another time after an evening of campaign drudgery he went to the town hall restaurant to have dinner, thinking some chile rellenos and cervezas were just what he needed. Late summer sunset dappled the trees and walls of the courtyard, and it was quiet. The food was good.

He had finished, and Delia had cleared away his plate and was bringing him a last cerveca, when Alfredo walked out of the city chambers across the yard. He was at the wrought iron gate when he saw Kevin. Kevin dropped his gaze to the table, but still saw Alfredo hesitate, gate in hand—then turn and walk over to him. Kevin's heart pounded.

"Mind if I sit?"

"Uh," Kevin said, unsure. Alfredo looked uncertain as well, and for an awkward moment they froze, both looking acutely uncomfortable. Finally Kevin jerked, shrugged, waved a hand, muttered, "Sure."

Alfredo pulled back one of the white plastic chairs and sat, looking relieved. Delia came out with Kevin's beer, and Alfredo ordered a margarita. Even in his distraction Kevin could see Delia struggling to keep surprise off her face. They really were the talk of the town.

When she was gone, Alfredo shifted onto the edge of his chair and put his elbows on the table. Staring down at his hands he said, "Listen, Kevin. I'm . . . real sorry about what's happened. With Ramona, you know." He swallowed. "The truth of the matter is . . ." He looked up to meet Kevin's gaze. "I love her."

"Well," Kevin said, looking away, intensely ill at ease. He heard himself say, "I believe it."

Alfredo sat back in his seat, looking relieved again. Delia brought his margarita and he drank half of it, looked down again. "I lost sight of it myself," he said in a low voice. "I'm sorry. I guess that's why all this happened, and, you know." He didn't seem to be able to finish the thought. "I'm sorry."

"There was more to it than that," Kevin said, and drank his beer. He didn't want to go any further into it. Talk about love between American men was a rare and uneasy event, even when they weren't talking about the same woman. As it was Kevin felt impelled to order a pitcher of margaritas, to cover the awkwardness.

"I know," Alfredo said, forging onward. "Believe me, I'm not trying to take anything away from you—from what happened, I mean. Ramona is really unhappy about what . . . well, about what us getting back together has meant for . . . you and her."

"Uhn," Kevin said, hating the babble the subject of love always seemed to generate.

"And I'm sorry too, I mean I never would've tried to do anything like what's happened. I was just . . ."

The margarita pitcher arrived, and they both set about busily filling and drinking the glasses, lapping up salt, their eyes not meeting.

"I was just a fool!" Alfredo said. "An arrogant stupid fool."

Again, as from a distance of several feet, Kevin heard himself say, "We all lose track of what's important sometimes." Thinking of Doris. "You do what you feel."

"I just wish it hadn't worked out this way."

Kevin shrugged. "It wasn't anyone's fault."

Had he said that? But it was as if he was taking something from Alfredo to say that, and he wanted to. He was by no means sure he believed any of the things he heard himself saying; yet out they came. He began to feel drunk.

Alfredo drank down his glass, refilled, drank more. "Hey, I'm sorry about that collision at third, too."

Kevin waved it away. "I was in the baseline."

"I shoulda slid, but I wasn't planning to when I came in, and I couldn't get down in time when I saw you were gonna stay there."

"That's softball."

They drank in silence.

"What—"

"I—"

They laughed awkwardly.

"What I was going to say," said Alfredo, "is that, okay, I'm sorry our personal lives have gotten tangled up, and for fucking up in that regard. And for the collision and all. But I still don't get it why you are so opposed to the idea of a really first-rate technical center on Rattlesnake Hill."

"I was gonna say the same thing in reverse," Kevin said. "Why you are so determined to build it up there on the hill?"

A long pause. Kevin regarded him curiously. Interesting to see Alfredo in this new light, knowing what he now knew about Heartech and the AAMT. "It doesn't make sense," he said, pressing harder. "If this center is all you say it is, then it could do well anywhere in town. But we only have one hill like that, still empty and left alone. It's a miracle it's still that way after all these years, and to take that away now! I just don't get it."

Alfredo leaned forward, drew incomprehensible diagrams in the condensation and salt and spilled liquor on the table. "It's just a matter of trying for the best. I like to do that, that's the way I am. I mean sure, the better the center does the better it'll be for me. I'm not free of that kind of thinking, but I don't see why I should be, either. It's part of trying for the best you can."

So interesting, to see him rationalize like that—to see the strain there, under the moustache, behind the eyes!

Kevin said, "Okay, I'd like to be a hundred myself, and I like to do good work too. But good work means doing it without wrecking the town you live in."

"It wouldn't be wrecking it! To have a center that combined high tech labs and offices with restaurants, an open deck with a view, a small amphitheater for concerts and parties and just looking at the view—man, that's been the goal of city planners for years and years. More people would use the hill than ever do now."

"More isn't better, that's the point. Orange County is perfect proof of that. After a certain point more is worse, and we passed that point long ago. It's gonna take years to scale things back down to where this basin is at the right population for people and the land. You take all the scaling back for granted, but you value the results of it too. Now you're getting complacent and saying it's okay for major growth to start again, but it isn't. That hill is open land, it's wilderness even if it's in our backyards. It's one of the few tiny patches of it left around here, and so it's worth much more as wilderness than it ever could be as any kind of business center."

Kevin stopped to catch his breath. To see how Alfredo would rationalize it.

Alfredo was shaking his head. "We have the whole back country, from Peter's Canyon Reservoir to Black Star Canyon, with Irvine Park too. Meanwhile, that hill is on the town side of things, facing the plain. Putting the center up there would make it the premiere small center in southern California, and that would do the town a lot of good!"

Suddenly Kevin could hear the echo in the argument. Surely this was exactly what the AAMT representatives had said to Alfredo when they were putting the arm on him.

Fascinating. Kevin only had to shake his head, and Alfredo was pounding the table, trying to get his point through, raising his voice: "It would, Kevin! It would put us on the map!"

"I don't care," Kevin said. "I don't want to be on the map."

"That's crazy!" Alfredo cried. "You don't care, exactly!"

"I don't care for your ideas," Kevin said. "They sound to me like ideas out of a business magazine. Ideas from somewhere else."

Alfredo blew out a breath. His eyebrows drew together, and he stared closely at Kevin. Kevin merely looked back.

"Well, hell," Alfredo said. "That's where we differ. I want El Modena on the map. I want on the map myself. I want to do something like this."

"I can see that." And behind the dispassion, the somehow scientific interest of watching Alfredo justify himself, Kevin felt a surge of strangely mixed emotion: hatred, disgust, a weird kind of sympathy, or pity. I want to do something like this. What did it take to say that?

"I just don't want to get personal about it," Alfredo said. He leaned forward, and his voice took on a touch of pleading: "I've felt what it's like when we take this kind of disagreement personally, and I don't like it. I'd rather dispense with that, and just agree to disagree and get on with it, without any animosity. I . . . I don't like being angry at you, Kevin. And I don't like you being angry at me."

Kevin stared at him. He took a deep breath, let it out. "That may be part of the price you pay. I don't like your plan, and I don't like the way you're keeping at it despite arguments against it that seem obvious to me. So, we'll just have to see what happens. We have to do what we have to do, right?"

Taken aback, Alfredo didn't answer. So used to getting his way, Kevin thought. So used to having everybody like him.

Alfredo shrugged. "I guess so," he said morosely, and drained his glass.

Dear Claire:

. . . My living room is coming together, I have my armchair with its reading light, set next to the fireplace, with a bookstand set beside it, piled high with beautiful volumes of thought. Currently I have a stack of "California writers" there, as I struggle to understand this place I have moved to—to cut through the legends and stereotypes, and get to the locals' view of things. Mary Austin, Jack London, Frank Norris, John Muir, Robinson Jeffers, Kenneth Rexroth, Gary Snyder, Ursula Le Guin, Cecelia Holland, some others . . . taken together, they express a vision that I am coming to admire more and more. Muir's "athlete philosopher," his "university of the wilderness," these ideas infuse the whole tradition, and the result is a very vigorous, clear literature. The Greek ideal, yes, love of the land, healthy mind in healthy body—or, as Hank says, moderation in all things, including moderation of course! You can be sure I will remain moderate in my enthusiasm for the more physical aspects of this philosophy. . . .

. . . Yes, the political battle here is heating up; a brush fire in the canyons to the east of town burned several hundred acres, including one structure, the house of Tom Barnard. The fire was not natural—someone started it, accidentally or deliberately. Which? No one can say. But now Barnard is planning to sail off with my wonderful Nadezhda.

Then again, few are as Machiavellian as I. The police, for lack of other evidence, have declared it a fire started by accident—with the file marked for the arson squad, in the event other questionable cases like this occur. In other words the Scottish verdict. It's the end of that, but I keep my suspicions.

Meanwhile the obvious parts of the battle continue apace. The mayor's party has started to do what is necessary to get a town referendum on the issue. If they get the referendum on the ballot (likely), and win it, then all our legal maneuvering will have been in vain.

I try to remain sanguine about it all. And I have assuaged my grief in the loss of Nadezhda by associating more with Fierce Doris. Yes, yes, just as you say, growing admiration and all that. She is still as hard as her bones, but she is sharp; and around here a little waspishness is not a bad thing. I have entertained her by taking her to see some of my more arcane pursuits, and behaving like a fool while engaged in them. Always my strong suit when it comes to pleasing people, as you know.

Doris responded in kind by taking me to see her new lab. Yes, this is the way her mind works. This was high entertainment. She has gotten a new position with a firm much like Avending, "but ahead in just the areas I'm most interested in." So, I said, her great sacrifice in quitting Avending was actually naked self-interest? Turned out that way, she said happily. Her new employer is a company called SSlabs, and they are developing an array of materials for room temperature superconducting and other remarkable uses, by making new alloys that are combinations of ceramics and metals—those metals known as the rare earths or lanthanides, I quote for your benefit as I know you will be interested. What do you call it when it is partly ceramic and partly metal? "Structured slurries"—and thus the company name. Exact elements and amounts in these slurries are, of course, closely guarded industrial secrets. Great portions of the lab were closed to me, and really all I got to see was Doris's office and a storage room, where she keeps rejected materials for use in her sculpting. Seeing the raw material of her art made me understand better what she had told me about allowing the shapes of the original objects to suggest the finished sculptures; the work is a kind of collaboration between her and the collective scientific/ industrial enterprise of which she is a part. The artist in her stimulated by what the scientist in her reveals. Results are wonderful. I will enclose a photo of the piece she gave me, so you can see what I mean.

. . . Romance here has gone badly awry for my friend Kevin, alas; his beloved Ramona has returned to her ex the mayor, leaving Kevin disconsolate. I have seldom seen such unhappiness. To tell you the truth I didn't think he had it in him, and it was hard to watch—somewhat like watching a wounded dog that cannot comprehend its agony.

Because of my own experience with E in the last year in Chicago, I felt that I knew what he was going through, and although I am not good at this kind of thing, I determined to help cheer him up. Besides, if I didn't, it seemed uncertain that my house would ever become habitable. Work on it has slowed to a remarkable degree.

So I decided to take him to the theater. Catharsis, you know. Yes, I was wrong—there is theater in Orange County—I discovered it some weeks ago. A last survivor down in Costa Mesa, a tiny group working out of an old garage. It only holds fifty or sixty people, but they keep it filled.

Kevin had never seen a play performed—they just aren't interested here! But he had heard of it, and I explained more of the concept to him on our way there. I even got a car, so we could arrive in clothes unsoaked by sweat. He was impressed.

The little company was doing *Macbeth*, but only by doubling and even tripling the parts. Kevin had heard the name, but was unfamiliar with the story. He was also unfamiliar with the concept of doubling, so that in the first two acts he was considerably confused, and kept leaning over to ask me why the witch was now a soldier, etc. etc.

But the way he fell into it! Oh Claire, I wish you could have seen it. This is a society of talkers, and Kevin is one of them; he understood the talkiness of the Elizabethans perfectly, the verbal culture, the notion of the soliloquy, the rambling on—it was like listening to Hank or Gabriela, it was perfectly natural to him.

And yet he had no idea what might happen next! And the company—small in number, young, inexperienced, they nevertheless had that burning intensity you see in theater people—and the two principals, a bit older than the rest but not much, were really fine: Macbeth utterly sympathetic, his desire to be king somehow pure, idealistic—and Lady Macbeth just as ambitious, but harder, hard and hot. The two of them together, arguing over whether or not to murder Duncan—oh it crackled, there was a heat in their faces, in the room! You really could believe it was the first time they had ever made this decision.

And for Kevin it was. I glanced over at him from time to time, and I swear it was like looking at a dictionary of facial expressions. How many emotions can the human face reveal? It was a kind of test. Macbeth had taken us into his inner life, into his soul, and we were on his side (this achievement is necessary for the play to succeed, I believe) and Kevin was sitting there rooting for him, at least at first. But then to watch him, following his ambition down into brutality, madness, monstrosity—and always that same Macbeth, still there, suffering at the insane choices he was making, appalled at what he had become! Fear, triumph, laughter at the lewd porter, apprehension, wincing pain, disgust, pity, despair at the skyrocket futility of all ambition: you could read it all on Kevin's face, twisting about into Greek masks, into Rodin shapes—the play had caught him, he watched it *as if it were really happening.* And the little company, locked in, absorbed, vibrant, burning with it—I tell you, I myself began to see it new! Thick shells of experience, expectation, and habit cracked, and near the end, when Macbeth stood looking down at Birnam Wood, wife dead, tomorrow and tomorrow and tomorrow, I sat in my chair shuddering as much as Kevin. Then Macduff killed him, but who could cheer? That was us, in him.

When the "house lights" came on Kevin slumped in his seat beside me, mouth open—pummeled, limp, drained. The two of us left the garage leaning against each other for support. People glanced at us curiously, half smiling.

On the drive home he said. My . . . Lord. Are there more like that?

None quite like that.

Thank God, he said.

But several of Shakespeare's plays are in the same class.

Are they all so *sad?*

The tragedies are very sad. The comedies are very funny. The problem plays are extremely problematic.

Whew, he said. I've never seen anything like that.

Ah, the power of theater. I blessed little South Coast Repertory in their little garage, and Kevin and I agreed we would go back again.

. . . I don't know whether to tell you about this or not. It was very odd. I don't know . . . how to think of it. The things that are happening to me!

One night I went out into the backyard, to pick some avocados. Suddenly I had an odd sensation, and as if compelled I looked back into the house. There under my lamps sat a couple, both reading newspapers, one on the couch, the other in my armchair. The woman had a Siamese cat in her lap.

I was startled—in fact, terrified. But then the man looked up, over his spectacles at the woman; and I felt a wave flow through me, a wave of something like calmness, or affection. It was so reassuring that all of a sudden I felt welcomed, somehow, and again as if impelled I went to the glass door to go inside, unafraid. But when I slid the door to the side, they were no longer visible.

I went in and felt the couch, and it was cold. But there was such a calmness in me! A kind of glow, an upwelling, as if I stood in an artesian well of kindness and love. I felt I was being welcomed to this house. . . .

Now I suppose I won't send this letter. You will think I am losing my mind. Certainly I have considered it. Too much sun out here, California weirdness, etc. etc. No doubt it is true. A lot of things seem to be changing in me. I who spent a night with geese and coyotes, I who saw crows burst out of a tree—But I didn't tell you about those things either. I'm not sure I could.

Still—and this is the important thing, yes?—I am happy. I am happy! You would know what an accomplishment that is. So if I have ghosts I welcome them, as they have welcomed me.

I suppose I can always cut this section and leave the rest.

... 10

For several nights running I barely slept, falling only into that shallow nap consciousness where part of the mind feels it is awake, while another part feels an hour passing between each thought. I would wake completely around three, feeling sick, unable to return even to the miserable half sleep. Toss and turn thinking, trying not to think, thinking.

At dawn I would get up and go to the canteen and drink coffee and try to write. All day I would sit there staring at the page, staring into the blank between my world and the world in my book. Until my hand would shake. Looking around me, looking at what my country was capable of when it was afraid. Seeing the headlines in the newspapers scattered around. Seeing my companions and the state they were in.

And one day I stood up with my notebooks and went outside, around the back of the canteen to the dumpsters. The book was in three thick spiral ring notebooks. I sat cross-legged on the concrete, and started ripping the pages away from the wire spiral, about ten at a time. I tore them up, first crossways, then lengthwise. When I had a little pile of paper I stood and threw the pieces into the dumpster. I did that until all the pages were gone. I tore the cardboard covers away from the spirals, and ripped them up too. The twisted wire spirals were the last things in.

No more utopia for me.

After that I returned to the canteen and sat just like before, feeling worse than ever. But there was no point in continuing, really there wasn't. The time has passed when a utopia could do anybody any good, even me. Especially me. The discrepancy between it and reality was too much.

So I sat there drinking coffee and staring out the window. One of my dorm mates, he sleeps a couple beds down, came by with his lunch. Hey Barnyard, he said, where's your book.

I threw it away.

Oh, no, he said, looking shocked. Hey, man. You can't do that.

Yes I can.

Next day, same time, he came by with a ballpoint and a gray lab notebook. Something from the hospital no doubt.

Here, man, you start writing again. Deadly serious look on his face. You got to tell what happens here! If you don't tell it, then who will? You got to, man. And he left the notebook and walked away.

So. I will not write that book. But here, now, I make these notes. To pass the time if nothing else. I observe: there is less desperation here than one would think. There is a refusal of despair. There is a state beyond panic. There is a courage that should shame the rest of us. There is a camp, an American internment camp, where every day people are taken to the hospital, where the others help them out, and carry on. There is a place where people on the edge of death make jokes, they help each other, they share what they have, they endure. In this hell they make their own "utopia."

Life at sea suited Tom. Nadezhda and he had a tiny cabin to bump around in, a berth barely wide enough to fit the two of them. At night the rhythmic pitch over the groundswell translated to the roll and press of her body against him, so that she became an expression of the sea, an embrace of wind and wave. He had forgotten the simple pleasure of sharing a bed. At dawn, if she was still sleeping, he rose and went on deck. The raw morning light. There he was, on the wide ocean's surface, where a few constants of light and color combined to create an infinity of blues. To sail on a blue salt world, ah, God, to think he had gone a lifetime without it, almost missed it! It made him laugh out loud.

At dawn he had the deck almost to himself. Those on watch were usually in the bridge, an enclosed glass-fronted compartment spanning the deck just before the mizzenmast. Once he came across a group that had stayed up all night, to see the green flash at sunrise.

The crew was about equally divided between men and women, and most of them were in their twenties. Their work, their play, and their education all spilled into one another. Partying and romance kept them up late every night; they were the most high-spirited group of young people Tom had ever seen, and he could see why. Quite a life. The young women were especially rambunctious. That first rush into an independent life! All youth responds to it, but some are aware it wasn't always like this, that even their parents didn't have such opportunity. So these women cavorted like the dolphins that surfed in the bow wave during certain magic dusks and dawns, tall, dark, hair and eyebrows thick and intensely black. Tom watched them like Ingres in the baths, laughing at their sexiness. Perfect dark skin, rounded limbs, heavy breasts, wide hips, like women from the Kama Sutra who had stepped off the page and forgotten their purpose, become as free as dolphins.

Occasionally he went down to the ship's communications room and called home. He talked to Kevin and learned of the latest developments there, and gave advice when he was asked. He also called Nylphonia and his other friends from time to time, and conferred with them about the search through Heartech's records. There were tendrils of association between Heartech and the AAMT, but they were tenuous. "We'd probably have to bust AAMT to get Heartech, and that won't be easy."

"I know. But try."

Thunderheads, slate below and blooming white above, showed how high the sky really was. A line of them lofted to the south like a stately row of galleons, and then the ship was underneath them. *Ganesh* rode waves like low hills, wind keening in the rigging. The sailors on watch wound the sails in on power reels, touching buttons on the bridge's huge control board. The masts' airfoil configurations shifted, metal parts squeaking together. Tom and Nadezhda sat in chairs behind and above the sailors, looking out the broad glass window. Their captain, Gurdial Behaguna, dropped by to look over the helmswoman's shoulder at the compass readout. He nodded at them, left. "He's pretty casual," Tom said.

Nadezhda laughed. "This is a small blow, Tom. You should see it in the North Pacific."

Tom watched spray explode away from the bow, then come whipping back on the wind and crash to invisibility against their window. "That's the return route, right? So I suppose I will."

She smiled, reached for his hand.

Another day later Tom went aloft with the bosun, Sonam Singh, who had on a tool belt and was going to do some repairs on a tackle block at the starboard end of the main moonsail yard—that is to say, the sixth and highest sail up the mainmast, above the main course, the topsail, the topgallant, the royal, and the skysail. It was as high on the ship as you could get, some two hundred and forty feet above the deck; to Tom it felt like a million. He looked down at the little mouse-sized people scurrying around the model ship down there, and felt his hands clutch at the halyard. They were climbing the weather side, so that the wind would blow them into the halyards rather than away from them. The mast's movement was a slow figure eight, with a couple of quick catches in it. Glancing behind he saw the broad V of the wake, its edges a startling white against the sea's brilliant blue. Fractal arabesques swirled away from the ship's sleek sides. The horizon was a long way away; the patch of world he could see was as round as a plate, and blue everywhere.

"Clip yourself onto this line," Singh told him, pointing to a cable bolted at intervals to the underside of the slender moonsail yard. "Now put your feet on the footrope"—which looped three or four feet under the yard—"and follow me out. And if you would please grab these handles on top of the yard. One step at a time. Okay? Okay."

Tom was in a harness like a rock-climber's, which was clipped to the line under the yard. Even if his foot slipped and his arm gave away, he would still be there, hanging by his chest, swinging far above the deck, but it beat the alternative. "I can't believe sailors used to climb out here without these," he said, shuffling down the footrope.

"Oh, yes, they were a dangerous bunch of men," Singh said, looking back at him, "Are you okay? Are you sure you want to be doing this?"

"Yes."

"Very good. Yes, they would be standing on the footrope and giving their hands to the sails, reefing them or letting them out, tying frozen gasket knots, and sometimes in most wicked weather. They were quite the athletes, there is no doubt of that. Rounding Cape Horn east to west, that would be a trial for anyone."

"Some of them must have fallen."

"Yes, they lost men overboard, no doubt of that. Once a ship lost every man aloft when it gusted hard south of Cape Horn—five men in all. Here we are, at the end. Look at this block, the little runner inside it has pulled itself away from the side. A case of poor manufacturing, if you ask me. Now the line is stuck, and if you tried to reel it in it would snap the line or short the reel. Here now, you can lean out in your harness if you are wanting, you don't have to hold on like that."

"Oh." Tom let go and leaned back in his harness, felt the wind and ground-swell swirl him about. Up here you could see the pattern the waves made on the sea's surface, long curving swells rippling the reflected sunlight. Blue everywhere. He watched the bosun repair the tackle block, asked him questions about it. "This line allows you to bring down this side of the sail. It is called bunting. Without it you can't use the sail at all."

Singh concentrated on his screwdriver and the block, swaying about as he worked. He explained some of the network of lines matted below them. "They

are beautiful patterns, aren't they? A very pretty technology indeed. Free loco-
motion for major freight hauling. Hard to believe it was ever abandoned."

"Wasn't it dangerous? I mean, that last generation of sailing ships, the big
ones with five and six masts, most of them came to grief, didn't they?"

"Yes, they did. The *Kopenhagen* and the *Karpfanger* disappeared from the
face of the sea. But so did a lot of diesel-driven tubs. As for that particular
generation of sailing ships, it was a matter of insufficient materials, and poor
weather forecasts, and carrying too much aloft. And some design flaws. It was
yet another case of false economies of scale—they built them too big. Bigger as
better, pah! When you're burning fuel to transport fuel, then it might look true.
Until the ship strikes a reef or catches fire. But if the fuel is the wind, if you're
interested in full employment, in safety, in a larger definition of efficiency, then
there is nothing like this beauty here. It is big but not too big. Actually it is as
big as those old six-masters were, but the design and the materials are much
improved. And with radio, and sonar to look at the bottom, and radar to look
at the surface, and satellite photos to look at the sky, and the computer to be
putting it all together. . . . Ah, it is a beauty, isn't it?"

They stopped in Corinto, Nicaragua, and had to wait a day to get to the docks,
anchored in a long line of ships like theirs. Tom and Nadezhda joined a group
going ashore, and they spent the day in the markets behind the docks, buying
fruit, an old-fashioned sextant, and clothing light enough to wear in the tropics. Tom sat for an hour in the bird market, fascinated by the vibrant coloration
of the tropical birds on sale. "Can they be real?" he said to Nadezhda.

"The parrots and the mynah birds and the quetzals are real. The New Guinea
lories are real, though they aren't native to the area. The rest are not real, not
in the way you mean. Haven't you ever seen gene-engineered hummingbirds?"

Flashes of saffron, violet, pink, silk blue, scarlet, tangerine. "No, I don't believe I have."

"You need to travel more." She laughed at the look on his face, kissed him,
took his arm and pulled him along. "Come on, they make some fine bikes here,
that's something you know about."

A day in a tropical market. Sharp smells of cinnamon and clove, the bleat-
ing of a pig, the clashing of amplified guitar riffs, the heat, dust, light, noise.
Tom followed Nadezhda's lead, dazed.

In the end they spent all the money they had brought ashore. The ship un-
loaded some microchips, titanium, manganese, and wine, and took on coffee,
stereo speakers, clothing, and gene-engineered seeds.

The following evening, the last before they embarked, they went back ashore
and danced the night away, sweating in the warm tropical air. Very late that

night they stood on the dance floor swaying slightly, arms around each other, foreheads pressed together, bodies all around them.

They set sail, headed west across the wide Pacific. Endless days in the blue of water and sky. Tom became a connoisseur of clouds. He took more of the geriatric drugs. He spent time in the foretop, he spotted whales and dreamed great dreams. They passed a coral atoll and he dreamed a whole life there, Polynesian sensuousness in the peace of the lagoon.

One balmy evening Nadezhda's class met on the foredeck, and Tom described his part in the struggle to make the international agreements curtailing corporations. "It was like trust busting in Teddy Roosevelt's time. In those days people agreed monopolies were bad because they were bad for business, basically—they cut at the possibility of free trade, of competition. But multinational corporations were a similar thing in a new format—they were big enough to make tacit agreements among themselves, and so it was a cartel world. Governments hated multinationals because they were out of government control. People hated them because they made everyone cogs in machines, making money for someone else you never saw. That was the combination needed to take them on. And even then we nearly lost."

"You talk like it was war," Pravi said scornfully. She was one of the sharpest of Nadezhda's students, well-read, quick-minded, skeptical of her teachers' memories and biases.

"It was war," Tom said, looking at her with interest. In the twilight the whites of her eyes looked phosphorescent, she seemed a dangerous young Hindu woman, a Kali. "They bought people, courts, newspapers—they killed people. And we really had to put the arm on the countries who decided that becoming a corporation haven would be a good source of revenue."

"Put the arm on them," Pravi said angrily. "You superpowers in your arrogance, ordering the world around again—what was it but another form of imperialism. Make the world do what you decide is right! A new kind of colonialism."

Tom shrugged, trying to see her better in the dusk. "People said that when the colonial powers lost sovereignty over their colonies, but kept the power by way of economic arrangements. That was called neo-colonialism, and I see the point of it. But look, the mechanisms of control and exploitation in the neo colonialist set-up were precisely the corporations themselves. As home markets were saturated it became necessary to invest abroad to keep profits up, and so the underdeveloped world was subsumed."

"Exactly."

"All right, all right. But then to cut the corporations up, distribute their assets down through their systems to constituent businesses—this amounted to a massive downloading of capital, a redistribution of wealth. It was new, sure, but to call it neo-colonialism is just to confuse things. It was actually the dismantling of neo-colonialism."

"By fiat! By the command of the superpowers, telling the rest of the world what to do, in imperial style! Putting the arm on them, as you put it!"

"Well look, we haven't always had the kind of international accords that now exist to take global action. The power of the United Nations is a fairly recent development in history. So some coercion by powerful countries working together was a political necessity. And at the time I'm speaking of capital was very mobile, it could move from country to country without restraint. If one country decided to become a haven, then the whole system would persist."

"At that point third world countries would have been in power, and the superpowers would have become colonies. You couldn't have had that."

"But the haven countries wouldn't have had the power. They might have skimmed away something in taxes, but in essence they would become functionaries of the corporations they hosted. That's how powerful corporate capitalism was. You just have no idea nowadays."

"We only know that once again you decided our fate for us."

"It took everyone to do it," Tom said. "A consensus of world opinion, governments, the press. A revolution of all the people, using the power of government—laws, police, armies—against the very small executive class that owned and ran the multinationals."

"What do you mean, a revolution?" another student asked.

"We changed the law so much, you see. We cut the corporate world apart. The ones that resisted and skipped to haven countries had their assets seized, and distributed to local parts. We left loose networks of association, but the actual profits of any unit company were kept within it in a collective fashion, nothing sucked away."

"A quiet revolution," Nadezhda said, trying to help out.

"Yes, certainly. All this took years, you understand. It was done in steps so that it didn't look so radical—it took two working generations. But it was radical, because now there's nothing but small businesses scattered everywhere. At least in the legal world. And that's a radical change."

Accusing, triumphant, Pravi pointed a finger at him. "So the United States went socialist!"

"No, not exactly. All we did was set limits on the more extreme forms of greed."

"By nationalizing energy, water, and land! What is that but socialism?"

"Yeah, sure. I mean, you're right. But we used it as a way to give everyone the opportunity to get ahead! Basic resources were made common property, but in the service of a more long-distance self-interest—"

"Altruism for the sake of self-interest!" Pravi said, disgusted. Her aggression, her hatred of America—it irritated Tom, made him sad. Enemies everywhere, still, after all these years, even among the young. What you sow you will reap, he thought. Unto the seventh generation.

"Sociobiologists say it's always that way," he said. "Some doubt the existence of altruism, except as a convoluted form of self-interest."

"Imperialism makes one cynical about human nature," Pravi said. "And you know as well as I that the human sciences are based on philosophical beliefs."

"No doubt." He shrugged. "What do you want me to say? The economic system was a pyramid, and money ran up to the top. We chopped the pyramid off and left only the constituent parts down at the base, and gave the functions that higher parts of the pyramid served over to government, without siphoning off money, except for public works. This was either altruism on the largest scale ever seen in modern times, or else very enlightened self-interest, in that with wealth redistributed in this way, the wars and catastrophes that would have destroyed the pyramid were averted. I suppose it is a statement of one's philosophy to say whether it was one or the other."

Pravi waved him away. "You saw the end coming and you ran. Like the British from India."

"You needn't be angry at us for saving you the necessity of violent revolution," Tom said, almost amused. "It might have been dramatic, but it wouldn't have been fun. I knew revolutionaries, and their lives were warped, they were driven people. It's not something to get romantic about."

Insulted, Pravi walked away, down the deck. The class muttered, and Nadezhda gave them a long list of reading assignments, then called it off for the night.

Later, standing up near the bowsprit, looking at stars reflected on the water, Tom sighed. The air was humid, the tropical night cloaked them like a blanket. "I wonder when we will lose the stigma," he said to Nadezhda softly.

"I don't know. We'll never see it."

"No." He shook his head, upset. "We did the best we could, didn't we?"

"Yes. When they shoulder the responsibility themselves, they'll understand."

"Maybe."

Another night he was called down to the communications room to receive a call from Nylphonia. She looked pleased, and said "I think you have Heartech and the AAMT in violation of Fazio-Matsui. Look here."

The AAMT had put Heartech's black account into a Hong Kong bank, but the funds were "washed but not dried," as Nylphonia put it. Still traceable. Some information had been stolen from the bank, and it corresponded perfectly with electronic money orders that had been recorded in passage through the phone system, going from Heartech to the AAMT. It would not be enough to convict them in court, but it would convince most people that the connection existed—that the accusation had not been concocted out of thin air. So it was sufficient for their purposes.

Tom nodded. "Good. Send a copy of this along to me, will you? And thanks, Nylphonia."

Well, he thought. Very interesting. Next time Kevin and Doris went into the council meeting, they could use this like a bomb. Make the accusation, present the evidence, show that the proposed development on Rattlesnake Hill had illegal funds behind it. End of that.

He thought of the little grove on the top of the hill, and grinned.

The next dawn he slipped out of their berth, dressed, and went on deck. They were tacking close-hauled to a strong east wind, and rode over the swells at an angle, corkscrewing with the pitch and yaw. The bow was getting soaked with spray, so Tom went to the midships rail, on the windward side. He wrapped an arm through the bottom of the mainmast halyards to steady himself. The cables were vibrating. Time after time *Ganesh* ran down the back of one swell and thumped its port bow into the steep side of the next, and white spray flew up from the bow, then was caught by the wind and blown over the bowsprit in a big, glittering fan. The sky was a pale limpid blue, and the sun caught the fans of bow spray in such a way that for a second or two each of them was transformed into a broad, intense rainbow. Giddy slide down a swell, dark blue sea, the jolt as they ran into the next swell, blast of spray out, up, caught in the wind and dashed to droplets, and then a still moment, the ship led by a pouring arch of vibrant color, red orange yellow green blue purple.

Captain Bahaguna was on the other side of the deck, helping a couple of crew members secure metal boxes over the rigging reels. It was tricky crossing the deck in such a swell. "What's up, Captain?"

"Storm coming." He looked disgruntled. "I've been trying to get around to the north of it for two days now, but it's swerving like a drunk."

Tom toed the box. "We'll need these?"

"Never can tell. I do it if we have the time. Ever been in a big storm?"

"That one off Baja."

Bahanguna looked up at Tom, smiled.

Below decks Sonam Singh was showing a group of sailors how to secure bulkheads. "Tom, go check out the bridge, you're in the way." The young sailors laughed as they worked, excited. Immersion in the world's violence, Tom thought, the primal thrill of being out in the wind. In the tempest of the world's great spin through space.

In the comm room Pravi was studying a satellite photo of the mid-Pacific. Pressure isobars overlaid on it contoured the mishmash of cloud patterns, drew attention to a small classic whirlpool shape. "Is it a hurricane?" Tom asked.

"Only a tropical storm," Pravi said. "It might get upgraded, though."

"Where are we?"

She jabbed at the map. Not far away from the storm.

"And which direction is it moving?"

"Depends on when you ask. It's coming our way now."

"Uh oh."

She laughed. "I love these storms."

"How many have you seen?"

"Two so far. But it's going to be three in a couple of hours."

Another thrill seeker. Revolution of the elements.

Tom returned to the deck, holding on to every rail. Things had changed in his brief stay below; the sea was running larger, and the horizon seemed to have extended away, as if they were now on a larger planet. *Ganesh* seemed smaller. It sledded down the long backs of the swells like a toboggan, shouldering deep into the trough and then rising like a cork to crash through the crest and hang in space. Then a free fall, until the bow crashed down onto the water, and they began another exuberant run on the back of the next swell. Except for this moment of skating, it felt like the ship's whole motion was up and down.

The wind still drove spray to the side in fanned white torrents, but the rainbows were gone, the sun too high and obscured by a high white film, which dulled the color of the sea. Off to the south the horizon was a black bar.

A bit dizzy, and fearful of seasickness, Tom found he felt best when he was facing the wind, and looking at the horizon. Seeing was important. He went to the mizzenmast halyards, wrapped his arms around a thick cable, and watched the sea get torn to tatters.

The wind picked up. Spray struck his face like needle pricks. It was loud. The swells had crest-to-trough whitecaps, which hissed and roared. The wind keened in the rigging at a score of pitches, across several octaves, from the bass thrum of the mast stays to the screaming of the bunting. Behind these noises was a kind of background rumble, which seemed to be the sound of the storm itself, disconnected from any source in wind or water: a dull low roar, like an immense submarine locomotive. Perhaps it was the wind in his ears, but it sounded more like the entire atmosphere, trying to leave the vicinity all at once.

Nadezhda appeared at his side, holding an orange rain jacket. "Put this on. Aren't you going below?"

"It made me dizzy!" They were shouting.

"We had one of these on the way over from Tokyo," Nadezhda said, looking at the long hog-backed hills of water surging by. "Lasted three days! You'll have to get used to being below."

"Not yet." He pointed to the black line on the southern horizon. "I'll have to when that arrives."

Nadezhda nodded. "Big squall."

"Pravi said it was almost a hurricane."

"I believe it." She laughed, licked salt off her upper lip. Face flushed and wet, eyes bright and watering. Fingers digging into his upper arm. "So wild, the sea! The place we can never ever tame."

Above them narrow rectangles of sail got even narrower. Most of the ship's sails were furled, and the ones out were down to their last reef. Still the ship was pushing well onto its side. They hung from the halyards as the ship plunged up and down. "Can you imagine having to go aloft!" Tom cried.

"No."

The ship shuddered through a thick crest. White water coursed down the lee rail of the deck. "We'd better get below," Nadezhda said. And indeed Sonam Singh was in the hatchway gesturing fiercely at them. As the ship skated down a swell they dashed for the hatchway, were pulled roughly down it.

"Keep inside," Singh ordered. "Go to the bridge if you want to see, but stay out of the way."

Crew members rushed by, dripping wet and bright with exhilaration. "They're going on deck?" Tom asked.

"Setting the sea anchor," Singh replied, and followed them out.

The passageways seemed narrower. You had to use the wall for support, or be banged against it. Up broad steps to the bridge, which was split into two rooms, one above the other. The top room was the cockpit of action; Captain Bahaguna and the helmsman were standing before the window watching the ship and waves through crazy patterns of water dashed against the glass. The fourth mast stood before them like a white tree. The lee railing, to starboard, was running just above the water, and crests boiled right over it and coursed back to the stern. That gave Tom a shock—the ship, buoyant as it was, still shouldered through the water like a submarine coming to the surface. The sky was a very dark gray now, and the broken white sea glowed strangely under it.

The captain watched the control terminal. It had a red light blinking among the greens. "We'll probably lose that sail," Bahaguna said, then saw Tom. "That block is stuck again. Here, get into the room below and get strapped into a seat. The real squall is about to hit."

The horizon had disappeared, replaced by a gray wall. They got to the room below holding on to rails with both hands, sat in empty chairs and fastened the seat belts.

They were headed straight into the waves. The bowsprit spiked an onrushing white hill of boiling water, lifted up a big mess of it that rushed down the deck, sluicing off both sides, until a wave some four feet high smashed into their window and erased the view. The light had a greenish cast in these blinded intervals. The ship moved sluggishly under the weight. Then the wave fell to the sides, and they could see gray clouds flying by just over the mast. Irregular thickets of water flew by, rain or spray, it was impossible to tell.

"The sea anchor's out," Nadezhda said. "That's what got us head on."

Soon Sonam Singh and part of the sea anchor detail came through, utterly drenched, moving as if in an acrobat's game. "We did it. Glad the storm lines are rigged on deck, I'll tell you."

So they were moving backwards in the storm, pulling a sea anchor. It was a tube of thick fabric, shaped like a wind sock, with its larger end connected to a cable that ran back to the ship's bow. As waves thrust the ship sternwards the sea anchor dragged before them, insuring that the bow faced into every wave, which was the only safe angle in seas like this. It was an ancient method, and still the most reliable.

The squall struck. The roar redoubled, the glass blurred completely. Nothing but patterns of gray on white. The sailors left the bridge like dancers on trampolines.

Bursts of wind stripped the water from the glass like a squeegee, and Tom saw a world transformed, no longer a place of air over water, atmosphere over ocean. Now the two were mixed in a bubbling white mass, and whole swells of foamy salt water were torn off the ocean surface and dashed through the air. The wind was trying to tear the surface of the ocean flat.

The bare masts themselves functioned as sails in a wind like this. All the rigging that extended forward was tauter than bowstrings, straight as theoretical lines of geometry; they gave off a thrumming that could be heard inside the bridge. On the other hand many of the lines supporting spars from the stern were slack, whipped back and forth so rapidly that they blurred in the middle. The masts and yards flexed in bows that were visible to the eye.

Another wave buried the window and it was back to the aquarium view, the murky green-black light.

Up and down the ship rode. They felt more than saw the bow shouldering through hills of water. The noise was unbelievable, like several jets taking off at once. Up and down, up and down, up and down. Tom got used to the motion, he was no longer dizzy, even in the weightless sweeps downward. Time passed. He fell into a bit of a trance, induced by the weird submarine light, interspersed with sudden glimpses of night-in-day chaos, seen with a strange clarity broken by lightning lines of water streaming over the glass. He was not getting used to the storm so much as being overwhelmed by it—making a psychic retreat from the infinity of watery assaults. The mind had to retreat from such mindless intensity.

A long time passed that way, with only occasional snatches of a view, always the same: flying mix of wind and water, under a black sky. Tom's hands and wrists were tired, weary from holding his chair arms. He needed to pee. Could he make it to the head?

Suddenly the noise dropped, the light grew. The motion of the ship eased, and when the window next cleared he saw white clouds scudding overhead. "The eye," Sonam Singh said, passing through on his way to the captain.

"I'm going to go to our berth and lie down," Nadezhda said. "I'm exhausted."

"Be careful getting there."

"I'll be wrapped to the rail."

"I'll come down later and see how you are."

"Fine." Off she went, balancing skillfully.

Up on the bridge they were discussing damage to the rigging. Tom stood carefully, staggered to the head. Peed with his shoulders banging wall to wall. The water in the bowl surged up and down. He felt battered, as if the little balancing mechanisms in his ears were still rattling about. Better to be seated, to have something to look at.

He got back to his seat and clipped in gratefully. Captain Bahaguna was giving rapid orders. "When it hits again it'll be from the southeast. We'll come about now." Crew members ran through. Pravi stopped to see how he was, said, "Don't you think the water surface is higher, like we're on a kind of hill? A kind of big, low waterspout under the low pressure, don't you think?"

Tom saw nothing of the sort. Green swells covered with white foam, white clouds stuffed with green rain. Off to the south was a black island: "Is that land!" Tom cried, frightened.

"Other side of the storm," she said. "We've got about twenty minutes."

The captain shouted at Singh about the sail that wouldn't furl. "It'll break the yard off and probably the pole too!"

"Nothing we can do about it, sir."

Then the explosive roar of the wind hit again. The ship heeled far to starboard; Tom thought they were going to turn turtle. It seemed a bomb was going off continuously. The window cleared and he saw the waves grown huge again, iron flecked with ivory, tops torn off, but still thirty, forty, perhaps fifty feet tall! When they were in a trough the next crest dwarfed the ship, it struggled up the side of the wave like a toy boat. "My God," Tom said, appalled. A wave engulfed them, and the glass showed only rushing darkness. The roar was muffled. They were underwater.

The ship shouldered up, broke to the surface and the howling wind.

Before them another wave as big as the one before, or bigger. Extending off to left and right as far as he could see. He was holding his breath, willing the ship to rise faster. The bowsprit seemed bent at a higher angle than before. The wave, a liquid hillside, a ridge collapsing on them, was dotted with a flurry of black dots.

"What are those!" he shouted, but no one heard him. Then they were flying up like the bob on a fishing line yanked from the water, up the wave hillside to the avalanching crest, inundated as if the wave were a broken dam, and Tom felt it through the chair: *whump.*

The ship was struggling in a different way. Sluggishly. The bow slewed off to port. Shouts came from above. Long minutes passed. Sonam Singh staggered by on hands and knees. "We hit something!" he cried at Tom.

"I saw it!" Tom said. "Wreckage—lumber, maybe."

He couldn't tell if Singh had heard, he was shouting something about the sea anchor.

Then the room rolled onto its side. Tom found himself hanging by his seat belt. Only his hipbones saved him from being cut in half. Muffled roar, underwater again. In the gloom people shouted. Singh was over on one wall. The ship shuddered violently, turned, righted itself. Some noise and light returned. Tom glanced through the window as he freed himself from the seat. Another white mountain smoking toward them, in the mind-numbing howl. Mainmast and second mast were both bent, held in a tangle of alloy and rope rigging. The deck around the foremast was twisted, perhaps buckled. The ship listed to port.

He got the seat belt undone and hung from the chair back. Time passed.

People behind him were shouting, but he couldn't turn his head to see. Then Sonam Singh grabbed him. Captain Bahaguna was crawling down the ladder from the bridge, followed by Pravi and the helmsman.

They had a shouted conference: "—lifeboats!" Singh said into the captain's ear. Then mouth collided with ear, hard, and they both cried out, held their heads.

"No lifeboat could survive in this!" Tom shouted loudly, suddenly afraid.

Singh shook his head. "They're submarine, remember? We go under. Then wait."

"The ship won't sink," Bahaguna said. He didn't like the idea.

"No, but we don't know what compartments might flood. The bows are breached, and the other masts might go. More dangerous here than in the boats. While the launch bay is still clear perhaps we should be getting out. We can come back when the storm has passed."

Inundated again. The ship listed far to port. Slowly water washed away from the glass. White foam, a moving hill of water. Under again. There were red lights all over the panel. The glass cleared and was instantly covered with water again.

A few more swells, sluggish response of the ship. Getting worse. A few more.

Finally the captain nodded, looking grim. "Okay. Abandon ship."

They all crawled to the passageway leading aft. Suddenly they were in the muffled dark again, crawling on the wall. Sonam Singh was cursing. "Damned lumber ships, they lose their deck loads—" He saw a group of tumbling bodies ahead, raised his voice to a bellow: "Slow down up there! Slow down! Everyone to launch bays!" But the bodies rushed on. The lifeboats were near the stern, Tom had remembered all about them. They would be fired out like ejection seats in an old jet fighter. He and Nadezhda had been given a tour—oh my God, he thought. Nadezhda!

Their cabin was just below and behind the second mast.

He turned down the steps to the tweendecks, ran forward on the meeting of wall and floor. He had been a sprinter most of his life, and now it all came back to him. A real scramble. He had done something to his left wrist, the hand wouldn't move well and the wrist hurt with a stabbing pain that went up his arm. He came to the passageway that led to their cabin. Several inches of water slopped over deck or wall, whichever was down. Thrown down, and on that hand again. He yanked open their door. The cabin was empty. Good. Water sloshed at knee height. The ship was permanently on its port side, but he needed to get starboard and aft, where the launch bays were. Storm muffled, ship underwater, he could hear his breath surging in and out of him in big gasps. Nadezhda must already be back there. This intersection of passageways didn't look familiar. Shit, he thought. Not a time to get lost! He held a railing, tried to recover his breath. Up steps, water sloshing, the compartment had been breached, or not sealed off from breached compartments further forward. Around a corner, down another passageway, up steps. Water followed him. Shocking to have water inside the ship. He cracked his forehead, a nice hard spot that, no harm done. Needed to get starboard, water at thigh level and his left hand didn't work. He was tired, arms and legs like blocks of wood, they didn't want to move. Okay, a long passageway fore and aft, hustle down it aft, almost there. Sonam Singh would be mad at him, but he had had to check.

The passageway turned and ended in a closed hatchway. Good enough, beyond that would be an unbreached compartment. But he had to get it open and get through. Warmish salt water foamed up around his waist as he worked the dogs of the hatch one-handed, left arm thrust under a railing to hold him. So many locks on these bulkhead doors! He was in danger of getting knocked over, drowned while inside the ship. Had to go under foam to get to the bottom dogs, and they were stiff as hell. Okay, last one. Flash of triumph as he put his weight on the handle and pushed out. The door was snatched from his good hand and the water behind him shoved him over the coping and right out the door—onto the open deck of the ship. Wrong hatch! He dug with his feet, trying to get a purchase and get back inside. Then water surged up around him and he was off and away, swept away helplessly. His leg hit something and he grasped for it. Caught it, had his grip torn away. Then he was tumbling underwater, thrashed in a soup as if body surfing. Instinctively he clawed upward, broke the surface with lungs bursting, took in a big gasp of air and foam, choked and was rolled under again.

Free of the ship, he thought. Probably so. Fear took all the air out of his lungs. Desperately he swam, up and up and up. He got to the surface and trod the boiling surface furiously. Yes, free of the ship. Couldn't see it anywhere. Overboard in a hurricane, "No!" he cried out, the word wrenched from him. Then under again and reeling, lungs burning as he held on. Drowned for sure, just a matter of time. He clawed madly to the surface, too frightened to let go. Another breath, another. He looked around for the ship, saw nothing. Too tired to move, and at the bottom of a trough with a wave forty feet high over his head. Hell.

Under again and somersaulting. Punched in the stomach. No way to tell up from down. This had happened to him body surfing as a kid, he had almost drowned three or four times. Swim to shore. He forced his eyes open. Green white black. He had to breathe, he couldn't breathe, he had to breathe and it was water he breathed; feeling it he choked in panic and thrashed upward and held his breath again, and then breathed in and out and in and out and in and out; and all of it water. Helpless to stop himself. He felt the water heavy inside him, lungs and stomach both, and marveled that he was still conscious, still thinking. You really do get a last moment, he thought. What do you know.

And indeed he felt an enormous liquid clarity growing in him, like a flash of something or other. It was quiet and blue black white, a riot of bubbles flying in every direction around him, glowing. Blue capture plate, white quarks. Done for. Relax. Concentrate. He cast his mind deliberately back to his wife, her face, his baby held easily in his hands, and then the images tumbled, a forested cliff over ocean, a window filled with blue sky and clouds, swirling like bubbles of nothing in the rich blue field of the life he had lived, every day of it his and Pamela's, and the crying out of his cells for oxygen felt like the pain of all that love given and lost, nothing of it saved, nothing but the implosion of drowning, the euphoria of release—and all the blue world and its blue beauty tumbled around him, flashed white and he snapped alert, wanting to speak, pregnant with a thought that would never be born.

... 11

O*ut.*
How I hugged that lawyer. He just looked tired. Lucky, he said. Procedural irregularity.

He drove me to a restaurant. Looking out the car window, stunned. Everything looked different. Fragile. Even America is fragile. I didn't know that before.

At the restaurant we drank coffee.

What will you do? the lawyer said.

I didn't have the faintest idea. I don't know, I said. Go to New York and meet my wife's ship when it comes in. Get cross country to my kid, find some kind of work. Survive.

There was a newspaper on the next table but I couldn't look at it. Crisis to crisis, we're too close to the edge, you can feel the slippage in the heat of the air.

And suddenly I was telling him about it, the heat, the barbed wire, the nights in the dorm, the presence of the hospital, the fear, the courage of all those inside. It's not fair, I said, my voice straining. They shouldn't be able to do that to them! I seized the newspaper, shook it. They shouldn't be able to do any of this!

I know, the lawyer said, sipping his coffee and looking at me. But people are afraid. They're afraid of what's happening, and they're afraid of the changes we would have to make to stop it from happening.

But we've got to change! I cried.

The lawyer nodded. Do you want to help?

What do you mean?

Do you want to help change things?

Of course I do! Of course, but how? I mean I tried, when I lived in California I tried as hard as I could. . . .

Look, Mr. Barnard, he said. Tom. It takes more than an individual effort. And more than the old institutions. We've started an organization here in Wash-

ington, DC, so far it's sort of a multi-issue lobbying group, but essentially we're trying to start a new political party, something like the Green parties in Europe.

He described what they were doing, what their program was. Change the law of the land, the economic laws, the environmental laws, the relationship between local and global, the laws of property.

Now there're laws forbidding that kind of change, I said. That's what they were trying to get me on.

We know. There are people afraid of us, you see. It's a sign we're succeeding. But there's a long way to go. It's going to be a battle. And we can use all the help we can get. We know what you were doing in California. You could help us. You shouldn't just go out there and survive, that would be a waste. You should stay here and help.

I stared at him.

Think about it, he said.

So I thought about it. And later I met with some of his colleagues, and talked about this new party, and met more people, and talked some more. And I saw that there is work here that I can do.

I'm going to stay. There's a job and I'll take it. Work for Pam, too. Talked to her on the ship-to-shore, and she sounded pleased. A job, after all, and her kind of work. My kind of work.

It didn't take all that much to convince me, really. Because I have to do something. Not just write a utopia, but fight for it in the real world—I have to, I'm compelled to, and talking with one of the people here late one night I suddenly understood why: because I grew up in utopia, I did. California when I was a child was a child's paradise, I was healthy, well fed, well clothed, well housed, I went to school and there were libraries with all the world in them and after school I played in orange groves and in Little League and in the band and down at the beach and every day was an adventure, and when I came home my mother and father created a home as solid as rock, the world seemed solid! And it comes to this, do you understand me—I grew up in utopia.

But I didn't. Not really. Because while I was growing up in my sunny seaside home much of the world was in misery, hungry, sick, living in cardboard shacks, killed by soldiers or their own police. I had been on an island. In a pocket utopia. It was the childhood of someone born into the aristocracy, and understanding that I understood the memory of my childhood differently; but still I know what it was like, I lived it and I know! And everyone should get to know that, not in the particulars, of course, but in the general outline, in the blessing of a happy childhood, in the lifelong sense of security and health.

So I am going to work for that. And if—if! if someday the whole world reaches utopia, then that dream California will become a precursor, a sign of things to come, and my childhood is redeemed. I may never know which it will be, it might not be clear until after we're dead, but the future will judge us! They will look back and judge us, as aristocrats' refuge or emerging utopia, and I want utopia, I want that redemption and so I'm going to stay here and fight for it, because I was there and I lived it and I know. It was a perfect childhood.

Kevin was working at Oscar's place when he heard the news. He was up on the roof finishing the seal and trim around the bedroom skylights, and Pedro, Ramona's father, came zooming up on his hill bike, skidding to a stop on the sidewalk. "Kevin?" he called.

"Yeah, Pedro! What's up?"

Serious look, hands on hips. "Get down here, I've got bad news."

Kevin hustled down the ladder, heart thumping, thinking something's happened to her, she's hurt and wants me there.

"It's Tom," Pedro said as he reached the ground. Kevin's heart leaped in a different direction. Just the look on Pedro's face told him. Deep furrow between his eyebrows. He grasped Kevin's upper arm. "Their ship was wrecked in a storm, and Tom—he was washed overboard."

"He what?"

It took some explaining, and Pedro didn't have all the particulars. Gradually it dawned on Kevin that they didn't matter. Killed by a storm. Lost at sea. Details didn't matter.

He sat on a workhorse. Oscar's front yard was cluttered with their stuff, dusty in the sun. He couldn't believe it.

"I thought ships didn't sink these days." Proud *Ganesh* flying away from Newport's jetties.

"It didn't really sink, but a lot of compartments flooded, and they judged it safer to get out into the lifeboats in case it did sink. It's still out there wrecked, dead in the water. I guess it was a typhoon, and they got hit by a load of lumber, tore the ship all up."

Pedro was holding his arm again. Looking up Kevin saw on his face the strain of telling him, the bunched jaw muscles. He looked as much like Ramona as a short gray-haired sixty-year-old man could, and suddenly a spasm of grief arrowed through Kevin's numbness. "Thanks for telling me." Pedro just shook his head. Kevin swallowed. From his Adam's apple down he was numb. He still had a putty knife in his hand. It was Pedro's kindness he felt most, it was that that would make him weep. He stared at the dirt, feeling the hand on his arm.

Pedro left.

He stood in Oscar's yard, looking around. Working alone this afternoon.

Was that better or worse? He couldn't decide. He was a lot more solitary than he used to be. He climbed back onto the roof, returned to work on the trim around the skylights. Putty. He sat on the roof, stared at it. When he was a kid he and Tom had hiked in the hills together, sun just up and birds in the trees. Bushwhacking while Tom claimed to be on an animal trail. They'd get lost and Kevin would say, "Animal trail, right Grandpa?" Seven years old and Tom laughing like crazy. Once Kevin tripped and skinned both knees bad and he was about to scream when Tom grabbed him up and exclaimed like it was a great deed, an extraordinary opportunity, and pulled up his own pantlegs to reveal the scars on his knees, then had taken out his Swiss army knife and nicked a scar on each knee, touched their four wounds together and then actually sucked blood from Kevin's shins, which had shocked Kevin, and spit it in four directions rattling out the nonsense words of an ancient Indian blood oath, until Kevin was strutting around glowing with pride at his stinging knees, badge of the highest distinction, mark of manhood and oneness with the hills.

That evening and the next day, the whole unwanted raft of condolences. He preferred swimming alone. Laps at the pool, thousands of yards.

He made calls to Jill and his parents. Jill gone as usual. He left a message, feeling bad. He got his mother on screen: weird moment of power and helplessness combined as he gave her the news. Suddenly he appreciated what Pedro had done, to come over and tell him like that. A hard thing to do. The little face on the screen, so familiar—shocked by the news, twisted with grief. After an awkward brief conversation they promised each other they would talk again soon.

Later that day he watched Doris cook a dinner for the house, when it was his turn. "You know we don't have any way to find those friends of his," she said. "I hope they'll get in touch with us."

"Yeah."

She frowned.

He was angry at the crew of *Ganesh*, angry at Nadezhda. Then she reached him on the phone and he saw her, arm in a sling, grim, distracted. He recalled what Tom had told him of her life, a tough one it sounded. She told him what she knew of the wreck. Four other crew members missing, apparently they had been trapped in a forward compartment and had tried to make their way back over the deck. Tom had disappeared in the chaos of the foundering, no one sure what had happened to him. Disappeared. Everyone had thought he was in one of the other lifeboats. She went on until Kevin stopped her. He asked her to come back to El Modena, he wanted her to return, wanted to see her. She said that she would, but she looked tired, hurt, empty. When the call was over he couldn't be sure if she would come or not. And then he really believed in the disaster. Tom was dead.

They finished the work on Oscar's house a couple of weeks later, in the burning heat of late September. They walked around it in their work boots and their greased, creased, and sawdusted work-shorts, brown as nuts, checking out every little point, the seal on the suntek and cloudgel, the paint, the computer (ask it odd questions it said "Sorry I fail the Turing test very quickly"), everything. Standing out in the middle of the street and looking at it, they shook Oscar's hand and laughed: it looked like a clear tent draped over one or two small dwellings, red and blue brick facades covered by new greenery. Oscar did a dance shuffle to the front door, singing "I'm the Sheik, of Ar—a—bee" in a horrible baritone. "And your love, belongs, to meee," pirouetting like the hippopotami in *Fantasia*, mugging Valentino-like swoops at Jody and Gabriela, who squeaked "Don't—stop—don't—stop" in unison, pushing him back and forth between them.

Inside they split up and wandered through the rooms, looking things over. Kevin came across Oscar and Hank standing together in the central atrium. Hank said, "These black pillars are neat. They give it an Egyptian Roman wrapped in plastic look that I like."

Oscar looked around dazed. "Egyptian Roman, wrapped in plastic," he murmured. "I always dreamed of it."

Kevin went back out front to get a beer from his bike basket.

Ramona appeared down on Laurinda, pedaled up to him. He waved and put down the dumpie, feeling strange. They had talked briefly several days before, after the news about Tom came in. Condolences.

"Hi," she said. "How are you?"

"Fine. We're just having a little celebration here."

"All done?"

"Yep."

"Hopefully Oscar will have a housewarming?"

"I think so, yeah. This is just an informal thing, the inside's still a mess."

She nodded. Pursed her lips. The furrow between her eyebrows appeared, reminding Kevin sharply of Pedro. "You okay?" Ramona said.

"Oh yeah, yeah."

"Can . . . can I have a talk with you?"

"Sure."

"Now's not a bad time?"

"No, no. Here, let's walk up the street, if you want."

She nodded gratefully, eyes to the ground. They walked up the bike path, her bike between them. She seemed nervous, awkward, uncomfortable—as she had been, in fact, ever since her birthday. It made Kevin weary. Looking at her, the long stride, the sun bouncing off glossy black hair, he felt an ache of desire for her *company*—just that, nothing more. That he would lose even her friendship. "Listen, Ramona, it's all right."

She shook her head. "It's not all right." Voice muffled. "I hate what's happened, Kevin, I wish it never would have."

"No!" Kevin said, shocked. "Don't say that! It's like saying . . ."

He didn't know how to finish, but she nodded, still looking down. All in a rush she said, "I know, I'm glad too, but I didn't ever want to hurt you and if it means I did and we can't be friends anymore, then I can't help but wish it hadn't happened! I mean, I love you—I love our friendship I mean. I want us to be able to be friends!"

"It's okay, Ramona. We can be friends."

She shook her head, unsatisfied. Kevin rolled his eyes, for the sake of himself alone, for his own internal audience (when had it appeared?). Here he was listening to himself say things again, completely surprised by what he heard coming out of his own mouth.

"Even if—even if . . ." She stopped walking, looked at him straight. "Even if Alfredo and I get married?"

Oh.

So that was it.

Well, Kevin thought, go ahead and say something. Amaze yourself again.

"You're getting married?"

She nodded, looked down. "Yes. We want to. It's been our whole lives together, you know, and we want to . . . do it all. Be a family, and . . ."

Kevin waited, but she appeared to have finished. His turn. "Well," he said. He thought to himself, you make a hell of a crowbar. "That's quite a bit of news," he said. "I mean, congratulations."

"Oh, Kevin—"

"No, no," he said, reaching out toward her, hand stopping; he couldn't bring himself to touch her, not even on the forearm. "I mean it. I want you to be happy, and I know you two are . . . a couple. You know. And I want us to go on being friends. I mean I really do. That's been the worst part of this, almost, I mean you've been acting so un*com*fortable with me—"

"I have been! I've felt terrible!"

He took a deep breath. This was something he had needed to hear, apparently; it lifted some weights in him. Just under the collarbones he felt lighter somehow. "I know, but . . ." He shrugged. Definitely lighter.

"I was afraid you would hate me!" she said, voice sharp with distress.

"No, no." He laughed, sort of: three quick exhalations. "I wouldn't ever do that."

"I know it's selfish of me, but I want to be your friend."

"Alfredo might not like it. He might be jealous."

"No. He knows what it means to me. Besides, he feels terrible himself. He feels like if he had been different before . . ."

"I know. I talked to him, a little."

She nodded. "So he'll understand. In fact I think he'll feel a lot better about it if we aren't . . . unfriendly."

"Yeah. Well . . ." It seemed he could make the two of them feel better than ever. Great. And himself?

Suddenly he realized that what they were saying now wouldn't really matter. That years would pass and they would drift apart, inevitably. No matter what they said. The futility of talk.

"You'll come to the wedding?"

He blinked. "You want me to?"

"Of course! I mean, if you want to."

He took a breath, let it out. A part of his mind under clamps sprang free and he wanted to say Don't, Ramona, please, what about me? Quick image of the long swing *no*. He couldn't afford to think of it. Find it, catch it, clamp it back down, lock it away. Didn't happen. Never. Never never never never never.

She was saying something he hadn't heard. His chest hurt, his diaphragm was tight. Suddenly he couldn't stand the pretense anymore, he looked back down the street, said "Listen, Ramona, I think maybe I should get back. We can talk more later?"

She nodded quickly. Reached out for his forearm and stopped, just as he had with her. Perhaps they would never be able to touch again.

He was walking back down the street. He was standing in front of Oscar's. Numbness. Ah, what a relief. No pleasure like the absence of pain.

Hank was around the side of the house, loading up his bike's trailer. "Hey, where'd you go?"

"Ramona came by. We were talking."

"Oh?"

"She and Alfredo are going to get married."

"Ah ha!" Hank regarded him with his ferocious squint. "Well. You're having quite a week, aren't you." Finally he reached into his trailer. "Here, bro, have another beer."

Alfredo and Matt's proposition got onto the monthly ballot, and one night it appeared on everyone's TV screens, a long and complex thing, all the plans laid out.

People interested typed in their codes and voted. Just under six thousand of the town's ten cared enough to vote, and just over three thousand of them voted in favor of the proposition. Development as described to be built on Rattlesnake Hill.

"Okay," Alfredo said at the next council meeting, "let's get back to this matter of re-zoning Rattlesnake Hill. Mary?"

Ingratiating as ever, Mary read out the planning commission's latest draft, fitted exactly to the proposition.

"Discussion?" Alfredo said when she was done.

Silence. Kevin stirred uncomfortably. Why was this falling to him? There were hundreds of people in town opposed to the plan, thousands. If only the indifferent ones had voted!

But Jean Aureliano was not opposed to the plan. Nor her party. So it was up to the people who really cared. The room was hot, people looked tired. Kevin opened his mouth to speak.

But it was Doris who spoke first, in her hardest voice. "This plan is a selfish one thrust on the community by people more interested in their own profit than in the welfare of the town."

"Are you talking about me?" Alfredo said.

"Of course I'm talking about you," Doris snapped. "Or did you think I had in mind the parties behind you putting up the capital? But they don't live here, and they don't care. It's only profits to them, more profits, more power. But the people who live here do care, or they should. That land has been kept free of construction through all the years of rampant development, to destroy it now would be disgusting. It would be a wanton act of destruction."

"I don't agree," Alfredo said, voice smooth. But he had been stung to speech, and his eyes glittered angrily. "And obviously the majority of the town's voters don't agree."

"We know that," Doris said, voice as sharp as a nail. "But what we have never heard yet from you is a coherent explanation of why this proposed center of yours should be located on the hill instead of somewhere else in the town, or in some other town entirely."

Alfredo went through his reasons again. The prestige, the aesthetic attraction of it, the increased town shares. On each point Doris assailed him bitterly. "You can't make us into Irvine or Laguna, Alfredo, if you want that you should move there."

Alfredo defended himself irritably. The other council members pitched in with their opinions. Doris mentioned Tom, started to tell them what Tom had been working on when he died—dangerous territory, Kevin thought, since they had never heard from Tom's friends. And since much of the material had been taken from Avending by Doris herself. But Alfredo cut her off before she got to any of that. "It was a great loss to all of us when Tom died. You can't bring him into this in a partisan way, he was simply one of the town's most important citizens, and in a way he belonged to all of us. I think it very well might be appropriate to name any center built on Rattlesnake Hill after him."

Kevin laughed out loud.

Doris cut through it, almost shouting: "When Tom Barnard died he was doing his damndest to stop this thing! To suggest naming the center after him when he opposed it is obscene!"

Alfredo said, "He never told me he opposed it."

"He never told you anything," Doris snarled.

Alfredo hit the tabletop, stung at last. "I'm tired of this. You're getting into the area of slander when you imply that there's illegal capital behind this venture—"

"Sue me!" Doris shouted. "You can't afford to sue me, because then your funding would be revealed for sure!" Kevin nudged her with his knee, but as far as he could tell she didn't even feel it. *"Go ahead and sue me!"*

Shocked silence. Clearly Alfredo was at a loss for words.

"Properly speaking," Jerry Geiger said mildly, "this is only a discussion of the zoning change."

"It's the zoning makes the rest of it possible!" Doris said. "If you want to go on record against the development, here's where you act."

Jerry shrugged. "I'm not sure that's true."

Matt Chung decided to follow that tack, and talked about how zoning gave them options. Alfredo and Doris hammered away at each other, both getting really angry. It went on for nearly an hour before Alfredo slammed his hand down and said imperiously, "We've been over this before, five or six times in fact. We have the testimony of the town, we know what people want! Time to vote!"

Doris nodded curtly. Showdown.

They voted by hand, one at a time. Doris and Kevin voted against the proposed zoning change. Alfredo and Matt voted for. Hiroko Washington voted against. Susan Mayer voted for. And Jerry voted for.

"Ah, Jerry," Kevin said under his breath. No rhyme nor reason, same as always. Might as well flip a coin.

So the zoning for Rattlesnake Hill was changed, from 5.4 (open space) to 3.2 (commercial).

Afterwards Kevin and Doris walked home. There it stood, a bubble of light in a dark orange grove, looking like a Chinese lantern. Behind and above it the dark bulk of the hill they had lost. They stopped and looked.

"Thanks for doing the talking tonight," Kevin said. "I really appreciate it."

"Damn it," Doris said. She turned into him, and he hugged her. He leaned his head down and put his face on the part of her straight black hair. Familiar fit, same as it ever was. "Damn it!" she said fiercely, voice muffled by his chest. "I'm sorry. I tried."

"I know. We all tried."

"It's not over yet. We can take it to the courts, or try to get the Nature Conservancy to help us."

"I know."

But they had lost a critical battle, Kevin thought. The critical battles. The *Flyer's* polls showed solid support for Alfredo. People thought he was doing a good job, dynamic, forward-looking. They wanted the town shares higher. Things were changing, the pendulum swinging, the Greens' day had passed. To fight business in America . . . it was asking for trouble, always. Kick the world, break your foot.

They walked into the house, arms around each other.

Kevin couldn't sleep that night. Finally he got up, dressed, left the house. Climbed the trail up the side of Rattlesnake Hill, moving slowly in the dark. Rustle of small animals, the light of the stars. In the little grove on top he sat, arms wrapped around his knees, thinking.

For a while he dozed. Uneasily he dreamed: he was in bed down in the house when a noise outside roused him, and he got up, went down the hall to the balcony window at the north end of the horseshoe. He looked down into the avocado grove, and there by the light of the moon he saw it again—the shape. It stood upright, on two legs, big and black, a node of darkness. It looked up at him, their gazes met and the moonlight flashed in its eyes, vertical slits of green like a big cat's eyes. Through the window he could hear the thing's eerie chuckle-giggle, and the hair on the back of his neck rose, and suddenly he felt as if the world were a vast, dark, windy place, with danger suffusing every part of its texture, every leaf and stone.

He jerked out of it. Too uneasy to wake up fully, he dove back below again, into sleep. Uneasy sleep, more dreams. A crowd on the hill.

When finally he woke to full consciousness, he got up and walked around the hilltop. It was just before dawn.

He found he had a plan. Somewhere in the night . . . he shivered, frightened by what he didn't know. But he had a plan. He thought about it until sunrise, and then, stiff and cold, he walked back down to home and bed.

The next morning he went to talk to Hank about his plan. Hank thought it was a good idea, and so did Oscar. So they went to talk to Doris. She laughed out loud. "Give me a couple of days," she told them. "I can make it by then."

"I'll let people know what's happening," Hank said. "We'll do it Sunday."

So on Sunday morning they held a memorial service for Tom Barnard, up on Rattlesnake Hill. Doris had cast a small plate, ceramic overlaid on a bronzelike alloy, with the overlay making a bas-relief border, and in the corners, animal figures: turtle, coyote, horse, cat. In the middle, a brief message:

> **In Memoriam, Thomas William Barnard**
> **Born, El Modena, California, March 22nd 1984**
> **Lost At Sea In The Pacific, August 23rd 2065**
> **There Will Never Come An End To the Good That He Has Done**

Hank conducted a brief ceremony. He was dressed in his Unitarian minister's shirt, and at first he looked like he was in costume, his face still lined and brick-red with sun, his hair still a tangle. And when he spoke it was in the same Hank voice, nothing inflated or ministerial about it. But he was a minister, in the Unitarian Church (also in the Universal Life Church, and in the World Peace Church, and in the Ba'hais), and as he talked about Tom, and the crowd continued to collect on the crown of the hill—older people who had known Tom all their lives, younger people who had only heard of him or seen him in the canyonlands, members of Hank's congregation, friends, neighbors, passersby, until there were two or three hundred people up there—all of them listened to what Hank had to say. Because there was a conviction in Hank, an intensity of belief in the importance of what they were doing, that could not be denied. Watching him Kevin lost his sense of Hank as daily partner and friend, the rapid voice tumbling words one over the next picked Kevin up and carried him along with the rest of them, into a shared sense of values, into a community. How Hank could gather them, Kevin thought. Such a presence. People dropping by the work sites to ask Hank about this or that, and he laughing and offering his advice, based on some obscure text or his own thoughts, whatever, there was never any pretense to it; only belief. It was as if he were their real leader, somehow, and the town council nothing at all. How did he do it? A matter of faith. Hank was certain they were all of them spiritual beings, in a spiritual community. And as he acted on that belief, those who had anything to do with him became a part of it, helped make it so.

"People die, rivers go on. Mountains go on."

He talked about Tom, told some of Tom's life story, incidents he had observed himself, other people's stories, Tom's stories, all in a rapid patter, a rhythm of conviction, affection, pleasure. "See one thing he does, know the rest. Now some of you know it and some of you don't, but this hilltop was nothing but prickly pear and dirt till Tom came up here. All these trees we stand under were planted by Tom when he was a boy, to give this hilltop some shade, to make it a good place to come up and look around, take a look for the ocean or the mountains or just down into town. And he kept coming up here for the rest of his life. So it's fitting that we make this little grove his memorial. It was a place he liked, looking over a place he loved. We don't have his body to bury, but that's not the important part of him anyway. Doris has cast a plaque and I've cut a flat spot into this big sycamore here, and all of us who care to, can help nail it in. Take a light whack so everyone can get a shot at it, and try not to miss and hit Doris's handiwork. It looks like the ceramic might break off."

"Are you kidding?" Doris said. "This is a new secret bonding, the ceramic and the metal interpenetrate each other."

"Like us and Tom's spirit, then. Okay, swing away."

And so they stood the plate against the largest sycamore in the grove, about head high, and passed out a few hammers from Hank's collection, and they swirled around the tree in a loose informal knot, chatting as they waited their turn to tap one of the four nails into the tree.

Wandering around greeting people Kevin saw Ramona, who gave him a big smile. He smiled back briefly, feeling serious, calm, content.

Ah. There down the slope a ways stood Alfredo, looking dark. Kevin felt a quick surge of bitter triumph. He decided that it wasn't a good time to talk to him. Best not to get into an argument at his grandfather's funeral.

But Alfredo brought the argument to him. Kevin was standing away from the crowd, watching it and enjoying the casual feel of it, the sense of neighborhood party. Tom would have liked that. Then Alfredo came up to him and said angrily, "I should think you'd be ashamed of using your grandfather's death like this."

Kevin just looked at him.

"How do you think it would make Tom feel?"

Kevin considered. "He would love it."

"This doesn't change anything, you know. We can build around it."

Kevin shook his head, looking past Alfredo, up at the grove. "This changes everything. And you know it." All of the people there would now think of the hill as a shrine, inviolate, and as they all had friends and family down below . . . Little ghost of his hatred: "Don't fuck with this hill any more, Alfredo. There's no one will like you if you do."

Then he saw who was standing before the memorial tree, about to take a swing with a hammer. He pointed. Alfredo turned around just in time to see Ramona smack a nail, then pass the hammer along.

That would make the difference. Alfredo would never dare cross Ramona on an issue this charged, not given everything else that had happened, the way it had all tangled together.

"Build it somewhere else," Kevin said harshly. "Build it down in town, by Santiago Creek or somewhere else nice. Tell your partners you gave it a try up here, and it didn't work. Whatever. But leave this hill alone."

Alfredo turned and walked away.

Later Kevin went to the tree to put the final knocks on all four nails: one for Nadezhda, one for his parents, one for Jill, one for himself. He touched the broken bark of the tree. Warm in the sunlight. This living tree. He couldn't think of a better memorial.

After the ceremony, Hank's idea of a wake: a party in Irvine Park, lasting all that afternoon. A lot of beer and hamburgers and loud music, flying frisbees, ecstatic dogs, barbeque smoke, endless innings of sloppy softball, volleyball without lines or scoring.

In the long summer twilight people drifted away, coasting down Chapman, their bike lights like a string of fireflies flickering between the trees. Kevin biked home alone, feeling the cool sage air rush over him. A good life, he thought. The old man had a good life. We can't ask for anything more.

So it came about that one morning Kevin Claiborne woke, under an orange tree in his house. Big day today: Ramona and Alfredo were getting married in the morning, and in the afternoon they were having the reception down in the park, next to the softball diamonds. Half the town would be there.

A late October day, dawning clear and cool. Hot in the afternoon. The best time of the year.

Kevin went down to their street project to work by himself for a while, leveling the new dirt. Filling in holes, thinking about the day and the summer. Thought like a long fast guitar solo, spinning away inside him. It was hard to focus on anything for more than a second or two.

Back home he dressed for the wedding, putting on his best shirt and the only dressy slacks he owned. Admittedly still casual, but not bad looking. Colorful, anyway: light green button-down shirt of the young exec style, and gray slacks, with creases and everything. No one could say he had underdressed for Ramona's wedding. Hopefully he wasn't overdressed.

He had given the matter of a wedding gift some thought. It was tough, because he wanted it to be nice without in any way suggesting that he was trying to intrude on their daily life, to remind them of him. Kitchen implements were therefore out, as well as a lot of other things. Nothing for the bedroom, thanks. He considered giving them something perishable, but that didn't seem right either. Might look like a comment in its own way, and besides, he did kind of want them to have something around, something Ramona might see from time to time.

Ornamental, then. He decided on a flowerpot made from scraps of the oakwork in Oscar's study. Octagonal, a neat bit of woodwork, but rough in a way that suggested outdoors. A porch pot. Bit sticky with the last coat of varnish, and he needed to get a plant for it. But it would do.

He biked to Santiago Creek Park with a trailer to carry everything. Okay, he told himself. No moping. No skeleton at the feast, for God's sake. Just put a good face on it. Otherwise better to not go at all.

He did fine. He found himself numb, and was thankful for that. He sat with the Lobos and they joked about the possibilities of playing with a pregnant shortstop and so on, and he never felt a twinge. The Sanchezes swept in beaming and the Blairs too, and Ramona walked down the path to the sound of Jody's guitar, by the stream in a long white Mexican wedding dress looking just like herself, only now it was obvious how beautiful she was. Kevin merely breathed deeply, felt his strength. He was numb. He understood now how actors could take on a role, play a part, as in *Macbeth*. They did it by erasing themselves, which allowed them to become what they played. He was learning that ability, he could do it.

Hank stood in the gazebo by the stream, in his minister's shirt again. His voice lifted and again he took them away, just as always. Kevin recalled him dusty in the yard, saying, "Ain't nothing written in stone, bro." Now he led Ramona and Alfredo through their marriage vows, "for as long as you both shall live." It's not stone, Kevin thought, we write these things in something both more fragile and more durable. Hank made him see it. You could believe in both because both were true. These were vows, sure enough. But vows were only vows. Intentions— and no matter how serious, public, heartfelt, they were still only vows. Promises. The future still loomed before them, able to take them anywhere at all. That was their great and terrible freedom. The weird emptiness of the future! How we long to fill it in, now, in the present; and how completely we are denied.

The wedding partners exchanged rings. Hers went on easily, her fingers were so slim. Blank out, Kevin, blank out. You don't know anything about her fingers. His they had trouble with; finally Hank muttered, "Let it stay there above the knuckle, the beer's getting warm." They kissed. At Hank's instigation the crowd applauded loudly, cheered. Kevin clapped hard, teeth clamped together. Hit his hands against each other as hard as he could, sure.

Picnic party in the park. Kevin set about getting unobtrusively drunk. The Lobos had a game to play but he didn't care. Danger to his long-forgotten hitting streak! He only laughed and refilled a paper cup with champagne. It didn't matter, it meant nothing. The laws of chance had bent in his corner of the world, but soon enough they would snap back, and neither the bend nor the snap would be his doing. He didn't care. He drank down his glass, refilled. Around him people were chattering, they made a sound like the sea.

He saw the wedding couple in an informal reception line, laughing together shoulder to shoulder. Handsome couple, no doubt about it. Both perfect. Not like him. He was a partner for someone like, say, Doris. Sure. He felt a surge of affection for Doris, for her bitter fight against Alfredo in the council meeting, for her pleasure in the plan for Tom's memorial. They had almost become partners, she had wanted it. How had they ever drifted apart? It had been his fault. Stupid man. He had learned enough to understand what her love had meant, he thought. Learned enough to deserve it, a little. Stupid slow learner, he was! Still, if something as flawed as the wedding couple could be made right . . . He refilled, went looking for Doris.

He spotted her in a group of Lobos, and watched her: small, round, neat, the sharp intelligence in that big laugh, the sense of fun. Wild woman. Down to earth. Could talk about anything to her. He walked over, feeling warmth fill him. Give her a hug and she would hug back, she would know what it meant and why he needed it.

And sure enough she did.

Then she was talking with Oscar, they were laughing hard at something. Oscar hopped up and began doing a ballerina routine on a bench. He wavered, she took a chop at the back of his knee. "Hey there." He hopped down, staggered gracefully her way, she leaned into him and pretended to bite his chest. They were laughing hard.

Kevin looked into his cup, retreated back to the drinks table. He looked back at Doris and Oscar. Hey, he thought. When did that happen? All the desire he had ever felt for Doris in the years they had been friends surged into a single feeling. She's mine, he thought sharply. It's me she liked, for years and years. What did Oscar think he was doing? Doris loved him, he had felt it that night in Bishop, or after the council fight, almost as strong as ever. If he started over, asserted himself, told Doris he was ready now, just like Alfredo had told Ramona—

. . . Oh. Well, it was true. Situations repeat themselves endlessly; there aren't that many of them, and there are a lot of lovers in this world. Perhaps everyone has been at every point of the triangle, sure.

Kevin walked behind a tree. He couldn't see his friends, could only hear their two voices, ragging each other vigorously, to the delight of the teammates nearby. When had they gotten to be such friends? He hadn't noticed. Last he knew they were sniping for real, and Doris seemed serious in her dislike. And Oscar was so fat!

He felt bad at that. Oscar was a good friend, one of his best. Oscar was great. He learned things from Oscar, he laughed and he made Oscar laugh. There was no one like Oscar. And if something was starting between him and Doris—

Again the intense burning flush. Jealousy, possessiveness. "Hey," he said to the tree. Feeling betrayed. "God damn." How many people, how many things could go wrong? He had thought his cup full, there.

He shook himself like a dog just out of the surf. Remembered how he had felt about Alfredo. He laughed shortly at himself. Raised his cup to the couple behind the tree. Drained it. Went to get more, feeling virtuous and morose.

It was a relief when the game started. Make-up for a postponed game, it was supposed to count but no one cared. Kevin pounced on the grounders that came his way, threw people out with a fierce pleasure in the act, in the efficiency and power of it. Mongoose jumping on cobras. *Third baseman Kevin Claiborne.* The phrase, spoken in a game announcer's voice, had resounded in his mind millions of times when he was a kid. Maybe billions. Why the appeal of those words? What makes us become what we become? Third base like a mongoose, this announcer had always said. Third base like a razor's edge. And here he was doing it. That broke her heart.

They were playing Hank's team, the poor Tigers, who rose above their heads to give them a challenge. Ramona, looking much more like herself in her gym shorts and T-shirt, played a sparkling shortstop, so that between them it was a defensive show. "We've got this side shut down entirely," she told him after another hot play. Low scoring game.

He hit as always. Walk to the plate and turn off the brain. Easy today. Swing away. Line drive singles, no problem. Not a thought.

Bottom of the last inning they were down a run, confident of a come-from-behind victory. But suddenly they were down to their last out, the tying run on first. Ramona was up, and Kevin walked out to the on-deck circle swinging a bat, and out of the blue he thought, if Ramona gets out then the game is over, and I'll have batted a thousand for a whole season.

He took a step back, shocked at himself. Where had that come from? It was a bad thought. Bad luck and maybe worse. It wasn't like him, and that frightened him. What makes us . . . ?

Ramona hit a single. Everyone yelling. Two on, two out, one run down.

Game on the line. If only that thought hadn't come into his head! He didn't mean it! It wasn't like him, he never thought like that. It wasn't his thought.

Into the batter's box, and the world slipped away. Make sure you touch the right home plate, he thought crazily. Tim, the Tigers' pitcher, nodded once at him, disdaining to walk the man who was batting a thousand. Kevin grinned, nodded back at him. Good for Tim, he thought—and that was his thinking, back in control. Good. Everything forgotten, the luck, the curse, the world. Tim's arm swung back and then under, releasing the ball. Up it lofted, into the blue sky, big and round, spinning slowly. All Kevin's faculties snapped together in that epiphany of the athlete, in the batter's pure moment of being, of grace. An eternal now later and the ball was dropping, he stepped forward with his lead foot, rocked over his hips, snapped his wrists hard. He barely felt the contact of bat and ball, right on the button and already it was shooting like a white missile over Damaso and out into right center. Clobbered it!

He ran toward first slowly, watching the ball. Hank, out in center field, had turned and was racing back; he put his head down and ran, thick short legs pumping like pistons. Forty-six years old and still running like that! And in his minister's shirt no less. He glanced over his shoulder, adjusted direction, ran an impossible notch faster, watched the ball all the way. It was over his head, falling fast to his backhand side—he sprinted harder yet, leaped up, snagged the ball at full extension, high in the air—fell, hit the ground and rolled. He stood up, glove high. And there in an ice-cream-cone bulge was the ball. Catch.

Kevin slowed down, approaching second. Confused. He had to laugh: he had forgotten how to leave the field after making an out. He stood there, feeling self-conscious. Game over, so there was no need to rush.

Hank had taken the ball from his glove. Now he was inspecting it with a curious pained expression on his face, as if he had, with a truly remarkable shot, killed a rabbit. After a while he jerked, shrugged, ran back in. He jogged up to Kevin and gave him the ball. "Sorry about that, Kev," he said rapidly, "but you know I figured you'd want me to give it a try."

"That was one hell of a try," Kevin said, and the crowd around them laughed.

"Well, what the hell—I guess batting nine-ninety-four for the year ain't such a bad average, anyhow."

Then everyone was cheering and clapping him on the shoulder. The Tigers mobbed Hank, and for a moment as they left the field Kevin was mobbed too, lifted up by the legs and carried on the shoulders of his teammates, so that he could look across at Hank, being carried the same way. Then he was back on the ground, in the dugout. Taking off his cleats.

Slowly the shoes slipped off.

Doris plopped beside him. "Don't feel bad, Kevin, it was a good hit. Hank made a super catch."

"It's not that," Kevin said, rubbing his forehead distractedly.

"Ah." She put an arm around his shoulder. "I understand."

She didn't, actually. But when people said that, it wasn't exactly what they meant. Kevin knew what she meant. He blew out a breath, feeling her arm over his back, and nodded at the dirty red concrete.

The reception rolled on through the afternoon, and the band set up and the dancing began. But after a few more drinks Kevin slipped away to his bike, uncoupled his trailer and rode off.

He was feeling low. Mostly because of Tom. He needed to talk to Tom, needed that grinning ancient face staring into his and telling him he was taking it all too seriously. Nine-ninety-four is actually *better* than a thousand, Tom would say. Could it really be true he would never talk to Tom Barnard again? The loss of that. Too much to imagine.

Biking down Redhill he gnawed at the thought, helpless before it. It was the worst of all the recent events, worst because it was irrevocable. Ain't nothing written in stone, bro—but death is written in stone, written in ceramic and bronze to outlive the generations of bodies, minds, spirits, souls—all gone, and gone for good. Lives like leaves. And he needed to talk to him, needed his advice and his jokes and his stories and his weirdness.

"Grandpa," he said, and shifted his hands down the handlebars to race position, and coasted for a second so he could yank up viciously on his toe clip straps, crushing his feet to the pedals. And he started to ride hard.

Wind blasted him, and the tops of his thighs groaned. They pulsed through the lactic build-up, a hot pain that slowly shifted to a fierce, machinelike pumping. His butt and the palms of his hands and the back of his neck bothered him as he settled through the other transient pains of hard biking. He breathed harder and harder, until his diaphragm and the muscles between his ribs were working almost as hard as his thighs, just to get the oxygen into him and the CO_2 out of him, faster and faster. Sweat dried on his forearms, leaving a whitish coating under the hairs. And all the while a black depression settled in his stomach, riding up and down rhythmically with every heave of his lungs, filling him from inside until he hurt, really hurt. Strange that emotion alone could make this kind of pain. That broke her heart. He was going to bike it out of him, the machine was nothing more than a rolling rack to expunge this pain, and the world that made it. He was south now, firing down Highway Five at full speed, dodging other traffic and taking the smooth curves of the downhill in tight, perfect lines. Toes pointed down to shift the calf muscles being used. Push down/pull up, push down/pull up, over and over and over and over and over, until the bike's frame squeaked under the stress. Fly south, flee that whole life, that whole world!

But in Dana Point he turned north, onto the Coast Highway. He wanted to ride within sight of the sea, and this was the best way. A moment of sharp mortal fear as he glanced down into the small boat harbor at Dana Point; something in the shape of it scared him. He fought it away, pushed harder up and down the roller coaster ride of the road, enjoying the pain. Eyes burning from sweat, thighs going wooden on him, his lungs heaved just as if he were sobbing, violently but rhythmically. Maybe this was the only way he could let himself sob so hard, and all without a tear, except those blown out by the harsh rush of salt wind scouring his face. Another moment of sharp fear as he passed the industrial complex at Muddy Canyon, like a vacuum in his heart, tugging everything inward. Harder, go harder, leave all that behind. Go harder, see what breaks first. Image of Ramona walking up the streamside path. That broke her heart.

On a whim he turned into Newport, onto Balboa Peninsula. It was a long sprint to the dead end at the Wedge, and he flew, final effort, killing himself on a bike. He came to the end of the road, slewed with braking, freed a cramping foot, put it down. The harbor channel, between its two stone jetties. Green scraps flying at the top of tall palm trees.

He freed the other foot, walked the bike to the concrete wall at the jetty's foot. His thighs felt ten feet around, he could barely walk. He was still gasping for air, and with the bike wind gone sweat poured out of him, ran down his burning face. All his muscles pulsed, bump bump bump with every hard knock of his heart. The whole world shifted and jumped with every heartbeat, bump bump bump, and things in the late afternoon sun had a luminous grainy quality, as if bursting with the internal pressure of their own colors. Ah yes: the end of a workout. Faint wash of nausea, fought, mastered, passed through, to something like sexual afterglow, only more total, more spread through the musculature—more in muscles than in nerves, some sort of beta-endorphin opiate high, the workout high, best of them all. Sure, he felt pretty good for a man in the first great multiple grief of his life. Except he was cooking. The afternoon sea breeze helped, but not enough. He trod through the sand, every step sinking deep, calves almost cramping.

He stripped to his shorts, walked out into the ocean. Water perfect, just over seventy degrees and clear as glass. He dove in, delicious coolness all over him. He swam around dragging his legs, which pulsed furiously. Lolled back into the shallows and leaped off the bottom to ride the little tubes until they dumped him on the sand. Could even catch a miniature Wedge effect, side wave backwashing across the incoming ones for an extra push. He had done this as a child, with Tom, an old man even then, doing the same beside him. Old bald man yelling, "Outside! Outside!" Green flags ripping above the lifeguard stands, the big stones of the jetty. They had done a lot together, Tom and he. Coronado to Lassen, Yuma to Eureka, there was no escaping that.

Cooled off and tired, Kevin sat on the wet sand just above the reach of the white soup. The salt wind dried him and he could feel the rime of it on his skin and in his hair, warping lick into tangles of curl. Late afternoon sun glassed the water. Salty light in the salty wind. Sand.

He put on his shirt and left it unbuttoned, dropped his shoes by his bike and walked out the jetty, feeling each warm stone with his toes. They had walked out here many times, he used to scare Tom with his leaps. He tried one, hurt his arch. Only kids could do it. His moods rushed up and down on a wild tide of their own, hitting new ebb records, then curious floods of euphoria. How he had loved his grandpa, what friends they had been. It was only by feeling that love that he could do justice to what had happened since. So he had to feel this good, and this bad. He stepped over a big gap between stones, landed perfectly. It was coming back, the art of it. You had to dance over them, keep committing yourself to something more than a normal step. Like life: like *that*, and *that*, and *that*.

The sun was obscured by a cloud for a moment, then burst out again. Big clouds like tall ships coasted in, setting sail for the mountains and the desert beyond. The ocean was a deep, rich, blue blue, a blue in blue within blue inside of blue, the heart and soul and center of blue. Blinding chips of sunlight bounced on the swelltops. Liquid white light glazed the apricot cliff of Corona del Mar, the needles of its torrey pines like sprays of dark green. Ironwood color of the sun-drenched cliff. Eye still jumping a bit here, oxygen starvation, then enrichment. What a glossy surface to the massive rocky substance of the world! These boulders under his feet were amazing pieces of work, so big and stony, like the broken marbles of giants.

He skipped from boulder to boulder, looking. From time to time his hands came together and swung the imaginary bat in its catlike involuntary swing.

He came to the end of the jetty, the shoulder-high lighthouse block. The wind rushed over him and the clouds sailed in, the waves made their myriad glugs and the sunlight packed everything, and he stood there balancing, feeling he had come to the right place, and was now wide awake, at the center of things. End of the world. Sun low on the water.

For a long time he stood there, turning round, staring at all of it, trying to take it all in. All the events of the summer filled him at once, flooding him from a deep well of physical sensation, spinning him in a slurry of joy and sorrow. There was a steel chisel someone had left behind. He kneeled, picked it up and banged it against the last granite rock of the jetty. The rock resisted, harder than he would have imagined. Stubborn stuff, this world. A chunk of rock about the size of two softballs was wedged between boulders, and he freed it for use as a hammer. Hammer and chisel, he could write something, leave his mark on the world. All of a sudden he wanted to cut something deep and permanent, something like I, Kevin Claiborne, was here in October of 2065 with oceans of clouds in the sky and in me, and I am bursting with them and everything has gone wrong! The granite being what it was, he contented himself with *KC*. He cut the figures as deep as he could.

When he was done he put down his tools. Behind him Orange County pulsed green and amber, jumping with his heart, glossy, intense, vibrant, awake, alive. His world and the wind pouring through it. His hands came together and made their half swing. If only Hank hadn't caught that last one. If only Ramona, if only Tom, if only the world, all in him all at once, with the sharp stab of our unavoidable grief; and it seemed to him then that he was without a doubt the unhappiest person in the whole world.

And at that thought (thinking about it) he began to laugh.

ACKNOWLEDGMENTS

For help on this one, many thanks to Anne Schneider, Joan Davis, Karen Fowler, Patrick Delahunt, Paul Park, Terry Bisson, and Beth Meacham.